IN PRAISE OF...
BERLIN GAME

"To read *Berlin Game* is to shrug off twenty-five years of acclimatization to the Cold War, and to recall what espionage fiction is about in the first place."

— *The Washington Post Book World*

"Mr. Deighton, as always, makes the familiar twists and turns of spy errantry new again, partly by his grip of narrative, partly by his grasp of character, and partly by his easy, sardonic tone."

— *The New Yorker*

MEXICO SET

"A bang-up spy thriller.... It's great fun to have an agent who can say, 'It's the game.... It's nothing to do with virtue or evil, or effort and reward, it's just a game.' An awfully good game it is too, the way Deighton plays it."

— *People*

"It crackles with excitement and surprises.... Deighton is a marvel."

— *Chicago Tribune*

LONDON MATCH

"Taut...splendid...first rate." — *The Wall Street Journal*

"Deighton is a master of the game.... His plots are serpentine and suspenseful without being impenetrable, his writing sharp, his pace breakneck. He has created characters who act from believable motivations, have real needs and desires."

— *San Francisco Chronicle*

LEN DEIGHTON

THREE COMPLETE NOVELS

LEN DEIGHTON

THREE COMPLETE NOVELS

BERLIN GAME

MEXICO SET

LONDON MATCH

WINGS BOOKS
NEW YORK • AVENEL, NEW JERSEY

This edition contains the complete and unabridged texts
of the original editions.

This omnibus was originally published in separate volumes under the titles:

Berlin Game, copyright © 1983 by B. V. Holland Copyright Corporation.
Mexico Set, copyright © 1984 by B. V. Holland Copyright Corporation.
London Match, copyright © 1985 by B. V. Holland Copyright Corporation.
Maps and illustrations copyright © 1986 by Century Hutchinson.

This 1993 edition is published by Wings Books,
distributed by Outlet Book Company, Inc., A Random House Company,
40 Engelhard Avenue, Avenel, New Jersey 07001,
by arrangement with Alfred A. Knopf, Inc.

Random House
New York • Toronto • London • Sydney • Auckland

Printed and bound in the United States of America

Library of Congress Cataloging-in-Publication Data

Deighton, Len, 1929–
[Novels. Selections]
Three complete novels / Len Deighton.
p.   cm.
Contents: Berlin game—Mexico set—London match.
ISBN 0-517-09272-7
1. Samson, Bernard (Fictitious character)—Fiction.   2. Spies—
Great Britain—Fiction.   3. Spy stories, English.   I. Title.
PR6054.E37A6   1993
823′.914—dc20   92-42528
CIP

8   7   6   5   4   3   2   1

CONTENTS

Preface

Is a man who betrays his wife a good and reliable business partner?
I was asked this question many years ago by an old friend who was
continually providing alibis for his partner's covert love affairs. The
idea stuck in my mind. Is a womanizer, or a promiscuous homosexual,
a reliable employee of government? That is a question discussed
endlessly by people for whom the wrong answer can be fatal. After
a lot of false starts and abandoned ideas I decided that I wanted to
use the theme of domestic and professional betrayal at some length,
and I wanted the domestic theme (and themes) to be at least as
important as the spy story element. I hoped that each aspect of the
story would strengthen the other (ie the more we know of Bernard
Samson's domestic problems the more concerned we are with his
professional difficulties and vice versa). I began to draft out my ideas
using the pictorial diagrams which are necessary for me when the
story is long or complex or both.

At first I'd planned to begin my story after the betrayal (at what
is now the beginning of *Mexico Set*) but as my planning continued it
became obvious that more description of the betrayer was needed. I
decided that the story needed a prologue. The 'prologue' draft got
longer and longer and eventually became *Berlin Game*.

The three stories take place over a year, so the action of each book
takes approximately four months. For an idea of this sort, the voice
of the first person seemed essential and I wanted that voice to be
highly subjective. Most importantly I wanted to use the first person
to establish Bernard Samson's character. Bernard is inclined to
complain and exaggerate so that we have to *interpret* the world around
him. For instance, Dicky Cruyer isn't the incompetent, cowardly,
self-seeking man Bernard describes, just as Bernard isn't the awesome
genius that he would have us think. This is an important aspect of
the book and readers who take Bernard's words literally are missing
a lot of the intended content.

But this is not to say that Bernard Samson's view of the world is any more biased than yours or mine. All the other characters – Bret, Dicky, Fiona, Gloria, Frank or even Stinnes – would offer equally subjective accounts. We'll never know exactly what happened that year, and Bernard's story is as near the truth as we can hope to get.

I decided not to edit, correct or modify the three texts; they are printed here as originally published. It was not an easy choice. Most authors become very dissatisfied with their work by the time the proofs come from the printer; I certainly do. So I was tempted to rewrite, or at least to cut and revise some of the beginnings and endings so it would all fit together more smoothly as one volume. When books are published at yearly intervals it is necessary to help the reader's memory here and there, both with descriptions of people and of places. However I had faced the problem of repetition right from the original planning stage, and I'd tried to bring variety and new information into the repeated passages.

So despite all the temptations I left the texts the way they were. I decided it would not be a good idea to have two versions of the same book, and I was influenced by the number of readers who wrote to tell me that they'd found it amusing, or instructive to examine the way in which the story was built. One man found that reading the three books in reverse order was the best way to discover the weaknesses of my longterm planning and he set his modern writing students the same task. I am told they all enjoyed it. I am glad.

Len Deighton

BERLIN GAME

I

'How long have we been sitting here?' I said. I picked up the field glasses and studied the bored young American soldier in his glass-sided box.

'Nearly a quarter of a century,' said Werner Volkmann. His arms were resting on the steering wheel and his head was slumped on them. 'That GI wasn't even born when we first sat here waiting for the dogs to bark.'

Barking dogs, in their compound behind the remains of the Hotel Adlon, were usually the first sign of something happening on the other side. The dogs sensed any unusual happenings long before the handlers came to get them. That's why we kept the windows open; that's why we were frozen nearly to death.

'That American soldier wasn't born, the spy thriller he's reading wasn't written, and we both thought the Wall would be demolished within a few days. We were stupid kids but it was better then, wasn't it, Bernie?'

'It's always better when you're young, Werner,' I said.

This side of Checkpoint Charlie had not changed. There never was much there; just one small hut and some signs warning you about leaving the Western Sector. But the East German side had grown far more elaborate. Walls and fences, gates and barriers, endless white lines to mark out the traffic lanes. Most recently they'd built a huge walled compound where the tourist buses were searched and tapped, and scrutinized by gloomy men who pushed wheeled mirrors under every vehicle lest one of their fellow-countrymen was clinging there.

The checkpoint is never silent. The great concentration of lights that illuminate the East German side produces a steady hum like a field of insects on a hot summer's day. Werner raised his head from his arms and shifted his weight. We both had sponge-rubber cushions under us; that was one thing we'd learned in a quarter of a century. That and taping the door switch so that the interior light didn't come on every time the car door opened. 'I wish I knew how long Zena will stay in Munich,' said Werner.

'Can't stand Munich,' I told him. 'Can't stand those bloody Bavarians, to tell you the truth.'

'I was only there once,' said Werner. 'It was a rush job for the Americans. One of our people was badly beaten and the local cops were no help at all.' Even Werner's English was spoken with the strong Berlin accent that I'd known since we were at school. Now Werner Volkmann was forty years old, thickset, with black bushy hair, black moustache, and sleepy eyes that made it possible to mistake him for one of Berlin's Turkish population. He wiped a spyhole of clear glass in the windscreen so that he could see into the glare of fluorescent lighting. Beyond the silhouette of Checkpoint Charlie, Friedrichstrasse in the East Sector shone as bright as day. 'No,' he said. 'I don't like Munich at all.'

The night before, Werner, after many drinks, had confided to me the story of his wife, Zena, running off with a man who drove a truck for the Coca-Cola company. For the previous three nights he'd provided me with a place on a lumpy sofa in his smart apartment in Dahlem, right on the edge of Grunewald. But sober, we kept up the pretence that his wife was visiting a relative. 'There's something coming now,' I said.

Werner did not bother to move his head from where it rested on the seatback. 'It's a tan-coloured Ford. It will come through the checkpoint, park over there while the men inside have a coffee and hotdog, then they'll go back in to the East Sector just after midnight.'

I watched. As he'd predicted, it was a tan-coloured Ford, a panel truck, unmarked, with West Berlin registration.

'We're in the place they usually park,' said Werner. 'They're Turks who have girlfriends in the East. The regulations say you have to be out before midnight. They go back there again after midnight.'

'They must be some girls!' I said.

'A handful of Westmarks goes a long way over there,' said Werner. 'You know that, Bernie.' A police car with two cops in it cruised past very slowly. They recognized Werner's Audi and one of the cops raised a hand in a weary salutation. After the police car moved away, I used my field glasses to see right through the barrier to where an East German border guard was stamping his feet to restore circulation. It was bitterly cold.

Werner said, 'Are you sure he'll cross here, rather than at the Bornholmerstrasse or Prinzenstrasse checkpoints?'

'You've asked me that four times, Werner.'

'Remember when we first started working for intelligence. Your dad was in charge then – things were very different. Remember Mr Gaunt – the fat man who could sing all those funny Berlin cabaret songs – betting me fifty marks it would never go up . . . the Wall, I mean. He must be getting old now. I was only eighteen or nineteen, and fifty marks was a lot of money in those days.'

'Silas Gaunt, that was. He'd been reading too many of those "guidance reports" from London,' I said. 'For a time he convinced me you were wrong about everything, including the Wall.'

'But *you* didn't make any bets,' said Werner. He poured some black coffee from his Thermos into a paper cup and passed it to me.

'But I volunteered to go over there that night they closed the sector boundaries. I was no brighter than old Silas. It was just that I didn't have fifty marks to spare for betting.'

'The cabdrivers were the first to know. About two o'clock in the morning, the radio cabs were complaining about the way they were being stopped and questioned each time they crossed. The dispatcher in the downtown taxi office told his drivers not to take anyone else across to the East Sector, and then he phoned me to tell me about it.'

'And you stopped me from going,' I said.

'Your dad told me not to take you.'

'But you went over there, Werner. And old Silas went with you.' So my father had prevented my going over there the night they sealed the sector. I didn't know until now.

'We went across about four-thirty that morning. There were Russian trucks, and lots of soldiers dumping rolls of barbed wire outside the Charité Hospital. We came back quite soon. Silas said the Americans would send in tanks and tear the wire down. Your dad said the same thing, didn't he?'

'The people in Washington were too bloody frightened, Werner. The stupid bastards at the top thought the Russkies were going to move this way and take over the Western Sector of the city. They were *relieved* to see a wall going up.'

'Maybe they know things we don't know,' said Werner.

'You're right,' I said. 'They know that the service is run by idiots. But the word is leaking out.'

Werner permitted himself a slight smile. 'And then, about six in the morning, you heard the sound of the heavy trucks and construction cranes. Remember going on the back of my motorcycle to see them stringing the barbed wire across Potsdamerplatz? I knew it would happen eventually. It was the easiest fifty marks I ever earned. I can't think why Mr Gaunt took my bet.'

'He was new to Berlin,' I said. 'He'd just finished a year at Oxford, lecturing on political science and all that statistical bullshit the new kids start handing out the moment they arrive.'

'Maybe you should go and lecture there,' said Werner with just a trace of sarcasm. 'You didn't go to university did you, Bernie?' It was a rhetorical question. 'Neither did I. But you've done well without it.'

I didn't answer, but Werner was in the mood to talk now. 'Do you ever see Mr Gaunt? What beautiful German he spoke. Not like yours and mine – *Hochdeutsch*, beautiful.'

Werner, who seemed to be doing better than I was, with his export loan business, looked at me expecting a reply. 'I married his niece,' I said.

'I forgot that old Silas Gaunt was related to Fiona. I hear she is very important in the Department nowadays.'

'She's done well,' I said. 'But she works too hard. We don't have enough time together with the kids.'

'You must be making a pot of money,' said Werner. 'Two of you senior staff, with you on field allowances. . . . But Fiona has money of her own, doesn't she? Isn't her father some kind of tycoon? Couldn't he find a nice soft job for you in his office? Better than sitting out here freezing to death in a Berlin side street.'

'He's not going to come,' I said after watching the barrier descend again and the border guard go back into his hut. The windscreen had misted over again so that the lights of the checkpoint became a fairyland of bright blobs.

Werner didn't answer. I had not confided to him anything about what we were doing in his car at Checkpoint Charlie, with a tape recorder wired into the car battery and a mike taped behind the sun visor and a borrowed revolver making an uncomfortable bulge under my arm. After a few minutes he reached forward and wiped a clear spot again. 'The office doesn't know you're using me,' he said.

He was hoping like hell I'd say Berlin Station had forgiven him for his past failings. 'They wouldn't mind too much,' I lied.

'They have a long memory,' complained Werner.

'Give them time,' I said. The truth was that Werner was on the computer as 'non-critical employment only', a classification that prevented anyone employing him at all. In this job everything was 'critical'.

'They didn't okay me, then?' Werner said, suddenly guessing at the truth: that I'd come into town without even telling Berlin Station that I'd arrived.

'What do you care?' I said. 'You're making good money, aren't you?'

'I could be useful to them, and the Department could help me more. I told you all that.'

'I'll talk to the people in London,' I said. 'I'll see what I can do.'

Werner was unmoved by my promise. 'They'll just refer it to the Berlin office, and you know what the answer will be.'

'Your wife,' I said. 'Is she a Berliner?'

'She's only twenty-two,' said Werner wistfully. 'The family was from East Prussia. . . .' He reached inside his coat as if searching for cigarettes, but he knew I wouldn't permit it – cigarettes and lighters are too damned conspicuous after dark – and he closed his coat again. 'You probably saw her photo on the sideboard – a small, very pretty girl with long black hair.'

'So that's her,' I said, although in fact I'd not noticed the photo. At least I'd changed the subject. I didn't want Werner quizzing me about the office. He should have known better than that.

Poor Werner. Why does the betrayed husband always cut such a ridiculous figure? Why isn't the unfaithful partner the comical one? It was all so unfair; no wonder Werner pretended his wife was visiting relatives. He was staring ahead, his big black eyebrows lowered as he concentrated on the checkpoint. 'I hope he wasn't trying to come through with forged papers. They put everything under the ultraviolet lights nowadays, and they change the markings every week. Even the Americans have given up using forged papers – it's suicide.'

'I don't know anything about that,' I told him. 'My job is just to pick him up and debrief him before the office sends him to wherever he has to go.'

Werner turned his head; the bushy black hair and dark skin made his white teeth flash like a toothpaste commercial. 'London wouldn't send you over here for that kind of circus, Bernie. For that kind of task they send office boys, people like me.'

'We'll go and get something to eat and drink, Werner,' I said. 'Do you know some quiet restaurant where they have sausage and potatoes and good Berlin beer?'

'I know just the place, Bernie. Straight up Friedrichstrasse, under the railway bridge at the S-Bahn station and it's on the left. On the bank of the Spree: Weinrestaurant Ganymed.'

'Very funny,' I said. Between us and the Ganymed there was a wall, machine guns, barbed wire, and two battalions of gun-toting bureaucrats. 'Turn this jalopy round and let's get out of here.'

He switched on the ignition and started up. 'I'm happier with her away,' he said. 'Who wants to have a woman waiting at home to ask you where you've been and why you're back so late?'

'You're right, Werner,' I said.

'She's too young for me. I should never have married her.' He waited a moment while the heater cleared the glass a little. 'Try again tomorrow, then?'

'No further contact, Werner. This was the last try for him. I'm going back to London tomorrow. I'll be sleeping in my own bed.'

'Your wife . . . Fiona. She was nice to me that time when I had to work inside for a couple of months.'

'I remember that,' I said. Werner had been thrown out of a window by two East German agents he'd discovered in his apartment. His leg was broken in three places and it took ages for him to recover fully.

'And you tell Mr Gaunt I remember him. He's long ago retired, I know, but I suppose you still see him from time to time. You tell him any time he wants another bet on what the Ivans are up to, he calls me up first.'

'I'll see him next weekend,' I said. 'I'll tell him that.'

2

'I thought you must have missed the plane,' said my wife as she switched on the bedside light. She'd not yet got to sleep; her long hair was hardly disarranged and the frilly nightdress was not rumpled. She'd gone to bed early by the look of it. There was a lighted cigarette on the ashtray. She must have been lying there in the dark, smoking and thinking about her work. On the side table there were thick volumes from the office library and a thin blue *Report from the Select Committee on Science and Technology,* with notebook and pencil and the necessary supply of Benson & Hedges cigarettes, a considerable number of which were now only butts packed tightly in the big cut-glass ashtray she'd brought from the sitting room. She lived a different sort of life when I was away; now it was like going into a different house and a different bedroom, to a different woman.

'Some bloody strike at the airport,' I explained. There was a tumbler containing whisky balanced on the clock-radio. I sipped it; the ice cubes had long since melted to make a warm weak mixture. It was typical of her to prepare a treat so carefully – with linen napkin, stirrer and some cheese straws – and then forget about it.

'London Airport?' She noticed her half-smoked cigarette and stubbed it out and waved away the smoke.

'Where else do they go on strike every day?' I said irritably.

'There was nothing about it on the news.'

'Strikes are not news any more,' I said. She obviously thought that I had *not* come directly from the airport, and her failure to commiserate with me over three wasted hours there did not improve my bad temper.

'Did it go all right?'

'Werner sends his best wishes. He told me that story about your Uncle Silas betting him fifty marks about the building of the Wall.'

'Not again,' said Fiona. 'Is he ever going to forget that bloody bet?'

'He likes you,' I said. 'He sent his best wishes.' It wasn't exactly true, but I wanted her to like him as I did. 'And his wife has left him.'

'Poor Werner,' she said. Fiona was very beautiful, especially when she smiled that sort of smile that women save for men who have lost their woman. 'Did she go off with another man?'

'No,' I said untruthfully, 'She couldn't stand Werner's endless affairs with other women.'

'Werner!' said my wife, and laughed. She didn't believe that Werner had affairs with lots of other women. I wondered how she could guess so correctly. Werner seemed an attractive sort of guy to my masculine eyes. I suppose I will never understand women. The trouble is that they all understand me; they understand me too damned well. I took off my coat and put it on a hanger. 'Don't put your overcoat in the wardrobe,' said Fiona. 'It needs cleaning. I'll take it in tomorrow.' As casually as she could, she added, 'I tried to get you at the Steigerberger Hotel. Then I tried the duty officer at Olympia but no one knew where you were. Billy's throat was swollen. I thought it might be mumps.'

'I wasn't there,' I said.

'You asked the office to book you there. You said it's the best hotel in Berlin. You said I could leave a message there.'

'I stayed with Werner. He's got a spare room now that his wife's gone.'

'And shared all those women of his?' said Fiona. She laughed again. 'Is it all part of a plan to make me jealous?'

I leaned over and kissed her. 'I've missed you, darling. I really have. Is Billy okay?'

'Billy's fine. But that damned man at the garage gave me a bill for sixty pounds!'

'For what?'

'He's written it all down. I told him you'd see about it.'

'But he let you have the car?'

'I had to collect Billy from school. He knew that before he did the service on it. So I shouted at him and he let me take it.'

'You're a wonderful wife,' I said. I undressed and went into the bathroom to wash and to brush my teeth.

'And it went well?' she called.

I looked at myself in the long mirror. It was just as well that I was tall, for I was getting fatter, and that Berlin beer hadn't helped matters. 'I did what I was told,' I said, and finished brushing my teeth.

'Not you, darling,' said Fiona. I switched on the Water-Pik and above its chugging sound I heard her add, 'You never do what you are told, you know that.'

I went back into the bedroom. She'd combed her hair and smoothed the sheet on my side of the bed. She'd put my pyjamas on the pillow.

They consisted of a plain red jacket and paisley-pattern trousers. 'Are these mine?'

'The laundry didn't come back this week. I phoned them. The driver is ill . . . so what can you say?'

'I didn't check into the Berlin office at all, if that's what's eating you,' I admitted. 'They're all young kids in there, don't know their arse from a hole in the ground. I feel safer with one of the old-timers like Werner.'

'Suppose something happened? Suppose there was trouble and the duty officer didn't even know you were in Berlin? Can't you see how silly it is not to give them some sort of perfunctory call?'

'I don't know any of those Olympia Stadion people any more, darling. It's all changed since Frank Harrington took over. They are youngsters, kids with no field experience and lots and lots of theories from the training school.'

'But your man turned up?'

'No.'

'You spent three days there for nothing?'

'I suppose I did.'

'They'll send you in to get him. You realize that, don't you?'

I got into bed. 'Nonsense. They'll use one of the West Berlin people.'

'It's the oldest trick in the book, darling. They send you over there to wait . . . for all you know, he wasn't even in contact. Now you'll go back and report a failed contact and you'll be the one they send in to get him. My God, Bernie, you are a fool at times.'

I hadn't looked at it like that, but there was more than a grain of truth in Fiona's cynical viewpoint. 'Well, they can find someone else,' I said angrily. 'Let one of the local people go over to get him. My face is too well known there.'

'They'll say they're all kids without experience, just what you yourself said.'

'It's Brahms Four,' I told her.

'Brahms – those network names sound so ridiculous. I liked it better when they had codewords like Trojan, Wellington and Claret.'

The way she said it was annoying. 'The postwar network names are specially chosen to have no identifiable nationality,' I said. 'And the number four man in the Brahms network once saved my life. He's the one who got me out of Weimar.'

'He's the one who is kept so damned secret. Yes, I know. Why do you think they sent you? And now do you see why they are going to make you go in and get him?' Beside the bed, my photo stared back at me from its silver frame. Bernard Samson, a serious young man with baby face, wavy hair and horn-rimmed glasses looked nothing like the wrinkled old fool I shaved every morning.

'I was in a spot. He could have kept going. He didn't have to come back all the way to Weimar.' I settled into my pillow. 'How long ago was that – eighteen years, maybe twenty?'

'Go to sleep,' said Fiona. 'I'll phone the office in the morning and say you are not well. It will give you time to think.'

'You should see the pile of work on my desk.'

'I took Billy and Sally to the Greek restaurant for his birthday. The waiters sang happy birthday and cheered him when he blew the candles out. It was sweet of them. I wish you'd been there.'

'I won't go. I'll tell the old man in the morning. I can't do that kind of thing any more.'

'And there was a phone call from Mr Moore at the bank. He wants to talk with you. He said there's no hurry.'

'And we both know what that means,' I said. 'It means phone me back immediately or else!' I was close to her now and I could smell perfume. Had she put it on just for me, I wondered.

'Harry Moore isn't like that. At Christmas we were nearly seven hundred overdrawn, and when we saw him at my sister's party he said not to worry.'

'Brahms Four took me to the house of a man named Busch – Karl Busch – who had this empty room in Weimar. . . .' It was all coming back to me. 'We stayed there three days and afterwards Karl Busch went back there. They took Busch up to the security barracks in Leipzig. He was never seen again.'

'You're senior staff now, darling,' she said sleepily. 'You don't have to go anywhere you don't want to.'

'I phoned you last night,' I said. 'It was two o'clock in the morning but there was no reply.'

'I was here, asleep,' she said. She was awake and alert now. I could tell by the tone of her voice.

'I let it ring for ages,' I said. 'I tried twice. Finally I got the operator to dial it.'

'Then it must be the damned phone acting up again. I tried to phone here for Nanny yesterday afternoon and there was no reply. I'll tell the engineers tomorrow.'

3

Richard Cruyer was the German Stations Controller, the man to whom I reported. He was younger than I was by two years and his apologies for this fact gave him opportunities for reminding himself of his fast promotion in a service that was not noted for its fast promotions.

Dicky Cruyer had curly hair and liked to wear open-neck shirts and faded jeans, and be the *Wunderkind* amongst all the dark suits and Eton ties. But under all the trendy jargon and casual airs, he was the most pompous stuffed shirt in the whole Department.

'They think it's a cushy number in here, Bernard,' he said while stirring his coffee. 'They don't realize the way I have the Deputy Controller (Europe) breathing down my neck and endless meetings with every damned committee in the building.'

Even Cruyer's complaints were contrived to show the world how important he was. But he smiled to let me know how well he endured his troubles. He had his coffee served in a fine Spode china cup and saucer, and he stirred it with a silver spoon. On the mahogany tray there was another Spode cup and saucer, a matching sugar bowl, and a silver creamer fashioned in the shape of a cow. It was a valuable antique – Dicky had told me that many times – and at night it was locked in the secure filing cabinet, together with the log and the current carbons of the mail. 'They think it's all lunches at the Mirabelle and a *fine* with the boss.'

Dicky always said *fine* rather than brandy or cognac. Fiona told me he'd been saying it ever since he was president of the Oxford University Food and Wine Society as an undergraduate. Dicky's image as a gourmet was not easy to reconcile with his figure, for he was a thin man, with thin arms, thin legs and thin bony hands and fingers, with one of which he continually touched his thin bloodless lips. It was a nervous gesture, provoked, said some people, by the hostility around him. This was nonsense of course, but I did dislike the little creep, I will admit that.

He sipped his coffee and then tasted it carefully, moving his lips while staring at me as if I might have come to sell him the year's crop. 'It's just a shade bitter, don't you think, Bernard?'

'Nescafé all tastes the same to me,' I said.

'This is pure chagga, ground just before it was brewed.' He said it calmly but nodded to acknowledge my little attempt to annoy him.

'Well, he didn't turn up,' I said. 'We can sit here drinking chagga all morning and it won't bring Brahms Four over the wire.'

Dicky said nothing.

'Has he re-established contact yet?' I asked.

Dicky put his coffee on the desk, while he riffed some papers in a file. 'Yes. We received a routine report from him. He's safe.' Dicky chewed a fingernail.

'Why didn't he turn up?'

'No details on that one.' He smiled. He was handsome in the way that foreigners think bowler-hatted English stockbrokers are handsome. His face was hard and bony and the tan from his Christmas in the Bahamas had still not faded. 'He'll explain in his own good time. Don't badger the field agents – that has always been my policy. Right, Bernard?'

'It's the only way, Dicky.'

'Ye gods! How I'd love to get back into the field just once more! You people have the best of it.'

'I've been off the field list for nearly five years, Dicky. I'm a desk man now, like you.' Like you have always been is what I should have said, but I let it go. 'Captain' Cruyer he'd called himself when he returned from the Army. But he soon realized how ridiculous that title sounded to a Director-General who'd worn a General's uniform. And he realized too that 'Captain' Cruyer would be an unlikely candidate for that illustrious post.

He stood up, smoothed his shirt, and then sipped coffee, holding his free hand under the cup to guard against drips. He noticed that I hadn't drunk my chagga. 'Would you prefer tea?'

'Is it too early for a gin and tonic?'

He didn't respond to this question. 'I think you feel beholden to our friend Bee Four. You still feel grateful about his coming back to Weimar for you.' He greeted my look of surprise with a knowing nod. 'I read the files, Bernard. I know what's what.'

'It was a decent thing to do,' I said.

'It was,' said Dicky. 'It was a truly decent thing to do, but that wasn't why he did it. Not only that.'

'You weren't there, Dicky.'

'Bee Four panicked, Bernard. He fled. He was near the border, at some godforsaken little place in Thüringerwald, by the time our people intercepted him and told him he wasn't wanted for questioning by the KGB – or anyone else, for that matter.'

'It's ancient history,' I said.

'We turned him round,' said Cruyer. It had become 'we' I noticed. 'We gave him some chickenfeed and told him to go back and play the outraged innocent. We told him to co-operate with them.'

'Chickenfeed?'

'Names of people who'd already escaped, safe houses long since abandoned . . . bits and pieces that would make Brahms Four look good to the KGB.'

'But they got Busch, the man who was sheltering me.'

Unhurriedly, Cruyer finished his coffee and wiped his lips with a linen napkin from the tray. 'We got two of you out. I'd say that's not bad for that sort of crisis – two out of three. Busch went back to his house to get his stamp collection. . . . Stamp collection! What can you do with a man like that? They put him in the bag of course.'

'The stamp collection was probably his life savings,' I said.

'Perhaps it was, and that's how they put him in the bag, Bernard. No second chances with those swine. I know that, you know that, and he knew it too.'

'So that's why our field people don't like Brahms Four.'

'Yes, that's why they don't like him.'

'They think he informed on that Erfurt network.'

Cruyer shrugged. 'What could we do? We could hardly spread the word that we'd invented that story to make the fellow *persona grata* with the KGB.' Cruyer walked across to his drinks cabinet and poured some gin into a large Waterford glass tumbler.

'Plenty of gin, not too much tonic,' I said. Cruyer turned to stare blankly at me. 'If that's for me,' I added. So there had been a blunder. They'd told Brahms Four to reveal old Busch's address, then the poor old sod had gone back for his stamps. And run into the arms of a KGB arrest squad.

Dicky put a little more gin into the glass, and added ice cubes gently so that they would not splash. He brought it, together with a small bottle of tonic, which I left unused. 'No need for you to concern yourself with this one any more, Bernard. You did your bit in going to Berlin. We'll let one of the others take over now.'

'Is he in trouble?'

Cruyer went back to the drinks cabinet and busied himself tidying away the bottle caps and stirrer. Then he closed the cabinet doors and said, 'Do you know the sort of material Brahms Four has been supplying?'

'Economics intelligence. He works for an East German bank.'

'He is the most carefully protected source we have in Germany. You are one of the few people ever to have seen him face to face.'

'And that was almost twenty years ago.'

'He works through the mail – always local addresses to avoid the censors and the security – posting his material to various members of the Brahms net. In emergencies he uses a dead-letter drop. But that's all – no microdots, no one-time pads, no codes, no micro transmitters, no secret ink. Very old-fashioned.'

'And very safe,' I said.

'Very old-fashioned and very safe, so far,' agreed Dicky. 'Even I don't have access to the Brahms Four file. No one knows anything about him except that he's been getting material from somewhere at the top of the tree. All we can do is guess.'

'And you've guessed,' I prompted him, knowing that Dicky was going to tell me anyway.

'From Bee Four we are getting important decisions of the Deutsche Investitions Bank. And from the Deutsche Bauern Bank. Those state banks provide long-term credit for industry and for agriculture. Both banks are controlled by the Deutsche Notenbank, through which come all remittances, payments and clearing for the whole country. Now and again we get good notice of what the Moscow Narodny Bank is doing and regular reports about the COMECON briefings. I think Brahms Four is a secretary or personal assistant to one of the directors of the Deutsche Notenbank.'

'Or a director?'

'All banks have an economic intelligence department. Being head of that department is not a job an ambitious banker craves for, so they get switched around. Brahms Four has been feeding us this sort of thing too long to be anything but a clerk or assistant.'

'You'll miss him. Too bad you have to pull him out,' I said.

'Pull him out? I'm not trying to pull him out. I want him to stay right where he is.'

'I thought . . .'

'It's his idea that he should come over to the West, not mine! I want him to remain where he is. I can't afford to lose him.'

'Is he getting frightened?'

'They all get frightened eventually,' said Cruyer. 'It's battle fatigue. The strain of it all gets them down. They get older and they get tired and they start looking for that pot of gold and the country house with the roses round the door.'

'They start looking for the things we've been promising them for twenty years. That's the truth of it.'

'Who knows what makes these crazy bastards do it?' said Cruyer. 'I've spent half my life trying to understand their motivation.' He looked out the window. Hard sunlight sidelighting the lime trees, dark blue sky with just a few smears of cirrus very high. 'And I'm still no nearer knowing what makes any of them tick.'

'There comes a time when you have to let them go,' I said.

He touched his lips; or was he kissing his fingertips, or maybe tasting the gin that he'd spilled on his fingers. 'Lord Moran's theory, you mean? I seem to remember he divided men into four classes. Those who were never afraid, those who were afraid but never showed it, those who were afraid and showed it but carried on with their job, and the fourth group – men who were afraid and shirked. Where does Brahms Four fit in there?'

'I don't know,' I said. How the hell can you explain to a man like Cruyer what it's like to be afraid day and night, year after year? What had Cruyer ever had to fear, beyond a close scrutiny of his expense accounts?

'Well, he's got to stay there for the time being, and there's an end to it.'

'So why was I sent to receive him?'

'He was acting up, Bernard. He threw a little tantrum. You know the way these chaps can be at times. He threatened to walk out on us, but the crisis passed. Threatened to use an old forged US passport and march out through Checkpoint Charlie.'

'So I was there to hold him?'

'Couldn't have a hue and cry, could we? Couldn't give his name to the civil police and send teleprinter messages to the boats and airports.' He unlocked the window and strained to open it. It had been closed all winter and now it took all Cruyer's strength to unstick it. 'Ah, a whiff of London diesel. That's better,' he said as there came a movement of chilly air. 'But he's still proving difficult. He's not giving us the regular flow of information. He threatens to stop altogether.'

'And you . . . what are you threatening?'

'Threats are not my style, Bernard. I'm simply asking him to stay there for two more years and help us get someone else into place. Ye gods! Do you know how much money he's squeezed out of us over the past five years?'

'As long as you don't want me to go,' I said. 'My face is too well known over there. And I'm getting too bloody short-winded for any strong-arm stuff.'

'We've plenty of people available, Bernard. No need for senior staff to take risks. And anyway, if things went really sour on us, we'd need someone from Frankfurt.'

'That has a nasty ring to it, Dicky. What kind of someone would we need from Frankfurt?'

Cruyer sniffed. 'No need to draw you a diagram, old man. If Bee Four really started thinking of spilling the beans to the Normannenstrasse boys, we'd have to move fast.'

'Expedient demise?' I said, keeping my voice level and my face expressionless.

Cruyer became a fraction uncomfortable. 'We'd have to move fast.

We'd have to do whatever the team on the spot thought necessary. You know how these things go. And XPD can never be ruled out.'

'This is one of our own people, Dicky. This is an old man who has served the Department for over twenty years.'

'And all we're asking,' said Cruyer with exaggerated patience, 'is for him to go on serving us in the same way. What happens if he goes off his head and wants to betray us is conjecture – pointless conjecture.'

'We earn our living from conjecture,' I said. 'And it makes me wonder what I would have to do to have "someone from Frankfurt" come along to get me ready for that big debriefing in the sky.'

Cruyer laughed. 'You always were a card!' he said. 'You wait until I tell the old man that one.'

'Any more of that delicious gin?'

He took the glass from my outstretched hand. 'Leave Brahms Four to Frank Harrington and the Berlin Field Unit, Bernard. You're not a German, you're not a field agent any longer, and you are far, far too old.'

He put a little gin in my glass and added ice, using claw-shaped silver tongs. 'Let's talk about something more cheerful,' he said over his shoulder.

'In that case, Dicky, what about my new car allowance? The cashier won't do anything without the paperwork.'

'Leave it to my secretary.'

'I've filled in the forms already,' I told him. 'I've got them with me, as a matter of fact. They just need your signature . . . two copies.' I placed them on the corner of his desk and gave him the pen from his ornate desk set.

'This car will be too big for you,' he muttered while pretending the pen was not marking properly. 'You'll be sorry you didn't opt for something more compact.' I gave him my plastic ballpoint, and after he'd signed I looked at the signature before putting the forms in my pocket. It was perfect timing, I suppose.

4

We'd arranged to visit Fiona's Uncle Silas for the weekend. Old Silas Gaunt was not really her uncle; he was a distant relative of her mother's. She'd never even met Silas until I took her to see him when I was trying to impress her, just after we'd first met. She'd come down from Oxford with all the expected brilliant results in philosophy, politics and economics – or 'Modern Greats' in the jargon of academe – and done all those things that her contemporaries thought smart: she studied Russian at the Sorbonne while perfecting the French accent necessary for upper-class young Englishwomen; she'd done a short cookery course at the Cordon Bleu; worked for an art dealer; crewed for a transatlantic yacht race; and written speeches for a man who'd narrowly failed to become a Liberal Member of Parliament. It was soon after that fiasco that I met her. Old Silas had been captivated by his newly discovered niece right from the start. We saw a lot of him, and my son Billy was his godchild.

Silas Gaunt was a formidable figure who'd worked for intelligence back in the days when such service was really secret. Back in the days when reports were done in copperplate hand-writing and field agents were paid in sovereigns. When my father was running the Berlin Field Unit, Silas was his boss.

'He's a silly little fart,' said Fiona when I related my conversation with Dicky Cruyer. It was Saturday morning and we were driving to Silas's farm in the Cotswold Hills.

'He's a dangerous little fart,' I said. 'When I think of that idiot making decisions about field people. . . .'

'About Brahms Four, you mean,' said Fiona.

' "Bee Four" is Dicky's latest contribution to the terminology. Yes, people like that,' I said. 'I get the goddamned shivers.'

'He won't let the Brahms source go,' she said. We were driving through Reading, having left the motorway in search of Elizabeth Arden skin tonic. She was at the wheel of the red Porsche her father had bought her the previous birthday. She was thirty-five and her father said she needed something special to cheer her up. I wondered how he was planning to cheer me up for my fortieth, coming in two weeks' time: I guessed it would be the usual bottle of Remy Martin, and wondered if I'd again find inside the box the compliments card of some office-supplies firm who'd given it to him.

'The Economics Intelligence Committee lives off that banking stuff that Brahms Four provides,' she added after a long silence thinking about it.

'I still say we should have stayed on the motorway. That chemist in the village is sure to have skin tonic,' I said. Although in fact I hadn't the faintest idea what skin tonic was, except that it was something my skin had managed without for several decades.

'But not Elizabeth Arden,' said Fiona. We were in a traffic jam in the middle of Reading and there was no chemist's shop in sight. The engine was overheating and she switched it off for a moment. 'Perhaps you're right,' she admitted finally, leaning across to give me a brief kiss. She was just keeping me sweet, because I was going to be the one who leaped out of the car and dashed off for the damned jar of magic ointment while she flirted with the traffic warden.

'Have you got enough space in the back, children?' she asked.

The kids were wedged each side of a suitcase but they didn't complain. Sally grunted and carried on reading her *William* book, and Billy said, 'How fast will you go on the motorway?'

'And Dicky is on the committee too,' I said.

'Yes, he claims it was his idea.'

'I lose count of how many committees he's on. He's never in his bloody office when he's needed. His appointment book looks like the *Good Food Guide*. Lately he's discovered "breakfast meetings". Now he gorges and guzzles all day. I don't know how he stays so thin.'

The traffic moved again, and she started up and followed closely behind a battered red double-decker bus. The conductor was standing on the platform looking at her and at the car with undisguised admiration. She smiled at him and he smiled back. It was ridiculous, but I couldn't help feeling a pang of jealousy. 'I'll have to go,' I said.

'To Berlin?'

'Dicky knows I'll have to go. The whole conversation was just Dicky's way of making sure I knew.'

'What difference can you make?' said Fiona. 'Brahms can't be forced to go on. If he's determined to stop working for us, there's not much anyone in the Department can do about it.'

'No?' I said. 'Well, you might be surprised.'

She looked at me. 'But Brahms Four is old. He must be due for retirement.'

'Dicky was making veiled threats.'

'Bluff.'

'Probably bluff,' I agreed. 'Just Dicky's way of saying that if I stand back and let anyone else go, they might get too rough. But you can't be sure with Dicky. Especially when his seniority is on the line.'

'You mustn't go, darling.'

'My being there is probably going to make no difference at all.'

'Well then . . .'

'But if someone else goes – some kid from the Berlin office – and something bad happens. How will I ever be sure that I couldn't have made it come out okay?'

'Even so, Bernard, I still don't want you to go.'

'We'll see,' I said.

'You owe Brahms Four nothing,' she said.

'I owe him,' I said. 'I know that, and so does he. That's why he'll trust me in a way he'll trust no one else. He knows I owe him.'

'It must be twenty years,' she said, as if promises, like mortgages, became less burdensome with time.

'What's it matter how long ago it was?'

'And what about what you owe me? And what you owe Billy and Sally?'

'Don't get angry, sweetheart,' I said. 'It's hard enough already. You think I want to go over there and play Boy Scout again?'

'I don't know,' she said. She was angry, and when we got on the motorway she put her foot down so that the needles went right round the dials. We were at Uncle Silas's farm well before he'd even opened the champagne for pre-lunch drinks.

Whitelands was a 600-acre farm in the Cotswolds – the great limestone plateau that divides the Thames Valley from the River Severn – and the farmhouse of ancient honey-coloured local stone with mullioned windows and lopsided doorway would have looked too perfect, like the set for a Hollywood film, except that summer had not yet come and the sky was grey, the lawn brown, and the rose-bushes trimmed back and bloomless.

There were other cars parked carelessly alongside the huge stone barn, a horse tethered to the gate, and fresh clots of mud on the metal grating of the porch. The old oak door was unlocked, and Fiona pushed her way into the hall in that proprietorial way that was permitted to members of the family. There were coats hanging on the wall and more draped over the settee.

'Dicky and Daphne Cruyer,' said Fiona, recognizing a mink coat.

'And Bret Rensselaer,' I said, touching a sleeve of soft camel hair. 'Is it going to be all people from the office?'

Fiona shrugged and turned so that I could help her take off her coat. There were voices and decorous laughter from the back of the house. 'Not all from the office,' she said. 'The Range Rover out front belongs to that retired general who lives in the village. His wife has the riding school – remember? You hated her.'

'I wonder if the Cruyers are staying,' I said.

'Not if their coats are in the hall,' said Fiona.

'You should have been a detective,' I said. She grimaced at me. It wasn't the sort of remark that Fiona regarded as a compliment.

This region of England has the prettiest villages and most beautiful countryside in the world, and yet there is something about such contrived perfection that I find disquieting. For the cramped labourer's cottages are occupied by stockbrokers and building speculators, and ye host in ye olde village pub turns out to be an airline pilot between trips. The real villagers live near the main road in ugly brick terraced houses, their front gardens full of broken motorcars.

'If you go down to the river, remember the bank is slippery with mud. And for goodness' sake wipe your shoes carefully before you come in for lunch.' The children responded with whoops of joy. 'I wish we had somewhere like this to go at weekends,' Fiona said to me.

'We do have somewhere like this,' I said. 'We have this. Your Uncle Silas has said come as often as you like.'

'It's not the same,' she said.

'You're damn right it's not,' I said. 'If this was our place, you'd not be going down the hall for a glass of champagne before lunch. You'd be hurrying along to the kitchen to scrape the vegetables in cold water.'

'Fiona, my darling! And Bernard!' Silas Gaunt came from the kitchen. 'I thought I recognized the children I just spotted climbing through the shrubbery.'

'I'm sorry,' said Fiona, but Silas laughed and slapped me on the back.

'We'll be eating very soon but there's just time to gulp a glass of something. I think you know everyone. Some neighbours dropped in, but I haven't been able to get them to stay for lunch.'

Silas Gaunt was a huge man, tall, with a big belly. He'd always been fat, but since his wife died he'd grown fatter in the way that only rich old self-indulgent men grow fat. He cared nothing about his waistline or that his shirts were so tight the buttons were under constant strain, or about the heavy jowls that made him look like a worried bloodhound. His head was almost bald and his forehead overhung his eyes in a way that set his features into a constant frown, which was only dispelled by his loud laughs for which he threw his head back and opened his mouth at the ceiling. Uncle Silas presided over his luncheon party like a squire with his farm workers, but he gave no offence, because it was so obviously a joke, just as his posture as a farmer was a joke, despite all the discarded rubber boots in the hall, and the weather-beaten hay rake disposed on the back lawn like some priceless piece of modern sculpture.

'They all come to see me,' he said as he poured Château Pétrus '64 for his guests. 'Sometimes they want me to recall some bloody fool thing the Department decided back in the sixties, or they want me to use my influence with someone upstairs, or they want me to sell some ghastly little Victorian commode they've inherited.' Silas looked round the table to be sure everyone present remembered that he had a partnership in a Bond Street antique shop. The taciturn American, Bret Rensselaer, was squeezing the arm of the busty blonde he'd brought with him. 'But I see them all – believe me I never get lonely.' I felt sorry for old Silas; it was the sort of thing that only very lonely people claimed.

Mrs Porter, his cook–housekeeper, came through the door from the kitchen bearing a roast sirloin. 'Good. I like beef,' said my small son Billy.

Mrs Porter smiled in appreciation. She was an elderly woman who had learned the value of a servant who heard nothing, saw nothing, and said very little. 'I've no time for stews and pies and all those mixtures,' explained Uncle Silas as he opened a second bottle of lemonade for the children. 'I like to see a slice of real meat on my plate. I hate all those sauces and purées. The French can keep their cuisine.' He poured a little lemonade for my son, and waited while Billy noted its colour and bouquet, took a sip, and nodded approval just as Silas had instructed him to do.

Mrs Porter arranged the meat platter in front of Silas and placed the carving knife and fork to hand before going to get the vegetables. Dicky Cruyer dabbed wine from his lips with a napkin. The host's words seemed to be aimed at him. 'I can't stand by and let you defame *la cuisine française* in such a cavalier fashion, Silas.' Dicky smiled. 'I'd get myself blackballed by Paul Bocuse.'

Silas served Billy with a huge portion of rare roast beef and went on carving. 'Start eating!' Silas commanded. Dicky's wife, Daphne, passed the plates. She worked in advertising and liked to dress in grandma clothes, complete with black velvet choker, cameo brooch and small metal-rim eyeglasses. She insisted on a very small portion of beef.

Dicky saw my son spill gravy down his shirt and smiled at me pityingly. The Cruyer boys were at boarding school; their parents only saw them at vacation time. It's the only way to stay sane, Dicky had explained to me more than once.

Silas carved into the meat with skilful concentration. There were ooos! and ahhs! from the guests. Dicky Cruyer said it was a 'sumptuous repast' and addressed Silas as 'mine host'. Fiona gave me a blank stare as a warning against provoking Dicky into more such comments.

'Cooking,' said Silas, 'is the art of the possible. The French have been brought up on odds and ends, chopped up and mixed up and disguised with flavoured sauces. I don't want that muck if I can afford some proper food. No one in their right mind would choose it.'

'Try *la cuisine nouvelle*,' said Daphne Cruyer, who was proud of her French accent. 'Lightweight dishes and each plate of food designed like a picture.'

'I don't want lightweight food,' growled Silas, and brandished the knife at her. '*Cuisine nouvelle*!' he said disdainfully. 'Big coloured plates with tiny scraps of food arranged in the centre. When cheap hotel restaurants did it, we called it "portion control", but get the public-relations boys on the job and it's *cuisine nouvelle* and they write long articles about it in ladies' magazines. When I pay for good food, I expect the waiter to serve me from a trolley and ask me what I want and how much I want, and I'll tell him where to put the vegetables. I don't want plates of meat and two veg carried from the kitchen by waiters who don't know a herring from a hot-cross bun.'

'This beef is done to perfection, Uncle Silas,' said Fiona, who was relieved that he'd managed to deliver this passionate address without the usual interjected expletives. 'But just a small slice for Sally . . . well-done meat, if that's possible.'

'Good God, woman,' he said. 'Give your daughter something that will put a little blood into her veins. Well-done meat! No wonder she's looking so damned peaky.' He placed two slices of rare beef on a warmed plate and cut the meat into bite-size pieces. He always did that for the children.

'What's peaky?' said Billy, who liked underdone beef and was admiring Silas's skill with the razor-sharp carving knife.

'Pinched, white, anaemic and ill-looking,' said Silas. He set the rare beef in front of Sally.

'Sally is perfectly fit,' said Fiona. There was no quicker way of upsetting her than to suggest the children were in any way deprived. I suspected it was some sort of guilt she shared with all working mothers. 'Sally's the best swimmer in her class,' said Fiona. 'Aren't you, Sally?'

'I was last term,' said Sally in a whisper.

'Get some rare roast beef into your belly,' Silas told her. 'It will make your hair curly.'

'Yes, Uncle Silas,' she said. He watched her until she took a mouthful and smiled at him.

'You're a tyrant, Uncle Silas,' said my wife, but Silas gave no sign of having heard her. He turned to Daphne. 'Don't tell me you want it well done,' he said ominously.

'*Bleu* for me,' she said. '*Avec un petit peu de moutarde anglaise.*'

'Pass Daphne the mustard,' said Silas. 'And pass her the *pommes de terre* – she could put a bit more weight on. It'll give you something to get hold of,' he told Cruyer, waving the carving fork at him.

'I say, steady on,' said Cruyer, who didn't like such personal remarks aimed at his wife.

Dicky Cruyer declined the Charlotte Russe, having had 'an elegant sufficiency', so Billy and I shared Dicky's portion. Charlotte Russe was one of Mrs Porter's specialities. When the meal was finished, Silas took the men to the billiards room, telling the ladies, 'Walk down to the river, or sit in the conservatory, or there's a big log fire in the drawing room if you're cold. Mrs Porter will bring you coffee, and brandy too if you fancy it. But men have to swear and belch now and again. And we'll smoke and talk shop and argue about cricket. It will be boring for you. Go and look after the children – that's what nature intended women to do.'

They did not depart graciously, at least Daphne and Fiona didn't. Daphne called old Silas a rude pig and Fiona threatened to let the children play in his study – a sanctum forbidden to virtually everyone – but it made no difference; he ushered the men into the billiards room and closed the ladies out.

The gloomy billiards room with its mahogany panelling was unchanged since being furnished to the taste of a nineteenth-century beer baron. Even the antlers and family portraits remained in position. The windows opened onto the lawn, but the sky outside was dark and the room was lit only by the green light reflected from the tabletop. Dicky Cruyer set up the table and Bret selected a cue for himself while Silas removed his jacket and snapped his bright red braces before passing the drinks and the cigars. 'So Brahms Four is acting the goat?' said Silas as he chose a cigar for himself and picked up the matches. 'Well, are you all struck dumb?' He shook the matchbox so that the wooden matches rattled.

'Well, I say – ' said Cruyer, almost dropping the resin he was applying to the tip of his cue.

'Don't be a bloody fool, Dicky,' Silas told him. 'The D-G is worried sick at the thought of losing the banking figures. He said you're putting Bernard in to sort it out for you.'

Cruyer – who had been very careful not to reveal to me that he'd mentioned me to the Director-General – fiddled with his cue to grant himself an extra moment of thought, then said, 'Bernard? His name was put up but I'm against it. Bernard's done his bit, I told him that.'

'Never mind the double talk, Dicky. Save all that for your committee meetings. The D-G asked me to knock your heads together this weekend and try to come up with a few sensible proposals on Monday . . . Tuesday at the latest. This damn business could go pop, you know.' He looked at the table and then at his guests. 'Now, how shall we do this? Bernard is no earthly good, so he'd better partner me against you two.'

Bret said nothing. Dick Cruyer looked at Silas with renewed respect. Perhaps until that afternoon he hadn't fully realized the influence the old man still wielded. Or perhaps he hadn't realized that Silas was just the same unscrupulous old swine that he'd been when he was working inside; just the same ruthless manipulator of people that Cruyer tried to be. And Uncle Silas had always emerged from this sort of crisis smelling of roses, and that was something that Dicky Cruyer hadn't always managed.

'I still say Bernard must not go,' insisted Cruyer, but with less conviction now. 'His face is too well known. Their watchers will be onto him immediately. One false move and we'll find ourselves over at the Home Office, trying to figure out who we can swop for him.' Like Silas, he kept his voice flat, and contrived the casual offhand tone in which Englishmen prefer to discuss matters of life and death. He was leaning over the table by this time, and there was silence while he put down a ball.

'So who *will* go?' said Silas, tilting his head to look at Cruyer like a schoolmaster asking a backward pupil a very simple question.

'We have short-listed five or six people we deem suitable,' said Cruyer.

'People who know Brahms Four? People he'll trust?'

'Brahms Four will trust no one,' said Cruyer. 'You know how agents become when they start talking of getting out.' He stood back while Bret Rensselaer studied the table, then without fuss potted the chosen ball. Bret was Dicky's senior but he was letting Dicky answer the questions as if he were no more than a bystander. That was Bret Rensselaer's style.

'Good shot, Bret,' said Silas. 'So none of them have ever met him?' He smoked his cigar and blew smoke at Cruyer. 'Or have I misunderstood?'

'Bernard's the only one who ever worked with him,' admitted Cruyer, taking off his jacket and placing it carefully on the back of an empty chair. 'I can't even get a recent photo of him.'

'Brahms Four.' Silas scratched his belly. 'He's almost my age, you know. I knew him back when Berlin was Berlin. We shared girlfriends and fell down drunk together. I know him the way you only know men you grew up with. Berlin! I loved that town.'

'As well we know,' said Cruyer with a touch of acid in his voice. He cleared the pocket and rolled the balls back along the table.

'Brahms Four tried to kill me at the end of 1946,' said Silas, ignoring Cruyer. 'He waited outside a little bar near the Alexanderplatz and took a shot at me as I was framed against the light in the doorway.'

'He missed?' said Cruyer with the appropriate amount of concern.

'Yes. You'd think even an indifferent shot would be able to hit a big fellow like me, standing full-square against the light, but the stupid bastard missed. Luckily I was with my driver, a military policeman I'd had with me ever since I'd arrived. I was a civilian in uniform, you see – I needed a proper soldier to help me into my Sam Browne and remind me when to salute. Well, he laid into Brahms Four. I think he would have maimed him had I not been there. The corporal thought he'd aimed at him, you see. He was damned angry about it.'

Silas drank a little port, smoked his cigar, and watched my inexpert stroke in silence. Cruyer dutifully asked him what had happened after that.

'The Russkies came running. Soldiers, regimental police, four of them, big peasant boys with dirty boots and unshaven chins. Wanted to take poor old Brahms Four away. Of course, he wasn't called Brahms Four then, that came later. Alexanderplatz was in their sector even if they hadn't yet built their wall. But I told them he was an English officer who'd had too much to drink.'

'And they believed you?' said Cruyer.

'No, but your average Russian has grown used to hearing lies. They didn't believe me but they weren't about to demonstrate a lot of initiative to disprove it. They made a feeble attempt to pull him away, but my driver and I picked him up and carried him out to our car. There was no way the Russians would touch a vehicle with British Army markings. They knew what would happen to anyone meddling with a Russian officer's car without permission. So that's how we brought him back to the West.'

'Why did he shoot at you?' I asked.

'You like that brandy, do you,' said Silas. 'Twenty years in the wood; it's not so easy to get hold of vintage brandy nowadays. Yes – well, he'd been watching me for a couple of days. He'd heard rumours that I was the one who'd put a lot of Gehlen's people in the bag, and his closest friend had got hurt in the roundup. But we talked about old times and he saw sense after a while.' I nodded. That vague explanation was Silas's polite way of telling me to mind my own business.

We watched Bret Rensselaer play, pocketing the red ball with a perfectly angled shot that brought the white back to the tip of his cue. He moved his position only slightly to make the next stroke. 'And you've been running him since 1946?' I said, looking at Silas.

'No, no, no,' said Silas. 'I kept him well away from our people in Hermsdorf. I had access to funds and I sent him back into the East Sector with instructions to lie low. He was with the Reichsbank during the war – his father was a stockbroker – and I knew that eventually the regime over there – Communist or not – would desperately need men with top-level banking experience.'

'He was your investment?' said Cruyer.

'Or, you might say, I was his investment,' said Silas. The game was slower now, each man taking more time to line up his shot as he thought about other things. Cruyer aimed, missed and cursed softly. Silas continued, 'We were both going to be in a position to help each other in the years ahead. That much was obvious. First he got a job with the tax people. Ever wondered how Communist countries first become Communist? It's not the secret police who do the deed, it's the tax collectors. That's how the Communists wiped out private companies: they increased the tax rate steeply according to the number of employees. Only firms with less than a dozen employees had a chance of surviving. When they'd destroyed private enterprise, Brahms Four was moved to the Deutsche Emissions und Girobank at the time of the currency reform.'

Dicky smiled triumphantly at me as he said to Silas, 'And that later became the Deutsche Notenbank.' Good guess, Dicky, I thought.

'How long was he a sleeper?' I asked.

'Long enough,' said Silas. He smiled and drank his port. 'Good port this,' he said, raising his glass to see the colour against the light from the window. 'But the bloody doctor has cut me back to one bottle a month – one bottle a month, I ask you. Yes, he was a sleeper all through the time when the service was rotten with traitors, when certain colleagues of ours were reporting back to the Kremlin every bloody thing we did. Yes, he was lucky, or clever, or a bit of both. His file was buried where no one could get at it. He survived. But, by God, I activated him once we'd got rid of those bastards. We were in bad shape, and Brahms Four was a prime source.'

'Personally?' said Dicky Cruyer. 'You ran him *personally*?' He exchanged his cue for another, as if to account for his missed stroke.

'Brahms Four made that a condition,' said Silas. 'There was a lot of that sort of thing at that time. He reported to me personally. I made him feel safer and it was good for me too.'

'And what happened when you were posted away from Berlin?' I asked him.

'I had to hand him over to another Control.'

'Who was that?' I asked.

Silas looked at me as if deciding whether to tell me, but he had already decided; everything was already decided by that time. 'Bret took over from me.' We all turned to look anew at Bret Rensselaer, a dark-suited American in his middle fifties, with fair receding hair and a quick nervous·smile. Bret was the sort of American who liked to be mistaken for an Englishman. Recruited into the service while at Oxford on a Rhodes scholarship, he'd become a dedicated Anglophile who'd served in many European stations before taking over as Deputy Controller of the European Economics desk, which later became the Economics Intelligence Committee and was now Bret's private empire. If Brahms Four dried up as a source, Bret Rensselaer's empire would virtually collapse. Little wonder he looked so nervous.

It was Bret's shot again. He balanced his cue as if checking its weight, then reached for the resin. 'I ran Brahms Four for years on a personal basis, just as Silas had done before me.'

'Did you ever meet him face to face?' I asked.

'No, I never went across to the East, and as far as I know, he never came out. He knew only my codename.' He finally finished with the resin and placed it carefully on the ledge of the scoreboard.

'Which you'd taken from Silas?' I said. 'What you're saying is that you carried on pretending to be Silas.'

'Sure I did,' said Bret, as if he'd intended to make this clear from the start. The only thing field men hate more than a Control change is a secret Control change with a name switch. It wasn't something any desk man would boast about. Bret had still not made his shot. He stood facing me calmly but speaking a little more rapidly now that he was on the defensive. 'Brahms Four related to Silas in a way no newcomer could hope to do. It was better to let him think his stuff was still coming to Silas.' He leaned over the table to make his shot. Characteristically it was faultless and so was his next, but the third pot went askew.

'Even though Silas had gone,' I said, moving aside and letting Silas see the table to choose his shot.

'I wasn't *dead*!' said Silas indignantly over his shoulder as he pushed past. 'I kept in touch. A couple of times, Bret came back here to consult with me. Frequently I sent a little parcel of forbidden goodies over to him. We knew he'd recognize the way I chose what he liked, and so on.'

'But after last year's big reshuffle he went soggy,' Bret Rensselaer added sadly. 'He went very patchy. Some great stuff still came from him but it wasn't one hundred per cent any more. He began to ask for more and more money too. No one minded that too much – he was worth everything he got – but we had the feeling he was looking for a chance to get out.'

'And now the crunch has come?' I asked.

'Could be,' said Bret.

'Or it could simply be the prelude for another demand for money,' said Silas.

'It's a pretty fancy one,' said Bret. 'A pretty damn complicated way of getting a raise in pay. No, I think he wants out. I think he really wants out this time.'

'What does he do with all this money?' I asked.

'We've never discovered,' said Bret.

'We've never been allowed to try,' said Cruyer bitterly. 'Each time we prepare a plan, it's vetoed by someone at the top.'

'Take it easy, Dicky,' said Bret in that kind and conciliatory tone a man can employ when he knows he's the boss. 'No point in upsetting a darn good source just in order to find he's got a mistress stowed away somewhere or that he likes to pile his dough into some numbered account in Switzerland.'

It was of course Silas who decided exactly how much it was safe to confide to me. 'Let's just say we pay it into a Munich bank to be credited to a publishing house that never publishes anything,' said Silas. If I was going over the wire, they'd make sure I knew only what they wanted me to know. That was the normal procedure; we all knew it.

'Hell, he wants a chance to spend his pay,' I said. 'Nothing wrong with that, is there?'

Silas turned to me with that spiteful look in his eye and said, 'Nothing wrong with that, unless you need the stuff he's sending us. Then there's everything wrong with it, Bernard. Everything wrong with it!' He cleared the pocket and sent the ball down the table with such violence that it rebounded all the way back to him. There was a cruel determination in him; I'd glimpsed it more than once.

'Okay, so you're trying to prove that I'm the only one who can go and talk to him,' I said. 'I guess that's what this friendly little game is all about. Or am I mistaken?' I fixed Silas with my stare and he smiled ruefully.

'You're not the right person,' said Bret unconvincingly. No one else spoke. They all knew I *was* the right person. This damn get-together was designed to show me the decision was unanimous. Dicky Cruyer touched his lips with the wet end of his cigar but did not put it into his mouth. Bret said, 'It would be like sending in the massed bands of the Brigade of Guards playing "Rule, Britannia!". Brahms Four will be terrified, and rightly so. You'll have a tail from the moment you go over.'

'I don't agree,' said Cruyer. They were talking about me as if I were not present; I had the feeling that this was the sort of discussion that would take place if I went into the bag, or got myself killed.

'Bernard knows his way about over there. And he doesn't have to be there very long – just a talk with him so that we know what's on his mind. And show him how important it is for him to stay in position for a couple of years.'

'What about you, Bernard?' Silas asked me. 'You haven't said much about it.'

'It sounds as if someone will have to go,' I said. 'And someone he knows would have a better chance of getting a straight answer.'

'And,' said Bret apologetically, 'there won't be much time. . . . Is that what you mean?'

Cruyer said, 'We sent a courier over by tour bus last month. He took the regular tourist bus over there and came back as easy as falling off a log.'

'Do they let the tourists from West Berlin get off the bus nowadays?' asked Silas.

'Oh, yes,' said Cruyer, smiling cheerfully. 'Things have changed since your day, Silas. They all visit the Red Army memorial. They even stop off for cakes and coffee – the DDR desperately needs Westmarks. Another good place for a meeting is the Pergamon Museum. Tour buses from the West go there too.'

'What do you think, Bernard?' said Bret. He fidgeted with his signet ring and stared at the table as if interested in nothing but Cruyer's tricky corner shot.

I found their sort of conjecture exasperating. It was the stuff of which long memos are made, the paperwork under which the Department is buried. I said, 'What's the use of my guessing? Everything depends upon knowing what he is doing. He's not a peasant, he's a scholarly old man with an important and interesting job. We need to know whether he's still got a happy marriage, with good friends who make speeches at the birth celebrations of his grandchildren. Or has he become a miserable old loner, at odds with the world and needing Western-style medical care. . . . Or maybe he's just discovered what it's like to be in love with a shapely eighteen-year-old nymphomaniac.'

Bret gave a short laugh and said, 'Two first-class tickets to Rio, and don't spare the champagne.'

'Unless the shapely one is working for the KGB,' I said.

Bret stared at me impassively. 'What would be the best way of "depositing" someone for this sort of job, Bernard?'

'I certainly wouldn't discuss with you guys the way I'd choose to go over there, except to say I wouldn't want any arrangements made from this end. No documents, no preparations, no emergency link, no local backup – nothing at all. I'd want to do it myself.' It was not the sort of private enterprise that the Department liked to encourage. I was expecting vociferous objections to this proposal, but none came.

'Quite right too,' said Silas.

'And I haven't agreed to go,' I reminded them.

'We leave it to you,' said Silas. The others, their faces only dimly seen in the gloom beyond the brightly lit table, nodded. Cruyer's hands, very white in the glare, crawled across the table like two giant spiders. He played the shot and missed. His mind wasn't on the game; neither was mine.

Silas pulled a face at Cruyer's missed stroke and sipped his port. 'Bernard,' he said suddenly. 'I'd better – ' He stopped mid-sentence. Mrs Porter had entered the room quietly. She was holding a cut-glass tumbler and a cloth. Silas looked up to meet her eyes.

'The phone, sir,' she said. 'It's the call from London.'

She didn't say who was calling from London because she took it for granted that Silas would know. In fact we all knew, or guessed, that it was someone urgently interested in how the discussion had gone. Silas rubbed his face, looked at me, and said, 'Bernard . . . help yourself to another brandy if you fancy it.'

'Thanks,' I said, but I had the feeling that Silas had been about to say something quite different.

Weekends with Uncle Silas always followed the same pattern: an informal Saturday lunch, a game of billiards or bridge until teatime, and a dress-up dinner. There were fourteen people for dinner that Saturday evening: us, the Cruyers, Rensselaer and his girlfriend, Fiona's sister Tessa – her husband away – to partner Uncle Silas, an American couple named Johnson, who were in England buying antique furniture for their shop in Philadelphia, a young trendy architect, who converted cottages into 'dream houses' and was making enough money at it to support a noisy new wife and a noisy old Ferrari, and a red-nosed local farmer, who spoke only twice the whole evening, and then only to ask his frizzy-haired wife to pass the wine.

'It was all right for you,' said Fiona petulantly when we were in the little garret room preparing for bed that night. 'I was sitting next to Dicky Cruyer. He only wants to talk about that beastly boat. He's going to France in it next month, he says.'

'Dicky doesn't know a mainsail from a marlinspike. He'll kill himself.'

'Don't say that, darling,' said Fiona. 'My sister Tessa is going too. And so is Ricky, that gorgeous young architect, and Colette, his amusing wife.' There was a touch of acid in her voice; she wasn't too keen on them. And she was still angry at being shut out of our conference in the billiards room.

'It must be a bloody big boat,' I said.

'It will sleep six . . . eight if you're all very friendly, Daphne told me. She's not going. She gets seasick.'

I looked at her quizzically. 'Is your sister having an affair with Dicky Cruyer?'

'How clever you are,' said Fiona in a voice from which any trace of admiration had been carefully eliminated. 'But you are behind the times, darling. She's fallen for someone much older, she told me.'

'She's a bitch.'

'Most men find her attractive,' said Fiona. For some reason Fiona got a secret satisfaction from hearing me condemn her sister, and was keen to provoke more of the same.

'I thought she was reconciled with her own husband.'

'It was a trial,' said Fiona.

'I'll bet it was,' I agreed. 'Especially for George.'

'You were sitting next to the antique lady – was she amusing?'

'A lady in the antique business.' I corrected her description, and she smiled. 'She told me to beware of dressers, they are likely to have modern tops and antique bottoms.'

'How bizarre!' said Fiona. She giggled. 'Where can I find one?'

'Right here,' I said, and jumped into bed with her. 'Give me that damned hot-water bottle.'

'There's no hot-water bottle. That's me! Oh, your hands are freezing.'

I was awakened by one of the farm dogs barking, and then from somewhere across the river there came the echoing response of some other dog on some other farm. I opened my eyes to see the time and found the bedside light on. It was four o'clock in the morning. Fiona was in her dressing gown drinking tea. 'I'm sorry,' she said.

'It was the dog.'

'I can never sleep properly away from home. I went downstairs and made tea. I brought up an extra cup – would you like some?'

'Just half a cup. Have you been awake long?'

'I thought I heard someone go downstairs. It's a creepy old house, isn't it? There's a biscuit if you want it.' I took just the tea and sipped some. Fiona said, 'Did you promise to go? Berlin – did you promise?' It was as if she felt my decision would reveal how important she was to me compared with my job.

I shook my head.

'But that's what your billiards game was all about? I guessed so. Silas was so adamant about not having any of us in there. Sometimes I wonder if he realizes that I'm senior staff now.'

'They're all worried about the Brahms Four business.'

'But why send you? What reason did they give?'

'Who else could go? Silas?' I told her the essence of the conversation that had taken place in the billiards room. The dogs began barking again. From downstairs I heard a door closing and then Silas trying to quieten the dogs. His voice was hoarse and he spoke to them in the same way he spoke to Billy and Sally.

'I saw the memo that Rensselaer sent to the D-G,' Fiona said, speaking more quietly now as if frightened that we might be overheard. 'Five pages. I took it back to my office and read it through.' I looked at her in surprise. Fiona was not the sort of person who disobeyed the regulations so flagrantly. 'I had to know,' she added.

I drank my tea and said nothing. I wasn't even sure I wanted to know what Rensselaer and Dicky Cruyer had in store for me.

'Brahms Four might have gone crazy,' she said finally. 'Bret and Dicky both suggest that as a real possibility.' She waited while the words took effect. 'They think he might have had some kind of mental breakdown. That's why they are worried. There's simply no telling what he might do.'

'Is that what it said in the memo?' I laughed. 'That's just Bret and Dicky covering their asses.'

'Dicky suggested that they let some high-powered medical people attempt a diagnosis on the basis of Brahms Four's reports but Bret squashed that.'

'It sounds just like one of Cruyer's bright ideas,' I said. 'Let the headshrinkers into a meeting and we'll be the front page of next week's Sunday newspapers' review section, complete with misquotes, misspellings and bits written "by our own correspondents". Thank Christ Bret killed that one. What form does the Brahms Four madness take?'

'The usual sort of paranoia: enemies round every corner, no one he can trust. Can he have a full list of everyone with access to his reports? Do we know there are top-level leaks of everything he sends us? The usual sort of loony stuff that people imagine when they're going round the bend.'

I nodded. Fiona didn't have the faintest idea of what an agent's life was like. Dicky and Bret had no idea either. None of these desk bastards knew. My father used to say, 'Eternal paranoia is the price of liberty. Vigilance is not enough.'

'Maybe Brahms Four is right,' I said. 'Maybe there *are* enemies round every corner over there.' I remembered Cruyer telling me the way the Department helped Brahms Four to ingratiate himself with the regime. He must have made a lot of enemies. 'Maybe he's not so loony.'

'And top-level security leaks too?' Fiona said.

'It wouldn't be the first time, would it?'

'Brahms Four asked for you. Did they tell you that?'

'No.' I concealed my surprise. So that was at the back of all their anxiety in the billiards room.

'He doesn't want any more contact with his regular Control. He's told them he'll deal with no one but you.'

'I'll bet that finally convinced the D-G that he was crazy.' I put the empty teacup on the side table and switched out my bedside light. 'I've got to get some sleep,' I told her. 'I wish I could manage on five hours a night like you, but I need a lot of sack time.'

'You won't go, will you? Promise you won't.'

I grunted and buried my face in the pillow. I always sleep face downwards; it stays dark longer that way.

5

On Monday afternoon I was in Bret Rensselaer's office. It was on the top floor not far from the suite the D-G occupied. All the top-floor offices were decorated to the personal taste of the occupants; it was one of the perks of seniority. Bret's room was 'modern', with glass and chrome and grey carpet. It was hard, austere and colourless, a habitat just right for Bret, with his dark worsted Savile Row suit and the crisp white shirt and club tie, and his fair hair that was going white, and the smile that seemed shy and fleeting but was really the reflex action that marked his indifference.

The nod, the smile, and the finger pointed at the black leather chesterfield did not interrupt the conversation he was having on his white phone. I sat down and waited for him to finish telling a caller that there was no chance of them meeting for lunch that day, next day, or any day in the future.

'Are you a poker player, Bernard?' he said even while he was putting the phone down.

'Only for matchsticks,' I replied cautiously.

'Ever wonder what will happen to you when you retire?'

'No,' I said.

'No plans to buy a bar in Málaga, or a market garden in Sussex?'

'Is that what you're planning?' I said.

Bret smiled. He was rich, very rich. The idea of him working a market garden in Sussex was hilarious. As for Málaga and its plebeian diversions, he'd divert the plane rather than enter its air space. 'I guess your wife has money,' said Rensselaer. He paused. 'But I'd say you're the type of inverted snob who wouldn't want to use any of it.'

'Would that make me an inverted snob?'

'If you were smart enough to invest her dough and double it, you'd do no one any harm. Right?'

'In the evenings, you mean? Or would that be instead of working here?'

'Every time I ask you questions, I find you asking me questions.'

'I didn't know I was being questioned,' I said. 'Am I being vetted?'

'In this business it does no harm to flip the pages of someone's bank account from time to time,' said Rensselaer.

'You'll find only moths in mine,' I said.

'No family money?'

'Family money? I was thirty years old before I got a nanny.'

'People like you who've worked in the field always have money and securities stashed away. I'll bet you've got numbered bank accounts in a dozen towns.'

'What would I put into them, luncheon vouchers?'

'Goodwill,' he said 'Goodwill. Until the time comes.' He picked up the short memo I'd sent him about Werner Volkmann's import-export business. So that was it. He was wondering if I was sharing the profit in Werner's business.

'Volkmann is not making enough dough to pay handsome kick-backs, if that's what you're thinking,' I said.

'But you want the Department to bankroll him?' He was still standing behind his desk; he liked being on his feet, moving about like a boxer, shifting his weight and twisting his body as if avoiding imaginary blows.

'You'd better get yourself some new bifocals,' I said. 'There's no suggestion that the Department give him a penny.'

Bret smiled. When he got tired of playing the shy Mr Nice Guy, he'd suddenly go for confrontation, accusation and insult. But at least he was unlikely to go behind your back. 'Maybe I read it hurriedly. What the hell is forfaiting anyway?'

Bret was like those High Court judges who lean over and ask what is a male chauvinist, or a mainframe computer. They know what they think these things are, but they want them defined by mutual agreement and written into the court record.

'Volkmann raises cash for West German companies so they can be paid promptly after exporting goods to East Germany.'

'How does he do that?' said Bret, looking down and fiddling with some papers on his desk.

'There's a hell of a lot of complicated paperwork,' I said. 'But the essential part of it is that they send details of the shipment and the prices to an East German bank. They sign them and rubber-stamp them and agree that it's all okay with the East German importers. They also agree on the dates of the payments. Volkmann goes to a bank, or a syndicate of banks, or any other source of cash in the West, and uses that "aval" to discount the cash that pays for the goods.'

'It's like factoring?'

'It's more complicated, because you're dealing with a lot of people, most of them bureaucrats.'

'And your pal Volkmann gets a margin on each deal. That's sweet.'

'It's a tough business, Bret,' I said. 'There are a lot of people offering to cut a fraction of a percentage off the next one, to get the business.'

'But Volkmann has no banking background. He's a hustler.'

I breathed in slowly. 'You don't have to be a banker to get into it,' I said patiently. 'Werner Volkmann has been doing these forfaiting deals for several years now. He has good contacts in the East. He moves in and out of the Eastern Sector with minimum fuss. They like him because they know he tries to do tie-in deals with East German exports – '

Bret held up his hand. 'What tie-in deals?'

'A lot of the banks just want to handle cash. Werner is prepared to shop around for a customer in the West who'll take some East German exports. In that way he can save them some hard currency or maybe even swing a deal where the export price equals the money due for the imports.'

'Is that so?' said Bret reflectively.

'Volkmann could be very useful for us, Bret,' I said.

'How?'

'Moving money, moving goods, moving people.'

'We do that already.'

'But how many people do we have who can go back and forth without question?'

'So what's Volkmann's problem?'

'You know what Frank Harrington is like. He doesn't get along with Werner, and never has.'

'And anyone Frank doesn't like, Berlin never uses.'

'Frank *is* Berlin,' I said. 'It's a small staff there now, Bret. Frank has to approve every damned thing.'

'And you want me to tell Frank how to run his Berlin office?'

'Do you ever read anything I send you, Bret? It says there that I just want the Department to approve a rollover guarantee of funds from one of our own merchant banks.'

'And that's money,' said Bret triumphantly.

'We're simply talking about one of our own banking outfits using their own expertise to give Werner normal facilities at current bank rates.'

'So why can't he get that already?'

'Because the sort of banks which best back these forfaiting deals want to know who Werner Volkmann is. And this Department has an old-fashioned rule that onetime field agents shouldn't go around giving the D-G as a reference, or saying that the way they got to learn about the forfaiting business was by running agents across the Wall since they were eighteen years old.'

'So tell me how Volkmann has stayed in business.'

'By going outside the regular banking network, by raising money from the money market. But that means trimming his agent's fee. It's making life tough for him. If he gives up the forfaiting business, we'll lose a good opportunity and a useful contact.'

'Suppose he fouls up on one of these deals and the bank doesn't get its money.'

'Oh, for Christ's sake, Bret. The boys in the bank are big enough to change their own nappies.'

'And they'll squeal bloody murder.'

'What do we have those lousy banks for, unless it's for this kind of job?'

'What kind of dough are we talking about?'

'A million Deutschemark rolling over would be about right.'

'Are you out of your tiny mind?' said Bret. 'A million D-mark? For that no good son of a bitch? No, sir.' He scratched the side of his nose. 'Did Volkmann put you up to all this?'

'Not a word. He likes to show me what a big success he is.'

'So how do you know he's strapped for cash?'

'In this business,' I said, 'it does no harm to flip the pages of someone's bank account from time to time.'

'One of these days you'll come unstuck doing one of your unofficial investigations into something that doesn't concern you. What would you do if the bells started ringing?'

'I'd just swear it was an *official* investigation,' I said.

'The hell you would,' said Rensselaer.

I started to leave the room. 'Before you go,' he said, 'what would you say if I told you that Brahms Four asked for you? Suppose I said he won't trust anyone else in the Department? What would you say about that?'

'I'd say he sounds like a good judge of character.'

'Okay, smart ass. Now let's have an answer for the record.'

'It could simply mean he trusts me. He doesn't know many Department people on personal terms.'

'Very diplomatic, Bernard. Well, downstairs in Evaluation they are beginning to think Brahms Four has been turned. Most people I've spoken with downstairs are now saying Brahms Four might have been a senior KGB man from the time Silas Gaunt first encountered him in that bar.'

'And most people downstairs,' I said patiently, 'wouldn't recognize a senior bloody KGB officer if he walked up to them waving a red flag.'

Rensselaer nodded as if considering this aspect of his staff for the first time. 'Could be you're right, Bernard.' He always said Bernard with the accent on the second syllable; it was the most American thing about him.

It was at that moment that Sir Henry Clevemore came into the room. He was a tall aloof figure, slightly unkempt, with that well-worn appearance that the British upper class cultivate to show they are not *nouveau riche*.

'I'm most awfully sorry, Bret,' said the Director-General as he caught sight of me. 'I had no idea you were in conference.' He frowned as he looked at me and tried to remember my name. 'Good to see you, Samson,' he said eventually. 'I hear you spent the weekend with Silas. Did you have a good time? What has he got down there, fishing?'

'Billiards,' I said. 'Mostly billiards.'

The D-G gave a little smile and said, 'Yes, that sounds more like Silas.' He turned away to look at Bret's desk top. 'I've mislaid my spectacles,' he said. 'Did I leave them in here?'

'No, sir. You haven't been in here this morning,' said Bret. 'But I seem to remember that you keep spare reading glasses in the top drawer of your secretary's desk. Shall I get them for you?'

'Of course, you're right,' said the D-G. 'The top drawer, I remember now. My secretary's off sick this morning. I'm afraid I simply can't manage when she's away.' He smiled at Bret, and then at me, to make it perfectly clear that this was a joke born out of his natural humility and goodwill.

'The old man's got a lot on his plate right now,' said Bret loyally after Sir Henry had ambled off along the corridor muttering apologies about interrupting our 'conference'.

'Does anyone know who'll take over when he goes?' I asked Bret. Goes ga-ga, I almost said.

'There's no date fixed. But could be the old man will get back into his stride again, and go on for the full three years.' I looked at Bret and he looked back at me, and finally he said, 'Better the devil you know than the devil you don't know, Bernard.'

6

The two sisters were not much alike. My wife, Fiona, was dark with a wide face and a mouth that smiled easily. Tessa, the younger one, was light-haired, almost blonde, with blue eyes and a serious expression that made her look like a small child. Her hair was straight and long enough to touch her shoulders, and she sometimes flicked it back behind her, or let it fall forward across her face so that she looked through it.

It was no surprise to find Tessa in my drawing room when I got back from the office. The two of them were very close – the result perhaps of having suffered together the childhood miseries that their pompous autocratic father thought 'character forming' – and Fiona had been working hard over the past year to patch together Tessa's marriage to George, a wealthy car dealer.

There was an open bottle of champagne in the ice bucket, and already the level was down as far as the label. 'Are we celebrating something?' I asked as I took off my coat and hung it in the hall.

'Don't be so bloody bourgeois,' said Tessa, handing me a champagne flute filled right to the brim. That was one of the problems of marrying into wealth; there were no luxuries.

'Dinner at eight-thirty,' said Fiona, embracing me decorously, her champagne held aloft so that she would spill none of it while giving me a kiss. 'Mrs Dias has kindly stayed late.'

Mrs Dias, our Portuguese cook, housekeeper and general factotum, was always staying late to cook the dinner. I wondered how much her labour was costing us. The cost, like so many other household expenses, would end up buried somewhere deep in the accounts and paid for out of Fiona's trust-fund income. She knew I didn't like it, but I suppose she disliked cooking even more than arguing with me about it. I sat down on the sofa and tasted the champagne. 'Delicious,' I said.

'Tess brought it with her,' explained Fiona.

'A gift from an admirer,' said Tessa archly.

'Am I permitted to ask his name?' I said. I saw Fiona glaring at me but I pretended not to be aware of it.

'All in good time, darling,' said Tessa. 'For the moment he remains incognito.'

'In flagrante delicto, did you say?'

'You sod!' she said, and laughed.

'And how's George?' I said.

'We live our own lives,' said Tessa.

'Don't upset Tessa,' Fiona told me.

'He's not upsetting me,' Tessa said, tossing her hair back with her bejewelled white hand. 'I like George and I always will like him. We're simply not able to live together without quarrelling.'

'Does that mean you're getting a divorce?' I asked, drinking a little more of the champagne.

'George doesn't want a divorce,' she explained. 'It suits him to use the house like a hotel during the week, and he has the cottage to take his fancy ladies to.'

'Does George have fancy ladies?' I said with no more than perfunctory interest.

'It has been known,' said Tessa. 'But he's making so much money these days, I don't think he has much time for anything but his business.'

'Lucky man,' I said. 'Everyone else I know is going broke.'

'Well, that's where George is so clever,' Tessa explained. 'He got the dealerships for smaller, cheaper cars years ago when no one seemed to want them.' She said it proudly. Even wives who quarrel with their husbands take pride in their achievements.

Fiona reached for the champagne. She wrapped it in a cloth and poured the rest of it into our glasses with the dexterity of a sommelier. She took care not to touch the bottle on the glass, and the cloth was crossed so as to leave the label still visible as she served. Such professional niceties came naturally to someone who'd grown up in a house with domestic servants. As she poured mine, she said, 'Tess wants me to help her find a flat.'

'And furnish it and do it up,' said Tessa. 'I'm no earthly good at anything like that. Look at the mess I made of the place I'm living in now. George never liked it there. Sometimes I think that was where our marriage began to go all wrong.'

'But it's a lovely house,' said Fiona loyally. 'It's just too big for the two of you.'

'It's old and dark,' said Tessa. 'It's a bit of a dump, really. I can understand why George hates it. He only agreed to buying it because he wanted to have an address in Hampstead. It was a step up from Islington. But now he says we can afford Mayfair.'

'And this new place,' I inquired. 'Is George going to like that?'

'Give over!' said Tessa, employing the jocular cockney accent that she thought particularly apt when talking to me. 'I haven't found a place yet – that's what I want help with. I go and see places but I can never make up my mind on my own. I listen to what these sharp estate agents tell me and I believe it – that's my trouble.'

Whatever kind of trouble Tessa had suffered in her life, it was not on account of her believing anything any man told her, but I did not contradict her. I nodded and finished my drink. It was almost time for dinner. The ever-cheerful Mrs Dias was an adequate cook but I wasn't sure I could face another plate of her feijoada.

'You wouldn't mind, darling, would you?' said Fiona.

'Mind what?' I said. 'Oh, you helping Tessa find a flat. No, of course not.'

'You're a sweetie,' Tessa told me, and to Fiona she said, 'You're lucky to have got your hands on Bernard before I saw him. I've always said he was a wonderful husband.'

I said nothing. Only Tessa could make being a wonderful husband sound like a carrier of pestilence.

Tessa leaned back on the sofa. She was wearing a smoky grey silk button-through dress that was shiny on the curves. One hand held her champagne and the other was toying with a real pearl necklace. Nervously she crossed and recrossed her legs and twisted the pearls tight against her white neck.

'Tessa wants to tell you something,' Fiona said.

'Any more of that champagne, darling?' I said.

'Tessa's Dom Pérignon is all finished,' said Fiona. 'You'll have to have Sainsbury's from the fridge.'

'Sainsbury's from the fridge sounds delicious,' I said, passing my empty glass to her. 'What do you want to ask me, Tessa?'

'Do you know a man named Giles Trent?' she said.

'Works for the FO. Tall man, grey wavy hair, low voice, upper-crust accent. Older than me, and not nearly so handsome.'

'Not exactly for the Foreign Office,' said Tessa archly. 'His office is in the FO, but he's a part of your organization.'

'Did he tell you that?' I said.

'Yes,' said Tessa.

'He shouldn't have,' I said.

'I know,' said Tessa. 'I was talking to Fiona about him, and she says that Giles Trent was working with your lot in Berlin back in 1978. She says he's quite important.'

Fiona came in with the champagne and poured a glass for me. I said, 'Well, if that's what Fiona says. . . .'

Fiona said, 'Tessa is my sister, darling. She's not going to go blurting out all your secrets to the Russians. Are you, Tess?'

'Not until the right Russian comes my way. Even then . . . I mean, did you ever see those photos of Russian ladies?' She held the pearl necklace in her mouth; it was a babyish gesture; she liked being a baby.

'What about Giles Trent?' I said.

Tessa toyed with the necklace again. 'I got to know him last summer. I met him at a dinner party given by some people who live down the road from us. He had tickets for Covent Garden – Mozart. I forget the name of the opera, but everyone was saying how difficult it was to get tickets, and Giles could get them. Well, it was heavenly. I'm not awfully keen on opera but we had a box and a bottle of champagne in the interval.'

'And you had an affair with him,' I finished it for her.

'He's a handsome brute, Bernie. And George was away watching the Japanese making motorcars.'

'Why not go with him?' I said.

'If you'd ever been on one of those trips that car manufacturers provide for the dealers, you wouldn't ask. Wives are superfluous, darling. There are hot and cold running girls in every bedroom.'

Fiona poured champagne for herself and Tessa, and said, 'Tess wants to tell you about Giles Trent. She doesn't want your advice on her marriage.' This admonition, like all such wifely admonitions, was delivered with a smile and a laugh.

'So tell me about Giles Trent,' I said.

'You were joking just now, I know. But Giles is older than you, Bernie, quite a bit older. He's a bachelor, very set in his ways. I thought he was queer at first. He's so neat and tidy and fussy about what he wears and what he eats and all that. In the kitchen – he has a divine house off the King's Road – all his chopping knives and saucepans are placed side by side, smallest on the left and biggest on the right. And it's so perfect that I was frightened to boil an egg and slice a loaf in case I spilled crumbs on the spotless tiled floor or marked the chopping board.'

'Tell me how you first discovered he wasn't queer,' I said.

'I said he wouldn't listen to me,' Tessa complained to Fiona. 'I said he'd just make sarcastic remarks all the time, and I was right.'

'It's serious, Bernard,' said my wife. She only called me Bernard when things were serious.

'You mean it's wedding bells for Tessa and Giles?'

'I mean Giles Trent is passing intelligence material to someone from the Russian Embassy.'

There was a long silence until finally I said, 'Shit.'

'Giles Trent has been in the service a long time,' said Fiona.

'Longer than I have,' I said. 'Giles Trent was lecturing at the training school by the time I got there.'

'In Berlin he was in Signals at one time,' said Fiona.

'Yes,' I said. 'And he compiled that training report for interrogators. I don't like the sound of that. Giles Trent, eh?'

'Giles Trent doesn't seem the type,' said Fiona. All the ladies had a soft spot for the elegant and gentlemanly Giles Trent. He raised his hat to them and always had a clean shirt.

'They never are the type,' I said.

'But no contact with field agents,' said Fiona.

'Well, let's be thankful for that at least,' I said. I looked at Tessa. 'Have you mentioned all this to anyone?'

'Only to Daddy,' said Tessa. 'He said forget all about it.'

'Good old Daddy,' I said. 'Always there when you need him.'

Mrs Dias came in bearing a large platter of shrimp fried in batter. 'Don't eat too many, sir,' she said in her shrill accent. 'Make you very fat.' The Portuguese are a lugubrious breed, and yet Mrs Dias was always smiling. I had the feeling that we were paying her too much.

'You're wonderful, Mrs Dias,' said my wife, smiling, although the smile faded when she recognized the shrimps as those she'd set aside in the kitchen to thaw for next day's lunch.

'She's a treasure,' said Tessa, taking a sample of the fried shrimp and burning her mouth so that she had to spit pieces of shrimp into her paper napkin. 'My God, it's hot,' she said, pulling a face.

Fiona, who hated anything fried in batter, waved a hand as I offered her the plate. I took one, blew on it, and ate it. It wasn't bad.

'We'll manage now, Mrs Dias,' said Fiona airily. I twisted round to see Mrs Dias standing at the door watching us with a big smile. She disappeared into the kitchen again. There was a cloud of smoke and a loud crash which we all pretended not to hear.

I said to Tessa, 'How do you know he's passing stuff to the Russians?'

'He told me,' she said.

'Just like that?'

'We'd started off in the middle of the afternoon drinking at some funny little club in Soho while Giles was watching the horses on TV. He won some money on one of the races and we went to the Ritz. We'd met a few friends by then, and Giles wanted to impress everyone by giving them dinner. I suggested Annabel's – George is a member. We stayed there late and Giles turned out to be a super dancer. . . .'

'Is this all leading up to something he told you in bed?' I said wearily.

'Well, yes. We went back to this dear little place he has off the King's Road. And I'd had a few drinks, and to tell you the truth I thought of George with all those Oriental popsies and I thought, what the hell. And I let Giles talk me into staying there.'

'What exactly did he say, Tessa? Because it's nearly half past eight and I'm getting hungry.'

'He woke me up in the middle of the night. It was absolutely ghastly. He sat up in bed and howled. It was positively orgasmic, darling. You've no idea. He howled for help or something. It was a nightmare. I mean, I've had nightmares and I've seen other people having nightmares – at school half the girls in the dorm had nightmares every night, didn't they, Fi? – but not like this. He was bathed in sweat and trembling like a leaf.'

'Giles Trent?' I said.

'Yes, I know. It's hard to imagine, isn't it? I mean he's so damned stiff-upper-lip and Grenadier Guards. But there he was shouting and having this nightmare. I had to shake him for ages before he awoke.'

Fiona said, 'Tell Bernie what he was shouting.'

'He shouted, "Help me! They made me do it," and "Please please please." Then I went and got him a big drink of Perrier water. He said that was what he wanted. He pulled himself together and seemed all right again. And then he suddenly asked me what I'd say if he told me he was a spy for the Russians. I said I'd laugh. And he nodded and said, well, it was true anyway. So I said, for money, do you do it for money? I was joking because I thought he was joking, you see.'

'So what did he say about money?' I asked.

'I knew he wasn't short of money,' said Tessa. 'He was at Eton and he knows anyone who's anyone. He has the same tailor as Daddy, and he's not cheap. And Giles is a member of so many clubs and you know how much club subscriptions cost nowadays. George is always on about that, but he has to take business people out, of course. But Giles never complains about money. His father bought him the freehold of this place where he lives and gave him an allowance that is enough to keep body and soul together.'

'And he has his salary,' I said.

'Well, that doesn't go far, Bernie,' said Tessa. 'How do you imagine you and Fiona would manage if all she had was your salary?'

'Other people manage,' I said.

'But not people like us,' said Tessa in a voice of sweet reasonableness. 'Poor Fiona has to buy Sainsbury's champagne because she knows you'll grumble if she gets the sort of champers Daddy drinks.'

Hurriedly Fiona said, 'Tell Bernie what Giles said about meeting the Russian.'

'He told me about meeting this fellow from the Trade Delegation. Giles was in a pub somewhere near the Portobello Road one night. He likes finding new pubs that no one knows about except the locals. It was closing time. He asked the publican for another drink and they wouldn't serve him. Then a man standing at the counter offered to take him to a chess club in Soho – Kar's Club in Gerrard Street. There's a members' bar there which serves drinks until three in the morning. This Russian was a member and offered to put Giles up for membership and Giles joined. It's not much of a place, from what I can gather – arty people and writers, and so on. He plays chess rather well, and it began to be a habit that he went there regularly and played the Russian, or just watched someone else playing.'

'When was the night of this nightmare?' I said.

'I don't remember exactly, but a little while ago.'

'And he's told you about the Russians on several occasions. Or just that once in the middle of the night?'

'I brought it up again,' said Tessa. 'I was curious. I wanted to find out if it was a joke or not. Giles Trent remembered your name, and he knows Fiona too, so I guessed that he was on secret work of some kind. Last Friday, we got back to his place very late and he was showing me this electronic chess-playing machine he'd just bought. I said that he wouldn't have to go to that chess club anymore. He said he liked going there. I asked him if he wasn't frightened that someone would see him with this Russian and suspect him of spying. Giles collapsed on the bed and muttered something about they might be right if that's what they suspected. He had been drinking a lot that night – mostly brandy, and I'd noticed before that it affects him in a way other drinks don't.'

By now Tessa had become very quiet and serious. It was a new sort of Tessa. I'd only known her in her role of uninhibited adventuress. 'Go on,' I prompted her.

Tessa said, 'Well, I still thought he was joking, and I was just making a gag out of it. But he wasn't joking. "I wish to God I could get out of it," he said. "But they've got me now and I'll never be free of them. I will end up at the Old Bailey sentenced to thirty years." I said, couldn't he escape? Couldn't he get on a plane and go somewhere?'

'What did he say?'

' "And end up in Moscow? I'd sooner be in an English prison listening to English voices cursing me than spend the rest of my life in Moscow. Can you imagine what it must be like?" he said. And he went on all about the sort of life that Kim Philby and those other two had in Moscow. I realized then that he must have been reading up all about it and worrying himself to death.'

Tessa sipped her champagne.

Fiona said, 'What will happen now, Bernie?'

'We can't leave it like this,' I said. 'I'll have to make it official.'

'I don't want Tessa's name brought into it,' said Fiona.

Tessa was looking at me. 'How can I promise that?' I said.

'I'd sooner let it drop,' said Tessa.

'Let it drop?' I said. 'This is not some camper who's trampled through your dad's barley field, and you being asked if you want to press charges for trespass. This is espionage. If I don't report what you've told me, I could be in the dock at the Old Bailey with him, and so could you and Fiona.'

'Is that right?' said Tessa. It was typical of her that she asked her sister rather than me. There was a simple directness about everything Tessa said and did, and it was difficult to remain angry with her for long. She confirmed all those theories about the second child. Tessa was sincere but shallow; she was loving but mercurial; she was an exhibitionist without enough confidence to be an actor. While Fiona displayed all the characteristics of elder children: stability, confidence, intellect in abundance, and that cold reserve with which to judge all the shortcomings of the world.

'Yes, Tess. What Bernie says is right.'

'I'll see what I can do,' I said. 'I can't promise anything. But I'll tell you this: if I am able to keep your name out of it and you let me down by breathing a word of this conversation to anyone at all, including that father of yours, I'll make sure you and he and anyone else covering up are charged under the appropriate sections of the Act.'

'Thank you, Bernie,' said Tessa. 'It would be so rotten for George.'

'He's the only one I'm thinking of,' I said.

'You're not so tough,' she said. 'You're a sweetie at heart. Do you know that?'

'You ever say that again,' I told Tessa, 'and I'll punch you right in the nose.'

She laughed. 'You're so funny,' she said.

Fiona went out of the room to get a progress report on the cooking. Tessa moved along the sofa to be closer to where I was sitting at the other end of it. 'Is he in bad trouble? Giles – is he in bad trouble?' There was a note of anxiety in her voice. It was uncharacteristically deferent to me, the sort of voice one uses to a physician about to make a prognosis.

'If he cooperates with us, he'll be all right.' It wasn't true of course, but I didn't want to alarm her.

'I'm sure he'll cooperate,' she said, sipping her drink and then looking at me with a smile that said she didn't believe a word of it.

'How long since he met this Russian?' I asked.

'Quite a time. You could find out from when he joined the chess club, couldn't you?' Tessa shook her glass and watched the bubbles rise. She was using some of the skills she'd learned at drama school the year before she'd met George and married him instead of becoming a film star. She leaned her head to one side and looked at me meaningfully. 'There's nothing bad in Giles, but sometimes he can be a fool.'

'I'll have to speak to you again, Tessa. You'll probably have to repeat it all to an investigating officer and write it out and sign it.'

She placed a finger on the rim of her glass and ran it round a couple of times. 'I'll help you on condition you go easy on Giles.'

'I'll go easy,' I promised. Hell, what else could I say?

Dinner was served on the Minton china and the table set with wedding presents: antique silver cutlery from Fiona's parents and a cut-glass vase that my father had discovered in one of the Berlin junk markets he visited regularly on Saturday mornings. The circular dining table was very big for three people, so we seated ourselves side by side, with Tessa between us. The main course was some sort of chicken stew, the quantity of it far too small for the serving dish in which it came to the table. Mrs Dias had a big gravy mark on her white apron and she was no longer smiling. After Mrs Dias had returned to the kitchen, Fiona whispered that Mrs Dias had broken the small serving dish and half the chicken stew had gone onto the kitchen floor.

'Why the hell are we whispering?' I said.

'I knew you'd start shouting,' said Fiona.

'I'm not shouting,' I said. 'I'm simply asking. . . .'

'We all heard you,' said Fiona. 'And if you upset Mrs Dias and we lose her. . . .' She left it unsaid.

'But why are you trying to make *me* feel guilty?' I said.

'He's always like this when something gets broken,' said Fiona. 'Unless, of course, he did it himself.'

I shared out what little there was of the chicken. I took plenty of boiled rice. Fiona had opened one of the few good clarets left in the cupboard, and I poured it gratefully.

'Would you like to come and stay with me while Bernard's away?' Fiona asked her sister.

'Where are you going?' Tessa asked me.

'It's not settled yet.' I said. 'I'm not sure I'm going anywhere.'

'Berlin,' said Fiona. 'I hate being here alone.'

'I'd love to, darling,' Tessa said. 'When?'

'I've told you, it's not arranged yet,' I said. 'I might not go.'

'Soon,' said Fiona. 'Next week, or the week following.'

Mrs Dias came in to remove the plates and solicit praise and gratitude for her cookery; these were provided in abundance by Fiona, with Tessa echoing her every superlative.

'Senhor Sam?' To her I was always Senhor Sam; she never said Senhor Samson. 'Senhor Sam . . . he like it?' She asked Fiona this question rather than addressing it to me. It was rather like hearing Uncle Silas and Bret Rensselaer and Dicky Cruyer discussing my chances of escaping from Berlin alive.

'Look at his plate,' said Fiona cheerfully. 'Not a scrap left, Mrs Dias.'

There was nothing left because my share was one lousy drumstick and the wishbone. The greater part of the chicken stew was now spread out on kitchen foil in the garden, being devoured by the neighbourhood's cat population. I could hear them arguing and knocking over the empty milk bottles outside the back door. 'It was delicious, Mrs Dias,' I said, and Fiona rewarded me with a beaming smile that vanished as the kitchen door closed. 'Do you have to be so bloody ironic?' said Fiona.

'It was delicious. I told her it was delicious.'

'Next time, you can interview the women the agency send round. Maybe then you'd realize how lucky you are.'

Tessa hugged me. 'Don't be hard on him, Fiona darling. You should have heard George when the au pair dropped his wretched video recorder.'

'Oh, that reminds me,' Fiona said, leaning forward to catch my attention. 'You wanted to record that W. C. Fields film tonight.'

'Right!' I said. 'What time was it on?'

'Eight o'clock,' said Fiona. 'You've missed it, I'm afraid.'

Tessa reached up to put her hand over my mouth before I spoke.

Mrs Dias came in with some cheese and biscuits. 'I told him to set the timer,' said Fiona, 'but he wouldn't listen.'

'Men are like that,' said Tessa. 'You should have said *don't* set the timer, then he would have set it. I'm always having to do that sort of thing with George.'

Tessa left early. She had arranged to see 'an old schoolfriend' at the Savoy Hotel bar. 'That must be some school!' I said to Fiona when she came back into the drawing room after seeing her sister to the door. I always let her see her sister to the door. There were always sisterly little confidences exchanged at the time of departure.

'She'll never change,' said Fiona.

'Poor George,' I said.

Fiona came and sat next to me and gave me a kiss. 'Was I awful tonight?' she asked.

'*Asinus asino, et sus sui pulcher* – an ass is beautiful to an ass, so is a pig to a pig.'

Fiona laughed. 'You were always using Latin tags when I first met you. Now you don't do that any more.'

'I've grown up,' I said.

'Don't grow up too much,' she said. 'I love you as you are.'

I responded by kissing her for a long time.

'Poor Tess. It had to happen to her, didn't it. She's so muddle-headed. She can't remember her own birthday let alone the dates she met Giles. I'm so glad you didn't start shouting at her or want to list it all in chronological order.'

'Someone will eventually,' I said.

'Did you have a terrible day?' she asked.

'Bret Rensselaer won't let Werner use the bank.'

'Did you have a row with him?' said Fiona.

'He had to show me how tough you get after sitting behind a desk for fifteen years.'

'What did he say?'

I told her.

'I've seen you punch people for less than that,' said Fiona, having listened to my account of Rensselaer's tough-guy act.

'He was just sounding me out,' I said. 'I don't take any of that crap seriously.'

'None of it?'

'Rensselaer and Cruyer don't think that Brahms Four has been turned – neither does the D-G, you can bet on that. If they thought he was working for the KGB, we wouldn't be debating which member of the London staff goes over there to put his neck in a noose. If they really thought Brahms Four was a senior KGB man, they'd be burying that Berlin System file now, not passing it around to get "Immediate Action" tags. They'd be preparing the excuses and half-truths they'd need to explain their incompetence. They'd be getting ready to stonewall the questions that come when the story hits the fan.' I took the wine that Tessa had abandoned and added it to my own. 'And they don't have any worries about me either, or they wouldn't let me within a mile of the office while this was on the agenda.'

'They've *got* to deal with you, Brahms Four insists. I told you that.'

'What they really think is that Brahms Four is the best damned source they've had in the last decade. As usual, they only came to this conclusion when it looked like they were losing him.'

'And what do you make of this ghastly business with Trent?'

I hesitated. I was guessing now, and I looked at her so that she knew this was just a guess. 'The approach to Trent might be a KGB effort to penetrate the Department.'

'My God!' said Fiona in genuine alarm. 'A Russian move to access the Brahms Four intelligence at this end?'

'To find out where it's coming from. Brahms Four is one of the best-protected agents we have. And that's only because he did a deal with old Silas, and Silas stuck to his word. The only way they would be able to trace him would be by seeing the material we're receiving in London.'

'That's unthinkable,' said Fiona.

'Why?' I said.

'Because Giles could never get his hands on the Brahms Four material – that's all triple A. Even I have never seen it, and you only get the odds and ends you need to know.'

'But the Russians might not know that Giles couldn't get hold of it. To them he's senior enough to see anything he asks for.'

Fiona stared into my eyes, trying to see what was in my mind. 'Do you think that Brahms Four might have got word of a KGB effort to trace him?'

'Yes,' I said. 'That's exactly what I think. Brahms Four's demand for retirement is just his way of negotiating for a complete change in the contact chain.'

'It gets more and more frightening,' said Fiona. 'I really don't think you should go there. This is not just a simple little day trip. This is a big operation with lots at stake for both sides.'

'I can't think of anyone else they can send,' I said.

Fiona became suddenly angry. 'You bloody well want to go!' she shouted. 'You're just like all the others. You miss it, don't you? You really like all that bloody macho business!'

'I don't like it,' I said. It was true but she didn't believe me. I put my arms round her and pulled her close. 'Don't worry,' I said. 'I'm too old and too frightened to do anything dangerous.'

'You don't have to do anything dangerous in this business to get hurt.'

I didn't tell her that Werner had phoned me and asked me how soon I'd go back there. That would have complicated everything. I just told her I loved her, and that was the truth.

7

It was cold; damned cold: when the hell would summer come? With my hands in my pockets and my collar turned up, I walked through Soho. It was early evening but most of the shops were closed, their entrances piled high with garbage awaiting next morning's collection. It had become a desolate place, its charm long lost behind a pox of porn shops and shabby little 'adult' cinemas. I welcomed the smoky warmth of Kar's Club, and I welcomed the chance of one of the hot spiced rum drinks that were a speciality of the place no less than the chess.

Kar's Club was not the sort of place that Tessa would have liked. It was below ground level in Gerrard Street, Soho, a basement that had provided storage space for a wine company before an incendiary bomb burned out the upper storeys in one of the heavy German air raids of April 1941. It was three large interconnecting cellars with hardboard ceilings and noisy central heating, its old brickwork painted white to reflect the lights carefully placed over each table to illuminate the chessboards.

Jan Kar was a Polish ex-serviceman who'd started his little club when, after coming out of the Army at war's end, he realized he'd never return to his homeland again. By now he was an old man with a great mop of fine white hair and a magnificent drinker's nose. Nowadays his son Arkady was usually behind the counter, but the members were still largely Poles with a selection of other East European émigrés.

There was no one there I recognized, except two young champions in the second room whose game had already attracted half a dozen spectators. Less serious players, like me, kept to the room where the food and drink were dispensed. It was already half full. They were mostly elderly men, with beards, dark-ringed eyes and large curly pipes. In the far corner, under the clock, two silent men in ill-fitting suits glowered at their game and at each other. They played impatiently, taking every enemy in sight, as children play draughts. I was seated in the corner positioned so that I could look up from the chessboard, my book of chess problems and my drink, to see everyone who entered as they signed the members' book.

Giles Trent came in early. I studied him with new interest. He was younger-looking than I remembered him. He took off his brown narrow-brimmed felt hat in a quick and nervous gesture, like a schoolboy entering the headmaster's study. His grey wavy hair was long enough to hide the tops of his ears. He was so tall that the club's low ceiling caused him to lower his head as he passed under the pink tasselled lampshades. He put his riding mac on the bentwood hanger and ran his fingers through his hair as if it might have become disarranged. He was wearing a Glen Urquhart check suit of the sort favoured by wealthy bookmakers. It came complete with matching waistcoat and gold watchchain.

'Hello, Kar,' Trent said to the old man seated near the radiator, nursing his usual whisky and water. Most of the members called him Kar. Only some of the older Poles who'd served with him in Italy knew that Kar was his family name.

Trent stayed at the counter where young Arkady dispensed cold snacks, the inimitable rum punch that his father was said to have invented under battle conditions in Italy, good coffee, warm beer, iced vodka, poor advice about chess and unpalatable tea. Trent took rum punch.

'Mr Chlestakov hasn't been in tonight,' the youth told Trent.

Trent grunted and turned to look round the room. I stared down at my chess problem. By resting my chin in my hand, I was able to conceal my face from him.

Trent's Russian arrived about ten minutes later. He was wearing an expensive camel-hair coat and handmade shoes. He only came up to Trent's shoulder, a potbellied man with big peasant hands and a jolly face. When he took his hat off, he revealed dark hair brilliantined and carefully parted high on the crown of his head. He smiled when he saw Trent and slapped him on the shoulder, asked him how he was, and called him 'tovarisch'.

I recognized the type; he was the sort of Soviet official who liked to show the happy friendly side of life in the USSR. The kind of man who never arrived at a party without a couple of bottles of vodka, and winked to let you know he was an incorrigible rogue who'd break any rule for the sake of friendship.

Trent must have asked him what he wanted to drink. I heard the Russian say loudly, 'Vodka. I only come here to drink my Polish friend's fine buffalo-grass vodka.' He spoke the smooth English that is the legacy of the teaching machine but lacked the rhythms that can only come from hearing it spoken.

They sat down at the table Trent had selected. The Russian drank several vodkas, laughed a lot at whatever Trent was telling him, and ate pickled herring with black bread.

There was a chessboard and a box of well-worn chess pieces on every table. Trent opened the board and set up the chess pieces. He did it in the measured, preoccupied way that people do things when they are worrying about something else.

The Russian gave no sign of being worried. He bit into his fish hungrily and chewed the bread with obvious delight. And every now and again he would call across the room to ask old Jan Kar what the weather forecast was, the rate of exchange for the dollar, or the result of some sporting fixture.

Old Jan had been in a Russian prison camp from 1939 until he was released to go into the General Ander's Polish Corps. He did not like Russians, and the answers he gave were polite but minimal. Trent's Russian companion gave no sign of recognizing this latent hostility. He smiled broadly at each answer and nodded sympathetically to acknowledge old Jan's flat-toned negative answers.

I got up from my seat and went over to the counter to get another drink – coffee, this time – and from there, keeping my back towards them, I was able to hear what Trent was saying.

'Everything is slow,' said Trent. 'Everything takes time.'

'This is just a crazy idea that comes now into my head,' said the Russian. 'Take everything you have down to the photocopying shop in Baker Street, the same place you got the previous lot done.'

The Russian had spoken quite loudly and, although I didn't look round, I had the feeling that Trent had touched his sleeve in an effort to quieten him. Trent's voice was softer. 'Leave it with me,' he said. 'Leave it with me.' The words came in the anxious tones of someone who wants to change the subject.

'Giles, my friend,' said the Russian, his voice slurred as if by the effects of the vodka. 'Of course I leave it with you.'

I took the coffee that Jan's son poured and went back to my table. This time I sat on another chair to keep my back turned to Trent and the Russian, but I could see them reflected faintly in a fly-specked portrait of General Pilsudski.

I continued to work my way through one of the Capablanca's games against Alekhine in the 1927 championships, although I did not understand the half of it. But by the time Capablanca won, Trent and the Russian had disappeared up the stairs and out into the street.

'Can I join you, Bernard?' said old Jan Kar as I tipped my chess pieces into their box and folded my board. 'I haven't seen you for years.'

'I'm married now, Jan,' I said. 'And I never was much of a chess player.'

'I heard about your dad. I'm sorry. He was a fine man.'

'It's a long time ago now,' I said.

He nodded. He offered me a drink, but I told him I would have to leave very soon. He looked round the room. It was empty. Everyone was in the room next door watching a game that had developed into a duel. 'Working, are you? It was that Russian, wasn't it?'

'What Russian?' I said.

'Insolent bastard,' said Jan Kar. 'You'd think they wouldn't go where they're not welcome.'

'That would seriously limit their movements.'

'I'll keep it to myself, of course. And so will my son.'

'I wish you would, Jan,' I said. 'It's very delicate, very delicate.'

'I hate Russians,' said old Jan.

Giles Trent's house was one of a terrace of narrow-fronted Georgian-style dwellings erected by speculative builders when the Great Exhibition of 1851 made Chelsea a respectable address for senior clerks and shopkeepers. Near the front door – panelled and black, with a brass lion's-head knocker – stood Julian MacKenzie, a flippant youth who'd been with the Department no more than six months. I'd chosen him to keep an eye on Trent because I knew he wouldn't dare ask me too many questions about it or expect any paperwork.

'He arrived home in a cab about half an hour ago,' MacKenzie told me. 'There's no one inside with him.'

'Lights?'

'Just on the ground floor – and I think I saw some lights come on at the back. He probably went into the kitchen to make himself a cup of cocoa.'

'You can go off duty now,' I told MacKenzie.

'You wouldn't like me to come in with you?'

'Who said I'm going in?'

MacKenzie grinned. 'Well, good luck, Bernie,' he said cheerfully, and gave a mock salute.

'When you've been with the Department for nearly twenty years and the probationers are calling you Bernie,' I said, 'you start thinking that maybe you're not going to end up as Director-General.'

'Sorry, sir,' said MacKenzie. 'No offence intended.'

'Buzz off,' I said.

I had to knock and ring three times before I could get Giles Trent to open the door to me. 'What the devil is it?' he said before the door was even half open.

'Mr Trent?' I said deferentially.

'What is it?' He looked at me as if I was a complete stranger to him.

'It would be better if I came inside,' I said. 'It's not something we can talk about on the doorstep.'

'No, no, no. It's midnight,' he protested.

'It's Bernard Samson, from Operations,' I said. Why the hell had I been worrying about Giles Trent recognizing me in the club? Here I was on his doorstep and he was treating me like a vacuum-cleaner salesman. 'I work on the German desk with Dicky Cruyer.'

I'd hoped that this revelation would bring about a drastic change of mood, but he just grunted and stood back, muttering something about being sure it could wait until morning.

The narrow hall, with Regency striped wallpaper and framed engravings by Dutch artists I'd never heard of, gave onto a narrow staircase, and through an open door I could see a well-equipped kitchen. The house was in a state of perfect order: no nicks in the paintwork, no scuffs on the wallpaper, no marks on the carpet. Everything was in that condition that is the mark of those who are rich, fastidious and childless.

The hall opened onto the 'divine' living room that Tessa had promised. There was white carpet and white walls and gleaming white leather armchairs with brass buttons. There was even an almost colourless abstract painting over the white baby grand piano. I could not believe it was an example of Giles Trent's taste; it was the sort of interior that is designed at great expense by energetic divorcées who don't take cheques.

'It had better be important,' said Trent. He was staring at me. He didn't offer me a drink. He didn't even invite me to sit down. Perhaps my sort of trench coat didn't look good on white.

'It is important,' I said. Trent had taken off the tie he'd been wearing at Kar's Club, and now wore a silk scarf inside his open shirt. He'd replaced his jacket with a cashmere cardigan and his shoes with a pair of grey velvet slippers. I wondered if he always dressed with such trouble between coming home and going to bed, or whether his informal attire accounted for the delay before he opened the door to me. Or was he expecting a visit from Tessa?

'I remember you now,' he said suddenly. 'You're the one who married Fiona Kimber-Hutchinson.'

'Were you at Kar's Club tonight?' I said.

'Yes.'

'Talking to a member of the Russian Embassy staff?'

'It's a chess club,' said Trent. He went across to the chair where he'd been sitting, placed a marker in a paperback of Zola's *Germinal,* and put it on the shelf along with hardback copies of Agatha Christie and other detective stories. 'I speak to many people there. I play chess with anyone available. I don't know what they do for a living.'

'The man you were with is described in the Diplomatic List as a first secretary but I think he's a KGB man, don't you?'

'I didn't think about it, one way or the other.'

'Didn't you? You didn't think about it? Okay if I quote you on that one?'

'Don't threaten me,' said Trent. He opened a silver box on the table where the book had been and took a cigarette and lit it, blowing smoke in a gesture that might have been repressed anger. 'I'm senior in rank and service to you, Mr Samson. Don't come into my home trying the bullyboy tactics that work so well with other people of your own sort.'

'You can't believe that being senior in service and rank gives you the unquestioned right to have regular meetings with KGB agents and discuss the merits of various photocopying services.'

Trent went red in the face. He turned away from me, but that of course only drew attention to his discomfiture. 'Photocopying? What the hell are you talking about?'

'I hope you're not going to say that you were only going to photocopy chess problems. Or that you were meeting that KGB man on the orders of the D-G. Or that you were engaged on a secret assignment for a person who's name you are not permitted to tell me.'

Trent turned and came towards me. 'All I'm going to tell you,' he said, tapping my chest with his finger, 'is to leave my house right away. Any further conversation will be done through my lawyer.'

'I wouldn't advise you to consult a lawyer,' I said in the friendliest tone I could manage.

'Get out,' he said.

'Aren't you going to tell me that you'll make sure I'm fired from the Department?' I said.

'Get out,' he said again. 'And you tell whoever sent you that I intend to take legal action to safeguard my rights.'

'You've got no rights,' I said. 'You sign the Act regularly. Have you ever bothered to read what it says on that piece of paper?'

'It certainly doesn't say I'm not entitled to consult a lawyer when I have some little upstart force his way into my house and accuse me of treason, or whatever it is you're accusing me of.'

'I'm not accusing you of anything, Trent. I'm just asking you some simple questions to which you are supplying very complicated answers. If you start dragging lawyers into this dialogue, our masters are going to regard it as a very unfriendly reaction. They are going to see it as a confrontation, Trent. And it's the sort of confrontation you can't win.'

'I'll win.'

'Grow up, Trent. Even if you went to law and did the impossible and got a verdict against the Crown so that you were awarded damages and costs, do you think they'd give you your job back? And where would you go to find another job? No, Trent, you've got to put up with being quizzed by menials like me because it's all part of the job, your job. Your one and only job.'

'Wait a minute, wait a minute. There are a couple of things I want to get straight,' he said. 'Who says I've been in regular contact with this Russian diplomat?'

'We've got this funny system in interrogation – you wrote one of the training books, so you'll know about this – that it's the interrogator that asks the questions and the man being investigated that answers them.'

'Am I being investigated?'

'Yes, you are,' I said. 'And I think you are as guilty as hell. I think you're an agent working for the Russians.'

Trent touched the silk scarf at his neck, loosening it with his fingers, as if he was too hot. He was frightened now, frightened in the way that such a man could never be by physical violence. Trent enjoyed physical exertion, discomfort and even hardship. He'd learned to deal with such things at his public school. He was frightened of something quite different: he was terrified that damage was going to be done to the grand illusory image that he had of himself. It was part of my job to guess what frightened a man, and then not to dwell on it but rather let him pick at it himself while I talked of other, tedious things, giving him plenty of opportunity to peel back the scab of fear and expose the tender wound beneath.

So I didn't tell Trent about the misery and disgrace that would be waiting for him. Instead I told him how simple it would be for me to drop this investigation, and destroy my notes and papers, in exchange for having him walking into my office the next morning and making a voluntary statement. In that way there would be no investigation; Trent would report an overture made to him from a Russian diplomat and we would brief him on how to react.

'And would the Department allow that? Would they agree to it being something that starts with a report from me?'

There was, of course, no report to change or destroy. I hadn't mentioned my conversation with Tessa to anyone at all. I nodded sagely. 'Use your imagination, Trent. What do you think the D-G would prefer? If we discover you in contact with the Russians, we've got a disaster on our hands. But if you can be described as one of our people feeding stuff to the Russians, we've got a minor triumph.'

'I suppose you're right.'

'Of course I'm right. I know how these things work.'

'You'd want me to continue my meetings with him?'

'Exactly. You'd be working for us. You'd be making a fool of him.'

Trent smiled; he liked that.

After I'd been through my piece a couple of times, Trent became friendly enough to press a couple of drinks on me and thank me for my kindness and consideration. He repeated my instructions earnestly and thankfully, and he looked up to wait for my nod of approval. For by now – in about an hour of conversation – I had established the role of father-confessor, protector and perhaps saviour too. 'That's right,' I said, this time letting the merest trace of warmth into my voice. 'You do it our way and you'll be fine. Everything will be fine. This could even mean a step up the promotion ladder for you.'

8

What wife, at some time or other, has not suspected her husband of infidelity? And how many husbands have not felt a pang of uncertainty at some unexplained absence, some careless remark or late arrival of his spouse? There was nothing definite in my fears. There was nothing more than confused suspicion. Fiona's embraces were as lusty as ever; she laughed at my jokes and her eyes were bright when she looked at me. Too bright, perhaps, for sometimes I thought I could detect in her that profound compassion that women show only for men who have lost them.

I'd been trying to read other people's minds for most of my life. It could be a dangerous task. Just as a physician might succumb to hypochondria, a policeman to graft, or a priest to materialism, so I knew that I studied too closely the behaviour of those close to me. Suspicion went with the job, the endemic disease of the spy. For friendships and for marriages it sometimes proved fatal.

I'd returned home very late after my visit to Giles Trent and that night I slept heavily. By seven o'clock next morning, Fiona's place alongside me in bed was empty. Balanced upon the clock-radio there was buttered toast and a cup of coffee, by now quite cold. She must have left very early.

In the kitchen I could hear the children and their young nanny. I looked in on them and took some orange juice while standing up. I tried to join in the game they were playing but they yelled derision at my efforts, for I'd not understood that all answers must be given in Red Indian dialect. I blew them kisses that they didn't acknowledge and, wrapped into my sheepskin car coat, went down into the street to spend fifteen minutes getting the car to start.

Sleet was falling as I reached the worst traffic jams, and Dicky Cruyer had parked his big Jag carelessly enough to make it a tight squeeze to get into my allotted space in the underground garage. Don't complain, Samson, you're lucky to have a space at all; Dicky – not having fully mastered the technique of steering – really needs two.

I spent half an hour on the phone asking when my new car was going to be delivered, but got no clear answer beyond the fact that delivery dates were unreliable. I looked at the clock and decided to call Fiona's extension. Her secretary said, 'Mrs Samson had an out-of-town meeting this morning.'

'Oh, yes – she mentioned it, I think,' I said.

Her secretary knew I was trying to save face; secretaries always guess right about that kind of thing. Her voice became especially friendly as if to compensate for Fiona's oversight. 'Mrs Samson said she'd be late back. But she'll phone me some time this morning for messages. She always does that. I'll tell her you called. Was there any message, Mr Samson?'

Was her secretary a party to whatever was going on, I wondered. Was it one of those affairs that women liked to discuss very seriously or was it recounted with laughter as Fiona had recounted to me some of her teenage romances? Or was Fiona the sort of delinquent wife who confided in no one? That would be her style, I decided. No one would ever own Fiona; she was fond of saying that. There was always a part of her that was kept secret from all the world.

'Can I give your wife a message, Mr Samson?' her secretary asked again.

'No,' I said. 'Just tell her I called.'

Bret Rensselaer liked to describe himself as a 'workaholic'. That this description was a tired old cliché didn't deter him from using it. He liked clichés. They were, he said, the best way to get simple ideas into the heads of idiots. But his description of himself was accurate enough; he liked work. He'd inherited a house in the Virgin Islands and a portfolio of stock that would keep him idling in the sun for the rest of his days, if that was his inclination. But he was always at his desk by 8.30 and had never been known to have a day off for sickness. A day off for other reasons was not unusual: Easter at Le Touquet, Whitsun at Deauville, the Royal Enclosure in June and the Dublin Horse Show in August were appointments marked in red pencil on Bret's year-planner.

Needless to say, Rensselaer had never served as a field agent. His only service experience was a couple of years in the US Navy in the days when his father was still hoping he'd take over the family-owned bank.

Bret had spent his life in swivel chairs, arguing with dictating machines and smiling for committees. His muscles had come from lifting barbells, and jogging around the lawn of his Thamesside mansion. And one look at him would suggest that it was a good way to get them, for Bret had grown old gracefully. His face was tanned in that very even way that comes from sun reflected off the *Pulver-*

schnee that only falls on very expensive ski resorts. His fair hair was changing almost imperceptibly to white. And the spectacles that he now required for reading were styled like those that California highway patrolmen hang in their pocket flap while writing you a ticket.

'Bad news, Bret,' I told him as soon as he could fit me into his schedule. 'Giles Trent is coming in this morning to tell us just what he's been spilling to the Russians.'

Bret didn't jump up and start doing press-ups as he was said to have done when Dicky brought him the news that his wife had walked out on him. 'Tell me more,' he said calmly.

I told him about my visit to Kar's Club and overhearing the conversation, and that I'd suggested that Trent report it all to us. I didn't say why I'd visited Kar's Club or mention anything about Tessa.

He listened to my story without interrupting me, but he got to his feet and spent a little time checking through his paperclip collection while he listened.

'Three Russians. Where were the other two?'

'Sitting in the corner, playing chess with two fingers, and saying nothing to anyone.'

'Sure they were part of it?'

'A KGB hit team,' I said. 'They weren't difficult to spot – cheap Moscow suits and square-toed shoes, sitting silent because their English isn't good enough for anything more than buying a cup of coffee. They were there in case the flashy one needed them. They work in threes.'

'Is there a Chlestakov on the Diplomatic List?'

'No, I invented that part of my story for Trent. But this one was a KGB man – expensive clothes but no rings. Did you ever notice the way those KGB people never buy rings in the West? Rings leave marks on the fingers that might have to be explained when they are called back home, you see.'

'But you said that in the club members' book they are all described as Hungarians. Are you sure they are Russians?'

'They didn't do a Cossack dance or play balalaikas,' I said, 'but that's only because they didn't think of it. This fat little guy Chlestakov – a phoney name, of course – was calling Trent "tovarisch". Tovarisch! Jesus, I haven't heard anyone say that since the TV reruns of those old Garbo films.'

Bret Rensselaer took off his glasses and fiddled with them. 'The Russian guy said, "This is just a crazy idea that comes into my head. Take everything down to the photocopying shop in Baker Street . . ."?'

I finished it for him: ' ". . . the same place you got the previous lot done." Yes, that's what he said, Bret.'

'He must be crazy saying that in a place where he could be overheard.'

'That's it, Bret,' I said, trying not to be too sarcastic. 'Like the man said, he's a KGB man who acts upon a crazy idea as soon as it comes into his head.'

Bret was toying with his spectacles as if encountering the technology of the hinge for the first time. 'What's eating you?' he said without looking up at me.

'Come on, Bret,' I said. 'Did you ever hear of a Russian making a snap decision about anything? Did you ever hear of a KGB man acting on a crazy idea that just came into his head?'

Bret smiled uneasily but didn't answer.

'All the KGB people I ever encounter have certain well-engrained Russian characteristics, Bret. They are very slow, very devious and very very thorough.'

Bret put his wire-frame glasses into their case and leaned back to take a good look at me. 'You want to tell me what the hell you're getting at?'

'They did everything except sing the "Internationale", Bret,' I said. 'And it wasn't Trent who did anything indiscreet. He played it close to the chest. It was the KGB man who came on like he was auditioning for Chekhov.'

'You're not telling me that these three guys were just pretending to be Russians?'

'No,' I said. 'My imagination doesn't stretch to the idea of anybody who is not Russian wishing to be mistaken for a Russian.'

'So you think these guys staged the whole thing for your benefit? You think they just did it to discredit Giles Trent?'

I didn't answer.

'So why the hell would Giles Trent confess when you confronted him?' said Bret, rubbing salt into it.

'I don't know,' I admitted.

'Just four beats to the bar, feller. Okay? Don't get too complicated. Save all that for Coordination. Those guys get paid to fit the loose ends together.'

'Sure,' I said. 'But meanwhile we'd better send someone along to turn Trent's place over. Not just a quick glance under the bed and a flashlight to see around the attic. A proper search.'

'Agreed. Tell my secretary to do the paperwork and I'll get it signed. Meanwhile assign someone to it – someone you can rely on. And by the way, Bernard, it's beginning to look as though we might have to ask you to go to Berlin after all.'

'I'm not sure I could do that, Bret,' I said with matching charm.

'It's your decision,' he said, and smiled to show how friendly he could be. Most of the time he was Mr Nice Guy. He opened doors for you, stood back to let you into the lift, laughed at your jokes, agreed with your conclusions, and asked your advice. But when all the pleasantries were over he made sure you did exactly what he wanted.

I was still thinking about Bret Rensselaer when I finished work that evening. He was different from any of the other Department heads I had to deal with. Despite those moments of brash hostility, he was more approachable than the D-G and more reliable than Dicky Cruyer. And Bret had that sort of laidback self-confidence that you have to be both rich and American to possess. He was the only one to defy the Departmental tradition that only the D-G could have a really big car, while the rest of the senior staff managed with Jaguars, Mercedes and Volvos. Bret had a bloody great Bentley limousine and a full-time uniformed chauffeur to go with it.

I saw Bret's gleaming black Bentley in the garage when I got out of the lift in the basement. The interior lights were on and I could hear Mozart from the stereo. Bret's driver was sitting in the back seat tapping his cigarette ash into a paper bag and swaying in time to the music.

The driver, Albert Bingham, was a sixty-year-old ex-Scots Guardsman whose enforced silence while driving resulted in a compulsive garrulity when off duty. 'Hello, Mr Samson,' he called to me. 'Am I parked in the way?'

'No,' I said. But Albert was out of his car and all ready for one of his chats.

'I wondered if you would be taking your wife's car,' he said. 'But on the other hand I guessed she'd be coming back here to collect it herself. I know how much she likes driving that Porsche, Mr Samson. We were having a chat about it only last week. I told her I could have it tuned up by a fellow I know at the place I get the Bentley serviced. He's a wizard, and he has a Porsche himself. A secondhand one, of course, not the latest model like that one of your wife's.'

'I'm going home in this elderly Ford,' I said, tapping the glass of it with my keys.

'I hear you're getting a Volvo,' he said. 'Just the right car for a family man.'

'We're too squeezed in my wife's Porsche,' I said.

'You'll be pleased with the Volvo,' said Albert in that tone of voice that marks the Bentley driver. 'It's a solid car, as good as the Mercedes any day, and you can quote me on that.'

'I might quote you on that,' I said, 'if I ever try trading it in for a Mercedes.'

Albert smiled and took a puff at his cigarette. He knew when he was being joshed and he knew how to show me he didn't mind. 'Your wife wanted to drive Mr Rensselaer in her Porsche, but he insisted on the Bentley. He doesn't like fast sports cars, Mr Rensselaer. He likes to be able to stretch his legs out. He was injured in the war – did you know he was injured?'

I wondered what Albert could be talking about. Fiona had arranged to go to Tessa's and sort through some house agents' offers. 'Injured? I didn't know.'

'He was in submarines. He broke his kneecap falling down a companionway – that's a sort of ladder on a ship – and it was reset while they were at sea. A sub doesn't return from patrol for a little matter of an ensign hurting his leg.' Albert laughed at the irony of it all.

Where had Rensselaer gone with my wife? 'So you nearly got an evening off, Albert.'

Gratified to see I hadn't climbed into the driving seat and fled from him, as most of the staff did when he started chatting, Albert took a deep breath and said, 'I don't mind, Mr Samson. I can use the overtime, to tell you the honest truth. And what do I care whether I'm sitting at home in my poky little bed-sitter or lying back in that real leather. It's Mozart, Mr Samson, and I'd just as soon listen to Mozart here in an underground garage as anywhere in the world. That stereo is a beautiful job. Come over and listen to it if you don't believe me.'

They couldn't have gone far, or Albert would not have brought the Bentley back to the garage to wait for them. 'Much traffic in town tonight, Albert? I have to go through the West End.'

'It's terrible, Mr Samson. One of these days, it's going to lock up solid.' This was one of Albert's standard phrases; he said it automatically while he worked out an answer to my question. 'Piccadilly is bad at this time. It's the theatres.'

'I never know how to avoid Piccadilly when I'm going home.'

Albert inhaled on his cigarette. I had given him the perfect opening on his favourite topic: shortcuts in central London. 'Well – '

'Take your journey tonight,' I interrupted him. 'How did you tackle it? You knew there would be heavy traffic . . . when did you leave . . . seven?'

'Seven-fifteen. Well, they went for a drink in the White Elephant Club in Curzon Street first. They could have walked from there to the Connaught, I know, but it might have started to rain and there'd be no cabs in Curzon Street at that time. The table at the Connaught Hotel Grill Room was for eight o'clock. No place for a big car like mine in Curzon Street. They're double-parked there by seven on some evenings at this time of year. I got there via Birdcage Walk, past Buckingham Palace and Hyde Park Corner . . . a long way round, you say. But when you've spent as many years driving in London as I have you . . .'

I let Albert's voice drone on as I asked myself why my wife told me she was spending the evening with Tessa when really she was having dinner in a hotel with Bret Rensselaer. 'Is that the time?' I said, looking at my watch while Albert was in full flow. 'I must go. Nice talking to you, Albert. You're a mine of information.'

Albert smiled. I could still hear *Così fan Tutte* from the Bentley's stereo when I was driving up the exit ramp.

I watched her as she took off her rain-specked headscarf. She wore a silk square only when she wanted to protect a very special new hairdo. She shook her head and flicked at her hair with her fingertips. Her eyes sparkled and her skin was pale and perfect. She smiled; how beautiful she seemed, and how far away.

'Did you eat out?' she said. She noticed the dining table with the unused place setting that Mrs Dias had left for me.

'I had a cheese roll in a pub.'

'That's the worst thing you could choose,' she said. 'Fat and carbohydrates: that's not good for you. There was cold chicken and salad prepared.'

'So did Tessa find another house?'

Alerted perhaps by my tone of voice, or by the way I stood facing her, she looked into my face for a moment before taking off her raincoat. 'I couldn't get to Tessa's tonight. Something came up.' She shook the raincoat and the raindrops flashed in the light.

'Work, you mean?'

She looked at me steadily before nodding. We had a tacit agreement not to ask questions about work. 'Something Rensselaer wanted,' she said, and kept looking at me as if challenging me to pursue it.

'I saw your car in the car park when I left but Security said you'd already gone.'

She walked past me to hang her coat in the hall. When she'd done that, she looked in the hall mirror and combed her hair as she spoke. 'There was a lot of stuff in the diplomatic bag this afternoon. Some of it needed translation and Bret's secretary has only A-level German. I went over the road and worked there.'

Claiming to be in the Foreign Office as an explanation of absence was the oldest joke in the Department. No one could ever be found in that dark labyrinth. 'You had dinner with Rensselaer,' I said, unable to control my anger any longer.

She stopped combing her hair, opened her handbag and dropped the comb into it. Then she smiled and said, 'Well, you don't expect me to starve, darling. Do you?'

'Don't give me all that crap,' I said. 'You left the building with Rensselaer at seven-fifteen. You were in his Bentley when he drove out of the garage. Then I discovered he'd left the reception desk at the Connaught as his contact number for the night-duty officer.'

'You haven't lost your touch, darling,' she said with ice in every syllable. 'Once a field man, always a field man – isn't that what they say?'

'It's what people like Cruyer and Rensselaer say. It's what people say when they are trying to put down the people who do the real work.'

'Well, now it's paid off for you,' she said. 'Now all your old expertise has enabled you to discover that I had dinner at the Connaught with Bret Rensselaer.'

'So why do you have to lie to me?'

'What lies? I told you I had to do some work for Rensselaer. We had dinner – a good dinner, with wine – but we were talking shop.'

'About what?'

She pushed past me into the front room and through into the dining room that opened from it in what designers call 'open plan'. She picked up the clean plates and cutlery that had been left for me. 'You know better than to ask me that.' She went into the kitchen.

I followed her as she put the plates on a shelf in the dresser. 'Because it's so secret?'

'It's confidential,' she said. 'Don't you have work that is too confidential to talk to me about?'

'Not in the grillroom of the Connaught, I don't.'

'So you even know which room we were in. You've done your homework tonight, haven't you.'

'What was I supposed to do while you're having dinner with the boss? Am I supposed to eat cold chicken and watch TV?'

'You were supposed to be having a beer with a friend, and then collecting the children from their visit to my parents' house.'

Oh, my God! I forgot. 'I clean forgot about the children,' I admitted.

'I phoned mother. I guessed you'd forget. She gave them supper and brought them here in a minicab. It's all right.'

'Good old Mum-in-law,' I said.

'You don't have to be bloody sarcastic about my mother,' said Fiona. 'It's bad enough trying to have an argument about Bret.'

'Let's drop it,' I said.

'Do what you like,' said Fiona. 'I've had enough talk for one night.' She switched off the light in the dining room, then opened the door of the dishwasher, closed it again, and turned it on. The sprays of the dishwasher beat on its steel interior like a Wagnerian drumroll. The noise made conversation impossible.

When I came from the bathroom, I expected to see Fiona tucked into the pillow and feigning sleep; she did that sometimes after we'd had a row. But this time she was sitting up in bed, reading some large tome with the distinctive cheap binding of the Department's library. She wanted to remind me that she was a dedicated wage slave.

As I undressed, I tried a fresh, friendly tone of voice. 'What did Bret want?'

'I wish you wouldn't keep on about it.'

'There's nothing between you, is there?'

She laughed. It was a derisory laugh. 'You suspect me . . . with Bret Rensselaer? He's nearly as old as my father.'

'He was probably older than the father of that cipher clerk – Jennie something – who left just before Christmas.'

Fiona raised her eyes from her book; this was the sort of thing that interested her. 'You don't think she . . . ? With Bret, you mean?'

'Internal Security sent someone to find out why she'd left without giving proper notice. She said she'd been having an affair with Bret. He'd told her they were through.'

'Good grief,' said Fiona. 'Poor Bret. I suppose the D-G had to be told.'

'The D-G was pleased to hear the girl had proper security clearance, and that was that.'

'How broad-minded of the old man. I'd have thought he would have been furious. Still, Bret isn't married. His wife left him, didn't she?'

'The suggestion was that Bret had sinned before.'

'And always with someone with proper security clearance. Well, good for Bret. So that's why you thought . . .' She laughed again. It was a genuine laugh this time. She closed her book but kept a finger in the page. 'He's going through the regular routine about the danger of security lapses.'

'I told him about Giles Trent,' I said. 'I kept Tessa out of it.'

'Bret has decided to talk to everyone personally,' said Fiona.

'Surely Bret doesn't suspect *you*?'

Fiona smiled. 'No, darling. Bret didn't take me to the Connaught to interrogate me over the bones of the last of this season's woodcock. He spent the evening talking about you.'

'About me?'

'And in due course of time he will take you aside and ask about me. You know how it works, darling. You've been at this business longer than I have.' She put a marker in her book before laying it aside.

'Oh, for Christ's sake.'

'If you don't believe me, darling, ask Bret.'

'I might do that,' I said. She waited until I got into bed, and then switched out the lights. 'I thought there was protein in cheese,' I said. She didn't answer.

9

Dicky Cruyer was in Bret Rensselaer's office when they sent for me on Wednesday. Cruyer had his thumbs stuck in the back pockets of his jeans and his curly head was tilted to one side as if he were listening for some distant sound.

Rensselaer was in his swivel chair, arms folded and feet resting on a leather stool. These relaxed postures were studied, and I guessed that the two of them had taken up their positions when they heard me at the door. It was a bad sign. Rensselaer's folded arms and Cruyer's akimbo stance had that sort of aggression I'd seen in interrogating teams.

'Bernard!' said Dicky Cruyer in a tone of pleasant surprise, as if I'd just dropped in for tea, rather than kept them waiting for thirty minutes in response to the third of his calls. Rensselaer watched us dispassionately, like a passing taxicab passenger might watch two men at a bus stop. 'Looks like another jaunt to Big B,' said Dicky.

'Is that so?' I said without enthusiasm. Bret was jacketless. This slim figure in white shirt, bow tie and waistcoat looked like the sort of Mississippi riverboat gambler who broke into song for the final reel.

'Not through the wire, or anything tricky,' said Dicky. 'Just a call into our office. An East German has just knocked on Frank Harrington's door with a bagful of paper and demands to be sent to London. Won't talk to our Berlin people, Frank tells me.' Dicky Cruyer ran his finger through his curls before nodding seriously at Rensselaer.

'Another crank,' I said.

'Is that what you think, Bernard?' said Rensselaer with that earnest sincerity I'd learned to disregard.

'What kind of papers?' I asked Dicky.

'Right,' said Cruyer. But he didn't answer my question.

Rensselaer took his time about describing the papers. 'Interesting stuff,' he stated cautiously. 'Most of it from here. The minutes of a meeting the D-G had with some Foreign Office senior staff, an appraisal of our success in tapping diplomatic lines out of London,

77

part of a report on our use of US enciphering machines. . . . A mixed bag but it's worth attention. Right?'

'*Well* worth our attention, Bret,' I said.

'What's that supposed to mean?' said Cruyer.

'For anyone who believes in Santa Claus,' I added.

'You mean it's a KGB stunt?' said Rensselaer. 'Yes, that's probably it.' Cruyer looked at him, disconcerted by his change of attitude. 'On the other hand,' said Rensselaer, 'it's something we ignore at our peril. Wouldn't you agree, Bernard?'

I didn't answer.

Dicky Cruyer moved his hands to grip the large brass buckle of his leather cowboy belt. 'Berlin Resident is worried – damned worried.'

'Old Frank is always worried,' I said. 'He can be an old woman, we all know that.'

'Frank's had a lot to worry about since he took over,' said Rensselaer, to put his loyalty to his subordinates on record. But he didn't deny that Frank Harrington, our senior man in Berlin, could be an old woman.

'All stuff from here?' I said. 'Identifiably from here? Verbatim? Copies of our documents? From here how?'

'It's no good asking Frank that,' said Dicky Cruyer quickly before anyone blamed him for not finding out.

'It's no good asking Frank anything,' I said. 'So why doesn't he send everything over here?'

'I wouldn't want that,' said Rensselaer, his arms still crossed, his eyes staring at the *Who's Who* on his bookshelf. 'If this is just the KGB trying to stir a little trouble for us, I don't want to get their man over here for interrogation. It would give them something to gloat over. Given that sort of encouragement, they'll try again and again. No, we'll take it easy. We'll have Bernard go over there and sort through this stuff and talk to their guy, and tell us what he thinks. But let's not overreact.' He snapped a desk drawer shut with enough force to make a sound like a pistol shot.

'It will be a waste of time,' I said.

Bret Rensselaer kicked his foot to swivel his chair and faced me. He uncrossed his arms for a moment, snapped his starched cuffs at me and smiled. 'That's exactly the way I want it handled, Bernard. You go and look it over with that jaundiced eye of yours. No good sending Dicky.' He looked at Dicky and smiled. 'He'd wind up talking to the D-G on the hot line.'

Dicky Cruyer thrust his hands deep into the pockets of his jeans, scowled and hunched his shoulders. He didn't like Rensselaer saying he was excitable. Cruyer wanted to be a cool and imperturbable sort of whizz kid.

Rensselaer looked at me and smiled. He knew he'd upset Cruyer and he wanted me to share the fun. 'Go through the Berlin telex and make a note of what references they quote. Then go and see the originals: read through the minutes of that meeting at the FO, and dig out that memo about the cipher machines, and so on. That way you'll be able to judge for yourself when you get there.' He glanced at Dicky, who was looking out the window sulking, and then at me. 'Whatever conclusion you come to, you'll tell Frank Harrington it's *Spielzeug* – garbage.'

'Of course,' I said.

'Take tomorrow's RAF flight and have a chat with Frank and calm him down. See this little German guy and sort through this junk he's peddling.'

'Okay,' I said. I knew Bret would find a way of getting me to what Dicky called 'Big B'.

'And what's the score with Giles Trent?' I asked.

'He's been taken care of, Bernard,' said Rensselaer. 'We'll talk about it when you return.' He smiled. He was handsome, and could turn on the charm like a film star. Of course Fiona could fall for him. I felt like spitting in his eye.

I caught the military flight to Berlin next day. The plane was empty except for me, two medical orderlies who'd brought a sick soldier over the day before, and a Brigadier with an amazing amount of baggage.

The Brigadier borrowed my newspaper and wanted to talk about fly fishing. He was an affable man, young-looking compared to most Brigadiers I'd ever met, but that was not much of a sampling. It wasn't his fault that he bore a superficial resemblance to my father-in-law, but I found it a definite barrier. I put my seat into the recline position and mumbled something about having had a late night. Then I stared out the window until thin wisps of cloud, like paint-starved brushstrokes, defaced the hard regular patterns of agricultural land that was unmistakably German.

The Brigadier began chatting to one of the medical orderlies. He asked him how long he'd been in the Army and if he had a family and where they lived. The private replied in an abrupt way that should have been enough to indicate that he'd prefer to talk football with his chum. But the Brigadier droned on. His voice too was like that of Fiona's father. He even had the same little 'huh?' with which Fiona's father finished each piece of reckless bigotry.

I remembered the first time I met Fiona's parents. They'd invited me to stay the weekend. They had a huge mansion of uncertain age near Leith Hill in Surrey. The house was surrounded by trees –

straggly firs and pines, for the most part. Around the house there were tree-covered hillsides so that Fiona's father – David Timothy Kimber-Hutchinson, Fellow of the Royal Society of Arts, wealthy businessman and farm owner, and prize-winning amateur watercolour painter – could proudly say that he owned all the land seen from the window of his study.

There is surely a lack of natural human compassion in a host who clears away Sunday breakfast at 10.30. Fiona's father did not think so. 'I've been up helping to feed the horses since six-thirty this morning. I was exercising my best hunter before breakfast.'

He was wearing riding breeches, polished boots, yellow cashmere roll-neck and a checked hacking jacket that fitted his slightly plump figure to perfection. I noticed his attire because he'd caught me in the breakfast room getting the last dry scrapings of scrambled egg from a dish on the electric hot plate while I was barefoot and clad in an ancient dressing gown and pyjamas. 'You're not thinking of taking that plate of oddments' – he came closer to see the two shrivelled rashers and four wrinkled mushrooms that were under the flakes of egg – 'up to the bedroom?'

'As a matter of fact, I am,' I told him.

'No, no, no.' He said it with the sort of finality that doubtless ended all boardroom discussion. 'My good wife will never have food in the bedrooms.'

Plate in hand, I continued to the door. 'I'm not taking it up there for your wife,' I said. 'It's for me.'

That very early encounter with Mr Kimber-Hutchinson blighted any filial bond that might otherwise have blossomed. But at that time the idea of marrying Fiona had not formed in my mind and the prospect of seeing Mr David Kimber-Hutchinson ever again seemed mercifully remote.

'My God, man. You've not even shaved!' he shouted after me as I went upstairs with my breakfast.

'You provoke him,' Fiona said when I told her about my encounter. She was in my bed, having put on her frilly nightdress, waiting to share the booty from the breakfast table.

'How can you say that?' I argued. 'I speak only when he speaks to me, and then only to make polite conversation.'

'You hypocrite! You know very well that you deliberately provoke him. You ask him all those wide-eyed innocent questions about making profits from cheap labour.'

'Only because he keeps saying he's a socialist,' I said. 'And don't take that second piece of bacon: one each.'

'You beast. You know I hate mushrooms.' She licked her fingers. 'You're no better, darling. What do you ever do that makes you more of a socialist than Daddy?'

'I'm not a socialist,' I said. 'I'm a fascist. I keep telling you that but you never listen.'

'Daddy has his own sort of socialist ideas,' said Fiona.

'He refuses to do business with the French, loathes the Americans, never employs Jews, thinks all Arabs are crooked, and the only Russian he likes is Tchaikovsky. Where is the brotherhood of man?'

'A lot of that tirade was directed at me,' said Fiona. 'Daddy's been angry ever since I got a reference from old Silas Gaunt. That's Mother's side of the family and Daddy's feuding with them.'

'I see.'

'When I hear my father going on as he did last night at dinner, I feel like joining the Communist Party, don't you?'

'No. I feel like suggesting your father join it.'

'No, seriously, darling.'

'The Communist Party?'

'You know what I mean: workers of the world unite and all that. Daddy pays lip service to the idea of socialism but he never does anything about it.'

'You wouldn't escape him by joining the CP,' I said. 'Your father would write out a cheque and buy it. And then he'd sell off its sports field as office sites.'

'Come back to bed,' said Fiona. 'Now that we've missed breakfast, there's nothing to get up for.'

Fiona rarely mentioned her father's politics – and was vague about her own beliefs. Political conversation at the dinner table usually had her staring vacantly into space, or prompted her to start a conversation about children or sewing or hairdressers. Sometimes I wondered if she was really interested in her job in the Department or if she just stayed there to keep an eye on me.

'We're about to land, old boy,' said the Brigadier. 'Make sure your seat belt is fastened.'

The plane was over Berlin now. I could see the jagged shape of the Wall as the pilot turned on to finals for the approach to RAF Gatow, the onetime Luftwaffe training college. Its runway ends abruptly at the Wall, except that here the 'Wall' is a wire-mesh fence and a sandy patch that intelligence reports say has been left without mines and obstacles in case the day should come when units of the adjoining Russian Army's tank depot would roll through it to take Berlin-Gatow with its runways intact and electronics undamaged.

10

Did you ever say hello to a girl you almost married long ago? Did she smile the same captivating smile, and give your arm a hug in a gesture you'd almost forgotten? Did the wrinkles as she smiled make you wonder what marvellous times you'd missed? That's how I felt about Berlin every time I came back here.

Lisl Hennig's hotel, just off Kantstrasse, in the Western Sector, was unchanged. No one had tried to repair or repaint the façade pockmarked by Red Army shell splinters in 1945. The imposing doorway, alongside an optician's shop, opened onto the same grandiose marble staircase. The patched carpet, its red now a faded brown, led up to the 'salon' where Lisl was always to be found. Lisl's mother had chosen the heavy oak furniture from Wertheim's department store at Alexanderplatz in the days before Hitler. And long before the grand old house became this shabby hotel.

'Hello, darling,' said Lisl as though I'd seen her only yesterday. She was old, a huge woman who overflowed from the armchair, her red silk dress emphasizing every bulge so that she looked like molten lava pouring down a steep hillside. 'You look tired, darling. You're working too hard.'

There had been few changes made in this 'salon' since Lisl was a child in a house with five servants. There were photos on every side: sepia family groups in ebony frames, faded celebrities of the thirties. Actresses with long cigarette holders, writers under big-brimmed hats, glossy film stars from the UFA studios, carefully retouched prima donnas of the State Opera, artists of the Dada movement, trapeze performers from the Wintergarten and nightclub singers from long-vanished clip joints. All of them signed with the sort of florid guarantees of enduring love that are the ephemera of show business.

Lisl's late husband was there, dressed in the white-tie outfit he wore to play Beethoven's Fifth Piano Concerto with the Berlin Philharmonic the night the Führer was in the audience. There were no photos of the bent little cripple who ended his days playing for *Trinkgeld* in a broken-down bar in Rankestrasse.

Some of these photos were of family friends; those who came to

Lisl's salon in the thirties and the forties when it was a place to meet the rich and famous, and those who came in the fifties to meet men with tinned food and work permits. There were modern pictures too, of long-term residents who endured the trials and tribulations: uncertain hot water and the noise of the central heating, and the phone messages that were forgotten and letters that were never delivered, and the bathroom lights that did not work. Such loyal clients were invited into Lisl's cramped little office for a glass of sherry when they settled the bill. And their photos were enshrined there over the cash box.

'You look terrible, darling,' she said.

'I'm fine, Tante Lisl,' I said. 'Can you find a room for me?'

She switched on another light. A large plant in an art-nouveau pot cast a sudden spiky shadow on the ugly brown wallpaper. She turned to see me better, and part of her pearl necklace disappeared into a roll of fatty muscle. 'There will always be a room for you, *Liebchen*. Give me a kiss.'

But I had already leaned over to give her a kiss. It was a necessary ritual. She had been calling me *Liebchen* and demanding kisses since before I could walk. 'So nothing changes, Lisl,' I said.

'Nothing changes! Everything changes, you mean. Look at me. Look at my ugly face and this infirm body. Life is cruel, Bernd, my sweetheart,' she said, using the name I'd been known by as a boy. 'You will discover it too: life is cruel.' Only Berliners can mock their own self-pity to produce a laugh. Lisl was one of life's most successful survivors and we both knew it. She roared with laughter and I had to laugh too.

She let her *Stuttgarter Zeitung* slide onto the carpet. She spent her life reading newspapers and talking about what she discovered in them. 'What has brought you to our wonderful city?' she asked. She rubbed her knee and sighed. Now that arthritis had affected her legs, she seldom went out except to the bank.

'Still selling tablets?' she asked. I'd always said that I worked for a pharmaceutical manufacturer that exported medicines to East and West. She didn't wait for a reply; in any case she'd never believed my story. 'And did you bring photos of your lovely wife and those beautiful children? Is everything all right at home?'

'Yes,' I said. 'Is the top room empty?'

'Of course it is,' she said. 'Who else but you would want to sleep there when I have rooms with balcony and bathroom en suite?'

'I'll go up and have a wash,' I said. The attic room had been my room when my father, a Major in the Intelligence Corps, was billeted here. The place was full of memories.

'I hope you're not going over the other side,' Lisl said. 'They have all the medicine they need over there in the East. They are getting very rough with medicine sellers.'

I smiled dutifully at her little joke. 'I'm not going anywhere, Lisl,' I said. 'This is just a holiday.'

'Is everything all right at home, darling? It's not that sort of holiday, is it?'

Frank Harrington, head of Berlin Station, arrived at Lisl's exactly on the dot of four. 'You got fed up with sleeping on that sofa at Werner's place, did you?'

I looked at him without replying.

'We are slow,' said Frank, 'but eventually we hear all the news.'

'You brought it?'

'I brought everything.' He put an expensive-looking black leather document case on the table and opened it. 'I even brought that A to Z street guide I borrowed from you in London. Sorry to have had it so long.'

'That's okay, Frank,' I said, throwing the London street guide into my open suitcase so that I wouldn't forget it. 'And where is the man who delivered this stuff?'

'He went back.'

'I thought he was staying so I could debrief him. That's what London wanted.'

Harrington sighed. 'He's gone back,' he said. 'You know how people are in situations like this. He got nervous yesterday and finally slipped off back over there.'

'That's a pity,' I said.

'I saw a lovely-looking girl downstairs talking to Lisl. Blonde. Couldn't have been more than about eighteen. Is she staying here?'

Frank Harrington was a thin sixty-year-old. His face was pale, with grey eyes and a bony nose and the sort of black blunt-ended stubble moustache that soldiers affect. His question was an attempt to change the subject, but Frank had always had an eye for the ladies.

'I couldn't tell you, Frank,' I said.

I began to sort through the papers he'd brought. Some of them were verbatim accounts of meetings that had taken place at the Foreign Office when our Secret Intelligence Service people went over there for special briefings. None of the material was of vital importance, but that it had got back to East German intelligence was worrying. Very worrying.

Frank Harrington sat by the tiny garret window from which I used to launch my paper aeroplanes, and smoked his foul-smelling pipe. 'You don't remember the time your father organized a birthday party for Frau Hennig?' Frank Harrington was the only person I knew who called Lisl Frau Hennig. 'He had a six-piece dance band downstairs in the salon and every black marketeer in Potsdamerplatz contributed food. I've never seen such a spread.'

I looked up from the papers.

He waved his pipe at me in a gesture of placation. 'Don't misunderstand me, Bernard. Your father had no dealings with the black market. The contributors were all Frau Hennig's friends.' He laughed at some thought passing through his mind. 'Your father was the last man to have dealings with the black market. Your father was a prude, so prim and proper that he made lesser mortals, like me, sometimes feel inadequate. He was a self-made man, your father. They are all like that – a bit unforgiving, unyielding and inclined to go by the book.' He waved his pipe again. 'Don't take offence, Bernard. Your dad and I were very close. You know that.'

'Yes, I know, Frank.'

'No proper education, your father. Left school when he was fourteen. Spent his evenings in the public library. Retired a Colonel, and ended up running the Berlin office, didn't he? Damned good going for a self-educated man.'

I turned over the next lot of papers to get to the memo on cipher machines. 'Is that what I'm like?' I asked him. 'Unforgiving, unyielding and inclined to go by the book?'

'Oh, come along, Bernard. You're not going to tell me you wish you'd been to university. You're *berlinerisch*, Bernard. You grew up in this funny old town. You were cycling through the streets and alleys before they built the Wall. You speak Berlin German as well as anyone I've ever met here. You go to ground like a native. That's why we can't bloody well find you when you decide you can't be bothered with us.'

'*Ich bin ein Berliner.*' I said. It was a joke. A *Berliner* is a doughnut. The day after President Kennedy made his famous proclamation, Berlin cartoonists had a field day with talking doughnuts.

'You think your father should have sent you back to England so that you could read politics and modern languages? You think it would have been better to have listened to Oxford academics telling you where Bismarck went wrong, and some young tutor explaining which prepositions govern the dative case?'

I said nothing. The truth was I didn't know the answer.

'Bloody hell, laddie, you know more about this part of the world than any Oxbridge graduate can learn in a lifetime.'

'Would you put that in writing, Frank?'

'You're still annoyed about young Dicky Cruyer getting the desk? Well, why wouldn't you be angry? I made my position clear from this end. That you can be sure of.'

'I know you did, Frank,' I said as I tapped the papers together to make them fit back into the brown paper envelope. 'But the fact is that you don't just learn about history and grammar at Oxford and Cambridge, you learn about the people you meet there. And in later life you depend upon those judgments. Knowing the streets and alleys of this dirty old town doesn't count for much when there is a desk falling vacant.'

Frank Harrington puffed at his pipe. 'And Cruyer was junior to you in service as well as younger.'

'Don't rub it in, Frank,' I said.

He laughed. I felt guilty about describing him as an old woman, but it would make no difference to his career whatever I said about him, because Frank was due to retire any time, and being pulled out of Berlin would be no hardship for him. He hated Berlin and made no secret of it. 'Let me write to the D-G,' said Frank as if suddenly inspired with a brilliant idea. 'The old man was a trainee with me back in the war.'

'For God's sake, no!' That was the trouble with Frank; just like Lisl, he always wanted to treat me as if I were a nineteen-year-old going after his first job. He wasn't so much an old woman as a well-meaning old auntie.

'So what do you make of all that wastepaper?' he said, poking a match into the bowl of his pipe as if searching for something.

'Garbage,' I said. 'It's just a lot of guesswork someone in Moscow has dreamed up to get us worried.'

Frank nodded without looking up at me. 'I thought you'd say that. You'd have to say that, Bernard. Whatever it was like, you'd have to say it was rubbish.'

'Can I buy you a drink?' I said.

'I'd better get back to the office and put that stuff into the shredder.'

'Okay,' I said. He'd guessed that London wanted it destroyed. Frank knew how their minds worked. Maybe he'd been here too long.

'You'll be wanting to go round town and see some of your play-mates, I suppose.'

'Not me, Frank.'

He smiled and puffed his pipe. 'You were always like that, Bernard. You never could bear letting anyone know what you were up to.' It was just the sort of thing I remember him saying to me when I was a child. 'Well, I'll look forward to seeing you for dinner tomorrow night. Just wear anything, it's only potluck.'

After he'd left, I went to my suitcase to get a fresh shirt. A folded piece of envelope, used as a bookmark, had fallen out of the street guide Frank had returned to me. It was addressed to Frau Harrington, but the address was no more than a postbox number followed by a post code. It was a damned weird way to get a letter to Frank's wife. I put it into my wallet.

The Russians got the State Opera, the Royal Palace, the government buildings and some of the worst slums; the Western Powers got the Zoo, the parks, the department stores, the nightclubs and the villas of the rich in Grunewald. And spiked through both sectors, like a skewer through a shish kebab, there is the East–West Axis.

The Bendlerblock, from where the High Command sent the German Army to conquer Europe, has now been converted to offices for a cosmetic manufacturer. The Bendlerstrasse has been renamed. Nothing here is what it seems, and that appeals to me. The Anhalter Bahnhof, a yellow brick façade with three great doors, was once the station for the luxury express trains to Vienna and all of southeast Germany. It is no longer a busy terminus. The great edifice stands upon a piece of waste ground long since abandoned to weeds and wild flowers. Werner Volkmann chose it as a meeting place as he had sometimes done before. It was usually a sign that he was feeling especially paranoid. He was carrying a small document case and wearing a big black overcoat with an astrakhan collar. On someone else it might have suggested an impresario or a nobleman, but it simply made Werner look like someone who bought his clothes at the flea market in the disused S-Bahn station on Tauentzienstrasse.

It was getting dark. Werner stopped and looked up the street. From over the high graffito-covered wall there was the reflected glare of bluish-green light that in any other city would have marked the position of a large stadium lit for an evening's football. But beyond this wall there was the large open space of the Potsdamerplatz. Once the busiest traffic intersection in Europe, it had now become a brightly lit *Todesstreifen*, a death strip, silent and still, with a maze of barbed wire, mines and fixed guns.

Werner loitered on the corner for a moment, turning to watch a dozen or more youngsters as they passed him and continued towards Hallesches Tor. They were attired in a weird combination of clothes: tight leotards, high boots and Afghan coats on the girls; studded leather sleeveless jackets and Afrika Korps caps on the men. Some of them had their hair dyed in streaks of primary colours. Werner was no more surprised by this sample of Berlin youth than I was. Berlin residents are exempt from military service, and there is a tendency among the young to celebrate it. But Werner continued to watch them, and waited, still staring, until a yellow double-decker bus stopped and took aboard everyone waiting at the bus stop. Only then did he feel safe. He turned abruptly and crossed the street at the traffic lights. I followed as if to catch the green.

He went into Café Leuschner and, after putting his hat on the rack, chose a seat at the rear. His document case he placed carefully on the seat next to him. I waved as if catching sight of him for the first time and went over to his table. Werner called to the waiter for two coffees. I sat down with a sigh. Werner had arrived late, an unforgivable sin in my business.

'It was one of Frank Harrington's people,' said Werner. 'I had to be sure I'd got rid of him.'

'Why would Frank have someone following you?'

'London has been kicking Frank's ass,' said Werner. 'There is talk of replacing him immediately.'

'What have you got to do with that? Why follow *you*?'

'Is there some kind of leak in London?' said Werner. Knowing it was unlikely that I'd answer him, he said, 'It's only fair you tell me. You ask me to go over the wire for you, it's only fair you tell me what's going on in London.'

'No leak,' I said. I might have added that no one had yet asked him to go 'over the wire' and that his regular visits to the East were a damned good reason for him knowing as little as possible about what was happening in London.

'And the money? Will London help me with the bank?'

'No money either,' I said.

Werner hunched lower over the table and nodded sorrowfully. I looked round the café. It was a roomy place, its gilt-framed mirrors supported by plaster cherubs and its plastic-topped tables fashioned to look like marble. There was a fine old counter that ran the whole length of the room. I'd known it when the Leuschners' father was serving behind it. Berlin kids could get genuine American ice cream here until Leuschner's daughter married her soldier and went to live in Arkansas.

The coffee arrived: two small electroplated pots, together with tiny jugs of cream, sugar wrapped in coloured paper advertising tea, and the usual floral cups and saucers. Floral-patterned cups and saucers: they reminded me of my childhood breakfasts when my father used to correct my mother's inadequate German. ' "*Es geht um die Wurst*","It depends on the sausage", means "Everything depends on it". But "*Mir ist alles Wurst*", or "It's all sausage to me", means "I really don't care".' My mother just smiled and poured more coffee into the floral-patterned cups. She had intended to say that there might not be enough sausage for all of us that evening. But my father was inclined to make everything more complicated than it need be. That too was a characteristic of the self-made man.

I said, 'Why did we go through all that business of meeting without being observed? I could just have met you in here.'

'And then we would have both been sitting here with Frank's watcher.'

'Have it your way, Werner,' I said.

'Frank Harrington is worried,' said Werner.

'What about?' I said, no longer entirely concealing my irritation. 'I thought Frank wouldn't let you near his office.'

Werner smiled one of the special oriental smiles that he thought made him appear inscrutable. 'I don't have to go into the office to hear the latest news from there. Frank is getting a lot of trouble from London. Rumours say there's a leak. Frank is frightened he'll be the scapegoat. He's frightened they'll get rid of him and find some way of not paying his pension.'

'Balls!'

'If Frank was recalled, do you think the Berlin office would start to use me again?'

'There is no leak of information.'

'Good,' said Werner, looking at me and nodding. There was nothing quite so disconcerting as Werner trying to be sincere. 'Max Binder went back. He had a wife and three kids, and he couldn't get a job. Finally he went back to the East.'

Max Binder was at school with us, a studious kid who sang the solo part in 'Silent Night' every Christmas and had a secret hoard of forbidden Nazi badges that we all coveted. I'd always liked him. 'Max is one of the best,' I said. 'His wife was from the East, wasn't she?'

'They got one of those "wedding cake" apartments on Stalinallee.' Werner still called the street by its old name. 'Nowadays people realize that those apartments are not so bad. At least they have high ceilings and lots of cupboards and storage space. The new places out at Marzahn are really jammed tight together. They've got families of four living in the space of Max's broom cupboard.'

'You've been across recently? You've seen Max?'

'I see Max from time to time. He has a good job now. He's in the customs service – chief clerk.'

There was something in Werner's voice that caught my attention. 'Are you in some racket with Max?'

'With Max?' Nervously he poured himself more coffee.

'I know you, Werner, and I know Max. What are you up to?'

'It's Max's office that handles the paperwork for some of my forfait deals, that's all.'

'The avalizing, you mean. The guarantee that the money will be paid. So that's it.'

Werner made no attempt to deny that there was some sort of fiddle going on. 'Look, Bernard. I saw Zena last week. She's promised to come back to me.'

He wanted my congratulations. 'That's good, Werner.'

'She was in Berlin . . . just a quick visit. We had lunch together. She wanted to know how I was.'

'And how were you?'

'I want her back, Bernie. I can't manage without her. I told her that.'

'And?'

'I told her I'd have more money. Money was always the problem with us. If I make a bit more money, she'd come back to me. She more or less promised.'

'I'll try again to get London to approve the money, Werner. Forget this mad idea of forging the avals or whatever it is you're doing. If you get into trouble in the East, they'll toss you into the cooler and throw away the key. It'll be "defrauding the people" or some such all-embracing charge, and they'll hammer you to make sure no one else pulls the same trick.'

Werner nodded. 'I'm just going to do it a couple of times so I have enough cash not to have to go crawling to the banks any more. Those money-market bastards are squeezing me, Bernie. They take the cream off every deal I do.'

'I said forget it, Werner.'

'I promised to take Zena to Spain for a really good holiday. Ever been to Marbella? It's wonderful. One day I'll buy a little place there and settle down. Zena needs some sunshine and a rest. So do I. Something like that would give us a new start. Maybe South America, even. It's worth taking a chance for a new start in life.'

Werner had finished two cups of black coffee and now he was holding the pot and shaking the last few drips from the spout. I said, 'Does Frank know about your import and export racket?'

'Frank Harrington? Good God, no. He goes out of his way to avoid me. Last month I was in that change office in Zoo station cashing traveller's cheques. Frank was there already. When he caught sight of me, he left the line and walked out. Frank Harrington is avoiding me. No. Hell, he's the last person I'd discuss it with.' He picked up the second coffeepot, swirling it to find out if there was coffee in it. 'Can I have the rest?'

I nodded. 'Why not tell Frank?'

This time Werner put cream into his coffee. He had the compulsive desire to drink and nibble that is often a sign of nervousness. 'I don't want him to know I'm going over there frequently.'

'Is there something you're not telling me?'

He became very concerned with his coffee, unwrapping another sugar cube, breaking it and putting half into his cup. Then he put the unused half in his mouth and chewed it noisily while he smoothed the wrapper flat with the edge of his hand. 'Don't mother me, Bernie. We grew up together. We both know what's what.'

'You're not playing footsie with those people in the East?' I persisted. 'You haven't come to some damn-fool arrangement with them?'

'So I can give away all your secrets, you mean?' He folded the sugar wrapper carefully and neatly to make a tiny paper dart. He flew it towards the salt and pepper in a test flight. 'What could I tell them? That Frank cuts me dead in the change office, that you come into town and stay at Lisl's? Shall I tell them that rumours say that London's chosen you to take over Berlin from Frank but Frank won't approve you as his successor?'

I looked at his paper dart. 'You could be useful to them, Werner. You've got an ear to the ground.' I picked up the dart and threw it back at him, but it didn't fly for me.

'Can't you understand?' he said in a low voice. 'No one gives me work any more. Frank has put the boot in. I used to get jobs from the Americans and your military intelligence people were always having something come up they couldn't handle. Now I don't get any of those jobs any more. I don't know enough to be a double, Bernie. I'm out of it. Your jobs are the only ones I get these days, and you only give me those for old times' sake – I know it and so do you.'

I didn't remind Werner that only a few minutes earlier he'd been insisting that it was 'only fair' to tell him everything I knew about the leaks in London. 'So they're saying that I'm to get Berlin? Maybe they are even saying who will get my job when I move.'

Werner picked up the dart. It flew well for him but only because he took his time refolding the wings and adjusting everything for optimum aerodynamics. 'You know what it's like in this town, people are always gossiping. I don't want you to think I believe any of that stuff.'

'Come on, Werner. You've got my attention now. You might as well tell me what you've heard. I'm not going to break down and weep about it.'

Those words appeared to have more meaning for him than I ever intended. We were speaking German and it is in the nature of German syntax that you have to compose the sentence in your mind before you start to say it. You can't start each sentence with a vague idea and change your mind halfway through, as people brought up to speak English do. So once Werner began he had to say it. 'There are rumours that your wife is taking over your job from you in London.'

'Now that's a neat twist,' I said. I still didn't guess what poor old Werner was trying to tell me.

He held the dart up to his face so that he could see it properly in the poor light of the café. He gave all his attention to it as he spoke rather hurriedly. 'They say you're splitting up, you and your wife. They say . . . they say that Rensselaer and your wife are . . .' He launched the dart, but this time it spiralled down into his saucer and the wings went brown with spilled coffee.

'Bret Rensselaer,' I said. 'He's nearly old enough to be her father. I can't imagine Fiona falling for Rensselaer.'

The expression on Werner's face let it be known that the failure of imagination was entirely mine. 'If Rensselaer felt guilty about giving Cruyer the German desk and taking your wife from you, he'd be smart to get Berlin for you. It would get you out of his way. The money is good and the unaccountable expenses are the best in the business. It's a job you'd dearly like, and be damned good at. You'd never turn it down, Bernie, you know that.'

I thought about it. It made me feel sick, but I was determined not to reveal that. 'And I wouldn't stand in Fiona's way if she got the chance of a senior post in Operations. She'd be the only woman on staff level there.' I smiled. 'It's neat, Werner. Like all good rumours it's neater than the truth. The fact is that Fiona can't stand Rensselaer, and the old man would never allow a woman in there, and no one's going to offer me Berlin when Frank goes.' I smiled, but my smile got stuck and he looked away.

'How can you be sure?' said Werner. 'I never thought my wife would go off to Munich with that Coca-Cola driver. I met him a couple of times. She told me he was the brother of a girl at her office. She said he sometimes gave her a lift home. He was in the apartment when I got back one evening. He was having a beer with her. I never suspected a thing. I was like you are now. She said he was a bit stupid. That's all it took to convince me there was nothing between them. It was just like you said just now. I thought she couldn't stand the guy, like you say your wife can't stand Rensselaer.' He unwrapped another sugar cube and began to fold himself another flying dart. 'Maybe the fact is that *you* can't stand him – just like I couldn't stand that truck driver – and so you can't imagine your wife going for him either.' He abandoned his half-made dart and drifted it into the ashtray. 'I've given up smoking,' he said mournfully, 'but I fidget a lot with my hands.'

'You didn't get me over here just to tell me all this stuff about Rensselaer having an affair with Fiona, did you, Werner?'

'No. I wanted to ask you about the office. You're the only person I know who sees Frank Harrington to talk to him on equal terms.'

'I don't see him on equal terms,' I said. 'Frank treats me like I'm a twelve-year-old child.'

'Frank is very patronizing,' said Werner. 'In Frank's day, they were all Cambridge pansies or Greek scholars, like Frank, who thought a little job in the intelligence service would be a good way to earn money while they wrote sonnets. Frank likes you, Bernard. He likes you very much. But he could never reconcile himself to the idea that a tough little Berlin street kid like you could take over the job he's doing. He's friendly with you, I know. But how do you think he really feels about taking orders from someone without a classical education?'

'I don't give him orders,' I said, to correct the record.

'You know what I mean,' said Werner. 'I just want to know what Frank has got against me. If I've done something to make him annoyed, okay. But if it's a misunderstanding, I want a chance to clear it up.'

'What do you care about clearing it up?' I said. 'You've got some racket going that's going to give you a villa in Marbella and Rioja and roses for the rest of your days. What the hell do you care about this clearing up misunderstandings with Frank?'

'Don't be *dumm*, Bernie,' he said. 'Frank could make a lot of trouble for me.'

'You're imagining things, Werner.'

'He hates me, Bernie, and he's frightened of you.'

'Frightened?'

'He's frightened at the idea of you taking over from him. You know too much – you'd ask too many questions, awkward questions. And all Frank cares about these days is keeping himself pure for his index-linked pension. He'll do nothing to prejudice that, never mind all that stuff he gives you about how friendly he was with your father.'

'Frank is tired,' I said. 'Frank has got the "Berlin blues". He doesn't hate anyone. He doesn't even hate the Communists any more. That's why he wants to go.'

'Didn't you hear me tell you that Frank Harrington has blocked your appointment here?'

'And didn't you hear me tell you that that was all bloody rubbish? I'll tell you why they don't use you any more, Werner. You've become a gossip, and that's the worst thing that can happen to anyone in this business. You tell me stupid rumours about this and about that, and you tell me that no one likes you and you can't understand why. You need to pull yourself together, Werner, because otherwise you'll have to add me to that long list of people who don't understand you.'

Werner was hunched over the table, the bulky overcoat and fur collar making him look even bigger than he really was. When he nodded, his chin almost touched the table. 'I understand,' he said. 'When I first realized my wife had betrayed me, I couldn't say a civil word to anyone.'

'I'll call you, Werner,' I said, getting to my feet. 'Thanks for the coffee.'

'Sit down,' said Werner. His voice was soft, but there vas an urgency that transcended our bickering. I sat down. Two men had entered the café. The younger Leuschner had been checking the levels of the bottles of drink arrayed under the big mirror. He turned round and smiled the sort of smile that is the legacy of ten years behind a bar. 'What's it to be?' Nervously he wiped the pitted marble counter, which was one of the very few things in the café that had survived the war as well as the Leuschner brothers. 'Would you like to eat? I can give you *Bratwurst* with red cabbage, or roast chicken with *Spätzle*.'

The men were thirty-year-old heavyweights, with robust shoes, double-breasted raincoats and hats with brims big enough to keep rain from dripping down the neck. I caught Werner's eye. He nodded; they obviously were policemen. One of them picked up the plastic-faced menu that had been put before them. Young Leuschner twirled the end of the big Kaiser Wilhelm moustache that he'd grown to make himself look older. Now, with his balding head, he didn't need it any more. 'Or a drink?'

'Chocolate ice cream,' said one of the men in a voice that dared anyone to be surprised.

'Schnaps,' said the other.

Leuschner chose from one of the half-dozen varieties of strong clear liquor and poured a generous measure. Then he put two scoops of ice cream into a dented serving dish and supplied napkin and spoon. 'And a glass of water,' mumbled the man, who'd already begun to gobble the ice cream. His companion turned to rest his back against the edge of the counter and look casually round the room as he sipped his drink. Neither man sat down.

I poured milk into my cup, in order to provide myself with something to do, and stirred it with care. The man eating the ice cream finished it in record time. The other muttered something inaudible, and both men came across to the table where I was sitting with Werner.

'You live near here?' said the chocolate ice cream.

'Dahlem,' said Werner. He smiled, trying to hide his resentment.

'That's a nice place to live,' said the ice-cream cop. It was difficult to decide how much was pleasantry and how much was sarcasm.

'Let's see your papers,' said the second man. He was leaning all his weight on the back of my chair and I could smell the Schnaps on his breath.

Werner hesitated for a moment, trying to decide whether anything was to be gained by making them prove they were policemen. Then he brought out his wallet.

'Open up the case,' said the ice cream, pointing to the document case Werner had placed on the seat beside him.

'That's mine,' I said.

'I don't care if it belongs to Herbert von Karajan,' said the cop.

'But I do,' I said. This time I spoke in English.

He glanced at my face and at my English clothes. I didn't have to spell it out that I was an officer of the 'protecting powers'. 'Identification?'

I passed to him the Army officer's card that identified me as a Major Bishop of the Royal Engineers. He gave me a bleak smile and said, 'This identification expired two months ago.'

'And what do you think might have happened since then?' I said. 'You think I've changed into someone else?'

He gave me a hard stare. 'I'd get your identification brought up to date if I was you, Major Bishop,' he said. 'You might find the next policeman you encounter suspects you of being a deserter or a spy or something.'

'Then the next policeman I encounter will make a fool of himself,' I said. But by that time both men were moving off across the room. The ice cream dropped a couple of coins onto the counter as he passed.

'Bloody Nazis,' said Werner. 'They picked me because I'm a Jew.'

'Don't be a fool, Werner.'

'Then why?'

'There could be a million reasons why a cop asks for papers. There could be some local crime . . . a recognized car nearby . . . someone with a description like you.'

'They'll get the military police. They'll come back and make us open the case. They'll do it just to show us who's the boss.'

'No, they won't, Werner. They'll go down the street to the next café or bar and try again.'

'I wish you weren't so damned obstinate.'

'About what?'

'Frank Harrington. This is the way he keeps the pressure up.'

'Have you ever stopped to think how much it costs to keep a man under surveillance? Four men and two cars on eight-hour shifts working a five-day week. We're talking about a minimum of six men and three cars. The cars must be radio-equipped to our wavelength, so that rules out rented ones. The men must be trained and vetted. Allowing for insurance and special pensions and medical schemes all Department employees have, each man would cost well over a thousand Deutschemark. The cars cost at least another thousand each. Add another thousand for the cost of backup and we're talking about Frank spending ten thousand marks a week on you. He'd have to hate you an awful lot, Werner.'

'Ask him,' said Werner sullenly. I had the feeling that he didn't want to be disillusioned about Frank's vendetta lest he have to face the fact that maybe Frank sacked him because he wasn't doing the job the way they wanted it done.

I raised my hands in supplication. 'I'll talk to him, Werner. But meanwhile you cut it out. Forget all this stuff about Frank persecuting you. Will you do that?'

'You don't understand,' said Werner.

I looked at the document case that I'd pretended was mine. 'And, just to satisfy my curiosity, what is in "my" case, Werner?'

He reached out to touch it, 'Would you believe nearly half a million Swiss francs in new paper?'

I looked at him but he didn't smile. 'Take care, Werner,' I said. Even when we'd been kids together, I never knew when he was fooling.

II

I remembered Frank Harrington's parties back in the days when my father took me along to the big house in Grunewald, wearing my first dinner jacket. Things had changed since then, but the house was still the same, and came complete with a gardener, cook, housekeeper, maid, and the valet who had been with Frank during the war.

I shared Frank's 'just wear anything, it's only potluck' evening with a dozen of Berlin's richest and most influential citizens. At dinner I was placed next to a girl named Poppy, recently divorced from a man who owned two breweries and an aspirin factory. Around the table there was a man from the Bundesbank and his wife; a director of West Berlin's Deutsche Opera, accompanied by its most beautiful mezzo-soprano; a lady museum director said to be a world authority on ancient Mesopotamian pottery; a Berlin Polizeipräsidium official who was introduced simply as ' . . . from Tempelhofer Damm'; and Joe Brody, a quietly spoken American who preferred to be described as an employee of Siemen's electrical factory. Frank Harrington's wife was there, a formidable lady of about sixty, with a toothy smile and the sort of compressed permanent wave that fitted like a rubber swimming hat. The Harringtons' son, a British Airways first officer on the Berlin route, was also present. He was an amiable young man with a thin blond moustache and a complexion so pink it looked as if his mother had scrubbed him clean before letting him come down to the dining room.

They were all dressed up to the nines, of course. The ladies wore long dresses and the mezzo-soprano had jewellery in her hair. The wife of the man from the central bank had diversified into gold and the lady museum director wore Pucci. The men were in dark suits with the sort of buttonhole ribbons and striped ties that provided all the information needed, to anyone entitled to know.

Over dinner the talk was of money and culture.

'There's seldom any friction between Frankfurt and Bonn,' said the man from the Bundesbank.

'Not while you are pouring your profits back to the government. Ten billion Deutschemark – is that what you're giving to the politicians again this year?' said Frank. Of course they must have guessed who Frank Harrington was, or had some idea of what he did for a living.

The Bundesbank man smiled but didn't confirm it.

The lady museum director joined in and said, 'Suppose you and Bonn both run short of money at the same time?'

'It's not the role of the Bundesbank to support the government, or to help with the economy, get back to full employment or balance trade. The Bundesbank's primary role is to keep monetary stability.'

'Maybe that's the way you see it,' said the mezzo-soprano, 'but it only requires a parliamentary majority in Bonn to make the role of the central bank anything the politicians want it to be.'

The Bundesbank official cut himself another chunk of the very smelly double-cream Limburger, and took a slice of black bread before answering. 'We're convinced that the independence of the Bundesbank is now regarded as a constitutional necessity. No government would affront public opinion by attempting to take us over by means of a parliamentary majority.'

Frank Harrington's son, who'd read history at Cambridge, said, 'Reichsbank officials were no doubt saying the same thing right up to the time that Hitler changed the law to let him print as much paper money as he needed.'

'As you do in Britain?' said the Bundesbank official politely.

Mrs Harrington hurriedly returned to the mezzo-soprano and said, 'What have you heard about the new *Parsifal* production?'

'*Du siehst, mein Sohn, zum Raum wird hier die Zeit.*' These words – 'You see, my son, time here turns into space' – provided Mrs Harrington, the mezzo-soprano and the ancient-pottery expert with an opportunity to pick the plot of *Parsifal* over for philosophical allusions and symbols. It was a rich source of material for after-dinner conversation, but I wearied of listening to it and found it more amusing to argue with Poppy about the relative merits of *alcool blanc* and whether *poire, framboise, quetsche* or *mirabelle* was the most delicious. It was an argument that dedicated experiment with Frank Harrington's sideboard array had left unresolved by the time Poppy got to her feet and said, 'The ladies are withdrawing. Come with me.'

The desire to flirt with her was all part of the doubts and fears I had about Fiona. I wanted to prove to myself that I could play the field too, and Poppy would have been an ideal conquest. But I was sober enough to realize that this was not the right time, and Frank Harrington's house was certainly not the place.

'Poppy dearest,' I said, my veins fired by a surfeit of mixed *eaux de vie*, 'you can't leave me now. I will never get to my feet unaided.' I pretended to be very drunk. The truth was that, like all field agents who'd survived, I'd forgotten what it was like to be truly drunk.

'*Poire* is the best,' she said, picking up the bottle. 'And a raspberry for you, my friend.' She banged the bottle of *framboise* onto the table in front of me.

She departed clutching the half-full bottle of pear spirit, her empty glass and discarded shoes to her bosom. I watched her regretfully. Poppy was my sort of woman. I drank two cups of black coffee and went across the room to corner Frank. 'I saw Werner last night,' I told him.

'Poor you,' said Frank. 'Let me top up your brandy if you are going to start on that one.' He stepped away far enough to get the brandy, but I put a hand over my glass. 'What an idiot I am,' said Frank. 'You're drinking that stuff the ladies are having.'

I ignored this barb and said, 'He thinks you've got it in for him.'

Frank poured some brandy for himself and furrowed his brow as if thinking hard. He put the bottle down on a side table before he answered. 'We have an instruction on his file. You know, Bernard, you've seen it.'

'Yes, I checked it out,' I said. 'It's been there five years. Isn't it time we let him try again?'

'Something not very sensitive, you mean. Umm.'

'He feels out of things.'

'And so he might,' said Frank. 'The Americans don't use him and he's never done anything much for anyone else here.'

I looked at Frank and nodded to let him know what a stupid answer that was: the Americans got copies of the sheet that said we were not using Werner. They would not use him without some very good reason. 'He thinks you have a personal grudge against him.'

'Did he say why?'

'He said he can't understand why.'

Frank looked round the room. The police official was talking to Poppy; he caught Frank's eye and smiled. Frank's son was listening to the mezzo-soprano, and Mrs Harrington was telling the maid – uniformed in the sort of white cap and apron that I'd seen otherwise only in old photos – to bring the semi-sweet champagne that would be so refreshing. Frank turned back to me as if regretting that nothing else demanded his immediate attention. 'Perhaps I should have told you about Werner before this,' he said. 'But I try to keep these things on a "need to know" basis.'

'Sure,' I said. Poppy was laughing at something the policeman told her. How could she find him so amusing?

'I put Werner in charge of the communications room security one night back in September 1978. There was a lot of signals traffic. The Baader–Meinhof gang had hijacked a Lufthansa Boeing, and Bonn was convinced they were flying it to Prague. . . . You ask your wife about it, she'll remember that night. No one got a wink of sleep.'

He sipped some of his brandy. 'About three o'clock in the morning, a cipher clerk came in with an intercept from the Russian Army transmitter at Karlshorst. It was a message from the commanding general requesting that some military airfield in southwest Czechoslovakia be kept operational on a twenty-four-hour basis until further notice. I knew what that message referred to because of other signals I'd seen, and I knew it wasn't anything to do with the Baader–Meinhof people, so I put a hold on that message. My interception unit was the only one to file that signal that night, and I've checked that one through NATO.'

'I'm not sure what you're getting at, Frank,' I said.

'That damned message went back through Karlshorst with "intercepted traffic" warnings on it. Werner was the only person who knew about it.'

'Not the only person, Frank. What about the cipher clerk, the operator, the clerk who filed the signal after you'd stopped it, your secretary, your assistant . . . lots of people.'

Artfully, Frank steered the conversation another way. 'So you were talking to dear old Werner last night. Where did this reunion take place – Anhalter station?'

The surprise showed on my face.

Frank said, 'Come along, Bernard. You used that old military identification card I let you have, and you were too damned idle to hand it back when it expired. You know those bogus cards have numbers that ensure we get a phone call when one turns up in a police report. I okayed it, of course. I guessed it was you. Who else would be in Leuschner's café at that time of night except drug pushers, pimps, whores and vagabonds, and that incurable romantic Bernard Samson?'

Joe Brady, the American 'from Siemen's' drifted over to us. 'What kind of caper are you two hatching up?' he said.

'We were talking about Anhalter station,' said Frank.

Joe Brody sighed. 'Before the war, that was the centre of the universe. Even now old-time Berliners walk out there to look at that slab of broken masonry and fancy they can hear the trains.'

'Joe was here in '39 and '40,' said Frank. 'He saw Berlin when the Nazis were riding high.'

'And came back with the US Army. And shall I tell you something else about Anhalter Bahnhof? When we got copies of Stalin's order to his Belorussian Front and his Ukraine Front for a converging attack that would take Berlin and end the war, the point at which those great armies would meet was specified as Anhalter Bahnhof.'

Frank nodded and said, 'Joe, tell Bernard what we did about that Karlshorst signal . . . the one about the airfield remaining open for the Russian commanding general. Do you remember?'

Joe Brody was a bright-eyed bald American who held his nose while he was thinking, like a man about to jump into deep water. 'What do you want to know, Mr Samson?'

Frank Harrington answered on my behalf. 'Tell him how we discovered who had divulged that interception.'

'You've got to realize that this wasn't a big deal,' Brody said slowly. 'But Frank thought it was important enough to suspend the clearance of everyone on duty that night until we got a lead on it.'

'We checked everyone who handled the message,' said Frank. 'I had nothing against Werner. I suspected the cipher clerk, as a matter of fact, but he came out clean.'

'Was Giles Trent handling signals traffic at that time?'

'Giles Trent? Yes, he was here then.'

'No, no,' said Brody. 'No chance you can pin this on Giles Trent. The way I understand it, he had no access to signals traffic.'

'Can you remember so well?' I said.

Brody's gold-rimmed glasses flashed as he turned his head to be sure he wasn't overheard. 'Frank gave me a free hand. He told me to dig as deep as I wanted. I guess Frank wanted me to go back to my people and tell them you Brits weren't about to paper over the cracks in the future.' Frank wet his lips and smiled to show he was still listening even if he had heard the story before. 'So I dug,' said Joe Brody. 'It was your guy Werner something . . .'

'Werner Volkmann,' I supplied.

'Volkmann. That's right!' said Brody. 'We eliminated the others, one by one. This other guy – Trent, Giles Trent – took a little extra time because London got sticky about letting us read his file. But he was in the clear.' He grabbed his nose again. 'Volkmann was the leak, believe me. I've done hundreds of these investigations.'

'And never made a mistake?' I asked.

'Not that kind of mistake,' said Brody. 'I don't go around ripping away a security clearance just to make myself feel six feet tall. This was Volkmann. Not Trent, nor any of the others – unless everyone was telling me lies. So you can tell your people in London the file is closed on that one.'

'Suppose I told you Trent is now an orange file?' I said.

'Holy cow!' said Brody without too much emotion. 'Is this going to become another one of those?'

'It looks as if it's nipped in the bud,' I said. 'But I would take a lot of convincing that Trent wasn't in on your problem too.'

'I know the feeling, young man,' said Brody. 'Research and investigation are no damn use if they don't support those prejudiced judgments we've already worked so hard on.'

'Anyone except Werner – that's it, isn't it?' said Frank.

'No!' I said too loudly. 'It's not that.'

'Bernard was at school with Werner,' Frank explained to Brody.

'Your loyalty does you credit, kid,' said Brody. 'Jesus, I know guys in your position who'd be trying to pin it on their wife.'

Frank Harrington laughed and so did Brody.

The next morning, I had breakfast with Lisl. We sat in the room she called her study. It had a tiny balcony that looked out on the traffic of Kantstrasse.

It was a wonderful room and I remembered it from the time I was small, and permitted inside when my father came to settle his monthly account. Apart from the walls covered with small framed photos, there were a thousand other wonders for a child's eye. There were small tables littered with ivory snuffboxes, a brass ashtray fashioned from a section of World War I shell-casing, the words A PRESENT FROM LEMBERG hammered into the brass, and Russian buttons soldered round its edge. There were two fans, open to reveal Japanese landscapes; a small china zeppelin with BERLIN-STAAKEN on its side; opera glasses made of yellowing ivory; and a silver carriage clock that didn't work. Most dazzling of all to the small boy I once was, a Prussian medal awarded to Lisl's grandfather, a magnificent piece of military jewellery suitably mounted on faded red velvet in a silver frame which Lisl's maids kept gleaming bright.

Breakfast was set on a small table against the window, which was open enough to move the lace curtain but not enough to move the starched linen table cloth. Lisl was seated in the high dining chair from which she could get up without assistance. I arrived exactly on time; I knew that nothing dooms a meeting with a German more completely than tardiness. '*Mein Liebchen*,' said Lisl. 'Give me a kiss. I can't jump up and down – it's this damned arthritis.'

I bent over and kissed her, careful to avoid the heavily applied rouge, powder and lipstick. I wondered how early she must have risen to have prepared her hair and makeup. 'Don't ever change it,' I said. 'Your glamorous room is still as enchanting as ever.'

She smiled. '*Nein, nein.*' That ummistakable Berlin accent: ny-yen, ny-yen. I knew I was home when I heard it.

'It's still the same as when my father was alive,' I said.

She liked to be complimented on the room. 'It's still exactly as it was when *my* father was alive,' she said. She looked round to be sure she was telling the truth. 'For a few years, we had a photo of the Führer over the fireplace – a signed photo – but it was a relief to put Kaiser Wilhelm back there.'

'Even if it's not signed,' I said.

'Naughty!' Lisl admonished, but she permitted herself a small smile. 'So, your work is complete and now you go home to your gorgeous wife and your dear children. When are you going to bring them to see me, darling?'

'Soon,' I said, helping myself to coffee.

'It had better be,' she said, and chuckled. 'Or your Tante Lisl will be pushing up the daisies.' She tore a piece from her bread roll and said, 'Werner says we Germans have too many words for death. Is that true?'

'In English we say "dead shot", "dead letter", a "dead fire", "dead calm", and so on. German is more precise, and has a different word for each meaning.'

'Werner says the Germans have a thousand different words for death, just as the Eskimos are said to have so many different words for snow. And the Jews have so many different words for idiot.'

'Do they?'

' "Schmo", "schlemiel", "schnook", "schmuck".' She laughed.

'Do you see a lot of Werner?'

'He's a good boy. I get lonely now I'm unable to get about on my feet, and Werner pops in to see me whenever he's passing. He's about the same age as you, you know.'

'He's a bit older, but we were in the same class at school.'

'I remember the night he was born. It was the 1st of March 1943. It was a bad air raid – fires in Bachstrasse and the Sigismundhof. Unter den Linden suffered and the passage through to the Friedrich-strassse was ruined. There were unexploded bombs in the grounds of the Italian Embassy and the house of the Richthofen family. A bomb stopped the church clock on Ku-Damn and it's stayed at seven-thirty ever since. Sometimes I say to him, "You stopped that clock the night you were born." Werner's mother was the cook for us. She lived with her husband in an attic just four doors along from here. I went and got her just before her contractions began. Werner was born in this house, did you know that? Of course you did. I must have told you a thousand times.'

'Werner,' I said. 'What kind of name is that for a nice Jewish boy?'

'One name for the world, another name for the family,' said Lisl. 'That's always the way it is for them.'

'Did you hide all the family, Lisl? What about his father?'

'His father was a big strong man – Werner inherited his build – and he worked as a gravedigger at the Jewish cemetery at Weissensee all through the war.'

'And was never arrested?'

She smiled the sort of smile I'd seen on other German faces, a look reserved for those who would never understand. 'So that the Nazis would have to assign Aryans to look after Jewish graves and bury Jewish dead? No, the workers at Weissensee cemetery were never arrested. When the Russians got here in '45 there was still a rabbi walking free. He was working there as a gravedigger with Werner's papa.' She laughed but I didn't. Only people who'd been here when the Russians arrived were permitted to laugh about it.

'It was after the war that Werner's father died. He died of not getting enough to eat for year after year.'

'Werner was lucky,' I said. 'Five-year-old orphans did not have much chance.'

'Is he in some sort of trouble?' said Lisl. She'd caught some careless inflection of my voice.

I hesitated. 'Werner can be headstrong,' I said.

'I've given him half my savings, *Liebchen*.'

'He wouldn't swindle you, Lisl.'

Her mascaraed eyelashes fluttered. 'I can't afford to lose it,' she said. 'I had it invested, but Werner said he could make more for me. I have it all in writing. I'm easy to handle, Werner knows that.' It was typical of her that she used the fashionable word '*pflegeleicht*', usually applied to non-iron clothes. But Lisl was not *pflegeleicht*: she was old-fashioned linen, with lots of starch.

'He won't swindle you, Tante Lisl. Werner owes you more than he can ever repay, and he knows it. But if he loses your money, there is nothing in writing that will get it back for you.'

'It's something to do with exports,' said Lisl, as if a measure of confession would persuade me to help her.

'I have to come back here,' I said. 'I'll talk to him on my next visit. But you should be more careful with your money, Lisl.'

She blew air through her teeth in a gesture of contempt. 'Careful? We have some of the oldest, biggest, richest corporations in Germany facing bankruptcy and you tell me to be careful. Where am I to invest my savings?'

'I'll do what I can, Lisl.'

'A woman on her own is helpless in these matters, darling.'

'I know, Lisl, I know.' I found myself thinking about Fiona again. I remembered phoning her from Berlin on the previous trip. I'd phoned her three or four times in the middle of the night and got no reply. She said the phone was out of order, but I went on wondering.

Watery sunshine trickled over the Persian carpet and made a golden buttress in the dusty air. Lisl stopped talking to chew her bread roll; the phone rang. It was for me: Frank Harrington. 'Bernard? I'm glad I caught you. I'm sending a car to take you to the airport this afternoon. What time do you want to leave Frau Hennig's? Do you want to stop off anywhere?'

'I've fixed up a car, Frank. Thanks all the same.'

'No, no, no. I insist.'

'I can't cancel it now, Frank.'

There was a pause at the other end before Frank said, 'It was like old times, seeing you again last night.'

'I should have thanked you,' I said, although I had already arranged for Mrs Harrington to receive a bunch of flowers.

'That conversation we had . . . about you know whom . . . I hope you won't be putting any of that in writing in London.'

So that was it. 'I'll be discreet, Frank,' I said.

'I know you will, old boy. Well, if you won't let me arrange a car . . .'

I knew 'the car' would turn out to be Frank, who would 'just happen to be going out that way' and would bend my ear until takeoff time. So I made regret noises and rang off.

'Frank Harrington?' said Lisl. 'Wanting some favour, no doubt.'

'Frank's always been a worrier. You know that.'

'He's not trying to borrow money, is he?'

'I can't imagine him being short of it.'

'He keeps a big house in England and his spectacular place here. He's always entertaining.'

'That's part of the job, Lisl,' I said. I was long since accustomed to Lisl's complaints about the wasteful ways of government servants.

'And the little popsie he's got tucked away in Lübars – is she part of the job too?' Lisl's laugh was more like a splutter of indignation.

'Frank?'

'I get to hear everything, darling. People think I am just a stupid old woman safely locked away up here in my little room, rubbing embrocation on my knees, but I get to hear everything.'

'Frank was in the Army with my father. He must be sixty years old.'

'That's the dangerous age, darling. Didn't you know that? You've got the dangerous sixties to look forward to too, *Liebchen*.' She spilled coffee trying to get it to her mouth without laughing.

'You've been listening to Werner,' I said.

Her lashes trembled and she fixed me with her steely eyes. 'You think you can get me to tell you where I heard it. I know your little tricks, Bernard.' A waggling finger. 'But it wasn't Werner. And I know all about Frank Harrington, who comes in here looking as if butter wouldn't melt in his mouth.' She used the equivalent Berlin expression about looking as if he wouldn't dirty a stream, and it seemed so apt for the impeccable Frank and his scrubbed-looking son. 'His wife spends too much time in England, and Frank has found other amusements here in town.'

'You're a fund of information, Tante Lisl,' I said. I kept my voice level to show her that I was not convinced about Frank's double life, and would not be too concerned even if I was convinced.

'A man in his line of business should know better. A man with a mistress in an expensive little house in Lübars is a security risk.'

'I suppose so.'

I thought she was going to change the subject, but she couldn't resist adding, 'And Lübars is so near the Wall. . . . You're damned near the Russkies right up there.'

'I know where Lübars is, Lisl,' I said grumpily.

'Happy birthday, darling,' she said as I reached the door.

'Thanks, Lisl,' I said. She never missed my birthday.

12

From the top of the brightly coloured apartment blocks of Märkisches Viertel, where sixty thousand West Berliners live in what the architects call 'a planned community' and its inhabitants call a 'concrete jungle', you can see across the nearby border, and well into the Eastern Sector.

'Some of them like it here,' said Axel Mauser. 'At least they say they do.' Axel had aged a lot over the last few years. He was three months younger than I was, but his pinched white face and large bald patch, and the way his years at desk and filing cabinet had bowed his head, made him look nearer to fifty than forty. 'They say they like having the shops and the church and the swimming pool and restaurants all built as part of the complex.'

I sipped a little beer and looked around the room. It was a barren place; no books, no pictures, no music, no carpet. Just a TV, a sofa, two armchairs and a coffee table with a vase of plastic flowers. In the corner, newspaper was laid out to protect the floor against oil. On it were the pieces of a dismantled racing bicycle that was being repaired to make a birthday present for his teenage son. 'But you don't?'

'Finish your beer and have another. No, I hate it. We've got twelve schools and fifteen kindergartens here in this complex. Twelve schools! It makes me feel like a damned termite. Some of these kids have never been downtown – they've never seen the Berlin we grew up in.'

'Maybe they are better off without it,' I said.

There was a snap and hiss as he opened a can of Export Pils. 'You're right, Bernd,' he said. 'What will kids find down there in the middle of the city except crime and dope and misery?' He poured half the can for himself and the other half for me. Axel was like that; he was a sharer.

'Well, you've got a view to beat anything.'

'It's amazing how far you can see on a really clear day. But I'd happily trade the view to be back in that old slum my grandfather had. I keep hearing about the "German miracle", but I don't see any of it. My father gave me a new bicycle for my twelfth birthday. What can I afford to give my eldest son? That damned secondhand one.'

'Kids don't think like that, Axel,' I said. 'Even I can see it's a special racing model. He'll like it all the more because you've worked so hard to get it ready for him.'

Axel Mauser had been one of the brightest kids in the school: top of the class at chemistry and mathematics, and so keen at languages that he used to lend me his bicycle in exchange for English conversation practice. Now he was working in the Polizeipräsidium records office as a senior clerk, and living in this cramped apartment with three children and a wife, who – even on a Saturday – worked in the nearby AEG factory to keep their secondhand BMW running and give them their regular package holiday in Ibiza. 'But where can I afford to move to? Do you know what rents people are paying in Berlin nowadays?'

'Your dad went back to live in the East.'

Axel smiled grimly. 'All because of that bloody fool Binder – Max Binder, remember that *Spieler*?'

Spieler: did he mean actor or gambler, I wondered. Max was a bit of both. 'I always liked Max,' I said.

Axel paused as if about to argue with me but then he went on: 'Max kept writing to Dad saying how much he was enjoying life over there. My dad believed it all. You know what Dad's like. He kept complaining about how it was over thirty years since he'd strolled down Unter den Linden. He'd wonder if he'd meet old friends on the Alexanderplatz – he was always on about that damned "Alex" – and he wanted to see the restoration job that's been done on the cathedral. And he'd get talking to Tante Lisl in that bar of hers when there were no customers in, and they'd be wallowing in nostalgia about seeing President Hindenburg in the Bristol and Lotte Lenya at the Wintergarten. . . .'

'And talking to Joseph Goebbels at the bar of the Kaiserhof,' I said. 'Yes, I've heard all those stories. I couldn't get enough of your dad's yarns when I was young. I saw a lot of him in those days when he was behind the bar at Lisl's.' From the next apartment there came the incessant sound of police sirens, shooting and the joyful shouts of children watching TV. Axel went across to the wall and thumped on it with the flat of his hand. This had no effect other than to make some of the plastic flowers quiver.

Axel shrugged at the continuing noise. 'And working for your dad too. Suppose they find out that he used to do those jobs for your dad? They'd throw him straight into prison.'

'Don't baby him, Axel. Rolf's a tough old bastard. He can look after himself.'

Axel nodded. 'So I said, "If you think you'll recapture your youth by going across the city, Dad, you go. And, take Tante Lisl with you. . . .'' When my mother was alive, she wouldn't listen to all those stories of his. She'd just tell him to shut up.'

'Well, he found a ready audience at that bar.'

'He was always complaining about working for Tante Lisl, wasn't he? But he loved standing behind the bar talking about "the real Berlin", in the days when there was a respect for Christian values – *eine christliche Weltanschauung*. And after a few customers had bought him drinks, he'd be talking about the *Kaiserzeit* as if he'd been a general in the first war instead of an artillery captain in the second.' Axel drank some beer. 'There's no fool like an old fool,' he said with unexpected vehemence, and looked at his beer so that I could not see his eyes. 'I'd hate anything to happen to him, Bernd.'

'I know,' I said. 'But don't worry about him. He's over sixty-five, so he is permitted to visit the West.'

'He sees Werner sometimes.' He looked at me. 'They're in some kind of racket together.'

It was more a question than a statement. 'Are they?'

'Are you still with the Army intelligence people?'

I nodded. It was my cover story for Berliners such as Axel who remembered my father and had seen me coming and going, and had given me the use of their sofas and their motorcars from time to time. It was not the sort of cover story that earned respect from Germans. Germany is the only country in the world where a job in any sort of intelligence-gathering organization is considered little better than pimping. It is a product of the postwar years when informers were everywhere.

'You're not after Dad?'

'Stop worrying about him, Axel,' I said. 'Rolf came right through the war, and then survived through the years that followed the war. I'm sure he's doing fine. In fact, I might be able to look him up next time I go into the East Sector. I'll take him something, if you like.'

'So what's it all about, Bernd?' said Axel. He got up and went to the window, staring eastwards to where the spike of the East German TV tower rose out of the Alexanderplatz. Once it was the heart of the city,' where pedestrians dodged bikes, bikes dodged cars, and cars dodged the trams that came through a five-way intersection at frightening speeds. Now the traffic had vanished and the 'Alex' was just an orderly concrete expanse, with red flags, flower boxes and slogans. 'You might as well come out with it,' said Axel, still staring out the window.

'With what?'

'It's nice to see you again, Bernd. But you work out of London nowadays, you say. With only a couple of days in the city and lots of old friends to visit, you didn't come to my little place to talk about how well I did in my chemistry exams, and have a can of beer – which I notice you drink very very slowly, as policemen do when they are on duty – and be interrupted by the shouting of the kids next door, and sit close to the heating because I can't afford to turn it up any higher. You must have had a reason to come here, and I think you are going to ask me a favour.'

'Remember a couple of years ago when I was looking for that kid who'd stolen a briefcase from an office near the Zoo station?'

'You asked me to look up a post-office box number and tell you who rented it. But that was an official request. That came through the British Army.'

'This one is more delicate, Axel.' I took from my pocket the envelope that Frank Harrington had left in my street guide. Axel took it reluctantly; even then he didn't immediately look at it. 'It's urgent, I suppose? These things are always urgent.' He read the address.

'It is, Axel. Otherwise I could have gone through the post office.'

He laughed scornfully. 'Have you tried getting anything out of our wonderful post office lately? Last week it took them four days to deliver a letter from a postbox in Tiergarten, and then it was nearly torn in two. And the price for a letter now. . . .' He read the numbers that were the address. 'One thousand is Berlin and twenty-eight is Lübars.'

'You said Polizeipräsidium kept copies of the forms the box renters sign. Could you get the name and address of the person who rents that box at Lübars post office? Could you get it even on a Saturday?'

'I'll phone from the bedroom.'

'Thanks, Axel.'

'It depends who's on duty this morning. I can't order anyone to do it. It's strictly forbidden . . . it's a criminal offence.'

'If I could clear up the inquiry immediately, I could go home.'

'We all thought you'd grow up to become a gangster,' said Axel. 'Did I ever tell you that?'

'Yes, Axel. You've told me that many times.'

'We asked Herrn Storch, the mathematics teacher, but he said all the English were like you.'

'Some of them are worse, Axel,' I said.

He didn't laugh; he nodded. He wanted me to know how much he disliked it. He wanted me to think twice before I asked him more such favours. When he went into the bedroom to phone, he turned the key in the door. He wanted to be sure that I could not get close enough to hear him.

The call took only five minutes. I suppose the Polizeipräsidium have such records on a computer.

'The addressee, Mrs Harrington, is the renter of the box. She gave an address in Lübars,' said Axel when he returned from the phone. 'I know exactly where it is. It's a street of beautiful houses with a view across open farmland. What wouldn't I give to live in such a place.'

'How difficult is it to get a postbox in a false name?' I asked.

'It depends who is on duty. But you don't have to provide much to get it in any name you wish. Many people have boxes under a nom de plume or a stage name, and so on.'

'I have not been to Lübars since we were kids. Is it still as pretty as it used to be?'

'Lübars village. We're quite close. If this window faced north, I could show you the street. They've preserved everything: the little eighteenth-century village church, the fire station and the village green with the fine chestnut trees. The farmhouses and the old inn. It's just a stone's throw away but it's like another world.'

'I'll get going, Axel,' I said. 'Thanks for the beer.'

'And what if on Monday they fire me? What then? You say how really sorry you are, and I spend the rest of my life trying to support a family on social welfare payments.'

I said nothing.

'You're irresponsible, Bernd. You always were.'

I would have expected Frank Harrington to have his mistress hidden away in a small anonymous apartment block somewhere in the French Sector of the city where no one notices what's happening. But the address Axel Mauser had provided was in the northernmost part of the Western Sector, a prong of land sandwiched between the Tegel Forest and the Wall. There were small farms here just a short way from the city centre, and tractors were parked on the narrow cobbled lanes among the shiny Porsches and four-litre Mercedes.

The big family houses were designed to look as though they'd been here since Bismarck, but they were too flawless to be anything but reconstructions. I cruised slowly down an elegant tree-lined road following three children on well-groomed ponies. It was neat and tidy and characterless, like those Hollywood back lots designed to look like anywhere old and foreign.

Number 40 was a narrow two-storey house, with a front garden big enough for two large trees and with a lot of empty space behind it. There was a sign on the chain fence, BELLEVUE KENNELS, and another that said BEWARE OF THE DOGS in three languages, including German. Even before I'd read it, the dogs began barking. They sounded like very big dogs.

Once through the inner gate, I could see a wired compound and a

brick outbuilding where some dogs were crowding at the gate trying
to get out. 'Good dog,' I said, but I don't think they heard me.

A young woman came from somewhere at the back of the house.
She was about twenty-two years old, with soft grey eyes, a tanned
sort of complexion, and jet-black hair drawn back into a bun. She
was wearing khaki-coloured cotton pants, and a matching shirt with
shoulder tabs and button-down pockets. It was all tailored to fit very
tight. Over it she had a sleeveless sheepskin jacket – fleece inwards
– with the sort of bright flower-patterned embroidery that used to be
a status symbol for hippies.

She looked me up and down long enough to recognize my Burberry
trench coat and Professor Higgins hat. 'Did you come to buy a dog?'
she said in good English.

'Yes,' I said immediately.

'We only have German shepherds.'

'I like German shepherds.' A big specimen of this breed emerged
from the house. It came within six feet of us, looked at the woman,
before hunching its shoulders and growling menacingly at me.

'You didn't come to buy a dog,' she said, looking at my face.
Whatever she saw there amused her, for she smiled to show perfect
white teeth. So did the dog.

'I'm a friend of Frank's,' I said.

'Of my Frank?'

'There's only one Frank,' I said. She smiled as if that were a joke.

'Has anything – ?'

'No, Frank is fine,' I said. 'In fact, he doesn't even know I've
come to see you.'

She'd been peering at me with eyes half closed, and now suddenly
she opened her mouth and gave a soft shout of surprise. 'You're
Werner's English friend, aren't you?'

We looked at each other, momentarily silenced by our mutual
surprise. 'Yes, I am, Mrs Volkmann,' I said. 'But I didn't come here
to talk about Werner.'

She looked around to see if her neighbours were in their garden
listening. But her neighbours were all safely behind their double-
glazing. 'I can't remember your name but you are the Englishman
who went to school with Werner. . . . Your German is perfect,' she
said, and changed into that language. 'No need for us to speak
English. I'll put Rudolf in the run and then we'll go inside and have
coffee. It's made already.' Rudolf growled. He did not want to go
into the run unless he took me with him.

'During the week, I have a girl to help me,' said Mrs Zena Volkmann while Rudolf submitted meekly to being pushed into the wired
compound. 'But at the weekend it is impossible to get anyone at any
price. They say there is unemployment but people just don't want to

work, that's the trouble.' Now her accent was more distinct. *Ostel-bisch*: Germans from anywhere east of the River Elbe. Everyone agrees it is not pejorative, but I never heard anyone say it except people who came from west of the River Elbe.

We entered the house through a pantry. Arranged in rows upon a purring freezer were twelve coloured plastic bowls containing measured amounts of bread and chopped meat. There was a mop and bucket in the corner, a steel sink unit and shelves with tins of dog food, and choke chains and collars hanging from a row of hooks on the wall. 'I can't go out for more than an hour or two because the puppies have to be fed four times a day. Two litters. One lot are only four weeks old and they need constant attention. And I'm waiting for another litter any day now. I wouldn't have started it all if I'd known what it was like.'

She went up a step and opened the door into the kitchen. There was the wonderful smell of freshly made coffee. There was no sign of anything connected with the dogs. The kitchen was almost unnaturally clean and tidy, with gleaming racks of saucepans, and glassware sparkling inside a cabinet.

She snapped off the switch of the automatic coffee-maker, grabbed the jug from the hot plate, put an extra cup and saucer on the tray, and tipped some biscuits onto a matching plate. The cup was as big as a bowl and decorated with the inevitable large brightly coloured flowers. We went to sit in the back room. The rear part of the house had been altered at some time to incorporate a huge window. It gave a panoramic view of a piece of farmland beyond the dog enclosures. There was a tractor making its way slowly across the field, disturbing a flock of rooks searching for food in the brown tilled earth. Only the grey line of the Wall marred this pastoral scene. 'You get used to it,' said Mrs Volkmann, as if in reply to the question that every visitor asked.

'Not everyone does,' I said.

She took a packet of cigarettes from the table, lit one and inhaled before replying. 'My grandfather had a farm in East Prussia,' she said. 'He came here once and couldn't stop looking at the Wall. His farm was nearly eight hundred kilometres from here but that was still Germany. Do you know how far from here Poland is now? Less than sixty. That's what Hitler did for us. He made Germany into the sort of tiny second-rate little country that he so despised.'

'Shall I pour out the coffee?' I said. 'It smells good.'

'My father was a schoolteacher. He made us children learn history. He said it would prevent the same things happening again.' She smiled. There was no humour in it; it was a small, polite, modest smile, the sort of smile you see models wearing in advertisements for expensive watches.

'Let's hope so,' I said.

'It will not prevent the same things happening. Look at the world. Can't you see Hitlers all round us? There is no difference between Hitler Germany and Andropov Russia. A hammer and sickle can look very like a swastika, especially when it is flying over your head.' She picked up the coffee I'd poured for her. I watched her carefully; there was a lot of hostility in her, even if it was hidden under her smiles and hospitality. 'Werner wants me back,' she said.

'He knows nothing of my coming here,' I said.

'But he told you where to find me?'

'Are you frightened of him?' I said.

'I don't want to go back to him.'

'He thinks you are living in Munich. He thinks you ran away with a Coca-Cola truck driver.'

'That was just a boy I knew.'

'He doesn't know you're still here in Berlin,' I said. I was trying to reassure her.

'I never go downtown. Anything I need from the big department stores I have delivered. I'm frightened I'll bump into him in the food department of KaDeWe. Does he still go there and eat lunch?'

'Yes, he still goes there.'

'Then why did Frank tell you where I was?'

'Frank Harrington didn't tell me.'

'You just worked it out?' she said sarcastically.

'That's right,' I said. 'I worked it out. There's nothing very difficult about finding people these days. There are bank balances, credit cards, charge accounts, car licences, driving licences. If Werner had guessed you were living in the city, he would have found you much more quickly than I did. Werner is an expert at finding people.'

'I write postcards and have a friend of mine post them from Munich.'

I nodded. Could a professional like Werner really fall for such amateur tricks?

I looked round the room. There were a couple of Berliner Ensemble theatre posters framed on the wall and a Käthe Kollwitz lithograph. The fluffy carpet was cream and the soft furnishings were covered in natural-finish linen with orange-coloured silk cushions. It was flashy but very comfortable – no little plastic bowls or gnawed bones, no sign anywhere of the existence of the dogs. I suppose it would have to be like that for Frank Harrington. He was not the sort of man who would adapt readily to smelly austerity. Through the sliding doors I glimpsed a large mahogany dining table set with a cut-glass bowl and silver centrepiece. The largest room had been chosen for dining. I wondered who came along here and enjoyed discreet dinners with Frank and his young mistress.

'It's not a permanent arrangement,' said Mrs Volkmann. 'Frank and I – we are close, very close. But it's not permanent. When he goes back to London, it will be all over. We both knew that right from the start.' She took a biscuit and nibbled at it in a way that would show her perfect white teeth.

'Is Frank going back to London?' I said.

She'd been sitting well forward on the big soft sofa, but now she banged a fist into a silk cushion before putting it behind her and resting against it. 'His wife would like him to get promoted. She knows that a posting to London would break up his affair with me. She doesn't care about Frank's promotion except that it would get him away from Berlin and away from me.'

'Wives are like that,' I said.

'But I won't go back to Werner. Frank likes to think I'd go back to Werner if and when that happens. But I'll never go back.'

'Why does Frank like to think that? Frank hates Werner.'

'Frank feels guilty about taking me away from Werner. At first, he really worried about it. That sort of guilty feeling often turns into hatred. You know that.' She smiled and smoothed her sleeve with a sensuous gesture, trailing her fingertips down her arm. She was a very beautiful woman. 'I get so bored at weekends,' she said.

'Where's Frank?'

'He's in Cologne. He won't be back until tomorrow night.' She smiled suggestively. 'He leaves me alone too much.'

I don't know if that was the invitation to bed that it sounded like, but I was not in the mood to find out. I was getting to the age when feelings of rejection linger. So I drank coffee, smiled, and looked at the grey line of the Wall. It was still early afternoon but it was getting misty.

'Then what have you come here for? I suppose London has sent you to buy me off. Do they want to give me money to leave Frank alone?'

'What kind of books do you read on those long lonely nights when Frank's not here, Mrs Volkmann? The days when people were paid money for *not* providing sexual favours went out with policemen in top hats.'

'Of course,' she said. A bigger smile this time. 'And that was fathers, not employers. What a shame. I was hoping you'd give me a chance to jump to my feet and say I'll never give him up, never, never, never.'

'Is that what you would have said?'

'Frank is a very attractive man, Mr – ?'

'Samson. Bernard Samson.'

'Frank is an inconsiderate swine at times but he's attractive. Frank is a real man.'

'Isn't Werner a real man?'

'Oohh, yes, I know. Werner is your friend. I have heard Werner talk of you. You are a mutual admiration society, the two of you. Well, Werner may be a fine friend, but you live with him for a year and you'd find out what he's like. He can't make up his mind about anything at all. He always wanted me to decide things: how, when, what, why. A woman marries a man to get away from all that, doesn't she?'

'Of course,' I said, and tried to make it sound as if I knew what she was talking about. The truth was, I wished like hell that I had a few more people in my life wanting to take orders instead of giving them.

'Have some more coffee,' she said sweetly. 'But then I must insist that you tell me what this is all about. Mysterious strangers can outstay their welcome too, you know.'

'You've been very patient with me, Mrs Volkmann and I appreciate that. My purpose in seeking you out was to tell you, unofficially, that under the circumstances my masters in London feel that you must be positively vetted.'

'A security check?'

'Yes, Mrs Volkmann. There will have to be a security check. You will be positively vetted.'

'This has already been done when I first married Werner.'

'Ah, well, this will be quite different. As you know, Frank Harrington is an important British official. We will have to make this what we call a Category Double X clearance. We hope you will understand why this has to be done and cooperate with the people assigned to the job.'

'I don't understand. Can't Frank arrange it?'

'If you pause a moment, Mrs Volkmann, you'll see how important it is that Frank doesn't know about it.'

'Frank will not be told?'

'Let Frank keep his private life secret. Frank's gone to a lot of trouble to do all this. . . .' I waved a hand vaguely in the air. 'How would he feel if young men from his own office had to compile reports on where you went, who you saw, how much you have in the bank? And how will he feel if he has to read reports about some old relationships that you have half forgotten and can only cause him pain?'

She inhaled on her cigarette, and looked at me through half-closed eyes. 'Are you telling me that this is the sort of thing that your investigators will pry into?'

'You're a woman of the world, Mrs Volkmann. You've obviously guessed that the investigation has already started. None of the agents assigned to you has actually reported to me yet, but you must have spotted my men following you during the past three or four weeks. We don't assign our most experienced people to these vetting jobs of course, and I'm not surprised that you realized what is in progress.'

I waited for her reaction, but she sat well back on the sofa and looked me in the eyes. She smoked but said nothing.

I said, 'I should have come to tell you about all this a month ago, but so much work piled up on my desk that I found it impossible to get away.'

'You bastard,' she said. There was no smile this time. I had the feeling that this was the real Zena Volkmann.

'I'm just carrying out my orders, Mrs Volkmann,' I said.

'So was Eichmann,' she said bitterly.

'Yes, well you know more about German history than I do, Mrs Volkmann, so I'll have to take your word for that.'

I gulped down the last of my coffee and got to my feet. She didn't move but she watched me all the time.

'I won't go out the back way if you don't mind,' I said. 'I don't want to disturb the dogs.'

'You're frightened that the dogs will tear you to pieces,' she said.

'Well, that's another reason,' I admitted. 'No need to show me to the door.'

'Frank will get you kicked out of the service for this,' she promised.

I stopped. 'I wouldn't mention any of this to Frank if I were you, Mrs Volkmann,' I said. 'This is a London decision, a decision made by Frank's friends. If it all became official, Frank would have to face a board of inquiry. He'd have a lot of explaining to do. The chances are he'd lose his job and his pension too. If that happened, Frank's friends might feel it was all your fault. And Frank has friends in Bonn as well as London – very loyal friends.'

'Get out!'

'Unless you've something to hide, they'll be no problem,' I said.

'Get out before I set the dogs on you.'

I went back to the car and waited. I decided to give it an hour and a half and see whether my hastily improvised story provoked any comings and goings. At that time on a Saturday afternoon there was not much traffic; something should happen soon, I told myself.

I could see the house from the driver's seat of the car. It was an hour and a quarter later that she came out carrying a big Gucci suitcase and an overnight bag. She was dressed in a leopard-skin coat with a matching hat. Real skin, of course. She was not the sort of lady who worried too much about leopards. The car arrived even before she closed the garden gate. She got into the front seat beside the driver and the car moved off immediately. I reached forward to turn the ignition key, but I had already recognized the car she climbed into. It was Werner's Audi and Werner was driving it. She was talking to him with much waving of the hands as the car passed mine. I ducked down out of sight but they were too involved in their discussion to notice me. So much for all her lies about Werner. And so much for all Werner's stories about her.

No point in chasing after them. Werner would be sure to see me if I tried to follow. In any case, Berlin is well covered. The security officers at the road checkpoints, the airport and the crossing places would be able to tell me where they went.

I went back to the house. I opened the pantry window with a wire coat hanger that I found in my car. She had left hurriedly. The coloured plastic bowls were piled up unwashed in the pantry sink. Frank wouldn't like that. In fact, he wouldn't like my putting his lady to flight if he found out what I'd done. There were lots of things he wouldn't like.

There was a note on the phone. It said simply that Zena had gone away for a few days because of a family crisis and she'd phone him at the office next week. It went on to say that a neighbour would feed the dogs, and would Frank leave one hundred marks on the hall table.

Whatever kind of racket Werner was in, it looked as if Zena was in it too. I wondered if it depended upon getting information from Frank, and what sort of information it was.

13

From Bret Rensselaer's top-floor office there was a view westwards that could make you think London was all greenery. The treetops of St James's Park, Green Park and the gardens of Buckingham Palace, and beyond that Hyde Park made a continuous woolly blanket. Now it was all sinking into the grey mist that swallowed London early on such afternoons. The sky overhead was dark, but some final glimmers of sunlight broke through, making streaky patterns on the emerald rectangles that were the squares of Belgravia.

Despite the darkness of the rain clouds, Rensselaer had not yet switched on the room lights. The thin illumination from the windows became razor-shape reflections in all the chromium fittings and made the glass-top desk shimmer like steel. And the same sort of metallic light was reflected up into Rensselaer's face, so that he looked more cadaverous than ever.

Dicky Cruyer was hovering over the boss, but moving around enough to see his face and be ready with an appropriate answer. Cruyer was well aware of his role; he was there whenever Rensselaer wanted witness, hatchet man, vociferous supporter or silent audience. But Cruyer was not a mere acolyte; he was a man who knew that 'to everything there is a season . . . a time to embrace and a time to refrain from embracing'. In other words, Cruyer knew exactly when to argue with the boss. And that was something I never did right. I didn't even know when to argue with my wife.

'You didn't tell Frank that it was all genuine material?' Cruyer asked me for the third time in thirty minutes.

'Frank doesn't give a damn whether it's genuine or not,' I said. They both looked at me with pained shock. 'As long as it didn't come dribbling out of his Berlin office.'

'You're hard on Frank,' Bret said, but he didn't argue about it. He took off his jacket and put it on a chairback, carefully arranging it so it wouldn't wrinkle.

'How would you like it wrapped up?' I said. 'You want me to tell you that he's sitting at home every night trying on false whiskers and working out new codes and ciphers just to keep in practice?' I suppose

I was angry at Werner's rumour about Frank not wanting me to inherit his job. I didn't believe it, but I was angry about it just the same. The friendship between Frank and me had always been ambivalent. We were friends only when I remembered my place; and sometimes I didn't remember my place.

'I don't want an eager beaver in the Berlin office,' said Bret Rensselaer, pausing long enough for me to register the personal pronoun that said Bret Rensselaer was the one who decided who got that coveted post. 'Frank Harrington' – the surname was used to distance Bret Rensselaer from his subordinate – 'went over there to sort out a mess of incompetence, and he did that. He's not a goddamned superstar, and we all knew it. He was a receiver, sent in to preside over a bankruptcy.' Bret Rensselaer had appointed Frank Harrington to Berlin and he resented anything said against his appointee.

'Frank did wonders,' said Dicky Cruyer. It was a reflex response, and while I was admiring it he added, 'You took a chance putting Frank into that job, Bret, and you did it with half the Department heads telling you it would be a disaster. Disaster!' Dicky Cruyer devoted a precious moment to making a clicking noise with his mouth that indicated his contempt for those amazingly shortsighted people who had questioned Bret Rensselaer's bold decision. He looked at me while he did it, for among those doubters I was numbered.

Rensselaer said, 'Did you notice anything else about the material that this fast-disappearing helper' – a glance at me as the person who'd let the helper slip through our hands – 'slammed down on Frank's desk?'

'You want me to answer, Bret?' I said. 'Or are we both going to wait for Dicky to say something?'

'Now, what the hell's this?' said Dicky anxiously. 'There are quite a few things about that material that I noticed. In fact, I'm in the process of writing a report about it.' Being in the process of writing a report about something was the nearest that Dicky ever came to admitting total ignorance.

'Bernard?' said Rensselaer, looking at me.

'That it all came through Giles Trent's office?'

Rensselaer nodded. 'Exactly,' he said. 'Every document that was in that bundle of material leaked to the Russians had, at some stage or other, passed through Trent's hands.'

'Well, let me hang this one on you,' I said. 'A few years ago – I have the dates and details – the Berlin office made an intercept that was reported back to Karlshorst within three days. Giles Trent was on duty there that night.'

'Then why the hell wasn't that on his file?' said Cruyer. I noticed that he was wearing a gold medallion inside his dark blue silk shirt. It went with his white denim trousers.

'He was completely cleared,' I said. 'Berlin decided who was responsible and took all necessary action.'

'But you don't believe it,' said Rensselaer.

I raised my hands in the sort of shrug of resignation that would have been over the top for a road-show actor's Shylock.

'But he was in the building?' said Rensselaer.

'He was on duty,' I said, avoiding the question. 'And he did handle everything that arrived in Berlin last week.'

'What do you think, Dicky?' said Rensselaer.

'Perhaps we're being *too* sophisticated,' said Dicky. 'Perhaps we've got a very straightforward case of Trent selling us out, but we insist upon looking for something else.' He smiled. 'Sometimes life is simple. Sometimes things are what they appear to be.' It was a cry from the heart.

I didn't say anything and neither did Rensselaer. He glanced at my face and didn't ask me what I thought. I guess I'm not as inscrutable as Cruyer.

When Rensselaer had finished with us, Dicky Cruyer invited me into his office. It was the sort of invitation I could decline at my peril, as Dicky's voice made clear, but I looked at my watch for long enough to make him open the drinks cabinet.

'All right,' he said as he put a big gin and tonic into my hand. 'What the hell is this all about?'

'Where do you want to begin?' I asked, and looked at my watch again. My difficulty in dealing with the stubborn and intractable mind of Bret Rensselaer was compounded by the myopic confusion that Dicky Cruyer brought to every meeting.

'Are you now trying to say that Giles Trent is innocent?' he said petulantly.

'No,' I said. I drank some of the very weak mixture while Cruyer was fishing around in his glass to scoop a fragment of tonic-bottle label from where it was floating among the ice cubes.

'So he is guilty?'

'Probably,' I said.

'Then I fail to understand why you and Bret were going through that rigmarole just now.'

'Can I help myself to a bit more gin?'

Cruyer nodded, and watched to see how much of it I poured. 'So why don't we just pull Trent in, and have done with it?'

'Bret wants to play him. Bret wants to find out what the Russkies want out of him.'

'Want out of him!' said Cruyer scornfully. 'Great Scott! They've been running him for all that time, and now Bret wants to give them more time. . . . How long before Bret is going to be quite sure what they want?' He looked up at me and said, 'They want to know what we do, say and think up here on the top floor. That's what they want.'

'Well, that's not so worrying. You could get everything important that is done, said or thought up here written on the back of a postage stamp, and still have room for the Lord's Prayer.'

'Never mind the wisecracks,' said Cruyer. He was right about Trent. There would be only one use for an agent who was so close to us; they'd use him to provide 'a commentary'. 'Trent's a Balliol man, like me,' said Dicky suddenly.

'Are you boasting, confessing or complaining?' I asked.

Dicky smiled that little smile with which all Balliol men like him confront the envy of lesser mortals. 'I'm simply pointing out that he's no fool. He'll guess what's going on.'

'Trent's no longer doing any harm,' I said. 'He's been debriefed and now we might as well play him for as long as we can.'

'I don't go along with all this damned double-agent, triple-agent, quadruple-agent stuff. You get to a point where no one knows what the hell is going on any more.'

'You mean it's confusing,' I said.

'Of course it's confusing!' said Cruyer loudly. 'Trent will soon have got to the point where he doesn't know which side he's working for.'

'As long as we know, it's all right,' I said. 'We're making sure that Trent only gets to hear the things we want Moscow to hear.'

Dicky Cruyer didn't resent my talking to him as if he were an eight-year-old; he appreciated it. 'Okay, I understand that,' he said. 'But what about this new leak in Berlin?'

'It's not a new leak. It's an incident dating from years ago.'

'But newly discovered.'

'No. Frank knew about it at the time. It's new only to us, and that only because he didn't think it was worth passing back here.'

'Are you covering for someone?' said Cruyer. However numb his brain, his antennae were alive and well.

'No.'

'Are you covering for Frank, or for one of your old Berlin schoolmates?'

'Let it go, Dicky,' I advised. 'It's for background information only. Frank Harrington has closed the file on this one. You go digging it all up again and someone is going to say you are vindictive.'

'Vindictive! My God, I ask for a few details about a security leak in Berlin and you start telling me I'm vindictive.'

'I said you'll run the risk of being accused of it. And Frank sees the D-G socially whenever he's in town. Frank is near enough to retirement to scream bloody murder if you do anything to make ripples on his pond.' Cruyer's face went a shade paler under his tan and I knew I'd touched a nerve. 'Do what you like,' I added. 'It's just a word to the wise, Dicky.'

He shot me a glance to see if I was being sardonic. 'I appreciate it,' he said. 'You're probably right.' He drank some of his gin and pulled a face as if he hated the taste. 'Frank lives in style, doesn't he? I was out at his country place last month. What a magnificent house. And he's got all the expense of living in Berlin as well.'

Two houses in Berlin, I felt tempted to say, but I sipped my drink and smiled.

Dicky Cruyer ran a finger along the waist of his white denim jeans until he felt the designer's leather label on his back pocket. Thus reassured, he said, 'The Harringtons are treated like local gentry in that village, you know. They have his wife presenting prizes at the village fête, judging at the gymkhana, and tasting the sponge cakes at the village hall. No wonder he wants to retire, with all that waiting for him. Have you been there?'

'Well, I've known him a long time,' I said, although why the hell I should find myself apologizing to Dicky for the fact that I'd been a regular guest at Frank's house ever since I was a small child, I don't know.

'Yes, I forget. He was a friend of your father's. Frank brought you into the service, didn't he?'

'In a way,' I said.

'The D-G recruited me,' said Dicky. My heart sank as he settled down into his Charles Eames leather armchair and rested his head back; it was usually the sign of Cruyer in reminiscent mood. 'He wasn't D-G then, of course, he was a tutor – not *my* tutor, thank God – and he buttonholed me in the college library one afternoon. We got to talking about Fiona. Your wife,' he added, just in case I'd forgotten her name. 'He asked me what I thought about the crowd she was running around with. I told him they were absolute dross. They were too! Trotskyites and Marxists and Maoists who could only argue in slogans and couldn't answer any political argument without checking back with Party headquarters to see what the official line was at that moment. Of course, it was years afterwards that I discovered Fiona was in the Department. Then of course I realized that she must have been mixing with that Marxist crowd on the D-G's orders all that time ago. What a fool she must have thought me. But I've always wondered why the D-G didn't drop a hint of what was really the score. Did you know Fiona infiltrated the Marxists when she was still only a kid?'

'Thanks for the drink, Dicky,' I said, draining my glass and deliberately putting it on his polished rosewood desk top. He jumped out of his chair, grabbed the glass and polished energetically at the place where it had stood. It never failed as a way of getting him back to earth from his long discursive monologues, but one day he was sure to tumble to it.

Having polished the desk with his handkerchief, and peered at the surface long enough to satisfy himself that it had been restored to its former lustre, he turned back to me. 'Yes, of course, I mustn't keep you. You haven't seen much of the family for the last few days. Still, you like Berlin. I've heard you say so.'

'Yes, I like it.'

'I can't think what you see in it. A filthy place bombed to nothing in the war. The few decent buildings that survived were in the Russian Sector and they got bulldozed to fill the city with all those ghastly workers' tenements.'

'That's about right,' I admitted. 'But it's got something. And Berliners are the most wonderful people in the world.'

Cruyer smiled. 'I never realized that you had a romantic streak in you, Bernard. Is that what made the exquisite and unobtainable Fiona fall in love with you?'

'It wasn't for my money or social position,' I said.

Cruyer took my empty glass, the bottle caps and the paper napkin I'd left unused and put them on to a plastic tray for the cleaners to remove. 'Could Giles Trent be connected to our problems with the Brahms net?'

'I've been wondering that myself,' I said.

'Are you going to see them?'

'Probably.'

'I'd hate Trent to get wind of your intention,' said Cruyer quietly.

'He's a Balliol man, Dicky,' I said.

'He could *inadvertently* pass it to his Control. Then you might find a hot reception waiting for you.' He finished his drink, wiped his lips and put his empty glass with the other debris on the tray.

'And Bret would lose his precious source,' I said.

'Don't let's worry about that,' said Cruyer. 'That's strictly Bret's problem.'

14

I collected Fiona from her sister's house that evening. She'd left a message asking me to take the car there, so she could bring back a folding bed that she'd lent to Tessa at a time when she'd decided to sleep apart from George. The bed had never been put to use. I always suspected that Tessa had used its presence as a threat. She was like that.

Tessa had prepared dinner. It was the sort of *nouvelle cuisine* extravaganza that Uncle Silas had been complaining of. A thin slice of veal with two tiny puddles of brightly coloured sauces, peas arranged inside a scooped-out tomato, and a few wafers of carrot with a mint leaf draped over them. Tessa had learned to prepare it at a cookery school in Hampstead.

'It's delicious,' said Fiona.

'He was yummy,' said Tessa when she'd finished eating. She never seemed to need more than a spoonful of food at any meal. *Nouvelle cuisine* was invented for people like Tessa, who just wanted to go through the pretence of eating a meal for the sake of the social benefits. 'He had these wonderful dark eyes that could see right through your clothes, and when he was demonstrating the cooking he'd put his arm round you and take your hands. "Like zis, like zis," he used to say. He was Spanish, I think, but he liked to pretend he was French of course.'

Fiona said, 'Tessa has cooked the most wonderful things for me while you were away.'

'Like zis?' I asked.

'And meals for the children,' said Fiona hurriedly, hoping to appeal to my feelings of obligation. 'She has given me a gallon of minestrone for the freezer. It will be so useful, Tess darling, and the children just love soup.'

'And how was Berlin?' said Tessa. She smiled. We understood each other. She knew I didn't like the tiny ladies' snack she'd prepared, or her supposed antics with the Spanish cookery teacher, but she didn't give a damn. Fiona was the peacemaker, and it amused Tessa to see her sister intercede.

'Berlin was wonderful,' I said with spurious enthusiasm.

'German food is more robust than French food,' said Tessa. 'Like German women, I suppose.' It was directed at me and more specifically at the buxom German girl I was with when Tessa first met me, back before I married Fiona.

'You know that German proverb: one is what one eats,' I said.

'Feast on cabbage and what do you become?' said Tessa.

'A butterfly?' I said.

'And if you eat dumplings?'

'At least you are no longer hungry,' I said.

'Give him some more meat,' Fiona told her sister, 'or he'll be bad-tempered all evening.'

When Tessa returned from the kitchen with my second helping of dinner, the plate no longer exhibited the finer points of *la nouvelle cuisine*. There was a chunky piece of veal and a large spoonful of odd-shaped carrot pieces that showed how tricky it was to slice thin even slices. There was only one kind of sauce this time, and it was poured over the meat. 'Where's the mint leaf?' I said. Tessa aimed a playful blow at the place between my shoulders, and it landed with enough force to make me cough.

'Did you notice anything different in the hall?' Tessa asked Fiona while I was wolfing the food.

'Yes,' said Fiona. 'The lovely little table, I was going to ask you about it.'

'Giles Trent. He's selling some things that used to belong to his grandmother. He needs the extra room and he has other things for sale. Anyone who could find space enough for a dining table. . . . Oh, Fiona, it's such a beautiful mahogany table, with eight chairs. I'd sell my soul for it but it would never fit here and this table belonged to George's mother. I dare not say I'd like to replace it.'

'Giles Trent?' I said. 'Is he selling up?'

'He's working with you now, isn't he?' said Tessa. 'He told me he has talked with you and everything is going to be all right. I'm so pleased.'

'What else is he selling?'

'Only furniture. He won't part with any of his pictures. I wish he'd decide to let me have one of those little Rembrandt etchings. I'd love one.'

'Would George agree?' asked Fiona.

'I'd give it to George for his birthday,' said Tessa. 'There's nothing a man can do if you buy something you want and say "Happy birthday" when he first sees it.'

'You're quite unscrupulous,' said Fiona without bothering to conceal her admiration.

'I'd go carefully on Rembrandt etchings,' I told her. 'There are lots of plates around, and the dealers just print a few off from time to time, and ease them into the market through suckers like Giles Trent.'

'Are they allowed to do that?' Tessa asked.

'What's to stop them?' I said. 'It's not forgery or faking.'

'But that's like printing money,' said Fiona.

'It's better,' I said. 'It's like using your husband's money and saying "Happy birthday".'

'Have you had enough veal?' said Tessa.

'It was delicious,' I said. 'What's for dessert – Chinese gooseberries?'

'Tess wants to watch the repeat of "Dallas" on TV tonight. We'd best be getting that bed downstairs and go home,' said Fiona.

'It's not heavy,' said Tessa. 'George carried it all by himself, and he's not very strong.'

I had the folding bed tied onto the roof rack of the car and we were on our way home by the time Tessa sat down to watch TV. 'Drive carefully,' said Fiona as we turned out of the entrance to the big apartment block where George and Tessa lived and saw the beginning of the snow. 'It's so good to have you home again, darling. I do miss you horribly when you're away.' There was an intimacy in the dark interior of the car and it was heightened by the bad weather outside.

'I miss you too,' I said.

'But it all went smoothly in Berlin?'

'No problems,' I said. 'Snow in April . . . my God!'

'But nothing to clear poor Giles?'

'Looks like he's even deeper in, I'm afraid.'

'I wish Tessa wouldn't keep seeing him. But there's nothing serious between them. You know that, don't you?'

'Why would he be selling his furniture?' I said.

'Antiques and furniture have been getting good prices lately. It's the recession, I suppose. People want to put their money into things that will ride with inflation.'

'Sounds like a good reason for hanging onto them,' I said. 'And if he must sell them, why not send them to a saleroom? Why sell them piece by piece?'

'Is there tax to be paid on such things? Is that what you mean?'

'The etchings are small. The lithographs can be rolled up,' I said. 'But the furniture is bulky and heavy.'

'Bernard! You don't think Giles would be idiot enough to run for it?'

'It crossed my mind,' I said.

'He'd be a fool. And could you imagine poor old Giles in Moscow, lining up to collect his vodka ration?'

'Stranger things have happened, darling. Surprises never end in this business.'

I turned onto Finchley Road and headed south. There was a lot of traffic coming the other way, couples who'd had an evening on the town and were now heading for their homes in the northern suburbs. The snow was melting as it touched the ground but the air was full of it, like a TV picture when an electric mixer is working. The flakes drifted past the neon signs and glaring shopwindows like coloured confetti. A few dabbed against the windscreen and clung for a moment before melting.

'I was talking to Frank about the old days,' I said. 'He told me about the time in 1978 when the Baader–Meinhof gang were in the news.'

'I remember,' said Fiona. 'Someone got the idea that there was to be a second kidnap attempt. I was quite nervous, I hadn't seen one of those security alerts before. I was expecting something awful to happen.'

'There was a radio intercept from Karlshorst. Something about an airport in Czechoslovakia.'

'That's right. I handled it. Frank was in one of his schoolmaster moods. He told me all about the intercept service, and how to recognize the different sorts of Russian Army signals traffic by the last but one group in the message.'

'Frank never passed that intercept back to London,' I said.

'That's very likely,' said Fiona. 'He always said that the job of the Berlin Resident is to ensure that London is not buried under an avalanche of unimportant material. Getting intelligence is easy, Frank said, but sorting it out is what matters.' She shivered and tried to turn up the heater of the car, but it was already fully on. 'Why? Is Frank having second thoughts? It's a long time ago – too late now for second thoughts.'

I wondered if she was thinking of other things; too late perhaps to be having second thoughts about a marriage. 'Look at that,' I said. A white Jaguar had skidded on the wet road and mounted the pavement so that its rear had swung round and into a shopwindow. There was glass all over the pavement, white like snow, and a woman with blood on her hands and her face. The driver was blowing into a plastic bag held by a blank-faced policeman.

'I'm glad I didn't take the Porsche over to Tessa's tonight. You don't stand a chance with the police if they find you behind the wheel of a red Porsche. When are you getting the new Volvo?'

'The dealer keeps saying next week. He's hoping my nerve will break and I'll take that station wagon he's trying to get rid of.'

'Go to some other dealer.'

'He's giving me a good trade-in price on this jalopy.'

'Why not have the station wagon, then?'

'Too expensive.'

'Let me give you the difference in price. Your birthday is coming up soon.'

'I'd rather not, darling. But thanks all the same.'

'It would be awfully useful for moving beds,' she said.

'I'm not going to give your father the satisfaction of using any of his money.'

'He'll never know.'

'But I will know, and I'm the one who told him where to put his dowry.'

'Where to put *my* dowry, darling.'

'I love you, Fiona,' I said, 'even if you do forget my birthday.'

She put her fingertips to her lips and touched my cheek. 'Where were you that night in 1978?' she said. 'Why weren't you at my side?'

'I was in Gdansk, involved in that meeting with the shipyard workers who never turned up. It was all a KGB entrapment. Remember?'

'I must have repressed the memory of it. Yes, Gdansk, of course. I was so worried.'

'So was I. My career has been one fiasco after another, from that time to this.'

'But you have always got out safely.'

'That's more than I can say for a lot of the others who were with me. We were in good shape in 1978 but there's not much left now.'

'You were always away on some job or other. I hated being in Berlin on my own. I hated the dark streets and the narrow alleys. I don't know what I would have done without dear old Giles to take me home each night and cheer me up with phone calls and books about Germany that he thought I should read to improve myself. Dear old Giles. That's why I feel so sorry for him now he's in trouble.'

'He took you home?'

'It didn't matter what time I finished work – even in the middle of the night when the panic was on – Giles would come up to Operations and have a cigarette and a laugh and take me home.'

I carried on driving, swearing at someone who overtook us and splashed filth on the windscreen, and only after a few minutes' pause did I say, 'Didn't Giles work over in the other building? I thought he'd need a red pass to come up to Operations.'

'Officially he did. But at the end of each shift – unless one of the panjandrums from London was there – people from the annex used to come into the main building. There was no hot water in the annex, and most of us felt we needed to wash and change after eight hours in that place.'

'But there was an inquiry. A man named Joe Brody questioned everyone about a leak that night.'

'Well, what are you supposed to say, darling? Do you think anyone is going to let Frank down? I mean, are you going to say that people from the annex come up and steal paper and pencils and take their girlfriends up to that sitting room on the top floor?'

'Well, I didn't know all that was going on.'

'Girls talk together, darling. Especially when there are just a few girls in a foreign town. And working in an office with the most disreputable lot of men.' She squeezed my arm.

'So everyone told lies to Joe Brody? Giles Trent *did* have access to the signals?'

'Brody is an American, darling. You can't let the old country down, can you?'

'Frank would throw a fit if he knew,' I said. It was appalling to think of all Frank's regulations, memoranda and complicated routines being flouted by everyone even when he was there in the office. In those days I'd spent most of my working hours off on the sort of assignment that the more artful executives avoid by pleading their German isn't fluent enough. Clever Dicky, stupid Bernard.

'Frank is just a selfish pig,' said Fiona. 'He likes the money and the prestige but he hates the actual work. What Frank likes is playing host to the jet set while the taxpayer gets the bill.'

'There has to be a certain amount of that,' I said. 'Sometimes I think the D-G only keeps Frank over there to pick up all the gossip. The D-G loves gossip. But Frank understands what is gossip and what is important. Frank has got a talent for anticipating trouble long before it arrives. I could give you a dozen examples of him pulling the coals out of the fire, acting only on gossip and those hunches he has.'

'Who will get Berlin when Frank retires?'

'Don't ask me,' I said. 'I suppose they will go to that computer and see if they can find someone who hates Berlin as much as Frank does, who wastes money as extravagantly as Frank does, who speaks that same *Kaiserliche* German that Frank does, and who looks like an Englishman on a package tour, as Frank manages to look.'

'You're cruel. Frank's so proud of his German too.'

'He'd get away with it if he didn't try writing out those instructions for the German staff and pinning them on the notice board. The only time I've ever seen Werner laughing, really laughing uncontrollably, was in front of the notice board in the front hall. He was reading Frank's German language instruction: "What to do in case of fire." It became a classic. There was a German security man who used to recite it at the Christmas party. One year Frank watched him and said, "It's jolly good the way these Jerries are able to laugh at the deficiences of their own language, what?" I said, "Yes, Frank, and he's got a voice a bit like yours, did you notice that?" "Can't say I did," said Frank. I never was quite sure if Frank understood what the joke was.'

'Bret said the D-G mentioned your name for the Berlin office.'

'Have you seen Bret much while I was away?'

'Don't start that all over again, darling. There is absolutely no question of a relationship between me and Bret Rensselaer.'

'No one's mentioned it to me,' I said. 'The job, I mean.'

'Would you take it?'

'Would you like to go back there?'

'I'd do anything to see you really happy again, Bernard.'

'I'm happy enough.'

'I wish you'd show it more. I worry about you. Would you like to go to Berlin?'

'It depends,' I said cautiously. 'If they wanted me to take over Frank's ramshackle organization and keep it that way, I wouldn't touch it at any price. If they let me reshape it to something better suited to the twentieth century . . . then it could be a job well worth doing.'

'And I can easily imagine you putting it to the D-G in those very words, darling. Can't you get it into your adorable head that Frank, Dicky, Bret and the D-G all think they are running a wonderful organization that is the envy of the whole world. They are not going to receive your offer to bring it into the twentieth century with boundless enthusiasm.'

'I must remember that,' I said.

'And now I've made you angry.'

'Only because you're right,' I said. 'Anyway, it's hardly worth discussing what I'd say if they offered me Frank's job when I know there is not the slightest chance they will.'

'We'll see,' said Fiona. 'You realize you've driven past our house, don't you? Bernard! Where the hell are we going?'

'There was a parked car . . . two men in it. Opposite our entrance.'

'Oh, but Bernard. Really.'

'I'll just drive around the block to see if there's any sort of backup. Then I'll go back there on foot.'

'Aren't you taking a parked car with two people in it too seriously? It's probably just a couple saying good night.'

'I've been taking things too seriously for years,' I said. 'I'm afraid it makes me a difficult man to live with. But I've stayed alive, sweetheart. And that means a lot to me.'

The streets were deserted, no one on foot and no occupied parked cars as far as I could see. I stopped the car. 'Give me five minutes.

Then drive along the road and into our driveway as if everything was normal.'

She looked worried now. 'For God's sake, Bernard. Do be careful.'

'I'll be okay,' I told her as I opened the door of the car. 'This is what I do for a living.'

I took a pistol from my jacket and stuffed it into a pocket of my raincoat. 'You're carrying a gun?' said Fiona in alarm. 'What on earth do you want with that?'

'New instructions,' I said. 'Anyone who regularly carries Category One papers has to have a gun. It's only a peashooter.'

'I hate guns,' she said.

'Five minutes.'

She reached out and gripped my arm. 'There's nothing between me and Bret,' she said. 'There's nothing between me and anyone, darling. I swear it. You're the only one.'

'You're only saying that because I've got a gun,' I said. It was a rotten joke, but she gave it the best sort of smile she could manage and then slid across to the driver's seat.

It was cold, and flakes of snow hit my face. By now the snowfall was heavy enough to make patterns on the ground, and the air cold enough to keep the flakes frozen so they swirled round in ever-changing shapes.

I turned into Duke Street, where we lived, from the north end. I wanted to approach the car from behind. It was safer that way; it's damned awkward to twist round in a car seat. The car was not one I recognized as being from the car pool, but on the other hand it wasn't positioned for a hot-rubber getaway. It was an old Lancia coupé with a radio-phone antenna on the roof.

The driver must have been looking in his rearview mirror because the door swung open when I got near. A man got out. He was about thirty, wearing a black leather zip-fronted jacket and the sort of brightly coloured knitted Peruvian hat they sell in ski resorts. I was reassured; it would be a bit conspicuous for a KGB hit team.

He let me come closer and kept his hands at his sides, well away from his pockets. 'Mr Samson?' he called.

I stopped. The other occupant of the car hadn't moved. He hadn't even turned in his seat to see me. 'Who are you?' I said.

'I've got a message from Mr Cruyer,' he said.

I went closer to him but remained cautious. I was holding the peashooter in the pocket of my coat and I kept it pointing in his direction. 'Tell me more,' I said.

He looked down at where the gun made a bulge and said, 'He told me to wait. You didn't leave a contact number.'

He was right about that. Fiona's request to move that damned bed had been waiting for me at home. 'Let's have it, then.'

'It's Mr Trent. He's been taken ill. He's in a house near the Oval. Mr Cruyer is there.' He motioned vaguely to the car. 'Shall I call him to say you're coming?'

'I'll go in my car.'

'Sure,' said the man. He pulled the knitted hat down round his ears. 'I'll ask Mr Cruyer to call you and confirm, shall I?' He was careful not to grin but my caution obviously amused him.

'Do that,' I said. 'You can't be too careful.'

'Will do,' he said, and gave me a perfunctory salute before opening the car door. 'Anything else?'

'Nothing else,' I said. I didn't let go of the gun until they'd driven away. Then I went indoors and poured myself a malt whisky while waiting for Cruyer's call. Fiona arrived before the phone rang. She gave me a tight embrace and a kiss from her ice-cold lips.

Cruyer was not explicit about anything except the address and the fact that he'd been trying to get me for nearly an hour, and would I please hurry, hurry, hurry. Not wanting to arrive there complete with folding bed, I lifted it from the roof rack before leaving. The exertion made me short of breath and my hands tremble. Or was that due to the confrontation with the man from the car? I could not be sure.

The part of south London that takes its name from the Surrey County cricket ground is not the smart residential district that some tourists might expect. The Oval is a seedy collection of small factories, workers' apartments and a park that is not recommended for a stroll after dark. And yet, tucked away behind the main thoroughfares, with their diesel fumes, stray cats and litter, there are enclaves of renovated houses – mostly of Victorian design – occupied by politicians and civil servants who have discovered how conveniently close to Westminster this unfashionable district is. It was in such a house that Cruyer was waiting for me.

Dicky was lounging in the front room reading *The Economist*. He habitually carried such reading matter rolled up in the side pocket of his reefer jacket which was now beside him on the sofa. He was wearing jeans, jogging shoes and a white roll-neck sweater in the sort of heavyweight wool that trawler-men require for deck duty in bad weather.

'I'm sorry you couldn't reach me,' I said.

'It doesn't matter,' said Dicky in a tone that meant it did. 'Trent has taken an overdose.'

'What did he take? How bad is he?' I asked.

'His sister found him, thank God,' said Dicky. 'She brought him here. This is her house. Then she called a doctor.' Dicky said doctor as another man might say pervert or terrorist. 'Not one of our people,' Dicky went on, 'some bloody quack from the local medical centre.'

'How bad is he?'

'Trent? He'll survive. But it's probably a sign that his Russian pals are turning the screws a bit. I don't want them tightening the screws to the point where Trent decides they can hurt him more than we can.'

'Did he say that? Did he say he's coming under pressure?'

'I think we should assume that he is,' said Dicky. 'That's why someone will have to tell him the facts of life.'

'For instance?'

'Someone is going to have to explain that we can't afford to have him sitting in Moscow answering the questions that a KGB debriefing panel will ask. Losing a few secret papers is one thing. Helping them build a complete diagram of our chain of command and the headquarters structure, and filling in personal details about senior officers for their files would be intolerable.' Dicky held the rolled-up magazine and slapped the open palm of his left hand with it. Ominously he added, 'And Trent had better understand that he knows too much to go for trial at the Old Bailey.'

'And you want me to explain all that?' I said.

'I thought you'd already explained it to him,' said Dicky.

'Did it occur to you that a suicide attempt might indicate that he's already been pressed too hard?'

Dicky became absorbed in the problem of rolling *The Economist* up so tightly that no light could be seen through it. After a long silence he said, 'I didn't tell the stupid bastard to sell out his country. You think because he's a Balliol man I want to go easy on him.' He got out his cigarettes and put one in his mouth unlit.

'I never went to college,' I said. 'I don't know what you're talking about.'

He heaved himself off the sofa and went to the mantelshelf where he rummaged for matches and pulled at a flower petal to see if the daffodils were plastic; they weren't. 'You didn't go to college but sometimes you hit the nail on the head, Bernard old friend. I've been thinking of that conversation you had with Bret Rensselaer this afternoon. It was only sitting here tonight that I began to see what you were getting at.' I'd never seen Dicky so restless. He found a matchbox on the shelf, but it was empty.

'Is that so?'

'You think everything's coming up too neat and tidy, don't you? You don't like the way in which that material implicating Trent has conveniently come into Frank's hands in Berlin. You're suspicious about his being on duty the night that damned radio intercept was filed. In short, you don't like the way everything points to Giles Trent.'

'I don't like it,' I admitted. 'When I get all my questions answered fully, I know I'm asking the wrong questions.'

'Let's cut out all this nebulous talk,' he said. He put the matchbox back on the shelf, having decided not to smoke. 'Do you think Moscow know we are on to Trent? Do you think Moscow intend to use him as a scapegoat?' Carefully he put his unlit cigarette back into the packet.

'It would be a good idea for them,' I said.

'To make us think every leak we've suffered for the last few years has been the work of Trent?'

'Yes, they could wipe the slate clean like that. We put Trent behind bars and heave a sigh of relief and convince ourselves that everything is fine and dandy.'

Now Dicky used the magazine to imprint red circles on his hand, examining the result with the sort of close scrutiny fortune tellers give the palms of wealthy clients.

'There would be only one reason for doing that,' said Dicky. He looked up from his hand and stared into my blank face. 'They'd have to have someone placed as well as Trent . . . someone who could continue to provide them with the sort of stuff they've been getting from Trent.'

'Better,' I said. 'Much better.'

'Why better?'

'Because Moscow Centre always like to get their people home. They'll spend money, arrest some poor tourist to use as hostage, or even spring from jail an agent serving a sentence to swop him. But they really try hard to get their people home.'

'I could tell you a few people who now find they don't like it "at home",' said Dicky.

'That doesn't make any difference,' I said. 'The motive that Moscow Centre play upon is getting them safely back to Russia . . . medals and citations and all that hero bullshit that Moscow do so well.'

'And there is no sign yet that they are going to try getting Trent back to Moscow.'

'And that will spoil their record,' I said. 'They'd have to have a really good reason for letting Trent fall off the tightrope. There's only one sort of motive they could have, and that's positioning or making more secure another agent. A better agent.'

'But maybe the Russians *don't* know we're on to him.'

'And maybe Trent doesn't want to go to Moscow. Yes, I thought of both those possibilities, and either could be true. But I think Trent is going to be deliberately sacrificed. And that would be very unusual.'

'This other person,' said Dicky. 'This other agent that Moscow might already have in position. . . . You're talking about someone at the very top? Am I right?'

'Look at the record, Dicky. We haven't run a good double agent in years and we haven't landed any of their important agents either. That adds up to one thing only: someone here is blowing everything we do,' I said. 'We've had a long string of miserable failures, and some of them were projects that Trent had no access to.'

'The record can be a can of worms – we both know that,' said Dicky. 'If they had someone highly placed, they wouldn't be stupid enough to act on everything he told them. That would leave a trail a mile wide. They are too smart for that.'

'Right,' I said. 'So the chances are that Moscow know even more than the evidence suggests.'

'Do you think it could be me?' said Dicky. He beat a soft but rapid tattoo on his hand.

'It's not you,' I said. 'Maybe it's not anyone. Maybe there is no pattern of betrayal – just incompetence.'

'Why not me?' Dicky persisted. He was indignant at being dismissed so readily as a suspect.

'If you'd been a Moscow agent, you would have handled the office differently. You would have kept your secretary in that anteroom instead of moving her inside where she can see what you are doing all the time. You'd make sure you know all kinds of current matters that you don't bother to find out. You wouldn't leave top-secret documents in the copying machine and cause a hue and cry all round the building the way you did three times last year. A Moscow agent wouldn't draw that kind of attention to himself. And you probably would know enough about photography not to make such a terrible mess of your holiday snapshots the way you do every year. No, you're not a Moscow man, Dicky.'

'And neither are you,' said Dicky, 'or you wouldn't have brought it up in the first place. So let's stick together on this one. You're going to Berlin to contact the Brahms net. Let's keep your reports of that trip confidential verbal ones. And from now on let's keep the wraps on Trent and everything we do, say or think about him. Between us, we can keep a very tight hold on things.'

'You mean, don't tell Bret?'

'I'll handle Bret. He'll be told only what he needs to be told.'

'You can't suspect Bret?' Immediately I thought of Fiona. If she was having an affair with Bret, any investigation of Bret would reveal it. Then there would be the very devil of a fuss.

'It can be anyone. You've said that yourself. It could be the D-G.'

'Well, I don't know, Dicky,' I said.

Dicky became agitated. 'Oh, I see what you're thinking. You think this might be a devious method of starving Bret of information. So that I can take over his job.'

'No,' I said, although that was exactly what had crossed my mind.

'Let's not kick off to a bad start,' said Dicky. 'We've got to trust each other. What do I have to do to make you trust me?'

'I'd want something in writing, Dicky. Something that I could produce just before they sentence me.'

'Then you'll do as I suggest?'

'Yes.' Now that Dicky had voiced my fears, I felt uneasy – or, rather, I felt frightened, bloody frightened. A Moscow agent in place endangered all of us, but if he was caught, maybe he'd leave the whole Department discredited and disbanded.

Dicky nodded. 'Because you know I'm right. You bloody well know I'm right. There is a Moscow agent sitting right at the top of the Department.'

I didn't remind Dicky that he'd started off by saying that it was my conversation with Bret that eventually made him see what I was getting at. It was better that Dicky thought it was all his own idea. Balliol men like to be creative.

There were footsteps and a knock at the door. The doctor came in. 'The patient is sleeping now, Mr Cruyer,' he said respectfully. Given the Victorian setting, I had expected a man with muttonchop whiskers and stovepipe hat. But the doctor was young, younger than Dicky, a wide-eyed boy, with long wavy hair that reached down to his stiff white collar, and carrying a battered black Gladstone bag that he must have inherited from some venerable predecessor.

'So what's the prognosis, Doc?' said Dicky.

The doctor put his bag down on the floor while he put his overcoat on. 'Suicide is no longer the rare tragedy it once was,' he said. 'In Germany, they have about fourteen thousand a year, and that's more than die there in traffic accidents.'

'Never mind the statistics,' said Dicky. 'Is our friend upstairs likely to try again?'

'Look, Mr Cruyer, I'm just a GP, not a soothsayer. But whether you like statistics or not, I can tell you that eight out of ten suicides speak of their intentions beforehand. If someone sympathetic had been available to your friend, he probably wouldn't have taken this desperate step. As to whether he'll try again, if you give him the care and attention he obviously requires, then you will know what he's going to do long before any quack like me gets called in to mop up the mess.'

Dicky nodded as if approving the doctor's little speech. 'Will he be fit by tomorrow?' said Dicky.

'By the weekend, anyway,' said the doctor. 'Thanks to Miss Trent.'

He moved aside to let Giles Trent's unmarried sister push past him into the room. 'Her time as a nurse served her well. I couldn't have done a better job myself.'

Miss Trent did not respond to the doctor's unctuous manner. She was in her late fifties, a tall thin figure like her brother. Her hair was waved and darkened and her spectacles decorated with shiny gems. She wore a cashmere cardigan and a skirt patterned in the Fraser tartan of red, blue and green. At the collar of her cotton blouse she wore an antique gold brooch. She gave the impression of someone with enough money to satisfy her modest tastes.

The furnishing of the room was like Miss Trent: sober, middle-class and old-fashioned. The carpets, bureau-bookcase and skeleton clock were valuable pieces that might have been inherited from her parents, but they did not fit easily there and I wondered if these were things Giles Trent had recently disposed of.

'I used my common sense,' she said, and rubbed her hands together briskly. There was a trace of the Highlands in her voice.

The young doctor bade us all goodnight and departed. Goodness knows what Dicky had told him but, despite his little outburst, his manner was uncommonly respectful.

'And you're the man my brother works for,' said Miss Trent.

'Yes, I am,' said Dicky. 'You can imagine how shocked I was to hear what had happened.'

'Yes, I can imagine,' she said frostily. I wondered how much she guessed about her brother's work.

'But I wish you hadn't called in your local doctor,' said Dicky. He gave her the card listing the Departmental emergency numbers. 'Much better to use the private medical service that your brother is entitled to.' Dicky smiled at her, and held his smile despite the stern look she gave both to the card and to Dicky. 'We'll get your brother into a nice comfortable room with a night nurse and medical attention available on the spot.' Again the smile, and again no response. Miss Trent's countenance remained unchanged. 'You've done your bit, Miss Trent.'

'My brother will stay here,' she said.

'I've made all the arrangements now,' said Dicky. He was a match for her; Dicky had the thick-skinned determination of a rhino. I was interested to watch the confrontation, but again and again my thoughts went back to Fiona. Morbidly I visualized her with Bret: talking, dancing, laughing, loving.

'Did you not hear what I said?' Miss Trent asked calmly. 'My brother needs the rest. You'll not be disturbing him.'

'That's a decision that neither of us need concern ourselves with,' said Dicky. 'Your brother has signed a contract under the terms of which his employers are responsible for his medical care. In situations like this' – Dicky paused long enough to raise an eyebrow – 'your brother must be examined by one of our own medical staff. We have to think of the medical insurance people. They can be devils about anything irregular.'

'He's sleeping.' This represented a slight retrenchment.

'If his insurance was revoked, your brother would lose his pension, Miss Trent. Now I'm sure you wouldn't want to claim that your medical knowledge is better than that of the doctor who examined him.'

'I did not hear the doctor say he could be moved.'

'He wrote it out for me,' said Dicky. He'd put the piece of paper between the pages of his magazine and now he leafed through it. 'Yes, here we are.' He passed the handwritten document to her. She read it in silence and passed it back.

'He must have written that when he first arrived.'

'Yes, indeed,' said Dicky.

'That was before he examined my brother. Is that what you were doing all the time before he came upstairs?'

'The ambulance will be here any moment, Miss Trent. Could I trouble you to put your brother's clothes into a case or a bag? I'll see you get it back of course.' A big smile. 'He'll need his clothes in a day or two, from what I understand.'

'I'll go with him,' she said.

'I'll phone the office and ask them,' said Dicky. 'But they almost always say no. That's the trouble with trying to get things done at this time of night. None of the really senior people can be found.'

'I thought you were senior,' she said.

'Exactly!' said Dicky. 'That's what I mean. No one will be senior enough to countermand my decision.'

'Poor Giles,' said the woman. 'That he'd be working for a man such as you.'

'For a lot of the time, he was left on his own,' said Dicky.

Miss Trent looked up suddenly to see what he meant, but Dicky's face was as blank as hers had been. Angrily she turned to where I was sitting holding a folded newspaper and pencil. 'And you,' she said. 'What are you doing?'

'It's a crossword,' I said. 'Six letters: the clue is "Married in opera but not in Seville". Do you get it?'

'I know nothing of opera. I hate opera, and I know nothing of Seville,' said Miss Trent. 'And if you've nothing more important than that to ask me, it's time you took yourself out of my house.'

'I've nothing more important than that to ask you, Miss Trent,' I said. 'Perhaps your brother will be able to solve it.'

Jesus, I thought, suppose Bret turned out to be a Moscow man and was trying to recruit Fiona to his cause. That would really be messy.

'It's not a crossword at all,' said Miss Trent. 'You're making up questions. That's the classified page.'

'I'm looking for another job,' I explained.

Dicky had Trent taken out to Berwick House, an eighteenth-century manor named after a natural son of James II and the sister of the Duke of Marlborough. It had been taken over by the War Office in 1940 and, like so many other good things seized temporarily by the government, it was never returned to its former owners.

The seclusion could hardly have been bettered had the place been specially built for us. Seven acres of ground with an ancient fifteen-foot-high wall that was now so overgrown with weeds and ivy that it looked more like a place that had been abandoned than one that was secret.

On the croquet lawn the Army had erected black creosoted Nissen huts, which now provided a dormitory for the armed guards, and two prefabricated structures which were sometimes used for lectures when there was a conference or a special training course in the main building. But, despite these disfigurements, Berwick House retained much of its original elegance. The moat was the most picturesque feature of the estate and it still had its bullrushes, irises and lilies. There was no sign of the underwater devices that had been added. Even the little rustic teahouse and gate lodge had been converted to guard posts with enough care to preserve their former appearance. And the infrared beams and sonic warning shields that lined the perimeter were so well hidden in the undergrowth that even the technicians who checked them did not find them of easy access.

'You've got a nerve,' said Giles Trent. 'It's kidnapping, no matter what fancy explanations Dicky gives me.'

'Your taking an overdose of sleeping tablets upset him,' I said.

'You're a sardonic bastard,' said Trent. We were in his cramped second-floor room: cream-painted walls, metal frame bed, and a print of Admiral Nelson dying at Trafalgar.

'You think I should feel sorry for you,' I said. 'And I don't feel sorry for you. That's why we are at odds.'

'You never let up, do you?'

'I'm not an interrogator,' I said cheerfully. 'And, unlike you, I never have been. You know most of our interrogation staff, Giles.

You trained some of them, according to what I saw on your file. Say who you'd like assigned to you and I'll do everything I can to arrange that you get him.'

'Give me a cigarette,' said Trent. We both knew that there was no question of Trent's being permitted anywhere near one of the interrogators. Such a confrontation would start rumours everywhere, from Curzon Street to the Kremlin. I passed him a cigarette. 'Why can't I have a couple of packets?' said Trent, who was a heavy smoker.

'Berwick House regulations forbid smoking in the bedrooms, and the doctor said it's bad for you.'

'I don't know what you wanted to keep me alive for,' said Trent in an unconvincing outburst of melancholy. He was too tall for the skimpy cotton dressing gown provided by the housekeeper's department, and he kept tugging at its collar to cover the open front of his buttonless pyjama jacket. Perhaps he remembered the interrogation training report in which he'd recommended that detainees should be made to suffer 'a loss of both dignity and comfort' while being questioned.

I said, 'They're not keeping you fit and well for the Old Bailey, if that's what you mean.'

He lit his cigarette with the matches I gave him and then hunched himself in order to take that very deep first breath that the tobacco addict craves. Only when he'd blown smoke did he say, 'You think not?'

'And have you centre stage for a publicity circus? You know too much, Giles.'

'You flatter me. I know only tidbits. When was I a party to any important planning?' I heard in his voice a note of disappointed ambition. Had that played a part in his treachery, I wondered.

'It's tidbits the government really hate, Trent. It's tidbits that are wanted for the papers and the news magazines. That's why you can never get into the Old Bailey through the crowds of reporters. They know their readers don't want to read those long reports about the Soviet economy when they could find out how someone bugged the bedroom of the Hungarian military attaché's favourite mistress.'

'If not the Old Bailey, then what – ?'

'I keep telling you, Giles. Just keep your friend Chlestakov happy.' I sat down on his bed. I wanted to show Trent that I was settling in for a long talk, and I knew that rumpling up his bed would irritate him. Irritation could make a man captious and indiscreet; that too was something I'd read in Trent's training report. I said, 'He had a sense of humour, your contact from the Embassy, calling himself Chlestakov. That was the name of the impostor in Gogol's *The Government Inspector*. He's the man who fills his pockets with bribes, seduces the prefect's daughter, lies, cheats and swindles all the corrupt officials of the town, and then gets away scot free as the curtain falls. He does get away scot free, doesn't he? Or does he get imprisoned at the end?'

'How should I know?'

'Gogol had a sense of humour,' I persisted.

'If not the Old Bailey, what?'

'Don't shout, Giles. Well, it's obvious, isn't it? Either they will feel you've cooperated and you'll be put out to grass, and finish your days with the senior citizens of some seaside resort on the south coast – or you refuse to cooperate, and you will end up in the ambulance with the flashing lights that doesn't get to the emergency ward in time.'

'Are you threatening me?'

'Well, I hope so,' I said. 'I'm trying like hell to get some sense into your brainless head.'

'Chlestakov, or whatever his real name is, suspects nothing. But if you keep me locked up in this place you'll certainly change that. Where are we, by the way? How long was I unconscious?'

'Don't keep asking the same thing, Giles. You know I can't answer. The immediate question is: when are you going to start telling us the truth?' There was no reaction from him except to examine his cigarette to see how many more puffs he had left. 'Let's go right back to that first interrogation. I was reading it this morning. . . .' He looked up. 'Oh, yes. I keep at it, Giles. I'm afflicted with the work ethic of the lower class. In that first interrogation you said you regularly went to the opera with your sister and Chlestakov, to pass photocopied documents to him. I was interested to notice that you used the word "*treff*".' I paused deliberately, wanting to see if my mention of his sister and the visits to the opera had any effect upon him. Now I watched him carefully as I prattled on. 'It's a spy word, *treff*. I can't say I remember ever using it myself, but I've often heard it used in films on TV. It has those romantic overtones that spying has for some people. *Treff!* German for meet, but also for strike or hit. And it has those irresistible military connotations: "battle", "combat", or "action". It means "line of battle" too. Did you know that, Giles?'

His vigorous puffing had already burned the cigarette down and now he was nursing it, holding it to his lips and trying to make it last. 'I never thought about it.'

'That's probably why Chlestakov used it on you. It made you both feel more daring, more rakish, more like men who change history. I once asked one of the KGB people why they gave their agents all those gadgets of the sort they gave you. The camera that looks like a cigarette lighter, the radio transmitter disguised like a video recorder and the one-time pads and all that. Chlestakov never asked you to use any of that junk – the KGB almost never do. Why would they bother, when all they have to do in a free society is have one of their hoodlums take a cab across town and have a chat or spend a couple of minutes in a photocopy shop? And this KGB man told me that it gave their agents confidence. Is that what it did for you, Giles? Did it make you feel more sure of yourself to have all that paraphernalia? It was fatal, of course. When we found all that stuff under the floorboards, you were sunk. Silly place, under the floorboards. Floorboards and attics – always the first place the searchers look. Was that Chlestakov's suggestion?'

'As a matter of fact, it was,' said Trent. He got to his feet and, pulling the belt of his dressing gown tighter, went to the door. He opened it and looked along the corridor. When he came back again, he muttered something about wanting a cup of tea. He said he thought he'd heard the nurse coming, but I knew I had him worried.

'To get back to the point, Giles. You said that you got opera tickets for Chlestakov and your sister, so that the three of you would look' – I paused – 'less conspicuous. That was a funny thing to say, Giles. I was thinking about that last night when I couldn't get to sleep. Less conspicuous than what, I thought. Less conspicuous than two men? It didn't make sense to me. Why would you take your sister along to the opera when you wanted to keep your meetings with Chlestakov as secret as possible? So I got up and started reading your transcript again. I found your descriptions of those visits to the opera. You quote your sister as saying that "Mr Chlestakov was a pleasant man, considering he was a Russian." I suppose you said that to emphasize the fact that your sister had no particular liking for Russians.'

'That's right,' said Trent.

'Or even that she was prejudiced against Russians.'

'Yes.'

'Whatever your sister's feelings about Chlestakov and his comrades, it certainly seems from your transcript that she was aware of his name and his nationality. Am I right?'

'Yes.' Trent had stopped pacing now. He stood by the little electric fire built into the fireplace and rubbed his hands together nervously. 'She loved the opera. Having her with us provided a reason for the meeting.'

'Your sister hasn't been entirely honest with you, Giles,' I said. 'Last night I invented a question that even the worst-informed opera buff in the world would have been able to answer. Your sister told me she didn't like opera. She said it vociferously. She said it as if she had some special reason for hating it.'

'I don't know what you're getting at.'

'Are you cold, Giles? You're shivering.'

'I'm all right.'

'We know the way it really happened, don't we, Giles? They got to you by means of your sister. Did Chlestakov, a nice gentleman of about the right age, go into that little wool shop your sister owns and ask help in choosing wool? For his mother? For his sister? For his daughter? Not for his wife – what had happened to her? Was he a widower? That's what they usually say. And then when the relationship had flowered – they're never in a hurry, the KGB, and I do admire that; we are always in a rush and the Americans even more so – eventually your sister suggests that you join their outings. And you say yes.'

'You make it sound so carefully planned.' He was angry, but his anger was not directed at me. It was not directed at anyone. It exploded with a plop, like a bullet thrown onto the fire.

'And you still want to believe it wasn't, eh? Well, I don't blame you. It must make a man angry to find he's performed his prescribed role in a play written in Moscow.'

'She nursed my father for ten years. She turned down good proposals of marriage. Was I supposed to crush her little chance of happiness?'

I shook my head in disbelief. 'Are you telling me that you thought it was all true? You thought Prince Charming had walked through the door of the wool shop, and your sister's foot just happened to fit the glass slipper? You thought it might be just a coincidence that he worked for the KGB and you worked for the Secret Intelligence Service?'

'He worked for the Soviet Trade Delegation,' growled Trent.

'Don't make jokes like that, Giles,' I said. 'You'll have me fall over laughing.'

'I wanted to believe it.'

'I know,' I said. 'Just like me and Santa Claus, but one day you have to ask yourself how he gets those bloody reindeer down the chimney.'

'What's the difference whether I went to the opera with them, or she came to the opera with us?'

'Now that's a question I can answer,' I said. 'The D-G wouldn't want to put you into the dock, for reasons we've already discussed. But there would be no such inhibitions about putting your sister there.'

'My sister?'

'With you as unnamed witness. You know how these things are done. You've read newspaper accounts of spy trials. In your circumstances, I'd have thought you'd read them with great care and attention.'

'She has nothing to do with this business.'

'You'd be silly to imagine that would be enough to keep her out of prison,' I said.

'You swine!'

'Think it over,' I said.

'I'll kill myself,' he said desperately. 'I'll make a good job of it next time.'

'And leave your sister to face the music alone? I don't think you will,' I said.

He looked so miserable that I gave him a couple of cigarettes and promised to have his clothes sent up to him. 'Have your regular medical check and take your tablets or whatever it is the nurse wants. Have lunch and then we'll have a stroll in the garden.'

'Garden? It's more like a jungle.'

'Be ready at two o'clock.'

'Be ready for what?'

'Be ready to come clean on your pal Chlestakov, and straighten out a few of the inconsistencies I've come across in your transcript.'

'What inconsistencies?'

'That would be telling, wouldn't it?'

There were gaps of blue sky, but the clouds were darkening to nimbostratus and there was rain in the air. Trent wore a short car jacket with a fur collar, which he turned up round his ears. On his head was a rather smart peaked cap that had come from an expensive hatter.

He seemed ill at ease in the country, and smoked another cigarette instead of breathing the fresh air. 'When will they let me out of here?' he asked. Having disposed of his cigarette, he picked up a twig, broke it into pieces and tossed them into the stagnant-looking moat.

'You go home tomorrow.'

'Is there someone who will cash a cheque for me?'

'See the cashier.' We walked alongside the moat until we came to a small wooden bridge and crossed it to where the shrubbery became neglected woodland. 'There was a postcard from Chlestakov,' I told him.

'At my home?'

'Where would you expect it to arrive?'

'He wants a meeting?'

'It says someone named Geof is having a fishing weekend. He caught four big fish of unspecified type and hopes to be back at work by two p.m. on the 16th of this month. I trust that means something to you.'

'It means nothing to you then?'

'It means only that the Moscow spy machine creaks along using the same antiquated ideas that have proved cumbersome for two decades or more.'

'It seems to work,' said Trent defiantly.

'When a huge police state devotes so much time, money and personnel to infiltrate the open society we have in the West, it gets results.'

'I don't like the Russians any more than you do,' said Trent. 'I was forced to work with them.'

'Because they threatened to report you to our security people. Yes, you told me all that.'

'You can sneer – you've no idea of what it's like.'

'But you knew how to handle it, didn't you? You did more and more spying. You grovelled before your pal Chlestakov and got him anything he wanted. For a man who doesn't like the Russians, you set an example of kindness and cooperation.'

'I knew that it wouldn't last for ever, that's why. I did many of the things they asked me but I took my time, and sometimes I said no. Sometimes I told Chlestakov that something wasn't possible. I played for time. I knew that eventually they would let me off the hook.'

'Why did you believe them? Why would any intelligence service let a well-placed agent off the hook?'

'Chlestakov guaranteed that, from the start.' Trent looked me in the eyes. 'And I believed him. It was just to be a temporary measure. He promised me that. I imposed other conditions too. He promised never to ask me about things that would endanger our own agents. He wanted general background information.'

'And a few little extra specifics,' I added.

'There were day-to-day things that Chlestakov needed for his official reports. He asked me about office routines and how the staff was rostered for duty. How old was Rensselaer, and did Cruyer own his house or have a mortgage? Many of his questions I couldn't answer, and some I didn't want to answer. But he told me that he had to have some such items that would impress Moscow.'

'He played on your sympathy, did he?' I asked sarcastically. 'If you didn't help poor old Chlestakov, he'd be moved to another assignment in some other town. And your sister wanted Chlestakov in London.'

'It may sound silly – '

'It sounds squalid,' I said. 'It sounds stupid and arrogant. Didn't you ever wonder if your treachery was worthwhile. Didn't you think your country was paying a high price for your sister's sex life?'

'Damn you.'

'Didn't you worry about being caught?'

'No.'

'Did Chlestakov not discuss with you the procedures he'd adopt if you came under suspicion? Didn't he tell you that he'd get you out of Britain if things went sour? Didn't he give you a number to phone if you had some security bloodhound asking you tricky questions?'

'I've told you all that before. We never talked about the possibility of my being caught.'

'And you've told me a pack of lies, Trent. Now I want some straight talking or you'll find yourself in another of our country houses, one where there won't be any walks in the garden or cigarettes with your lunch. Do I make myself clear?'

'You make yourself clear,' said Trent. My threats produced no real signs of fear in him – just suppressed anger. I could see a physical strength in him that matched his mental toughness. It was not the strength of the athlete but just the natural power of a man who'd grown up tall and strong. It was odd to think of Trent attempting suicide; still stranger to think of him failing to do it once his mind was made up, but I did not pursue the subject. We picked our way through the brambles and the bracken. There was the crack of twigs underfoot and the squelch of mud. Once a rabbit sprang out of the undergrowth and startled both of us.

It was Trent who spoke. 'I told them I could never go to Moscow. I'd sooner be in prison in England than go to Russia and die an exile. Chlestakov said that was all right. He said it would suit them. He said it was better that I'd told them that right from the start, because then he could make sure that I never got any information that could embarrass the KGB if said in court.'

'Embarrass the KGB! Is that the word he used? They put sane dissidents into lunatic asylums, consign thousands to their labour camps, they assassinate exiles and blackmail opponents. They must surely be the most ruthless, the most unscrupulous and the most powerful instrument of tyranny that the world has ever known. But dear old Chlestakov is frightened you might embarrass them.'

'The past is past,' said Trent defensively. 'Tell me what you want of me now and I'll do it.'

'What does the postcard mean?'

'I'm to meet Chlestakov next Tuesday evening. I must phone Monday afternoon at three to be told the details.'

'I think it would be better if you cut through that one. Get hold of him and tell him it's an emergency. Tell him you were brought here and questioned after taking an overdose. Keep as near the true facts as you can.'

'Shall I say you questioned me?'

'Yes,' I said. 'Tell him you're frightened. Tell him the game's up. Tell him you're scared, really scared.'

Trent nodded.

'He'll ask you if anyone else has been questioned, and you'll say that everyone is being questioned. He'll ask you if we had any evidence, and you'll think about that and reluctantly admit that there was none.'

'None at all?'

'He'll tell you that it was the overdose that made us take you into custody, and you'll admit that that's probably true. I want it so that Chlestakov is reassuring you. So you keep whining. He'll ask you who is in charge of the investigation, and you'll give him my name. He'll tell you that I'm not senior enough to make this a really important investigation. And he'll tell you that for something on the scale that you two are doing we'd bring investigators in from outside. Got all that?'

'You've made it quite clear.'

'And when the dust has settled on that exchange, you'll tell Chlestakov what a pity it is that you were silly enough to take that overdose, because you're now in a position to get something really big. Tell him you were going to write a report on the Berlin System – all the Berlin networks, every damn thing we are doing over there. That should make his mouth water.'

'I've never heard of the Berlin System.'

'He will have heard of it.'

'But now I won't be able to get it? Is that what I tell him?'

'Softly, softly. It will take time. You want to be quite sure you're no longer under any sort of suspicion. But this is really big stuff, tell him. This file contains all the facts and figures back for ten years and there will be all the CIA contacts and exchanges too.'

'And eventually you'll give me material to pass to him?' asked Trent. 'It's better if I know right at the start.'

'We won't let you down, Giles. We'll give you something that will make him happy and keep comrade Chlestakov where he can get his slippers warmed.'

'Keep my sister out of this.'

'Okay. I'll keep her out of it. But you'd better give me two hundred percent.'

'I will,' he said.

We came back through the shrubbery and onto the little hump-backed bridge. Trent stopped to light another cigarette, ducking into his coat collar to shelter the flame. I said, 'There's something I want to ask you. It's not important to the debriefing, I'm just curious.'

His head emerged in a cloud of blue smoke. He tossed the spent matchstick into the moat. Two ducks swam quickly towards it but, discovering it wasn't edible, moved away sedately. 'What then?' He was looking at the moat, with the dead leaves moving slowly on the current and the patches of weed swaying to the movement of the ducks.

'One night in September 1978 – '

'In 1978 I was in Berlin,' he said as if that would mean the end of the question.

'We all were,' I said. 'Fiona was there, Frank was there, I was there. Dicky was working in Frankfurt and he used to come to Berlin whenever he got the chance. Bret too. I want to ask you about a radio intercept that Signals got one night during the Baader–Meinhof panic. Remember?'

'The airliner hijack – I remember that clearly enough. Frank Harrington seemed to think it had all been done to discredit him.' Trent smiled. It was as near as he came to making a joke.

'There was a special inquiry about this Russian Army signal.'

Trent turned to look at me. 'Yes, I remember that. Frank let an American do the questioning. It was a fiasco.'

'A fiasco?'

Trent shrugged but said nothing.

'You went into the main building,' I said, 'and into Operations at the end of your duty shift. You saw the signal . . . maybe on Fiona's desk.'

'The night of the big panic? Who said I was in Operations?'

'Fiona. You went up to collect her and take her home.'

'Not that night, I didn't.'

'Are you sure? You're not telling me you weren't permitted in Operations?'

'Well, officially I wasn't, but anyone who wore a badge could get into the main building. I'm not denying I gate-crashed Operations regularly. But I didn't do it when I knew Frank was up there holding court and laying down the law. Hell, you know what Frank is like. I've seen him blast a senior man because he'd moved a fire extinguisher out of his office.'

'Frank's a bit obsessed about fire precautions,' I said. 'We all know that.'

'Well, he's obsessed about a few other things, including people from the annex going into Operations without an Ops pass. No, I didn't go up there that night. The word went round that Frank was throwing a fit because Bonn thought the mayor of Berlin was going to be kidnapped, and we all stayed well away from him.'

'It was just a signal intercept from Karlshorst. . . .'

He nodded. 'News of which got back to Karlshorst within three days, and they changed codes and wavelengths. Yes, I know all about it. That American fellow . . . Joe something – "Just call me Joe," he kept saying – '

'Joe Brody.'

'Joe Brody. He explained the whole thing.'

'Let's make it off the record,' I said.

'Off the record, on the record – it makes no difference. I didn't go up there that night.'

'Fiona told me you did.'

'Then Fiona is not telling you the truth.'

'Why should she lie about it?' I said.

'That's something you'll have to ask Fiona.'

'Did you get the information by some other means? I'm determined to press this point, Giles. You may as well come clean.'

'Because your pal Werner Volkmann did it? And you'd like to clear him?'

'How did Werner get into Operations that night? He's never worked in Operations. He's always been a street man.'

'Werner Volkmann wasn't up there. He was Signals Security One. He brought it from Signals to Ciphers that night.'

'That's all? But Werner would have to be some wizard to decipher a message while he's travelling five blocks in the back of a car.'

Trent smoked reflectively. 'The theory was that Werner Volkmann was hanging around the cipher room that night. He could have seen the deciphered message. Anyway, he didn't have to decipher it in order to tell the Russians that their traffic was being intercepted. He only had to recognize the heading or the footing codes and the time and the Karlshorst Army transmitter identification. The Russians would know exactly what had been intercepted without Werner ever knowing what the message was.'

'Do you believe it was Werner?'

'Brody is a very careful investigator. He gave everyone a chance to speak their piece. Even Fiona was interrogated. She handled the message. I never saw the report, of course, but it concluded that Volkmann was the most likely person of those who could have done it.'

'I said, did you believe Volkmann did it.'

'No,' said Trent. 'Werner's too lazy to be a double agent – too lazy to be a single agent, from what I saw of him.'

'So who could have done it?'

'Frank hates Werner, you know. He'd been looking for a chance to get rid of him for ages.'

'But someone still has to have done it. Unless you think Frank leaked his own intercept just as a way of putting the blame on Werner.'

'It's possible.'

'You can't be serious.'

'Why not?'

I said, 'Because if Frank wants to get rid of Werner, he's only got to fire him. He doesn't have to go to all the trouble of leaking an intercept to the Russians.'

'It wasn't a vitally important piece of intelligence,' said Trent. 'We've seen more important things than that used as *Spielzeug* just to boost the reputation of a double agent.'

'If Frank wanted to fire him, he could have fired him,' I repeated.

'But what if Frank wanted him discredited?'

I stared at Trent and thought about it. 'I suppose you're right,' I said.

'Werner Volkmann spread stories about Frank.'

'Stories?'

'You've heard Werner when he's had a few beers. Werner is always able to see scandal where none exists. He had stories about Frank fiddling money from the non-accountable funds. And stories about Frank chasing the typists around the filing cabinets. I suppose Frank got fed up with it. You keep telling stories like that and finally people are going to start believing them. Right?'

'I suppose so,' I said.

'Someone leaked it,' said Trent. 'If it wasn't Volkmann or Frank, then Moscow had someone inside Operations that night. And it certainly wasn't me.'

'God knows,' I said, as if I'd lost interest in the mystery. But now I was sure that the Karlshorst intercept was vitally important, because it was the only real slip Moscow's well-placed man had made.

'What do you think will happen?' said Trent. What was going to happen to him, he meant.

'You've had a long time in this business,' I reminded him. 'Longer than I have. You know how these things work. Do you know how many people just as guilty as you are have retired from the service with an unconditional pardon and a full pension?'

'How many?' said Trent. He knew I couldn't answer and that amused him.

'Plenty,' I said. 'People from Five, people from Six, a couple of Special Branch people, and those three from Cheltenham that you helped to interrogate last year.'

Trent said nothing. We watched four men as they came out of the house and went down the gravel path towards the gate lodge. One of them skipped half a pace in order to keep step with the others. They were security guards, of course. Only such men are that anxious to keep in step with their fellows. 'I hate prisons,' he said. He said it conversationally, as a man might remark upon his dislike of dinner parties or sailing.

'You've never been inside, have you?'

'No.'

'It's not like this, believe me. But let's hope it won't come to that – not for you, not for anyone.'

'That's called "leaving the door open",' said Trent. It was a subheading in his training report.

'Don't dismiss it on that account,' I said. But we both knew that Trent had written: 'Promise the interviewee anything. Promise him freedom. Promise him the moon. He'll be in no position to argue with you afterwards.'

16

People made jokes about 'the yellow submarine', but Fiona seemed to like going down to the Data Centre, three levels below Whitehall. So did I sometimes, for a brief spell. Down there, where the air was warmed, dehydrated, filtered and purified, and the sky was always light blue, you had the feeling that life had temporarily halted to give you a chance to catch your breath and think your own unhurried thoughts. That's why the staff down there are so bloody slow. And why, if I wanted anything urgently, I went down and got it myself.

The Data Centre can only be entered through the Foreign Office. Since this entrance was used by so many others, it was difficult for enemy agents to identify and target our computer staff. The Centre occupied three underground levels: one for the big computers, one for the software and its servicing staff, and the lowest and most secret level for data.

I went through the security room on the ground floor. I spent the usual three minutes while the uniformed guard got my picture, and a physical description, on his identity-check video screen. He knew me of course, the old man on the desk, but we went through the procedures just the same. The higher your rank, the longer it took to satisfy the security check, the men on the desk were more anxious to impress the senior staff. I'd noticed the way some of the junior employees seemed to get past with no more than a nod or a wink.

He punched a code to tell the computer I was entering the Centre, and smiled. 'Here we are, sir.' He said it as if he'd been more impatient than I had. 'Going to see your wife, sir?'

'It's our anniversary tonight,' I told him.

'Then it'll be champagne and roses, I suppose.'

'Two lagers and an Indian take-away,' I said.

He laughed. He preferred to believe I wore these old suits because I was a spy.

Fiona was on level 3 in Secret Data. It was a very big open room like a well-lit car park. Along one wall, the senior staff had been allotted spaces marked out by means of a tiny rug, a waist-high bookcase and a visitor's chair for visitors who never came. There was endless metal shelving for spools and, facing that, some disk-drive units. Underfoot was the special anti-static carpet, its silver-grey colour reflecting the relentless glare of the fluorescent lighting.

She didn't see me as I came along the glass-sided corridor that ran the length of the Centre. I pushed through the transparent door. I looked around: there was no one in sight except my wife. There was a hum of electricity and the constantly whirring disk drives. Then came the sudden whine of a machine going into high speed before modulating into a steady pattern of uneven heartbeats.

Fiona was standing at one of the machines, waiting for it to whine down to a complete standstill. Then she pressed the button, and a drawer purred open. She dropped a cover over the disk and snapped the catches before closing the machine again. It was Fiona's boast that she could stand in for any one of the Data Centre staff. 'That way they can't tell you it's a long job, or any of the other fairy stories they invent to get home early.'

I went to the nearby terminal, a typewriter keyboard with a swivel display screen and printer. There was a roller-foot typist's chair pulled close to it, and a plastic bin spilling over with the wide, pale green paper of the terminal's printer.

'You remembered,' said Fiona. Her face lit up as she saw me. 'You remembered. That's wonderful.'

'Happy anniversary, darling,' I said.

'You know we're going to the school to watch our son win his race?'

'Even that I remembered.' It was a convention of our marriage that I was the one who was overworked and forgetful, but Fiona gave more hours to her work than I ever did. She was always making mysterious journeys and having long late meetings with people she did not identify. At one time I'd simply felt proud of having a wife senior enough to be needed so much. Now I was no longer sure of her. I wondered who she was with and what she did on those nights when I was alone in my cold bed.

She kissed me. I held her tight and told her how much I loved her, and how I missed her when we were apart. A girl wheeling a trolley loaded with brown boxes of new magnetic tapes saw us, and thought she'd discovered some illicit romance. I winked at her and she smiled nervously.

Fiona began tidying the papers spread across her metal desk; behind her, shelves of files, books and operator manuals were packed to capacity. She had to move a pile of papers before she could sit down. She began to speak, but changed her mind and waited as a nearby tape suddenly went into high speed and then ran down to silence. 'Did you phone Nanny and tell her to give the children early dinner?'

'She was doing something in the garden. I told Billy to tell her.'

'You know how Billy gets everything mixed up. I wish she would stay with the children. I don't want her doing something in the garden.'

'She was probably doing something about the children's clothes.'

'We have a perfectly good tumble dryer,' said Fiona.

Nanny preferred to hang the clothes to dry in the garden, but I decided not to mention this. The dryer was an endless source of disagreement between the two women. 'Phone her again if you like,' I said.

'Are you going to be long?'

'No. Just one personnel printout,' I said.

'If you're going to be here for half an hour or more, there's work I could do.'

'Ten minutes,' I said. I sat down at the terminal and entered OPEN. The machine purred and the screen lit up with 'Please type your name, grade and department.' I typed that and the screen went blank while the computer checked my entry against the personnel file. Then 'Please ensure that no other person can see the screen or the console. Now type your secret access number.' I complied with that request and the screen said 'Please type the date and time.' I did it. The machine requested 'Today's code number, please.' I entered it.

'What time does this sports show begin?' Fiona called across to me. She was hunched over her desk giving all her attention to the task of painting her nails Passion Red.

The screen said 'Program?'; I responded with KAGOB to enter the KGB section. 'Seven-thirty, but I thought we'd have a quick drink in that pub opposite.'

The same girl who'd seen us kissing came past carrying a huge bundle of computer output clutched to her bosom. There were plenty of other boxes for secret waste, but she obviously wanted to have a closer look at the lovers.

I typed in the other codes, 'Redland Overseas' and the name of 'Chlestakov', and the screen asked 'Screen only?' It was a 'default query', which meant the material was typed on the printer unless the operator specified otherwise. I pressed START.

The terminal made a loud buzzing noise. It was running background, which meant it was rejecting millions of words that were not about Chlestakov. Then suddenly the printer cleared its throat, hiccupped twice, and rattled off four lines of text before the machine settled into background again. 'And don't tug at the printout,' Fiona called to me. 'The new lot of continuous tracking paper has got something wrong with the sprocket holes. We've had three printouts jam this afternoon.'

'I never tug at the printout.'

'If it doesn't feed, dial 03 on the internal for the duty engineer.'

'And say goodbye to being anywhere before midnight.'

'Don't tug at it and it won't jam,' she said. She still hadn't raised her eyes from peering closely at her nails.

The printer suddenly came to life and produced a long section of data on Chlestakov, the daisy wheel whizzing backwards and forwards. It always amazed me the way it printed every second line backwards. It was a little like Leonardo da Vinci mirror writing. No doubt its designers wanted to make human operators feel inferior. The run ended with a little tattoo of end codes to show that all the relevant data had been searched, and the printer was silent. The red light on the console came on to SYSTEMS BUSY, which is computer language for doing nothing.

Fiona walked from her desk waving her extended fingers at me in a manner I would have regarded as threatening had I not seen her drying her nails before. 'You had nice weather for your jaunt to Berwick House. You should have taken the Porsche.'

'Everybody expects such big tips when they see a car like that.'

'How was poor Giles?'

'Feeling sorry for himself.'

'Did he take a lethal dose or was it a cry for help?'

'A cry for help? You've been mixing with sociologists again.'

'But was it?'

'Who can tell? The bottle of tablets was empty, but it might have only had a couple of tablets in it. Thanks to his sister's quick action, he vomited before the tablets all dissolved.'

'And the doctor didn't say?'

'He was only a kid, and Dicky had obviously filled his head with dark hints about the secret service. I don't think he knew what he was doing. It was Trent's sister who did the medical treatment. She only called in the doctor because nurses – even ex-nurses – are brainwashed to believe that they must have a doctor to nod at them while they make the decisions and do all the work.'

'Do you think he'll try again?' said Fiona. She blew on her nails.

'Not if he knows what's good for his sister. I told him I'd make sure she stood trial if he did a bolt in any direction.'

'You hate him, don't you? It's a long time since I saw you like this. I'll bet you scared the daylights out of poor Giles.'

'I doubt that very much.'

'You don't know how frightening you can be. You make all those bad jokes of yours and your face is like a block of stone. That's what made me fall for you, I suppose. You were so damned brutal.'

'Me?'

'Don't keep saying "Me?" darling. You know what a tough bastard you can be.'

'I hate the Giles Trents of this world. And if that's what you call being tough, I wish like hell there were more tough people like me. I hate the Communists and the stupid sods in this country who play their game and think they are just being "caring, sharing, wonderful people". I've seen them at close quarters. Never mind the smooth-talking little swines that come over here to visit the TUC or give talks on international friendship. I've seen them back where they come from, back where they don't have to wear the plastic smiles or hide the brass knuckles.'

'You can't run the Soviet Union as though it were the Chelsea Flower Show, darling.'

I grunted. It was her usual reply to my tirades about the KGB. Fiona, for all her talk of social justice and theories about alleviating Third World poverty, was happy to let the end justify the means when it suited her arguments. In that I could recognize the teachings of her father.

'But Trent's not really KGB material, is he?' she said.

'They told Trent that they'd only need him for three years.'

'I suppose that was just to make it easier for him.'

'Trent believed it.'

She laughed. 'I can't imagine that Trent's saying he believed it cut much ice with you.'

'He's not a complete idiot. I think they meant it.'

'Why? How would that make sense?'

'And his KGB contact told him to put that radio under the floorboards. That slipped out when we were talking – I'm sure *that* was true.'

'So what?'

'Floorboards? I'd only tell one of my agents that if I was hoping he'd get caught. You might as well take a full page in the local paper as hide a clandestine radio under the floor.'

'I'm still not following you.'

'They didn't give Trent any goodbye codes,' I said.

'What are they?'

'Numbers he can phone if he's being followed, or his home has been burgled, or he finds a security man going through his desk one morning when he arrives a bit early. They didn't even promise to get him away if anything went wrong.'

'Can you see Giles Trent living in Moscow? Really, darling!'

'KGB procedures are laid down in Moscow. They don't let any local man decide what he thinks will suit the personality of the agent he runs. You don't understand the bloody Russians. *All* KGB agents have goodbye codes.'

'Perhaps they have decided to change things.'

'They never change anything.'

She touched a painted nail very carefully to be sure it was dry. 'I'm ready when you are.'

'Okay.' I got to my feet and read the Chlestakov data again.

'Don't be tempted to take that computer printout from the building,' she warned. 'Security will go mad.'

'On our wedding anniversary? I wouldn't dare.' I fed the computer printout into a shredder and watched the paper worms tumble into the clear plastic bag.

'I'll buy it,' said Fiona. 'Why no goodbye codes or whatever they are?'

'I think Trent has been prepared as a scapegoat. I think they wanted us to catch him. I think they know everything we're saying to him.'

'Why?'

'The lack of any preparations for escape, the mention of three years, and then having him hide the radio – a radio he didn't need and was never trained to operate – under the floor. I think he was set up.'

'What for?'

'The only reason I can think of is to hide the fact that they have someone amongst us already.'

I was expecting her to laugh, but she didn't; she frowned. 'You're serious, aren't you?'

'Someone at the top.'

'Have you told Bret this theory?'

'Dicky thinks we should keep it to ourselves.'

'So Dicky's in on it.'

'Whatever's wrong with Dicky, no one could believe he might be a double agent. The Russians would never employ a twit like him. So I've agreed to keep everything on Trent confidential.'

'Everything?'

'Everything relevant.'

She moved her head as if trying to see me in a new light. 'You're hiding material from Bret? Why, that means you're hiding it, in effect, from the D-G and the committee.'

'In effect, yes.'

'You've gone crazy, darling. They have a name for what you're doing. They call it treason.'

'It's Dicky's idea.'

'Oh, that's different,' she said with heavy irony. 'If it's Dicky's idea, that's all you need say.'

'You think it's that crazy?'

She shook her head as if lost for words. 'I can't believe all this is happening. I can't believe I'm standing here and listening to you spout this absolute and ridiculous nonsense.'

'Let's go and see our son win the Olympics,' I said.

She said, 'Poor little Billy, he's convinced he's going to win.'

'But you're not,' I said.

'He's a sweet child,' said Fiona, 'but I'm sure he'll finish last.'

'You don't have a drinks cabinet on this level, do you?'

'No alcohol in the yellow submarine, by order of the D-G,' said Fiona.

'For my next birthday,' I said, 'a hip flask.'

Fiona pretended she hadn't heard.

17

We got to Billy's school at 7.45 so I went inside without that drink I'd promised myself. It was a typical state school, designed in the sixties by the sort of architect who worked with the radio going. It was a giant shoebox that would have been totally featureless but for the cracks in the hardboard and the rust dribbles down the walls.

This evening of sporting events took place in a huge glass-fronted building adjoining the exercise yard. About three dozen dutiful parents, having purchased programmes, were perched on metal folding chairs at the chilliest end of the gymnasium. The young bearded headmaster, wearing the colourful and voluminous scarf of some provincial university, told us to hurry because we were late and reminded us that it was forbidden to walk on the wooden floor without gym shoes. Since I had neglected to equip myself with the right shoes, I walked round the gym while the senior boys performed knee bends to the sound of Pink Floyd on a tape recorder that hissed.

There was no room for us with the other parents, so I helped Fiona onto a vaulting horse and got up there alongside her. The headmaster gave me a disapproving look, as if he had decided I was the sort of man who might walk back across his polished floor.

The first event was the junior relay race. There was a lot of shouting, shoving and jumping up and down in mock excitement. Fiona put her head close to mine and said, 'I was thinking about Giles Trent. Was he expecting his sister to call, that night he took the overdose?'

'They both say no, but maybe they are both lying.'

'Why would they lie?'

'Him because he's too public-school macho to admit that he'd pull a stunt like that.'

'Why would the sister lie?'

'If she admitted that Trent was expecting her, she'd have to start wondering whether that "cry for help" was her brother's way of telling her to lay off.'

'A drastic way of telling her, wasn't it? Couldn't he tell her over a cup of tea?'

'His sister is a formidable lady. She is not the sort of woman who would admit that her brother need sell his soul to provide her with a man. She would have grunted and shrugged and ignored whatever he said.'

'But by that time serious pressure was coming from the Department and from his Russian contact. Did he think a suicide attempt would make the Russians lay off?'

'Maybe,' I said. I watched the race. Good grief, the energy those kids had; it made me feel very old.

'Or did he think the suicide attempt would make the Department lay off?' Fiona had started thinking about the Giles Trent problem now that it had sexual and emotional aspects. I guess all women are like that.

'I don't know, darling,' I said. 'I'm just guessing.'

'Your guesses can be pretty good.'

'How many married men get an accolade like that from their wives?'

'I'm just lulling you into a false sense of security,' she said.

She looked up to watch the hurdles being positioned for the next race. The bearded headmaster was well in evidence. He had a tape measure. He checked the position of everything and marked his approval or disapproval with nods or headshakes. Fiona watched the children parade until she was quite sure that Billy was not anywhere in the teams. Then she returned to the subject of Trent. 'Giles did it for the sake of his sister. He didn't have to get into it at all, did he? You said the Russian targeted him through the sister.'

'But don't imagine that they hit him when he was cold. Don't think the KGB go to all the trouble they went to without being confident he would buy their proposition.'

'I didn't think of it like that.'

'You think a woman goes after a married man just on the off-chance that he's fed up with his wife? No, she checks out her chances of success.' I'd almost said Tessa but I'd recovered myself just in time.

'What sort of signs would she look for?'

'Some people find it fascinating to think about doing the worst thing they can think of. What would it be like to murder someone? What would it be like to post this stuff off to the Russians? How would it feel to have a vulgar noisy mistress tucked away in a flat in Bayswater? At first they toy with it because it's so crazy. But one day that impossible idea starts to take shape. How would I start to do it, they ask themselves, and step by step the practical planning begins.'

'I take due note of the fact that you haven't told me what signs a woman looks for when she's after a married man.'

I smiled and applauded the winning hurdler.

She didn't let the subject drop. 'You think Giles got beyond the fantasy stage even before the Russians approached his sister?' she asked.

'Maybe not, but he didn't come running into the security office on the day he discovered exactly what his sister's boyfriend did for a living.'

'Because he'd thought about it?'

'Everyone thinks about it,' I said.

'Mistresses, or selling secrets?'

'It's only human to think about such things.'

'So where did Giles go wrong?' she asked.

'He envisaged himself sinning and found he could live with that image of himself.' I took out my cigarettes but the headmaster came over and, smiling, shook his head, so I put them away again.

'And you couldn't live with the image of yourself snuggled up with the noisy girl in Bayswater?'

'You can't have everything,' I said. 'You can't have the fantasies *and* the reality. You can't have the best of both worlds.'

'You've just blown a hole in the Liberal Party election platform.'

'No one can serve two masters. You'd think even a bean-brained public-school man like Trent would have known that.'

'There was never anything between Bret and me,' said Fiona, and touched my hand.

'I know,' I said.

'Really know?'

'Yes, really know.' I wanted to believe it. It was a failing in me, I suppose.

'I'm so pleased, darling. I couldn't bear the idea of you worrying about me.' She turned to look into my eyes. 'And Bret, of all people . . . I could never fancy him. When is Billy coming on?'

I looked at the programme. 'It must be the next but one: the junior obstacle race.'

I leaned closer to Fiona and whispered how much I loved her. I could smell the faint perfume of her shampoo as I nuzzled against her hair.

'No one thought it would last,' she said. She hugged me. 'My mother said I'd leave you within six months. She even had a room ready for me right up until Billy was born. Did you know that?'

'Yes.'

'Tessa was the only one who encouraged me to marry you. She could see how much I loved you.'

'She could see how you wrapped me around your finger.'

'What a lovely thought.' She laughed at the idea of it. 'I've always been frightened that some clever little lady will come along and find out how to wrap you around her finger, but I've seen no sign of it so far. The truth of it is, darling, that you're unwrappable. You're just not a ladies' man.'

'What does a ladies' man have to do?'

'You can't be bothered with women. I never worry about you leading a double life. You'd never go to all the trouble needed to tuck that "vulgar noisy mistress" away in Bayswater.'

'You sound like Giles Trent. The other day he told me that Werner Volkmann could never be a double agent because he was too lazy.'

'No one could accuse you of being lazy, my darling, but you certainly don't go out of your way to be nice to women – not to me, not to Tessa, or even your mother.'

I found these criticisms unreasonable. 'I treat women just as I treat men,' I said.

'For goodness' sake, my darling thickheaded husband. Can't you understand that women don't want to be treated just like you treat men? Women like to be fussed over and cherished. When did you ever bring home a bunch of flowers or a surprise gift? It never occurs to you to suggest we have a weekend away.'

'We're always having weekends away.'

'I don't mean with Uncle Silas and the children – that's just to give Nanny a break. I mean a surprise weekend in Paris or Rome, just the two of us in some lovely little hotel.'

I never cease to wonder about what goes on in a woman's brain. 'Whenever I've asked you to come along on a trip, you say you've got too much work to do.'

'I'm not talking about going with you on one of those damned jobs of yours. You think I want to walk around Berlin while you go off to see some old crony?'

'I'll have to go back there,' I said.

'I heard Dicky talking to Bret about it.'

'What did they say?'

It was typical of Fiona's caution that she looked round to be quite sure that no one was in earshot. She needn't have bothered. Some of the parents were talking to the head, some were out in the dark windswept yard calling for their children, while the rest remained in their seats stoically watching the races. 'The D-G apparently said there was no one else experienced enough to send. Dicky said that they'd soon have to wind up the Brahms net. Bret pretended to agree, but Bret won't survive as a Department head without his Brahms Four source. But, for the time being, Dicky and Bret have compromised on the idea that they'll squeeze a couple more years out of him. They think you're the only person who could persuade the network to keep working a little while longer.'

'Keep them working until Bret is retired and Dicky is moved to another desk. Is that what they mean?'

'I daresay it's at the back of their minds. When the Brahms Four material stops, there'll be a big reshuffle. Someone will have to take the blame. Even if it's just a stroke of fate, they'll still want someone to take the blame.'

'I'm not convinced the Brahms Four stuff is so bloody earthshaking,' I said. 'Now and again he's given us some juicy items, but a lot of it is self-evident economic forecasts.'

'Well, Bret guards it with his life, so I don't suppose either of us has seen more than a fraction of the stuff he sends.'

'Even Bret admits that a lot of his messages are simply corroboration of intelligence we already have from other sources. From Brahms Four we usually have good notice of the Soviet grain deals, but often it arrives after we know the new shipping contracts the Russians have signed. The type of ships they charter always gives us clear notice of how much grain they'll buy from Argentina and how much they'll be shipping via the Gulf of Mexico. We didn't need Brahms Four telling us about the Moscow Narodny Bank buying Argentine peso futures. But what did he tell us about the Russian tanks going into Afghanistan? Not a damned whisper.'

'But, darling, you're so unreasonable. The Russians don't need any help from their state bank in order to invade Afghanistan. Brahms Four can only give us banking intelligence.'

'You think the Russians weren't pouring money into Kabul for weeks before the soldiers went in? You think they weren't buying intelligence and goodwill in Pakistan? And the sort of people you buy in that part of the world don't take Diners Club cards. The KGB must have used silver and gold coins in the sort of quantity that only a bank can supply.' They were placing boxes and rubber tyres on the floor for the next race.

'Is this Billy?' said Fiona. 'What's all that for?'

'Yes, this is Billy. He's in the obstacle race.' Obstacle race! Only a son of mine would choose that.

She said, 'Anyway, darling, you and I both know it doesn't matter how good the Brahms material is. That source of information, from somewhere in the Soviet-controlled banking world, is the sort of intelligence work that even a politician can understand. You can't explain to the Minister about electronic intelligence gathering, or show him pictures taken by spy satellites. It's too complicated, and he knows that all that technological hardware belongs to the Americans. But tell the Minister that we have a man inside the Moscow Narodny and on their Economic Intelligence Committee, and he'll get excited. Form a committee to process that intelligence, and the Minister can talk to the Americans on his own terms. We all know Bret has built an empire on the strength of the Brahms source, so don't start saying it's anything less than wonderful. Or you'll become very unpopular.'

'That would be a new experience for me.'

She smiled that sweet sort of smile that she used only when she was sure I'd ignore her advice, and said, 'I mean really unpopular.'

'I'll take a chance on that,' I said angrily. 'And if your friend Bret doesn't like my opinions, he can get stuffed.' I overreacted of course. She knew I was still suspicious of her relationship with Bret. It would have been far smarter just to make soft noises and let her think I suspected nothing.

Then I spotted Billy. I waved but he was too shy to wave back; he just smiled. He was marching round the gym with all the other juniors. I suppose even clumsy boys like Billy were allowed in the obstacle race.

It was a relay race and for some unexplained reason Billy was first in his team. He scrambled through two rubber tyres, zigzagged round a line of plastic cones, and then climbed on a box before beginning his final sprint back to his number 2. He skidded at speed and went full length. When he got up, his face was covered with blood, and blood was spattered on his white vest. His teammates were shouting at him and he wasn't quite sure which way he was facing. I knew the feeling very well.

'Oh, my God,' said Fiona.

I prevented her jumping down and running to him. 'It's just his nose,' I said.

'How do you know?' said Fiona.

'I just know,' I said. 'Leave him alone.'

18

Rolf Mauser always turned up where and when he was least expected. 'Where the hell have you sprung from?' I said, unhappy to be dragged out of bed by a phone call in the early hours of the morning. Unhappy too to be standing ankle-deep in litter, drinking foul-tasting coffee from a machine in London's long-distance bus station at Victoria.

'I couldn't wait until morning, and I knew you lived nearby.' I'd known Rolf Mauser since I was a schoolboy and he was an unemployed onetime Wehrmacht captain who scratched a living from the Berlin black market and ran errands for my father. Now he was sixty-six years old but he'd not changed much since the last time we'd met, when he was working as a barman in Lisl Hennig's hotel.

'Your son Axel said you were in East Berlin.'

'In a manner of speaking, I still am,' said Rolf. 'They let us old people out nowadays, you know.'

'Yes, I know. Have you seen Axel? He worries about you, Rolf.'

'Rolf now, is it? I remember a time when I was called Herr Mauser.'

'I can remember a time when you were called Hauptmann Mauser,' I reminded him. It was my father who, noting that Mauser's promotion to captain had come only three weeks before the end of the war, had addressed him as Hauptmann Mauser. Rolf had glowed with pride.

'Hauptmann Mauser.' He smiled dutifully, the sort of smile that family groups provide for the amateur photographer. 'Yes, your father knew how to play on a young man's vanity.'

'Did he, Rolf?'

He heard the resentment in my voice and didn't reply. He looked round the bus station as if seeing it for the first time. He wore a brown leather overcoat of the sort that they sold on East Berlin's Unter den Linden in the shops where only rich Western tourists could afford to buy. Like so many Germans, he liked his clothes tightly fitted. The belted overcoat on this big round-shouldered man, and the pointed nose that twitched each time he spoke, made him look like an affluent armadillo standing on its hind legs. His face was round and he had pale skin and tired eyes, the legacy of years of dark bars, late hours, tobacco smoke and alcohol. There was little sign now of that tough young artillery officer who won the oak leaves to his Knight's Cross at Vinnitsa on the River Bug in the Red Army's spring offensive of 1944.

'Going far, Rolf?'

'Did you bring everything?'

'You've got your goddamned nerve, Rolf.'

'You owe me a favour, Bernd.'

A bus arrived, the sound of its diesel engine amplified by the low entrance arch. It backed carefully into its designated position under the signs and half a dozen weary travellers scrambled down to get their luggage, yawning and scratching as if not yet fully awake. 'You'll be conspicuous in your loden hat and leather coat once you get into the British hinterland,' I told Mauser. He didn't react to this advice. The driver of the bus got out and wound the roller to change the destination plate to Cardiff.

'Give me the packet, Bernd. Save the lectures for young Werner.' He twitched his nose. 'Getting nervous about this sort of thing? I don't remember you getting nervous in the old days.'

'What the hell do you want with a gun, Rolf?' I felt like saying that I was only nervous because I didn't trust Rolf to know what he was doing with a gun. In the 'old days' Rolf had run messages and told stories of his exploits both in the war and after. God only knows what dark deeds he might once have committed. But for many years he'd done little more than hide letters and packets under his bar counter and give them to strangers who knew the right password.

'Did I ask you what you wanted with the motorcycle that day in Pankow?' he said.

It seemed a silly comparison but Rolf obviously thought it appropriate. Funny that he'd not mentioned some of the other favours he'd done for me. He hadn't risked his life but he'd risked his job for me more than once, and laying down a job for a friend comes high on my friendship scale.

He said, 'Do I get the briefcase or are you going to unpack it all here in the middle of the bus station?' As a child, I'd been intimidated by Rolf Mauser's appearance and by the big bushy eyebrows that turned up at the outer ends to give him a fierce demonic appearance. When I'd realized that he brushed his straggly eyebrows upwards to keep them out of his eyes, my fears of Rolf Mauser had vanished and I saw in him a lonely old man who liked to wallow in memories of his youth.

'Suppose I told you I had no money?' I said.

Behind us a thin Negro wielded a gigantic broom, sweeping fried chicken bones, ice-cream wrappers and brightly coloured litter before him. Rolf turned and tossed his empty paper cup into the heap as the man brushed it slowly past us. 'All British senior staff have five hundred pounds in used notes available at home at all times. That's been the regulations for years now, Bernd. We both know that.'

'The briefcase is for you.' I passed it to him.

'You were always considerate, Bernd.'

'I don't like it, Rolf.'

'Why?'

'What do you want with a gun, Rolf?'

'Who taught you to crack a safe?'

'That wasn't a safe, Rolf. That strongbox where they kept the school reports could have been opened with a knife and fork.'

'My son Axel said you were a good friend, Bernd.'

'Did you need Axel to confirm it, Rolf?'

'We both know you are a good friend.'

'Or did you decide I was the only one fool enough to give you money and a gun and ask no questions?'

'Good friend. I appreciate it. We all do.'

'Who are "we all"?'

Rolf Mauser smiled. 'We all do, Bernd; me, Axel, Werner and the others. And now we owe you something.'

'Maybe,' I said cautiously. Rolf was the sort of man whose favours could get you into a lot of trouble.

He put the briefcase down on the ground and held it upright between his ankles while he undid his magnificent leather coat. When he rebuttoned it, he belted it more tightly as if he hoped that would make him warmer.

'Who is Brahms Four, Bernd? What's his name?'

'I can't tell you, Rolf.'

'Is he still in Berlin?'

'No one knows,' I said. It wasn't true of course, but it was the nearest I could go.

'Rumours say Brahms Four is not working for you any longer. We want to know if he's left Berlin.'

'What does it matter to you?' I asked.

'Because when Brahms Four is *kaputt* you'll pay off the Brahms network and close us down. We need to know in advance. We need to get ready.'

I looked at him for a moment without replying. Rolf Mauser's participation in Brahms was – as far as my information went – recent and minimal. Then the penny dropped: 'Because of your rackets, you mean? Because London is supplying you with things you need to keep Werner's import-export racket functioning?'

'You haven't reported that, have you, Bernd?'

'I have enough of my own problems without trying to find more,'

I said. 'But London Central aren't here to help you run rackets in East Germany, or anywhere else.'

'You didn't always talk that way, Bernd. I remember a time when everyone agreed that Brahms was the best source in Berlin System. The best by far.'

'Times change, Rolf.'

'And now you'd throw us to the wolves?'

'What are you saying?'

'You think we don't know that you have a KGB spy here in London Central. Brahms net is going to be blown any minute.'

'Who says so? Did Werner say it? Werner is not a member of the network. He's not employed by the Department at all. Do you know that?'

'It doesn't matter who said it,' replied Rolf.

'So it was Werner. And we both know who told him, don't we, Rolf?'

'I don't know,' said Rolf staunchly, although his eyes said different.

'That bloody wife of his. That bloody Zena,' I said. I cursed Frank Harrington and his womanizing. I knew Frank too well to suspect him of revealing to her anything really important. But I'd seen enough of Zena Volkmann to know that she'd trade on her relationship with Frank. She'd make herself sound important. She'd feed Werner any wild guesses, rumours and half-truths. And Werner would believe anything he heard from her.

'Zena worries about Werner,' said Rolf defensively.

'You must be very stupid, Rolf, if you really believe that Zena worries about anything but herself.'

'Perhaps that's because no one else worries about her enough,' said Rolf.

'You'll break my bloody heart, Rolf,' I said.

I'm afraid we parted on a note of acrimony. When I looked back, he'd still not boarded the bus. I suspected that he had no intention of boarding any bus. Rolf Mauser could be a devious devil.

19

Some of the most secret conversations I'd ever heard took place not in any of the debugged 'silent rooms' under the Department's new offices but in restaurants, St James's clubs or even in the backs of taxicabs. So there was nothing surprising about Dicky Cruyer's suggestion that I go to his house about nine 'for a confidential chat'.

A man repairing the doorbell let me in. Dicky's wife, Daphne, was working at home that morning. A large layout pad occupied most of the corner table in the front room. A jam jar of coloured felt-tip pens was balanced on the TV, and scattered across the sofa were scribbled roughs for advertising a new breakfast food. Daphne's art-school training was everywhere evident; brightly painted bits of folk art and crudely woven cushion covers, a primitive painting of Adam and Eve over the fireplace and a collection of matchbox covers displayed in an antique cabinet. The only personal items in the room were photos: a picture of the Cruyers' two sons amid a hundred other grim-faced, grey-uniformed boys in front of the huge Gothic building that was their boarding school; and, propped on the mantelshelf, a large shiny colour photo of Dicky's boat. There was some very quiet Gilbert and Sullivan leaking out of the hi-fi. Dicky was humming.

Through the 'dining area' I could see Daphne in the kitchen. She was pouring hot milk into large chinaware mugs. Looking up she said '*Ciao!*' with more than her usual cheerfulness. Did she know her husband had been having an affair with my sister-in-law? Her hair was that straggly mess that only comes from frequent visits to very expensive hairdressers. From what little I knew about women, that might have been a sign that she did know about Dicky and Tessa.

'Traffic bad?' said Dicky as I threw my raincoat onto a chair. It was his subtle way of saying I was late. Dicky liked to have everyone on the defensive right from the start. He'd learned such tactics in a book about young tycoons. I secretly borrowed it from his office bookshelf one weekend so that I could read it too.

'No,' I lied. 'It only took me ten minutes.'

He smiled and I wished I'd not got into the game.

Daphne brought cocoa on a dented tin tray advertising Pears soap. My cup celebrated the silver jubilee of King George V. Dicky complimented Daphne on the cocoa and pressed me to have a biscuit, while she gathered up her pens and paper and retreated upstairs. I sometimes wondered how they managed together; secret intelligence was a strange bedfellow for a huckster. It was better to be married to a Departmental employee; I didn't have to ask her to leave the room every time the office came through on the phone.

He waited until he heard his wife go upstairs. 'Did I tell you the Brahms network was going to fall to pieces?'

It was, of course, a rhetorical question; I was expected to confirm that he'd predicted that very thing with uncanny accuracy a million times or more, but I looked at him straight-faced and said, 'You may have done, Dicky. I'm not sure I remember.'

'For Christ's sake, Bernard! I told Bret only two days ago.'

'So what's happened?'

'The people have scattered. Frank is here.'

'Frank is here?'

'Don't just repeat what I say. Yes, dammit. Frank is here.'

'In London?'

'He's upstairs taking a bath and cleaning up. He arrived last night and we've been up half the night talking.' Dicky was standing at the fireplace with fingers tapping on the mantelshelf and one cowboy boot resting on the brass fender.

'Aren't you going into the office?' I cradled the cocoa in my hands, but it wasn't very hot so I drank it. I hate cold cocoa.

Dicky tugged at the gold medallion hanging round his neck on a fine chain. It was a feminine gesture and so was the artful smile with which he answered my question.

I said, 'Bret will know Frank is in London. If you are missing from the office, he'll put two and two together.'

'Bret can go to hell,' said Dicky.

'Are you going to drink your cocoa?'

'It's real chocolate, actually,' said Dicky. 'Our neighbours across the road brought it back from Mexico and showed Daphne how the Mexicans make it.'

I recognized Dicky's way of saying he didn't like it. 'Here's health,' I said, and drank his cocoa too. His mug was decorated with rodents named Flopsy, Mopsy, Cottontail and Peter. It was smaller than mine; I suppose Daphne knew he didn't much like cocoa the way the Mexicans fixed it.

'Yes. Bret can go to hell,' repeated Dicky. The gas fire wasn't on. He gently kicked the artificial log with the tip of his boot.

If Dicky was hell-bent on a knock-down-drag-out fight my money would be on Bret Rensselaer. I didn't say that; I didn't have to. 'This is all part of your plan to keep Bret out of things?'

'Our plan,' said Dicky. '*Our* plan.'

'I still haven't had that confidential memo you promised me.'

'For God's sake. I'm not going to let you down.' From upstairs there came the sound of the Rolling Stones. 'It's Daphne,' explained Dicky. 'She says she works better to music.'

'So what is Frank up to? Why come here to whisper in your ear? Why not report to the office?'

Again came Dicky's artful smile. 'We both know that, Bernard. Frank is after my job.'

'Frank is a hundred years old and waiting for retirement.'

'But retiring from my desk would give him another few thousand a year on his pension. Retiring from my desk, Frank would be sure of a CBE or even a K.'

'Have you been encouraging Frank to think he's getting your job? There's not a chance of it at his age.'

Dicky frowned. 'Well, don't let's rake that over, at least not for the time being. If Frank has unspoken ambitions, it's not for us to make predictions about them. You follow me, don't you?'

'Follow you, I'm way ahead of you. Frank helps you to get rid of Bret Rensselaer. Then you get Bret's job and Frank gets yours – except that Frank won't get yours.'

'You've got an evil mind,' said Dicky without rancour. 'You always think the worst of everyone around you.'

'And the distressing thing about that is the way I'm so often proved right.'

'Well, take it easy on Frank. He's shaken.'

Dicky was of course exaggerating wildly, both about the disintegration of the Brahms net and about Frank Harrington's morale. Frank came downstairs ten minutes later. He looked no worse than I would have looked after sitting up with Dicky all night. He was freshly shaved, with two tiny cuts where he'd trimmed the edges of his blunt-ended moustache. He wore a chalk-stripe three-piece suit, clean shirt and oxford shoes polished to a glasslike finish, and he was waving that damned pipe in the air. Frank was tired and hoarse with talking, but he was an expert at making the best of himself and I knew he'd display no sign of weakness in front of Dicky and me.

Frank seemed pleased to see me. 'I'm glad you're here, Bernard. Has Dicky put you in the picture?'

'I've told him nothing,' said Dicky. 'I wanted him to hear it from you. Drinking chocolate, Frank?'

Frank looked quickly at his gold wristwatch. 'A small gin and tonic wouldn't go amiss, Dicky, if it's all the same to you.'

'It's cocoa, Frank,' I said. 'Made the way they drink it in Mexico.'

'You said you liked it,' said Dicky defensively.

'I loved it,' I said. 'I drank two of them, didn't I.'

'If you've got Plymouth gin,' said Frank, 'I'll have it straight or with bitters.' He went over to the fireplace and knocked out his pipe.

When Dicky came back from the drinks wagon and saw the charred tobacco ashes in the hearth, he said, 'Christ, Frank! Can't you see that that's a gas fire.' He handed Frank the gin and then went down on his knees at the fireplace.

'I'm awfully sorry,' said Frank.

'It looks just like a real open fire,' said Dicky as he used one of Daphne's discarded breakfast-food roughs to marshal the pipe dottle into a tiny heap that could be hidden under the artificial log.

'I'm sorry, Dicky. I really am,' said Frank as he sat back on the sofa with a yellow oilskin tobacco pouch on his knees. He looked at me and nodded before sipping his gin. Then, in a different sort of voice, he said, 'It could become bad, Bernard. If you're going over there, this would be the time to do it.'

'How bad?'

Dicky got to his feet and slapped his hands against his legs to get rid of any ash on his fingers. 'Bloody bad,' said Dicky. 'Tell him how you first found out what was going on.'

'I'm not sure I know what *is* going on yet,' said Frank. 'But the first real sign of trouble came when I had a call from the police liaison chap in Bonn. The border guards at Hitzacker in Lower Saxony had fished a fellow out of the Elbe. He'd got over the Wall and across all those damned minefields and border obstacles and into the river. He was just about done in, but he wasn't injured in any way. From the West German police report I gather there'd been no sounds of shooting or anything from the other side. It was as near as you can get to a perfect escape.'

'Lucky man,' said Dicky.

'Or a well-informed one,' said Frank. 'The border runs along the northeast bank of the river there, so the East Germans can't put obstacles and mantraps in the water. That's why the DDR keep bellyaching about the way the border should run along the middle of the Elbe. Meanwhile it's a good place to try an escape.'

'A border crossing? Why did Bonn get involved and why did anyone call you?'

'Bonn got interested when the interrogator at the reception centre found that the escapee was an East German customs official.'

Frank looked at me as if expecting a reaction. When I gave none, he spent a few moments trying to light his pipe. 'An East German customs official,' he said again, and waved the match in the air to extinguish it. He almost tossed the dead match into the fireplace but remembered in time and placed it on the large Cinzano ashtray that

Dicky had put at his elbow. 'Max Binder. One of our people. A Brahms network man.'

Dicky had had a whole night of Frank's measured story-telling and now he tried to hurry things along. 'When Frank put in the usual "contact string" for the rest of the Brahms network next morning, he got no response from anyone.'

'I didn't say that, Dicky,' said Frank pedantically. 'I got messages from two of them.'

'You didn't get messages,' said Dicky even more pedantically. 'You got two "out of contact" signals.' Dicky had decided that the failure of the Brahms network was his big chance, and he was determined to write the story his own way.

Frank grunted and sipped his gin.

Dicky said, 'Those bastards have been working a racket with the import bank credits, and making a fortune out of it. And Bret's probably been authorizing false papers and the contacts and everything they needed.'

'Werner keeps complaining about the false papers,' I said.

'That was just to put us off the scent,' said Frank. 'The false papers were what they needed more than anything else.'

'We've had a lot of unofficial complaints from the DDR about "antisocial elements given aid and assistance",' I said.

Frank looked up from his pipe and said sharply, 'I resent that, Bernard. You know only too well that those East Germans keep up a regular bombardment of complaints along those lines. How the hell was I to know that this time their cocktail-party diatribes were based on fact?'

Dicky could not restrain a grim smile, and he turned away to hide it. The Brahms network being no more than a criminal gang manipulating the Department for its own profit must surely be enough to bring Bret Rensselaer crashing to the ground. And into the bargain Bret would lose his Brahms Four source. 'Frank says he expects the DDR to prefer murder charges against them,' Dicky added.

'Who? Where?' I said. I immediately thought of Rolf Mauser and was sufficiently surprised to allow my consternation to show. I'd been worrying about the way I'd urged Bret to okay a rollover loan for Werner. Would he suspect that I was a part of this racket? To cover myself, I got up and went over to the drinks wagon. 'Okay if I pour myself a drink, Dicky?'

'Has anyone been in touch with you?' Frank asked me. 'Rolf Mauser's son thinks he went to Hamburg. My bet would be London.'

'Anyone else?' I said, holding up the gin bottle. 'No. No one's contacted me up to now.'

Frank returned my gaze for a moment before shaking his head. 'No,' he said, 'I only said that murder charges would be the next step if the net's been penetrated. It's a device the DDR use for fugitives,' he explained. 'A murder charge automatically makes a fugitive Category One. It gets their descriptions circulated by tele-printer and the call goes out to the armed forces, as well as all the police services and the border guards. And of course there is always more chance of a murderer being reported by the public. These days the man in the East German street has become rather tolerant of black marketeers.' Frank looked at me again. 'Right, Bernard?'

I sipped a little of the gin I'd poured for myself and wondered to what extent Frank guessed that I'd seen Rolf or one of the network. Dicky wasn't suspicious; he could obviously think of nothing except how to use this new situation for his own advancement, but Frank had known me since I was a child. It was not so easy to fool Frank. 'It had to come,' said Frank. 'Brahms have been no use to us except to channel back material from Brahms Four. They've got into mischief, and now they're in trouble. We've seen it happen before, haven't we?'

'You say they're running, without backup or any support or anything from us?'

'No. That's Dicky's interpretation. They might simply be taking cover for a couple of days,' said Frank. 'It's what they do when the security forces are having a routine shakeout.'

'But no matter how routine the shakeout,' I said, 'they might be picked up. And Normannenstrasse will give them an offer they can't resist and maybe blow another network or so. Is that what you're thinking, Frank?'

'What kind of offer they can't resist?' said Dicky.

I didn't answer but Frank said, 'The Stasis will make them talk, Dicky.'

Dicky poured himself a drink. 'Poor bastards. Max Binder, old Rolf Mauser – who else?'

'Let's leave the mourning until we know they are in the bag,' I said. 'Where's Max Binder now?'

'He's still in the reception centre in Hamburg. The interrogation people won't let us have him until they are through.'

'I don't like that, Frank,' said Dicky. 'I don't like some little German interrogator grilling one of our people. Get him out of there right away.'

'We can't do that,' said Frank. 'We have to go through the formalities.'

'Our Berlin people don't go into the reception centre,' said Dicky.

Patiently Frank explained, 'Berlin is still under Allied military occupation, so in Berlin we can do things our way. But things that happen in the Federal Republic have to go through the state BfV office and then through Cologne, and these things take time.'

'When did you see him, Frank?'

Daphne Cruyer tapped and put her head round the door. 'I'm off to the agency now, darling. We're auditioning ten-year-olds for the TV commercial. I can't leave my assistant to face that horde of little monsters on her own.' She was wearing a broad-brimmed hat, long blue cloak and shiny boots. She had changed her image since her visit to Silas in floral pinafore and granny glasses.

'Bye, bye, darling,' said Dicky, and kissed her dutifully. 'I'll phone you at the office if I'm working late again.'

Daphne gave me an affectionate kiss too. 'You men are always working late,' she said archly. Now I was convinced she knew about Dicky and Tessa. I wondered if her amazing outfit was also a reaction to Dicky's infidelity.

Only after we'd all watched Daphne climb into her car and drive away did Frank answer my question.

'The positive identification was enough for me,' said Frank. 'No sense in me trailing all the way out to some godforsaken hole in Lower Saxony. I wasted all next day trying to contact the rest of them.'

'Daphne's forgotten to take her portfolio,' said Dicky, picking up a flat leather folder from the table where she'd put it while kissing him. 'I'll phone her office and tell them to send a motorcycle messenger.' It was the sort of solicitude shown only by unfaithful husbands.

Dicky left the room to make his phone call from the hall. His loud voice was muffled by the frosted glass panel.

'You'd better tell me the real story,' I told Frank. 'While Dicky's phoning.'

'What do you mean?'

'A DDR customs man swimming across the Elbe would excite the police liaison man in Bonn like a plate of cold dumplings. And even if this discovery did get him so animated, why would he think of you as someone who must be told immediately?' Frank didn't respond, so I pushed. 'Police liaison in Bonn aren't given any phone numbers for SIS Berlin, Frank. I thought even Dicky would sniff at that one.'

'They went to Max Binder's home to arrest him.'

'On what charge?'

'We don't know. It must have been something to do with their forfait racket. His wife was home. She got a message to him and he cleared out quickly.'

'You got this from Max Binder?'

'I got it from someone who was told by Werner,' admitted Frank. 'Werner is in no danger. There's no evidence that anyone but Binder was involved. And Max Binder escaped by swimming the Elbe at

Hitzacker, just as I described. He's still in the reception centre. I want to contact Brahms Four, but no one will tell me how.'

From the hall I could still hear Dicky's voice. He had explained in considerable detail what the portfolio contained and from where it had to be collected, but now he was worrying if a motorcycle messenger would be able to carry it. The doorbell rang twice and Dicky shouted to tell the electrician to stop testing it. 'You got it from someone who told Werner,' I repeated. 'And who was that, Frank?'

'Zena told me,' said Frank, prodding about in the bowl of his pipe so that he wouldn't have to meet my stare. 'She's a captivating creature, and I adore the little thing. She has to see Werner from time to time. She filled in some details of this Max Binder story.' He sucked at his pipe but no smoke came.

'I see.'

'You know about me and Zena Volkmann, don't you?' He probed into the bowl of his pipe. When he was sure that the tobacco was not alight, he put the pipe into his top pocket and took a swig at his drink.

'Yes, I know, Frank. I guess she gave you that box of papers that I came to Berlin to look at.'

'It was genuine,' said Frank.

'All too bloody genuine,' I agreed. 'It was straight from Moscow Centre. Top-grade stuff, carefully selected to make it look as if Giles Trent was their only man in London. Where did she get it from?'

'Zena knows a lot of people,' said Frank.

'She knows too many people, Frank. Too many of the wrong people.'

'It's better that we don't go into all that with Bret, and everyone at London Central.'

'Zena is obviously in on this racket that Brahms have been running.'

'It's possible,' said Frank. He finished his gin and licked his lips.

'It's not *possible*, Frank. It's all too bloody obvious. That girl's been making a fool of you. She's been in league with Werner and all the others all the time.'

'You're trying to tell me that your pal Werner was pimping for his own wife?' Frank's voice was harsh; he was determined to forgo his own illusions only by destroying mine too.

'I don't know,' I said. 'Perhaps the breakup with Werner came first. Then she found herself with something she could sell to the Brahms net and Werner was the only contact with them she had.'

'Sell what to the Brahms net?' Frank was uneasy now. He clipped and unclipped the flap of his yellow tobacco pouch and studied the tobacco as if it was of great interest to him.

'Information, Frank.'

'You're not suggesting that I told her anything that could become critical?'

'We'd better find out, Frank,' I said. 'We'd better find out damned soon. We've got field agents who must be warned if Zena Volkmann has been providing your pillow talk to men who might wind up in Normannenstrasse.'

'Don't let's overreact,' said Frank. 'I get information from her; she gets none from me.'

'It won't seem like overreaction to me, Frank,' I said. 'Because I'm going to be there. I'm going to be on the wrong side of Charlie pulling your chestnuts out of the fire, and trying to dance quickly enough to keep the Stasis a jump or two behind me. So just to make sure Zena doesn't hear about my travel plans, I'm going to keep well clear of you and your extramarital activities, Frank.'

'Don't be a fool, Bernard. Do you think any of those clowns you drink with in Steglitz would know how to get you through the wire safely? Do you think any of those kids you were at school with know the town as well as I know it? I've spent most of my life reading about, looking at and talking to Berliners. I get my information from a million different sources and I study it. That's what I do all day long, Bernard. I know Berlin like a librarian knows his shelves of books, like a dentist knows a patient's mouth, like a ship's engineer knows the bits and pieces of his engine. I know every square inch of that stinking town, from palace to sewer.'

'You know the town, Frank. You know it better than anyone, I'll admit that.'

Frank looked at me quizzically. 'For God's sake!' he said suddenly. 'You're not saying you don't trust me.' He stood up to face me and banged his chest with a flattened hand. 'This is Frank Harrington you're talking to. I've known you since you were a tiny tot.'

'Let it go, Frank,' I said.

'I won't,' said Frank. 'I told your father I'd look after you. I told him that when you joined the Department, and I told him it at the very end. I said I'd look after you, and if you're going over the other side, you're going to do it my way.'

I'd never seen Frank get so emotional. 'Let me think about it,' I said.

'I'm serious,' said Frank. 'You go my way or you're not going.' It was a way of avoiding it, and for a moment I felt like taking the opportunity. 'My way or I'll veto it.'

From the hall I could hear Dicky telling the electrician that he was charging too much to fix the bell. Then Dicky put his head round the door and borrowed a fiver from me. 'It's the black economy,' explained Dicky as he took the money. 'You can only get things done if you pay spot cash.'

'Okay, Frank,' I said when Dicky had gone. 'We'll do it your way.'

'Just you and me,' said Frank. 'I'll get you over there.' He didn't promise to get me back again, I noticed.

'Dicky is keeping everything very tight,' I said. 'Did he tell you that?'

Frank was examining his oilskin pouch again to see how much tobacco he had left. 'You can't go wrong that way,' he said.

'Not even Bret,' I said.

'It's coming from someone,' said Frank. 'It's coming from someone with really good access to material.'

I didn't say anything. Such a remark from Frank was *lèse-majesté* and I could think of nothing to reply.

I looked at the clock over the fireplace and wondered aloud if that was really the time. I told Frank to come and have dinner with us some time, and he promised to phone if he could fit it in. Then I shouted goodbye to Dicky, who was still on the phone explaining that Daphne's folio of breakfast-food roughs was vitally important. It was a contention that someone on the other end of the phone seemed to doubt.

Of the Departmental safe houses in which to meet Giles Trent I had chosen the betting shop in Kilburn High Road. The girl behind the counter nodded as I came in. I pushed past three men who were discussing the ancestry of a racehorse, and went through a door marked 'staff only' and upstairs to a small front room. Its window overlooked the wide pavement, where a number of secondhand bathtubs and sinks were displayed.

'You're always in time for the coffee,' said Trent. He was standing at a wooden bench. Upon it there was a bottle of Jersey milk, a catering-size tin of Sainsbury's powdered coffee and a bag of sugar from which the handle of a large spoon protruded. Trent was pouring boiling water from an electric kettle into a chipped cup with the name Tiny painted on it in nail varnish. 'No matter how long I wait for you, the moment I decide to make coffee, you arrive.'

'Something came up,' I said vaguely. For the first time I could see Trent as the handsome man who was so attractive to Tessa. He was tall, with a leonine head. His hair was long and wavy. It was not greying in that messy mousy way that most men's hair goes grey; it was streaked with silver, so that he looked like the sort of Italian film star who got cast opposite big-titted teenagers.

'I really don't think it's necessary for us to go through this amazing rigmarole of meeting here in this squalid room.' His voice was low and resonant.

'Which squalid room would you prefer?' I said, taking a cup from those arranged upside down on the draining board of the sink. I put boiling water, coffee powder, sugar and milk into it.

'My office is no distance from yours,' said Trent. 'I come across to that building several times a week in the normal course of my work. Why the devil should I be making myself conspicuous in this filthy betting shop in Kilburn?'

'The thing I don't like about powdered coffee,' I said, 'is the way it makes little islands of powder. They float. You get one of those in your mouth and it tastes horrible.'

'Did you hear what I said?'

'I didn't realize you wanted an answer,' I said. 'I thought you were just declaiming about the injustice of life.'

'If you put the coffee in first, then poured the hot water on it a little at a time, it would dissolve. Then you put the cold milk in.'

'I was never much good at cooking,' I said. 'First of all, you are not nearly as conspicuous going into a broken-down betting shop in Kilburn as you like to think. On race days, that shop downstairs is crowded with men in expensive suits who put more on a horse than you or I earn in a year. As to your point that it would be better security procedure for us to meet in my office or yours, I can only express surprise at your apparent naiveté.'

'What do you mean?'

'Security from who?' I said. 'Or, as you might put it, from whom? What do you think is secure about meeting in that office of yours, with all those Oxford graduates staring at us with wide eyes and open mouths? You think I've forgotten the way I had a procession of chinless crustaceans coming in and out of your office the last time I was over there? Each one staring at me to see if people from SIS wore their six-shooters on the hip or in shoulder harness.'

'You imagine things,' said Trent.

'I do,' I said. 'That's what I'm paid to do: imagine things. And I don't need to spend a lot of time imagining what could happen to you if things went sour with Chlestakov. You might be a world authority on making instant coffee but you'll be safer if you leave the security arrangements to me.'

'Don't give me that security lecture all over again,' he said. 'I don't want a twenty-four-hour guard on my home or special locks on the doors and windows.'

'Then you're a bloody fool,' I said. We were both standing by the wooden table as we talked. There were only hard little wooden chairs in the room; it was more restful to stand up.

'Chlestakov didn't turn up,' said Trent. He was looking out the window, watching a young woman with a baby in her arms. She was stopping people as they walked past. Most of them walked on with tight embarrassed expressions on their faces. 'She's begging,' said Trent. 'I thought those days had gone for ever.'

'You spend too much time in Mayfair,' I said. 'So who came?'

'And no one gives her anything. Do you see that?'

'So who came?'

'To the meeting at Waterloo station? No one came.'

'They always send someone,' I said. 'And keep well back from the window. Why do you think we put net curtains up?'

'No one arrived. I did it exactly by the book. I arrived under the big four-faced clock at seven minutes past the hour. And then went back two hours later. Still no one. Then I went to the standby rendezvous.'

'Where was that?'

'Selfridge's food department, near the fresh fish counter. I did it exactly as arranged.'

'Moscow Centre like to stick to the tried and true methods,' I said. 'We arrested one of their people under that damned clock back in 1975.' I went to the window where he stood and watched the woman begging. A man wearing a dark raincoat and grey felt hat was reaching into his inside pocket.

'She's had luck at last,' said Trent. 'I wondered why she didn't stand outside Barclays Bank, but I suppose a betting shop is better.'

'Can't you spot a plainclothes cop when you see one?' I said. 'To beg or gather alms in a public place is an offence under the Vagrancy Act of 1824, and by having the baby with her she can be charged under the Children and Young Persons Act too.'

'The bastard,' said Trent.

'The plainclothes cop is there because this is a safe house,' I said. 'He doesn't know that, of course, but he knows that this is Home Office notified premises. The woman doesn't beg regularly or she'd have learned to keep clear of betting shops, because betting shops attract crooks and crooks bring cops.'

'Are you saying the woman is working for the KGB, and they are keeping this SIS safe house under observation?'

I didn't answer his question. 'They must have thought you were being followed, Trent. That's the only explanation for Chlestakov failing to show up. The Russians always show up at a rendezvous. Tell me again about the previous meeting.'

'You're right, a police car's arrived and they're putting her into it.' He looked at me and said, 'It went very well. I told Chlestakov that I might be able to get my hands on the Berlin System, and he went crazy at the thought of it. He took me to dinner at some fancy club in Curzon Street and insisted that we order a big meal and very expensive claret. I'm not all that fond of fancy French food, but he obviously wanted to keep me sweet. That's why I can't understand why the Embassy have cut me.'

'Not the Embassy,' I said. 'Just the KGB Section of the Embassy. They have a motive – you can be quite sure that the Russians always have a motive for everything they do.'

'You said they work out of Moscow for everything.'

'Did I? Well, if I said that, I was right. The London Section Chief wouldn't change his underwear until Moscow Centre have approved the kind of soap the laundry use.'

'But why would Moscow tell them to cut me? And if they were going to drop me, why not tell me so?'

'I don't know, Giles old friend.'

'Don't call me Giles old friend in that sarcastic way.'

'You'll have to put up with me calling you Giles old anything in any way I choose for the time being,' I said. 'Because if Moscow Centre have decided to drop you, it might not simply be a matter of them leaving you off the list of people invited along for vodka and caviar, and a film show about the hydroelectric plant at Kuibyshev.'

'No?'

'It might mean they will get rough,' I told him.

He took this suggestion very calmly. 'Would you like to hear what I think?'

'I'd like to hear it very much,' I said. I was being sarcastic but Trent didn't notice.

'I think you had Chlestakov picked up.'

'Picked up? By Special Branch, you mean?'

'Special Branch or your own duty arresting officer. Or perhaps by some agency or department distanced from you.'

'What sort of agency "distanced" from us could I have used to "pick up" Chlestakov?'

'The CIA.'

'You're talking like an eighteen-year-old anti-nuke demonstrator. You know we'd not let the bloody CIA pick up anyone in this country. And you know very well that there are no agencies distanced from us, or undistanced from us, that could take a Russian national into custody.'

'No one ever gets a straight answer from you bullyboys,' said Trent.

'Are you drunk, Trent?' I said, going closer to him.

'Of course not.'

'Christ, it's not even lunchtime.'

'Why the hell shouldn't I have a drink if I fancy one? I'm doing all your dirty work for you, aren't I? Who will get a medal and promotion if we pull the wool over the eyes of old Chlestakov? You will, you and Dicky bloody Cruyer and all that crowd.'

I grabbed him by the lapel and shook him until his head rolled. 'Listen to me, you creep,' I said softly. 'The only dirty work you're doing is clearing up your own shit. If you take another drink before I give you my permission, I'll get a custody order and lock you away where you can't put agents' lives at risk.'

'I'm not drunk,' he said. He had in fact sobered up now that I'd shaken his brains back into operation.

'If I lose one agent, I'll kill you, Trent.'

He said nothing; he could see I was serious. 'They're your friends, aren't they,' he said. 'They're your Berlin schoolfriends. Ahhh!'

I shouldn't have hit him at all but it was only a little jab in the belly and it helped him to sober up still more.

I picked up the phone and dialled our Federal emergency number. I recognized the voice at the other end. 'Peter? This is Bernard. I'm in the Coach and Horses.' All our safe houses had pub names. 'And I need someone to get a male drunk home and look after him while he sobers up. And I don't want anyone whose heart can be broken by a sob story.'

I put the phone down and looked at Trent. He was sitting on one of the hard chairs, holding his belly and crying silently.

'You'll be all right,' I told him. 'Save your tears for Chlestakov. If he's no longer any use to them, they'll send him home and give him the sort of job that will encourage the ones still here to work harder.'

20

As usual, Rolf Mauser arrived at a bad time. I was watching a very good BBC documentary on model railways, the children were upstairs playing some kind of jumping game, and Fiona was in the kitchen arguing with the nanny about her wages.

I bought Rolf Mauser into the living room and offered to take his leather overcoat from him but he waved me away testily. 'Are you all right, Rolf?' I said.

'Give me a whisky.'

He looked pale. I gave him a big scotch and he sat down and stared at the trains on TV with unseeing eyes. Light spilling from the table lamp beside him showed a fresh cut on his ear. Even as I noticed that, his hand went up to touch his head. He winced with pain as he found some tender places.

'You all right, Rolf?' All his self-confidence seemed to have gone; even those demonic eyebrows were sagging a little.

'I'm sixty-six years old, Bernd, and I'm still alive.'

'You're a tough old bastard, Rolf.' His shoes were scuffed and his leather coat had dirty marks on the front. He took paper tissues from a box on the table and cleaned himself up a bit.

The little trains on TV were making a lot of noise. I used the remote control to switch the sound off. Rolf Mauser looked round furtively and then pulled a brown paper bag from his pocket. He passed it to me. 'You said you'd get rid of it.'

I took a bundle from the bag. Unwinding a heavy woollen scarf, I found my revolver inside. I broke it and sniffed at the breech. There was no smell except that of fresh thin oil. It had been scrubbed clean. Rolf must have been a good soldier.

'You said you'd get rid of it,' he repeated. I shook the bag. Inside there were three bullets and three used brass cases.

'What have you been doing, Rolf?'

'Get rid of it, I say.'

I put the gun and the scarf into the brown paper bag again. And I locked it into the desk where I kept unpaid bills, Fiona's jewellery and letters from the bank about my overdraft.

Rolf turned to watch what I was doing. He said, 'I'm going back tonight. Could you lend me a car to get to Harwich?'

'I'd better know what it's all about,' I said.

'Yes or no?' he said.

'There's a blue Mini outside. What time do you have to be there?'

'Give me a strong envelope and I'll put the keys in the post to you, and tell you where it's parked.'

'You're too late for the Hamburg boat,' I said. He looked up at me without replying. I doubt if he had any intention of leaving via the cross-Channel ferry from Harwich. Rolf's way of keeping secrets was to confide endless untruths to anyone who'd listen. 'I'll get the keys,' I said. 'It's the nanny's car, so be careful with it.'

'Can you find a hat for me, Bernd? I've lost mine.'

I came back with a selection of headgear. He took a cloth cap and tried it on. It fitted him well enough to hide his cuts and shadow his face. 'You stole the car,' I said as I pulled the hat down lower on his head. 'You came to see me, found the keys in the car, and drove away without coming to the door.'

'Sure, Bernd, sure.'

'No one will believe you, but stick to that story and I'll do the same.'

'I said yes,' he said irritably.

'What's happening to the Brahms net?'

'Nothing.'

'Max Binder swam the Elbe.'

'Max lost his nerve,' he said.

'Who else lost their nerve?'

'Not me,' he said, looking me in the eyes. Confidence or no confidence, he was still as ferocious as ever. 'I deal with problems as they come up. I don't go swimming across the Elbe and leaving my wife and kids to face the music.'

'The rest of Brahms all in place? London are worried.'

'A slight hiccup,' he said. 'Brahms had that slight hiccup that the economists talk about when their miscalculations have thrown half a million people out of work.' It was the sort of bitter joke for which he permitted himself a twisted smile.

'Let's hope the hiccup doesn't become whooping cough.'

It was 'gasping cough' in German. Rolf Mauser nodded. 'We took precautions,' he said. 'We've long ago learned that London cannot protect us.'

I let the criticism go. The Brahms net was old and tired. It should have been dismantled years before. Just as the information from Brahms Four was all that made them worthwhile to London, so this damned import-export racket was their sole reason to continue going through the motions. It was a marriage of convenience and, like all such marriages, it depended upon the self-interest of both parties.

Rolf helped himself to another drink – a large one. Then he got to his feet, buttoned up his coat and announced his departure.

'Don't stop and ask a cop which way to go,' I advised. 'Breathe that booze over him and you'll end up in a police cell.'

'I'll take my chances,' he said. 'I like being on my own, Bernd. I never did like doing things the way it's written in the book. Your father knew that.'

'Have you got English money?'

'Go back to your TV,' he said. 'And tell your wife I'm sorry I couldn't stay.'

'She'll understand,' I said.

He smiled his twisted little smile again. Even from before I married her, he'd never been able to get along with Fiona.

Rolf had been gone three hours or more by the time the phone rang with the call from Dicky. 'Where are you?' he said.

'Where am I? Where the hell do you think I am? I'm at home. I'm sitting in front of the TV trying to decide whether to switch the heating back on and watch the late-night movie.'

'The way they patch these calls, you can't be sure where anyone is these days,' grumbled Dicky vaguely.

'What is it?' I said. The film had already started and I didn't want a long chat with him about my Berlin expenses or the new car.

'Has anyone been in touch with you?' he asked. On the TV screen the titles gave place to a small steamer chugging across a bright blue lake.

'No one.'

'You called someone from Security to take Giles Trent back to his home today.'

At the bow of the steamer were three men in white suits leaning over the rail peering into the water. 'Trent had been drinking,' I said. 'He was being abusive and accusing us of arresting Chlestakov, his Embassy contact.'

'Who answered the phone?'

'In the security office? That kid with the moustache – Peter. I don't know his last name.'

'Did he have any trouble with Trent?'

'Look, Dicky,' I said. 'I decide when someone with an orange file needs to be picked up and taken home. Trent can complain to the D-G if he wants, but if I get any more flak from that bastard I'll lock him up again. And there's nothing anyone can do about that except take me off it. And that's a development I wouldn't mind at all. I don't enjoy it, you know.'

'I know all that,' said Dicky.

'And if they move me it will be egg on your face, Dicky.'

'Don't get hot under the collar,' said Dicky placatingly. 'No one is blaming you. You did everything that could be done, everyone is agreed on that.'

'What are you talking about, Dicky?'

'This fiasco with Trent. The bloody newspapers will start implying that we did it. You know that. And the only way we can argue with them is by telling them more than we want Moscow to know.'

'Would you start again, please?' I said.

'Didn't anyone phone to tell you that Trent's been killed?'

'When? How?'

'Late this afternoon or early evening. Someone climbed over the garden wall at the back and shinned up the drainpipe to get into an upstairs window that had been left unlocked. Special Branch let us have someone to write up a preliminary docket.'

'Trent is dead?'

'Shot. He was in the shower. The curtain was drawn across to save any chance of blood splashing on the killer, or at least that's what the Special Branch detective says. None of the neighbours heard the shot. With the television showing nothing but cops and robbers, you could use a machine gun nowadays without anyone noticing the noise.'

'Any idea who did it?'

Dicky gave a tiny derisive hoot. 'Are you joking? The report says the bullets hit the bathroom wall with abnormally low velocity. The ballistics boys say the bullets had been specially prepared by experts – they'd had a proportion of their powder removed. Well, that sounds like a laboratory job, eh? That's our KGB friends, I think. Why do they do that, Bernie?'

'So they don't go through the next two or three houses and spoil the neighbours' television. Who found him?'

'His sister. She let herself in with her own key. She'd come to see if he was okay after that business with the sleeping pills. If it hadn't been for that, we wouldn't have discovered the body until tomorrow morning. I'd always suspected that Trent was queer, didn't you? I mean, him never being married. But giving the sister a key to the house makes that unlikely, wouldn't you say?'

'Anything else, Dicky?'

'What? No. But I thought I should ask you if he was acting normally when he left you this morning.'

'I can't help you, Dicky,' I said.

'Well, I know you've got an early start in the morning. Frank says wrap up well. It's cold in Berlin.'

After I rang off, I returned to my desk. When I unwrapped the pistol, I found a series of holes in the woollen scarf. Rolf Mauser had wrapped the gun in it before shooting Trent. A revolver can't be silenced any other way. I had to use a magnifying glass for a clear sight of the marks left on the bullet cases by the process of hand-loading. There was no doubt that the bullets had been specially prepared by someone with gunsmith's tools and powder measure.

I sat down and looked at the TV before switching off. The steamer was sinking; the men were drowning. I suppose it was some kind of comedy.

21

It was very very dark and Frank Harrington was being ultra cautious, using the electric lamp only to show me a safety well into which I might fall, or large puddles, or the rails when we had to get across to the other side of the railway track.

There is a curious smell in Berlin's underground railway system. It brings to mind the stories about engineers blasting the locks of the canal between Schöneberger and Möckern bridges in those final hours of the war, so that the tunnels flooded to drown civilians, German soldiers and Russians alike. Some say there was no flooding – just leaks and water that came through the damaged bulkhead that guards the Friedrichstrasse U-Bahn station from the cold waters of the Spree. But don't deny those nightmares to anyone who has picked his way over the cross-ties in the darkness after the trains have stopped, for he will tell you about the ghosts down there. And the curious smell remains.

Frank moved forward very slowly, talking softly all the while so that I would know where he was. 'Half the passengers on the underground trains going from Moritzplatz to Voltastrasse don't even realize that they actually go under East Berlin and back into the West again.'

'Are we under the East Sector yet?' I asked.

'On this section of line, they do know of course. The trains stop at Friedrichstrasse station and the passengers are checked.' He stopped and listened, but there was only the sound of dripping water and the distant hum of the electric generators. 'You'll see the marks on the tunnel wall when we get that far. There's red paint on the wall to mark the boundary.' He flashed his light on the side of the tunnel to show me where the marks would be. There was nothing there except bundles of wires sagging from support to support and blackened with decades of filth. As he switched off his lamp, Frank stumbled into a piece of broken drain and cursed. It was all right for him; he had rubber boots on, and wore old clothes under his railway-engineer's overalls. The clothes I wore under my overalls were all I had for my time in East Berlin. And we'd both decided that carrying a case or a parcel in the small hours was asking to be stopped and searched.

We walked slowly along the track for what seemed like hours. Sometimes Frank stopped to listen, but there was only the sudden scratching sounds of rats and the ceaseless hum of electricity.

'We'll wait here for a bit,' said Frank. He held his wristwatch close to his face. 'Some nights there are East Berlin railway engineers going down the track to check the apparatus at the terminal – what used to be Kaiserhof station. Thälmannplatz, they call it nowadays. The Communists like to name the streets and stations after heroes, don't they?' Frank switched on his lamp long enough to show a recessed space in the wall of the tunnel, containing a yellow-painted metal box with a telephone in it. This was one of the places the drivers had to come to if their train stopped between stations. There was a bench there too, and Frank sat down. We were not far below street level and I could feel a cold draft coming down the air shaft.

'Ever wonder why the Berlin Wall follows that absurd line?' said Frank. 'It was decided at a conference at Lancaster House in London while the war was still being fought. They were dividing the city up the way the Allied armies would share it once they got here. Clerks were sent out hotfoot for a map of Berlin but the only thing Whitehall could provide was a 1928 city directory, so they had to use that. They drew their lines along the administrative borough boundaries as they were in 1928. It was only for the purposes of that temporary wartime agreement, so it didn't seem to matter too much where it cut through gas pipes, sewers and S-Bahn or these underground trains either. That was in 1944. Now we're still stuck with it.' We were sitting in the dark. I knew Frank was dying for a puff at that damned pipe, but he didn't succumb to the temptation. He talked instead.

Frank said, 'Years back, when the Communists started building that incredible great satellite city at Marzahn, they wanted it to have its own administration and become a *Stadtbezirk*, a city borough in its own right. But the Communist lawyers sat down with the men from Moscow and went through those old wartime agreements. The outcome was that they were told on no account to create a new *Bezirk*. By breaking the old agreement, they would open the way for the Western Powers to make changes too.'

'Lawyers run the world,' I said.

'I'm going to let you out into the street at Stadtmitte station,' Frank said. He'd told me all about it, shown me a map and photos, but I didn't interrupt him when he told me everything all over again. 'Stadtmitte is an intersection. East German trains and West German trains both pass through. On different levels, of course.'

'How long now, Frank?'

'Relax. We must wait until we're sure the East Germans are not repairing their track. They're not armed but they sometimes have radios to talk to the men who switch off the juice. They have to be sure the lengthmen won't be electrocuted when they start work.'

We waited in the darkness for what seemed an age. Then we walked slowly along the tunnel again. 'In 1945, the Red Army – fighting their way into the city – were held up at Stadtmitte U-Bahn station,' said Frank. 'The station was being used as headquarters by the SS Division Nordland. They were the last German regulars holding out, and they weren't very German. Nordland had become a collection of foreign volunteers, including three hundred Frenchmen who'd been sent from another unit. The Germans were shooting from about where we are standing now and the Russians couldn't get down onto the track. You know that old saying about one man can hold off an army if he fights his battle in a tunnel. Well, the Germans were fighting their final battle and it was in a tunnel.'

'What happened?'

'The Russians manhandled a field-artillery piece down the entrance steps, along the platform, and onto the tracks. Then they fired along the tunnel here, and that was the end of the story.' Frank stopped suddenly and held his hand outstretched as a warning to be silent.

He must have had superhuman hearing, for it was only after we'd stood there for a moment or two that I could hear the sounds of voices and a muffled hammering. Frank put his head close to mine and whispered, 'Sounds travel a long way in these old tunnels. Those men are probably no nearer than the old disused platform at Französischestrasse.' He looked round. 'This is where you leave me.' He pointed up to another air shaft. At the top there was the faintest glimmer of grey light seen through a grating. 'But move quietly.'

I stripped off the overalls and passed them to Frank; then I climbed up the narrow air shaft. There were iron rungs set into the brickwork. Some of them were rusted and broken, but I had nothing to carry and I got to the top easily enough. The grating was held in place with rusting bars. It looked immovable.

'Lift it,' said Frank from below me. 'Lift it until you can see the street is clear. Then choose your moment and go.'

I put my hand to the grating and it moved easily enough. It hadn't been cleaned and oiled – Frank was too subtle for anything so obvious – but it had been removed recently and made ready for me to push aside.

'Good luck, Bernard.'

I tossed my working gloves back down the shaft, and then went through the manhole as quickly as I could, but I need not have worried. The Friedrichstadt – the governmental centre of old Berlin – is empty and silent by Western standards, even during the working day. Now there was no one in sight, just the distant sounds of traffic somewhere to the east of the city. For Stadtbezirk Mitte is a Communist fist punched into the West. It is bordered on three sides by the 'anti-Fascist protection barrier', or what the rest of the world calls the Wall. It was close by. Endless batteries of glaring lights kept the open strip of borderland as bright as day, and the scattered light made the darkness overhead grey, like the mist that creeps inland from an ice-cold sea.

Frank had chosen my route with care. The entrance to the air shaft was hidden from passers-by. There was a pile of sand and big heaps of rubble, some building equipment and a small generator trailer belonging to the Electricity Authority. Berlin's cast-iron manhole covers are very heavy, and by the time this one was back in place I was red-faced and out of breath. I paused for a moment before walking up Charlottenstrasse, intending to cut along the back of the State Opera House parallel to Unter den Linden. I would have to cross the Spree. There was no way of avoiding those bridges, for just as the Wall enclosed this part of Mitte on two sides, the River Spree made up the other two sides of what was virtually a box.

As I got nearer to the State Opera, I saw lights and people. Doors at the back of the building were open and men were carrying huge scenery flats and the statue of a horseman that was recognizably from the last act of *Don Giovanni*. I crossed the street to keep in the shadows but two policemen walking towards me from the direction of the old Reichsbank building – now the offices of the Central Committee – made me change my mind quickly. If only we hadn't had to wait until the underground trains stopped, I could have mingled with the tourists and those groups of Western visitors who go through Checkpoint Charlie just to visit the theatres or the opera houses for the evening. Some of them were dressed in dinner suits and stiff-fronted shirts, or the flamboyant mess kit of a garrisoned regiment. With them came women in long evening dresses and expensive hairdos. Such visitors provided a glimpse of Western decadence for the bored locals. None of those visitors ever gets asked for papers on the street, but such dress would be rather conspicuous amongst the workers where I was going.

There were very few people to be seen anywhere. I walked north and stopped under the arch at Friedrichstrasse station. There were a couple of noisy men arguing about the satirical cabaret across the road, some railway workers waiting for their shift to begin and some silent African tourists staring at everything. The Weidendamm bridge would be my best bet. It was darker there than on the bridges that went over to the island; too many government buildings being guarded on that side of the city.

There were memories everywhere I looked, and there was no getting away from the war. The last escapers from the Führerbunker had come this way, crossing the river by the footbridge when all else failed, and leaving Martin Bormann dead by the river.

The Charité Hospital. In the mortuary of that grim building, the Red Army found the bodies of the men who had tried to overthrow Hitler in the July 1944 plot. Their bodies had been kept in the cold room there on Hitler's personal orders.

A policeman came walking up from the old Brecht theatre beside the Spree. He hurried his pace as he saw me. My papers were in order but I realized too late that I didn't know how to talk to a policeman. 'Hey, you,' the policeman called.

How did East Berliners address a policeman nowadays? This wasn't the USA. Being too familiar would be just as suspicious as being too respectful. I decided to be a little drunk, a shift-worker who'd had a couple of vodkas before heading home. But how many vodkas could a man have these days before he risked being taken to the police station?

'What are you doing here?' The policeman's voice was shrill, and his accent revealed his home to be somewhere in the north: Rostock, Stralsund or Rügen Island, perhaps. On this side of the Wall there was a theory that out-of-town recruits were more reliable than Berliners.

I kept walking. 'Get up,' the policeman said. I stopped and turned round. He was talking to a couple of men sitting on the ground in the shadow of the bridge. They didn't get up. The cop said, 'Where are you from?'

The elder of the two, a bearded man wearing overalls and a battered leather jacket, said, 'And where are *you* from, sonny?'

'Let's get you home,' said the cop.

'Get me home,' said the bearded man. 'That's right. You get me home to Schöneberg.' He laughed. 'Yorckstrasse, please, right near the railway.'

The younger man got to his feet unsteadily, 'Come on,' he said to his companion.

'Yorckstrasse, Schöneberg,' said the bearded man again. 'Only two stops from here on the S-Bahn. But you've never heard of it and I'll never see it again.' He began to sing tunelessly. *'Das war in Schöneberg im Monat Mai.'* His singing voice revealed the extent of his drunkenness in a way that his speech did not.

The policeman was less conciliatory now. 'You'll have to get off the street,' he said. 'Stand up. Show me your papers.'

The drunk gave an artful little laugh. His companion said, 'Leave him alone – can't you see he's not well,' in a voice so slurred that his words were almost incomprehensible.

'If you're not on your way home in two minutes, I'll run you along to the police station.'

'Er ist polizeiwidrig dumm,' said the bearded man, and laughed. It

meant criminally stupid, and it was a joke that every German policeman had heard.

'Come along with me,' said the cop.

The man began singing again, louder this time: '*Das war in Schöneberg im Monat Mai. . . .*'

I hurried on lest the policeman call for help with his two difficult drunks. Even when I was a hundred metres or more down the road, I could still hear the drunken old man singing about the little girl who had so often and gladly kissed the boys as they did in Schöneberg so long ago.

At Oranienburger Tor, where the Chausseestrasse leads up to the football stadium, I turned into the dark labryinth of side streets. I'd forgotten what it was like to be a newly 'deposited' field agent with false papers and a not very convincing cover story. I was too old for it; once I was safely back behind my desk in London, I wouldn't fret to move again.

More than a century old, these grim-looking apartment blocks, five and six storeys high, had been built to shelter peasants who came to the city looking for jobs in the factories. They had changed very little. Rolf Mauser lived on the second floor in a rambling, tumbledown apartment building in Prenzlauer Berg. He was bleary-eyed and barefoot when he opened the door, a red silk dressing gown over his pyjamas.

'What the hell are you doing here?' he said as he took the chain off the door. It was his turn to be surprised in the middle of the night, and I rather relished it.

He motioned me into the sitting room and I sank down on a soft chair without removing either coat or hat. 'A change of plan, Rolf,' I said. 'I had a feeling that it wasn't good on the street tonight.'

'It's never good on the street,' he said. 'Do you want a bed?'

'Is there room for me?'

'Rooms are all I have in abundance. You can take your choice of three different ones.' He put a bottle of Polish vodka on the table alongside me and then opened the white porcelain stove to poke the ashes over. 'The rents over this side of the Wall are more or less the same, whether you've got a two-room flat or a huge house. So why move?' The acrid smell of burning coal filled the room.

'I wondered whether you'd be here, Rolf.'

'Why not? After what happened in London, this is the safest place, isn't it?'

'How do you figure that, Rolf?' I said.

'The evidence will be in London. That's where they'll be looking for the culprit.'

'I hope so, Rolf,' I said.

'I had to do it, Bernd. I had to bring him round the corner, you know. That man in London was going to blow the whole network.'

'Let's forget it,' I said, but Mauser was determined to have my approval for his deed.

'He'd already told Berlin KGB to have personnel and solitary prison accommodation ready for up to fifty arrests. The Brahms network would have been *kaputtgemacht*. And several other networks too. Now do you understand why I had to do what I did?'

'I understand it, Rolf. I understand it even better than you do.' I poured myself a shot of Rolf's fruit-flavoured vodka and drank it down. It was too fiery for the fruit flavouring to soften it much.

'I had to execute him, Bernd.'

'*Um die Ecke bringen* – that's gangster talk, Rolf. Let's face the truth. You murdered him.'

'I assassinated him.'

'Only public officials can be assassinated; and even then the victims have to be tyrants. Executions are part of a process of law. Face it: you murdered him.'

'You play with words. It's easy to be clever now that the danger has been removed.'

'He was a weak and foolish man, riven by guilt and fear. He knew nothing of importance. He'd never heard of Berlin System until last week.'

'Yes,' said Rolf. 'Berlin System – that's what he promised them. I asked Werner about it. He said that it was a complete breakdown of all networks and contacts, including emergency contacts and interservice contacts, for the whole Berlin area. We were very worried, Bernd.'

'Where did you get Trent's name and address?' I asked.

He didn't answer.

'From Werner. Who got it from that bloody Zena. Right?'

'You were asking Frank Harrington questions about some mix-up in 1978. Frank guessed that this man Trent was being investigated.'

'And he told Zena?'

'You know Zena. She got it out of him.'

'How many times do I have to tell you that Werner is not employed by the Department. Why didn't you get in touch with Olympia Stadion?'

'Not enough time, Bernd. And Werner is more reliable than your people at Olympia. That's why you use him, isn't it?'

'Why didn't you tell me what you were going to do that night in London?'

'We didn't want London Central to know,' said Rolf. He poured himself a shot of vodka. He was beginning to sweat, and it wasn't with the heat from the stove.

'Why not?'

'So where was this man Trent getting his Berlin System from? Answer me that. He was going to get it from someone in London, Bernd.'

'Damn right,' I said angrily. 'He was going to get it from *me*.' I looked at him, wondering how much to confide to him.

'From you, Bernd? Never.'

'It was all part of a play, you fool. I told him to promise it to Moscow. I promised him the System because I wanted to keep him on the hook while I reeled him in.'

'It was an official play, you mean?'

'You bloody fool, Rolf.'

'I killed the poor bastard for nothing?'

'You messed up my plan, Rolf.'

'Oh, my God, Bernd.'

'You'd better show me where I'm to sleep, Rolf. I have a busy day tomorrow.'

He stood up and mopped the sweat from his brow with a red handkerchief. 'I won't get to sleep, Bernd. It's a terrible thing I have done. How can I sleep with that on my conscience?'

'Think of all the poor bastards you killed in those artillery bombardments, Rolf, and add one.'

22

The next morning was very sunny. Even Prenzlauer Berg looked good. But Rolf Mauser's second-floor apartment faced out onto a cobbled courtyard almost entirely filled by a large soot-caked chestnut tree. The greenish light reflected from its young leaves made it seem as if the whole place was under water.

Only a few stunted bushes grew in the yard. But there were bicycles there by the dozen and prams double-parked. Rows of rubbish bins too, their contents distributed far and wide by hungry cats that woke me in the night with their angry screeches. The narrow peeling stucco walls of the courtyard, which had brought the chestnut into early bud, echoed every sound. Everyone could hear the admonitions, arguments and shouted greetings of two women who were throwing pailfuls of water onto the mess and scrubbing energetically with stiff brooms.

'It's not exactly the Kaiserhof in its heyday,' said Rolf, serving himself from a dented pot of coffee and leaving me to do the same. He had the bluff manner of a soldier, the self-centred ways of a man who'd lived alone too long. 'Those damned cats kept me awake.'

'Cobbler's Boys,' I said, picking up one of the triangular wholemeal rolls that Berliners eat at breakfast time. 'I slept very well. Thanks for the bed, Rolf. I'll push on today.'

'It's difficult to get them now,' said Rolf. 'All bread prices are controlled. None of these lazy swines of bakers want the extra work of making anything but ordinary bread.' He'd recovered from his self-doubts of the night before, as all soldiers must renew their conscience with every dawn.

'It's the same everywhere,' I said.

'Stay a week if you want to. I get a bit fed up being here alone. The couple who let me share it are away visiting their married daughter.' He took his cup of coffee from the tray he'd brought, put milk into it, and sat down on the bed while I finished shaving. 'But you'll have to take your turn carrying coal from the cellar.'

'I hope I won't need a week, Rolf.'

'You're going to see Brahms Four?'

'Probably.'

'Is there really a person called Brahms Four?'

'I hope so, Rolf.'

'I always thought it was the code name for a syndicate. Why else would the Brahms Four material always be kept separate from everything else we sent?'

'Nothing so unusual about that.'

'Officially he's in the Brahms network.' He paused to let me know he was about to say something significant. 'But no one in the Brahms network has ever seen him.'

'How do you know that?' I said sharply. 'Damn it, Rolf, you should know better than to discuss named agents with third parties.'

'Even if the third parties are also agents?'

'Especially then, because the chances of them being interrogated are that much greater.'

'You've been a long time away, Bernd. You've been sitting behind a desk in London too long. Now you talk like one of those memos that Frank Harrington likes to write.'

'Save some of that coffee for me, Rolf,' I complained.

He stopped filling his cup, and looked up and grinned at me. 'Suppose you find he doesn't exist?' he said, pouring the last of the coffee into my cup, dregs and all. 'Suppose you find he's just a postbox in the KGB building and you've been made a fool of for years and years?'

'Is that your guess, Rolf?'

He bit off a mouthful of roll and chewed it. 'No. I'm just being devil's advocate.'

Rolf Mauser was right: although not a Department employee, I trusted Werner Volkmann more than anyone Berlin Station could provide. He had a car he used on the East side of the Wall. He was waiting for me at that part of Schönhauserallee where the underground trains come up into the daylight and rattle along the antiquated construction that patterns the whole street with shadows.

I opened the door and got in beside him. Without a word of greeting, he started up and headed north.

'No wonder Brahms Four is getting jumpy,' I said. 'Too many people are becoming curious about him.'

'He'll not go undetected for another six months,' said Werner.

'London were hoping to squeeze another two years out of him.'

He made a noise that expressed his contempt for London Central and all their plans and ambitions. 'With Brahms network channelling his reports?'

'Other ways could be tried,' I said.

'Such as VHF radio, just powerful enough to transmit to Olympia Stadion?' said Werner with an unmistakable edge to his voice.

'That was mentioned,' I admitted. It had been Dicky's one and only contribution to a very long meeting the previous month.

'By a fool,' said Werner.

'But what's the alternative? Putting him into a different network?'

'It could be done, couldn't it?'

'You've never had a job of introducing an agent into a network,' I said. 'Most of the nets are run by temperamental prima donnas. I couldn't face all the arguments and anxieties that go with these damned shotgun marriages.'

'Put him in contact with another network and you'll slow up the delivery,' said Werner. He was guessing, of course; he had no knowledge of what other networks we had with access to Berlin. But in fact his guess was right. There are lots of men like Werner; they just can't stop working, pay or no pay. It was probably Werner who'd held Brahms together so long.

'And you increase the number of people who know he exists,' I said.

'Does he exist?' said Werner. 'Sometimes I wonder.'

'Have you been talking to Rolf Mauser?'

'Of course I have,' admitted Werner. 'Do you imagine the network can handle material for years and not wonder where it's coming from? Especially when we get bombarded with priority demands for immediate handling.'

'I'm seeing him as soon as possible,' I said.

Werner looked away from the road for long enough to study my face. 'You're sharing secrets today, are you? That's out of character, Bernie. Why would you tell me you're seeing him?'

'Because you've guessed already.'

'No, no, no,' said Werner. 'That's not it.'

'Because we might have to get him out of East Berlin fast, Werner.'

'I'll take you to wherever you want to go,' offered Werner. 'Down-town? I have nothing to do.'

'I'll need the car, Werner. You've got *plenty* to do. I want you to take the London flight and be back here by evening.'

'What for?'

'When it happens, it will happen very fast.'

'When what happens?'

'Suppose, Werner . . .' It was hard saying it out loud. 'Suppose it's Fiona who's the KGB agent in London.'

'Your wife?'

'Well, think about it. Everything fits: the Giles Trent fiasco, and the way she tried to pin the leak of that Karlshorst signal on him. Bret wasn't in Berlin at the time in question. Dicky never saw the signal. Fiona is the only one in the right place at the right time, every time.'

'You can't be serious, Bernie.'

'I want to be wrong, Werner. But if it is Fiona and she decides to run for it, she'll take the children too.' I wanted him to say I was talking nonsense.

'But, Bernie, the duty officer at the airport would probably recognize her. Going out alone, she could say she was working. But with two kids I'd say any airport duty officer would be bound to check back with the office before letting her through.'

'So what will she do?' I said.

'If she really is KGB, she'll have them arrange about getting your children out separately. Jesus, Bernie. It's too awful to think about. It couldn't be Fiona, could it?'

'We'll have to trust Dicky,' I said. 'He'll give you whatever you need. Take the children over to my mother. Make it all sound normal. I don't want Fiona to know I suspect her. But have someone with them all the time – guards, I mean, people who will know what has to be done, not just security men – and arrange things so I can swear I know nothing about it, Werner. Just in case I'm wrong about Fiona.'

'I'm sure you're wrong about her, Bernie.'

'You'd better get going. I'll drop you at a taxi rank and then take your car. I've got a busy day. See you at Rolf's tonight.'

'I'm sure you're wrong about Fiona,' said Werner, but every time he said it he sounded less and less convinced that I was wrong.

23

I went to see Brahms Four at his office in Otto-Grotewohl-Strasse. It used to be Wilhelmstrasse in the old days, and just down the street beyond the Wall it still was. The building too had changed its name, for this was the huge and grandiose Air Ministry block that Hermann Göring had built for his bickering bureaucrats. It was one of the few Nazi government buildings that survived the fighting here in the centre of the city.

After filling in the requisite form for the clerk on the reception desk, I was shown upstairs. Here was the man who'd come back from what Dicky described as 'some godforsaken little place in Thüringerwald' to dig me out of my hideout in a narrow alley behind the Goethe Museum in Weimar just minutes before they came to get me. I'd never forget it.

Goodness knows what clerk in London Central had named the network Brahms or by what chance this man had become its number 4. But it had been put on his documents decades ago and, for their purposes, it was his name still. His real name was Dr Walter von Munte but, living in the proletarian state of the German Democratic Republic, he'd long since dropped the 'von'. He was a tall gloomy man of about sixty, with a lined face, gold-rimmed glasses and grey closely cropped hair. He was frail-looking despite his size, and his stooped shoulders and old-fashioned good manners made him seem servile by the standards of today's world. The black suit he wore was carefully pressed but, like the stiff collar and black tie, it was well worn. And he wrung his hands like a Dickensian undertaker.

'Bernd,' he said. 'I can't believe it's you . . . after all these years.'

'Is it so long?'

'You were not even married. And now, I hear, you have two children. Or have I got it wrong?'

'You've got it right,' I said. He was standing behind his desk watching me as I went over to the window. We were close to the Wall: here I could almost see the remains of Anhalter railway station; perhaps from a higher floor I'd see the Café Leuschner. I carelessly touched the telephone junction box on the windowsill, and glanced up at the light fittings before going back again.

He guessed what I was doing. 'Oh, you need not worry about hidden microphones here. This office is regularly searched for such devices.' He smiled grimly.

Only when I sat down on the moulded plastic chair did he sit down too. 'You want to get out?' I said softly.

'There is not much time,' he said. He was very calm and matter of fact.

'What's the hurry?'

'You know what the hurry is,' he said. 'One of your people in London is reporting regularly to the KGB. It's only a matter of time. . . .'

'But you're special,' I said. 'You are kept apart from everything else we do.'

'They have a good source,' he said. 'It must be someone at the top in London.'

'London want you to stay on,' I said. 'For two years at least.'

'London is Oliver Twist. London always wants more. Is that why you came here? To tell me to stay on?'

'It's one of the reasons,' I admitted.

'You've wasted your time, Bernd. But it's good to see you, just the same.'

'They'll insist.'

'Insist?' While he considered the idea of London forcing him to stay on, he carefully tore the edging from a block of postage stamps. 'How can they insist on anything? If I ceased to report to them, what could they do about that? If they betrayed me, the word would soon get around and your whole service would suffer.'

'There would be no question of London betraying you. You know that.'

'So what sanction do they have? How could they insist?' Having made the postage stamps look more tidy, he rolled up the stamp edging to make it into a ball.

I said, 'You'd have to give up all thoughts of going to the West. And I think you want to go to the West.'

'My wife wants to go. She wants to see her brother's grave. He was killed in Tunisia in the war. They were very close as children. But if it proves impossible, then so be it.' He shrugged and unrolled the stamp edging, smoothing it flat again.

'And you want to see your son in São Paulo.'

He said nothing for a long time, toying with the stamp edging as if he were thinking of nothing else. 'You are still as painstaking as you used to be, Bernd. I should have guessed you'd trace the payments.'

'A holding company in Luxembourg that receives money from Bayerische Vereinsbank in Munich, and transfers money to the São Paulo office of the Banco Nacional is not exactly deep cover,' I said. 'That publishing-company account isn't active enough to fool anyone for long.'

'Who else knows that?' He opened the brass flap on his ornate pen stand and looked at the dried-up sediment in the inkwell.

'I have told no one.'

'I appreciate that, Bernd.'

'You got me out of Weimar,' I said.

'You were young. You needed help.'

He screwed up the stamp edging a second time and tossed it into the dry inkwell with commendable accuracy before closing the brass flap. 'They arrested Busch the very next day.'

'That was a long time ago.'

'I gave them his address.'

'I know.'

'Who could have guessed the poor old fellow would go back home again?'

'I would have done the same,' I said.

'Not you, Bernd. You're made of harder stuff.'

'That's why they sent me to tell you to hang on,' I said.

He didn't smile. Without looking up from his desk, he said, 'Suppose I could help you find the traitor in London?'

So that was it. So that's what all the messages and the difficulties had been leading up to. I said nothing. Munte knew nothing about London except the identity of Silas, who'd been his friend and run him so long ago. And nowadays Silas had little contact with the day-to-day running of London Central. Surely Silas couldn't be one of them.

He spoke again, still fidgeting with the pen stand. 'I couldn't name him, but I could identify him positively to your satisfaction. And provide evidence that would satisfy even a law court, if that's the course that London decided upon.'

Giles Trent, perhaps. I had to find out if he was trying to sell me something I already had. 'How would you do that? What sort of evidence?'

'Could you get me out?'

'You alone?'

'Me and my wife. Together. It would have to be the two of us together. We wouldn't be separated.'

I felt sure that he was going to tell me about Giles Trent. If the KGB had discovered that we were playing Trent, I'd like to know. But I couldn't pull Munte out just for that.

Perhaps he guessed the sort of thoughts that were running through my mind. 'I'm talking about someone with access to London Data Centre,' he said, staring at me, knowing that I would be surprised to hear he even knew such a place existed. 'Someone with pass-codes prefixed "Knee jerk".'

I sat very still and tried to look impassive. Now there was no longer any way of avoiding the awful truth. The 'Knee jerk' codes were used only by a handful of specially selected top personnel in London Central. Used in the Data Centre's computer, they accessed the automatic link – hence 'Knee jerk' – to CIA data files. If they'd seen printout with 'Knee jerk' marks here in East Berlin, there was no limit to what might have been betrayed. It was not Giles Trent we were talking about; it was someone senior, someone very close to Operations. 'How soon could you get this evidence?'

'This evening.'

'When would you want to travel?' This development changed everything. If Brahms Four could help identify such a well-placed Soviet agent, London would want him there to give evidence.

'You know what women are like, Bernd. My wife would probably need a few days to think about it.'

'Tomorrow. I'll take you back with me. But let me make this clear. Unless you produce irrefutable evidence that enables me to identify the person who is supplying this material, the deal is off.'

'I'll bring you four handwritten pages of data. Would that satisfy you?'

'Handwriting? Then it's certainly not genuine. No agent would be that stupid.'

'Is that what you think, Bernd? Sometimes – when it's late, and one is tired – it becomes very difficult to take all the necessary precautions. Blame the KGB controller in the London Embassy who forwarded the original instead of making a copy. Or blame the clerks here in Berlin who have left the document in the file, Bernd. I feel sorry for the agent. I know exactly how he felt.'

'Handwritten? And no one here remarked on it?'

'Lots of our papers are handwritten. We are not quite so automated as you are in the West. It's a distinctive hand – very neat with curly loops.'

'From London?' Fiona's writing. But could it all be a plant?

'We are only a bank. Our security precautions are not very elaborate. It was a very interesting and most secret report about proposed Bank of England support for sterling. I recognized what it was only because I was looking for such things.'

'By tonight, you say?'

'I know where the report is.'

'Your wife must understand that she can't take anything with her except what she can wear and put in her pockets.'

'We have talked about it many times, Bernd.'

'No friends or relatives, no small dogs or parrots or albums of family photos.'

'She understands,' he said.

'It doesn't get easier,' I said. 'Don't frighten her, but make sure your wife understands that she's risking her life.'

'She will not be frightened, Bernd.'

'Very well.'

'I will see you at nine o'clock, my friend. Can you find the Pioneer House at Wühlheide near Köpenick? It's a twenty-five-minute ride on the S-Bahn from here. Room G-341. I'll have the papers.'

'I'll find it.'

He stood up and, with both hands on his hips, tilted his head back and sighed like a man awakening from a long sleep. 'At last the decision is made,' he said. 'Can you think what that means to me, Bernd?'

'I'll need to phone my wife in London,' I said. 'She gets anxious if I don't keep in contact. Can I direct-dial on a secure phone?'

'Use this one. I call the West several times every day. Dial nine and then the number,' he said. 'There is no monitoring of calls, but it will be logged. Be discreet, Bernd.'

'We have a prearranged code,' I explained. 'Just domestic chat. I'll mention the handwritten paper. She'll understand what's happened.'

24

The Pioneer Park is a lavish example of the priority that East Germany gives to sport and leisure. Two square miles of parkland are landscaped into a complex of sports stadiums, running tracks, football and athletic fields, baths, swimming pools, and even a course for trotting races. I found the main building, and inside its gleaming interior I picked my way past well-equipped gyms and huge indoor pools that came complete with everything from diving instructors to rows of buzzing hair-dryers.

I found G-341 on the third floor and looked through the glass panel before entering. It was a small rehearsal room, beautifully panelled in contrasting wood, and occupied by four elderly men playing Schubert's 'Death and the Maiden' quartet. Dr Munte was sitting at a grand piano but he was not playing. His head was cocked and his eyes closed as he listened to the performance. Suddenly he got up and said, 'No, gentlemen, no. There is no grace there.' He saw me looking through the door but gave no sign of recognition. 'Perhaps we've had too much Schubert tonight. Let's see how well you remember the Haydn Seventy-seven C Major.' He beckoned me into the room and greeted me with a bow and formal handshake while the players sorted out the parts for the quartet.

'This is only our third attempt,' he said apologetically. One of the men dropped his music on the floor and had to go on his knees to gather the sheets together again.

'It's a difficult work,' I said.

Munte started them playing, using a delicate movement of both hands; then after watching them with a proprietorial satisfaction, he took me to a room beyond. This second room was larger, its walls lined with neat steel lockers for musical instruments and wooden lockers for clothes.

'You missed "The Trout",' he said. 'I play the piano part for that.'

'Did you get the document?'

He bent his head, still listening to the music coming from the next room. 'The first violin is not up to it any more,' he admitted sadly.

'He's having heat treatment for his finger joints, but I fear it's not helping him a great deal.'

'The document,' I said impatiently. 'Did you bring it?'

'No,' he said. 'I didn't.'

'Why not?'

Before he could answer, the door from one of the other adjoining rehearsal rooms swung open. A plump man came in dragging a small child and a cello, one in each hand. 'Now here's Dr Munte,' said the fat man to his son. 'Ask him how long you need every day.' He turned to us and said, 'Getting the little devil to practise would try the patience of a saint. All he thinks about is American jazz. Talk to him, Dr Munte. Tell him he's got to practise. Tell him he must play real music, German music.'

'If the interest is lacking, the child will never love music, Herr Spengler. Perhaps you should let him do what he wants.'

'Yes, that's the modern way, isn't it,' said the fat man, not bothering to hide his annoyance at Munte's lack of support. 'Well, I don't believe in the modern way. This is not California. . . .' He looked at my appearance and seemed to guess that I was not an East Berliner. But, having decided that I was not a foreigner, he continued: 'We are Germans, aren't we? This is not California – *yet*. And may the Lord protect us from the sort of things that go on over there in the West. If I say my son is going to practise the cello, he'll do it. Do you hear that, Lothar? You'll practise every night for an hour *before* you go out to play football with your friends.'

'Yes, *Väterchen*,' said the boy with affection. He held his father's hand tightly until the man unclasped it in order to get keys from his pocket. The boy seemed reassured by his father's dictum.

The fat man put the cello into a locker and closed the door. Then he locked it with a padlock. 'You're not strong enough for football,' he said loudly as they went out. The little boy grabbed his father's hand again.

'We Germans find reassurance in tyranny,' said Munte sadly. 'That's always been our downfall.'

'The document.'

'The file containing the document you want is now with the clerk to the head of the bank's Economic Committee.'

'Why?' Was the Berlin KGB office already in action?

'It's a big file, Bernd. There could be many perfectly ordinary reasons for his taking it away.'

'Can you get it back from him tomorrow?'

'The normal way is to ask the records office, and wait while they find out where it is. Eventually such files turn up on the desk.'

'You're not suggesting that we wait while the slow wheels of Communist bureaucracy turn for us?'

'I'm not suggesting anything,' said Munte sharply. He obviously identified himself with the slow wheels of bureaucracy and was offended.

'Go to wherever it is tomorrow. Remove this damned handwritten document and bring it to me.'

'How will I explain such an action? The files – even the most ordinary ones – are signed in and out. What would the head of the Economic Committee say if his clerk tells him that I've taken the file – or even come into the office to look at it?'

'For God's sake,' I said angrily. I wanted to shout at him, but I kept my voice low. 'What do you care how extraordinary such actions are? What do you care how suspicious anyone gets? We're talking about one last thing you do before we get you out of here.'

'Yes, you're talking about it,' he said. 'But suppose you see this document and decide it's not something you want. Then you say thank you, and leave me to go back into the office and face the music, while you return to London and tell them I had nothing worthwhile to offer.'

'Very well,' I said. 'But I can't give you an absolutely firm undertaking to get you out until London agree to my request. I can't get you out on my own, you know that. I could tell you a pack of lies but I'm telling you the truth.'

'And how long will that take?'

I shrugged.

'The slow wheels of Western bureaucracy?' he asked sarcastically. He was angry. Fear does that to some people, especially to such introspective sober-faced old men as Munte. It was odd to think of him fearlessly enduring all the dangers of spying for years and then getting so frightened at the idea of living in the West. I'd seen it in other men: the prospect of facing a highly competitive, noisy, quick-moving, kaleidoscopic society and braving its dangers – sickness, crime, poverty – could be traumatic. He needed reassurance. And if I did not reassure him quickly and properly he might suddenly decide he didn't want to go to the West after all. Such things had happened before, not once but many times.

'Preparations must be made,' I said. 'You and your wife will not go to a reception centre for refugees. You'll be VIPs, looked after properly, so that you have no worries. You'll go to Gatow, the military airport, and fly directly to London on an RAF plane – no customs or immigration nonsense. But for all that you'll need documentation, and such things take time.' I said nothing of the dangers of crossing the Wall.

'I'll get it tomorrow,' he said. 'Will Silas Gaunt be there?'

'He'll be there, I'm sure.'

'We were close friends in the old days. I knew your father too.'

'Yes, I know.' Next door there was a pause in the music before the slow movement began.

'Haydn speaks an everlasting truth,' he said.

'You'll be all right once you're there,' I said. 'You'll see old friends and there will be a lot to do.'

'And I will see my son.'

I knew they wouldn't let Munte go to Brazil so readily. There would be long debriefings, and even after six months or so, when trips abroad are sometimes permitted, they wouldn't want him to go to Brazil, with its German colony so infiltrated by East German agents. 'We might be able to get your son to London for you,' I said.

'One step at a time,' he replied. 'I'm not even in London yet.'

'You'll soon be there.' I said it glibly while wondering which route to take back to the centre of the city.

'Will I?' said Munte in a voice that made me give him my whole attention. 'You've told London that I want to get out. And, guessing the real meanings behind the conversation you had with your wife on my phone, they now know about the evidence I'm providing for you to pinpoint the traitor there.'

'Yes?' I said doubtfully. From the next room there came the solemn melodies of the quartet, the first violin wringing a plaintive song from under his stiffening fingers.

'Are you really such a fool? Someone in London is worrying what you will discover here. They will make quite certain that they hear any news you supply to London. They will then take measures to eliminate both of us.'

'You worry too much,' I said. 'There will be no official report of what I told my wife.'

'I don't believe you. Someone will have to take responsibility for the task of getting us out.'

'My immediate superior. He'll be the only person told. Rest assured that he is not the man we are after.'

'I'm not going home tonight.'

'Then where are you going?'

'We've got a *Laube*. It's just two tiny rooms and a kitchen but we have electricity, and I won't lie awake all night worrying about policemen knocking on the door. My wife went out there earlier today. She will have some hot soup waiting.'

'Where?'

'At Buchholz, behind the church. It's a huge spread of allotments. Hundreds of people go out there at the weekend even at this time of year.'

'Tonight? It's a long journey to Buchholz. Do you want a ride? I've got a car.'

'You're very kind. It's not such an easy journey by bus and the S-Bahn is quite far away from us.'

I realized that Munte had deliberately introduced the topic with the hope of getting a ride there. 'How soon will you be ready?'

'I must wait for the end of the Haydn. I must tell my friend that his fingers are getting better. It's not true of course, but it's the sort of lie one expects from a good friend.' He smiled bleakly. 'And I will not see any of my friends again, will I?'

First I took Munte to his home in Erkner, a village surrounded by lakes and forests on the extreme eastern edge of the city. I waited in the car ten minutes or more. He returned carrying a small case.

'Family photos, old letters and my father's medals,' he explained apologetically. 'I suddenly realized that I will never return here.'

'Don't take too much with you,' I cautioned.

'I'll throw most of it away,' he promised. 'I should have done that years ago but I never seemed to have enough time.'

I drove north from Erkner on the autobahn with which Fritz Todt – Hitler's chief engineer – had ringed Berlin. The road was in poor condition and more than once the traffic was diverted to single-lane working. Near the Blumberg exit we were waved down by an army motorcyclist, and military policemen signalled frantically with their special flashlight-batons and ran about shouting in the imperious way that all military policemen learn at training school. Civilian traffic was halted while a Russian Army convoy passed us. It took ten minutes for the heavy trucks – some carrying tanks and others with missiles – to pick their way around the broken sections of roadway. It was during this delay that Munte told me a joke. He not only told me a joke, he told me it was a joke before he started it.

'There is a joke that East Berliners have about these neglected autobahns,' he said. 'People say why can't those *verdammten* Nazis come back and keep their *Autobahnen* in good order.'

'It's a good joke,' I said.

We waited a long time while the Russian trucks splashed through the rain puddles and thumped their suspensions on the potholes. Munte watched them with unseeing eyes. 'I was driving along here during the Berlin fighting,' he said suddenly. 'It was towards the end of April 1945. The reports said that tanks of the 1st White Russian Front were moving into the northwest part of Charlottenburg and had halted at Bismarckstrasse. And there were unconfirmed reports of Red Army infantry in Moabit. In the car with me I had my younger brother and two of his schoolfriends. We were trying to get to my parents' home near Wannsee before the Russians got that far south. What an idiot I must have been! We didn't know the Russians coming from the southwest had already got to Wannsee. They were past Grunewald and fighting in the streets of Friedenau by that time.'

He was silent until I finally said, 'Did you get there?'

'I was on this same road, this same piece of autobahn. Stopped, just as we're stopped, but by some motorized SS unit. They drained every last drop of gas from my car and pushed it off the road. They were doing that with every car and truck that came along here. I even saw them commandeer two Luftwaffe fuel tankers at gunpoint.'

'You walked home?'

'When the SS men got us out of my car, they looked at our papers. I had my Reichsbank pass and they accepted that without comment. But the three children were ordered to join an assorted collection of soldiers who were being pressed into battle. I objected but they shut me up by threatening to send me into the fighting too.' He cleared his throat. 'I never saw any of those boys again.'

'It's nearly forty years ago,' I reminded him. 'You're not still blaming yourself?'

'I should have stayed with him. He was only fifteen years old.'

'You did what you thought was right,' I said.

'I did what I was told,' said Munte. 'I did it because I was frightened. I've never admitted that to anyone else, but I will tell you truthfully I was frightened.'

The Russian convoy passed and our lane of cars started moving again. Munte sat back in his seat with his head resting against the window. He did not speak again for the rest of the journey, except to warn me when we were getting near to the autobahn interchange for Pankow.

It was late when we reached Buchholz, a village that has become a suburb. The tramlines end in front of the church in a street that is wide enough to be a village square. It was dark and the only light came from a *Weinstube* where a waiter was sweeping the floor of an empty bar.

Munte told me to turn off at the church. We bumped along a narrow country lane alongside a cemetery. It was dark, but by the headlights' beams I could see that there were trees and bushes on each side of a track that was only just wider than the car. Marking these plots of cultivated land were elaborate little wrought-iron gates, neatly painted fences and trimmed hedges displaying an individuality of taste that bordered on caricature.

Against a horizon faintly pink with the advertising lights of the Western Sector of the city I could make out the squat shapes of the houses and hutments on each patch of ground. Lovingly fashioned by dedicated owners, this was the only sort of private house ownership permitted in the Democratic Republic. And selling such improved property provided a rare opportunity for officially tolerated capitalism.

Munte held out his hand to show me where to stop. I welcomed the careful directions he gave me how to get out of this maze of narrow tracks, for there was not space enough to turn the car or even to avoid another on the same path.

I said, 'Your material is kept quite separate from everything else, Dr Munte. Even if there is a traitor in London, you needn't fear that you'll be betrayed.' The old man got out of the car with a stiff-limbed difficulty that he'd not shown before. It was almost as if he'd aged during the short car journey.

He bent down to look at me. I leaned over the front passenger seat and wound the window down so that I could hear him. 'You have no need to be so devious, Bernd,' he said. 'I intend to go to my office in the morning. I will get the document for you. I am not afraid.'

I said nothing. I noticed that he was wringing his hands again, the way he had in his office earlier that day.

'I never go that way,' he added as if he owed me an explanation. 'No matter how much longer it takes me or where I want to get to, I never go that way. Until tonight, I haven't been back on that section of autobahn since it happened.'

'I'm sorry if it upset you, Dr Munte.'

'I should have done it years ago,' he said. 'At last I've got rid of those terrible old nightmares.'

'That's good,' I said, although I knew he'd only exchanged old ones for new.

I was tired by the time I got back to Rolf Mauser's place in Prenzlauer Berg. But I observed the customary precautions and parked Werner's Wartburg round the corner and sat in it for a few moments scanning the area before locking up.

The streets were empty. The only sounds came from the elevated railway trains on Schönhauserallee and the occasional passing car or bus. There was no parking problem where Rolf Mauser lived.

A glimmer of light in the entrance to the apartment building was provided by a low-power bulb situated too high to be cleaned. It illuminated the broken floral-patterned floor tiles and, on the wall, a dozen or more dented metal boxes for mail. On the left was a wide stone staircase. To the right a long narrow corridor led to a metal-reinforced door that gave on to the courtyard at the rear of the building. At night the metal door was locked to protect the tenants' bicycles, and to prevent anyone disturbing the peace by using the rubbish bins or the ash-cans.

I knew there was someone standing there even before I saw the slight movement. And I recognized the sort of movement it was. It was the movement a man made when his long period of waiting is at last near an end.

'Don't do anything,' said a whispered voice.

I inched back into the shadow and reached in my pocket for a knife, the only weapon I would risk in a town where stop searches were so common.

'Bernie?' It was Werner, one of the few Germans who called me anything other than Bernd.

'What is it?'

'Did anyone see you come in?'

'No. Why?'

'Rolf's got visitors.'

'Who?'

There came the sound of two cars arriving. When two cars arrive together at a residential block in Prenzlauer Berg, it is not likely to be a social call. I followed Werner quickly down the narrow corridor, but he could not get the door to the courtyard open. Two uniformed policemen and two men in leather overcoats came into the entrance and shone their flashlights at the names on the mailboxes.

'Mauser,' said the younger of the uniformed cops, directing the beam of his torch on one of the boxes.

'Master detective,' growled a leather-coated man in mock admiration. As he turned, the light of the torch showed him to be a man of about thirty-five with a small Lenin-style goatee beard.

'You said number nineteen,' said the young policeman defensively. 'I took you to the address you gave me.' He was very young, and had the sort of Saxon accent that sounds comical to most German ears.

'The boss ordered me to be here fifteen minutes ago,' growled Lenin in the hard accent of working-class Berlin. 'I should have walked.'

'You still would have ended up at the wrong address,' said the cop, his Saxon accent stronger than before.

The leather-coated man turned on him angrily. 'Maybe someone told you it's a softer touch being drafted into the police service than into the Army. I don't care that your daddy is a Party bigshot. This is Berlin. This is my town. Shut up and do as you're told.' Before the young conscript could reply, the leather-coated man started up the stairs. The other three followed him, and his harangue continued. 'Wait till this KGB Colonel arrives. You'll jump then, boys, you'll jump then.'

Werner was still twisting the handle of the door to the yard when he realized that the cops were not going to shine their lights and discover us at the end of the corridor. 'That was a close thing,' he said.

'What's going on?'

'Two of them; Stasis. Upstairs in Rolf's apartment. They got here about three hours ago. You know what that means.'

'They're waiting for someone.'

'They're not waiting for *someone*,' said Werner grimly. 'They're waiting for *you*. Did you leave anything in the apartment?'

'Of course not.'

'Let's get out of here,' said Werner.

'Do you think they'll have a guard posted outside?'

'Let me go first. My papers are good ones.'

'Hold it a minute.' I could see a shadow, and then a cop came into view. He moved into the doorway as if he might have heard our voices, and then went outside again.

We waited a few more minutes and then the four security policemen brought Rolf Mauser downstairs to the car. Rolf was making a lot of noise; his voice came echoing down the stairwell long before he came into sight.

'Let me go. What's all this about? Answer my questions. How dare you handcuff me! This could wait till morning. Let me go!'

Rolf's angry shouting must have been heard in every apartment in the building. But no one came to the door. No one came to see what was happening.

The front door crashed closed and we heard Rolf's voice in the empty street before the sound of the cars' engines swallowed his protests.

Only after the police had departed with their prisoner did the apartment doors upstairs open. There were whispered questions, and even quieter answers, for a few minutes before all went completely quiet.

'That's the only way to do it,' I said. 'A silent prisoner might just as well confess. Rolf's shouting might make them pause to think. That might give us a chance to do something to help him.'

'He didn't shout to convince them he was innocent,' said Werner. 'He was shouting to warn you off.'

'I know,' I said. 'And there's nothing we can do to help him, either.' Was Rolf Mauser Fiona's first victim, I wondered. And would I be the next one?

25

Officially, Werner Volkmann had no accommodation in East Berlin, but his riverside warehouse in Friedrichshain, with an office on the ground floor, contained four upstairs rooms that he had converted into comfortable living quarters, complete with tiny kitchen and a sitting room. It was against government regulations for him to stay overnight there – no one could let a guest stay the night without police permission – but because Werner was earning foreign exchange nothing was ever said about his little 'home'.

Werner unlocked the massive warehouse door using three keys. 'Refrigerators, colour TV sets, real – made in the USA – blue jeans, Black and Decker drills, all the most sought-after delights of the decadent West are stored here from time to time,' he said, explaining the need for the complex locks.

'Black and Decker drills?'

'To improve and enlarge living accommodation. Or, better still, fix up some little weekend place that they are legally permitted to sell.' He went up a steep staircase and unlocked another door.

'Plenty of Black and Decker here,' I said looking at the newly decorated hall hung with two well-framed watercolours: a contorted nude and a crippled clown. I bent closer to see them. German Expressionist painters, of course. There is something in their tragic quality that touches the soul of Berliners.

'Nolde and Kirchner,' said Werner, taking off his coat and hanging it on an elaborate mahogany hallstand. 'Not your sort of thing, I know.'

'But worth a packet, Werner,' I said. I looked round and saw some fine pieces of antique furniture. Werner had always been a clever forager. At school he'd been able to get American candy bars, pieces of broken tanks, military badges, roller-skate wheels and all the other treasures that schoolboys wanted then.

'Westmarks will buy anything on this side of the wall. And there are still mountains of treasures locked away in cellars and attics.'

I put my hat and coat alongside Werner's and followed him into the next room. Light came in through the window. Werner went across the room and looked out. Here was the River Spree. Bright moonlight fell on a grimy stretch of riverside land. Drawn against the sky was the complex ironwork of the elevated railway, chopped off abruptly on its way to the West, and left to rust. Nearer was a roofless factory building, derelict and untouched since the fighting stopped in 1945. To the right I could see along the dark river to the glaring arc lights of the Oberbaum bridge, one of the border crossing points, for here the river is the boundary between the East and West Sectors.

Werner closed the curtains abruptly and switched on the table lamps. 'We need a drink,' he said. There being no opposition from me, he produced a bottle of German brandy and some glasses. Then he got ice and a jug of water from a refrigerator alongside his big stereo TV.

'That's a sure sign of a separated man,' I said. 'A man with ice available in his living room. Married men have to go to the kitchen to get ice in their booze.'

'And what about a bachelor?'

'Ice in the bedroom,' I said.

'You've always got an answer,' said Werner. 'That used to irritate me when we were kids.'

'I know,' I said. 'I'm good at irritating people.'

'Well, you certainly irritated Zena,' he said.

'Why didn't you tell me you knew where she was?'

'And have you think she was having an affair with Frank Harrington?'

'Wasn't she having an affair with Frank Harrington?' I said cautiously. I sipped my brandy without the water that Werner was waving in the air.

'You drink too much. Do you know that?'

'Yes, I know because my wife keeps telling me.'

'I'm sorry,' said Werner. 'I didn't mean to criticize. But right now you can't afford to blunt your mind.'

'If that's what it does, give me another,' I said.

He poured more brandy into my glass, and said, 'No, that place in Lübars is a safe house. Zena was doing an undercover job for Frank Harrington. She's never been unfaithful to me. She would have told me more but she knows how much I've always disliked Frank.'

'Is that what she told you? An undercover job.'

'I've got her back,' said Werner. 'She's explained everything to me and we've started afresh. Sometimes there has to be a really bad disagreement before two people understand each other.'

'Well, here's to you, Werner,' I said.

'It was you who really got us back together again,' said Werner. 'You frightened her.'

'Any time, Werner,' I offered.

He smiled the sort of smile that showed me he was not amused. 'I did what you wanted. I went to London today and saw Dicky. It was a rush. I only just caught the flight back.'

'All okay? No problems at the checkpoint?'

'Was I followed, you mean? Listen, the East Germans don't give a shit about my going to London and straight back here again. London is now at the centre of the forfaiting market. I'm always in and out. How the hell do you think I get these deals for them? None of the West German banks are very keen to go into a syndicate unless I've got some nice juicy London or New York bank in it too.'

'That's good.'

'The DDR need Westmarks, Bernie. They're desperate for hard currency. They're squeezed between the Russians and the West. They need oil from Russia, but they also need Western technology. And all the time, the squeeze is getting tighter and tighter. I don't know what's going to happen over here in a decade from now. And by the way, I paid Lisl back the money I borrowed – and interest too.'

'Don't sound so worried, Werner.'

'These people are Germans, Bernie. Of course I'm worried about what happens here.'

'Sure,' I said.

'Don't give me that look,' he complained.

'What look was I giving you?'

'That "Why do you Jews always have to get so emotional?" look.'

'Stop being so paranoid,' I said. 'And why are you being so bloody mean with your brandy? It's not even French.'

He pushed the bottle over to me this time. 'I saw Dicky Cruyer, just as you said, and he agreed that I put you on tomorrow's truck. Your wife had spoken with you on the phone by then, so Dicky fixed it right away. As soon as you are in the Federal Republic, we'll bring your precious Brahms Four out.' Werner smiled. He knew that Dicky had sent me to Berlin to keep Brahms Four active and in place.

'Sounds good,' I said.

'I'll feel much easier when you're back in the West,' said Werner. 'There are too many people who could recognize your face.'

'And what if they do?'

'Don't be childish,' said Werner. He picked up the brandy, recorked the bottle, and put it back into an antique lacquer cabinet decorated with Chinese mountain scenery.

'Was that cabinet something else you picked up for a pair of Levis?' I asked, irritated by the way he closed the door of it.

'If some smart little bastard from the Stasis recognizes you, they'll take you in for interrogation. You know too much to be running round loose over here. I don't know why London permitted it.'

'Well, you don't know everything, Werner,' I said. 'There are a couple of things now and again that the D-G doesn't check out with you.'

'You don't think that was some kind of routine visit that the Stasis made to Rolf Mauser tonight? They know you're here, Bernie. They're looking for you – it's obvious.'

'Let me do the worrying, Werner,' I said. 'I've had more practice.'

Werner got to his feet and said, 'Let's go downstairs and I'll show you the truck you'll be hiding in.'

I got up and drained the dregs from my glass.

'Drinking makes you bad-tempered,' said Werner.

'No,' I said. 'It's having the bottle taken away that does that.'

The warehouse, which Werner leased from the Foreign Trade Ministry, was big. There were two thirty-ton trucks parked downstairs and there was still plenty of room for packing cases and workbenches and the office with two desks, three filing cases and an ancient Adler typewriter.

'We bolt you in,' said Werner, climbing into the back of the trailer. His voice echoed in the confined space. 'The first couple of times we did it, we welded that section after the people were inside, but we burned someone's leg doing it, so now we bolt it up and paint it with quick-drying paint. I hope you don't suffer from claustrophobia.' He pointed to the place at the front of the cargo compartment where two metal sheets had been opened to reveal a narrow compartment. 'Plenty of air holes, but they are not visible because of the baffles. These two brackets hold a small wooden seat, and we'll fix a soft cushion on it because you'll be a long time in here.'

'How long?'

'Those bastards at the customs don't work a long hard day,' said Werner. 'Ten minutes of writing out forms and they have to sit down and recuperate for an hour or so.'

'How long altogether?'

'Sometimes the trucks are parked in the compounds for two days before the officials even look up and nod. Drivers have been known to go crazy in the waiting room. Maybe that's the idea.'

'Three days, maximum?'

'We're talking about a game of chance, Bernie. Relax, and take along something to read. I'll fix a light for you. How about that? It could be they'll wave us through.'

'I won't be the one travelling in this metal box,' I said.

'I knew that,' said Werner in a voice that was more annoyed than self-satisfied.

'What did you know?'

'Right from the start, I thought, that bastard is going to pull some kind of switch. And here it is. So who is going?'

'Brahms Four goes first. He wants to take his wife. You could fit two people in here, couldn't you? It's better they go on the first trip.'

'That's not the reason. That's just calculated to break my heart and make me think you're a wonderful fellow.'

'I *am* a wonderful fellow,' I said.

'You're a devious bastard,' said Werner.

'You told Dicky?'

'I did it just the way you wanted. No one knows except Dicky Cruyer . . . and anyone he tells.'

'And my kids?' Finally I had to ask the question I'd been avoiding.

'You're worrying unnecessarily, Bernie. It can't be Fiona.'

'Twenty-four-hour cover? Three men and two cars each shift?'

'I did it just the way you said. Your kids are watched night and day. I was surprised that Dicky Cruyer okayed it.'

'Thanks, Werner,' I said.

'Does Fiona know where this place is?' So now even he was truly convinced.

'Not from me, she doesn't.'

'She wouldn't let you get arrested, Bernie. You're the father of her kids.' He spoke of Fiona apologetically. Why does the betrayed partner always get treated like a leper? It's damned unfair. But it was no different from the way I'd treated Werner all through his sufferings with *his* disloyal wife.

'So you'll put two seats in here?' I said, rapping the metal sheet of the hidden compartment.

'Where do we pick them up?'

'We'll have to think carefully about that, Werner,' I said. 'Not a good idea to let them come here. You don't want some little creep writing down your address in a debriefing sheet that gets circulated to NATO intelligence officers.' Werner shuddered and said nothing. I said, 'But we don't want a big truck like this going off the main roads. It would stick out like a sore thumb in some back street in Pankow.'

'Müggelheimer Damm,' suggested Werner. It was a long, almost straight road through the forest that bordered the Grosser Müggelsee – a big lake just outside the city. 'There are no houses all the way from Alstadt to Müggelheim – just the forest road. And it's convenient from here.'

'Which way will you go? Through Russian Army HQ Karlshorst? Or past the Red Army memorial at Treptow?' Both places were always well provided with sharp-eyed traffic police and plainclothes security men.

'What does it matter? We'll be clean at that stage of the journey.'

'A halted truck on that long forest road?' I said doubtfully.

'It will look as if the driver has gone behind a tree,' said Werner.

'Where on the Müggelheimer Damm?'

'Keep driving till you see me,' said Werner. 'It's better that I choose somewhere I like the look of. You'll find me. There won't be many bright yellow thirty-ton articulated trucks parked along that section of road on a weekday.'

'At twelve-thirty,' I said. 'We'll hope the traffic cops will be having lunch.'

'Do you think his wife might be claustrophobic? A lot of women are. There was a case some years ago, I remember, where an escapee started beating on the floor of a car to get out. She just couldn't stand being locked in the luggage compartment. They were all arrested. If I gave Brahms Four a needle, could we rely on him to give her a shot?'

'If necessary.'

'I knew you wouldn't go first,' said Werner. 'I knew you'd want to get Brahms Four out before you went yourself.'

'What made you think so, Werner?'

'You wouldn't put yourself into a position where London Central could have a change of mind and you not be able to do much about it.'

'Go to the top of the class, Werner,' I said.

'*Fait accompli*, that's your style. It always has been.' He jumped down from the truck.

'One more thing,' I said. 'Just to be on the safe side, I want Brahms Four under observation right from the time he gets on the streetcar at Buchholz to go to work tomorrow.'

'No problem,' said Werner.

'Any divergence from what I've told him to do and we'll scrub the whole thing.'

'I like you, Bernie. You're the only man I know who's more suspicious than I am, and that reassures me.'

'Any divergence at all,' I said.

'You won't tell him about Müggelheimer Damm before he gets there?'

'I won't even answer if he says good morning.'

'Even if it is Fiona,' said Werner, 'she can't act on this day-to-day information without making it obvious that she's the KGB agent.'

'Moscow might decide it's worthwhile. Brahms Four is a good source – maybe the only really big leak they haven't been able to plug.'

'That's why you want him to go first. Moscow will let the first one through even if they know about it. They'll let it go believing it's you and thinking the second escape will be their only chance of getting Brahms Four. It's a dangerous game, Bernie. If you are right, you'll get caught.'

'But maybe I'm wrong,' I said.

26

'Don't worry, Frau Doktor von Munte,' I said. 'Your husband will soon be back.' I looked out the window. The little gardens of fruit and vegetables stretched in every direction across the flat land, and the curious assortment of hutments and sheds looked even more bizarre by daylight. On every side there were heaps of sand, bags of cement, and piles of bricks, blocks and timber for more amateur building work.

Now May was here. Fruit trees, climbing flowers, shrubs and bushes were engulfing the buildings. There was lilac – the smell of it was everywhere – and cherry trees in snowy bloom, tubs of roses and dwarf rhododendrons. But the vegetation was not enough to hide the one-storey building that the next-door neighbour had painted bright red, and laboriously drawn wobbly lines of yellow upon, to produce the effect of a medieval castle.

The little house that the Muntes owned was more restrained. Painted dark green, to blend with the surroundings, its wooden window shutters bore old-fashioned flower designs. On the side of it there was a tiny lean-to greenhouse with pots of herbs, boxes of lettuce plants and some carnations, all crowded together to catch the sunshine. The garden too was more in keeping with the elderly couple; everything neat and tidy, like an illustration from a gardening manual.

'Why did you tell him to say he wasn't feeling well?' she asked. Mrs Munte was a severe-looking woman, in a black dress with a white lacy collar. Her hair was drawn back tight into a bun and her face had the high cheekbones and narrowed eyes that marked the German communities of the Baltic States. Blue eyes and reddish-flaxen hair are common in Estonia. 'Why did you?' It was an inscrutable face but it was calm too, the sort of face that, apart from a few wrinkles and spots, remains unchanged from early teens to old age.

'So that no one will be surprised when he's away from the office for a couple of days.'

'I wish we had stayed at the apartment in Erkner. Here we have no TV. I get so bored here.'

'Your neighbour is sunning himself. Why don't you spend half an hour outside?' The owner of the *Schloss* next door had stretched a blanket on his minuscule lawn. Now he was applying lotion to his bare chest and searching the sky for dark clouds, a wary frown upon his face.

'No. He'll chatter to me,' said Mrs Munte. 'He's a retired bus driver. He's on his own. Once he starts talking, you can't stop him. He grows tulips. I hate tulips, don't you? They look like plastic.' She was standing at the tiny window looking out at her rhododendrons and roses. 'Walter has worked so hard on his flowers. He'll miss them when we're somewhere else.'

'There'll be other roses and rhododendrons,' I said.

'Even this morning he went out to spray the roses. I said it was silly but he insisted on doing it.'

'They need it at this time of the year,' I said. 'Mine have got black spots.'

'Will you go with us?'

'I follow on.'

'You've done this sort of thing before, I suppose?'

'You'll be quite safe, Frau von Munte. It's uncomfortable but not dangerous.'

'Of course you'd say that,' she said peevishly. 'It's your job to encourage us.'

'By the time Dr von Munte gets back here, it will be time to think about leaving.'

'Why do you make him come all the way back here before we leave? Why couldn't we meet him in town?'

'It's the way it's been planned,' I said.

She looked at me and shook her head. 'It's so that you can look at those papers he's bringing you. It's to give you a chance to cancel everything. Walter told me what you said.'

'Why not read your book?' I said. It was an anthology called *More Short Stories from Poland*. Twice or three times she'd started to read it and then put it down. Her mind was on other things. I said, 'There is nothing to be gained from letting these thoughts go round and round in your mind.'

'How do I know my husband isn't already on his way?'

'To the West?'

'Yes. How do I know he's not already on his way?'

'He wouldn't go anywhere without you, Frau von Munte.'

'Perhaps that disappointed you,' she said. There was a hard note of satisfaction in her voice. 'You wanted Walter to go on his own, didn't you?'

'No,' I said.

'Oh, yes, you did. You made the arrangements for just one person. You were going to leave me here.'

'Is that what Dr von Munte told you?'

'He confides in me. That is what our marriage has always been.'

'What else has he confided to you?' I asked. I smiled to soften my question.

'I know what he's gone back to his office for, if that's what you mean.'

'Tell me, then.'

'A paper of some kind, handwritten by a communist agent. Someone very highly placed in the London intelligence service.'

I didn't deny that she was right.

'Yes,' she said. 'And you'll recognize the handwriting and you'll know who it is.'

'I hope so,' I said.

'But what will you do then, I wonder. Will you reveal who it is or will you use it for your own purposes?'

'Why do you say that?'

'It's obvious to me,' she said. 'If you wanted only to reveal the truth, you could have had the papers sent to London. But you want to look at them. You want to be the one who has the power.'

'Would you make some more coffee, please?'

'My husband is too nice,' she said. 'He'd never use the sort of power he has to advance himself. He does what he does because of his beliefs.' I nodded. She went to a tiny sink, which could be closed inside the cupboard when not in use, filled the electric kettle and switched it on. 'We bought this *Laube* during the war. Walter said the bombs were less dangerous in the soft earth. We grew potatoes, leeks and onions. There was no electricity then, of course, and we had to go a long walk to get drinking water.' She talked compulsively, her arms akimbo as she stared at the kettle. I noticed her small red hands and her red bony elbows as she rubbed her arms as if she felt cold. She had concealed her nervousness until now, but it is often accompanied by such bodily chills. She waited until the kettle came to the full boil before pouring the water into the pot. 'Do you have a wife?' she asked. She'd put a felt cover on the coffee pot and now she clasped it with her open hands to feel the warmth of it. 'Does she sit at home all day getting bored?'

'She goes to work,' I explained. 'She works with me.'

'Is that how you met? I met Walter at the big house his parents had near Bernau. They are an old important family, you know.'

'I met your husband's father once,' I said. 'He was a remarkable old man. I was only a small child, but he spoke to me as an equal. And a few days later, he sent me a leather-bound copy of *Die schöne Müllerin*. It had come from his library, and had his name embossed in gold on the cover and an engraved bookplate inside. My father told me that only a dozen books from his library had survived the war. I have it still.'

'You lived in Berlin as a child. That explains your perfect Berlin accent.' She seemed more relaxed now that she knew I'd met old von Munte. 'Hundreds of local people went to the old gentleman's funeral. They had it out there at the house where all the rest of the family had been buried. My father was a country physician. He attended the old man right until the end. What did your father do for a living?'

'He started out as a clerk. In the thirties he was unemployed for a long time. Then he went into the Army. The war began and he became an officer. After the war he stayed in the Army.'

'I'm Walter's second wife, of course. Ida was killed in one of the very first air raids.' She poured coffee for us. 'Do you have children?'

'Two: a boy and a girl.'

'It's Ida's child, of course – the one he wants to see.' She pushed the large cup of black coffee across the table to me in a gesture that contained an element of rejection.

'In São Paulo?'

'There's only the one child. That's why Walter dotes on him so much. I hope and pray he is not disappointed.'

'Disappointed how?'

'It's such a long time,' she said as if on that account the chances of the two men disappointing each other were self-evident.

'He's sure to be grateful,' I said. 'Walter has given him so much.'

'He's given his son everything,' she said. 'He's given him every penny he's earned from you. He's given him the life that was rightfully mine.' She drank some coffee. Her words were bitter but her face was calm.

'And now his son will be able to thank you both.'

'We'll be strangers to him. His son won't want the burden of looking after us. And Walter has no chance of earning any more.'

'It will be all right,' I promised vaguely.

'Our presence will remind him of his obligation, and he will resent that. Then he'll start feeling guilty about such feelings and associate us with that guilt.' She drank more coffee. She'd obviously been thinking about it a great deal. 'I'm always a pessimist. Is your wife a pessimist?'

'She had to be an optimist to marry me,' I said.

'You haven't told me how you met,' said Mrs Munte.

I mumbled something about meeting her at a party, and went over to look out the window. She'd arrived with two other girls. Dicky Cruyer knew her name, and so I immediately approached her with a bottle of Sancerre and two empty glasses. We'd danced to music from an old broken record player and discussed our host, a Foreign Office junior clerk who was celebrating a posting to Singapore.

Fiona was typing letters for a travel company in Oxford Street. It was a temporary job, due to finish the next week. She asked me if I knew of any really interesting work for someone with a good degree who could type and take shorthand in three languages. I didn't think she was serious at first. Her clothes and jewellery made her look anything but desperate for employment.

'She told me she was out of work,' I said.

At the time, Bret Rensselaer was setting up an undercover operation that worked out of an office block in Holborn and processed selected data from the Berlin office. We needed staff and Bret had already decided that we would not go through the normal civil-service recruitment procedure. It took too long and involved too much form-filling and interviewing; to make matters worse, the civil service only sent us applicants that the Foreign Office had already decided were not good enough for them.

'What was she wearing?' said Mrs Munte.

'Nothing special,' I said. It was a tight sweater of angora wool. I remember it because it took two dry cleanings and a lot of brushing to remove the final fluffs of wool from my only good suit. I asked her where she'd learned shorthand and typing and she cracked some silly joke that made it clear that she was an Oxford graduate, and I pretended not to understand such subtlety. Dicky Cruyer tried to cut in on our dancing at that point, but Fiona said couldn't he see that she was dancing with the most handsome man in the room?

'But you saw her again?' said Mrs Munte.

I had a date with her the very next evening. And I wanted to be able to say I had a job for her. It was an attractive idea to have her in the same office with me. Bret Rensselaer didn't much like the idea of taking on someone we hadn't properly vetted, but when we found out that she was related to Silas Gaunt – who'd become something of a legend in the Department – he gave me a grudging okay. At first it was conditional on her working only out of my office, and not having access to the really sensitive material or any contact with our Berlin people. But in a few years, hard work and long hours gave her a series of promotions that put her in line for an Operations desk.

'I got her a job,' I said.

'Perhaps it was the job, rather than you, she was after,' said Mrs Munte, tilting her head on one side to show me it was not a serious suggestion.

'Perhaps it was,' I said.

I was watching two men at the far end of the narrow lane that led up from the Buchholz church. They were both in civilian clothes, but unmistakably Stasis. It was government policy that the secret police never wore beards or moustaches, and dressed in plain clothes of a type that made them immediately recognizable to every East German who saw them. Everyone except the most naive realized that there were other plainclothes policemen who weren't so easy to spot, but where the hell were they? 'Frau von Munte,' I said matter of factly, 'there are a couple of policemen coming up the lane checking each of the houses in turn.' I kept watching them. Now I could see that there were two more men – one in police uniform – and, behind them, a black Volvo negotiating the narrow lane with great care. Beyond that came a minibus with a light fixed to the roof. 'Four policemen,' I said. 'Perhaps more.'

She came over to the window, but had the good sense to stand well back from it. 'What kind of policemen?' she asked.

'The kind who get Volvos,' I said. With the scarcity of any sort of hard currency, only senior ranks or special squads could get an imported car.

'What do we do?' She gave no sign of fear. Married to a spy for a couple of decades, I suppose she'd lived through this nightmare times without number.

'Get two boxes of those seedlings from the greenhouse,' I said. 'I'll just look round in here before we leave.'

'Where are we going?'

'Back to my car.'

'We'll have to go past them.'

'They'll see us whichever way we go. Better to brazen it out.'

She put on an absurd fez-like felt hat and fastened it into her hair with ferocious-looking hatpins. She looked round the room. There were obviously many things she'd planned to take with her, but she grabbed only a fur coat from a box under the bed and put it on. She went out to the greenhouse, came back, and handed me a box of seedlings and kept one for herself. As we went out, I smiled to the neighbour stretched out on a blanket in front of his castle. He shut his eyes and pretended to be asleep. Closing the little garden gate carefully after Mrs Munte, I followed her down the lane towards the policemen.

They were working systematically, a two-man team on each side of the lane. One man to go into the garden and knock at the door, the other to watch the back. The driver of the car would be ready to take a potshot at anyone trying to run for it. In the back of the Volvo there was another man. It was Lenin, the senior officer of the team that had arrested Rolf Mauser. He was sprawled across the back seat ticking off names and addresses from papers on a clipboard.

'Who are you, where are you going?' said one of the policemen as we got near. It was the young Saxon conscript again. He'd been given the job of plodding along the lane to hold back the bushes that might scratch the paintwork of the car.

'None of your business, young man,' said Mrs Munte. She made an incongruous figure, standing there in the sunshine holding the plants and wearing her fur coat and *Kaffeeklatsch* hat.

'Do you live here?' He moved out to block the path. I noticed that the flap of his pistol holster was undone. His arms were folded across his body, a gesture that policemen like to think looks friendly.

'Live here?' said Mrs Munte. 'What do you think we are, squatters?'

Even the policemen smiled. Whatever Mrs Munte looked like, she could not be mistaken for one of the dirty long-haired squatters seen so frequently on TV news from the West Sector. 'Do you know anyone here named Munte?'

'I don't know any of these people,' she said disdainfully. 'I come to this dreadful place only to buy things I can't get elsewhere. My son is helping me with these carnations. It's his day off and he's brought his car here. Ten marks for these few seedlings. It's disgraceful. You should be concerning yourself with the profiteers that are flourishing here.'

'We are,' said the policeman. He still smiled but didn't move.

She leaned close to him. 'What are you doing?' she whispered loudly. 'Is it wife swoppers you are after? Or have the whores moved in here again?'

He grinned and stood aside. 'You're too young to know about that kind of thing, *Mutti*,' he said. He turned round and watched us as we staggered along with the boxes of plants. 'Make way for the busy gardeners,' he called to the policemen behind him. And they stood aside too. The man in the back of the Volvo stared at his papers and said nothing. He probably thought our papers had been checked.

27

My box of carnation plants was heavy enough to make me sweat by the time we got to the church at Buchholz, but Mrs Munte was not complaining. Perhaps she was much stronger than she looked. Or perhaps she'd chosen a lighter one for herself.

Buchholz marks the end of the number 49 tram route. In the cobbled village square were the bicycles of commuters who lived beyond the terminus. There were hundreds of them, racked, stacked, hanging and piled; the narrow pathways that gave access to them made an intricate maze. Within this maze a man was standing. He had a newspaper in his hands and he was reading from it in a preoccupied way that permitted him to glance round him, and to look down the street as if waiting for the tram to arrive. It was Werner Volkmann; there was no mistaking the big bearlike torso and short legs, and the hat that was planted right on top of his large head.

He gave no sign of seeing me, but I knew he'd chosen that spot so he could keep the car in his line of vision. I unlocked the doors and put the plants in the boot and Mrs Munte in the back seat. Only then – when Mrs Munte was shut in the car and couldn't hear us – did Werner cross the road to talk to me.

'I thought you'd be across the other side of town,' I said quietly, stifling the impulse to scream at him.

'It's probably okay,' said Werner. He turned to look up the street. There was a police car outside the post office, but the driver was showing no interest in us. He was talking to a cop in one of the long white coats that only traffic police wear. 'Four plainclothes cops visited your man's office this morning. It was nothing more than a few polite inquiries, but it scared hell out of him.'

'The same team who arrested Rolf Mauser are now raking through the *Lauben* and asking if anyone knows him.'

'I know. I saw them arrive.'

'Thanks, Werner.'

'No sense in me rushing in there to get arrested with you,' said Werner defensively. 'I can be more help to you free.'

'So where is he?'

'Brahms Four? He left his office soon after arriving at work. He came into the street holding a small attaché case and wearing a pained look. I didn't know what to do – no phone here to reach you. So I had one of my people grab him. I stayed clear. He doesn't know me. I didn't want him to see the warehouse, so I had someone drive him out to Müggelsee. The truck will go separately. Then I came up here to ask you whether we should still go ahead.'

'At least let's make the kind of attempt that will look good on the report,' I said. 'Let's take this old lady over to Müggelsee and put her in the truck.'

'You kept your man well wrapped up,' said Werner. 'Twenty years at least he's been operating in this town, and I'd never seen him until today.'

'Deep cover,' I said, imitating the voice of Frank Harrington at his most ponderous.

Werner smiled. He enjoyed any joke against Frank.

Werner got in the driver's side and took the wheel. He started up and turned the car south for Berlinerstrasse and the city centre. 'For Müggelsee the autobahn will be quicker, Werner,' I said.

'That would take us out of the East Sector and into the Zone,' said Werner. 'I don't like crossing the city boundaries.'

'I came that way to get here. It's quicker.'

'This is Himmelfahrt – Ascension Day. A lot of people will be taking the day off to swim and sun. It's not an official holiday, but there's a lot of absenteeism. That's the only kind of "ism" that's really popular here. There will be cops on the roads that lead out of town. They'll be taking names and arresting drunks and generally trying to discourage people from having a holiday whenever they feel like goofing off.'

'You talked me out of it, Werner.'

Mrs Munte leaned forward between the seats. 'Did you say we're going to Müggelsee? That will be crowded. It's popular at this time of year.'

'Me and Bernie used to swim out there when we were kids,' said Werner. 'The Grosser Müggelsee is always the first to warm up in summer and the first to freeze for ice skating. It's shallow water. But you're right, gnädige Frau, it will be crowded out there today. I could kick myself for forgetting about the holiday.'

'My husband will be there?'

I answered her: 'Your husband is there already. We'll join him and you'll be across the border by nightfall.'

It was not long before we saw the first revellers. There were a dozen or more men in a brewer's dray. Such horse-drawn vehicles, with pneumatic tyres, are still common in Eastern Europe. But this one was garlanded with bunches of leaves and flowers and coloured

paper. And the fine dapple-grey horses were specially groomed with
brightly beribboned manes. The men in the dray wore funny hats –
many of them black toppers – and short-sleeved shirts. Some wore
the favourite status symbol of Eastern Europe: blue jeans. And inevitably there were Western T-shirts, one blazoned 'I love Daytona
Beach, Florida' and another *'Der Tag geht . . . Johnnie Walker kommt'*.
The horses were going very slowly and the men were singing very
loudly between swigging beer and shouting to people in the street
and catcalling after girls. They gave a loud cheer as our car went past
them.

There were more such parties as we got to Köpenick. Groups of
men stood under the trees at the edge of the road, smoking and
drinking in silence with a dedication that is unmistakably German.
Other men were laughing and singing; some slept soundly, neatly
arranged like logs, while others were being violently ill.

Werner stopped the car well down the Müggelheimer Damm.
There were no other vehicles in sight. Plantations of tall fir trees
darkened the road. This extensive forest continued to the lakes on
each side of the road and far beyond. There was no sign of Werner's
big articulated truck, but he'd spotted its driver standing at the
roadside. He was near one of the turnoffs, narrow tracks that led to
the edge of the Müggelsee.

'What is it?' Werner asked him anxiously.

'Everything is in order,' said the man. He was a big beefy red-
necked man, wearing bib-and-brace overalls and a red and white
woollen hat of the sort worn by British football supporters. 'I had
the truck here, as we arranged, but a crowd of these lunatics . . .'
He indicated some small groups of men standing in a car park across
the road. 'They began climbing all over it. I had to move it.' He had
the strongest Berlin accent I'd ever heard. He sounded like one of
the old-style comedians, who can still be heard telling Berliner jokes
in unlicensed cabarets in the back streets of Charlottenburg.

'Where are you now?' said Werner.

'I pulled off the road into one of these firebreaks,' said the driver.
'The earth's not so firm – all that bloody rain last week. I'm heavy,
you know. Get stuck and we're in trouble.'

'This is the other one,' said Werner, moving his head to indicate
Mrs Munte in the back seat.

'She doesn't look too heavy,' said the driver. 'What do you weigh,
Fräulein? About fifty kilos?' He grinned at her. Mrs Munte, who
obviously weighed twice that, didn't answer. 'Don't be shy,' said the
driver.

'And the man?' said Werner.

'Ah,' said the driver, 'the Herr Professor.' He was the sort of
German who called any elderly well-dressed fellow-countryman

'Professor'. 'I sent him up to that lakeside restaurant to get a cup of coffee. I told him someone would come for him when we are ready.'

While he was saying that, I saw the black Volvo and the mini-bus coming down the road from the direction of Müggelheim. They would have made good time on the autobahn, flashing their lights to get priority in the traffic or using their siren to clear the fast lane.

'Get the professor,' said Werner to me. 'I'll drive the old lady down to where the truck is parked, and come back to meet you here.'

As I hurried along the woodland path towards the lake, I could hear a curious noise. It was the regular roaring sound that waves make as they are sucked back through the pebbles on a long stony beach. It got louder as I approached the open-air restaurant, but that did not prepare me for the scene I found there.

The indoor restaurant was closed on weekdays, but there were hundreds of men milling around the lakeside *Biergarten* in inebriated confusion. They were mostly young workers dressed in bright shirts and denim pants, but some wore pyjamas and some had Arab head-dress, and many of them had brought the black top hat that is traditional for Himmelfahrt. I could see no women, just men. There were long lines of them waiting at a serving hatch marked '*Getränke*' and an equally long line at a hatch marked '*Kaffee*', where only beer, in half-litre plastic cups, was being served. Tables were crammed with dozens and dozens of empty plastic cups stacked together, and there were more empties scattered in the flower beds and lined up along the low dividing walls.

'*Heiliger bim-bam!*' said a drunk behind me, as surprised as I was at the sight.

The roars of sound were coming from the throats of the men as they watched a rubber ball being kicked high into the air. It went up over their heads and cut an arc in the blue sky before coming down to meet yet another skilfully placed boot that sent it back up again.

It took me a few minutes to spot Munte. By some miracle he'd found a chair and was sitting at a table at the edge of the lake where it was a little less crowded. He seemed to be the only person drinking coffee. I sat down on the low wall next to him. There were no other chairs in sight; prudent staff had no doubt removed them from the danger zone. 'Time to go,' I said. 'Your wife is here. Everything is okay.'

'I got it for you,' he said.

'Thanks,' I said. 'I knew you would.'

'Half the clerks in my department have taken the day off too. I had no trouble walking into the chief's office, finding the file and helping myself.'

'I'm told you had a visit from the police.'

'The office had a visit from the police,' he corrected me. 'I left before they found me.'

'They came out to Buchholz,' I said.

'I was trying to think of some way of warning you when a man came up to me in the street and brought me here.' He reached into his pocket and produced a brown envelope. He put it on the table. I left it there for a moment. 'Aren't you going to open it and look inside?' he asked.

'No,' I said. Not far away from us, a six-piece wind band had assembled. Now they were making all those sounds musicians have to make before playing music.

'You want to see the writing. You want to see who is the traitor in London Central.'

'I know who it is,' I said.

'You've guessed, you mean.'

'I know. I've always known.'

'I risked my freedom to get it this morning,' he said.

'I'm sorry,' I said. I picked up the envelope and toyed with it as I reasoned out what to do. Finally I handed it back to him. 'Take it to London,' I said. 'Give it to Richard Cruyer – he's a slim fellow with curly hair and chewed fingernails – make sure no one else gets it. Now we must go. The police seem to have traced us here. They're the same ones who went to Buchholz.'

'My wife – is she safe?' He got to his feet in alarm. As he did so, the wind band began playing a drinking song.

'Yes, I told you. But we must hurry.' I could see them arriving now. I could see Lenin, with his long brown leather overcoat and his little beard. He was wearing a brown leather cap too, and metal-rimmed glasses. His face was hard and his eyes were hidden behind the bright reflections of his lenses. Alongside him was the young Saxon conscript, white-faced and anxious, like a child lost in a big crowd. It was unusual to have a conscript in such a team. His father's influence must be considerable, I thought. The four policemen had stopped suddenly at the end of path, surprised, just as I had been upon first catching sight of the multitude.

The band music was loud. Too loud to make conversation easy. I grabbed Munte's arm and moved him hurriedly into a crowd of men who had linked arms and were trying to dance together. One of them – a muscular fellow with a curly moustache – was wearing striped pyjamas over his clothes. He grabbed Munte and said, 'Komm, Vater. Tanzen.'

'I'm not your father,' I heard Munte say as I stood on tiptoe to see the policemen. They had not moved. They remained on the far side of the beer garden, bewildered at the task of finding anyone in such a crowd. Lenin tapped one of the older men and sent him down the line of men waiting to buy beer. He sent the fourth man back along the path; no doubt he was going to bring more men from the minibus.

For the second time, Munte disengaged his arm from that of the man in pyjamas. 'Ich bin vaterlos,' said the man sorrowfully. The 'fatherless' man pretended to cry. His friends laughed and swayed in time with the om-pah-pah music. I grabbed Munte and pushed through the dancers. Looking back, I caught sight of the leather-capped Lenin, who was clambering onto a tub of flowers to see over the heads of the crowd. Around him the dancing had stopped and the football went rolling down the steps unheeded.

'Walk that way, through the trees,' I told Munte. 'You'll meet a broad-shouldered man, about my age, wearing a coat with an astra-khan collar. In any case, keep going along the road until you see a very big truck with a bright yellow tarpaulin marked "Underberg". Stop the truck and get in. Your wife will be there already.'

'What about you?'

'I'll try to delay the police.'

'That's dangerous, Bernd.'

'Get going.'

'Thank you, Bernd,' said the old man soberly. We both knew that, after Weimar, it was what I had to do for him.

'Walk, not run,' I called as he ambled away. His dark suit ensured that he would soon be swallowed up by the gloom of the forest.

I pushed my way along to the edge of the lake. A number of men had walked out on the little pier and climbed into a small sailing boat. Now someone was trying to untie the mooring ropes, but it was proving difficult for the maladroit drunk. One of the restaurant staff was shouting at the men, but they paid no heed.

A very loud cheer brought my attention round to the beer garden again. Three young drunks were walking along the top of a low wall. Each carried a pitcher of beer and wore a black top hat, and each was otherwise naked. Every few paces they stopped, bowed deeply to acknowledge the applause, and then drank from the jugs.

Lenin had his three cohorts at his side as he elbowed his way through the muttering crowd of holiday makers, their exuberance stifled by his presence. Thinking the policemen were there to check absentees from work, and were about to arrest the streakers, the onlookers were resentful. Intoxication emboldened them enough to show their resentment. There were catcalls. The four policemen were jostled and pushed. They were confronted by a particularly big opponent, a bearded man in sweat shirt and jeans, who seemed determined to bar their way. But they were trained to deal with such situations. Like all cops, they knew that quick action, with a nicely judged degree of violence, is what crowd control depends upon. One of the uniformed cops felled the bearded man with a blow of his truncheon. Lenin blew three blasts on his whistle – to suggest that many more policemen were on call – and they plunged on through a crowd which parted to make way for them.

By now Munte was a hundred yards or more into the forest and out of sight, but Lenin had obviously spotted him for, once through the thickest part of the crush of men, he began running.

I ran, too, choosing a path that would converge on the policemen's. I ran alongside them through the springy undergrowth of the dark forest. Lenin looked round to see who was chasing him, saw me, and looked to his front again. 'This way!' I shouted, and headed down a path that led back to the lakeside.

For a moment Lenin and his three subordinates continued going the way that Munte had gone. Surely the old man had heard them coming after him by now. 'You four!' I shouted with the sort of arrogance that was calculated to convince them of my seniority. 'This way, you bloody fools. He's heading for the boat!'

Still the men raced after Lenin, while I continued on the path. This was my last chance. 'Do you hear me, you idiots?' I shouted breathlessly. 'This way, I say!'

My desperation must have been the convincing factor, for Lenin changed direction and came thumping across the forest floor, his ammunition boots shaking the earth, his eyeballs dilated and his face bright red with exertion. 'The boat is hidden,' I shouted to account for what I guessed would be the complete absence of any boat when they reached the water. I waved the uniformed cops past me and then went back up the path as if expecting more policemen who might need guidance.

But by the time I was fifty yards up the track, Lenin had got to the waterfront and found no boats or places along the lake's edge where any could be hidden. He'd sent the young Saxon conscript back to find me.

'Stop, sir,' said the cop in that unmistakable accent.

'This way!' I shouted, bluffing to the end.

'Stop, sir,' said the cop again. 'Stop or I shoot.' He had his pistol in his hand. I reasoned that a conscript lad who argued with the leader of his arrest team might well be the type who would pull the trigger. I stopped. 'Your identification, please, sir,' said the cop.

I could see Lenin plodding back up the path, breathing heavily and wriggling his fingers in anger. The game was up. 'I was just trying to help,' I said. 'I saw him come this way.'

'Search him,' said Lenin to the Saxon boy. He paused to catch his breath. 'Then take him back and lock him up.' To the other cop he said, 'We'll go to the Müggelheimer Damm, but we've probably lost them. They must have had a car waiting there.' He came very close to me and stared me in the eyes. 'We'll find out all about it from this one.'

28

They locked me in an office of the police barracks. It had a barred window and a mortice lock; they figured I wasn't dangerous enough to need a prison cell. In a perverse way I resented that. And I resented the fact that Lenin sent the Saxon kid in to do the first interrogation. 'What's your name and who employs you?' – all that sort of crap. And always that accent. I kept trying to guess the exact location of his hometown, but it was a game he wouldn't join. I think he was from some little town in the German backwoods where Poland meets Czechoslovakia. But I got him off guard by talking about his accent and his family. And when I suddenly switched the topic of conversation to the fiasco at Müggelsee, he let slip that the Muntes had got away. I nodded and asked him for something to eat so quickly afterwards that I don't think he even noticed what he'd said.

After the Saxon kid had finished, they left a blank-faced young cop sitting in the office with me, but he wouldn't respond to my conversation. He didn't say anything, or even watch me, when I went to look out the window. We were on the top floor of what the international intelligence community calls 'Normannenstrasse', East Germany's State Security Service block in Berlin-Lichtenberg.

From this side of the building I could look down on Frankfurter-allee. This wide road is Berlin's main highway eastwards and there was a steady stream of heavy traffic. The weather had turned colder now, and the only people on the street were clerical staff from the State Security Ministry filing down the steps into Magdalenenstrasse U-Bahn station at the end of the working day.

Lenin joined in the fun about midnight. They'd taken my wrist-watch, of course, along with my money, a packet of French cigarettes, and my Swiss Army knife, but I could hear a church or a municipal clock striking each hour. Lenin was amiable. He even laughed at a joke I made about the coffee. He was older than I had estimated: my age perhaps. No wonder that chase through the forest had made him puff. He wore a brown corduroy suit with button-down top pocket and braided edges to the lapels. I wonder if he'd designed it himself or had picked it up from some old village tailor in a remote part of

Hungary or Rumania. He liked travelling; he told me that. Then he talked about old American films, the time he'd spent seconded to the security police in Cuba, and his love for English detective stories.

He brought out his tiny cheroots and offered me one; I declined. It was the standard interrogator's ploy.

'I can't smoke them,' I told him. 'They give me a sore throat.'

'Then I suggest that we both smoke the French cigarettes we took from you. Permit?'

I was in no position to object. 'Okay,' I said. He produced my half-empty packet of Gauloises from his coat and took one before sliding one across to me.

'I found those Western cigarettes on the U-Bahn train,' I said.

He smiled. 'That's what I wrote in the arrest report. You think I don't listen to what you say?' He threw his cigarette lighter to me. It was of Western origin, an expendable one with visible fuel supply. It was very low but it worked. 'Now we destroy the evidence by burning, you and me. Right?' He winked conspiratorially.

Lenin, who said his real name was Erich Stinnes, had an encyclopedic memory; he was able to recite endlessly the names of his favourite authors – for they were many and varied – and he seemed to know in bewildering detail every plot they'd written. But he spoke of the fictional characters as if they were alive. 'Do you think,' he asked me, 'that Sherlock Holmes, coming across a criminal of some foreign culture, would find detection more difficult? Is it perhaps true that he is effective only when working against a criminal who shares the creed of the English gentleman?'

'They're just stories,' I said. 'No one takes them seriously.'

'I take them seriously,' said Lenin. 'Holmes is my mentor.'

'Holmes doesn't exist. Holmes never did exist. It's just twaddle.'

'How can you be such a philistine,' said Lenin. 'In *The Sign of Four*, Holmes said that when you have eliminated the impossible, whatever remains, no matter how improbable, must be the truth. Such perception cannot be dismissed lightly.'

'But in *A Study in Scarlet* he said almost the opposite,' I argued. 'He said that when a fact appears opposed to a long train of deductions, it invariably proves to be capable of bearing some other interpretation.'

'Ah, so you are a believer,' said Lenin. He puffed on the Gauloise. 'Anyway, I don't call that a contradiction.'

'Look, Erich,' I said. 'All I know about Sherlock bloody Holmes is the curious incident of the dog in the night-time.'

Lenin waved a hand to silence me, sat back with hands placed fingertips together, and said, 'Yes, "Silver Blaze".' A frown came as he tried to remember the exact words: 'The dog did nothing in the night-time. That was the curious incident.'

'Exactly, Erich, old pal,' I said. 'And, as one Sherlock Holmes fan to another, would you mind explaining to me the equally curious absence of any proper bloody attempt to interrogate me.'

Lenin smiled a tight-lipped little smile, like a parson hearing a risqué joke from a bishop. 'And that's just what I would say in your position, Englishman. I told my superior that a senior security man from London will wonder why we are not following the normal procedure. He will begin to hope that he'll get special treatment, I said. He'll think we don't want him to know our interrogation procedure. And he'll think that's because he's going home very soon. And once a prisoner starts thinking along those lines, he closes his mouth very tight. After that it can take weeks to get anything out of him.'

'And what did your superior say?' I asked.

'His exact words I am not permitted to reveal.' He shrugged apologetically. 'But as you can see for yourself, he paid no heed to my advice.'

'That I should be interrogated while still warm?'

He half closed his eyes and nodded; again it was the mannerism of a churchman. 'It's what should have been done, isn't it? But you can't tell these desk people anything.'

'I know,' I said.

'Yes. You know what it's like, and so do I,' he said. 'Both of us work the tough side of the business. I've been West a few times, just as you've come here. But who gets the promotions and the big wages – desk-bound Party bastards. How lucky you are not having the Party system working against you all the time.'

'We have got it,' I said. 'It's called Eton and Oxbridge.'

But Lenin was not to be stopped. 'Last year my son got marks that qualified him to go to university, but he lost the place to some kid with lower marks. When I complained, I was told that it was official policy to favour the children of working-class parents against those from the professional classes, in which they include me. Shit, I said, you victimize my son because his father was clever enough to pass his exams? What kind of workers' state is that?'

'Are you recording this conversation?'

'So they can put me into prison with you? Do you think I'm crazy?'

'I still want to know why I'm not being interrogated.'

'Tell me,' he said, suddenly leaning forward, drawing on his cigarette, and blowing smoke reflectively as he formed the question in his mind. 'How much per diem do you get?'

'I don't understand.'

'I'm not asking you what you do for a living,' he said. 'All I want to know is how much do they pay you for daily expenses when you are away from home.'

'One hundred and twelve pounds sterling per day for food and lodging. Then we get extra expenses, plus travel expenses.'

Lenin blew a jet of smoke in a gesture that displayed his indignation. 'And they won't even pay us a daily rate. The cashier's office insists upon us writing everything down. We have to account for every penny we've handled.'

'That's the sort of little black book I wouldn't like to keep,' I said.

'Incriminating. Right. That's it exactly. I wish I could get that fact into the heads of the idiots who run this bureau.'

'You're not recording any of this?'

'Let me tell you something in confidence,' said Lenin. 'I was on the phone to Moscow an hour ago. I pleaded with them to let me interrogate you my way. No, they said. The KGB Colonel is on his way now, Moscow says – they keep saying that, but he never arrives – you are ordered not to do anything but hold the prisoner in custody. Stupid bastards. That's Moscow for you.' He inhaled and blew smoke angrily. 'Quite honestly, if you broke down and gave me a complete confession about having an agent in Moscow Central Committee, I'd yawn.'

'Let's try you,' I said.

He grinned. 'What would you do in my place? This KGB Colonel will take over your file when he gets here tomorrow morning. Do you think he'll give me any credit for work done before he arrives? Like hell he will. No, sir, I'm not going to dig anything out of you for those Party bigshots.'

I nodded but I was not beguiled by his behaviour. I'd long ago learned that it is only the very devout who toy with heresy. It's only the Jesuit who complains of the Pope, only the devoted parent who ridicules his child, only the super rich who pick up pennies from the gutter. And in East Berlin it is only the truly faithful who speak treason with such self-assurance.

They took me downstairs at seven o'clock the next morning. I'd heard cars arriving shortly before, and men shouting in the way that guard commanders shout when they want to impress some visiting hotshot.

It was a plush office by East European standards: modern-design Finnish desk and chairs and a sheepskin rug on the floor. A faint aroma of disinfectant mingled with the cheap perfume of the floor polish. This was the smell of Moscow.

Fiona was not sitting behind the desk; she was standing at the side of the room. My friend Lenin was standing stiffly at her side. He'd obviously been briefing her, but Fiona's authority was established by the imperious way in which she dismissed him. 'Go to your office and get on with it. I'll call if I want you,' she said in that brisk Russian that I'd always admired. So the so-called Erich Stinnes was a Russian – a KGB officer no doubt. Well, he spoke bloody good Berlin German. Probably he'd grown up here, the son of an occupier, as I was.

Fiona straightened her back as she looked at me. 'Well?' she said.

'Hello, Fiona,' I said.

'You guessed?' She looked different; harder perhaps, but confident and relaxed. It must have been a relief to be her real self after a lifetime of deception. 'Sometimes I was sure you'd guessed the truth.'

'What guessing was needed? It was obvious, or should have been.'

'So why did you do nothing about it?' Her voice was steel. It was as if she were pushing herself to be as robotic as a weighing machine.

'You know how it is,' I said vaguely. 'I kept thinking of other explanations. I repressed it. I didn't want to believe it. You didn't make any mistakes, if that's what you mean.' It wasn't true, of course, and she knew it.

'I should never have handwritten that damned submission. I knew those fools would leave it in the file. They promised. . . .'

'Is there anything to drink in this office?' I asked. Now that I had to face the truth, I found it easier than dealing with the dread of it. Perhaps all fear is worse than reality, just as all hope is better than fulfilment.

'Maybe.' She opened the drawers in the desk and found an almost full bottle of vodka. 'Will this do?'

'Anything will do,' I said, getting a teacup from a shelf and pouring myself a measure of it.

'You should cut down on the drinking,' she said impassively.

'You don't make it easy to do,' I said. I gulped some and poured more.

She gave me the briefest of smiles. 'I wish it hadn't ended like this.'

'That sounds like a line from Hollywood,' I said.

'You make it hard on yourself.'

'That's not the way I like it.'

'I always made it a condition that nothing would happen to you. Every mission you did after that business at Gdynia I kept you safe.'

'You betrayed every mission I did, that's the truth of it.' That was the humiliating part of it, the way she'd protected me.

'You'll go free. You'll go free this morning. It made no difference that Werner demanded it.'

'Werner?'

'He met me with a car at Berlin-Tegel when my plane landed. He held me at pistol point. He threatened me and made me promise to release you. Werner is a schoolboy,' she said. 'He plays schoolboy games and has the same schoolboy loyalties you had when I first met you.'

'Maybe that was my loss,' I said.

'But not my gain.' She came closer to me, for one last look. 'It was a good trick to say you'd cross first. It made me think I might get here in time to catch Brahms Four; your precious von Munte.'

'Instead you caught me,' I said.

'Yes, that was clever, darling. But suppose I hang on to you?'

'You won't do that,' I said. 'It wouldn't suit you to have me around. In a Soviet prison I'd be an impediment to you. And an imprisoned husband wouldn't suit that social conscience you care so much about.'

'You're right.'

'At least you're not trying to find excuses,' I said.

'Why should I bother? You wouldn't understand,' she said. 'You just *talk* about the class system and make jokes about the way it works. I do something about it.'

'Don't explain,' I said. 'Leave me something to be mystified about.'

'You'll always be the same arrogant swine I met at Freddy Spring-field's party.'

'I'd like to think I was just a little smarter than the man you made a fool of then.'

'You've got nothing to regret. You'll go back to London and get Dicky Cruyer's desk. By the end of the year you'll be running Bret Rensselaer out of his job.'

'Will I?'

'I've made you a hero,' she said bitterly. 'You made me run for cover, and at a time when no one else suspected the truth. Until you phoned about the handwritten report, I thought I could keep going for ever and ever.'

I didn't answer. I kicked myself for not acknowledging the truth years before – that I had been Fiona's greatest asset. Who would believe that Bernard Samson would be married to a foreign agent and not realize it? Her marriage to me had made her life more compli-cated, but it had kept her safe.

'And you rescued your precious agent. You got Brahms Four home safely enough to make all your other agents breathe easily once more.'

I still said nothing. She might be leading me on. Until I was sure that the Muntes were safe, I preferred to play dumb on the subject.

'Oh, yes. You're a professional success story, my darling. It's only your domestic life that is a disaster. No wife, no home, no children.'

She was gloating. I knew she wanted to provoke me into an outburst of bad temper. I recognized that tone of voice from other times, other places and other arguments. It was the tone of voice she sometimes used to criticize Werner, my grammar, my accent, my suits, my old girlfriends.

'Can I go now?'

'The arresting officer – Major Erich Stinnes – is taking you to Checkpoint Charlie at nine o'clock. The arrangements are all made. You'll be all right.' She smiled. She was enjoying the chance to show me how much authority she had. She was a KGB Colonel; they would treat her well. The KGB look after their own, they always have done. It's only the rest of the world they treat like dirt.

I turned to go, but women won't let anything end like that. They always have to sit you down at the table for a lecture, or write you a long letter, or make sure they have not just the last word but the last thought too.

'The children will go to the best school in Moscow. It was part of the arrangements I made. I might be able to arrange that you have a safe passage to see them now and again, but I can't promise.'

'Of course not,' I said.

'And I can't send them to England on visits, darling. I just couldn't trust you to send them back, could I?'

'No,' I said. 'You couldn't. Now can I go?'

'I paid off the overdraft and put six hundred into your account to pay off Nanny. And one hundred for some outstanding bills. I wrote it all down and left the letter with Mr Moore, the bank manager.'

'Okay.'

'The D-G will send for you, of course. You can tell him that the official policy at this end will be one of no publicity about my defection. I imagine that will suit him all right, after all the scandals the service has suffered in the past year.'

'I'll tell him,' I promised.

'Goodbye then, darling. Do I get one final kiss?'

'No,' I said. I opened the door; Lenin was waiting on the landing, leather cap in hand. He saw Fiona standing behind me. He didn't smile in the presence of a senior officer. I wondered if he knew she was my wife. She'd probably be working out of Berlin. Poor Erich Stinnes.

When we got to the ground floor, I walked past him and he hurried to catch up with me as I marched to the front door to get out of that foul building. 'Is there anything else?' Lenin asked as he signalled for the car.

'For instance?' I said.

I sat in the black Volvo and looked out at the sunny streets: Stalinallee that had become Karl-Marx-Allee one night when all the street signs were changed before daybreak. The Alex, left onto Unter den Linden, and then left again so that Checkpoint Charlie was to be seen at the bottom of Friedrichstrasse.

'I'll take you right through the checkpoint,' said Stinnes. The driver touched the horn. The frontier police recognized the car, put the booms up and we drove through without stopping.

The American soldier in the glass-sided hut on the Western side gave us no more than a glance. 'Far enough,' I said. 'I'll get one of these cabs.' But in fact I'd already caught sight of Werner. He was seated in the car over the road where we always parked when we waited at Checkpoint Charlie. The Volvo turned and stopped. I got out and took a deep breath of that famous *Berliner Luft*. I wanted to run down to the canal and follow it to Lützowplatz and then to Dad's office on Tauentzienstrasse. I would open his desk and take the chocolate bar that was his ration. I'd climb up the mountain of rubble that filled half the street, and slide down the other side in a cloud of dust. I'd run through the carefully swept ruins of the clinic, where cleaned bottles, dusted bricks and salvaged pieces of charred timber were arranged so proudly. At the shop on the corner I'd ask Mr Mauser if Axel could come out to play. And we'd go and find Werner and maybe go swimming. It was that sort of day. . . .

'Did it go all right, Werner?'

'I phoned England an hour ago,' said Werner. 'I knew it would be the first thing you'd ask. There's an armed police guard around your mother's house. Anything the Russians try won't work. The children are safe.'

'Thanks Werner,' I said. Thinking about the children made it easier not to think about Fiona. Better still would be not having to think at all.

MEXICO SET

I

'Some of these people *want* to get killed,' said Dicky Cruyer, as he jabbed the brake pedal to avoid hitting a newsboy. The kid grinned as he slid between the slowly moving cars, flourishing his newspapers with the controlled abandon of a fan dancer. 'Six Face Firing Squad'; the headlines were huge and shiny black. 'Hurricane Threatens Veracruz.' A smudgy photo of street fighting in San Salvador covered the whole front of a tabloid.

It was late afternoon. The streets shone with that curiously bright shadowless light that precedes a storm. All six lanes of traffic crawling along the Insurgentes halted, and more newsboys danced into the road, together with a woman selling flowers and a kid with lottery tickets trailing from a roll like toilet paper.

Picking his way between the cars came a handsome man in old jeans and checked shirt. He was accompanied by a small child. The man had a Coca Cola bottle in his fist. He swigged at it and then tilted his head back again, looking up into the heavens. He stood erect and immobile, like a bronze statue, before igniting his breath so that a great ball of fire burst from his mouth.

'Bloody hell!' said Dicky. 'That's dangerous.'

'It's a living,' I said. I'd seen the fire-eaters before. There was always one of them performing somewhere in the big traffic jams. I switched on the car radio but electricity in the air blotted out the music with the sounds of static. It was very hot. I opened the window but the sudden stink of diesel fumes made me close it again. I held my hand against the air-conditioning outlet but the air was warm.

Again the fire-eater blew a huge orange balloon of flame into the air.

'For us,' explained Dicky. 'Dangerous for people in the cars. Flames like that, with all these petrol fumes . . . can you imagine?' There was a slow roll of thunder. 'If only it would rain,' said Dicky. I looked at the sky, the low black clouds trimmed with gold. The huge sun was coloured bright red by the city's ever-present blanket of smog, and squeezed tight between the glass buildings that dripped with its light.

'Who got this car for us?' I said. A motorcycle, its pillion piled high with cases of beer, weaved precariously between the cars, narrowly missing the flower seller.

'One of the embassy people,' said Dicky. He released the brake and the big blue Chevrolet rolled forward a few feet and then all the traffic stopped again. In any town north of the border this factory-fresh car would not have drawn a second glance. But Mexico City is the place old cars go to die. Most of those around us were dented and rusty, or they were crudely repainted in bright primary colours. 'A friend of mine lent it to us.'

'I might have guessed,' I said.

'It was short notice. They didn't know we were coming until the day before yesterday. Henry Tiptree – the one who met us at the airport – let us have it. It was a special favour because I knew him at Oxford.'

'I wish you hadn't known him at Oxford; then we could have rented one from Hertz – with air-conditioning that worked.'

'So what can we do . . .' said Dicky irritably '. . . take it back and tell him it's not good enough for us?'

We watched the fire-eater blow another balloon of flame while the small boy hurried from driver to driver, collecting a peso here and there for his father's performance.

Dicky took some Mexican coins from the slash pocket of his denim jacket and gave them to the child. It was Dicky's faded work suit, his cowboy boots and curly hair that had attracted the attention of the tough-looking woman immigration officer at Mexico City airport. It was only the first-class labels on his expensive baggage, and the fast talking of Dicky's Counsellor friend from the embassy, that saved him from the indignity of a body search.

Dicky Cruyer was a curious mixture of scholarship and ruthless ambition, but he was insensitive, and this was often his undoing. His insensitivity to people, place and atmosphere could make him seem a clown instead of the cool sophisticate that was his own image of himself. But that didn't make him any less terrifying as friend or foe.

The flower seller bent down, tapped on the window glass and waved at Dicky. He shouted 'Vamos!' It was almost impossible to see her face behind the unwieldy armful of flowers. Here were blossoms of all colours, shapes and sizes. Flowers for weddings and flowers for dinner hostesses, flowers for mistresses and flowers for suspicious wives.

The traffic began moving again. Dicky shouted 'Vamos!' much louder.

The woman saw me reaching into my pocket for money and separated a dozen long-stemmed pink roses from the less expensive marigolds and asters. 'Maybe some flowers would be something to give to Werner's wife,' I said.

Dicky ignored my suggestion. 'Get out of the way,' he shouted at the old woman, and the car leaped forward. The old woman jumped clear.

'Take it easy, Dicky, you nearly knocked her over.'

'*Vamos!* I told her; *vamos*. They shouldn't be in the road. Are they all crazy? She heard me all right.'

'*Vamos* means "Okay, let's go",' I said. 'She thought you wanted to buy some.'

'In Mexico it also means scram,' said Dicky driving up close to a white VW bus in front of us. It was full of people and boxes of tomatoes, and its dented bodywork was caked with mud in the way that cars become when they venture on to country roads at this rainy time of year. Its exhaust-pipe was newly bound up with wire, and the rear panel was removed to help cool the engine. The sound of its fan made a very loud whine so that Dicky had to speak loudly to make himself heard. '*Vamos*; scram. They say it in cowboy films.'

'Maybe she doesn't go to cowboy films,' I said.

'Just keep looking at the street map.'

'It's not a street map; it's just a map. It only shows the main streets.'

'We'll find it all right. It's off the Insurgentes.'

'Do you know how big Mexico City is? The Insurgentes is about thirty-five miles long,' I said.

'You look on your side and I'll look this side. Volkmann said it's in the centre of town.' He sniffed. 'Mexico, they call it. No one here says "Mexico City". They call the town Mexico.'

I didn't answer; I put away the little coloured town plan and stared out at the crowded streets. I was quite happy to be driven round the town for an hour or two if that's what Dicky wanted.

Dicky said, "Somewhere in the centre of town" would mean the Paseo de la Reforma near the column with the golden angel. At least that's what it would mean to any tourist coming here for the first time. And Werner Volkmann and his wife Zena are here for the first time. Right?'

'Werner said it was going to be a second honeymoon.'

'With Zena I would have thought one honeymoon would be enough,' said Dicky.

'More than enough,' I said.

Dicky said, 'I'll kill your bloody Werner if he's brought us out from London on a wild-goose chase.'

'It's a break from the office,' I said. Werner had become my Werner I noticed and would remain so if things went wrong.

'For you it is,' said Dicky. 'You've got nothing to lose. Your desk will be waiting for you when you get back. But there's a dozen people in that building scrambling round for my job. This will give Bret just the chance he needs to take over my work. You realize that, don't you?'

'How could Bret want to take your job, Dicky? Bret is senior to you.'

The traffic was moving at about five miles an hour. A small dirty-faced child in the back of the VW bus was staring at Dicky with great interest. The insolent stare seemed to disconcert him. Dicky turned to look at me. 'Bret is looking for a job that would suit him; and my job would suit him. Bret will have nothing to do now that his committee is being wound up. There's already an argument about who will have his office space. And about who will have that tall blonde typist who wears the white sweaters.'

'Gloria?' I said.

'Oh? Don't say you've been there?'

'Us workers stick together, Dicky,' I said.

'Very funny,' said Dicky. 'If Bret takes over my job, he'll chase your arse. Working for me will seem like a holiday. I hope you realize that, old pal.'

I didn't know that the brilliant career of Bret was taking a downturn to the point where Dicky was running scared. But Dicky had taken a PhD in office politics so I was prepared to believe him. 'This is the Pink Zone,' I said. 'Why don't you park in one of these hotels and get a cab?'

Dicky seemed relieved at the idea of letting a cab driver find Werner Volkmann's apartment but, being Dicky, he had to argue against it for a couple of minutes. As he pulled into the slow lane the dirty child in the VW smiled and then made a terrible face at us. Dicky glanced at me and said, 'Are you pulling faces at that child? For God's sake, act your age, Bernard.' Dicky was in a bad mood, and talking about his job had made him more touchy.

He turned off the Insurgentes on to a side-street and cruised east-wards until we found a car-park under one of the big hotels. As we went down the ramp into the darkness he switched the headlights on. This was a different world. This was where the Mercedes, Cadillacs and Porsches lived in comfort, shiny with health, smelling of new leather and guarded by two armed security men. One of them pushed a ticket under a wiper and lifted the barrier so that we could drive through.

'So your school chum Werner spots a KGB heavy here in town. Why did Controller (Europe) insist that I come out here at this stinking time of year?' Dicky was cruising very slowly round the dark garage, looking for a place to park.

'Werner didn't spot Erich Stinnes,' I said. 'Werner's wife spotted him. And there's a departmental alert for him. There's a space.'

'Too small; this is a big car. Alert? You don't have to tell me that, old boy. I signed the alert, Remember me? Controller of German Stations? But I've never seen Erich Stinnes. I wouldn't know Erich Stinnes from the man in the moon. You're the one who can identify him. Why do I have to come?'

'You're here to decide what we do. I'm not senior enough or reliable enough to make decisions. What about there, next to the white Mercedes?'

'Ummmmm,' said Dicky. He had trouble parking the car in the space marked out by the white lines. One of the security guards – a big poker-faced man in starched khakis and carefully polished high boots – came to watch us. He stood arms akimbo, staring, while Dicky went backwards and forwards trying to squeeze between a white convertible and a concrete stanchion that bore brightly coloured patches of enamel from other cars. 'Did you really make out with that blonde in Bret's office?' said Dicky as he abandoned his task and reversed into another space marked 'reserved'.

'Gloria? I thought everyone knew about me and Gloria,' I said. In fact I knew her no better than Dicky did but I couldn't resist the chance to needle him. 'My wife's left me. I'm a free man again.'

'Your wife defected,' said Dicky spitefully. 'Your wife is working for the bloody Russkies.'

'That's over and done with,' I said. I didn't want to talk about my wife or my children or any other problems. And if I did want to talk about them Dicky would be the last person I'd choose to confide in.

'You and Fiona were very close,' said Dicky accusingly.

'It's not a crime to be in love with your wife,' I said.

'Taboo subject, eh?' It pleased Dicky to touch a nerve and get a reaction. I should have known better than to respond to his taunts. I was guilty by association. I'd become a probationer once more and I'd remain one until I proved my loyalty all over again. Nothing had been said to me officially, but Dicky's little flash of temper was not the first indication of what the department really felt.

'I didn't come on this trip to discuss Fiona,' I said.

'Don't keep bickering,' said Dicky. 'Let's go and talk to your friend Werner and get it over and done with. I can't wait to be out of this filthy hell-hole. January or February; that's the time when people who know what's what go to Mexico. Not in the middle of the rainy season.'

Dicky opened the door of the car and I slid across the seat to get out his side. '*Prohibido aparcar*,' said the security guard, and with arms folded he planted himself in our path.

'What's that?' said Dicky, and the man said it again. Dicky smiled and explained, in his schoolboy Spanish, that we were residents of the hotel, we would only be leaving the car there for half an hour, and we were engaged on very important business.

'*Prohibido aparcar*,' said the guard stolidly

'Give him some money, Dicky,' I said. 'That's all he wants.'

The security guard looked from Dicky to me and stroked his large black moustache with the ball of his thumb. He was a big man, as tall as Dicky and twice as wide.

'I'm not going to give him anything,' said Dicky. 'I'm not going to pay twice.'

'Let me do it,' I said. 'I've got small money here.'

'Stay out of this,' said Dicky. 'You've got to know how to handle these people.' He stared at the guard. '*Nada! Nada! Nada! Entiende?*'

The guard looked down at our Chevrolet and then plucked the wiper between finger and thumb and let it fall back against the glass with a thump. 'He'll wreck the car,' I said. 'This is not the time to get into a hassle you can't win.'

'I'm not frightened of him,' said Dicky.

'I know you're not, but I am.' I got in front of him before he took a swing at the guard. There was a hard, almost vicious, streak under Dicky's superficial charm, and he was a keen member of the Foreign Office judo club. Dicky wasn't frightened of anything; that's why I didn't like working with him. I folded some paper money into the guard's ready hand and pushed Dicky towards the sign that said 'Elevator to hotel lobby'. The guard watched us go, his face still without emotion. Dicky wasn't pleased either. He thought I'd tried to protect him against the guard and he felt belittled by my interference.

The hotel lobby was that same ubiquitous combination of tinted mirror, plastic marble and spongy carpet underlay that international travellers are reputed to admire. We sat down under a huge display of plastic flowers and looked at the fountain.

'Machismo,' said Dicky sadly. We were waiting for the top-hatted hotel doorman to find a taxi driver who would take us to Werner's apartment. 'Machismo,' he said again reflectively. 'Every last one of them is obsessed by it. It's why you can't get anything done here. I'm going to report that bastard downstairs to the manager.'

'Wait until after we've collected the car,' I advised.

'At least the embassy sent a Counsellor to meet us. That means that London has told them to give us full diplomatic back-up.'

'Or it means Mexico City embassy staff – including your pal Tiptree – have a lot of time on their hands.'

Dicky looked up from counting his traveller's cheques. 'What do I have to do, Bernard, to make you remember it's Mexico? Not Mexico City; Mexico.'

2

This was a new Werner Volkmann. This was not the introverted Jewish orphan I'd been at school with, nor the lugubrious teenager I'd grown up with in Berlin, nor the affluent, overweight banker who was welcome on both sides of the Wall. This new Werner was a tough, muscular figure in short-sleeved cotton shirt and well-fitting Madras trousers. His big droopy moustache had been trimmed and so had his bushy black hair. Being on holiday with his twenty-two-year-old wife had rejuvenated him.

He was standing on the sixth-floor balcony of a small block of luxury apartments in downtown Mexico City. From here was a view across this immense city, with the mountains a dark backdrop. The dying sun was turning the world pink, now that the stormclouds had passed over. Long ragged strips of orange and gold cloud were torn across the sky, like a poster advertising a smog-reddened sun ripped by a passing vandal.

The balcony was large enough to hold a lot of expensive white garden furniture as well as big pots of tropical flowers. Green leafy plants climbed overhead to provide shade, while a collection of cacti were arrayed on shelves like books. Werner poured a pink concoction from a glass jug. It was like a watery fruit salad, the sort of thing they pressed on you at parties where no one got drunk. It didn't look tempting, but I was hot and I took one gratefully.

Dicky Cruyer was flushed; his cowboy shirt bore dark patches of sweat. He had his blue-denim jacket slung over his shoulder. He tossed it on to a chair and reached out to take a drink from Werner.

Werner's wife Zena held out her glass for a refill. She was full-length on a reclining chair. She was wearing a sheer, rainbow-striped dress through which her suntanned limbs shone darkly. As she moved to sip her drink, German fashion magazines, balanced on her belly, slid to the ground and flapped open. Zena cursed softly. It was the strange, flat-accented speech of eastern lands that were no longer German. It was probably the only thing she'd inherited from her impoverished parents, and I had the feeling she would sometimes have been happier without it.

'What's in this drink?' I said.

Werner recovered the magazines from the floor and gave them to his wife. In business he could be tough, in friendships outspoken, but to Zena he was always indulgent.

Werner raised money from Western banks to pay exporters to East Germany, and then eventually collected the money from the East German government, taking a tiny percentage on every deal. 'Avalizing' it was called. But it wasn't a banker's business; it was a free-for-all in which many got their fingers burned. Werner had to be tough to survive.

'In the drink? Fruit juices,' said Werner. 'It's too early for alcohol in this sort of climate.'

'Not for me it isn't,' I said. Werner smiled but he didn't go anywhere to get me a proper drink. He was my oldest and closest friend; the sort of close friend who gives you the excoriating criticism that new enemies hesitate about. Zena didn't look up; she was still pretending to read her magazines.

Dicky had stepped into the jungle of flowers to get a clearer view of the city. I looked over his shoulder to see the traffic still moving sluggishly. In the street below there were flashing red lights and sirens as two police cars mounted the pavement to get around the traffic. In a city of fifteen million people there is said to be a crime committed every two minutes. The noise of the streets never ceased. As the flow of homegoing office workers ended, the influx of people to the Zona Rosa's restaurants and cinemas began. 'What a madhouse,' said Dicky.

A malevolent-looking black cat awoke and jumped softly down from its position on the footstool. It went over to Dicky and sank a claw into his leg and looked up at him to see how he'd take it. 'Hell!' shouted Dicky. 'Get away, you brute.' Dicky aimed a blow at the cat but missed. The cat moved very fast as if it had done the same thing before to other gringos.

Wincing with pain and rubbing his leg, Dicky moved well away from the cat and went to the other end of the balcony to look inside the large lounge with its locally made tiles, old masks and Mexican textiles. It looked like an arts and crafts shop, but obviously a lot of money had been spent getting it that way. 'Nice place you've got here,' said Dicky. There was more than a hint of sarcasm in his remark. It was not Dicky's style. Anything that departed much from Harrod's furniture department was too foreign for him.

'It belongs to Zena's uncle and aunt,' explained Werner. 'We're taking care of it while they're in Europe.' That explained the notebook I'd seen near the telephone. Zena had neatly entered 'wine glass', 'tumbler', 'wine glass', 'small china bowl with blue flowers'. It was a list of breakages, an example of Zena's sense of order and rectitude.

'You chose a bad time of year,' complained Dicky. 'Or rather Zena's uncle chose a good one.' He drained the glass, tipping it up until the ice cubes, cucumber and pieces of lemon slid down the glass and rested against his lips.

'Zena doesn't mind it,' said Werner, as if his own opinions were of no importance.

Zena, still concentrating on her magazine, said, 'I love the sun.' She said it twice and continued to read without losing her place.

'If only it would rain,' said Werner, 'It's this build-up to the storms that makes it so unbearable.'

'So you saw this chap Stinnes?' said Dicky very casually, as if that wasn't the reason that the two of us had dragged ourselves four thousand miles to talk to them.

'At the Kronprinz,' said Werner.

'What's the Kronprinz?' said Dicky. He put down his glass and used a paper napkin to dry his lips.

'A club.'

'What sort of club?' Dicky stuck his thumbs into the back of his leather belt and looked down at the toes of his cowboy boots reflectively. The cat had followed Dicky and looked as if it was about to reach up above his boot to put a claw into his thin calf again. Dicky aimed a vicious little kick at it but the cat was too quick for him. 'Get away,' said Dicky, more loudly this time.

'I'm sorry about the cat,' said Werner. 'But I think Zena's aunt only let us use the place because we'd be company for Cherubino. It's your jeans. Cats like to claw at denim.'

'It bloody hurts,' said Dicky, rubbing his leg. 'You should get its claws clipped or something. In this part of the world cats carry all kinds of diseases.'

'What's it matter what sort of club?' said Zena suddenly. She closed the magazine and pushed her hair back. She looked different with her hair loose; no longer the tough little career girl, more the lady of leisure. Her hair was long and jet black and held with a silver Mexican comb which she brandished before tossing her hair back and fixing it again.

'A club for German businessmen. It's been going since 1902,' said Werner. 'Zena likes the buffet and dance they have on Friday nights. There's a big German colony here in the city. There always has been.'

'Werner said there would be a cash payment for finding Stinnes,' said Zena.

'There usually is,' said Dicky slyly, although he knew there would be no chance of a cash payment for such a routine report. It must have been Werner's way of encouraging Zena to cooperate with us. I looked at Werner and he looked back at me without changing his expression.

'How do you know it really is Stinnes?' said Dicky.

'It's Stinnes all right,' said Werner stoically. 'His name is on his membership card and his credit at the bar is in that name.'

'And his cheque book,' said Zena. 'His name is printed on his cheques.'

'What bank?' I asked.

'Bank of America,' said Zena. 'A branch in San Diego, California.'

'Names mean nothing,' said Dicky. 'How do you know this fellow is a KGB man? And, even if he is, what makes you so sure that this is the johnny who interrogated Bernard in East Berlin?' A brief movement of the hand in my direction. 'It might be someone using the same cover name. We've known KGB people do that. Right, Bernard?'

'It has been known,' I said, although I was damned if I could recall any examples of such sloppy tactics by the plodding but thorough bureaucrats of the KGB.

'How much?' said Zena. And, when Dicky looked at her and raised his eyebrows, she said, 'How much are you going to give us for reporting Stinnes? Werner said you want him badly. Werner said he was very important.'

'Steady on,' said Dicky. 'We don't have him yet. We haven't even positively identified him.'

'Erich Stinnes,' said Zena as if repeating a prepared lesson. 'Fortyish, thinning hair, cheap specs, smokes like a chimney. Berlin accent.'

'Beard?'

'No beard,' said Zena. Hastily she added, 'He must have shaved it off.' She did not readily abandon her claims.

'So you've spoken with him' I said.

'He's there every Friday,' said Werner. 'He's a regular. He works at the Soviet Embassy, he told Zena that. He says he's just a driver.'

'They're always drivers,' I said. 'That's how they account for their nice big cars and going wherever they want to go.' I poured myself some more of Werner's fruit punch. There was not much of it left, and the bottom of the jug was a tangle of greenery and soggy bits of lemon. 'Did he talk about books or American films, Zena?'

She swung her legs out of the reclining chair with a display of tanned thigh. I saw the look in Dicky Cruyer's face as she smoothed her dress. She had that sexy appeal that goes with youth and health and boundless energy. And now she knew she had the right Stinnes her pearly grey eyes sparkled. 'That's right. He loves old Hollywood musicals and English detective stories . . .'

'Then that's him,' I said, without much enthusiasm. Secretly I'd hoped it would all come to nothing and I'd be able to go straight back to London and my home and my children. 'Yes, that's "Lenin";

that's the one who took me down to Checkpoint Charlie when they released me.'

'What will happen now?' said Zena. She was short; she only came up to Dicky's shoulder. Some say short people are aggressive to compensate for their small stature, but look at Zena Volkmann and you might start thinking that aggressive people are made short lest they take over the whole world. Either way Zena was short and the aggression inside her was always bubbling along the edges of the pan like milk before it boils over. 'What will you do about him?'

'Don't ask,' Werner told her.

But Dicky answered her, 'We want to talk to him, Mrs Volkmann. No rough stuff, if that's what you are afraid of.'

I swallowed my fruit punch and got a mouthful of tiny pieces of ice and some lemon pips.

Zena smiled. She wasn't frightened of any rough stuff; she was frightened of not getting the money for arranging it. She stood up and twisted her shoulders, slowly stretching her arms above her head one after the other in a lazy display of overt sexuality. 'Do you want my help?' she said.

Dicky didn't answer directly. He looked from Zena to Werner and back again and said, 'Stinnes is a KGB major. That's too low a rank for the computer to offer much on him. Most of what we know about him came from Bernard, who was interrogated by him.' A glance at me to stress the unreliability of uncorroborated intelligence from any source. 'But he's senior staff in Berlin. So what is he doing in Mexico? Must be a Russian national. What's his game? What's he doing in this German club of yours?'

Zena laughed. 'You think he should have joined Perovsky's?' She laughed again.

Werner said, 'Zena knows this town very well, Dicky. She has aunts and uncles, cousins and a nephew here. She lived here for six months when she first left school.'

'Where, what, how or why is Perovsky's?' said Dicky. He was German Stations Controller. He didn't like being laughed at, and I could see he was taking a little time getting used to Werner calling him Dicky.

'Zena is joking,' explained Werner. 'Perovsky's is a big, rather run-down club for Russians near the National Palace. The ground floor is a restaurant open to anyone. It was started after the revolution. The members used to be dukes and counts and people who'd escaped from the Bolsheviks. Now it's a pretty mixed crowd but the anti-communist line is still *de rigueur*. The people from the Soviet Embassy give it a wide berth. If a man such as Stinnes went in there and spoke out of turn he might never get out.'

'Really never get out?' I said.

Werner turned to look at me. 'It's a rough town, Bernie. It's not all *margaritas* and *mariachis* like the travel posters.'

'But the Kronprinz Club is not so particular about its membership?' persisted Dicky.

'No one goes there to talk politics. It's the only place in town where you can get real German draught beer and good German food,' explained Werner. 'It's very popular. It's a social club; you get a very mixed crowd there. A lot of them are transients: airline pilots, salesmen, ships' engineers, businessmen, priests even.'

'And KGB men?'

'You Englishmen avoid each other when you are abroad,' said Werner. 'We Germans like to be together. East Germans, West Germans, exiles, expatriates, men avoiding tax, men avoiding their wives, men avoiding their creditors, men avoiding the police. Nazis, monarchists, communists, even Jews like me. We like to be together because we are Germans.'

'Such Germans as Stinnes?' said Dicky sarcastically.

'He must have lived in Berlin. His German is as good as Bernie's,' said Werner, looking at me. 'Even more convincing in a way, because he has the sort of strong Berlin accent you seldom hear except in some workers' bar in the city. It was only when I began to listen to him really carefully that I could detect something that was not quite right in the background of his voice. I'll bet everyone in the club thinks he's German.'

'He's not here to get a tan,' said Dicky. 'A man like that is sent here only for something special. What's your guess, Bernard?'

'Stinnes was in Cuba,' I said. 'He told me that when we talked together. Security police. I went back to the continuity files and began to guess he was there to give the Cubans some advice when they purged some of the bigwigs in 1970. It was a big shake-up. Stinnes must have been some kind of Latin America expert even then.'

'Never mind old history,' said Dicky. 'What's he doing now?'

'Running agents, I suppose. Guatemala is a KGB priority, and it's not so far from here. Anyone can walk through; the border is just jungle.'

'I don't think that's it,' said Werner.

I said, 'The East Germans backed the Sandinista National Liberation Front long before it looked like winning and forming a government.'

'The East Germans back anybody who might be a thorn in the flesh of the Americans,' said Werner.

'But what do you really think he's doing?' Dicky asked me.

I was stalling because I didn't know how much Dicky would want me to say in front of Zena and Werner. I kept stalling. I said, 'Stinnes speaks good English. Unless the cheque book is a deliberate way of throwing us off the scent, he might be running agents into California. Handling data stolen from electronics and software research firms perhaps.' I was improvising. I didn't have the slightest idea of what Stinnes might be doing.

'Why would London give a damn about that sort of caper?' said Werner, who knew me well enough to guess that I was bluffing. 'Don't tell me London Central put out an urgent call for Stinnes because he's stealing computer secrets from the Americans.'

'It's the only reason I can think of,' I said.

'Don't treat me like a child, Bernard,' said Werner. 'If you don't want to tell me, just say so.'

As if in response to Werner's acrimony, Zena went across to the fireplace and pressed a hidden bellpush. From somewhere in the labyrinth of the apartment there came the sound of footsteps, and an Indian woman appeared. She had that chin-up stance that makes so many Mexicans look as if they are ready to balance a water jug on their heads, and her eyes were half closed. 'I knew you'd want to sample some Mexican food,' said Zena. Personally it was the last thing I'd ever want to sample, but without waiting to hear our response she told the woman we would sit down immediately. Zena used her poor Spanish with a fluent confidence that made it sound better. Zena did everything like that.

'She can understand German perfectly and a certain amount of English too,' said Zena after the woman had gone. It was a warning to guard our tongues. 'Maria has worked for my aunt for over ten years.'

'But you don't talk to her in German,' said Dicky.

Zena smiled at him. 'By the time you've said tortillas, tacos, guacamole and quesadillas, and so on, you might as well add *por favor* and get it over with.'

It was an elegant table, shining with solid-silver cutlery, hand-embroidered linen and fine cut-glass. The meal had obviously been planned and prepared as part of Zena's pitch for a cash payment. It was a good meal, and not too damned ethnic, thank God. I have a very limited capacity for the primitive permutations of tortillas, bean-mush and chillies that numb the palate and sear the insides from Dallas to Cape Horn. But we started with grilled lobster and cold white wine, and not a refried bean in sight.

The curtains were drawn back so that air could come in through the open windows, but the air was not cool. The cyclone out in the Gulf had not moved nearer the coast, so the threatened storms had not come but neither had much drop in temperature. By now the sun had gone down behind the mountains that surround the city on every side, and the sky was mauve. Pin-pointed like stars in a planetarium were the lights of the city, which stretched all the way to the foothills of the distant mountains until like a galaxy they became a milky blur. The dining room was dark; the only light came from tall candles that burned brightly in the still air.

'Sometimes London Central can get in ahead of our American friends,' said Dicky, suddenly spearing another grilled lobster tail. Had he really spent so long thinking up a reply for Werner? 'It would give us negotiating power in Washington if we had some good material about KGB penetration of anywhere in Uncle Sam's backyard.'

Werner reached across the table to pour more wine for his wife. 'This is Chilean wine,' said Werner. He poured some for Dicky and for me and then refilled his own glass. It was Werner's way of telling Dicky he didn't believe a word of it, but I'm not sure Dicky understood that.

'It's not bad,' said Dicky, sipping, closing his eyes and tilting his head back to concentrate all his attention on the taste. Dicky fancied his wine expertise. He'd already made a great show of sniffing the cork. 'I suppose, with the peso collapsing, it will get more and more difficult to get any sort of imported wine. And Mexican wine is a bit of an acquired taste.'

'Stinnes only arrived here two or three weeks ago,' said Werner doggedly. 'If London Central is interested in Stinnes, it won't be on account of anything he might be planning to do in Silicon Valley or in the Guatemala rain forest; it will be on account of all the things he did in Berlin during the last two years.'

'Do you think so? said Dicky, looking at Werner with friendly and respectful interest, like a man who wanted to learn something. But Werner could see through him.

'I'm not an idiot,' said Werner, using the unemotional tone but exaggerated clarity with which a man might specify decaffeinated coffee to an inattentive waiter. 'I was dodging KGB men when I was ten years old. Bernie and I were working for the department when the Wall was built in 1961 and you were still at school.'

'Point taken, old boy,' said Dicky with a smile. He could afford to smile; he was two years younger than either of us, with years' less time in the department, but he'd got the coveted job of German Stations Controller against tough competition. And – despite rumours about an imminent reshuffle in London Central – he was still holding on to it. 'But the fact is that the people in London don't tell me every last thing they have in mind. I'm just the chap chipping away at the coal-face, right? They don't consult me about building new nuclear power stations.' He poured some warm butter over his last piece of lobster with a care that suggested he had no other concern in his mind.

'Tell me about Stinnes,' I said to Werner. 'Does he come along to the Kronprinz Club trailing a string of KGB zombies? Or does he come on his own? Does he sit in the corner with his big glass of *Berliner Weisse mit Schuss,* or does he sniff round to see what he can ferret out? How does he behave, Werner?'

'He's a loner,' said Werner. 'He probably would never have spoken to us in the first place except that he mistook Zena for one of the Biedermann girls.'

'Who are the Biedermann girls?' said Dicky. After the remains of the lobster course had been removed, the Indian servant brought an elaborate array of Mexican dishes: refried beans, whole chillies and the tortilla in its various disguises: enchiladas, tacos, tostadas and quesadillas. Dicky paused for long enough to have each one identified and described but he took only a tiny portion on his plate.

'Here in Mexico the chilli has sexual significance,' said Zena, directing the remark to Dicky. 'The man who eats hot chillies is thought to be virile and strong.'

'Oh, I love chillies,' said Dicky, his tone of voice picking up the hint of mockery that was to be detected in Zena's remark. 'Always have had a weakness for chillies,' he said, as he reached for a plate on which many different ones were arranged. I glanced at Werner who was watching Dicky with interest. Dicky looked up to see Werner's face. 'It's the tiny, dark-coloured ones that blow your head off,' Dicky explained. He took a large, pale-green cayenne and smiled at our doubting faces before biting a section from it.

There was a silence after Dicky's mouth closed upon the chilli. Everyone except Dicky knew he'd mistaken the cayenne for one of the very mild *aji* chillies from the eastern provinces. And soon Dicky knew it too. His face went red, his mouth half opened, and tears shone in his eyes. He fought against the pain but he had to take it from his mouth. Then he fed himself lots and lots of plain rice.

'The Biedermanns are a wealthy Berlin family,' said Zena, carrying on as if she'd not noticed Dicky's desperate discomfort. 'They are well known in Germany. They have interests in German travel companies. The newspapers said the company had borrowed millions of dollars to build a holiday village in the Yucatan peninsula. It's never been finished. Erich Stinnes thought I looked just like the younger sister Poppy who's always in the newspaper gossip columns.'

There was a silence as we all waited for Dicky to recover. Finally he leaned back in his chair and managed a rueful smile. There was perspiration on his forehead and he was breathing with his mouth open. 'Do you know these Biedermann people, Bernard?' said Dicky. He sounded hoarse.

'Have an avocado,' said Werner. 'They are very soothing.' Dicky took an avocado pear from the bowl and began to eat some.

I said, 'When my father was attached to the military government in Berlin he gave old Biedermann a licence to start up his bus service again. It was one of the first after the war; it started the family fortune, I suppose. Yes, I know them. Poppy Biedermann was having dinner at Frank Harrington's the last time I was in Berlin.'

Dicky was eating the avocado quickly with his teaspoon, using it to heal the burning in his mouth. 'That was bloody hot,' he confessed finally.

'There's no way you can be sure which are hot and which are mild,' said Zena in a gentle tone that surprised me. 'They cross-pollinate; even on the same plant you can get fiery ones and mild ones.' She smiled.

'Could these Biedermann people be interesting to Stinnes?' said Dicky. 'For instance, might they own a factory that's making computer software in California? Or something like that? What do you know about that, Bernard?'

'Even if that was the case, no point in making contact with the boss,' I said. I could see that Dicky had focused on the idea of Silicon Valley and it was not going to be easy to shake him off it. 'The approach would be made to someone in the microchip laboratory. Or someone doing the programs for the software.'

'We need to know the current situation from the California end,' said Dicky with a sigh. I knew that sigh. Dicky was just getting me prepared for a sweaty week in Mexico City while he went to swan around in southern California.

'Talk to the Biedermanns,' I said. 'It's easier.'

'Stinnes asked about the Biedermanns,' said Werner. 'He asked if I knew them. I used to know Paul very well, but I told Stinnes I knew the family only from the newspapers.'

'Werner, you didn't tell me you know the Biedermanns,' Zena interjected excitedly. 'They are always in the gossip columns. Poppy Biedermann is beautiful. She just got divorced from a millionaire.'

Dicky looked at me and said, 'Better you talk to Biedermann. No sense in me showing my face. Keep it informal. Find out where he is; go and see him. Would you do that, Bernard?' It was an order in the American style: disguised to sound like a polite inquiry.

'I can try.'

Dicky said, 'I don't want to channel this through London, or get Frank Harrington to introduce us, or the whole world will know we're interested.' He poured himself some iced water and sipped a little. He was recovering some of his composure, when suddenly he screamed, 'You bastard!', his eyes fixed on poor Werner and his head thrust forward low over the table. Werner looked perplexed until Dicky, still leaning forward with his head almost on his plate, yelled, 'That bloody cat.'

'Cherubino, you're very naughty,' said Zena mildly as she bent down to disengage the cat's claws from Dicky's leg. But by that time Dicky had delivered a kick that sent Cherubino across the room with a howl of pain.

Zena stood up, flushed and furious. 'You've hurt her,' she said angrily.

'I'm awfully sorry,' said Dicky. 'Just gave way to a reflex action, I'm afraid.'

Zena said nothing. She nodded and left the room in search of the cat.

'Paul Biedermann is approachable,' said Werner, to cover the awkward silence. 'He arranged a bank guarantee for me last year. It cost too much but he came through when I needed him. He has an office in town and a house on the coast at Tcumazan.' Werner looked at the door but there was no sign of Zena.

'There you are, then,' said Dicky. 'Get on to him, Bernard.'

I knew Paul Biedermann too; I'd exchanged hellos with him recently in Berlin and hardly recognized him. He'd smashed himself up driving a brand-new Ferrari back to Mexico from a drunken party in Guatemala City. At 120 miles an hour the car had gone deep into the roadside jungle. It took the rescuers a long time to find him, and a long time to cut him free. The girl with him had been killed, but the inquiry had glossed over it. Whatever the truth of it, now one of his legs was shorter than the other and his face bore the scar tissue of over a hundred neat stitches. These infirmities didn't help me overcome my dislike of Paul Biedermann.

'Just a verbal report. Nothing in writing for the time being. Not you, not me, not Biedermann.' Dicky was keeping all the exits covered. Nothing in writing until Dicky heard the results and arranged the blames and the credits with godlike impartiality.

Werner shot me a glance. 'Sure thing, Dicky,' I said. Dicky Cruyer was such a clown at times, but there was another, very clever Dicky who knew exactly what he wanted and how to get it. Even if it did sometimes mean giving way to one of those nasty little reflex actions.

3

The jungle stinks. Under the shiny greenery, and the brightly coloured tropical flowers that line the roadsides like the endless window displays of expensive florists, there is a squelchy mess of putrefaction that smells like a sewer. Sometimes the road was darkened by vegetation that met overhead, and strands of creeper fingered the car's roof. I wound the window closed for a moment, even though the air-conditioning didn't work.

Dicky wasn't with me. Dicky had flown to Los Angeles, giving me a contact phone number that was an office in the Federal Building. It was not far from the shops and restaurants of Beverly Hills, where by now he would no doubt be sitting beside a bright blue pool, clasping an iced drink, and studying a long menu with that kind of unstinting dedication that Dicky always gave to his own welfare.

The big blue Chevvy he'd left for me was not the right sort of car for these miserable winding jungle tracks. Imported duty-free by Tiptree, Dicky's embassy chum, it didn't have the hard suspension and reinforced chassis of locally bought cars. It bounced me up and down like a yo-yo in the pot-holes, and there were ominous scraping sounds when it hit the bumps. And the road to Tcumazan was all pot-holes and bumps.

I'd started very early that morning, intending to cross the Sierra Madre mountain range and be in a restaurant lingering over a late lunch to miss the hottest part of the day. In fact I spent the hottest part of the day crouched on a dusty road, with an audience of three children and a chicken, while I changed the wheel of a flat tyre and cursed Dicky, Henry Tiptree and his car, London Central and Paul Biedermann, particularly the last for having chosen to live in such a God-forsaken spot as Tcumazan, Michoacan, on Mexico's Pacific coast. It was a place to go only for those equipped with private planes or luxury yachts. Getting there from Mexico City in Tiptree's Chevvy was not recommended.

It was early evening when I reached the ocean at a village variously called 'Little San Pedro' or 'Santiago', according to who directed you. It was not on the map under either name; even the road leading there

was no more than a broken red line. Santiago consisted only of a
rubbish heap, some two dozen huts constructed of mud and old
corrugated iron, a prefabricated building surmounted by a large cross
and a cantina with a green tin roof. The cantina was held together
by enamelled advertisements for beer and soft drinks. They had been
nailed, sometimes upside-down or sideways, wherever cracks had
appeared in the walls. More adverts were urgently needed.

The village of Santiago is not a tourist resort. There were no
discarded film packets, paper tissues or vitamin containers to be seen
littering the streets or even on the dump. From the village there was
not even a view of the ocean; the waterfront was out of sight beyond
a flight of wide stone steps that led nowhere. There were no people
in sight; just animals – cats, dogs, a few goats and some fluttering
hens.

Alongside the cantina a faded red Ford sedan was parked. Only
after I pulled in alongside did I see that the Ford was propped up
on bricks and its inside gutted. There were more hens inside it. As
I locked up the Chevvy, people appeared. They were coming from
the rubbish heap: a honeycomb of tiny cells made from boxes,
flattened cans and oil-drums. It was a rubbish heap, but not exclusively so. No women or children emerged from the heap; just short,
dark-skinned men with those calm, inscrutable faces that are to be
seen in Aztec sculpture: an art form obsessed with brutality and
death.

The smell of the jungle was still there, but now there was also the
stink of human ordure. Dogs – their coats patchy with the symptoms
of mange – smelled each other and prowled around the garbage. One
outside wall of the cantina was entirely covered with a crudely painted
mural. The colours had faded but the outline of a red tractor carving
a path through tall grass, with smiling peasants waving their hands,
suggested that it was part of the propaganda for some long-forgotten
government agricultural plan.

It was still very hot, and my damp shirt clung to me. The sun was
sinking, long shadows patterned the dusty street, and electric bulbs,
which marked the cantina doorway, made yellow blobs in the blue
air. I stepped over a large mongrel dog that was asleep in the doorway
and pushed aside the small swing-doors. There was a fat, mousta-
chioed man behind the bar. He sat on a high stool, his head tipped
forward on to his chest as if he was sleeping. His feet were propped
high on the counter, the soles of his boots pushed against the drawer
of the cash register. When I entered the bar he looked up, wiped his
face with a dirty handkerchief and nodded without smiling.

There was an unexpected clutter inside; a random assortment of
Mexican aspirations. There were sepia-coloured family photos, the
frames cracked and wormeaten. Two very old Pan-American Airways

posters depicted the Swiss Alps and downtown Chicago. Even the girlie pictures revealed the ambivalent nature of machismo: Mexican film stars in decorous swimsuits and raunchy *gringas* torn from American porno magazines. In one corner there was a magnificent old jukebox but it was for decoration only; there was no machinery inside it. In the other corner there was an old oil-drum used as a urinal. The sound of Mexican music came quietly from a radio balanced over the shelf of tequila bottles that, despite their varying labels, looked as if they'd been refilled many times from the same jug.

I ordered a beer and told the *cantinero* to have one himself. He got two bottles from the refrigerator and poured them both together, holding two bottles in one hand and two glasses in the other. I drank some beer. It was dark, strong and very cold. '*Salud y pesetas*,' said the bartender.

I drank to 'health and money' and asked him if he knew anyone who could mend my punctured tyre. He didn't answer immediately. He looked me up and down and then craned his neck to see my Chevvy, although I had no doubt he'd watched me arrive. There was a man who could do such work, he said, after giving the matter some careful thought. It might be arranged, but the materials for doing such jobs were expensive and difficult to obtain. Many of the people who claimed such expertise were clumsy, inexpert men who would fix patches that, in the hot sun and on the bad roads, would leak air and leave a traveller stranded. The brakes, the steering and the tyres: these were the vital parts of a motor car. He himself did not own a car but one of his cousins had a car and so he knew about such things. And on these roads a stranded traveller could meet bad people, even *bandidos*. For a puncture I needed someone who could make such a vital repair properly.

I drank my beer and nodded sympathetically. In Mexico this was the way things were done; there was nothing to be gained by interrupting his explanation. It was for this that he got his percentage. He shouted loudly at the faces looking in through the doorway and they went away. No doubt they went to tell the man who fixed flats that his lucky day had finally come.

We each had another beer. The *cantinero's* name was Domingo. Awakened by the sound of the cash register, the dog looked up and growled. 'Be quiet, Pedro,' said the bartender and edged a small plate of chillies across the counter towards me. I declined. I left some money on the counter in front of me when I asked him how far it was to the Biedermann house. He looked at me quizzically before answering. It was a long, long way by road, and the road was very bad. Rain had washed it out in places. It always did at this time of year. On a motorcycle or even in a jeep it was possible. But in my Chevvy, which Domingo called my double bed – *cama matrimonial* –

there would be no chance of driving there. Better to take the track and go on foot, the way the villagers went. It would take no more than five minutes, maybe ten. Fifteen minutes at the most. If I was going up to the Biedermann house everything was okay.

Mr Biedermann owed me some money, I explained. Might I encounter trouble collecting it?

Domingo looked at me as if I'd just arrived from Mars. Didn't I know that Señor Biedermann was *muy rico, muy, muy rico*?

'How rich?' I asked.

'For no one does what he gives seem little, or what he has seem much,' said the bartender, quoting a Spanish proverb. 'How much does he owe you?'

I ignored his question. 'Is he up at the house now?' I fiddled with the money on the counter.

'He's not an easy man to get along with,' said Domingo. 'Yes, he's up at the house. He's there all alone. He can't get anyone to work for him any more, and his wife is seldom with him nowadays. He even does his own laundry. No one round here will work for him.'

'Why?'

Domingo put the tip of his thumb in his mouth and upended his fist to show me that Biedermann was a heavy drinker. 'He can get through two or three bottles of it when he's in one of his rages. Tequila, mezcal, aguardiente or imported whisky, it's all the same to him once he starts guzzling. Then he gets rough with anyone who won't drink with him. He hit one of the workmen mending the floor; the youngster had to go to the dispensary. Now the men refuse to finish the work.'

'Does he get rough with people who collect money?' I asked.

Domingo didn't smile. 'When he is not drinking he is a good man. Maybe he has troubles; who knows?'

We went back to talking about the car. Domingo would arrange for the repair of my tyre and look after the car. If the beer-delivery truck arrived it would perhaps be possible to deliver the car to the Biedermann house. No, I said, it was better if the car remained where it was; I'd seen a few beer-delivery drivers on the road.

'Is the track to the Biedermann house a good one?' I asked. I pushed some money to him.

'Whatever path you take, there is a league of bad road,' said Domingo solemnly. I hoped it was just another proverb.

I got my shoulder-bag from the car. It contained a clean shirt and underclothes, swimming trunks and towel, shaving kit, a big plastic bag, some string, a flashlight, some antibiotics, Lomatil and a half-bottle of rum for putting on wounds. No gun. Mexico is not a good place for gringos carrying guns.

I took the path that Domingo had shown me. It was a narrow track made by workers going between the crops and the village. It climbed steeply past the flight of stone steps that Domingo said was all that remained of an Aztec temple. It was sunny up here while the valleys were swallowed in shadow. I looked back to see the villagers standing round the Chevvy, Domingo parading before it in a proprietorial manner. Pedro cocked his leg to pee on the front wheel. Domingo looked up, as if sensing that I was watching, but he didn't wave. He wasn't a friendly man; just talkative.

I rolled down my shirt-sleeves against the mosquitoes. The track led along the crest of a scrub-covered hill. It skirted huge rocks and clumps of yucca, with sharp leaves that thrust into the skyline like swords. It was hard going on the stony path and I stopped frequently to catch my breath. Through the scrub-oak and pines I could see the purple mountains over which I'd driven. There were many mountains to the north. They were big, volcanic-looking, their distance – and thus their exact size – unresolved, but in the clear evening air everything looked sharp and hard, and nearer than it really was. Now and again, as I walked, I caught sight of the motor road that skirted the spur and came in a long detour up the coast. It looked like a damned bad road; I suppose only the Biedermanns ever used it.

It took me nearly an hour to get to the Biedermann house. I was almost there before I came over the ridge and caught sight of it. It was a small house of modern design, built of decorative woods and matt black steel, its foundations set into the rocks upon which the Pacific Ocean dashed huge breakers. One side of the house was close to a patch of jungle that went right to the water's edge. There was a little pocket of sandy beach there, and from it ran a short wooden pier. There was no boat in sight, no cars anywhere, and the house was dark.

A chainlink fence that surrounded the grounds of the house had been damaged by a landslide, and the wire was cut and bent up to provide a gap big enough to get through. The makeshift track continued after the damaged fence and ended in a steep scramble up to a patch of grass. There were flowers here; white and pink camellias and floribunda and the inevitable purple bougainvillaea. Everything had been landscaped to hide the place where a new macadam road ended at the double garage and shaded carport. But there were no cars to be seen, and wooden crates blocked the white garage doors.

So Paul Biedermann had taken flight despite the appointment I'd made with him. I was not surprised. There had always been a streak of cowardice in him.

I had no difficulty getting inside the house. The front door was locked but a ladder left on the grass reached to one of the balconies. The sliding window, secured only by a plastic clip, was easy enough to force.

There was still enough daylight coming through the window for me to see that the master bedroom had been tidied and cleaned with that rigorous care that is the sign of leave-taking. The huge double bed was stripped of linen and covered with clear plastic covers. Two small carpets were rolled up and sealed into bags that would protect them from termites. Torn up and in the waste-paper basket I found half a dozen Mexico City airport luggage tags dating from some previous journey, and three new and unused airline shoulder-bags not required for the next. The sort of airline bags that come free with airline tickets were not something that the Biedermanns let their servants carry. I stood listening, but the house was completely silent. There was only the sound of the big Pacific Ocean waves battering against the rocks below the house and roaring their displeasure.

I opened one of the wardrobes. It smelled of moth repellent. There were clothes there: a man's cream-coloured linen suits, brightly coloured pants and sweaters, handmade shoes – treed and in shoe-bags embroidered 'P.B.' – and drawers filled with shirts and underclothes.

In the other wardrobe, a woman's dresses, expensive lingerie folded into tissue paper and a multitude of shoes of every type and colour. On the dressing table there was a photo of Mr and Mrs Biedermann in swimsuits standing on a diving board and smiling self-consciously. It had been taken before the car accident.

The three guest bedrooms on the top floor – each with separate balcony overlooking the ocean and private bathroom – had all been stripped bare. Inside the house, a gallery that gave access to the bedrooms was open on one side to overlook the big lounge downstairs. All the furniture was covered in dustsheets, and to one side of the lounge there was a bucket of dirty water, a trowel, some adhesive and dirty rags marking a place where a large section of flooring was being retiled.

Only when I got to Biedermann's study, built to provide a view of the whole coastline, was there any sign of recent occupancy. It was an office; or, more exactly, it was a room furnished with that special sort of luxury furniture that can be tax-deducted as office equipment. There was a big puffy armchair, a drinks cabinet, and a magnificent wood-inlay desk. In the corner there was that sort of daybed that Hollywood calls a 'casting couch'. On it there were blankets roughly folded and a soiled pillow. A big waste-bin contained computer print-out and some copies of the *Wall Street Journal*. More confidential print-out was now a tangle of paper worms in the clear plastic bag of the shredder. But the notepads were blank, and the expensive desk diary – the flowers of South America, one for every week of the year in full colour, printed in Rio de Janeiro – never used. There were no books apart from business reference books and phone and telex directories. Paul Biedermann had never been much of a reader at school but he'd always been good at counting.

I tried the electric light but it did not work. A house built out here on the edge of nowhere would be dependent upon a generator operating only when the house was occupied. By the time I had searched the house and found no one, the daylight was going fast. The sea had turned the darkest of purples and the western skyline had almost vanished.

I went back up to the top floor and chose the last guest room along the gallery as a place to spend the night. I found a blanket in the wardrobe and, choosing one of the plastic-covered beds, I covered myself against the cold mist that rolled in off the sea. It soon became too dark to read and, as my interest in the *Wall Street Journal* waned, I drifted off to sleep, lulled by the sound of the waves.

It was 2.35 when I was awakened by the car. I saw its lights flashing over the ceiling long before I heard its engine. At first I thought it was just a disturbed dream, but then the bright patch of light flashed across the ceiling again and I heard the diesel engine. It never struck me that it might be Paul Biedermann or any of the family coming home. I knew instinctively that there was danger.

I slid open the glass door and went outside on to the balcony. The weather had become stormy. Thin ragged clouds raced across the moon, and the wind had risen so that its roar was confused with the sound of the breakers on the rocks below. I watched the car. The headlights were high and close together, a configuration that suggested some jeep-like vehicle, as did the way it negotiated the bad road. It was still going at speed as it swung round the back to the garage area. The driver had been here before.

There were two voices; one of the men had a key to the front door. I went through the guest bedroom and crouched on the interior gallery so that I could hear them speaking in the lounge below.

'He's run away,' said one voice.

'Perhaps,' said the other, as if he didn't care. They were speaking in German. There was no mistaking the Berlin accent of Erich Stinnes, but the other man's German had a strong Russian accent.

'His car is not here,' said the first man. 'What if the Englishmen arrived before us and took him off with them?'

'We would have passed them on the road,' said Stinnes. He was perfectly calm. I heard the sound of him putting his weight on to the big sofa. 'That's better.' A sigh. 'Take a drink if you want it. It's in the cabinet in his study.'

'That stinking jungle road. I could do with a bath.'

'You call that jungle?' said Stinnes mildly. 'Wait till you go over to the east coast. Wait until you go across to the training camp where the freedom fighters are trained, and cut your way through some real tropical rain forest with a machete, and spend half the night digging chiggers out of your backside. You'll find out what a jungle is like.'

'What we came through will do for me,' said the first man.

I raised my head over the edge of the gallery until I could see them. They were standing in the moonlight by the tall window. They were wearing dark suits and white shirts and trying to look like Mexican businessmen. Stinnes was about forty years old: my age. He had shaved off the little Lenin-style beard he'd had when I last saw him but there was no mistaking his accent or the hard eyes glittering behind the circular gold-rimmed spectacles.

The other man was much older, fifty at least. But he was not frail. He had shoulders like a wrestler, cropped head and the restless energy of the athlete. He looked at his watch and then out of the window and then walked over to the place where the tiles were being repaired. He kicked the trowel so that it went skidding across the floor and hit the wall with a loud noise.

'I told you to have a drink,' said Stinnes. He did not defer to the other man.

'I said you should frighten Biedermann. Well, you've frightened him all right. It looks as if you've frightened him so much that he's cleared out of here. That's not what they wanted you to do.'

'I didn't frighten him at all,' said Stinnes calmly. 'I didn't take your advice. He's already too frightened. He needs reassurance. But he'll surface sooner or later.'

'Sooner or later,' repeated the elder man. 'You mean he'll surface after you've gone back to Europe and be someone else's problem. If it was left to me, I'd make Biedermann a number-one priority. I'd alert every last KGB team in Central America. I'd teach him that an order is an order.'

'Yes, I know,' said Stinnes. 'It's all so easy for you people who sit at desks all your life. But Biedermann is just one small part of a complicated plan . . . and neither of us knows exactly what the plan is.'

It was a patronizing reproach, and the elder man's soft voice did not conceal the anger in him. 'I say he's the weak link in the chain, my friend.'

'Perhaps he is supposed to be just that,' said Stinnes complacently. 'One day maybe the Englishwoman will put *you* in charge of one of her crazy schemes, and then you'll be able to ignore orders and show everyone what a clever man you are in the field. But until that time you'll do things the way you're ordered to do them, no matter how stupid it all seems.' He got to his feet. 'I'll have a drink, even if you don't want one. Biedermann has good brandy.'

Stinnes passed below me out of sight and I heard him go into the study and pour drinks. When he returned he was carrying two glasses.

'It will calm you, Pavel. Have patience; it will work out all right. You can't rush these things. You'll have to get used to that. It's not like chasing Moscow dissidents.' He gave the elder man a glass and they both drank. 'French brandy. Schnapps and beer are not worth drinking unless they come from a refrigerator.' He drank. 'Ah, that's better. I'll be glad to be back in Berlin, if only for a brief spell.'

'I was in Berlin in 1953,' said the elder man. 'Did you know that?'

'So was I,' said Stinnes.

'In '53? Doing what?'

Stinnes chuckled. 'I was only ten years old. My father was a soldier. My mother was in the army too. We were all kept in the barracks during the disturbances.'

'Then you know nothing. I was in the thick of it. The bricklayers and builders working on those Stalinallee sites started all the trouble. It began as a protest against a ten per cent increase in work norms. They marched on the House of Ministries in Leipzigerstrasse and demanded to see the Party leader, Ulbricht.' He laughed. It was a low, manly laugh. 'But it was the poor old Mining Minister who was sent out to face them. I was twenty. I was with the Soviet Control Commission. My chief dressed me up like a German building worker and sent me out to mix with the mob. I was never so frightened in all my life.'

'With your accent you had every cause to be frightened,' said Stinnes.

His colleague was not amused. 'I kept my mouth shut; but I kept my ears open. That night the strikers marched across to the RIAS radio station in West Berlin and wanted their demands to be transmitted over the Western radio. Treacherous German swine.'

'What were their demands?' asked Stinnes.

'The usual: free and secret elections, cuts in the work norms, no punishment for the trouble-makers.' The older man drank some more. He was calmer now that he'd had a drink. 'I advised my people to bring our boys out to clear the streets the way we'd cleared them in 1945. I told them to announce an immediate curfew and give the army shoot-on-sight orders.

'But they didn't,' said Stinnes.

'I was only twenty years old. The men who'd fought in the war had no time for kids like me. The Control Commission was not taken seriously. So they sat up all night hoping that everything would be all right in the morning.'

'The disturbances spread next day.'

'By 11 a.m. on 17th June they were tearing the red flag down from the Brandenburg Gate and ransacking the Party offices.'

'But the army sat on it, didn't they?'

'Eventually they had to. There were strikes all over the country:

Dresden, Leipzig, Jena and Gera, even in Rostock and the Baltic island of Rügen. It took a long time before things settled down. They should have acted immediately. Since then I've had no sympathy for people who tell me to have patience because everything will come out all right.'

'And that's what you'd like me to do now?' asked Stinnes mockingly. 'Bring our boys out to clear the streets the way we cleared them in 1945? Announce an immediate curfew and give the army shoot-on-sight orders?'

'You know what I mean.'

'You have no idea what this business is all about, Pavel. You've spent your career running typewriters; I've spent mine running people.'

'What do you mean?'

'You rush in like a rapist when we are in the middle of a seduction. Do you really think you can march agents up and down like Prussian infantry? Don't you understand that men such as Biedermann have to be romanced?'

'We should never use agents who are not politically dedicated to us,' said Pavel.

Stinnes went to the window and I could see him clearly in the moonlight as he looked at the sea. Outside, the wind was roaring through the trees and making thumping noises against the windows. Stinnes held his drink up high and swirled it round to see the expensive brandy cling to the glass. 'You've still got that passion that I once had,' said Stinnes. 'How do you hang on to all your illusions, Pavel?'

'You're a cynic,' said the elder man. 'I might as well ask how you continue doing your job without believing in it.'

'Believing?' said Stinnes, drinking some of the brandy and turning back to face his companion. 'Believing what? Believing in my job or believing in the socialist revolution?'

'You talk as if the two beliefs are incompatible.'

'Are they compatible? Can a "workers' and peasants' state" need so many secret policemen like us?'

'There is a threat from without,' said the elder man, using the standard Party cliché.

'Do you know what Brecht wrote after the 17th June uprising? Brecht I'm talking about, not some Western reactionary. Brecht wrote a poem called "The Solution". Did you ever read it?'

'I've no time for poetry.'

'Brecht asked, would it not be easier for the government to dissolve the people, and vote itself another?'

'Do you know what people say of you in Moscow?' the older man asked. 'They say, is this man a Russian or is he a German?'

'And what do you say when people ask that question of you, Pavel?'

'I had never met you,' said the elder man, 'I knew you only by reputation.'

'And now? Now that you've met me?'

'You like speaking German so much that sometimes I think you've forgotten how to speak Russian.'

'I haven't forgotten my mother tongue, Pavel. But it is good for you to practise German. Even more you need Spanish, but your appalling Spanish hurts my ears.'

'You use your German name so much, I wonder if you are ashamed of your father's name.'

'I'm not ashamed, Pavel. Stinnes was my operational name and I have retained it. Many others have done the same.'

'You take a German wife and I wonder if Russian girls were not good enough for you.'

'I was on active service when I married, Pavel. There were no objections then as I remember.'

'And now I hear you talk of the June '53 uprising as if you sympathized with the German terrorists. What about our Russian boys whose blood was spilled restoring law and order?'

'My loyalty is not in question, Pavel. My record is better than yours, and you know that.'

'But you don't believe any more.'

'Perhaps I never did believe in the way that you believe,' said Stinnes. 'Perhaps that's the answer.'

'There's no half-way,' said the elder man. 'Either you accept the Party Congress and its interpretation of Marxist-Leninism or you are a heretic.'

'A heretic?' said Stinnes, feigning interest. '*Extra ecclesiam nulla salus*; no salvation is possible outside the Church. Is that it, Pavel? Well, perhaps I am a heretic. And it's your misfortune that the Party prefers that, and so does the service. A heretic like me does not lose his faith.'

'You don't care about the struggle,' said the elder man. 'You can't even be bothered to search the house.'

'There's no car, and no boat at the dock. Do you think a man such as Biedermann would come on foot through the jungle that frightens you so much?'

'You knew he wouldn't be here.'

'He's a thousand miles away by now,' said Stinnes. 'He's rich. A man like that can go anywhere at a moment's notice. Perhaps you haven't been in the West long enough to understand how difficult that makes our job.'

'Then why did we drag out here through that disgusting jungle?'

'You know why we came. We came because Biedermann told us

the Englishman phoned and said he was coming here. We came because the stupid woman in Berlin sent a priority telex last night telling us to come here.'

'And you wanted to prove Berlin was wrong. You wanted to prove you know better than she knows.'

'Biedermann is a liar. We have found that over and over again.'

'Then let's get on the road back,' said the older man. 'You've proved your point; now let's get back to Mexico City, back to electric light and hot water.'

'The house must be searched. You are right, Pavel. Take a look round. I will wait here.'

'I have no gun.'

'If anyone kills you, Pavel, I will get them.'

The elder man hesitated as if about to argue, but he went about his task, nervously poking about with his flashlight, while Stinnes watched him with ill-concealed contempt. He came upstairs too but he was an amateur. I stepped outside to avoid him. I need not have bothered even to do that, for he did little more than shine a light through the doorway to see if the bed was occupied. After no more than ten minutes he was back in the lounge telling Stinnes that the house was empty. 'Now can we go back?'

'You've gone soft, Pavel. Is that why Moscow sent you to be my assistant?'

'You know why Moscow sent me here,' the elder man grumbled.

Stinnes laughed briefly and I heard him put his glass down on the table. 'Yes, I read your personal file. For "political realignment". Whatever did you do in Moscow that the department thinks you are not politically reliable?'

'Nothing. You know very well that that bastard got rid of me because I discovered he was taking bribes. One day his turn will come. A criminal like that cannot survive for ever.'

'But meanwhile, Pavel, you suit me fine. You are politically unreliable and so the one man I can be sure will not report my unconventional views.'

'You are my superior officer, Major Stinnes,' said the older man stuffily.

'That's right. Well, let's head back. You'll drive for the first couple of hours. I will drive when we reach the mountains. If you see anything in the road drive over it. Too many people get killed on these roads swerving to avoid eyes they see shining in the headlights.'

4

I didn't sleep again after they departed. I dozed fitfully but imagined I could hear their diesel car returning, with the alternate roars and screams that a really bad surface racks from a small engine. But it was just the wind, and then, as dawn came and the storm passed over, I was kept awake by the screeching and chattering of the animals. They came right down to the water through the thick undergrowth that bordered one side of the house. There was a stream there; it passed close by a window of Paul Biedermann's study. I suppose he liked to watch the animals. It was an aspect of Biedermann's character that I'd not yet encountered.

Dawn shone its hard grey light and made the sea look like granite. I went down to the kitchen and found some canned food: beans and tomatoes. I could find no way of warming the mixture so I ate a plateful cold. I was hungry.

From the kitchen window there was a view back towards the village. That way the sky was light pink. I counted seven vultures, circling very high and looking for breakfast. Nearer to the house there were birds in the trees making a lot of noise, and monkeys scrambling about in the lower branches with occasional forays into the garden.

I would have given a lot for a cup of coffee, but instant powder stirred into cold tinned milk did not appeal. I made do with a shot of Biedermann's brandy. It was everything Stinnes said about it. So good, in fact, that I took another.

Fortified by the strong drink, and one of Biedermann's fancy striped sweaters chosen from his wardrobe, I went outside. The sky was overcast to give a cold shadowless light and, although the black clouds had gone, there was still a cold wind from the ocean. The tyre marks of the jeep were to be seen on the roadway. I followed the new macadam road to the entrance gate. It was open, its chain freshly cut. Despite the borrowed sweater I was cold, and colder still as I circled the house completely, crossed the patio that was sheltered from the wind, and climbed up the hill at the back to the highest point of rock. I couldn't see the road or the village but there was a haze of woodsmoke rising from where I guessed the village must be. I couldn't see any sign of Biedermann or his car. That was the first time I'd noticed the swimming pool. It was about two hundred metres from the house and hidden by a line of junipers planted by some landscape gardener for that purpose.

The pool was big, and very blue. And full length on the bottom, at the deep end, was a human figure. At first I thought it was a drowning case. Wrapped in cheap grey blankets, the figure made a shapeless bundle that almost disappeared in the dark depths of blue shade. It was only when I got past the wooden building that housed four changing rooms and filtering and heating equipment that I was sure that the pool was dry and drained.

'Hey!' I shouted at the inert figure. '*Tu que haces?*'

Very slowly the blankets became unravelled to reveal a man dressed in badly wrinkled white trousers and a T-shirt advertising Underberg. One of his bare sunburned arms bore a lacework of neat white scar tissue, and so did one side of his face. He blinked and squinted into the light, trying to see me against the glaring sky.

'Paul Biedermann,' I shouted. 'What the hell are you doing in the pool?'

'You came,' he said. His voice was hoarse and he coughed to clear his throat. 'The others have gone? How did you get here?'

'It's Bernd,' I said. 'We spoke on the phone; Bernd Samson. I walked. Yes, the other two drove away hours ago.' He must have been watching the road. My approach along the track had gone unobserved from wherever he'd been hiding.

Wrapped into his blanket I could see a hunting rifle. Biedermann pushed it away as he bent his head forward almost to his knees and stretched his arms. Then he rubbed his legs and arms, trying to restore his circulation. It must have been very uncomfortable on the hard, cold surface of the concrete pool all night. He looked up and then smiled as he recognized me. It was a severe smile, twisted by the puckered scars that marked one side of his face.

'Bernd. Are you alone?' he said, trying to make it sound as if it meant no more to him than how many cups of coffee to order. His face and arms were blue; it was the light reflected from the painted sides of the pool.

'They've gone,' I said. 'Come and switch the electricity on, and make me a cup of coffee.'

He slung the rifle on his shoulder and climbed up the ladder of the empty pool. He left the blanket where it was. I wondered if he intended to spend another uncomfortable night here.

He moved about like an automaton. Once inside the house he showed me all the things I should have found for myself. There was bottled gas for cooking, a generator for lighting, and a battery-powered Sony short-wave radio. He boiled water and measured out coffee in silence. It was as if he wanted to take as long as he could to defer the start of the conversation. Even when we were both seated in his study, hands clasped round cups of strong black coffee, he still didn't offer any explanation about his curious behaviour. I said nothing. I waited for him to speak. It was usually better that way and I wanted to see how he would start, and even more importantly what he would avoid.

'I've got everything,' said Paul Biedermann. 'Plenty of money, my health, and a wife who stood by me after the accident. Even after that girl was killed in my car.' It was hard to believe that this was the nervous schoolboy I'd known in Berlin. It was not just the strong American accent he'd acquired at his expensive East Coast school but something in his poise and his manner too. Paul Biedermann had become unreservedly American in a way that only Germans are able to do.

'That was a nasty business,' I said.

'I was unconscious three days. I was in hospital almost six months altogether, counting the convalescence. Six months; and I hate hospitals.' He drank some coffee. It was a heavy Mexican coffee that Biedermann had made into a devil's brew that made my teeth tingle. 'But then I got entangled with those bastards and I haven't slept properly ever since. Do you know that, Bernd? It's the literal truth that I haven't slept really well since the start of it.'

'Is that so,' I said. I didn't want to sit there with my tongue hanging out. I wanted to sound casual; bored, almost. But I wanted to know, especially after I'd heard Stinnes and his pal talking about Biedermann as if he was a KGB agent.

'The Russians,' said Biedermann, 'spies and all that. You know what I'm talking about, don't you?' He was looking over my shoulder as if he wanted to see the animals and birds in the trees outside.

'I know what you're talking about, Paul,' I said.

'Because you're in all that, aren't you?'

'In a manner of speaking,' I said

'I was talking to my sister Poppy. She met you at a dinner party at the house of one of the big Berlin spy chiefs. You're one of them, Bernd. You probably always have been. Was that why your father sent you to school in Berlin, instead of sending you back to England the way the other British families sent their kids back there to go to school?'

'Who were they, Paul? Who were those men who came in the night?'

'I didn't see you arrive. I was out with the gun, shooting lizards. I hate lizards, don't you? Those Russkies are like lizards, aren't they?

Especially the one with glasses. I knew they would come, and I was right.'

'How well do you know them?'

'They pass me around like a parcel. I've dealt with so many different Russians that I've almost lost count. These two were sent from Berlin. The one with the strong Berlin accent calls himself Stinnes but he's not really a German, he's a Russian. The other one calls himself Pavel Moskvin. It sounds like a phoney name, doesn't it? I still haven't figured out if they work from Moscow or are part of the East German intelligence service. What do you think, Bernd?'

'Moskvin means "man from Moscow". It could be a genuine name. Do they have diplomatic cover?'

'They said they do.'

'Then they are Russians. The KGB give almost all their people diplomatic cover. The East Germans don't. They work mostly in West Germany and infiltrate their agents among the refugees going there.'

'Why?'

'It's part of the overall contingency plan. East German agents in West Germany are hard to find. They don't need the cover. And in other parts of the world East German networks survive after Russians with diplomatic cover are discovered and kicked out.'

'They never answer any questions. I thought they'd leave me alone, now that I spend most of the year in Mexico.' Not most of the time but most of the year. Most of the financial year; it was a fiscal measurement of time.

'How did you get entangled with the Russians, Paul?' I asked, carefully using his own words.

'What am I supposed to do? I've got half my family still living over there in Rostock. Am I supposed to tell them to go to hell so that they take it out on my aunts and uncles?'

'Yes, that's what you're supposed to do,' I said.

'Well, I didn't,' said Biedermann. 'I played along with them. I told them I'd do nothing serious but I played along when they asked for run-of-the-mill jobs.'

'What did they get you to do?'

'Laundering money. They never asked me to give them money – they seem to have plenty of that to throw around. They wanted Deutschmarks changed into dollars, Swedish kronor changed into Mexican pesos and vice versa, Latin American currencies changed into Dutch guilders.'

'They could have all that done at a money exchange in West Berlin.'

He smiled and stared at something beyond me and drank his coffee. '*Ja*,' he said, forgetting for a moment that we were speaking English. He touched the side of his face as if discovering the terrible scars for the first time. 'There was a difference; the money was sent to me in large cash transfers and I had to pass it on in small contributions and donations.'

'Pass it on how?'

'By mail.'

'In small amounts?'

'One hundred dollars, two hundred dollars. Never more than five hundred dollars – or the equivalent amount in whatever currency.'

'Cash?'

'Oh yes, cash. Strictly no cheques.' He shifted uneasily in his seat, and I had the feeling that he now regretted this confession. 'High-denomination notes in plain envelopes. No registered letters; that would mean a lot of names and addresses and post-office forms. Too risky, that sort of thing, they said.'

'And where has all this money been going to?'

He put his coffee on the table and began searching the pockets of his pants as if looking for a cigarette. Then he stood up and looked round. Eventually he found a silver box on the table. He took one for himself. Then he offered the open box to me. It was, of course, that sort of evasive temporizing that armchair psychologists call 'displacement activity'. Before he could repeat the whole performance in pursuit of matches, I threw him mine. He lit his cigarette and then waved the smoke away from his face nervously. 'You know where it's been going to, Bernd. Trade unions, peace movements, "ban the bomb" groups. Moscow can't be seen making donations to them. The money has to come from "little people" all over the world. You weren't born yesterday, Bernd. We all know the way it's done.'

'Yes, we all know the way it's done, Paul.' I swung round to see him. On the side-table there was the bottle of brandy that Stinnes and I had plundered. I wondered if that was what had attracted his gaze when he had stared over my shoulder. He wasn't looking at it now; he was looking at me.

'Don't damn well sneer at me. I've got my relatives to worry about. And if I hadn't koshered their bloody contributions someone else would do it for them. It's not going to change the history of the world, is it?' He was still moving round the room, looking at the furnishings as if seeing them for the first time.

'I don't know what it's going to do, Paul. You're the one that had the expensive education: schools in Switzerland, schools in America and two years' postgraduate studies at Yale. You tell me if it's going to change the history of the world.'

'You weren't so high and mighty in the old days,' said Biedermann. 'You weren't so superior when you sold me that old Ferrari that kept breaking down.'

'It was a good car. I had no trouble with it,' I said. 'I only sold it

because I went to London. You should have looked after it better.'
What a memory he had. I'd quite forgotten selling him that car.
Maybe that's how the rich got richer – by remembering in resentful
detail every transaction they made.

He kept his cigarette in his mouth and, still standing, fingered the
keys of the computer as if about to use it. 'It's getting more and more
difficult,' he said. He turned to look at me, the smoke of the cigarette
rising across his face like a fine veil and going into his eyes so that
he was squinting. 'Now that the Mexicans have nationalized the
banks, and the peso has dropped through the floor, there are endless
regulations about foreign exchange. It's not so easy to handle these
transactions without attracting attention.'

'So tell your Russians that,' I suggested.

'I don't want them to solve my problems. I want to get out of the
whole business.'

'Tell them that.'

'And risk what happens to my relatives?'

'You talk as though you are some sort of master spy,' I said. 'If
you tell them you've had enough of it, that will be the end of it.'

'They'd kill me,' he said.

'Rubbish,' I said. 'You're not important enough for them to waste
time or effort on.'

'They'd make an example of me. They'd cut my throat and make
sure everyone knew why.'

'They'd not make an example of you,' I said. 'How could they?
The last thing they want to do is draw attention to their secret
financing network. No, as long as they thought you'd keep their
secrets, they'd let you go, Paul. They'd huff and puff and shout and
threaten in the hope you'd get frightened enough to keep going. But
once they saw you were determined to end it they'd reconcile themselves to that.'

'If only I could believe it.' He blew a lot of smoke. 'One of the
new clerks in my Mexico City office – a German fellow – has been
asking me questions about some of the money I sent out. It's just a
matter of time . . .'

'You don't let the staff in your office address the envelopes, do
you?'

'No, of course not. But I do the envelopes on the addressing
machine. I can't sit up all night writing out envelopes.'

'You're a fool, Paul.'

'I know,' he said sadly. 'This German kid was updating the address
lists and he noticed these charities and trade unions that were all
coded in the same way. It was in a different code from all the other
addresses. I said it was part of my Christmas charity list but I'm not
sure he believed me.'

'You'd better transfer him to one of your other offices,' I said.

'I'm going to send him to Caracas but it won't really solve the problem. Some other clerk will notice. I can't address the envelopes by hand and have handwritten evidence all over the place, can I?'

'Why are you telling me all this, Paul?'

'I've got to talk it over with someone.'

'Don't give me that,' I said.

He stubbed out his cigarette and said, 'I told the Russians that the British secret service was becoming suspicious. I invented stories about strangers making inquiries at various offices.'

'Did they believe that?'

'Phone calls. I always said the inquiries were phone calls. So I didn't have to describe anyone's physical appearance.' He went over to the side-table and picked up the bottle of brandy. He put it into a cupboard and shut the door. It looked like the simple action of a tidy man who didn't want to see bottles of booze standing around in his office.

'That was clever,' I said, although I thought such a device would sound very unconvincing to any experienced case officer.

'I knew they'd have to give me a respite if I was under surveillance.'

'And talking to me is a part of that scheme? Did you tell them about my phone call? Was it that that gave you the idea? Is that why they came here last night?'

He didn't answer my question, and that convinced me that my guess was right. Biedermann had thought up all this nonsense about the British becoming suspicious only after I'd phoned him. He said, 'You're something in the espionage business, you've admitted that. I realize you're not in any sort of senior position, but you must know people who are. And you're the only contact I have.'

I grunted. I didn't know whether that was Paul Biedermann's sincere opinion or whether he was hoping to provoke me into claiming power and influence.

'Does that mean you can help?' he said.

I finished the coffee and got to my feet. 'You copy that list of addresses for me – London might be interested in that – and I'll make sure that Bonn is told that we are investigating you. You'll become what NATO intelligence calls "sacred". None of the other security teams will investigate you without informing us. That will get back to your masters quickly enough.'

'Wait a moment, Bernd. I don't want Bonn restricting my movements or opening my mail.'

'You can't have it both ways, Paul. "Sacred" is the lowest category we have. There's not much chance that Bonn will find that interesting enough to do anything: they'll leave you to us.'

Biedermann didn't look too pleased at the idea of his reputation suffering, but he realized it was the best offer he was likely to get. 'Don't double-cross me,' he said.

'How would I do that?'

'I'm not up for sale to the highest bidder. I want out. I don't want to exchange a master in Moscow for a master in London.'

'You make me laugh, Paul,' I said. 'You really think you're a master spy, don't you? Are you sure you want to get out, or do you really want to get in deeper?'

'I need help, Bernd.'

'Where did you hide your car?'

'You can drive along the beach when the tide is out.'

I should have thought of that one. The tide comes in and washes away the tyre tracks. It had fooled Stinnes and his pal too. Sometimes amateurs can teach the pros a trick or two. 'The tide is out now,' I said. 'Get it and give me a lift into the village, will you, before someone starts renting my Chevvy out as a bijou residence.'

'Keep the sweater,' he said. 'It looks good on you.'

5

'*Muy complicado*,' said Dicky. We were elbowing our way through a huge cobbled plaza that twice a week became one of Mexico City's busiest street markets, and he was listening to my account of the trip to Paul Biedermann's house. It was what Dicky called combining business with pleasure. '*Muy* bloody *complicado*,' he said reflectively. That was Dicky's way of saying he didn't understand.

'Not *very* complicated,' I said. I'd found Biedermann's story depressingly simple – too simple, perhaps, to be the whole truth – but not complicated.

'Biedermann hiding in the bloody pool all night clasping a gun?' said Dicky with heavy irony. 'No, not complicated at all, of course.' He'd been chewing the nail of his little finger and now he inspected it. 'You're not telling me you believed all that stuff?'

The sun was very hot. Towering cumulus clouds were building up to the east and the humidity was becoming intolerable. We were walking down a line of vendors selling secondhand hardware that varied from ancient spark plugs to fake Nazi medals. Dicky stopped to look at some broken pottery figurines that a handwritten notice said were ancient Olmec. Dicky picked one up and looked at it. It looked too new to be genuine, but then so did many of the fragments in the National Museum.

Dicky passed it to me and walked on. I put it back on the ground with the other junk. I had too many broken fragments in my life already. I found Dicky looking at a basketful of silver-plated bracelets. 'I must get some little presents to take back to London,' he said.

'Which parts of Biedermann's story do you think were not true?' I asked him.

'Never mind the exam questions,' snapped Dicky. He didn't want to be in Mexico; he wanted to be in London making sure his job was secure. In some perverse way he blamed me for his situation, although, God knows, no one would have waved goodbye to him with more pleasure.

He began bargaining with the Indian squatting behind the folk-art jewellery. After a series of offers and counter-offers, Dicky agreed to buy six of them. He crouched down and solemnly began to sort through all of them to find the best six.

'I'm asking you what you believe and what you don't believe,' I said. 'Hell, Dicky. You're in charge. I need to know.'

Still crouched down, he looked at me from under the eyelashes that made him the heart-throb of the typing pool. He knew I was goading him. 'You think I've been swanning around in Los Angeles wasting my time and the department's money, don't you?' Dicky was looking very Hollywood since his return from California. The faded jeans had gone, replaced by striped seersucker trousers and a short-sleeved green safari shirt with loops to hold rhino bullets.

'Why would I think that?'

Satisfied with his choice of bracelets, he sorted out his Mexican money and paid for them. He smiled and put the bracelets in the pocket of his shirt. 'I saw Frank Harrington in LA. You didn't know I was going to see Frank, did you?'

Frank Harrington headed the Berlin Field Unit. He was an old experienced Whitehall warrior with influence where it really counted: at the very top. I didn't like the idea of Dicky sliding off to meetings with him, especially meetings from which I was deliberately excluded. 'No, I didn't know.'

'Frank was attending some CIA powwow and I buttonholed him to talk about Stinnes.' We'd got to the end of the line and Dicky turned to go up the next row of stalls; brightly coloured fruit and vegetables on one side and broken furniture on the other. 'This is not just another Mexican street market,' said Dicky, who'd insisted that we come here. 'This is a *tiangui* – an Indian market. Not many tourists get to see them.'

'It might have been better to have come earlier. It's always so damned hot by lunchtime.'

Dicky chuckled scornfully. 'If I don't jog and have a decent breakfast I can't get going.'

'Perhaps we should have found a hotel right here in town. Going backwards and forwards to Cuernavaca eats up a lot of time.'

'A couple of miles jogging every morning would do you good, Bernard. You're putting on a lot of weight. It's all that stodge you eat.'

'I like stodge,' I said.

'Don't be ridiculous. Look at all these wonderful fresh vegetables and delicious fruit. Look at those great heaps of chillies. There must be fifty different kinds. I wish I'd brought the camera with me now.'

'Does Frank know anything about Stinnes?'

'Ye gods. Frank knows everyone in Berlin. You know that, Bernard. Frank says Stinnes is one of their brightest people. Frank has a fat file on him, and all his activities from one end of the world to the other.'

I nodded. Frank always claimed to have fat files on everything when he was away from his office. It was only when you were with him in Berlin that the 'fat file' turned out to be a small pink card with 'Refer to Data Centre' scribbled on it. 'Good old Frank,' I said.

This end of the market beyond the vegetables was occupied by food stalls. Almost everyone in the market seemed to be eating. They were eating and buying, eating and selling, eating and chatting, and even eating as they smoked and drank. Some of the more dedicated were sitting down to eat, and for these aficionados seats were provided. There were chairs and stools of every kind, age and size, with nothing in common but their infirmity.

Most of the stalls had steaming pots from which stewed mixtures of rice, chicken, pork and every variety of beans were being served. There were charcoal grills too, laden with pieces of scorching meat that filled the air with smoke and appetizing smells. And the ever-present tortillas were being eaten as fast as they could be kneaded, rolled out and cooked. An old lady came up to Dicky and handed him a tortilla. Dicky was disconcerted and tried to argue with her.

'She wants you to feel the texture and admire the colour,' I said.

Dicky gave her one of his big smiles, fingered it as if he was going to have it made up into a three-piece suit, and handed it back with a lot of '*Gracias, adios*'.

'Stinnes speaks excellent Spanish,' I said. 'Did Frank tell you anything about that?'

'You were right about Stinnes. He went to Cuba to sort out some of their security problems. He did so well that he became the KGB's Caribbean trouble-shooter all through the early seventies. He's been to just about all the places where the Cubans have sent soldiers; and that's a lot of travelling.'

'Does Frank know why Stinnes is here?'

'I think you've answered that already,' said Dicky. 'He's here running your friend Biedermann.' He looked at me and, when I didn't respond, said, 'Don't you think so, Bernard?'

'Arranging a little money to prop up a trade union or finance an anti-nuke demo? Not exactly something for one of the KGB's brightest people, is it?'

'I'm not so sure,' said Dicky. 'Central America is a top KGB priority, you can't deny that, Bernard.'

'Let me put it another way,' I said. 'Covert financing of that sort is an administration job. It's not something for Stinnes with his languages and years of field experience.'

'Ho ho,' said Dicky. 'Hint, hint, eh? You mean, you chaps with field experience and fluent languages are wasted on the sort of job that administrators like me can manage?'

It was exactly what I thought, but since it wasn't what I'd intended to say I denied it. 'Why the German name?' I said. 'And why does a man like that work out of Berlin? He must be forty years old; a crucial age for an ambitious man. Why isn't he in Moscow where the really big decisions are made?'

'*Si, maestro*,' said Dicky very slowly. He looked at me quizzically and ran a fingertip along his thin bloodless lips as if trying to prevent himself smiling. Instead of concealing my own feelings, I'd subconsciously identified with Stinnes. For I was also forty years old and I wanted to be where the big decisions are made. Dicky nodded solemnly. He might be a little slow on languages and fieldwork but in the game of office politics he was seeded number one. 'Frank Harrington had an answer for that one. Stinnes – real name Nikolai Sadoff – married a German girl who couldn't master the Russian language. They lived in Moscow for some time but she was miserable there. Stinnes finally asked for a transfer. They live in East Berlin. Frank Harrington thinks a Mexico City assignment will probably be a quick in and out for Stinnes.'

'Yes, he talked as if he was going soon – "*when I've gone back to Europe*", he said.'

'He said the Englishwoman had put him in charge of one of her crazy schemes, didn't he?'

'More or less,' I said.

'And we both know who the Englishwoman is, don't we? Your wife is running this operation. It was your wife who sent the telex from Berlin that they grudgingly obeyed. Right?'

I said nothing.

Dicky stared at me, his mouth pursed, his eyes narrowed. 'Is it right or not?' He smiled. 'Or do you think they might have some other Englishwoman running the KGB office in Berlin.'

'Probably Fiona,' I said.

'Well, I'm glad we agree on that one,' said Dicky sarcastically. It was only when I heard the contempt in his voice that I realized that he hated working on this job with me as much as I did with him. In the London office our relationship was tolerable; but on this type of job every little difference became abrasive. Dicky turned away from me and took a great interest in the various pots of stew. One of the stallholders opened the lids so that we could sniff. 'Smell that,' I said 'There's enough chilli in there to put you into orbit.'

'Obit, you mean,' said Dicky, moving on quickly. 'Put you into the *Times* obit column.' His dinner with the Volkmanns had lessened his appetite for the chilli. 'Our friend Paul Biedermann is going soggy on them. He starts making up stories about British spies telephoning him, and who knows what other sort of nonsense he's been telling them. So they get nervous and Stinnes is sent over here to kick arses and get Biedermann back into line.'

'Is that also what Frank says?'

'No, that's what *I'm* saying. It's obvious. I don't know why you are being so baroque about it. Maybe it's not a very big deal. But these KGB people like a nice little jaunt to Mexico, fresh lobster salad and a swim in the Pacific to brighten up their working days. Stinnes is no different.'

'It doesn't feel right. Biedermann is rich and successful; he is woolly-minded and flabby with it. He doesn't have the motivation, and he certainly doesn't need the money.'

'So what? Biedermann was frightened for his family. Shall we eat here? Some of this food looks really good. Look at that.' He read the sign. 'What are carnitas?'

'Stewed pork. He's serving it on chicharrones: pork crackling. You eat the meat, then eat the plate. Biedermann wouldn't give that plate of pork for his family, and especially not for distant relatives in Rostock.'

'We'll walk to the end and see what else there is and then come back here and try some,' Dicky suggested. Dicky could always surprise me. Just as I had decided he was the archetypal gringo tourist, he wanted to have lunch at a *fonda*. 'So what's your theory?'

'I have no theory,' I said. 'Agents come in many shapes and sizes. Some are waiting for the socialist millennium, some hate their parents, some get angry after being ripped off by a loan company. Some simply want more money. But usually it begins with opportunity. A man finds himself handling something secret and valuable. He starts thinking about using that opportunity to get more money. Only then does he become a dedicated communist agent. So how does Biedermann fit into that? Where are his secrets? What's his motivation?'

'Guilt,' said Dicky. 'He feels guilty about his wealth.'

'If you'd ever met Paul Biedermann you'd know what a good joke that is.'

'Blackmail, then?'

'About what?'

'Sex.'

'Paul Biedermann would pay to have people say he was a sex maniac. He thinks of himself as a rich playboy.'

'You let your acute dislike of Paul Biedermann spill over into your judgements, Bernard. The fact of the matter is that Biedermann is an agent. You heard the two KGB people talking. He is an agent; it's no good your trying to convince yourself he's not.'

'Oh, he's an agent,' I said. 'But he's not the sort of agent that a man such as Stinnes would be running. That's what puzzles me.'

'Your experience makes you over-estimate what qualities an agent needs. Try and see it from their point of view: rich US businessman – someone the local cops would be reluctant to upset – isolated house on a lonely stretch of beach in western Mexico, not too far by road from the capital. And not too far by sea from Vladivostok.'

'Landing guns, you mean?'

'A man with a reputation for drinking who gets so rough with his servants that he's left all alone in the house. Wife and children often away. Convenient beach, pier big enough for a big motor boat.'

'Come along, Dicky,' I said. 'This is just a holiday cottage by Biedermann's standards. This is just a place he goes to read the *Wall Street Journal* and spend the weekend dreaming up a quick way to make a million or two.'

'So for half the year the house is completely empty. Then Stinnes and his pals have the place all to themselves. We know guns go from Cuba to Mexico's east coast and onwards by light plane. So why not bring them across the Pacific from the country where they are manufactured?' We'd got to the end of the food stalls and Dicky became interested in a stall selling pictures. There were family group photos and coloured litho portraits of generals and presidents. All of the pictures were in fine old frames.

'It doesn't smell right,' I said. But Dicky had put together a convincing scenario. If it was the house they were interested in, it didn't matter what kind of aptitude Biedermann had for being a field agent. Yes, London Central would love a report along those lines. It had the drama they liked. It had the geopolitic that called for maps and coloured diagrams. And, as a bottom line, it could be true.

'If it doesn't smell right,' said Dicky with heavy irony, 'I'll tell London to forget the whole thing.' He stood up straight as he looked at the selection of pictures for sale, and I realized he was studying his reflection in the glass-fronted pictures. He was too thin for a large, bright-green safari shirt. It made him look like a lollipop. 'Is it going to rain?' he said, looking at the time. He'd bought a new wrist-watch too. It was a multi-dial black chronometer that kept perfect time at 50 fathoms.

'It seldom rains in the morning, even during the rainy season.'

'It will bucket down on the stroke of noon, then,' said Dicky, looking up at the clouds that were now turning yellowish.

'I'm still not sure what London wants with Stinnes,' I said.

'London want Stinnes enrolled,' he said, as if he'd just remembered it. 'Shall we walk back to where the pork is? What did you say it's called – carnitas?'

'Enrolled?' It could mean a lot of things from persuaded to defect, to knocked on the head and rolled in a carpet. 'That would be difficult.'

'The bigger they are the harder they fall,' said Dicky. 'You said yourself that he's forty years old and passed over for promotion. He's been stuck in East Berlin for ages. Berlin is a plum job for Western intelligence but it's the boondocks for their people. A smart KGB major left to rot in East Berlin is sure to be fretting.'

'I suppose his wife likes it there,' I said.

'What's that got to do with it?' said Dicky. 'Would I take an intelligence job in Canada because my wife liked ice hockey?'

'No, Dicky, you wouldn't.'

'And this fellow Stinnes will see what's good for him. Frank Harrington thought the chances were good.'

'You talked about all this with Frank?'

'Sure. Frank has to be in on it because Stinnes is based in Big B. Stinnes is very much in his territory, Bernard.' A nervous movement of fingers through curly hair. 'The worst difficulty is that the Data Centre showed that Stinnes has an eighteen-year-old son. That might prove sticky.'

'Christ, Dicky,' I said, as I came to terms with this bombshell. 'Did you know all this when we left London?'

'Enrolling Stinnes, you mean?'

'Yes, enrolling Stinnes I mean.'

'It looked as if it might go that way.' That was Dicky on the defensive. He'd known all along, that was obvious. I wondered what else he knew that he was not going to tell me about until it happened. 'London Central put out a departmental alert for him, didn't they?' We had reached the carnitas stand by now. He selected a chair that didn't wobble and sat down. 'I'll have mine wrapped in a tortilla; pork skin is very fattening.'

'London Central puts out departmental alerts for clerks who make off with the petty cash.'

'But they don't send senior staff, like us, to identify them when they are spotted,' said Dicky.

'Enrolled,' I said, considering all the implications. 'A hot-shot like Stinnes. You and me? It's madness.'

'Only if you start thinking it's madness,' said Dicky. 'My own opinion . . .' Pause. 'For what's it's worth . . .' A modest smile. '. . . is that we stand an excellent chance.'

'And when did you last enrol a KGB major?'

Dicky bit his lip. We both knew the answer to that one. Dicky was a pen-pusher. Stinnes was the first KGB officer Dicky had ever come this close to, and he hadn't seen Stinnes yet.

'Isn't London proposing to send someone over here to help? This is a complicated job, Dicky. We need someone who has experience.'

'Nonsense. We can do it. I don't want Bret Rensselaer breathing down my neck. If we can pull this one off, it will be a real coup.' He smiled. 'I didn't expect you to start asking London for help, Bernard. I thought you were the one who always liked to do everything on his own.'

'I'm not on my own,' I said. 'I'm with you.' The stallholder was stirring his cauldron of pork and arranging suitable pieces on a large metal platter.

'And you'd prefer to work with your friend Werner, eh?'

I could hear danger signals. 'We were at school together,' I said. 'I've known him a long time.'

'Werner Volkmann isn't even employed by the department. He hasn't been employed by us for years.'

'Officially that's right,' I said. 'But he's worked for us from time to time.'

'Because you give him jobs to do,' said Dicky. 'Don't try to make it sound as if the department employs him.'

'Werner knows Berlin,' I said.

'You know Berlin. Frank Harrington knows Berlin. Our friend Stinnes knows Berlin. There is no great shortage of people who know Berlin. That's no reason for employing Werner.'

'Werner is a Jew. He was born in Berlin when the Nazis were running things. Werner instinctively sees things in people that you and I have to learn about. You can't compare his knowledge of Berlin and Berliners with anything I know.'

'Calm down. Everyone knows Werner is your alter ego, and so mustn't be criticized.'

'What do you want? You can have "lean meat", "pure meat", "meat without fat" or "a bit of everything".'

'What's the difference between . . .'

'Don't let's get into semantics,' I said. 'Try *surtido*, that's a bit of everything.' Dicky nodded his agreement.

Dicky, who always showed a remarkable aptitude for feeding himself, now discovered that a carnitas stand is always conveniently close to those that sell the necessary accompaniments. He provided us with salsas and marinated cactus, and was now discovering that tortillas are sold by the kilo. 'A kilo,' he said as the tortilla lady disappeared with the payment and left him with a huge pile of them. 'Do you think they'll keep if I take them back for Daphne?' He wrapped some of the pork into the top tortilla. 'Delicious,' he said as he ate the first one and took a second tortilla to begin making another. 'What are all those pieces?'

'That's ear, and those pieces are intestine,' I said.

'You just wait until Daphne hears what I've been eating; she'll throw up. Our neighbours came out to Mexico last year and stayed in the Sheraton. They wouldn't even clean their teeth unless they had bottled water. I wish I had my camera so you could photograph me eating here in the market. Now what is it again – carnitas? I want to get it exactly right when I tell them.'

'Carnitas,' I said. '*Surtido.*'

Dicky wiped his mouth on his handkerchief and stood up and looked round the market square. Just from where we were sitting I could see people selling plastic toys, antique tables and gilt mirrors, cheap shirts, brass bedsteads, dog-eared American film magazines and a selection of cut-glass stoppers that always survive long after the decanters. 'Yes,' said Dicky. 'It's really quite a place, isn't it? Fifteen million people perched at seven thousand feet altitude with high mountain tops all round them and thick smog permanently overhead. Where else could you find a capital city with no river, no coastline and such lousy roads? And yet this is one of the oldest cities the world has ever known. If that doesn't prove that the human race is stone-raving mad, nothing will.'

'I hope you don't think I'm going to walk right up to Stinnes and offer him a chance to defect,' I said.

'I've been thinking about that,' said Dicky. 'The Volkmanns already know him. Shall we let them make the first overtures?'

'Werner doesn't work for the department. You just told me that.'

'Correction,' said Dicky. 'I said that Werner's knowledge of Berlin is not sufficient reason for using him in Berlin. Let's remember that Werner has had a "non-critical employment only" tag on his file.'

'You can be a spiteful bastard, Dicky,' I said. 'You're talking about that signals leak in 1978. You know very well that Werner was completely cleared of suspicion.'

'It was your wife who did it,' said Dicky. Suddenly he was angry. He was angry because he'd never suspected Fiona of leaking secrets, and now I realized that Dicky saw me as someone who had helped to deceive him rather than as Fiona's principal victim.

The sky was darkening with stormclouds now and there was the movement of air that precedes a storm. I never got used to the speedy effects of the heat and humidity. The sweet smell of fresh fruits and vegetables had filled the air when we first arrived at the market. Now it was already giving way to the smells of putrefaction as the spoiled, squashed and broken produce went bad.

'Yes, it was my wife who did it. Werner was innocent.'

'And if you'd listened you'd have heard me say that Werner has *had* a "non-crit" tag on his file. I didn't say it was still there.'

'And now you're going to ask Werner to enrol Stinnes for you?'

'I think you'd better put it to him, Bernard.'

'He's on holiday,' I said. 'It's a sort of second honeymoon.'

'So you told me,' said Dicky. 'But my guess is that they are both

getting a bit bored with each other. If you were on your honeymoon
– first, second or third – you wouldn't want to spend the evenings in
some broken-down German club in a seedy part of town, would you?'

'We haven't seen the club yet,' I reminded him. 'Perhaps it's
tremendous.'

'I love the way you said that, Bernard. I wish I could have recorded
the way you said "tremendous". Yes, it might be Mexico's answer
to Caesar's Palace in Vegas, or the Paris Lido, but don't bank on it.
You see, if it was me on a second honeymoon with that delectable
little Zena, I'd be in Acapulco, or maybe finding some sandy little
beach where we could be undisturbed. I wouldn't be taking her along
to the Kronprinz club to see who's winning the bridge tournament.'

'The way it's turned out,' I said, 'you're not taking the delectable
little Zena anywhere. I thought I heard you saying you didn't like
her. I remember you saying that one honeymoon with Zena would
be enough for you.' From the sulphurous yellow sky there came a
steady drum-roll of thunder, an overture for a big storm.

Dicky laughed. 'I admit I was a little hasty,' he said. 'I hadn't
been away from home for very long when I said that. The way I feel
now, Zena is looking sexier and sexier every day.'

'And you think talking to Stinnes about Western democracy and
the free world will give the Volkmanns a new interest in life,' I said.

'Even allowing for your sarcasm, yes. Why don't you put it to
them and see what they say?'

'Why don't *you* put it to them and see what they say?'

'Look at those children and the donkey and the old man with the
sombrero. That would make the sort of photo that wins prizes at the
Photo Club. I was so stupid not to bring a camera. But have you
seen the sort of price you have to pay for a camera in this country?
The Americans are really putting the squeeze on the peso. No, I
think *you* should put it to them, Bernard. You get hold of Werner
and talk with him, and then he could go along to the Kronprinz Club
tonight and see if Stinnes is there.' He stopped at a stall to watch a
man making *chiles rellenos*, putting meat fillings into large peppers.
Each one got a big spoonful of chopped chillies before being deep-
fried and put in a garlicky tomato sauce. Just looking at it made me
feel queasy.

'Werner will have to know what London is prepared to offer
Stinnes. I assume there will eventually be a big first payment, a salary
and contractual provisions about the size of the house they'll get and
what sort of car and so on.'

'Is that the way it's done?' said Dicky. 'It sounds like a marriage
contract.'

'They like it defined like that because you can't buy houses in East

Europe and they don't know the prices of cars and so on. They usually want to have a clear idea of what they are getting.'

'London will pay,' said Dicky. 'They want Stinnes; they really want him. That's just between us, of course; that's not for Werner Volkmann to know.' He touched the side of his nose in a conspiratorial gesture. 'No reasonable demand will be refused.'

'So what does Werner say to Stinnes?' On the cobbled ground there were shiny black spots appearing one after the other in the grey dust. The rain had come.

'Let's keep it all very soft-sell, shall we?' said Dicky. His wife Daphne worked in a small advertising agency. Dicky told me that it had very aggressive methods with really up-to-date selling techniques. Sometimes I got the feeling that Dicky would like to see the department being run on the same lines. Preferably by him.

'You mean we don't brief Werner?'

'Let's see how the cookie crumbles,' said Dicky. It was an old advertising expression that meant put your head in the sand, your arse in the air and wait for the explosion.

My prediction that the rain came only in the afternoons was only just right. It was a few minutes after one o'clock when the rain started. Dicky took me in the car as far as the university, where he was to see one of his Oxford friends, and there – on the open plaza – let me out into steady rain. I cursed him, but there was no hostility in Dicky's self-interest; he would have done the same thing to almost anyone.

It was not easy to get a cab but eventually an old white VW beetle stopped for me. The car's interior was battered and dirty, but the driver's position was equipped like the flight deck of a Boeing jet. The dashboard was veneered in walnut and there was an array of small spanners and screwdrivers and a pen-shaped flashlight as well as a large coloured medallion of the shrine of the Virgin of Guadalupe. In contrast to the derelict bodywork of the little car, the young driver was dressed in a freshly starched white shirt with a dark-grey tie and looked more like a stockbroker than a cab driver. But Mexico is like that.

The traffic moved slowly through the heavy rain but it didn't make less noise. There were two-stroke motorcycles and cars with broken mufflers and giant trucks – some so carefully painted up that every bolt-head, rivet and wheel-nut was picked out in different colours. Here on the city's outskirts, the wide boulevard was lined with a chaos of broken walls, goats grazing on waste ground, adobe huts, rubbish tips, crudely painted shop-fronts in primary colours and corrugated-iron fences defaced with political slogans and ribaldry.

Despite the rain, drunks sprawled full-length on the pavement and the barbecue fires hissed and flared at the taco counters.

By the time we got near to Werner Volkmann's apartment, the rainstorm was flooding the gutters and making great lakes through which the traffic splashed, and in which it sometimes stalled. There was a constant racket of car horns and engines being over-revved by nervous drivers. The cab moved slowly, and I watched drenched and dirty kids offering dry, clean lottery tickets that were protected inside clear plastic bags. And plenty of well-dressed shoppers had chauffeurs who could hold an umbrella in one hand and open the door of a limousine with the other. I couldn't imagine Zena Volkmann anywhere but here in the Zona Rosa. Within the area contained by the Insurgentes, Sevilla and Chapultepec there are the big international hotels, smart restaurants, the shops with branches in Paris and New York. And in the crowded cafés that spill out on to the pavement are to be heard every new rumour, joke and scandal that this outrageous town provides in abundance.

Zena Volkmann could live anywhere, of course. But she preferred to live in comfort. She'd learned to respect wealth, and the wealthy, in a way that only a poverty-stricken childhood teaches. She was a survivor who'd climbed up the ladder without benefit of any education beyond reading and writing and painting her face, plus a natural ability to count. Perhaps I did her an injustice but sometimes I had the feeling that she would do anything if the price was high enough, for she still had that fundamental insecurity that one bout of poverty can inflict for a lifetime, and no amount of money remedy.

She made no secret of her feelings. Even amid the contrasts of Mexico she showed no great interest in the plight of the hungry. And like so many poor people she had only contempt for socialism in any of its various forms, for it is only the rich and guilty who can afford the subtle delights of egalitarian philosophies.

Zena Volkmann was only twenty-two years old but she'd lived with her grandparents for much of her childhood. From them she'd inherited a nostalgia for a Germany of long ago. It was a Protestant Germany of aristocrats and *Handküsse*, silvery Zeppelins and student duels. It was a *kultiviertes* Germany of music, industry, science and literature; an imperial Germany ruled from the great cosmopolitan city of Berlin by efficient, incorruptible Prussians. It was a Germany she'd never seen; a Germany that had never existed.

The elaborate afternoon *Kaffee-Trinken* that she'd prepared was a manifestation of her nostalgia. The delicate chinaware into which she poured the coffee, and the solid-silver forks with which we ate the fruit tart, and the tiny damask napkins with which we dabbed our lips were all parts of a ceremony that was typically German. It was a scene to be found in the prosperous suburbs of any one of a hundred West German towns.

Zena's brown silk afternoon dress, with embroidered collar and hem below the knee, made her look like a dedicated hausfrau. Her long dark hair was in two plaits and rolled to make the old-fashioned 'earphone' hairstyle virtually unknown outside Germany. And Werner, sitting there like an amiable gorilla, had gone to the extent of putting on his tan-coloured tropical suit and a striped tie too. I was only too aware that my old rain-wet open-necked shirt was not exactly *de rigueur*, as I balanced the coffee-cup on the knee of my mud-splashed nylon pants.

While Zena had been in the kitchen I'd told Werner about my trip to Biedermann's house, about the Russians I'd seen there and Biedermann's confession to me. Werner took his time to answer. He turned to look out of the window. On a side-table the broken fragments of a cup and saucer had been arranged in a large ashtray. Werner moved the ashtray to the trolley that held the TV. From this sixth-floor apartment there was a view across the city. The sky was low and dark now, and the rain was beating down in great shimmering sheets, the way it does only in such tropical storms. He still hadn't answered by the time Zena returned from the kitchen.

'Biedermann always was a loner,' said Werner. 'He has two brothers, but Paul makes all the business decisions. Did you know that?'

It was small talk, but now Zena was with us and I was undecided about how much to say in front of her. 'Are both his brothers in the business?'

Werner said, 'Old Biedermann gave equal shares to all five of them – two girls and three boys. But the others leave all the decisions to Paul.'

'And why not?' said Zena, cutting for me a slice of fruit tart. 'He knows how to make money. The other four have nothing to do but spend it.'

'You never liked him, did you, Bernie?' said Werner. 'You never liked Paul.'

'I hardly knew him,' I said. 'He went off to some fancy school. I remember his father. His father used to let me steer the trucks round their yard while he operated the accelerator and brakes. I was only a tiny child. I really liked the old man.'

'It was a filthy old yard,' said Werner. He was telling Zena rather than me. Or perhaps he was retelling it to himself. 'Full of junk and rubbish. What a wonderland it was for us children who played there. We had such fun.' He took a piece of tart from Zena. His slice was small; she was trying to slim him down. 'Paul was a scholar. The old man was proud of him but they didn't have much in common when

Paul came back with all those college degrees and qualifications. Old Mr Biedermann had had no proper education. He left school when he was fourteen.'

'He was a real Berliner,' I said. 'He ran the transport business like a despot. He knew the names of all his workers. He swore at them when he was angry and got drunk with them when there was something to celebrate. They invited him to their marriages and their christenings and he never missed a funeral. When the union organized a weekend outing each year they always invited him along. No one would have wanted to go without the old man.'

'You're talking about the road transport business,' said Werner. 'But that was only a tiny part of their set-up.'

'It was the business the old man started, and the only part of the Biedermann empire he ever really liked.' A timer began to ping somewhere in the kitchen but Zena didn't move. Eventually it stopped. I guessed the Indian woman was there but banished to the back room.

'It was losing money,' said Werner.

'So, when Paul Biedermann came back from his American business management course, the first thing he did was to sell the transport company and pension his father off.'

'You sound very bitter, Bernie. That couldn't be why you hate Paul so much, could it?'

I drank some more coffee. I began to have the feeling that Zena didn't intend to leave us alone to talk about the things we had to talk about. I kept the small talk going. 'It killed old Biedermann,' I said. 'He had nothing to live for after the yard closed and the company was being run from New York. Do you remember how he used to sit in Leuschner's café all day, talking about old times to anyone who would listen, even to us kids?'

'It's the way things are now,' said Werner. 'Companies are run by computers. Profit margins are sliced thin. And no manager dare raise his eyes from his accounts long enough to learn the names of his staff. It's the price we pay for progress.'

Zena picked up the ashtray containing the broken cup and saucer. I could tell that Werner had broken it by the way she averted her eyes from him. She took the coffee-pot too and went to the kitchen. I said, 'Dicky saw Frank Harrington in LA. Apparently London have decided to try enrolling Erich Stinnes.' I had tried to make it unhurried but it came out in a rush.

'Enrolling him?' I was interested to see that Werner was as dismayed and surprised as I had been. 'Is there any background?'

'You mean, have there been discussions with Stinnes before. I was wondering the same thing myself but from what I got out of Dicky I think the idea is to go in cold.'

Werner leaned his considerable weight back in the armchair and blew through his pursed lips. 'Who's going to try that?'

'Dicky wants you to try,' I said. I drank some of my strong coffee and tried to sound very casual. I could see that Werner was torn between indignation and delight. Werner desperately wanted to become a regular departmental employee again. But he knew that being chosen for this job was no tribute to his skills; he was simply the man closest to Stinnes. 'It's a great opportunity,' said Werner resentfully, 'a great opportunity for failure. So Frank Harrington, and all those people who've been slandering me all these years, can have a new excuse and start slandering me all over again.'

'They must know the chances are slim,' I said. 'But if Stinnes went for it, you'd be the talk of the town, Werner.'

Werner gave me a wry smile. 'You mean both East and West sides of it?'

'What are you talking about?' said Zena, returning with the coffee. 'Is this something to do with Erich Stinnes?'

Werner glanced at me. He knew I didn't want to discuss it in front of Zena. 'If I'm going to try, Zena will have to know, Bernie,' he said apologetically. I nodded. The reality was that Werner told her everything I told him, so she might as well hear it from me.

Zena poured more coffee for us and offered us a selection of *Spritzgebäck*, little German biscuits that Werner liked. 'It is about Stinnes, isn't it?' she said as she picked up her own coffee – she drank it strong and black – and sat down. Even in this severe dress she looked very beautiful; her big eyes, very white teeth and the high cheekbones in that lightly tanned face made her look like the work of some Aztec goldsmith.

'London want to enrol him,' said Werner.

'Recruit him to work for London, do you mean?' said Zena.

'You recruit ordinary people to become spies,' Werner explained patiently. 'But an enemy security officer, especially one who might help you break his own networks, is "enrolled".'

'It's the same sort of thing,' said Zena brightly.

'It's very different,' said Werner. 'When you recruit someone, and start them spying, you paint romantic pictures for them. You show them the glamour and make them feel courageous and important. But the agent you enrol knows all the answers already. Enrolment is tricky. You are telling lies to highly skilled liars. They're cynical and demanding. It's easy to start it off but it usually goes sour some way along the line and everyone ends up mad at everyone else.'

'You make it sound like getting a divorce,' said Zena.

'It's a bit like that,' I said. 'But it can get more violent.'

'More violent than a divorce?' Zena fluttered her eyelashes. 'You're only going to offer Erich Stinnes a chance to defect to the West.

Can't he do that any time he wants? He's in Mexico. Why go back to Russia if he doesn't want to?' There was something deliciously feminine about Zena and her view of the world.

'It's not as easy as that,' said Werner. 'Not many countries will allow East European nationals to defect. Seamen who jump ship, passengers or Aeroflot crew who leave their planes at refuelling stops, or Soviet delegates who walk into foreign police stations and ask for asylum find it's not so easy. Even right-wing governments send them right back to Russia to face the music.' He bit into a biscuit. 'Good *Spritzgebäck*, darling,' he said.

'I couldn't get hazelnuts but I tried this other sort; with honey. They're not bad, are they? Why won't they let them defect? They send them back to Russia? That's disgusting,' said Zena.

'Encouraging defectors upsets the Russians for one thing,' said Werner. 'If Stinnes said he wanted to stay in Mexico, the Soviet ambassador would go running along to the Foreign Secretary and start pressurizing the Mexican authorities to hand him back.'

'In which case doesn't Stinnes just say go to hell?' said Zena.

'The ambassador then says that Stinnes has stolen the cash box or that he's wanted to face criminal charges in Moscow. The Mexicans then find themselves accused of harbouring a criminal. And don't forget that someone has to pay the defector a salary or find him a job.' Werner reached for another biscuit.

'This is Mexico,' said Zena. 'What do they care about the Russians?'

Werner was fully occupied with the biscuits. I said, 'The Russians have a lot of clout in this part of the world, Mrs Volkmann. They can stir up trouble by getting neighbouring countries to apply pressure. Cuba will always oblige, since its economy depends totally on Soviet money. They can apply economic sanctions. They can influence United Nations committees and all the rigmarole of Unesco and so on. And all of these countries have to contend with a domestic Communist Party organization ready to do whatever the Russians want done. Governments don't offend the Soviet Union without very good reason. Providing asylum for a defector is seldom reason enough.'

'There are still plenty of defectors, though,' persisted Zena.

'Yes,' I said. 'Many defectors are sponsored by the USA, the way that famous musicians or performers are, because of the bad publicity their escapes make for the communist system. And they can earn their own living easily enough. The remainder have to bring something worthwhile with them as the price of entry.'

'Secrets?'

'That depends on what you call secrets. Usually a country provides asylum to someone bringing information about the way the Soviets have been spying on the host country. For that sort of information a government is usually prepared to withstand Russian pressures.'

'And for that reason,' said Werner, 'most of the decent Russians can't defect and the KGB bastards can. Put all the defectors together and you'd have a ballet company and orchestra, some sports stars and a vast army of secret policemen.'

Zena looked at me with her big grey eyes and said archly, 'But if you two are right about Erich Stinnes, he's a KGB man. So he could provide some secrets about spying on Mexico. So he would be allowed to stay here without your help.'

'Would you like to live in Mexico for the remainder of your life, Mrs Volkmann?' I said.

She paused for a moment as if thinking the idea over. 'Perhaps not,' she admitted.

'No, a man such as Stinnes would want a British passport.'

'Or a US passport?' said Zena.

'American citizenship provides no right to travel abroad. A British passport identifies a British subject, and they have the right to leave the country any time they wish. Stinnes will give us quite a list of requirements if he decides to defect. He'd need a lot of paperwork so that he has a completely new identity. I mean an identity that is recorded in such a way that it will withstand investigation.'

'What sort of things?' said Zena.

I said, 'Things that require the cooperation of many different government departments. For instance, he'll need a driving licence. And we don't want that to materialize out of nowhere, not for a forty-year-old with no other driving experience on file and no record of passing a driving test. He'd need to have some innocuous-looking file in his local tax office. He'll want a credit card; what does he put on the application? Then there are documents for travelling. He'll probably want some freedom of movement and that's always a headache. Incidentally he must give us some identity photos for his passport and so on. One good full-face picture will be enough. A picture of his wife too. I'll get the copies done at the embassy.'

Werner nodded. He realized that this was his briefing. I was talking around the sort of offer he would be able to make to Stinnes. 'You're assuming that he would live in England?' said Werner.

'Certainly for the first year,' I said. 'It will be a long debriefing. Would that be a problem?'

'He's always spoken of Germany as the only place he'd ever want to be. Isn't that true, Zena?'

'That's what he's always said,' Zena agreed. 'But it's the sort of thing everyone says at the Kronprinz Club. Everyone is drinking German beer and exchanging news of the old country. It is natural to talk of Germany with great affection. We all do. But when you are offering someone a chance to retire in comfort, England wouldn't be too bad, I think.' She smiled.

I said, 'Dicky thinks Stinnes will jump at any decent offer.'

'Does he?' said Werner doubtfully.

'London thinks Stinnes has been passed over for promotion. They think he's been stuck away in East Berlin to rot.'

'So why is he here in Mexico?' said Werner.

'Dicky thinks it's just a nice little jaunt for him.'

'It's a convenient thing to say when you can't think of any convincing answer,' said Werner. 'What do you think, Bernie?'

'I'm convinced he's here in connection with Paul Biedermann,' I said cautiously. 'But why the hell would he be?'

Werner nodded. He didn't take me seriously. He knew I disliked Biedermann and thought this was clouding my judgement. 'What makes you think that, Bernie?' he said.

'Stinnes and his pal didn't know I was listening to them out at the Biedermann house. They said they were running Biedermann and I believe it.'

'Paul Biedermann has been koshering cash for the KGB,' Werner told Zena. 'And sending it off for them too.'

'What a bastard,' said Zena. The family property in East Prussia, which Zena had failed to inherit because it was now a part of the USSR, made her unsympathetic to people who helped the KGB. But she didn't put much venom into her condemnation of Biedermann; her mind was on Stinnes. 'What's so special about Stinnes?' she asked me.

'London wants him,' I said. 'And London Central moves in strange and unaccountable ways.'

'It's all Dicky Cruyer's idea,' she said, as if she'd had a sudden insight. 'I'll bet it's not London at all. Dicky Cruyer went off to Los Angeles and had a meeting with Frank Harrington. Then he returned with the electrifying news that London wants Erich Stinnes, and he's to be coaxed into defection.'

'He couldn't do that,' said Werner, who hated to have his faith in London Central undermined. 'It's a London order, isn't it, Bernie? It must be.'

'Don't be silly, Werner,' his wife argued. 'It was probably made official afterwards. You know that anyone could talk Frank Harrington into anything.'

Werner grunted. Zena's brief love affair with the elderly Frank Harrington was something that was never referred to, but I could see it was not forgotten.

Zena turned to me. 'I'm right. You know I am.'

'A successful enrolment would do wonders for Dicky's chances of holding on to the German Desk,' I said. I got up and walked over to the window. I had almost forgotten that we were in Mexico City, but the mountains just visible behind a veil of mist, the dark ceiling of clouds, the flashes of lightning and the tropical storm that was thrashing the city were not like anything to be seen in Europe.

'When do we get the money for finding him?' Zena said. My back was to her and I pretended to think that she was asking Werner.

It was Werner who replied. 'It will work out, darling. These things take time.'

Zena came across to the window and said to me, 'We'll not do any more to help until we've been paid some money.'

'I don't know anything about the money,' I said.

'No, no one knows anything about the money. That's how you people work, isn't it?'

Werner was still sitting heavily in his chair, munching his biscuits. 'It's not Bernie's fault, darling. Bernie would give us the crown jewels if it was only up to him.' The crown jewels had always been Werner's idea of ultimate wealth. I remembered how, when we were at school, various prized possessions of his had all been things he wouldn't exchange for the crown jewels.

'I'm not asking for the crown jewels,' said Zena demurely. I turned to look her in the face. My God but she was tough, and yet the toughness did not mar her beauty. I suddenly saw the fatal attraction she had for poor Werner. It was like having pet piranhas in the bath, or a silky rock python in the linen cupboard. You could never tame them but it was fun to see what effect they had on your friends. 'I'm asking to be paid for finding Erich Stinnes.' She picked up a notepad by the phone and entered the cup and saucer on to her list of breakages.

I looked at Werner but he was trying on some new inscrutable faces, so I said, 'I don't know who told you that there was a cash payment for reporting the whereabouts of Erich Stinnes but it certainly wasn't me. The truth is, Mrs Volkmann, that the department never pays any sort of bounty. At least I've never heard of such a payment being made.' She stared at me with enough calm, dispassionate interest to make me worry whether my coffee was poisoned. 'But I probably could sign a couple of vouchers that would reimburse you for air fares, first class, return trip.'

'I don't want any charity,' she said. 'I want what is due to me.' It wasn't 'us', I noticed.

'What sort of fee would you think appropriate?' I asked.

'It must be worth sixteen thousand American dollars,' she said. So she'd decided what she wanted. At first I wondered how she'd come to such an exact figure, but I then realized that it had not been quantified by the job she'd done; it was the specific amount of money she wanted for something or other. That was the way Zena's mind worked; every step she took was on the way to somewhere else.

'That's a lot of money, Mrs Volkmann,' I said. I looked at Werner. He was pouring himself more coffee and concentrating on the task as if oblivious of everything around him. It suited him to to have Zena giving me hell. I suppose she was voicing the resentment that had been building up in Werner in all the years he'd suffered from the insensitive double-dealing of the birdbrains at London Central. But I didn't enjoy having Zena bawl me out. I was angry with him and he knew it. 'I will see that your request is passed on to London.'

'And tell them this,' she said. She was still speaking softly and smiling so that a casual observer might have thought we were chatting amicably. 'You tell them unless I get my money I'll make sure that Erich Stinnes never trusts a word you say.'

'How would you achieve that, Mrs Volkmann?' I asked.

'No, Zena . . .' said Werner, but he'd left it too late.

'I'd tell him exactly what you're up to,' she said. 'I'd tell him that you'll cheat him just as you've cheated me.'

I laughed scornfully. She seemed surprised. 'Have you been sitting in on this conversation, and still not understood what Werner and I are talking about, Mrs Volkmann? Your husband earns his money from avalizing. He borrows money from Western banks to pay in advance for goods shipped to East Germany. The way he does it requires him to spend a lot of time in the German Democratic Republic. It's natural that the British government might use someone such as Werner to talk to Stinnes about defecting. The KGB wouldn't like that, of course, but they'd swallow it, the same way we swallow it when they use trade delegates to contact trouble-makers and float some ideas we don't like.'

I glanced at Werner. He was standing behind Zena now, his hands clasped together and a frown on his face. He'd been about to interrupt but now he was looking at me, waiting to hear what I was going to say. I said, 'Everyone likes a sportsman who can walk out into the middle of a soccer field, exchange a joke with the linesmen and flip a coin for the two team captains. But "enrolling" doesn't just mean offering a man money to come to the other side; it can mean beating him over the head and shipping him off in a crate. I don't say that's going to happen, but Werner and I both know it's a possibility. And if it does happen I want to make sure that the people in the other team keep thinking that Werner is an innocent bystander who paid the full price of admission. Because if they suspect that Werner is the kind who climbs the fence and throws beer cans at the goalkeeper they might get rough, Mrs Volkmann. And when the KGB get rough, they get very rough. So I advise you most sincerely not to start talking to Erich Stinnes in a way that makes it sound as if Werner is closely connected with the department, or there's a real risk that they'll do something nasty to you both.'

Werner knew I was going to spell it out for her. I suppose he didn't want her to understand the implications in case she worried.

I looked at her. She nodded. 'If Werner wants to talk to Stinnes, I won't screw it up for you,' she promised. 'But don't ask me to help.'

'I won't ask you to help,' I said.

Werner went over to her and put his arm round her shoulder to comfort her. But she didn't look very worried about him. She still looked very angry about not getting the money.

6

'If Zena ever left me, I don't know what I'd do,' said Werner. 'I think I'd die, I really would.' He fanned away a fly using his straw hat.

This was Werner in his lugubrious mood. I nodded, but I felt like reminding him that Zena had left him several times in the past, and he was still alive. He'd even survived the very recent time when she'd set up house with Frank Harrington – a married man more than old enough to be her father – and had looked all set to make it permanent. Only Zena was never going to make anything permanent, except perhaps eventually make Werner permanently unhappy.

'But Zena is very ambitious,' said Werner. 'I think you realize that, don't you, Bernie?'

'She's very young, Werner.'

'Too young for me, you mean?'

I worded my answer carefully. 'Too young to know what the real world is like, Werner.'

'Yes, poor Zena.'

'Yes, poor Zena,' I said. Werner looked at me to see if I was being sarcastic. I smiled.

'This is a beautiful hotel,' said Werner. We were sitting on the balcony having breakfast. It was still early in the morning, and the air was cool. The town was behind us, and we were looking across gently rolling green hills that disappeared into gauzy curtains of morning mist. It could have been England; except for the sound of the insects, the heavy scent of the tropical flowers, and the vultures that endlessly circled high in the clear blue sky.

'Dicky found it,' I said.

Zena had let Werner off his lead for the day, and he'd come to Cuernavaca – a short drive from Mexico City – to tell me about his encounter with Stinnes at the Kronprinz Club. Dicky had decided to 'make our headquarters' in this sprawling resort town where so many Americans came to spend their old age and their cheap pesos. 'Where's Dicky now?' said Werner.

'He's at a meeting,' I said.

Werner nodded. 'You're smart to stay here in Cuernavaca. This side of the mountains it's always cooler and you don't have to breathe that smog all day and all night.'

'On the other hand,' I said, 'I do have Dicky next door.'

'Dicky's all right,' said Werner. 'But you make him nervous.'

'I make him nervous?' I said incredulously.

'It must be difficult for him,' said Werner. 'You know the German Desk better than he'll ever know it.'

'But he got it,' I said.

'So did you expect him to turn a job like that down?' said Werner. 'You should give him a break, Bernie.'

'Dicky does all right,' I said. 'He doesn't need any help. Not from you, not from me. Dicky is having a lovely time.'

Dicky had lined up meetings with a retired American CIA executive named Miller and an Englishman who claimed to have great influence with the Mexican security service. In fact, of course, Dicky was just trying out some of the best local restaurants at the taxpayer's expense, while extending his wide circle of friends and acquaintances. Dicky had once shown me his card-index files of contacts throughout the world. It was quite unofficial, of course; Dicky kept them in his desk at home. He noted the names of their wives and their children and what restaurants they preferred and what sort of house they lived in. On the other side of each card Dicky wrote a short résumé of what he estimated to be their wealth, power and influence. He joked about his file cards; 'he'll be a lovely card for me,' he'd say, when someone influential crossed his path. Sometimes I wondered if there was a card there with my name on it and, if so, what he'd written on it.

Dicky was a keen traveller, and his choice of bars, restaurants and hotels was the result of intensive research through guidebooks and travel magazines. The Hacienda Margarita, an old ranchhouse on the outskirts of town, was proof of the benefits that could come from such dedicated research. It was a charming old hotel, its cool stone colonnades surrounding a courtyard with palmettos and pepper trees and tall palms. The high-ceilinged bedrooms were lined with wonderful old tiles, and there were big windows and cool balconies, for this place was built long before air-conditioning was ever contemplated, built at the time of the conquistadores if you could bring yourself to believe the plaque over the cashier's desk.

Meanwhile I was enjoying the sort of breakfast that Dicky insisted was the only healthy way to start the day. There was a jug of freshly pressed orange juice, a vacuum flask of hot coffee, canned milk – Dicky didn't trust Mexican milk – freshly baked rolls and a pot of local honey. The tray was decorated with an orchid and held a copy of *The News*, the local English-language newspaper. Werner drank orange juice and coffee but declined the rolls and honey. 'I promised Zena that I'd lose weight.'

'Then I'll have yours,' I said.

'You're overweight too,' said Werner.

'But I didn't make any promises to Zena,' I said, digging into the honey.

'He was there last night,' said Werner.

'Did he go for it, Werner? Did Stinnes go for it?'

'How can you tell with a man like Stinnes?' said Werner. 'I told him that I'd met a man here in Mexico whom I'd known in Berlin. I said he had provided East German refugees with all the necessary papers to go and live in England. Stinnes said did I mean genuine papers or false papers. I said genuine papers, passports and identity papers, and permission to reside in London or one of the big towns.'

'The British don't have any sort of identity papers,' I said. 'And they don't have to get anyone's permission to go and live in any town they like.'

'Well, I don't know things like that,' said Werner huffily. 'I've never lived in England, have I? If the English don't need papers, what the hell are we offering him?'

'Never mind all that, Werner. What did Stinnes say?'

'He said that refugees were never happy. He'd known a lot of exiles and they'd always regretted leaving their homeland. He said they never properly mastered the language, and never integrated with the local people. Worst of all, he said, their children grew up in the new country and treated their parents like strangers. He was playing for time, of course.'

'Has he got children?'

'A grown-up son.'

'He knew what you were getting at?'

'Perhaps he wasn't sure at first, but I persisted and Zena helped. I know she said she wouldn't help, Bernie, but she did help.'

'What did she do?'

'She told him that a little money solves all kinds of problems. Zena said that friends of hers had gone to live in England and loved every minute of it. She told him that everyone likes living in England. These friends of hers had a big house in Hampshire with a huge garden. And they had a language teacher to help them with their English. She told him that these were all problems that could be solved if there was help and money available.'

'He must have been getting the message by that time,' I said.

'Yes, he became cautious,' said Werner. 'I suppose he was frightened in case I was trying to make a fool of him.'

'And?'

'I had to make it a little more specific. I said that this friend of mine could always arrange a job in England for anyone with experience of security work. He'd just come down here for a couple of weeks' holiday in Mexico after travelling through the US, recruiting security experts for a very big British corporation, a company that did work for the British government. The pay is very good, I told him, with a long contract optional both sides.'

'I wish you really did have a friend like that, Werner,' I said. 'I'd want to meet him myself. How did Stinnes react?'

'What's he going to say, Bernie? I mean, what would you or I say, in his place, faced with the same proposition?'

'He said maybe?'

'He said yes . . . or as near as he dared go to yes. But he's frightened it's a trap. Anyone would be frightened of its being a trap. He said he wanted more details, and a chance to think about it. He'd have to meet the man doing the recruiting. I said I was just a go-between of course . . .'

'And he believed you are just the go-between?'

'I suppose so,' said Werner. He picked up the orchid and examined it as if seeing one for the first time. 'You can't grow orchids in Mexico City, but here in Cuernavaca they flourish. No one knows why. Maybe it's the smog.'

'Don't just suppose so, Werner.' He made me angry when he avoided important questions by changing the subject of conversation. 'I wasn't kidding last night . . . what I said to Zena. I wasn't kidding about them getting rough.'

'He believed me,' said Werner in a tone that indicated that he was just trying to calm me down.

'Stinnes is no amateur,' I said. 'He's the one they assigned to me when I was arrested over there. He had me taken to the Normannenstrasse building and sat with me half the night, discussing the more subtle aspects of Sherlock Holmes and laughing and smoking and making it clear that if he was in charge of things they'd be kicking shit out of me.'

'We've both seen a lot of KGB specimens like Erich Stinnes,' said Werner. 'He's affable enough over a stein of beer but in other circumstances he could be a nasty piece of work. And not to be trusted, Bernie. I kept my distance from him. I'm no hero, you know that.'

'Was there anyone with him?'

'An older man – fifty or so – built like a tank, cropped hair, can't seem to speak any language without a strong Russian accent.'

'Sounds like the one who went with him to the Biedermann house. Pavel, he called him. I told you what they said, didn't I?'

'I guessed it was him. Luckily Pavel isn't really fluent in German, expecially when Stinnes and I got going. Stinnes got rid of him as soon as he realized the drift my conversation was taking. I thought that might have been a good sign.'

'I can use all the good signs we can get, Werner.' I drank some coffee. 'It's all right telling him about language lessons in Hampshire, but he knows the real score would be him sitting in some lousy little safe house blowing KGB networks. And drinking half a bottle of Scotch every night in an effort to forget what damage he's doing to his own people, and that he's going to have to start doing it all over again next morning. Hey, don't look so worried, Werner.'

He looked at me, biting his lip. 'He knows you're here, Bernie, I'm sure he does.' There was a note of anxiety now. 'He asked if I knew an Englishman who was a friend of Paul Biedermann. I said Paul knew lots of Englishmen. He said yes, but this one knew all the Biedermann family and had done for years.'

'That description fits lots of people,' I said.

'But it doesn't fit anyone else who's in Mexico City,' said Werner. 'I think Stinnes knows you're here. And if he knows you're here, that's bad.'

'Why is it bad?' I said, although I knew what he was going to say. I'd known Werner so long that our minds ran on the same tracks.

'Because it sounds like he got it from Paul Biedermann.'

'Maybe,' I said.

'If Stinnes was worried about Biedermann, the way he sounded worried from that conversation you overheard, then he's likely to put him through the wringer. You know, and I know, that Biedermann couldn't take much punishment before he started to recount everything he knows, plus a few things he only guesses at.'

'So what could Biedermann tell them? That I sell secondhand Ferraris that keep breaking down?'

'You're smiling. But Biedermann could tell them quite a lot. He could tell them about you working for the SIS. He could tell them about Frank Harrington in Berlin and the people Frank sees.'

'Don't be ridiculous, Werner. The KGB know all about Frank Harrington. He's been "Berlin Resident" for a long time, and he was no stranger to Berlin before he took the job. As for knowing who I work for, we were discussing rates of pay that night Stinnes had me in Normannenstrasse.'

'I think he wants to talk to you, Bernie. He did everything except spell out your name.'

'Eventually he'll have to see me. And he'll recognize me. Then he'll telex Moscow and have them send a computer print-out of whatever they know about me. That's the way it is, Werner. There's nothing we can do about that.'

'I don't like it, Bernie.'

'So what am I going to do – glue on a false beard and put a stone in my shoe to make me limp?'

'Let Dicky do it.'

'Dicky? Are you joking? Dicky enrol Stinnes? Stinnes would run a mile.'

'He'll probably run a mile when you try,' said Werner. 'But Dicky has no record of work as a field agent. It's very unlikely that they'd do anything really nasty to Dicky.'

'Well, that's another reason,' I said.

'It's not something to joke about, Bernie. I know you were painting a rosy picture for Zena yesterday. And I appreciate you trying to set her mind at rest. But we both know that the best way to prevent an enrolment is to kill the enroller . . . and we both know that Moscow shares that feeling.'

'Did you fix a time and place?'

'I still don't like it, Bernie.'

'What can happen? I tell him how lovely it is living in Hampshire. And he tells me to get stuffed.'

Music started from the big patio below our balcony. Some of the hotel staff were erecting a stage, arranging folding chairs and decorating the columns with coloured lanterns in preparation for the concert I'd seen advertised in the lobby. Sitting under the tall, spiky palmetto trees on the far side of the patio were six men and a flashy-looking girl. One of the men was strumming a guitar and tuning it. The girl was smiling and humming the tune, but the other men sat very still and completely impassive, as the natives of very hot countries learn to do.

Werner followed the direction of my gaze and leaned over to see what was happening. The man strumming the guitar picked out a melody everyone in Mexico knows, and quietly sang:

> Life is worth nothing, life is worth nothing,
> It always starts with crying and with crying ends.
> And that's why, in this world, life is worth nothing.

Werner said, 'Stinnes says he's frightened of this man Pavel. He says Pavel is desperate to get back to Moscow and that his only way of doing that is to get back into favour. Stinnes is frightened that Pavel will make trouble at the first opportunity.'

'It sounds like a cosy chat, Werner. He said he's frightened?' Stinnes was not the type who was easily frightened, and certainly not the type to say so.

'Not like I'm telling you,' said Werner. 'It was all wrapped up in euphemisms and double-meanings but the meaning was clear.'

'What is the end result?'

'He wants to talk to you but it's got to be somewhere completely safe. Somewhere that can't be bugged or have witnesses hidden.'

'For instance?'

'Biedermann's boat. He'll meet my contact on Biedermann's boat, he says.'

'That sounds sensible,' I said. 'You did well, Werner.'

'Sensible for him, but not so sensible for you.'

'Why?'

'Are you crazy? He's sure to have Biedermann with him. They'll cruise out into the Pacific and dump you over the side. They'll say you had cramp while swimming. The local cops are sure to be in Biedermann's pocket, and so is the local doctor who'll issue a death certificate, if that's the way they decide to play it.'

'You've got my demise all worked out, haven't you, Werner?'

'If you're too stupid to see the danger for yourself, then it's as well I spell it out for you.'

'I don't see them going to all that trouble to do something that can be more easily achieved by a hit-and-run traffic accident as I hurry across the Reforma one morning.'

'Of course, I don't know what kind of back-up you'll be arranging. For all I know you'll have a Royal Navy frigate out there, with a chopper keeping you on radar. I realize you don't tell me everything.'

There were times when Werner could drive me to the point of frenzy. 'You know as well as I do that I tell you all you need to know. And if I'm going out to meet Stinnes on this bloody boat I won't even be carrying my Swiss army knife . . . Royal Navy frigate . . . Good God, Werner, the ideas you come up with.' Below us the guitar player sang:

 . . . Only the winner is respected.
 That's why life is worth nothing in Guanajuato . . .

'Do whatever you want,' said Werner mournfully. 'I know you won't take my advice. You never have in the past.'

I seem to have spent half my life listening to Werner handing out advice. And engraved on my memory there was a long list of times when I heartily regretted taking it. But I didn't tell him this. I said, 'I'll be all right, Werner.'

'You *think* you're all right,' said Werner. 'You think you're all right because your wife defected to the Russians. But that doesn't make you any safer, Bernie.'

I didn't understand what he was getting at. 'Make me safer? What do you mean?'

'I never got along with Fiona, I'll admit that any time. But it was more because of her attitude than because of mine. When you married her I was ready to be friends. You know that, Bernie.'

'What are you trying to say, Werner?'

'Fiona works for the KGB nowadays. Well, I'm not saying she's going to send a KGB hit team after the father of her children. But don't imagine you will enjoy complete immunity for ever and ever. That's not the way the KGB work, you know that, Bernie.'

'Isn't it?'

'You're on different sides now, you and Fiona. She's working against you, Bernie. Remember that always. She'll always be working against you.'

'You're not saying that Fiona sent Stinnes to Mexico in the hope that you might come here on holiday? Instead of going to Spain, for which you'd already booked tickets when you read in *Time* magazine about Mexico being even cheaper. That she did that because she hoped you would spot Stinnes and report it to London Central. Then she figured that they would send me here with an offer to enrol him. I mean that would be a lot of "ifs", wouldn't it? She'd have to be a magician to work that one out in advance, wouldn't she?'

'You like to make me sound ridiculous,' said Werner. 'It makes you feel good, doesn't it?'

'Yes, it does. And since you like to feel sorry for yourself we have the perfect symbiotic relationship.' It was getting warmer in the morning sunshine, and the sweet scents of the flowers hung in the air. And yet these were not the light, fresh smells of Europe's country-side. The flowers were big and brightly coloured; the sort of blooms that eat insects in slow motion in nature films on TV. And the heavy cloying perfumes smelled like an airport duty-free shop.

'I'm simply saying what's obvious. That you mustn't think that you'll continue to have a charmed life just because Fiona is working for them.'

'*Continue* to have? What do you mean?'

Werner leaned forward. 'Fiona made sure nothing happened to you during all those years when she was an active agent inside London Central. That's what you said yourself. It's no good denying it; you told me that, Bernard. You told me just after they let you go.'

'I said *maybe* she had a deal like that.'

'But she's not going to be doing that any more. She's running Stinnes – and whatever he's doing with Biedermann – from a desk in East Berlin. Moscow is going to be watching every move she makes, and she's got to show them that she's on their side. Even if she wanted to protect you she'd not be allowed to. If you go out on Paul Biedermann's boat with the idea that nothing can happen to you, because the KGB will play it the way Fiona wants, you might not come back.'

'Well, perhaps this would be a good chance to find out what the score is,' I said. 'I'll go out on the boat with Stinnes and see what happens.'

'Well, don't say you weren't told,' said Werner.

I didn't want to argue, especially not with Werner. He was worried for my safety, even if he was clucking like a mother hen. But I was nervous about what Stinnes could have in store for me. And Werner, voicing my fears, was making me twitchy. My argument with Werner was an attempt to allay my own fears but the more we argued the less convincing I sounded. 'Put yourself in his place, Werner,' I said. 'Stinnes is doing exactly what you or I would do. He is reserving his position, asking for more information, and playing it very safe. He doesn't care whether we will find it easy or convenient to rendezvous on Biedermann's boat. If we don't overcome our reservations, our fears and our difficulties he'll know we're not serious.'

Werner pushed his lower lip forward as if in thought. And then, to consolidate this reflective pose, he pinched his nose between thumb and forefinger while closing his eyes. It was a more elaborate version of the faces he'd pulled at school when trying to remember theorems. 'I'll go with you,' he said. It was a noble concession; Werner hated boats of any shape or size.

'Would Stinnes permit that?'

'I'll just turn up there. We'll say you had trouble with the traffic cops. We'll say they wanted a notarized affidavit from the legal owner of the car you're using. That's the law here. We'll say you couldn't get one, so I had to drive you in my car.'

'Will he believe that?' I said.

'He'll think the cops were trying to wring a big bribe from you – it's common for cops to stop cars with foreigners in and demand a bribe from the driver – and he'll think you were too dumb to understand what they really wanted.'

'When is this meeting to be?'

'Tomorrow. Okay?'

'Fine.'

'Very early.'

'I said okay, Werner.'

'Because I have to phone him and confirm.'

'Codes or anything?'

'No, he just wants me to phone and say if my friend will be able to go on the fishing trip.'

'Good. A lot of mumbo-jumbo with codes would have made me uneasy. It's the way the Moscow desk men would want it done.'

Werner nodded. The guitar player was still singing the catchy melody:

. . . Christ on your hill, on the mountain ridge of Cubilete,
Console those who suffer, you're worshipped by the people,
Christ on your hill, on the mountain ridge of Cubilete.

'It's a popular song,' said Werner. 'Did you know that the Cubilete is a mountain ridge shaped like a dice-cup? But why is life worth nothing?'

'It means life is cheap,' I said. 'The song is about the way that people are killed for nothing in this part of the world.'

'By the way,' said Werner, 'if you could let us have the return air fares you mentioned, I'd appreciate it.'

'Sure,' I said. 'I can do that on my own authority. Two first-class air tickets Berlin to Mexico City and return. I'll give you a voucher that any big airline will cash.'

'It would be useful,' said Werner. 'The peso is cheap but we get through a lot of money one way and the other.'

7

It was still night when we got to Santiago, but there was enough moonlight to see that Biedermann's gate was locked. I noticed that a new chain had been found to replace the one that had been sawn through on my previous visit. There was no response to pressing the button of the speaker-phone.

'If that bastard doesn't turn up . . .' I said and kicked the gate.

'Calm down,' said Werner. 'We're early. Let's stroll along the beach.'

We left Werner's pick-up truck at the entrance and walked to the beach to watch the ocean. The storms had cleared and the weather was calm, but close-to the noise of the ocean was thunderous. The waves hitting the beach exploded across the sand in reat galaxies of sparkling phosphorescence. Everywhere the coast was littered with flotsam: broken pieces of timber from boats and huts and limbs of trees torn apart by the great winds.

Over the salty putrefaction that is the smell of the ocean there came a whiff of woodsmoke. Along the water's edge, at the place where a piece of jungly undergrowth came almost to the sand, there was a flickering light of a fire. Werner and I walked along to see it, and round the corner of the rocks we saw blanketed shapes huddled around a dying fire.

Here in the shelter of the rocks and vegetation there was less noise from the sea but I could feel the pounding surf underfoot and there was spray in the air that made beads of moisture on my spectacles.

Nearer to the fire, perched with his back against a rock, there was a man. Now and then the fire flared enough to show his bearded face and the hair tied in a pony-tail. He was a muscular youth, darkly tanned, wearing old swimming trunks and a clean T-shirt that was too small for him. He was smoking and staring into the fire. He seemed not to see us until we were almost on top of him.

'Who's that?' he called in English. His voice was high-pitched; he sounded nervous.

'We live near by,' I said. 'We're going out fishing. We're waiting for the boat.'

There was a snuffling sound coming from one of the huddled shapes. At first it was a soft warbling muffled by the blankets. 'Shut up, Betty,' said the bearded man. But the sound didn't cease. It became more nasal, almost stertorous, until it was recognizably a girl sobbing. 'Shut up, I say. There are people here. Try and go back to sleep.' The bearded boy inhaled deeply on his cigarette. There was the sweet smell of marijuana smoke in the air.

But the girl sat up. She was about eighteen years old, pretty if you made allowances for the spots on her face that might have been a sign of adolescence or bad diet. Her hair was cut short, shorter in fact than that of the bearded man. As the blanket fell away from her shoulders I could see that she was wearing only a bra. Her body was badly sunburned. She stopped sobbing and wiped the tears from her eyes with her fingertips. 'Have you got a cigarette?' she asked me. 'An American cigarette?'

I offered her my packet. 'Can I take two?' she whispered.

'Keep the packet,' I said. 'I'm trying to give it up.'

She lit the cigarette immediately and passed the packet to the bearded boy who used the joint he'd been smoking to light up a Camel instead. Behind him one of the other sleepers moved. I had the feeling that all of them were awake and listening to us.

'Have you just arrived?' I said. 'I don't remember you being here last week.'

The boy seemed to feel that some explanation was necessary. 'There were seven of us, four guys and three girls.' He leaned forward and used a piece of wood to prod the fire. There were tiny burned fragments of unprocessed film there and the boy prodded them into the ashes until they burned. 'We met and got together waiting for a bus way north of here in Mazatlan. We're back-packing along the coast, and heading down towards Acapulco. But one of the guys – Theo – slept under a manzanillo tree the night before last, and the sap is poisonous. That was at our previous camp, a long way up the coast from here. We made good mileage since then. But Theo was shook. He cut away inland to look for a clinic.' The bearded boy rubbed his arm where the dark suntan was made even darker by a long stain of iodine that had treated a bad cut on his forearm.

'Have you seen a power boat in the last few hours?' I asked.

'Sure,' said the bearded boy. 'It's anchored on the other side of the headland. We were watching it this afternoon. It's a ritzy son of a bitch. Is that the one you're going on? She came up the coast and tried to get into the little pier, but I guess the tide was wrong or something because finally they had to use the dinghy to land a couple of guys.' He turned his head to look at the waves striking the beach. They came racing towards us, making a huge, shimmering sheet of polished steel until the water lost its impetus and sank into the darkened sand.

'We haven't seen her yet,' I said. 'A good boat, is it?'

'That boat's a ship, man,' he said. 'What are you going after – marlin or sailfish or something?'

'We're after anything that's out there,' I said. 'Are you hiking all the way?'

'We thumb a ride now and again. And twice we took a Mexican second-class bus, but along this piece of coast the highway runs too far inland. We like to keep near the ocean. We like to swim, and catching fish to eat saves dough. But it's heavy going along this section. We've chopped our way through for the last five miles or so.'

They were all obviously awake now, all six of them. But they remained very still so that they heard everything being said. I could see that they'd made a little encampment here in the shelter of a rocky outcrop. There were seven back-packs perched up on the rocks and kept fastened against rats and monkeys. Someone had tried to build a *palapas*, the hut that local people make as a temporary shelter using the coconut palms. But making them was not so easy as it looks, and this one had fallen to pieces. The wood framework had collapsed at one end, and split palm fronds were scattered across the beach. Laundry was hanging to dry on some bushes: a man's T-shirt, a pair of jeans and underpants. A yellow plastic jug was rigged up in a tree to make a shower bath. Two tin plates were bent almost double.

'Someone's tried to eat their plate,' I said.

'Yeah,' said the bearded boy. 'We tried to dig a well without a spade. It's tough going. There's no water here. We'll have to move on tomorrow.'

'Where will you meet your friend?' I said.

The boy looked at me long enough to let me know I was asking too many questions, but he answered. 'Theo decided to head back home. He left his back-pack with us. He didn't want to go on down to Acapulco.'

'That's tough,' I said.

'Those manzanillo trees really burn a piece out of you, man.'

'I'll watch out for them,' I said.

'Do that,' said the boy. The rocks here were volcanic, teeth riddled with cavities so that the sea gurgled and gulped and vented spray that hissed before falling back, in a flash of fluorescent light, on to the sharp, black molars.

'Thanks for the cigarettes,' the girl said very quietly as we moved away. There was another girl alongside her. She put her arm round the girl who'd been crying and, as we moved away, she said, 'Try and go to sleep, Betty. Tomorrow we must move on.'

Werner and I strolled back along the beach and then got into the little pick-up truck. It had four-wheel drive and had managed the final section of road without much trouble. Werner had borrowed it. He had an amazing ability to get almost anything at any time anywhere. I didn't ask where it had come from. He looked at his watch. 'Stinnes should be here any minute,' he said.

'A man like that is usually early,' I said.

'If you've got any doubts . . .'

'No, we'll hang on.'

'Did you wonder who those people were on the beach? Did you guess they were hippies?'

'I'm still wondering,' I said. I could taste the salt spray on my lips and I polished my glasses again to get rid of the marks.

'What the girl was crying about? Is that what you're wondering?'

'Six people back-packing through miles of scrub but there's seven packs?'

'One belongs to the kid who went looking for the clinic. Hell, you know the crazy things people do.'

'An injured kid abandons his back-pack? That's like saying he's abandoned all his belongings.'

'It's possible,' said Werner.

'And the other six carry an extra back-pack? How do you do that, Werner? Never mind cutting your way through the scrub at the same time. How do you carry a back-pack when you're already wearing one? Try it some time.'

'So what are you saying?'

'If those kids had an extra pack to carry they would take it to pieces and distribute it. More likely – seeing those kids – they would sell it in the local village where a decent pack would get them some stores or something to smoke or whatever they wanted.'

'And the boy had a bad cut on his arm,' said Werner.

'A bad cut in exactly the right place, Werner, the left forearm. And there were cuts on his hand too. Maybe more cuts under the borrowed T-shirt. The girl was sobbing like her heart was broken. And the other girl was comforting her.'

'Someone had taken a shower bath.'

'Yes, and washed one set of clothes,' I said. 'Four men and three girls, sleeping on the beach each night. It's a recipe for trouble.'

'Why dig for water? There must be water in the village,' said Werner.

'Sure. And you can bet that Biedermann didn't start building his house until he found water there.'

'If we're guessing right, we should tell the police,' said Werner.

'Oh, sure,' I said. 'That's all we need, the local cops quizzing us all night and walking all over Stinnes and Biedermann too. I can't think of any surer way of ending any chance of enrolling Stinnes than having him walk into a murder investigation that we've made sure coincided exactly with his expected time of arrival.'

'I don't like the idea of just doing nothing about it,' said Werner. 'Sometimes, Werner, you amaze me.'

He didn't answer. I'd seen him like this before. Werner was in a self-righteous sulk. He thought I should report my suspicions to the police and I had no doubt that he was preparing a lecture to which I would be subjected when he had it word-perfect. We sat in the car, watching the eastern sky lighten and thinking our own thoughts, until, half an hour later, we saw the headlights of two cars bumping along the track towards us.

Stinnes was in one car and Paul Biedermann in the other. One of the cars had got stuck on the final stretch of bad road. Biedermann opened the gate without more than a mumbled greeting and we all drove up to the house.

'I'm sorry about the locked gate,' said Biedermann. There had been no formal introductions. It was as if by tacit consent this was to be a meeting that never took place. 'The servants must have forgotten what I told them.'

The 'servants' were a man and boy who, judging by the state of their boots, had recently arrived by the footpath that I had taken on the previous visit. They gave us mugs of the very sweet coffee made from the sugar-coated coffee beans that Mexicans like. They wore checked shirts and jeans. One of them was little more than a child. I guessed they were also the 'crew' of Biedermann's motor boat. They treated Biedermann with a surly deference that might have been the result of the drunken rages that he was reputed to indulge in. But now Biedermann was sober and withdrawn. The four of us stood on the patio looking at the sun-streaked dawn sky and down to where a forty-foot cabin cruiser was at anchor a hundred metres offshore.

I took this opportunity to look at Stinnes, and I suppose he was making the most of this chance to study me. It was only his perfect German and the Berlin accent that made it possible for Stinnes to be mistaken for a native Berliner. Such thin, wiry bodies and Slavic faces are common on the streets of Moscow. He'd removed his straw hat and revealed a tall forehead and hair that was thinning enough to show the shape of his skull. His eyes flittered behind small, circular, gold-rimmed spectacles that now he took off to polish while he looked around. He'd been in the sun, and the chin from which he'd shaved a small beard was darkened. But his complexion was sallow and without pigment enough to tan evenly. In the Mexican sun his cheekbones and nose had turned a yellowish brown like the nicotine-stained fingers of a heavy smoker. And his cotton suit – so light in colour as to be almost white – was ill fitting and wrinkled by the car journey. And yet, for all that, Stinnes had the quick intelligent eyes and tough self-confidence that makes a man attractive to his fellow humans.

'Let's get going,' said Biedermann impatiently. He was nervous. He made sure he never met my gaze. 'Leave the coffee. Pedro and his son will make more on the boat if you want it. We're taking food with us.' He fussed about us like a tour guide, leading the way as we went down to the pier. He was telling us to mind the steps and to watch out for the mud or the slippery wooden boards. I looked along the coast to see the hippies on the beach, but it was too far and they were hidden by the rocks. I looked back over my shoulder. Stinnes was at the very rear, picking his way down the steps with exaggerated care, his straw hat, old-fashioned spectacles and creased white suit making him look like a character from Chekhov. Not the muddled, avuncular Chekhov of the Western stage but the cold, arid class enemy that the Soviet theatre depicts.

The sun was coming through the haze now, its yellowish glare like a melted blob of butter oozing through a tissue-paper wrapping. No one had commented on Werner's presence, and I was grateful to him for being there. Either they didn't plan to get rough, or they planned to get so rough that one extra victim would make no difference.

It was named *Maelstrom* and was the sort of boat that the Paul Biedermanns of this world love. It stood high out of the water with a top deck used for spotting and an awning-covered stern and a big 'dentist's chair' for the man who was fishing. The lounge was lined with expensive veneering and had a stereo hi-fi, a big TV and a wet bar with refrigerator. Steps up from there gave on to a big 'bridge' where a swivel seat provided the captain with a panoramic view through the wrap-around windscreen. There was even a yachting cap with the word 'captain' entwined in crossed anchors and embroidered in fine gold wire. But Pedro the Mexican didn't wear the captain's hat; his long greasy hair would have stained it. He sat at the controls like a long-distance bus driver waiting at a depot. He rested on the wheel, toying with a wrapped cheroot that he never lit. There was a cheap transistor radio jammed behind the sun visor. He tuned it to a local station that played only Mexican music, and then turned the volume down so that it couldn't be heard in the lounge.

The big engines throbbed with a note so low that the sound was less apparent than the vibrations through the soles of my shoes. Stinnes looked round without much sign of delight or admiration. I suppose it was everything a communist hated. Even a lapsed fascist like me found it a bit too rich.

'Now who would like a drink?' asked Biedermann, in a voice that had the cheerful vibrancy of the perfect host. He had unlocked the bar and was pulling various bottles of drink from the cupboard. 'Scotch. Brandy. English gin.' He held up a bottle and shook it, 'Robert Brown – that's Mexican whisky, and if you've never tried it it's quite an experience.'

Stinnes walked across the lounge and very quietly said, 'Better if you took Mr Volkmann back up to the house, Paul. If Pedro shows me the controls I can handle the boat.' It was a typical KGB trick; carefully planned but unexpected. They could not learn spontaneity but they contrived ways to do without it.

Paul Biedermann looked up at him and blinked. 'Sure. If that's the way you want it.'

'It's the way I want it,' said Stinnes. He took off his straw hat and smoothed his sparse hair by pressing the flat of his hand against his skull.

'And I'll take Pedro and his kid too. Or do you want them with you?' When Stinnes didn't reply, Biedermann gave a nervous smile and got to his feet. 'Pedro. Show Mr Stinnes how to manage the boat.'

I was sitting on the far side of the lounge, watching Biedermann carefully. Either he was scared of Stinnes or it was a very good act. Werner was watching the whole scene too. Typically he was hunched in an armchair with his eyes half closed. It was always like that with Werner; he liked to know everything that was going on, and guess the things he didn't know. But he liked to look half asleep. Werner would have made a very successful gossip columnist, except that he would have missed a lot of deadlines.

Stinnes looked at me and, although his expression didn't change, he waited for me to nod before going up to take over the controls. 'And, Paul,' said Stinnes. 'No drinking, Paul. Better we all kept clear heads.'

'Oh, sure,' said Paul Biedermann. 'I just thought somebody. . . .'

'Better lock it away,' said Stinnes. 'You take Mr Volkmann up to the house and have more coffee.'

'Before you lock it away,' I said, 'leave a little something to one side, would you?'

I poured myself a good measure of malt whisky from the bottle Biedermann had put aside for me and sipped it neat. I never really trust drinking water anywhere but Scotland; and I've never been to Scotland.

I heard the whine of the electric motor that brought the anchor up and felt the boat wallow as the current took a hold. Through the porthole I could see the dinghy containing Werner and Paul Biedermann and the two Mexicans returning to the pier. It was being tossed about. I wondered if Werner was feeling okay. He hated the sea in any shape or form. It was a notable gesture of friendship that he should offer to come along.

The engines vibrated right through the boat as Stinnes – sitting upstairs at the controls – increased the revs and engaged the screws. The sound of waves pounding against the hull changed to the noise of water rushing past it, and a large patch of sunlight raced across the veneered bulkhead as Stinnes turned the wheel and headed the boat out to the open sea.

I let Stinnes play with the controls while I continued to drink my malt and ask myself what I was doing out at sea in this floating Cadillac in the hurricane season with a KGB major at the helm. He pushed up the revs after a few minutes, and soon there was the crash of shipped water spewing across the deck, and the boat heeled over so that green ocean dashed against the glass for long enough to darken the cabin. Stinnes corrected the steering, more gently this time. He was learning. Best to leave him alone for a few minutes.

I left him for what seemed a long time. By the time I went across the cabin to pour myself a second drink, I had to plant my feet wide apart because the boat was reeling. We'd reached the point where the cool equatorial stream of the Pacific was affected by the very warm summer currents that follow the coast. I held tight to my drink as I went upstairs to where Stinnes was at the controls. The sunlight was behind him, turning his sparse hair into a bright halo and edging his white cotton jacket with a rim of gold. There was the muffled sound of Mexican music coming from the little plastic radio.

'Suppose I take you seriously?' said Stinnes, greeting my appearance on the bridge. 'Suppose I say, yes I'd like to defect? Is it some kind of joke? Or are you really able to negotiate?'

'Where are you taking us?' I said with some alarm. 'We're out of sight of land.' I had to talk loudly to be heard over the noise of the sea and the music from the radio.

'I know what I'm doing,' said Stinnes. 'Biedermann has radar and sonar and depth-finding gear and every other luxury.'

'Does he have anything to cure a fatal drowning?' I said.

'Volkmann says you have some sort of deal,' said Stinnes. He glanced down at the instruments and rapped the barometer with his knuckles.

'Are you just crazy about Mexican music, or are you waiting for a hurricane warning?' I said. He turned down the volume of the little radio until it was only a whisper heard faintly against the sound of the wind and the throb of the engines. 'There is a deal,' I said. 'Ready and waiting.'

'Why me?' said Stinnes.

I'd asked myself that already and got no answer. 'Why not?' I said.

'Your government has not sent you all this way without a motive, a good motive.'

No mention of Dicky Cruyer, I noticed. Did that mean that Dicky was unknown to him? It could be useful. 'There were other reasons for my being here.'

He looked at me and his face was blank but I knew he didn't believe me. He was suspicious, just as I would have been in his place. There could be no half-measures. I would have to work very hard to land this one. He was like me, too damned old and too damned cynical to fall for anything but innocent sincerity or a cynicism even more profound than his own. 'You are targeted,' I said. 'Starred by London as an exceptional enemy agent.'

The sun was brighter now, coming over his shoulder and falling on the instrument panel so that I could see the controls reflected in the lenses of his spectacles. 'Is that so?' His voice was flat, but I had the feeling he believed me and was proud to be starred by London. This was probably the right way to tackle him. It would be like a love affair; and Stinnes had reached that dangerous age when a man was only susceptible to an innocent little cutie or to an experienced floozy. And the stock-in-trade of both was flattery.

'London are like that sometimes,' I said. 'They decide they want someone and then it's rush, rush, rush. I hate this sort of job.'

'I want no mention of all this in your signals traffic,' said Stinnes. 'Especially not in your embassy signals from Mexico City. I insist on that right from the start.'

I didn't want him to think London was *too* keen. If Stinnes said no we might have to snatch him and I didn't want him prepared for that sort of development. I kept it very cool. 'We'll have to act quickly,' I said. 'If we don't get everything settled in the next week or so London might lose interest and drop the idea. It's the way they are.'

It was fully daylight now and, although the sun had still to eat through the morning haze, there were no clouds. It was going to be a very hot day. The wind was at about eight to ten knots, so that the waves were lengthening and breaking here and there to make scattered white horses. On the westerly horizon I could see two ships. I watched the compass. Was Stinnes going to turn the tables on me. Were they Russian trawlers, waiting for Stinnes to deliver me to the ship's side, with a KGB interrogation team leaning over the rails? Perhaps Stinnes understood what was going through my mind, for he swung the wheel gently to head well south of them. As he changed the heading, an extra big wave broke over the bow and dashed spray so that the air was full of the taste of it. 'Your people are clever, Samson . . . Is that your true name – Samson?'

'It's my name. Are they clever?'

He smiled a humourless little smile. 'I'm forty, and still a major. Slim chance now for a colonel's badges. I'm not a wunderkind, Samson. I won't end up a general with a department to myself and a nice big office in Moscow, and a big car and driver who takes me home each night. Even I have begun to admit that to myself.'

'I thought you liked Berlin,' I said.

'I've been there long enough. I've had enough of Berlin. I've had enough of sitting in my cramped little house watching West German television advertise all the things my wife wants and can't get.' Another wave broke across the bow. He throttled back so that the boat just rode the waves with enough power to hold the heading. The boat slid about, tossed from wave to wave, and I had to grab a rail to hold myself steady. 'I'm going to get a divorce,' he said, suddenly occupying himself with the controls so that it seemed to be an aside without importance. 'Did London know anything about that?'

'No,' I said.

'No, of course not. Even my own people don't know yet. The Directorate don't like divorce . . . instability, they call it. Domestic instability. Anything that goes wrong in a marriage is categorized as "domestic instability". It can be child beating, wife beating, keeping a mistress or habitual drunkenness. It's called "domestic instability" and it gets a black mark. It gets you the sort of black mark that results in long talks with investigating officers, and some-times leads to a short "leadership course" with political indoctrination and physical training. Wives of KGB officers get to depend on it, Samson.'

'I don't like physical training,' I said. Perhaps London are clever, I thought. Perhaps they did know. That's why they were in such a hurry. I wondered if Dicky had been told. I wondered too how many of those black marks Stinnes was eligible for; not child beating, wife beating possibly, mistress keeping highly likely. He was the sort of man who would attract some women. I looked at that hard, unyielding face, smooth like a carefully carved netsuke handled by generations of collectors, and darkening as elephant tusk darkens when locked away and deprived of light.

'You wouldn't like this sort of physical training,' said Stinnes. 'The KGB Field Officers' Leadership School is nearly one hundred miles from the nearest town on Sakhalin Island in the Sea of Okhotsk. I went there once when I was a young lieutenant. I was part of a two-man armed escort. It was in September 1964. A captain from my unit had been assigned to the school for the four-month course. He was sent there because when very drunk one night he told a roomful of officers that Nikita Khrushchev was not fit to be Prime Minister and certainly should not be First Secretary of the Soviet Communist Party. It's a grim place, Samson; I was only there two hours but that was enough for me. Unheated rooms, cold-water showers and "candidates" have to run everywhere. Only the staff are permitted to walk. Not the sort of place that you or I like. The funny thing was that a few weeks later Khrushchev was denounced in far stronger terms and replaced by Brezhnev and ousted.' Stinnes gave a brief, humourless smile. 'But the captain wasn't released. He served his full sentence . . . that is to say he did the whole leadership course. I wouldn't like to be sent there.'

'It sounds like a strong argument for marital fidelity,' I said.

'Yes, I haven't officially asked for a divorce. I was only thinking about it. But everyone knows that I no longer get along so well with my wife Inge. I am bored with her and she is bored with me and there is nothing to be done except that I must get out before I begin to loathe her. Do you understand?' He looked at me. We both knew what had happened to my wife: she'd become his boss. And he didn't seem like a man who would enjoy working for a woman boss. I wondered if that was a part of the real story.

'Have you got any other children?' I asked.

'No, just the boy, eighteen years old. He is at an age when he realizes how I fall short of the Daddy he once revered. At first it made me angry, then it made me sad. Now I've come to see it as the natural progress of youth.'

'You married a German,' I said.

'I was lonely. Inge was only a few months younger than me. You know that special sort of magic Berlin girls can wield. Sunshine, strong beer, short skirts, long lazy evenings, sailing boats on the Muggelsee. It shouldn't be allowed.' Stinnes laughed, a short dry bitter laugh, as if he still was in love with her and resented it.

'Coming to the West would solve all your problems,' I said. I didn't want to rush him; any suggestion of haste now could make him change his mind. Maybe he would come to us, maybe he was just humouring me, but I knew it was important to keep pressing forwards. I knew what sort of ideas must be going through his mind. There would be so many things he would have to do. There would be good people he'd want to transfer away so they weren't tainted by his treachery.

'What a wonderful offer. How could anyone resist a future without problems.'

'It's your life,' I said. For a moment I didn't care what he did but immediately my professionalism overcame my anger. It was my job to enrol Erich Stinnes and I would do everything I could to land him. 'But say no and I doubt if London will come back to you again. It's now or never.'

'Very well,' said Stinnes. 'You tell your people that I said no. I want that to go to London through your Mexico City embassy in the usual coding.' I nodded and tried not to show my surprise that the Russians had broken our codes. In future we'd have to make sure that everything important went to London via Washington and used the NSA's crypto-ciph B machines.

He waited until I grunted my assent. He knew he'd given me an important piece of intelligence.

'I will report an approach. I won't identify you, Samson. I'll make it vague enough for Moscow to think it's some low-grade local agent trying to make a name for himself. But you go back to London and tell whoever is the desk man on this one that they've got a deal.'

'What will the timing be?'

'There are things I have to do. I'll need a month.'

'Yes,' I said. He'd want to get his hands on some secret paperwork, so that he'd have something to bring. He'd want some time with his wife, a last talk with his son, a meal with his family, a drink with his secretary, an evening with old friends. He'd want to imprint them upon his memory. 'I understand.'

I felt the hot sun on my arm; it was on the starboard bow. Only now did I notice that he'd been turning the helm in tiny expert movements that had brought the boat round until it was heading back home again. Stinnes did everything with that same professional stealth. It made me uneasy.

'My people will be impatient,' I warned.

'We all know what desk men are like. You'll keep them warm?'

'I'll try,' I promised. 'But you'd better bring something good with you.'

'I'm not a beginner, Samson. That's what I need a month to arrange.' He got a small black cigar from his top pocket and took his time lighting it. Once he got it well alight he took the cheroot from his mouth and nodded as if confirming something to himself.

If he really intended to come to us he'd be grabbing as many secret documents as he could find, and locking them away somewhere, a Swiss bank vault perhaps. Only a fool would come without having some extras tucked away somewhere. And Stinnes was no fool.

'What sort of material are they looking for?' he asked.

'They'll expect you break a network,' I said.

He thought about it. 'Is that what London says?'

'It's what I'm saying. You know they'll expect it. It's what you'd want if you had me in Moscow.'

'Yes.'

'I'll give you a word of advice,' I said. 'Don't withdraw a net and then come over to us with a list of people who have left no forwarding address. That would just make everyone bad-tempered, and they'll start to think you're still on salary from Moscow. Understand?'

He blew evil-smelling cigar smoke. 'It's a pleasure to do business with you, Samson. You make everything very clear.'

'So let me make this clear too. If you try to turn me round, if you try any tricks at all, I will blow you away.'

8

By midday we'd been waiting nearly three hours, and our plane had still not arrived. Other departures were also delayed. The official explanation was the hurricanes. Mexico City airport was packed with people. There were Indian women clasping sacks of flour and a sequin-suited rock group guarding their amplifiers. All found some way to deal with the interminable delay: mothers suckled babies, boys raced through the concourse on roller-skates, a rug pedlar – burdened under his wares – systematically pitched his captive audience, tour guides paced resolutely, airline staff yawned, footsore hikers snored, nuns told their rosaries, a tall Negro – listening to a Sony Walkman – swayed rhythmically, and some Swedish school kids were gambling away their last few pesos.

Dicky Cruyer had excess baggage, and some parcels of cheap tin decorative masks that he insisted must go as cabin baggage. From where I sat I could see Dicky focusing all his charm on to the girl at the check-in desk. There were no seats available so I was propped on one of Dicky's suitcases talking to Werner. I watched Dicky gesturing at the girl and running his hands back through his curly hair in the way he did when he was being shy and boyish.

'Don't trust him,' said Werner.

'Dicky? Don't worry, I won't.'

'You know who I mean,' said Werner. 'Don't trust Stinnes.' Werner was sitting on another of Dicky's many cases. He was wearing a *guyavera*, the traditional Mexican shirt that is all pleats and buttons, and with it linen trousers and expensive-looking leather shoes patterned with ventilation holes. Although Werner complained of Mexico's heat and humidity, the climate seemed to suit him. His complexion was such that he tanned easily, and he was more relaxed in the sunshine than ever he'd seemed to be in Europe.

'There's nothing to lose,' I said.

'For London Central, you mean? Or nothing to lose for you?'

'I'm just doing what London want me to do, Werner . . . Theirs not to make reply, Theirs not to reason why, Theirs but to do and die . . . You know how London expect us to work.'

'Yes,' said Werner, who'd had this same conversation with me many times before. 'It's always *easier* to do and die than it is to reason why.'

'I don't trust him; I don't distrust him,' I said as I thought about Werner's warning. 'I don't give a damn about Stinnes. I don't begrudge him his opportunity to squeeze a bigger cash payment from the department than any loyal employee ever got. More money, I'd guess, than the wife and kids of any of the department's casualties ever collected. But it makes me wonder, Werner. It makes me wonder what the hell it's all about.'

'It's the game,' said Werner. He too was slumped back against the wall with a plastic cup of warm, weak coffee in his hand. 'It's nothing to do with virtue and evil, or effort and reward; it's just a game. You know that, Bernie.'

'And Stinnes knows how to play it better than we do?'

'It's not a game of skill,' said Werner. 'It's a game of chance.'

'Is there nothing that lights up and says "tilt" when you cheat?'

'Stinnes isn't cheating. He's just a man in the right place at the right time. He's done nothing to entice London to enrol him.'

'What do you make of him, Werner?'

'He's a career KGB officer. We've both seen a million of them. Stinnes holds no surprises for me, Bernie. And, providing you don't trust him, no surprises for you either.'

'He didn't ask enough questions,' I said. 'I've been thinking of that ever since the boat trip. Stinnes didn't ask me any important questions. Not the sort of questions I'd be asking in his place.'

'He's a robot,' said Werner. 'Did you expect him to engage you in a political argument? Did you expect a detailed discussion about the deprivation of the Third World?'

'I suppose I did,' I admitted.

'Well, this is the right country for anyone looking for political arguments,' said Werner. 'If ever there was a country poised on the brink of revolution, this is it. Look around; two-thirds of the Mexican population – about fifty million people – are living at starvation level. You've seen the *campesinos* struggling to grow crops in volcanic ash or rock, and bringing to market half a dozen onions or some such pathetic little crop. You've seen them scratching a living here in the city in slums as bad as anywhere in the world. Four out of ten Mexicans never drink milk, two out of ten never eat meat, eggs or bread. But the Mexican government subsidizes Coca Cola sales. The official explanation is that Coca Cola is nutritious.' Werner drank some of the disgusting coffee. 'And, now that the IMF have forced Mexico to devalue the peso, big US companies – such as Xerox and Sheraton – can build factories and hotels here at rock-bottom prices, but sell to hard-currency customers. Inflation goes up. Unemployment figures go up. Taxes go up. Prices go up. But wages go down. How would you like it if you were Mexican?' It was quite a speech for Werner.

'Did Stinnes say that?'

'Haven't you been listening to me? Stinnes is a career KGB officer. Stinnes doesn't give a damn about the Mexicans and their problems, except how and when it affects his career prospects. I started talking about all this to him at the club one evening. Stinnes knows nothing about Mexico. He's not even had the regular briefing that all East European diplomatic services give to their personnel.'

'Why?' I said.

'Why? said Werner irritably, thinking I merely wanted to change the subject. 'How could I know?'

'Think about it, Werner. The first thing it indicates is that he came here at short notice. Even then, knowing the KGB, they would have arranged for him to have political indoctrination here in Mexico City.'

Werner shifted his weight uncomfortably on Dicky's suitcase and looked around to see if there was anywhere else to sit. There wasn't; in fact the whole place was getting more and more crowded. Now there was a large group of young people carrying bright orange shoulder-bags that announced them to be a choir from New Zealand. They were seating themselves all along the corridor. I hoped they wouldn't start singing. 'I suppose you're right,' said Werner.

'I am right,' I said. 'And I'll tell you something else. The complete absence of political indoctrination suggests to me that Stinnes is not here to run agents into California, nor to supervise Biedermann's funnelling of Moscow money to local organizations.'

'Don't keep me in suspense,' said Werner wearily.

'I haven't got the answer, Werner. I don't know what Stinnes is doing here. I don't even know what *I'm* doing here. Stinnes could be positively identified without having me along.'

'London didn't send you along so that you could identify Stinnes,' said Werner. 'London sent you along so that Stinnes could identify you.'

'No anagrams, Werner. Keep it simple for me.'

'What do you think was the first thing that came into his mind the other night when I started telling him about freezers, videos and the acceleration a Porsche 924 turbo gives you from a standing start?'

'Entrapment?'

'Well, of course. He was terrified that I was a KGB employee who was going to provide the evidence that would put him into a Siberian penal battalion for twenty years.'

'Ummm. But he could be sure that I was an SIS agent from London because he'd actually had me under arrest in East Berlin. I suppose you're right, Werner. I suppose Bret had that all figured out.'

'Bret Rensselaer, was it? Of all the people in London Central he's the most cunning one. And right now he's very keen to prove the department needs him.'

'Dicky is frightened that Bret will get the German Desk,' I said.

'*Stuhlpolonaise*,' said Werner.

'Exactly. Musical chairs.' Werner's use of the German word called to mind the prim formality and the slow rhythm of the promenading couples that exactly described London Central's dance when some big reshuffle was due. 'And Bret has sent Dicky marching four thousand miles away from the only chair, and Dicky wants to get back to London before the music stops.'

'But he doesn't want to return without news of a great success,' said Werner.

'You see that, do you?' I said admiringly. Werner didn't miss much. 'Yes, Bret has contrived a quandary that alarms even Dicky. If he waits here long enough to land Stinnes, Bret will be the man who congratulates him and sends him off on another assignment. On the other hand, if Dicky rushes back there without a conclusion to the Stinnes operation, someone is going to say that Dicky is not up to the job.'

'But you're both going back,' said Werner. He looked round the crowded lounge. Outside, the apron was empty and the regular afternoon rainstorm was in full fury. There was not much evidence that anyone was going anywhere.

'I'm now the file officer. Dicky is writing a report that will explain the way in which he has brought the Stinnes operation to the brink of a successful conclusion before handing everything over to me.'

'He is a crafty little bastard,' said Werner.

'Now tell me something I don't know.'

'And, if Stinnes doesn't come over, Dicky will say you messed it up.'

'Go to the top of the class, Werner. You're really getting the hang of it.'

'But I think there's only a slight chance that we'll get Stinnes over.'

'Why?' I agreed with Werner but I wanted to hear his views.

'He's still frightened, for one thing. If Stinnes really trusted you, he wouldn't tell you to send a negative signal to London. He'd let you tell London anything you liked.'

'Don't tell Dicky I told you about the compromised signal traffic,' I said. 'He'll say it's a breach of security.'

'It is a breach of security,' said Werner. 'Strictly speaking I shouldn't be told that sort of top-grade item unless it's directly concerned with my work.'

'My God, Werner. Am I glad you don't have the German Desk in London. I think you'd shop me if you thought I was breaking security.'

'Maybe I would,' said Werner complacently. I grabbed him by the throat and pretended to throttle him. It was a spectacle that interested one of the nuns enough for her to nudge her companion and nod towards me. I gave them both a sinister scowl and Werner put his tongue out and rolled his eyes.

After I'd released Werner and let him drink some more of that awful coffee, I said, 'You said Stinnes knows I'm kosher on account of interrogating me.'

'That could be a double ploy,' said Werner. 'If you were really working for Moscow, then you would be quite happy to let yourself get arrested in East Berlin. Then you'd be perfectly placed to trap Stinnes.'

'But Stinnes isn't important enough for Moscow to play out that sort of operetta.'

'Stinnes probably thinks he is important enough. It's human, isn't it? We all think we are important enough for anything.'

Werner could be exasperating. 'That's what Hollywood calls "moronic logic", Werner. It's the sort of nit-picking insanity that can't be faulted but is only too obviously stupid.'

'So explain why it's stupid.'

I took a deep breath and said, 'Because if Moscow had a well-placed agent in London whose identity was so closely guarded that Stinnes could not possibly suspect him, then Moscow would not bring him to Berlin and get him arrested just so as to get the confidence of Stinnes so that months later in Mexico City he could be enticed into agreeing to a defection plan. I mean . . . ask yourself, Werner.'

He smiled self-consciously. 'You're right, Bernie. But Stinnes will continue to be suspicious, you mark my words.'

'Sure, but he'll be suspicious of London and whether those tricky desk men will keep their promises. He won't be worrying if I'm a KGB plant. A man like Stinnes can probably recognize a KGB operator at one hundred paces just as we can recognize one of our people.'

'Talking of recognizing one of our own at one hundred paces, Dicky is heading this way,' said Werner. 'Is the man with him SIS?'

Dicky Cruyer was still wearing his Hollywood clothes; today it was blue striped seersucker trousers, sea-island cotton sports shirt and patent-leather Gucci shoes. He was carrying a small leather pouch that was not, Dicky said, a handbag, or anything like one.

Dicky had his friend from the embassy in tow. They'd been at Balliol together and they made no secret of their intense rivalry. Despite their being the same age, Henry Tiptree looked younger than Dicky. Perhaps this was because of the small and rather sparse moustache that he was growing, or his thin neck, bony chin and the awkward figure he cut in his Hong Kong tropical suit and the tightly knotted old school tie.

Dicky told me how his friend Henry had been made Counsellor at the very early age of thirty-eight and was now working hard to reach Grade 3. But the diplomatic service is littered with brilliant Counsellors of all ages, and a large proportion of them get shunted off to the Institute for Strategic Studies or given a fellowship at Oxford, where they could write a lot of twaddle about Soviet aims and intentions in East Europe, while people like me and Werner actually dealt with them.

'Henry has arranged everything about the baggage,' said Dicky.

'There was nothing to arrange about my baggage,' I said. 'I checked it through when we first got here.'

Dicky ignored my retort and said, 'It will go air freight. But because we have first-class tickets they'll put it on the same plane we're on.'

'And which plane is that?' I asked.

Henry looked at his watch and said, 'They say it's coming in now.'

'You don't believe that, do you?' said Dicky. 'Ye gods, these airline buggers tell lies more glibly than even the diplomatic service.'

'Haw haw,' said Henry dutifully. 'But I think this time it's probably true. There are lots of delays at this time of year but eventually they come lumbering in. Three hours is about par for the course. That's why I thought I'd better be here to see you off.' Henry pronounced it 'orrf', he had that sort of ripe English accent that he'd need for becoming an ambassador.

'Plus the fact that you had to be here because it's bag day,' said Dicky. Henry smiled.

Werner said, 'Bag day?'

'The courier with the diplomatic bag is coming in on this plane,' I explained.

'Even so, your presence is much appreciated, Henry,' Dicky told him. 'I'll make sure the Prime Minister's Private Secretary hears about the cooperation you gave us.' They both laughed at Dicky's little joke but there was a promise of some undefined help when the opportunity came. Balliol men were like that; or so Dicky always said.

I could see that Werner was eyeing Henry with interest, trying to decide whether he was actually employed by the SIS within the embassy staff. It seemed possible. I winked at Werner. He grinned as he realized that I'd known what was in his mind. But we untutored men were like that; or so I always said.

'Dicky says that you're the man who holds the department toge-ther,' said Henry.

'It's not easy,' I said.

Dicky, who had expected me to deny that I held the department together, said, 'Henry loaned us the car.'

'Thanks, Henry,' I said.

'I don't know how you managed with that damned air-conditioning not working,' said Henry. 'But I suspect you chaps are going to charge full Hertz rates on your expenses, eh?'

'Not Dicky,' I said.

'Haw haw,' said Henry.

Dicky changed the subject hurriedly. 'Strawberries and freshly caught salmon,' said Dicky. 'This is the time to be in England, Henry. You can keep the land of tacos and refried beans.'

'Don't be a sadist, Dicky,' said the man from the embassy. 'I'm hoping my transfer comes through. Else I might be stuck here until Christmas or New Year. I have no chance of leave.'

'You shouldn't have joined,' said Dicky.

'I mustn't complain. I had an enjoyable six months learning the lingo and I get up to Los Angeles now and again. Mind you, these Mexicans are a rum crowd. It doesn't take much to make them awfully cross.' Henry said 'crorss'.

'No matter. You won't be here for ever. And now you're Grade 4 you're certain to end your career with a K,' said Dicky enviously. It was Dicky's special grievance that equivalently graded SIS employees could not count on such knighthoods or even lesser honours. Every-thing depended upon where you ended up.

'As long as I don't spill drinks over the President's wife or start a war or something.' He laughed again.

Quietly I asked Dicky if he'd told the embassy about their inter-cepted signals.

'Ye gods,' said Dicky. 'Bernie has just reminded me of something for your very private ear. Something for your Head of Station's very private ear, in fact.'

Henry raised an eyebrow. Head of Station was the senior SIS officer in the embassy.

Dicky said, 'Strictly off the record, Henry old bean, we have reasons to believe that the Russians are listening to your Piccolo machinery and have learned to read the music.'

'I say,' said Henry.

'I suggest he tells your Head of Mission immediately. But he must make it clear that it's only a suspicion.'

'I don't get to talk to the boss all that often, Dicky. The top brass stagger off to Acapulco every chance they get.' He went to the window and said, 'It's coming in now. She'll turn round quickly. Better get your luggage checked through.'

'It might be a hoax,' said Dicky. 'But we hope to be in a position to confirm or deny within a couple of weeks. If there's anything to it you'll hear officially through the normal channels.'

'You London Central people really do see life,' said Henry. 'Have you really been doing a James Bond caper, Dicky? Have you been crossing swords with the local Russkies?'

'Mum's the word,' said Dicky. 'We'd better get some of these airline chappies to haul this baggage over to the check-in.'

'But where will we sit then?' said ever-practical Werner.

Dicky ignored this question and snapped his fingers at a passing slave, who readily and instantly responded by tipping Werner off his perch and grabbing Dicky's other cases to swing on to his shoulder.

Dicky stroked his expensive baggage as if he didn't like to see it go. 'Those three are very fragile – *muy fragil. Comprende usted?*'

'Sure thing,' said the porter. 'No problem, buddy.'

'So those Russian buggers are reading the Piccolo radio traffic,' mused Henry. 'Well, that might explain a lot of things.'

'For instance?' said Dicky, counting his cases as the porter heaved them on to a trolley.

'Just little things,' said Henry vaguely. 'But I'd say your tip-off is no hoax.'

'One up for Mr Stinnes,' said Werner.

The TV monitor flashed a gate number for our flight, and we hurriedly said goodbye to Henry and Werner so that Dicky could follow closely behind the porter to be sure his cases didn't go astray.

'Henry did modern languages,' said Dicky, once we were airborne and heading home with a glass of champagne in our fists and a smiling stewardess offering us small circular pieces of cold toast adorned with fish eggs. 'He was a damned fine bat; and Henry's parties were famous, but he's not very brainy and he wasn't exactly a hard worker. He got this job because he knows all the right people. To tell you the truth, I never though he'd stick to the old diplomatic grind. It's not like Henry to have a regular job and say yes sir and no sir to everyone in sight. Poor sod, sweating out his time in that hell-hole.'

'Yes, poor Henry,' I said.

'He's desperately keen to get into our show but quite honestly, Bernard, I don't think he's right for us, do you?'

'From what you say I think he's exactly right for us.'

'Do you?' said Dicky.

Dicky had arranged everything the way he liked it. He'd put his three fragile parcels on to a vacant seat and secured them with the safety-belt. He'd taken off his shoes and put on the slippers he'd taken from his briefcase. He'd swallowed his motion-sickness tablets and made sure the Alka Seltzer and aspirin were where he could find them easily. He'd read the safety leaflet and checked the position of the emergency exits and reached under his seat to be sure that the advertised life-jacket was really there. 'These airline blighters speak their own language,' said Dicky. 'Have you noticed that? Stewardesses are hostesses; it makes you wonder whether to call the stewards "hosts". Safety-belts are lap-straps, and emergency exits are safety exits. Who thought up all that double-talk?'

'It must have been the same PR man who renamed the War Office the Ministry of Defence.'

I held up my glass so that the stewardess could pour more champagne. Dicky put his hand over his glass. 'We've a long journey ahead,' he said with an admonitory note in his voice.

'Sounds like a good reason to have another glass of champagne,' I said.

Dicky put down his glass and slapped his thigh lightly, like a chairman bringing a meeting to order, and said, 'Well, now I've got you to myself at last, perhaps we can talk shop.'

The only reason we'd not spent a lot of time talking shop was because Dicky had spent every available moment eating, drinking, shopping, sightseeing and extending his influence. Now he was going to find out what work I'd been doing so that he'd be able to persuade his superiors that he'd been working his butt off. 'What do you want to know, Dicky?'

'What are the chances that Comrade Stinnes will come over to us?'

'You're skipping the easy ones, are you?'

'I know you hate making guesses, but what do you think will happen? You've actually met with Stinnes. What sort of fellow is he? You've handled this sort of defection business before, haven't you?'

I didn't hate making guesses at all; I just hated confiding them to Dicky, since he so enjoyed reminding me of the ones I got wrong. I said, 'Not with a really experienced KGB official, I haven't. The defectors I've dealt with have been less important.'

'Stinnes is only a major. You're making him sound like a a member of the Politburo. I seem to remember you were involved with that colonel . . . the air attaché who dithered and dithered and finally got deported before we could get him.'

'Rank for rank, you're right. But Stinnes is very experienced and very tough. If we get him we'll have a very good source. He will keep the debriefing panel scribbling notes for months and months and give us some good data and first-class assessments. But our chances of getting him are not good.'

'You told me he said yes,' said Dicky.

'He's bound to say yes just to hear what we say.'

'Is it money?' said Dicky.

'I can't believe that money will play a big part in his decision. Men such as Stinnes are very thoroughly indoctrinated. It's always very difficult for such people to make the change-over to our sort of society.'

'He's a hard-nose communist, you mean?'

'Only inasmuch as he knows he mustn't rock the boat. I'd be surprised to find he's a real believer.' I drank my champagne. Dicky waited for me to speak again. I said, 'Stinnes is a narrow-minded bigot. He's one of a top-level elite in a totalitarian state where there are no agonizing discussions about capital punishment, or demos about pollution of the environment or the moral uncertainties of having atomic weapons. A KGB major like Stinnes can barge into the office of a commanding general without knocking. Here in the West no one has the sort of power that he enjoys.'

'But we're offering him a nice comfortable life. And, from what you say about his wanting a divorce, the offer comes at exactly the right time.'

'Giving up such power will not be easy. As a defector he'll be a nobody. He's probably seen defectors and the way they live in the Soviet Union. He'll have no illusions about what it will be like.'

'How can you compare the life of a defector going to the East with that of a defector coming to the West? All they have to offer is a perverted ideology and a medieval social system based on privilege and obedience. We have a free society; a free press, freedom to protest, freedom to say anything we like.'

'Stinnes has spent a long time in the upper layers of an authoritarian society. He won't want to protest or demonstrate against government – whatever its creed – and he'll have precious little sympathy for those who do.'

'Then give him a handful of cash and take him round the shops and show him the material benefits that come from free enterprise and competition.'

'Stinnes isn't the sort of man who will sell his soul for a mess of hi-fi components and a micro-wave oven,' I said.

'Sell his soul?' said Dicky indignantly.

'Don't turn this into a political debate, Dicky. You asked me what chance we stand, and I'm telling you what I think is in his mind.'

'So what sort of chance *do* we stand?' persisted Dicky. 'Fifty fifty?'

'Not better anyway,' I said.

'I'll tell the old man fifty fifty,' said Dicky as he mentally ticked off that question. I don't know why I tried to explain things to Dicky. He preferred yes-or-no answers. Explanations confused him.

'And what about this Biedermann chap?'

'I don't know.'

'He's as rich as Croesus. I looked him up when I got to Los Angeles.'

'I can't see how he can be important to us, so how can he be important to Stinnes? That's what puzzles me.'

'I'll put him into my report,' said Dicky. Although it sounded like a statement of intent, it was Dicky's way of asking me to okay it.

'By all means. I've got the list of people he forwarded the money to. You could probably get one of the bright young probationers to build that into something that sounded impressive.'

'Are we going to do anything about Biedermann?'

'There's not much we can do,' I said doubtfully, 'except keep an eye on him, and rough him up from time to time to let him know he's not forgotten.'

'Gently does it,' said Dicky. 'A man like that could make trouble for us.'

'I've known him since I was a kid,' I said. 'He's not going to make trouble for us, unless he thinks he can get away with it.'

'Getting Stinnes is the important thing,' said Dicky. 'Biedermann is nothing compared with the chance of bringing Stinnes over to us.'

'I'll stroke my lucky rabbit's foot,' I said.

'If we do manage to land Stinnes, you'll get all the credit for it.'

'Will I?' I said. It seemed unlikely.

'That's one of the things I told Bret before we left London. I told him that this was really your operation. You let Bernard handle things his way, I told him. Bernard's got a lot riding on this one.'

'And what did Bret say to that?' I found that, if you scraped the ancient airline caviar off the little discs of toast, the toast didn't taste too bad.

'Have you upset Bret?'

'I'm always upsetting him.'

'You've got a lot riding on this one, Bernard. You need Bret. You need all the help you can get. I'm right behind you all the way, of course, but if Bret takes over my desk you'd get no support from him.'

'Thanks, Dicky,' I said doubtfully. It was just Dicky's way of getting me to help him in his power struggle against Bret, but I was flattered to think that Dicky thought I had enough clout to make any difference.

'You know what I'm talking about, don't you, Bernard?'

'Sure,' I said, although in fact I didn't know. I settled back in my seat and looked at the menu. But from the corner of my eye I could see Dicky wrapping his fountain pen in a Kleenex tissue, although we were already at 35,000 feet and if his pen was going to leak it would have leaked already.

'Yes,' said Dicky. 'This one will be make or break for you, Bernard.' He laid the bandaged pen to rest in his handbag, like a little Egyptian mummy that was to stay in its tomb for a thousand years.

'Thank God there's no in-flight movie,' said Dicky. 'I hate in-flight movies, don't you?'

'Yes,' I said. It was one of the very few things upon which Dicky and I could have unreserved agreement.

Now that we were above the clouds, the sunlight was blinding. Dicky, seated at the window, pulled down the tinted shield. 'You don't want to read or anything, do you?'

I looked at Dicky and shook my head. He smiled, and I wondered what sort of game he was playing with all his talk of this being my operation. He'd certainly taken his time before revealing this remarkable aspect of our jaunt to me.

We reached London Sunday mid-morning. The sun was shining in a clear blue sky but there was a chilly wind blowing. In response to two telex messages and a phone call made from Mexico, the duty officer had arranged for a car to meet us. We loaded it to the point where its suspension was groaning and went to Dicky's house. Once there I accepted Dicky's offer to go inside for a drink.

Dicky's wife was waiting for us with a chilled bottle of Sancerre in the ice bucket and coffee on the warmer. Daphne was an energetic woman in her early thirties. I found her especially attractive standing there in the kitchen surrounded by wine and food. Daphne had radically changed her image; floral pinafores and granny glasses were out, and pale-yellow boiler suits were in. Her hairstyle had changed too, cut in a severe pageboy style with fringe, so that she looked like the art student Dicky had married so long ago. 'And Bernard, darling. What a lovely surprise.' She had the loud voice and upper-class accent that go with weekends in large unheated country houses, where everyone talks about horses and reads Dick Francis paperbacks.

Daphne was in the middle of preparing lunch. She had a big bowl on the table in front of her and a spring scale upon which half a pound of warm butter was being weighed. Her hands were covered in flour, and she was wiping them on a towel that bore a printed picture of the Eiffel Tower. She picked up a collection of bracelets and bangles and slipped them all on to her wrist before embracing Dicky.

'You're early, darling,' she said as she kissed him and gave me a peck too.

Dicky brushed flour from his shirt and said, 'The plane arrived on time. I didn't allow for that.'

She asked Dicky if he wanted coffee or wine but she didn't ask me. She took a glass from the cupboard and an opened bottle of chilled wine from the ice bucket and poured me a generous measure. It was delicious.

Dicky, rummaging through the kitchen cupboard, said, 'Where are the blue Spode cups and saucers?'

'They're in the dishwasher. We only have three left now. You'll have to use a mug.'

Dicky sighed the way he did when one of the clerks returned to him top-secret papers he'd left in the copying machine. Then he poured himself a mug of black coffee and we sat down round the kitchen table.

'I'm sorry we can't go into the sitting room,' said Daphne. 'It's out of use for the time being.' She looked up at the kitchen clock before deciding it was okay to pour a glass of wine for herself.

'Daphne's left her ad agency,' said Dicky. 'I didn't tell you, did I? They lost the breakfast food account and had to cut staff. They offered Daphne a golden handshake; five thousand pounds. Not bad, eh?' Dicky was pressing his ears and gulping, the way he always did after a flight.

'What are you doing now, Daphne?' I asked.

Dicky answered for her. 'She's stripping. She's gone into it with another girl from the agency.' Daphne smiled the sort of smile that showed she'd heard this joke before but she let Dicky squeeze it dry. 'There's money in stripping, Daphne says.' Dicky smiled broadly and put his arm on his wife's shoulder.

'Furniture,' said Dicky. 'The lounge is stacked to the ceiling with antique furniture. They'll strip the paint off it and polish it up and sell it for a fortune.'

'Not *antique* furniture,' said Daphne. 'Bernard already regards us as philistines. I don't want him to think I'm a complete barbarian, ruining antiques. It's second-hand odds and ends, kitchen chairs and tables and so on. No use going round the little shops in Camden Town looking for it. Liz and I go into the country banging on doors. It's rather fun. You meet the oddest people. Apparently you just dip the furniture into caustic soda and the paint falls off. We're starting that next week when I've got some gloves to protect my hands.'

'I tried it once,' I said. 'It was a wooden fireplace. It fell to pieces. It was only fifty years of paintwork that was holding it together.'

'Oh, don't say that, Bernard,' said Daphne. She laughed. 'You're discouraging me.' She poured more wine for me. She didn't seem at all discouraged.

'Take no notice of Bernard,' said Dicky. 'He can't fix an electric plug without fusing all the lights.'

'We won't be selling the furniture as perfect,' said Daphne.

'It's what all the newly weds are looking for,' said Dicky. 'At least it's one of the things.' He gave his wife a wink and an affectionate hug. 'And it looks good. I mean that. It looks very good. Once the girls get decent premises they'll make a fortune, you mark my words. They were going to call the shop "The Strip Joint" but now we hear someone is using that already.'

'You're not very tanned, Dicky,' she said, looking closely at his face. 'Considering where you've been. I thought you'd come back much more tanned than that. Neither is Bernard,' she added, glancing at me.

'We've been working, old thing, not sunning. Right, Bernard?' He picked up the cork from the wine Daphne had served me and sniffed at it.

'Right, Dicky.'

'And I saw Henry Tiptree, darling. You remember Henry. He was at Balliol with me.'

'The one who left the BBC because they were all poofs?'

'No, darling; Henry. Tall, thin, reddish hair. Looks a bit of a twit. His cousin is a duke. Henry's the one who always used to bring you those huge boxes of Belgian handmade chocolates, remember?'

'No,' said Daphne.

'And you always took the chocolates to your mother. Then Henry was posted off somewhere and you made me buy them for her. Belgian chocolates. They cost me a fortune.'

'Yes, and then when we got married you told her the shop didn't sell them any more and you got her Black Magic instead.'

'Well, they cost an absolute fortune,' said Dicky. 'Anyway Henry is in Mexico now and let us borrow his car. And I managed to get a trip to Los Angeles and I got you everything on your list except the pillowcases from Robinson's. They didn't have the exact colour of the sample you gave me. They were more purple than mauve, so I didn't buy them.'

'You are sweet, darling,' said Daphne. 'He is so sweet,' she told me.

'I know,' I said.

'And I got a dozen of those masks the Mexicans make out of old tin cans, and I got six silver-plated bracelets in the market. So that's the Christmas-present list taken care of.'

'I ordered a whole salmon for Thursday,' said Daphne. 'But I can't think of an extra girl for Bernard.'

'I should have told you,' said Dicky, turning to me. 'You're invited for dinner Thursday. Are you free?'

'I imagine I am,' I said. 'Thanks.'

'And don't worry about an extra girl for him,' said Dicky. 'He's having it away with one of the girls in the office.' There was a note of bitterness in Dicky's voice. Daphne detected it too. She looked at him sharply; for Dicky's affections had wandered lately and Daphne had discovered it. She drained her wineglass.

'How nice,' Daphne said icily, pouring herself another drink. 'What's her name, Bernard?'

'Her name is Gloria,' said Dicky before I replied.

'Is that the one you wanted as your secretary?' said Daphne. She stood with the bottle in her hand, waiting for the reply.

'No, no, no,' said Dicky. 'It was Bret who wanted to foist her on to me but I wasn't having her.' Having tried to appease Daphne, he turned to me and said, 'No offence to you, old man. I'm sure she's a very nice girl.'

'That's perfect,' said Daphne. She poured me some more wine. 'It will be nice to meet her. I remember Dicky saying she was a wonderful typist.' I could tell that Daphne was far from convinced of Dicky's innocence.

'She'll come to dinner, your friend Gloria?' Dicky asked, watching me carefully.

'Gloria? Oh, of course she will,' I said. 'She'll go anywhere for a free meal.'

'That's not very gallant of you, Bernard,' said Daphne.

'We'll be here,' I heard myself saying. I don't know why I say such things, except that Dicky always brings out the worst in me. I hardly knew Gloria. I'd only spoken to her twice, and then it was only to tell her to hurry up with my typing.

9

It was good to be back in London again. First I opened the shutters in every room and let in the afternoon sunlight. I just couldn't get used to going home to a dark, silent house. It seemed such a short time ago that it was echoing with the sound of the children, nanny and Fiona my wife.

For lunch I made myself a cup of tea and balanced the contents of a tin of sardines on two very stale wholemeal biscuits. It was hot and airless in the top-floor room I used as a study. I opened the window and let in the sounds of London on a Sunday afternoon. I could hear the distant cries of children playing in the street, and the recorded carillon of an ice-cream pedlar. I phoned the office and told them I was home. The duty clerk sounded tired and bored but I resisted his attempt to engage me in conversation about the climate of Mexico at this time of year.

While eating my sardines I opened the stack of mail. Apart from bills for gas, electricity and wine, most of the mail was coloured advertising brochures; head waiters leered at credit cards, famous chefs offered a 'library' of cookbooks, pigskin wallets came free with magazine subscriptions, and there was a chance to hear all the Beethoven symphonies as I'd never heard them before. On my desk-pad the Portuguese cleaning lady – Mrs Dias – had pencilled a list of people who'd phoned during her daily visits. Her handwriting was rather uncertain, but I recognized no one there I felt like phoning except for my mother. I called her and chatted. I had a word with the children too. They seemed happy enough but I could hear the nanny prompting them from time to time.

'Did you like it in Mexico?' said Sally.

'It was very hot,' I said.

'Grandma said you'd take us to the seaside when you got back.'

'Is that where you want to go?'

'You've been away a long time, Daddy.'

'I'll take you to the seaside.'

'When?'

'As soon as I can.'

'Billy said you'd say that.'
'I'm sorry,' I said. 'I'm a rotten father.'
'Are we coming home?'
'Yes, very soon.'

It was only after I'd showered and changed my clothes that I noticed the cream-coloured envelope propped in front of the clock. Mrs Dias would naturally think of the clock as the place to which the human eye most readily returned.

Phone me home or office as soon as you return. Many matters to discuss. David.

It had been delivered by hand. The envelope bore a bright-red 'Urgent' sticker and the message was written in ink on a heavy handmade paper that matched the envelope. I recognized the stationery even without the engraved address and the artistic picture of the house that adorned it. The prospect of a discussion with my father-in-law, Mr David Timothy Kimber-Hutchinson, philanthropist, philosopher, tycoon and Fellow of the Royal Society of Arts, was not my idea of a welcome home. But I couldn't think of any excuse for avoiding it so I phoned him and agreed to drive down to him without delay.

His house was built on a tree-covered hillside not far from the place where the ancient Roman highway of Stane Street surmounted the Downs. It was a Jacobean mansion, so restored over the ages that very little of the original sixteenth-century building remained. But priority had been given to the corporeal things of life, so that the roof never leaked and the plumbing, the heating and the electricity supply always provided a level of comfort rarely encountered in English country houses.

Sometimes I wondered how much money went through his hands for him to be able to run this place with its desirable living accommodation for the servants, a self-contained wing for his guests and heated stabling for his horses. I parked my battered Ford between Kimber-Hutchinson's silver Rolls and his wife's Jaguar. The Kimber-Hutchinsons wouldn't have a foreign car. It wasn't simply a matter of patriotism, the old man once told me; it would upset some of his customers. Poor fellow, he needed handmade shoes because of his 'awkward feet' and Savile Row suits because he wasn't lucky enough to have the figure for ready-made ones. Cheap wine played havoc with his stomach so he drank expensive ones, and because he couldn't fit into economy-size airline seats he was forced to go everywhere first class. Poor David, he envied people like me, he was always telling me so.

David – he liked me to call him David; 'father-in-law' being too specific, 'father' too inaccurate, 'Mr Kimber-Hutchinson' too cumbersome and 'Kimber' a form of address reserved for his intimates – was waiting for me in the studio. The studio was a luxuriously converted barn. At one end there was a huge north-facing window and an easel where he liked to stand and paint water-colours that were snapped up at good prices by executives of the companies with which he did business. Under the skylight there was a. large wooden rostrum that was said to have come from the Paris studio of Maillol, a sculptor who'd devoted his life to loving portrayals of the female nude. I'd once asked David what he used it for but got only the vaguest of answers.

'Come in and sit down, Bernard old chap.' He was working on a painting when I got there, but he was not at the easel. He was seated at a small table, a drawing board resting on his knees, while he pencilled in the outlines of a landscape with horses. On the table there were half a dozen enlarged photos of the same view, photos of horses and a sheet of tracing paper from which he'd worked. 'You've discovered my little secret,' he said without looking up from his sketch. 'I always start off from photographs. No sense in not using all the help you can get. Michelangelo would have used a camera when doing the Sistine Chapel ceiling had he got the chance.'

Since David Kimber-Hutchinson showed no sign of revealing more about Michelangelo's frustrated technological aspirations, I grunted and sat down while he finished drawing the horse. Although it was a faithful reproduction of the horse in the photo, David's traced drawing of it looked wooden and stunted. He was obviously aware of this, for he was redrawing the outline to extend its legs, but that didn't seem to improve it.

He was wearing a dark-blue artist's smock over his yellow cashmere rollneck and riding breeches. His face was flushed. I guessed he'd just got back from a canter over the Downs. It was rather as if he'd arranged things so that I would see him tracing his pictures. Perhaps he thought I would admire such acquired trickery more than mere talent. A man could not take credit for talent in the way he could for cunning.

Eventually he abandoned his attempt and put the pencil down on the table in front of him. 'I can never draw horses,' he said. 'It's just not fair. No artist loved horses as I do, or knew as much about them. But even when I use photos I can't damn well draw them. It's not fair.'

I'd never heard him appeal to equity before. Usually he upheld the ultimate justice of market forces and even the survival of the fittest.

'Perhaps it's because you trace photos,' I said. 'Maybe you should trace paintings.'

He looked at me, trying to decide whether to take offence, but my face was blank and he said, 'I might try that. Trace a Stubbs or something, just to get some idea of the trade secrets. Ummm. It's all tricks, you know. A Royal Academy painter admitted that to me once. Painting is just learning a set of tricks, just like playing the stock exchange.'

'They are tricks I will never master,' I admitted.

'Easy enough to do, Bernard. Easy enough to do.' He took off his artist's smock and smiled. He liked to hear that his achievements were beyond other men; especially he liked to be praised about his skills with horses. He was up every morning grooming his horses and he endured the long drive to his London office for the sake of seeing his horses. More than once he'd told me that he liked horses better than he liked people. 'They never lie to you, horses,' he said. 'They never try to swindle you.'

He spoke without looking up from his board. 'So you're still driving that old Ford,' he said. 'I thought you were going to get a Volvo.'

'I cancelled the order,' I said. 'I don't need a big car now.'

'And a big car costs money, more than you can afford,' he said with that directness that you could always count upon. 'You should see the bills I pay on that Rolls. I had to replace the fire-extinguisher last month and that cost me seventy-eight pounds.'

'It might be worth that if you are on fire,' I said.

'Have a drink, Bernard. It's a tiring drive from London. How did you come, Kingston bypass? Full of weekend drivers, was it? "Murder mile" they call it, that bit south of Kingston Vale. I've seen a dozen cars crunched together on that stretch of road. The lights change at Robin Hood Gate and they go mad.'

'Coming in this direction it wasn't too bad,' I said.

He went over to an old cupboard that contained jars full of brushes and tubes of paint and bottles of turpentine and linseed oil for the times when he worked in oils. From a compartment in the cupboard he got a glass and a bottle of drink. 'You're a whisky and soda man, as I remember. Lots of soda and lots of whisky.' He laughed and poured a huge Scotch. He had me summed up nicely. 'Teacher's all right?' He handed it to me without waiting for a reply. 'No ice over here.'

'Thanks.' It was a cheap tumbler, not the Waterford he used at his dinner table. This David who painted here in his studio was a different David – an artist, a plain man with earthy pleasures and simple tastes.

'Yes,' he said. 'A big car is no use to you now that you're on your own. The big house will be a burden too. I've scribbled out some figures to show you.'

'Have you?' I said.

He got a piece of paper from the table and sank down on the sofa, studying the piece of paper as if he'd never seen it before. 'You bought the house four years ago, and property has been sticky ever since then. I warned you about that at the time, as I remember. The way the market is now, you'll be lucky to get your money back.' He looked at me.

'Really,' I said.

'And when you take into account inflation and loss of earnings on capital it's been a bad investment. But you'll have to grin and bear it, I'm afraid. The important thing is to reduce your outgoings. Get on to a house agent first thing in the morning, Bernard. Get that house on the market. And find yourself a small service flat; bedroom, sitting room and a kitchen, that's all you need. In fact, I wonder if you really need a kitchen.' When I didn't respond, he said, 'I've jotted down the phone numbers of a couple of house agents I do business with. You don't want to go to the first people you happen upon. Too many Jews in that line of business.' A smile. 'Oh, I forgot, you like Jews, don't you?'

'No more than I like Scotsmen or Saudi Arabians. But I always suspect that whatever is being done to Jews this week is likely to be done to me next week. In any case, I have decided to hang on to the house. At least for the time being.'

'That would be absurd, Bernard. You'll have only your salary in future. You won't have Fiona's trust fund, the children's trust funds or Fiona's salary.'

'The trust funds were used solely for Fiona and the children,' I pointed out to him.

'Of course, of course,' said David. 'But the fact remains that your household will have far less money. And certainly not enough to keep up a rather smart little house in the West End.'

'If I moved into a service flat there would be no room for the children.'

'I was coming to that, Bernard. The children – and I think you will agree unreservedly about this – are the most important single factor in this whole tragic business.'

'Yes,' I said.

He looked at me. 'I think I'll have a drink myself,' he said. He got up and went to the cupboard and poured himself a gin and tonic with plenty of tonic. 'And let me do something about yours too, Bernard.' He took my glass and refilled it. After he'd sipped his drink he started again but this time from another angle. 'I'm a socialist, Bernard. You know that; I've never made a secret of it. My father worked hard all his life and died at his work-bench. Died at his work-bench. That is something I can't forget.'

I nodded. I'd heard it all before. But I knew that the work-bench was to David's father what David's easel was to him. David's father had owned half of a factory that employed 500 people.

'But I've never had any dealings with communists, Bernard. And when I heard that Fiona had been working for the Russians all these years I said to my wife, she's no daughter of ours. I said it just like that. I said she's no daughter of ours, and I meant it. The next morning I sent for my lawyer and I disowned her. I wrote and told her so; I suppose the lawyers handling her trust fund have some sort of forwarding address . . .' He looked at me.

'I don't know,' I said. 'I haven't contacted them. I daresay the department has contacted them but I don't know anything about a forwarding address.'

'Whether she'll ever get my letter or not I don't know.' He came over to where I was sitting and, lowering his voice, he added in a voice throbbing with emotion, 'And personally, Bernard, I don't care. She's no daughter of mine. Not after this.'

'I think you were going to say something about the children,' I prompted him.

'Yes, I was. Fiona has gone for good, Bernard. She's never coming back. If you're holding on to the house in the hope that Fiona comes back to you, forget it.'

'If she came back,' I said, 'she'd face a very long term in prison.'

'Yes, I thought of that,' he said. 'Damn it, that would be the final disgrace. Her mother would die of shame, Bernard. Thank God the story was never picked up by the newspapers. As it is I've cut back on visits to my clubs, in case I see someone who's in the know about such things. I miss a lot of my social life. I haven't had a round of golf since the news reached us.'

'It hasn't exactly made life easy for me,' I said.

'In the department? I suppose they think you should have got on to her earlier, eh?'

'Yes, they do.'

'But you were the one who finally worked out what was going on. You were the one who discovered she was the spy, eh?'

I didn't answer.

'You needn't worry, Bernard. I don't hold that against you. Someone had to do it. You just did your duty.' He drank some of his drink and gave a grim, manly smile. I suppose he thought he was being magnanimous. 'But now we have to face the mess that she's left behind her. My wife and I have discussed the whole thing at great length . . .' A smile to share with me the difficulties that always come from discussions with women. '. . . and we'd like to have the children. The nanny could come too so we'd preserve the essential continuity. I've spoken to a friend of mine about the schools. Billy has to change his school this year anyway . . . '

'I'm keeping the children with me,' I said.

'I know how you feel, Bernard,' he said. 'But in practical terms it's not possible. You can't afford to keep up the mortgage payments on the house the way the interests rates are going. How would you be able to pay the nanny? And yet how could you possibly manage without her?'

'The children are with my mother at present.'

'I know. But she's too old to deal with young children. And her house is too small; there's only that little garden.'

'I didn't know you'd been there,' I said.

'When I heard you were away in Mexico I made it my business to see the children and make sure they were comfortable. I took some toys for them and gave your mother some cash for clothes and so on.'

'That was none of your business,' I said.

'They're my grandchildren,' he said. 'Grandparents have rights too, you know.' He said it gently. He didn't want to argue; he wanted to get his way about the custody of the children.

'The children will stay with me,' I said.

'Suppose Fiona sends more Russians and tries to kidnap them?'

'They have a twenty-four-hour armed guard,' I said.

'For how much longer? Your people can't provide a free armed guard for ever, can they?'

He was right. The guards were still there only because I'd had to go to Mexico. As soon as I got back to the office there would be pressure to withdraw that expensive facility. 'We'll see,' I said.

'I won't see the children's trust funds squandered on it. My lawyer is a trustee for both the children; perhaps you're overlooking that. I'll make sure you don't use that money for security guards or even for the nanny's wages. It wouldn't be fair to the children; not when we can offer them a better life here in the country with the horses and farm animals. And do it without taking their money.'

I didn't answer. In a way he was right. This rural environment was better than anything I could offer them. But the bad news would be having the children grow up with a man like David Kimber-Hutchinson, who hadn't exactly made a big success of bringing up Fiona.

'Think it over,' he said. 'Don't say no. I don't want to find myself fighting for custody of the children through the law courts. I pay far too much money to lawyers anyway.'

'You'd be wasting your money,' I said. 'In such circumstances a court would always give me custody.'

'Don't be so sure,' he said. 'Things have changed a lot in the last few years. I'm advised that my chances of legal custody are good. The trouble is – and I'm going to be absolutely frank with you about this – that I don't fancy paying lawyers a lot of money to tell the world what a bad son-in-law I have.'

'So leave us alone,' I said. I'd feared I was heading into a confrontation like this right from the moment I saw the cream-coloured envelope in front of the clock.

'But I wouldn't be the only loser,' he continued relentlessly. 'Think what your employers would say to having your name, and my daughter's name, dragged through the courts. They wouldn't keep that out of the newspapers in the way they've so far been able to do with Fiona's defection.'

He was right, of course. His legal advisers had earned their fees. The department would keep this out of the courts at all costs. I'd get no support from them if I tried to hang on to my children. On the contrary; they'd press me to accept my father-in-law's sensible offer of help.

Beyond him, through the big studio windows, I could see the trees made gold by the evening sunlight and the paddock where Billy and Sally liked to explore. Money isn't everything, but for people such as him it seemed as if it could buy everything. 'I'd better be getting along,' I said. 'I didn't get much sleep on the plane and there'll be a lot of work waiting for me on my desk tomorrow morning.'

He put his hand on my shoulder. 'Think about it, Bernard. Give it a couple of weeks. Take a look at some of the bills coming in and jot down a few figures. Look at your net annual income and compare it with your expenditure last year. Even if you pare your expenses right down you still won't have enough money. Work it out for yourself and you'll see that what I've said makes sense.'

'I'll think about it,' I promised, although my mind was made up already, and he could discern that from the tone of my voice.

'You could come down here any time and see them, Bernard. I'm sure I don't have to tell you that.'

'I said I'd think about it.'

'And don't go reporting Fiona's Porsche as stolen. I sent my chauffeur to get it and it will be advertised for sale in next week's *Sunday Times*. Better to get rid of it. Too many unhappy memories for you to want to use it. I knew that.'

'Thanks, David,' I said. 'You think of everything.'

'I do but try,' he said.

10

Despite my tiredness I didn't sleep well after my return from Leith
Hill. The air was warm and I left the bedroom window open. I was
fully awakened by the ear-piercing screams of turbo-fans, and the
thunder of aircraft engines, throttles opening wide to compensate for
flap drag. The approach controllers at London Heathrow like to send
a few big jets roaring over the rooftops about 6.30 each morning, just
in case any inhabitants of the metropolis oversleep.

The radio alarm clock was tuned to Radio 3 so that I could hear
the seven o'clock news bulletin and then spend fifteen minutes on
the exercise bike to the sounds of Mozart and Bach. Since living
alone I'd connected the coffee-machine to a time-switch so that I
could come downstairs to a smell of fresh coffee. I opened a tin of
Carnation milk and found a croissant in the bread-bin. It was old and
dried and shrivelled like something discovered in a tomb of the
Pharaohs. I chewed it gratefully. I hadn't had a decent meal since
well before getting on the plane. But I wasn't hungry. My mind was
fully occupied with thoughts of the children and the conversation I'd
had with my father-in-law. I didn't want to believe him but his
warnings about money worried me. He was seldom, if ever, wrong
about money.

I was outside in the street, unlocking the door of my car, when
the girl approached me. She was about thirty, maybe younger, dark-
skinned and very attractive. She was wearing a nurse's uniform
complete with dark-blue cloak and a plain blue handbag. 'My damned
car won't start,' she said. Her accent was unmistakably West Indian;
Jamaica, I guessed. 'And matron will kill me if I'm not at St Mary
Abbots Hospital at eight forty-five. Are you going anywhere in that
direction? Or to somewhere I can get a taxi?'

'St Mary Abbots Hospital?'

'Marloes Road near Cromwell Road, not far from where the air
terminal used to be.'

'I remember now,' I said.

'I'm sorry to trouble you,' she said. 'I live across the road at
number forty-seven.' It was a large house that some speculator had

converted into tiny apartments and then failed to sell. Now there was always a 'For rent' sign on the railings and a succession of short-term tenants. I suppose it was the sort of place that my father-in-law would like to put me in. She said, 'There is something wrong with the starter, I think.'

I got in and leaned across and opened the passenger door for her. 'The staff nurse is a bitch,' she said. 'I daren't be late again.'

'I can go through the park,' I said.

She decorously wrapped her cloak around her legs and put her handbag on her lap. 'It's very kind of you. It's probably miles out of your way.'

'No,' I said. In fact it was a considerable detour but the prospect of sitting next to her for twenty minutes was by no means unwelcome.

'You'd better fasten your seat belt,' she said. 'It's the law now, isn't it?'

'Yes,' I said. 'Let's not break the law so early in the morning.'

She fastened her own seat belt and said, 'Do you follow the cricket?'

'I've been away,' I said.

'I'm from Kingston, Jamaica,' she explained. 'I had five brothers. I had to become interested in cricket; it was all they ever talked about.'

We were still talking about cricket when I came out of the park and, no right turn being permitted, continued south into Exhibition Road. As I stopped at the traffic lights by the Victoria and Albert Museum she broke into my chatter about England's poor bowling against Australia last winter by saying, 'I'm sorry to have to do this to you, Mr Samson. But you're going to turn west on to Cromwell Road when we've been round this one-way system.'

'Why? What do you mean?' I turned my head and found her staring at me. She didn't answer. I looked down and saw that she was holding a hypodermic on her lap. Its needle point was very close to my thigh. 'Keep your eyes on the road. Just do as I say and everything will be all right.'

'Who the hell are you?'

'We'll drive out along the Cromwell Road extension to London Airport. There's something I have to do. When it's done you'll be free to go wherever you have to go.' She reached up with her free hand and tilted the driving mirror so that I could not see the traffic behind.

'And if I slam on the brakes suddenly?'

'Don't do that, Mr Samson. I am a qualified nurse. My papers are in order, my story is prepared. What I have in this syringe will take effect within seconds.' She still had the West Indian accent but it was less pronounced now, and there was a change in her manner too.

Less of the Florence Nightingale, more of the Jane Fonda. And she didn't say 'sorry' or 'thank you' any more.

I was constrained by the seat belt. I could see no alternative to driving to Heathrow. She switched on the car radio. It was tuned to Radio 4 so we both listened to 'Yesterday in Parliament'.

'I'll say this again,' she said. 'No harm is intended to you.'

'Why the airport?'

'You'll understand when we get there. But don't think there is any plan to abduct you. This just concerns your children and your work.' We were driving behind a rusting old car that was emitting lots of black smoke; on the back window there was a sticker saying 'Nuclear Power – No Thanks'.

When we got to the airport she directed me to Terminal 2, used by non-British airlines mostly for European services. We passed the terminal main entrance and the multi-storey car-park that serves it, and continued until we came to a piece of road that leads on to Terminal 3. Despite the yellow lines and 'No parking' signs, there were cars parked there. 'Stop here,' she said. 'And don't look round.' Carefully, and without releasing her hold of the hypodermic or looking away from me, she reached back to unlock the nearside rear door.

We were double-parked near two dark-blue vans. I heard my car door open and felt the movement of the suspension as it took the weight of another passenger. 'Drive on. Slowly,' said the nurse. I did as I was told. 'We'll go back through the tunnel. Then down to the motorway roundabout, keep going round it and back to Terminal 2 again. Do you understand that?'

'I understand,' I said.

'He's all yours,' the nurse said to the person in the back seat, but she kept her eyes on me.

'It's me, darling,' said a voice. 'I hope I didn't terrify you.' She couldn't eliminate that trace of mockery. Some people didn't hear it but I knew her too well to miss that touch of gloating pride. It was my wife. I was numb. I'd always prided myself on being prepared for anything – that's what being a professional agent meant – but now I was astonished.

'Fiona, are you mad?'

'To come here? There is no warrant for my arrest. I have changed my appearance and my name . . . no, don't look round. I don't want you unconscious.'

'What's it all about?' To keep me driving was a good idea; it limited my chances of doing anything they didn't want me to do.

'It's about the children, darling. Billy and Sally. I went to see them. I waited on the route between your mother's house and the school. They looked so sweet. They didn't see me, of course. I had to watch out for your bloodhounds, didn't I? They both wore matching outfits; acid green with shiny yellow plastic jackets. I'm sure Daddy sent them. Only my father has that natural instinct for the sort of vulgarity that children always love.'

'Have you seen your father?'

She laughed. 'I'm not here on holiday, Bernard darling. And, even if I were, I'm not sure that visiting my father would be on the itinerary.'

'So what is all this about?'

'Don't be surly. I had to talk to you and I couldn't phone you without the risk of being recorded on that damned answering machine.' She paused for a moment. I could hear the deep rapid breathing – hyperventilation almost – that was always a sign of her being excited or nervous, or both. 'I don't want the children's lives made miserable, any more than you do.'

'What are you proposing?'

'I'll give you an undertaking to leave the children here in England for a year. It will give them a chance to lead normal lives. It's perfectly ghastly to have them going to school in a car with two security men and having armed guards hanging around them day and night. What sort of life is that for a child.'

'For a year?' I said. 'What then?'

'We'll see. But I'll promise nothing beyond a year.'

'And you'd want me to leave them unguarded?'

'The department will call them off before long anyway. You know that as well as I do. And you can't afford to pay for such security.'

'I'd manage.' I stopped at the roundabout until there was a break in the traffic and then moved off. It was tricky driving without the rear-view mirror.

'Yes, you'd arrange some sort of protection using your old friends.' She managed to imbue the word with all her distaste for them. 'I can imagine what the result would be. Your pals sitting around getting drunk, and talking about what they'd do if I tried to get the children away from you.'

'And you want nothing in return?'

'I'd certainly expect you drop this absurd business with poor old Erich Stinnes.'

'What has Stinnes got to do with us?'

'He's my senior assistant. That's what he's got to do with us. You won't tempt Erich with any offers of the good life waiting in the West. He's too committed and too serious for that. But I know you, and I know the department. I know you're likely to kidnap him if all else fails.'

'And that would look bad for you,' I said. We were coming to the airport tunnel. I wondered if the sudden darkness would give me a chance to disable the nurse before she had a chance to jab me but I decided it wouldn't. 'Terminal 2?'

'Yes, Terminal 2,' said Fiona. 'If you persist with this pursuit of Erich Stinnes, I will consider any undertaking about the children null and void. Be reasonable, Bernard. I'm trying to do what's best for Billy and Sally. How do you think I feel about the prospect of not seeing them? I'm trying to prove my goodwill to you. I'm asking nothing in return except that you don't kidnap my senior assistant. Is that asking too much?'

'It won't be my decision, Fiona.'

'I realize that. But you have influence. If you really want them to drop it, they'll drop it. Don't make Erich a part of your personal vendetta against me.'

'I have no vendetta against you,' I said.

'I did what I knew I had to do,' she said. It was the nearest I'd ever heard her get to apologizing.

'You're running the KGB office over there now, are you?'

I could hear the amusement in her voice. 'I'm giving it a completely new organization. It's so old-fashioned, darling. But I'll soon have it in shape. Aren't you going to wish me good luck?'

I didn't answer. At least she hadn't asked me to join her. Even Fiona knew better than that. And yet it was not like her not to try. Was it because she knew there was no chance of suborning me, or because she had other plans – such as kidnapping or even removing me permanently?

'Stop behind this taxi,' said the nurse. It was the first time she'd spoken since Fiona got into the car. I stopped.

'Erich Stinnes will not defect voluntarily,' said Fiona. 'Tell your people that.'

'I've told them that already,' I said.

'Then we won't quarrel. Goodbye, darling. Best not tell the children you've seen me. It will only upset them. And don't report our meeting to anyone at London Central.'

'Or what?'

'Or I won't contact you again, will I? Use your brains, darling.'

'Goodbye, Fiona.' I still could hardly believe what had happened – I suppose she counted on the surprise – and by the time I'd said goodbye the door had opened. It slammed loudly and she was gone. I remembered how she'd broken the hinge on the old Ford by always slamming the door too hard.

'Keep your eyes this way,' said the nurse. 'It's not all over yet.' I saw her look at her watch. She had it pinned to the bib of her apron the way all nurses do.

'What is it?' I said. 'The Aeroflot flight to Moscow or the Polish Airlines flight to Warsaw? That transits in East Berlin, doesn't it?'

'We'll return on the A4,' she said, 'not the motorway, in case you got some brilliant idea about doing something very brave on the way back.'

'I haven't had a brilliant idea for a long time,' I said. 'And you can ask anyone about that.'

11

Bret Rensselaer sent for me that morning. I wasn't there. He sent for me again and continued to send for me until finally I arrived back from my detour to the airport. Bret was in his usual office on the top floor. It was elegantly furnished – grey carpet, glass-and-chrome desk, and black leather Chesterfield – in a monochrome scheme that so well suited Bret's hand-ground carbon steel personality.

Bret was a hungry-looking American in his mid-fifties, with fair hair that was turning white, and a smile that could slice diamonds. Rumours said that he had applied for British citizenship to clear the way for the knighthood he'd set his heart on. Certainly he had never had to pine for the material things of life. His family had owned a couple of small banks which had been absorbed into a bigger banking complex, and that into another, so that now Bret's shares were worth more money than he needed for his very British understated lifestyle.

'Sit down, Bernard.' He always put the accent on the second syllable of my name. Had it not been for that, and the talc he used on his chin and the ever-present fraternity ring, I think I might sometimes have overlooked his American nationality, for his accent was minimal and his suits were Savile Row. 'You're late,' he said. 'Damned late.'

'Yes, I am,' I said.

'Do I rate an explanation?'

'I was having this wonderful dream, Bret. I dreamed I was working for this nice man who couldn't tell the time.'

Bret was reading something on his desk and gave no sign of having heard me. He was wearing a starched white Turnbull and Asser shirt with exaggerated cuffs, monogrammed pocket and gold links. He wore a waistcoat that was unbuttoned and a grey silk bow-tie. His jacket was hung on a chair that seemed to be there only so that Bret would have somewhere to hang his jacket. Finally he looked up from the very important paper he was reading and said, 'You probably heard that I'm taking a little of the load off Dicky Cruyer's shoulders for the time being.'

'I've been away,' I said.

'Sure you have,' he said. He smiled and took off his reading glasses to look at me and then put them on again. They were large, with speed-cop-style frames, and made him look younger than his fifty-five years. 'Sure you have.' So Bret had staked a claim to a chunk of Dicky's desk. I couldn't wait to see how Dicky was taking that. Bret said, 'I just took on this extra work while Dicky went to Mexico. Just because I'm senior to Dicky, that doesn't mean he's not in charge of the desk. Okay?'

'Okay,' I said. It was pure poetry. Just in case anyone thought Bret was assisting Dicky he was going to precede everything he did by pointing out that he was senior to Dicky. But that was only because he wanted everyone to know that he wasn't after Dicky's job. Who could have thought of anything as Byzantine as that except helpful unassuming old Bret Rensselaer.

'So you talked with this guy Stinnes?'

'I talked with him.'

'And?'

I shrugged.

Bret said, 'Do I have to drag every damned word out of you? What did he say? What do you think?'

'What he said and what I think are two very different things,' I said.

'I spoke with Dicky already. He said Stinnes will come over to us. He's in a dead-end job and wants to leave his wife anyway. He wants a divorce but is frightened of letting his organization know about it, in case they get mad at him.'

'That's what he said.'

'Does that fit in with what we know about the KGB?'

'How do I find out what "we" know about the KGB?'

'OK, smart ass. Does it fit in with what you know about them?'

'Everything depends upon what his personal dossier says. If Stinnes has been sleeping around – with other men's wives, for instance – and the divorce is the result of that . . . then maybe it would blow up into trouble for him.'

'And what would happen to him?'

'Being stationed outside Russia is considered a privilege for any Russian national. For instance, army regulations prevent any Jew, of any rank, serving anywhere but in the republics. Even Latvians, Lithuanians, Estonians, Crimean Tartars and people from the western Ukraine are given special surveillance when serving in foreign posts, even in communist countries such as the DDR or Poland.'

'But Stinnes is not in any of those categories?'

'His marriage to the German girl is unusual. Not many Russians marry foreigners. They know only too well that it will make them into second-class citizens. Stinnes is an exception, and it's worth noting the confidence he showed in doing it. His use of a German name is also curious. It made me wonder at first if he had come from one of the German communities.'

'Do German communities still exist in Russia? I thought Stalin liquidated them back in the forties.' He swung his chair round and got to his feet so that he could look out of the window. Bret Rensselaer was a peripatetic man who could not think unless his body was in motion. Now he hunched his shoulders like a prize fighter and swayed as if avoiding blows. Sometimes he raised his foot to bend the knee that was said to have troubled him since he was a teenage US Navy volunteer in the final months of the Pacific war. But he never complained of his knee. And it didn't give him enough trouble to interfere with his skiing holidays.

'The big German communities on the Volga were wiped out by executions and deportations back in 1941. But there are still Germans scattered across Russia from one end to the other.' His back was still turned to me but I was used to him and his curious mannerisms so I continued to talk. 'Many German communities are established in Siberia and the Arctic regions. Most big cities in the USSR have a German minority, but they keep a low profile, of course.'

He turned to face me. 'How can you be sure that Stinnes is not from one of those German communities?' He tugged at the ends of the grey silk bow-tie to make sure it was still neat and tidy.

'Because he is stationed in East Germany. The army and the KGB have an inflexible rule that no one of German extraction serves with army units in Germany.'

'So if Stinnes applies for a divorce the chances are that he'll be sent to work in Russia?'

'And probably to some remote "new town" in Central Asia. It wouldn't be the sort of posting he'd want.'

'No matter how he beefs about Berlin. Right.' This thought cheered him up. 'So that makes Stinnes a good prospect for our offer.'

'Whatever you say, Bret,' I told him.

'You're a miserable critter, Bernard.' Now he took his reading glasses off and put them on the desk while he had a good look at me from head to toe.

'Forget enrolling Stinnes,' I said. 'The chances are it will never happen.'

'You're not saying we should drop the whole business?'

'I'm not saying you should drop it. If you and Dicky have nothing better to do, go ahead. There are lots of other – even less promising – projects that the department are putting time and money into. Furthermore I'd say it would be good for Dicky to get some practical experience at the sharp end of the business.'

'Is that gibe intended for me too?'

'No reason why you shouldn't get into the act. You've never seen a Russian close to, except over the smoked-salmon sandwiches at embassy tea parties,' I said. 'Stinnes is a real pro. You'll enjoy talking to him.'

Bret didn't like comments on his lack of field experience any more than any of the others did, but he kept his anger in check. He sat down behind his desk and swung his glasses for a moment. Then he said, 'We'll leave that for the time being because there's some routine stuff I have to go through with you.' I said nothing. 'It's routine stuff about your wife. I know you've been asked all this before, Bernard, but I have to have it from you.'

'I understand,' I said.

'I wish I was sure you did,' said Bret. He slumped down into his chair, picked up his phone but before using it said to me, 'Frank Harrington is in town. I think it might be a good idea to have him sit in on this one. You've no objection, I take it?'

'Frank Harrington?'

'He's very much involved with all this. And Frank's very fond of you, Bernard. I guess I don't have to tell you that.'

'Yes, I know he is.'

'You're a kind of surrogate son for him.' He toyed with the phone.

'Frank has a son,' I pointed out.

'An airline pilot?' said Bret scornfully, as if that career would automatically preclude him from such paternity. He pushed a button on the phone and said, 'Ask Mr Harrington to step in.' While we were waiting for Frank to arrive he picked up a piece of paper. I could see it was a single page from his loose-leaf notebook. He turned it over, made sure there was no more of his tiny handwritten notes on the back of it, and then placed it on a pile of such pages under a glass paperweight. Bret was methodical. He ran his forefinger down the next page of notes and was still reading them when Frank came in.

Frank Harrington was the head of the Berlin Field Unit, the job my father had held long long ago. He was a thin, bony sixty-year-old, dressed in a smooth tweed three-piece suit and highly polished Oxford shoes. Seen on the street he might have been mistaken for the colonel of a rather smart infantry regiment, and sometimes I had the feeling that Frank cultivated this resemblance. Yet despite the pale but weather-beaten face, the blunt-ended stubble moustache and the handkerchief tucked into his cuff, Frank had never been in the army except on short detachments. He'd come into the department largely on the strength of his brilliant academic record; *Literae Humaniores* was said to demand accurate speech, accurate thought and a keen and critical intellect. Unfortunately 'Greats' provides no inkling of the modern world and no clue to the mysteries of present-day politics or economics. And such classical studies could warp a young man's grasp of modern languages, so that even now Frank's spoken German had the stilted formality of a *kaiserliche* proclamation.

Without a word of greeting Bret pointed a finger at the black leather chesterfield. Frank smiled at me and sat down. We were both used to Bret's American style of office procedure.

'As I said, this is just a recap, Bernard, so let's get it over and done with,' said Bret.

'That suits me,' I said. Frank took his pipe from his pocket, fondled it and then blew through it loudly. When Bret glanced at him, Frank smiled apologetically.

'Obviously . . .' Bret looked at me to see how I reacted to his question '. . . you never suspected your wife of working for the KGB prior to your mission to East Berlin.'

'That's correct,' I said. I looked at Frank. He had brought a yellow oilskin tobacco pouch on to his knee and was rummaging through it to fill his pipe. He didn't look up.

'Even if we go back years and years?' said Bret.

'Especially if we go back years and years,' I said. 'She was my wife. I was in love with her.'

'No suspicions. None at all?'

'She'd been cleared by the department. She'd been cleared by Internal Security. She had been vetted regularly . . .'

'*Touché*,' said Bret. Frank Harrington nodded to no one in particular but didn't smile.

'If you're making notes,' I told Bret, 'make a note of that. My failure was no greater than the department's failure.'

Bret shook his head. 'Don't be stupid, Bernard. She was your wife. You brought her to me and suggested that I gave her a job. You were married to her for twelve years. She's the mother of your children. How can you compare your failure to know what she truly was with ours?'

'But finally I did know,' I said. 'If I hadn't flushed her out she'd still be working here, and still be passing your secrets back to Moscow.'

'*Our* secrets,' said Bret Rensselaer. 'Let's rather say our secrets, unless you are thinking of leaving us too.'

I said, 'That's a bloody offensive thing to say, Bret.'

'Then I withdraw it,' said Bret. 'I'm not trying to make life more difficult for you, Bernard, really I'm not.' He moved his small pages about on the desk. 'You didn't ever hear any phone conversations, or find correspondence which, in the light of what we know now, has a bearing on your wife's defection?'

'Do you think I wouldn't have said so. You must have read the transcript of my formal interview. It's all there.'

'I know it is, Bernard, and I've already apologized for going through all this once more. But that interview was for Internal Security. This is to go on your report.' Each year a report on every member of the staff was filed to the Personnel Department by his or her immediate superior. The fact that Bret was completing mine this year was just another sign of the way he was edging into Dicky Cruyer's department.

'To go on my report?'

'Well, you didn't imagine we'd be able to overlook your wife's defection, did you? I'm supposed to report on your . . . ' A glance down at his notes. '. . . judgement, political sense, power of analysis and foresight. Almost every report has some sort of mention of an employee's wife, Bernard. There is nothing special about that. The whole British Civil Service has exactly the same system of reports, so don't get paranoid.'

Frank finished filling his pipe. He leaned back and said, 'The department looks after its own, Bernard. I don't have to tell you that.' He still hadn't lit his pipe, but he put it into his mouth and chewed at the stem of it.

I said, 'I don't think I know what you're talking about, Frank.'

Frank Harrington had spent a long time in the department, and this gave him certain privileges, so that now he didn't defer to Bret Rensselaer despite Bret's senior ranking. 'I'm trying to explain to you that Bret and I want this to come out well for you, Bernard.'

'Thanks, Frank,' I said, without much warmth.

'But it's got to look right on paper too,' said Bret. He stood up, put his hands in his pockets and jingled his small change.

'And how does it look on paper now?' I said. 'Without you and Frank putting all your efforts into making it come out well for me.'

Bret looked at Frank with a pained expression in his eyes. He was practising that look, so that he could turn it on me if I continued to be insubordinate. Bret was standing by the window. He looked at the view across the park and without turning round said, 'The department's got a lot of enemies, Bernard. Not only certain socialist Members of Parliament. The Palace of Westminster has plenty of publicity hounds who'd love to get hold of something like this so they could pontificate on "Panorama", get a few clips on TV news and be interviewed on "Newsnight". And there are many of our colleagues in Whitehall who always enjoy the sight of us wriggling under the microscope.'

'What is it we're trying to hide, Bret?' I asked.

Bret rounded on me angrily. 'For Christ's sake . . .' He went across the room, picked up his jacket and draped it over his arm. 'Talk to him, Frank,' he said. 'I'm stepping outside for a moment. See if you can talk some sense into the man, will you?'

Frank said nothing. He held the unlit pipe in his teeth for a moment before taking it from his mouth and staring at the tobacco. It was something to do while Bret Rensselaer went out and closed the door. Even then Frank took his time before saying, 'We've known each other a long time.'

'That's right,' I said.

'Berlin: 1945. You were just beginning to walk. You were living at the top of Frau Hennig's house. Your father was one of the first officers to get his family out to occupied Germany. I was touched by that, Bernard. So many of the other chaps preferred to be away from their families. They had the plush life of the conqueror. Big apartments, servants, booze, women – everything was available for a few cigarettes or a box of rations. But your father was an exception, Bernard. He wanted you and your mother there with him, and he moved heaven and hell to get you over there. I liked him for that, Bernard. And for much more.'

'What is it you want to tell me, Frank?'

'This business with your wife was a shock. It was a shock for you, and a shock for me. The whole department was caught napping, Bernard, and they are still smarting from the blow.'

'And blaming me? So that's it?'

'No one's blaming you, Bernard. As you told Bret just now, you're the one who tipped us off. No one can blame you.'

'But . . . Can I hear a "but" coming?'

Frank fiddled with his pipe. 'Let's talk about this chap Stinnes,' he said. 'He was the officer who arrested you in East Berlin at the time of your wife's defection?'

'Yes,' I said.

'And he was the interrogation officer too?'

'I've been through all that with you, Frank,' I said. 'There was no proper interrogation. He'd had orders from Moscow to wait for Fiona to arrive.'

'Yes, I remember,' said Frank. 'The point I'm making is that Stinnes is a senior officer with the KGB's Berlin office.'

'No doubt about that,' I agreed.

'Your wife is now working for the KGB in that same office?'

'The current guess is that she's in charge of it,' I said.

'And Stinnes is certain to be one of her senior staff members, wouldn't you say?'

'Of course.'

'So Stinnes is the one person who knows about your wife's defection and her present occupation. It's even possible that he was concerned with her debriefing.'

'Don't keep going round and round in circles, Frank. Tell me what you're trying to say.'

Frank brandished the pipe at me and closed his eyes while he formulated his response. It was probably a mannerism that dated all the way back to his time at Oxford. 'This chap Stinnes knows all about your wife's defection and subsequent employment and he interrogated you. Since that time there has been a departmental alert for him. When he's located in Mexico City why does Dicky Cruyer – the German Stations Controller, no less – go out there to look him over?'

'We both know the answer to that one, Frank. Dicky loves free trips to anywhere. And this one got him out of the way while Bret chiselled a piece out of Dicky's little empire.'

'Very well,' said Frank, in a way that made it clear that he didn't agree with my interpretation of those events. 'So why send you?'

'Because I work with Dicky. With both of us out of the way Bret had a better excuse for "taking over some of the workload".' I imitated Bret's voice.

'You're barking up the wrong tree,' said Frank. 'They want to enrol Stinnes. That was a decision of the steering committee, and it's been given urgent priority. They want Stinnes over here, spilling the beans to a debriefing panel.'

'About Fiona?'

'Yes, about your wife,' said Frank. I noticed he always said 'your wife' since her defection. He couldn't bring himself to use her name any more. 'And about you.'

'And about me?'

'How long before the penny drops, Bernard? How long is it going to take you to understand that you must remain a suspect until you are cleared by first-class corroborative evidence?'

'Wait a minute, Frank. Remember me? The one who tipped off the department about Fiona's activities.'

'But she'd made mistakes, Bernard. If you hadn't raised the alarm, someone else would have done so sooner or later. So why not have you tell the department about her. And have it done the way Moscow Centre wanted it done?'

I thought about it for a moment. 'It doesn't hold water, Frank.'

'The way you did it gave her a chance to escape. She got away, Bernard. You sounded the alarm but don't forget that in the event she had time enough to make her escape.'

'There were a few sighs of relief at that, Frank. Some people around here would have done anything to avoid all the publicity of another spy trial. And putting Fiona on trial would have blown a hole in the department.'

'Anyone heaving such sighs of relief is a bloody fool,' said Frank. 'She's taken a pot full of gold with her. No secret papers, as far as we know, but her experience here will be worth a lot to them. You know that.'

'And people are saying that I deliberately arranged her escape?' I was indignant and incredulous.

Frank could see how furious I was, and hastily he said, 'No one is accusing you of anything, but we must examine every possibility. *Every* possibility. That's our job, Bernard. If your wife was due to go into the bag anyway, why not arrange for you to tell us? In that way the KGB lose one highly placed agent but have another in position in the same office. And the second agent's credentials are gilt-edged; didn't he even turn in his own wife?'

'Is that why they want to enrol Stinnes?'

'I thought you'd understand that right from the start. Bringing Stinnes in for interrogation is the one way that you can prove that everything went the way you say it went.'

'And if I don't bring him in?'

Frank tapped the bowl of his pipe against his thumbnail. 'You're not doing yourself any good by saying that Stinnes can't be enrolled. Surely you see that.'

'I'm just saying what I believe.'

'Well, dammit, Bernard, stop saying what you believe. Or the department will think you don't want us to get our hands on Stinnes.'

'The department can think what the hell it likes,' I said.

'That's foolish talk, Bernard. Stinnes would be a plum defector for us. But the real reason that the department is spending all this time and money is because they think so highly of you. It's principally because they want to keep you that they are pushing the Stinnes enrolment.'

Frank had the diplomatic touch, but it didn't change the underlying facts. 'It makes me bloody angry, Frank.'

'Don't be childish,' said Frank. 'No one really suspects you. It's just a formality. They haven't even put you on a restricted list for secret information. So much of the difficulty arises from the way that you and Fiona had such a happy marriage, that's the absurd thing about it. One only had to see you together to know that you were both in love. Happy marriage; promising career; delightful children. If you'd had constant arguments and separations, it would be easier to see you as the wronged party – and politically uninvolved.'

'And if we don't enrol Stinnes? What then, if we don't enrol him?'

'It will be difficult to keep you in Operations if we don't enrol Stinnes.'

'And I know what that implies.' I remembered a few employees whom Internal Security considered unsuitable for employment in Operations. It was chilling to remember those people who'd had their security ratings downgraded in mid-career. The periodic routine checks were usually the cause. That's what turned up the discreet homosexuals who weekended with young Spanish waiters, and lesbians sharing apartments with ladies who turned out not to be their cousins. And there were younger people who'd conveniently forgotten being members of international friendship societies while students. Societies which had the words 'freedom', 'peace' and 'life' in their articles so that anyone who opposed them would be associated with incarceration, war and death. Or had joined other such innocuous-sounding gatherings, which locate themselves conveniently near universities and provide coffee and buns and idealistic talk from respectably dressed foreign visitors. I knew that such downgraded rejects found themselves working the SIS end of an embassy in Central Africa or checking Aeroflot cargo manifests at London Airport.

'I wouldn't worry about having to leave Operations,' said Frank. 'You'll get Stinnes. Now you understand what's involved, you'll get him. I'm confident of that, Bernard.'

There seemed to be nothing more to say. But as I got up from my chair Frank said, 'I had a word with the D-G last night. I was having drinks at his place and a number of things came into the conversation . . .'

'Yes?'

'We're all concerned about you and the problem of looking after the children, Bernard.'

'The only problem is money,' I said sharply.

'We all know that, Bernard. It's money I'm talking about. The D-G has looked into the possibility of giving you a special allowance. The diplomatic service has something called "Accountable Indirect Representational Supplement". Only a bureaucrat could think up a name like that, eh? It reimburses the cost of a nanny, so that children are taken care of while diplomats and wives attend social functions. Diplomats also have "Boarding School Allowance". I'm not sure how much that would come to, but it would probably ease your financial situation somewhat. It might take a bit of time to come through; that's the only snag.'

'I'm not sending the children to boarding school.'

'Relax, Bernard. You're too damned prickly these days. No one is going to come snooping round you to find out what kind of school your children are attending. The D-G simply wants to find a way to help. He wants a formula that's already acceptable. An *ex gratia* payment would not be the way he'd want to do it. If anyone discovered an *ex gratia* payment going directly to an employee, it could blow up into a scandal.'

'I'm grateful, Frank.'

'Everyone is sympathetic, Bernard.' He put his tobacco pouch in his pocket. His pipe was still unlit. 'And, by the way, Stinnes is back in Berlin. He's been in the West Sector to visit your friends the

Volkmanns . . . Mrs Volkmann, in particular. I thought you'd like to know that.'

Frank Harrington had had an affair with Zena Volkmann and there was bad feeling between him and Werner that dated from long before. I wondered if Frank was telling me about Stinnes as some sort of reproach to Werner, who'd not reported it. 'Yes, I'll follow that up, Frank. I will have to go to Berlin. It's just a matter of fitting it in.'

I left Frank to tell Bret that he'd done what was wanted. He'd drawn a diagram so simple that even I could understand it. Then he'd written detailed captions under all the component parts.

I went to my office and sent for a young probationer named Julian MacKenzie. 'Well?' I said.

'No, the nurses at St Mary Abbots don't wear the uniform you described and they don't change shifts at eight forty-five. And there is no coloured woman, of any age, known to the residents of the block opposite your house.'

'That was very quick, MacKenzie.'

'I thought it was pretty good myself, boss.' MacKenzie was an impertinent little sod who'd come down from Cambridge with an honours in modern languages, got the A1 mark that the Civil Service Selection Board usually reserve for friends and relations, and had been a probationer with the department for a few months. It was a record of achievement made even more remarkable by the fact that MacKenzie, despite his Scottish name, had a strong Birmingham accent. His ambition was such that he would work hard and long, and never ask questions nor expect me to give him signed authorizations for each little job. Also his insubordinate attitude to all and sundry amused me.

'I'd really like to get into fieldwork. How can I start on that? Any hints and tips, boss?' This had now become a standard inquiry.

'Yes, comb your hair now and again, change your shirt every day and introduce an obsequious note into your social exchanges with the senior staff.'

'I'm not joking.'

'Neither am I,' I assured him. 'But, while you're here, what's the last name of that girl Gloria. That typist who used to work for Mr Rensselaer?'

'The gorgeous blonde job with the big knockers?'

'You have such a delicate way of phrasing everything, MacKenzie. Yes, that's who I mean. I haven't seen her lately. Where is she working now?'

'Her name's Kent, Gloria Kent. Her father is a dentist. She's very keen on ballroom dancing and water skiing. But she's not a typist, she's a Grade 9 executive officer. She's hoping to fiddle one of those departmental grants to go to university. And what's more she speaks fluent Hungarian.' He grinned. 'Ambition drives us all. I'd say Miss Kent is hankering after a career in the service, wouldn't you?'

'You're a mine of information, MacKenzie. Is her father Hungarian?'

'You guessed. And she lives with her parents, miles out in the sticks. No joy for you there, I'm afraid.'

'You're an impertinent little sod, MacKenzie.'

'Yes, I know, sir. You told me that the other day. She's working in Registry at present, the poor little thing. It's only my daily trips down there to see her among the filing cabinets that keeps her sane.'

'Registry, eh?' It was the most unpopular job in the department and nearly one-third of all the staff were employed there. The theory was that the computer in the Data Centre would gradually replace the thousands of dusty files, and Registry would eventually disappear. But, true to the rules of all bureaucracy, the staff at the Data Centre grew and grew but the staff in Registry did not decrease.

'She'd like working up here with you, sir. I know she'd give anything for a job with any member of the Operations staff.'

'Anything?'

'Almost anything, sir,' said MacKenzie. He winked. 'According to what I hear.'

I phoned the old dragon who ran Registry and told her I wanted Miss Kent to work for me for a few days. When she came up to the office I showed her the great pile of papers due for filing. They'd been stacking up in the cupboard for months, and my own secretary was pleased to see the task taken off her hands.

Gloria Kent was tall. She was slim and long-legged and about twenty years old. Her hair was the colour of pale straw. It was wavy but loose enough to fall across her forehead, short but long enough to touch the roll neck of her dark-brown sweater. She had large brown eyes and long lashes and a wide mouth. If Botticelli had painted the box top for a Barbie doll the picture would have looked like Gloria Kent. And yet she was not doll-like. There was nothing diminutive about her. And she didn't bow her head, the way so many tall women do to accommodate themselves to the egos of shorter men they find around them. And it was her straight-backed posture – for her use of make-up was minimal – that gave her the appearance of a chorus girl rather than a civil servant.

She'd been sorting out the files for about an hour when she said, 'Will I be going back to work in Registry?'

'It's nothing to do with me, Miss Kent,' I said. 'We're both working for Mr Cruyer. He makes all the decisions.'

'He's the Controller of German Stations,' she said, giving Dicky his official title. 'So that's my department, is it?'

'The German Desk, we usually call it,' I said. 'Everything's in a turmoil up here at present, I'm afraid.'

'I know. I was working for Mr Rensselaer. But that only lasted ten days. Then his Economics Intelligence Committee had no more work for me. I did odd bits of typing for people on the top floor, then I was sent down to Registry.'

'And you don't like Registry?'

'No one likes it. There's no daylight and the fluorescent lighting makes me so tired. And you get so dirty handling those files all day. You should see my hands when I go home at night. When I get home I can't wait to strip right off and have a bath.'

I took a deep breath and said, 'You won't get so dirty up here, I hope.'

'It's a treat to see the daylight, Mr Samson.'

'No one round here calls me anything but Bernard,' I said. 'So it might be easier if you did the same.'

'And I'm Gloria,' she said.

'Yes, I know,' I said. 'And by the way, Gloria, Mr Cruyer always likes to meet his staff socially. Every now and again he has a few members of the staff along to his house for an informal dinner and a chat.'

'Well, I think that's very nice,' said Gloria. She smoothed her skirt over her hips.

'It is,' I said. 'We all appreciate it. And the fact is that he has one of these dinners on Thursday. And he made a special point of saying that he'd like you to be there.'

'Thursday. That's rather short notice,' she said. She moved her head to let her hair swing and touched it as if already calculating when to go to the hairdresser's.

'If you have something more important to do, I know he'll understand.'

'It would sound terrible, though, wouldn't it?'

'No, it wouldn't sound terrible. I'd explain to him that you had some other appointment that you couldn't give up.'

'I'd better come,' she said. 'I'm sure I can rearrange things. Otherwise . . .' She smiled. 'I might spend the rest of my life in Registry.'

'He'd like us there at seventy forty-five, for drinks. They sit down to eat at eight thirty. If you live too far away, I'm sure Mrs Cruyer will be happy to let you have a room to change. Come to that,' I said, 'you could have a drink at my house and change there. Then I could drive you over there. His house is rather difficult to find.'

I saw a look of doubt come into her face. I feared for a moment that I'd overplayed my hand but I busied myself with my work and said no more.

Dicky's dinner party was very successful. Daphne had worked for three days preparing the meal, and I realized that she'd not invited me for lunch the previous Sunday because she had been trying out on Dicky the same cucumber soup recipe, and the same wild rice, and the same gooseberry fool that she served for the dinner party. Only the boiled salmon was an experiment; its head fell on the kitchen floor as it was coming out of the fish kettle.

There were eight of us. If Gloria Kent had expected it to be a gathering of departmental staff she gave no sign of disappointment at meeting the Cruyers' new neighbours and a couple named Stephens, the wife being Liz Stephens who was Daphne's partner in the stripping business. Dicky couldn't resist his joke about Daphne making money from stripping, although it was clear that only Gloria had not been told it before. Gloria laughed.

The conversation at table was confined to the usual London dinner-party small talk; listing foreign ski resorts, local restaurants, schools and cars in descending order of desirability. Then there was talk about the furniture stripping. The first attempt had gone badly. No one had told them not to try it with bentwood furniture and the first lot of chairs had disintegrated in the soda bath. The two women were able to laugh about it but their husbands exchanged looks of mutual resignation.

The neighbours from across the road – whose schoolgirl babysitter had to be home very early – left after the gooseberry fool. The Stephenses departed soon afterwards after just one hurried cup of coffee. This left the four of us sitting in the front room. Dicky had the hi-fi playing Chopin very quietly. Gloria asked Daphne if she could help with the washing up and, being told no, admired the primitive painting of Adam and Eve that was hanging over the fireplace. Daphne had 'discovered' it in a fleamarket in Amsterdam. She was always pleased when someone admired it.

'A damn fine meal, darling,' said Dicky as his wife brought the second pot of coffee and chocolate-covered after-dinner mints. His voice was a fruity imitation of Silas Gaunt, one of the old-timers of the department. He pushed his cup forward for a refill.

Daphne glanced at him, smiled nervously and poured the hot coffee on to the polished table. I had the feeling that these dinners were nightmares for Daphne. She had been a pushy, self-confident career girl when Dicky married her, but she knew her limitations as a cook and she knew how critical Dicky (onetime President of Oxford

University Wine and Food Society) Cruyer could be when he was playing host to people he worked with. Sometimes she seemed physically frightened of Dicky and I knew enough about his sudden fits of bad temper to sympathize.

After a competition to see who could use the most Kleenex tissues to clean up the spilled coffee – which Daphne won by using a large handful of them to conceal and smuggle out of the room a box of very wet cigars – Gloria said, 'You have such a beautiful house, Mrs Cruyer.'

'*Daphne*. Daphne, for God's sake. It's a pigsty,' said Daphne with modest self-confidence. 'Sometimes it gets me down.'

I looked round to see any sign of the furniture that Daphne had stored in there but it had all been removed. Poor Daphne. Their cars were parked in the street. I suppose all the furniture was now stacked in the garage.

'And lovely to see you both,' said Dicky, passing coffee to Gloria. Dicky put a lot of meaning into the word 'both'; it was almost carnal. She smiled nervously at Dicky and then looked at me. 'Yes,' said Dicky, passing a cup of coffee to me, 'Bernard has talked about you so much.'

'When?' said Gloria. She was no fool. She guessed immediately what was behind Dicky's remarks.

'When we were in Mexico,' said Dicky.

'Mexico City,' I said.

'They call it Mexico,' said Dicky.

'I know,' said Gloria, as if her mind was on other things. 'My mother and father went there two years ago, on a package holiday. They brought back a lot of home movies. That's my father's hobby. It looked awful.' She turned to me and smiled; sweet smile but cold eyes. 'I didn't know you were talking about me when you were in Mexico, Bernard,' she said.

I drank some of my coffee.

Gloria turned her attention to Daphne. 'As long as I don't have to go back to working in Registry, Mrs Cruyer,' she said. 'It's absolute hell.' Daphne nodded. It was brilliant of her to say it to Daphne. Had she said it to Dicky or to me, I think Daphne would have made sure Gloria went back into Registry the following morning. 'Couldn't you ask your husband to let me work somewhere else?'

Daphne looked uncertain. She said, 'I'm sure he'll do what he can, Gloria. Won't you, Dicky?'

'Of course I will,' said Dicky. 'She can work upstairs. There's always extra work to do and I've had to ask Bret Rensselaer to share his secretary with one of the Deputy Desk people. Gloria could help my secretary and Bernard's secretary and do the occasional job for Bret.'

So Dicky was fighting back. Good old Dicky. Share his secretary; that should make Bret retire to a neutral corner and shake the tears from his eyes.

'That would be wonderful, Mr Cruyer,' said Gloria, but she smiled at Daphne. It was becoming clear to me that Gloria had a great career ahead of her. What was that joke about Hungarians going into a revolving door behind you, and coming out ahead of you.

'We're all one happy family in Dicky's department,' I said.

Dicky smiled at me scornfully.

'But we'd better be moving along,' I said. And to meet Dicky's gaze I added, 'Gloria has left her clothes at my place.'

'Oh, doesn't that sound awful,' said Gloria. 'Bernard let me change at his house. My parents live too far away for me to go home to change.'

When we'd said our goodnights and were in my old Ford, Gloria said, 'What nice people they are.'

'Yes,' I said.

'Mr Cruyer is a very interesting man,' she said.

'Do you think so?'

'Don't you?' she said, as if worried that she'd said the wrong thing.

'Very interesting,' I said. 'But I was surprised you got on to that so quickly.'

'He was at Balliol,' she said wistfully. 'All the very brightest people go to Balliol.'

'That's true,' I said.

'Where did you go to, Bernard?'

'You can call me Mr Samson if you like,' I said. 'I didn't go anywhere. I left school when I was sixteen and started work.'

'Not for the department?'

'Sort of,' I said.

'You can't take the Civil Service exam at sixteen.'

'It all happened in a foreign country,' I said. 'My father was the Berlin Resident. I grew up in Berlin. I speak Berlin German like a native. I know the town. It was natural that I should start working for the department. The paperwork was all done afterwards. I never took the selection board.' It sounded more defensive than I had intended it should.

'I got five A levels,' said Gloria proudly. Gone was the *femme fatale*; all of a sudden she was the sixth-form schoolgirl running home with her school report.

'Here we are,' I said. 'Do you want to come inside and have a drink?'

To my surprise she tilted her head back until it was on my shoulder. I could smell her perfume and the warmth of her body. She said, 'I don't want this evening to end.'

'We'll keep it going as long as possible,' I said. 'Come and have a drink.'

She smiled lazily. She hadn't had much wine or I might have suspected that she was drunk. She put her hand on my arm and turned her face to me. I kissed her on the forehead and opened the door. 'Come along, then.' She giggled and got out of the car. As she slid from the seat her skirt rode up to expose a lot of leg. She tugged at it and smiled modestly.

Once inside the house she sat down on the sofa and again said what a wonderful evening it had been. 'Brandy?' I said. 'Liqueur? Scotch and soda?'

'A very tiny brandy,' she said. 'But I'll miss my last train if we don't go very soon.' I poured two huge Martell brandies and sat down next to her.

'Will your parents worry?' I gave her a decorous kiss on the cheek. 'If you miss your train, would they really worry?'

'I'm a big girl now,' she said.

'You are indeed, Gloria,' I said admiringly. 'You're a wonderful girl.' I put my arm round her and pulled her close. She was soft and warm and big. She was just what I wanted.

'What were you saying about me when you were in Mexico City?' Her voice was dreamy and softened by the way she was nibbling my ear.

'Mexico. You heard what Dicky said. They always call it Mexico.'

She murmured, 'Did you bet Dicky Cruyer that you'd get me into bed?'

'Of course not,' I said.

'You said you'd already had me in bed? Ummm?'

'Good Lord, no,' I said. 'We were talking about staffing. We weren't talking about any one member of the staff in particular. We were talking about the office . . . the workload.'

She nuzzled her face against my ear. 'You're a terrible liar, Bernard. Did anyone ever tell you that? You are a completely hopeless liar. How did you ever survive as a secret agent?' She was kissing my cheek now. As I hugged her she murmured, 'Admit it, you told Dicky we were lovers.' As she said it she turned her head to offer me her lips and we kissed. When she broke away she purred, 'You did, didn't you?'

'I might have said something that gave him the wrong impression,' I admitted. 'You can see what Dicky's like.'

She kissed me again. 'I must go home,' she said.

'Must you?'

'I must. My parents *might* worry.'

'You're a big girl now,' I reminded her. But she pushed me away and got to her feet. 'Perhaps some other time,' she said. She was alert now, and I could see she had decided to leave. 'I'll go upstairs and get my bag. But you·. . .' She took me by the hand and pulled me to the front door. 'You will go out and start the car and take me to the station.'

When I showed little inclination to do this, she marched upstairs to get the clothes she'd left there and, over her shoulder, said, 'If I miss my train at Waterloo you'll have to drive me all the way to Epsom, Mr Samson. And that's a miserable drive at this time of night. And my parents always wait up to see who I've been with. I hate to make them angry.'

'Okay, Gloria,' I said. 'You talked me round.' I didn't relish facing the wrath of a Hungarian dentist in the small hours of the morning.

I took her to Waterloo Station in time to catch her train and I returned to my lonely bed.

It was only next morning that I discovered that she'd used the scissors from the bathroom cupboard to cut all my underpants in two. And it was only when daylight came that I could see that she'd written 'You are a bastard Mr Samson' in lipstick on the bedroom window. I spent ages removing the lipstick marks, and hiding my pieces of underwear, before Mrs Dias the cleaning lady arrived. I was not in a hurry to repeat that experience with Gloria. It seemed as if there might be something of deep psychological significance about the retribution she'd wreaked upon my linen for what seemed to me a harmless little joke.

12

'That bloody Werner has been seeing Stinnes,' said Dicky. He was pacing up and down chewing at the nail of his little finger. It was a sign that he was agitated. He was often agitated lately. Sometimes I wondered that Dicky had any nails left.

'So I hear,' I said calmly.

'Ah,' said Dicky. 'I thought so. Have you been going behind my back again?'

I salaamed; a low bow in a gesture of placation, 'Oh, master. I hear this only from Harrington sahib.'

'Cut out the clowning,' said Dicky. He sat down behind his huge rosewood table. He didn't have a real desk in his office; just a few fine pieces of antique furniture including this rosewood table that he used as a desk, a Charles Eames chair for him to sprawl in, and a couple of easy chairs for visitors. It was big room with two windows facing across the park. At one time he'd shared this room with his secretary, but once he'd annexed the office next door for her he spread himself.

'No one tells me anything,' said Dicky. He was sitting on his hard little chair, legs and knees pressed together and arms folded tight across his chest. It was an illustration from a textbook that tells you how to deal with sulking children. 'Bret's determined to take over my job. Now I suppose he's going to cut off all my communications with my stations.'

'Werner Volkmann doesn't officially work for the department. You wouldn't give him any money in Mexico City. You remember I asked you, and you said over your dead body.'

'He's got no right to have meetings with Stinnes without keeping me informed.'

'He can't have had many meetings in Berlin,' I said. 'He's only been back there five minutes.'

'He should have asked permission,' said Dicky.

'Werner doesn't owe us anything; we owe him.'

'Who owes him?' said Dicky contentiously.

'The department owes him. Werner located Stinnes for us and then you wouldn't okay a payment. What can you expect?'

'So your pal Werner is out to teach us a lesson. Is that his game?'

I sank down deep in Dicky's Charles Eames armchair; it was very relaxing. Little wonder Dicky never got any work done. 'Werner is one of those strange people who like to work in intelligence. He makes a good living from his banking activities but he wants to work for us. You put Werner back on the payroll and he'd be the most enthusiastic agent on your books. Give him a little money and even his wife would start getting interested.'

'She's mercenary. That Zena is very mercenary.'

So even Dicky had noticed. 'Yes, she is,' I said. 'But if they both are seeing Stinnes, my advice is to keep her sweet.'

Dicky grunted and continued biting his nail.

'Zena keeps her ears and eyes open. And Stinnes seems to like her. She might be able to guess what's in his mind before anyone else does.'

Dicky pouted. He was always like this about approving extra payments to any field agents. Normally I would have arranged any discussion about money for some day when Dicky was in one of the upward phases of his manic lifestyle. 'If Werner Volkmann makes a complete cock-up of everything, and he's not on the payroll, I can disown him,' explained Dicky, who tackled every task by deciding how he'd extricate himself from it if disaster ensued.

'I'll take personal responsibility for him,' I said.

Dicky brightened at the idea of that. 'That might be a way of doing it,' he said. The wall behind Dicky was almost completely covered with framed photos of Dicky smiling and shaking hands with important people. This form of self-advertisement, more usually found in the offices of extrovert American film producers, was considered bad form when Dicky first began his collection. But Dicky had made it into a prank, a droll collegiate form of fun, so that now he was able to have his joke and eat it too. One of the photos showed Dicky in Calcutta, while on a tour with Sir Henry Clevemore, the Director-General. It was a large colour photo in a gold frame. The two men were standing in front of a stall displaying crude lithographic posters. By looking closely you could recognize portraits of John Lennon, Napoleon, Marilyn Monroe, Lenin and John F. Kennedy. Somehow I always thought of Dicky as that young man in the photo, smiling at his boss amid a galaxy of successful people. 'I've told Berlin that I want Werner over here immediately. He'll be on the morning plane. I've sent a car to the airport so he will be here about three. We'll sit him down and find out what the hell it's all about. Okay, Bernard?'

'I hope you'll start off by offering him a proper contract,' I said.

'He's not your employee. He can just tell you to get stuffed and phone his lawyer.'

Dicky bit his lip. 'We've just been through all that. You said you'd take responsibility for him.'

'Then let me offer him a proper contract,' I said. Dicky looked doubtful. I said, 'Distancing yourself from Werner in case everything goes wrong might be sound reasoning. But don't distance yourself from him so far that he's out of sight. Don't distance yourself so far from Werner that you'll get no credit if everything goes well.'

Dicky took out a handkerchief and blew his nose. 'I'm getting a cold,' he said woefully. 'It's coming back here after the hot weather in Mexico.'

I nodded. I recognized the signs. When Dicky displayed the symptoms of the common cold it was usually because he was expecting some work he couldn't handle, or questions he didn't want to answer. 'Let me see Werner,' I said. 'Let me draft a contract. Don't bring him up here to the office. Tell me what you want him to do and I'll keep you in touch with him. Run him through me. Then you'll have the best of both worlds.'

'Very well,' said Dicky. He blew his nose again, trying to conceal his relief behind his big white handkerchief.

'But I'll need money,' I said. 'Not a handful of small change; ten grand at least, Dicky.'

'Ten grand?'

'It's only money, Dicky.'

'You're irresponsible, Bernard. Two thousand maybe, not ten.'

'It's not your money, Dicky.'

'That's just the sort of thing I'd expect you to say,' said Dicky. 'You think the department has money to burn.'

'Money is a part of our armoury,' I said. 'It's what we use to do our job. We can conserve the department's money by sitting on our arses and staring into space.'

'I knew you'd have an answer,' said Dicky.

I nodded. I knew it was an answer which Dicky would be noting down for future use the next time the cashier's office queried Dicky's profligate expense accounts.

'Very well then, ten thousand. On account, mind you. I shall want every penny of it accounted for.'

'I think Werner should go over into East Berlin and see what he can find out about Stinnes on his home ground.'

Dicky took his little finger and bit into the nail with a dedication that made our conversation a secondary matter. 'Dangerous,' said Dicky between nibbles. 'Dangerous for all concerned.'

'Let Werner be the judge of that. I won't force him to go.'

'No, you'll just give him the money, and tell him he's getting a contract. And then you'll ask him if he wants to go over there. You're a ruthless bastard, Bernard. I thought Werner was your friend.'

'He is my friend. Werner won't go unless he thinks he can do it without getting into trouble.' But was it true, I wondered? Was I really planning to manipulate Werner in such a cynical way? If so, would I even have realized it without Dicky's rejoinder?

'Ten thousand pounds,' mused Dicky. 'Couldn't I use a windfall like that. I don't know how I'm going to afford the boys' school fees next year. I just had a long letter from the headmaster. I don't blame the school; their expenses are rocketing.'

'The government say that inflation is down again,' I said. I wondered what Dicky would say if he got to hear that I was getting a supplementary 'Boarding School Allowance' and the money for the nanny.

'What do the bloody politicians care?' said Dicky. 'The first thing those bastards do when they get into office is to vote themselves some astronomical rise in salaries and allowances.'

'Yes,' I said. 'To the barricades.' So discontent was running through the ranks of Whitehall, despite index-linked pensions and all the rest of it.

'Yes,' said Dicky. 'Well, I daresay you have your own financial worries.'

'Yes, Dicky. I do.'

'So where shall I tell the driver to dump Werner when he brings him from the airport? You say you don't want to see him up here. And if he's in and out of the East all the time it's just as well he stays at arm's length.'

'Shall I tell your secretary to type out a chit for the money?'

'Yes, yes, yes, yes, yes,' said Dicky irritably. 'I said yes. I'm not going to go back on my promise to your precious Werner. Get the chit and I'll sign it.'

I went back to my office with the chit. I wouldn't put it past Dicky to retrieve the signed form from his secretary's tray and start having second thoughts about it. My secretary had gone to early lunch but Gloria Kent was there. I had the feeling that she was slowing down on the filing so she could make sure she stayed upstairs.

'Take this money order along to the cashier's office. Tell them I want a cheque made out to cash. And I want it before lunch.'

'The cashier's office is awfully busy, Bernard,' she said.

'Stay there until you get it. And make yourself a nuisance while you're waiting.'

'How do I do that?' said Gloria.

'Talk to them,' I suggested. 'Or, better still, read all the paperwork you can find, and comment on what payments are going out to whom. That always makes them jumpy.'

'I'm never sure when you are joking,' said Gloria.

'I never joke about money,' I said.

No sooner had she gone down the corridor than my phone rang. It was the operator telling me there was an outside call from Mrs Kozinski. I was always puzzled in the same way when I heard that name Kozinski. I never thought of Fiona's sister as being Mrs Kozinski, and I certainly never thought of dear old George, my brother-in-law, with his cockney accent and his terrible jokes, as George Kozinski.

'Bernard here.'

'Oh, Bernard, I've been trying to get you for ages. Your people there guard you so well, darling. How I wish I had such suspicious guardians looking after me. It's like trying to get through to Buckingham Palace. Worse, in fact, because George has several customers in the royal household and I've seen him get through to them in no time at all.' It was the breathless syntax of the gossip column.

'How are you, Tessa?' So it was my amazing, sexy, scatterbrained, wanton sister-in-law. 'Is anything wrong?'

'Nothing I could possibly talk about over the telephone, darling,' she said.

'Oh, really,' I said, wondering if the call was being monitored by Internal Security. After everything that Frank Harrington had told me, it would have been very stupid of me to imagine I was not under some sort of surveillance, however perfunctory.

'Bernard. Are you free for lunch? Today, I mean. Right now, in fact. If you have an appointment, change it. I must see you, darling.' She was able to say this with strong emphasis upon each phrase and yet not convey any note of real urgency. I had the feeling that even if her house was on fire, Tessa would shout a stylish 'fire' in a manner that sounded more fashionable than desperate.

'I'm free for lunch.'

'Super.'

'Where would you like to go?' I knew that Tessa had always got some place she wanted to go to for lunch. Too many times I'd heard her acerbic descriptions of inadequate lunches in unfashionable places.

'Oh.' Only the English middle class have the gliding diphthong that makes them able to say 'Oh' like that. Tessa could make 'Oh' into a Bach cantata. Having had time to think, she said, 'I'm too bored with all these frightfully twee little restaurants run by young male couples who've been to Bocuse on holiday. What about the Savoy, darling? When you get right down to it, it's the only place in London with any real class. Everywhere is full of advertising people these days.'

'I'll see if I can get a table,' I promised.

'The Restaurant, darling, not the Grill. I never see any of my friends when I go to the Grill. Shall we say one o'clock? When you phone, ask for the chef, Mr Edelmann. George knows him awfully well. Mention George.'

'Is it just social, Tessa? Or is there really something special?'

'I had dinner with Daddy last night, Bernard. I must talk to you. It's about you-know-who and the children, darling. I heard about your visit to Leith Hill.'

'Yes, David wanted to see me.'

'I know all about it. We'll have a lovely lunch and we'll talk about everything. There's so much to tell you, Bernard. It seems ages since we last had a proper talk together.'

'And George is well?'

'George is always well when he's making money, darling. You know that.'

'I'm glad to hear he's making money,' I said.

'He has the Midas touch, darling. We've got an apartment in Mayfair now. Did you know that? No, of course you didn't. The change-of-address cards don't go out until next week. You'll love it; it's adorable. And so central.'

'We'll talk about it over lunch,' I said as I spied Dicky coming in.

'Savoy Restaurant, one o'clock sharp,' said Tessa. She was muddle-headed and vague about most things, but she was making sure there would be no mistake about our lunch. I suppose anyone who had the number of illicit love affairs and assignations that Tessa enjoyed would have to be methodical and precise about appointments.

'See you there,' I said.

'Who was that?' said Dicky.

I felt like saying it was none of his damn business but I answered him truthfully. 'Tessa Kozinski,' I said. 'My sister-in-law.'

'Oh,' said Dicky. As I understood it from Fiona, Tessa had had a brief mad affair with Dicky. I watched his face and decided it was probably true. 'I've met her. She's a nice little woman.'

Nice little woman was not the description that usually came to mind when a man met Tessa Kozinski. 'Some people think she's a sex bomb,' I said.

'I wouldn't say that,' said Dicky very coolly.

'Was there something you wanted?'

'Werner. Where shall I send him?'

'Send him along to the Savoy Restaurant,' I said. 'I'm lunching there with my sister-in-law.'

'I thought you were short of money,' said Dicky.

'Werner is joining me for coffee,' I said.

'Oh no you don't,' said Dicky. 'You're not going to charge that lunch. It's not on.'

'The Restaurant,' I said. 'Not the Grill. Tessa never sees any of her friends in the Grill.'

Tessa arrived looking magnificent. She was thirty-three years old but she looked ten years younger than that. Whatever Tessa was doing, it seemed to be good for her. She had wonderful skin and light fair hair that she wore long so that it broke over her shoulders. George's income, to say nothing of the allowance she got from her father, was to be seen in every expensive stitch of the dark-blue Chanel suit, the Hermès handbag and Charles Jourdan shoes. Even the most blasé waiter turned his head to watch her as she kissed me with extravagant hugs and sighs before sitting down.

She kicked off a shoe under the table and swore softly as she rubbed her foot. 'What a wonderful table you've got for us. With that lovely view of the river. They must know you.'

'No,' I said truthfully. 'I mentioned George's name as you suggested.'

She smiled dutifully as at an oft-repeated joke. She waved away the menu without looking at it and ordered an Ogen melon and a grilled sole with a small mixed salad. When she saw me looking down the wine list she said, 'Would you think me awful if I asked you to order a bottle of Bollinger, darling? My doctor has told me to avoid red wines and all other sorts of booze.'

'A bottle of Bollinger,' I told the waiter.

'I saw David,' she said. She rubbed her foot again. 'He's an absolute bastard, isn't he?'

'We've never got along very well together,' I said.

'He's a bastard. You know he is. And now he's trying to get the children. I hope you told him to go straight to hell.'

'I wouldn't like him to have the children,' I said.

'I wouldn't allow the old bastard to run a zoo,' said Tessa. 'He ruined my life and I blame him for what happened to Fiona.'

'Do you?'

'Well, don't they say all these spies and traitors are just reacting to the way they hate their parents?'

'It is a popular theory,' I said.

'And my father is living evidence of the truth of it. Who could imagine poor old Fi working for the rotten commies unless she'd been driven to it by David?'

'I'm keeping the children with me,' I said. 'It will be difficult to afford it, but no more difficult than it was for my father.'

'Good for you, Bernie. I was hoping you'd say that, because I'm going to help you, if you'll let me.' She looked at me with a stern expression that I found so appealing. It was impossible not to compare her with the diamond-hard Zena. But despite her sophisticated life-style and smart back-chat Tessa was insecure. Sometimes I wondered if her casual love affairs were attempts to reassure herself, just as some people use drink or mirrors. I'd always had a weak spot for her, no matter how exasperating she was. She was shallow, but she was spontaneously generous. I'd find it easy to fall in love with her but I was determined not to. She smiled demurely, and then looked out of the window. The River Thames was high, the water gleaming like oil. Against the current, a string of barges, piled high with rubbish, moved very slowly and were devoured piecemeal by an arch of Waterloo Bridge.

'I'll let you, Tessa. I can use any help I can get.'

'I phoned your mother. She worries about you.'

'Mothers always worry,' I said.

'She said the children are coming back to Duke Street. Nanny is still with them, that's one good thing. She's been wonderful, that girl. I didn't think she had it in her. It's probably very uncomfortable for her, cramped up in that little house of your mother's. Anyway I thought I'd come over to Duke Street with my cleaning woman and get everything ready for them. Okay?'

'It's nice of you, Tessa. But I'm sure it will be all right.'

'That's because you're a man and you've got no idea of what has to be done in a house when two young children are moving in. They'll need the rooms aired, clean clothes ready, beds made, food prepared, groceries in the cupboard and some cooked meals in the freezer.'

'I suppose you're right,' I said.

'Well, of course I'm right, darling. You don't think all these things get done by magic, do you?'

'I've got Mrs Dias,' I explained.

'Mrs Dias,' said Tessa. She laughed, drank some champagne, eyed the waiter and pointed to our glasses to get more. Then she laughed again at the thought of Mrs Dias. 'Mrs Dias, darling, is about as much use as a spare whatnot at a wedding, if you know what I mean.'

'I know what you mean,' I said. 'But Fiona always managed with Mrs Dias.'

'Because Fiona always did half the housework herself.'

'Did she? I didn't know that.'

'Of course you didn't. Men don't know anything. But the fact remains that you'll have to get the house properly organized if you are to hang on to your children. It won't be easy, Bernard. But I'll do everything I can.'

'It's very kind of you, Tessa.'

'I'm determined that David won't get his hands on them.' The waiter brought the food. Tessa held up her glass and said, 'Good luck, Bernard.' Leaning across the table to me, she said, 'Champagne – real French champagne – is not fattening. I'm going to this perfectly wonderful doctor who's put me on a diet.'

'I'm glad to hear the wonderful news about champagne,' I said. 'How fattening is cheap red Spanish plonk?'

'Don't start all that working-class-boy-makes-good stuff. I've heard it all before. Now let's get this straight; I'll send a car to bring your nanny and the children from your mother's house on Saturday morning. George can always find a car from one of the showrooms, and a spare driver.'

'Thanks,' I said. 'Was there something else you wanted to talk to me about?'

'No, no, no,' she said. 'Just about the house. I'll get it in some sort of order. Give me your door key. I know you keep a spare one in your office desk.'

'Is there anything you don't know?' I said.

She looked up and reached across the table to touch the back of my hand with her outstretched finger. Her touch made me shiver. 'Quite a lot of things I don't know, Bernard.' she said. 'But all in good time, eh?'

13

Werner did not arrive at three o'clock. He did not get Dicky's message until after lunch. The plane on which he was due to fly out of Berlin-Tegel had some mechanical malfunction. Since the old agreements specify that German airliners may not use the airlanes between Berlin and West Germany, there was a delay while another British Airways plane was brought into service. When eventually the plane did arrive in London, Werner was not aboard.

Werner did not arrive the following day. I phoned his apartment in Berlin-Dahlem but the phone was unanswered.

By the third day Dicky was uttering threats and dark suspicions. 'But the Berlin office sent a car,' said Dicky plaintively. 'And arranged his air ticket, and had one hundred pounds in sterling left with the driver. Where the hell has the bloody man gone?'

'There's probably a good explanation,' I said.

'It had better be a bloody show-stopper,' said Dicky. 'Now even the Deputy D-G has started asking about Stinnes. What am I supposed to say? Tell me that, will you?' It was not a rhetorical question; he stared at me and waited for an answer. When none came he pulled out his handkerchief and dabbed his eyes. He stood for a moment, breathing deeply as if preparing to sneeze, and then finally blew his nose. 'I still haven't shaken off that cold,' he said.

'A couple of days at home might be the best way of curing it,' I said.

He shot me a suspicious glance and then said, 'It might come to that. I'm beginning to think I might be infectious.'

'Give Werner until the weekend,' I said. 'Then perhaps we should put out some sort of alert or a contact string to find out where he is.'

'Did you phone Frank Harrington?'

'Yes, but he's only just got back to Berlin. And Werner isn't one of his agents. He has no contact number for Werner.'

'Only for Zena?' said Dicky sarcastically. Such caustic remarks about senior staff – let alone their misconduct – were most unusual. I began to wonder if Dicky was running a fever.

★

Werner phoned me that evening, just as I was about to leave the office. The whole floor was almost empty; Dicky had gone home, Gloria Kent had gone home, my secretary had gone home. The switchboard staff had already connected the outside lines to the duty office but luckily Werner came through on my private phone. 'Where the hell have you been?' I asked him angrily. 'I've had Dicky kicking my arse all round the office about you.'

'I'm sorry,' said Werner. He could be mournful without sounding apologetic. 'But you'd better get over here right away.'

'Where are you? Berlin?'

'No, I'm in England. I'm in that old safe house you used to use . . . the one near the sea at Bosham.'

'Chichester? What are you doing there, Werner? Dicky will be furious.'

'I can't talk. I'm using a call phone in a pub. There is someone waiting. I'll meet you at the house.'

'It's about seventy miserable miles, Werner. I hate that road. It will take an hour or more.'

'See you then. You remember how to find it?'

'I'll see you there,' I said without enthusiasm.

Bosham, which the English – as a part of their chronic conspiracy to baffle foreigners – pronounce 'Bozzam', is a collection of cottages, old and new, crowded on to a peninsula between two tidal creeks that give on to inland waters, and eventually to the Channel. Here are sailing boats of every shape and size, and sailing schools and sailing clubs. And here are pubs crammed with nautical junk, and clocks that chime ships' bells at closing time. And noisy men in sailor's jerseys who tow their boats behind their cars.

The safe house was not too far from Bosham's little church. It was a neat little 'two up and two down' with a freshly painted weather-boarded front, and bright orange roof-tiles. Even in the years of depressed property prices such little weekend cottages with their view of the boats, and sometimes even a glimpse of the water between them, had kept their value.

Summer had gone but it had been a fine day for those lucky enough to spend it sailing. But now there was an offshore wind and when I arrived and got out of my car the air was chilly and I needed the coat I'd thrown on to the back seat. It was twilight when I arrived. The yellow lights of the houses were reflected in the water and there were still people on some of the boats, folding their sails and trying to prolong the perfect day. Werner was waiting for me, sitting at the wheel of a Rover 2000 that was parked close up against the house. He opened the car door and I got in beside him.

'What's the story, Werner?'

'A black girl . . . woman, I should say. West Indian. Was married to an American airman stationed in Germany. She's divorced. Lives in Munich; very active political worker, very vocal communist. Then two years ago she became very quiet and very respectable. You know what I mean?'

'She was recruited by the KGB?'

'It looks that way. Last week she came to Berlin for a briefing. I followed Stinnes one evening after I'd noticed him looking at his watch all through dinner. Then I followed her. She came here.' Werner smiled. He was a boy scout. He loved the whole business of espionage, as other men are obsessed with golf, women or stamp collections.

'I believe we met,' I said.

'Came here,' said Werner.

'To England. Yes, I know.'

'Came *here*,' said Werner. He had the car keys in his hand, and now he tapped them against the steering wheel to emphasize his words. 'To this house.'

'How is that possible? This is a departmental safe house.'

'I know,' said Werner. 'I followed her here and I recognized it. You sent me here. It was a long time ago. I brought a parcel of documents for someone being held here.'

'Is she in there now?'

'No, she's gone.'

'Have you tried to get in?'

'I've been inside. I came out again. There's a body upstairs.'

'The girl?'

'It looked like a man. I couldn't find the main switch for the electricity. You can't see much with only a flashlight.'

'What sort of body?'

'The shutters were closed so there was no daylight and I didn't want to trample through the house leaving marks everywhere.'

'We'd better take a look,' I said. 'How did you get in before?'

'Kitchen window. It's very messy, Bernard. Really messy. Blood on the floor. I've left footmarks, I'm afraid. Blood on the floor. Blood on the walls. Blood on the ceiling.'

'What happened? Do you have an idea?'

'Looks like the body's been there a couple of days. Gun-shot wound. High-velocity head shot. You know what happens.'

'We'd better take a look,' I said. I got out of the car. From somewhere near by I could hear merry holiday-makers leaving the pub, their voices raised in song.

As Werner had already found, it was not difficult to get the kitchen window open, but my forced entry was not the demonstration of expertise that I'd intended. Werner did not comment on the way my shoes left mud in the sink and my elbow knocked a teacup to the floor, and for that restraint I was grateful to him.

I let Werner in through the front door and went to the cupboard under the stairs to find the fuse box and put the lights on. Nothing much had changed since I'd last visited the house. We'd had an East German scientist there for a long debriefing session. I'd taken my turn on the rota with him. To alleviate the misery of his internment he'd been allowed some sailing trips. The house brought back happy memories for me. But since that time two Russian air-force officers had been held here. One of them had eventually returned to the USSR. Despite the way in which all such internees were brought here in a closed vehicle, there had been fears about the address being compromised.

Officially the house had not been used for such defectors for some years but, such was the dogged plod of departmental housekeeping, all the arrangements about its upkeep had obviously continued. Not only was the electricity still connected and paid for; the house was clean and tidy. There were signs of use: crockery on the draining board and fresh groceries in evidence on the shelf.

I went upstairs to the front bedroom first. I opened the doors and switched on the light. It was just as messy as Werner had described. The pale-green floral wallpaper was spattered with blood, there was more on the ceiling and a sticky pool of it on the floor. Exposure to the air had discoloured the blood so that it was no longer bright red but brownish and in places almost black.

It was small room, with a single bed made up with loose covers and cushions to look like a sofa. In the corner there was a dressing table with a large mirror in which was reflected the body of a man sprawled across the cheap Indian carpet. He had been thrown forward from a small kitchen chair in which he'd been sitting. The chair was on its side; its back-rest showed bare white wood where a bullet had torn a large splinter from it.

'Do you recognize him?'

'Yes,' I said. 'It's one of our people, a probationer. A bright kid. His name is Julian MacKenzie.' The light shone on a circular disc of plastic and I picked it up from the floor. It was a watch glass with a scratch on it. I recognized it as the one from my old Omega. After it stopped I'd put the watch and the crystal in an envelope and never taken it for repair. I wondered who had found it and where.

'Did you know he was coming here?' Werner asked.

I switched off the light and pulled the door closed on the dead boy. I looked into the next room. It was another bedroom, with another single bed. 'Single bed,' I said, trying to keep my mind from thinking about MacKenzie's body. 'No one could believe that this was a weekend cottage. Weekend cottages are always crammed with beds.'

There was a dressing table in the corner, this time littered with torn pieces of wrappers, some face powder and the smudge marks of spilled liquids. There was a large plastic box on the bed. I opened it carefully and found a set of electric hair-curlers. I closed the lid again and wiped the places I'd touched. A waste-paper basket held a collection of plastic bottles: shampoo, moisturizing cream, hair conditioner, hair colouring and a lot of screwed-up tissues and tufts of cotton wool. There was more evidence of occupation in the bathroom: long hairs in the bath where someone – probably a woman – had washed her hair, and towels draped unfolded on the rack so that they would dry easily.

'That's right,' said Werner. 'It's not like a weekend cottage; it's like a safe house.' He followed me downstairs. I looked round the kitchen. 'Did you discover where the booze is kept when you first got in?'

'There's no booze.'

'Don't be idiotic, Werner. There is always booze in a safe house.'

'There's a bottle of something in the refrigerator.' Werner took a chair and sat astraddle it, leaning his elbow on the chairback, his hand propped under his wide jaw. He watched me, his black eyes glowering under those bushy black eyebrows, and his forehead wrinkled in a disapproving frown. Sometimes I didn't notice what a huge bear of a man he was, but now, his shoulders hunched and his feet spread wide apart, he looked almost like a Sumo wrestler.

He stared at me while I found some glasses in a cabinet and got the drink – a large square-shaped green bottle of *Bokma oude jenever* – from the refrigerator. It had no doubt come from some sailing trip to the Dutch coast. Still standing, I poured some for myself and one for Werner. He waved it away at first, but when I drank some of mine he picked it up and sniffed it suspiciously before sipping some and pulling a face.

'Poor MacKenzie,' I said. I didn't sit down with him. I went round the room with bottle and glass in my hands, looking at all the pictures, the fittings and the furniture, remembering the time I'd spent here.

'A probationer, was he? He hadn't learned when to be afraid.'

'The black girl was dressed as a nurse. She got a ride in my car. She said she was late for work. She pulled a hypodermic needle on me. The seat belt held me. I felt a bloody fool, Werner. But what could I do?'

'She must have slept in the second bedroom. There is a nurse's uniform in the wardrobe and a box of medical equipment including a couple of hypodermics and some drugs with labels that I don't understand.'

'She said she was from Jamaica. They probably chose her because she has a British passport.' I sat down and put my glass on the table with the bottle.

'Yes, I saw her go through immigration with UK passport holders.'

'But why this house, Werner? If she was a KGB agent, why this departmental safe house? They have their own places, houses we don't know about.'

Werner pulled a face to show me he didn't know the answer.

'I sent MacKenzie off to find her.'

'Looks like he found her,' said Werner.

'You followed the black girl here. What then?'

'I went back to London. Zena was in London, just for two days. I didn't want to leave her on her own. She frets when left alone.'

'You're a bloody wonderful agent, Werner.'

'I didn't know it was important,' said Werner. His flushed face and the anger in his voice were indications of embarrassment. 'How could I guess it was going to turn out like this?'

'But you came back. Then what?'

'The black girl's car had gone. I saw a Ford Fiesta parked down near the pub. It had a radio telephone. I recognized the fittings and the antenna.'

'MacKenzie. Yes. None of the senior staff have the standard radio-telephone fittings nowadays. It's too conspicuous.'

'I climbed in here. I found the body. I phoned you. End of story.'

'I appreciate it, Werner.'

'Smart boy, your MacKenzie. How did he get on to her? She's not easy to follow, Bernard. What did she do that led your boy right here?'

'I don't know, Werner.'

'And he didn't phone in to tell you what he was doing?'

'What are you trying to say, Werner?'

'Your MacKenzie was one of them, wasn't he? It's the only explanation that fits. He was a KGB employee. He told you nothing. He helped them do whatever they had to do, then the black girl silenced him.'

'It's a tempting theory, Werner. But I don't buy it. Not yet anyway. I'd need more than that to believe that MacKenzie was a KGB employee.'

'So how did he track them down? Was it just luck?'

'You saw the body upstairs, Werner. It's not pretty, is it? You and I have seen plenty of that sort of thing, but you went a bit green and I needed a drink. I don't see it as a woman's deed. She fires a gun; splashes a lot of blood. There are screams and cries and a man mortally wounded. She sees his death agonies. She fires again; more spurting blood. Then again. Then again.' I rubbed my face. 'No. I don't think a woman would do it that way.'

'Then perhaps you don't know much about women,' said Werner feelingly.

'*Crime passionel*, you mean. But this is not the case of a woman who surprises her lover in bed with her rival. This was cold-blooded murder. MacKenzie was seated on a chair in the middle of the room. No evidence of any sexual motive. The bed was not even rumpled.'

'If not the black woman, who?'

'It wasn't done by a woman. It was a man; men probably, a KGB hit team.'

'Killing one of their own people,' said Werner, resolutely holding to his theory.

'If the KGB had recruited MacKenzie at Cambridge and then he was able to get a job in the department, they'd be keeping him in deep cover and waiting for him to get a desk for himself. They wouldn't kill him.'

'So, if he wasn't a KGB agent, whatever secret did your MacKenzie discover that made it necessary to kill him?'

'MacKenzie was no great detective, Werner. He was just a sharp young kid with a brilliant academic record from Cambridge. He wasn't even an ex-copper; no investigative experience, no training, and he wasn't a natural the way you are a natural. He'd never be able to trace an experienced KGB agent to a safe house. He was lured here, Werner. Someone was providing him with clues he had to fall over.'

'Why?'

'It was our safe house, Werner. A closely guarded departmental secret. The KGB bastards wanted to show us how clever they are.'

'And murder your probationer to rub salt in?' Werner was not convinced. He drank some more gin, looking at it after he sipped it as if he thought it might be poisoned. 'Strange-flavoured stuff this . . .' He read the label. '. . . *oude jenever*. It's not like real schnapps.'

'Hollands; it's supposed to taste like that,' I said. 'It was used as a medicine when they first concocted it.'

'You'd have to be damned ill to need it,' said Werner, pushing it aside. 'A deliberate murder?'

'He was seated in that chair in the middle of the room, Werner. His executioner was behind him. The pistol held against the top of the spine. It's the way the Okhrana executed Bolshevik revolutionaries in the time of the Tsar. In the nineteen-twenties the Tcheka hunted down white Russian émigré's in Paris and Berlin. Some of them were killed in that fashion. In the Spanish Civil War, Stalin's NKVD went to Catalonia and executed dozens of Trotskyites like that.'

'But why would a KGB hit team be so theatrical? And what did the black girl come here to do?'

'She came to see me. Or, more accurately, she saw me when she came to London.'

'What did she come to see you about?'

I hesitated about my reply. I poured myself another shot of gin and drank some. I'd always liked the curious malty flavour of Hollands gin and now I welcomed the fiery path it blazed to my stomach.

'You'll have to tell me,' said Werner. 'We're both too deep into this one to hold back any secrets.'

'Fiona sent a message. She says she'll let me keep the children here for a year, but she wants me to prevent the Stinnes enrolment.'

'Prevent it?'

'Not encourage it.'

'Why? Did it really come from her, or is it a KGB move?'

'I don't know, Werner. I keep trying to put myself in her place. I keep trying to guess what she might do. She loves the children, Werner, but she'll want to impress her new masters. She's given her whole life to them, hasn't she, her career, her family, her marriage? She's given more of herself to Moscow than she ever gave to the children.'

'Stinnes is involved,' said Werner. 'The black girl was briefed by Stinnes. I saw them together.'

'Let's not jump to conclusions. Maybe Stinnes isn't told the whole plan. If they know he's seeing you when he comes West they might deliberately keep him in the dark.' I took off my glasses and cupped my hands over my eyes to spend a moment in the dark. I felt very tired. Even the prospect of a drive back to London was daunting. Surely the existence of this safe house must have been something that Fiona had revealed to them. What else had she told them, and what else might she tell them? MacKenzie was upstairs dead, but I still had trouble believing it. My stomach was knotted with tension, and even the drink didn't relax me, or remove from my mouth the rancid taste of fear.

A sudden noise outside made me jump. I got to my feet and listened, but it was only one of the revellers falling over a rubbish bin. I sat down again and sipped my drink. I closed my eyes for a moment. Sleep was what I needed. When I woke up it would all be different. MacKenzie would be alive, and Fiona would be at home with the children, waiting for me.

'You can't just sit here all night draining that bottle of gin, Bernard. You'll have to tell the department.'

'The trouble is, Werner, I didn't tell them about the black girl.'

'But you told MacKenzie to find her.'

'I kept it all unofficial.'

'You're a bloody fool, Bernie.' Werner had always believed that he could do my job better than I did it, and every now and again something happened to encourage him in that delusion. 'A bloody fool.'

'Now you tell me.'

'You make trouble for yourself. Why didn't you tell them?'

'I went into the office fully intending to. Then Bret started droning on, and Frank Harrington was there to play the heavy father. I just let it slide.'

'This is murder. A departmental employee, in a safe house, with KGB involvement. You can't let this one slide, Bernard.'

I looked at Werner. He'd described the situation concisely, and in just the way the KGB operation planners had no doubt seen it. Well, the only thing they didn't allow for is that I might avoid the consequences by keeping my mouth tightly shut. 'That's not all of it,' I said. 'The black girl made me drive out to London Airport. When I was there Fiona got into the back of the car. I couldn't get a look at her but it was her, no doubt of that. I'd recognize her voice anywhere. The stuff about the kids came from her direct. The black girl was with her. She heard what was said, so I suppose it was all KGB-approved.'

I expected Werner to be as astonished as I'd been but he took it very calmly. 'I guessed it might be something like that.'

'How did you guess?'

'You saw the electric hair-rollers upstairs. Rollers to change a hairstyle. There were a lot of cosmetics too. Cosmetics no black girl could use. And hair dye. When you didn't draw attention to them I realized that you knew there was another woman. It had to be Fiona. She came here to make her hair curly, and colour it so she wouldn't be recognized.'

'You're not just a pretty face, Werner,' I said with genuine admiration.

'You don't really imagine you're going to be able to prevent all this emerging from an investigation of MacKenzie's death?'

'I don't know, Werner. But I'll try.' Werner stared at me, trying to see if I was frightened. I was scared stiff but I did everything I could to conceal it.

I wished that Werner would change the subject, but he persisted. 'And when MacKenzie got here he'd be sure to recognize Fiona. That would be sufficient reason why he was killed. They didn't want him to report her. They wanted you to do it. Or maybe wanted you to not report her so that the eventual consequences would be worse for you.'

'Let's not get too subtle. The KGB are not noted for subtlety.'

'You'd better rethink that one,' said Werner. 'Your wife is working for them now and she's rewriting the book.'

'Do you see evidence of that?'

'Bernie, she knows that she could never get you to defect, so she's not wasting any time trying. Instead she's doing the next best thing; she's persuading the department that you've already changed sides. In that way she will get you removed from Operations and maybe removed from the department completely.'

'Because the KGB see me as their most dangerous enemy?' I said sarcastically.

'No, because Fiona sees you as her most dangerous enemy. You know her better than anyone. You know how she thinks. You're the obstacle, the one person who is likely to understand what she gets up to.'

Perhaps Werner was right. Just as I was frightened of how Fiona could use all her knowledge of me against me, so I suppose she had the same fear of what I might do against her. The trouble was that, while our marriage had left her well aware of all my weaknesses, it had taught me only that she had none. I said, 'That's why I don't feel like reporting any of this to London Central. They'll say it's evidence of my being pressured and they'll keep asking me what I was under pressure about and eventually I'll find myself telling them about Fiona meeting me at the airport. And then I'll be suspended from duty pending investigations.' I put the cap on the gin bottle, wiped it clean of prints, then washed up the glasses and put them back. I wanted to be active; sitting there talking to Werner was making me twitchy. 'You can see this place is regularly maintained. Someone will find the body and report through the normal channels. Much better that way, Werner.'

But Werner was unrelenting. 'I'll do whatever you ask, Bernie. But I think you should go back to London Central and tell them everything.'

'Have you left any marks anywhere?'

'A few places. But I know which places.'

'Look at that,' I said, holding up the watch crystal. 'Some bastard planted it upstairs near the body so it would be found by the investigating officer.'

'I saw you pick it up. Yours, is it?'

I nodded and put the watch glass back into my pocket. 'Let's clean up and get out of here, Werner. Suppose we take the flight to Berlin tomorrow morning. Would that suit you? This will be a good time for me to be away from the office.'

Werner looked at me and nodded. I was frequently complaining of the way Dicky absented himself from the office at any sign of trouble. The way in which I was now running away from trouble offended Werner's sense of duty.

'What else?' said Werner suspiciously. 'I can see there's something more. You might as well tell me now.' He massaged his cheek as if trying to keep awake.

It was not easy to hide my thoughts from Werner. 'London Central want to put you back on their payroll. Ten thousand sterling on account; regular monthly payments plus expenses against signature. You know the score, Werner.'

The sloppy cement of Werner's face set into that inscrutable concrete expression he wore to prevent anyone discovering that he was happy. 'And?'

'They want you to take a short reconnaissance into the East and see what you can find out about Stinnes.'

'For instance?'

'His marriage; is it really on the rocks? What is his reputation? Was he really passed over for promotion or is that just a yarn?'

'Is that all?' said Werner with heavy sarcasm. His face was very mobile now, and he moved his lips to wet them, as if his mouth had gone suddenly dry at the thought of the risks. 'Any advice from London Central about how I should go about discovering all the intimate secrets of the KGB? This is not a US base on visitors' day. They don't have press officers over there, handing out typewritten releases and glossy photos you can reproduce without fee, and maps of the military installations in case visitors get lost.' He took a mouthful of the gin. Necessity had overcome his dislike of the flavour.

I couldn't argue with him. He knew more about the difficulties of such a job than I did, and we both knew infinitely more than those people at London Central who were going to sign the report and get the credit. 'Do what you can,' I said. 'Take the money and do what you can.'

'It won't be much,' said Werner.

'The money won't be much either,' I said. 'So don't do anything silly.' Werner emptied his glass and gave me another one of his deadpan faces. He knew I was frightened.

14

I drove back to London listening to Ingrid Haebler playing Mozart piano concertos. I turned the car's tape player up very loud as I tried to disentangle the thoughts and theories whirling endlessly in my brain. Had I been less tired, and less concerned with the death of MacKenzie, I might have taken reasonable precautions when entering my home. As it was, what should have been adequate warning for any man – the mortise unlocked and the letterbox flap still partly open after some hand had gripped the door to push it – did not register upon my thoughts. I walked through the front door and found all the downstairs lights burning.

I walked through the hall. There was no one to be seen in the front room so I pushed the door of the kitchen and stepped back. There was a figure lost in the gloom of the tiny pantry beyond. I touched the butt of the pistol in my pocket.

'Who's there?'

'Bernard darling. I wasn't sure if you were home or not.'

'Tessa. How did you get in?'

'You gave me a door key, Bernard. Surely you remember.'

'Of course.'

'I'm putting frozen soup and fish fingers into the freezer, my love. Your children are coming home tomorrow. Or have you forgotten that?' She spoke over her shoulder. I could see her more clearly now in the dark shadows of the pantry. Her long fair hair was falling over her face as she stretched forward to reach into the freezer, the dark pantry ceiling made a firmament by the glittering diamond rings on her fingers. And around her there was the swirling 'smoke' of frozen air.

'No,' I said. But I had forgotten.

'I spoke on the phone with your nanny. She's a good girl but she'll need food for them. You wouldn't want her to go out shopping and leave the children at home. And she won't want to drag them round the shops.'

'It's very kind of you, Tessa.'

She put the last packet into place and then closed the lid of the freezer chest with a loud thump. 'So what about a drink?' she said. She slapped her hands to remove the crystals of dry ice. She was dressed in a loose-fitting button-through dress of natural cotton, and under it a shiny pink blouse that went so well with her fair hair.

I looked at my watch. It was nearly midnight. 'What would you like, Tessa?'

'Did I see a bottle of champagne in the fridge? Or is that being kept for a tête-à-tête with the gorgeous Gloria?'

'News travels fast,' I said, taking off my coat and getting glasses and the bottle of champagne. I put the contents of the ice tray into the champagne bucket and put the bottle into it with water.

'It's so stylish to have a proper ice bucket,' said Tessa. 'Did I tell you that George bought a solid-silver one and someone swiped it.'

'Stole it? Who?'

'We never found out, darling. It was a party we had for car people. Some bastard stole the champagne bucket. I wondered if they knew it was solid silver or if they just took it for a lark. Oh, yes, I heard all about the exotic creature you took over there to dinner. I had coffee with Daphne.'

'Daphne Cruyer? I thought you and Daphne . . . That is, I thought . . .'

'Spit it out, Bernard darling. You mean you thought Daphne and I should be at each other's throats since I had a little fling with Dandy Dicky?'

'Yes,' I gave all my attention to the champagne cork. After some difficulty it opened with a bang and I spilled some before pouring.

'Daphne's not like that, darling. Daphne is a lovely person. I wouldn't have done it if I'd thought that Daphne would be hurt.'

'Wasn't she hurt?'

'Of course not. Daphne thinks it's all a most wonderful hoot.'

'Why would Daphne think it's a hoot for you to have an affair with Dicky?'

'An affair. How romantic. It wasn't an affair, darling. No one could have an affair with Dicky; he's having an imperishable love affair with himself. What woman could compete with Dicky's first and only love?'

'So what was it?' I passed her the glass.

'It was a whim. A caprice. A sudden fancy. It was all over in a couple of weeks or so.'

'Fiona said it lasted nearly three months.'

'Not at all.'

'Fiona had a good memory for that sort of thing. I'm sure it was three months.'

'Well, three months. Don't go on about it. Three months, how long is that? I can't believe Daphne worried. She knew I wasn't going to run off with him. Could you imagine me running off with Dicky? And now Daphne has him right under her thumb.'

'Does she?'

'Of course she does, darling. He's feeling as guilty as hell, and so he should. He can't do enough for Daphne nowadays; he even buys her flowers. Umm, that's delicious champagne. I told you my doctor has put me on a special diet – lots of champagne but no other sort of alcohol and no sugar or fat.' She turned the bottle so that she could read the lable. 'Bollinger, and vintage too. My very favourite champagne. How extravagant you are becoming. Is this something to do with Gloria?'

'I wish you'd shut up about Gloria,' I said. 'That bottle of Bollinger is the last bottle from the case you gave us as a present last Christmas.'

'How silly I am,' said Tessa. 'How too too embarrassing.'

'It was very kind of you, Tessa. And thank you for bringing the food for the children.' I held up the glass as if in toast, and then drank to her.

'But that's not everything,' said Tessa, who had a childlike need for praise. 'I've had their room cleaned, and brought some new toys, and bedlinen patterned with huge dragons breathing fire. Pillows too. You should see them, Bernard. I wish they made them adult-bed size. Dragons; I would love them on my bed, wouldn't you, darling?'

'Talking of bed . . .'

'Am I keeping you up, Bernard? You look tired. I'm sorry to come over here so late but I can't let my bridge partner down. We were playing until past eleven. And he's the one with the frozen-food wholesale place where I get all this stuff. He put it in the back of his car. It was all packed with dry ice. You needn't worry.'

'I'm not worrying.'

'Can I have a splash more of that champagne?' She poured it without waiting for a reply. 'Oh, there's lots. More for you? Then I really must go home.'

'Thanks, Tessa. Yes.'

We both drank and then suddenly, as if seeing me for the first time, she said, 'Bernard. Where have you been, darling? You look absolutely ghastly.'

'I've been working. What do you mean?'

She stared at me. 'You look positively ill, darling. You've changed. If I hadn't seen it with my own eyes, I wouldn't have believed it. In just a couple of days you've aged ten years, Bernard. Are you ill?'

'Easy does it, Tessa.'

'Seriously, my love. You look frightful. You haven't had an accident in the car? You haven't run over someone or something like that?'

'Of course not.'

'George had a bad accident a couple of years ago and I remember he went quite grey-haired overnight. And he looked as you do; green, darling. You look green and quite old.'

I picked up the champagne and said, 'If we're going to finish this bottle we might as well sit down and talk in comfort.' I led the way into the front room, switched on the lights and we sat down. I said, 'I'm just a bit tired, that's all.'

'I know. All this business with Fiona; it must be absolutely rotten for you. And now, with Daddy making himself an absolute arsehole about the children, you must be having quite a time of it. And money must be a problem too. Daddy says you're selling this house. You're not, are you?' Tessa seemed tired too; at least she was not her usual high-spirited self. She let her hair swing across her face as if she wanted to hide behind it, like a child behind a curtain playing peekaboo.

'Not for the time being.'

'Hang on to it, Bernard. Daddy says it's too big. But it's a sweet little house and you must have a playroom for the children as well as a bedroom. And if nanny didn't have that large bedroom, she'd want a sitting room too.'

'Your father said it was too big because he wants the children with him at Leith Hill.'

'I know. I told him it was a stupid idea.' Her face twitched and for a moment I wondered if she was going to cry but she pushed her knuckle against her face and recovered her composure. 'He'd never tolerate the noise the children make, and can you imagine him playing with them or reading to them at bedtime?'

'No,' I said.

'He just wants the children as ornaments. Just like those suits of armour in the hall, and that ridiculous library, filled with expensive first editions that he never looks at, except when he calls a valuer in to renew the insurance. And then he goes off to tell everyone at his club what a wonderful investment he made.'

'I suppose he has his good points,' I said, more because of the distress she was showing than because I could think of any.

'He keeps them well hidden,' she said, and laughed as if shaking off her sudden bout of sadness. She got to her feet, reached for the champagne bottle and filled her glass and mine before going back to the sofa. Then she slipped off her shoes and, leaning one elbow on the sofa end, tucked her feet under herself.

'Do you want to phone George?' I offered. 'Does he know where you are?'

'The answer is no to both questions,' she said. 'And the answer to the next question is that he doesn't care either.'

'Are things all right between you and George?'

'George doesn't love me any more. George hates me. He's just looking for some way to get rid of me so that he can go off with someone else.'

'Does George have someone else? Does he have affairs?'

'How can I be sure? Sex is like crime. Only one per cent motivation and ninety-nine per cent opportunity.' She drank some wine. 'I can't blame him, can I? I've been the worst wife any man ever had. George always wanted children.' She rummaged through her handbag to get a handkerchief. 'Oh, don't look so alarmed, Bernard. I'm not going to start sobbing or anything.' Despite this assurance she dabbed her eyes and gave every sign of doing so. 'Why did I marry him?'

'Why did you?'

'He asked me. It's as simple as that.'

'I'm sure many other men asked you.'

'George asked me when I was feeling low. He asked me at a time when I suddenly wanted to be married. You wouldn't understand; men never feel like that. Men just get married for peace and comfort. They never feel frightened of not being married the way women do sometimes.'

I was embarrassed by the intensity of her feelings. 'How do you know George has someone else? Has he told you so?'

'A wife doesn't have to be told. It's obvious that he doesn't love me. He has someone else; of course he does.' She wiped her eyes with the handkerchief before looking up at me. She blinked and gave a brave little smile. 'He's taking her off to South Africa.'

'Women always tend to imagine men have other women,' I said. 'If he hasn't mentioned another woman, there possibly isn't one.'

'George might have begun to hate all women. Is that what you mean? Maybe George just wants a bit of peace and quiet away from me? Away from all women. Drinking and laughing with his friends in the car business.'

It was exactly what I thought. 'No,' I said. 'Of course not. But George is very wrapped up in his work. He always has been, you know that. And the economy is still not picking up the way everyone hoped it would. Perhaps he needs to give a lot of thought to his business.'

'You men always stick together.'

'I hardly know George, but he always seemed a decent sort of chap. But you've led him a merry dance, Tess. It can't have been easy for him. I mean you haven't exactly been discreet with these little affairs, have you?'

'And, if you were George, the chance of being in South Africa, a few thousand miles away from me, would be a wonderful opportunity. And certainly not one to be marred by taking a wife along with you. I mean, women are everywhere, aren't they? You can rent them by the hour. Or rent them by the dozen. There are women available from the Arctic to the Pacific, from Persia to Peking.'

'Women are available everywhere,' I said. 'But marriages, reasonably happy marriages, are extremely rare.'

'I've been a fool, Bernard. George has always been a good husband. He's never made a fuss about money, and until last week I never thought of George with other women.'

'What happened last week?'

'Did I tell you he went to Italy, the Ferrari factory, last week? He's been there before and I know the hotel he always stays in. So I phoned them and asked if Mrs Kosinski was staying there. The switchboard girl said Mr and Mrs Kosinski were not in their room but there was another gentleman occupying the second bedroom of the suite if I'd like to speak with him or leave a message with him.'

'And did you speak with this "him"?'

'No, I got scared and rang off.'

'Who was the other man?'

'One of the people from the factory, or perhaps it was George's general manager. He goes along on these trips sometimes.'

'And have you tackled George about it?'

'I tried a little test. He's going to South Africa on some business deal. I've never been to South Africa so I said I'd go with him. He gave me a strange look and said he couldn't change the arrangements, and he is going alone.'

'Is that all?'

'He's going with a woman. Surely that's obvious. He's taking her to South Africa with him.'

'He's always going off on business trips. Are you saying he's always taken women with him?'

'I don't know. I've hardly ever gone with him on a business trip before. It's always so boring to meet all these car salesmen. It was bad enough when he brought them home. All they ever talk about is delivery dates, advertising schedules and profit margins. They never talk about motor cars unless it's rally driving or the Grand Prix. Have you ever been to a motor race, Bernard?'

'I don't think so. I don't remember it.'

'Then you haven't been to one. Because if you'd been to a motor race you'd never forget it. George took me to the Monte Carlo one year. It sounded as if it might be fun. George got a suite at the Hotel de Paris, and a girl I was at school with lives in Monte Carlo with her family. Well, Bernard, I knew I'd done the wrong thing when I phoned my friend and her maid told me that they always leave town when the race is on. Because the noise is deafening and it goes on non-stop day and night. Endless, darling. I put a pillow over my head and screamed.'

'You didn't stay in your hotel room all through the race?'

'I'm not a complete ninny, Bernard. George had the best seats anyone could have. But after the race has been on for ten minutes, there is no way of telling which of the wretched cars is in front and which is at the back. All you see is these stinking little machines driving past you, and you choke on the petrol fumes and get deafened by the noise. And when you try to get back to your hotel you run into the Monaco policemen who are just about the most asinine gorillas in the whole world. It's their big opportunity to scream and shout and push people around and they take full advantage of it. Don't ever go, Bernard, it's absolutely ghastly.'

'I take it that was the last business trip you did with George.'

'And you guessed right, darling.' She looked at me. Her eyes were wide and very blue.

'And now you are convinced that George has found some lady who likes the noise and petrol fumes, and thinks the Monaco police are wonderful.'

'Well, it looks like that, doesn't it? My mother always said I should go with him everywhere. Mummy never lets David out of her sight. She hated the idea of my letting George go away alone. That's always how trouble starts, my mother says.' Tessa put her face into her hands and wept in a rather restrained way. I felt sorry for her. The weeping was straight out of drama school. But I could see that, beyond the abandoned-little-woman act, she was genuinely distressed.

'It's not the end of the world, Tessa.'

'I've got no one to turn to,' she said between sobs. 'You're the only one I can talk to now that Fi has gone.'

'You have a thousand friends.'

'Name one.'

'Don't be silly. You have so many friends.'

'Is that your polite way of saying lovers, Bernard? Lovers are not friends. Not my sort of lovers anyway. The men in my life have never been friends. My love affairs have always been jokes . . . schoolgirl jokes. Silly pranks that no one took seriously. A squeeze, a hug, a couple of hours between the sheets in a very expensive hotel room. A weekend stay in the country house of odd people I hardly knew. Passionate embraces in ski chalets and quick cuddles in parked cars. All the flushed excitement of infatuation and then it's all over. We knew it couldn't last, didn't we? Goodbye, darling, and don't look back.'

'You always seemed so happy, Tessa.'

'I was, darling. Happy, confident Tessa, full of fun and always making jokes about my love life. But that was while I had George to go home to. Now I don't have George to go home to.'

'Do you mean . . . ?'

'Don't look so alarmed, Bernard. I don't mean literally, darling. I don't mean that I'm moving in here with you. You should see your face.'

'I didn't mean that,' I said. 'If you leave George you can always use the boxroom. There's a bed there that we've used when my mother came to stay. It's not very comfortable.'

'Of course it's not comfortable, darling. It's a room made for mothers to stay in. It's a horrid, dark little room that would exactly suit a sister-in-law who came to stay, and who might otherwise stay too long.' She gave all her attention to the bubbles rising through the champagne and ran her fingertip down the glass to trace a line through the condensation.

'Sounds like you're determined to feel sorry for yourself.'

'But I am, darling. Why shouldn't I feel sorry for myself? My husband doesn't want me any more, and the only man I've always loved keeps looking at his lovely new watch and yawning.'

'Go back home and tell George you love him,' I said. 'You might find that everything will come out all right.'

'You must be Mrs Lonelyheart. I read your column every week.'

I picked the bottle out of the bucket and divided the last of the champagne between our two glasses. The bottle dripped icy water down my arm. She smiled. This time it was a more convincing smile. 'I've always adored you, Bernard. You know that, don't you?'

'We'll talk about that some other time, Tessa. Meanwhile do you think you can drive home, or shall I phone for a cab?'

'They don't have alcohol at the bridge club, that's the worst thing about it. No, I'm as sober as a judge. I will drive home and leave you in peace.'

'Talk to George. The two of you can sort it out.'

'You're a darling,' she said. I helped her into her smart suede car coat and she gave me a decorous kiss. 'You're the only one I can talk to.' She smiled. 'I'll be over here when nanny arrives. You get on with your work. No need to worry.'

'I'm flying to Berlin in the morning.'

'How wretched for you, Bernard. You won't be here to welcome the children.'

'No, I won't be here.'

'Don't worry. I'll go to Gloriette – opposite Harrods – and get them a superb chocolate cake with "Love from Daddy" written on the top, and I'll tell them how sorry you are to be away.'

'Thanks, Tessa.'

I opened the front door for her but she didn't leave. She turned to me and said, 'I dreamed about Fiona the other night. I dreamed that she phoned me, and I said was she speaking from Russia, and she said never mind where she was speaking from. Do you ever dream about her, Bernard?'

'No,' I said.

'It was so vivid, my dream. She said I was to meet her at London Airport. I was to tell no one. She wanted me to bring her some photos.'

'Photos?'

'Photos of your children. It's so silly when you think of it. Fiona must have taken photos with her when she went. In this dream she desperately wanted these photos of the children. I dreamed she was shouting down the phone at me the way she did when we were children and she couldn't get her own way. Wake up, she shouted. It was such a silly dream but it upset me at the time. She wanted photos of you too.'

'What photos of me?'

'It was only a dream, darling. Oh, photos of you she left at my house a couple of months ago. She forgot to take them with her one night. Photos taken recently, for your passport, I should think. Awfully dull photos, I think, and portraits of the children. Isn't it odd how one dreams such silly trivial things?'

'Which terminal?'

'What do you mean?'

'In the dream. Which terminal at London Airport did she ask you to go to?'

'Terminal 2. Don't let it upset you, Bernard. I wouldn't have mentioned it if I'd known. Mind you, it upset me at the time. It was very early in the morning and I dreamed I answered the phone and the operator asked me if I'd accept a reverse-charge call from Bosham. I ask you, darling. From what deep dark confines of my brain-box did I dredge Bosham? I've never been there.' She laughed. 'George was awfully cross when I woke him up and told him. If the phone had really rung, I would have heard it, wouldn't I, he said. And then I realized it was all a dream. Mind you, the phone often rings without George hearing it, especially if he's been boozing at his club as he had that night.'

'I'd just try and forget about it,' I said. 'It's not unusual to get strange dreams after something like that happens.'

She nodded and I squeezed her arm. Her sister's betrayal had affected her deeply. For her, as for me, it was a personal betrayal that required a fundamental rethinking of their whole relationship. And that meant a fundamental rethinking of oneself. Perhaps she knew what was in my mind, for she looked up at me and smiled as if at some secret we shared.

'Forget it,' I said again. I didn't want Tessa to worry, and, on the practical level, I didn't want her to phone the telephone exchange and check if there really was a reverse-charge call from Bosham. It could only lead on to inquiries I was trying to avoid. I could follow Fiona's reasoning. By reversing the charges, she made sure the call didn't appear on the telephone bill of the house in Bosham and thus implicate her sister.

I kissed Tessa again and told her to look after herself. I didn't like the idea of Fiona wanting passport pictures of me. She didn't want them to go beside her bed.

I watched Tessa get into her silver VW. She lowered the car window so that she could blow me a kiss. The way the headlights flashed a couple of times, and the direction indicators winked, as she backed out of the tiny parking space, made me wonder if she was telling the truth about the availability of alcohol at her bridge club.

But when I went upstairs to bed I saw MacKenzie sprawled across the floor with his brains spattered over the wallpaper. It was some sort of hallucination. But just for a moment, as I switched on the bedroom light, his image was as clear and as real as anything I've ever seen. It was the shock and the drink and the tiredness and the anxiety. Poor little sod, I thought; I sent him to his death. If he'd been an experienced agent perhaps I'd not have felt so guilty about it, but MacKenzie was not much more than a child, and a novice at the spy game. I felt guilty, and as I prepared for bed I began to suffer the delayed reaction that my body had deferred and deferred. I shook uncontrollably. I didn't want to admit, even to myself, that I was frightened. But that image of MacKenzie kept blurring into an image of myself, and my guilt was turning into fear. For fear is so unwelcome that it comes only in disguise, and guilt is its favourite one.

15

There was a time when Lisl Hennig's house seemed gigantic. When I was small child, each marble step of that grand staircase was a mountain. Scaling mountains had then required an exertion almost beyond me, and I'd needed a moment's rest when each summit was won. And that was how it now was for Frau Lisl Hennig. The staircase was something she tackled only when she felt at her best. I watched her as she inched her way into the 'salon' and berthed in a huge gilt throne, plumped up with velvet cushions so she didn't put too much strain upon her arthritic knees. She was old, but the brown dyed hair, big eyes and the fine features in her wrinkled face made it difficult to guess exactly how old.

'Bernd,' she said, using the name by which I'd been known at my Berlin school. 'Bernd. Put my sticks on the back of the chair where I can find them if I want them. You don't know what it's like to be crippled in this way. Without my sticks I am a prisoner in this damned chair.'

'They are there already,' I said.

'Give me a kiss. Give me a kiss,' she said testily. 'Have you forgotten Tante Lisl? And how I used to rock you in my arms?'

I kissed her. I had been in Berlin for three days, waiting for Werner to come back from his 'short reconnaissance' to the East Sector, but every day Lisl greeted me as if seeing me after a long absence.

'I want tea,' said Lisl. 'Find that wretched girl Klara and tell her to bring tea. Order some for yourself if you'd like to.' She had always had this same autocratic demanding manner. She looked around her to be sure that everything was in its rightful place. Lisl's mother had chosen these hand-carved pieces of oak furniture, and the chandelier that had been hidden in the coal cellar in 1945. In Lisl's childhood this room had been softened by lacework and embroidery as befits a place to which the ladies retired after dining in the room that now contained the hotel reception desk. This 'salon' was where where Lisl's mother gave the fine ladies of Berlin afternoon tea. And on fine summer days the large windows were opened to provide a view from the balcony as the Kaiser Alexander Guard Grenadiers went marching back to their barracks behind their band.

It was Lisl who first called it a 'salon' and entertained here Berlin's brightest young architects, painters, poets, writers and certain Nazi politicians. To say nothing of the seven brawny cyclists from the Sports Palace who arrived one afternoon with erotic dancers from one of the city's most notorious *Tanzbars* and noisily pursued them through the house in search of vacant bedrooms. They were here still, many of those celebrities of what Berlin called 'The Golden Twenties'. They were crowded together on the walls of this salon, smiling and staring down from sepia-toned photos that were signed with the overwrought passions that were an expression of the reckless decade that preceded the Third Reich.

Lisl was wearing green silk, a waterfall rippling over her great shapeless bulk and cascading upon her tiny, pointed, strap-fronted shoes. 'What are you doing tonight?' she asked. Klara – the 'wretched girl' who was about sixty and had worked for Lisl for about twenty years – looked round the door. She nodded to me and gave a nervous smile to show that she'd heard Lisl demanding tea.

'I have to see Werner,' I said.

'I was hoping you'd play cards,' she said. She rubbed her painful knee and smiled at me.

'I would have liked that, Lisl,' I said, 'but I have to see him.'

'You hate playing cards with your old Tante Lisl. I know. I know.' She looked up and, as the light fell on her, I could see the false eyelashes and the layers of paint and powder that she put upon her face on the days she went outside. 'I taught you to play bridge. You were only nine or ten years old. You loved it then.'

'I would have loved it now,' I protested untruthfully.

'There is a very nice young Englishman whom I want you to meet, and old Herr Koch is coming.'

'If only I didn't have to see Werner,' I said, 'I would have really liked to spend an evening with you.' She smiled grimly. She knew I hated card games. And the prospect of meeting a 'very nice young Englishman' was rivalled only by the idea of spending the evening listening to the oft-repeated reminiscences of old Mr Koch.

'With Werner?' exclaimed Lisl, as if suddenly remembering. 'There was a message for you. Werner is delayed and can't see you tonight. He'll phone you early tomorrow.' She smiled. 'It doesn't matter, *Liebchen*. Tante Lisl won't hold you to your word. I know you have more interesting things to do than play bridge with an ugly old crippled woman like me.'

It was game, set and match to Lisl. 'I'll make up a four,' I said with as much grace as I could muster. 'Where was Werner phoning from?'

'*Wundervoll*,' said Lisl with a great smile. 'Where was he phoning from, darling? How would I know a thing like that?' I think she'd guessed that Werner was in the East Sector, but she didn't want to admit it, not even to herself. Like so many other native Berliners she tried not to remember that her town was now a small island in the middle of a communist sea. She referred to the communist world by means of jokes, half-truths and euphemisms, the same way that 300 years earlier the Viennese had shrugged off the besieging Ottoman Turks. 'You don't really understand the bidding,' said Lisl. 'That's why you'll never be a good bridge player.'

'I'm good enough,' I said. It was stupid of me to resent her remark, since I had no ambition to become a good bridge player. I was piqued that this old woman was able to trap me into an evening's bridge using the same obvious tactics that she'd used on me when I was an infant.

'Cheer up, Bernd,' she said. 'Here is the tea. And I do believe there is cake. No lemon needed, Klara. We drink it English style.' The frail Klara set the tray down on the table and went through the ritual of putting out the plates, forks and cups and saucers, and the silver bowl that held the tea-strainer. 'And here is my new English friend,' said Lisl, 'the one I was telling you about. Another cup and saucer, Klara.'

I turned to see the man who'd entered the salon. It was Dicky's college chum from Mexico City. There was no mistaking this tall, thin Englishman with his brown, almost ginger, hair brushed flat against his skull. His heart-shaped face still showed the effects of the fierce Mexican sun. His ruddy complexion was marked in places by freckles that, together with his awkwardness, made him look younger than his thirty-eight years. He was wearing grey flannels and a blue blazer with large decorative brass buttons and the badge of some cricket club on the pocket. 'Bernard Samson,' he said. He stretched out his hand. 'Henry Tiptree. Remember?' His handshake was firm but furtive, the sort of handshake that diplomats and politicians use to get through a long line of guests. 'What good luck to find you here. I was talking to a chap named Harrington the other night. He said you knew more about this extraordinary town than any other ten people.' His voice was cultured, throaty and rather penetrating. The sort of voice the BBC assign to reading the news the night someone very important dies. 'Extra . . . awwwrdinary town,' he said again, as if practising. This time he held the note even longer.

'I thought you worked in Mexico City.'

'*Und guten Tag, gnädige Frau*,' he said to Lisl, who had been wrinkling her brow as she concentrated enough to understand this sudden onslaught of English. Henry Tiptree bent over to kiss the bejewelled hand which she lifted for him. Then he bowed again and smiled at her with that sort of sinister charm that baritones show in Hollywood musicals about old Vienna. He turned to me. 'You thought I worked in Mexico City. And so did I. Haw haw. But when you've worked in the diplomatic service for a few years, you start to know that the chap you last heard of doing the Korean language course in Seoul will next be seen working as an information officer in the embassy in Paris.' He scratched the side of his nose reflectively. 'No, some guru in the Personnel Department considered that my schoolboy German was just what was needed for me to be attached to you chaps for an undecided period of time. No explanation, no apologies, no time to get ready. Wham, bam, and here I am. Haw haw.'

'Quite a surprise,' I said. 'I believe we're playing cards together this evening.'

'I'm so pleased you're joining us,' said Henry, and seemed genuinely pleased. 'This is what I call the real Berlin, what? The beautiful and cultured Frau Hennig here, and this wonderful chap Koch whom she's told me all about. These are the people one wants to meet, not the free-loading johnnies who come knocking at the door of your average embassy.'

Lisl was smiling; she understood enough English to know that she was beautiful and cultured. She tapped my arm. 'And wear a jacket and a tie, will you, *Liebchen*? Just to make your old Lisl happy. Just for once wear a nice suit, the one you always wear to see Frank Harrington.' Lisl knew how to make me look a bloody fool. I looked at Tiptree; he smiled.

We played cards in Lisl's study, a small room crammed with her treasures. This was where she did the accounts and collected the money from her guests. She kept her bottle of sherry here in a cupboard otherwise filled with china ornaments. And here, with its prancing angels and winged dragons, was the grotesque ormolu mantel clock that could sometimes be heard throughout the house chiming away the small hours. There was a picture of Kaiser Wilhelm over the fireplace; around it a slight brightness of the wallpaper showed it was the place where a larger signed photo of Adolf Hitler had hung for a decade that had ended with the family home becoming this hotel.

'I think the cards need a good shuffle,' said Lisl plaintively as she arranged in front of her the few remaining counters for which we gave fifty pfennigs each. Lisl's losses could not possibly come to more than the price of the bottle of sherry that between us we'd almost consumed, but she didn't like losing. In that respect and many others she was very *berlinerisch*.

The four of us were arranged round the circular-topped mahogany tripod table, at which Lisl usually sat to take her breakfast. The four chairs were also mahogany; superbly carved with Venetian-style figure-of-eight backs, they were all that was left of the sixteen dining chairs that her mother had so cherished. Lisl had been talking about the European royal families and the social activities of their surviving members. She was devoted to royalty and convinced of the divine right of kings, despite her frequently proclaimed agnosticism.

But now Lothar Koch had started one of his long stories. 'So what was I saying?' said Koch, who was incapable of shuffling cards and talking at the same time.

'You were telling us about this most interesting secret report on the Dutch riots,' prompted Henry.

'Ah, yes,' he said. Lothar Koch was a small motheaten man, with dark-ringed troubled eyes and a nose far too large for his small sunken face. Mr Koch had a large gold Rolex wrist-watch and liked to wear spotted bow-ties in the evening. But his expensive-looking suits were far too big for him. Lisl said that they fitted him before he lost weight, and now he refused to buy any more clothes. I'm far too old to buy new suits, he'd told Lisl when he celebrated his seventieth birthday in a suit that was already too baggy. Now he was eighty-five, still shrinking, and he still hadn't bought any new clothes. Lisl said he stopped buying overcoats when he was sixty. '*Ja, ja, ja*. There had been riots in Amsterdam. That was the start of it. That was 1941. Brandt came into my office soon after the riots . . .'

'Rudolf Brandt,' explained Lisl. 'Heinrich Himmler's secretary.'

'Yes,' said Koch. He looked at me to be sure I was listening. He knew I'd heard all his stories before and that my attention was apt to wander.

'Rudolf Brandt,' I confirmed. 'Heinrich Himmler's secretary. Yes, of course.'

Having confirmed that I was paying attention, Koch said, 'I remember it as if it was yesterday. Brandt dumped on to my desk this report. It had a yellow front cover and consisted of forty-three typewritten pages. Look what that fool Bormann has come up with now, he said. He meant Hitler, but it was customary to blame Bormann for such things. It's true Bormann had countersigned each page, but he was just the Head of the Party Chancellery, he had no political power. This was obviously the Führer. What is it? I asked. I had enough paperwork of my own to read; I wasn't looking for another report to occupy my evening. Brandt said, the whole population of Holland is to be resettled in Poland.'

'Good God,' said Henry. He took a minuscule sip of his sherry and then wiped his lips with a paper napkin advertising König Pilsener. Lisl got them free. Tiptree had changed his clothes. Perhaps in response to Lisl's sartorial demands of me, he was wearing a white shirt, old school tie and a dark grey worsted suit of the type that is issued to really sincere employees by some secret department of the Foreign Office.

'Yes,' said Lisl loyally. She'd heard the story more times than I had.

'Eight and half million people. The first three million would include "irreconcilables", which was Nazi jargon for anyone who wasn't a Nazi and not likely to become one. Also there would be market-garden workers, farmers and anyone with agricultural training or experience. They would be sent to Polish Galicia and there create a basic economy to support the rest of the Dutch, who would arrive later.'

'So what did you tell him?' said Henry. He pinched the knot of his tie between finger and thumb, and shook it as if trying to remove a small striped animal that had him by the throat.

Mr Koch looked at me. He realized that I was the 'irreconcilable' part of his audience. 'So what did you say, Mr Koch?' I asked.

He looked away. My display of intense interest had not convinced him I was listening, but he continued anyway. 'How can we put this impossible strain upon the Reichsbahn? I asked him. It was useless to appeal to these people on moral grounds, you understand.'

'That was clever,' said Henry.

'And the *Wehrmacht* was preparing for the attack on the USSR,' said Mr Koch. 'The work that involved was terrible . . . especially train schedules, factory deliveries and so on. I went across to see Kersten that afternoon. It was showery and I went out without coat or umbrella. I remember it clearly. There was a lot of traffic on Friedrichstrasse and I was drenched by the time I got back to my office.'

'Felix Kersten was the personal medical adviser to Heinrich Himmler,' explained Lisl.

Koch said, 'Kersten was a Finnish citizen, born in Estonia. He wasn't a doctor but he was an exceptionally skilled masseur. He'd lived in Holland before the war and had treated the Dutch royal family. Himmler thought he was a medical genius. Kersten was especially sympathetic to the Dutch and I knew he'd listen to me.'

'Why don't you deal the cards,' I suggested. Koch looked at me and nodded. We both knew that if he tried to do it while continuing his story he would get his counting hopelessly muddled.

'It's a fascinating story,' said Henry. 'What did Kersten say?'

'He listened but didn't comment,' said Koch, tapping the edges of the pack against the table-top. 'But afterwards his memoirs claimed that it was his personal intervention that saved the Dutch. Himmler suffered bad stomach cramps and Kersten warned him that such a vast scheme as resettling the entire population of Holland would not only be beyond the capabilities of the German railways but, since it would be Himmler's responsibility, it could mean a breakdown in his health.'

'They dropped it?' said Henry. He was a wonderful audience, and Mr Koch basked in the attention Henry was providing.

Koch riffled the cards so that they made a sound like a short burst of fire from a distant MG 42. He smiled and said, 'Himmler persuaded Hitler to postpone it until after the war. By this time, you see, our armies were fighting in Yugoslavia and Greece. I knew there was no chance of it ever happening.'

'I say, that's extraordinary,' said Henry. 'You should have got some sort of medal.'

'He did get a medal,' I said. 'You did get a medal, didn't you, Herr Koch?'

Koch riffled the cards again and murmured assent.

'Mr Koch got the *Dienstauszeichnung*, didn't you, Mr Koch?'

Mr Koch gave me a fixed mirthless smile. 'Yes, I did, Bernd.' To Henry he said, 'Bernd thinks it amusing that I was given the Nazi long-service award for ten years in the Nazi Party. But as he also knows . . .' A finger was raised and waggled at me. '. . . my job and my grade in the Ministry of the Interior made it absolutely necessary that I joined the Party. I was never an active Party worker, everyone knows that.'

'Herr Koch was an irreconcilable,' I said.

'You are a trouble-maker, Bernd,' said Mr Koch. 'If I hadn't been such a close friend of your father I would get very angry at some of the things you say.'

'Only kidding, Lothar,' I said. In fact I remained convinced that old Lothar Koch was an irredeemable Nazi who read a chapter from *Mein Kampf* every night before going to sleep. But he always showed a remarkable amiability in the face of my remarks and I admired him for that.

'What's all this "Bernd" nonsense, Samson?' said Henry with a puzzled frown on his peeling red forehead. 'You're not a German, are you?'

'Sometimes,' I said, 'I feel I almost am.'

'This woman should have a medal,' said Koch suddenly. He indicated Lisl Hennig. 'She hid a family of Jews upstairs. She hid them for three years. Do you know what would have happened if the Gestapo had found them – echhh.' Mr Koch ran his index finger across his throat. 'She would have gone into a concentration camp. You were a mad fool, Lisl, my dear.'

'We were all mad fools in one way or another,' said Lisl. 'It was a time of mad foolishness.'

'Didn't your neighbours know you were hiding them?' asked Tiptree.

'The whole street knew,' said Koch. 'The mother of the hidden family was her cook.'

'Once we had to push her into the refrigerator,' said Lisl. 'She was so frightened that she struggled. I'll suffocate, she shouted, I'll suffocate. But the kitchen maid – a huge woman, long since dead, God bless her – helped me, and we put all the food on the table and pushed Mrs Volkmann inside.'

'The Gestapo men were here, searching the house,' said Mr Koch.

'Just three of them,' said Lisl. 'Jumped-up little men. I took them to the bar. That is as far as they wanted to search.'

'And the woman in the refrigerator?' said Henry.

'When the level of the schnapps went half-way down the bottle we decided it would be safe to get her out. She was all right. We gave her a hot-water bottle and put her to bed.'

'That was Werner's mother,' said Lisl to me.

'I know, Lisl,' I said. 'You were very brave.'

Often after such bridge games Lisl had provided a 'nightcap' on the house, but this time she let us pay for our own drinks. I think she was still smarting because my inexpert bridge had won me five marks while she ended up losing three. She was in one of her petulant moods and complained about everything from the pain in her knees to the tax on alcohol. I was thankful that Lisl decided to go early to bed. I knew she wouldn't sleep. She'd read newspapers and perhaps play her old records until the small hours. But we said our goodnights to her and soon after that Lothar Koch phoned for a taxi and departed.

Henry Tiptree seemed anxious to prolong the evening, and with a bottle of brandy on the table in front of us I was happy to answer his questions. 'What an extraordinary old man,' said Henry, after Koch said goodnight and tottered off down the stairs to his waiting taxi.

'He saw it all,' I said.

'Did he really have to become a Nazi because he worked in the Ministry?'

'It was because he was a Nazi that he got a job in the Ministry. Prior to 1933 he was working at the reception desk of the Kaiserhof. That was a hotel that Hitler used a great deal. Lothar knew most of the Nazi big-shots. Some of them came in with their girlfriends, and the word soon went round that if you needed to rent a room by the hour then Lothar – the one with the Party badge on the lapel of his coat – was the right clerk to see.'

'And for that he got a job in the Ministry of the Interior?'

'I don't know that that was the only reason, but he got the job. It wasn't, of course, the high-ranking post that Lothar now likes to remember. But he was there and he kept his ears open. And he closed his eyes to such things as Lisl hiding Werner's parents.'

'And are his stories true?'

'The stories are true. But Lothar is prone to change the cast so that the understudy plays leading man now and again.'

Henry studied me earnestly before deciding to laugh. 'Haw haw,' he said. 'This is the real Berlin. Gosh. The office wanted to put me into the Kempinski or that magnificent new Steigenberger Hotel but your friend Harrington told me to install myself in here. This is the real Berlin, he said. And, by gosh, he's right.'

'Mind if I pour myself a little more of that brandy?' I said.

'Oh, I say. Let me.' He poured me a generous measure while taking only a small tot for himself.

'And I guess you're here for some damned cloak-and-dagger job with Dicky?'

'Wrong twice,' I said. 'Dicky is safely tucked up in bed in London and I am only here to collect a bag of documents to carry back to London. It's a courier's job really, but we're short of people.'

'Damn,' said Henry. 'And I was persuading myself that the worried look on your brow all evening was you fretting about some poor devil out there cutting his way through the barbed wire, what?' He laughed and drank some brandy. From Lisl's room I heard one of her favourite records playing. It was scratchy and muffled.

> . . . No one here can love and understand me,
> Oh what hard-luck stories they all hand me . . .

'I'm sorry to disappoint you,' I said.

'Couldn't we compromise?' said Henry cheerfully. 'Couldn't you tell me that there is at least one James Bond johnny out there risking his neck among the Russkies?'

'There probably is,' I said. 'But no one has told me about him.'

'Haw haw,' said Henry, and drank some brandy. At first he'd been drinking very sparingly but now he abandoned some of that caution.

'Tell me what you're doing here,' I said.

'What am I doing here? Yes, what indeed. It's a long story, my dear chap.'

'Tell me anyway.' I looked at my watch. It was late. I wondered where Werner had phoned from. He was in a car with East German registration. That always made it more complicated; he wouldn't bring that car into the West. He'd planned to return through the Russian Zone and on to the autobahn that comes from Helmstedt.

I'd never liked that method; the autobahns were regularly patrolled to prevent East Germans meeting West German transients at the roadside. I'd arranged for someone to be at the right place at the scheduled time this morning. Now I had no idea where he was, and I could do nothing to help him. Lisl's record started again.

> Pack up all my cares and woe.
> Here I go, singing low,
> Bye-bye, blackbird . . .

'Do you have time to hear my boring life story?' said Henry. He chuckled. We both knew that Henry Tiptree was not the sort of man who confided his life story to anyone. Never complain, never explain, is the public-school canon.

'I have the time,' I said, 'and you have the brandy.'

'I thought you were going to say: I have the time if you have the inclination, as Big Ben said to the leaning tower of Pisa. What? Haw haw.'

'If you're working on something secret . . .' I said.

He waved away any such suggestion. His hand knocked against his glass and spilled some of his drink, so he poured more. 'My immediate boss is working on one of those interminable reports that will be called something like "Western Negotiating Policy and Soviet Military Power". He will have his name on the front and get promoted on the strength of it. I'm just the chap who, after doing all the legwork, will wind up with my name lost in a long list of acknowledgements.' This thought prompted him to drink more seriously.

'And what will it say, your long study?'

'I say, you are polite. You know what it will say, Samson. It will say all those things we all know only too well but that politicians are desperately keen we should forget.'

'Such as?'

'That eighty per cent of all armaments established in Central Europe since 1965 belong to the Warsaw Pact countries. It will say that between 1968 and 1978 American military spending was cut by forty per cent, and during the same period Soviet military spending increased by seventy-five per cent. It will record how Western military strength was cut by fifty thousand men, while during the same period the East increased its forces by one hundred and fifty thousand men. It will tell you nothing that you don't already know.'

'So why write it?'

'Current theory has it that we must look for the motives behind the huge Soviet military build-up. Why are the Russkies piling up these enormous forces of men, and gigantic stockpiles of armaments? My master feels that an answer can be found by looking at the detailed tactical preparations made by Russian army units in the front line, units that are facing NATO ones.'

'How will you do that?' I asked. Lisl's record was now playing for the third time.

'It's a long and arduous process. We have people who regularly talk with Russian soldiers – on day-to-day matters – and we interrogate deserters and we have reports from cloak-and-dagger outfits.' He bared his teeth. 'Have some more brandy, Samson. I heard you're quite a drinker.'

'Thanks,' I said. I wasn't sure I liked having that reputation but I wasn't going to spare his brandy to disprove it. He poured a large measure for both of us and drank quite a lot of his.

'I'm mostly with your people,' he said. 'But I'll be spending time with other outfits too. Dicky arranged all that. Awfully good fellow, Dicky.' A lock of ginger hair fell forward across his face. He flicked it back as if annoyed by a fly. And when it fell forward again pushed it back with enough force to disarrange more hair. 'Cheers.'

'What will you be doing with them?' I said.

He spoke more slowly now. 'Same damn thing. Soviet Military Power and Western . . . what did I say it was called?'

'Something like that,' I said. I poured out more brandy for both of us. We were near the bottom of the bottle now.

'I know what you're doing, Samson,' he said. His voice was pitched high, as a mother might speak to a baby, and he raised a fist in a joking gesture of anger. 'At least . . . I know what you're trying to do.' His words were slurred and his hair in disarray.

'What?'

'Get me drunk. But you won't do it, old chap.' He smiled. 'I'll drink you under the table, old fellow.'

'I'm not trying to make you drunk,' I said. 'The less you drink the more there is for me.'

Henry Tiptree considered this contention carefully and tried to find the flaw in my reasoning. He shook his head as if baffled and drained the brandy bottle, dividing it between us drip by drip with elaborate care. 'Dicky said you were cunning.'

'Then here's to Dicky,' I said in toast.

'Cheers to Dicky,' he responded, having misheard me. 'I've known him a long time. At Oxford I always felt sorry for him. Dicky's father had investments in South America and lost most of his money in the war. But the rest of Dicky's family were well off. Dicky had to watch his cousins dashing about in sports cars and flying to Paris for weekends when Dicky didn't have the price of a railway ticket to London. It was damned rotten for him, humiliating.'

'I didn't know that,' I said.

'Chaps at Oxford said he was a social climber . . . and he was, and still is . . . But that's what spurred Dicky into getting such good results. He wanted to show us all what he could do . . . and, of course, having no money meant he had a lot of time on his hands.'

'He has a lot of time on his hands now,' I said.

Henry Tiptree looked at me solemnly before giving a sly grin. 'What about another bottle of this stuff?' he offered.

'I think we've both had enough, Henry,' I said.

'On me,' said Henry. 'I have a bottle in my room.'

'Even if it's on you, we've had enough,' I said. I got to my feet. I was in no hurry. I wasn't drunk but my response times were down and my coordination poor. What time in the morning would Werner phone, I wondered. It was stupid of me to tell Werner that he would be going on the payroll. Now he'd be determined to show London Central what they'd been missing for all those years. With Werner that could be a surefire recipe for disaster. I'd seen Werner when he wanted to impress someone. When we were at school there had been a pretty girl named Renate who lived in Wedding. Her mother cleaned the floor at the clinic. Werner was so keen to impress Renate that he tried to steal an American car that was parked outside the school. He was trying to force the window open with wire when the driver, an American sergeant, caught him. Werner was lucky to get away with a punch in the head. It was ridiculous. Werner had never stolen anything in his life before. A car – Werner didn't have the slightest idea of how to drive. I wondered if he'd had trouble in the Sector or out in the Zone. If anything happened to him I'd blame myself. There'd be no one else to blame.

Henry Tiptree was sitting rigidly in his seat, his head facing forward and his body very still. His eyes flicked to see about him; he looked like a lizard watching an unsuspecting fly. A less tidy man would not have appeared so drunk. On the impeccable Henry Tiptree such slightly disarranged hair, the tie knot shifted a fraction to one side and the jacket rumpled by his attempts to fasten the wrong button made him look comic. 'You won't get away with it,' he said angrily. He was going through the various stages of drunkenness from elation to depression via happiness, suspicion and anger.

'Get away with what?' I asked.

'You know, Samson. Don't play the innocent. You know.' This time his anger enabled him to articulate clearly.

'Tell me again.'

'No,' he said. He was staring at me with hatred in his eyes.

I knew then that Tiptree played some part in spinning the intricate web in which I was becoming enmeshed. On every side I was aware of suspicion, anger and hatred. Was it all Fiona's doing, or was it something I had brought upon myself? And how could I fight back when I didn't know where to find my most deadly enemies, or even who they were?

'Then goodnight,' I said. I drank the rest of the brandy, got up from the chair and nodded to him.

'Goodnight, Mr bloody Samson,' said Tiptree bitterly. 'Champion bloody boozer and secret agent extraordinary.'

I knew he was watching me as I walked across the room so I went carefully. I looked back when I got as far as the large folding doors that divided the salon from the bar. He was struggling to get to his feet, reaching right across to grip the far edge of the table. Then, with whitened knuckles, he strained to pull himself up. He seemed well on the way to succeeding, but when I got to the stairs I heard a tremendous crash. His weight had proved too much and the table had tipped up.

I returned to the bar where Henry Tiptree had fallen full-length on the floor. He was breathing very heavily and making slight noises that might have been groans, but he was otherwise unconscious. 'Come along, Henry,' I said. 'Let's get out of here before Lisl hears us. She hates drunks.' I knew if he was found there in the morning Lisl would blame me. No matter what I said, anything that happened to this 'English gentleman' would be my fault. I put the table back into position and hoped that Lisl hadn't heard the commotion.

As I dragged Tiptree up on to my shoulder in a fireman's lift, I began to wonder why he'd come here. He'd been sent, surely, but who had sent him? He wasn't the sort who came to stay in Tante Lisl's hotel, and went down the corridor for a bath each morning and then found there was no hot water. The Tiptrees of this world prefer downtown hotels, where everything works, even the staff – places where the silk-attired jet-setters of all sexes line up bottles of Louis Roederer Cristal Brut, and turn first to those columns of the newspaper that list share prices.

Henry Tiptree had the glossy polish that the best English boarding schools can sometimes provide. Such boys quickly come to terms with bullies, cold showers, corporal punishment, homosexuality, the classics and relentless sport, but they acquire the hardness that I'd seen in Tiptree's face. He had a mental agility, plus a sense of purpose, that his friend Dicky Cruyer lacked. But of the two I'd take Dicky any time. Dicky was just a free-loader, but behind all the haw haws and the schoolboy smiles this one was an expensively educated storm-trooper.

As I crossed the salon, with Tiptree's whole weight upon me, I swayed and so did the mirror, the floor and the ceiling, but I steadied myself again and paused before going past the door that led to Lisl's room.

Her record was still playing and I could imagine her propped up amid a dozen lace pillows nodding her head to the music:

> Make my bed and light the light,
> I'll arrive late tonight.
> Blackbird, bye-bye.

16

It was cold. Featureless grey cloud stretched across the flat country-side as far as the horizon. Rain continued relentlessly so that the last of those villagers who'd been huddled in cottage doorways waiting for a respite now hurried off and got wet. All the gutters were spilling and the rain gurgled down the drainpipes and overflowed the drains. Slanted sheets of it rebounded from the cobblestone village street to make a phantom field of wheat through which occasional motor cars or delivery vans slashed their way like harvesters.

The message from Werner had told me to come to the Golden Bear, and I had come here, and I had waited two days. On the second day a young Oberstabsmeister had arrived at breakfast time. I recognized the dark green VW Passat station wagon. It bore the badge of the *Bundesgrenzschutz*. For West Germany had border guards too, and one of their jobs was investigating strangers who came to border villages and spent too much time staring eastwards at the barbed wire and the towers that marked the border where people on excursions from the German Democratic Republic got shot dead.

The border guard NCO was a white-faced youth with fair hair that covered the tops of his ears and curled out from under his uniform hat. 'Papers,' he said without the formality of a greeting or introduction. He knew I'd watched him as he came in. I'd seen him check the hotel register and exchange a few words with the proprietor. 'How long do you plan to stay?'

'About a week. I go back to work next Monday.' I'd booked the room for seven days. He knew that. 'I'm from Berlin,' I said obsequiously. 'Sometimes I feel I must get away for a few days.'

He grunted.

I showed him my papers. I was described as a German citizen, resident in Berlin, and working as a foreman in a British army stores depot. He stood for a long time with the papers in his hand, looking from the documentation to me and then back again. I had the impression he did not entirely believe my cover story, but plenty of West Berliners came down the autobahn and took their vacations

423

here on the easternmost edge of West Germany. And if he contacted the army my cover story would hold up.

'Why here?' said the border guard.

'Why not here?' I countered. He looked out of the window. The rain continued relentlessly. Across the road, workmen were demolishing a very old half-timbered building. They continued working despite the rain. As I watched, a wall fell with a crash of breaking laths and plaster and a shower of rubble. The bleached plaster went dark with raindrops and the cloud of dust that rolled out of the wreckage was quickly subdued. The fallen wall revealed open fields beyond the village, and a shiny strip that was a glimpse of the wide waters of the great Elbe river that divided East from West. The Elbe had always been a barrier; it had even halted Charlemagne. Throughout history it had divided the land: Lombard from Slav, Frank from Avar, Christian from Barbarian, Catholic from Protestant, and now communist from capitalist. 'It's better than over there,' I said.

'Anywhere is better than over there,' said the guard with ill-humour, as if I'd avoided his question. Beyond him I saw the proprietor's son Konrad come into the breakfast room. Konrad was a gangling eighteen-year-old in blue jeans and a cowboy shirt with fringes. He was unshaven but I had yet to decide whether this was a deliberate attempt to grow a beard or a part of the casual indifference he seemed to show for all aspects of his morning ablutions. He began setting the tables for lunch. On each he put cutlery and wineglasses, linen napkins and cruet, and finally a large blue faience pot of special mustard for which the Golden Bear was locally famous. Despite the care and attention he gave to his task I had no doubt that he'd come into the room to eavesdrop.

'I walk,' I said. 'The doctor said I must walk. It's for my health. Even in the rain I walk every day.'

'So I heard,' said the guard. He dropped my identity papers on to the red-checked tablecloth alongside the basket containing breakfast rolls. 'Make sure you don't walk in the wrong direction. Do you know what's over there?'

He was looking out of the window. One hand was in his pocket, the thumb of the other hooked into his belt. He looked angry. Perhaps it was my Berlin accent that annoyed him. He sounded like a local; perhaps he didn't like visitors from the big city, and whatever Berliners said it could sound sarcastic to a critic's ear. 'Not exactly,' I said. Under the circumstances it seemed advisable to be unacquainted with what was 'over there'.

The white-faced Oberstabsmeister took a deep breath. 'Starting from the other side you first come to the armed guards of the *Sperrzone*. People need a special pass to get into that forbidden zone, which is a five-kilometre-wide strip of ground, cleared of trees and bushes, so that the guards can see everything from their towers. The fields there can only be worked during daylight and under the supervision of the guards. Then comes a five-hundred-metre-deep *Schutzstreifen*. The fence there is three metres high and made of sharp expanded metal. The tiny holes are made so that you can't get a hold on it, and if your fingertips are so small that they can go into the gaps – a woman's or a child's fingers, for instance – the metal edge will cut through the finger like a knife. That marks the beginning of the "security zone" with dog patrols – free running dogs sometimes – and searchlights and minefields. Then another fence, slightly higher.'

He pursed his lips and closed his eyes as if remembering the details from a picture or a diagram. He was speaking as a child recites a difficult poem, prompted by some system of his own rather than because he really understood the meaning of what he said. But for me his words conjured a vivid memory. I'd crossed such a border zone one night in 1978. The man with me had been killed. Poor Max, a good friend. He'd screamed very loudly so that I thought they'd be sure to find us but the guards were too frightened to come into the minefield and Max took out the searchlight with a lucky shot from his pistol. It was the last thing he did; the flashes from the gun showed them where he was. Every damn gun they had was fired at him. I'd arrived safely but so shattered that they took me off the field list and I'd been a desk man ever since. And now, listening to the guard, I did it all again. My face felt hot and there was sweat on my hands.

The guard continued. 'Then a ditch with concrete sides that would stop a tank. Then barbed wire eight metres deep. Then the *Selbstschussgeräte* which are devices that fire small sharp pieces of metal and are triggered by anyone going near them. Then there is a road for patrol cars that go up and down all the time. And on each side of that roadway there's a carefully raked strip that would show a footmark if anyone crossed it. Only then do you get to the third and final strip: the *Kontrollstreifen* with another two fences, very deep barbed wire, more minefields and observation towers manned by machine-gunners. I don't know why they bother to man the towers in the *Kontrollstreifen*; as far as we know, no escaper along this section has ever got within a hundred metres of it.' He gave a grim little chuckle.

I had continued to butter my bread roll and eat it during this long litany, and this seemed to annoy him. Now that his description had finally ended I looked up at him and nodded.

'Then of course there is the river,' said the guard.

'Why are you telling me all this?' I said. I drank some coffee. I desperately needed a drink, a proper drink, but the coffee would have to do.

'You might as well understand that your friend will not be coming,' said the guard. He watched me. My hand trembled as I brought the cup down from my mouth and I spilled coffee on the tablecloth.

'What friend?' I dabbed at the stain.

'We've seen your sort before,' said the border guard. 'I know why you are waiting here at the Golden Bear.'

'You're spoiling my breakfast,' I said. 'If you don't leave me in peace I'll complain to the Tourist Bureau.'

'Walk west in future,' he said. 'It will be better for your health. No matter what your doctor might prescribe.' He grinned at his joke.

After the guard had departed, the proprietor's son came over to me. 'He's a bastard, that one. He should be "over there", that one.' *Drüben*; over there. No matter which side of the border it was, the other side was always *drüben*. The boy spread a tablecloth on the table next to mine. Then he laid out the cutlery. Only when he got to the cruet did he say, '*Are* you waiting for someone?'

'I might be,' I said.

'Nagel. That's his name. Oberstabsmeister Nagel. He would make a good communist guard. They talk to the communists every day. Do you know that?'

'No.'

'One of the other guards told me about it. They have a telephone link with the border guards on the other side. It's supposed to be used only for river accidents, floods and forest fires. But every morning they test it and they chat. I don't like the idea of it. Some bastard like Nagel could easily say too much. Your friend won't try swimming, will he?'

'Not unless he's crazy,' I said.

'Sometimes at night we hear the mines exploding,' said Konrad. 'The weight of a hare or a rabbit is enough to trigger them. Would you like more butter, or more coffee?'

'I've had enough, thanks, Konrad.'

'Is he a close friend, the one you're expecting?'

'We were at school together,' I said.

Konrad crossed himself, flicking his fingers to his forehead and to his shoulders with a quick gesture that came automatically to him.

Notwithstanding Oberstabsmeister Nagel's warning, I strolled along the river that morning. I was buttoned into my trenchcoat against the ceaseless rain. It is flat this land, part of the glaciated northern lowlands. To the west is Holland, to the north an equally flat Denmark, to the south the heathland of Lüneburg. As to the east, a man could walk far into Poland before finding a decent-sized hill. Except that no man could walk very far east.

Near the river there was a battered enamel notice: '*Halt. Zonengrenze.*' It was an old sign that should have been replaced a long time ago. The Soviet Union's military-occupation zone of Germany was now fancifully called the German Democratic Republic. But like Werner I could not stop calling it the Russian Zone. Perhaps we should have been replaced a long time ago too.

I walked on through grass so high that it soaked the legs of my trousers right up to the knees. I knew I would be no nearer to Werner out on the river bank but I could not stay cooped up in the Golden Bear. The Elbe is very wide here, meandering as great rivers do on such featureless terrain. And on both banks there are marshy fields, bright green with the tall, sharp-bladed grass that flourishes in such water meadows. And, although the far bank of the river had been kept clear of all obstruction, on this side there were young willow and alder, trees which are always thirsty. From across the river there came a sudden noise: the fierce rattle of a heron taking to the air. Something had flushed it out – the movement of some hidden sentry, perhaps. It flew over me with leisurely beats of its great wings, its legs trailing in the soft air as a child might trail its fingers from a boat.

A light wind cut into me but did not disperse the grey mist that followed the river. The sort of morning when border guards get jumpy and desperate men get reckless. Only working men were abroad, and working boats too. Barges, long strings of them, brown phantoms gliding silently on the almost colourless water. They slid past, following the dredged channel that took them on a winding course, sometimes near to the east bank and sometimes near the west one. All communist claims to half the river had faltered on the known difficulties of the deep water channel. Even the East German patrol boats, specially built with shallow-draught hulls, could not keep to the half of the river their masters claimed. There were West German boats too; a police cruiser and a high-speed Customs boat puttering along this deserted stretch of river bank.

I spotted another heron, standing in the shallow water staring down. It was absolutely still, except that it swayed slightly as the reeds and rushes moved in the wind. 'The patient killer of the marshland' my schoolbook had called it – waiting for a fish to swim into range of that spearlike beak. Now and again the wind along the water gusted enough to make the the mist open like curtains. On the far bank a watchtower was suddenly visible. An opened window – mirrored to prevent a clear view of the gunmen – flashed as the daylight was reflected in its copper-coloured glass. And then, as suddenly, the mist closed and the tower, the windows, the man, everything vanished.

When I reached the remains of the long-disused ferry pier I saw activity on the far side of the river. Four East German workmen were repairing the fencing. The supports were tilting forwards, their foundations in the marshy river bank softened further by the heavy rain. While the four men worked, two guards – *kasernierte Volkspolizei* – stood by with their machine-pistols ready, and looked anxiously at the changing visibility lest their charges escaped into the mist. Such 'barracks police' were considered more trustworthy than men who went home each night to their wives and families.

More barges passed. Czech ones this time, heading down to where the river crossed the border into Czechoslovakia. Sitting on the hatch cover there was a bearded man drinking from a mug. He had a dog with him. The dog barked at a patch of undergrowth on the far side of the river, and ran along the boat to continue its protest.

As I got to the place at which the dog had barked I saw what had attracted its attention. There were East German soldiers, three of them, dressed in battle order complete with camouflaged helmets, trying to conceal themselves in the tall grass. They were *Aufklärer*, specially trained East German soldiers, who patrolled the furthermost edge of the frontier zone, and sometimes well beyond it. They had a camera, they always had cameras, to keep the capitalists observed and recorded. I waved at their blank faces and pulled my collar up across my face.

I walked for nearly two hours, looking at the river and thinking about Stinnes and Werner and Fiona, to say nothing of George and Tessa. Until ahead of me I saw a dark green VW Passat station wagon parked. Whether it was Oberstabsmeister Nagel or one of his associates I did not want to find out. I cut back across the field where the car could not follow and from there back to the village.

It was lunchtime when I arrived at the Golden Bear. I changed out of my wet shoes and trousers and put on a tie. As I was polishing the rain spots from my glasses there was a knock at my door. 'Herr Samson? Konrad here.'

'Come in, Konrad.'

'My father asks if you are having lunch.'

'Are you expecting a rush on tables?'

Konrad smiled and rubbed his chin. I suppose his unshaven face itched. 'Papa likes to know.'

'I'll eat the *Pinkel* and kale if that's on the menu today.'

'It's always on the menu; Papa eats it. A man in this village makes the *Pinkel* sausage. He makes *Brägenwurst* and *Kochwurst* too. *Pinkel* is a Lüneburg sausage. But people come from Lüneburg, even from Hamburg, to buy them in the village. My mother prepares it with the kale. Papa says cook can't do it properly.' Having heard my lunch order he didn't depart. He was looking at me, the expression on his face a mixture of curiosity and nervousness. 'I think your friend is coming,' he said.

I draped my wet trousers over the central-heating radiator. 'And some smoked eel too; a small portion as a starter. Why do you think my friend is coming?'

'Mother will press the wet trousers if you wish.' I gave them to him. 'Because there was a phone call from Schwanheide. A taxi is bringing someone here.'

'A taxi?'

'It is a frontier crossing point,' explained Konrad, in case I didn't know.

'My friend would not phone to say he was coming.'

Konrad smiled. 'The taxi drivers phone. If they bring someone here, and a room is rented, they get money from my father.'

Schwanheide was a road crossing point not far away, where the frontier runs due north, away from the river Elbe. I gave the boy my trousers. 'You'd better make that two lots of *Pinkel* and kale,' I said.

Werner arrived in time for lunch. The dining room was a comfortable place to be on such a damp, chilly day. There was a log fire, smoke-blackened beams, polished brass and red-checked tablecloths. I felt at home there because I'd found the same bogus interior everywhere from Dublin to Warsaw and a thousand places in between, with unashamed copies in Tokyo and Los Angeles. They came from the sort of artistic designer who paints robins on Christmas cards.

'How did it go?' I asked. Werner shrugged. He would tell me in his own good time. He always had to get his thoughts in order. He ordered a tankard of Pilsener. Werner never seemed to require a strong drink no matter what happened to him, and he still hadn't finished his beer by the time the smoked eel and black bread arrived. 'Was there any trouble?'

'No real trouble,' said Werner. 'The rain helped.'

'Good.'

'It rained all night,' said Werner. 'It was about three o'clock in the morning when I came through Potsdam . . .'

'What the hell were you doing in Potsdam, Werner? That's to hell and gone.'

'There were road repairs. I was diverted. When I came through Potsdam it was pouring with rain. There was not a soul to be seen anywhere; not one car. Not even a police car or an army truck until I got to the centre of town; Friedrich Ebert Strasse . . . Do you know Potsdam?'

'I know where Friedrich Ebert Strasse is,' I said. 'The intelligence report I showed you said that there has lately been a traffic checkpoint at the Nauener Tor after dark.'

'You read all that stuff, do you?' said Werner admiringly. 'I don't know how you find time enough.'

'I hope you read it too.'

'I did. But I remembered too late. There was a checkpoint there last night. At least there was an army truck and two men inside it. They were smoking. I only saw them because of the glow of their cigarettes.'

'Were your papers okay? How did you account for being over there? That's a different jurisdiction.'

'Yes, it's *Bezirk* Potsdam,' said Werner. 'But I would have talked my way out of trouble. The diversion signs are not illuminated. I should think a lot of people get lost trying to find their way back to the autobahn. But the rain was very heavy and those policemen decided not to get wet. I slowed down and almost stopped, to show I was law-abiding. The driver just wound down the window of the truck and waved me through.'

'It didn't use to be like that, did it, Werner? There was a time when everyone over there did everything by the book. No more, no less; always by the book. Even in hotels the staff would refuse tips or gifts. Now it's all changed. Now no one believes in the socialist revolution, they just believe in Westmarks.'

'These were probably conscripts,' said Werner, 'counting out their eighteen months of compulsory service. Maybe even *Kampfgruppen*.'

'*Kampfgruppen* are keen,' I said. 'Unpaid volunteers, they would have been all over you.'

'Not any longer,' said Werner. 'They can't get enough volunteers. The factories pressure people to join nowadays. They make it a condition of being promoted to foreman or supervisor. The *Kampf-gruppen* have gone very slack.'

'Well, that suits me,' I said. 'And when you were coming through Potsdam with papers that say you have limited movement in the immediate vicinity of Berlin, I suppose that's all right with you too.'

'It's not just the East,' said Werner defensively. He regarded any criticism of Germans and Germany as a personal attack upon him. Sometimes I wondered how he reconciled this patriotism with wanting to work for London Central. 'It's the same everywhere: bribery and corruption. Twenty or more years ago, when we first got involved in this business, people stole secrets because they were politically committed or patriotic. Moscow's payments out were always piddling little amounts, paid to give Moscow a tighter grip on agents who would willingly have worked for nothing. How many people are like that nowadays? Not many. Now both sides have to pay dearly for their espionage. Half the people who bring us material would sell to the highest bidder.'

'That's what capitalism is all about, Werner.' I said it to needle him.

'I'd hate to be like you,' said Werner. 'If I really believed that I wouldn't want to work for London.'

'Have you ever thought about your obsession with working for the department?' I asked him. 'You're making enough money; you've got Zena. What the hell are you doing schlepping around in Potsdam in the middle of the night?'

'It's what I've done since I was a kid. I'm good at it, aren't I?'

'You're better at it than I am; that's what you want to prove, isn't it, Werner?' He shrugged as if he'd never thought about it before. I said, 'You want to prove that you could do my job without tarnishing yourself the way that I tarnish myself.'

'If you're talking about the hippies on the beach . . .'

'Okay, Werner. Here we go. Tell me about the hippies on the beach. I knew we'd have to talk about it sooner or later.'

'You should have reported your suspicions to the police,' said Werner primly.

'I was in the middle of doing a job, Werner. I was in a foreign country. The job I do is not strictly legal. I can't afford the luxury of a clear conscience.'

'Then what about the house in Bosham?' said Werner.

'I do things my way, Werner.'

'You started this argument,' said Werner. 'I have never criticized you. It's your conscience that's troubling you.'

'There are times when I could kill you, Werner,' I said.

Werner smiled smugly, then we both looked round at the sound of laughter. A party of people were coming into the dining room for lunch. It was a birthday lunch given for a bucolic sixty-year-old. He'd been celebrating before their arrival, to judge by the way he blundered against the table and knocked over a chair before getting settled. There were a dozen people in the party, all of them over fifty and some nearer seventy. The men were in Sunday suits and the women had tightly waved hair and old-fashioned hats. Twelve lunches: I suppose that's why the kitchen wanted my order in advance. 'Two more Pilsener,' Werner called to Konrad. 'And my friend will have a schnapps with his.'

'Just to clean the fish from my fingers,' I said. The boy smiled. It was an old German custom to offer schnapps with the eel and use the final drain of it to clean the fingers. But like lots of old German customs it was now conveniently discontinued.

The birthday party occupied a long table by the window but they were too close for Werner to continue his account. So we chatted about things of no importance and watched the celebration.

Konrad brought our *Pinkel* and kale, a casserole dish of sausage and greens, with its wonderful smell of smoked bacon and onions. And, having decided that I was a connoisseur of fine sausage, his mother sent a small extra plate with a sample of the *Kochwurst* and *Brägenwurst*.

The birthday party were eating a special order of *Schlesisches Himmelreich*. This particular 'Silesian paradise' was a pork stew flavoured with dried fruit and hot spices. There was a cheer when the stew, in its big brown pot, first arrived. And another cheer for the bread dumplings that followed soon after. The portions were piled high. The ladies were tackling it delicately, but the men, despite their years, were shovelling it down with gusto, and their beer was served in one-litre-size tankards which Konrad replaced as fast as they were emptied.

Osmund, the red-faced farmer whose birthday was being celebrated, kept proposing joke toasts to 'celibacy' and 'sweethearts and wives – and may they never meet' and then, more seriously, a toast for Konrad's mother who every year cooked this fine meal of Silesian favourites.

But the party did not become more high-spirited as the celebration progressed. On the contrary, everyone became more dejected, starting from the time that Osmund proposed a toast to 'absent friends'. For these elderly Germans were all from Breslau. Their beloved Silesia was now a part of Poland and they would never see it again. I'd caught their accents when they first entered the room, but now that memories occupied their minds, and alcohol loosened their tongues, the Silesian accents became far stronger. There were quick asides and rejoinders that used local words and phrases I didn't know.

'Our Germany has become little more than a gathering place for refugees,' said Werner. 'Zena's family are just like them. They have these big family gatherings and talk about the old times. They talk about the farm as if they left only yesterday. They remember the furniture in every room of those vast houses, which fields never yielded winter barley and which had the earliest crop of sugar-beet, and they can name every horse they've ever ridden. And they do what these people at the next table are doing: they eat the old dishes, talk about long dead friends and relatives. Eventually they will probably sing the old songs. It's another world, Bernie. We're big-city kids. People from the country are different from us, and these Germans from the eastern lands knew a life we can't even guess at.'

'It was good while it lasted.'

'But when it ended it ended for ever,' said Werner. 'Her family got out just ahead of the Red Army. The house was hit by artillery fire before they would face the reality of it and actually start moving westwards. And they came out with virtually only what they stood up in – a handful of cash, some jewellery and a pocketful of family photos.'

'But Zena is young. She never saw the family estates in East Prussia, did she?'

'Everything was blown to hell. Someone told them that there's a fertilizer factory built over it now. But she grew up listening to these fairy stories, Bernie. You know how many kids have fantasies about really being born aristocrats or film stars.'

'Do they?' I said.

'Certainly they do. I grew up wondering whether I might really be the son of Tante Lisl.'

'And who does Zena grow up thinking her mother might be?'

'You know what I mean, Bernie. Zena hears all these stories about her family having dozens of servants, horses and carriages . . . and about the Christmas balls, hunting breakfasts, ceremonial banquets and wonderful parties with military bands playing and titled guests dancing outside under the stars . . . Zena is still very young, Bernard. She doesn't want to believe that it's all gone for ever.'

'You'd better persuade her it is, Werner. For her sake, and for your own sake too.'

'She's a child, Bernie. That's why I love her so much. It's because she believes in all kinds of fairy stories that I love her.'

'She doesn't really think of going back, does she?'

'Going back in time, yes. But not going back to East Prussia.'

'But she has the accent,' I said.

Werner looked at me as if I'd mentioned some intimate aspect of his wife that I should not have known about. 'Yes, she's picked it up from her parents. It's strange, isn't it?'

'Not very strange,' I said. 'You've more or less told me why. She's determined to hang on to her dreams.'

'You're right,' said Werner, who'd gone through the usual teenage dalliance with Freud, Adler and Jung. 'The desire is in her subconscious but the fact that she chooses speech as the characteristic to imitate shows that she wants that secret desire to be known.'

Oh my God, I thought. I've started him off now. Werner lecturing on psychology was among the most mind-numbing experiences known to science.

I looked across to where the birthday party was having the dessert dishes cleared away, and ordering the coffee and brandy that would be served to them in the bar. But Osmund was not to be hurried. He had his glass raised and was proposing yet another toast. He nodded impatiently at Konrad's suggestion that they retire to the next room. 'The words of our immortal Goethe,' said Osmund, 'speak to every German soul when he says, "*Gebraucht der Zeit. Sie geht so schnell von hinnen; doch Ordnung lehrt euch Zeit gewinnen.*" '

There were murmurs of agreement and appreciation. Then they all drank to Goethe. As they all trooped off to the bar, I said to Werner, 'I never feel more English than when I hear someone quoting your great German poets.'

'What do you mean?' said Werner, with more than a trace of indignation.

'Such ideas would win few converts in England at any level of intellect, affluence or political thought. Consider what our friend just proclaimed so proudly. In English it would become something like "Employ each hour which so quickly glides away . . ." So far, so good. But then comes ". . . but learn through order how to conquer time's swift flight." '

'It's a rotten translation,' said Werner. 'In the context *gewinnen* is probably meant as "reclaim" or "earn".'

'The point I'm making, my dear Werner, is the natural repulsion any Englishman would feel at the notion of inflicting order upon his time. Especially inflicting order upon his leisure time or, as is possibly implied here, his retirement.'

'Why?'

'For Englishmen order does not go well with leisure. They like muddle and disarray. They like "messing about in boats", or dozing in a deckchair on a beach, or pottering about in the garden, or reading the newspapers or some paperback book.'

'Are you trying to persuade me that you are very English?'

'That fellow Henry Tiptree is in Berlin,' I said. 'He's that tall friend of . . .'

'I know who he is,' said Werner.

'Tiptree asked me if I was German.'

'And are you German?'

'I feel very German when I'm with people like Tiptree,' I said. Konrad came to the table brandishing his menu. He was looking at Werner with great interest.

'So if Tiptree starts quoting Goethe at you, you'll have a nervous collapse,' said Werner. 'Do you want a dessert? I don't want a dessert, and you're getting too fat.'

'Just coffee,' I said. 'I don't know what I am. I see those people from Silesia. You tell me about Zena's family. I look at myself and I wonder where I can really call home. Do you know what I mean, Werner?'

'Of course I know what you mean. I'm a Jew.' He looked at Konrad. 'Two coffees; two schnapps.'

Konrad did not hurry us to leave the dining room after he brought the order. He poured the coffees and brought tiny glasses of clear

schnapps and then left the bottle on the table. It was of local manufacture. Konrad seemed to think that anyone who'd come from 'over
there' would need an ample supply of alcohol. But I had to wait until
we were quite alone before I could get down to business. I looked
round the room to be sure there was no one who could hear us. There
was no one. From the next room came the loud voices of the Silesians.
'What about Stinnes?'

Werner rubbed his hands together and then sniffed at them. There
was still the fishy smell of the smoked eel. He splashed some of the
alcohol on his napkin and rubbed his fingers with the dampened
cloth. 'When I went over there I thought it would be a waste of time.'

'Did you, Werner?'

'I thought if London Central want me to go there and cobble up
some sort of report I would oblige them. But I didn't believe I could
find out very much about Stinnes. Furthermore I was pretty well
convinced that Stinnes had been leading us up the garden path.'

'And now?'

'I've changed my mind on both scores.'

'What happened?'

'You're concerned about him aren't you?' said Werner.

'I don't give a damn. I just want to know.'

'You identify with him.'

'Don't be ridiculous,' I said.

'He was born in 1943, the same year that you were born. His father
was in the occupying army in Berlin, just as your father was. He
went to a German civilian school just as you did. He is a senior-grade
intelligence officer with a German speciality, just as you are a British
one. You identify with him.'

'I'm not going to argue with you, Werner, but you know as well
as I do that I could prepare a list a mile long to show you that you're
talking nonsense.'

'For instance?'

'Stinnes has also had a Spanish-language speciality for many years,
and seems to be a KGB expert on Cuba and all things Cuban. I'll
bet you that if Stinnes was lined up for a job in Moscow it was to be
on their Cuba Desk.'

'Stinnes didn't originally go to Cuba just because he could speak
Spanish,' said Werner. 'He went there primarily because he was one
of Moscow's experts on Roman Catholicism. He was in the Religious
Affairs Bureau; Section 44. Back in those days the Bureau was just
two men and a dog. Now, with the Polish Church playing a part in
politics, the Bureau is big and important. But Stinnes has not worked
for Section 44 for many years. His wife persuaded him to take the
Berlin job.'

'That's good work, Werner. His marriage?'

'Stinnes has always been a womanizer. It's hard to believe when you look at him but women are strange creatures. We both know that, Bernie.'

'He's getting a divorce?'

'It all seems to be exactly as Stinnes described. They live in a house – not an apartment, a house – in the country, not far from Werneuchen.'

'Where's that?'

'North-east, outside the city limits. It's the last station on the S-Bahn. The electric trains only go to Marzahn but the service continues a long way beyond.'

'Damned strange place to live.'

'His wife is German, Bernie. She came back from Moscow because she couldn't learn to speak Russian. She'd not want to live with a lot of Russian wives.'

'You went out there?'

'I saw the wife. I said I was compiling a census for the bus service. I asked her how often she went into Berlin and how she travelled.'

'Jesus. That's dangerous, Werner.'

'It was okay, Bernie. I think she was glad to talk to someone.'

'Don't do anything like that again, Werner. There are people who could do that for you, people with papers and back-up. Suppose she'd sent for the police and you'd had to show your papers?'

'It was okay, Bernie. She wasn't going to send for anyone. She was nursing a bruised face that was going to become a black eye. She said she fell over but it was Stinnes who hit her.'

'What?'

'Now do you see why it's better I do these things myself? I talked to her. She told me that she was hoping to move back to Leipzig. She came from a village just outside Leipzig. She has a brother and two sisters living there. She can't wait to get back there. She hates Berlin, she told me. That's the sort of thing a wife says when she really means she hates her husband. It all fits together, Bernie.'

'So you think Stinnes is on the level? He has been passed over for promotion and he does want a divorce?'

'I don't know about the promotion prospects,' said Werner, 'but the marriage is all but over. I went to all the houses in that little street. The neighbours are all German. They talked to me. They've heard Stinnes and his wife arguing, and they heard them shouting and things breaking the night before I saw her with a battered face. They fight, Bernie. That's an established fact. They fight because Stinnes runs around with other women.'

'Let me hang this one on you. This business – the arguments with his wife, his womanizing and his being in a dead-end job – is all arranged by the KGB as part of a cover story. At best, they will lead us on into this entrapment to see what we're going to do. At worst, they'll try to grab one of us.'

'Grab one of us? They won't grab me; I've just been twice through the checkpoints. I see no reason to think they are going to grab Dicky. When you say grab one of us, you mean grab Bernie Samson.'

'Well, suppose I do mean that?'

'No, Bernie. It's not just a cover story. Stinnes punched his wife in the face. You're not telling me that he did that as part of his cover story too?'

I didn't answer. I looked out of the window. Already the workmen were back from lunch and at work on the demolition. I looked at my watch; forty-five minutes exactly. That's the way it was in Germany.

Werner said, 'No one would go home and hit his wife just to fit in with a story his boss invented.'

'Suppose it was all part of some bigger plan. Then perhaps it would be worth while.'

'Why don't you admit you are wrong, Bernie? Even if they thought they were going to get the greatest secrets in the world, Stinnes did not punch his wife for *that* reason.'

'How can you be sure?'

'Bernie,' said Werner gently. 'Have you calculated the chances of my going out to that house and seeing her with a bruised face? A million to one? If we were discussing rumours, I might go along with you. If I had only the reports of the neighbours, I might go along with you. But a man doesn't smash his wife's face in on the million-to-one chance that an enemy agent would take what you describe as a dangerous chance.'

'You're right, Werner.'

He looked at me a long time. I suppose he was trying to decide whether to say the rest of it. Finally he said, 'If you want to hear what I really think, it comes closer to home.'

'What do you really think, Werner?' Now that the last remaining wall was down, they started to bulldoze the rubble into piles.

'I think Stinnes was in charge in Berlin until your wife took over his department. She told you Stinnes was her senior assistant . . .'

'That was obviously not true. If Stinnes was her senior assistant the last person she'd tell would be me.'

'I think she threw Stinnes out. I think she sent him off to Mexico to get him out of her way. It's the same when anyone takes over a new department; a new boss gets rid of all the previous top staff and their projects.'

'Maybe.' I looked at the workmen. I'd always thought that old buildings were better made than new ones. I'd always thought they were solid and well built but this one was just as flimsy as any of the new ones that greedy speculators threw together.

'You know what Fiona is like. She doesn't like competition of the sort that Stinnes would give her. It's just what Fiona would do.'

'I've been giving a lot of thought to what Fiona might do,' I said. 'And I think you're right about her wanting to get rid of Stinnes. Maybe she's decided to get rid of him for good and all.' Werner looked up and waited for the next bit. 'Get rid of him to us by letting him get enrolled.'

Werner closed his eyes and pinched his nose between thumb and forefinger. He said, 'A bit far-fetched, Bernie. She went to England to warn you off. You told me that.' His eyes remained shut.

'That might be the clever part of it. She warns me to lay off Stinnes; she knows that it will have no effect on me.'

'And her threats to kidnap the children?'

'There were no threats to kidnap the children. I was thinking back to the conversation. She offered to let things stay as they are for a year.'

He opened his eyes and stared at me. 'Providing Stinnes was left alone.'

'Okay, but it was all very negative, Werner, and Fiona is not negative. Normally I would have expected her to say what I must do and she'd say what she'd do in return. That's the sort of person she is; she makes deals. I think she wants us to enrol Stinnes. I think she'd like to get rid of him permanently. If she really wanted to stop us enrolling him she'd send him to some place where we couldn't get our hands on him.'

'And killing the boy, MacKenzie. How does that fit into the theory?'

'She had a witness with her all the time – the black girl – and there were others too. That's why she was talking in riddles. She didn't want to see me alone so there was no chance of them suspecting her of double-crossing them. I think the MacKenzie murder was a decision made by someone else; the back-up team. She'd have a back-up team with her. You know how they work.'

Werner sat motionless for a moment as he thought about it. 'She's ruthless enough for it, Bernie.'

'Damn right she is,' I said.

He waited a moment. 'You still love her, don't you?'

'No, I don't.'

'Whatever you want to call it, something prevents you thinking about her clearly. If it came to the crunch, that something would prevent you doing what needed to be done. Maybe that wouldn't matter so much except that you are determined to believe that she feels the same way about you. Fiona is ruthless, Bernie. Totally dedicated to doing whatever the KGB want done. Face it, she'd eliminate MacKenzie without a qualm and, if it comes to it, she'll eliminate you.'

'You're an incurable romantic, Werner,' I said, making a joke of it, but the strength of his feelings had shaken me.

Now Werner had said what he thought about Fiona, he was embarrassed. We sat silent, both looking out of the window like strangers in a railway carriage. It was still raining. 'That Henry Tiptree,' said Werner eventually. 'What does he want?

'He doesn't like super-luxury hotels such as the Steigenberger, with private baths, and room service, disco and fancy food. He likes the real Berlin. He likes to rough it at Lisl's.'

'Crap,' said Werner.

'He tried to get me drunk the other night. He probably thought I was going to bare my soul to him. Why crap? I like Lisl's and so do you.'

Werner didn't bother to answer my question. We both knew that Henry Tiptree was not like us and was unlikely to share our tastes in anything from music and food to cars and women. 'He's spying on you,' said Werner. 'Frank Harrington's sent him to Lisl's to spy on you. It's obvious.'

'Don't be silly, Werner.' I laughed. It wasn't funny. I laughed just because I was sitting across the table from Werner, and Werner was sitting there safe and sound. I said, 'To hear you talk, Frank Harrington rules the world. Frank is only the Berlin Resident. All he's interested in is nursing the Berlin Field Unit along until he retires. He's not training his spies to chase me across the world from Mexico City to Tante Lisl's in order to get me drunk and see what secrets he can winkle out of me.'

'You always try to make me sound ridiculous.'

'Frank isn't out to get you. And he's not trying to get me either.'

'So who is this Henry Tiptree?'

'Just another graduate of the Foreign Office charm school,' I said. 'He's helping to write one of those reports about the Soviet arms build-up. You know the sort of thing; what are the political intentions and the economic consequences.'

'You don't believe any of that,' said Werner.

'I believe it. Why wouldn't I believe it? The department is buried under the weight of reports like that. Forests are set aside to provide the pulp for reports like that. Sometimes I think the entire staff of the Foreign Office does nothing else but concoct reports like that. Do you know, Werner, that in 1914 the Foreign Office staff numbered a hundred and seventy-six people in London plus four hundred and fifty in the diplomatic service overseas. Now that we've lost the empire they need six thousand officials plus nearly eight thousand locally engaged staff.'

Werner looked at me with heavy-lidded eyes. 'Take the Valium and lie down for a moment.'

'That's nearly fourteen thousand people, Werner. Can you wonder why we have Henry Tiptrees swanning round the world looking for something to occupy them?'

'I don't like him,' said Werner. 'He's out to make trouble. You'll see.'

'I'll ask Frank who he is,' I offered. 'I'll have to make my peace with Frank. I'll need his help to keep London off my back.' I tried to make it sound easy, but in fact I dreaded all the departmental repercussions that would emerge when I surfaced again. And I was far from sure whether Frank would be able to help. Or whether he would want to help.

'Are you driving back to Berlin? I had to leave the car in the East, of course. I'll phone Zena and say I'll be back for dinner. Are you free for dinner?'

'Zena will want you all to herself, Werner.' Surely Frank Harrington would stand by me. He'd always helped in the past. We had a father-and-son relationship, with all the stormy encounters that that so often implies. But Frank would help. Within the department he was the only one I could always rely upon.

'Nonsense. We'll all have dinner,' said Werner. 'Zena likes entertaining.'

'I'm not too concerned about Tiptree,' I said. It wasn't true, of course. I *was* concerned about him. I was concerned about the whole bloody tangled mess I was in. And the fact that I'd denied my concern was enough to tell Werner of those fears. He stared at me; I suppose he was worried about me. I smiled at him and added, 'You only have to spend ten minutes with Tiptree to know he's a blundering amateur.' But was he really such a foolish amateur, I wondered. Or was he a very clever man who knew how to look like one?

'It's the amateurs who are most dangerous,' said Werner.

17

Zena Volkmann could be captivating when she was in the mood to play the gracious hostess. This evening she greeted us wearing tight-fitting grey pants with a matching shirt. And over this severe garb she'd put a loose silk sleeveless jacket that was striped with every colour in the rainbow. Her hair was up and coiled round her head in a style that required a long time at the hairdresser. She had used some eyeshadow and enough make-up to accentuate her cheekbones. She looked very pretty, but not like the average housewife welcoming her husband home for dinner, more like a girlfriend expecting to be taken out to an expensive night-spot. I delivered Werner to the apartment in Berlin-Dahlem ready to forget his invitation. But Zena said she'd prepared a meal for the three of us and insisted earnestly enough to convince me to stay, loudly enough for Werner to be proud of her warm hospitality.

She held his upper arms and kissed him carefully enough to preserve her lipstick and make-up and then straightened his tie and flicked dust from his jacket. Zena knew exactly how to handle him. She was an expert on how to handle men. I think she might even have been able to handle me if she'd put her mind to it but luckily I was not a part of her planned future.

She asked Werner's advice about everything she didn't care about, and she enlisted his aid whenever there was a chance for her to play the helpless woman. He was called to the kitchen to open a tin and to get hot pans from the oven. Werner was the only one who could open a bottle of wine and decant it. Werner was asked to peer at the quiche and sniff at the roast chicken and pronounce it cooked. But since virtually all the food had come prepared by the Paul Bocuse counter of the Ka De We food department, probably the greatest array of food on sale anywhere in the world, Zena's precautions seemed somewhat overwrought. Yet Werner obviously revelled in them.

Had I read all the psychology books that Werner had on his shelf I might have started thinking that Zena was a manifestation of his desire for a daughter, or a reflection of childhood suspicions of his mother's chastity. As it was I just figured that Werner liked the dependent type and Zena was happy to play that role for him. After all, I was pretty sure that Zena hadn't read any of those books either.

But you don't have to read books to get smart, and Zena was as smart as a street urchin climbing under the flap of a circus tent. Certainly Zena could teach me a thing or two, as she did that evening. The apartment itself was an interesting indication of their relationship. Werner, despite his constant declarations of imminent bankruptcy, had always been something of a spender. But before he met Zena this apartment was like a student's pad. It was entirely masculine: an old piano, upon which Werner liked to play 'Smoke Gets in Your Eyes', and big lumpy chairs with broken springs, their ancient floral covers perforated by carelessly held cigarettes. There was even a motheaten tiger's skin which – like so much of Werner's furnishings – had come from the fleamarket in the abandoned S-Bahn station on Tauentzienstrasse. In those days the kitchen was equipped with little more than a can-opener and a frying pan. And glasses outnumbered cups by five to one. Now it was different. It wasn't like a real apartment any more; it was like one of those bare-looking sets that are photographed for glossy magazines. The lights all shone on the ceiling and walls, and the sofa had a serape draped over it. Green plants, little rugs, cut flowers and a couple of books were strategically positioned, and the chairs were very modern and uncomfortable.

We were sitting round the dining table, finishing the main course of chicken stuffed with truffles and exotic herbs. Zena had told Werner what wonderful wine he'd chosen, and he asked her what she'd been doing while he was away.

Zena said, 'The only outing worth mentioning is the evening I went to the opera.' She turned to me and said, 'Werner doesn't like opera. Taking Werner to the opera is like trying to teach a bear to dance.'

'You didn't go alone?' asked Werner.

'That's just what I was going to tell you. Erich Stinnes phoned. I didn't tell him you were not here, Werner. I didn't want him to know you were away. I don't like anyone to know you're away.'

'Erich Stinnes?' said Werner.

'He phoned. You know what he's like. He had two tickets for the opera. One for you, Werner, and one for me. I thought it was very nice of him. He said it was in return for all the dinners he'd eaten with us.'

'Not so many,' said Werner glumly.

'He was just being polite, darling. So I said that you would be late back but that I would love to go.'

I looked at Werner and he looked at me. In some other situation, such looks exchanged between two men in some other line of work might have been comment on a wife's fidelity. But Werner and I were thinking other thoughts. The alarm on Werner's face was registering the fear that Stinnes knew Zena was alone because he had had him followed over there in the East Sector of the city. Zena looked from one to the other of us. 'What is it?' she said.

'The opera,' said Werner vaguely, as his mind retraced his movements from Berlin and across the dark countryside to the frontier and tried to remember any persisting headlights on the road behind, a shadow in a doorway, a figure in the street or any one of a thousand slips that even the best of agents is prey to.

'He sent a car,' said Zena. 'I started worrying when it was due to arrive. I thought it might drive up to the front door with a Russian army driver in uniform, or with a hammer-and-sickle flag on the front of it.' She giggled.

'You went to the East?'

'We saw Mozart's *Magic Flute*, darling. At the Comic Opera. It's a lovely little theatre; have you never been? Lots of people from the West go over for the evening. There were British officers in gorgeous uniforms and lots of women in long dresses. I felt under-dressed if anything. We must go together, Werner. It was lovely.'

'Stinnes is married,' said Werner.

'Don't be such a prude, Werner, I know he's married. We've both heard Erich talking about his failed marriage at length enough to remember that.'

'It was a strange thing for him to do, wasn't it?' Werner said.

'Oh, Werner, darling. How can you say that? You heard me saying how much I liked the opera. And Erich asked you if you liked opera and you said yes you did.'

'I probably wasn't listening,' said Werner.

'I know you weren't listening. You almost went to sleep. I had to kick you under the table.'

'You must be very careful with Erich Stinnes,' said Werner. He smiled as if determined not to become angry with her. 'He's not the polite gentleman that he likes to pretend to be. He's KGB, Zena, and all those Chekists are dangerous.'

'I've got apple strudel, and after that I've got chocolates from the Lenotre counter at Ka De We, the ones you like. Praline. Do you want to skip the strudel? What about you, Bernard?'

'I'll have everything,' I said.

'Whipped cream with the strudel? Coffee at the same time?' said Zena.

'You took the words right out of my mouth,' I said.

'Stinnes is playing a dangerous game,' Werner told her. 'No one knows what he's really got in mind. Suppose he held you hostage over there in the East?'

Zena hugged herself, grimaced, and said, 'Promises, promises.'

'It's not funny,' said Werner. 'It could happen.'

'I can handle Erich Stinnes,' said Zena. 'I understand Erich Stinnes better than you men will ever understand him. You should ask a woman to help if you really want to understand a man like that.'

'I understand him all right,' Werner called after her as she disappeared into the kitchen to get the apple strudel and switch on the coffee-machine. To me in a quieter voice he added, 'Perhaps I understand him too bloody well.'

The phone rang. Werner answered it. He grunted into the mouthpiece in a way that was unusual for the amiable Werner. 'Yes, he's here, Frank,' he said.

Frank Harrington. Of the whole population of Berlin I knew of only one that Werner really disliked, and that was the head of the Berlin Field Unit. It did not portend well for Werner's future in the department. For Werner's sake I hoped that Frank retired from the service soon.

I took the phone. 'Hello, Frank. Bernard here.'

'I've tried everywhere, Bernard. Why the hell don't you phone my office when you get into town and give me a contact number.'

'I'm at Lisl's,' I said. 'I'm always at Lisl's.'

'You're not always at Lisl's,' said Frank. He sounded angry. 'You're not at Lisl's now, and you haven't been at bloody Lisl's for the last two nights.'

'I haven't been in Berlin for two nights,' I said. 'You don't want me to phone you every night wherever I am, anywhere in the world, do you? Even my mother doesn't expect that, Frank.'

'Dicky says you left London without even notifying him you were going anywhere.'

'Dicky said that?'

'Yes,' shouted Frank. 'Dicky said that.'

'Dicky's got a terrible memory, Frank. Last year he took one of those mail-order memory courses you see advertised in the newspapers. But it didn't seem to make much difference.'

'I'm not in the mood for your merry quips,' said Frank. 'I want you in my office, tomorrow morning at ten o'clock, without fail.'

'I was going to contact you anyway, Frank.'

'Tomorrow morning, my office, ten o'clock, without fail,' said Frank again. 'And I don't want you drinking all night in Lisl's bar. Understand?'

'Yes, I understand, Frank,' I said. 'Give my best regards to your wife.' I rang off.

Werner looked at me.

'Frank reading the Riot Act,' I explained. 'Don't get drunk in

Lisl's bar, he said. It sounds as if he's been talking to that fellow Henry Tiptree.'

'He's spying on you,' said Werner, in a voice of feigned weariness. 'How long is it going to take before you start believing me?'

Zena reappeared with a tray upon which stood my slice of apple strudel, whipped cream, the coffee and a small plate of assorted chocolates. 'Who was on the phone?' she asked.

'Frank Harrington,' said Werner. 'He wanted Bernie.'

She nodded to show she'd heard and she arranged the things from the tray on the table. Then, when she'd finished her little task, she looked up and said, 'They're offering Erich a quarter of a million dollars to defect.'

'What?' said Werner, thunderstruck.

'You heard me, darling. London Central are offering Erich Stinnes a quarter of a million dollars to defect.' She was aware of what a bombshell she'd thrown at us. I had the impression that her main motive in persuading me to stay to dinner was to have me present when she announced this news.

'Ridiculous,' said Werner. 'Do you know anything about that, Bernie?'

Zena gave me no chance to steal her thunder. She said, 'That is a gross sum that would include his car and miscellaneous expenses. But it wouldn't be subject to tax and it wouldn't include the two-bedroom house they'll provide for him. He'll be on his own anyway. He's decided not to ask his wife to go with him. He's not even going to tell her about the offer. He's frightened she'll report him. They don't get along together; they quarrel.'

'A quarter of a million dollars,' said Werner. 'That's . . . nearly seven hundred thousand marks. I don't believe it.'

Zena put the strudel in front of me and placed the whipped cream to hand. 'Do you want whipped cream in your coffee, Werner?' She poured a cup of coffee and passed it to her husband. 'Well, it's true, whether you believe it or not. That's what they've offered him.'

'I haven't heard anything about it, Zena,' I said. 'I'm supposed to be handling the whole business but I've heard nothing yet about a big lump sum. If they were going to offer him a quarter of a million dollars I think they'd tell me, don't you?'

It was intended as a rhetorical question but Zena answered it. 'No, my dear Bernard,' she said. 'I'm quite sure they *wouldn't* tell you.'

'Why not?' I said.

'Use your imagination,' said Zena. 'You're senior staff at London Central, maybe more important than a man such as Stinnes . . .'

'Much more important,' I said between mouthfuls of strudel.

'Exactly,' said Zena. 'So if Erich is worth a quarter of a million dollars to London Central you'd be worth the same to Moscow.'

It took me a moment or two to understand what she meant. I grinned at the thought of it. 'You mean London Central are frightened in case I discover what I'm worth and then defect to Moscow and price myself at the same fee?'

'Of course,' said Zena. She was twenty-two years old. To her it had the elegant simplicity that the world had for me when I was her age.

'I'd need more than a quarter of a million dollars to soften the prospect of having to spend the rest of my days in Moscow,' I said.

'Don't be evasive,' said Zena. 'Do you really think that Erich will spend the rest of his days in London?'

'You tell me,' I said. I finished my strudel and sipped at my coffee. It was very strong. Zena liked strong black coffee but I floated cream on mine. So did Werner.

Werner rubbed his face and took his coffee over to the armchair to sit down. He looked very tired. 'You can see what Zena means, Bernie.' He looked from me to Zena and back again, hoping to find a way of keeping the peace.

'No,' I said.

'Extending this idea just for the sake of argument,' he said apologetically, 'Moscow would simply want to debrief you in depth. What are we talking about: six months? Twelve months at the outside.'

'And after that?' I said. 'Continuing to extend this for the sake of argument, what would happen to me after that?'

'A new identity. Now that the KGB have that new forgery factory near the airport at Schönefeld they can provide papers that pass damned near any sort of scrutiny. German workmanship, you see.' He smiled a tiny smile; just enough to make it all a bit of a joke.

'German workmanship,' I said. The Russians had been at it since 1945. They'd gathered together the scattered remnants of SS unit *Amt* VI F, which from Berlin's Delbruckstrasse – and using the nearby Spechthausen bei Eberswalde paper factory, and forgers housed in the equally nearby Oranienburg concentration camp – had supervised the manufacture of superb forgeries of everything from Swedish passports to British five-pound notes. 'Perfect papers and a new identity. Plus an unlimited amount of forged paper money. That would be lovely, Werner.'

Werner looked up from under his heavy eyelids and said, 'Defectors to Moscow wind up in weird places, Bernie. You and I both know certain residents of Cape Town, Rome and . . . where was that last one: some place in Bolivia? . . . who have changed their names and occupations suddenly and successfully since the last time we saw them.'

'For a quarter of a million dollars?' I said. 'And spend the rest of your life in Cape Town, Rome or Bolivia?'

'Zena didn't mean that you'd do that for a quarter of a million dollars, Bernie.'

'Didn't she? What did you mean, Zena?' I said.

Zena said, 'No need to get touchy. You heard what I said, and you know it's true. I said that London Central were afraid of what you might do. I didn't say that I felt the same way. London Central trust no one. They don't trust Werner, they don't trust you, they don't trust me.'

'Trust you how?' I said.

Zena touched her necklace and smoothed the collar of her silk jacket, preening herself while looking away across the room as if half occupied with other, more important matters. 'They don't trust me to be their contact for Stinnes. I asked Dicky Cruyer. He ignored the question. Earlier this evening I put the same idea to you. You changed the subject.'

'Do you know for certain that Erich Stinnes has only the one child?' I said.

'Not a child exactly,' said Zena. 'He has just the one son who is eighteen years old. Perhaps nineteen by now. He failed to get into Berlin University last year in spite of having very high marks. They have a system over there that gives priority to the children of manual workers. Erich was furious.'

I got up from the table and went to look out of the window. It was dusk. Werner's apartment in the fashionable Berlin suburb of Dahlem looked out on to other expensive apartment blocks. But between them could be seen the dark treetops of the Grunewald, parkland that stretched some six kilometres to the wide water of the Havel. On a sunny day – with the windows open wide – the sweet warm air would endorse every claim made for that famous *Berliner Luft*. But now it was almost dark and the rain was spattering against the glass.

Zena's provocative remarks made me jumpy. Why had London not told me what they'd offered to Stinnes. I wasn't just the 'file officer' on a run-of-the-mill operation. This was an enrolment – the trickiest game in the book. The usual procedure was to keep 'the enroller' informed about everything that happened. I wondered if Dicky knew about the quarter of a million dollars. It took no more than a moment to decide that Dicky must know; as German Stations Controller he'd have to sign the chits for the payment. The quarter of a million dollars would have to be debited against his departmental outgoings, until the cashier adjusted the figures by means of a payment from central funding.

Street gutters overflowing with rain-water reflected the street lamps and made a line of moons that were continually shattered by passing traffic. Any one of the parked cars might have contained a surveillance team. Any of the windows of the apartment block across the street might have concealed cameras with long-focal-length lenses, and microphones with parabolic reflectors. At what point does sensible caution become clinical paranoia. At what point does a trusted employee become 'a considered risk', and then finally a 'non-critical employment only' category. I closed the curtains and turned round to face Zena. 'How furious?' I said. 'Is Stinnes furious enough to send his son to university in the West?'

'It's nothing to do with me,' said Zena. 'Ask him for yourself.'

'We need all the help we can get,' Werner told her gently.

'The son has gone to live with Stinnes's first wife. He's gone to live in Russia.'

'You're way ahead of us there, Zena,' I admitted. 'There was nothing about a first wife on the computer.'

She showed obvious pleasure at this. 'He's had only one child. The first wife was Russian. The marriage was dissolved a long time ago. For the last year or so the son has been living with Stinnes and his second wife. He wanted to learn German. Now he's gone back to live with his mother in Moscow. She has a relative who thinks he can get the boy a place at Moscow University, so the boy rushed off to Moscow immediately. He's obviously frantic to go to university.'

'If you were him you'd be frantic too,' I said. 'Secondary-school graduates who fail to get a place in a university are sent to do manual or clerical work in any farm or factory where workers are needed. Furthermore he'd become liable for military service; but university students are exempted.'

'The mother has contacts in Moscow. She'll get her son a place.'

'Is Stinnes attached to the boy?' I said. I was amazed at how much she'd been able to wheedle out of the taciturn Erich Stinnes. 'They quarrel a lot,' said Zena. 'He is at the age when sons quarrel with their fathers. It is nature's way of making the fledglings fly from the nest.'

'So you think Stinnes will come?' said Werner. His attitude to the Stinnes enrolment was still ambivalent.

'I don't know,' said Zena. I could see she resented the way in which Werner had pressed her to reveal these things about Stinnes. She felt perhaps that it was all information that London Central should pay for. 'He's still thinking about it. But if he doesn't come it won't be because of his wife or his son.'

'What will be the deciding factor, then?' I said. I picked up the coffee-pot. 'Anyone else for more coffee?'

Werner shook his head. Zena pushed her cup towards me but my casual attitude didn't make her any happier about providing me with free information. 'He's forty years old,' said Zena. 'Isn't that the age when men are supposed to suffer some mid-term life crisis?'

'Is it?' I said.

'Isn't it the age at which men ask themselves what they have achieved, and wonder if they chose the right job?' said Zena.

'And the right wife? And the right son?' I said.

Zena gave a sour smile of assent.

'And don't women have the same sort of mid-term life crisis?' asked Werner.

'They have it at twenty-nine,' said Zena and smiled.

'I think he'll do it,' said Werner. 'I've been telling Bernie that. I've changed my mind about him. I think he'll come over to us.' Werner still didn't sound too happy at the prospect.

'You should offer him a proper job,' said Zena. 'For a man like Stinnes a quarter-million-dollar retirement plan is not much better than offering him a burial plot. You should make him feel he's coming over to do something important. You must make him feel needed.'

'Yes,' I said. Such psychology had obviously worked well for her with Werner. And I remembered the way in which my wife had been enrolled with the promise of colonel's rank and a real job behind a desk with people like Stinnes to do her bidding. 'But what could we offer him? He's not spent the last ten years as a capitalist mole. If he comes to the West it will be because he is apolitical. He likes being a policeman.'

'Policeman?' said Zena with a hoot of derision. 'Is that what you all call yourselves? You think you're just a lot of fat old cops helping old ladies across the road and telling the tourists how to get back to the bus station.'

'That will do,' said Werner in one of his rare admonitions.

'You're all the same,' said Zena. 'You, Bernie, Stinnes, Frank Harrington, Dicky Cruyer . . . all the ones I've ever met. All little boys playing cowboys.'

'I said cut it out,' said Werner. I suspected he was angry more because I was present to witness her outburst than because she hadn't said it all before many times.

'Bang, bang,' said Zena, playing cowboys.

'A quarter of a million dollars,' said Werner. 'London must want him awfully badly.'

'I found something in Stinnes's car,' said Zena.

'What did you find?' said Werner.

'I'll show you,' said Zena. She went across to the glass-fronted cabinet in which Werner used to keep his scale model of the Dornier Do X flying boat. Now, like all his aircraft models, it was relegated to the storeroom in the basement, and Zena had a display of china animals there. From behind them she got a large brown envelope. 'Take a look at that,' she said, pulling some typed sheets from the envelope and sliding them across the table. I took one and passed another to Werner, who was sitting on the sofa.

There were five sheets of grey pulp paper. Both sides were covered with single-spaced typing. The copies were produced on a stencil duplicator of a type seldom seen nowadays in Western countries but still commonly used in the East. I studied the sheets under the light, for some of the lettering was broken and on the grey paper I found it difficult to read, but such Russian security documents were predictable enough for me to guess at the parts I could not read or couldn't understand.

'What is it about?' said Zena. 'I can't read Russian. Does that mean secret?'

'Where exactly did you get this?' I asked her.

'From Stinnes's car. I was sitting in the back and so I felt inside all those pockets those old-fashioned cars have. I found old pencils and some hairpins and these papers.'

'And you took it?'

Werner looked up expectantly.

'I put it in my handbag. No one saw me, if that's what's worrying you. Does that mean secret?' she asked again. She pointed to a large, red-inked, rubber-stamp mark that had been applied to the copies.

'Yes, secret,' I said. 'But there is nothing here that makes it worth phoning the White House and getting the President out of bed.'

'What is it?'

'The top heading says "Group of Soviet Forces in Germany", which is the official name for all the Russian army units there, and the reference number. The second line is the title of the document: "Supplementary Instructions Concerning Counter-Intelligence Duties of State Security Organs". Then there comes this long preamble which is standard for this sort of document. It says, "The Communist Party of the Soviet Union traces the Soviet people's way in the struggle for the victory of communism. The Party guides and directs the forces of the nation and the organs of state security." '

'What's it about?' said Zena impatiently.

'It's half-way down the page before it gets down to business. These numbered paragraphs are headed "Instructions for KGB unit commanders in their relationship with commanders of army units to which they are attached". It says be firm and polite and cooperate . . . that sort of crap that all government clerks everywhere churn out by the ream. Then the next lot of paragraphs is headed "Duties of Special Departments" and it instructs KGB officers about likely means that imperialist intelligence forces are currently using to obtain Russian secrets.'

'What sort of methods?' said Zena.

'Two of the paragraphs give details of people discovered spying.

One was in a factory and the other near a missile site. Neither example is what would normally be called espionage. One is a man who seems to have run into a forbidden zone after his dog, and the other case is a man taking photos without a permit.'

'You're trying to say that this paper I've brought you is just rubbish. I don't believe you.'

'Then ask Werner. Your husband knows more Russian than I do.'

'Bernie has translated it perfectly,' said Werner.

'So you think it's rubbish too,' said Zena. Her disappointment had made her angry.

Werner looked at me, wondering how much he was permitted to say. Knowing that he'd tell her anyway, I said, 'This is a regular publication; it is published every month. Copies go to the commanders of certain KGB units throughout the German Democratic Republic. You see that number at the top; this is number fifteen of what is probably a total of not more than one hundred. It's secret. London like to have copies of them if they can get them. I doubt if we've got a complete collection of them on our files, although perhaps the CIA have. The Americans like to have everything complete – the complete works of Shakespeare, a complete dinner service of Meissen, a complete set of lenses for the Olympus camera, and garages crammed with copies of the *National Geographic* going back for twenty-five years.'

'And?' said Zena.

I shrugged. 'It's secret, but it's not interesting.'

'To you. It's not interesting to you, that's what you mean.'

'It's not interesting to anyone except archive librarians.'

I watched Werner getting out of the sofa. It was a very low sofa and getting out of it was no easy thing to do. I noticed that Zena never sat in it; she kneeled on it so that she could swing her legs down to the floor and get to her feet with comparative ease.

'I found it in the car,' said Zena. 'I guessed the stamp meant secret.'

'You should have left it where it was,' said Werner. 'Think what might have happened if they'd searched the car as you went through the crossing point.'

'Nothing would have happened,' said Zena. 'It wasn't my car. It was an official car, wasn't it?'

'They're not interested in such subtle distinctions over there,' said Werner. 'If the border guards had found that document in the car they would have arrested you and the driver.'

'You worry too much,' said Zena.

Werner tossed the document pages on to the table. 'It was a mad thing to do, Zena. Leave that sort of risk to the people who get paid for it.'

'People like you and Bernie, you mean?'

'Bernie would never carry a paper like that through a checkpoint,' said Werner. 'Neither would I. Neither would anyone who knew what the consequences might be.'

She had been expecting unstinting praise. Now, like a small child, she bit her red lips and sulked.

I said, 'Even if the Vopos had done nothing to you, do you realize what would happen to Stinnes if they knew he'd been careless enough to leave papers in his car when it came into West Berlin? Even a KGB officer couldn't talk his way out of that one.'

She looked at me evenly. There was no expression on her face, but I had the feeling that her reply was calculated. 'I wouldn't cry for him,' she said.

Was this callous rejection of Stinnes just something she said to please Werner, I wondered. I watched Werner's reaction. But he smiled sadly. 'Do you want this stuff, Bernie?' he asked, picking up the papers.

'I don't want it,' I said. It was an understatement. I didn't want to hear about Zena's crazy capers. She didn't understand what kind of dangers she was playing with, and she didn't want to know.

It was only when Werner had gone into his study that Zena realized what he intended. But by that time we could hear the whine of the shredder as Werner destroyed the pages.

'Why?' said Zena angrily. 'Those papers were valuable. They were mine.'

'The papers weren't yours,' I said. 'You stole them.'

Werner returned and said, 'It's better that they disappear. Whatever we did with them could lead to trouble for someone. If Stinnes suspects you've taken them he'll think we put you up to it. It might be enough to make him back out of the deal.'

'We could have sold them to London,' said Zena.

'London wouldn't be keen to have papers that were so casually come by,' I explained. 'They'd wonder if they were genuine, or planted to fool them. Then they'd start asking questions about you and Stinnes and so on. We don't want a lot of London desk men prying into what we're doing. It's difficult enough to do the job as it is.'

'We could have sold them to Frank Harrington,' said Zena. Her voice had lost some of its assertion now.

'I'm trying to keep Frank Harrington at arm's length,' I said. 'If Stinnes is serious we'll do the enrolment from Mexico. If we do it from here, Frank will want to mastermind it.'

'Frank's too idle,' said Zena.

'Not for this one,' I said. 'I think Frank has already begun to see the extent of London's interest. I think Frank will want to get into the act. This would be a feather in his cap – something good for him to retire on.'

'And Mexico City is a long way from London,' said Werner. 'Less chance of having London Central breathing down your neck if you are in Mexico. I know how your mind works, Bernie.'

I smiled but said nothing. He was right, I wanted to keep London Central as far away as possible. I still felt like a mouse in a maze; every turn brought me to another blank wall. It was difficult enough to deal with the KGB but now I was fighting London Central too and Fiona was thrown into the puzzle to make things even more bewildering. And what was going to be waiting at the end of the maze – a nasty trap like the one that I'd sent MacKenzie to walk into?

'I still say we should have sold the papers to Frank,' said Zena.

Werner said, 'It might have proved dangerous. And the truth is, Zena darling, that we can't be absolutely sure that Stinnes didn't leave it there for you to find. If it all turned out that way, I wouldn't want you to be the person who took them to Frank.'

She smiled. She didn't believe that Stinnes had left the papers in the car to trick her. Zena had difficulty in believing that any man could trick her. Perhaps her time with Werner had lulled her into a false sense of security.

18

I'd known Frank Harrington for a lifetime; not his lifetime, of course, but mine. So when the car collected me from Lisl's the next morning I was not surprised that it took me to Frank Harrington's house rather than to the SIS offices at the Olympic Stadium. For when Frank said '*the* office' he meant the stadium that Hitler had built for the 1936 Games. But '*my* office' meant the room he used as a study in the large mansion out at Grunewald that was always at the disposal of the 'Berlin Resident' and that Frank had occupied for two long stints. It was a wonderful house which had been built for a relative of a banker named Bleichroder, who'd extended to Bismarck the necessary credit for waging the Franco-Prussian War. The garden was extensive, and there were enough trees to give the impression of being deep in the German countryside.

I was marched into the room by Frank's valet, Tarrant, a sturdy old man who'd been with Frank since the war. Frank was behind his desk, brandishing important-looking papers. He looked up at me under his eyebrows, as a commanding officer looks at a recruit who has misbehaved.

Frank was wearing a dark-grey three-piece suit, a starched white shirt and a tightly knotted Eton school tie. Frank's 'colonel of the regiment' act was not confined to his deportment. It was particularly evident in this study. There was rattan furniture and a buttoned leather bench that was so old and worn that the leather had gone almost white in places. There was a superb camphor-wood military chest, and on it an ancient typewriter that should have been in a museum. Behind him on the wall there was a large formal portrait of the Queen. It was all like a stage set for a play about the last days of the British Raj. This impression of being in an Indian army bungalow was heightened by the way in which a hundred shafts of daylight came into Frank's dark study. The louvred window shutters were closed as a precaution against sophisticated microphones that could pick up vibrations from window panes, but the slats of Berlin daylight that patterned the carpet might have come from some pitiless Punjab sun.

'Good God, Bernard,' said Frank. 'You do try my patience at times.'

'Do I, Frank? I don't mean to; I'm sorry.'

'What the hell were you doing at Lüneburg?'

'A meeting,' I said.

'An agent?'

'You know better than to ask me that, Frank,' I said.

'There's the very deuce of a fuss in London. One of your chaps was murdered.'

'Who was that?'

'MacKenzie. A probationer. He worked for you sometimes, I understand.'

'I know him,' I said.

'What do you know about his death?'

'What you've told me.'

'No more than that?'

'Is this a formal inquiry?'

'Of course not, Bernard. But it's not the right moment to conceal evidence either.'

'If it was the right moment, would you tell me so, Frank?'

'I'm trying to help, Bernard. When you go back to London you'll walk into more pointed questions than these.'

'For instance?'

'Don't you care about this poor boy?'

'I do care. I care very much. What would I have to do to convince you about that?' I said.

'You don't have to convince me about anything, Bernard. I've always stood behind you. Since your father died I've considered myself *in loco parentis*, and I've hoped that you would come to me if in trouble in the same way that you'd have gone to your father.'

Was this what Frank had been so keen to talk to me about. I couldn't decide. And now I turned the heat on to Frank. 'Is Henry Tiptree one of your people, Frank?' I kept my voice very casual.

'Tiptree? The chap staying at Frau Hennig's?' He touched his stubble moustache reflectively.

Frank was virtually the only person I knew who called Lisl 'Frau Hennig' and it took me a moment to respond to his question. 'Yes. That's the one,' I said.

I'd caught Frank on the hop. He reached into a drawer of his desk and found a packet of pipe tobacco. He took his time in tearing the wrapper open and sniffing at the contents to see how fresh it had stayed in his drawer. 'What did Tiptree say he's doing?'

'He gave me a lot of hogwash. But I think he's from Internal Security.'

Frank became rather nervous. He stuffed tobacco into the bowl of his pipe carelessly enough to spill a lot on the otherwise very tidy desk-top. 'You're right, Bernard. I'm glad you tumbled to him. I wanted to tip you the wink but the signals from London were strictly for me only. The D-G told me not to tell anyone, but now that you've guessed I might as well admit it . . .'

'What's his game, Frank?'

'He's an ambitious young diplomat who wants to have some cloak-and-dagger experience.'

'In Internal Security?'

'Don't sound so incredulous. That's where they put such people. We don't want them at the sharp end, do we, Bernard?'

'And why did Internal Security send him here?'

'Internal Security never tell us lesser mortals what they are doing, or why they're doing it, Bernard. I'm sure he guesses that anything he tells me is liable to get back to you.'

'And why should that matter?'

'Let me rephrase that.' Frank forced a grin on to his reluctant face. 'I meant that anything he told me is liable to get back to any member of the Berlin staff.'

'Is that bastard investigating me?' I said.

'Now don't get excited, Bernard. No one knows what he's doing. Internal Security are a law unto themselves, you know that. But even if he is poking his nose into your affairs, you've no cause to be surprised. We all get investigated from time to time. And you have . . .'

'I have a wife who defected. Is that what you were going to say, Frank?'

'It's not what I was going to say but, now that you've brought it into the conversation, it is a factor that Internal Security is bound to find relevant.'

I didn't answer. At least I had Frank on the defensive. It was better than him giving me a hard time about MacKenzie. Now that his pipe was filled with tobacco I gave him enough time to light up. 'Yes, you're sure to have them breathing down your neck for a little while. But these things eventually blow over. The service is fair-minded, Bernard. You must admit that.' He sucked at his pipe in short rapid breaths that made the tobacco flare. 'Do you know of even one case of a departmental employee being victimized?'

'I don't know of one,' I said, 'for the very good reason that the lid is kept tightly clamped upon such things.'

'Couldn't have chaps writing letters to *The Times* about it, could we?' said Frank. He smiled but I looked at him blankly, and watched him as he held the matchbox over the bowl of his pipe to increase the draft. I never knew whether he was so very bad at getting his pipe lit, or whether he deliberately let it go out between puffs, to give him something to do while thinking up answers to awkward questions.

'I might not need back-up on the Stinnes business, Frank,' I said, choosing my words carefully. 'I might want to handle it well away from the city, maybe not in Germany anywhere.'

Frank recognized the remark for what it was; a departmental way of telling him to go to hell. Official notice that I was going to keep the Stinnes operation well away from him and all his doings. 'It's your show, lad,' said Frank. 'How is it going?'

'Did you know that London have offered Stinnes a cash payment?'

Only his eyes moved. He looked up from his pipe but held it to his mouth and continued to fuss with it. 'No. At least not officially.'

'But you did hear?'

'The D-G told me that there might be a payment made. The old man always tells me if such things happen here on my patch. Just by way of courtesy.'

'Is the D-G taking a personal interest?'

'He is indeed.' An artful little grin. 'That's why so many of our colleagues are giving it such close attention.'

'Including you?'

'I came into the service with Sir Henry Clevemore. We trained together – although he was rather older than me – and we've become close friends. But Sir Henry is the Director-General, and I'm just the poor old Berlin Resident. He doesn't forget that, Bernard, and I make sure that I never forget it either.' This was Frank's way of reminding me that I was too damned insubordinate. 'Yes. If Sir Henry is taking a close personal interest in any particular enterprise, I also take an interest in it. He's no fool.'

'The last time I saw him he was in bad shape.'

'Sick?' said Frank, as if hearing that suggestion for the first time.

'Not just sick, Frank. When I spoke to him he was rambling.'

'Are you suggesting that the old man's *non compos mentis*?'

'He's completely fruit-cake, Frank. You must know that if you've seen him lately.'

'Eccentric, yes,' said Frank cautiously.

'He's one of the most powerful men in Britain, Frank. Let's not quibble about terminology.'

'I wouldn't like to think you're encouraging anyone to think the D-G is in anything but vigorous mental and physical health,' said Frank. 'He's been under a heavy strain. When the time is ripe he'll go, of course. But we're all very keen that it should not look like a response to the government's request.'

'Are the government asking for his head?'

'There are people in the Cabinet who'd like someone else sitting in the D-G's chair,' said Frank.

'You mean some particular someone else?'

'They'll put a politician in there if they get a chance,' said Frank. 'Virtually every government since the war has cherished the idea of having a "reliable" man running us. Not just the socialists; the Tories also have their nominees. For all I know, the Liberals and Social Democrats have ideas about it too.'

'Is it a job you'd like?'

'Me?'

'Don't say you've never thought about it.'

'Berlin Resident to D-G would be a giant step for man.'

'We all know that you came back here to straighten out a mess. Had you stayed in London you could have been the old man's deputy by now.'

'Perhaps,' said Frank.

'Has the idea been mentioned?' I persisted.

'With varying degress of seriousness,' admitted Frank. 'But I've set my mind on retirement, Bernard. I don't think I could take on the job of running the whole department at my age. I've said that if the old man got really sick I'd go in and hold the fort until someone permanent was appointed. It would be simply a way of keeping a political nominee out. But I couldn't do the reorganization job that is really required.'

'That is desperately overdue,' I said.

'That some think is desperately overdue,' agreed Frank. 'But the general consensus is that, if the worst came to the worst, the department can manage better with an empty D-G's office than with no Berlin Resident.'

'The D-G's office is already empty a lot of the time,' I said. 'And the Deputy D-G has an ailing wife and a thriving law business. It's a time-consuming combination. Not much sign of him on the top floor nowadays.'

'And what does the gossip say will happen?' said Frank.

'Now that Bret Rensselaer has lost his empire he's become one of the hopefuls.'

Frank took the pipe from his mouth and grimaced. 'Bret will never become D-G. Bret is American. It would be unacceptable to the government, to the department, and to the public at large if it ever got out.'

'Bret is a British subject now. He has been for some years. At least that's what I've heard.'

'Bret can arrange what paperwork he likes. But the people who make the decisions regard Bret as an American, and so he's American. And he'll always remain American.'

'You'd better not tell Bret.'

'Oh, I don't mean he won't get his knighthood. Actors, comics and footballers get them nowadays, so why not Bret? And that's what he really wants. He wants to go back to his little New England town and be Sir Bret Rensselaer. But he wouldn't be allowed to go back and tell them that he's just become Director-General of MI6, would he? So what's the point?'

'You're a bit hard on Bret,' I said. 'He's not simply in it for a K.' I wondered whether Frank's sudden dislike of Bret had something to do with his becoming a contender for the D-G's job. I didn't believe Frank's modest disclaimers. Given a chance, Frank would fight tooth and nail for the D-G's chair.

Frank sighed. 'A man has no friends in this job, Bernard. The Berlin Field Unit is the place where London sends the people it wants to get rid of. This is the Siberia of the service. They send you over here to handle an impossible job, with inadequate staff and insufficient funding. And, all the time you're trying to hold things together, London throws shit at you. There is one thing upon which London Central Policy Committee and Controller Europe always agree. And that is that every damn cock-up in London is because of a mistake made here in the Berlin Field Unit. Bret only put me here to get me out of the way when it looked as if I might be getting the Economics Desk which he later parlayed into an empire.'

'All gone now, Frank,' I said. 'You had the last laugh on that one. Bret lost everything when they brought Brahms Four out and closed him down. These days Bret is fighting for a piece of Dicky's desk.'

'Don't write Bret off. He won't become D-G, but he's smooth, very bright and well provided with influential supporters.' Frank got up from behind his desk and went over to switch on the lamp that was balanced over his ancient typewriter. The lampshade was green glass and the light coming through it made Frank's pinched face look sepulchral. 'And if you enrol Stinnes there will be a mighty reassessment of everyone's performance over the last decade.' Frank's voice was more serious now, and I had the feeling that he might at last tell me what had prompted this urgent meeting.

'Will there?' I said.

'You can't have overlooked that, Bernard. His interrogation will go on for ever. They'll drag out every damned case file that Stinnes ever heard of. They'll read every report that any of us ever submitted.'

'Looking for another mole?'

'That might well be the excuse they offer. But there is no mole. They will use Stinnes to find out how well we've all done our jobs over the past decade or so. They'll be able to see how well we guessed what was going on over the other side of the hill. They'll read our reports and predictions with all the advantage of hindsight. And eventually they will give us our end-of-term school reports.'

'Is that what the D-G plans to do with Stinnes?' I said.

'The D-G is not quite the crackpot you like to think he is, Bernard. Personally I'm too near to retirement for it to affect me very much. But the Stinnes debriefing will leave a lot of people with egg on their faces. It will take time, of course. The interrogators will have to check and double-check and then submit their reports. But eventually the exam results will arrive. And some of them might be asked to see the headmaster and discreetly told to find another school.'

'But everyone at London Central seems to want Stinnes enrolled.'

'Because they are all convinced that Stinnes will show how clever they are. You have to be an egomaniac to survive in the London office. You know that.'

'Is that why I've survived there?' I asked.

'Yes.' Frank was still standing behind me. He hadn't moved after switching on the lamp. On the wall there was a photograph – a signed portrait of Duke Ellington. It was the only picture in the room apart from the portrait of the Queen. Frank had one of the world's largest collections of Ellington recordings, and listening to them was the only leisure activity he permitted himself, apart from his sporadic love affairs with unsuitable young women. 'How it will affect you I don't know,' said Frank. He touched my shoulder in a gesture of paternal reassurance.

'Nothing will come to light that might affect *my* chances of becoming D-G,' I said.

'You're still angry about Dicky Cruyer getting the German Desk, aren't you?'

'I thought it would go to someone who really knew the job. I should have known that only Oxbridge men would be short-listed.'

'The department has always been like that. Historically it was sound. Graduates from good universities were unlikely to be regicides, agrarian reformers or Luddites. One day it will all change, but change comes slowly in England.'

'It was my fault,' I said. 'I knew the way it worked but I told myself that this time it would be different. There was no reason for thinking it would.'

'But you never thought of leaving the service?' said Frank.

'For a week I thought of nothing else except leaving. Twice I wrote out my resignation. I even talked to a man I used to know about a job in California.'

'And what made you decide to stay?'

'I never did decide to stay. But I always seemed to be in the middle of something that had to be finished before I could leave. Then when that was done I'd already be involved with a new operation.'

'You talked to Fiona about all this?'

'She never took it seriously. She said I'd never leave the department. She said that I'd been threatening to leave since the first time she found out what I did for a living.'

'You've always been like a son to me, Bernard. You know that. I daresay you're fed up with hearing me tell you. I promised your Dad I would look after you, but I would have looked after you anyway. Your Dad knew that, and I hope you know it too.' Frank was still behind me. I didn't twist round; I stared at Duke Ellington dressed in white tails some time back in the thirties. 'So don't be angry at what I'm going to say,' said Frank. 'It's not easy for me.' The photo was of a very young Duke but it had been signed for Frank during Ellington's West Berlin visit in 1969. So long ago. Frank said, 'If you have any doubts about what the Stinnes debriefing will turn up . . . better perhaps to get out now, Bernard.'

It took me a long time to understand what he was trying to tell me. 'You don't mean defect, Frank?'

'Letting Stinnes slip through our hands will be no solution,' said Frank. He gave no sign of having heard my question. 'Because after Stinnes there will come another and after that another. Not perhaps as important as Stinnes but contributing enough for Coordination to put the pieces together.' His voice was soft and conciliatory as if he'd rehearsed his piece many times.

I swung round to see him. I was all ready to blow my top but Frank looked drained. It had cost him a lot to say what he'd said and so despite my anger I spoke softly. 'You think I'm a Soviet agent? You think that Stinnes will blow my cover, and so I'm deliberately obstructing his enrolment? And now you're advising me to run? Is that it, Frank?'

Frank looked at me. 'I don't know, Bernard. I really don't know.' He sounded exhausted.

'No need to explain to me, Frank,' I said. 'I lived with Fiona all those years without knowing my own wife was a Soviet agent. Even at the end I had trouble believing it. Sometimes I wake up in the middle of the night and I think it's all a nightmare, and I'm relieved it's all over. Then as I become fully awake I realize that it's not over. The nightmare is still going on.'

'You must get Stinnes. And get him soon,' said Frank. 'It's the only way that you'll prove to London that you're in the clear.'

'He'll freeze if he's hurried,' I said. 'We've got to let him talk himself into coming. There was an old man who used to live up in Reinickendorf. He was a swimmer who'd been a competitor in the 1936 Olympics but he'd lost a foot to frostbite in the war. He taught a lot of the kids to swim. One year I took my son Billy to him and he had him swimming in no time at all. I asked him how he did it, because Billy had always been frightened of the water. The old man said he never told the kids to go into the water. He let them come along and watch the others. Sometimes it took ages before a child would summon up the courage to get into the pool but he always let them make their own decision about it.'

'And that's what you're doing with Stinnes?' Frank came back to his desk and sat down.

'He'll have to break a KGB network to prove his bona fides, Frank. You know that, I know it, and he knows it too. Stop and think what it means. He'll be turning his own people over to us. Once a network breaks, there's no telling how it will go. Scribbled notes, a mislaid address book or some silly reply to an interrogator and another network goes too. We both know the way it really happens, no matter what the instruction books ordain. These are his people, Frank, men and women he works with, people he knows, perhaps. He's got to come to terms with all that.'

'Don't take too long, Bernard.'

'If London hadn't meddled by making the big cash offer we might have him by now. The cash will make him feel like a Judas. Mentioning the cash too early is the most stupid thing we could do with a man like Stinnes.'

'London Central are trying to help you,' said Frank. 'And that's the worst thing that can happen to any man.'

'It's taking a longer time than usual because we went to him; he didn't come to us. Those idiots in London are trying to compare Stinnes to the sort of defector who comes into West Berlin, picks up a phone and says, let's go. For them you just send a military-police van and start on the paperwork. Stinnes hasn't been nursing this idea for years and waiting for a chance to jump. He's got to be tempted; he's got to be seduced. He's got to get accustomed to it.'

'Surely to God he knows what he wants by now,' said Frank.

'Even after he's decided, he'll want to put his hands on a few documents and so on. It's a big step, Frank. He has a wife and a grown-up son. He'll never see them again.'

'I hope you don't adopt this maudlin tone with him.'

'We'll get him, Frank. Don't worry. Is there anything else you wanted to talk about?'

Frank stared at me before saying, 'No, I just thought it appropriate to tell you personally about the death of your man MacKenzie. The department are keeping it all very low-key.'

'I appreciate it, Frank,' I said. The true reason for the meeting – the suggestion that I might want to walk through Checkpoint Charlie and disappear for ever – was now a closed book, a taboo subject that would probably never be mentioned again.

The door opened as if by magic. I suppose Frank must have pressed some hidden signal to summon old Tarrant, his valet and general factotum. 'I appreciate it very much, Frank,' I said. He'd risked what was left of his career, and a magnificent pension, to fulfil the promise he'd made to my father. I wondered if I would have shown such charity and confidence to him had our positions been reversed.

'Tarrant, tell the driver that my guest is leaving. And have his coat ready, would you?' said Frank.

'Yes, sir,' said Tarrant in loud sergeant-major style. After Tarrant had gone marching off along the hall, Frank said, 'Do you ever get lonely, Bernard?'

'Sometimes,' I said.

'It's a miserable affliction. My wife hates Berlin. She hardly ever comes over here nowadays,' said Frank. 'Sometimes I think I hate it too. It's such a dirty place. It's all those bloody coal-fired stoves in the East. There's soot in the air you breathe; I can taste it on bad days. I can't wait to get back to England. I get so damned bored.'

'No outside interests, Frank?'

His eyes narrowed. I always overstepped the mark with Frank but he always responded. Sometimes I suspected that I was the only person in the world who talked to him on an equal footing. 'Women, you mean?' There was no smile; it was not something we joked about.

'That sort of thing,' I said.

'Not for ages. I'm too old for philandering.'

'I find that hard to believe, Frank,' I said.

Suddenly the phone rang. Frank picked it up. 'Hello?' He didn't have to say who he was; this phone was connected only to his private secretary here in the house. He listened for a time and said, 'Just telex the usual acknowledgement and say we're sending someone, and, if London want to know what we're doing, tell them that we are handling it until they give instructions otherwise. Phone me if anything develops. I'll be here.'

He put the phone down and looked at me. 'What is it?' I asked.

'You'd better close the door for a moment, while we sort this out,' said Frank. 'Paul Biedermann has been arrested by a security officer.'

'What for?'

'We're not exactly sure yet. He's in Paris, Charles de Gaulle airport. We've just had it on the printer. The signal said "Mikado" and that's a NATO code word for any sort of secret documents.'

'What's it got to do with us?' I said.

Frank gave a grim smile. 'Nothing, except that some bloody idiot in London has given Biedermann a "sacred" tag. At present no one in London is admitting to it, but eventually they'll find out who authorized it. You can't put a tag on anyone without signing the sheet.'

'That's right,' I said. I suddenly went very cold. I was the idiot in question.

Frank sniffed. 'And if Biedermann is carrying stolen secret papers while getting protection from someone in London there will be a hell of a row.' He looked at me and waited for my response.

'It doesn't sound as if he got much protection. You said he was arrested.'

'A spot check. No tag could save him from a spot check. But people with "sacred" tags are supposed to be under some sort of surveillance, no matter how perfunctory.' He smiled again at the thought of someone in London getting into hot water. 'If he's got NATO secrets, they'll go mad. Do you know Paul Biedermann?'

'Of course I do. We were both on that cricket team you tried to get going for the German kids.'

'Cricket team. Ah, that's going back a long time.'

'And I met his sister Poppy here in this house not so long ago. The last time you had me over for dinner.'

'Poppy's a darling. But Paul is a shifty bastard. Didn't you sell him that Ferrari of yours?'

'Shifty? And is that an opinion you've reached since the phone rang?' I asked. 'Yes, I sold him my car. I often wish I'd kept it. He's been through half a dozen since that one, and even with my car allowance I can't even afford a new Volvo.'

'I've always wondered if young Biedermann was in the spy game. He's perfectly placed; all that travelling. And he's egoistical enough to want to do it. But it sounds as if the other side got in first.'

'He's a creep,' I said.

'Yes, I know you hate him. I remember your lecturing me about the way he sold his father's transport yard. How would you like to go to Paris and sort this one out? It will just be a matter of a preliminary talk with the people who are holding him. By that time London will have got hold of whoever signed the "sacred" tag. Whoever signed the tag will have to go to Paris, that's the drill, isn't it?'

'Yes, it is,' I said. I had a cold feeling of foreboding. Whoever had signed the 'sacred' tag would have to go to wherever Biedermann was being held. There was no way out of that; it was mandatory. Anyone who knew I'd signed that 'sacred' tag could make me go anywhere they wanted me to go; all they had to do was to have Biedermann arrested, and put the NATO signal on the line. I hadn't thought of that when making Biedermann 'sacred', and now it was too late to change anything.

'Are you all right, Bernard? You've gone a nasty shade of green.'

'It was the breakfast I had at Lisl's,' I said hastily. 'I can't digest German breakfasts any more.'

Frank nodded. Too much of an explanation. That was the trouble when dealing with Frank and Werner; they knew me too well. That was the trouble when dealing with Fiona too. 'Just hold the fort in

Paris until London sends whoever signed that tag. I'm very short of people this week, and since you're on your way back to London anyway . . . You don't mind, do you?'

'Of course not,' I said. I wondered whether the person who had masterminded this one had known I'd be with Frank today, or whether that was just a lucky coincidence for them. Either way the result was the same. Sooner or later I would have to go to Paris. I was the mouse in the maze; start running, mouse. 'Can you let me have a hand-gun, Frank?'

'Now? Right away? You do come up with some posers, Bernard. The army look after our hardware nowadays, and it takes a day or two to get the paperwork through channels and make an appointment with the duty armoury officer. I could have it by the end of the week. What exactly do you want? I'd better write it down so that I don't get it wrong.'

'No, don't bother,' I said. 'I just wanted to know what the score was, in case I was here and needed a gun some time.'

Frank smiled. 'I thought for one moment you were thinking of taking a gun to Paris. That would mean one of those non-ferrous jobs – airport guns they call them nowadays – and I'm not sure we have any available.' He was relieved, and now he placed a hand on the phone as he waited for it to ring again. 'My secretary will be phoning back with all the details, and then the car can get you to the airport in time for the next plane.' He consulted his gold wrist-watch. 'Yes, it will all fit together nicely. What a good thing you were here when it happened.'

'Yes,' I said. 'What a good thing I was here when it happened.'

Frank must have heard the bitterness in my voice, for he looked up to see my face. I smiled.

19

Charles de Gaulle is the sort of futuristic airport that you might find inside a Christmas cracker that was made in Taiwan a long time ago. Overhead the transparent plastic was discoloured with brown stains, moving staircases no longer moved, carpeting was threadbare, and the imitation marble had cracked here and there to reveal a black void into which litter had been thrown. There were long lines to get coffee and even longer ones to get a drink, and the travellers who liked to eat while sitting down were sprawled on the floor amid the discarded plastic cups and wrappings from microwave-heated sandwiches.

I was lucky. I avoided the long lines. A uniformed CRS man met me as I stepped from the plane. He took my bag and conducted me through customs and immigration, with no more than a perfunctory wave to the CRS officer in charge there. Now he opened a locked door that admitted me to another world. For behind the chaotic slum that the traveller knows as an airport there is another spacious and leisurely world for the staff. Here there is an opportunity to rest and think and eat and drink undisturbed, except for the sound of unanswered telephones.

'Where are you holding him?' I asked the CRS man as he held the door open for me.

'You'll have to talk to Chief Inspector Nicol first,' said the CRS man. We were in a small upper section of the main building that is used by the police. Most of the offices on this corridor were used by the Compagnie Républicaine de Sécurité who manned the immigration desks. But the office into which I was taken was not occupied by a man who checked passports. Chief Inspector Gérard Nicol was a well-known personality of the Sûreté Nationale. 'The cardinal' they called him, and he was senior enough to have his own well-furnished office in the Ministry building on the rue des Saussaies. I'd met him several times before.

'Chief Inspector Nicol; I'm Samson,' I said as I went into his office. I kept it very formal. French policemen demand politeness from colleagues and prisoners alike.

He looked me up and down as if deciding it was really me. 'It's a long time, Bernard,' he said finally. He was dressed in that uniform that Sûreté officers wear when they are not wearing uniform: dark trousers, black leather jacket, white shirt and plain tie.

'Two or three years,' I said.

'Two years. It was the security conference in Frankfurt. There was talk of you getting a big promotion.'

'Someone else got it,' I said.

'You said you wouldn't get it,' he reminded me.

'But I didn't believe it.'

He protruded his lower lip and shrugged as only a Frenchman shrugs. 'So now they are sending you to charm us into letting you have custody of our prisoner?'

'What is he charged with?' I asked.

By way of answer, Nicol picked up a transparent bag by the corner so that the contents fell on to the desk-top. A US passport crammed with immigration stamps of everywhere from Tokyo to Portugal, a bunch of keys, a wrist-watch, a crocodile-skin wallet, a gold pencil, a bundle of paper money – German and French – and coins, a plastic holder containing four credit cards, a packet of paper handkerchiefs, an envelope defaced with scribbled notes, a gold lighter and a packet of the German cigarettes – Atika – that I'd seen Biedermann smoking. Nicol picked up the credit cards. 'Biedermann, Paul,' he said.

'Identification from a credit card?' I sorted quickly through Biedermann's possessions.

'It's more difficult to get a credit card these days than to get a *carte de séjour*,' said Nicol sorrowfully. 'But there's a California driving licence with a photo if you prefer it. We haven't charged him with anything yet. I thought we'd wait until you arrived.'

'That's most considerate of you,' I said. I put the packet of German cigarettes into my pocket. If Nicol saw me do so he made no comment.

'We always try to oblige,' said Nicol. There is no habeas corpus in French law. There is no method whereby a man unlawfully detained may be set free. The Prefect of Police doesn't need a formal charge or evidence that any crime has been committed; he needs no judicial authority to search houses, issue warrants and confiscate letters in the post. He can order the arrest of anyone without even having evidence that any crime has been committed. He can interrogate them and then hand them over for trial, release them or send them to a lunatic asylum. No wonder French policemen look so relaxed.

'May I see what he was carrying?' I asked.

'He had that small shoulder-bag containing shaving things and some underwear, a newspaper and aspirins and so on. That's over

there. I found nothing of interest in it. But he was also carrying this.'
Nicol pointed to a hard brown leather case on the side-table. It was
an expensive piece of luggage without any manufacturer's labels, a
one-suiter with separate spaces for shoes, shirts and socks. I suppose
the factory made it to the maximum regulation size for cabin baggage,
but it was large enough to get anyone into a lot of arguments with
officious check-in clerks.

One compartment inside the lid was intended for business papers.
It even had special places for pens, pencils and a notebook. Inside
the zippered section there were four lots of typed pages, each neatly
bound into varying-coloured plastic folders. I flipped through the
pages quickly. It was all in English, but it was unmistakably American
in presentation and content. The way in which these reports had been
prepared – with coloured charts and captioned photos – made them
look like the sort of elaborate pitch that an advertising agency might
make to a potential client.

The introduction said, 'The German yard Howaldtswerke Deutsche
Werft at Kiel has dominated the market in small- and medium-size
diesel submarines for more than 15 years. Two Type 209 (1400 t.)
submarines are being fitted out and Brazil has ordered two of the
same displacement. Work on these will start almost immediately.
Two larger (1500 t.) boats are already begun for delivery to India.
These will not be stretched versions of the Type 209 but specially
designed to a new specification.'

Soon, however, the detailed descriptions became more technical:
'The Type 209s carry Krupp Atlas passive/active sonar in the sail but
the TR 1700 also have a passive-ranging sonar of French design. The
fire-control system made by Hollandse Signaal-Apparaten is standard,
but modifications are being incorporated following the repeated
failure of the Argentine submarine *San Luis* in attacks against the
Royal Navy task force.'

'It doesn't look like you've captured a master spy,' I said.

'It's marked secret,' said Nicol defensively.

'But so are a lot things in the museum archives,' I said.

'Never mind the archives, this is dated last month. I don't know
anything about submarines, but I know the Russians give a high
priority to updating their knowledge of the world's submarines. And
I know that these diesel ones are the hunter-killers that would have
to be used to find their nuclear-powered ones.'

'You've been watching too many TV documentaries,' I said.

'And I've learned enough at NATO security conferences to know
that a report like this that reveals secrets about submarines built in
German yards for the Norwegian and Danish navies will get everyone
steamed up.'

'There's no denying that,' I said. 'We think Biedermann is a small-time KGB agent working out of Berlin. Where was he going?'

'I can't tell you.'

'Can't tell me, or don't know?' I said.

'He arrived from Paris in a taxi cab and hadn't yet bought a ticket. Look for yourself.' Nicol indicated Biedermann's personal possessions which were still on the desk.

'So it was a tip-off?'

'A good guess,' said Nicol.

'Don't give me that, Gérard,' I said. 'You say he hadn't bought a ticket. And he hadn't arrived by plane. So he wasn't going through Customs, immigration or a security check when you found the papers. Who tipped you off to search him?'

'Tipped off?'

'The only reason you know all that printed junk is secret is because you were tipped off.'

'I hate policemen, don't you, Bernard? They always have such nasty suspicious minds. I never mix with them off-duty.'

'American passport. Have you told the embassy?'

'Not yet,' he said. 'Where is Biedermann resident?'

'Mexico. He has companies registered there. For tax purposes, I suppose. Is he talking?'

'He helped us a little with some preliminary questions,' admitted Nicol.

'A *passage à tabac*?' I said. It was delicate police euphemism for the preliminary roughing up that was given to uncooperative prisoners under interrogation.

He looked at me blank-faced and said, 'That sort of thing doesn't happen any more. That all stopped fifty years ago.'

'I was only kidding,' I said, although I could have opened my shirt and showed him a few scars that proved otherwise. 'What's the official policy? Are you holding on to the prisoner, or do you want me to take him away?'

'I'm waiting for instructions on that,' said Nicol. 'But it's been agreed that you talk to him.'

'Alone?'

Nicol gave me a mirthless grin. 'Providing you don't get rough with him and try and blame it on to our primitive police methods.'

So my taunt did find its mark. 'Thanks,' I said. 'I'll do the same for you some time.'

'It was a tip-off. It was phoned through to my office, so it was someone who knew how the Sûreté works. The caller said a man would be at the Alitalia desk; a scarred face, walks with a limp. A clerk took the call. There's no chance of identifying the voice or tracing the call but you can talk to the clerk if you wish. A man; perfect French, probably a Paris accent.'

'Thanks,' I said. 'Sounds like you've already narrowed it down to eight million suspects.'

'I'll get someone to take you downstairs.'

They were holding Paul Biedermann in the specially built cell block that is one floor below the police accommodation. It is a brickbuilt area with a metal-reinforced ceiling. In 1973 – by which time airports had become a major attraction for hijackers, assassins, demonstrators and lunatics and criminals of every kind – the cell block was tripled in size and redesigned to provide twenty-five very small solitary cells, eight cells with accommodation for three prisoners each (current penology advising that four prisoners together fight, and two get too friendly), and four rooms for interrogating prisoners in secure conditions. Three cells for women prisoners were also built at that time.

Paul Biedermann was not in a cell of any sort. They were holding him in one of the interrogation rooms. Like most such rooms it had a small observation chamber large enough for two or three people. The door to that was unlocked and I stepped inside it and watched Paul Biedermann through the mirrored glass panel. There was all the usual recording equipment here but no sign of its being recently used.

The interrogation room in which Biedermann was being held had no bed; just a table and two chairs. Nothing to be broken, bent or used as a weapon. The door was not a cell door; there was no iron grill or bolts, and it was secured only by a heavy-duty mortise lock. After I'd had a good look at him I opened the locked door and went inside.

'Bernd. Am I glad to see you.' He laughed. The scars down the side of his face puckered, and his smile was so broad that his twisted face looked almost demented. 'Jesus. I was hoping it would be you. They said that someone was coming from Berlin. I can explain every-thing, Bernd. It's all a crazy mistake.' Even under stress he still had that low-pitched hoarse voice and the strong American accent.

'Easy does it, Paul,' I said. I looked around the white-tiled room but I couldn't see any obvious signs of hidden microphones. If the observation chamber was not in use they were probably not recording us. Finally I decided not to worry too much about it.

'I did everything you told me to do, Bernd. Everything.' He was wearing expensive linen pants and open-neck brown shirt with a scarf tied at the neck. There was a soft brown cashmere jacket thrown carelessly on to one of the chairs. 'Have you got a cigarette? They even took away my cigarettes. How do you like that.'

I offered him the pack of Atika cigarettes. They were his own cigarettes from the things on Nicol's desk. He took one and I put the pack on the table. There was a tacit understanding that he'd get them if he was good. I lit his cigarette and he inhaled greedily. 'Were you carrying all that secret junk I saw upstairs?'

'No,' he said.

'You weren't carrying it? You never saw it before?'

'Yes. That is to say, yes and no. I was carrying it. But I don't know . . . submarines.' He laughed briefly. 'What do I know about submarines?'

'Sit down. Relax for a moment. Then tell me exactly how you got the papers,' I said.

He exhaled smoke, and waved it away with his hand as if trying to dispel the smoke in case a guard came and took the cigarette away from him. 'I always travel light. I was flying to Rome. I have a holiday place on Giglio – that's an island . . .'

'I know where Giglio is,' I said. 'Tell me about the papers.'

'I travel light because a car always collects me at the airport and the only clothes I'll need will be those that I keep there.'

'What a life you have, Paul. Is that what they call *la dolce vita* down there in Giglio.'

He gave me a fleeting smile that was no more than a grimace. 'So I just carry a little shoulder-bag that is well under regulation size for cabin baggage.'

'Just clothes inside it?'

'Hardly anything inside it; shaving stuff and a change of linen in case I get delayed somewhere.'

'So what about the brown leather case?'

'I paid off the taxi outside the arrivals hall and went in through the main entrance, and before I got anywhere near the Alitalia desk the taxi driver came running after me. He gave me the brown case and said I'd forgotten it. I said it wasn't mine but he was already saying that he was illegally parked and he pushed it to me and disappeared – it was very crowded – and so I thought I'd better take it to the police.'

'You thought it was a genuine mistake? What did the cab driver say when he gave it to you?'

'He said, I'm the cab driver. Here's the bag you left behind.'

'Give it a minute's thought, Paul. I'd really like to get it right.'

'That's what he said. He said, I'm the cab driver. Here's the bag you left behind.' Biedermann waited, looking at my face. 'What's the matter with that?'

'It could be all right, I suppose. But if I was a cab driver and someone had just paid me off, I wouldn't feel the need to say who I was, I'd be egoistical enough to think he'd know who I was. And neither would I be inclined to tell him what the bag was. I'd expect my passenger to recognize it immediately. I'd expect him to fall over with excited appreciation. And I'd hang around long enough for him to manifest that appreciation in the time-honoured way. Right, Paul?'

'Yeah . . . It seemed all right at the time. But I was flustered.'

'Are you quite sure that the man who gave you the case was the man you paid off in the cab?'

Paul Biedermann's face froze. Then he inhaled again and thought about it. 'Jesus. You're right, Bernd. The cab driver was wearing a leather jacket the same colour as one I've got, and a dark-blue shirt. I noticed his sleeve while he was driving.'

'And the one who gave you the case?'

'He was in shirt-sleeves. I thought my driver had taken his jacket off. But the second man's shirt was white. Jesus, Bernd, you're a genius. Some bastard planted that bag on me. I was going to find the police office when they arrested me.'

'You were near the Alitalia desk,' I said. 'Don't get careless, Paul. Who would have known you would be at the Alitalia desk?'

'Can you get me out of here?' he said. His voice had that soft, whispery quality that I'd heard from other desperate men.

'I'll try,' I promised. 'Who'd know you'd be at the Alitalia desk?'

'Only the girl in the hotel reception. She phoned them for me. Was it your people who forced the case on me? Is it a way of getting me to work for you?'

'Don't be stupid, Paul.'

'Why would the Russians do it? I mean they could have asked me to take the bloody case and I would have taken it. I've taken other things for them, I told you that.' He stubbed out his cigarette. He had that American habit of stubbing them out half smoked.

'Yes,' I said, although he hadn't told me about carrying packages for them. There was a long silence. Biedermann fidgeted.

'Why did they do that?' said Biedermann. 'Why? Tell me why.'

'I don't know,' I said. 'I wish I did know.' Nervously he reached for another cigarette and I lit it for him. 'I'll go and talk to the chief inspector again. London have asked for you. He's waiting to hear if Paris will release you into my custody.'

'I hope to God they do. Trying to sort this out in the French courts will take years.'

I unlocked the door with the key Nicol had given me. Biedermann, as if anxious to do me some extra service, for which I might pay in goodwill, said, 'Watch out for that guy Moskvin. He's an evil old bastard. The other one is almost human at times, but Moskvin is a fink. He's really a fink.'

'I'll do what I can for you, Paul,' I promised.

I went out and locked the door. I went back along the corridor to the stairs to speak again with Nicol. I was at the top of the stairs when I almost bumped into a woman in a blue overall coat. She was quite young, about twenty-five, and carrying a tiny plastic tray upon which there was a coffee with froth on it and a dried-up sandwich. 'With the compliments of Chief Inspector Nicol,' the woman said in a shrill working-class accent. 'It's for the man being held in custody. The inspector said you had the key.'

'Yes, I have. Do you want it?'

'Will you take the coffee to him?' she said nervously. 'Inspector Nicol wouldn't approve of you giving the key to anyone – bad security.'

'Very well,' I said.

'Don't be too long. The inspector has to go to a meeting.'

'I'll be right with him,' I promised.

I spent no more than a minute giving Paul Biedermann the coffee and sandwich. 'They gave me lunch,' he said looking at the miserable sandwich. 'But I'd love the coffee.' It had that bitter smell of the high-roast coffee that the French like so much.

I locked him up again and went upstairs to see Nicol. He was still behind his desk. He was speaking on the phone but he beckoned me inside and ended his conversation abruptly. 'Did you get anything out of him, Bernard?' A vase of cut flowers was now on his desk. It was the undefinable Gallic touch; that little *je ne sais quoi* that the French like to think makes them human.

'He says the case was planted on him.' I said. I put the door key on Nicol's desk. I noticed that the desk had been tidied and the contents of Biedermann's pockets were now back inside the plastic bag.

'By a cab driver? He got that taxi cab from a rank in the Rivoli? How would you arrange for him to select that particular cab? Not very convincing, is it?'

'I think it was another person who gave him the case. I think he might have been set up.'

'Why would anyone do that? You said he was a small-time agent.'

'I can't think why they'd do it,' I admitted.

'Paris still hasn't replied, but they should come through any time now. Since we've got to sit here, can I send out for a drink for you?'

'A *grand crème* like the one you just sent to your prisoner would be most acceptable. Do you do that with all the prisoners, or was that just to impress me?'

'And a brandy with it? That's what I'm going to have.'

'You talked me into it. Thanks.'

He reached for the internal phone but before he grasped it said, 'What coffee that I sent down for him?'

'You sent a coffee and sandwich down to him, didn't you?'

'A coffee? What do you think this is, the Ritz? I don't send coffee down for prisoners. Not here; not anywhere.'

'You didn't?'

'Are you mad? A prisoner can break a cup and slash his wrists. Don't they teach you anything in England?'

I stood up. 'A young woman gave it to me. She was wearing a blue overall coat. She looked like a secretary but she spoke like a truck driver. She had a very strong Paris accent. She said the coffee and sandwich came with your compliments and would I give it to the man in custody. She said you had to go to a meeting . . .'

'She wanted to get you out of the way,' said Nicol. He picked up the key and shouted for the uniformed man who was sitting at a desk in the next room. He took the staircase at one leap and I was right behind him.

It was too late, of course. Paul Biedermann was on his knees in the corner, his forehead on the floor like a Muslim at prayer. But his contorted position was due to the muscular contractions that had twisted his body, put a leer on his face and stopped his heart.

Nicol held Biedermann's wrist, trying to believe there was a pulse still beating there, but it was obvious that all signs of life had gone. 'Get the doctor,' Nicol told his uniformed man. A police officer may presume death but not pronounce it.

Nicol picked up the coffee-cup, sniffed it and put it down again. The sandwich was untouched. It was a miserable, dried-up sandwich. It obviously wasn't part of the plan that he should eat the sandwich.

'We'll be up all night,' said Nicol. He had gone white with anger. 'My people will be furious when they hear. When prisoners die in custody it's always police brutality. Everyone knows that. You told me that yourself, didn't you? Can you imagine what the communists will make of this? There'll be hell to pay.'

'The Russians?'

'Never mind the Russians,' said Nicol. 'I've got all the communists I need right here in the National Assembly. I've got more than I need, in fact.'

'It's my fault,' I said, once we were back in his office.

'You're damned right it is,' said Nicol, his anger unabated by this appeasement. 'And that's the way it's going to go down on paper. Don't expect me to cover up for you.' He got a few sheets of lined paper from the drawer and pushed it across his desk towards me. 'You'll have to give me a written statement. I know you'll say you can't; but you'll have to write out something.'

I looked at the blank paper for a long time. Statements are always on lined paper. The police don't trust anyone to write in straight lines. Nicol uncapped a ball-point pen and banged it down on to the paper to hurry me along.

'You're not going to ask me to stay here?'

'Stay here? Me? Keep you here? And explain to my Minister that I let some foreigner go down and murder my prisoner? Write a statement and get out of here, and stay out. The sooner I'm rid of you, the better pleased I'll be. Go and explain it all to your people in London. Although how the hell you will explain it I can't begin to guess.'

The curious rigmarole with the phoney taxi driver began to make sense. The KGB were determined to frame me. It would look as if I put a 'sacred' tag on Biedermann, when there was no real investigation in progress, to help him work as a KGB courier. And then, they'd say, the murder was done to silence him.

Now the big conundrum was finally answered. Now I knew what Stinnes had been doing in Mexico City. He'd been sent there to set up Biedermann, and Biedermann was being made ready for this murder for which I'd be blamed. Of course they'd not let Stinnes know the whole plan; that was not the KGB way. Communism has never escaped that conspiratorial climate in which it was born, and in the field even senior KGB officers are kept to their individual tasks. But what care and attention they put into their tasks. Even while I was sitting there frozen with anxiety, and twisted up with indecision, I had to admire the scheme that had trapped me. The KGB were not noted for their brilliant ideas, but their dogged planning, determination and attention to detail could often make something out of a lousy idea.

Well, the mouse was nearing the end of the maze. Now I knew what trap faced me. But surely to God no one in London Central would believe that I could be a KGB agent, and certainly not one who'd murder Biedermann or MacKenzie in cold blood. But then I remembered the way that Frank had wrung out his conscience to give me a chance to run off to Moscow. There could be nothing more sincere than that; Frank had risked his job, his chances of a K and his pension for me. Even Frank believed I might be guilty, and he'd known me since I was in my cradle. I wouldn't get the benefit of the doubt from those stoney-faced Oxbridge men in London Central.

20

And when finally I got back to London I was surprised to find a woman in my bed. Well, that's not precisely true. The woman was Tessa my sister-in-law, and she wasn't exactly in my bed; she was sleeping in the spare room. And I wasn't surprised either; there was a note on the hall-stand telling me she was sleeping there.

It was early in the morning. She came downstairs in her magnificent floral dressing gown to find me in the front room. Her long blonde hair was dishevelled and her eyelids were still heavy with sleepiness. There is a curious intimacy about seeing a woman's face without make-up. Tessa looked pale, especially round her eyes where there was usually shadow and darkened eyebrows and blackened lashes. It was the face of a sleepy child but no less attractive for that. I'd never before realized how beautiful she was; George was a lucky man, but there were too many other men equally lucky.

'Bernard. We thought you were never coming back. The children keep asking me . . .'

'I'm sorry, Tessa. I've come straight from the airport.'

'Nanny gets nervous here on her own, then the children recognize that, and they get frightened too. It's stupid, but she's such a good girl with the children. She doesn't get much time to herself. I moved into the boxroom. You said that I could use it.'

'Of course I did. Any time. Thanks for looking after them,' I said. I took off my hat and coat and threw them on to an armchair. Then I sat down on the sofa.

'Did they give you breakfast on the plane?'

'Nothing fit for human consumption.'

'Do you want coffee?' She fiddled with her hair as if suddenly aware that it was disarrayed.

'Desperately.'

'And orange juice? It will take time for the coffee to drip through.'

'Does David know I'm away so much?'

'He was furious. He threatened to come here and take the children. That was another reason why I stayed here. Nanny wouldn't be able to stand up to him.' Furtively she looked at herself in the mirror and straightened the dressing gown. 'I'm planning to take the children to my cousin's house on Friday . . . perhaps you'd prefer that I didn't, now that you're home.' Hastily she added, 'She has three children, big garden, lots of toys. We were going to stay there over the school holiday.'

'I have to go back to Mexico,' I said. 'Don't change your plans.'

She bent over me and touched my face in a gesture of great affection. 'I know you love the children. They know it too. You have to do your work, Bernard. Don't worry.' She went into the kitchen and rattled bottles and glasses and cups and saucers. When she came back she was holding a tray with a half-filled bottle of champagne. There was also a jug containing water into which a can-shaped slug of frozen orange juice was trying to melt. 'How do you like your orange juice?' she said. 'Diluted with champagne or straight?'

'Champagne? At this time in the morning I thought they served it in ladies' slippers.'

'It was in the fridge, left over from last night. I split a bottle with nanny but we didn't finish it. The bubbles stay if you put it straight back into the fridge after pouring. I brought a case with me when I came. I had a big bust-up with George and I thought, why leave all the champers there?'

'A permanent bust-up?'

'Who knows? George was shouting. He doesn't often shout.'

'Did he go to South Africa?'

She poured some champagne for both of us. 'I told you all that, didn't I? . . . Phoning the hotel in Italy and asking for Mrs Kosinski. Was it terribly tiresome of me to burden you with all that?'

'Did he go?' I stirred the frozen juice and poured some into both glasses. I was too damned puritanical to drink champagne so early in the morning, but adding the orange juice made it seem permissible.

'No, he sent his general manager instead. It shows that there must have been another woman.'

'I don't follow the logic of that,' I said. I tasted the champagne mixture.

'The other woman would have been furious had he turned her down and taken his wife instead. His only way out of trouble was not to go at all.'

'I wish I could help,' I said.

'I'm not sure that you could, Bernard.' She looked at her watch. 'The coffee will only take a moment or so.'

'I'll speak to George.'

'I'm sure you've got all sorts of worries of your own.'

'No,' I said resolutely. Good old Bernard, always has time to help his fellow humans no matter what threatens. Or was I just trying to convince myself?

'George is being such a fool, Bernard. I mean, he knows that I've been tempted by other men.'

She paused. 'Ummm,' I said. I nodded and admired her choice of words. Only a woman could describe such a long succession of reckless love affairs as being tempted, without any clear admission that she'd submitted to the temptations.

'I didn't go to great trouble to hide it from him. You know that, Bernard. So he's left it a bit late, hasn't he? You'd have thought he would have said something before deciding to go off with other women. It's not like him.'

'Was it one particular relationship that might have made George angry?'

'Oh, Bernard,' she said. Her voice was loud, louder than she intended perhaps, for she looked round, wondering if the nanny had heard but the nanny's room was at the top of the house next to the children. 'Bernard, really. You are exasperating.' She drank. 'That's good,' she said.

I hated to annoy anyone without understanding why. 'What have I done, Tessa?' I asked.

'Surely it's obvious. Even to a thick-headed idiot like you it must be evident.'

'What?'

'Evident that I adore you, Bernard. It's you that George is always making such a fuss about.'

'But we've . . . I mean I never.'

She gave a short, sardonic chuckle. 'You've gone red, darling. I didn't know I could make you blush. You're always so damned cool. That's what makes you so adorable.'

'Now stop all this nonsense, Tessa. What is it all about?'

'It's George. He's convinced that we're having a red-hot love affair, and nothing I tell him makes any difference.'

'Oh, really. I'll have to talk to him.'

'I wish you luck, darling. He takes no notice of anything I tell him.'

'And he knows you're here now?'

'Well, of course he does. That's what really got him steamed up. He called me some horrible names, Bernard. If you were really my lover you'd go round there and punch him on the nose. I told him that.'

'You told him what?'

'I said, if Bernard was really my lover he'd come round here and give you a good thrashing.'

'Oh my God, Tessa. Whatever made you say that?'

'I was angry.' She laughed as she remembered the scene with her husband. But I didn't join in the laughter. 'I told him you had lots of women. I told him you don't need me.'

'I haven't got lots of women.' I didn't want her spreading such stories. 'I haven't got any women, to tell you the truth.'

'Now don't overdo it, Bernard. No one expects you to live the life of a hermit. And that Secret de Vénus in the bathroom is not something you got from the supermarket to make you smell lovely.'

'Secret of what?'

'Bath oil from Weil of Paris. It costs an absolute fortune and I know Fi never used it.'

'I let someone from the office change here.'

'Gorgeous Gloria. I know all about her from Daphne Cruyer. She left it here, did she? Her mind was on other things in store. You are a quiet one, Bernard. How many others are there?'

My inclination was to rebut her charges but, knowing that was exactly what she wanted, I let it go. 'Poor George,' I said. 'I'll have to straighten it out.'

'He won't believe you. We may as well go straight upstairs, jump into bed, and make all his suspicions come true.'

'Don't joke about it,' I said.

'Come over here on the sofa and I'll show you if I'm joking or not.' She inched back the hem of her dressing gown to expose her thigh. It was a jokey gesture, the sort of antic she'd probably copied from some ancient film, but I could see she was naked under the dressing gown. I took a deep breath and devoted all my attention to the drink. That 'sweet disorder in the dress' made it difficult to concentrate on anything but Tessa; she was disturbingly attractive.

I gulped my drink and got to my feet. 'I'll go up to the children,' I said. 'We'll all have breakfast together.'

Tessa smiled.

'And I'll talk to George. I'll phone him this morning.'

'I'm sure you have more important things to do,' she said. She stood up too. 'Do you want me to clear out?'

'I thought you wanted to go back to George.'

'I don't know what I want,' she said. 'I need time to think.'

'You don't need time to think,' I said. 'You must either go back to George or leave him and make a clean break. You'll both be miserable if you let things go on like this. You have to decide whether you love him or not. That's all that really matters.'

'Is it? Are you still in love with Fiona?'

'No,' I said. 'And I never was.'

'You can't just wipe out the past, Bernard. I know how happy Fi was when you asked her to marry you. She adored you, you both were happy. I don't know what happened but don't say you never loved her.'

'That Fiona I knew was only part of a person, an actress who never let me see the real person. She lived a lie and I'm glad she's gone to where she wanted to be.'

'Don't be bitter. George could say the same thing about me. He could say that I have never truly given him my real self.'

'I can't help you make up your mind, Tessa.'

'Don't kick me out, Bernard. I'll look after the children and I'll keep out of your way. While you've been away I've been sitting upstairs watching nanny's television with her, and I use her little kitchen to make breakfast and we eat it in the nursery. We hardly ever come down here. I won't be in the way when you bring people home.'

'I have no plans for bringing people home, if by that you mean women.'

'Are you going into the office this morning?'

'Eventually,' I said. We stood close together. Neither of us had anything to say but we didn't want to move. We were lonely, I suppose.

She said, 'I can hear the bath-water running for the children. Why don't you go and say hello to them? They will be so excited to see you.'

'I'll have to have a talk with George,' I warned her.

'But not right at this moment,' she pleaded.

'I'll phone him when I get to the office,' I said. 'I hate misunderstandings.'

When I got upstairs the children greeted me vociferously. I told them that Tessa was going to take them away to the country.

'Nanny too?' Billy asked.

Nanny gave a shy smile. Billy was in love with his nanny I think. 'Of course,' I said.

'Auntie Tessa lets us drink champagne,' said Sally. Billy glared at her because she was revealing a secret. They had never asked me about their mother. I wondered what they thought about her sudden disappearance but it seemed better to let it go until they asked questions.

Pinned up on their board there was a coloured drawing of a red-faced man sitting on a pointed box strumming a guitar. Across the vivid blue sky it said 'Wellcom Daddy' in big letters. 'Is that me?' I said.

'We copied it from a picture of Mick Jagger,' Billy told me. 'And then we drew your glasses on afterwards. I did the outline and Sally filled in the colours.'

'And that's a pyramid in Mexico,' said Sally. 'We copied it from the encyclopedia.'

'It's beautiful,' I said. 'Can I keep it?'

'No,' said Billy. 'Sally wants to take it to school.'

I went into the little room where I keep my typewriter, books and unpaid bills. I looked up 'fink' in my dictionary of American slang.

fink n. 1 A company spy, secret informer or strike breaker. (Orig. Pink, contraction of Pinkerton man.)

I wondered how Pavel Moskvin fitted to that definition and what else Paul Biedermann had been about to tell me about it.

21

I knew what to expect. That was why I lingered over breakfast, spent a little extra time with the children and chose a dark suit and sober tie. Bret Rensselaer chose to see me in the number 3 conference room. It was a small top-floor room that was normally used when the top brass wanted to have a cozy chat far away from the noise of the typewriters, the smell of copying machines and the sight of the workers drinking tea from cups without saucers.

There was a coffin-shaped table there and Bret was in the chairman's seat at the head of it. I was at the other end. The rest of them – Dicky Cruyer and his friend Henry Tiptree, together with Frank Harrington and a man named Morgan, who was general factotum and hatchet man for the D-G – were placed so that they were subject to Bret's authority. Quite apart from anything that might happen to me, Bret was going to stage-manage things to get maximum credit and importance. Bret was a 'department head' looking for a department, and there was no more dangerous animal than that stalking through the corridors of Whitehall. He was wearing a black worsted suit – only a man as trim as Bret could have chosen a fabric that would show every spot of dust and hair – and a white shirt with stiff collar and the old-fashioned doubled-back cuffs that require cuff-links. Bret's cuff-links were large and made from antique gold coins, and his blue-and-white tie was of a pattern sold only to Concorde passengers.

'I've listened,' said Bret. 'You can't say I haven't listened. I'm not sure I'm able to understand much of it but I've listened to you.' He looked at his watch and noted the time in the notebook in front of him. Bret had gone to great pains to point out to me how informal it all was; no stenographer, no recording and no signed statements. But this way was better for Bret, for there would be no record of what had been said except what Bret wrote down. 'I've got a hell of a lot of questions still to ask you,' he said. I recognized the fact that Bret was ready for any sort of showdown; 'loaded for bear' was Bret's elegant phrase for it.

I was trying to give up smoking but I reached for the silver-plated cigarette box that was a permanent feature of top-floor conference rooms, and helped myself. No one else wanted a cigarette. They didn't want to be associated with me by thought, theory or action. I had the feeling that if I'd declared abstinence they'd all have rushed out to get drunk. I lit up and smiled and told Bret that I'd be glad to do things any way he wanted.

There were no other smiles. Frank Harrington was fiddling with his gold wrist-watch, pushing a button to see what time it was in Timbuctoo. Henry Tiptree, having written something that was too private to say, was now showing it to Morgan. Bret seemed to have hidden away the little notepads and pencils that were always put at each place on the table. That had effectively prevented note-taking except for the freckle-faced Tiptree, who'd brought his own notepad. Dicky Cruyer was wearing his blue-denim outfit and a sea-island cotton sports shirt open enough to reveal a glimpse of gold chain. Now it was obvious that Dicky had known all along that Henry Tiptree was an Internal Security officer. I'd never forgive him for not warning me back in Mexico City when Tiptree first came sniffing around.

Bret Rensselaer took off the big, wire-frame, speed-cop-style glasses that he required for reading and said, 'Suppose I suggested that you were determined that Stinnes would never be enrolled? Suppose I suggested that everything you've done from the time you went to Mexico City – and maybe before that, even – has been done to ensure that Stinnes stays loyal to the KGB?' He raised a hand in the air and waved it around as though he was trying to get someone to bid for it. 'This is just a hypothesis, you understand.'

I took my time answering. 'You mean I threatened him? Are you "suggesting" that I told him that I worked for the KGB and that I'd make sure that any attempt to defect would end in disaster for him?'

'Oh, no. You'd be far too clever for a crude approach like that. If it was you, you wouldn't tell Stinnes anything about your job with the KGB. You'd just handle the whole thing in an incompetent fumbling way that would ensure that Stinnes got scared. You'd make sure he was too damned jumpy to make any move at all.'

I said, 'Is that the way you think it was handled, Bret? In an incompetent fumbling way?' No hypothesis now, I noticed. The incompetence was neatly folded in.

Mexico City had been Dicky's operation and Dicky was quick to see that Bret was out to sink him. 'I don't think you have all the necessary information yet,' Dicky told Bret. Dicky wasn't going to be sunk, even if it meant keeping me afloat.

'We were taking it slowly, Bret,' I said. 'The brief implied that London wanted Stinnes gung-ho, and ready to talk. We didn't want to push hard. And you said London Debriefing Centre wouldn't want to find themselves dragging every word out of him. Frank will remember that.'

Bret realized that he could get caught in the fallout. Defensively he said, 'I didn't say that. What the hell would I know about what the Debriefing Centre want?'

Dicky leaned forward to see Bret and said, 'Words to that effect, Bret. You definitely said that Bernard was to use his own judgement. He decided to do things slowly.'

'Maybe I did,' said Bret and, having pacified Dicky, turned the heat back on to me. 'But how slow is slow? We don't want Stinnes to die of old age while you're enrolling him. We want to speed things up a little.'

I said, '*You* wanted to speed things up. So you applied the magic speed-up solution, didn't you? You offered Stinnes a quarter of a million dollars to help him make up his mind. And you did it without even informing me, despite the fact that I am the enroller. I'm going to make an official objection to that piece of clumsy meddling.' I turned to the D-G's personal assistant and said, 'Have you got that, Morgan? I object to that interference with my operation.'

Morgan was a white-faced Welshman whose only qualifications for being in the department were an honours degree in biology and an uncle in the Foreign Office. He looked at me as if I were an insect floating in his drink. His expression didn't change and he didn't answer. On the day I leave the department I'm going to punch Morgan in the nose. It is a celebration I've been promising myself for a long time.

Bret continued hurriedly, as if to cover up for the way I'd made a fool of myself. 'We were in a hurry to debrief Stinnes for reasons that must be all too clear to you.'

'To question him about Fiona's defection?' I said. 'Would you push that ashtray down the table, please?'

'It wasn't a defection, buddy. To defect means to leave without permission. Your wife was a KGB agent passing secret information to Moscow.' He slid the heavy glass ashtray along the polished table with that violent aplomb with which bartenders shove bourbon bottles in cowboy films.

I took the ashtray, tapped ash into it and said, 'Whatever it was she did, you wanted to question Stinnes about it?'

'We wanted to question him about your role in that move. There are people downstairs who've always thought that you and your wife were working together as a team.' I saw Frank edge his chair back an inch from the table, his subconscious prompting him to dissociate himself from anyone who thought that.

I said, 'But when she ran I was already there. I was in East Berlin. Why would I come back here to put my head in a noose?'

Bret held one of his cuff-links and twisted his wrist in the starched white cuff. His eyes were fixed on me. He said, 'That was the cunning of it. What guilty man would come running back to the department he betrayed? The fact that you came back was the most ingenious defence you could have contrived. What's more, Bernard, it's very you.'

'I say, Bret. Steady on,' said Frank Harrington. Bret looked at Frank for long enough to remind him who'd given him his present posting and who could no doubt get him a staff job in Iceland if he felt inclined. Frank turned his objection into a cough and Bret looked down the table to me.

'Very me?' I said.

'Yes,' said Bret. 'It's exactly the kind of double-bluff that you excel at. And you are one of the few people who could swing it. You are cool; very cool.'

I inhaled on my cigarette and tried to be as cool as he said I was. I knew Bret; he worked on observation. It was his standard method to throw his weight around and then see how people reacted to him. He even did it with the office clerks. 'You can invent some exciting yarns, Bret,' I said. 'But this particular parable leaves out one vitally important event. It leaves out the fact that I was the one who flushed Fiona out. It was my phone call to her that made her run.'

'That's your version of events,' said Bret. 'But it conveniently overlooks the fact that she got away. I'd say that your phone call warned her in time for her to get away safely.'

'But I told Dicky too.'

'Only because you wanted him to stop her taking your children.'

'Leaving my motivation aside,' I said, 'the fact is that I stampeded her into immediate flight. Even the report says that she seems to have taken no papers or anything of importance with her.'

'She took nothing because she was determined to be clean for Customs and immigration. The way the British law stands, there were no legal grounds for preventing her leaving the country with or without a passport. She knew that if she had nothing incriminating with her we would have had to wave goodbye with a smile on our faces when she took off.'

'I don't want to be side-tracked into a discussion about the British subject's rights of exit and re-entry,' I said primly, as if Bret was trying to evade the subject of discussion. 'I'm just telling you that she was unprepared. With proper warning she could have dealt us a bad blow.'

Bret was all ready for that one. 'She was a burned-out case, Bernard, and she'd run her course. The evidence that would incriminate her was there. If you hadn't stampeded her, the next agent in would have done. But, by having you do it, Moscow were going to make you a golden boy here in London. That's what chess players call a gambit, isn't it? A piece is sacrificed to gain a better position from which to attack.'

'I don't know much about chess,' I said.

'I'm surprised,' said Bret. 'I would have thought you'd be good at it. But you'll remember that next time you're playing – about losing a piece to get into a better position – won't you?'

'Since my duplicity was so bloody obvious, Bret, why didn't you arrest me then, as soon as I got back here?'

'We weren't sure,' said Bret. He shuffled in his seat. Bret was a shirt-sleeve man. He didn't look right sitting there with his jacket on like a shop-window dummy.

'You didn't ask me to face a board. There wasn't even an inquiry.'

'We wanted to see what you would do about enrolling Stinnes.'

'That's not very convincing, Bret. The fact that you wanted to enrol Stinnes, and question him, was a measure of your doubt about my guilt.'

'Not at all. This way, we could confirm or deny your loyalty and have Stinnes as a bonus. Dicky and I talked that one over. Right, Dicky?' Bret obviously felt that Dicky wasn't giving him the support he needed.

Dicky said, 'I've always said that there was insufficient evidence to support any action against Bernard. I want to make that clear to everyone round this table.' Dicky looked round the table making it clear to everyone.

Well, good old Dicky. So he's not just a pretty face either. He'd realized that this might well turn out to be the opportunity he'd been waiting for; the opportunity to dump a bucket of shit over Bret's head. Dicky was going to sit on the sidelines, but he'd be cheering for me now that Bret had adopted the role of my prosecutor. And, if I proved to be guilty, Dicky would still be able to wriggle free. The present company were well equipped to understand every nuance of Dicky's carefully worded communiqué to the future. He'd said there was insufficient evidence to support any action against me. Dicky wasn't going to stick his neck out and say I wasn't guilty.

Seeing that Bret was momentarily disconcerted by his remark, Dicky followed with a quick right and left to the body. 'And if Bernard didn't manage to persuade Stinnes to defect that would prove his guilt?' Dicky asked. He used a rather high-pitched voice and a little smile. It was Dicky's idea of the droll Oxford don that he'd once hoped to be, but it ill fitted a man in trendy faded denim and Gucci shoes. Dicky persisted, 'Is that it? It sounds like those medieval witch trials. You throw the accused into a lake and if he comes up you know he's guilty so you execute him.'

'Okay, Dicky, okay,' said Bret, holding up a hand and admiring his signet ring, his fraternity ring and his manicure. 'But there are still a lot more questions unanswered. Why did Bernard make Biedermann sacred?'

It was a good tactic to address the question to Dicky Cruyer, but Dicky leaped aside like a scalded cat. He knew that being cast as my counsel was just one step away from being my accessory. 'Well, what about that, Bernard?' said Dicky, turning his head towards me with an expression that said he'd gone as far as any man could go to help me.

I said, 'I was at school with Biedermann. I knew him all his life. He was never of any importance.'

'Would you like to see a rough listing of Biedermann's business holdings?' said Bret. 'Not a bad spread for a nothing.'

'No, I wouldn't. I'm talking about what he did as an agent. He was of no importance.'

'How can you be so sure?' said Bret.

'Biedermann's death is a red herring. He could never be anything more than a very small piece of the KGB machinery. There is nothing to suggest that Biedermann has ever had access to any worthwhile secrets.' They all looked at me impassively; they all knew that I'd play down Biedermann whatever he was.

Tiptree spoke for the first time. He used his hand to smooth his well-brushed ginger hair and then fingered his thin moustache as if making sure it was still gummed on. He was like a nervous young actor just about to make his first stage appearance. He said, 'Carrying secrets this time though, eh?'

'I'll wait for the official assessment before saying anything about that,' I said. 'And, even if it's worthwhile material, I'll bet you that it will reveal nothing about the Russians.'

'Well, of course it will reveal nothing about the Russians,' said Tiptree in his measured, resonant voice. 'This chap was a Soviet agent, what?' He looked round the table and smiled briefly.

Morgan spoke for the first time. He explained to Tiptree what I was getting at. 'Samson means that we'll learn nothing about Soviet aims or intentions from the submarine construction report that was being carried by Biedermann.'

'The only thing we'll learn from it', I added, 'is that the KGB chose a document that will involve the maximum number of security organizations: France, Denmark, Norway, Britain, several Latin American customers. Mexico where he was resident and the US because of his passport.'

'But the material was important enough for him to be killed,' said Tiptree.

'He was killed to incriminate me,' I said.

'Well,' said Tiptree with studied patience. 'There's no avoiding the fact that you gave him the drink that poisoned him.'

'But I didn't know what it was. We've been through all that. Just before we came in here Bret told me that the Sûreté have even found someone who identified the girl who gave me the poisoned coffee.'

Bret fidgeted in his chair. He liked to swing round in his swivel chair in his office. This wasn't a swivel chair but Bret kept throwing his weight from one side to the other as if hoping that it might become one. He corrected me. 'I said, the Sûreté found someone in the building who remembered seeing the girl you described. Hardly the same thing, Bernard. Hardly the same thing.'

'You say that Biedermann was of no account,' said Tiptree, still exhibiting that mannered patience with which great minds untangle ignorance. 'I wish you could give us just one reason for believing that.'

'Biedermann was so unimportant that the KGB killed him just to implicate me. Doesn't that prove something?'

Bret said, 'It proves nothing, as well you know. For all we can figure, Biedermann was in this up to his neck and you were working with him. That sounds a more likely motive for his murder. That explanation shows why you made him sacred without putting his name on our copy of the filing sheets.'

'I wanted a favour from him. I was preparing the way for it.'

'What favour?'

'I wanted him to help me persuade Stinnes.'

Bret said, 'What help were you going to get from the unimportant little jerk you described?'

'Stinnes was in contact with Biedermann. I thought Stinnes would choose to work through him instead of Werner Volkmann.'

'Why?'

'It's what I would have done.'

'So why didn't Stinnes do it through Biedermann?'

'I think he planned to do it that way but that the KGB began to get worried about what was happening and stopped him.'

'Play that back at half-speed,' said Bret.

'I think Moscow encouraged Stinnes to tease us a little at first. But then Stinnes realized he had the perfect cover for coming over to us. But Moscow never trusts anyone, so I think they are monitoring Stinnes and his contacts with us. He has an assistant – Pavel Moskvin – who might be someone assigned by Moscow Centre to spy on him. It could well be that they have other people spying on him. We all know that Moscow likes to have spies who spy on spies who spy on spies. I think someone higher up told Stinnes not to use Biedermann as the go-between. They had other plans for Biedermann. He was to be murdered.'

Bret fixed me with his eyes. We both knew that by 'someone higher up' I meant Fiona. I half expected him to say so. Once I'd suspected him of being Fiona's lover. Even now I'd not entirely dismissed the idea. I wonder if he knew that. He said, 'So you thought Biedermann would be valuable to us. That's why you made him sacred?'

'Yes,' I said.

'Wouldn't it be simpler, and more logical, to think you covered for Biedermann because he was a buddy?'

'Are we looking for simplicity and logic?' I said. 'This is the KGB we're talking about. Let's just stick to what is likely.'

'Then how likely is this?' said Bret. 'Biedermann is your KGB contact. You make him sacred to keep everyone else off his back. That way you'll be the first to hear if he attracts the attention of any NATO intelligence agency. And your excuse for contacting him, any time you want, night or day, is that you are continuing the investigation into his activities.'

'I didn't like Biedermann. I've never liked him. Anyone will tell you that.' It was a feeble response to Bret's convincing pattern and he ignored it.

'That sort of cover – investigation – has been used before.'

'Biedermann was killed in order to frame me for his murder, and because while he was alive his evidence would support everything I've told you. There's no other reason for what was otherwise a completely gratuitous killing.'

'Oh, sure,' said Bret. 'All to get you into deep trouble.'

I didn't answer. The KGB's operational staff had done their work well. Given all the facts against some other employee of the department, I too would have been as suspicious as Bret was.

Dicky stopped biting his nail. 'Shall I tell you what I think,' said Dicky. His voice was high and nervous but it wasn't a question; Dicky was determined to share his theory. 'I think Stinnes never gave a damn about Biedermann. That night in Mexico, when he first made contact with the Volkmanns, he apparently went across to the table because he mistook Zena Volkmann for the Biedermann girl. I say Stinnes was after Zena Volkmann. Hell, she's a stunner, you know, and Stinnes has a reputation as a woman chaser. I think we're making too much of Biedermann's role in all this.'

'Well, think about this one,' I said. 'Suppose Stinnes was sent to Mexico City only because Zena and Werner were already there. He told them that he'd been there a few weeks but we have no proof of that. We've been congratulating ourselves on the way that we put out an alert and then the Volkmanns spotted him. But suppose it's the other way round? Suppose Stinnes knew exactly who the Volkmanns were that night when he went over to their table in the Kronprinz

Club? Suppose the whole scenario had been planned that way by the KGB operational staff.'

I looked around. 'Go on,' said Bret. 'We're all listening.'

I said, 'How could he mistake Zena Volkmann for Poppy Bieder-mann? No one could mistake one for the other; there's no resemblance. He pretended to mistake Zena for the Biedermann girl in order to bring Biedermann into the conversation, knowing that we'd find out Paul Biedermann was in Mexico and that we'd make contact with him. Suppose they were thinking of involving Biedermann right back when we started?'

'With what motive?' said Dicky and then regretted saying it. Dicky liked to nod things through as if he knew everything. He touched his bloodless lips as if making sure his mouth was shut.

'Well, he's not done too badly, has he?' I said. 'He's got everyone here jumping up and down with excitement. You're accusing me of being a KGB agent and of murdering Biedermann on KGB instructions. Not bad. We'd be very proud to have the KGB floundering about like this, trying to find out who's on which side.'

Bret frowned; my accusation of floundering found a target. Frank Harrington leaned forward and said, 'So how far will they go? Send Stinnes here to give us a lot of misinformation?'

'I doubt if he could sustain a prolonged interrogation.'

'Then why the hell would they bother?' said Bret.

'To get me to run, Bret,' I said.

'Run to Moscow?'

'It fits. They send Stinnes to Mexico so that Volkmann will spot him because they guess that I'll be the chosen contact. And then they plan Biedermann's murder so that they can incriminate me. They might even have guessed I'd make Biedermann NATO sacred – it's been done before: we all know that – and now they want to pin his murder on me.' There were all sorts of other things – from the black girl's clumsy approach, to MacKenzie's murder – that supported my theory but I had no intention of revealing those. 'The whole thing adds up to a way of making me run.'

'That's what physicians call a "waste-paper basket diagnosis",' said Bret. 'You throw all the symptoms into the pot and then invent a disease.'

'Then tell me what's wrong with it,' I said.

'I'd want to see you completely cleared of suspicion before I started racking my brains about why they might be framing you,' said Bret. 'And we've still got a long way to go on that one.'

Frank Harrington looked round the table and said, 'It would be worth a lot to them to have Bernard there asking for political asylum. I think we have to take into account the way that Bernard has stayed here and faced the music.' Until that moment I'd wondered if Frank's offer to let me run off to Checkpoint Charlie had been in response to some directive from London. But now I decided that Frank had done it on his own. I was more than ever grateful to him. And if Frank seemed lukewarm in his contribution to this meeting that might be because he could offer more support to me behind the scenes if he showed no partisanship.

To me Bret said, 'That's your considered opinion, is it; that all this evidence against you is part of a Moscow plan to have you running over there?' He paused, but no one said anything. Sarcastically Bret added, 'Or could it just be your paranoia?'

'I'm not paranoid, Bret,' I said. 'I'm being persecuted.'

Bret exploded with indignation. 'Persecuted? Let me tell you – '

Frank put a hand on Bret's arm to calm him. 'It's a joke, Bret,' he said. 'It's an old joke.'

'Oh, I see. Yes,' said Bret. He was embarrassed at losing self-control if only for a moment. 'Well, it's hard to imagine KGB Operations cooking that one up.'

I said, 'I could tell you some even more stupid ideas that we've followed through.'

Bret didn't invite me to tell him any of the stupid ideas. He said, 'But what you describe would be a change of style, wouldn't it? The sort of thing someone new might dream up, to show what a genius they were.' Everyone round the table knew what he meant but when he remembered there were no notes or recordings he said it anyway. 'Someone like your wife?'

'Yes. Fiona. She could have had a hand in something like that.'

'She makes you run. She gets you and gets your kids. Ummm,' said Bret. He had a gold ball-point pen in his fist, and he clicked the top two or three times to show us he was thinking. 'Would Fiona think you could be stampeded that way? She knows you well. Why would she guess wrong? Is she wrong?'

'Hold it, Bret,' I said. 'Just four beats to the bar.'

Bret said, 'Because we still have another unreported incident.' He looked at Tiptree.

Tiptree continued right on cue. Maybe it hadn't been rehearsed but this interview had obviously been discussed in detail. Tiptree looked at me and said, 'A black woman asked for a lift in your car and you took her to London Airport. There you both had a brief exchange of words with a second woman.'

I looked at Tiptree and then at Bret. I was shaken. They'd caught me off-guard with that one. And bringing it up so late was a part of the effect it had. 'That was nothing to do with the department.'

'Well, I say it *was* to do with the department,' said Bret.

'We're all allowed a private life, Bret,' I reminded him. 'Or are we starting a new game? We all come in on Monday mornings and discuss each other's private lives as revealed by the surveillance teams. Do you want to start right away?' Bret, who wasn't above taking some of the more shapely secretaries to his riverside mansion for a cosy weekend, was not keen to get into an exchange of confidences.

To take the pressure off Bret, Henry Tiptree said, 'By that time we were checking your journeys between home and the office. You were under suspicion from the time you returned, Bernard. Surely you must have guessed that.'

'No, I didn't. At least, I didn't think you were sending Internal Security teams to follow me home.'

'So who was she?' said Tiptree.

'It was a neighbour. She has a friend who works at the airport and I was going to employ her to look after the children. She's a qualified nurse who wanted to earn some extra money on her days off. But, the way things are now, I have to have someone full-time.'

It was a hasty improvisation and I was by no means sure that Tiptree believed me. Tiptree looked at me for a long time and I stared back at him in mutual antipathy. 'Well, we'll leave that for the time being,' he said, as if making a concession to me. I wondered if he too had been trying to trace the black girl with rather less luck than poor old MacKenzie. 'Let's move on to MacKenzie,' said Tiptree, as if reading my thoughts. 'Tell me what he was doing for you at the time of his death.'

Was it a trick? 'I don't know the time of his death,' I said. 'I just know what the doctor estimated it might have been.'

Tiptree smiled grimly. 'If you don't know the time of his death,' he said, carefully inserting that proviso as if not believing it, 'tell me about MacKenzie. You gave him quite a few errands. From what I hear of you, it's not like you to use a probationer. You're the one who's always complaining about the lack of experience around here. You're the one who won't tolerate amateurism. Why MacKenzie, then?'

I kept as near to the truth as possible. 'He wanted to be a field agent,' I told them. 'He really wanted that.' They nodded. We'd all seen lots of probationers who wanted to be field agents, even though the various selection boards tried to screen out anyone with that perverted ambition. Soon even the most headstrong such probationer came to realize that his chances of being sent off to operate as a field agent were very slim. Field agents were seldom chosen from recruited staff. Field agents didn't get sent anywhere. Field agents were there already.

'You used him a lot,' said Tiptree.

I said, 'He would always find time to help. He'd type reports when all the bloody typing pool had refused to work overtime. He'd stand in the rain all night and never ask questions about the premises he'd watched. He'd go into municipal offices and spend hours rummaging through boxes of old birth certificates or ratings slips or voters' lists. And because he was a particularly rude and badly dressed probationer, and spoke ungrammatical English with a regional accent, he had no trouble convincing anyone that he was a reporter on one of our great national newspapers. That's why I used him.'

Morgan, a man with a Welsh accent who had briefly tried his hand at being a reporter for one of our great national newspapers, allowed a ghost of a smile to haunt his face.

'That hardly explains what he was doing in a departmental safe house in Bosham,' said Tiptree.

'Oh, we all know what he was doing there,' I said. 'He was lying there dead. He was lying there dead for seven days before anyone from that highly paid housekeeping department of ours bothered to check the premises.'

'Yes, those bastards,' said Bret. 'Well, I shafted those lazy sons of bitches. We won't have that trouble any more.'

'That will be very comforting for me next time I walk into a safe house and sit down in a chair so that some KGB hood can put a .44 Magnum into my cranium.'

'How do you know what kind of pistol it was,' said Henry Tiptree as casually as he was able.

'I *don't* know what kind of pistol it was, Mr Tiptree,' I said. 'I just know what kind of bullet it was; a hollow-point one that mushrooms even when the muzzle velocity is high, so it blows people apart even when it's not well aimed. And, before you ask me the supplementary question that I can see forming on your lips right now, I got that out of the ballistics sheet that was part of the file on MacKenzie's death. Maybe that's something you should read, since you are so keen to find the culprit.'

'No one is blaming you for MacKenzie's death,' said Frank gently.

'Just for Biedermann's,' I said. 'Well, that's nice to know.'

'You don't have to stand up and sing "Rule Britannia",' said Bret. 'There's been no suggestion of opening an orange file on you. We're simply trying to get at the truth. You should be more keen than anyone that we do that.'

'Then try this one on for size,' I said. 'Suppose everything is the way I say it is – and so far you've produced nothing to prove I'm wrong – and suppose my slow way of enrolling Stinnes is the best way. Then perhaps there are people in the department who'd like to see my attempt to enrol Stinnes fail.' I paused to let the words sink in. 'Suppose those people hope that, by hurrying me along and interfering with what I do, they'll keep Stinnes where he is on the other side.'

'Let me hear that again,' said Bret. His voice was hard and unyielding.

'You heard what I said, Bret. If Stinnes goes into London Debriefing Centre in the way I want him to go there – relaxed and cooperative – he'll sing. I'm telling you that there might be people, not a thousand miles from here, who are not musically inclined.'

'It's worth thinking about, Bret,' said Frank. I had voiced what Frank had already said to me in Berlin. He looked at me and gave an almost imperceptible wink.

'You're not including me?' Bret said.

'I don't know, Bret. Talk it over with your analyst. I only deal in facts.'

'No one is trying to muzzle you, wise guy,' said Bret. He was talking directly to me now, as if there was no one else in the room.

'You could have fooled me, Bret. The way I was hearing it, I'd handled the Stinnes enrolment with fumbling incompetence. People are throwing money at him, without even keeping me informed. I'd begun to think that perhaps I was not doing this exactly the way you wanted it done.'

'Don't talk to me like that,' said Bret.

'You listen to me, Bret old buddy,' I said. 'I'll talk to you any way I choose to talk. Because I'm the file officer on the Stinnes investigation. And, just in case you've forgotten, we have an old-fashioned system in this department; once an agent is assigned to a file he has full powers of decision. And he continues with his task until he closes the file or hands it over. Either way he does it of his own volition. Now you put me here in the hot seat and rig this kangaroo court to intimidate me. But I've been over there where intimidation is done by experts. So you don't frighten me, Bret. You don't frighten me at all. And if this pantomime was staged to make me abandon the Stinnes file it's been a waste of time. I'll get Stinnes. And he'll come back here and talk like a rescued castaway.'

They were embarrassed at my outburst. The lower ranks must not complain. That was something any decent school taught a chap in his first term. Frank coughed, Morgan tipped his head back to look at the ceiling, Tiptree stroked his hair, and Dicky had all his fingers arrayed along the edge of the table, selecting one to make a meal from.

'But if anyone present thinks the Stinnes file should be taken away from me, now is the time to stand up and say so.' I waited. Bret looked at me and smiled derisively. No one spoke.

I stood up and said, 'Then I'll take it as unanimously agreed that I remain file officer. And now I'm leaving you gentlemen to write up the minutes of this meeting any way you like, but don't ask me to sign them. If you want me during the next few minutes I'll be with the D-G. I'm exercising my rights under another old-fashioned rule of this department; the right to report directly to the Director-General on matters of vital concern to the service.'

Bret started to get to his feet. I said, 'Don't see me out, Bret. And don't try to head me off from seeing the old man. I made the appointment this morning and he's waiting for me right now.'

I'd got as far as the door before Bret recovered himself enough to think of a rejoinder. 'You'd better get Stinnes,' he said. 'You screw up on Stinnes and I'll have you working as a file clerk in Registry.'

'Why not?' I said. 'I've always wanted to read through the senior staff's personal files.'

I took a deep breath when I got out in the corridor. I'd come out of the belly of the whale, but there was still a rough sea.

The meeting with the D-G was the sort of civilized formality that any meeting with him always was. I wasn't, of course, reporting anything of vital concern to the service. I was just imposing on the D-G's goodwill in order to say hello to him. I always tried to have an important appointment to escape to when I suspected that a meeting would go on too long.

His room was dim and smelled of leather chairs and dusty books that were piled upon them. The D-G sat by the window behind a small desk crowded with family photos, files, trays of paperwork and long-forgotten cups of tea. It was like entering some old Egyptian tomb to chat with an affable mummy.

'Of course I remember you,' said the D-G. 'Your father, Silas Gaunt, was Controller (Europe) when I first came here.'

'No, Silas Gaunt is a distant relative but only by marriage,' I said. 'My father was Colonel Samson; Berlin Resident when Silas was Controller (Europe).'

The D-G nodded vaguely. 'Controller (Europe), the Iberian Desk . . . such ridiculous titles. I've always thought we sound like people running the overseas service of the BBC.' He gave a little chuckle. It was a joke he'd made many times before. 'And everything is going well, is it?'

The D-G didn't look like a man who would like to hear that anything was going less than well. I had the feeling that if I implied that all was not going well, the D-G would throw himself through the window without pausing to open it. I suppose everyone had the same protective feeling when talking with the D-G. That's no doubt why the department was something of a shambles. 'Yes, sir,' I said. 'Everything is going very well.' A brave man, that Bernard Samson, and truthful to a fault.

'I like to keep in touch with what's happening,' said the D-G. 'That's why I sent for you.'

'Yes, sir,' I said.

'The wretched doctor won't let me drink at all. But it doesn't look as if you're enjoying that lemon tea. Why don't you go and pour yourself a decent drink from my cupboard. What was that you said?'

'Thank you, sir.'

'I've all the time in the world,' said the D-G. 'I'd love to hear what's happening in Washington these days.'

'I've been in Berlin, sir. I work on the German Desk.'

'No matter, no matter. Tell me what's happening in Berlin. What did you say your name was again?'

'Samson, sir. Bernard Samson.'

He looked at me for a long time. 'Samson, yes, of course. You've had this frightful problem about your wife.'

'Yes, sir.'

'Mr Harrington explained your difficulties to me. Did he tell you we're hoping to get some supplementary payment for you?'

'Yes, sir. That would be most helpful.'

'Don't worry about the children. They'll come to no harm, I guarantee it.' The D-G smiled. 'Promise, now. You'll stop worrying about the children.'

'Yes, sir. I promise.'

'Samson. Yes, of course. I've always had a knack for remembering names,' he said.

After leaving the D-G's office I went into the toilet and found myself sharing a hot-air drier with Frank Harrington.

'Feeling better now, Bernard?' he said humorously.

'Better than I was before? Or better than the people at that meeting of Bret's?'

'Oh, you left us in no doubt about that, my dear fellow. You made your superiority more than clear to everyone present. What did you do to the D-G, ask him for his resignation?' He saw me look round and added. 'It's quite all right; there's no one else here.'

'I said what needed saying,' I said defensively.

'And you said it very well. Bret went home to change his underpants.'

'That will be the day,' I said.

'You underestimate the effect of your passionate outbursts, Bernard. Bret has only himself to blame. Your little dig about a kangaroo court went home. Bret was distressed; he even told us he was distressed. He spent ten minutes singing your praises to convince us all that it wasn't anything of the kind. But, Bernard, you're inclined to the overkill.'

'Is that a warning, Frank?'

'Advice, Bernard. Advice.'

'To guard my tongue?'

'Not at all. I always enjoy your tantrums except when I'm on the receiving end of them. I enjoyed seeing you scare them half to death in there.'

'Scare them?'

'Of course. They know how easily you can make a fool of them. Bret still hasn't forgotten that joke you made about his visit to Berlin last year.'

'I've forgotten what I said.'

'Well, he hasn't forgotten. You said he went up the steps at Checkpoint Charlie and looked over the Wall. He didn't like that, Bernard.'

'But that's what he did do. He lined up behind a busload of tourists and went up the steps to look over the God-damned Wall.'

'Of course he did. That's why he didn't join in the laughter. If Dicky had said it, or anyone else in the office without field experience, it wouldn't have mattered. But coming from you it caused Bret a loss of dignity; and dignity means a lot to Bret.' All the time Frank was smiling to show me what a good joke it all was.

'But?'

'But one at a time, Bernard, old friend. Don't antagonize a whole roomful of people all at once. It's a dangerous sport, old lad. They get together when they have something in common. Just one at a time in future. Right?'

'Right, Frank.'

'Your father would have enjoyed that shindig you put on for us. He wouldn't have approved, of course. Not your father's style; we both know that. But he would have enjoyed it, Bernard.'

Why did that last remark of Frank's please me so much? Do we never shed the tyranny of our father's love?

22

By the time I had finished my day at the office I was not in the right mood to face an aggrieved husband, even a mistakenly aggrieved one. But I'd suggested to George that we had a drink together and it was better to get it over soon. He suggested that we meet at the new apartment he'd bought in Mayfair, so I went there directly from the office.

It was a huge place on two floors of a house in Mount Street towards the Hyde Park end. Although I knew that it was still unoccupied. I was unprepared for the bare floorboards and the smell of the newly plastered walls.

George was there already. He was only thirty-six years old but he seemed to do everything he could to make himself appear at least ten years older than that. Born in Poplar, where the River Thames made a mighty loop that was the heart of London's dockland, he'd left school at fifteen to help support his crippled father. By the time he was twenty-one he was driving a Rolls Royce, albeit an old one he was trying to sell.

George's small stature contributed to the impression of restless energy as he moved from room to room in short paces, stooping, tapping, measuring and checking everything in sight. He had heavy spectacles that constantly slipped down his nose, wavy hair that was silver grey at the temples, and a large moustache. From his appearance it was easy to believe that his parents were Polish immigrants, but the flattened vowels of his East London accent, and his frequently dropped aitches, always came as a surprise. Sometimes I wondered if he cultivated this cockney voice as some sort of asset for his car deals.

'Well, there you are, Bernard,' he said. 'Good to see you. Very nice.' He greeted me more like a prospect than like someone he suspected of dalliance with his wife.

'It's quite a place you have here, George,' I said.

'We'll go for a drink in a moment. I must get the measuring done before the daylight goes. There's no juice here yet, see.' He clicked the electricity switch to prove it.

He was dressed in a flashy dark-blue suit with a pattern of chalk stripes that made him look even shorter than he really was. It was all obviously expensive – the silk shirt and floral Cardin tie, and the black brogue shoes – for George liked everyone to see immediately that he was the poor boy who'd made good. 'I want to talk to you about Tessa,' I said.

'Uh-huh.' George could make that sound mean anything; 'yes', 'no' or 'maybe'. He was measuring the length of the room. 'Hold that,' he said, giving me the end of the tape measure to hold against one side of the fireplace. 'Pale-gold carpet in here,' he said. 'What do you think?'

'Very elegant,' I said. I crouched to help him measure the hearth. 'I'm grateful that you've let her help take care of the children while I was away,' I said in what I thought was a diplomatic approach.

'She didn't ask me,' said George. 'She never asks me anything. She just does what she wants.' He wound up the tape suddenly so that it slipped from my fingers.

I stood up. 'The nanny doesn't like being alone at night,' I explained.

George stood up suddenly and stared into my eyes with a pained expression on his face. 'Five foot six inches,' he said. He rolled up the last few inches of tape, using the little handle, and then tucked it under his arm while he wrote the measurement on his hand in bright-blue ball-point pen. 'Do you mind?' he said. He gave me the end of the tape and was already backing across the room to measure the width of it.

'I thought I should have a word with you,' I said.

'What about?'

'About Tessa.' I reached down to hold the end of the tape against the wall. He pulled it taut and peered closely at the tape in the fast-disappearing daylight.

'What about Tessa?' said George, writing on his hand again.

'She's been sleeping round at my place. I thought I should say thank you.'

He looked at me and gave a wry smile.

'I like Tessa,' I said. 'But I wouldn't like you to get the wrong idea.'

'What idea would be the wrong one?'

'About me and Tessa,' I said.

'Your intentions are strictly honourable, are they?' said George, pronouncing the aitch as if determined to get it wrong. He walked to the other end of the room and tested a floorboard with his heel. It creaked as he put his weight on it. He pulled a face and then went to the window and looked down into the street. 'I just like to make sure the car is all right,' he explained.

'I don't have any intentions,' I said. I was getting irritated with him and I allowed it into my voice.

'Just talk, is it?' His voice was only a shade louder, but from the other end of the room it seemed to pick up some echo and was resonant in the large empty room. 'You and Tessa: you just chat together. Companionship, is it?'

'Of course we talk,' I said.

'Talk about me, I suppose. You give her advice about me, I imagine. How to make our marriage work. That sort of thing.'

'Sometimes,' I admitted.

'Well, that's worse,' he said without raising his voice. 'How would you like it if it was your wife talking to other men about how to handle you? How would you like it, eh?'

'I don't know,' I admitted. Put like that it made me feel bad.

'I'd rather you jumped into bed with her. A quick impersonal frolic like that can be overlooked.' He came nearer and stroked the marble fireplace. 'I put that fireplace in,' he said. 'Marble. It came out of a beautiful old house in Bristol.' Carefully he tested the newly plastered patch on the wall where the antique fireplace had been installed. And then he stepped close to say, 'But she has the gall to tell me how much she likes talking with you. It's a bloody cheek, Bernard.'

It was almost as if he was having two conversations with two different people. He turned to stroke the newly prepared wall. In a quieter voice he said, 'Pale-grey stripes this wallpaper will be, Regency pattern. It will go well with our furniture. Remember that lovely Georgian commode – the serpentine-fronted piece? It's hidden in the hall now; you can't get a proper look at. Well, that's going in a place of honour, on that far wall. And over it there'll be an oval mirror – Georgian rococo, a great wreath of gilded leaves – a beautiful piece that I bought at Sotheby's last week. Original mirror; the frame has been restored, but really well done. I paid a damned sight too much for it but I was bidding against a dealer. I never mind taking anything one bid beyond a dealer. After all, he's going to mark it up fifty per cent, isn't he?'

'I suppose so,' I said.

'Of course he is.'

'I'd like to be good friends with you, George,' I said. 'Good friends with you both.'

'Why?' said George.

'Why?' I repeated.

'We're not exactly blood relations, are we? We only met because we married two birds who are sisters. You don't care about me, and I don't care about you. Why should you want to be friends with me?'

'Okay,' I said angrily. 'So let's not be friends. But I'm not screwing your wife and I've got no plans to try. And if you're too bloody dumb to appreciate what I'm trying to say, you can go to hell.'

'Dark-blue tiles in the dining room,' said George, opening a sliding door and stepping through it. 'Imported from Italy. Some people say tiles make a room too noisy. But in a dining room I like a bit of a rumpus. We'll keep the same dining table. It's an old piece of Victorian junk but it was the first piece of furniture my parents ever owned. My Dad bought it when they got married.' He pushed his glasses up with his forefinger. ''Course getting rid of the house in Hampstead won't be any picnic. The property game is tough right now. I'll lose money on it.'

'I'm sure you explained that to the people you bought this place from,' I said.

He gave a quick, appreciative grin. 'Ah, you're right. Property is always a good investment, Bernard. And when the market is depressed a sensible man should buy the most valuable things he can afford. I'll drop anything up to twenty-five grand on the Hampstead place but I reckon I'm getting this at about eighty grand less than it would go for in normal times. And I'll do it through my own company's pension fund and save a lot on tax.'

'Tessa thinks you don't love her any more.'

'She's led me a dance, Bernard. No need to tell you that. She's been a rotten wife.'

It was true. What could I say to him. 'Perhaps things could be different. She feels neglected, George. Perhaps you give too much time to your work.'

'My business is all I've got,' he said. He raised the tape and measured the dining-room window for no reason except to have something to do with his hands. 'She's a cruel woman. You don't know how cruel.' He stepped through the doorway into the kitchen and his voice echoed in the smaller space. 'I'm putting self-cleaning American ovens in here. The bloody fool who's supplying them was practically telling me the German ovens were better.'

'And are the German ovens better?'

'I don't care what they're like; don't expect me to buy anything German. My Dad would turn in his grave. Bad enough selling bloody Jap cars. Anyway, that idiot didn't know an oven from a vacuum cleaner. You don't think I go into a shop and ask the opinion of the people selling the goods, do you?'

'Don't you?'

'It would be like expecting someone to come into one of my show-rooms asking me what's the best sort of car. The best sort of car is the one that pays me the biggest mark up. No, the Americans are the only people who can design self-cleaning ovens.' He sniffed. 'She's suddenly decided that she can't drink anything but champagne.

It's costing me a fortune but I don't stop her – she's only doing it to make me angry. She thinks it's very funny.'

'Oh, I don't know about that. She drinks champagne at my house too.'

'She drinks it at a lot of houses but it's always my champagne she drinks.'

'Perhaps you're right,' I said.

'She needn't have made such a show of it,' he said sadly. 'She could have been discreet. She didn't have to make me a laughing stock, did she?' He opened the door of the high-level oven and looked inside. 'She's a good cook, Tessa. She likes to pretend she's a bad cook but she can make use of a decent kitchen.'

'Perhaps she didn't realize . . .'

He closed the oven door and then studied the complicated array of dials and the clock that controlled the cooking. 'She realized. Women realize everything, everything to do with love affairs and those antics. Women realize that, all right. She realized that she was hurting me. Don't make any mistake about that, Bernard.' He said it without any rancour, as if discussing some particular feature of the oven.

'I didn't know you felt so bitter,' I said.

'I'm not bitter. Look at this apartment. Does it look as if I'm bitter?'

'Tessa is worried that you went to Italy with someone else,' I said tentatively.

'I know she is. Let her worry.'

'If it's serious, George, you should tell her. It would be better for both of you.'

He sighed. 'My brother Stefan and his wife were on holiday in Rome. We spent a couple of days in the same hotel. Got it?'

'So when Tessa asked for Mrs Kosinski the hotel thought she meant your sister-in-law? Why don't you tell Tessa that?'

'She never asked me,' said George. 'She lectures me and argues. She never asks me anything.'

'Women are like that,' I said. 'You're not thinking of a divorce, then?'

'No, Bernard, I'm not thinking of a divorce.' He stepped into another small room that had obviously been used as a laundry room. Even the plumbing for the washing-machine was still in the wall. The room was painted white with a grey-tiled floor and a central drain. 'This would make a nice little darkroom, wouldn't it?'

'I suppose so,' I said.

'But Tessa says she'd like a little room for sewing. Sounds a funny idea to me, having a room just for sewing, but that's what she wants, so I said okay. There's a bathroom that I can make into a darkroom.

In a way it's a shame to use a room with a good window for photography when I can easily make do with one of the inside rooms.' He moved into the next room and tried the switch, even though he knew that there was no electricity. 'The feelings I had for her have died, of course. There's no love that can survive the battering that a constantly unfaithful wife gives.' The daylight was disappearing and his face was rimmed with a reddish-gold line. He looked out of the window to get another glimpse of his parked car.

I said, 'It sounds like a grim prospect, George, living with someone you don't love.'

'Does it? It would to you, of course. But I'm a Catholic.' Of course, how could I have forgotten? I felt a fool for having mentioned divorce, and George must have known that, for he quickly added, 'No crucifix in the living room, no gold cross dangling round my neck, but I'm a Catholic and my faith is important to me. I'm up before six in the morning, so I can be at seven o'clock mass and not be late for work. My Dad and Mum were the same. Until Dad fell into the hold of a ship and smashed his legs and spent the rest of his days in the wheelchair. After that she took him to a later mass. Back in Poland both my mother's brothers are priests. I wasn't brainy enough for the priesthood but my faith is strong.' He smiled. I suppose by now he knew how surprising such announcements could be to people who thought of him as a cockney capitalist who would bow only before Mammon. 'It will be easier for me here. I'll go to mass at Farm Street. I am Jesuitical . . .' He smiled. 'Always have been. And its only a few steps along the road. It's a wonderful little church and I'll get an extra few minutes in bed every morning.' He smiled artfully but I couldn't imagine anyone for whom an extra few minutes in bed would make so little difference.

'She's insecure,' I said. 'Tessa is insecure.'

'Is that what she told you?'

'She's very vulnerable, George. She needs reassurance. You surely realize that all that flamboyance conceals a terrible lack of self-confidence. Fiona always said it was the second-child syndrome. And now I see it happening with my own children too. Tessa grew up in the shadow of a brilliant, strong-willed sister.'

'You missed out the domineering father,' said George. He took his hat from the ladder where he'd left it and said, 'You've thought about it a lot, I can see. Perhaps we married the wrong sisters. Perhaps you could have stopped Tessa going off the rails in a way that I failed to do.' It was difficult to know if he was being sarcastic or serious.

'And you could have stopped Fiona going off the rails in a way that I failed to do. Is that what you mean?'

'Who knows?' said George.

'I'm beginning to think Fiona hates me,' I said. I don't know why

I suddenly confided to him something I'd admitted to no one else, except that George had the dispassionate manner of a highly paid medical specialist. And, I suppose, of the confessional.

'You're a reproach to her,' he said unhesitatingly. Perhaps he'd thought about it before. 'You make her feel small. You make her feel cheap.'

'You think that's how she sees it?'

'Betraying your country is like betraying your partner. And when a marriage breaks up it can't count as a success for either party; it's a mutual failure. How can Fiona bear to think of you continuing, business as normal with the job, the kids and the home. It makes her look silly, Bernard. It makes her look like a spoiled little girl playing at politics, no better than any of these loud-mouthed film actresses who like to pretend they're political activists. Of course Fiona hates you.' He had been toying with his hat but now he put it on his head, as a signal that he wanted to change the subject. 'Now if you'd still like a drink, let's go round to the Connaught. I prefer hotels and a comfortable place to sit down. I'm not very keen on pubs for pleasure. I see too much of them when I'm doing business. A sandwich too, if you like. I've nothing to go home for.'

'It was my invitation,' I reminded him. 'Let me buy you dinner, George.'

'That's very decent of you, Bernard. I see you're still running that old Ford. I wish you'd let me fix you up with something better.'

'As a prospect, George, I'm a pushover.'

'Good. Good. There's nothing I enjoy more than selling a man a car,' said George, and he seemed quite serious. He was relaxed now; a changed person now that our difficult conversation was over. Perhaps he'd been dreading it as much as I had. 'And I've got a set of wheels that would be right up your street, Bernard. A couple of villains bought a car from me and got her ready for a big payroll hold-up. The brakes and steering are superb and she gave me a hundred and sixty up the motorway without a murmur of complaint. She'd come cheap, Bernard. Interested?'

'Why cheap, George?'

'The bodywork's in poor condition and it's not worth my while to do anything about that. When people come to buy cars they don't want to know about brakes and steering, and not one in ten wants to look at the engine, Bernard. I buy and sell bodywork. I tell all my workpeople that.'

'I'm interested.'

'Of course you are. A battered-looking car that will kick sand into the face of a Mercedes 450 is just your style. Come and have a look at it some time. I'll keep it for you.'

'Thanks, George.'

'I've had a funny sort of day today,' he volunteered. 'The police phoned up this morning and said they'd recovered a solid-silver wine cooler we'd had stolen. Not so very old, but it's a lovely piece, very ornate. I thought I'd never see it again. A youngster who used to work for me as a mechanic had tried to sell it to an antique dealer at the Portobello Road market. The dealer guessed it was stolen and told the police.'

Tessa's 'ice bucket' was George's 'wine cooler', I noticed. It was the same with so many things. They seemed to have so little in common that it was a wonder they'd ever got married. 'You were lucky to get it back,' I said.

He took a last proud look at his new apartment before double-locking the front door and then turning the mortise lock as well. 'The kid thought it was silver-plated Britannia metal; he didn't recognize it as solid silver. Stupid, eh? That would make anyone suspicious. He was a good little worker too, only nineteen years old but I was paying him a very good salary. Strange thing to do; to steal something from a man's home, isn't it?'

'Yes, it is.'

But the 'Jesuitical' George debated against himself. 'On the other hand, I exposed him to temptation, didn't I? I invited him to a house with such valuable things on show. I have to bear some measure of guilt. I told the police constable that.'

'What did he say?'

'He said he couldn't get into a discussion about ethics and morality; he had quite enough trouble trying to understand the law.' George laughed. 'Criminal activity is one per cent motivation and ninety-nine per cent opportunity. You must have heard me say that, Bernard.'

'It sounds familiar, George,' I said.

The prospect of returning to Mexico – even without Dicky – was daunting. I wanted to stay here; to see more of the children, get a bellyful of home cooking and an earful of Mozart. Instead I was headed for a round of plastic hotels, 'international cuisine' and Muzak.

I got home before midnight, having spent a pleasant evening dining with George. He'd gone on about what he described as exactly the right car for me: 'Shabby appearance but a lot of poke under the bonnet.' Was that what George felt about me, or subconscious reflections upon his own shortcomings?

I couldn't go to bed until the duty messenger arrived with my airline tickets. Feeling sorry for myself, I wandered into the nursery and fingered Sally's 'Joke Book': 'How do you catch a monkey? – Hang upside-down in a tree and make a noise like a banana.' And in Billy's book of children's verse I found Kipling:

> Five and twenty ponies,
> Trotting through the dark –
> Brandy for the Parson,
> 'Baccy for the Clerk;
> Laces for a lady, letters for a spy,
> Watch the wall, my darling, while the Gentlemen go by!

And I'd promised to get batteries for their radio-controlled racing car and try to mend Sally's Donald Duck alarm clock. I'd missed both their birthdays this year and now they were packed off to Tessa's cousin. I felt guilty about them, but I couldn't refuse to go back to Mexico. I needed the department's backing.

If I said goodbye to the department I had no qualifications that would get me a comparable pay packet elsewhere. The department wouldn't fix a job for me. On the contrary, there would be those who'd say my resignation showed I was implicated in Fiona's activities. That had been made clear enough at the meeting. There was no choice but to be an exemplary employee of the department, a reliable professional, who produced solid results while the others produced empty rhetoric. And if, as I did my job without fear or favour and cleared myself of suspicion, some of the department's more outstanding incompetents got trampled underfoot, that would suit me fine.

The doorbell rang. 11.45. My God, but they took their time. There had been no sound of a motorcycle, and that was unusual for deliveries at this time of night. Bearing in mind Werner's ominous warnings about KGB hit teams, I opened the door very cautiously and stood well back in the shadows.

'Good evening, Mr Samson. What's the matter?'

It was Gloria Kent. 'Nothing.'

'You were expecting a motorcycle messenger, were you?'

She was damned quick on the uptake. 'Yes, I was.'

'Can I come in for a moment? I'm on my way home from seeing my boyfriend.'

'You've missed your last train,' I said sourly. 'Yes, come in.'

She was wearing a fur hat and a tan suede coat, trimmed with brown leather. Its big fur collar was buttoned up to the gold-coloured scarf at her throat. The coat was cut to emphasize her hips, and the flare of its hem meant you couldn't miss the shiny leather boots. I noticed the McDouglas Paris label as I took the coat from her to hang up. It was lined with some expensive-looking fur. It wasn't a coat you could afford on the salary of a Grade 9 executive officer. I supposed those people in Epsom must have had very well-cared-for teeth.

She sat down without invitation. She had a small case with her and she kept this by her side. 'I wanted to say thank you,' she said.

'What for?'

'For not sending me back down to Registry. For letting me stay upstairs and help your secretary. I thought you'd be angry. I thought you'd get rid of me.'

'I wouldn't want you to suffer for my error of judgement,' I said.

She smiled. 'Could you spare a very small glass of that delicious brandy I had last time? Martell, I think it was.'

'Sure.' I poured small measures into two glasses and gave her one. 'Did you leave some bath oil here? Secret of Venus?'

'Oh, good. Did you find it?'

'My sister-in-law did.'

'Oh dear.' Gloria laughed and drank half of her brandy in one go, and then all but coughed. 'It's cold tonight,' she said. She put the glass down and got the case on to her knees. 'I wanted to tell you that I'm sorry about what happened. I felt the least I could do was to make up for the damage I did.' She opened the case. It contained men's undershirts and underpants, all new and in transparent wrappings.

I wasn't going to let her make a fool of me a second time. I wondered if some of the other girls in the office were in on the joke. 'It's not my size,' I snapped.

She looked dismayed. 'But it is. "Marks and Spencer's; Cotton; Large." I noticed when I was . . . when I was cutting them up. I'm terribly sorry about that, Mr Samson. It was a childish thing to do.'

'We were both childish,' I said. She didn't smile, but I was still uncertain about her.

'But I was the one who did the damage.'

'I've replaced them. I don't need them.'

'I thought about that. But Marks and Sparks are very good at changing things. They even let you have cash refunds . . .' She looked at my face as she took a large manilla envelope from the case. 'Your tickets for Mexico City are here, and there's three hundred pounds in traveller's cheques. The tickets and cheques are made out in the name of Samson but I could change them first thing in the morning if you are on some other passport. If you want to use them, the traveller's cheques should be signed right away; the cashier's office hates letting them go out of their hands blank like this. Your secretary wasn't sure about what name or passport you'd be using. She said you preferred to keep that sort of information to yourself.'

'Thanks, Gloria. Samson will be fine.'

'Will you let me put these things away for you?' she said. She got to her feet, gulped the rest of her brandy and made for the stairs. I was going to say no but she was already on her way.

I shrugged.

She'd been upstairs about five minutes when I heard a heavy thump that made me think she'd knocked over the bedside TV set. I hurried upstairs and went into the bedroom. It was dark, but by the light of the bedside lamp I could see Gloria's clothes and silk underwear trailed across the room. Gloria was on the far side of the bed. She was stark naked. She'd just finished righting the heavy chair she'd knocked on its side. Now she stood arms akimbo as if about to do her morning gymnastics. 'What the hell . . . ?' I said. I switched on the other bedside light.

'It was the only way I could think of getting you up here,' she said. 'It would have been corny to call to you.'

'Cut it out, Gloria. You said you've just come from your boyfriend.' She had a magnificent figure, and I found it impossible not to stare at her.

'There's no boyfriend. I said that in case you had some woman here already.'

'What's the joke?'

'No joke. I want a second chance on what I declined the other day. I was thinking about it. I was silly.' She climbed into bed and pulled the duvet over her up to her neck. She shivered. 'Hey, this bed is freezing cold. Haven't you ever heard of electric blankets? Come and warm me up.'

I hesitated.

'No security risk, Bernard. I've been vetted and cleared for all categories of documents.' She smiled dreamily and shook her head so that her hair shone in the lamplight. 'Come along, action man. Office talk says you are impulsive and instinctive.' She must have seen something in my face, for she quickly added. 'No, no one at the office knows. Your secretary thinks I gave the tickets to the duty messenger. It's not a joke, I swear it.'

She was irresistible. She was so young and so earnest. I undressed. She said nothing but she watched me, smiling to share the absurdity of our folly. As I got into bed she stretched right over me to switch off the light. I wanted her; I grabbed her.

Afterwards, long afterwards, I found myself staring at the bedside table that stood at what had once been my wife's side of the bed. There was a glimmer of light coming from the hall. I could see a history book that Fiona had never read beyond page 30, a comb and a packet of aspirins. She always combed her hair as she got out of bed in the morning. It was almost a reflex action, done before she was fully awake.

'Don't go to sleep,' said Gloria.

'I've never been more awake.'

'Are you thinking about your wife . . . your children.'

'The children are away.'

'I know that, you fool. I know everything about you, now that I work with your secretary.'

'Have you been prying?' I said with pretended severity.

'Of course I have. It's what we do, isn't it?'

'Not to each other.'

'Sometimes to each other,' she corrected me.

'Yes, sometimes to each other,' I said.

'I wish you trusted me . . . really trusted me.'

'Why?'

'Because I love you,' she said.

'You don't love me. I'm old enough to be your father.'

'What's that got to do with love?'

'It could never come to anything; you and me . . . it could never come to anything serious, Gloria.'

'Do you hate that name – Gloria?'

'No, of course not.'

'Because you say it as if you hated it. My family call me Zu, its short for Zsuzsa.'

'Well, Zu, I don't hate the name Gloria . . .'

She laughed and hugged me, and bent her head to bite my shoulder in mock anger. Then suddenly she was serious and, stroking the blue-striped cotton duvet, she said, 'Have you been in this bed with other women? Since your wife left you, have you?'

I didn't answer.

'I didn't realize that. It was insensitive of me.'

'No, it's good. I can't stay celibate for the rest of my life.'

'You still love her?'

'I miss her. You live with someone, you have children and watch them grow up. You worry together, you share bad times . . . she's a part of my life.'

'Will she come back, do you think?'

'It's not something we should be discussing,' I said. 'There was an official reminder circulated in the office about her. My wife's disappearance is now covered by the Official Secrets Act.'

'I don't care about the office, Bernard. I care about you . . .' A long pause. 'And about me.'

'She won't come back. They never come back.'

'You're angry,' she said. 'You're not sad, you're angry. It's not the political betrayal, it's the personal betrayal that is making you so bitter.'

'Nonsense,' I said.

I could see clearly now as my eyes adjusted to the dim light from the hall. She propped herself up on her elbow to see my face better. The bed covering slid from her shoulders and the light traced the lines of her nakedness. 'It's not nonsense. Your wife didn't defect because she read *Das Kapital*. She must have worked on a one-to-one basis with a Soviet case officer. For years she did that. It was an assignment; a romance, a seduction. No matter how chaste the physical relationship between them, your wife was seduced.'

'It's a romantic idea, Zu, but that's not exactly the way these things work.'

'Women have personal relationships. They don't give loyalty to abstractions the way that men do.'

'You're letting your imagination run away with you because this particular Soviet agent is a woman. Most spies are men.'

'Most spies are homosexuals,' she said. And that stopped me short. So many of the ones placed in Western society were homosexuals – latent or active – and it is true that the KGB depended upon regular and frequent personal contact. Our people in the East could not move so easily, and personal contact was confined to emergencies.

'Homosexuals are the most socially mobile element in Western society,' I said glibly.

'Promiscuous, you mean. Cabinet Minister one night, laboratory technician the next. Is that what you mean?'

'That's what I mean.'

'I hope you don't think I'm promiscuous,' she said, moving from the general to the personal in that way that women so often do.

'Aren't you?' I said.

'Don't be beastly, darling.' She put her hand out and touched my face. 'What are you thinking about?'

I remembered what Stinnes had told the clumsy Pavel Moskvin in the empty Biedermann beach-house in Mexico. You rush in like a rapist when we are in the middle of a seduction, he said. On more than one occasion I'd spoken in the same terms. I'd warned Dicky that Stinnes was not being recruited, he was being enrolled. Recruiting is a seduction, I'd told him, but enrolment is a divorce. You recruit an agent by glamorizing that innocent's future. But an enemy agent like Stinnes is not susceptible to romance. You bring him over by promises of house, motor car and payments of alimony. 'Nothing,' I answered.

'You can be so distant,' she said suddenly. 'You make me feel as if I was no longer here. No longer necessary.'

'I'm sorry,' I said. I reached and pulled her close to me. Her body was cold as she snuggled against me, and I pulled the bedclothes up almost over our faces. She kissed me. 'You're here; you're necessary,' I said.

'I do love you, Bernard. I know you think I'm immature but I love you desperately.'

'I think you're very mature,' I said, caressing her.

'Oh, yes,' she said dreamily. And then, as the thought came to her, 'You won't hide me from your children, will you?'

'No, I won't.'

'Promise?'

'Of course.'

'I'm good with children.'

'You're good with grown-ups too,' I said.

'Oh, yes,' she said. She snuggled down in the bed and cuddled me. I stayed awake as long as I could. I was frightened of going to sleep in case I had another nightmare about MacKenzie and woke up screaming and bathed in sweat the way I had two or three times before. But eventually I dozed off. I didn't dream at all. Gloria was good for me.

24

It was like stepping into a sauna bath to get off the plane into the heat of Mexico City. I arrived on a particularly bad day, when the humidity and temperature had reached a record-breaking high. Like a city under bombardment, the steamy streets echoed with constant rolls of distant thunder that never got louder. And black-headed cumulo-nimbus clouds, poised over the mountains, did not bring the threatened rainstorms. Such weather played upon the nerves of even the most acclimatized inhabitants, and the police statistics show a pattern of otherwise unaccountable violence that peaks at this time of year.

'I'll have to talk with Stinnes,' I told Werner. 'I've got to see him face to face.' We were in the apartment that belonged to Zena's uncle. The list of breakages hanging by the phone had grown much longer. Perhaps that was another sign of the way the oppressive weather made everyone so jumpy. I was reluctant to move away from the air-conditioner, but the air coming through it was warm, and the noise of the motor was so loud that it was difficult to hear what Werner was saying in reply. I cupped my ear.

'He'll be ready to go on Friday,' said Werner, raising his voice as he said it a second time. 'Just as London requested. Friday; no sooner and no later.' Even Werner, who seemed to enjoy the hot weather, had finally succumbed to the high humidity. He was shirtless and continually gulping deep draughts of iced lemonade. I'd told him that it would not help but he persisted. Werner could be very stubborn at times.

I said, 'London will not authorize the payment of such a large sum of money until someone on the spot checks with the recipient and okays it, and I am the someone on the spot.'

Zena came into the room bringing more iced lemonade. She said, 'His embassy has restricted everyone's movements. It's not so easy for them to go strolling in and out as they used to do.'

'I find that difficult to believe,' I said. 'Stinnes is a KGB man. He doesn't have to take any notice of anything the embassy says; he can tell the ambassador to drop dead.'

Zena interpreted my response as a sign of nervousness. 'It will be all right,' she said, and smiled at me in the patronizing way she did so often with Werner.

'It won't be all right,' I said. 'London won't authorize the money . . . not this kind of money.'

'Then tell London that they must authorize it,' said Zena.

'My standing with London Central is not so good that they will take my orders so readily,' I explained. 'They'll want some questions answered.'

'What questions?' said Werner.

'They'll ask why Stinnes is so insistent upon having the money up front.'

'Why not?' said Zena, who would be surprised at anyone wanting money any other way.

'What's the hurry?' I said. 'Why won't Stinnes wait until he's in the UK? What's Stinnes going to do in the middle of Mexico City with a suitcase full of pound notes?'

'American dollar bills,' said Zena. 'That's what he asked for, used hundred-dollar bills.'

Zena's manner annoyed me and I snapped at her. 'Golden sovereigns, zlotys, shark teeth or cowrie shells . . . what's the difference?' I said. 'Why carry a case filled with cash through a rough town like this? What's wrong with a bank transfer or a letter of credit or even a bearer bond?

'I wonder if Erich thought of sovereigns,' said Zena. 'Do you know, I think he might have preferred sovereigns or krugerrands, even, to US paper. How heavy would it be in gold?'

I ignored her question. 'Whatever he chooses to have as a payment, he'll still have it with him when he gets into the car, won't he? So if we were acting in bad faith we could easily take it away from him. I can't see what's in his mind.'

'I don't think he'll have it with him,' said Zena very casually, as if wondering whether the storm would come and the rain cool the streets. 'Erich is clever. He'll put it away somewhere where no one else can get their hands on it.'

'Will he?' I said.

'That's what I'd do,' said Zena.

'Nip into the bank, and give it to the cashier?' I said mockingly.

She rose to my bait. 'Or give it to someone he trusts,' said Zena.

I laughed. 'He gives his money to someone he trusts, but delivers his body to people he doesn't trust? I'd say anyone who followed that line of reasoning is an imbecile.' I looked at her to see what made her so sure about what Stinnes had in mind. There was no doubt that she had great influence over him. Now I began to wonder if

Zena was thinking of delivering him to us, and then stealing his money from him. Poor Erich Stinnes.

'No doubt you do,' she said haughtily. 'That's because, now your wife has left you, you have no faith or trust in anything or anyone. But there are trustworthy people in this world.'

'Yes,' I said. 'There are trustworthy people in this world, but you have to take such unacceptable risks to find out who they are.'

She smiled as if pitying me and with unmuted sarcasm said, 'Life is difficult, isn't it? You have to risk what you need to get what you want.' She picked up the coffee-cups from the table and put them on a tray, making more noise than was necessary. 'I have to go out, Werner,' she said, as if by adding his name I would not be privy to this item of information.

'Yes, darling,' said Werner.

'Goodbye, Mrs Volkmann,' I said. 'It was nice to talk with you.' She glared at me. She knew I'd come back to the apartment with Werner only because I knew she had an appointment.

'I wish you and Zena got along better,' said Werner after she had gone.

'You mean you wish I'd be more polite to her.'

'She's not the easiest of people to get along with,' said Werner. 'But you always seem to say the wrong things.'

'Did you get the gun for me, Werner?'

I did my best. I followed him over to the big bookcase in which chinaware was displayed. He opened a locked drawer. Reaching into it, and groping about behind the cloth-wrapped silver cutlery, he got a Colt .38 Detective Special. He handed it to me. I took it from the fancy tooled-leather holster and examined it. Its nickel finish had almost all worn off; it must have been a quarter of a century old. At some recent time it had been fitted with a hammer shroud to reduce the chance of its discharging accidentally and shooting a hole in someone's foot. 'I know you wanted a small automatic with a silencer but this is all I could get at such short notice,' said Werner apologetically.

'It's fine,' I said. I tried to say something nice about it other than it might be a valuable antique. 'These steel-frame guns are easier to hold against the recoil the short barrel gives. I just want it to wave about, in case Stinnes suddenly has a change of mind.'

'Only one box of bullets, but they are not too ancient.'

'It's Stinnes. I just don't like the feel of it, Werner,' I said. I stuck the gun in the waist of my trousers and almost fell to the floor with the weight of it. I needed the box of bullets in my pocket to balance me. 'It's almost as if Zena doesn't want me to see Stinnes.'

'She's become protective about him. She thinks London Central are out to swindle everyone. And frankly, Bernard, you don't do very much to lessen her suspicions.'

'And what about you?' I asked. 'Do you share the suspicions?'

'If *you* were promising Stinnes the money, I'd be sure he was going to get it. But they're keeping you out of all that, aren't they?'

'They'll have to send me the money soon. They'll have to have it here by Friday or they can't expect me to get him on to the plane.'

Werner pinched his nose with his finger and thumb. 'Well, I'm not sure London will send you the money,' he said.

'What do you mean, Werner?'

'Your friend Henry Tiptree arrived here in the city. What would you bet me that he's not arranging the cash payment. They'll keep you out of it, Bernard.'

'Tiptree? How do you know?'

'I know,' said Werner. 'Perhaps it's just as well. Let him play his secret games if that's what London wants him to do. It's right what you said, Bernie. It's dangerous to carry a bagful of cash across this town. There are plenty of people here who'll knife you for fifty centavos. Plenty of them.'

'But I still don't understand why Zena is so keen to prevent me meeting Stinnes,' I said. 'We can't go on with this absurd business of me talking to you and Zena, and then you bringing messages back from Stinnes. It was all right at the beginning but now time is tight.'

'What difference does it make?' said Werner. 'You talking to him; me talking to him; Zena talking to him. What's the difference?'

'If Stinnes pulls out at the last moment. Or if there is some other kind of cock-up . . . and it's quite possible that something will go wrong . . . then I'd like to think it was my fault rather than yours.'

'It will be all right,' said Werner. 'But Erich is very nervous. He has enemies there in the office with him; it's dangerous for him.'

He was 'Erich' now to both the Volkmanns. I didn't like that; it was too personal. Better to keep a doctor–patient relationship in this sort of operation just in case it got very rough. 'He should have thought of that when he was vacillating,' I said.

'It's a big step, Bernie.'

'Yes, it is.' I went over to the air-conditioner. I held my hand in front of the outlet but the air was still not much cooled.

'It makes a lot of noise but doesn't work very well,' explained Werner. 'The Mexicans call them "politicians".'

'And if I have to finally submit to London a report about a cock-up, they are immediately going to ask me why the hell I didn't insist on seeing Stinnes for myself.'

'Erich knows what's at stake,' said Werner. 'He's an experienced agent. It will be just as if we were doing it. We'd make sure we got it right, wouldn't we?'

'He'd better get it right,' I said. 'He won't be able to go back to his embassy and say he's had a change of mind.'

'Why won't he?' said Werner. 'We've known that to happen before, haven't we? I thought that's why London were so keen to load him on to the plane and get him away.'

'London have thought of that one,' I said. 'As soon as they get the telex to say that we have Stinnes, they'll leak a story to one of the news agencies. It will say that we have a high-grade KGB defector who has been supplying information for some years. And the chosen reporter will even have some details of the intelligence that good old Stinnes is said to have provided to them.'

Now Werner pinched the cloth of his undershirt between finger and thumb and pulled it away from his body to let some air get to him. 'Erich Stinnes has never passed anything back to London, has he?'

'What do you think?'

'I'd think that's just London Central dropping him into the dirt so he doesn't dare think about going back again ever.'

'Fantastic, Werner,' I said with mock admiration. 'You got it at first guess. But for God's sake don't let Stinnes get wind of it.'

'Who came up with that nasty little idea? Bret Rensselaer?'

'Well, we both know it couldn't be Dicky,' I said. 'Dicky never had an idea.'

'Where do you want to meet Erich?' Werner asked.

'I'll have to see him,' I said. 'Face to face, and well before Friday. Today if possible. If he wants to confide in Zena, or anyone else for that matter, that's up to him. That's a decision I can't take for him. The information about Friday's rendezvous is for him alone, Werner.'

'You're going to keep Zena out of it, are you? Are you going to keep me out of it too?'

'You've done your bit, and so has Zena. Let's get it over with. I want to get out of this city. The rain and the heat . . . and the smell. It's not my idea of a holiday.'

'Zena's uncle and aunt are due back from their vacation at the weekend, so we'll also be leaving. But I won't be sorry,' said Werner. 'I'll never complain about Berlin weather again after this damned humidity. Three times I've had someone in to look at that air-conditioner and they keep telling me it's working fine. They say it's too hot outside for the machine to cope with it.'

I looked at him and nodded.

'Okay,' said Werner. 'I'll get you together with Erich Stinnes. He's going to phone about six. I'll bring him anywhere you want him.'

'I'll need to talk to him. Somewhere safe. Angel's body shop; that car repair place out near the Shrine of Guadalupe. Remember? It's painted in very bright red and yellow.'

'What time?'

'Drive straight in, through the workshop and out the back. There's a yard. I'll be parked there. Oh, say seven o'clock.'

'I'll be there.'

'No Zena,' I said.

Werner drank some lemonade. 'I've never seen her like this before,' he said sadly. 'She really likes Erich. She's worrying about him.'

'Keep her out of it, Werner.'

'Bernie. You don't think Zena could be infatuated with Erich Stinnes, do you?'

'You know her better than I do,' I said, to avoid the question. Or rather to avoid the answer, which was simply that I knew only one thing that Zena was infatuated with. And Erich Stinnes was about to take delivery of a quarter of a million of them.

'But do I?' said Werner, as if he doubted it. 'You never see the person you love, except through tinted spectacles. Sometimes I expect too much of her. I love her. I'd give her the crown jewels.'

'She'd like the crown jewels, Werner.'

He smiled without putting much effort into it. 'I love her too much, I know that. You're a friend; you can see it better than I can.'

'It's no good asking me about Zena,' I said. 'It's no good expecting me to understand anything about any woman. Whatever Zena feels about Erich Stinnes, there's not much chance that either of us will ever discover what it is. I thought she hated Russians.'

'She talks about him a lot. She kept one of those passport photos he sent to you. She keeps it in the pages of her own passport. I noticed her remove it when we went through immigration at the airport.'

'That's not very significant,' I said.

'If she ran off with Stinnes I'd die,' said Werner.

'She's not going to run off with Stinnes,' I said. 'And, even in the unlikely event that she did, you wouldn't die, Werner. You'd feel miserable but you wouldn't die.' I felt like grabbing him and shaking him out of his despondent mood but I knew it wouldn't work. I'd tried such measures before.

'When we left Berlin this time, she took all her jewellery across to her sister.'

Shit, I thought, don't say there's another Zena. But I smiled and said, 'Has she got much jewellery?'

'Quite a bit; some diamond rings, a three-strand necklace of pearls and a platinum bracelet set with large diamonds. And there's a heavy gold necklace that cost me nearly ten thousand marks. Then there are things from her mother; pendants, a watch set with diamonds and pearls. She likes jewellery. You must have seen her wearing it.'

'I may have done,' I said. 'I didn't notice.'

'She took it to her sister.'

'She was frightened of burglars,' I said.

'She never leaves it in the apartment when we're away.'

'Well, there you are. She wanted to make sure it was safe. There'd be no point in bringing it to Mexico. You'd be asking for trouble with the Customs. And taking it out again would be even more difficult.'

'But usually she asks me to put it in my safe-deposit box. This time she took it round to her sister.'

'You could always ask her about it,' I said, and tried to think of a way to change the subject.

'I did ask her,' said Werner. 'She said she thought her sister might like to wear it while we're away.'

'There you are, then. That's the explanation.'

'Her sister never goes anywhere she could wear stuff like that.'

'So why do you think she took it to her sister?'

'If Zena was going to run off with Erich Stinnes, it would be a good thing to do. She likes that jewellery better than anything in the world.'

'It will be better that Zena doesn't know exactly what's happening on Friday,' I said.

'You mean I refuse to tell her?' I could see Werner anticipating the fight he was going to have about it.

'Better that neither of you know,' I said.

'She won't be satisfied with a refusal,' said Werner. 'She's followed this one through right from the beginning. She'll want to be in on the final act.'

'We'll think of something to tell her,' I said. 'By the way, how do you know that Henry Tiptree has arrived here?'

'He phoned me. He gave me a lot of flattery about what a wonderful reputation I had. Then he arranged a meeting. He said he wanted to pick my brains. But he phoned up later and put the meeting off. He'll phone again, he said.'

'Why did he cancel?'

'Is it important?'

'I'm just curious.'

'I can't tell you why. Zena took the call. He didn't give any reason as far as I know. Zena said he just phoned up and cancelled the meeting.' I nodded. Werner said, 'Don't mention the gun to Zena. She hates guns.'

So Zena had been talking to Tiptree. Or he'd been talking to her. Either way I didn't like it. And I didn't like the way they'd kept Werner out of it. They were a bad combination: the tough, dedicated little Zena, and Tiptree, the ambitious diplomat trying his hand at a cloak-and-dagger job. They were amateurs. Amateurs keep their eyes on the target instead of looking over their shoulders.

25

You look out for the *tacheria* which always has smoke from the open fire and a line of people waiting for the fresh tacos. Across the road there are the buses that bring pilgrims to the Shrine of Guadalupe. Buses of all shapes and sizes and colours. Huge air-conditioned monsters that bring people from the big international hotels down-town and bone-rattling old wrecks which convey pilgrims from across the mountains. But the customers buying tacos are not all from the shrine; locals come here too.

Next door to the smoky *tacheria* is the place where I was to meet Stinnes. It is a large, shed-like building with a ramshackle frontage. Across the bright-red overhang, 'Angel – body shop' is crudely lettered in bloody script. Inside there are trucks and motor cars in various stages of repair and renovation. And always there is the intense flashing light, and the intermittent hiss of the welding torch. There is always work for skilled car-repair men in Mexico City.

I got there early, drove through the workshop, and parked in the backyard. Angel Morales, a small, sad-eyed man with dark skin and a carefully trimmed moustache, came out to see who it was. 'I'm meeting someone, Angel,' I said. 'It's business.' I passed him an envelope containing money.

Angel nodded mournfully. Angel was a friend of a friend of mine but we'd put things on a proper business footing from the time we first met. It was better than using any of the safe houses that the SIS people at the embassy would provide for me. He took the envelope and tucked it into a pocket of his oily overalls without looking inside it. 'I want no trouble,' said Angel. That must have been the only English that Angel knew, for he'd said the same words to me on the two previous meetings.

'There'll be no trouble, Angel,' I said, giving him the sort of wide smile that I'd seen on carefree men with easy minds.

He nodded and went back to shout abuse at an Indian youth who was bolting a new section of metal on to the back of a badly broken truck.

They arrived exactly on time. Stinnes was driving his own car. He stopped the car in the yard and got out but didn't switch off the engine. Then Werner got into the driver's seat and – waiting only long enough for Stinnes to get clear – he gave a brief wave of the hand before reversing back. Carelessly he knocked the rear fender against the wall. Embarrassed, he swung the car round and accelerated loudly to drive away. It was arranged that Werner would return with the car in half an hour. I wondered if Werner was angry at being excluded from the meeting. But then I dismissed that idea from my mind. Werner was enough of a pro not to let that bother him.

Stinnes was dressed in a green tropical suit which repeated washings had faded to a very light colour. The collar of his white shirt was buttoned, but he wore no tie. It gave the impression of an absent-minded man who'd dressed hurriedly, but I knew that Stinnes was not absent-minded, and the way in which he'd dragged out the arrangements for his enrolment was the mark of a man who never hurried.

Stinnes was solemn as he got into the car. 'There is nothing wrong, I hope,' he said, when the greetings were over.

'What sort of a game are you playing, Erich?' I said. 'I wish I knew.'

'What games are there?'

'There are many different ones,' I said. 'There is the Moscow game in which you lead us by the nose, and then say no thanks.'

'I know only the Bernard Samson game,' he said. 'I do as you propose. I get my money and a few months of interrogation and I retire in comfort.'

'What about the Erich Stinnes game? You grab the money and you take off on your own and disappear.'

'You'll find a way to prevent that, I'm sure. That's your job, isn't it?'

'What have you arranged with London behind my back, Erich?' I said.

'That's what really annoys you; the way your own department have behaved. You have no complaint against me. I have kept my word all along the line.'

'We haven't gone very far yet,' I pointed out.

'The London game, that's what you haven't mentioned,' said Stinnes.

I said nothing. He was trying to rile me in order to see what he could discover. It was to be expected; it was what I would do to him under the same circumstances.

'The London game . . .' said Stinnes. 'You take the blame for all their mistakes. Is that perhaps the London game, Mr Samson?'

'I don't know,' I said. I was tired of this silly conversation.

But Stinnes persisted. He said, 'If you disappear, it would leave your people in London with a convenient scapegoat for all their failures, wouldn't it?'

'No. They'd have a lot of explaining to do,' I said, with more bravado than I could spare.

'Not if the money also disappeared with you.'

'What are you telling me, Erich?' I kept it light and tried to act as if I found his suggestions amusing. 'That London would murder me and make the money vanish and pretend that I'd been a KGB agent for many years?'

He smiled but gave no reply.

'And how would you fit into that scenario? Me dead. Money gone. Erich Stinnes where?'

'I'll keep to my agreement. I've told you that. Do you have any reason to doubt?' I followed Stinnes's gaze. The ground sloped up at the back of the yard. On a grubby white wall a youth in faded jeans and a purple T-shirt was spraying a slogan on the tall stucco wall: *La revolución no tiene fronteras* – the revolution has no frontiers. It was to be seen all over Central America, wherever they could afford the paint.

'We're still on opposing sides, Erich. On Friday we'll be meeting under different circumstances. But until then I'm treating you with great suspicion.'

He turned his head to look at me. 'Of course. Perhaps you're waiting for some gesture of good faith from me. Is that what you're saying?'

'It would raise my morale.'

'This particular gesture of good faith might not,' said Stinnes. He reached into his pocket and got a Russian passport. He gave it to me. There was nothing special about it – it had been issued two years before and was convincingly marked and dog-eared – except that the photo and physical description were mine. I went cold. 'Keep it,' said Stinnes. 'As a souvenir. But don't use it. The serial numbers are ones that will alert the frontier police. And there are invisible marks that when seen under fluorescent light will mean a phone call to Moscow.' He smiled, inviting me to join in the fun.

'There was a plan to kidnap me?'

'A silly contingency plan that has long since been abandoned . . . on my instructions.'

'And no one suspects you might be coming to us?'

'A frustrated fool suspects, but he had cried wolf too often with too many others.'

'Take care, Erich.'

'Take care? How safe is this place? Angel's body shop. Can we be sure we're not observed.'

I said, 'Werner knows his job. And Angel's yard is as safe as anywhere in this dangerous town.'

'Do you observe what those men over there are doing with that chisel?' he asked. 'They are cutting the number from that truck engine. They are criminals. The police probably have this workshop under observation. You must be mad to bring me to such a place.'

'You've got a lot to learn about the West, Erich. This fellow Angel regularly works on transforming American trucks and cars that are stolen in Texas and California. The first time I came here I walked into the office and saw him with a box of US licence plates that had been ripped off cars before they were resprayed.'

'And?'

'Well, you don't think he can go on doing that year after year without attracting the attention of the police, do you?'

'Why isn't he in prison?'

'He bribes the police, Erich. What do they call them here – "the biting ones" – come regularly to collect their fees. This is the safest place in the whole town. No cop would dare come in here and disturb our peaceful conversation. He'd have the whole force at his throat.'

'I can see I have much to learn about the West,' said Stinnes with heavy sarcasm. It was interesting that he chose to pretend that bribery and corruption was not plaguing the Eastern bloc. He took off his spectacles and blinked. 'It was hard to say goodbye to my son,' he said, as if thinking aloud. 'He asked me if I'd ever thought of defecting to the West . . . He'd never said such a thing before. Never. It was very strange, almost like telepathy. I had to say no, didn't I?'

For the first time I felt sorry for him, but I made sure it didn't show. 'We'll meet in Garibaldi Square,' I said. 'Take a cab there and pretend you want to listen to the musicians. But stay in the cab. Arrive at nine o'clock. The time might change if the plane is late. Phone the number I gave you between six and seven to confirm. Whoever answers will give a time but no place. That means Garibaldi Square. No baggage. Wear something that won't look too conspicuous in England.'

'I'll be there.'

'And don't tell Mrs Volkmann.'

'Don't tell her where I'm meeting you?'

'Don't tell her anything.'

'She's with your people, isn't she? I thought I'd be travelling on the plane with her.'

'Don't tell her anything.'

'Are you sure that you're in charge of this operation?'

'As one pro to another, Erich, let me admit to you that these jobs make me nervous. You will not be armed; understand? I *will* be armed. And the moment I see any sign of KGB heavies, or any other evidence of a stake-out, I will blow a hole in you so big that daylight will shine through you from the other side. No offence, Erich, but I felt it better to tell you that in advance.'

'As one pro to another,' said Stinnes with more than a trace of sarcasm, 'I appreciate your frankness.' He wasn't looking at me as he spoke. He was looking right through the open doors of the work-shop to where a jeep had stopped in the street. There were three military policemen in it, all wearing US-army-style equipment complete with helmets painted white. One of the MPs climbed out of the jeep and came through into the yard where we were parked. He stared right at us for a long time. Stinnes stopped talking until the MP turned round and went back inside. We watched him go into the large crate that Angel used as an office. The outside of the crate was covered in girlie pictures, calendars and travel posters; one said, 'Sheraton Hotels let you move to the rhythm of Latin America.'

After a few minutes the military policeman reappeared, buttoning his top pocket. He grinned to his driver as the jeep drove away.

'It's the same everywhere in this town. Cops even prey on the cabs taking the tourists to the airport,' I said. 'Everyone pays off.'

Stinnes looked at his watch to see how long it would be before Werner returned. He said, 'You realize how much you need my goodwill, don't you?'

'Do I?'

'London Central want to know one thing above all else. They want to know if you are Moscow's man. If I say "yes" you'll be finished.'

'If you say I'm Moscow's man, they will discover you are lying,' I said calmly.

'Perhaps they would; perhaps they wouldn't.'

'The debriefing panel are not stupid,' I said, with more conviction than I truly felt. 'They don't use thumbscrews or electric prodders or even a bread-and-water diet, but they'll discover the truth.'

'Eventually, perhaps. But that might come too late to do you any good.'

'They won't take me out and shoot me,' I said.

'No, they won't. But you'd be removed from your job and discredited. If they cleared you afterwards you wouldn't be rehabili-tated and reinstated.'

'If I thought this was all a KGB plot to discredit me, I'd kill you now, Stinnes.'

'That would make matters worse for you. If I was killed, you would immediately be suspected. Your position would be worse than having me slander you. With me alive you could argue against me, but London Central would see my dead body as convincing proof of your guilt.'

'Is that how it looks to you?'

'It's how it *is*,' said Stinnes. 'Is there anything else?'

'Did my wife arrange the death of the boy at Bosham?'

'Why?'

'I have to know.'

'He recognized her.'

'But did she kill him?'

'Your wife? Of course not.'

'Did she authorize it?'

'No, it was a local decision. Your wife was not consulted.'

I looked at him, trying to see into his brain. 'You'd say that anyway,' I said.

I could see by his face that he could not be bothered to discuss the matter. But then he seemed to realize that from now onwards he might have to get used to doing things our way. 'Pavel Moskvin, one of my people, was trying to make himself famous.'

'By murdering one of our junior staff?'

'Moskvin was using my name; he was in England impersonating me. He got the idea that MacKenzie was you.'

'What?'

'He knows nothing about you, except your name and that you wanted to get into contact with me. He was in England on a routine task; he was no more than a back-up for your wife's team. But, when MacKenzie arrived, Moskvin couldn't resist it. He pretended he was me.'

'What a fiasco,' I said.

'Moskvin is a meddling fool. He thinks it's all so easy. Finally he killed your man rather than have to report what a mess he'd made of everything. No, your wife was not involved. Your wife is furious about it.' A workman wheeled a trailer pump from the shop and started the motor. It made a loud thumping sound until the pressure built up. Then the man began to spray a car door. The spray gun hissed loudly as clouds of pink paint came rolling across the yard.

'You came here *after* the Volkmanns arrived, didn't you?'

'I told her you'd guess that. Chronology is always the first element of deduction.'

'The Volkmanns arrived here, and then you came and let them discover you here.'

'Your wife was sure her scheme would make you run.'

'Was she?' I had my doubts about whether she'd discuss such things with Stinnes, or with anyone else. It was not Fiona's style.

'She thought London Central would be flaying you alive by now. Instead you seem to have have talked your way out of trouble there. And instead of you fleeing East I am coming West. It will be a double defeat for her, and there are people in Moscow who'll not allow her to escape without blame. She will have within her an anger that only women know. She will take revenge upon you, Samson. I would not like to be in your shoes when she seeks retribution.'

'You win some; you lose some.' I could smell the paint now. It had that acrid taste of cheap boiled sweets that all such quick-drying paints have.

'You say that because you are a man,' said Stinnes.

'I say it because I'm a pro. Just as you are one, and just as my wife is. Professionals don't take revenge; they have enough trouble doing their job.'

'You may be a good agent,' said Stinnes. 'But you have a lot to learn about women.'

'The only thing a man has to know about women is that he'll never know anything about them. Now let me back up the car before the radiator goes pink.'

I started up the car and moved it out of the way of the mad sprayman. Stinnes said, 'Are you still in love with your wife?'

'No,' I said. I was getting fed up with everyone concerning themselves about how much I loved Fiona. 'Are you still in love with Mrs Volkmann?' I retorted.

Stinnes was startled. His head moved as if I'd given him a slap in the face.

'You'd better tell me,' I said. 'It could have a bearing on the enrolment.'

'How?'

'Have you arranged to go to England with Mrs Volkmann?'

'She arranged it. Your people approved.'

'Did they, by God.'

'She told them it must be a condition. I *am* in love with her. And she's in love with me.'

'Are you serious, Erich?'

'I love her. Have you never been in love?'

'Not with Zena Volkmann.'

'Don't try to change anything. It's too late now. We're going to start a new life together in England. If you tell her husband or try to interfere I will not go ahead.'

'You must be a bloody fool,' I said. 'A man like you, listening to the sweet talk of a little chiseller like Zena Volkmann. She wants to get her hands on the money. Can't you see that?'

'It's my business,' he said peevishly.

'Your fight with your wife . . . her bruised face. Was that something to do with Zena Volkmann? You didn't punch her in the face just to make it all look right, did you?'

'When I told Inge there was another woman she became hysterical. I didn't want to hurt her but she tried to kill me. She had a metal poker.' He sighed. 'Zena said I must tell her. Zena insisted upon a clean break. Otherwise, she said, Inge might keep trying to find me. This way, perhaps she'll forget me and marry again.'

'You didn't tell your wife that you were going to defect?'

'I am in love, but I am not insane. No, of course I didn't tell her.'

'Then stay sane about Zena too,' I said. 'I'll give Zena a ticket to London, for the flight after yours. You make sure you arrive alone on Friday. Or I'll have to get rid of Zena the hard way.'

Stinnes seemed not to take my threat seriously. He said, 'I suppose every tourist going to London wants to see 221B Baker Street.'

'What's in Baker Street?' I said. But even before I'd finished saying it I recognized it as the fictitious address of Sherlock Holmes. 'Oh, yes, of course. We'll go along there together,' I promised.

'It's something I've always wanted to see,' said Stinnes. But before he could get started about Holmes, Werner arrived in Stinnes's car. He got out, leaving the door open, and walked over to us.

'Are you finished?' said Werner. 'Or do you want me to give you a little more time?'

Stinnes looked at me. I said, 'We're all through, Werner.'

As Stinnes got out of the car he touched his forehead in a salutation. '*Auf Wiedersehen*,' he said, with a more than a trace of mockery in his voice. I noticed the way he abruptly introduced the subject of Sherlock Holmes; he hadn't promised not to bring Zena with him.

'*Sayonara*,' I said. I still didn't know what to make of him.

'What's biting you?' said Werner as he got into the car alongside me. I looked in the mirror until Stinnes had got into his car and driven away. Then I gave Werner the Russian passport to look at. 'Holy Christ,' said Werner.

'Yes, they were going to snatch me.'

'And Stinnes prevented it?'

'He's bound to want the credit,' I said. 'They might just have dropped it in favour of other plans.'

'London would have thought you'd gone voluntarily,' said Werner. 'It's a smart idea.'

'Yes, Moscow are having a lot of smart ideas about me lately.'

'Fiona, you mean?'

'It's tempting to think it's all coming from her,' I said. 'But I don't want to become obsessed about it.'

'Did he say anything about Zena?' said Werner.

'We've been all through that, Werner. You make sure Zena is kept busy on Friday. You tell her nothing is planned and you're flying her to Acapulco for a long weekend and swim and get a tan. Send her off on her own on Friday morning so you can be my back-up at the airport on Friday night. Then fly out on the late plane to join her.'

'She won't fall for that, Bernie. She knows it's getting close.'

'You convince her that you both could do with a couple of days off. Make it sound right, Werner. You know what this one means to me. I need Stinnes in London.'

'And I need Zena here with me,' said Werner grimly.

'Stinnes thinks Zena is eloping with him.'

'Eloping?'

'You know what I mean,' I said.

'Zena is just stringing him along,' said Werner. 'She's trying to help you, Bernie.'

'She's bloody devious, Werner. She's your wife, I know. But she's too bloody devious.'

Werner didn't deny it. 'She's seen that man Tiptree,' said Werner.

'Seen him?'

'That's where she went this afternoon when we were talking. She went to meet Henry Tiptree. She told me when she got back.'

'What are London playing at?' I said wearily.

'Why put up with it?' said Werner. 'Why don't you go and see Tiptree? Tell him to either take over the whole operation or stay out of it.'

'I thought of that, Werner,' I said. 'But Tiptree is sure to say he'll take over. And we both know that Tiptree might well make a botch of it. I'm convinced that Erich Stinnes is serious. If he turns up on Friday I'll deliver him to the bloody plane; at gunpoint if necessary. I'll get him to London or die in the attempt. If I hand it over to Tiptree, and it all goes wrong, London will say I deliberately abandoned the operation because I didn't want Stinnes debriefed in London.'

Werner turned away from me and wound down the window as if suddenly interested in something else. He was avoiding my eyes. I suppose he was upset at the prospect of losing Zena.

'Zena's not going anywhere with Stinnes,' I promised him. 'You'll be at the airport, Werner. You can stop her if she tries.' He didn't reply. I started up the car and turned round in the yard. Then I drove through the workshop. The flashes of the acetylene torch lit up the wrecked cars like the flashguns of a thousand paparazzi. Outside a blue-and-white police car was parked. The driver was inside talking to Angel.

26

Garibaldi Square is to Mexican musicians what the Galapagos Archipelago is to wildlife. Even in the small hours of the night the square was crowded with people and the air was filled with the sound of two or three dozen groups singing and playing different songs. There is no pop, rock, soul or punk to be heard; no Elvis, no Beatles, no Elton John. This is Mexican music and, if you don't like it, you can go somewhere else.

'I've only been here before in the morning. I had no idea what it was really like. It's fantastic,' said Henry Tiptree, as we walked past five musicians in serapes and sombreros singing '. . . life is worth nothing in Guanajuato'. Tiptree halted for a moment to listen. 'It's not even spoiled by tourists; almost everyone here is Mexican.'

'It's right for what we want,' I said. 'It's ill-lit, noisy and crowded.' And smelly too. Trapped by the surrounding mountains, the still air was pressed down upon the city, trapping the petrol fumes and woodsmoke so that the air offended the nose and stung the eyes.

'I'm not working against you, Samson,' said Henry Tiptree suddenly.

'If you say so,' I said. Tiptree stopped to look around the square. There was music coming from every direction, and yet the effect was polyphony rather than discord. Or was I becoming inured to chaos?

Tiptree continued to look round the square. He fingered the moustache that never seemed to grow, and spoke with that sort of confidential manner that people use to assert their self-importance. 'You must understand,' he said, 'that the success of this operation will be measured according to whether we get our man to London; nothing else counts for much. That's why London Central is determined that we do everything right.'

'We all are,' I said. 'But who knows best what's right?'

'Very philosophical,' said Tiptree flatly.

'I am very philosophical,' I said. 'You get philosophical after London Central screws up for you a few times.'

'London Central have confirmed that I'm in charge,' said Tiptree.

'I want that understood before we go a step further. You will take Stinnes to London, but here in the city we're doing things my way.'

'You're in charge,' I agreed. London Central? Who'd put this idiot in charge? Dicky? Bret? Morgan, perhaps. Tiptree seemed to be on very good terms with Morgan, the D-G's factotum, who could have caught the D-G in a weak moment and got a signature from him.

Tiptree shot me a suspicious glance. He knew my glib pledge counted for little or nothing. I didn't risk my neck taking orders from learners. He stopped to watch another group of musicians. They were singing a song about a man who'd lost his heart to a girl from Veracruz. The men were illuminated by a hissing acetylene lamp placed at their feet. The lead singer – a very old man with a face like a walnut and a *bandido* moustache – had a fine bass voice that was racked with emotion. There is a passionate soul in every Mexican, so that love or revolution dominates his whole being; but only for a few minutes at a time.

'What have you arranged about his money?' I asked.

From the corner of my eye I could see that Tiptree was looking at me, trying to decide how to answer. 'Mrs Volkmann is meeting us at the bank,' he said finally. 'Stinnes wants the money paid to her.'

Only with a great effort did I prevent myself from jumping up and down and shrieking with rage. This idiot was keeping Zena better informed than me. But very calmly I said, 'What bank is open in Garibaldi Square at this hour?'

'So there are things that even you don't know, eh, Samson?'

He went along the pavement to find a *pulqueria* where even the barman looked drunk. The fermenting sap of the maguey plant smells like rancid nut-oil, but it's the cheapest way to oblivion, and like so many such bars this one was packed. After pushing his way between the customers right to the very back, Tiptree opened a door and held it open for me. I followed him into a narrow hallway, then he started to go up a steep flight of creaking stairs.

'Wait a minute,' I said. I stopped at the bottom of the stairs to look around. There was only a dim electric bulb to illuminate a passage that led out to the the backyard and the urinals. 'Where are we going?' My voice echoed as I closed the door behind me. The customers in the bar were kicking up so much noise that I could only faintly hear the music from Garibaldi Square. There was a lot about this place that I didn't like.

'I'm meeting Stinnes in the square,' I protested.

'Don't be so nervous,' said Tiptree. 'The plan has been changed. Stinnes knows.' He smiled to reassure me, but it only made me see what a conceited fool he was. He knew how much I resented this change of plan and the way that Zena had already been made a party to it. 'It's all arranged.'

I touched the butt of the old pistol to be sure it was still there and then followed him up the narrow stairs. Rat-trap, fire-trap, mantrap; it was the sort of place I didn't like at any time. But I especially didn't like it for this sort of business. Narrow stairway with a wide well, so that a man with a Saturday-night special at the top of the house could plink an army one by one.

Tiptree stopped on the first-floor landing. There was just enough light to see that the door looked new. It was the only new-looking object anywhere in sight. He pressed the buzzer and waited for a small panel to open. It provided someone inside with a view of Tiptree's Eton tie. But he bent lower to see inside and whispered something that resulted in the sound of well-oiled bolts being slid back.

'I don't like surprises,' I told Tiptree. 'I arranged to meet Stinnes in the square.'

'I've sent a message to him,' said Tiptree. 'He'll meet us here. It's too damned public, that square.'

When the door was opened, by a slight Mexican boy who wore a straw hat, brim curled cowboy-style, I noticed there was a sheet of steel layered into the woodwork of the door. Another boy stood behind him, studying us warily. He recognized Tiptree and nodded.

'This is the bank,' announced Tiptree. It was a large room that overlooked the square, but the blinds had been pulled down. The room, with its ornate Victorian wallpaper and brass light-brackets, had the atmosphere of some Wild West saloon a century ago. Three almost identical men sat at three almost identical old tables. The men were dressed in white short-sleeved shirts with black trousers and black ties and black well-polished shoes: the uniform used throughout the world by men who wish to be entrusted with money. Each man was equipped with half a dozen ledgers, a small cash-box, a scribbling pad and a Japanese calculator. Through a half-open door I could see another room where girls were typing on the wide-platen typewriters that are required for account sheets.

'It's a money-change office,' I said.

'Three partners; brothers. They used to run a loan company . . . One that was always ready to change money too. But, when the government nationalized all the banks, larger horizons opened.'

'Is it a legal bank?' I asked.

'Strictly speaking it's not legal and it's not a bank,' said Tiptree. 'But it's right for what we want. I've spent a lot of time in Mexico, Samson. I know how things work here.'

I looked at the old man sitting inside the door with a shotgun across his knees. The teenage boys who'd let us in looked like blood relations. Perhaps it was a family business.

Tiptree greeted Zena. She was sitting on a wooden bench and

nodded politely to both of us. Despite the heat, she was dressed in a linen suit with Paris labels, and her make-up and the low-heeled shoes made her look like someone who'd prepared for a journey. There was no sign of Werner.

'Is this where the money is supposed to be?' I asked.

Tiptree smiled at the doubt he heard in my voice. 'Don't be misguided by appearances. A quarter of a million dollars is a bagatelle to these people, Samson. They could have ten million, in any of the world's major currencies, laid out across the floor within an hour.'

'You've got it all worked out,' I said.

'You're the muscle; I'm the brains,' said Tiptree, without expending too much energy to persuade me it was a joke.

Tiptree exchanged polite, British-style greetings with one of the partners and formally introduced me. The senior partner was called Pepe, a soft-spoken man with white hair, a pock-marked face and a pocket full of pens. Tiptree told him that Zena was the one to whom the money was to be paid. I looked at Zena and she smiled.

When they were ready to count the money, Zena went to the table to watch the man piling the hundred-dollar bills on the table. I went to watch too. They were used notes; 250 of them in each thick bundle. They were held together by heavy-duty red rubber bands into which torn scraps of paper had been inserted with '$25,000' scrawled on each of them. There were ten bundles.

Perhaps in some other bank, in some other town, the money might then have been passed across the table. But this was Mexico and these were men well accustomed to the mistrust that peasants show for bankers. It all had to be counted a second time note by note. Despite Pepe's fumbling, it took only a few minutes.

When he'd finished counting, Pepe opened a cupboard to get a cardboard box for the money. There were many other boxes, of all shapes and sizes, stacked in the cupboard. On the side of this box it said 'Flat fillets of anchovies 50 tins – 2 oz.' I wonder who first discovered that fifty tins of anchovies fit into exactly the same space as a quarter of a million dollars. Or vice versa.

Perhaps I should have given more attention to Pepe's nervous manner and to the clumsiness he showed in handling the notes but I was too concerned with the prospect of Zena departing with the money before Stinnes arrived. I looked at my watch and I looked at the clock on the wall. Stinnes was late. Something had gone wrong. All my professional intuition said leave, and leave right away. But I stayed.

While Pepe was putting strapping-tape on the box, Zena went to the window. She was holding back the edge of the blind to see down into the square when Pepe told me and Tiptree to put our hands on our heads.

'I'm sorry,' said Pepe, whose drawn white face, the stubble of tomorrow's beard already patterning his chin, bore a frown of desolate unhappiness. 'I'm doing only what I must do.'

Tiptree, despite his excellent Spanish, did not understand Pepe's soft instruction.

'Put your hands on your head,' I said. 'Do as he says.' Even then I think Tiptree would not have understood except that he saw me put my hands on my head. 'Someone got here ahead of us.'

'Your friends?' said Tiptree, looking round the room.

'How I wish they were,' I said. But I had no time for Tiptree's stupid suspicions. I was trying to decide what role the old man with the shotgun was playing in this business, and whether the two boys with him were armed.

Now Zena also had her hands on her head. She'd been pulled away from the window in case her shadow on the blind was seen by someone in the street. 'What's happening?' said Zena.

It was then that a burly, dark-suited man came from the next room. Beside him there was a Mexican boy with a machine-pistol. I didn't like machine-pistols. Especially cheap machine-pistols like this one. Hoping to survive a false move against a man with a machine-pistol was like shouting abuse at a man with a garden hose and hoping not to get wet. I looked at it carefully. It was a Model 25, a Czech design that dated from the time before they changed over to Soviet calibres. An old, cheap gun, but the boy liked waving it around, and he kept the metal stock folded forward to make this easier to do.

I recognized the dark-suited man from the night I'd spent at Biedermann's house. It was Stinnes's companion, the man who called himself Pavel Moskvin; the 'fink' – a tough-looking fifty-year-old with a cropped head and the build of a debt-collector. 'You,' he said to me in his abominable German. 'You make sure your friends know that no one will harm them if they do as they are told.'

'What's it all about?' I said.

He looked at me but didn't answer. 'Tell them,' he said.

Zena and Tiptree had heard for themselves. Tiptree said, 'Is this your doing, Samson?'

'Don't be stupid,' I said. 'It's a KGB stake-out. They are waiting for Stinnes. They might leave us out of it if we behave.'

'What will they do?' said Tiptree. 'Are they going to kill him?'

I shrugged. We could only wait and see. The door-buzzer sounded, and Moskvin nodded to tell Pepe to open the spy-hole.

Pepe looked through and after a brief muttering through the hatch said it was a woman who wanted to change some US one-dollar bills into Mexican money. 'Do you recognize her?' Moskvin asked Pepe.

'We have a lot of people asking for change: waiters, hotel workers, shop workers. I don't know. I can't see much through the hatch.'

'Tell her to return tomorrow. Say you've run out of money.' Moskvin's Spanish was even worse than his German. To get a job in the Soviet foreign service with so little aptitude for languages, a man would have to be a very loyal Party supporter.

Pepe sent the woman away and then we all settled down to wait. It was a nerve-racking business. Moskvin had prepared it well. It was the right place. He had all the evidence he needed to nail Stinnes, and this way he'd have the dollars too. There was nothing the KGB liked better than rubbing our noses in it. I cursed Tiptree for changing the rendezvous. It wouldn't have been so easy for Moskvin out there in the dark crowded square.

I looked at Pepe. His business made it unlikely that he had Communist Party connections. Probably the KGB had had Tiptree under observation when he came here to make arrangements about the money.

In such a situation almost everything is guesswork. I guessed the old man was the regular guard for the bank, simply because he did not look like the sort of tough whom Moskvin would bring in. And I guessed from the way he held the double-barrelled gun that Moskvin had removed the shells. And the despondent expressions of the faces of the young boys and the envy with which they eyed the machine-pistol convinced me that they were unarmed. I could take the old man and the kids, I could probably handle Moskvin at the same time, but the machine-pistol tilted the balance.

I kept my hands on my head and tried to look very frightened. It was not difficult, especially when I saw the way the kid with the machine-pistol was flourishing it and caressing the trigger lovingly. 'I want everyone to remain still,' said Moskvin. He said it frequently and in between saying it he was looking at his wrist-watch. 'And stay away from the windows.'

Pepe made a harmless move to get a handkerchief from his pocket. Moskvin was angry. He punched Pepe in the back with a force that knocked him to his knees. 'The next person to move without permission will be shot,' he promised, and gave Pepe a spiteful kick to emphasize this warning.

There were just the two of them, it seemed, and it was unlikely that they had worked together before. One machine-pistol and probably some kind of handgun in Moskvin's pocket. Against them, one person alone would stand little chance.

I looked round the room, deciding what to do when and if Stinnes pressed the buzzer. They'd have to open the door because otherwise the steel door-lining would both protect and hide him. Did they have someone downstairs in the bar, I wondered. Or someone outside in the street to watch for Stinnes's arrival. The crowded bar would make a perfect cover.

I looked at the three partners, the three guards and the two women clerks who'd been brought in from the next room. They all kept their hands on their heads, and they all had that patient and passive visage that makes the people of Latin America so recognizably different from the Latin people of Europe.

It was while I was musing on this question that I heard the bang of the downstairs door. Under normal circumstances the sounds of footsteps on the staircase would not have been audible, but the circumstances were not normal; everyone in the room was wound up tight.

The boy with the machine-pistol pulled the bolt back to cock the gun for firing. There was a click as the sear engaged the sear-notch in the bolt. It was enough to snap some mechanism within Zena's mind. 'You promised,' she shouted. 'You promised not to hurt him.'

She was shouting at Moskvin, but he smiled without even bothering to look back at her. So that was how it had been done. Moskvin had been monitoring the whole thing through Zena. But she wasn't KGB material. There was no need to ask what she was getting out of it; the box of money. Nice going, Moskvin. But if my wife Fiona wasn't behind that notion I'd eat the money bill by bill.

We could hear the footsteps as someone reached the top of the stairs and paused on the landing. 'You promised,' said Zena. She was almost incoherent with anger. 'I love him. I told you.' She stiffened as she recognized their total indifference, and her face had gone livid under the bright make-up.

Neither Moskvin nor his machine-gun man bothered with Zena. Their eyes were on the door where Stinnes was expected any minute.

There is always some damned possibility that lies beyond every probability. Perhaps the only thing I'd never considered was that Zena could be infatuated with Stinnes. There was a strong streak of romanticism in her complex personality, and there was that old Prussian rectitude that made her record every broken teacup in a notebook. Zena would allow Stinnes to be betrayed but not killed.

Ignoring the machine-pistol, Zena flung herself across the room like a human cannon-ball. She collided with the boy, her feet kicking and fingernails gouging. He bent, and almost fell, under the momentum of her attack, and there was a crash as their two bodies smashed against the wall. Trying to defend himself against her fingernails, the boy dropped his machine-gun and tried to grab her hands. An ear-splitting bang echoed round the room as the bullet in the chamber was fired by the impact. But by that time Zena had her nails into the boy's face and he was yelling at her to stop. He was frightened of her, and it was to be heard in his yells. Thus encouraged, she stopped only long enough to grab his long hair and use it to swing his head against a sharp corner of a filing cabinet.

Had Moskvin reached into his pocket for a pistol, or stooped to pick up the machine-gun, he might have regained control. But he used his huge fists. It was the reflex action of a man who'd spent his life throwing his weight around both literally and figuratively. He gave Zena's small body a mighty blow to the kidneys and followed it with a left hand to the side of her head.

The punches landed with sickening force. They took care of little Zena all right. She was only half conscious as she fell to the floor, arms flailing. Then Moskvin could not resist a kick at her. But it took time. There was lots of time, and I pushed my pistol back into my belt as I watched Tiptree bring a small Browning automatic from his pocket and with commendable speed fire two shots at Moskvin. The first bullet went wild – I heard it ricochet and hit a typewriter in the next room – but his second bullet hit Moskvin in the leg. Moskvin stopped kicking Zena and screamed. I guessed he was an amateur. Now he demonstrated the way in which an amateur is efficient only while all goes well for him. Once injured, Moskvin lost interest in killing Stinnes. He lost interest in the money. He lost interest in the boy who'd had his face shredded by Zena's nails and his cranium gashed on the sharp corner of the filing cabinet. He even lost interest in the machine-pistol on the floor.

The Mexicans all remained very still, hands on heads and their faces impassive. I put my hands back on my head too. There was no sense in getting killed, but I got ready for the aftermath by stepping slowly to one side so that I could plant my foot on the machine-pistol. That was the trump card.

Moskvin fell back on to a chair and pressed his palm against the copious bleeding. He nursed his pain and wanted everything to stop. He clamped his hands to his wounded leg and crooned and wept with the pain of it. The pain could not have been very great but he was frightened. He'd probably convinced himself he was going to die. Even people hardened to the sight of blood can be very deeply affected by a glimpse of their own.

Now Tiptree found time enough to look around to see where I'd gone. 'Open the door,' he told me, with a superiority that bordered on contempt. 'And take your hands off your head. It's all over.' When I didn't move fast enough, he looked down to where I had my foot on the machine-pistol and said, 'Oh, you've got that, have you? Good.'

Loudly Moskvin said, 'I must go to hospital. I'm bleeding to death.'

'Shut up,' I said.

Despite the changed situation, the Mexicans kept their hands on their heads. They were taking no chances. I picked up the machine-gun, went to the door and slid back the hatch, expecting to see

Stinnes. Instead, a small child whispered, 'I have a message. It is only for Señor Samson.'

'I'm Señor Samson,' I said.

The child looked at me for a long time before deciding to confide his very guarded message. He whispered, 'Your friend is waiting for you at the place you arranged.'

'Thank you,' I said.

'You are to give me one hundred pesos,' said the child. Stinnes knew how to get his messages delivered. I passed a note through the hatch to him, and then closed it.

'I must go to hospital,' said Moskvin. His voice became lower and more forceful as a little of his confidence returned to him.

'If he says another word about anything, shoot him,' I told Tiptree in English. 'They won't ask him questions in the morgue.'

Tiptree nodded solemnly. I think he would have done it too; you never can be sure with enthusiasts like Tiptree.

Moskvin went suddenly quiet. He obviously understood enough English to know what was good for him.

The onetime machine-gunner was sitting on the floor covered in blood. He was only half conscious and his eyes were closed with the pain. He'd discovered that the filing cabinet can be a formidable weapon.

'What's next?' said Tiptree. His voice was shrill. He was excited and over-confident and still waving his pistol around.

'You're staying here to make sure no one leaves until I phone you from you know where.'

'Wait a minute,' said Tiptree, his voice revealing a sudden concern. 'This all has to be sorted out. This Russian shot, the Mexican boy badly hurt and the girl unconscious. The police may come. How do I explain the guns?'

I dialled the freight office at the airport. Werner answered immediately. 'We're ready this end,' he said. 'Is everything all right with you?'

I looked at Zena. There was no point in alarming Werner; there was nothing he could do. 'So far, so good,' I said, and hung up the phone. To Tiptree I said, 'The success of this operation will be measured according to whether we get our man to London; nothing else counts for much. You told me that. London are relying on you, Henry. Don't let them down. I'll get someone to call you at this number to tell when we are safely airborne. Meanwhile keep them here. This is your big chance. They're very dangerous agents.'

'I'll go. You stay,' suggested Tiptree.

'You don't know where I arranged to meet our friend,' I said.

'And you won't tell me,' said Tiptree.

I didn't bother to answer. I looked at them. The stupid peasant

Moskvin, with his trouser-cuff rolled up, winding his tie round his leg to stop the bleeding, and frightened for his life. And the onetime machine-gunner, now sitting on the floor groaning, eyes closed, staunching blood from his lacerated face and head with a great handful of paper tissues.

And there was tiny Zena, the astounding little fireball whom I would never understand. How typical that as she began to regain consciousness her fingers were searching out the rips and torn seams in her expensive Paris suit.

Well, even Tiptree should be able to deal with those 'dangerous agents'. But how he'd deal with the police was something I didn't intend to stay long enough to find out.

'You're right,' said Tiptree, with a sudden smile. Luckily the adrenalin was marring his judgement and his self-esteem did the rest. 'I'll take care of this. Tell London that my report will follow in due course.'

'I'll tell them,' I said.

I went downstairs and out into the backyard, climbing over a tall stack of beer-crates to surmount a wall and from there jumping down into the alley, just in case Moskvin had another friend waiting in the bar. Stinnes was waiting in a cab on the corner. He opened the door for me and I slid in beside him. I was expecting him to ask immediately where Zena was but he said, 'What was the delay?' He leaned forward to the driver. 'Airport,' he told him. The driver started the engine.

'Freight side,' I said. I dropped the box of money on to Stinnes's knees but, after taking a moment to recognize what it was, he put it aside without opening it.

'I don't want the money,' he said, as if he'd been thinking about it for a long time. 'I didn't do it for the money.'

'I know you didn't,' I said. 'But take it anyway. You'll have no trouble getting rid of it.'

The taxi pulled away from the curb, slowly at first to avoid hitting the strolling musicians and the revellers. Stinnes sank back into his seat. To think that I'd been getting ready to prevent him at pistol point from racing up there to his beloved Zena.

'Freight side,' said Stinnes. 'Another change of plan. And when we get to the airport freight-yard, what new idea then? A bus to Los Angeles?'

'Maybe,' I said.

'You're late,' he said, looking at his watch.

'Your man Moskvin turned up. Apparently he couldn't bear to be parted from you.'

'Moskvin,' said Stinnes. 'Yesterday I found him rifling through my desk. He found nothing, of course, but I should have told you about him.'

'Your lady friend was reporting everything back to Moskvin. Everything.'

'She was talking to Moskvin?'

'How else did she come to be there?' There were other answers to that question but Stinnes didn't know them. And this wasn't the right time to tell him that Zena had risked her life to save him.

He was silent as we drove through Garibaldi Square. At the intersection he leaned aside and ducked his head to see the 'bank'. Perhaps he needed to see the building, and the lights behind the drawn blinds, to come to terms with Zena's treachery. 'You were right about her,' he said sadly. 'I could tell from your face when you said what a fool I was. You made me see sense.'

There was heavy traffic, but I'd allowed for some delay; I'd even allowed time for the traffic jam. The traffic slowed and then came to a complete standstill. The fire-eater was still at work. He blew a fierce tongue of flame into the air. It was darker now and the flame lit up all the cars, rippled in the paintwork and shone in all the windows. 'It's fantastic the things some people do for a living,' said Stinnes. He wound down the car window and gave the child collecting the money 200 pesos.

When the traffic had started moving again, he got a small black cheroot from his pocket and put it in his mouth. When he searched his pockets for a light I watched him carefully, but it was only matches that he brought from his pocket.

'Tell me,' I said, 'as well as the boy with the message, did you also send that old woman?' I appreciated such extreme caution. It was what any real pro would do.

He lit the little cigar with the studied care a man might lavish upon a fine double Corona. 'Yes, I sent the old woman too.' He blew smoke, and the car filled with a strong smell of the over-fermented tobacco leaf that Stinnes seemed to like. 'Yes,' he said. 'I wanted to know what was happening. I had no intention of going up there all on my own. The blinds were down; narrow stairs, crowded bar. It didn't look healthy. What happened?'

'Nothing much,' I said. 'Moskvin's a desk man, is he?'

'Yes,' said Stinnes. 'And I hate desk men.'

'So do I,' I said feelingly. 'They're bloody dangerous.'

LONDON MATCH

I

'Cheer up, Werner. It will soon be Christmas,' I said.

I shook the bottle, dividing the last drips of whisky between the two white plastic cups that were balanced on the car radio. I pushed the empty bottle under the seat. The smell of the whisky was strong. I must have spilled some on the heater or on the warm leather that encased the radio. I thought Werner would decline it. He wasn't a drinker and he'd had far too much already, but Berlin winter nights are cold and Werner swallowed his whisky in one gulp and coughed. Then he crushed the cup in his big muscular hands and sorted through the bent and broken pieces so that he could fit them all into the ashtray. Werner's wife Zena was obsessionally tidy and this was her car.

'People are still arriving,' said Werner as a black Mercedes limousine drew up. Its headlights made dazzling reflections in the glass and paintwork of the parked cars and glinted on the frosty surface of the road. The chauffeur hurried to open the door and eight or nine people got out. The men wore dark cashmere coats over their evening suits, and the women a menagerie of furs. Here in Berlin Wannsee, where furs and cashmere are everyday clothes, they are called the Hautevolee and there are plenty of them.

'What are you waiting for? Let's barge right in and arrest him now.' Werner's words were just slightly slurred and he grinned to acknowledge his condition. Although I'd known Werner since we were kids at school, I'd seldom seen him drunk, or even tipsy as he was now. Tomorrow he'd have a hangover, tomorrow he'd blame me, and so would his wife, Zena. For that and other reasons, tomorrow, early, would be a good time to leave Berlin.

The house in Wannsee was big; an ugly clutter of enlargements and extensions, balconies, sun deck and penthouse almost hid the original building. It was built on a ridge that provided its rear terrace with a view across the forest to the black waters of the lake. Now the terrace was empty, the garden furniture stacked, and the awnings rolled up tight, but the house was blazing with lights and along the front garden the bare trees had been garlanded with hundreds of tiny white bulbs like electronic blossom.

'The BfV man knows his job,' I said. 'He'll come and tell us when the contact has been made.'

'The contact won't come here. Do you think Moscow doesn't know we have a defector in London spilling his guts to us? They'll have warned their network by now.'

'Not necessarily,' I said. I denied his contention for the hundredth time and didn't doubt we'd soon be having the same exchange again. Werner was forty years old, just a few weeks older than I was, but he worried like an old woman and that put me on edge too. 'Even his failure to come could provide a chance to identify him,' I said. 'We have two plainclothes cops checking everyone who arrives tonight, and the office has a copy of the invitation list.'

'That's if the contact is a guest,' said Werner.

'The staff are checked too.'

'The contact will be an outsider,' said Werner. 'He wouldn't be *dumm* enough to give us his contact on a plate.'

'I know.'

'Shall we go inside the house again?' suggested Werner. 'I get a cramp these days sitting in little cars.'

I opened the door and got out.

Werner closed his car door gently; it's a habit that comes with years of surveillance work. This exclusive suburb was mostly villas amid woodland and water, and quiet enough for me to hear the sound of heavy trucks pulling into the Border Control point at Drewitz to begin the long haul down the autobahn that went through the Democratic Republic to West Germany. 'It will snow tonight,' I predicted.

Werner gave no sign of having heard me. 'Look at all that wealth,' he said, waving an arm and almost losing his balance on the ice that had formed in the gutter. As far as we could see along it, the whole street was like a parking lot, or rather like a car showroom, for the cars were almost without exception glossy, new, and expensive. Five-litre V-8 Mercedes with car-phone antennas and turbo Porsches and big Ferraris and three or four Rolls-Royces. The registration plates showed how far people will travel to such a lavish party. Businessmen from Hamburg, bankers from Frankfurt, film people from Munich, and well-paid officials from Bonn. Some cars were perched high on the pavement to make room for others to be double-parked alongside them. We passed a couple of cops who were wandering between the long lines of cars, checking the registration plates and admiring the paintwork. In the driveway – stamping their feet against the cold – were two *Parkwächter* who would park the cars of guests unfortunate enough to be without a chauffeur. Werner went up the icy slope of the driveway with arms extended to help him balance. He wobbled like an overfed penguin.

Despite all the double-glazed windows, closed tight against the cold of a Berlin night, there came from the house the faint syrupy whirl of Johann Strauss played by a twenty-piece orchestra. It was like drowning in a thick strawberry milk shake.

A servant opened the door for us and another took our coats. One of our people was immediately inside, standing next to the butler. He gave no sign of recognition as we entered the flower-bedecked entrance hall. Werner smoothed his silk evening jacket self-consciously and tugged the ends of his bow tie as he caught a glimpse of himself in the gold-framed mirror that covered the wall. Werner's suit was a hand-stitched custom-made silk one from Berlin's most exclusive tailors, but on Werner's thickset figure all suits looked rented.

Standing at the foot of the elaborate staircase there were two elderly men in stiff high collars and well-tailored evening suits that made no concessions to modern styling. They were smoking large cigars and talking with their heads close together because of the loudness of the orchestra in the ballroom beyond. One of the men stared at us but went on talking as if we weren't visible to him. We didn't seem right for such a gathering, but he looked away, no doubt thinking we were two heavies hired to protect the silver.

Until 1945 the house – or *Villa*, as such local mansions are known – had belonged to a man who began his career as a minor official with the Nazi farmers organization – and it was by chance that his department was given the task of deciding which farmers and agricultural workers were so indispensable to the economy that they would be exempt from service with the military forces. But from that time onwards – like other bureaucrats before and since – he was showered with gifts and opportunities and lived in high style, as his house bore witness.

For some years after the war the house was used as transit accommodation for US Army truck drivers. Only recently had it become a family house once more. The panelling, which so obviously dated back to the original nineteenth-century building, had been carefully repaired and reinstated, but now the oak was painted light grey. A huge painting of a soldier on a horse dominated the wall facing the stairs and on all sides there were carefully arranged displays of fresh flowers. But despite all the careful refurbishing, it was the floor of the entrance hall that attracted the eye. The floor was a complex pattern of black, white and red marble, a plain white central disc of newer marble having replaced a large gold swastika.

Werner pushed open a plain door secreted into the panelling and I followed him along a bleak corridor designed for the inconspicuous movement of servants. At the end of the passage there was a pantry. Clean linen cloths were arranged on a shelf, a dozen empty champagne bottles were inverted to drain in the sink and the waste bin was filled with the remains of sandwiches, discarded parsley, and some broken glass. A white-coated waiter arrived carrying a large silver tray of dirty glasses. He emptied them, put them into the service elevator together with the empty bottles, wiped the tray with a cloth from under the sink, and then departed without even glancing at either of us.

'There he is, near the bar,' said Werner, holding open the door so we could look across the crowded dance floor. There was a crush around the tables where two men in chef's whites dispensed a dozen different sorts of sausages and foaming tankards of strong beer. Emerging from the scrum with food and drink was the man who was to be detained.

'I hope like hell we've got this right,' I said. The man was not just a run-of-the-mill bureaucrat; he was the private secretary to a senior member of the Bonn parliament.

I said, 'If he digs his heels in and denies everything, I'm not sure we'll be able to make it stick.'

I looked at the suspect carefully, trying to guess how he'd take it. He was a small man with crew-cut hair and a neat Vandyke beard. There was something uniquely German about that combination. Even amongst the over-dressed Berlin social set his appearance was flashy. His jacket had wide silk-faced lapels, and silk also edged his jacket, cuffs and trouser seams. The ends of his bow tie were tucked under his collar and he wore a black silk handkerchief in his top pocket.

'He looks much younger than thirty-two, doesn't he?' said Werner.

'You can't rely on those computer printouts, especially with listed civil servants or even members of the Bundestag. They were all put onto the computer when it was installed, by copy typists working long hours of overtime to make a bit of spare cash.'

'What do you think?' said Werner.

'I don't like the look of him,' I said.

'He's guilty,' said Werner. He had no more information than I did, but he was trying to reassure me.

'But the uncorroborated word of a defector such as Stinnes won't cut much ice in an open court, even if London will let Stinnes go into a court. If this fellow's boss stands by him and they both scream blue murder, he might get away with it.'

'When do we take him, Bernie?'

'Maybe his contact will come here,' I said. It was an excuse for delay.

'He'd have to be a real beginner, Bernie. Just one look at this place

– lit up like a Christmas tree, cops outside, and no room to move – no one with any experience would risk coming into a place like this.'

'Perhaps they won't be expecting problems,' I said optimistically.

'Moscow know Stinnes is missing and they've had plenty of time to alert their networks. And anyone with experience will smell this stakeout when they park outside.'

'He didn't smell it,' I said, nodding to our crew-cut man as he swigged at his beer and engaged a fellow guest in conversation.

'Moscow can't send a source like him away to their training school,' said Werner. 'But that's why you can be quite certain that his contact will be Moscow-trained: and that means wary. You might as well arrest him now.'

'We say nothing; we arrest no one,' I told him once again. 'German security are doing this one; he's simply being detained for questioning. We stand by and see how it goes.'

'Let me do it, Bernie.' Werner Volkmann was a Berliner by birth. I'd come to school here as a young child, my German was just as authentic as his, but because I was English, Werner was determined to hang on to the conceit that his German was in some magic way more authentic than mine. I suppose I would feel the same way about any German who spoke perfect London-accented English, so I didn't argue about it.

'I don't want him to know any non-German service is involved. If he tumbles to who we are, he'll know Stinnes is in London.'

'They know already, Bernie. They must know where he is by now.'

'Stinnes has got enough troubles without a KGB hit squad searching for him.'

Werner was looking at the dancers and smiling to himself as if at some secret joke, the way people sometimes do when they've had too much to drink. His face was still tanned from his time in Mexico and his teeth were white and perfect. He looked almost handsome despite the lumpy fit of his suit. 'It's like a Hollywood movie,' he said.

'Yes,' I said. 'The budget's too big for television.' The ballroom was crowded with elegant couples, all wearing the sort of clothes that would have looked all right for a ball at the turn of the century. And the guests weren't the desiccated old fogies I was expecting to see at this fiftieth birthday party for a manufacturer of dishwashers. There were plenty of richly clad young people whirling to the music of another time in another town. *Kaiserstadt* – isn't that what Vienna was called at a time when there was only one Emperor in Europe and only one capital for him?

It was the makeup and the hair-dos that sounded the jarring note of modernity, that and the gun I could see bulging under Werner's beautiful silk jacket. I suppose that's what was making it so tight across the chest.

The white-coated waiter returned with another big tray of glasses. Some of the glasses were not empty. There was the sudden smell of alcohol as he tipped cherries, olives, and abandoned drinks into the warm water of the sink before putting the glasses into the service lift. Then he turned to Werner and said respectfully, 'They've arrested the contact, sir. Went to the car just as you said.' He wiped the empty tray with a cloth.

'What's all this, Werner?' I said.

The waiter looked at me and then at Werner and, when Werner nodded assent, said, 'The contact went to the suspect's parked car . . . a woman at least forty years old, maybe older. She had a key that fitted the car door. She unlocked the glove compartment and took an envelope. We've taken her into custody but the envelope has not yet been opened. The captain wants to know if he should take the woman back to the office or hold her here in the panel truck for you to talk to.'

The music stopped and the dancers applauded. Somewhere on the far side of the ballroom a man was heard singing an old country song. He stopped, embarrassed, and there was laughter.

'Has she given a Berlin address?'

'Kreuzberg. An apartment house near the Landwehr Canal.'

'Tell your captain to take the woman to the apartment. Search it and hold her there. Phone here to confirm that she's given the correct address and we'll come along later to talk to her,' I said. 'Don't let her make any phone calls. Make sure the envelope remains unopened; we know what's in it. I'll want it as evidence, so don't let everybody maul it about.'

'Yes, sir,' said the waiter and departed, picking his way across the dance floor as the dancers walked off it.

'Why didn't you tell me he was one of our people?' I asked Werner.

Werner giggled. 'You should have seen your face.'

'You're drunk, Werner,' I said.

'You didn't even recognize a plainclothes cop. What's happening to you, Bernie?'

'I should have guessed. They always have them clearing away the dirty dishes; a cop doesn't know enough about food and wine to serve anything.'

'You didn't think it was worth watching his car, did you?'

He was beginning to irritate me. I said, 'If I had your kind of money, I wouldn't be dragging around with a lot of cops and security men.'

'What would you be doing?'

'With money? If I didn't have the kids, I'd find some little pension in Tuscany, somewhere not too far from the beach.'

'Admit it; you didn't think it was worth watching his car, did you?'

'You're a genius.'

'No need for sarcasm,' said Werner. 'You've got him now. Without me you would have ended up with egg on your face.' He burped very softly, holding a hand over his mouth.

'Yes, Werner,' I said.

'Let's go and arrest the bastard . . . I had a feeling about that car – the way he locked the doors and then looked round like someone might be waiting there.' There had always been a didactic side to Werner; he should have been a school-teacher, as his mother wanted.

'You're a drunken fool, Werner,' I said.

'Shall I go and arrest him?'

'Go and breathe all over him,' I said.

Werner smiled. Werner had proved what a brilliant field agent he could be. Werner was very very happy.

He made a fuss of course. He wanted his lawyer and wanted to talk to his boss and to some friend of his in the government. I knew the type only too well; he was treating us as if *we'd* been caught stealing secrets for the Russians. He was still protesting when he departed with the arrest team. They were not impressed; they'd seen it all before. They were experienced men, brought in from the BfV's 'political office' in Bonn.

They took him to the BfV office in Spandau, but I decided they'd get nothing but indignation out of him that night. Tomorrow perhaps he'd simmer down a little and get nervous enough to say something worth hearing before the time came when they'd have to charge him or release him. Luckily it was a decision I wouldn't have to make. Meanwhile, I decided to go and see if there was anything to be got out of the woman.

Werner drove. He didn't speak much on the journey back to Kreuzberg. I stared out of the window. Berlin is a sort of history book of twentieth-century violence, and every street corner brought a recollection of something I'd heard, seen, or read. We followed the road alongside the Landwehr Canal, which twists and turns through the heart of the city. Its oily water holds many dark secrets. Back in 1919, when the Spartakists attempted to seize the city by an armed uprising, two officers of the Horse Guards took the badly beaten Rosa Luxemburg – a Communist leader – from their headquarters at the Eden Hotel, next to the Zoo, shot her dead and threw her into the canal. The officers pretended that she'd been carried off by angry rioters, but four months later her bloated corpse floated up and got jammed into a lock gate. Now, in East Berlin, they name streets after her.

But not all the ghosts go *into* this canal. In February 1920 a police sergeant pulled a young woman out of the canal at the Bendler Bridge. Taken to the Elisabeth Hospital in Lützowstrasse, she was later identified as the Grand Duchess Anastasia, the youngest daughter of the last Czar of All the Russias and only survivor of the massacre.

'This is it,' said Werner, pulling into the kerb. 'Good job there's a cop on the door, or we'd come back to find the car stripped to the chassis.'

The address the contact had given was a shabby nineteenth-century tenement in a neighbourhood virtually taken over by Turkish immigrants. The once imposing grey stone entrance, still pitted with splinter damage from the war, was defaced by brightly coloured graffiti sprays. Inside the gloomy hallway there was a smell of spicy food and dirt and disinfectant.

These old houses have no numbered apartments, but we found the BfV men at the very top. There were two security locks on the door, but not much sign of anything inside to protect. Two men were still searching the hallway when we arrived. They were tapping the walls, prizing up floorboards, and poking screwdrivers deep into the plaster with that sort of inscrutable delight that comes to men blessed by governmental authority to be destructive.

It was typical of the overnight places the KGB provided for the faithful. Top floors: cold, cramped and cheap. Perhaps they chose these sleazy accommodations to remind all concerned about the plight of the poor in the capitalist economy. Or perhaps in this sort of district there were fewer questions asked about comings and goings by all kinds of people at all kinds of hours.

No TV, no radio, no soft seats. Iron bedstead with an old grey blanket, four wooden chairs, a small plastic-topped table and upon it black bread roughly sliced, electric ring, dented kettle, tinned milk, dried coffee, and some sugar cubes wrapped to show they were from a Hilton hotel. There were three dog-eared German paperback books – Dickens, Schiller, and a collection of crossword puzzles, mostly completed. On one of the two single beds a small case was opened and its contents displayed. It was obviously the woman's baggage: a cheap black dress, nylon underwear, low-heeled leather shoes, an apple and orange, and an English newspaper – the *Socialist Worker*.

A young BfV officer was waiting for me there. We exchanged greetings and he told me the woman had been given no more than a brief preliminary questioning. She'd offered to make a statement at first and then said she wouldn't, the officer said. He'd sent a man to get a typewriter so it could be taken down if she changed her mind again. He handed me some Westmarks, a driving licence, and a passport; the contents of her handbag. The licence and passport were British.

'I've got a pocket recorder,' I told him without lowering my voice.

'We'll sort out what to type and have it signed after I've spoken with her. I'll want you to witness her signature.'

The woman was seated in the tiny kitchen. There were dirty cups on the table and some hairpins that I guessed had come from a search of the handbag she now held on her lap.

'The captain tells me that you want to make a statement,' I said in English.

'Are you English?' she said. She looked at me and then at Werner. She showed no great surprise that we were both in dinner suits complete with fancy cuff links and patent-leather shoes. She must have realized we'd been on duty inside the house.

'Yes,' I said. I signalled with my hand to tell Werner to leave the room.

'Are you in charge?' she asked. She had the exaggerated upper-class accent that shop girls use in Knightsbridge boutiques. 'I want to know what I'm charged with. I warn you I know my rights. Am I under arrest?'

From the side table I picked up the bread knife and waved it at her. 'Under Law 43 of the Allied Military Government legislation, still in force in this city, possession of this bread knife is an offence for which the death sentence can be imposed.'

'You must be mad,' she said. 'The war was almost forty years ago.'

I put the knife into a drawer and slammed it shut. She was startled by the sound. I moved a kitchen chair and sat on it so that I was facing her at a distance of only a yard or so. 'You're not in Germany,' I told her. 'This is Berlin. And Decree 511, ratified in 1951, includes a clause that makes information gathering an offence for which you can get ten years in prison. Not spying, not intelligence work, just collecting information is an offence.'

I put her passport on the table and turned the pages as if reading her name and occupation for the first time. 'So don't talk to me about knowing your rights; you've got no rights.'

From the passport I read aloud: 'Carol Elvira Miller, born in London 1930, occupation: schoolteacher.' Then I looked up at her. She returned my gaze with the calm, flat stare that the camera had recorded for her passport. Her hair was straight and short in pageboy style. She had clear blue eyes and a pointed nose, and the pert expression came naturally to her. She'd been pretty once, but now she was thin and drawn and – in dark conservative clothes and with no trace of makeup – well on the way to looking like a frail old woman. 'Elvira. That's a German name, isn't it?'

She showed no sign of fear. She brightened as women so often do at personal talk. 'It's Spanish. Mozart used it in *Don Giovanni*.'

I nodded. 'And Miller?'

She smiled nervously. She was not frightened, but it was the smile of someone who wanted to seem cooperative. My hectoring little speech had done the trick. 'My father is German . . . was German. From Leipzig. He emigrated to England long before Hitler's time. My mother is English . . . from Newcastle,' she added after a long pause.

'Married?'

'My husband died nearly ten years ago. His name was Johnson, but I went back to using my family name.'

'Children?'

'A married daughter.'

'Where do you teach?'

'I was a supply teacher in London, but the amount of work I got grew less and less. For the last few months I've been virtually unemployed.'

'You know what was in the envelope you collected from the car tonight?'

'I won't waste your time with excuses. I know it contained secrets of some description.' She had the clear voice and pedantic manner of schoolteachers everywhere.

'And you know where it was going?'

'I want to make a statement. I told the other officer that. I want to be taken back to England and speak to someone in British security. Then I'll make a complete statement.'

'Why?' I said. 'Why are you so anxious to go back to England? You're a Russian agent; we both know that. What's the difference where you are when you're charged?'

'I've been stupid,' she said. 'I realize that now.'

'Did you realize it before or after you were taken into custody?'

She pressed her lips together as if suppressing a smile. 'It was a shock.' She put her hands on the table. They were white and wrinkled with the brown freckle marks that come with middle age. There were nicotine stains, and the ink from a leaky pen had marked finger and thumb. 'I just can't stop trembling. Sitting here watching the security men searching through my luggage, I've had enough time to consider what a fool I've been. I love England. My father brought me up to love everything English.'

Despite this contention she soon slipped back into speaking German. She wasn't German; she wasn't British. I saw the rootless feeling within her and recognized something of myself.

I said, 'A man was it?' She looked at me and frowned. She'd been expecting reassurance, a smile in return for the smiles she'd given me and a promise that nothing too bad would happen to her. 'A man . . . the one who enticed you into this foolishness?'

She must have heard some note of scorn in my voice. 'No,' she said. 'It was all my own doing. I joined the Party fifteen years ago.

After my husband died I wanted to keep myself occupied. So I became a very active worker for the teachers union. And one day I thought, well, why not go the whole hog.'

'What was the whole hog, Mrs Miller?'

'My father's name was Müller; I may as well tell you that because you will soon find out. Hugo Müller. He changed it to Miller when he was naturalized. He wanted us all to be English.' Again she pressed her hands flat on the table and looked at them while she spoke. It was as if she was blaming her hands for doing things of which she'd never really approved.

'I was asked to collect parcels, look after things, and so on. Later I began providing accommodation in my London flat. People were brought there late at night – Russians, Czechs, and so on – usually they spoke no English and no German either. Seamen sometimes, judging by their clothing. They always seemed to be ravenously hungry. Once there was a man dressed as a priest. He spoke Polish, but I managed to make myself understood. In the morning someone would come and collect them.'

She sighed and then looked up at me to see how I was taking her confession. 'I have a spare bedroom,' she added, as if the propriety of their sleeping arrangements was more important than her services to the KGB.

She stopped talking for a long time and looked at her hands.

'They were fugitives,' I said, to prompt her into talking again.

'I don't know who they were. Afterwards there was usually an envelope with a few pounds put through my letterbox, but I didn't do it for the money.'

'Why did you do it?'

'I was a Marxist; I was serving the cause.'

'And now?'

'They made a fool of me,' she said. 'They used me to do their dirty work. What did they care what happened to me if I got caught? What do they care now? What am I supposed to do?'

It sounded more like the bitter complaint of a woman abandoned by her lover than of an agent under arrest. 'You're supposed to enjoy being a martyr,' I said. 'That's the way the system works for them.'

'I'll give you the names and addresses. I'll tell you everything I know.' She leaned forward. 'I don't want to go to prison. Will it all have to be in the newspapers?'

'Does it matter?'

'My married daughter is living in Canada. She's married to a Spanish boy she met on holiday. They've applied for Canadian citizenship but their papers haven't come through yet. It would be terrible if this trouble I'm in ruined their lives; they're so happy together.'

'And this overnight accommodation you were providing for your Russian friends – when did that all stop?'

She looked up sharply, as if surprised that I could guess that it had stopped.

'The two jobs don't mix,' I said. 'The accommodation was just an interim task to see how reliable you were.'

She nodded. 'Two years ago,' she said softly, 'perhaps two and a half years.'

'Then?'

'I came to Berlin for a week. They paid my fare. I went through to the East and spent a week in a training school. All the other students were German, but as you see I speak German well. My father always insisted that I kept up my German.'

'A week at Potsdam?'

'Yes, just outside Potsdam, that's right.'

'Don't miss out anything important, Mrs Miller,' I said.

'No, I won't,' she promised nervously. 'I was there for ten days learning about shortwave radios and microdots and so on. You probably know the sort of thing.'

'Yes, I know the sort of thing. It's a training school for spies.'

'Yes,' she whispered.

'You're not going to tell me you came back from there without realizing you were a fully trained Russian spy, Mrs Miller?'

She looked up and met my stare. 'No, I've told you, I was an enthusiastic Marxist. I was perfectly ready to be a spy for them. As I saw it, I was doing it on behalf of the oppressed and hungry people of the world. I suppose I still am a Marxist-Leninist.'

'Then you must be an incurable romantic,' I said.

'It was wrong of me to do what I did; I can see that, of course. England has been good to me. But half the world is starving and Marxism is the only solution.'

'Don't lecture me, Mrs Miller,' I said. 'I get enough of that from my office.' I got up so that I could unbutton my overcoat and find my cigarettes. 'Do you want a cigarette?' I said.

She gave no sign of having heard me.

'I'm trying to give them up,' I said, 'but I carry the cigarettes with me.'

She still didn't answer. Perhaps she was too busy thinking about what might happen to her. I went to the window and looked out. It was too dark to see very much except Berlin's permanent false dawn: the greenish white glare that came from the floodlit 'death strip' along the east side of the Wall. I knew this street well enough; I'd passed this block thousands of times. Since 1961, when the Wall was first built, following the snaky route of the Landwehr Canal had become the quickest way to get around the Wall from the neon glitter of the Ku-damm to the floodlights of Checkpoint Charlie.

'Will I go to prison?' she said.

I didn't turn round. I buttoned my coat, pleased that I'd resisted the temptation to smoke. From my pocket I brought the tiny Pearlcorder tape machine. It was made of a bright silver metal. I made no attempt to hide it. I wanted her to see it.

'Will I go to prison?' she asked again.

'I don't know,' I said. 'But I hope so.'

It had taken no more than forty minutes to get her confession. Werner was waiting for me in the next room. There was no heating in that room. He was sitting on a kitchen chair, the fur collar of his coat pulled up round his ears so that it almost touched the rim of his hat.

'A good squeal?' he asked.

'You look like an undertaker, Werner,' I said. 'A very prosperous undertaker waiting for a very prosperous corpse.'

'I've got to sleep,' he said. 'I can't take these late nights any more. If you're going to hang on here, to type it all out, I'd rather go home now.'

It was the drink that had got to him, of course. The ebullience of intoxication didn't last very long with Werner. Alcohol is a depressant and Werner's metabolic rate had slowed enough to render him unfit to drive. 'I'll drive,' I said. 'And I'll make the transcription on your typewriter.'

'Sure,' said Werner. I was staying with him in his apartment at Dahlem. And now, in his melancholy mood, he was anticipating his wife's reaction to us waking her up by arriving in the small hours of the morning. Werner's typewriter was a very noisy machine and he knew I'd want to finish the job before going to sleep. 'Is there much of it?' he asked.

'It's short and sweet, Werner. But she's given us a few things that might make London Central scratch their heads and wonder.'

'Such as?'

'Read it in the morning, Werner. We'll talk about it over breakfast.'

It was a beautiful Berlin morning. The sky was blue despite all those East German generating plants that burn brown coal so that pale smog sits over the city for so much of the year. Today the fumes of the *Braunkohle* were drifting elsewhere, and outside the birds were singing to celebrate it. Inside, a big wasp, a last survivor from the summer, buzzed around angrily.

Werner's Dahlem apartment was like a second home to me. I'd

known it when it was a gathering place for an endless stream of Werner's oddball friends. In those days the furniture was old and Werner played jazz on a piano decorated with cigarette burns, and Werner's beautifully constructed model planes were hanging from the ceiling because that was the only place where they would not be sat upon.

Now it was all different. The old things had all been removed by Zena, his very young wife. Now the flat was done to her taste: expensive modern furniture and a big rubber plant, and a rug that hung on the wall and bore the name of the 'artist' who'd woven it. The only thing that remained from the old days was the lumpy sofa that converted to the lumpy bed on which I'd slept.

The three of us were sitting in the 'breakfast room', a counter at the end of the kitchen. It was arranged like a lunch counter with Zena playing the role of bartender. From here there was a view through the window, and we were high enough to see the sun-edged treetops of the Grunewald just a block or two away. Zena was squeezing oranges in an electric juicer, and in the automatic coffee-maker the coffee was dripping, its rich aroma floating through the room.

We were talking about marriage. I said, 'The tragedy of marriage is that while all women marry thinking that their man will change, all men marry believing their wife will never change. Both are invariably disappointed.'

'What rot,' said Zena as she poured the juice into three glasses. 'Men do change.'

She bent down to see better the level of the juice and ensure that we all got precisely the same amount. It was a legacy of the Prussian family background of which she was so proud, despite the fact that she'd never even seen the old family homeland. For Prussians like to think of themselves not only as the conscience of the world, but also its final judge and jury.

'Don't encourage him, Zena darling,' said Werner. 'That contrived Oscar Wilde-ish assertion is just Bernard's way of annoying wives.'

Zena didn't let it go; she liked to argue with me. 'Men change. It's men who usually leave home and break up the marriage. And it's because they change.'

'Good juice,' I said, sipping some.

'Men go out to work. Men want promotion in their jobs and they aspire to the higher social class of their superiors. Then they feel their wives are inadequate and start looking for a wife who knows the manners and vocabulary of that class they want to join.'

'You're right,' I admitted. 'I meant that men don't change in the way that their women want them to change.'

She smiled. She knew that I was commenting on the way she

had changed poor Werner from being an easygoing and somewhat bohemian character into a devoted and obedient husband. It was Zena who had stopped him smoking and made him diet enough to reduce his waistline. And it was Zena who approved everything he bought to wear, from swimming trunks to tuxedo. In this respect Zena regarded me as her opponent. I was the bad influence who could undo all her good work, and that was something Zena was determined to prevent.

She climbed up onto the stool. She was so well proportioned that you only noticed how tiny she was when she did such things. She had long, dark hair and this morning she'd clipped it back into a ponytail that reached down to her shoulder blades. She was wearing a red cotton kimono with a wide black sash around her middle. She'd not missed any sleep that night and her eyes were bright and clear; she'd even found time enough to put on a touch of makeup. She didn't need makeup – she was only twenty-two years old and there was no disputing her beauty – but the makeup was something from behind which she preferred to face the world.

The coffee was very dark and strong. She liked it like that, but I poured a lot of milk into mine. The buzzer on the oven sounded and Zena went to get the warm rolls. She put them into a small basket with a red-checked cloth before offering them to us. '*Brötchen*,' she said. Zena was born and brought up in Berlin, but she didn't call the bread rolls *Schrippe* the way the rest of the population of Berlin did. Zena didn't want to be identified with Berlin; she preferred keeping her options open.

'Any butter?' I said, breaking open the bread roll.

'We don't eat it,' said Zena. 'It's bad for you.'

'Give Bernie some of that new margarine,' said Werner.

'You should lose some weight,' Zena told me. 'I wouldn't even be eating bread if I were you.'

'There are all kinds of other things I do that you wouldn't do if you were me,' I said. The wasp settled in my hair and I brushed it away.

She decided not to get into that one. She rolled up a newspaper and aimed some blows at the wasp. Then with unconcealed ill-humour she went to the refrigerator and brought me a plastic tub of margarine. 'Thanks,' I said. 'I'm catching the morning flight. I'll get out of your way as soon as I'm shaved.'

'No hurry,' said Werner to smooth things over. He had already shaved, of course; Zena wouldn't have let him have breakfast if he'd turned up unshaven. 'So you got all your typing done last night,' he said. 'I should have stayed up and helped.'

'It wasn't necessary. I'll have the translation done in London. I appreciate you and Zena giving me a place to sleep, to say nothing of the coffee last night and Zena's great breakfast this morning.'

I overdid the appreciation I suppose. I'm prone to do this when I'm nervous, and Zena was a great expert at making me nervous.

'I was damned tired,' said Werner.

Zena shot me a glance, but when she spoke it was to Werner. 'You were drunk,' she said. 'I thought you were supposed to be working last night.'

'We were, darling,' said Werner.

'There wasn't much drinking, Zena,' I said.

'Werner gets drunk on the smell of a barmaid's apron,' said Zena. Werner opened his mouth to object to this put-down. Then he realized that he could only challenge it by claiming to have drunk a great deal. He sipped some coffee instead.

'I've seen her before,' said Werner.

'The woman?'

'What's her name?'

'She says it's Müller, but she was married to a man named Johnson at one time. Here? You've seen her here? She said she lives in England.'

'She went to the school in Potsdam,' said Werner. He smiled at my look of surprise. 'I read your report when I got up this morning. You don't mind, do you?'

'Of course not. I wanted you to read it. There might be developments.'

'Was this to do with Erich Stinnes?' said Zena. She waved the wasp away from her head.

'Yes,' I said. 'It was his information.'

She nodded and poured herself more coffee. It was difficult to believe that not so long ago she'd been in love with Erich Stinnes. It was difficult to believe that she'd risked her life to protect him and that she was still having physiotherapy sessions because of injuries she'd suffered in his defence.

But Zena was young; and romantic. For both of those reasons, her passions could be of short duration. And for both those reasons, it could well be that she had never been in love with him, but merely in love with the idea of herself in love.

Werner seemed not to notice the mention of Erich Stinnes's name. That was Werner's way – *honi soit qui mal y pense*. Evil to him who evil thinks – that could well be Werner's motto, for Werner was too generous and considerate to ever think the worst of anyone. And even when the worst was evident, Werner was ready to forgive. Zena's flagrant love affair with Frank Harrington – the head of our Berlin Field Unit, the Berlin Resident – had made me angrier with her than Werner had been.

Some people said that Werner was the sort of masochist who got a perverse pleasure from the knowledge that his wife had gone off to live with Frank, but I knew Werner too well to go in for that sort of instant psychology. Werner was a tough guy who played the game by his own rules. Maybe some of his rules were flexible, but God help anyone who overstepped the line that Werner drew. Werner was an Old Testament man, and his wrath and vengeance could be terrible. I know, and Werner knows I know. That's what makes us so close that nothing can come between us, not even the cunning little Zena.

'I've seen that Miller woman somewhere,' said Werner. 'I never forget a face.' He watched the wasp. It was sleepy, crawling slowly up the wall. Werner reached for Zena's newspaper, but the wasp, sensing danger, flew away.

Zena was still thinking of Erich Stinnes. 'We do all the work,' she said bitterly. 'Bernard gets all the credit. And Erich Stinnes gets all the money.' She was referring to the way in which Stinnes, a KGB major, had been persuaded to come over to work for us and given a big cash payment. She reached for the jug, and some coffee dripped onto the hotplate making a loud, hissing sound. When she'd poured coffee for herself, she put the very hot jug onto the tiles of the counter. The change of temperature must have made the jug crack, for there was a sound like a pistol shot and the hot coffee flowed across the counter top so that we all jumped to our feet to avoid being scalded.

Zena grabbed some paper towels and, standing well back from the coffee flowing onto the tiled floor, dabbed them around. 'I put it down too hard,' she said when the mess was cleared away.

'I think you did, Zena,' I said.

'It was already cracked,' said Werner. Then he brought the rolled newspaper down on the wasp and killed it.

2

It was eight o'clock that evening in London when I finally delivered my report to my immediate boss, Dicky Cruyer, Controller German Stations. I'd attached a complete translation too, as I knew Dicky wasn't exactly bilingual.

'Congratulations,' he said. 'One up to Comrade Stinnes eh?' He shook the flimsy pages of my hastily written report as if something might fall from between them. He'd already heard my tape and had my oral account of the Berlin trip so there was little chance that he'd read the report very thoroughly, especially if it meant missing his dinner.

'No one in Bonn will thank us,' I warned him.

'They have all the evidence they need,' said Dicky with a sniff.

'I was on the phone to Berlin an hour ago,' I said. 'He's pulling all the strings that can be pulled.'

'What does his boss say?'

'He's spending his Christmas vacation in Egypt. No one can find him,' I said.

'What a sensible man,' said Dicky with admiration that was both sincere and undisguised. 'Was he informed of the impending arrest of his secretary?'

'Not by us, but that would be the regular BfV procedure.'

'Have you phoned Bonn this evening? What do BfV reckon the chances of a statement from him?'

'Better we stay out of it, Dicky.'

Dicky looked at me while he thought about this and then, deciding I was right, tried another aspect of the same problem. 'Have you seen Stinnes since you handed him over to London Debriefing Centre?'

'I gather the current policy is to keep me away from him.'

'Come along,' said Dicky, smiling to humour me in my state of paranoia. 'You're not saying you're still suspect?' He stood up from behind the rosewood table that he used instead of a desk and got a transparent plastic folding chair for me.

'My wife defected.' I sat down. Dicky had removed his visitors' chairs on the pretext of making more space. His actual motive was to provide an excuse for him to use the conference rooms along the corridor. Dicky liked to use the conference rooms; it made him feel important and it meant that his name was exhibited in little plastic letters on the notice board opposite the top-floor lifts.

His folding chairs were the most uncomfortable seats in the building, but Dicky didn't worry about this as he never sat in them. And anyway, I didn't want to sit chatting with him. There was still work to clear up before I could go home.

'That's all past history,' said Dicky, running a thin bony hand through his curly hair so that he could take a surreptitious look at his big black wristwatch, the kind that works deep under water.

I'd always suspected that Dicky would be more comfortable with his hair cut short and brushed, and in the dark suits, white shirts and old school ties that were de rigueur for senior staff. But he persisted in being the only one of us who wore faded denim, cowboy boots, coloured neckerchiefs, and black leather because he thought it would help to identify him as an infant prodigy. But perhaps I had it the wrong way round; perhaps Dicky would have been happier to keep the trendy garb and be 'creative' in an advertising agency.

He zipped the front of his jacket up and down again and said, 'You're the local hero. You are the one who brought Stinnes to us at a time when everyone here said it couldn't be done.'

'Is that what they were saying? I wish I'd known. The way I heard it, a lot of people were saying I did everything to avoid bringing him in because I was frightened his debriefing would drop me into it.'

'Well, anyone who was spreading that sort of story is now looking pretty damned stupid.'

'I'm not in the clear yet, Dicky. You know it and I know it, so let's stop all this bullshit.'

He held up his hand as if to ward off a blow. 'You're still not clear on paper,' said Dicky. 'On paper . . . and you know why?'

'No, I don't know why. Tell me.'

Dicky sighed. 'For the simple but obvious reason that this Department needs an excuse to hold Stinnes in London Debriefing Centre and keep on pumping him. Without an ongoing investigation of our own staff, we'd have to hand Stinnes over to MI5. . . . That's why the Department haven't cleared you yet: it's a department necessity, Bernard, nothing sinister about it.'

'Who's in charge of the Stinnes debriefing?' I asked.

'Don't look at me, old friend. Stinnes is a hot potato. I don't want any part of that one. Neither does Bret . . . no one up here on the top floor wants anything to do with it.'

'Things could change,' I said. 'If Stinnes gives us a couple more winners like this one, then a few people will start to see that being in charge of the Stinnes debriefing could be the road to fame and fortune.'

'I don't think so,' said Dicky. 'The tip-off you handled in Berlin was just for openers . . . a few quick forays before Moscow tumble what's happening to their networks. Once the dust settles, the interrogators will take Stinnes through the files . . . right?'

'Files? You mean they'll be poking into all our past operations?'

'Not *all* of them. I don't suppose they'll go back to discover how Christopher Marlowe discovered that the Spanish Armada had sailed.' Dicky permitted himself a smile at this joke. 'It's obvious that the Department will want to discover how good our guesses were. They'll play all the games again, but this time they'll know which ones have a happy ending.'

'And you'll go along with that?'

'They won't consult me, old son. I'm just German Stations Controller; I'm not the D-G. I'm not even on the Policy Committee.'

'Giving Stinnes access to department archives would be showing a lot of trust in him.'

'You know what the old man's like. Deputy D-G came in yesterday on one of his rare visits to the building. He's enraptured about the progress of the Stinnes debriefing.'

'If Stinnes is a plant . . .'

'Ah, if Stinnes is a plant . . .' Dicky sank down in his Charles Eames chair and put his feet on the matching footstool. The night was dark outside and the windowpanes were like ebony reflecting a perfect image of the room. Only the antique desk light was on; it made a pool of light on the table where the report and transcript were placed side by side. Dicky almost disappeared into the gloom except when the light reflected from the brass buckle of his belt or shone on the gold medallion he wore suspended inside his open-neck shirt. 'But the idea that Stinnes is a plant is hard to sustain when he's just given us three well-placed KGB agents in a row.'

He looked at his watch before shouting 'Coffee' loudly enough for his secretary to hear in the adjoining room. When Dicky worked late, his secretary worked late too. He didn't trust the duty roster staff with making his coffee.

'Will he talk, this one you arrested in Berlin? He had a year with the Bonn Defence Ministry, I notice from the file.'

'I didn't arrest him; we left it to the Germans. Yes, he'll talk if they push him hard enough. They have the evidence and – thanks to Volkmann – they're holding the woman who came to collect it from the car.'

'And I'm sure you put all that in your report. Are you now the official secretary of the Werner Volkmann fan club? Or is this something you do for all your old school chums?'

'He's very good at what he does.'

'And so we all agree, but don't tell me that but for Volkmann, we wouldn't have picked up the woman. Staking out the car is standard procedure. Ye gods, Bernard, any probationary cop would do that as a matter of course.'

'A commendation would work wonders for him.'

'Well, he's not getting any bloody commendation from me. Just because he's your close friend, you think you can inveigle any kind of praise and privilege out of me for him.'

'It wouldn't cost anything, Dicky,' I said mildly.

'No, it wouldn't cost anything,' said Dicky sarcastically. 'Not until the next time he makes some monumental cock-up. Then someone asks me how come I commended him; then it would cost something. It would cost me a chewing out and maybe a promotion.'

'Yes, Dicky,' I said.

Promotion? Dicky was two years younger than me and he'd already been promoted several rungs beyond his competence. What promotion did he have his eye on now? He'd only just fought off Bret Rensselaer's attempt to take over the German desk. I'd thought he'd be satisfied to consolidate his good fortune.

'And what do you make of this Englishwoman?' He tapped the roughly typed transcript of her statement. 'Looks as if you got her talking.'

'I couldn't stop her,' I said.

'Like that, was it? I don't want to go all through it again tonight. Anything important?'

'Some inconsistencies that should be followed up.'

'For instance?'

'She was working in London, handling selected items for immediate shortwave radio transmission to Moscow.'

'Must have been bloody urgent,' said Dicky. So he'd noticed that already. Had he waited to see if I brought it up? 'And that means damned good. Right? I mean, not even handled through the Embassy radio, so it was a source they wanted to keep very very secret.'

'Fiona's material probably,' I said.

'I wondered if you'd twig that,' said Dicky. 'It was obviously the stuff your wife was betraying out of our day-to-day operational files.'

He liked to twist the knife in the wound. He held me personally responsible for what Fiona had done; he'd virtually said so on more than one occasion.

'But the material kept coming.'

Dicky frowned. 'What are you getting at?'

'It kept coming. First-grade material even after Fiona ran for it.'

'This woman's transmitted material wasn't all from the same

source,' said Dicky. 'I remember what she said when you played your tape to me.'

He picked up the transcript and tried to find what he wanted in the muddle of *humms* and *hahhs* and 'indistinct passage' marks that are always a part of transcripts from such tape recordings. He put the sheets down again.

'Well anyway, I remember there were two assignment codes: JAKE and IRONFOOT. Is that what's worrying you?'

'We should follow it up!' I said. 'I don't like loose ends like that. The dates suggest that Fiona was IRONFOOT. Who the hell was JAKE?'

'The Fiona material is our worry. Whatever else Moscow got – and are still getting – is a matter for Five. You know that, Bernard. It's not our job to search high and low to find Russian spies.'

'I still think we should check this woman's statement against what Stinnes knows.'

'Stinnes is nothing to do with me, Bernard. I've just told you that.'

'Well, I think he should be. It's madness that we don't have access to him without going to Debriefing Centre for permission.'

'Let me tell you something, Bernard,' said Dicky, leaning well back in the soft leather seat and adopting the manner of an Oxford don explaining the law of gravity to a delivery boy. 'When London Debriefing Centre get through with Stinnes, heads will roll up here on the top floor. You know the monumental cock-ups that have dogged the work of this Department for the last few years. Now we'll have chapter and verse on every decision made up here while Stinnes was running things in Berlin. Every decision made by senior staff will be scrutinized with twenty-twenty hindsight. It could get messy; people with a history of bad decisions are going to be axed very smartly.'

Dicky smiled. He could afford to smile; Dicky had never made a decision in his life. Whenever something decisive was about to happen, Dicky went home with a headache.

'And you think that whoever's in charge of the Stinnes debriefing will be unpopular?'

'Running a witch-hunt is not likely to be a social asset,' said Dicky.

I thought 'witch-hunt' was an inaccurate description of the weeding out of incompetents, but there would be plenty who would favour Dicky's terminology.

'And that's not only my opinion,' he added. 'No one wants to take Stinnes. And I don't want you saying we should have responsibility for him.'

Dicky's secretary brought coffee.

'I was just coming, Mr Cruyer,' she said apologetically. She was a mousy little widow whose every sheet of typing was a patchwork of white correcting paint. At one time Dicky had had a shapely twenty-five-year-old divorcee as secretary, but his wife, Daphne, had made him get rid of her. At the time, Dicky had pretended that firing the secretary was his idea; he said it was because she didn't boil the water properly for his coffee. 'Your wife phoned. She wanted to know what time to expect you for dinner.'

'And what did you say?' Dicky asked her.

The poor woman hesitated, worrying if she'd done the right thing. 'I said you were at a meeting and I would call her back.'

'Tell my wife not to wait dinner for me. I'll get a bite to eat somewhere or other.'

'If you want to get away, Dicky,' I said, rising to my feet.

'Sit down, Bernard. We can't waste a decent cup of coffee. I'll be home soon enough. Daphne knows what this job is like; eighteen hours a day lately.' It was not a soft, melancholy reflection but a loud proclamation to the world, or at least to me and his secretary who departed to pass the news on to Daphne.

I nodded but I couldn't help wondering if Dicky was scheduling a visit to some other lady. Lately I'd noticed a gleam in his eye and a spring in his step and a most unusual willingness to stay late at the office.

Dicky got up from his easy chair and fussed over the antique butler's tray which his secretary had placed so carefully on his side table. He emptied the Spode cups of the hot water and half filled each warmed cup with black coffee. Dicky was extremely particular about his coffee. Twice a week he sent one of the drivers to collect a packet of freshly roasted beans from Mr Higgins in South Molton Street – chagga, no blends – and it had to be ground just before brewing.

'That's good,' he said, sipping it with all the studied attention of the connoisseur he claimed to be. Having approved the coffee, he poured some for me.

'Wouldn't it be better to stay away from Stinnes, Bernard? He doesn't belong to us any longer, does he?' He smiled. It was a direct order; I knew Dicky's style.

'Can I have milk or cream or something in mine?' I said. 'That strong black brew you make keeps me awake at night.'

He always had a jug of cream and a bowl of sugar brought in with his coffee although he never used either. He once told me that in his regimental officers' mess, the cream was always on the table but it was considered bad form to take any. I wondered if there were a lot of people like Dicky in the Army; it was a dreadful thought. He brought the cream to me.

'You're getting old, Bernard. Did you ever think of jogging? I run three miles every morning – summer, winter, Christmas, every morning without fail.'

'Is it doing you any good?' I asked as he poured cream for me from the cow-shaped silver jug.

'Ye gods, Bernard. I'm fitter now than I was at twenty-five. I swear I am.'

'What kind of shape were you in at twenty-five?' I said.

'Damned good.' He put the jug down so that he could run his fingers round the brass-buckled leather belt that held up his jeans. He sucked in his stomach to exaggerate his slim figure and then slammed himself in the gut with a flattened hand. Even without the intake of breath, his lack of fat was impressive. Especially when you took into account the countless long lunches he charged against his expense account.

'But not as good as now?' I persisted.

'I wasn't fat and flabby the way you are, Bernard. I didn't huff and puff every time I went up a flight of stairs.'

'I thought Bret Rensselaer would take over the Stinnes debriefing.'

'Debriefing,' said Dicky suddenly. 'How I hate that word. You get briefed and maybe briefed again, but there is no way anyone can be debriefed.'

'I thought Bret would jump at it. He's been out of a job since Stinnes was enrolled.'

Dicky gave the tiniest chuckle and rubbed his hands together. 'Out of a job since he tried to take over my desk and failed. That's what you mean, isn't it?'

'Was he after your desk?' I said innocently, although Dicky had been providing me with a blow-by-blow account of Bret's tactics and his own counterploys.

'Jesus Christ, Bernard, you know he was. I told you all that.'

'So what's he got lined up now?'

'He'd like to take over in Berlin when Frank goes.'

Frank Harrington's job as head of the Berlin Field Unit was one I coveted, but it meant close liaison with Dicky, maybe even taking orders from him sometimes (although such orders were always wrapped up in polite double-talk and signed by Deputy Controller Europe or a member of the London Central Policy Committee). It wasn't exactly a role that the autocratic Bret Rensselaer would cherish.

'Berlin? Bret? Would he like that job?'

'The rumour is that Frank will get his K. and then retire.'

'And so Bret plans to sit in Berlin until his retirement comes round and hope that he'll get a K. too?' It seemed unlikely. Bret's social life centred on the swanky jet setters of London South West One. I couldn't see him sweating it out in Berlin.

'Why not?' said Dicky, who seemed to get a flushed face whenever the subject of knighthoods came up.

'Why not?' I repeated. 'Bret can't speak the language, for one thing.'

'Come along, Bernard!' said Dicky, whose command of German was about on a par with Bret's. 'He'll be running the show; he won't be required to pass himself off as a bricklayer from Prenzlauer Berg.'

A palpable hit for Dicky. Bernard Samson had spent his youth masquerading as just such lowly coarse-accented East German citizens.

'It's not just a matter of throwing gracious dinner parties in that big house in the Grunewald,' I said. 'Whoever takes over in Berlin has to know the streets and alleys. He'll also need to know the crooks and hustlers who come in to sell bits and pieces of intelligence.'

'That's what you say,' said Dicky, pouring himself more coffee. He held up the jug. 'More for you?' And when I shook my head he continued: 'That's because you fancy yourself doing Frank's job . . . don't deny it, you know it's true. You've always wanted Berlin. But times have changed, Bernard. The days of rough-and-tumble stuff are over and done with. That was okay in your father's time, when we were a de facto occupying power. But now – whatever the lawyers say – the Germans have to be treated as equal partners. What the Berlin job needs is a smoothie like Bret, someone who can charm the natives and get things done by gentle persuasion.'

'Can I change my mind about coffee?' I said. I suspected that Dicky's views were those prevailing among the top-floor mandarins. There was no way I'd be on a short list of smoothies who got things done by means of gentle persuasion, so this was goodbye to my chances of Berlin.

'Don't be so damned gloomy about it,' said Dicky as he poured coffee. 'It's mostly dregs, I'm afraid. You didn't really think you were in line for Frank's job, did you?' He smiled at the idea.

'There isn't enough money in Central Funding to entice me back to Berlin on any permanent basis. I spent half my life there. I deserve my London posting and I'm hanging on to it.'

'London is the only place to be,' said Dicky. But I wasn't fooling him. My indignation was too strong and my explanation too long. A public school man like Dicky would have done a better job of concealing his bitterness. He would have smiled coldly and said that a Berlin posting would be 'super' in such a way that it seemed he didn't care.

I'd only been in my office for about ten minutes when I heard Dicky coming down the corridor. Dicky and I must have been the only ones still working, apart from the night-duty people, and his footsteps sounded unnaturally sharp, as sounds do at night. And I could always recognize the sound of Dicky's high-heeled cowboy boots.

'Do you know what those stupid sods have done?' he asked, standing in the doorway, arms akimbo and feet apart, like Wyatt Earp coming into the saloon at Tombstone. I knew he would get on the phone to Berlin as soon as I left the office; it was always easier to meddle in other people's work than to get on with his own.

'Released him?'

'Right,' he said. My accurate guess angered him even more, as if he thought I might have been party to this development. 'How did you know?'

'I didn't know. But with you standing there blowing your top it wasn't difficult to guess.'

'They released him an hour ago. Direct instructions from Bonn. The government can't survive another scandal, is the line they're taking. How can they let politics interfere with our work?'

I noted the nice turn of phrase: 'our work'.

'It's all politics,' I said calmly. 'Espionage is about politics. Remove the politics and you don't need espionage or any of the paraphernalia of it.'

'By paraphernalia you mean us. I suppose. Well, I knew you'd have some bloody smart answer.'

'We don't run the world, Dicky. We can pick it over and then report on it. After that it's up to the politicians.'

'I suppose so.' The anger was draining out of him now. He was often given to these violent explosions, but they didn't last long providing he had someone to shout at.

'Your secretary gone?' I asked.

He nodded. That explained everything – usually it was his poor secretary who got the brunt of Dicky's fury when the world didn't run to his complete satisfaction. 'I'm going too,' he said, looking at his watch.

'I've got a lot more work to do,' I told him. I got up from my desk and put papers into the secure filing cabinet and turned the combination lock. Dicky still stood there. I looked at him and raised an eyebrow.

'And that bloody Miller woman,' said Dicky. 'She tried to knock herself off.'

'They didn't release her too?'

'No, of course not. But they let her keep her sleeping tablets. Can you imagine that sort of stupidity? She said they were aspirins and that she needed them for period pains. They believed her, and as soon as they left her alone for five minutes she swallowed the whole bottle of them.'

'And?'

'She's in the Steglitz Clinic. They pumped her stomach; it sounds as if she'll be okay. But I ask you . . . God knows when she'll be fit enough for more interrogation.'

'I'd let it go, Dicky.'

But he stood there, obviously unwilling to depart without some further word of consolation. 'And it would all happen tonight,' he added petulantly, 'just when I'm going out to dinner.'

I looked at him and nodded. So I was right about an assignation. He bit his lip, angry at having let slip his secret. 'That's strictly between you and me of course.'

'My lips are sealed,' I said.

And the Controller of German Stations marched off to his dinner date. It was sobering to realize that the man in the front line of the western world's intelligence system couldn't even keep his own infidelities secret.

When Dicky Cruyer had gone I went downstairs to the film department and took a reel of film from the rack that was waiting for the filing clerk. It was still in the wrapping paper with the courier's marks on it. I placed the film in position on the editing bench and laced it up. Then I dimmed the lights and watched the screen.

The titles were in Hungarian and so was the commentary. It was film of a security conference that had just taken place in Budapest. There was nothing very secret; the film had been made by the Hungarian Film Service for distribution to news agencies. This copy was to be used for identification purposes, so that we had up-to-date pictures of their officials.

The conference building was a fine old mansion in a well-kept park. The film crew had done exactly what was expected of them: they'd filmed the big black shiny cars arriving, they'd got pictures of Army officers and civilians walking up the marble steps and the inevitable shot of delegates round a huge table, smiling amicably at each other.

I kept the film running until the camera panned around the table. It came to a nameplate FIONA SAMSON and there was my wife – more beautiful than ever, perfectly groomed, and smiling for the cameraman. I stopped the film. The commentary growled to a halt and she froze, her hand awkwardly splayed, her face strained, and her smile false. I don't know how long I sat there looking at her. But suddenly the door of the editing room banged open and flooded everything with bright yellow light from the corridor.

'I'm sorry, Mr Samson. I thought everyone had finished work.'

'It's not work,' I said. 'Just something I remembered.'

3

So Dicky, having scoffed at the notion that I was being kept away from Stinnes, had virtually ordered me not to go near him. Well, that was all right. For the first time in months I was able to get my desk more or less clear. I worked from nine to five and even found myself able to join in some of those earnest conversations about what had been on TV the previous evening.

And at last I was able to spend more time with my children. For the past six months I had been almost a stranger to them. They never asked about Fiona, but now, when we'd finished putting up the paper decorations for Christmas, I sat them down and told them that their mother was safe and well but that she'd had to go abroad to work.

'I know,' said Billy. 'She's in Germany with the Russians.'

'Who told you that?' I said.

I hadn't told him. I hadn't told anyone. Just after Fiona's defection, the Director-General had addressed all the staff in the downstairs dining room – the D-G was an Army man with undisguised admiration for the late Field Marshal Montgomery's techniques with the lower ranks – and told us that no mention of Fiona's defection was to be included in any written reports, and it was on no account to be discussed outside the building. The Prime Minister had been told, and anyone who mattered at the Foreign Office knew by means of the daily report. Otherwise the whole business was to be 'kept to ourselves'.

'Grandpa told us,' said Billy.

Well, that was someone the D-G hadn't reckoned with: my irrepressible father-in-law, David Kimber-Hutchinson, by his own admission a self-made man.

'What else did he tell you?' I asked.

'I can't remember,' said Billy. He was a bright child, academic, calculating and naturally inquisitive. His memory was formidable. I wondered if it was his way of saying that he didn't much want to talk about it.

'He said that Mummy may not be back for a long time,' said Sally. She was younger than Billy, generous but introverted in that mysterious way that so many second children are, and closer to her mother. Sally was never moody in the way Billy could be, but she was more sensitive. She had taken her mother's absence much better than I'd feared, but I was still concerned about her.

'That's what I was going to tell you,' I said. I was relieved that the children were taking this discussion about their mother's disappearance so calmly. Fiona had always arranged their outings and gone to immense trouble to organize every last detail of their parties. My efforts were a poor substitute, and we all knew it.

'Mummy is really there to spy for *us* isn't she, Daddy?' said Billy.

'Ummm,' I said. It was a difficult one to respond to. I was afraid that Fiona or her KGB colleagues would grab the children and take them to her in East Berlin or Moscow or somewhere, as she once tried to. If she tried again, I didn't want to make it easier for her to succeed, and yet I couldn't bring myself to warn them against their own mother. 'No one knows,' I said vaguely.

'Sure, it's a secret,' said Billy with that confident shrug of the shoulders used by Dicky Cruyer to help emphasize the obvious. 'Don't worry, I won't tell.'

'It's better just to say she's gone away,' I said.

'Grandpa said we're to say Mummy's in hospital in Switzerland.'

It was typical of David to invent his own loony deception story and involve my children in it.

'The fact is that Mummy and I have separated,' I said in a rush. 'And I've asked a lady from my office to come round and see us this afternoon.'

There was a long silence. Billy looked at Sally and Sally looked at her new shoes.

'Aren't you going to ask her name?' I said desperately.

Sally looked at me with her big blue eyes. 'Will she be staying?' she said.

'We don't need anyone else to live here. You have Nanny to look after you,' I said, avoiding the question.

'Will she use our bathroom?' said Sally.

'No. I don't think so,' I said. 'Why?'

'Nanny hates visitors using our bathroom.'

This was a new insight into Nanny, a quiet plump girl from a Devon village who spoke in whispers, was transfixed by all TV programmes, ate chocolates by the truckload, and never complained. 'Well, I'll make sure she uses my bathroom,' I promised.

'Must she come today?' said Billy.

'I invited her for tea so that we could all be together,' I said. 'Then, when you go to bed, I'm taking her to dinner in a restaurant.'

'I wish we could all go out to dinner in a restaurant,' said Billy, who had recently acquired a blue blazer and long trousers and wanted to wear them to good effect.

'Which restaurant?' said Sally.

'The Greek restaurant where Billy had his birthday.'

'The waiters sang "Happy Birthday" for him.'

'So I heard.'

'You were away.'

'I was in Berlin.'

'Why don't you tell them it's your girlfriend's birthday,' said Sally. 'They'll be awfully nice to her, and they'd never find out.'

'She's not my girlfriend,' I said. 'She's just a friend.'

'She's his boyfriend,' said Billy. Sally laughed.

'She's just a friend,' I said soberly.

'All my lovers and I are just good friends,' said Sally, putting on her 'Hollywood' voice.

'She heard that in a film,' Billy explained.

'Her name is Gloria,' I said.

'We've nothing for tea,' said Sally. 'Not even biscuits.'

'Nanny will make toast,' said Billy to reassure me. 'She always makes toast when there's nothing for tea. Toast with butter and jam. It's quite nice really.'

'I believe she will be bringing a cake.'

'Auntie Tessa brings the best cakes,' said Sally. 'She gets them from a shop near Harrods.'

'That's because Auntie Tessa is very rich,' said Billy. 'She has a Rolls-Royce.'

'She comes here in a Volkswagen,' said Sally.

'That's because she doesn't want to be flash,' said Billy. 'I heard her say that on the phone once.'

'I think she's *very* flash,' said Sally in a voice heavy with admiration. 'Couldn't Auntie Tessa be your girlfriend, Daddy?'

'Auntie Tessa is married to Uncle George,' I said before things got out of hand.

'But Auntie Tessa isn't faithful to him,' Sally told Billy. Before I could contradict this uncontradictable fact, Sally after a glance at me added, 'I heard Daddy tell Mummy that one day when I shouldn't have been listening.'

'What kind of cake will she bring?' said Billy.

'Will she bring chocolate layer cake?' said Sally.

'I like rum babas best,' said Billy. 'Especially when they have lots of rum on them.'

They were still discussing their favourite cakes – a discussion that can go on for a very long time – when the doorbell rang.

Gloria Zsuzsa Kent was a tall and very beautiful blonde, whose twentieth birthday was soon approaching. She was what the service called an 'Executive Officer' which meant in theory that she could be promoted to Director-General. Armed with good marks from school and fluent Hungarian learned from her parents, she joined the Department on the vague promise of being given paid leave to go to university. It probably seemed like a good idea at the time. Dicky Cruyer had got his Army service – and Bret his studies at Oxford – credited towards promotion. Now financial cutbacks made it look as if she was stuck with nothing beyond a second-rate office job.

She took off her expensive fur-lined suede coat and the children gave whoops of joy on discovering that she'd brought the rum babas and chocolate layer cake that were their favourites.

'You're a mind reader,' I said. I kissed her. Under the children's gaze I made sure it was no more than the sort of peck you get along with the Legion of Honour.

She smiled as the children gave her a kiss of thanks before they went off to set the table for tea. 'I adore your children, Bernard.'

'You chose their favourite cakes,' I said.

'I have two young sisters. I know what children like.'

She sat down near the fire and warmed her hands. Already the afternoon light was fading and the room was dark. There was just a rim of daylight on her straw-coloured hair and the red glow of the fire's light on her hands and face.

Nanny came in and exchanged amiably noisy greetings with Gloria. They had spoken on the phone several times and the similarity in their ages gave them enough in common to allay my fears about Nanny's reaction to the news that I had a 'girlfriend'.

To me Nanny said, 'The children want to make toast by the fire in here, but I can easily do it in the toaster.'

'Let's all sit by the fire and have tea,' I said.

Nanny looked at me and said nothing.

'What's wrong, Nanny?'

'It would be better if we eat in the kitchen. The children will make a lot of crumbs and mess on the carpets and Mrs Dias won't come in again to clean until Tuesday.'

'You're a fusspot, Nanny,' I said.

'I'll tidy up, Doris,' Gloria told Nanny. Doris! Good grief, those two were getting along too nicely!

'And Mr Samson,' said Nanny tentatively. 'The children were invited to spend the evening with one of Billy's school friends. The Dubois family. They live near Swiss Cottage. I promised to phone them before five.'

'Sure, that's okay. If the children want to go. Are you going too?'

'Yes, I'd like to. They have *Singin' in the Rain* on video, and they'll serve soup and a snack meal afterwards. Other children will be there. We'd be back rather late, but the children could sleep late tomorrow.'

'Well, drive carefully, Nanny. The town's full of drunk drivers on a Saturday night.'

I heard cheers from the kitchen when Nanny went back and announced my decision. And tea was a delight. The children recited 'If' for Gloria, and Billy did three new magic tricks he'd been practising for the school Christmas concert.

'As I remember it,' I said, 'I'd promised to take you to the Greek restaurant for dinner, have a drink or two at Les Ambassadeurs, and then drive you home to your parents.'

'This is better,' she said. We were in bed. I said nothing. 'It is better, isn't it?' she asked anxiously.

I kissed her. 'It's madness and you know it.'

'Nanny and the children won't be back for hours.'

'I mean you and me. When will you realize that I'm twenty years older than you are?'

'I love you and you love me.'

'I didn't say I loved you,' I said.

She pulled a face. She resented the fact that I wouldn't say I loved her, but I was adamant; she was so young that I felt I was taking advantage of her. It was absurd, but refusing to tell her that I loved her enabled me to hang onto a last shred of self-respect.

'It doesn't matter,' she said. She pulled the bedclothes over our heads to make a tent. 'I know you love me, but you don't want to admit it.'

'Do your parents suspect that we're having an affair?'

'Are you still frightened that my father will come after you?'

'You're damned right I am.'

'I'm a grown woman,' she said. The more I tried to explain my feelings to her, the more amused she always got. She laughed and snuggled down in the bed, pressing against me.

'You're only ten years older than little Sally.'

She grew tired of the tent game and threw the bedclothes back. 'Your daughter is eight. Apart from the inaccurate mathematics of that allegation, you'll have to come to terms with the fact that when your lovely daughter is ten years older she will be a grown woman too. Much sooner than that, in fact. You're an old fogy, Bernard.'

'I have Dicky telling me that I'm fat and flabby and you telling me that I'm an old fogy. It's enough to crush a man's ego.'

'Not an ego like yours, darling.'

'Come here,' I said. I hugged her tight and kissed her.

The truth was that I was falling in love with her. I thought of her too much; soon everyone at the office would guess what was between

us. Worse, I was becoming frightened at the prospect of this impossible affair coming to an end. And that, I suppose, is love.

'I've been filing for Dicky all week.'

'I know, and I'm jealous.'

'Dicky is such an idiot,' she said for no apparent reason. 'I used
to think he was so clever, but he's such a fool.' She was amused and
scornful, but I didn't miss the element of affection in her voice.
Dicky seemed to bring out the maternal instinct in all women, even
in his wife.

'You're telling me. I work for him.'

'Did you ever think of getting out of the Department, Bernard?'

'Over and over again. But what would I do?'

'You could do almost anything,' she said with the adoring intensity
and the sincere belief that are the marks of those who are very young.

'I'm forty,' I said. 'Companies don't want promising "young" men
of forty. They don't fit into the pension scheme and they're too old
to be infant prodigies.'

'I shall get out soon,' she said. 'Those bastards will never give me
paid leave to go to Cambridge, and if I don't go up next year I'm not
sure when I'll get another place.'

'Have they told you they won't give you paid leave?'

'They asked me if unpaid leave would suit me just as well. Morgan,
actually; that little Welsh shit who does all the dirty work for the D-
G's office.'

'What did you say?'

'I told him to get stuffed.'

'In those very words?'

'No point in beating about the bush, is there?'

'None at all, darling,' I said.

'I can't stand Morgan,' she said. 'And he's no friend of yours
either.'

'Why do you say that?'

'I heard him talking to Bret Rensselaer last week. They were talking
about you. I heard Morgan say he felt sorry for you really because
there was no real future for you in the Department now that your
wife's gone over to the Russians.'

'What did Bret say?'

'He's always very just, very dispassionate, very honourable and
sincere; he's the beautiful American, Bret Rensselaer. He said that
the German Section would go to pieces without you. Morgan said the
German Section isn't the only Section in the Department and Bret
said, "No, just the most important one".'

'How did Morgan take that?'

'He said that when the Stinnes debriefing is completed Bret might
think again.'

'Jesus,' I said. 'What's that bastard talking about?'

'Don't get upset, Bernie. It's just Morgan putting the poison in. You know what he's like.'

'Frank Harrington said Morgan is the Martin Bormann of London South West One.' I laughed.

'Explain the joke to me.'

'Martin Bormann was Hitler's secretary, but by controlling the paperwork of Hitler's office and by deciding who was permitted to have an audience with Hitler, Bormann became the power behind the throne. He decided everything that happened. People who upset Bormann never got to see Hitler and their influence and importance waned and waned.'

'And Morgan controls the D-G like that?'

'The D-G is not well,' I said.

'He's as nutty as a fruitcake,' said Gloria.

'He has good days and bad days,' I said. I was sorry for the D-G; he'd been good in his day – tough when it was necessary, but always scrupulously honest. 'But by taking on the job of being the D-G's hatchet man – a job no one else wanted – Morgan has become a formidable power in that building. And he's done it in a very short time.'

'How long has he been in the Department?'

'I don't know exactly – two years, three at the most. Now he's talking to old-timers like Bret Rensselaer and Frank Harrington as man to man.'

'That's right. I heard him ask Bret about taking charge of the Stinnes debriefing. Bret said he had no time. Morgan said it wouldn't be time-consuming; it was just a matter of holding the reins so that the Department knew what was happening, from day to day, over at London Debriefing Centre. You'd have thought Morgan was the D-G the way he was saying it.'

'And how did Bret react to that?'

'He asked for time to think it over, and it was decided that he'd let Morgan know next week. And then Bret asked if anyone knew when Frank Harrington was retiring, and Morgan said nothing was fixed. Bret said, "Nothing?" in a funny voice and they laughed. I don't know what that was about.'

'The D-G has a knighthood to dispose of. Rumour says it will go to Frank Harrington when he retires from the Berlin office. Everyone knows that Bret would give his right arm for a knighthood.'

'I see. Is that how people get knighthoods?'

'Sometimes.'

'There was something else,' said Gloria. 'I wasn't going to tell you this, but Morgan said the D-G had decided it would be just as well for the Department if you didn't work in Operations as from the end of this year.'

'Are you serious,' I said in alarm.

'Bret said that Internal Security had given you a clean bill of health – that's what he said, "a clean bill of health". And then Morgan said it was nothing to do with Internal Security; it was a matter of the Department's reputation.'

'That doesn't sound like the D-G,' I said. 'That sounds like Morgan.'

'Morgan the ventriloquist,' said Gloria.

I kissed her again and changed the subject. It was all getting too damned depressing for me.

'I'm sorry,' she said, responding to my change of mood. 'I was determined not to tell you.'

I hugged her. 'How did you know the children's favourite cakes, you witch?'

'I phoned Doris and asked her.'

'You and Nanny are very thick,' I said suspiciously.

'Why don't you call her Doris?'

'I always call her Nanny. It's better that way when we're living in the same house.'

'You're such a prude. She adores you, you know.'

'Don't avoid my question. Have you been plotting with Nanny?'

'With Nanny? About what?'

'You know about what.'

'Don't do that. Oh, stop tickling me. Oh oh oh. I don't know what you're talking about. Oh stop it.'

'Did you connive with Nanny so that she and the children were out for the evening? So that we could go to bed?'

'Of course not.'

'What did you give her?'

'Stop it. Please. You beast.'

'What did you give her?'

'A box of chocolates.'

'I knew it. You schemer.'

'I hate Greek food.'

4

Taking the children to see Billy's godfather was an excuse for a day in the country, a Sunday lunch second to none, and a chance to talk to 'Uncle Silas', one of the legends of the Department's golden days. Also it gave me a chance to tie up some loose ends in the arrested woman's evidence. If Dicky didn't want it done for the Department, then I would do it just to satisfy my own curiosity.

The property had always fascinated me; Whitelands was as surprising as Silas Gaunt himself. From the long drive, with its well-tended garden, the ancient stone farmhouse was as pretty as a calendar picture. But over the years it had been adapted to the tastes of many different owners. Adapted, modified, extended and defaced. Across the cobbled yard at the back there was a curious castellated Gothic tower, its spiral staircase leading up to a large, ornately decorated chamber which once had been a mirrored bedroom. Even more incongruous in this cottage with its stone floors and oak beams was the richly panelled billiards room, with game trophies crowding its walls. Both architectural additions dated from the same time, both installed by a nineteenth-century beer baron to indulge his favourite pastimes.

Silas Gaunt had inherited Whitelands from his father, but Silas had never been a farmer. Even when he left the Department and came to live here in retirement, he still let his farm manager make all the decisions. Little wonder that Silas got lonely amid his six hundred acres on the edge of the Cotswolds. Now all the soft greenery of summer had gone. So had the crisp browns of autumn. Only the framework of landscape remained: bare tangles of hedgerow and leafless trees. The first snow had whitened rock-hard ridges of the empty brown fields: crosshatched pieces of landscape where magpies, rooks and starlings scavenged for worms and insects.

Silas had had few guests. It had been a hermit's life, for the conversation of Mrs Porter, his housekeeper, was limited to recipes, needlework, and the steadily rising prices of groceries in the village shop. Silas Gaunt's life had revolved round his library, his records and his wine cellar. But there is more to life than Schiller, Mahler and Margaux, which trio Silas claimed as his 'fellow pensioners'. And so he'd come to encourage these occasional weekend house parties at which departmental staff, both past and present, were usually represented along with a sprinkling of the artists, tycoons, eccentrics and weirdos whom Silas had encountered during his very long and amazing career.

Silas was unkempt; the wispy white hair that made a halo on his almost bald head did not respond to combs or to the clawing gesture of his fingers that he made whenever a strand of hair fell forward across his eyes. He was tall and broad, a Falstaffian figure who liked to laugh and shout, could curse fluently in half a dozen languages, and who'd make reckless bets on anything and everything and claimed – with some justification – to be able to drink any man under the table.

Billy and Sally were in awe of him. They were always ready to go to Whitelands and see Uncle Silas, but they regarded him as a benevolent old ruffian of whose sudden moods they should constantly be wary. And that was the way I saw him myself. But he'd had a fully decorated Christmas tree erected in the entrance hall. Under it there was a little pile of presents for both children, all of them wrapped in bright paper and tied neatly with big bows. Mrs Porter's doing no doubt.

Like all old people, Silas Gaunt felt a need for unchanging ritual. These guest weekends followed a firmly established pattern: a long country walk on Saturday morning (which I did my best to avoid), roast beef lunch to follow, billiards in the afternoon, and a dress-up dinner on Saturday evening. On Sunday morning his guests were shepherded to church and then to the village pub before coming back to lunch which was locally obtained game or, failing that, poultry. I was relieved to find that duckling was on the menu this week. I did not care for Silas's selection of curious little wild birds, every mouthful with its portion of lead shot.

'Surprised to see Walter here?' Uncle Silas asked me again as he sharpened his long carving knife with the careless abandon of a butcher.

I had registered my surprise on first arriving, but apparently I'd inadequately performed my allotted role. 'Amazed!' I said, putting all my energies into it. 'I had no idea. . . .' I winked at von Munte. I knew him even better than I knew Uncle Silas; once long ago he'd saved my life by risking his own. Dr Walter von Munte smiled, and even the staid old Frau Doktor gave the ghost of a smile. Living with extroverted, outspoken Silas must have come as something of a shock after their austere and tight-lipped life in the German Democratic Republic, where even the von in their name had been taken from them.

I knew that the von Muntes were staying there – it was my job to know such things. I'd played a part in bringing them out of the East. Their presence was, to some extent, the reason for my visit, but their whereabouts was considered a departmental secret and I was expected to register appropriate surprise.

Until a few short weeks ago this lugubrious old man had been one of our most reliable agents. Known only as Brahms Four he'd supplied regular and carefully selected facts and figures from the Deutsche Notenbank, through which came banking clearances for the whole of East Germany. From time to time he'd also obtained for us the decisions and plans of COMECON – the East Bloc Common Market – and memos from the Moscow Narodny bank too. At the receiving end, Bret Rensselaer had built an empire upon the dangerous work of von Munte, but now von Munte had been debriefed and left in the custodial care of his old friend Uncle Silas, and Bret was desperately seeking new dominions.

Silas stood at the end of the long table and dismembered the duck, apportioning suitable pieces to each guest. He liked to do it himself. It was a game he played: discussing and arguing what each and every guest should have. Mrs Porter watched the cameo with an expressionless face. She arranged the pile of warmed plates, positioned the vegetables and gravy, and, at exactly the right psychological moment, brought in the second roasted duckling. 'Another one!' said Silas as if he hadn't ordered the meal himself and as if he didn't have a third duckling in the oven for extra portions.

Before pouring the wine, Silas lectured us about it. Château Palmer 1961, he said, was the finest claret he'd ever tasted, the finest perhaps of this century. He still hovered, looking at the wine in the antique decanter as if now wondering whether it would be wasted on the present company.

Perhaps von Munte sensed the hesitation for he said, 'It's generous of you to share it with us.'

'I was looking through my cellar the other day.' He stood up straight, looking out across the snow-whitened lawn as if oblivious of his guests. 'I found a dozen bottles of 1878 port down there. My grandfather bought them for me, to mark my tenth birthday, and I'd completely forgotten them. I've never tasted it. Yes, I've got a lot of treasures there. I stocked up when I had the money to afford it. It would break my heart to leave too much magnificent claret behind when I go.'

He poured the wine carefully and evoked from us the sort of compliments he needed. He was like an actor in that and many other respects – he desperately needed regular and earnest declarations of love. 'Label uppermost, always label uppermost; when you store and when you pour.' He demonstrated it. 'Otherwise you'll disturb it.'

I knew it would be a predominantly masculine lunch, a departmental get-together, Silas had warned me beforehand, but I still came. Bret Rensselaer and Frank Harrington were both there. Rensselaer was in his middle fifties; American-born, he was trim almost to the point of emaciation. Although his hair was turning white, there was still enough of the blond colouring left to prevent him looking old. And he smiled a lot and had good teeth and a face that was bony so that there weren't many wrinkles.

Over lunch there was the usual seasonal discussion about how quickly Christmas was approaching and the likelihood of more snow. Bret Rensselaer was deciding upon a place to ski. Frank Harrington, our senior man in Berlin, told him it was too early for good snow, but Silas advised Switzerland.

Frank argued about the snow. He liked to think he was an authority on such matters. He liked skiing, golfing and sailing, and generally having a good time. Frank Harrington was waiting for retirement, something for which he'd been strenuously practising all his life. He was a soldierly-looking figure with a weather-beaten face and a blunt-ended stubble moustache. Unlike Bret, who was wearing the same sort of Savile Row suit he wore to the office, Frank had come correctly attired for the upper-class English weekend: old Bedford cord trousers and a khaki sweater with a silk scarf in the open neck of his faded shirt. 'February,' said Frank. 'That's the only time for any decent skiing anywhere worth going.'

I observed the way Bret was eying von Munte, whose stream of high-grade information had taken Bret into the very top ranks of the Department. Bret's desk was now closed down and his seniority had been in peril ever since the old man had been forced to flee. No wonder the two men watched each other like boxers in a ring.

Talk became more serious when it touched upon that inevitable subject in such company, the unification of Germany. 'How deeply ingrained in East Germans is the philosophy of Communism?' Bret asked von Munte.

'Philosophy,' said Silas, interrupting sharply. 'I'll accept that Communism is a perverted sort of religion – infallible Kremlin, infallible Vatican – but philosophy, no.' He was happier with the von Muntes here, I could tell from the tone of his voice.

Von Munte didn't take up Silas's semantic contention. Gravely he said, 'The way in which Stalin took from Germany Silesia, Pomerania and East Prussia made it impossible for many of us Germans to accept the USSR as a friend, neighbour, or example.'

'That's going back a long while,' said Bret. 'Which Germans are we talking about? Are young Germans interested in the tears and cries of pain we hear about the lost territories?' He smiled. This was Bret being deliberately provocative. His charming manner was frequently used like this – the local anaesthetic that accompanied the lancet of his rude remarks.

Von Munte remained very calm; was it a legacy of years of banking or years of Communism? Either way, I'd hate to play poker against him. 'You English equate our eastern lands with Imperial India. The French think we who talk about reasserting Germany's border to the frontiers of East Prussia are like the *pieds-noirs*, who hope once again to have Algeria governed from Paris.'

'Exactly,' said Bret. He smiled to himself and ate some duckling.

Von Munte nodded. 'But our eastern provinces have always been German and a vital part of Europe's relationship with the East. Culturally, psychologically and commercially, Germany's eastern lands, not Poland, provided the buffer and the link with Russia. Frederick the Great, Yorck and Bismarck – and indeed all those Germans who instituted important alliances with the East – were *ostelbisch*, Germans from the eastern side of the River Elbe.' He paused and looked round the table before going on with what was obviously something he'd said time and time again. 'Czar Alexander I and Nicolas who succeeded him were more German than Russian, and they both married German princesses. And what about Bismarck who was continually defending Russian interests even at the expense of Germany's relations with the Austrians?'

'Yes,' said Bret sardonically. 'And you have yet to mention the German-born Karl Marx.'

For a moment I thought von Munte was going to reply seriously to the joke and make a fool of himself, but he'd lived amid signals, innuendoes, and half-truths long enough to recognize the joke for what it was. He smiled.

'Can there ever be lasting peace in Europe?' said Bret wearily. 'Now, if I'm to believe my ears, you say Germany still has territorial aspirations.' For Bret it was all a game, but poor old von Munte could not play it.

'For our own provinces,' said von Munte stolidly.

'For Poland and pieces of Russia,' said Bret. 'You'd better be clear on that.'

Silas poured more of his precious Château Palmer in a gesture of placation for all concerned. 'You're from Pomerania, aren't you, Walter?' It was an invitation to talk rather than a real question, for by now Silas knew every last detail of von Munte's family history.

'I was born in Falkenburg. My father had a big estate there.'

'That's near the Baltic,' said Bret, feigning interest to make what he considered a measure of reconciliation.

'Pomerania,' said von Munte. 'Do you know it, Bernard?' he asked me, because I was the closest person there to being a fellow-countryman.

'Yes,' I said. 'Many lakes and hills. They call it Pomeranian Switzerland, don't they?'

'Not any longer.'

'A beautiful place,' I said. 'But as I remember it, damned cold, Walter.'

'You must go in the summer,' said von Munte. 'It's one of the most enchanting places in the world.' I looked at Frau Doktor von Munte. I had the feeling that the move to the West was a disappointment for her. Her English was poor and she keenly felt the social disadvantage she suffered as a refugee. With the talk of Pomerania she brightened and tried to follow the conversation.

'You've been back?' Silas asked.

'Yes, my wife and I went there about ten years ago. It was foolish. One should never go back.'

'Tell us about it,' said Silas.

At first it seemed as if the memories were too painful for von Munte to recount, but after a pause he told us about his trip. 'There is something nightmarish about going back to your homeland and finding that it's occupied exclusively by foreigners. It was the most curious experience I've ever had – to write "birthplace Falkenburg" and then "destination Zlocieniec".'

'The same place, now given a Polish name,' said Frank Harrington. 'But you must have been prepared for that.'

'I was prepared in my mind but not in my heart,' said von Munte. He turned to his wife and repeated this in rapid German. She nodded dolefully.

'The train connection from Berlin was never good,' von Munte went on. 'Even before the war we had to change twice. This time we went by bus. I tried to borrow a car, but it was not possible. The bus was convenient. We went to Neustettin, my wife's home town. We had difficulty finding the house in which she'd lived as a child.'

'Couldn't you ask for directions?' said Frank.

'Neither of us speaks much Polish,' said von Munte. 'Also, my wife had lived in Hermann-Göring-Strasse and I did not care to ask the way there.' He smiled. 'But we found it eventually. In the street where she lived as a girl we even found an old German woman who remembered my wife's family. It was a remarkable stroke of luck, for there are only a handful of Germans still living there.'

'And in Falkenburg?' said Silas.

'Ah, in my beloved Zlocieniec, Stalin was more thorough. We could find no one there who spoke German. I was born in a house in the country, right on the lake. We went to the nearest village and the priest tried to help us, but there were no records. He even lent me a bicycle so that I could go out to the house, but it had completely disappeared. The buildings have all been destroyed and the area has been made into a forest. The only remains I could recognize were a couple of farm buildings a long way distant from the site of the house where I was born. The priest promised to write if he found out any more, but he never did.'

'And you never went back again?' asked Silas.

'We planned to return, but things happened in Poland. The big demonstrations for free trade unions and the creation of Solidarity was reported in our East German newspapers as being the work of reactionary elements supported by western fascists. Very few people were prepared to even comment on the Polish crisis. And most of the people who did talk about it said that such "troubles", by upsetting the Russians, made conditions worse for us East Germans and other peoples in the Eastern Bloc. Poles became unpopular and no one went there. It was as if Poland ceased to exist as a next-door neighbour and became some land far away on the other side of the world.'

'Eat up,' said Silas. 'We're keeping you from your lunch, Walter.'

But soon von Munte took up the same subject again. It was as if he had to convert us to his point of view. He had to remove our misunderstandings. 'It was the occupation zones that created the archetype German for you,' he said. 'Now the French think all Germans are chattering Rhinelanders, the Americans think we are all beer-swilling Bavarians, the British think we are all icy Westphalians, and the Russians think we are all cloddish Saxons.'

'The Russians,' I said, having downed two generous glasses of Silas's magnificent wine as well as a few aperitifs, 'think you are all brutal Prussians.'

He nodded sadly. 'Yes, *Saupreiss*,' he said, using the Bavarian dialect word for Prussian swine. 'Perhaps you are right.'

After lunch the other guests divided into those who played billiards and those who preferred to sit huddled round the blazing log fire in the drawing room. My children were watching TV with Mrs Porter.

Silas, giving me a chance to speak privately with von Munte, took us to the conservatory to which, at this time of year, he had moved his house plants. It was a huge glass palace, resting against the side of the house, its framework gracefully curved, its floor formed of beautiful old decorative tiles. In these cold months the whole place was crammed full of prehensile-looking greenery of every shape and size. It seemed too cold in there for such plants to flourish, but Silas said they didn't need heat so much as light. 'With me,' I told him, 'it's exactly the opposite.'

He smiled as if he'd heard the joke before, which he had because I told it to him every time he trapped me into one of these chats amid his turnip tops. But Silas liked the conservatory, and if he liked it, everyone else had to like it too. He seemed not to feel the cold.

He was jacketless, with bright red braces visible under his unbuttoned waistcoat. Walter von Munte was wearing a black suit of the kind that was uniform for a German government official in the service of the Kaiser. His face was grey and lined and his whitening hair cropped short. He took off his gold-rimmed glasses and polished them on a silk handkerchief. Seated on the big wicker seat under the large and leafy plants the old man looked like some ancient studio portrait.

'Young Bernard has a question for you, Walter,' said Silas. He had a bottle of Madeira with him and three glasses. He put them on the table and poured a measure of the amber-coloured wine for each of us, then lowered his weight onto a cast-iron garden chair. He sat between us, positioned like a referee.

'It is not good for me,' said von Munte, but he took the glass and looked at the colour of it and sniffed it appreciatively.

'It's not good for anyone,' said Silas cheerfully, sipping his carefully measured portion. 'It's not *supposed* to be good for you. The doctor cut me down to one bottle per month last year.' He drank. 'This year he told me to cut it out altogether.'

'Then you are disobeying orders,' said von Munte.

'I got myself another doctor,' said Silas. 'We live in a capitalist society over here, Walter. I can afford to get myself a doctor who says it's okay to smoke and drink.' He laughed and sipped a little more of his Madeira. 'Cossart 1926, bottled fifty years later. Not the finest Madeira I've ever encountered, but not at all bad, eh?' He didn't wait for our response, but selected a cigar from the box he'd brought under his arm. 'Try that,' he said, offering the cigar to me. 'That's an Upmann grand corona, one of the best cigars you can smoke and just right for this time of day. Walter, what about one of those petits that you enjoyed last night?'

'Alas,' said von Munte, holding up his hand to decline. 'I cannot afford your doctor. I must keep to one a week.'

I lit the cigar Silas had given me. It was typical of him that he had to select what he thought suitable for us. He had well-defined ideas about what everyone should have and what they shouldn't have. For anyone who called him a 'fascist' – and there were plenty who did – he had the perfect response: scars from Gestapo bullets.

'What do you want to ask me, Bernard?' said von Munte.

I got the cigar going and then I said, 'Ever hear of MARTELLO, HARRY, JAKE, SEE-SAW or IRONFOOT?' I'd put in a few extra names as a means of control.

'What kind of names are these?' said von Munte. 'People?'

'Agents. Code names. Russian agents operating out of the United Kingdom.'

'Recently?'

'It looks as if one of them was used by my wife.'

'Yes, recently. I see.' Von Munte sipped his port. He was old-fashioned enough to be embarrassed at the mention of my wife and her spying. He shifted his weight on the wicker seat and the movement produced a loud creaking sound.

'Did you ever come across those names?' I asked.

'It was not the policy to let my people have access to such secrets as the code names of agents.'

'Not even source names?' I persisted. 'These are probably not agent names; they're the code names used in messages and for distribution. No real risk there, and the material from any one source keeps its name until identified and measured and pronounced upon. That's the KGB system and our system too.'

I glanced round at Silas. He was examining one of his plants, his head turned away as if he weren't listening. But he was listening all right; listening and remembering every last syllable of what was being said. I knew him of old.

'Source names. Yes, MARTELLO sounds familiar,' said von Munte. 'Perhaps the others too, I can't remember.'

'Two names used by one agent *at the same time*,' I said.

'That would be unprecedented,' said von Munte. He was loosening up now. 'Two names, no. How would we ever keep track of our material?'

'That's what I thought,' I said.

'This was from the woman arrested in Berlin?' said Silas suddenly. He dropped the pretence of looking at his plants. 'I heard about that.' Silas always knew what was happening. In earlier days, while the D-G had been settling in, he'd even asked Silas to monitor some of the operations. Nowadays Silas and the D-G kept in touch. It would be foolish of me to imagine that this conversation would not get back to the Department.

'Yes, the woman in Berlin,' I said.

Walter von Munte touched his stiff white collar. 'I was never allowed to know any secrets. They gave me only what they thought I should have.'

I said, 'Like Silas distributing his food and cigars, you mean?' I kept wishing that Silas would depart and leave me and von Munte to have the conversation I wanted. But that was not Silas's way. Information was his stock in trade, it always had been, and he knew how to use it to his own advantage. That's why he'd survived so long in the Department.

'Not as generously as Silas,' said von Munte. He smiled and drank some of the Madeira and then shifted about, deciding how to explain it all. 'The bank's intelligence staff went over to the Warschauer Strasse office once a week. They would have all the new material in trays waiting for us. Old Mr Heine was in charge there. He'd produce for us each item according to subject.'

'Raw?' I said.

'Raw?' said von Munte. 'What does that mean?'

'Did they tell you what the agent said or did they merely tell you the content of his message?'

'Oh, the messages were edited, but otherwise as received. They had to be; the staff handling the material didn't know enough about economics to understand what it was about.'

'But you identified different sources?' I asked yet again.

'Sometimes we could, sometimes that was easy. Some of it was total rubbish.'

'From different agents?' I persisted. My God, but it was agony to deal with old people. Would I be like this one day?

'Some of their agents sent only rumours. There was one who never provided a word of good sense. They called him "Grock". That wasn't his code name or his source name; it was our joke. We called him "Grock", after the famous clown, of course.'

'Yes,' I said. But I'm glad von Munte had told me it was a joke; that gave me the cue to laugh. 'What about the good sources?' I said.

'You could recognize them from the quality of their intelligence and from the style in which it was presented.' He sat back in his chair. 'Perhaps I should explain what it was like in the Warschauer Strasse office. It wasn't our office. It is supposed to be an office belonging to Aeroflot, but there are always police and security guards on the door, and our passes were carefully scrutinized no matter how often we visited there. I don't know who else uses the building, but the economic intelligence staff met there regularly, as I said.'

'And you were included in "economic intelligence staff"?'

'Certainly not. They were all KGB and security people. My superior was only invited to attend when there was something directly affecting our department. Other bank officials and Ministry people came according to what was to be discussed.'

'Why didn't the briefing take place at the KGB offices?' I asked. Silas was sitting upright on his metal chair, his eyes closed as if he were dozing off to sleep.

'The Warschauer Strasse office was – perhaps I should say is – used at arm's length by the KGB. When some Party official or some exalted visitor has enough influence to be permitted to visit the KGB installation in Berlin, they are invariably taken to Warschauer Strasse rather than to Karlshorst.'

'It's used as a front?' said Silas opening his eyes and blinking as if suddenly coming awake from a deep slumber.

'They wouldn't want visitors tramping through the offices where the real work was being done. And Warschauer Strasse has a kitchen and dining room where such dignitaries can be entertained. Also there is a small lecture hall where they can see slide shows and demonstration films and so on. We liked going over there. Even the coffee and sandwiches served were far better than anything available elsewhere.'

'You said you could tell the source from the quality and the style. Could you enlarge on that?' I asked.

'Some communications would begin an item with a phrase such as "I hear that the Bank of England" or whatever. Others would say, "Last week the Treasury issued a confidential statement." Others might put it, "Fears of an imminent drop in American interest rates are likely to bring . . .". These different styles are virtually sufficient for identification, but correlated with the proved quality of certain sources, we were soon able to recognize the agents. We spoke of them as people and joked about the nonsense that certain of them sometimes passed on to us.'

'So you must have recognized the first-class material that my wife was providing.'

Von Munte looked at me and then at Silas. Silas said, 'Is this official, Bernard?' There was a note of warning in his voice.

'Not yet,' I said.

'We're sailing a bit close to the wind for chitchat,' Silas said. The choice of casual words, and the softness of his voice, did nothing to hide the authority behind what he said; on the contrary, it was the manner in which certain classes of Englishmen give orders to their subordinates. I said nothing and von Munte watched Silas carefully. Then Silas drew on his cigar reflectively and, having taken his time, said, 'Tell him whatever you know, Walter.'

'As I told you, I only saw the economic material. I can't guess what proportion of any one agent's submissions that might be.' He looked at me. 'Take the material from the man we called "Grock". It was rubbish, as I said. But for all I know, Grock might have been sending wonderful stuff about underwater weaponry or secret NATO conferences.'

'Looking back at it, can you now guess what my wife was sending?'

'It's only a guess,' said von Munte, 'but there was one tray of material that was always well written and organized in a manner one might call academic.'

'Good stuff?'

'Very reliable but inclined towards caution. Nothing very alarming or exciting; mostly confirmations of trends that we could guess at. Useful, of course, but from our point of view not wonderful.' He looked up at the sky through the glass roof of the conservatory. '*Eisenguss*,' he said suddenly and laughed. '*Nicht Eisenfuss; Eisenguss*. Not iron foot but cast iron or pig iron; *Gusseisen*. Yes, that was the name of the source. I remember at the time I thought he must be some sort of government official.'

'It means poured iron,' said Silas, who spoke a perfect and pedantic German and couldn't tolerate my Berlin accent.

'I know the word,' I said irritably. 'The audiotypist was careless, that's all. None of them are really fluent.' It was a feeble excuse and quite untrue. I'd done it myself. I should have listened more carefully when I was with the Miller woman or picked up my mistranslation when typing from the tape recording.

'So now we have a name to connect Fiona with the material she gave them,' said Silas. 'Is that what you wanted?'

I looked at von Munte. 'Just the one code word for Fiona's tray?'

'It all came under the one identification,' said von Munte. 'Why would they split it up? It wouldn't make sense, would it?'

'No,' I said. I finished my drink and stood up. 'It wouldn't make sense.'

Upstairs I could hear the children growing noisy. There was a limit to the amount of time that TV kept them entertained. 'I'll go and take charge of my children,' I said. 'I know they tire Mrs Porter.'

'Are you staying for supper?' said Silas.

'Thanks, but it's a long journey, Silas. And the children will be late to bed as it is.'

'There's plenty of room for you all.'

'You're very kind, but it would mean leaving at crack of dawn to get the children to school and me to the office.'

He nodded and turned back to von Munte. But I knew there was more to it than simple hospitality. Silas was determined to have a word with me in private. And on my way downstairs, after I'd told the children that we'd be leaving soon after tea, he emerged from his study and, with one hand on my shoulder, drew me inside.

He closed the study door with great care. Then, in a sudden change of mood that was typical of him, he said, 'Do you mind telling me what the bloody hell this is all about?'

'What?'

'Don't what me, Bernard. You understand English. What the hell are you cross-questioning von Munte about?'

'The arrested woman . . .'

'Mrs Miller,' he interrupted me, to show how well informed he was.

'Yes, Mrs Carol Elvira Johnson, née Miller, father's name Müller, born London 1930, occupation schoolteacher. That's the one.'

'That was quite uncalled for,' said Silas, offended at my reply. 'Well, what about her?'

'Her testimony doesn't fit what I know of KGB procedures and I wanted to hear about von Munte's experience.'

'About using multiple code names? Did the Miller woman say they used multiple code names?'

'She handled two lots of exceptionally high-grade intelligence material. There were two code names, but the Department is happy to believe that it all came from Fiona.'

'But you incline to the view that it was two lots of material from two different agents?'

'I didn't say that,' I said. 'I'm still trying to find out. It can't hurt to improve upon our knowledge, can it?'

'Have you spoken to anyone at the office about this?'

'Dicky Cruyer knows.'

'Well, he's a bright lad,' said Silas. 'What did he say?'

'He's not interested.'

'What would you do in Dicky Cruyer's place?'

'Someone should check it with Stinnes,' I said. 'What is the point of debriefing a KGB defector if we don't use him to improve upon what we already know?'

Silas turned to the window; his lips were pressed tight together and his face was angry. From this first-floor room there was a view across the paddock all the way to the stream that Silas called his 'river'. For a long time he watched the flecks of snow spinning in the air. 'Drive slowly. It will freeze hard tonight,' he said without looking round at me. He'd suppressed his anger and his body relaxed as the rage drained out of him.

'No other way to drive in that old banger of mine.'

When he turned to me he had his smile in place. 'Didn't I hear you telling Frank that you're buying something good from your brother-in-law?' He never missed anything. He must have had super-human hearing and, in defiance of the laws of nature, it improved with every year he aged. I had been telling Frank Harrington about it, and, in keeping with our curious father–son sort of relationship, Frank had told me to be very careful when I was driving it.

'Yes,' I said. 'A Rover 3500 saloon that a couple of tearaways souped up to do one hundred and fifty miles an hour.'

'With a V-8 engine that shouldn't be too difficult.' His eyes narrowed. 'You'll surprise a few Sunday drivers with that one, Bernard.'

'Yes, that's what Tessa's husband said. But until it's ready I have to manage with the Ford. And in that I can't surprise anyone.'

Silas leaned close and his manner was avuncular. 'You've come out of the Kimber-Hutchinson business with a smile on your face, Bernard. I'm pleased.' I couldn't help noticing that his distant relative Fiona was now referred to by her maiden name, thus distancing both of us from her.

'I don't know about the smile,' I said.

He ignored my retort. 'Don't start digging into that all over again. Let it go.'

'You think that's best?' I said, to avoid giving him the reassurance he was asking for.

'Leave all that to the people at Five. It's not our job to chase spies,' said Silas and opened the door of his study to let me out onto the landing.

'Come along, children,' I called. 'Tea and cake and then we must leave.'

'The Germans have a word for the results of such overenthusiasm, don't they,' said Silas, who never knew when to stop. '*Schlimmbesserung*, an improvement that makes things worse.' He smiled and patted my shoulder. There was no sign of anger now. Silas had become Uncle Silas again.

5

'Why does *anyone* have to go to Berlin,' I asked Dicky resentfully. I was at home: warm and comfortable and looking forward to Christmas Day.

'Be sensible,' said Dicky. 'They're getting this Miller woman's body out of the Hohenzollern Canal. We can't leave it to the Berlin cops, and a lot of questions will have to be answered. Why was she being moved? Who authorized the ambulance? And where the hell was she being moved to?'

'It's Christmas, Dicky,' I said.

'Oh, is it?' said Dicky feigning surprise. 'That accounts for the difficulty I seem to be having getting anything done.'

'Don't Operations know that we have something called the Berlin Field Unit?' I said sarcastically. 'Why isn't Frank Harrington handling it?'

'Don't be peevish, old boy,' said Dicky, who I think was enjoying the idea of ruining my Christmas. 'We showed Frank how important this was by sending you over to supervise the arrest. And you interrogated her. We can't suddenly decide that BFU must take over. They'll say we're unloading this one onto them because it's the Christmas holiday. And they'd be right.'

'What does Frank say?'

'Frank isn't in Berlin. He's gone away for Christmas.'

'He must have left a contact number,' I said desperately.

'He's gone to some relatives in the Scottish Highlands. There have been gales and the phone lines are down. And don't say send the local constabulary to find him because when I track him down, Frank will point out that he has a deputy on duty in Berlin. No, you'll have to go, Bernard. I'm sorry, but there it is. And after all, you're not married.'

'Hell, Dicky. I've got the children with me and the nanny has gone home for Christmas with her parents. I'm not even on stand-by duty. I've planned all sorts of things over the holiday.'

'With gorgeous Gloria, no doubt. I can imagine what sort of things you planned, Bernard. Bad luck, but this is an emergency.'

'Who I spend my Christmas with is my personal business,' I said huffily.

'Of course, old chap. But let me point out that you introduced the personal note into this conversation. I didn't.'

'I'll phone Werner,' I said.

'By all means. But you'll have to go, Bernard. You are the person the BfV knows. I can't get all the paperwork done to authorize someone else to work with them.'

'I see,' I said. That was the real reason, of course. Dicky was determined that he would not go back into the office for a couple of hours of paperwork and phoning.

'And who else could I send? Tell me who could go and see to it.'

'From what you say, it's only going to be a matter of identifying a corpse.'

'And who else can do that?'

'Any of the BfV men who were in the arrest team.'

'That would look very good on the documentation, wouldn't it,' said Dicky with heavy irony. 'We have to rely on a foreign police service for our certified identification. Even Coordination would query that one.'

'If it's a corpse, Dicky, let it stay in the icebox until after the holiday.'

There was a deep sigh from the other end. 'You can wriggle and wriggle, Bernard, but you're on this hook and you know it. I'm sorry to wreck your cosy little Christmas, but it's nothing of my doing. You have to go and that's that. The ticket is arranged, and cash and so on will be sent round by security messenger tomorrow morning.'

'Okay,' I said.

'Daphne and I will be pleased to entertain the children round here, you know. Gloria can come round too, if she'd like that.'

'Thanks, Dicky,' I said. 'I'll think about it.'

'She'll be safe with me, Bernard,' said Dicky, and did nothing to disguise the smirk with which he said it. He'd always lusted after Gloria. I knew it and he knew I knew it. I think Daphne, his wife, knew it too. I hung up the phone without saying goodbye.

And so it was that, on Christmas Eve, when Gloria was with my children, preparing them for early bed so that Santa Claus could operate undisturbed, I was standing watching the Berlin police trying to winch a wrecked car out of the water. It wasn't exactly the Hohenzollern Canal. Dicky had got that wrong; it was Hakenfelde, that industrialized section of the bank of the Havel River not far from where the Hohenzollern joins it.

Here the Havel widens to become a lake. It was so cold that the police doctor insisted the frogmen must have a couple of hours' rest to thaw out. The police inspector had argued about it, but in the end the doctor's opinion prevailed. Now the boat containing the frogmen had disappeared into the gloom and I was left with only the police inspector for company. The two policemen left to guard the scene had gone behind the generator truck, the noise of which never ceased. The police electricians had put flood lamps along the wharf to make light for the winch crew, so that the whole place was lit with the bright artificiality of a film set.

I stepped through the broken railing at the place where the car had gone into the water. Looking down over the edge of the jetty I could just make out the wobbling outline of the car under the dark oily surface. The winch, and two steadying cables, held it suspended there. For the time being, the car had won the battle. One steel cable had broken, and the first attempts to lift the car had ripped its rear off. That was the trouble with cars, said the inspector – they filled with water, and water weighs a ton per cubic metre. And this was a big car, a Citroën ambulance. To make it worse, its frame was bent enough to prevent the frogmen from getting its doors open.

The inspector was in his mid-fifties, a tall man with a large white moustache, its ends curling in the style of the Kaiser's soldiers. It was the sort of moustache a man grew to make himself look older. 'To think,' said the inspector, 'that I transferred out of the Traffic Department because I thought standing on point duty was too cold.' He stamped his feet. His heavy jackboots made a crunching sound where ice was forming in the cracks between the cobblestones.

'You should have kept to traffic,' I said, 'but transferred to the Nice or Cannes Police Department.'

'Rio,' said the inspector, 'I was offered a job in Rio. There was an agency here recruiting ex-policemen. My wife was all in favour, but I like Berlin. There's no town like it. And I've always been a cop; never wanted to be anything else. I know you from somewhere, don't I? I remember your face. Were you ever a cop?'

'No,' I said. I didn't want to get into a discussion about what I did for a living.

'Right from the time I was a child,' he continued. 'I'm going back a long time now to the war and even before that. There was a traffic cop, famous all over Berlin. Siegfried they called him; I don't know if that was his real name but everyone knew Siegfried. He was always on duty at the Wilhelmplatz, the beautiful little white palace where Dr Goebbels ran his Propaganda Ministry. There were always crowds of tourists there, watching the well-known faces that went in and out, and if there was any kind of crisis, big crowds would form there to try and guess what was going on. My father always pointed out Siegfried, a tall policeman in a long white coat. And I wanted a big white coat like the traffic police wear. And I wanted to have the ministers and the generals, the journalists and the film stars, say hello to me in that friendly way they always greeted him. There was a kiosk there on the Wilhelmplatz which sold souvenirs and they had postcard photos of all the Nazi bigwigs and I asked my father why there wasn't a photo card of Siegfried on sale there. I wanted to buy one. My father said that maybe next week there would be one of Siegfried, and every week I looked but there wasn't one. I decided that when I grew up I'd be the policeman in the Wilhelmplatz and I'd make sure they had my photo on sale in the kiosk. It's silly, isn't it, how such unimportant things change a man's life?'

'Yes,' I said.

'I know you from somewhere,' he said, looking at my face and frowning. I passed the police inspector my hip flask of brandy. He hesitated and took a look round the desolate yard. 'Doctor's orders,' I joked. He smiled, took a gulp, and wiped his mouth on the back of his hand.

'My God, it's cold,' he said as if to explain his lapse from grace.

'It's cold and it's Christmas Eve,' I said.

'Now I remember,' he said suddenly. 'You were in that football team that played on the rubble behind the Stadium. I used to take my kid brother along. He was ten or eleven; you must have been about the same age.' He chuckled at the recollection and with the satisfaction of remembering where he'd seen me before. 'The football team; yes. It was run by that crazy English colonel – the tall one with glasses. He had no idea about how to play football; he couldn't even kick the ball straight, but he ran round the pitch waving a walking stick and yelling his head off. Remember?'

'I remember,' I said.

'Those were the days. I can see him now, waving that stick in the air and yelling. What a crazy old man he was. After the match he'd give each boy a bar of chocolate and an apple. Most of the kids only went to get the chocolate and apple.'

'You're right,' I said.

'I knew I'd seen you somewhere before.' He stood looking across the water for a long time and then said, 'Who was in the ambulance? One of your people?' He knew I was from London and guessed the rest of it. In Berlin you didn't have to be psychic to guess the rest of it.

'A prisoner,' I said.

It was already getting dark. Daylight doesn't last long on clouded Berlin days like this in December. The warehouse lights made little puff balls in the mist. Around here there were only cranes, sheds, storage tanks, crates stacked as high as tenements, and rusty railway tracks. Facing us far across the water were more of the same. There was no movement except the sluggish current. The great city around us was almost silent and only the generator disturbed the peace. Looking south along the river I could see the island of Eiswerder. Beyond that, swallowed by the mist, was Spandau – world-famous now, not only for its machine guns but for the fortress prison inside which the soldiers of four nations guarded one aged and infirm prisoner: Hitler's deputy.

The police inspector followed my gaze. 'Not Hess,' he joked. 'Don't say the poor old fellow finally escaped?'

I smiled dutifully. 'Bad luck getting Christmas duty,' I said. 'Are you married?'

'I'm married. I live just round the corner from here. My parents lived in the same house. Do you know I've never been out of Berlin in all my life?'

'All through the war too?'

'Yes, all through the war I was living here. I was thinking of that just now when you gave me the drink.' He turned up the collar of his uniform greatcoat. 'You get old and suddenly you find yourself remembering things that you haven't recalled in about forty years. Tonight for instance, suddenly I'm remembering a time just before Christmas in 1944 when I was on duty very near here: the gasworks.'

'You were in the Army?' He didn't look old enough.

'No. Hitler Youth. I was fourteen and I'd only just got my uniform. They said I wasn't strong enough to join a gun crew, so they made me a messenger for the air defence post. I was the youngest kid there. They only let me do that job because Berlin hadn't had an air raid for months and it seemed so safe. There were rumours that Stalin had told the Western powers that Berlin mustn't be bombed so that the Red Army could capture it intact.' He gave a sardonic little smile. 'But the rumours were proved wrong, and on December fifth the Americans came over in daylight. People said they were trying to hit the Siemens factory, but I don't know. Siemensstadt was badly bombed, but bombs hit Spandau, and Pankow and Oranienburg and Weissensee. Our fighters attacked the *Amis* as they came in to bomb – it was a thick overcast but I could hear the machine guns – and I think they just dropped everything as soon as they could and headed home.'

'Why do you remember that particular air raid?'

'I was outside and I was blown off my bicycle by the bomb that dropped in Streitstrasse just along the back of here. The officer at the air-raid post found another bike for me and gave me a swig of schnapps from his flask, like you did just now. I felt very grown up. I'd never tasted schnapps before. Then he sent me off on my bike with a message for our headquarters at Spandau station. Our phones had been knocked out. Be careful, he said, and if another lot of bombers come, you take shelter. When I got back from delivering the message there was nothing left of them. The air defence post was just rubble. They were all dead. It was a delayed action bomb. It must have been right alongside us when he gave me the schnapps, but no one felt the shock of it because of all the racket.'

Suddenly his manner changed, as if he was embarrassed at having told me his war experiences. Perhaps he'd been chafed about his yarns by men who'd come back from the Eastern Front with stories that made his air-raid experiences seem no more than minor troubles.

He tugged at his greatcoat like a man about to go on parade. And then, looking down into the water at the submerged car again, he said, 'If the next go doesn't move it, we'll have to get a big crane. And that will mean waiting until after the holiday; the union man will make sure of that.'

'I'll hang on,' I said. I knew he was trying to provide me with an excuse to leave.

'The frogmen say the car is empty.'

'They wanted to go home,' I said flippantly.

The inspector was offended. 'Oh, no. They are good boys. They wouldn't tell me wrong just to avoid another dive.' He was right, of course. In Germany there was still a work ethic.

I said, 'They can't see much, with the car covered in all that oil and muck. I know what it's like in this sort of water; the underwater lamps just reflect in the car's window glass.'

'Here's your friend,' said the inspector. He strolled off towards the other end of the wharf to give us a chance to talk in private.

It was Werner Volkmann. He had his hat dumped on top of his head and was wearing his long heavy coat with the astrakhan collar. I called it his impresario's coat, but today the laugh was on me, freezing to death in my damp trench coat. 'What's happening?' he said.

'Nothing,' I said. 'Nothing at all.'

'Don't bite my head off,' said Werner. 'I'm not even getting paid.'

'I'm sorry, Werner, but I told you not to bother to drag out here.'

'The roads are empty, and to tell you the truth, being a Jew I feel a bit of a hypocrite celebrating Christmas.'

'You haven't left Zena alone?'

'Her sister's family are with us – four children and a husband who works in the VAT office.'

'I can see why you came.'

'I like it all up to a point,' said Werner. 'Zena likes to do the whole thing right. You know how it is in Germany. She spent all the afternoon decorating the tree and putting the presents out, and she has real candles on it.'

'You should be with them,' I said. In Germany the evening before

Christmas Day – *heiliger Abend* – is the most important time of the holiday. 'Make sure she doesn't burn the house down.'

'I'll be back with them in time for the dinner. I told them you'd join us.'

'I wish I could, Werner. But I'll have to be here when it comes out of the water. Dicky put that in writing and you know what he's like.'

'Are you going to try again soon?'

'In about an hour. What did you find out at the hospital this morning?'

'Nothing very helpful. The people who took her away were dressed up to be a doctor and hospital staff. They had the Citroën waiting outside. From what the people in the reception office say, the ambulance was supposed to be taking her to a private clinic in Dahlem.'

'What about the cop guarding her?'

'For him they had a different story. They told him they were clinic staff. They said they were just taking her downstairs for another X-ray and would be back in about thirty minutes. She was very weak and complained bitterly about being moved. She probably didn't realize what was going to happen.'

'That she was going into the Havel, you mean?'

'No. That they were a KGB team, there to get her away from police custody.'

I said, 'Why didn't the clinic reception phone the police before releasing her?'

'I don't know, Bernie. One of them said that she was taken out using the papers of a patient who was due to be moved that day. Another one said there was a policeman outside with the ambulance, so it seemed to be all in order. We'll probably never find out exactly what happened. It's a hospital, not a prison; the staff don't worry too much about who's going in and out.'

'What do you make of it, Werner?'

'They knew she was talking, I suppose. Somehow what she was telling us got back to Moscow and they decided there was only one way of handling it.'

'Why not take her straight back into East Berlin?' I said.

'In an ambulance? Very conspicuous. Even the Russians are not too keen on that sort of publicity. Snatching a prisoner from police custody and taking her across the wire would not look good at a time when the East Germans are trying to show the world what good neighbours they can be.' He looked at me. I pulled a face. 'It's easier this way,' added Werner. 'They got rid of her. They were taking no chances. If she had talked to us already, they'd be making sure she couldn't give evidence.'

'But it's a drastic remedy, Werner. What made them get so excited?'

'They knew she was handling the radio traffic your wife provided.'

'Right,' I said. 'And Fiona is over there. So why would they be worried about what she might tell us?'

'Fiona is behind it? Is that what you mean?'

'It's difficult not to suspect her hand is in it.'

'But Fiona is safe and sound. What has she got to worry about?'

'Nothing, Werner, she's got nothing to worry about.'

He looked at me as if puzzled. Then he said, 'The radio traffic then. What did Dicky think about the multiple codes?'

'Dicky didn't seem to be listening. He was hoping the Miller woman would just fade away, and he's forbidden me to speak with Stinnes.'

'Dicky was never one to go looking for extra work,' said Werner.

'No one is interested,' I said. 'I went down to talk to Silas Gaunt and von Munte and neither of them were very interested. Silas waggled his finger at me when I brought the matter up with von Munte. And he told me not to rock the boat. Don't start digging into all that again, he said.'

'I don't know old Mr Gaunt the way you do. I just remember him in the Berlin office at the time when your dad was Resident. We were about eighteen years old. Mr Gaunt bet me that the Wall would never go up. I won fifty marks from him when they built the Wall. And fifty marks was a lot of money in those days. You could have an evening out with all the trimmings for fifty marks.'

'I wish I had one mark for every time you've told me that story, Werner.'

'You're in a filthy mood, Bernie. I'm sorry you got this rotten job, but it's not my fault.'

'I'd really looked forward to a couple of days with the kids. They're growing up without me, Werner. And Gloria is there too.'

'I'm glad that's going well . . . you and Gloria.'

'It's bloody ridiculous,' I said. 'I'm old enough to be her father. Do you know how old she is?'

'No, and I don't care. There's an age difference between me and Zena, isn't there? But that doesn't stop us being happy.'

I turned to Werner so that I could look at him. It was dark. His face was visible only because it was edged with light reflected from the array of floodlights. His heavy-lidded eyes were serious. Poor Werner. Was he really happy? His marriage was my idea of hell. 'Zena is older than Gloria,' I said.

'Be happy while you can, Bernie. It's nothing to do with Gloria's age. You still feel bad about losing Fiona. You haven't got over her running away yet. I know you, and I can tell. She was a sort of anchor for you, a base. Without her you are restless and unsure of yourself. But that's only temporary. You'll get over it. And Gloria is just what you need.'

'Maybe.' I didn't argue with him; he was usually very perceptive about people and their relationships. That was why he'd been such a good field agent back in the days when we were young and carefree, and enjoyed taking risks.

'What's really on your mind? Code names are just for the analysts and Coordination staff. Why do you care how many code names Fiona used?'

'She used *one*,' I snapped. 'They all use one. Our people have one name per source and so do their agents. That's what von Munte confirmed. Fiona was *Eisenguss* – no other names.'

'How can you be so sure?'

'I'm not one hundred per cent sure,' I told him. 'Special circumstances come up in this business; we all know that. But I'm ninety-nine per cent sure.'

'What are you saying, Bernie?'

'Surely it's obvious, Werner.'

'It's Christmas, Bernie. I had a few drinks just to be sociable. What is it you're saying?'

'There are two major sources of material that the Miller woman handled. Both top-grade intelligence. Only one of them was Fiona.'

Werner pinched his nose between thumb and forefinger and closed his eyes. Werner did that when he was thinking hard. 'You mean there's someone else still there? You mean the KGB still have someone in London Central?'

'I don't know,' I said.

'Don't just shrug it off,' said Werner. 'Don't hit me in the face with that kind of custard pie and then say you don't know.'

'Everything points to it,' I said. 'But I've told them at London Central. I've done everything short of drawing a diagram and no one gives a damn.'

'It might just be a stunt, a KGB stunt.'

'I'm not organizing a lynching party, Werner. I'm just suggesting that it should be checked out.'

'The Miller woman might have got it wrong,' said Werner.

'She might have got .it wrong, but even if she got it wrong, that still leaves a question to be answered. And what if someone reads the Miller transcript and starts wondering if I might be the other source?'

'Ahh! You're just covering your arse,' said Werner. 'You don't really think there's another KGB source in London Central, but you realized that you'd have to interpret it that way in case anyone thought it was you and you were trying to protect yourself.'

'Don't be stupid.'

'I'm not stupid, Bernard. I know London Central and I know you. You're just running round shouting fire in case someone accuses you of arson.'

I shook my head to say no, but I was wondering if perhaps he was right. He knew me better than anyone, better even than Fiona knew me.

'Are you really going to hang on until they get that motor car out of the water?'

'That's what I'm going to do.'

'Come back for a bite of dinner. Ask the police inspector to phone us when they start work again.'

'I mustn't, Werner. I promised Lisl I'd have dinner with her at the hotel in the unlikely event of my getting away from here in time.'

'Shall I phone her to say you won't make it?'

I looked at my watch. 'Yes, please, Werner. She's having some cronies in to eat there – old Mr Koch and those people she buys wine from – and they'll get fidgety if she delays dinner for me.'

'I'll phone her. I took her a present yesterday, but I'll phone to say Happy Christmas.' He pulled the collar of his coat up and tucked his white silk scarf into it. 'Damned cold out here on the river.'

'Get back to Zena,' I told him.

'If you're sure you're not coming. . . . Shall I bring you something to eat?'

'Stop being a Jewish mother, Werner. There are plenty of places where I can get something. In fact, I'll walk back to your car with you. There's a bar open on the corner. I'll get myself sausage and beer.'

It was nearly ten o'clock at night when they dragged the ambulance out of the Havel. It was a sorry sight, its side caked with oily mud where it had rested on the bottom of the river. One tyre was torn off and some of the bodywork ripped open where it had collided with the railings that were there to prevent such accidents.

There was a muffled cheer as the car came to rest. But there was no delay in finishing the job. Even while the frogmen were still packing their gear away, the car's doors had been levered open and a search was being made of its interior.

There was no body inside – that was obvious within the first two or three minutes – but we continued to search through the car in search of other evidence.

By eleven-fifteen the police inspector declared the preliminary forensic examination complete. Although they'd put a number of oddments into clear-plastic evidence bags, nothing had been discovered that was likely to throw any light on the disappearance of Carol Elvira Miller, self-confessed Russian agent.

We were all very dirty. I went with the policemen into the toilet facilities at the wharfside. There was no hot water from the tap, and only one bar of soap. One of the policemen came back with a large pail of boiling water. The rest of them stood aside so that the inspector could wash first. He indicated that I should use the other sink.

'What do you make of it?' said the inspector as he rationed out a measure of the hot water into each of the sinks.

'Where would a body turn up?' I asked.

'Spandau locks, that's where we fish them out,' he said without hesitation. 'But there was no one in that car when it went into the water.' He took off his jacket and shirt so that he could wash his arms where mud had dribbled up his sleeve.

'You think not?' I stood alongside him and took the soap he offered.

'The front doors were locked, and the back door of the ambulance was locked too. Not many people getting out of a car underwater remember to lock the doors before swimming away.' He passed me some paper towels.

'It went into the water empty?'

'So you don't want to talk about it. Very well.'

'No, you're right,' I said. 'It's probably just a stunt. How did you get the information about where to find it?'

'I looked at the docket. An anonymous phone call from a passer-by. You think it was a phony?'

'Probably.'

'While the prisoner was taken away somewhere else.'

'It would be a way of getting our attention.'

'And spoiling my Christmas Eve,' he said. 'I'll kill the bastards if I ever get hold of them.'

'Them?'

'At least two people. It wasn't in gear, you notice, it was in neutral. So they must have pushed it in. That needs two people; one to push and one to steer.'

'Three of them, according to what we heard.'

He nodded. 'There's too much crime on television,' said the police inspector. He signalled to the policeman to get another bucket of water for the rest of them to wash with. 'That old English colonel with the kids' football team. . . . he was your father, wasn't he?'

'Yes,' I said.

'I realized that afterwards. I could have bitten my tongue off. No offence. Everyone liked the old man.'

'That's okay,' I said.

'He didn't even enjoy the football. He just did it for the German kids; there wasn't much for them in those days. He probably hated every minute of those games. At the time we didn't see that; we wondered why he took so much trouble about the football when he couldn't even kick the ball straight. He organized lots of things for the kids, didn't he. And he sent you to the neighbourhood school instead of to that fancy school where the other British children went. He must have been an unusual man, your father.'

Washing my hands and arms and face had only got rid of the most obvious dirt. My trench coat was soaked and my shoes squelched. The mud along the banks of the Havel at that point is polluted with a century of industrial waste and effluents. Even my newly washed hands still bore the stench of the riverbed.

The hotel was dark when I let myself in by means of the key that certain privileged guests were permitted to borrow. Lisl Hennig's hotel had once been her grand home, and her parents' home before that. It was just off Kantstrasse, a heavy grey stone building of the sort that abounds in Berlin. The ground floor was an optician's shop and its bright façade partly hid the pockmarked stone that was the result of Red Army artillery fire in 1945. My very earliest memories were of Lisl's house – it was not easy to think of it as a hotel – for I came here as a baby when my father was with the British Army. I'd known the patched brown carpet that led up the grand staircase when it had been bright red.

At the top of the stairs there was the large salon and the bar. It was gloomy. The only illumination came from a tiny Christmas tree positioned on the bar counter. Tiny green and red bulbs flashed on and off in a melancholy attempt to be festive. Intermittent light fell upon the framed photos that covered every wall. Here were some of Berlin's most illustrious residents, from Einstein to Nabokov, Garbo to Dietrich, Max Schmeling to Grand Admiral Dönitz, celebrities of a Berlin now gone for ever.

I looked into the breakfast room; it was empty. The bentwood chairs had been put up on the tables so that the floor could be swept. The cruets and cutlery and a tall stack of white plates were ready on the table near the serving hatch. There was no sign of life anywhere. There wasn't even the smell of cooking that usually crept up through the house at night-time.

I tiptoed across the salon to the back stairs. My room was at the top – I always liked to occupy the little garret room that had been my bedroom as a child. But before reaching the stairs I passed the door of Lisl's room. A strip of light along the door confirmed that she was there.

'Who is it?' she called anxiously. 'Who's there?'

'It's Bernd,' I said.

'Come in, you wretched boy.' Her shout was loud enough to wake everyone in the building.

She was propped up in bed; there must have been a dozen lace-edged pillows behind her. She had a scarf tied round her head, and on the side table there was a bottle of sherry and a glass. All over the bed there were newspapers; some of them had come to pieces so that pages had drifted across the room as far as the fireplace.

She'd snatched her glasses off so quickly that her dyed brown hair was disarranged. 'Give me a kiss,' she demanded. I did so and noticed the expensive perfume and the makeup and false eyelashes that she applied only for very special occasions. The *heiliger Abend* with her friends had meant a lot to her. I guessed she'd waited for me to come home before she'd remove the makeup. 'Did you have a nice time?' she asked. There was repressed anger in her voice.

'I've been working,' I said. I didn't want to get into a conversation. I wanted to go to bed and sleep for a long time.

'Who were you with?'

'I told you, I was working.' I tried to assuage her annoyance. 'Did you have dinner with Mr Koch and your friends? What did you serve them – carp?' She liked carp at Christmas; she'd often told me it was the only thing to serve. Even during the war they'd always somehow managed to get carp.

'Lothar Koch couldn't come. He had influenza and the wine people had to go to a trade party.'

'So you were all alone,' I said. I bent over and kissed her again. 'I'm so sorry, Lisl.' She'd been so pretty. I remember as a child feeling guilty for thinking she was more beautiful than my mother. 'I really am sorry.'

'And so you should be.'

'There was no way of avoiding it. I had to be there.'

'Had to be where – Kempinski or the Steigenberger? Don't lie to me, *Liebchen*. When Werner phoned me I could hear the voices and the music in the background. So you don't have to pretend you were working.' She gave a little hoot of laughter, but there was no joy in it.

So she'd been in bed here working herself up into a rage about that. 'I was working,' I repeated. 'I'll explain tomorrow.'

'There's nothing you have to explain, *Liebchen*. You are a free man. You don't have to spend your *heiliger Abend* with an ugly old woman. Go and have fun while you are young. I don't mind.'

'Don't upset yourself, Lisl,' I said. 'Werner was phoning from his apartment because I was working.'

By this time she'd noticed the smell of the mud on my clothes, and now she pushed her glasses into place so that she could see me more clearly. 'You're filthy, Bernd. Whatever have you been doing?

Where have you been?' From her study there came the loud chimes of the ornate ormolu clock striking two-thirty.

'I keep telling you over and over again, Lisl. I've been with the police on the Havel getting a car from the water.'

'The times I've told you that you drive too fast.'

'It wasn't anything to do with me,' I said.

'So what were you doing there?'

'Working. Can I have a drink?'

'There's a glass on the sideboard. I've only got sherry. The whisky and brandy are locked in the cellar.'

'Sherry will be just right.'

'My God, Bernd, what are you doing? You don't drink sherry by the tumblerful.'

'It's Christmas,' I said.

'Yes. It's Christmas,' she said, and poured herself another small measure. 'There was a phone message, a woman. She said her name was Gloria Kent. She said that everyone sent you their love. She wouldn't leave a phone number. She said you'd understand.' Lisl sniffed.

'Yes, I understand,' I said. 'It's a message from the children.'

'Ah, Bernd. Give me a kiss, *Liebchen*. Why are you so cruel to your Tante Lisl? I bounced you on my knee in this very room, and that was before you could walk.'

'Yes, I know, but I couldn't get away, Lisl. It was work.'

She fluttered her eyelashes like a young actress. 'One day you'll be old, darling. Then you'll know what it's like.'

6

Christmas morning. West Berlin was like a ghost town; as I stepped into the street the silence was uncanny. The Ku-damm was empty of traffic and, although some of the neon signs and shop lights were still shining, there was no one strolling on its wide pavements. I had the town virtually to myself all the way to Potsdamer Strasse.

Potsdamer Strasse is Schöneberg's main street, a wide thoroughfare that is called Hauptstrasse at one end and continues north to the Tiergarten. You can find everything you want there and a lot of things you've been trying to avoid. There are smart shops and slums, kebab counters and superb nineteenth-century houses now listed as national monuments. Here is a neobaroque palace – the *Volksgerichtshof* – where Hitler's judges passed death sentences at the rate of two thousand a year, so that citizens found guilty of telling even the most feeble anti-Nazi jokes were executed.

Behind the Volksgerichthof – its rooms now echoing and empty except for those used by the Allied Travel Office and the Allied Air Security Office (where the four powers control the air lanes across East Germany to Berlin) – was the street where Lange lived. His top-floor apartment overlooked one of the seedier side streets. Lange was not his family name, it was not his name at all. 'Lange' – or 'Lofty' – was the descriptive nickname the Germans had given to this very tall American. His real name was John Koby. Of Lithuanian extraction, his grandfather had decided that 'Kubilunas' was not American enough to go over a storefront in Boston.

The street door led to a grim stone staircase. The windows on every landing had been boarded up. It was dark, the stairs illuminated by dim lamps protected against vandals by wire mesh. The walls were bare of any decoration but graffiti. At the top of the house the apartment door was newly painted dark grey and a new plastic bell push was labelled JOHN KOBY – JOURNALIST. The door was opened by Mrs Koby and she led me into a brightly lit, well-furnished apartment. 'Lange was so glad you phoned,' she whispered. 'It was wonderful that you could come right away. He gets miserable sometimes. You'll cheer him up.' She was a small thin woman, her face pale like the faces of most Berliners when winter comes. She had clear eyes, a round face, and a fringe that came almost down to her eyebrows.

'I'll try,' I promised.

It was the sort of untidy room in which you'd expect to find a writer or even a 'journalist'. There were crowded bookshelves, a desk with an old manual typewriter, and more books and papers piled on the floor. But Lange had not been a professional writer for many years, and even in his newspaper days he'd never been a man who referred to books except as a last resort. Lange had never been a journalist, Lange had always been a streetwise reporter who got his facts at firsthand and guessed the bits in between. Just as I did.

The furniture was old but not valuable – the random mixture of shapes and styles that's to be found in a saleroom or attic. Obviously a big stove had once stood in the corner, and the wall where it had been was covered in old blue-and-white tiles. Antique tiles like those were valuable now, but these must have been firmly affixed to the wall, for I had the feeling that any valuable thing not firmly attached had already been sold.

He was wearing an old red-and-gold silk dressing gown. Under it there were grey flannel slacks and a heavy cotton button-down shirt of the sort that Brooks Brothers made famous. His tie bore the ice-cream colours of the Garrick Club, a London meeting place for actors, advertising men, and lawyers. He was over seventy, but he was thin and tall and somehow that helped to give him a more youthful appearance. His face was drawn and clean-shaven, with a high forehead and grey hair neatly parted. He had a prominent bony nose and teeth that were too yellow and irregular to be anything but his own natural ones.

I remembered in time the sort of greeting that Lange gave to old friends – the *Handschlag*, the hands slapped together in that noisy handshake with which German farmers conclude a sale of pigs.

'A Merry Christmas, Lange,' I said.

'It's good to see you, Bernie,' he said as he released my hand. 'We were in the other house the last time we saw you. The apartment over the baker's shop.' His American accent was strong, as if he'd arrived only yesterday. And yet Lange had lived in Berlin longer than most of his neighbours. He'd come here as a newspaperman even before Hitler took power in 1933, and he'd stayed here right up to the time America got into World War II.

'Coffee, Bernard? It's already made. Or would you prefer a glass of wine?' said Gerda Koby, taking my coat. She was a shy withdrawn woman, and although I'd known her since I was a child, she'd never called me 'Bernie'. I think she would have rather called me 'Herr Samson', but she followed her husband in this matter as in all others.

She was still pretty. Rather younger than Lange, she had once been an opera singer famous throughout Germany. They'd met in Berlin when he returned here as a newspaperman with the US Army in 1945.

'I missed breakfast,' I said. 'A cup of coffee would be great.'

'Lange?' she said. He looked at her blankly and didn't answer. She shrugged. 'He'll have wine,' she told me. 'He won't cut down on it.' She looked too small for an opera singer, but the ancient posters on the wall gave her billing above title: Wagner in Bayreuth, *Fidelio* at the Berlin State Opera, and in Munich a performance of *Mongol Fury* which was the Nazis' 'Aryanized' version of Handel's *Israel in Egypt*.

'It's Christmas, woman,' said Lange. 'Give us both wine.' He didn't smile and neither did she. It was the brusque way he always addressed her.

'I'll stick to coffee,' I said. 'I have a lot of driving to do. And I have to go to Police HQ and sign some forms later today.'

'Sit down, Bernie, and tell me what you're doing here. The last time we saw you you were settled in London, married, and with kids.' His voice was hoarse and slurred slightly in the Bogart manner.

'I am,' I said. 'I'm just here for a couple of days on business.'

'Oh, sure,' said Lange. 'Stuffing presents down the chimneys: then you've got to get your reindeer together and head back to the workshops.'

'The children must be big,' said Mrs Koby. 'You should be with them at home. They make you work at Christmas? That's terrible.'

'My boss has a mean streak,' I said.

'And you haven't got a union by the sound of it,' said Lange. He had little love for the Department and he made his dislike evident in almost everything he said about the men in London Central.

'That's right,' I said.

We sat there exchanging small talk for fifteen minutes or maybe half an hour. I needed a little time to get used to Lange's harsh, abrasive style.

'Still working for the Department, eh?'

'Not any longer,' I said.

He ignored my denial; he knew it counted for nothing. 'Well, I'm glad I got out of it when I did.'

'You were the first man my dad recruited in Berlin, at least that's what people say.'

'Then they've got it right,' said Lange. 'And I was grateful to him. In 1945 I couldn't wait to kiss the newspaper business goodbye.'

'What was wrong with it?'

'You're too young to remember. They dressed reporters up in fancy uniforms and stuck "War Correspondent" badges on us. That was so all those dumb jerks in the Army press departments could order us about and tell us what to write.'

'Not you, Lange. No one told you what to do.'

'We couldn't argue. I was living in an apartment that the Army had commandeered. I was eating US rations, driving an Army car on Army gas, and spending Army occupation money. Sure, they had us by the balls.'

'They tried to stop Lange seeing me,' said Mrs Koby indignantly.

'They forbade all Allied soldiers to talk to any Germans. Those dummies were trying to sell the soldiers their crackpot non-fraterniz- ation doctrine. Can you imagine me trying to write stories here while forbidden to talk to Germans? The Army fumed and threw kids into the stockade, but when you've got young German girls walking past the GIs patting their asses and shouting "*Verboten*", even the Army brass began to see what a dumb idea it was.'

'It was terrible in 1945 when I met Lange,' said Gerda Koby. 'My beautiful Berlin was unrecognizable. You're too young to remember, Bernard. There were heaps of rubble as tall as the tenement blocks. There wasn't one tree or bush left in the entire city; the Tiergarten was like a desert – everything that would burn had long since been cut down. The canals and waterways were all completely filled with rubble and ironwork, pushed there to clear a lane through the streets. The whole city stank with the dead; the stench from the canals was even worse.'

It was uncharacteristic of her to speak so passionately. She came to a sudden stop as if embarrassed. Then she got up and poured coffee for me from a vacuum flask and poured a glass of wine for her husband. I think he'd had a few before I arrived.

The coffee was in a delicate demitasse that contained no more than a mouthful. I swallowed it gratefully. I can't get started in the morning until I've had some coffee.

'*Die Stunde Null*,' said Lange. 'Germany's hour zero – I didn't need anyone to explain what that meant when I got here in 1945. Berlin looked like the end of the world had arrived.' Lange scratched his head without disarranging his neatly combed hair. 'And that's the kind of chaos I had to work in. None of these Army guys, or the clowns who worked for the so-called Military Government, knew the city. Half of them couldn't even speak the language. I'd been in Berlin right up until 1941 and I was able to renew all those old contacts. I set up the whole agent network that your dad ran into the East. He was smart, your dad, he knew I could deliver what I promised. He assigned me to work as his assistant and I told the Army where to stick their "War Correspondent" badge, pin and all.' He laughed. 'Jesus, but they were mad. They were mad at me and mad at your dad. The US Army complained to Eisenhower's intelligence. But your dad had a direct line to Whitehall and that trumped their ace.'

'Why did you go to Hamburg?' I said.

'I'd been here too long.' He drank some of the bright red wine.

'How long after that did Bret Rensselaer do his "fact-finding mission"?' I asked.

'Don't mention that bastard to me. Bret was just a kid when he came out here trying to "rationalize the administration".' Lange put heavy sarcastic emphasis on the last three words. 'He was the best pal the Kremlin ever had, and I'll give you that in writing any time.'

'Was he?' I said.

'Go to the archives and look . . . or better still, go to the "yellow submarine".' He smiled and studied my face to see if I was surprised at the extent of his knowledge. 'The yellow submarine – that's what I hear they call the big London Central computer.'

'I don't know. . . .'

'Sure, sure,' said Lange. 'I know, you're not in the Department any more; you're over here to conduct a concert of Christmas carols for the British garrison.'

'What did Bret Rensselaer do?'

'Do? He dismantled three networks that I was running into the Russian Zone. Everything was going smoothly until he arrived. He put a spanner into the works and eventually got London to pack me off to Hamburg.'

'What was his explanation?' I persisted.

'Bret didn't provide any explanations. You know him better than that. No one could stop him. Bret was only on temporary attachment to us at that time, but he'd been given some piece of paper in London Central that said he could do anything.'

'And what did my father do?'

'Your father wasn't here. They got him out of the way before Bret arrived. I had no one to appeal to; that was part of the setup.'

'Setup? Were you set up?' I said.

'Sure I was set up. Bret was going out to get me. Mine was the only desk in Berlin that was getting good material from the Russians. Jesus. I had a guy in Karlshorst who was bringing me day-to-day material from the Russian commandant's office. You can't do better than that.'

'And he was stopped?'

'He was one of the first we lost. I went across to the US Army to offer them what I had left, but Bret had already been there. I got the cold shoulder. I had no friends there because of the showdown I'd had with them during the early days. So I went to Hamburg just as London Central wanted.'

'But you didn't stay.'

'In Hamburg? No, I didn't stay in Hamburg. Berlin is my town, mister. I just went to Hamburg long enough to work my way through my resignation and then I got out. Bret Rensselaer had got what he wanted.'

'What was that?'

'He'd showed us what a big shot he was. He'd denazified the Berlin office and wrecked our best networks. "Denazified", that's what he called it. Who the hell did he think we could find who would risk their necks prying secrets from the Russkies – Socialists, Communists, left-wing liberals? We had to use ex-Nazis; they were the only pros we had. By the time your dad came back and tried to pick up the pieces, Bret was reading philosophy at some fancy college. Your dad wanted me to work with him again. But I said, "No dice." I didn't want to work for London Central, not if I was going to be looking over my shoulder in case Bret came back to breathe fire all over me again. No, sir.'

'It was my fault, Bernard,' said Mrs Koby. Again she spoke my name as if it was unfamiliar to her. Perhaps she always felt self-conscious as a German amongst Lange's American and British friends.

'No, no, no,' said Lange.

'It was my brother,' she persisted. 'He came back from the war so sick. He was injured in Hungary just before the end. He had nowhere to go. Lange let him stay with us.'

'Nah!' said Lange angrily. 'It was nothing to do with Stefan.'

'Stefan was a wonderful boy.' She said it with heartfelt earnestness as if she was pleading for him.

'Stefan was a bastard,' said Lange.

'You didn't know him until afterwards. . . . It was the pain, the constant pain that made him so ill-natured. But before he went off to the war he was a kind and gentle boy. Hitler destroyed him.'

'Oh, sure, blame Hitler,' said Lange. 'That's the style nowadays. Everything was Hitler's fault. How would Germans manage without the Nazis to blame everything on?'

'He was a sweet boy,' said Mrs Koby. 'You never knew him.'

Lange gave a sardonic laugh that ended as a snort. 'No, I never knew any sweet boy named Stefan, and that's for sure.'

Mrs Koby turned all her attention to me and said, 'Lange gave him a bedroom. At that time Lange was working for your people. We had a big apartment in Tegel, near the water.'

'He came there,' said Lange. 'Bernie came there many times.'

'Of course you did,' said Mrs Koby. 'And you never met my brother Stefan?'

'I'm not sure,' I said.

'Bernie wouldn't remember Stefan,' said Lange. 'Bernie was just a kid when Stefan died. And for years Stefan hardly ever left that damned bedroom!'

'Yes, poor Stefan. His life was so short and time passes so quickly,' said Mrs Koby.

Lange explained to me. 'My wife thinks that everybody cut her dead because Stefan had been a Waffen-SS officer. But in those days most Germans were too damned busy trying to find a handful of potatoes to feed their families. No one cared about their neighbours' "regimental histories".'

'They cared,' said Mrs Koby feelingly. 'I am a German. People said things to me that they wouldn't have said to you or to any American or British officer. And there were looks and murmurs that only a German would understand.'

'Stefan was in the SS,' said Lange contemptuously. 'He was a major . . . what did they call SS majors – *Obergruppenführer* . . . ?'

'*Sturmbannführer*,' supplied Mrs Koby wearily. Lange knew what an SS major was called, but he preferred a word that sounded cumbersome and comical to his ears. 'They picked on Stefan because he was once an adjutant at Sepp Dietrich's headquarters.'

'Nah!' said Lange. 'He was only there a couple of weeks. He was an artillery man.'

'They wanted Stefan to give evidence at the trial of General Dietrich, but he was too sick to go.' It had become an argument now, the sort of quiet ritualistic dispute that couples indulge in only when visitors are there to sit in judgement.

'Your brother had the bad luck to be in a division that bore the name of Adolf Hitler. Had he been in some other SS division, such as *Prinz Eugen* or the SS cavalry division *Maria Theresa*, he wouldn't have attracted any comment at all.' He smiled and drank some more of his blood-red wine. 'Have a glass of wine, Bernie. Plum wine; Gerda makes it. It's delicious.'

'People can be so cruel,' said Mrs Koby.

'She means all those wonderful "liberals" who crawled out of the woodwork when Germany lost the war.'

'It hurt Lange too,' said Mrs Koby. 'Bret Rensselaer came to the apartment one day and told him to get rid of Stefan. But Lange was brave; he told Rensselaer to go to hell. I loved him for that.' She turned to her husband. 'I loved you for that, Lange.' I had the feeling that in all the years that had passed, she'd never told him before.

'I don't have creeps like Bret Rensselaer telling me who I can have in my apartment,' growled Lange. 'And where would Stefan have gone? He needed attention all the time. Sometimes Gerda was up all night with him.'

Mrs Koby said, 'It was a terrible row . . . shouting. I thought Lange would hit him. Bret Rensselaer never forgave Lange after the argument. He said that Allied officers shouldn't be sheltering SS war criminals. But Stefan wasn't a criminal, he was just a soldier, a brave soldier who'd fought for his country.'

'Bret loses his temper sometimes, Mrs Koby,' I said. 'He says things he doesn't really mean.'

'He was just a kid,' said Lange again. Bret's youthfulness had obviously added to Lange's humiliation. 'Having a rich father got junior a fancy intelligence assignment.'

'It was the Russian woman,' said Mrs Koby. 'I always said she was behind it.'

'Nah,' said Lange.

'What Russian woman?' I said.

'She called herself a princess,' said Lange. 'Tall, dark . . . she'd obviously been a great-looking doll when she was young. She was much older than Bret, but he was the sort of American who goes for all that aristocracy junk. She knew everyone in the city and Bret liked that. He moved her into the apartment he grabbed for himself and lived with her all the time he was here. They had two servants and gave smart little dinner parties and Frank Harrington and Silas Gaunt and the D-G were entertained there. She spoke perfect English, and a dozen more languages. Her father had been a Russian general killed in the Revolution. Or so the story went.'

'And she was a Nazi,' Mrs Koby prompted.

'That's the real joke,' said Lange. 'His White Russian "princess" was a well-known figure in Berlin. She was always being photographed at the night spots and the parties. She was someone the top Nazis always invited along to their parties and balls. Yeah, it was Bret who was really getting close to the Nazis, not me.'

'Is any of this stuff on Bret's file?' I said.

With a flash of the insight for which he was famous, Lange said, 'Are you vetting Rensselaer? Are you checking the bastard out for some new job?'

'No,' I said truthfully.

'This goddamned conversation always seems to get back to Rensselaer, the way conversations do when people from London Central call here.'

I got to my feet. 'And a Merry Christmas to you both,' I said acidly.

'Sit down, kid, for Christ's sake. You're like your dad; too damned prickly for your own good.' He finished his wine and gave his wife the empty glass. 'Have a glass of wine, Bernie. No one can make it like Gerda. I didn't mean *you*, kid. Shit, you were with Max when he died. Max was one of my best guys. Now was he a Nazi?'

'Max was one of the best,' I said.

'I never heard how it happened,' said Lange.

For a moment or more I hesitated. Then I said, 'We'd been in the East nearly three weeks. It was at the time when a lot of things were going wrong for us. A KGB arrest team came for him in a safe house we used in Stendal. I was there with him. It was about nine o'clock in the evening. Max got a car; God knows where he found it. Neither of us had papers; they were in a suitcase at the station.'

'You should have got the papers. No one in their right mind tries the Wall.'

'Railway station?' I said. 'Don't you remember what an East German railway station is like? They're full of cops and soldiers. There's someone asking you for your papers every step of the way. And by that time the luggage office was probably staked out. No, there was no way but through the wire. We decided to try the border down near Wolfsburg. We chose that section because the Wall was being repaired there, and I'd seen a drawing of it. Okay, no one in their right mind tries the Wall, but the guards were getting to feel the same way and they can be slack on a cold night.

'The *Sperrzone* was easy; at that place it was mostly agricultural land still being worked. We spotted the bunkers and the towers and followed the ditch by the road the workers use. We had tools to cut the fences and everything was okay until we were crawling through the *Kontrollstreifen*. And the night was dark, really dark. Everything went fine at the start. But we must have hit a wire or some alarm because suddenly there was a commotion. They began shooting before they could really get a bead on us. You know how they are; they shoot just to show their sergeant that they're on the ball. We were okay until we got to the road that they use for the patrol cars. We stopped worrying about disturbing the pattern in the naked strip and ran across into the mine field. The guards chasing us stopped at the edge of the mine field. It was too dark for them to see us so they had to get the searchlight – we were too far into the mine field for their hand lamps to be much use to them. We crawled and stopped. Crawled and stopped. Max was an old man; the crawling was difficult for him. A couple of times the big light in the tower came across us without stopping. We stayed still for a few minutes, but then they got systematic about it and began to sweep the area bit by bit. Max took careful aim and took out the light with two shots. But they saw the flash of his gun. The machine gunner in the tower just fired at the place he'd seen the flash. He kept his finger on the trigger so that Max must have been torn to pieces. I ran. It was a miracle. In the darkness and the general confusion I got right through.'

Just thinking about it made me tremble.

'Months later, Frank Harrington got hold of the Vopo guard commander's report. It confirmed that Max had been killed by the machine gunner. They'd decided to say there was only one escaper, and thus make their success rate one hundred per cent.' I took a drink of coffee. 'Max saved my life, Lange. He must have guessed what would happen. He saved me.' Why had I suddenly blurted out this story to Lange? I hadn't talked about it to anyone since it happened in 1978.

'Hear that, Gerda?' said Lange softly. 'You remember dear old Max, don't you? What a drinker. Remember how angry you used to get because he never wanted to go home? Then next day he always sent flowers and you forgave him.'

'Of course I do, darling,' she said. I understood now why I suddenly had to say it. I couldn't say it to Max. Max was dead. The next best thing was to say it to Lange who loved him.

'He was a good man,' said Lange. 'He was a Prussian of the old school. I recruited him back in 1946.'

Mrs Koby gave me a glass of her bright red homemade plum wine and gave another one to Lange.

'Didn't you ever feel like going back to the States, Lange?' I said. I drank some of the wine. It was a fierce fruity concoction that made me purse my lips.

'Nah. Berlin is where I want to be.' He watched me drinking the wine without commenting. I had the feeling that drinking a glass of Gerda's plum wine was a test that visitors were expected to endure without complaining.

'They wouldn't let us go to America, Bernard,' said Mrs Koby in contradiction to her husband's bluff dismissal of the idea. 'We got all ready to leave, but the Embassy wouldn't give us a visa.'

'But you're a citizen, Lange,' I said.

'No, I'm not. When I started working for your dad, he rushed through a British passport for me. Even if they let me in, we'd both be aliens in the US. I'm not sure I'd even get Social Security payments. And when I talked to one of our Embassy people he had the nerve to tell me that "working for a foreign intelligence service" would count against me with the Immigration Department. How do you like that?'

'He was kidding you, Lange,' I said. Lange looked at me and said nothing and I didn't press it. I drained my wine glass and got to my feet again. 'I must go,' I said.

'I didn't mean anything, Bernie. I know you weren't sent here by London Central.'

'No offence taken, Lange. But I'm taking Lisl to Werner Volkmann's place for a meal. You know how Lisl is about people being late.'

'It's going to be a Jewish Christmas, is it? What's he serving you – gefilte fish and turkey noodle soup?'

'Something like that,' I said. I didn't care for Lange's jokes.

Lange got up too. 'I hear Frank is retiring,' he said. It was an obvious attempt to draw me out. 'Jesus, he's said goodbye enough times, hasn't he?'

'Sinatra?' I said facetiously.

'Frank *Harrington*,' said Mrs Koby, to put me right.

Lange gave his snorty little laugh and said, 'And I hear that some guy named Cruyer is calling the shots in London these days.'

I pulled my trench coat on. 'Cruyer?' I said. 'That name doesn't ring any bells for me.'

'You've got a great sense of humour, Bernie,' said Lange, without disguising the bitterness he felt at being excluded from the latest gossip about London Central.

7

It was still early when I left Lange and walked north to the Tiergarten and what is the most mysterious part of the present-day city of Berlin. The park was empty, its grass brown and dead and glazed with frost. The trees were bare, like scratchy doodles upon the low grey sky. Rising from behind the trees, like a gilt-tipped rocket set for launching, the *Siegessäule* column. Its winged Victoria – which Berliners call 'golden Elsie' – celebrates the last war that Germany won, some hundred and ten years ago.

And as you turn the corner, you see them – stranded along the edge of the Tiergarten like the gigantic hulks of a rusting battlefleet. They are the embassy buildings that until 1945 made this 'diplomatic quarter' the centre of Berlin's most exclusive and extravagant social life – Berlin is not the capital of West Germany; Bonn enjoys that distinction. So these roofless, derelict buildings standing on the sacrosanct foreign ground of other governments have been left untouched for almost forty years.

The ruined embassies had always fascinated me, ever since we had trespassed there to play dangerous games in my school days. There was the window from which Werner launched his model glider and fell thirty feet into the stinging nettles. Through the broken shell I could see the rafters I'd climbed as a dare and won from a boy named Binder one out of his coveted collection of forbidden Nazi badges. The roof was high and the rafters rickety. I looked at the dangers now and shuddered. I looked at many such previously encountered dangers now and shuddered; that's why I was no longer suitable for employment as a field agent.

I went round the *Diplomatenviertel* not once but twice. I wanted to be quite sure that I was being followed; it's so easy to become paranoid. He was not a real professional; he wasn't quick enough, for one thing, and what professional would wear a distinctive beard and short tartan-patterned coat? He was carrying a large brown-paper parcel, trying to look like someone taking a Christmas present across town, but he wasn't delivering a present to somewhere across town; he was following me; there was no doubt about that. I stopped and peered up at the old Italian Embassy. Some rooms at the back seemed to be occupied, and I wondered who would live in such a place. The bearded man stopped and seemed to wonder too.

My decision to visit Lange this morning was a spontaneous one, so my follower must have been with me since I left Tante Lisl's before breakfast, and that meant he'd probably been outside the hotel all night. All night on Christmas Eve; where do you find such dedication these days? From Tante Lisl's he must have used a car, otherwise I would have spotted him earlier. He'd have found it easy enough to anticipate the speed and direction of a solitary walker in the almost empty streets. I should have noticed the car right from the start. I was becoming too old and too careless. He stopped again; he must have guessed he'd been spotted, but he was still sticking to the book, ducking out of sight and keeping his distance. He was inexpert but diligent. It was easy to guess that he'd hoped to do the whole job from inside a car, hence the brightly coloured car coat, but now that I'd come poking about in the Tiergarten, he'd had to get out of the car and earn his money. Now he was conspicuous, especially with that big parcel under his arm.

I looked back. I couldn't see his car but he hadn't had many alternatives about where to leave it. I walked west, uncertainly changing direction but heading southward enough to keep him hoping that I would return to where he'd left the car. Was he alone? I wondered. Surely no professional would try to tail a suspect without any assistance whatsoever. But it was Christmas and perhaps all he had to do was to report my movements. He wasn't a private eye; whatever their shortcomings, they can all follow an errant husband and stay out of sight. And if he wasn't a KGB man and he wasn't a private eye, what was left? One of our own people from the Berlin Field Unit? Even my advanced paranoia couldn't believe that one of those lazy bastards could be persuaded into action on Christmas Day. Now I strolled back towards the park. I stopped to examine the trunk of a tree where someone had carved a hammer and sickle that was bent to become a swastika. I used the chance to watch him out of the corner of my eye. The parcel slipped from his grasp and he took his time about picking it up. He was right-handed; well, that was a useful thing to bear in mind.

I paused again at the little river in the park. But today the famous *Berliner Luft* was too cold for water to survive in. There were two people skating on the ice. A man and a woman, elderly judging by their stately posture and the way they skated side by side, long overcoats, flowing scarfs, and heads held high, like an illustration from some nineteenth-century magazine.

I hurried along the path as if suddenly remembering an appointment. Then I stooped down to hide. It wouldn't have worked with anyone more experienced, so it was really a test of his expertise. I still had no measure of him and couldn't guess what his motives might be. As it was, he walked right into it. That is to say, he walked right into me. It was the hurrying that did it; it often stampedes the pursuer into incautious and impulsive actions. That was how Hannibal won the Battle of Lake Trasimene after crossing the Apennines. All it needed was that sudden dash towards Rome to make Flaminius chase after him and blunder right into his ambush. Hannibal would probably have had the makings of a good field agent.

'Don't move,' I said. I had him from behind, my arm round his throat and the other twisting hell out of his right arm while he was still looking for me far down the path. He grunted. I was holding his neck too tight. 'I'm going to release you,' I said, 'but if you move carelessly after that, I'll have to really hurt you. You understand, don't you?'

He still didn't answer properly so I relaxed my hold on his throat a bit more to let him breathe. When I let him go he bent double and I thought he was going to collapse on me. I looked at him with surprise. The arm seam of his coat was torn and his hat was knocked off. He was making terrible noises. I suppose I'd grabbed him too tightly; I was out of practice. But he shouldn't have been gasping; a young man like him, well under thirty, should have been in better physical shape. Still bent over he clutched his middle, taking very deep breaths.

'Who the hell are you?' I said.

'We'll ask the questions, Mr Samson!' There was another of them, a slim bespectacled man in a flashy brown-suede overcoat with fur collar. He was holding a gun and not bothering too much about who saw it. 'Hands behind your back, Samson. You know how these things are done.' I cursed my stupid overconfidence. I should have guessed that such clumsiness as the bearded man displayed was all part of the trick. They'd now made me play Flaminius to their Hannibal.

The bearded one – still gasping for breath – rubbed me down quickly and thoroughly and said, 'He has nothing.'

'No gun, Samson? This is not the expert we've heard so much about. You're getting old and careless.'

I didn't answer. He was right. I'd chosen not to go to Lange with a gun under my arm because it would have made it harder to deny my connection with London Central.

'Here he comes,' said the man. 'It took him long enough, didn't it.' He was watching a dented panel truck trundling over the brown grass. The skaters were nowhere to be seen now: they were all part of the same team sent to get me.

The rear doors of the van opened to reveal a gleaming wheel chair.

They pushed me up onto the chair and strapped my ankles and neck to the steel framework. Then they blindfolded me as the van drove away. It was all over in five minutes.

The roads were empty. The journey took no more than twenty minutes. The blindfold was good enough to prevent me seeing where I was, but I was bumped up steps and the gates of an elevator were carelessly slammed against my arm.

They unstrapped me and locked me in a room. I was left to remove my own blindfold, not so easy when one's arms are cuffed behind one's back. It was impossible not to admire their efficiency and to deplore my own unpreparedness. There was no doubt where they'd brought me: I was in East Berlin, just a few minutes' walk from Checkpoint Charlie. But from this side of the Wall, it's a long walk back.

There were two windows. It was an anteroom – really a place where people waited. But the people who waited here had to have bars on the windows and heavy locks on the doors, and the window glass was frosted to make it difficult to see out. At the top of each window there was a small ventilation panel. I could reach that far only by putting a stool on the tabletop. With hands cuffed behind me I almost toppled as I scrambled up. Now through the narrow gap – the panel opened only as far as the bars permitted – I could see across the city. There was no movement: no cars, no trucks, no people. I recognized the massive USSR Embassy in the Linden from the shape of the roof. Nearby there was the last remaining section of the Adlon Hotel; a few cramped rooms in the rear that in the thirties were used only for the personal servants of the hotel's clients. And there were the parking lot and the hillock that marked the site of the *Führerbunker* where Hitler had fought his last battles against marriage and the Red Army and, defeated by both Venus and Mars, blew out his troubled brains. Now I knew where I was: this was Hermann Göring's old Air Ministry, one of the few examples of Nazi architecture to escape both Anglo-American bombers and Soviet planners.

I went back to the hard wooden chair and sat down. It was Christmas Day – not a festival that any sincere Communist cares to celebrate, but there were enough insincere ones to empty the building. It was silent except for the occasional, distant sounds of a slammed door or the hum of the lift. I looked round the room: no books or papers, the only printed item a brightly coloured poster that was a part of the Kremlin's contribution to the anti-nuke debate. But the missile to be banned was labelled 'NATO'. There was no mention of Russian missiles – just a handsome young Communist and a snarling GI. There was a second door in the room. It had a glass panel over which had been stuck patterned translucent paper. Such paper was commonly used in the East Bloc where frosted glass was sometimes in short supply. Standing with my back to the door I was able to peel a little of it back from the corner. A sticky compound remained on the glass, but I scratched it away with my fingernail.

By resting my face close against the glass it was possible to see into the next room. There were two people there, a man and a woman. Both wore white linen: a doctor and nurse. The woman was about forty; over her greying hair she wore a small starched cap. The man was younger, twenty-five or so. His white jacket was unbuttoned and there was a stain on the lapel that might have been blood. A stethoscope hung from his neck. He stood by the door writing in a small notebook. He consulted his wristwatch and then wrote more. The nurse was leaning against a two-tier bunk bed looking at something bundled there on the lower bed. She looked back to catch the doctor's eye. He looked up from his writing and she shook her head. The movement was almost imperceptible, as if she'd been shaking her head all morning. She was Russian, I had no doubt of that. She had the flat features, narrowed eyes, and pale colouring that are typical of people from Russia's eastern Arctic. She turned back to the bundle of clothes and touched it tenderly. It was too small to be a person – except a very small person. She leaned closer, fussing in the way that mothers do when babies sleep face down. But this was too big for a baby. She moved a trifle. It was a child – a red woolly striped hat had slipped from its head. Swaddled in thick blankets an elbow protruded from between. A yellow sleeve – an anorak. And shiny boots. Jesus Christ, they had Billy! Little Billy. Here in Berlin.

The scene wobbled, my pulse raced, and my throat was suddenly dry. Only by steadying myself against the wall was I able to prevent myself fainting. Billy! Billy! Billy! I leaned close to the peephole again. The nurse moved away to get a small enamel tray from the table. She carried it carefully to the sink and took from it a hypodermic syringe. She put the needle into a glass of pink-coloured liquid. I felt ill. No matter how much my brain told me to remain calm, my emotions took over. Now I knew why men with wives and families were so seldom used as field agents.

They are watching, they are watching you, now, at this moment, I told myself for the hundredth time. This is all a well-prepared act to disorient you and soften you up for what comes next. But it didn't help much. I could think of nothing except my son and what these bastards might do to him. Surely to God, Fiona knows about this. Surely she would stop them hurting her own son. But suppose Fiona doesn't know?

There was the sudden noise of a key being inserted into the lock. Someone was entering from the corridor. There was enough time for me to get back to the bench and sit down. There was enough time for me to look relaxed and unconcerned, but I'm not sure I managed that.

'Herr Samson!' We knew each other. He was a great bull of a man, about fifty years old, with a big peasant frame upon which years of manual labour had layered hard muscle. His skull shone through close-cropped hair. His large nose was surmounted by a big broad forehead. Pavel Moskvin. The London Central computer described him as a KGB 'political adviser'. That could mean anything. Political advisers were sometimes the brightest of bright graduates, multilingual polymaths who could quote Groucho as readily as Karl Marx. Such men used a stretch with the KGB as a finishing school. But Moskvin was long past all that. I had him marked down as the sort of untalented plodder who'd graduated from the factory floor having discovered that the Party always looks after its own. The USSR was filled with men like him; their unthinking loyalty was what held the whole creaky system together.

'Where is my wife?' I asked him. It wasn't a textbook opening or anything that London Central would have approved, but I knew they'd have me on a tape and there seemed a good chance that Fiona would be monitoring the dialogue.

'Your wife? Why would you want to know that, Herr Samson,' said Moskvin mockingly. His German was awkward and ungrammatical but his manner said everything.

'My people know I'm here, Moskvin,' I said. 'They'll be putting out a red alert any time now.'

'Are you trying to frighten me?' he said. 'Your people know nothing, and they don't care. It is Christmas. You are all alone, Herr Samson, all alone. Your people in London will be eating pudding, watching your Queen speaking on television and getting drunk!'

'We'll see,' I muttered ominously, but his version of what London Central might be doing sounded only too likely.

'Why don't you behave sensibly, Samson?'

'For instance?'

There were footsteps in the corridor. He half turned towards the door, his head cocked to listen. The break in his attention gave me the chance I'd been praying for. With both hands cuffed behind me, I grasped the backrest of the chair. Then, with head bowed low to counter the weight, I twisted my body and with all my force heaved the chair in his direction.

It was too heavy for me. It hit him in the legs instead of on the side of the head, but the violence of it caught him unprepared so that he staggered back cursing and spluttering with rage.

He kicked the chair aside. 'I'll teach you . . .' he said and stepped forward to punch me. He didn't aim anywhere; he hit me as an angry drunk might pound a wall. But Moskvin was a heavyweight. His blows didn't have to be aimed; they hit like sledgehammers and I was slammed against the wall so hard that I lost my balance and slid to the floor. 'You crazy fool!' he growled and wiped his mouth with the reddened knuckles of his fist. 'If you want a fight I'll take you downstairs and kill you with my bare hands.'

Slowly I scrambled to my feet and he kicked the chair over to me again with the side of his boot. I sat down on it and closed my eyes. I had a terrible pain inside me, as though molten lead was pouring through my lungs.

When Moskvin spoke again, he'd recovered some of his former composure. 'Be sensible. Face the truth. Your wife has chosen to work with us of her own free will. Do you really believe that we are holding her captive? Is that what your bosses in London have told you? Forget it. She is one of us, Samson. She does not wish to return to the West; she will never go back there. Never.' He watched me carefully and I stared back at him. 'Do you want a cigarette?' he asked finally.

'No,' I said, although I needed one desperately. We both knew the way it went; you accept a cigarette, you say thank you, and the next thing you're chatting away and reaching for the writing paper. 'I don't smoke.'

He smiled. He knew all about me. With Fiona working for the KGB, there was little about me that they couldn't find out. The pain lessened a little as I shifted my position and controlled my breathing, but one of his punches seemed to have torn a ligament and the big trapezius muscle of my back sent sharp pains right up to my neck.

'Why make life miserable for both of you?' said Moskvin in what he obviously thought a friendly manner. His German was better now; perhaps this was a text he'd prepared and practised. 'While you are working for the German Stations Controller in London and your wife is here in Berlin, the two of you must be permanently unhappy.'

'What are you proposing?' I said. I tried not to look at the glass-panelled door but it was difficult. Moskvin watched me carefully. He knew I'd seen into the next room. His arrival was too prompt to be anything but a reaction from a man watching what I did. Yes, I could see it now; the camera was behind that damned anti-nuke poster. A circular patch of the lettering was dull – open-weave cloth through which a focused camera could see clearly.

'There would be nothing for you here, Samson. We know everything you could tell us.'

I nodded. Had they really given up hope of enrolling me, or was this some subtle way of trying to get me to prove I knew more than they thought. 'You're right,' I said.

'So why not an overseas posting?' said Moskvin. He had both hands in the pockets of his greatcoat, fidgeting with something metallic that clanked. When he brought his hands into view there were three clips of pistol ammunition in his fingers. He fiddled with them. When he saw me looking at him he said, 'Don't have any more of those stupid ideas, Samson. The gun is downstairs in my safe.' Lots of bullets; it was characteristic of this violent primitive.

'Overseas?'

'You know Washington; you like Americans.'

'Lots of people want to go to Washington,' I said to gain time. 'Who knows when a vacancy will come.'

Moskvin continued to play with the clips. 'Washington gossip says London Central will fill two vacancies in the next month or two. Two senior jobs – that's what our Washington office tells us.'

Through the blur of pain my memory said he was right: sickness and a promotion had created two unexpected vacancies in the Washington Embassy. I'd seen the signal on Bret's desk. I was senior enough to apply for either. 'No,' I said.

'Think about it,' said Moskvin. Under his silky voice I could hear the hatred and contempt that he was trying to hide.

'Or what?'

'No threats,' said Moskvin. 'But surely it would be more civilized?'

'More civilized than staying in London to undo some of the harm of my wife's treachery?'

'Be more sophisticated and less arrogant, Herr Samson. Can you really believe that your contribution to the work at London Central will make any difference?'

I shrugged – but it hurt.

'What are you trying to prove, Samson? We've got an operations file on you that's that thick.' He indicated with finger and thumb. 'And that's without all the dangerous tricks you've done undetected. How long can you go on trying to prove you're a field agent? Until you get yourself killed, is that it?'

'You wouldn't understand,' I said.

'Because I'm a desk man?' He almost lost control over his rage. 'Vanity, is that it? Prove yourself over and over again so you can be sure you're not a coward? Just as the repressed homosexual becomes a womanizer to prove he's really a man?' Was that some reference to his ex-colleague Stinnes? If it was, he gave no further evidence of it. He put away his playthings and stood, hands on hips, his long black greatcoat open to reveal an ill-fitting grey suit and dark roll-neck sweater. He looked like someone who'd dressed in response to a fire alarm.

'Start life again, Herr Samson. Forget the pain of the past.' He saw me glance towards the door. 'What do I have to do to persuade you?' He smiled and I could see the sadistic glee in his face. He knew I'd seen into the next room.

'I'll think about it,' I told him. Was Billy still there, I wondered? It was torture carrying on this conversation.

'Don't think about it,' said Moskvin softly. His voice rose to a shout as he added, 'Do it!'

'I said I'd think about it.'

'Then think about this too,' he yelled. He snatched the door open and stood in the doorway. With hands cuffed, I'd stand no chance against him – he'd already proved that. But I pushed close to see over his shoulder.

'Billy!' I called but the bundled figure made no response. 'Why drug the child?' I said. I couldn't keep the weariness and defeat from my voice. The doctor and nurse had gone. Even the disinfectant, the hypodermic and the enamel tray had gone. 'Where's the doctor?' I asked.

'Doctor?' said Moskvin. 'What doctor? Are you mad?' He went striding across the room to the bunk bed. 'Think about this, Samson,' he yelled over his shoulder. He raised his arm, his massive fist clenched over the bed.

'No, don't!' It was a plea now, the fight had gone out of me. But he paid no heed to my call. His punch almost broke the wooden frame of the bed, with such force did it descend. The terrible blow swept everything across the room: blankets, the pathetic wollen hat, the boots and anorak. It all clattered to the floor in a heap.

Moskvin laughed. 'What did you think, Samson? Did you think we had your son in here?' Now I could see that these were not Billy's clothes: just clothes like them.

I leaned against the wall. I felt the bile rising in my throat. I closed my lips tight, determined not to give him the satisfaction of seeing me throw up. But it was not possible. I leaned forward and vomited my breakfast across the floor along with a generous measure of Mrs Koby's homemade wine.

Moskvin really laughed then. It was the first spontaneous human reaction I'd ever seen from him. He unlocked my handcuffs. 'We'll get a car and take you back to the West, Samson. Where would you like to go, Frau Hennig's hotel?'

I nodded and used a handkerchief to wipe my face and my clothes. The sweet-sour smell of the vomit was in my nostrils.

'You'll need to wash and change,' said Moskvin. 'But you just remember this, clever Mr Field Agent: any time we want you, we'll pick you up as easily as we did today. And not just you, Samson; your children, your mother, your friend Volkmann . . . any time we want you. You remember that, my friend.' He laughed again. I could hear him laughing as he marched off down the corridor and shouted for the driver. I looked back at the TV monitor. Was Fiona watching? And did she feel proud of herself?

★

When I got back to Tante Lisl's I took a long hot bath and examined my cuts and bruises. Then I changed my clothes to take Lisl to the Volkmanns' for what we both thought was to be a quiet sit-down meal. We were wrong.

It was a ferocious event; the sort of frantic party you find only in Berlin and New York. The hi-fi was playing 'Hello, Dolly!' as I went in, and the guests were in that restrained sort of fancy dress that provides a chance to wear jewellery and expensive hair-dos. It was noisy and crowded and the air was blue with tobacco smoke and there was the fragrance of French perfumes and Havana cigars.

Tante Lisl showed little surprise at the mad scene to which I'd brought her. She'd brought up little Werner after his parents died, and she felt for him that compassionate condescension that motherhood brings. She sat in the corner on the thronelike chair that Werner had thoughtfully placed there for her. She sipped her champagne and surveyed the antics of the guests with a wry superiority, like a tribal chief watching the sort of ceremonial dances that end in human sacrifice. She'd prepared carefully for the party: false eyelashes and real pearls; Tante Lisl's ultimate accolade.

I went to the buffet table in the dining room to assemble a plate of food for her. The room, like every other room in the apartment, was crowded. In front of me there was a tall thin Mephistopheles. He was engaged in earnest conversation with a man in a white-silk roll-neck sweater. He said in uncertain English, 'We Germans are so very like you Americans! That's why there is this constant friction. Both our countrymen respond to ideology, both seek always to improve the world, and both often want to improve it by means of military crusades.'

'And both like clean toilets,' said the American in the roll-neck sweater. 'Germany is the only god lamned country in Europe that doesn't have filthy bathrooms.'

'Anal oriented, we psychiatrists say,' Mephistopheles told him. 'In other countries people just want to get in there, do what has to be done, and get out again as soon as possible. But you Americans and we Germans like to have toilets we can spend time in. One glance in any of these home-improvement magazines will confirm that.'

A movement of the crowd around the buffet allowed me to push forward to the table near the window and reach the stack of empty plates and silverware. I looked round me. Only in Berlin would they have a party like this in daylight. Outside it was gloomy, but to the west there was even a little sunlight breaking through the clouds. The food was disorienting too. It was not exactly what I'd think of as Christmas Day lunch, but it was a magnificent display of luxuries. Although a great deal had already been eaten, new plates of food kept appearing, brought by waitresses in neat black dresses and fancy lace aprons. This was a *Fresserei*, a feast where people gobble like animals. There were lobster tails in mayonnaise and crab claws in wine sauce. There was caviar and cold salmon, foie gras with truffles, and a dozen types of sliced sausage.

'There's blood on your face,' said a woman with diamond-studded spectacles, reaching past me to get more *Leberwurst* and potato salad. 'Naughty boy. You look as if you'd been fighting.'

'I have,' I said. 'I found Santa Claus in my sitting room helping himself to my whisky.' In the Tiergarten the bearded man's sleeve buttons had cut my cheek, and when I dabbed the place, I found it had been bleeding again.

The diamond spectacles discovered a dish of smoked eel garnished with jelly. Uttering a whoop of joy she heaped her plate with eel and black bread and moved away.

I put a selection of food onto two plates and, balancing them carefully, moved off through the crowd. Enough space had been cleared in the centre of the floor for a dozen or more people to dance, but they had to hug really close. Berliners give themselves wholeheartedly to everything they do: Berlin opera and concert audiences cheer, boo, jeer or applaud with a mad tenacity unknown elsewhere. And so it was with parties; they sang, they danced, they gobbled and guzzled, hugging, arguing and laughing as if this party were the final expression of everything they'd ever lived for.

A very handsome young black man, dressed in the shiny silk shorts and brightly coloured singlet of a boxer – and with gloves suspended from his neck in case anyone missed the point – was talking to Zena Volkmann, his hostess, while both were picking at one plate of food.

Zena Volkmann was wearing glittering gold pants and a close-fitting black shirt upon which a heavy gold necklace and a gold flower brooch showed to good effect, as did her figure. Her face was still tanned dark from her recent trip to Mexico and her jet-black hair was loose and long enough to fall over her shoulders. She saw me and waved a fork.

'Hello, Zena,' I said. 'Where's Werner?'

'I sent him to borrow ice from the people downstairs,' she answered. And immediately turned back to her companion, saying, 'Go on with what you were saying.'

I saw other people I knew. In the corner there was Axel Mauser who'd been at school with me and Werner. He was wearing a beautifully tailored white-silk jacket with black pants, bow tie and frilly shirt. He was talking to a woman in a silver sheath dress and waving his hands as he always did when telling a story. 'Tante Lisl's here,' I told him as I went past. 'She'd love you to say hello, Axel.'

'Hello, you old bastard,' said Axel, getting me into focus. 'You look terrible. Still up to your tricks?'

'Just say hello,' I said. 'She'll be hurt if you forget her.'

'Okay, Bernd, I won't forget. You know my wife, don't you?'

I said hello. I hadn't recognized the woman in the silver dress as Axel's wife. Every other time I'd seen her she'd been in a grimy apron with her hands in the sink.

By the time I took the plates of food, cutlery, and black bread to Lisl, I was too late. Old Lothar Koch had already brought a plate for her. He was sitting beside her, embarrassed perhaps to see her here and explaining his sudden recovery from the influenza that had prevented him dining with her the previous evening. Koch was a shrunken little man in his middle eighties. His ancient evening suit was far too big for him, but he'd long ago declared that his life expectancy precluded him wasting money on new clothes. I said hello to him. 'Miracle drugs,' said Lothar Koch to me and to Lisl and to the world at large. 'I was at death's door last night, Bernd. I was just telling Frau Hennig the same thing.' I called her 'Lisl' and he called her 'Lisl', but when he talked to me about her she had to be 'Frau Hennig', even when she was sitting there with us. He was like that. He wiped his large nose on a crisp linen handkerchief.

I decided to abandon both plates of food. What I really needed was a drink. I joined a big crowd at the table where an overworked waitress was dispensing champagne.

'That's a bloody good costume,' remarked a very young sheriff doffing his ten-gallon hat to a man dressed as a Berlin cop. But the man dressed as the cop was not amused. He *was* a Berlin cop, desperately trying to find someone who'd left a light-blue Audi blocking the entrance to the underground garage.

'Cocktails to the right, champagne to the left,' said a waitress trying to disperse the crowd.

I moved forward and got a bit nearer to the drinks. In front of me there was an elderly architecture lecturer talking with a delicate-looking female student. I knew them both as people I'd met with the Volkmanns. The lecturer was saying '. . . leaving politics to one side, Hitler's plans for a new Berlin were superb.'

'Really,' said the pale girl; she was a history student. 'I think the plans were grotesque.'

'The Anhalter and Potsdam railway stations were to be rebuilt to the south of Tempelhof so that the centre of the city could have an avenue three miles long. Palaces, magnificent office buildings, and a huge triumphal arch. On the northern side there was to be a meeting hall with a dome eight hundred and twenty-five feet across with space inside for one hundred and fifty thousand people.'

'I know. I went to your lectures about it,' said the girl in a bored voice. 'Afterwards I went to the library. Did you know that the only part of Hitler's plan ever put into effect was the planting of deciduous trees in the Tiergarten? And that only restored the old mixed forest that Frederick the Great had felled to help pay for the Silesian Wars.'

The lecturer seemed not to have heard. He said, 'City planning needs firm central government. The way things are going, we'll never see a properly planned town anywhere.'

'Thank God for that,' said the bored girl. She picked up two glasses of champagne and moved away. He recognized me and smiled.

As soon as I'd got my champagne I began looking for somewhere to sit. Then I saw Werner. He was standing in the doorway that led to his bedroom. He was looking harassed. I went across. 'Quite a party, Werner,' I said in admiration. 'I was expecting a small sit-down for eight or ten.'

He ushered me into the bedroom. Now I saw how enough space had been cleared for the dancing. Furniture was packed into the bedroom so that it was piled almost to the ceiling. There was only just space enough for Werner and me to stand. He closed the bedroom door.

'I just have to have a few minutes to myself,' he explained. 'Zena says we need more ice, but we've got tons of ice!'

'Well, it's a hell of a spread, Werner. I saw Axel . . . Axel Mauser dressed up like I'd never believe. Is he still working for the police?'

'Axel's wife got a big promotion in AEG. She's some kind of executive now and they're moving out of that lousy apartment in Märkisches Viertel to a place near the forest in Hermsdorf.'

'You'd better give Tante Lisl a kiss and a formal greeting,' I said. 'She keeps asking where you are. In her day, the host and hostess stood at the door and shook hands with everyone as they were announced.'

'Zena loves this sort of party,' said Werner, 'but it's too noisy for me. I come and hide. I don't know half those people out there. Would you believe that?' He wrung his hands and said, 'Did you go and see Lange?' He straightened some of the dining-room chairs that were stacked one upon the other. Then he looked at me, 'Are you all right?'

'I phoned him and went across there this morning.'

Werner nodded mournfully. 'He's still the same, isn't he? Still bad-tempered. Remember how he used to shout at us when we were kids?' Werner wasn't looking at me. Stuck under the seats of the dining chairs there were manufacturers' labels. Werner suddenly began reading one as if deeply interested in the dates and codes.

'I didn't realize how much he hates Bret Rensselaer,' I said. 'Lange still blames Bret for his having to leave the Department.'

Werner abandoned his study of the label and gave me a little smile that showed no sympathy for Lange. 'He only says that because he's been on the shelf ever since. When Lange resigned from the

Department he thought he was going to get a wonderful job some-where else and go back and show your dad and all the rest of them what a big success he was.'

'I don't know what he lives on,' I said.

'His wife inherited her parents' apartment in Munich. They lease it out and live on the income from it.'

'I was followed this morning, Werner,' I said. I drank the rest of my champagne. What I needed was something stronger.

He looked up sharply and raised his eyebrows. I told him about the bearded man and the way I'd been kidnapped and held in East Berlin.

'My God!' said Werner. He went white. 'And then they released you?'

'I wasn't really worried,' I told him untruthfully. 'It was obviously just to throw a scare into me.'

'Perhaps taking a job in Washington would be the best course.'

'You've never worked in an embassy,' I reminded him. 'Those people live in a fantasy world . . . Ritz crackers, white wine and randy wives. I had six months of that; never again.'

'Do you think it was Fiona's idea? What was behind it?'

'I just can't decide,' I said.

'A doctor and a nurse . . . pretending they had your son . . . too bizarre for Fiona. It smells like Moscow.'

'I'd prefer to think that.'

'You'll report it, of course,' said Werner.

'I don't come out of it too well, do I?'

'You must report it, Bernie.'

'How did they get to hear about the vacancies coming up in Wash-ington?' I said.

'The word gets round quickly,' said Werner cautiously. He guessed what I was going to say.

'You know who automatically gets first notice of any changes in Washington, don't you?' I said.

Werner came closer to where I was standing and lowered his voice. 'You're not getting some sort of obsession about Bret Rensselaer are you?' he asked.

'Obsession?'

'You keep on about him. First it was those code names . . . about how no agent ever had two names. And you try to persuade me that there is still a KGB man in London Central.'

'I've told you no more than facts,' I said.

'No one can argue with facts, Bernie. But the Bret Rensselaer role you're trying to write into this script of yours is not something that has emerged from calm and rational reasoning; it's personal.'

'I don't give a damn about Bret,' I said.

'You know that's not true, Bernie,' said Werner in a sweet and reasonable voice. 'You went round to Lange knowing that he hates Bret. You wanted to hear someone say that Bret was some kind of monster who deliberately wrecked the early networks. You knew what Lange was going to say before you went; we've both heard all that rigmarole from him a hundred times. If you're trying to put a noose round Bret's neck, you'll need something a damn sight more reliable than Lange's gossip or news about vacancies in Washington. You try and prove Bret a bad security risk and you're going to make a fool of yourself.'

'Why would I want to do that?' I protested.

'There was a time when you suspected he was having an affair with Fiona. . . .'

'I was wrong,' I said quickly. Werner looked up; I'd said it too damned quickly. 'There was no substance in that,' I added, more calmly this time.

'You resent Bret. No matter how irrational that might be, you resent him.'

'Why should I?'

'I don't know. He's rich and charming and something of a ladies' man. I resent him too; he's too damned smooth, and he has a cruel streak in him. But keep your head, Bernie.'

'I'll keep my head.'

Werner was not convinced. 'Bret has everything going for him. Bret is an Anglophile: everything British is wonderful. The British like hearing that kind of praise – it's exactly what they believe – and so Bret is very popular. You won't find it easy to move against him.'

'I've already discovered that,' I said. 'For all Silas Gaunt's caustic remarks and Dicky Cruyer's bitter envy of him, neither of them would be happy to see Bret facing a board of enquiry.'

'Bret's an old-fashioned US gentleman – honest and brave.'

'Is that the way you see him?'

'It's the way he is, Bernie. He's not KGB material. Promise me you'll think about what I'm telling you, Bernie. I don't give a damn about Bret. It's you I'm thinking of. You know that, don't you?'

'Sure I do, Werner. Thanks. But I'm not gunning for Bret. I just want to talk with Stinnes and get a few ends tidied away.'

'Did you wonder if the Stinnes defection might be a KGB stunt?'

'Yes, lots of times, but he's given us some good ones; not wonderful, but good,' I said. 'And now it looks like the Miller woman was murdered. She was a long-term agent, Werner. Would they really kill one of their own just to make Stinnes look kosher?'

'We haven't found her body yet,' said Werner.

'Leaving it inside the ambulance would make it too easy for us,' I said. But Werner was right: until we had an identified corpse, there was always the chance that she was alive.

'Then what about the chances of Brahms Four being a KGB plant?'

I thought about it before answering. 'I don't think so.'

But Werner noticed my hesitation and followed it up. 'Did von Munte really need to be brought out of the East? He was an old man and so was his wife. How long before he'd be old enough to make one of those permitted visits to the West?'

'Don't be stupid, Werner. Officials with his sort of confidential information are not permitted to come West on visits, even if they live to be a hundred years old.'

'But suppose von Munte *was* a plant? Sent to give us dud information. You said Silas Gaunt was difficult and protective when you tried to question him. Suppose London Debriefing Centre have already detected that he's a KGB plant. Suppose they've lodged him with Silas Gaunt to keep him on ice and make sure he doesn't do any damage.'

'That would require a faith in the brilliance of the London Debriefing Centre staff that I just can't muster,' I said.

'That's what I mean, Bernie. You're determined to see it the way you want it.'

8

Christmas was gone but, having been on duty, I had my Christmas leave to come. I took the children to the circus and to the theatre. We did the things they wanted to do. We inspected the model ships and real planes on the top floors of the Science Museum, the live reptiles in the Regent's Park zoo and the plaster dinosaur skeleton in the hall of the Natural History Museum. The children had seen it all before, over and over again, but they were creatures of habit and they chose the things they knew so well so that they could tell me about them, instead of me telling them. I understood this pleasure and shared it. The only thing that marred these delightful events was that Gloria had no leave days to enjoy and I missed her.

I took the children to see George Kosinski, their uncle and my brother-in-law. The place we visited was not one of his swanky motor-car showrooms but a dirty cobbled yard in Southwark. One-time marshland, the district was now a grimy collection of slums and sooty factories interspersed with ugly new office blocks as rent increases drive more and more companies south of the River Thames.

George Kosinski's repair yard was a derelict site; a place that had been hit by a German bomb in 1941 and never subsequently built upon. Next to the yard was a heavy and ornate block of Victorian flats that had become slums. Across the road, more recent municipal housing was even worse.

George's yard was protected by a high wall into which broken glass had been cemented to discourage uninvited callers. For those more difficult to discourage there were two guard dogs. Along the other side of the yard there was a railway viaduct. Two arches of the viaduct had been bricked up and converted to repair shops, but one section of the arched accommodation had been made into an office.

George was sitting behind a table. He was wearing his hat and overcoat, for the small electric fan-heater did little to warm the cold damp air. The ceiling curved over his head and nothing had been done to disguise or insulate the ancient brickwork of the arch. In a cardboard box in the corner there were empty beer and wine bottles, cigarette butts, broken glass and discarded Christmas decorations.

Through the thin partition that separated this makeshift office from the workshop there came the sound of rock music from a transistor radio.

George Kosinski was thirty-six years old, although most people would have thought him five or even ten years older than that. He was a small man with a large nose and a large moustache, both of which looked inappropriate, if not false. The same could be said of his strong cockney accent to which I had to get freshly attuned each time I saw him. His suit was expensive: Savile Row, with the lapels stitched a little too tight so as to make the handwork evident. His shirt, his shoes, which were resting on the table amid the paperwork, and his tie were all as expensive as can be. His hair was curly, and greying at the temples to give him the distinguished appearance that is the result of regular visits to the hairdresser. Whatever he economized on, it was not his clothes or his transport, for outside there stood his gleaming new Rolls.

'Well, here we are. You've come to beard your Uncle George in his den, have you?' He took his feet off the table with a sigh. I had the feeling that he'd contrived that posture for our entrance. He liked to think of himself as unconventional.

The children were too awed to reply. Leaning back in his chair George banged on the wall with the side of his fist. Someone next door responded to this command, for the radio was immediately turned down.

'Your father's come to buy a beautiful car from me – did he tell you that?' He looked up at me and added, 'It's not arrived yet.' A glance at his watch. 'Any minute now.'

'We're a bit early, George,' I said.

'Can't give you a drink or anything. I don't keep anything of any value here. You can see what it's like.'

I could see. The cracked lino on the floor and the bare walls said it all. As well as that, there was a notice that said WE DON'T BUY CAR RADIOS. He saw me looking at it and said, 'All day long there are people in and out of here trying to sell me radios and tape recorders.'

'Stolen?'

'Of course. What would these tearaways be doing with an expensive car stereo except that they've ripped it out of some parked car? I never touch anything suspect.'

'Do you spend much time here?' I asked.

He shrugged. 'I call in from time to time. You run a business, any sort of business, you have to see what's happening. Right, Bernard?'

'I suppose so.' George Kosinski was a rich man, and I wondered how he endured such squalor. He wasn't mean – his generosity was well known and admitted even by those with whom he struck the tough bargains for which he was equally well known.

'Rover 3500; you'll not be sorry you bought it, Bernard. And if I'm wrong, bring it back to me and I'll give you your money back. Okay?'

'Okay,' I said. He was saying it to the children as much as to me. He liked children. Perhaps his marriage would have been happier if he'd had children of his own.

'I saw it yesterday morning. Dark green, a beautiful respray, just like a factory finish, and the people doing the waxing job are the best in the country. You've got a vintage car there, Bernard. Better than that: a special. The V-8 engine has scarcely been used.'

'It's not another one of those cars that's been owned by that old lady who only used it to go shopping once a week and was too nervous to go more than twenty miles an hour?' I said.

'Naughty,' said George with a smile. 'Your dad is naughty,' he told the children. 'He doesn't believe what I'm telling him. And I've never told a fib in my life.' Suddenly there came a thunderous roar. Billy flinched and Sally put her hands on her head. 'It's the trains,' said George. 'They're only just above our heads.'

But George's boast had captured Billy's imagination and when the sound of the train diminished he said, 'Have you really never told a fib, Uncle George? Never ever?'

'Almost never,' said George. He turned to me. 'I have a friend of yours calling in this morning. I told him you'd be here.'

'Who?'

'It's not a secret or anything?' said George. 'I won't get into trouble for telling somebody where you are, will I?' It was a jest, but not entirely a jest. I'd heard the same sort of resentment in the voices of other people who had only a rough idea of what I did for a living.

He screwed his face up in an expression that was somewhat apologetic. 'There are people who know I know you . . . people who seem to know more about what you do for a living than I know.' Nervously George pushed his glasses up, using his forefinger. He was always doing that when he became agitated. The spectacle frames were too heavy, I suppose, or perhaps it was perspiration.

'People try to guess what I do,' I said. 'Better they're not encouraged, George. Who is it?'

'Posh Harry they call him. Do you know who I mean? He's something in the CIA, isn't he? He seems to know you well enough. I thought it would be all right to say I was seeing you.'

'It was a long time ago that he worked for the CIA,' I said. 'But Harry is all right. He's coming here, you say?'

'He wants to see you, Bernard. He reckons he's got something you'll like.'

'We'll see,' I said. 'But you know what he's like, George. I never meet him without wondering if he's going to wind up selling me a set of encyclopedias.'

Posh Harry arrived on time. He was a pristine American, whose face, like his suits and linen, seemed never to wrinkle. He was of Hawaiian extraction, and although in a crowd he would pass as European, he had the flat features, small nose, and high cheekbones of Oriental peoples. He spent half his life on planes and had no address except hotels, shared offices and box numbers. He was an amazing linguist and he always knew what was happening to whom, from Washington to Warsaw and back again. He was what the reporters call 'a source' and always had something to add about the latest spy scandal or trial or investigation whenever the media ran short of comment. His brother – much older than Harry – was a CIA man whose career went back to OSS days in World War II. He'd died in some lousy CIA foul-up in Vietnam. Sometimes it was suggested that Harry was a recognized conduit through whom the CIA leaked stories they wanted to make public, but it was difficult to reconcile that with Harry's family history. Harry was not an apologist for the CIA; he'd never completely forgiven them for his brother's death.

Harry was exactly the kind of man that Hollywood casts as a CIA agent. His voice was just right too. He had the sort of low, very soft American voice that is crisp, clear and attractive; the voice that sports commentators use for games that are very slow and boring.

Harry arrived wearing those English clothes you can only find in New York City. A dark-grey cotton poplin raincoat, calfskin oxford shoes, tweedy jacket, and a striped English old school tie that had been invented by an American designer. The hat was a giveaway though; a plaid sports cap that few Englishmen would wear, even on a golf course.

'Good to see you again, George,' he said as he took George's hand. Then he gave me the same sort of greeting, in that low gravelly voice, and shook my hand with a firm, sincere grip.

'I'll go and see if your motorcar has arrived,' said George. 'Come on, kids.'

'I spoke on the phone to Lange,' explained Harry. 'He really enjoyed meeting with you again.'

'What did Lange have to say?'

'Nothing I didn't already know. That you're still working hard, following up orders from London Central.'

'What else?'

'Something about Bret Rensselaer,' said Harry. 'I didn't pay too much attention.'

'That's the best way with Lange,' I agreed. 'He has a bee in his bonnet about Bret Rensselaer.'

'So it's not true that Bret's being specially vetted?'

'Not as far as I know,' I said.

'I'm no special buddy of Bret's, as you probably know. But Bret is one hundred per cent okay. There's no chance Bret would do anything disloyal.'

'Is that so?' I said, keeping it all very casual.

'For years your people kept Bret away from any US sensitive material in case it compromised his loyalty, but he was never any kind of undercover man for the Agency. Bret is your man, you can rest assured on that one.'

I nodded and wondered where Posh Harry had got the idea that Bret was suspected of leaking to the Americans. Was that Lange's misinterpretation or Harry's? Or was it simply that no one could start to envisage him doing anything as dishonourable as spying for the Russians? And if that was it, was I wrong? And, if he was guilty of such ungentlemanly activities, who was going to believe it?

'What have they got against Bret anyway?' asked Harry.

'Better you contact me through the office, Harry,' I said. 'I don't like getting my relatives involved.'

'Sure, I'm sorry,' said Harry, giving no sign of being sorry. 'But this is something better done away from the people across the river there.' He gave a nod in the vague direction of Westminster and Whitehall.

'What is it?'

'I'm going to give you something on a plate, Bernard. It will give you a lot of kudos with your people.'

'That's good,' I said without sounding very keen. I'd suffered some of Harry's favours in the past.

'And that's the truth,' said Harry. 'Take a look at that.' He passed me a photocopy of a typewritten document. There were eight pages of it.

'Do I have to read it? Or are you going to tell me what it's all about?'

'That's a memo that was discussed by the Cabinet about three or four months ago. It concerns the security of British installations in West Germany.'

'The British Cabinet? This is a British Cabinet memo?'

'Yessir.'

'Is there anything special about it?'

'The special thing about it was that one copy at least ended up in the KGB files in Moscow.'

'Is that where this photocopy came from?'

'KGB; Moscow. That is exactly right,' he smiled. It was the sales-man's smile, broad but bleak.

'What has this got to do with me, Harry?'

'This could be the break you need, Bernard.'

'Do I need a break?'

'Come on, Bernard. Come on! Do you think it's a secret that your people are nervous about employing you?'

'I don't know what you're talking about, Harry,' I said.

'Okay. When your wife defected it was swept under the carpet. But don't imagine there were no off-the-record chats to the boys in Washington and Brussels. So what do you think those people were likely to say? What about the husband, they asked. I'm not going to baby you along, Bernie. Quite a few people – people in the business, I mean – know what happened to your wife. And they know that you are under the microscope right now. Are you going to deny it?'

'What's your proposition, Harry?' I said.

'This memo is a hot potato, Bernie. What son of a bitch leaked that one? Leaked it so that it didn't stop moving until it got to Moscow?'

'An agent inside Ten Downing Street? Is that what you're selling me?'

'Number Ten is your neck of the woods, old buddy. I'm suggesting you take this photocopy and start asking questions. I'm saying that a big one like this could do you a power of good right now.'

'And what do you want out of it?'

'Now come on, Bernie. Is that what you think of me? It's a present. I owe you a couple of favours. We both know that.'

I folded the sheets as best I could and put it all into my pocket. 'I'll report it, of course.'

'You do whatever you choose. But if you report it, that paper will go into the box and you'll never hear another thing about it. The investigation will be directly handed over to the security service. You know that as well as I do.'

'I'll think about it, Harry. Thanks anyway.'

'A lot of folks are rooting for you, Bernard.'

'Where did you get it, Harry?'

Posh Harry had a foot on the chair and was gently scraping a mud spot from his shoe with his fingernail. 'Bernard!' he said reproach-fully. 'You know I can't tell you that.' He wet his fingertips with spittle and tried a second time.

'Well, let's eliminate a few nasties,' I said. 'This wasn't taken from any CIA office, was it?'

'Bernard, Bernard.' He was still looking at his shoe. 'What a mind you've got!'

'Because I don't want to carry a parcel that's ticking.'

He finished the work on his shoe and put his feet on the floor and looked at me. 'Of course not. It's raw, it's hot. It hasn't been on any desks.'

'Some kind of floater then?'

'What do you think I am, Bernard? A part-time pimp for the KGB? Do you think I've lasted this long without being able to smell a KGB float?'

'There's always a first time, Harry. And any one of us can make a mistake.'

'Well, okay, Bernard. I've got no real provenance on this one, I'll admit that. It's a German contact who's given me nothing but gold so far.'

'And who pays him?'

'He's not for sale, Bernard.'

'Then it's no one I know,' I said.

He gave a little mirthless chuckle as a man might acknowledge the feeble joke of a valuable client. 'You're getting old and embittered, Bernard. Do you know there was a time when you'd get angry at hearing a crack like that? You'd have given your lecture about idealism, and politics, and freedom, and people who have died for what they believe in. Now you say it's no one you know.' He shook his head. It was mockery, but we both knew he was right. We both knew plenty of people who had never been for sale, and some of them had died proving it.

'Is George selling you a car?' I said to change the subject.

'I lease from George. I've done that for years. He lets me change cars, see? You knew that, didn't you?' He meant that George let him have a succession of cars when he was keeping someone under observation and didn't want the car he used recognized.

'No,' I said. 'George observes the discretion of the confessional. I didn't even know he knew you.'

'And nice kids, Bernie.' He slapped me on the back. 'Don't look so worried, pal. You've got a lot of good friends. A lot of people owe you. They'll see you through.'

Posh Harry was in the middle of saying all this when the door of the office crashed open. In the doorway there was a woman, thirtyish and pretty in the way that women become pretty if they use enough expensive makeup. She wore a full-length fur coat and hugged a large handbag to herself as if it contained a lot of valuables.

'Hon-ee,' she called petulantly. 'How much longer do I have to sit around in this dump?'

'Coming, sweetheart,' said Posh Harry.

'Har-ree! We're going to be so late,' she said. Her voice was laden with magnolia blossoms, the sort of accent that happens to ladies who watch *Gone With the Wind* on TV while eating chocolates.

Harry looked at his watch. Then we went through the usual routine of exchanging phone numbers and promising to meet for lunch, but neither of us put much enthusiasm into it. After Harry had finally said goodbye, George Kosinski returned with the kids.

'Everything all right, Bernard?' he said. He looked at me expectantly. I suppose for George all meetings were deals or potential deals.

'Yes, it was all right,' I said.

'Your Rover is there. The kids like it.' He put his briefcase on the table and began to rummage through it to find the registration book, but he only found it after dumping the contents of his case on the table. There was a bundle of mail ready to be posted, a biography of Mozart, and an elaborately bound Bible. 'A present for my nephew,' he said, as if the presence of the Bible required some sort of explanation. He also found a copy of the *Daily Telegraph*, an assortment of car keys with large labels attached, an address book, some foreign coins, and a red silk scarf. He waved the Mozart book at me. 'I've become interested in music lately,' he said. 'I've been going to concerts with Tessa. Mozart had a terrible life, did you know that?'

'I'd heard rumours,' I said.

'If ever you wanted to prove that there is no relationship between effort and reward in this world, you've only got to read the life of Mozart.'

'You don't even have to do that,' I said. 'You can come and work in my office and find that out.'

'The piano concertos,' said George. He pushed his glasses up again. 'It's the piano concertos that I really like. I've gone right off pop music since discovering Mozart. This morning I've ordered the complete quintets from the record shop. Wonderful music, Bernard. Wonderful.'

'Is Tessa sharing this musical enthusiasm?' I asked.

'She goes along with it,' said George. 'She's an educated woman, of course. Not like me; left school at fourteen hardly able to write. Tessa knows about music and art and that sort of thing. She learned it at school.'

He saw me glancing out of the window at what was going on in the yard. 'The children are all right, Bernard. My foreman is letting them help him with a decoking job. All kids are keen on mechanical things; you probably know that already. You just can't keep boys away from motorcars. I was like that when I was young. I loved cars. Most of the cars pinched are taken by kids too young to get a driving licence.' He sighed. 'Yes, Tessa and me are getting along. We've got to, Bernard. She's getting too old for running after other men; she's realized that herself.'

'I'm glad,' I said. 'I've always liked Tessa.'

George stopped this rambling conversation. He looked at me and spent a moment thinking about what he was going to say. 'I owe you an apology, Bernard. I know that.'

He'd virtually accused me of having an affair with his wife Tessa at a time when he was suspecting every man who knew her of the same thing. Now he'd had a chance to see things in perspective.

'It's never been like that,' I said. 'In fact, I never really knew her until Fiona left me. Then Tessa did everything to help . . . with the children and getting the house sorted out and arguing with her father and so on. I appreciate it and I like her, George. I like her very much. I like her so much that I think she deserves a happy marriage.'

'We're trying,' said George. 'We're both trying. But that father of hers. He hates me, you know. He can't bear anyone he knows hearing that I'm his son-in-law. He's ashamed of me. He calls himself a socialist, but he's ashamed of me because I don't have the right accent, the right education, or the right family background. He really hates me.'

'He's not exactly crazy about me,' I said.

'But you don't have to meet him in your club or fall over him in restaurants when you've got a client in tow. I swear he's screwed up a couple of good deals for me by barging in when I'm in the middle of lunch and making broad hints about my marriage. Life's difficult enough, Bernie. I don't need that kind of treatment, especially when I'm with a client.'

'He may not have done it deliberately,' I said.

'Of course he does it deliberately. He's teaching me a lesson. I go round telling everyone that I'm his son-in-law, so he goes round telling everyone that I can't control my wife.'

'Does he say that?'

'If I caught him . . .' George scowled as he thought about it. 'He hints, Bernard. He hints. You know what that man can imply with a wink and a nod.'

'He's got some strange ideas,' I said.

'You mean he's dead stupid. Yes, well I know that, don't I. You should hear his ideas about how I should run my business.' George stopped putting his possessions back into the briefcase, placed his hands on his hips, and cocked his head to one side in the manner of my father-in-law. His voice was that of David Kimber-Hutchinson too: 'Go public, George. Look for export opportunities, George. Better still, create a chance to merge with one of the really big companies. Think big. You don't want to be a car salesman all your life, do you?' George smiled.

The egregious David Kimber-Hutchinson was inimitable, but it was a good impersonation. And yet there is no better opportunity of seeing deep into a person's soul than to watch him impersonate someone else. A deep hurt had produced in George a resentment that burned bright. If it came to a showdown, I wouldn't care to be in Kimber-Hutchinson's shoes. And because I was already ranged against my father-in-law, I noted this fact with interest.

'And yet he makes a lot of money,' I said.

'They look after each other, the Davids of this world.'

'He wanted the children. He thought he'd adopt them. . . .'

'And make them into little Kimber-Hutchinsons. I know. Tessa told me all about it. But you'll fight him, Bernard?'

'Every inch of the way.'

My enemy's enemy . . . there is no finer basis for friendship, according to the old proverb. 'Do you see him often?' I asked.

'Too damned often,' said George. 'But I'm determined to be nice to Tessa so I go down there with her and listen to the old man rabbiting on about what a big success he is.' George put his Mozart book into his case. 'He wants to buy a new Roller from me and he's determined to trade in the old one at a good price. He's taken me all round the paintwork and upholstery three times. Three times!'

'Wouldn't that be good business, George? A new Rolls-Royce must cost quite a packet.'

'And have him on my doorstep whenever it didn't start on the first turn of the key? Look, I'm not a Rolls dealer, but I buy and sell a few in the course of the year. They're good, the ones I sell, because I won't touch a dodgy one. It's a tricky market; a customer can't deduct much of the price from his tax allowances these days. But you know, and I know, that no matter what kind of brand new Rolls I get for that old bastard, it will start giving him trouble from the moment I deliver it. Right? It's some kind of law of nature; the car I get for him will give trouble. And he'll immediately decide that it's not straight from the factory at all; he'll say it's one I got cheap because there was something wrong with it.' He snapped the case shut. 'I don't want all that hassle, Bernard. I'd rather he went off and bought one in Berkeley Square. I've told him that, but he won't bloody well believe that there's anyone in this world who turns down a business opportunity.'

'Well, it's not like you, George.'

He grinned ruefully. 'I suppose not, but it's the way I feel about him.'

'Let's go and look at my new car,' I said. But he didn't move from behind the table.

'Posh Harry said you're in trouble. Is that right, Bernard?'

'Posh Harry makes his living by selling snippets of information. What he doesn't know he guesses, what he can't guess he invents.'

'Money trouble? Woman trouble? Trouble at work? If it's money I might be able to help, Bernard. You'd be better borrowing from me than from a High Street bank. I know you don't want to move from the house. Tessa explained all that to me.'

'Thanks, George. I think I'm going to manage the money end. Looks like they're going to give me some special allowance to help with the kids and the nanny and so on.'

'Couldn't you take the children away for a bit? Get a leave of absence and have a rest? You look damned tired these days.'

'I can't afford it,' I said. 'You're rich, George. You can do whatever you fancy doing. I can't.'

'I'm not rich enough to do anything I want to do. But I know what you mean; I'm rich enough to avoid doing the things I don't want to do.' George took off his heavy spectacles. 'I asked Posh Harry what he had to see you about. He didn't want to tell me, but I pressed him. He has to keep in with me, I do him a lot of favours one way and the other. And he wouldn't find many people who'd wait so patiently to be paid. I said, "What do you want with Bernard?" He said, "I'm helping him; he's in trouble." "What kind of trouble?" I said. "His people think he's working for the other side," said Harry. "If they prove it, he'll go to jail for about thirty years; they can't let him walk the streets; he knows too damned much about the way his people work." ' George stopped for a moment.

' "Bernard Samson wouldn't work for the Russians," I said. "I know him well enough to know that, and if the people he works for can't see that they must be stupid." ' George scratched his neck as he decided how to go on with his story. ' "Well, his wife worked for them," said Harry, "and if he's not working for them too, the Russians are not going to leave him alone either." "What do you mean?" I asked Posh Harry. "That's the bind he's in," said Posh Harry, "that's why he needs help. Either the Brits will jail him for thirty years or the Russians will send a hit team to waste him." ' George put his glasses on again and looked at me as if seeing me for the first time.

'Posh Harry earns a living selling stories like that, George. It's good dramatic stuff, isn't it? It's like the films on TV.'

'Not when you know one of the cast,' said George. Another train rolled slowly across the viaduct, its noise enough to prevent any conversation. 'Bloody trains,' said George after the sound had died away. 'We had trains making that kind of a racket right alongside the house where I grew up. I swore I'd never have to endure that kind of thing again once I made enough money . . . and here I am.' He looked round his squalid little office as if seeing it through the eyes of a visitor. 'Funny, isn't it?'

'Let's go and look at my car,' I suggested again.

'Bernard,' said George, fixing me with a serious stare. 'Do you know a man named Richard Cruyer?'

'Yes,' I said, vaguely enough to suddenly deny it if that became necessary.

'You work with him, don't you?'

I tried to remember if George and Tessa had ever had dinner at my home with the Cruyers as fellow guests. 'Yes, I work with him. Why?'

'Tessa has had to see him a couple of times. She says it was in connection with this children's charity she's doing so much work for.'

'I see,' I said, although I didn't see. I'd never heard Tessa mention any sort of charity she was doing any work for and I couldn't imagine what role Dicky Cruyer would play in any charity that wasn't devoting its energies to his own well-being.

'I can't help being suspicious, Bernard. I've forgiven her and removed from my mind a lot of the bad feeling that was poisoning our relationship. But I still get suspicious, Bernard. I'm only human.'

'And what do you want to know?' I asked, although what he wanted to know was only too evident. He wanted to know if Dicky Cruyer was the sort of man who would have an affair with Tessa. And the only truthful answer was an unequivocal 'Yes'.

'What's going on. I want to know what's going on.'

'Have you asked Tessa?'

'It would mean a flare-up, Bernard. It would destroy all the work we've both done trying to put the marriage together. But I've got to know. It's racking me; I'm desperate. Will you find out for me? Please?'

'I'll do what I can, George,' I promised.

9

I identified with Stinnes. He was a cold fish and yet I thought of him as someone like myself. His father had been a Russian soldier with the occupation forces in Berlin and he'd been brought up like a German, just as I had. And I felt close to him because of the way our paths had overlapped since that day he had me arrested in East Berlin. I'd talked him into coming over to us; I'd reassured him about his treatment, and I'd personally escorted him to London from Mexico City. I respected his professionalism, and that coloured all my thoughts and my actions. But I didn't really like him, and that affected my judgement too. I couldn't completely understand the undoubted success he enjoyed with women. What the devil did they see in him? Women were always attracted by purposeful masculine strength, organizing ability, and the sort of self-confidence that leaves everything unsaid. Stinnes had all that in abundance. But there were none of the other things one usually saw in womanizers: no fun, no flamboyance, no amusing stories, none of the gesturing or physical movements by which women so often remember the ones they had once loved. He had none of those warm human characteristics that make a love affair so easy to get into and so hard to escape, no self-mockery, no admitted failings; just the cold eyes, calculating mind and inscrutable face. He seemed especially cold-blooded about the work he did. Perhaps that was something to do with it. For the womanizer is destructive, the rock upon which desperate women dash themselves to pieces.

But there was no denying the dynamic energy that was evident in that seemingly inert body. Stinnes had an actor's skill, an almost hypnotic will that is turned on like a laser beam. Such heartless dedication is to be seen in the great Hollywood stars, in certain very idealistic politicians, and even more often as a brutal streak in comedians who frighten their audience into laughing at their inadequate jokes.

I didn't feel like that about Bret Rensselaer, who was an entirely different personality. Bret wasn't the hard-eyed pro that Stinnes was. Quite apart from his inadequate German, Bret could never have been a field agent; he would never have been able to endure the squalor and discomfort. And Bret could never have been a good field agent for the same reason that so many other Americans failed in that role: Bret liked to be seen. Bret was a social animal who wanted to be noticed. The self-effacing furtiveness that all Europeans have been taught, in a society still essentially feudal, does not come readily to Americans.

Bret seemed to have had endless women since his wife left him, but his ability to charm was easy to understand, even for those who were impervious to it. Despite his age, he was physically attractive, and he was generous with money and was amusing company. He liked food and wine, music and movies. And he did all those things that rich people always know how to do: he could ski and shoot and sail and ride a horse; and get served in crowded restaurants. I'd had my share of differences with Bret; I'd suffered his insulting outbursts and grudgingly admired his stubbornness, but he was not a heartless apparatchik. If you got him at the right moment, he could be informal and approachable in a way that none of the other senior staff were. Most important of all, Bret had the uniquely American talent of flexibility, the willingness to try anything likely to get the job done. Yet Bret got jobs done, and for that I gave him due credit; it was on that account that I trod warily when I first began to wonder about his loyalties.

Bret Rensselaer had the jutting chin and the rugged ageless features of a strip-cartoon hero. Like most Americans Bret was concerned with his weight and his health and his clothes to an extent that his English colleagues regarded as unacceptably foreign. The public-school senior staff at London Central spent just as much money on their Savile Row suits and handmade shirts and Jermyn Street shoes, but they wore them with a careless scruffiness that was a vital part of their snobbery. A real English gentleman never tries; that was the article of faith. And Bret Rensselaer tried. But Bret had a family that went back as far as the Revolutionary War, and what's more, Bret had money, lots of it. And with any kind of snob, money is the trump card if you play it right.

Bret was already in his office when I arrived. He always started work very early – that was another of his American characteristics. His early arrival and punctuality at meetings were universally admired, though I can't say he started a trend. This morning a meeting had been arranged between me, Dicky Cruyer, Morgan – the D-G's stooge – and Bret Rensselaer in Bret's office. But when I arrived on time – growing up in Germany produces in people a quite unnatural determination to be punctual – Morgan was not there and Dicky had not even arrived in his office, let alone in Bret's office.

Bret Rensselaer's office accommodated him on the top floor along with all the other men who mattered at London Central. From his desk there was a view across that section of London where the parks are: St James's Park, Green Park, the garden of Buckingham Palace, and Hyde Park were all lined up to make a continuous green carpet. In the summer it was a wonderful view. Even now, in winter, with a haze of smoke from the chimneys and the trees bare, it was better than looking at the dented filing cabinets in my room.

Bret was working. He was sitting at his desk, reading his paperwork and trying to make the world conform to it. The jacket of his suit, complete with starched white linen handkerchief in his top pocket, was placed carefully across the back of a chair that Bret seemed to keep for no other purpose. He wore a grey-silk bow tie and a white shirt with a monogram placed so that it could be seen even when he wore his waistcoat. The waistcoat – 'vest', he called it, of course – was unbuttoned and his sleeves rolled back.

He'd had his office furnished to his own taste – that was one of the perquisites of senior rank – and I remember the fuss there'd been when Bret brought in his own interior decorator. A lot of the obstructive arguments about it had come from someone in Internal Security who thought interior decorators were large teams of men in white overalls with steam hammers, scaffolding and pots of paint. In the event it was a delicate bearded man, wearing a denim jacket embroidered with flower patterns over a 'No Nukes' sweatshirt. It took a long time to get him past the doorman.

But the result was worth it. The centrepiece of the office was a huge, chrome, black-leather-and-glass desk, specially ordered from Denmark. The carpet was dark grey and the walls were in two shades of grey too. There was a long black chesterfield for visitors to sit on while Bret swivelled and rocked in a big chair that matched the chrome and leather of the desk. The theory was that the clothes of the occupants of the room provided all the necessary colour. And as long as the colourful bearded designer was in the room, it worked. But Bret was a monochrome figure and he blended into the decor as a chameleon matches its natural habitat, except that chameleons only match their surroundings when they're frightened.

'I'm taking over Stinnes,' he announced when I went into the room.

'I heard they were trying to hang that on you!' I said.

He grinned to acknowledge my attempt to put him down. 'No one hung it on me, buddy. I'm very happy to handle this end of the Stinnes debriefing.'

'Well, that's just great then,' I said. I looked at my watch. 'Have I arrived too early?'

We both knew that I was just poisoning the well for Dicky Cruyer and Morgan, but Bret went along with it. 'The others are late,' he said. 'They're always goddamned late.'

'Shall we start?' I said. 'Or shall I go and have a cup of coffee?'

'You sit where you are, smart ass. If you need coffee so urgently, I'll get some brought here.' He pressed a button on his white phone and spoke into a box while staring at the far side of the room with his eyes unfocused.

They sent coffee for four and Bret got to his feet and poured out all four cups so that Cruyer's coffee and Morgan's coffee were getting cold. It seemed a childish revenge, but perhaps it was the only one Bret could think of. While I drank my coffee Bret looked out of his window and then looked at things on his desk and tidied it up. He was a restless man who, despite an injured knee, liked to duck and weave and swing like a punch-drunk boxer. He came round and sat on the edge of his desk to drink his coffee; it was a contrived pose of executive informality, the kind that chairmen of big companies adopt when they're being photographed for *Forbes* magazine.

Even after Bret and I had been sitting there for ten minutes drinking in silence the other two had still not turned up. 'I saw Stinnes yesterday,' Bret finally volunteered. 'I don't know what they do to people at that damned Debriefing Centre, but he was in a lousy uncooperative mood.'

'Where have they put him, Berwick House?'

'Yes. Do you know that the so-called London Debriefing Centre has premises as far away as Birmingham?'

'They were using a place in Scotland until last year, when the D-G said we couldn't spare the travelling time for our staff going backwards and forwards.'

'Well, Stinnes isn't having a ball. He did nothing but complain. He said he's given us all he's going to give us until he gets a few concessions. The first concession is to go somewhere else. The Governor – the one you don't like: Potter – says Stinnes has threatened to escape.'

'How would you feel, restricted to Berwick House for week after week? It's furnished like a flophouse and the only outdoor entertainment is walking around the garden close to the walls to see how many alarms you can trigger before they order you back inside again.'

'It sounds as if you've been locked up there,' said Bret.

'Not there, Bret, but places very like it.'

'So you wouldn't have put him there?'

'Put him there?' I couldn't help smiling, it was so bloody ridiculous. 'Have you taken a look at the staff of the London Debriefing Centre lately?' I asked. 'Do you know where they recruit those people? Most of them are redundant ex-employees of Her Majesty's famous Customs and Excise Department. That fat one who is now officially designated the Governor – stop me if you're laughing so much it hurts – came from the Income Tax office in West Hartlepool. No, Bret, I wouldn't have put the poor bastard into Berwick House. I wouldn't have put Stalin there either.'

'So let's have it,' said Bret with studied patience. He slid off the edge of the desk and stretched his back as if he was getting stiff.

'I haven't given it a lot of thought, Bret. But if I wanted anyone to cooperate, I'd put him somewhere where he felt good. I'd put him into the Oliver Messel suite at the Dorchester Hotel.'

'You would, eh?' He knew I was trying to needle him.

'And do you know something, Bret? The Dorchester would cost only a fraction of what it's costing the taxpayer to hold him at Berwick House. How many guards and clerks do they have there nowadays?'

'And what's to stop him walking out of the Dorchester?'

'Well, Bret, maybe he wouldn't want to escape from the Dorchester the way he wants to get out of Berwick House.'

Bret leaned forward as if trying to see me better. 'I listen to everything you say, but I'm never quite sure how much of this crap you believe,' he said. I didn't reply. Then Bret said, 'I don't remember hearing any of these theories when Giles Trent was being held in Berwick House. You're the one who said he mustn't be allowed to smoke and arranged for him to have small-size pyjamas with buttons missing and a patched cotton dressing gown without a cord.'

'That's all standard drill for people we're interrogating. Jesus, Bret, you know the score, it's to make them feel inadequate. It wasn't my idea; it's old hat.'

'Stinnes gets the Oliver Messel suite and Trent didn't even get buttons for his "pj's"? What are you giving me?'

'Stinnes isn't a prisoner. He's come over to us voluntarily. We should be flattering him and making him feel good. We should be getting him into a mood so that he wants to give us one hundred per cent.'

'Maybe.'

'And Stinnes is a pro . . . he's an ex-field agent, not a pen pusher like Trent. And Stinnes knows his job from top to bottom. He knows that we're not going to rip out his fingernails or give him the live electrodes where it hurts most. He's sitting pretty, and until we play ball with him he'll remain *stumm*.'

'Have you discussed this with Dicky?' asked Bret.

I shrugged. Bret knew that Dicky didn't want to hear about Stinnes; he'd made that clear to everyone. 'No sense in letting the rest of the coffee get cold,' I said. 'Mind if I take Dicky's cup?'

He pushed the coffee towards me and looking at the door again said, 'It wouldn't have to be a great idea to be an improvement on what's happening at present.'

'Isn't he talking at all?'

'The first two weeks were okay. The senior interrogator – Ladbrook, the ex-cop – knows what he's doing. But he doesn't know much about our end of the business. He got out of his depth and since the Berlin arrest Stinnes's become very difficult. He is very disillusioned, Bernard. He's been through the honeymoon and now he is in that post-honeymoon gloom.'

'No, don't tell me, Bret.' I held one hand to my head as if on the verge of remembering something important. 'The "honeymoon" and the "post-honeymoon gloom" . . . I recognize the magical syntax . . . there's a touch of Hemingway there, or is it Shelley? What golden-tongued wordsmith told you that Stinnes was in the – how was it he put it? – "post-honeymoon gloom"? I must write that down in case I forget it. Was that the Deputy Governor, the bearded one with the incontinent dachshund that craps on his carpet? Jesus, if I could only get stuff like that into my reports, I'd be D-G by now.'

Bret looked at me and chewed his lip in fury. He was mad at me, but he was even madder at himself for repeating all that garbage that London Debriefing staff trot out to cover their manifold incompetence. 'So where can we move him to? Technically, London Debriefing have custody of him.'

'I know, Bret. And this is the time that you tell me again about how necessary it is to keep up the pretence that he's being questioned about my loyalty, in case the Home Office start making noises about him being transferred to MI5 facilities.'

'It's the truth,' said Bret. 'Never mind how much you don't like it, the truth is that you're our only excuse for holding onto Stinnes.'

'Bullshit,' I said. 'Even if the Home Office started asking for him today, the paperwork would take three months going through normal channels, four or five months if we were deliberately slow.'

'That's not so. I could tell you of three or four people handed over to Five within two or three weeks of entering the UK.'

'I'm talking about the paperwork, Bret. Until now we've mostly let them go because we don't want them. But the paperwork that makes the transfer necessary takes an average of three months.'

'I won't argue with you,' said Bret. 'I guess you see more of the paperwork from where you sit.'

'Oh boy, do I.'

He looked at his watch. 'If they don't arrive by nine, we'll have to do this later in the day. I'm due at a meeting in the conference room at nine forty-five.'

But as he said it, Dicky Cruyer and Morgan came through the door, talking animatedly and with exhilarant friendliness. I was disconcerted by this noisy show, for I detested Morgan in a way I didn't dislike anyone else in the building. Morgan was the only person there whose patronizing superiority came near driving me to physical violence.

'And what happens if I get you home later than midnight?' said Dicky with that fruity voice he used after people had laughed at a couple of his jokes. 'Do you turn into a pumpkin or something?' They both laughed. Perhaps he wasn't talking about Tessa, but it made me sick in my stomach to think of her being with Dicky Cruyer and of George being miserable about it.

Without a word of greeting Bret pointed a finger at the black-leather chesterfield and the two of them sat down. This seemed to sober them and Dicky was even moved to apologize for being late. Morgan had a blue cardboard folder with him; he balanced it on his knees and brought out a plain sheet of paper and a slim gold pencil. Dicky had the Gucci zipper case that he'd brought back from Los Angeles. From the case he brought a thick bundle of mixed papers that looked like the entire contents of his in-tray. I suspected that he intended dumping it upon me; it was what he usually did. But he spent a moment getting them in order to show how prepared he was for business.

'I have an important appointment in just a little while,' said Bret, 'so never mind the road show; let's get down to business.' He reached for the agenda sheet and, after adjusting his spectacles, read it aloud to us.

Bret was determined to establish control of the meeting right away. He had unchallenged seniority, but he had everything to fear from both of them. The insidious tactics of Morgan, who used his role of assistant to the D-G to manipulate all and sundry, were well known. As for Dicky Cruyer, Bret had been trying to take over the German desk from him and been rebuffed at every stage. Watching the way that Dicky was ingratiating himself with Morgan I began to see how Bret had been outmanoeuvred.

'If you have to get away, Bret, we can adjourn to my office and finish off,' offered Morgan affably. His face was very pale and rotund, with small eyes, like two currants placed in a bowl of rice pudding. He had a powerful singsong Welsh accent. I wondered if it had always been like that or whether he wanted to be recognized as the local boy who'd made good.

'Who would sign the minutes?' said Bret in an elegant dismissal of Morgan's attempt to shed him. 'No, I'll make certain we'll finish off in the allotted time.'

It was a run-of-the-mill meeting to decide some supplementary allocations to various German Stations. They'd been having a tough time financially, since appropriations hadn't been revised through countless upward revaluations of the Deutschemark. Bret put on his glasses to read the agenda and pushed the meeting along at breakneck speed, cutting into all Dicky's digressions and Morgan's questions. When it was all over, Bret got to his feet. 'I've accepted the D-G's invitation to supervise the Stinnes interrogation,' he announced, although by that time everyone in the room – if not everyone in the building – knew that. 'And I'm going to ask for Bernard to assist me.'

'That's not possible,' said Dicky, reacting like a scalded cat. Dicky suddenly glimpsed the unwelcome prospect of actually having to do the work of the German desk, instead of passing it over to me while he tried to find new things to insert into his expense accounts. 'Bernard has a big backlog of work. I couldn't spare him.'

'He'll have time enough for other work as well,' said Bret calmly. 'I just want him to advise me. He's got some ideas I like the sound of.' He looked at me and smiled, but I wasn't sure what he was smiling about.

Morgan said, 'When I offered help, I didn't mean senior staff. Certainly not technical people such as Bernard.'

'Well, I didn't know *you* ever offered me anything,' said Bret coldly. 'I was under the impression that the D-G still ran the Department.'

'A slip of the tongue, Bret,' said Morgan smoothly.

'Bernard is the only person who can unlock the problems Debriefing Centre is having with Stinnes.' Bret was establishing the syntax. The problems with Stinnes would remain LDC's problems, not Bret's, and a continuing failure to unlock those problems would be my failure.

'It's just not possible,' said Dicky Cruyer. 'I don't want to seem uncooperative, but if the D-G keeps pushing this one, I'll have to explain to him exactly what's at stake.' Translated, this meant that if Bret didn't lay off, he'd get Morgan to pretend the order to lay off came from the D-G.

'You'll have to tackle your problem by getting some temporary help, Dicky,' said Bret. 'This particular matter is all settled. I talked to the D-G at the Travellers' Club yesterday – I ran into him by accident and it seemed a good chance to talk over the current situation. The D-G said I could have anyone. In fact, I'm not sure it wasn't Sir Henry who first brought Bernard's name into the conversation.' He looked at his watch and then smiled at everyone and removed his speed-cop glasses. He got to his feet, and Dicky and Morgan stood up too. 'Must go. This next one is a really important meeting,' said Bret. Not like this meeting he was leaving, which by implication was a really unimportant one.

It was Morgan's turn to be obstructive. 'There are one or two things you are overlooking, Bret,' he said, his lilting Welsh accent more than ever in evidence. 'Our story to the world at large is that we are holding Stinnes only in order to investigate Bernard's possible malfeasance. How can we explain Bernard's presence at Berwick House as one of the investigating officers?'

Bret came round from behind his desk. We were all standing close. Bret seemed at a loss for words. He rolled his sleeves down slowly and gave all his attention to pushing his gold cuff links through the holes. Perhaps he'd not reckoned with that sort of objection.

Although until this point I'd had reservations about joining Bret Rensselaer's team, now I saw the need to voice my own point of view, if only for self-preservation. 'What lies you are telling in order to hold Stinnes is your problem, Morgan,' I said. 'I was never consulted about them, and I can't see that operating decisions should be made just to support your insupportable fairy stories.'

Bret took his cue from me. 'Yes, why should Bernard roll over and play possum to get you out of the hole?' he said. 'Bernard's the only one who's been close to Stinnes. He knows the score, like none of the rest of us. Let's not have the tail wagging the dog. Eh?' The 'eh' was addressed to Morgan in his role as tail.

'The D-G will be unhappy,' threatened Morgan. He smoothed his tie. It was a nervous gesture and so was the glance he gave in Dicky's direction. Or what would have been Dicky's direction, except that Dicky had returned to the sofa and become very busy collecting together, and counting, the bundle of papers that we hadn't got round to discussing. Even if they were just papers that Dicky carried with him in order to look overworked, on contentious occasions like this he knew how to suddenly become occupied and thus keep apart from the warring factions.

Bret went to the chair where his jacket was arrayed and took his time about putting it on. He shot his cuffs and then adjusted the knot of his tie. 'I talked this over with him, Morgan,' said Bret. He took a deep breath. Until now he'd been very calm and composed, but he was about to blow his top. I knew the signals. Without raising his voice very much Bret said, 'I never wanted responsibility for the Stinnes business; you know that better than anyone because you've been the one pestering me to take it on. But I said okay and I've started work.' Bret took another breath. I'd seen it all before; he didn't need the deep breath so it gave nervous onlookers the impression that he was about to start throwing punches. In the event, he prodded Morgan in the chest with his forefinger. Morgan flinched. 'If you screw this up I'll rip your balls off. And don't come creeping back here with some little written instruction that the old man's initialled. The only thing you'll succeed in changing is that I'll hand your lousy job right back to you, and it's not the job upon which careers are built. You'll discover that, Morgan, if you're misguided enough to try taking it over.'

'Steady on, Bret,' said Dicky mildly, looking up briefly from his papers but not coming within range of Bret's wrath.

Bret was really angry. This was something more than just a Bret tantrum, and I wondered what else might be behind it. His face was drawn and his mouth twitched as if he was about to go further, and then he seemed to change his mind about doing so. He reached his fingers into his top pocket to make sure his spectacles were there and strode from the room without looking back at anyone.

Morgan seemed shaken by Bret's outburst. He'd seen these flashes of temper before, but that wasn't the same as being on the receiving end of them, as I well knew. Dicky counted his papers yet again and held on tight to his neutral status. This round went to Bret, but only on points, and Bret was not fool enough – or American enough – to think that a couple of quick jabs to the body would decide a match against these two bruisers. Winning one little argument with the public-school mafia at London Central was like landing a blow on a heavy leather punching sack – the visible effect was slight, and two minutes later the pendulum swung the whole contraption back again and knocked you for six.

There was a silence after Bret departed. I felt like Cinderella abandoned by the fairy godmother to the mercies of the ugly sisters. As if to confirm these fears Dicky gave me the papers, which were indeed the contents of his in-tray, and said would I have a look at them and bring them back this afternoon. Then Dicky looked at Morgan and said, 'Bret's not himself these days.'

'It's understandable,' said Morgan. 'Poor Bret's had a tough time of it lately. Since he lost the Economics Intelligence Committee he's not been able to find his feet again.'

'Rumour says Bret will get Berlin when Frank Harrington resigns,' said Dicky.

'Not without your say-so, Dicky,' said Morgan. 'The D-G would never put into Berlin someone whom you'd find it difficult to work with. Do you want Bret in Berlin?'

Ah! So that was it. It was obvious what Dicky might gain from keeping Morgan sweet, but now I saw what Morgan might want in exchange. Dicky muttered something about that all being a long way in the future, which was Dicky's way of avoiding a question that Morgan was going to ask again and again, until he finally got no for an answer.

10

'When you're felling a forest, the chips must fly,' said Bret. He was quoting Stinnes, but he might have been referring to the brush he'd had with Morgan that morning and to what might come of it. We were sitting in the back of his chauffeur-driven Bentley purring along the fast lane to visit Stinnes. 'Is that a Russian proverb?' he asked.

'Yes,' I said. 'But a Russian remembers it also as the widely used excuse for the injustices, imprisonments, and massacres by Stalin.'

'You're a goddamned encyclopedia brain, Samson,' said Bret. 'And this guy Stinnes is a tricky little shit.'

I nodded and leaned back in the real leather. For security reasons the senior staff were expected to use the car pool for duty trips, and the only chauffeur-driven car was that provided to the Director-General, but Bret Renssellaer cared nothing for all that. The Belgravia residence his family had maintained in London since before World War I came complete with servants and motorcars. When Bret became a permanent fixture at London Central there was no way to ask him to give up his pampered lifestyle and start driving himself around in some car appropriate to his departmental rank and seniority.

'And here we are,' said Bret. He'd been reading the transcript of his previous talks with Stinnes and now he put the typewritten pages back into his case. His reading hadn't left him in a very happy mood.

Berwick House, a fine old mansion of red brick, was built long before that building material became associated with new and undistinguished provincial colleges. It was an eighteenth-century attempt to imitate one of Wren's country mansions. But the War Office official who chose to commandeer the whole estate just after World War II started was no doubt attracted by the moat that surrounded the house.

The house couldn't be seen from the road; it only came into view after the car turned in at the weathered sign that announced that Berwick House was a Ministry of Pensions training school. I suppose that was the most unattractive kind of establishment that the occupiers could think of. There was a delay at the gate lodge. We went through the outer gate and then pulled into the gravel patch where there were detection devices to check every vehicle. They knew we were coming and Bret's shiny black Bentley was well known to them, but they went through the formal procedure. Ted Riley even wanted to see our identification and that of Albert the chauffeur. Ted was an elderly man who had long ago worked for my father. I knew him well but he gave no sign of recognition.

'Hello, Ted.'

'Good morning, sir.' He was not a man who would presume on old friendships.

Ted had been an Intelligence Corps captain in Berlin after the war, but he got involved with some black-market dealers in Potsdamer Platz and my father had transferred him out uncomfortably quickly. Ted had given my mother whole Westphalian hams from time to time, and when my father discovered that Ted had dabbled in the black market, he was furious at what he thought was some kind of attempt to involve us. Ted was white-haired now, but he was still the same man who used to give me his chocolate ration every week when I was small. Ted Riley waved us through. The second man opened the electric gates and the third man phoned to the guard box at the house.

'They're rude bastards,' said Bret, as if his definition was something I should write down and consult at future visits.

'They have a bloody awful job, Bret,' I said.

'They should use Defence Ministry police down here. These people are full of crap. Identity. They know me well enough.'

'Ministry of Defence police look like cops, Bret. The whole idea is that these people wear civilian clothes and look like civilians.'

'This bunch look like civilians, all right,' said Bret scornfully. 'They look like senior citizens. Can you imagine how they'd handle a real attempt to break into this place?'

'At least they're reliable and don't attract attention locally. They're all carefully vetted, and Ted Riley, who's in charge, is a man I'd stake my life on. The number-one priority here is that we have people on guard duty who won't take bribes from newspaper reporters or smuggle gin for the inmates.' When he didn't answer I added, 'They're not supposed to be able to repulse an armoured division.'

'I'm glad you told me,' said Bret sarcastically. 'That makes me feel much better about them.' He stared out as we passed the Nissen huts where the guards lived and at the slab-sided grey structures that were sometimes used for conferences. The landscape was brown and bare, so that in places the alarms and wires had become visible.

We went over the old bridge across the moat. It was only when the car turned into the courtyard at the rear of the building that its true condition could be seen. It was like a film set: the east wing was little more than a façade supported by huge slabs of timber. This side of the house had been burned to the ground by incendiary bombs jettisoned by a Luftwaffe pilot trying desperately to gain height. He'd failed and the Heinkel crashed, six miles away after taking a small section of steeple from the village church.

London Debriefing Centre was an updated version of what used to be called the 'London District Cage', the place where the War Crimes Investigation Unit imprisoned important Nazis awaiting trial. Signs of those days hadn't entirely disappeared: there were still the remnants of old wartime posters to be seen in some of the offices, and defacing the walls of some of the subterranean 'hard-rooms' – a polite departmental euphemism for prison cells – there were the curious runelike marks that prisoners use to keep track of time.

The LDC senior administration staff were all there when we arrived. Their presence was no doubt due to the fact that Bret had now taken over liaison duties. On my previous visits to Berwick House I'd wandered in and out with only a perfunctory hello and scribbled signature, but Bret was important enough for both the Governor and Deputy Governor to be in their offices.

The Governor, still in his middle thirties, was a huge man with heavy jowls, black hair brushed tight against his skull, and a carefully manicured hairline moustache, the sort of thing Valentino wore when being a rotter. To complete the effect, he was smoking a cigarette in an amber cigarette holder. Like his Deputy, he was dressed in black pants, white shirt and plain black tie. I had the feeling that they would both have preferred the whole staff to be in uniform, preferably one with plenty of gold braid.

The Governor's office was in fact a large panelled room with comfortable armchairs and an impressive fireplace. The only justification for calling it an office was a small desk in the corner together with two metal filing cabinets and a box of small file cards on the windowsill. He offered us a drink and wanted us to sit down and chat about nothing in particular, but Bret declined.

'Let me see,' said the Governor, reaching for his little file cards and walking his fingertips along the edges of them as if Stinnes wasn't the only person they were holding. 'Sadoff . . . ah, here we are: Sadoff, Nikolai.' From the box he plucked a photo of Erich Stinnes and slapped it on the desk top with the air of a man winning a poker game. The photo showed Stinnes staring into the camera and holding across his chest a small board with a number.

'He usually calls himself Stinnes,' I said.

The Governor looked up as if seeing me for the first time. 'We don't let people indulge their fantasies here at the Debriefing Centre. Let them use a pseudonym and you invite them to invent the rest of it.' He put down his cigarette and pulled a card out of the box far enough to read the handwriting on it, but he'd kept his little finger in position so that he hadn't lost the place. I suppose you learn little tricks like that when you spend a lifetime counting paper clips.

'When was he last interviewed?' Bret asked.

'We are letting him stew for a few days,' said the Governor. He smiled. 'He began to be very tiresome.'

'What did he do?' Bret asked.

The Governor looked at his bearded Deputy who said, 'He shouted at me when I took some books away from him. A childish display of temper, no more than that. But you have to let him see who's the boss.'

'Is he locked up?' I said.

'He's confined to his room,' said the Governor.

'We're trying to get information from him,' I explained patiently. 'We're in a hurry.'

'Life and death, is it?' the Governor asked with a not quite hidden edge of sarcasm in his tone.

'That's right,' I said, responding in the same manner.

He was smoking the cigarette in the amber holder again. 'It always is with you chaps,' said the Governor, smiling like an adult playing along with a children's game. 'But you can't hurry these things. The first thing is to establish the relationship between the staff and the prisoner. Only then can you get down to the real nub of the intelligence.' He sat down in a chair that was far too small for him and crossed his legs.

'I'll try and remember that,' I said.

He didn't look at me; he looked at Bret and said, 'If you want to see him, you can, but I prefer him not to be permitted out of his room.'

'And there was the medical,' the bearded Deputy reminded his boss.

'Ah, yes.' The Governor's voice was sad as he put the cards and photo away. 'He twice refused to let the doctor examine him. We can't have that. If anything happened to him, there'd be hell to pay, and you chaps would put the blame on me.' Big smile. 'And you'd be right to do so.'

'So what's the position now?' Bret asked.

'The doctor refused to attempt an examination unless Sadoff was willing and cooperative. So we've deferred it until next week. But meanwhile we don't even have a note of his height and weight and so on.' He looked up at us. I suppose both Bret and I were looking worried. The Governor said, 'It's nothing new to us. We've seen all this before. By next week he'll be willing enough, have no fear.'

Bret said, 'It sounds as if it's developed into a contest of wills.'

'I don't enter into contests,' said the Governor with a closed-mouth smile. 'I'm in charge here. The detainees do as I say. And certainly I won't allow any one of them to avoid a physical examination.'

'We'll have a word with him,' said Bret.

'I'll come with you,' said the Governor. He heaved himself to his feet.

'That won't be necessary,' said Bret.

'I'm afraid it will,' said the Governor.

I could see that Bret was becoming more and more angry, so I said to him, 'I'm not sure the Governor's security clearance would be sufficient, considering the subject to be discussed.'

There was of course no particular subject on the agenda, but Bret got the idea quickly enough. 'That's quite true,' said Bret. He turned to the Governor and said, 'Better we keep to the regulations, Governor. From what you say, Stinnes might well make a written complaint about something or other. If that happens, I'd like to make sure you're completely in the clear.'

'In the clear?' said the Governor indignantly. But when Bret made no supplementary explanation, he sat down heavily, moved some papers around, and said, 'I've got a great deal of work to get through here. If you're quite sure you can manage on your own, by all means carry on.'

I went in alone. Erich Stinnes looked content – as much as anyone locked up in Berwick House and left to the mercies of the Governor and his Deputy could have looked content. I knew which room they'd choose for him. It was up on the second floor; cream-painted walls and a plain metal-frame bed, with a print of a naval battle on the wall. That was the room that had the microphones. And the mirror over the sink could be changed so that a TV camera in the next room could film through it.

They'd replaced the light cotton suit he'd worn in Mexico with a heavier English one. It wasn't a perfect fit but it looked good enough. His spectacles flashed with the light from the window as he turned round to see me. 'Oh, it's you,' he said, with no emotion to reveal whether he was happy or disappointed to see me. He'd been standing near the window sketching.

Stinnes was forty years old, a thin bony figure with Slavic features and circular gold-rimmed glasses behind which quick intelligent eyes glittered, and made an otherwise nondescript face hard. He might have been taken for an absent-minded professor, but Sadoff – who preferred his operational name of Stinnes – had been until a few weeks ago a KGB major. Married twice, with a grown-up son who was trying to get into Moscow University, he'd defected and thus got rid of a troublesome wife and been paid a quarter of a million dollars for his services. For such a man, time was not pressing; he was youngish and he was Russian. It was imbecilic to think that 'letting him stew for a few days' would have any effect upon him. I'd never seen him looking more relaxed.

I went to look at his drawing. He must have spent most of the daylight hours at the window. There was a copy of the *Reader's Digest Book of British Birds* with scraps of paper to mark some of the pages. A school notebook was crammed with his spiky writing. He'd diligently recorded the birds he'd sighted.

A bird identification book was the first thing he'd asked for when he arrived at Berwick House. He'd also asked for a pair of binoculars, a request that was denied. There had been a discussion about whether Erich's birdwatching was genuine or whether he had some other reason for wanting the binoculars. If it was a pretence, he'd certainly devoted a lot of time and energy to it. There were sketches of the birds too, and notes about their songs.

But his observations were not confined to ornithology. He'd pinned a piece of paper to a removable shelf, that was propped against the window frame. It made a crude easel so that he could draw the landscape as seen from his room. The paper was some sort of brown wrapping paper, and to draw he was using the stub end of an old pencil and a fountain pen.

'I didn't know you were an artist, Erich . . . the perspective looks spot on. Your trees are a bit shaky though.'

'Trees are always difficult for me,' he confessed. 'The bare ones are easy enough, but the evergreens are difficult to draw.' Thoughtfully he added a couple of extra touches to the line of trees that surmounted the hill beyond the village. 'Do you like it?' he asked, indicating the drawing with his hand and not looking up from it.

'I love it,' I said. 'But they won't like it downstairs.'

'No?'

'They'll think you're compromising security by making a drawing of the moat and grounds and the walls and what's beyond them.'

'Then why put me on the second floor? If you don't want me to see over the wall, why put me here?'

'I don't know, Erich. It's not my idea to hold you here at all.'

'You'd put me into a four-star hotel, I suppose?'

'Something like that,' I said.

He shrugged to show that he didn't believe me. 'This is good enough. The food is good, the room is warm, and I can have as many hot baths as I wish. It is what I expected . . . better than I feared it might be.' This was not in line with what Bret had said about Stinnes and his complaints.

Without preamble I said, 'They released the male secretary. It was political: Bonn. We had enough evidence, but it was a political decision to let him go. We picked up the courier too. I thought we'd got a case officer at first, but it was just the courier.'

'What name?' said Stinnes. He was still looking at his landscape drawing.

'Müller – a woman. Do you know her?'

'I met her once. A Party member, a fanatic. I don't like using people like that.' He held up the pencil to show me. 'Do you have a penknife?'

'Radio operator,' I prompted him. I wondered if he liked holding some bits of information back so that I would feel clever at getting them out of him. Certainly he gave no sign of reticence at telling me the rest of what he knew.

'Correct. She came over to Potsdam for the course. That was when I met her. She didn't know I was from the Command Staff, needless to say.'

'She was working out of London, probably handling my wife's material,' I said.

'Are you sure?' He took my Swiss Army knife from me and sharpened his pencil very carefully. 'If I use my razor blade, it's no good for shaving. They only give one blade per week and always take the old one away.'

'It's a guess,' I admitted. 'Grow a beard.'

'It's probably a good guess. In our system we keep Communications completely separated from Operations, so I can't tell you for sure.' He passed the knife back to me and tried out the pencil on the edge of his picture. He made a lot of little scribbles, wearing it down to give the pencil an especially sharp point. Then he had another go at the trees.

'With two code names?' I said. 'One agent with two codes? Is that likely?'

Stinnes stopped toying with his drawing and looked at me, frowning, as if trying to understand what I was getting at. 'Of course, Communications staff are a law unto themselves. They have all sorts of crazy ideas, but I have never heard of such a thing.'

'And material kept coming after my wife defected,' I said.

He smiled. It was a grim smile that didn't extend to his cold eyes. 'The Müller woman is telling you this?'

'Yes, she is.' I kept it in the present tense. I didn't want him to know that the woman was lost to us.

'She is mad.' He looked at his drawing again. I said nothing. I knew he was reflecting on it all. 'Oh, she might have had more material, but operators never know the difference between top-rate material and day-to-day rubbish. The Müller woman is fooling you. What is it she is trying to get from you?' He made the trees a little taller. It looked better. Then he shaded the wall darker.

'Think, Erich. It's important.'

He looked at me. 'Important? Are you trying to persuade yourself that there is another one of our people deeply embedded in London Central?'

'I want to know,' I said.

'You want to make a name for yourself. Is that what you mean?' He looked into my eyes and smoothed his thinning hair against the top of his head. It was wispy hair and the light from the window made it into a halo.

'That would be a part of it,' I admitted.

'I would have been told.' He pricked the sharp pencil point against the palm of his hand, not once but again and again like a sapper cautiously feeling for buried mines. 'If there was another well-placed agent in London Central, I would have been told.'

'Suppose the Müller woman had regular traffic direct with Moscow.'

'That's quite possible. But they would have told me. I was the senior man in Berlin. I would have known.' He stopped fidgeting with the pencil and put it into his top pocket. 'The Müller woman is trying to make you go round and round in circles. I'd advise you to disregard any suggestions about another KGB agent in London. It's the sort of thing that Moscow would like to start you wondering about.'

'Do you have enough to read?'

'I have the Bible,' he said. 'They gave me a Bible.'

'Is that what you're reading, the Bible?'

'It's always interested me, and reading it in English helps me learn. I am beginning to think that Christianity has a lot in common with Marxist-Leninism.'

'For instance?'

'God is dialectical materialism; Christ is Karl Marx; the Church is the Party, the elect is the proletariat, and the Second Coming is the Revolution.' He looked at me and smiled.

'How do heaven and hell fit into all that?' I asked.

He thought for a moment. 'Heaven is the socialist millennium, of course. I think hell must be the punishment of capitalists.'

'Bravo, Erich,' I said.

'You know I used to be with Section 44?'

Section 44 was the KGB's Religious Affairs Bureau. 'It was in your file,' I said. 'You left at the wrong time, Erich.'

'Because of Poland, you mean? Yes, the man running Section 44 these days is a general. But I would never have got that sort of promotion. They would have slotted less expert people in above me. Had I stayed there, I would still be a lieutenant. It's the way things are done in Russia.'

'It's the way things are done everywhere,' I said. 'So the Bible is enough for you?'

'A few books would be welcome.'

'I'll see what I can do,' I said. 'And I'll see if I can get you moved to somewhere more comfortable, but it might take time.' I took from my pocket five small packets of cheroots. They were evil smelling and I didn't want to give him a chance to light up before I left the room.

'What is time?' He displayed the palms of both hands. There was no humour in his gesture: just contemptuous mockery.

'Did you have to tell him that Bonn ordered the release of that guy?' said Bret. He was standing in the surveillance room with a set of headphones in his hands. 'That's lousy security, Bernard. We took a lot of trouble keeping that out of the newspapers.' It was a tiny dimly lit room with just enough space for the radio and TV equipment, although today there was nothing in use but the bugging equipment wired here from the second floor.

'Maybe you did, but every reporter in town knows about it, so don't think Moscow is puzzling. It's a two-way traffic, Bret. Stinnes has got to feel he's a part of what's going on.'

'You should be pushing harder. That's what I wanted you for, to help push the interrogation along faster.'

'I will, but I'm not the interrogator and I can't undo weeks of stupidity in one short interview, Bret,' I said. 'Easy does it. Let me move him out of here and establish a working relationship.'

'Hardly worth the journey down here,' Bret complained, putting the headphones on the shelf and switching off the light. 'I could have got a lot done this afternoon.'

'That's what I told you, but you insisted on coming with me.'

'I never know what you're likely to get up to when you're on your own.' The only light came from a small grimy skylight and Bret's face was completely in shadow. He put his hands into his trouser pockets so that his dark melton overcoat was held open. This aggressive stance, the clothes, and the lighting made him look like a still photo from some old gangster film.

'That makes me wonder why you chose me to work with you on this one,' I said. That much was true, very true.

He looked at me as if deciding whether to bother with a proper reply. Then he said, 'There's no one in the German Section with field experience comparable to yours. You're bright as hell, despite your lack of proper schooling and the chip you have on your shoulder about it. For most things concerning the German Section, you've got your own unofficial sources of information, and often you dig out material that no one else can get. You are straight. You make up your own mind, and you write your reports without giving a damn what anyone wants to hear. I like that.' He paused and just slightly flexed his leg as if his bad knee was troubling him. 'On the other hand, you put yourself and your personal problems before the Department. You're damned rude and I don't find your sarcastic remarks as amusing as some of the others do. You're insubordinate to the point of arrogance. You're selfish, reckless, and you never stop complaining.'

'You must have been reading my mail, Bret,' I said. It was interesting to see that Bret made no comment about what Stinnes had said about the Müller woman or about the suggestion that the KGB had another agent working inside London Central. Perhaps he thought it was just my way of drawing Stinnes out.

II

The Science Museum was quiet that morning. It was Saturday. The giggling, chewing, chatting, scuffling battalions of school children who are shepherded through it by glassy-eyed teachers on weekdays do not choose to visit such institutions in their own time. Especially when there's a football match on TV.

I was with the children and Gloria. It had become a regular Saturday routine: a visit to one of the South Kensington museums followed by lunch at Mario's restaurant in Brompton Road. Then she came back home with me and stayed until Sunday night, or sometimes Monday morning.

The aviation gallery on the top floor of the Science Museum was empty. We stood on the overhead walkway that provided a chance to be up among the old planes suspended from the roof. The children had run ahead to stare at the Spitfire, leaving me and Gloria with the dusty old Vickers Vimy that made the first non-stop flight across the Atlantic. We hadn't been talking about work, but I suddenly said, 'Do you know the sort of chits they fill out when someone has to go across to the Cabinet Office and ask questions? Pale green chits with lines and a little box for a rubber stamp. You know what I mean?'

'Yes,' she said. She leaned over the balcony of the walkway trying to see where the children were.

'Have you ever dealt with anyone in the Cabinet Office? Do you know anyone over there?'

'From time to time I have to deal with some of them,' she said. She still was giving the conversation only perfunctory attention. She had picked up the phone handpiece to get a recorded account of the exhibit and I had to wait until she had finished. Then she offered the phone to me but I shook my head.

'It's going to rain,' she said. 'I should have brought an umbrella.' She had just come from the hairdresser's and rain is the hairdresser's friend. I looked out through the big windows. You could see across the rooftops of West London from here. The clouds were dark grey so that inside the hall it was gloomy. The huge planes were casting dark shadows on the exhibits below us.

When she'd put the earpiece down I said, 'Do you know anyone in the Cabinet Office? Do you know anyone I could talk to without official permission?'

'You want to go over there and make enquiries?' she said. She was alert now and turned to watch my face. 'I suppose so, if that's what you want.' She smiled.

It was her immediate cheerful complaisance that made me feel guilty. 'No, forget it,' I said. I heard the children clattering down the stairs at the far end and watched them emerge from under the walkway. Billy made straight for the aero engines. He'd always liked the engines, even when he was small.

'Of course I'll do it,' Gloria put her arms through mine and hugged me. 'Look at me, darling. I'll do it for you. It's the easiest thing in the world.'

'No. It's a stupid idea,' I said, turning away from her. 'If they insist upon having the chit, it could end up with you getting fired.' The Cabinet Office was for us the most sensitive of government departments. We were controlled from the Cabinet Office. When the D-G was put upon the carpet – as he was now and again – it was the carpet of the Cabinet Office that he was put on.

'Why not go through ordinary channels?' she said. She touched her pale blonde hair. The sky had grown even darker and it was beginning to rain; the raindrops could be heard beating against the glass panels of the roof.

'Shall we just forget it?'

'No need to get angry. I said I'd do it. But tell me why.'

'This isn't the time or the place . . . and in any case I don't want to discuss it. Forget it.'

She hugged my arm. 'Tell me why, Bernard. You'd want to know why if it was you arranging it for someone else, wouldn't you?'

It was reasonable. But it was damned difficult to explain it all to her without sounding like a lunatic. 'There's a technical input of material that opens the possibility of another KGB penetration of the Department.'

She gave a little laugh. It was a lovely laugh. Her laugh was always enough to make me fall in love with her all over again, even when it contained so much derision. 'How very departmental. I've never heard you using all that jargon. You sound like Mr Cruyer. Is that a very pompous way of saying that the woman you went off to see in Berlin said we have a mole in the office?'

'Yes, it's a pompous way of saying that.'

'And you believe her, Bernard? A mole? Who do you think it might be?'

'I don't believe her, but it should be followed up.'

'So why not tell Mr Cruyer. . . . My God, you don't think it's Dicky Cruyer, do you?'

I played it down, of course. 'The woman is not a very high-ranking source. She's just a low-grade radio operator. It's a matter of code words and radio procedures. Even if she's told us the whole truth, there could easily be some other explanation.'

Gloria was still looking at me and waiting for an answer. 'No, it's not Dicky,' I said. 'But it's no good talking to him about it. Dicky doesn't want to get involved. I've mentioned it to him, but he doesn't want to know.'

Of course, she couldn't resist the temptation to play spies. Who can resist it? I can't. 'What if his indifference is simply a cover?' she said, like a child guessing the answer to a riddle.

'No. He's too busy with his clubs and his expense-account lunches and his girlfriends to have time for his work, let alone being a double.'

'But what if . . .?'

'Look, sweetheart. How many times have you taken a pile of work in to Dicky and had him tell you to bring it straight across to me, without even going through it to see what was there?'

'I see what you mean,' she said.

'Don't sound so disappointed,' I said. 'No, it's not Dicky. The chances are, it's not anyone.'

'But if there was someone, that someone would be in the German Section?'

'Yes. I think so.'

'So it's Bret.' She was quick.

'It's probably not anyone.'

'But it's Bret you're concerned about. Your request to go over to the Cabinet Office and ask questions would have to go through Bret. It's him you want to avoid, isn't it?'

'For the time being, yes.'

'But that's absurd, darling. Bret is . . . well, he's . . .'

'He's so honourable. I know. That's what everyone says. I'm getting sick of hearing about how honourable he is.'

'Do you have anything else that points to Bret?'

'Some silly little things. A man in Berlin reckons that when Bret went there many years ago, he dismantled the networks we were running to the Russian Zone.'

'And did he do that?'

'I don't know.'

She hugged me and rested her head against my cheek. 'Don't be stupid, darling,' she whispered. 'I know you too well. You must have double-checked that one in the archives. How could you resist it. And you were in there only yesterday.'

'The official explanation is that Bret was expediting the denazification programme in line with top-level Anglo-American agreements of that time.'

'And do you believe that's what Bret was doing?'

'Bret was sent to Berlin to do a job. I can't find any evidence that he did anything wrong.'

'But he has lots of little bits of mud sticking to him?'

'That's right,' I said.

'And now there's something else,' she said. 'A bigger piece of mud?'

'What makes you think so?'

'Because so far there's nothing that would account for you wanting to talk to the Cabinet Office staff.'

'Yes,' I said. 'Something else has come up. I've got hold of one of our secret documents. . . . It's suggested that it's come from Moscow.'

'And you've got it?'

'A photocopy,' I said.

'And you haven't told anyone at the office? That's awfully dangerous, Bernard. Even I know that you can go to prison for that.'

'Who should I tell?'

'And it points at Bret?'

'Even if there was a leak, it's not necessarily one of the staff. We lose papers by theft and accident. Material goes astray and winds up on the other side.'

'If you did find something against Bret, it wouldn't be difficult to convince Morgan . . . he'd use any little thing to roast Bret. He hates him, you know. They had an argument the other day. Do you know about it?'

'Yes, I know.'

'Morgan is determined to bring Bret Rensselaer down.'

'Well, I don't want to help Morgan do that. But I have to follow this line to wherever it leads. I don't like Cabinet memos being sent to newspapers and I don't like them going directly to Moscow either.'

'What do you want to find out?'

'I want to talk to someone who knows how the Cabinet Office works. Someone who knows how their paperwork circulates.'

'I know a woman in the chief whip's office. She's nice and she knows everyone. There'll be no problem. She could tell you all that. That would be easier than the Cabinet Office.'

'Look at Billy explaining about the engine to Sally. He looks like an old man, doesn't he?'

'Of course he doesn't,' she said. 'How sweet the children are together.'

'We mustn't be late at Mario's; they get crowded at lunchtime on Saturday.'

'Relax. Mario won't turn you away,' she said. 'But take it easy on that *pappardelle* you keep eating. You're getting plump, darling.'

It was only a matter of time. The urge to reform the male is something no woman can resist. I said, '*Pappardelle con lepre* – they only have it in winter. And they run out of it if you're late.'

'Did I say plump?' she said. 'I meant big. Have two lots, Bernard. I like my men colossal.'

I aimed a playful blow at her, but she was ready for it and jumped aside.

It was still raining when we came out of the Science Museum. There are never any taxicabs available in Exhibition Road at midday on Saturday, they are all working the West End or the airport or taking a day off. Mario's is not very far, but we were all rather wet by the time we arrived.

Mario was there, of course; laughing, shouting and doing a lot of those things I don't like the school kids doing when they're in the museums. We always went to Mario's to eat; that's not quite true, of course – not always but often. There were lots of reasons. I'd known Mario for ages – everyone in London knew him – but his new restaurant had only just opened by the time Fiona defected. I'd never been there with her; it had no unhappy memories for me. And I liked Mario. And I couldn't help remembering the time that little Billy had vomited all over his lovely tiled floor and Mario had laughed and made no fuss about it. They don't make people like Mario any more, or if they do, they're not running restaurants.

The children ordered *spaghetti carbonara* followed by chicken. It was their regular favourite. Gloria thought I was a bad influence on their eating habits but, as I always pointed out to her, they never demanded salad when I had salad.

When I ordered the *pappardelle* it was Gloria who said, 'Give him a big portion; he hasn't eaten for a couple of days.'

Mario's face was inscrutable, but I said, 'Mario knows that's not true. I had lunch here yesterday with Dicky Cruyer.'

'You swine,' said Gloria. 'You told me you were going to diet.'

'I had to come,' I said. 'It was work. And Dicky was paying.'

Billy went off to the toilet. Mario had imported the urinals at tremendous expense from Mexico, and Billy liked to check them out whenever he visited the place.

Sally went with Mario to choose an avocado for Gloria. Sally considered herself a connoisseur of avocados. It was while we were on our own that Gloria said, 'Is Dicky Cruyer having an affair with your sister-in-law?'

'Not as far as I know,' I said truthfully, although not totally truthfully since George had told me she might be. 'Why?'

'I saw them in a Soho restaurant that night when my father took me to dinner to quiz me about why I wasn't sleeping at home at weekends.'

'It couldn't have been Tessa,' I said. 'She won't eat anywhere except at the Savoy.'

'Don't be flippant,' she said. She grinned and tried to slap my hand, but I pulled it away so that she made the cutlery jingle. 'Answer me. Am I right?'

'What did your father say that evening? You never told me about it.'

'Why don't you just answer my question?' she said.

'Why don't you answer *my* question?' I replied.

She sighed. 'I should never have fallen in love with a spy.'

'Ex-spy,' I said. 'I've given up spying a long time ago.'

'You never do anything else,' she said. It was a joke, but it wasn't a joke.

We had to go out to dinner – to George and Tessa Kosinski's – that evening. But you can't go out to dinner after rain has reduced your hair to rat-tails. It was a special event, their housewarming, and we'd promised to go; but Gloria wailed that she couldn't. That was the predicament that faced us that Saturday afternoon. Had my wife, Fiona, ever been so childish and petulant, I would have dismissed such protests angrily, or at least with bad-tempered sarcasm. But Gloria was little more than a child, and I found the manner in which she treated such minor incidents as crises both silly and funny. How wonderful to be so young, and so unaware of the terror that the real world holds, that disarrayed hair can bring tears. How gratifying when one quick phone call and the price of a repair job at a crimping salon in Sloane Street can bring such a gasp of joy.

And if you'd told me that my reactions were the sign of a fundamental flaw in our relationship, if you'd told me that these aspects of my love affair with her were only what could be expected when a man of forty falls in love with a woman young enough to be his daughter, I'd have agreed with you. I worried about it constantly and yet I always ended up asking myself whether such elements of paternalism weren't to be found everywhere. Maybe not in every happy marriage, but certainly in every blissful affair.

I was still careful, not to say wary, about the places I took her to and the people we mixed with. Not that I had an infinity of choices. A man without a wife discovers all kinds of things about his friends. When my wife first left me I'd expected that all my friends and acquaintances would be inviting me out – I'd heard so many wives complaining about how difficult it was to find that 'extra man' for dinner. But it doesn't work like that; at least, it didn't for me. A man separated from his lawful wife becomes a leper overnight. People – that is to say one's married friends – act as if a broken marriage is some kind of disease that might prove contagious. They avoid you, the party invitations dry up, the phone doesn't ring, and when you finally do get an invitation, you're likely to find yourself entertained alone on an evening when their attractive teenage daughters are not in the house.

The Kosinski's housewarming party was amusing enough. I suspected that this was a result of practice, for it was rumoured that George and Tessa were staging a series of such gatherings and representing each as the one and only. But the evening was none the worse for that. The guests, like the food, were decorative and very rich. The cooking was elaborate and the wines were old and rare. Tessa was amusing and George was friendly in a way that suggested that he liked to see me with Gloria; perhaps seeing us together removed any last feelings he had about me coveting his wife.

George's Mayfair flat was a glittering display of tasteful extravagance. The old Victorian dining table that had once belonged to George's poor immigrant parents was the only modest item of furniture to be seen. And yet this long table, so necessary for a big family and now fully extended, provided George with a chance to play host to sixteen guests with enough room at each place setting for three large polished wine glasses, lots of solid-silver knives and forks, and a big damask napkin. The other guests were a glamorous mixture that emphasized the different worlds in which George and Tessa moved: a bald stockbroker who, sniffing the claret admiringly, dropped his monocle into it; a heavily lacquered TV actress who would eat only vegetables; a Japanese car designer who drank nothing but brandy; a grey-haired woman who looked like a granny, ate everything, and drank everything and turned out to be a particularly fearless rally driver; a Horse Guards subaltern with shrill young deb; and two girls who owned a cooking school and had sent a prize student to cook for Tessa that evening.

None of the women – not even the gorgeous Tessa, flaunting a new green-silk dress that was all pleats and fringe – could compare with mine. Gloria's hair was perfect, and she wore a choker of pearls and a very low-cut white dress that was tight-fitting enough to do justice to her wonderful figure. I watched her all the evening as she effortlessly charmed everyone, and I knew beyond a doubt that I was seriously in love with her. Like all such London dinner parties it ended rather

early and we were home and undressing for bed before midnight. We
didn't read.

It was dark. I looked at the radio clock and saw that it was three-
twenty in the morning as I became fully awake. I'd been sleeping
badly for some time. I had a recurring dream in which I was swept
away in the filthy swirl of some wide tropical river – I could see the
palm trees along the distant banks – and as I drowned I choked on
the oily scum. And as I choked I woke up.

'Are you all right?' said Gloria sleepily.

'I'm all right.'

'I heard you coughing. You always cough when you wake up in
the night like this.' She switched on the light.

'It's a dream I have sometimes.'

'Since that boy Mackenzie was killed.'

'Maybe,' I said.

'No maybe about it,' she said. 'You told me that yourself.'

'Switch the light off. I'll be all right now. I'll go back to sleep.'

I tried to sleep, but it was no use. Gloria was awake too, and after
more time had passed she said, 'Is it about Bret? Are you worrying
about Bret?'

'Why should I worry about him?'

'You know what I mean.'

'I know what you mean.' It was dark. I wanted a cigarette very
badly, but I was determined not to start smoking again. Anyway
there were no cigarettes in the house.

'Do you want to tell me about it?'

'Not particularly,' I replied.

'Because I might be the mole?'

I laughed. 'No, not because you might be the mole,' I said. 'You've
only been in the Department five minutes. You're very recently
vetted. And with a Hungarian father you'd get a specially careful
scrutiny. You're not the mole.'

'Then tell me.'

'The Cabinet memo that ended up in Moscow was about the
security of certain very sensitive British establishments in West
Germany. The Prime Minister had asked how secure they were, and
some bright spark got the idea of asking us to attempt penetrations
of them. So that's what we eventually did. We assigned reliable people
in West Germany to target those establishments. Operation Vitamin
they called it. Then there was a report compiled so that security could
be improved.'

'So what?'

'It was a looney idea, but they say the PM liked the report. It was written up like an adventure story. It was simple. So simple that even the politicians could understand it. No one over here liked it, of course. The D-G was against it all along. He said we were creating a dangerous precedent. He was frightened that we'd be continually asked to waste our resources checking out the security of our overseas installations.'

'What then?'

'MI5 were furious. Even though it was all done overseas, they felt we were treading on their toes. The Defence Ministry made a fuss too. They said they had enough problems keeping the Communists and protesters out without us making trouble for them too. And they said that the existence of that report constituted a security risk. It was a blueprint for Moscow, an instruction manual telling anyone how to breach our most secret installations.'

'And Bret signed the Vitamin report?'

'I didn't say that.' There *were* cigarettes in the house; there was an unopened packet of twenty Benson & Hedges that someone had left on the hall table. I'd put them in the drawer there.

'You didn't have to say it.'

'See why it's important? My wife saw the memo probably, but the report was done after she'd gone. Moscow had the memo; but has Moscow seen the full report? We really must know.'

She switched the light on and got out of bed. She was wearing a blue nightdress with a lacy top and lots of tiny silk bows. 'Would you like a cup of tea? It wouldn't take a minute.' The dim glow from the bedside lamp made a golden rim around her. She was very desirable.

'It might wake up the children and Nanny.' Maybe one cigarette wouldn't start me off again.

'Even if the report did get to Moscow, it might not have been Bret Rensselaer's fault.'

'His fault or not his fault, if that report got to Moscow the blame will be placed on Bret.'

'That's not right.'

'Yes it is. Not fair, you mean? Maybe not, but he masterminded our end of the Vitamin operation. Any breach in its security will be his, and this one could be the end of Bret's career in the Department.' Damn. Now I remembered giving the cigarettes to the plumber who fixed the immersion heater. I'd had no money for a tip for him.

She said, 'I'll make tea; I'd like a cup myself.' She was very close to me, standing in front of the mirror. She glanced at her reflection as she straightened her hair and smoothed her rumpled nightdress. It was thin, almost transparent, and the light was shining through it.

'Come here, duchess,' I said. 'I don't feel like tea just yet.'

12

My Department has been called a 'ministry without a minister'. That description is never used by our own staff. It's a description applied to us by envious civil servants suffering at the hands of their own political masters. In any case, it isn't true. Such a condition would equate the D-G with the career permanent secretaries who head up other departments, and permanent secretaries leave when aged sixty. One glance at the D-G and you'd know he was far, far over that hill, and there was still no sign of him departing.

Though in the sense that we didn't have a political boss, that fanciful description was true. But we had something worse; we had the Cabinet Office, and that was not a place I cared to tread uninvited. So I gladly accepted Gloria's suggestion that her friend in the government chief whip's office would answer all my questions about the distribution of Cabinet paperwork.

Downing Street is, of course, not a street of houses. It's all one house – that is to say it's all part of one big block of government offices, so that you can walk right through it to the Horse Guards, or maybe even to the Admiralty if you know your way upstairs and downstairs and through the maze of corridors.

Number Twelve, where the Whip's Office was situated, was quiet. In the old days, when the socialists were running things, you could always count on meeting someone entertaining over there. Obscure party officials from distant provincial constituencies, trade-union leaders swapping funny stories between mouthfuls of beer or whisky and ham sandwiches, the air full of smoke and slander.

It was more sedate nowadays. The PM didn't like smoking, and Gloria's friend, Mrs Hogarth, had only weak tea and ginger biscuits to offer. She was about forty, an attractive red-haired woman with Christian Dior spectacles and a hand-knitted cardigan with a frayed elbow.

She took me into one of the rather grand panelled offices at the back, explaining that her own office in the basement was cramped. She normally used this one when the politicians were on holiday, and that meant for much of the year. She gave me tea and a comfortable chair and took her place behind the desk.

'Any of the lobby correspondents could tell you that,' she said, in answer to my question about who saw Cabinet memos. 'It's not a secret.'

'I don't know any lobby correspondents,' I said.

'Don't you?' she said, examining me with real interest for the first time. 'I would have thought you'd have known a lot of them.'

I smiled awkwardly. It was not a compliment. I had a feeling she'd smelled the whisky on my breath. Through the window behind her there was a fine view of the Prime Minister's garden and beyond its wall the parade ground of the Horse Guards, where certain very privileged officials had parked their cars.

'I haven't got a lot of time for chatting,' she said. 'People think we've got nothing to do over here when the House isn't sitting, but I'm awfully busy. I always am.' She smiled as if confessing to some shameful failing.

'It's good of you to help me, Mrs Hogarth,' I said.

'It's all part of my job,' she said. She measured one spoon of sugar into her tea, stirred very gently so it didn't spill, and then drank some unhurriedly. 'Cabinet memos.' She looked at the photocopy I'd given her and read some of it. 'There were eight copies of this one. I remember it, as a matter of fact.'

'Could you tell me who got them?' I said. I dipped my biscuit into my tea before eating it. I wanted to see how she'd take it.

She saw me, but looked away hurriedly and became engrossed in her notepad. 'One for the Prime Minister, of course; one for the Foreign Secretary; one for the Home Secretary; one for Defence; one for the leader of the Commons; one for the government chief whip; one for the Lords; one for the Cabinet secretary.'

'Eight?' Two men had come into the garden carrying roses still wrapped in the nursery packing in a large box. One of them kneeled down and prodded the soil with a trowel. Then he put some of the soil into his hand and touched it to see how wet it was.

Mrs Hogarth swung round to see what I was looking at. 'It's a wonderful view in the summer,' she said. 'All roses. The PM's very fond of them.'

'It's a bit late to be planting roses,' I said.

'It's been too wet,' she said. She turned to watch the men. 'I planted some in November, but they're not doing well at all. Mind you, I live in Cheam – there's a lot of clay in the soil where I live.' The gardeners decided that the soil was right for planting roses. One of them started to dig a line of holes to put them in, while the second man produced bamboo canes to support the rosebushes that were already established.

Mrs Hogarth coughed to get my attention again. 'This memo was drafted by the Defence Ministry. I don't know who did it, but junior ministers will have seen it in the early stages. Perhaps it was drafted many times. That could add up.'

'I'm interested in who saw the document or a copy of it,' I said.

'Well, let's look at what might have happened to those eight copies of the memo,' she said briskly. 'In each minister's private office there is his principal private secretary plus one or two bright young men. Additionally, there will be an executive officer and a couple of clerical officers.'

'Would all those people normally see a memo like this?'

'Certainly the PPS would read it. And one of the clerical staff, or perhaps an executive officer, will file it. It depends how keen and efficient the others are. I think you should assume that all of the people in each minister's private office would have a good idea of the content, just in case the minister started shouting for it and they had to find it.'

'Sounds like a lot of people,' I said. The gardeners were lining up the newly planted roses, using a piece of white string.

'We're not finished yet. The Cabinet Office, the Home Office and the Foreign Office would all have executive responsibilities arising from this document.'

'Not the Home Office,' I corrected her gently.

'That's not the way they'd see it,' she said. Obviously, she too had had dealings with the Home Office, who assumed executive responsibility over everyone and everything.

'You're right,' I said. 'Please go on.'

'So in those departments the memo would go to the permanent secretary, and to his private office, and then to the appropriate branch to be dealt with.'

'Two more administrative officials and at least one executive or clerical officer,' I said.

'In the Cabinet Office add one private secretary and one executive or clerical officer. From there to the Defence Secretariat, which would mean three administrators and one executive or clerical officer.'

'It's quite a crowd,' I said.

'It adds up.' She drank some tea.

A man came in through the door. 'I didn't know you were in here, Mabel. I was just going to use the phone.' Then he caught sight of me. 'Oh, hello, Samson,' he said.

'Hello, Pete,' I said. He was a baby-faced thirty-year-old, with light-brown wavy hair and a pale complexion upon which his cheeks seemed artificially reddened. For all his Whitehall attire – pinstripe trousers and black jacket – Pete Barrett was a very ambitious career policeman who'd taken a law degree at night school. He'd adapted to local costume in just the way I would have expected when I'd first met him about five years earlier. Barrett was a Special Branch man who'd been desperate to get into the Department. He'd failed to do so and despite this soft job he'd found, he was bitter about it.

'Is that man bothering you, Mrs Hogarth?' he enquired with his ponderous humour. He was cautious about baiting me, but it was a diffidence laced with contempt. He went round to the window, looked out at the garden as if he might be checking on the gardeners, and then looked at the papers on the desk. She closed the spiral notebook in which she'd been doing her figuring. It had a double red stripe on the cover; such notebooks are for classified information with all the pages numbered.

She kept her hand on the closed notebook. 'A routine enquiry,' she answered, in a studied attempt to discourage his interest.

But he was not to be deterred. 'A routine enquiry?' He gave a forced chuckle. 'That sounds like Scotland Yard, Mabel. That sounds like what I'm supposed to say.' He leaned forward to read the document on the desk in front of her. He held his tie against his chest so that it wouldn't fall against her. This stiff posture, hand flat on chest, his wavy hair and red cheeks made him look more than ever like a puppet.

'If you're after tea, you're unlucky. My girl is off sick, I made it myself this afternoon. And my ginger biscuits are all finished.'

Barrett didn't respond to this at all. In other circumstances I would have told him to go away in no uncertain terms, but this was his territory and I had no authority to be asking questions here. And I could think of no convincing reason for having this copy of the memo. Furthermore I had the feeling that Barrett had known I was in the room before coming in.

'A Cabinet memo no less,' he said. He looked at me and said, 'What exactly is the problem, Bernie?'

'Just passing the time,' I said.

He stood upright, a puppet on parade now, chin tucked in and shoulders held well back. He looked at me. 'You're on my patch now,' he said with mock severity. Outside, the two gardeners had dug the line of holes for the roses, but one of them was looking up at the sky as if he'd felt a spot of rain.

'It's nothing you'd be interested in,' I said.

'My office received no notice that you were coming,' he said.

Mrs Hogarth was watching me. She was biting her lip, but I don't know whether this was in anger or anxiety.

'You know the drill, Bernie,' he persisted. 'A Cabinet memo . . . that's a serious line of enquiry.'

Mrs Hogarth stopped biting her lip and said, 'I wish you'd stop reading the papers on my desk, Mr Barrett.' She put the photocopy memo I'd given her into the tray with other papers. 'That particular paper was nothing to do with my visitor and I find your reading it aloud a most embarrassing breach of security.'

Barrett went red. 'Oh . . .' he said. 'Oh. Oh, I see.'

'Use the phone next door. There's no one in there. I really must get on now. Perhaps you're not busy, but I am.'

'Yes, of course,' said Barrett. 'I'll see you around, Bernie.'

I didn't answer.

'And please shut the door,' Mrs Hogarth called after him.

'Sorry,' he said as he came back to close it.

'Now where were we,' she said. 'Ah, yes: Number Ten. Here in Number Ten such a memo would be handled by two private secretaries. And one executive or clerical officer must have seen it. And I think you should consider the possibility that the press office and policy unit were interested enough to read it. That would be quite normal.'

'I'm losing track.'

'I have a note of it. I haven't added the Defence Ministry people. . . .' She paused for a moment to write something on her pad, murmuring as she wrote, '. . . private office, let's say two; permanent secretary's office, another two . . . and policy branch, plus clerical. Let's say eleven at the Defence Ministry.'

'Eleven at the Defence Ministry? But they had no executive action.'

'Don't you think they would want to notify their units in an effort to keep these SIS intruders out?'

'Yes, I suppose they might. But they shouldn't have done it. That wasn't the idea at all. The plan was intended to test the security.'

'Don't be silly. This is Whitehall. This is politics. This is power. The Defence Ministry is not going to stand there and wait patiently and do nothing while you cut their balls off.' She saw the surprise in my face. She smiled. She was a surprising lady. 'And if you're going to do a thorough investigation, you must take into account that some ministers have private secretaries who would handle all papers that cross their ministers' desks. And the way that papers are filed in a registry sometimes means that the registry clerks handle them too.'

'It's a hell of a lot of people,' I said. 'So even the most secret secrets are not very secret.'

'I'm sure I don't have to mention that papers like this are left on desks and are sometimes seen by visitors to the various offices as well as by the staff. And I haven't included your own staff who handled this particular one.' She tapped the photocopy lightly with her fingertips.

'That particular one? What do you mean?'

'Well, this is a photocopy of the Cabinet secretary's copy. You knew that, didn't you?'

'No, I didn't. The number and date have been blanked out. How can you tell?'

She took a biscuit and nibbled it to gain time. 'I'm not sure if I'm permitted to tell you that,' she said.

'It's an investigation, Mrs Hogarth.'

'I suppose it's all right, but I can't give you the details. I can only tell you that when sensitive material like this is circulated, the word processor is used so that the actual wording of its text is changed. Just the syntax, you understand; the meaning is not affected. It's a precaution . . .'

'So that if a newspaper prints a quote from it, the actual copy can be identified.'

'That's the idea. They don't talk about that very much, of course.'

'Of course. And this is the one that went to the Cabinet Office?'

'Yes. I wouldn't have wasted your time with all that detail if I'd known that's all you wanted. I naturally thought you'd photocopied your own copy and were trying to trace one that had been stolen.' She passed the photocopy to me.

'It's natural that you'd think that,' I said as I put it back into my pocket. 'It was stupid of me not to make it all clear.'

'Oh yes, that's made from your Department's copy,' said Mrs Hogarth.

She got to her feet, but for a moment I sat there, slowly coming to terms with the idea that the document Bret Rensselaer had been given for action was the one copied for Moscow's KGB archives. I'd gone on hoping that her answer would be different, but now I would have to look the facts straight in the eye.

'I'll come with you to the door,' she prompted. 'We're getting very security conscious nowadays. Would you like to go out through the Number Ten door? Most people do, it's rather fun, isn't it?'

'You're quite certain?' I said. 'No chance you've got it wrong?'

'No chance at all. I checked it twice against my list. I can't show it to you, I'm afraid, but I could get one of the security people to confirm it. . . .'

'No need for that,' I said.

It was raining now and the gardeners had abandoned the idea of planting the roses. They'd put the plants back into their box and were heading towards the house for shelter.

Mrs Hogarth watched them sorrowfully. 'It happens every time they start on the garden. It's almost like a rainmaking ceremony.'

In the front hall of Number Ten there was a bored-looking police inspector, a woman in an overall distributing cups of tea from a tray, and a man who opened the door for me while holding his tea in one hand. 'I appreciate your help, Mrs Hogarth,' I said. 'I'm sorry about not having the official chit.'

She shook hands as I went out onto that famous doorstep and said, 'Don't worry about the chit. I have it already. It came over this morning.'

13

'It's our anniversary,' said Gloria.

'Is it?' I said.

'Don't sound so surprised, darling. We've been together exactly three months tomorrow.'

I didn't know from what event she'd started counting, but out of delicacy I didn't enquire. 'And they said it wouldn't last,' I said.

'Don't make jokes about us,' she said anxiously. 'I don't mind what jokes you make about me, but don't joke about us.'

We were in the sitting room of an eleventh-floor flat near Notting Hill Gate, a residential district of mixed races and lifestyles on the west side of central London. It was eight-thirty on a Monday evening. We were dancing very very slowly in that old-fashioned way in which you clasped each other tight. The radio was tuned to Alan Dell's BBC programme of big-band jazz, and he was playing an old Dorsey recording of 'Tea for Two'. She was letting her hair grow longer. It was a pale-gold colour and now it was breaking over her shoulders. She wore a dark-green ribbed polo-neck sweater, with a chunky necklace and a light-brown suede skirt. It was all very simple, but with her long legs and generous figure the effect was stunning.

I looked around the room: gilded mirror, silk-lined lamp-shades, electric-candle wall lights and red velvet hangings. The hi-fi was hidden behind a row of fake books. It was the same elaborate clutter of vaguely nineteenth-century brothel furnishings that's to be seen in every High Street furniture shop throughout Britain. The curtains were open, and it was better to look through the window and see the glittering patterns of London by night. And I could see us reflected in the windows, dancing close.

Erich Stinnes was thirty minutes overdue. He was to stay here, with Ted Riley in the role of 'minder'. Upstairs, where Stinnes would spend most of his time, there was a small bedroom and study, and a rather elaborate bathroom. It was a departmental house, not exactly a 'safe house' but one of the places used for the clandestine accommodation of overseas departmental employees. It was the policy that such people were not brought into the offices of London Central. Some of them didn't even know where our offices were.

I had come here to greet Stinnes on his arrival, double-check that Ted Riley was in attendance, and take Stinnes out to dinner to celebrate the new 'freedom' he'd been so reluctantly granted. Gloria was with me because I'd convinced Bret, and myself, that her presence would make Stinnes more relaxed and soften him up for the new series of interrogations that were planned.

'What happened about that chit for Number Ten?' I said as we danced. 'Your friend over there said she'd already had one. How could she have got a chit? I didn't even apply for one.'

'I told her a tale of woe. I said that after it was all signed and approved I'd lost it. I told her that I'd get the sack if she didn't cover for me.'

'You wicked girl,' I said.

'There's so much paperwork. If we didn't bend the rules now and again, we'd never get everything done.' As we danced she reached out and stroked my head. I didn't like being stroked like a pet poodle, but I didn't complain. She was only a child and I suppose such corny little manifestations of endearment were what she thought appropriate to her role as a femme fatale. I wondered what she'd really like *me* to do – bury her in long-stem red roses and ravish her on a sable rug in front of a log fire in the mountains, with gypsy violins in an adjoining room?

'You're worrying about Bret Rensselaer, aren't you?' she asked softly.

'You're always saying that, and I'm always replying that I don't give a damn about him.'

'You're worried about what you discovered,' she said. She accepted my little bursts of bad temper with equanimity. I wondered if she realized how much I loved her for doing that.

'I'd feel a hell of a lot better without having discovered it,' I admitted. The music came to an end and there was some chat about trumpet and the tenor-sax solos before the next record started: Count Basie playing 'Moonglow'. She threw her head back, twisting her head so that her long pale hair flashed in the light. We began dancing again.

'What are you going to do about it? Report it?' she asked.

'There's not much I can report. It's all very slight and circumstantial except for the Cabinet memo, and I'm not going to stride into the D-G's office and report that. They'll want to know why I didn't report it when I first got it. They'll ask who gave it to me, and I don't want to tell them. And they'll start digging deep into all kinds of things. And meanwhile I'll be suspended from duty.'

'Why not tell them who gave it to you?'

'All my sources of information and goodwill would dry up overnight if I blew one of them. Can you imagine what sort of grilling Morgan would arrange for the man who'd got hold of Bret's copy of the memo?'

'In order to get rid of Rensselaer?'

'Yes, to get rid of Rensselaer.'

'He must be a wonderful man, your contact,' she said wistfully. I hadn't told her anything about Posh Harry and she resented my secrecy.

'He's a slippery bastard,' I said. 'But I wouldn't deliver him to Morgan.'

'It might be him or you,' she said with that ruthless simplicity that women call feminine logic.

'It's not him or me yet. And it's not going to be him or me for a long time to come.'

'So you'll do nothing?'

'I haven't decided yet.'

'But how can it be Bret?' she asked. It was the beginning of the same circle of questions that whirled round in my head day and night. 'Bret takes your advice all the time. He's even agreed to moving Stinnes here from Berwick House at your suggestion.'

'Yes, he has,' I said.

'And you're having second thoughts about his coming here. I know you are. Are you worried that Bret might try to kill him or something?'

'At Berwick House they have guards and alarms and so on. They're not installed there solely to keep the inmates in; they keep nasty people out.'

'So send him back there.'

'He'll be here any minute.'

'Send him back tomorrow.'

'How can I do that? Think what a damned fool I'd look going into Bret's office, cap in hand, to tell him I've changed my mind about it.'

'And think what a damned fool you'd look if something happened to Stinnes.'

'I have thought about that,' I said with what I thought was masterful restraint.

She smiled. 'It *is* funny, darling. I'm sorry to laugh, but you have brought it on yourself by telling Bret how incompetent the Debriefing Centre staff are.'

'I'm wondering to what extent Bret manoeuvred me into that one,' I said.

She hooted. 'That'll be the day, beloved. When you're manoeuvred into one of your tirades.'

I smiled too. She was right, of course; I had walked right into this one, and the consequences were entirely of my own making.

She said, 'But if Bret is a KGB agent . . .'

'I've told you there's nothing . . .'

'But let's play "if",' she persisted. 'He's placed himself into a wonderful position of power.' She hesitated.

Her hesitation was because any conjecture about Bret and Stinnes inevitably made me look a fool. 'Go on,' I said.

'If Bret Rensselaer is a KGB agent, he's done everything just right. He's been pushed into taking over the Stinnes debriefing without showing any desire to get the job. Now he's going to isolate the best intelligence source we've had for years and do it at your suggestion. All the Stinnes intelligence will pass through him, and if anything goes wrong, he has you as the perfect scapegoat.' She looked at me but I didn't react. 'Suppose Bret Rensselaer knows you have the photocopy of that Cabinet memo? Did you think of that, Bernard? Maybe Moscow knows what's happened. If he's a KGB agent, they would have told him.'

'I did think of that,' I admitted.

'Oh, Bernard, darling. I'm so frightened.'

'There's nothing to be frightened about.'

'I'm frightened for you, darling.'

I heard the apartment front door bang and an exchange of voices as Ted Riley let Stinnes step past him into the hallway and then double-locked the door.

I let go of Gloria and said, 'Hello, Ted.'

Ted Riley said, 'Sorry we're late. Those bloody Berwick House people can't even understand their own paperwork.' He went across to the window and closed the curtains. Ted was right of course; I should have kept them closed when the lights were on. We were high in the sky and not overlooked, but a sniper's rifle could do the job all right. And Moscow would think Stinnes worth that kind of trouble.

Erich Stinnes watched us with solemn and sardonic respect. Even when he was introduced to Gloria his reaction was a polite smile and a bow in the German fashion. Over his grey suit he wore a stiffly new raincoat and a soft felt hat, its brim turned down all round in a way that made him look very foreign.

'You'll probably be anxious to get away to your gut-bash,' said Riley, throwing his coat onto a chair and looking at his watch.

'It won't be crowded,' I said. 'It's just a little family place.' Stinnes looked up, realizing that I was warning him not to expect a banquet. My available expenses did not extend to a lavish treat, and with Gloria along, the modest dinner for three was going to sound like a big dinner for two if I was going to reclaim it all.

Before we left I took Stinnes upstairs to show him his study. There was a small desk there with an electric typewriter and a pile of paper. On the wall there was a map of the world and over his desk a map of Russia. There was a shelf of assorted books – mostly Russian-language books including some fiction and English-Russian and English-German dictionaries. On his desk there was the current copy of *The Economist* and some English and German newspapers. There was a small shortwave radio receiver too, a Sony 2001 with preset and scan tuning. Instead of using batteries it was plugged into the mains via a power adapter and I warned him that if he unplugged it there was a danger that the adapter would burn out, but he seemed to know that already. Not surprising since the 2001 had long since been standard issue for KGB agents.

'Eventually you'll be able to go out alone,' I told him. 'But for the time being, Ted Riley will have to accompany you wherever you want to go. But if he says no, it's no. Ted's in charge.'

'You have gone to a lot of trouble, Samson,' Stinnes said as he surveyed the room. The suspicion that was to be seen in his eyes was in his voice too.

'It wasn't easy to arrange, so don't let me down,' I said. 'If you bolt, I'll get all the blame . . . all the blame.' I said it twice to emphasize the truth of it.

'I have no plans to bolt,' he said.

'Good,' I said, and we went downstairs to where Ted was unpacking his overnight bag and Gloria was holding the curtain aside, staring out at the London skyline. Bad security, but you can't live your entire life by rules and regulations. I know: I'd tried.

'We won't be late, Ted,' I promised.

Ted looked at Gloria who closed the curtains and put on her coat. Ted helped her into it. 'At midnight he turns into a frog,' he told her, indicating me with a movement of his head.

'Yes, I know, but he's seeing someone about it,' she said affably.

Ted laughed. He guessed that I'd asked for him to do this job and it seemed to have given him a new lease on life.

To entertain Erich Stinnes, my first choice would have been a German restaurant or, failing that, a place that served good Russian food. But London, almost alone among the world's great cities, has neither Russian nor German restaurants. Gloria suggested a Spanish place she knew in Soho, but my dislike of Spanish and Portuguese cooking is exceeded only by my dislike of the fiery stodge of Latin American. So we went to an Indian restaurant. Erich Stinnes needed guidance through the menu. It was an unusual admission; Stinnes was not the sort of man who readily admitted to needing assistance in any circumstance, but he was a great ladies' man and I could see he liked having Gloria describe to him the difference between the peppery *vindaloos* and the milder *kormas*. Gloria was what gossip columnists call a 'foodie': she liked talking about food and discussing restaurants and recipes even more than she liked eating. So I let her order the whole spread, from the thick puree of *dhal* to crispy fried *papadoms* and the big bowl of boiled rice that comes decorated with nuts and dried fruit and edible bits of something that looks like silver paper.

I watched them, heads close together, as they went muttering their way through the long menu. For a moment I felt a pang of jealousy. Suppose Erich Stinnes was a KGB plant – I'd never entirely dismissed the idea, even when he was at his most cooperative – then what an extra laugh for Fiona if I lost my girlfriend to one of her field agents. Gloria was fascinated by him, I could see that. It was strange that this sallow-complexioned man with his hard face and balding head could attract women so effortlessly. It was his evident energy, of course, but now and again, when he thought I wasn't observing him, I could see signs of that energy flagging. Stinnes was growing tired. Or old. Or frightened. Or maybe all three. I knew the feeling.

We drank beer. I preferred an Indian meal partly because no one was expected to drink anything strong with a curry. This wasn't going to be the right time to get Stinnes boozed to the point of indiscretion. And it wasn't going to be the right expense account either. At this first outing, Stinnes would be wary of such tactics, but his first sip of the fizzy water that the British call lager allayed all such fears. He pursed his lips in distaste, but didn't complain about the watery beer or anything else.

The decor was typical of such places: red-flock wallpaper and a dark-blue ceiling painted with stars. But the food was good enough, flavoured with ginger and paprika and the milder spices. Erich Stinnes seemed to enjoy it. He sat against the wall with Gloria next to him, and although he supplied his due amount of small talk, his eyes moved constantly, looking to see whether any of the other customers, or even staff, looked like departmental employees. That's the way Moscow would have done it; they always have watchers to watch the watchers.

We had been talking about books. 'Erich likes reading the Bible,' I announced for no real reason other than to keep the conversation going.

'Is that true?' she said, turning to Erich Stinnes.

Before he could answer, I explained, 'He was with Section 44 back in the old days.'

'Do you know what that is?' he asked her.

'The KGB's Religious Affairs Bureau,' she said. It wasn't easy to catch her out; she knew her way around the files. 'But I don't know exactly what they do.'

'I'll tell you something they do,' I said to her, ignoring the presence of Stinnes for a moment. 'They desecrate graves and spray swastikas on the walls of synagogues in NATO countries so that the Western press can make headlines speculating about the latest upsurge of neo-Nazi activity and get a few extra votes for the left-wingers.'

I watched Stinnes, wondering if he'd deny such outrages. 'Sometimes,' he said gravely. 'Sometimes.'

I'd finished eating, but now she picked up a crisp *papadom* I'd not eaten and nibbled at it. 'Do you mean you've become a dedicated Christian?'

'I'm not a dedicated anything,' said Stinnes. 'But one day I will write a book comparing the medieval Church to applied Marxist-Leninism.'

This was just the sort of talk she liked: an intellectual discussion, not the bourgeois chitchat, office gossip, and warmed-up chunks of *The Economist* that I served her. 'For instance?' she said. She furrowed her brow; she looked very young and very beautiful in the dim restaurant lighting, or was that British lager stronger than I thought.

'The medieval Church and the Communist state share four basic dictums,' he said. 'First and foremost comes the instruction to seek the life of the spirit: seek pure Marxism. Don't waste your efforts on other trivial things. Gain is avarice, love is lust, beauty is vanity.' He looked round at us. 'Two: Communists are urged to give service to the state, as Christians must give it to the Church – in a spirit of humility and devotion, not in order to serve themselves or to become a success. Ambition is bad: it is the result of sinful pride . . .'

'But you haven't . . .' said Gloria.

'Let me go on,' said Stinnes quietly. He was enjoying himself. I think it was the first time I'd seen him looking really happy. 'Three: both Church and Marx renounce money. Investment and interest payments are singled out as the worst of evils. Four, and this is the most important similarity, there is the way in which the Christian faithful are urged to deny themselves all the pleasures of this world to get their reward in paradise after they die.'

'And Communists?' she asked.

He smiled a hard close-lipped smile. 'If *they* work hard and deny themselves the pleasures of this world, then after they die their children will grow up in paradise,' said Stinnes. He smiled again.

'Very good,' said Gloria admiringly. There wasn't much left on the plates or dishes that covered the table. I'd already had enough to eat – a little curry goes a long way with me – so she picked up the dish of chicken *korma* and divided the last of it onto their two plates.

Stinnes took the dishes of the rice and the eggplant and, when I declined, divided the food between them.

'You missed out number five,' I said, while they were tucking into their final helpings. Both of them looked at me as if they'd forgotten I was there with them. 'Victory over the flesh. Both Church and Communist state preach that.'

I was serious, but Gloria dismissed it. 'Very funny,' she said. She wiped her lips with the napkin. To Stinnes she said, 'Was the Church *very* opposed to capitalism? I know it objected to loaning money and collecting interest, but it wasn't opposed to trading.'

'You're wrong,' said Stinnes. 'The medieval Church preached against any sort of free competition. All craftsmen were forbidden to improve tools or change their methods lest they take advantage of their neighbours. They were forbidden to undersell; goods had to be offered at a fixed price. And the Church objected to advertising, especially if any trader compared his goods with inferior goods offered by another trader at the same price.'

'It sounds familiar,' said Gloria. 'Doesn't it, Bernard?' she asked, politely drawing me into the conversation as she looked into a tiny handbag-mirror to see that her lips were wiped clean of curry.

'Yes,' I said. '*Homo mercator vix aut numquam potest Deo placare* – a man who is a merchant will never be able to please God – or please the Party Congress. Or please the Trades Union Congress either.'

'Poor merchants,' said Gloria.

'Yes,' said Stinnes.

The waiter came over to our table and began clearing the dishes away. He offered us a selection of those very sweet Indian-style desserts, but no one wanted anything but coffee.

Stinnes waited until the table was completely cleared. It was as if this action prompted him to change the conversation: he leaned forward, arms on the table, and said, 'You were asking about code words . . . radio codes . . . two names for one agent.' He stopped there to give me time to shut him up if I didn't want Gloria to hear the rest of the conversation.

I told him to go on.

'I said it was impossible. Or at least unprecedented. But I've been thinking about it since then. . . .'

'And?' I said after a long pause during which the waiter put the coffee on the table.

'I told you it was nonsense, but now I think you may be correct. There was a line of intelligence material that I was not permitted to see. It was handled by our radio room, but it went directly to Moscow. None of my staff ever saw it.'

'Was that unusual?' I asked.

'Very unusual, but there seemed no reason to think that we were missing anything very good. I thought it was some Moscow deskman trying to make a name for himself by working on one narrow field of interest. Senior staff in Moscow do that sometimes; then suddenly – choosing their moment carefully – they produce a very thick file of new material and before the cheers die down they get the promotion they've had their eye on.'

'How did you find out about it?'

'It was kept separate, but it wasn't given any special high security rating. That might have been a very cunning idea – it didn't attract so much attention like that. People handling it would just have thought it applied to some boring technical file. How did I come across it? It came onto my desk by accident. It was the second of February of last year. I remember the date because it was my son's birthday. The decoded transcripts were put on my desk with a pile of other material. I looked through it to see what was there and found this stuff with an agent name I didn't recognize but a London coding. I thought it must be a mistake. I thought a typing error had given it the five-letter group for London. It's not often that the typists there make such an error, but it's not unknown. It was only last week that I remembered it in the light of what you were asking me about agents with two code names. Any use to you?'

'It might be,' I said. 'What else can you remember?'

'Nothing. Except that it was very long and it seemed to be about some sort of intelligence exercise that your people had carried out in West Germany.' He looked at me but I gave no reaction. 'You'd sent your own agents breaking into your data-gathering installations. Some sort of security report and a lot of electronics. . . . I can't understand electronics, can you?'

'No,' I said. So that was it. The long message couldn't be anything other than the full report for the PM that resulted from the Cabinet memo. Bret had supervised and signed that report. If Moscow's copy of the memo had come through Bret's hands – and I had Mrs Hogarth's evidence that it did – then it was reasonable to suppose that the full report that followed had also been supplied by Bret. My God, it was shattering, even when I was partly prepared for it. More shattering perhaps because when you begin to be convinced of something, you expect some damned law of averages to start providing a bit of contradictory evidence. Bret. Could it be true?

'You've gone very quiet,' said Stinnes.

'It's that damned *dhal*,' I said. 'It really slows me down.'

Gloria glanced at me. She said nothing, but she began looking through her handbag as if looking for something she'd mislaid. It was her attempt to appear bored by the conversation. Maybe Stinnes was fooled, but I doubt it.

14

The relaxed evening in the curry restaurant with Stinnes brought quick results. By the following Saturday morning I was drinking Bret Rensselaer's gin and tonics and listening to Bret's congratulations. The fact that Bret's congratulations were delivered in a way that could have an inattentive onlooker thinking he was singing his own praises did not distress me. First, because I was accustomed to Bret's habits and manners, and, secondly, because there were no onlookers.

'It sure paid off,' said Bret. 'Everything I said okay to paid off.' He was dressed in casual wear: dark open-neck sports shirt and white linen pants. I'd seldom seen Bret wearing anything other than his Savile Row suits, but then I'd seldom been honoured with an invitation to go to his Thames-side mansion in off-duty hours. Bret had his own circle of friends – minor aristocracy, international jet-setters, merchant bankers, and business tycoons. No one from the Department got regular invitations here except perhaps the D-G and the Deputy, and maybe the Cruyers if Bret needed a favour from the German desk. Other than that, the guest list was confined to a few particularly sexy girls from the office who got invited for the weekend to look at Bret's art collection.

I'd driven from London in dry weather with the sun shining through a gap of blue sky, but now the sky was clouding over and the colour drained from the landscape. From where I sat there was a view across a long lawn, brown after the harsh winter frosts, and then, at the bottom of his garden, the Thames. Here in Berkshire it was just a weedy stream a few yards across. Despite the river's huge loops, it was difficult to believe that we were in the Thames Valley, a short distance from London's dockland where oceangoing ships could navigate on these same waters.

Bret walked round the back of the sofa where I was sitting and poured more gin into my glass. It was a large room. Three soft, grey-leather sofas of modern Italian design were arranged round the glass-topped coffee table. There was an unpainted wooden fireplace where a log fire flickered and occasionally filled the room with a puff of wood smoke that made my eyes water. The walls were plain white to provide a background against which Bret's paintings could be seen at their best. One on each wall: a Bratby portrait, a Peter Blake pop-art bearded lady, a Hockney swimming pool and a wood abstract by Tilson over the fireplace. The best of British painters were there. It would have to be British for him; Bret was the sort of Anglophile who took it all seriously. Other than the sofas, the furniture was English, antique and expensive. There was a Regency chest of dark mahogany with a glass-domed skeleton clock on it, and a secretaire-bookcase behind whose glass doors some pieces of Minton porcelain were displayed. No books; all the books were in the library, a room Bret liked to preserve for his own exclusive use.

'The interrogator is pleased, of course. The D-G is pleased. Dicky Cruyer is pleased. Everyone is pleased, except perhaps the staff at London Debriefing Centre, but the D-G is smoothing things over with them. Some sort of letter congratulating them on their skilful preparation is the sort of thing I thought appropriate.'

Would this be a time when I could start cross-questioning Bret about his apparent involvement with the KGB? I decided not and drank some more gin and tonic. 'Good,' I said.

'In just two days Stinnes has given us enough to break a network that's operating out of the Ministry of Defence research laboratory at Cambridge. Apparently they've known there's been a leak for months and months, and this will provide a chance to clear that one up.'

'England?' I said. 'Cambridge, England? Hold the phone, Bret – we can't go into a KGB network operating in Britain. That's Home Office territory. That's MI5's job. They'll go ape.'

He went to the fire and squatted at it to prod the burning log with his fingertips. It made sparks. Then he wiped his fingers on a paper tissue before sinking into the soft leather opposite me. He smiled his wide, charming, Hollywood smile. It was a calculated gesture to make his explanation more dramatic. Everything he did was calculated, and he liked drama to the point of losing his temper with anyone in sight if the mood took him. 'We're legitimately holding Erich Stinnes. The Home Office have responded to the D-G's notification and agreed that we do some preliminary interrogations so that we can make sure that our own people are in the clear.'

'You mean hold him while I'm being investigated,' I said.

'Of course,' said Bret. 'You know perfectly well we're using you as the excuse. It's wonderful. Don't suddenly go temperamental on me, Bernard. It's just a formality. Hell, do you think they'd let you anywhere near Stinnes if you were really suspect?'

'I don't know, Bret. There are some damned funny people in the Department.'

'You're in the clear, so forget it.'

'And you're going to infiltrate some poor sod into the Cambridge network and try to blow it? You don't stand a chance. Can't we investigate it on a formal basis – questioning and so on?'

'It would take too long. We've got to move fast. If we go for a formal investigation, MI5 will take it over when Stinnes is transferred and they'll make the arrests and get the glory. No, this is urgent. We'll do it ourselves.'

'And you'll get the glory,' I said.

Bret didn't take offence. He smiled. 'Take it easy, Bernard,' he said mildly. 'You know me better than that.' He spoke to the ceiling for he was sitting deep down in the soft cushions of the sofa, his head resting back, and his suede moccasins plonked on the glass-topped table so that he was stretched as straight as a ruler. Outside the sky was getting darker and even the white walls couldn't stop the room becoming gloomy.

I didn't pursue that particular line. I didn't know him better than that. I didn't know him at all. 'You'll have to tell Five,' I said.

'I told them last night,' he said.

'The night-duty officer on a Friday night? That's too obvious, Bret. They'll be hopping mad. When are you putting your man in?'

'Tonight,' he said.

'Tonight!' I almost snorted my drink down my nose. 'Who's running him? Are Operations in on this? Who gave the okay?'

'Don't be so jittery, Bernard. It will be all right. The D-G gave me the go-ahead. No, Operations are not a party to the plan; it's better that they don't know about it. Secrecy is of paramount importance.'

'Secrecy is of paramount importance? And you've left a message with the night-duty officer at Five? You realize that probationers – kids just down from college – are likely to get weekend duties like that. Whoever he is, he'll want to cover himself, so now he's phoning everyone in his contact book and trying to think of more names.'

'You're becoming paranoid, Bernard,' Bret said. He smiled to show me how calm he was remaining. 'Even if he is an inexperienced kid from college – and I know kids from college are not high on your all-time Hit Parade – the messages he'll leave with maids, au pair girls and receptionists at country hotels won't explicitly describe our operation.'

He was a sarcastic bastard. 'For God's sake, grow up, Bret,' I said. 'Can't you see that a flurry of activity like that – messages being left in all sorts of non-departmental places for the urgent attention of senior MI5 staff – is enough to compromise your operation?'

'I don't agree,' he said, but he stopped smiling.

'Some smart newspaper man is likely to get the smell of that one. If that happens, it could blow up in your face.'

'In *my* face?'

'Well, what are those messages going to be saying? They are going to be saying that we're just about to go blundering into matters that don't concern us. They're going to say we're stealing Five's jobs from them. And they'll be right.'

'This isn't a hot tip on a horse; they'll be sensible,' said Bret.

'It's going to be all over town,' I said. 'You're putting your man into danger, real danger. Forget it.'

'MI5 are not going to let newsmen get hold of secrets like this.'

'You hope they're not. But this isn't *their* secret, it's ours. What will they care if your Boy Scout comes a cropper? They'll be delighted. It would teach us a lesson. And why would they be so fussy about newspaper men getting the story? If it made headlines that said we were treading on their territory, it would suit their book.'

'I'm not sure I want to listen to this any more,' said Bret huffily. This was Bret getting ready for his knighthood – loyal servant of Her Majesty and all that. 'I trust MI5 to be just as careful with secret information as we are.'

'So do I, if it's *their* information. But this is not their information. This is a message – a message from you; not a message about one of their operations but about one of ours. What's more, it was given out on a Friday evening in what is a transparent trick to hamper any efforts they might make to stop us. How can you believe they'll play it your way and help you score?'

'It's too late now,' said Bret. He took two ice cubes from a container that was painted to look like a side drum from the band of the Grenadier Guards, complete with battle honours, and dropped them into his drink. Bret could make one drink last a long time. It was a trick I'd never mastered. He offered ice to me but I shook my head. 'It's all approved and signed for. There's not going to be any pussyfooting about trying to infiltrate them. There's an office in Cambridge which contains files on the whole network. It's coded, Stinnes says, coded to read like normal office files. But that shouldn't be a big problem. We're putting a man in there this evening. He's coming here to meet you.'

'Beautiful, Bret,' I said sarcastically. 'That's all I need – for your tame gorilla to get a good look at me before he gets rolled in a carpet and shipped to Moscow.'

Bret permitted himself a ghost of a smile. 'It's not that kind of operation, Bernard. This is the other side of the job. We'll be in England. If there's any interference, we'll be putting the handcuffs on those bastards, not the other way around.'

I weakened. I should have remained cynical about it, but I weakened because I began to feel that it might prove as simple as Bret Rensselaer said it would be. 'Okay. What do you want me to do?'

'Run him up to Cambridge and play nurse.' So that was it. I should have guessed that you don't get invited to Bret's for nothing. My heart sank into my guts. I felt the way some of those girls must have felt when they realized there were more works of art that lined the stairs all the way to Bret's bedroom. He saw it in my face. 'Did you think I was going to try to do it myself?'

'No, I didn't.'

'If you really think I can do it, Bernard, I'll try.' He was restless. He got up again and poured more gin for me. It was only then that I realized that I'd gulped the rest of my drink without even noticing that I'd done so. 'But I think our man deserves the best help we can find for him. And you're the best.'

He went back and sat down. I didn't reply. For a moment we both sat there in that beautiful room thinking our own thoughts. I don't know what Bret was thinking of, but I was back to trying to decide what his relationship with my wife had been.

At one time I'd felt sure that Fiona and Bret had been lovers. I looked at him. She was right for him, that very beautiful woman from a rich family. She was sophisticated in a way that only wealthy people can be. She had the confidence, stability, and intellect that nature provides for the first-born child.

The suspicion and jealousy of that time, not so long ago, had never gone away, and my feelings coloured everything I had to do with Bret. There was little chance I would ever discover the truth of it, and I was not really and truly sure that I wanted to know. And yet I couldn't stop thinking about them. Had they been together in this room?

'I'll never understand you, Bernard,' he said suddenly 'You're full of anger.'

I felt like saying that that was better than being full of shit, but in fact I didn't think that of Bret Rensselaer. I'd thought about him a lot over the past few months. First because I thought he was jumping into bed with Fiona, and now because the finger of treason was pointed at him. It all made sense. Put it all together and it made sense. If Bret and Fiona were lovers, then why not co-conspirators too?

I had never faced an official enquiry, but Bret had tried to make me admit that I'd been in league with my wife to betray the Department's secrets. Some traces of the mud he'd thrown had stuck to me. That would be a damned smart way to cover his own tracks. No one had ever accused Bret of being a co-conspirator with Fiona. No one had even suspected that they were having a love affair. No one, that is, except me. I had always been able to see how attractive he'd be for her. He was the sort of man I'd had as rivals when I'd first met her; mature, successful men, not Oxbridge graduates trying to hack a career in a merchant bank, but men much older than Fiona, men with servants and big shiny cars who paid for everything by just signing their name on the bill.

It was very dark in the room now and there was a growl of thunder. Then more thunder. I could see the clock's brass pendulum catching the light as it swung backwards and forwards. Bret's voice came out of the gloom. 'Or is it sadness? Anger or sadness – what's bugging you, Samson?'

I didn't want to play his silly undergraduate games, or sophisticated jet-set games, or whatever they were. 'What time is this poor bastard arriving?' I said.

'No fixed time. He'll be here for tea.'

'That's great,' I said. Tea! Earl Grey no doubt, and I suppose Bret's housekeeper would be serving it in a silver teapot with muffins and those very thin cucumber sandwiches without crusts.

'You talked to Lange,' he said. 'And he bad-mouthed me the way he always does? Is that it? What did he say this time?'

'He was talking about the time you went to Berlin and made him dismantle his networks.'

'He's such a crook. He's still resenting that after all these years?'

'He thinks you dealt a blow to a good system.'

'The "Berlin System", the famous "Berlin System" that Lange always regarded as his personal creation. It was Lange who ruined it by bringing it into such discredit that London Central sent me there to salvage what I could from it.'

'Why you?' I said. 'You were very young.'

'The world was very young,' said Bret. 'Britain and the US had won the war. We were going to be arm in arm together while we won the peace too.'

'Because you were American?'

'Right. An American could look at what was going on in Berlin and be impartial about it. I was to be the one who went there and unified the Limeys and the Yanks and made them into a team again. That was the theory; the fact was that the only unification came from the way they all hated and despised me. The Berlin intelligence community got together just to baffle and bamboozle me. They led me a merry dance, Bernard; they made sure that I couldn't get to the people I wanted, get the documents I wanted, or get competent office help. I didn't even have a proper office, did you know that? Did Lange tell you how he made sure that no German would work for me?'

'The way I heard it, they gave you a big apartment and two servants.'

'Is that the way Lange tells it? By now he probably even believes it. And what about the Russian princess?'

'He mentioned her.'

'The real story is that those bastards made sure the only office space I had was shared with a clerk who went through my files every day and told them what I was doing. When I tried to get other accommodation they blocked every move I made. Finally I contacted a friend of my mother's. She wasn't young, she wasn't a princess, and she had never been in Russia, although her mother was distantly related to White Russian aristocracy. She had a big apartment in Heerstrasse, and by offering half of it to me she was able to prevent it being commandeered for use by some other Allied military outfit. I used that place as an office and I got her neighbour to do my typing.'

'Lange said she was a Nazi, your friend.'

'She'd lived in Berlin right through the war and her folks had been murdered by the Bolsheviks, so I guess she didn't go around waving any red flags. But she had close friends among the July twentieth conspirators. When Hitler was blown up in 1944 she was taken in for questioning by the SD. She spent three nights in the cells at Prinz-Albrecht Strasse. It was touch and go whether they sent her to a camp, but there were so many suspected persons to be detained that they grew short of cells to hold them, so they let her go.'

'There was a row about Lange's brother-in-law,' I said.

'Damn right there was. If Lange had learned how to keep his head down and his mouth shut, maybe it wouldn't have blown up like that. But Lange has to be the big man on campus. And he particularly resented me because I was a fellow American. He wanted the exclusive title of tame Yank, and he'd got a lot of leeway playing that role. The office let him get away with all kinds of tricks because they thought it was just another example of good old Yankee know-how and the unconventional American way of tackling things.'

'So he resigned?'

'It was tough for him, but he'd been told enough times about that woman he married. There was no way I could ignore an SS man living in Lange's parlour while I was lowering the boom on guys who'd done nothing more than joining the party to save their school-teaching jobs.'

I didn't answer. I tried to reconcile Bret's version of these events with Lange's burning hatred. 'They were not good times,' I said.

'Did you ever hear of CROWCASS?' said Bret.

'Vaguely. What is it?'

'Right after the fighting ended, SHAEF started building a file of suspected war criminals. CROWCASS was the Central Registry of War Criminals and Security Suspects. Maybe it was a muddle, the way everyone said it was afterwards, but at the time CROWCASS was gospel, and Lange's brother-in-law had his name on that registry.'

'Did Lange know that?'

'Sure he did.'

'When did he find out?'

'I don't know when he found out, but he knew about the brother-in-law having served in the Waffen-SS before he got married. I know that because I found in the file a copy of the letter he'd been sent warning him not to go ahead. And all ex-members of the SS and Waffen-SS were automatically arrested unless they'd already faced an enquiry and been cleared. But Lange didn't care about any of that. He was playing the American card again. He let the British think he'd got special dispensation from the Americans and vice versa. He's a slippery one; I guess you know that.'

'Didn't you know it?' I said.

'I know that, and I knew it then. But everyone was telling me what a wonderful network he was running. They wouldn't let me see anything he was producing, of course – security wouldn't permit. So I just had to take their word for it.'

'He brought us some good people. He'd been in Berlin before the war. He knew everybody. He still does.'

'So what was I to do?' said Bret defensively. 'His goddamned brother-in-law was running around with a *Kenn-karte* that identified him as a payroll clerk with a building company. It had a denazification stamp. He liked to tell everyone he'd been a Navy medic. He was picked up brawling in a bar in Wedding. He was stinking drunk and still fighting when they took him downtown and threw him into the drunk tank. They put these drunks under the cold showers to cool them off, and a cop who'd got hit on the nose began wondering how this Navy medic came to have an SS blood-group tattoo under his arm.'

Outside, the river and the fields beyond were obliterated by grey mist and rain was beating against the window. Bret was lost in the shadows and his voice was impersonal, like a recording machine delivering some computer judgement.

'I couldn't ignore it,' he said. 'It was a police report. It was delivered to the office, but no one there wanted a hot potato like that on their desk. They sent it right along to me. It was probably the only piece of paperwork that they forwarded to me in the proper way.' I said nothing. Bret realized that his explanation was convincing and he pursued it. 'Lange thought himself indispensable,' said Bret. 'It's tempting to think that at any time, but it was especially tempting for someone heading up several networks – good networks, by all accounts. But no one is indispensable. The Berlin System managed without Lange. Your dad put the pieces together.'

'Lange thinks my father would have helped him. He thinks my father was deliberately moved out of Berlin so that you could go in there and get rid of him.'

'That's crap and Lange knows it. Your dad had done very well in Berlin. Silas Gaunt was his boss and when Silas got a promotion in London he brought your father back to London with him. Nothing was ever written on paper, but it was understood that your dad would go up the ladder with Silas. He had a fine career waiting for him in London Central.'

'So what happened?' I said.

'When Lange got sore, he tried to sell all his networks to the US Army. They wouldn't touch him, of course.'

'He had good networks,' I said.

'Very good, but even if they'd been twice as good, I doubt if he could have sold the Counter Intelligence Corps on the idea of taking them over.'

'Why?'

'The CIC weren't concerned with what was happening in the Russian Zone. Their task was security. They were looking for Nazis, neo-Nazi groups, and Communist subversives operating in the West.'

'So why not pass Lange on to some other department?'

'In those days the US had no organization spying on the Russians. Congress wanted America to play Mr Nice Guy. There were a few retreads from the old OSS and they were working for something that called itself the War Department Detachment, which in turn was a part of something called the Central Intelligence Group. But this was amateur stuff; the Russians were laughing at it. Lange tried everywhere, but no one wanted his networks.'

'It sounds like a meat market.'

'And that's the way the field agents saw it when the news filtered through to them. They were demoralized, and Lange wasn't very popular.'

'So my father came back to Berlin to sort it out?'

'Yes, your dad volunteered to come back and sort it out even though he knew he'd lose his seniority in London. Meanwhile Lange was sent to Hamburg to cool off.'

'But he didn't cool off?'

'He got madder and madder. And when your dad wouldn't take him back unless he completely separated himself from his Waffen-SS brother-in-law, Lange resigned.'

'Are you saying my dad sacked Lange?'

'Look in the records. It's not top secret.'

'Lange blames you,' I said.

'To you he blames me,' said Bret.

'He blames my father?'

'In the course of the years Lange has blamed everyone from the records clerk to President Truman. The only one Lange never blames is himself.'

'It was a tough decision,' I said. 'SS man or no SS man, I admire the way Lange stood by him. Maybe he did the right thing. Turning his brother-in-law out onto the street would have wrecked his marriage, and that marriage still works.'

'The reason Lange wouldn't turn his brother-in-law out was because that brother-in-law was making anything up to a thousand dollars a week in the black market.'

'Are you kidding?'

'That fateful night the cops picked him up in Wedding, he had nearly a thousand US dollars in his pocket and another thousand bucks in military scrip. That's what got the cops so excited. That's why I had to do something about it. It's in the police report; take a look at it.'

'You know I can't take a look at it. They never put those old files onto the computer, and no one can find anything that old down in Registry.'

'Well, ask anyone who was there. Sure, Lange was on the take from his brother-in-law. Some people said Lange was setting up some of his deals for him.'

'How?' I said, but the answer was obvious.

'I don't know. But I can guess. Lange hears about a black-market deal through one of his agents. Instead of busting them, he cuts his brother-in-law into the deal.'

'He'd never survive if he pulled tricks like that.'

'Don't play the innocent, Samson, it doesn't suit you. You know what the city was like during those days. You know how it worked. Lange would just say that he wanted the black-market deal to continue because one of the dealers was an important Soviet agent. His brother-in-law would play the role of Lange's stoolie. They'd all make money with no chance of arrest. It's a foolproof system. No one could touch him.'

There was a ring at the front door. I heard the housekeeper going down the hall.

'This will be our man for the break-in tonight,' said Bret. 'It will be like old times for you, Bernard.'

And then through the door walked Ted Riley.

15

'Why did you get yourself into this crock?' I asked Ted Riley for what must have been the hundredth time. For the hundredth time he failed to give me any proper explanation. He was in no hurry. He was drinking Powers Irish whiskey, and it was having an effect upon him, for when he spoke his voice had the lilt of Kerry, a brogue that makes everything into a song. I remembered that voice from my childhood, and it brought back to me all Ted's stories.

There was the one about his grandfather piling his freshly cut peat into 'stooks' and how, 'in the soft pink light of each and every morning', he found that some of his peat had been stolen. The thefts continued for years until one day Grandfather Riley tucked gunpowder into the turf and a neighbour's cottage burned to the ground. It was to avoid the violent retribution threatened by the injured man's relatives that the Rileys moved to County Kerry where Ted was born. How many of Ted's stories were true, how many embroidered, and how many invented just to amuse a wide-eyed little boy, I'll never know. But Ted was a part of my childhood, like climbing Berlin's rubble piles and ice skating on the Muggelsee.

'Ahhhh.' Ted's yawn was a symptom of anxiety. For all God's creatures, fear brings a drowsiness, a self-preserving urge to snuggle down somewhere out of sight and go to sleep.

We were sitting in the sort of room in which I seem to have spent half my adult life. It was a hotel room in Cambridge, but this was not the Cambridge of Gothic spires or cloistered dons, this was a shopping street on the wrong side of town, a shabby hotel with cracked lino on the floor, a bathroom a long way down the hall, and a sink where a dripping tap had resisted all my efforts to silence it.

It was late evening, but we'd kept the room lights switched off. The curtain remained open and the room's only light came from the street lamps, the bilious yellow sodium glow reflected from the rain-wet road to make patterns on the ceiling. I could make out the shape of Ted Riley slumped on the bed, still wearing his damp raincoat. His hat was pulled down to cover his face. He only moved it back when he drank.

I was standing near the window, looking through the net curtain at the premises across the street. It was an old four-storey building, its fascia stained and in places broken. According to the brass plates alongside the front door, it housed a firm of architects and an industrial designer as well as the solicitor's office we were to break into. On the top floor was the flat for the caretaker, but tonight according to Ted's research the caretaker was away visiting his son's family in London. The whole building was dark.

'Ah, now . . .! You know . . .!' Ted said, and raised his glass to me. That was supposed to answer all my questions.

Ted Riley was trying to tell me that no matter how carefully he tried to explain things, I'd not understand. We were a generation apart, and what was more important, Ted's generation had fought a war while my generation had not. Ted was a friend of my father and everything in Ted's gesture told me that my father would have never asked him that question; my father would have known the answer. That's why Ted didn't reply. It was a convenient thing for Ted to believe.

I poured myself some more whiskey and took the bottle across to the bed. Ted held up his glass to me without removing the hat from his face. I poured him another good measure. He'd need it.

'Thanks, my boy,' he said.

No matter how close I felt to Ted Riley, he saw me as the little boy who'd made good. Those who got their feet under a desk at London Central were regarded as a race apart by the men and women who had done the real work in those lonely places where the real work was done.

'When your man makes a suggestion, I'm in no position to turn it down,' said Ted. 'I'm employed on sufferance. The Department has told me so in those very words.' He meant Bret, of course, and Bret was 'my man' because I'd accompanied him to Berwick House in his big car.

I stepped back to the window to watch the street. I didn't have to move far; the room was no bigger than a large cupboard. 'That was a long time ago,' I heard myself saying, just as everyone kept saying it to me when they thought I needed reassurance about my past. Time used to be the panacea for everything, but nowadays our sins are remembered on computers, and random-accessed memories do not fade.

A police car passed. Not quite slowly enough to be observing our target but not quite fast enough to be merely passing by. I decided not to mention it to Ted; he was jumpy enough already.

'There's no statute of limitations on blackmail,' said Ted with no special bitterness in his voice. 'It's written down somewhere in some secret file, to be used against me whenever I'm anything less than exemplary.'

For a moment I thought there was some double meaning there. I thought he was telling me that I was in the same position. But that wasn't the Department's style. How can you blackmail anyone about something that has become common knowledge? No, just as Ted Riley's disgrace had been so assiduously concealed, so would any lingering suspicion about me be kept buried deep in the boneyard. I said, 'For God's sake, Ted. Hams or cheese or booze or something . . . it's too long ago for anyone to care about it.'

'I was young and very stupid. It wasn't so much the little black-market deals. Everyone was frightened that I'd been forced to reveal military information too. I never thought of it like that at the time.'

'Not Dad,' I said. 'Dad would have trusted you with his life.'

Ted grunted to show how silly I was. 'Your dad signed the note for the enquiry. I could have kept it covered up until your dad found out. Your dad packed me off to London to face the music.'

For a moment I felt sick. Ted was not only a very close colleague of my father, but a friend of the family. He was always in and out when we were living at Lisl Hennig's place. Ted was one of the family. Our German maidservant would keep a spare set of cutlery and a napkin handy just in case Ted arrived for dinner unannounced. 'I'm sorry, Ted. I had no idea.'

Ted gave another grunt. 'I don't blame your dad; I blame myself. Your dad made no secret of what he did to staff who broke the rules, and I was senior staff. Your dad did the only thing he could do. He made an example of me. I bear him no grudge, Bernard.'

His voice was that of the slim young officer who'd so effortlessly hoisted me onto his shoulder and galloped down the corridor to put me into the bath. But in the gloom I could see that the voice was coming from a fat disappointed old man.

'Dad was bloody inflexible,' I said. I went and sat on the bed. The tired old springs groaned and the mattress sagged under my weight.

'God rest him,' said Ted. He stretched out and touched my arm. 'You had the finest father anyone could wish for. He never asked us to do anything he wouldn't do himself.' Ted's voice was strained. I'd forgotten that Ted was one of the sentimental breed of Irishmen.

'Dad was something of a Prussian at times,' I said to ease the tension. Ted was getting to the kind of maudlin mood in which he'd start singing 'Come back to Erin, mavourneen, mavourneen . . .' in the tear-jerking baritone that he always produced at the Christmas parties we used to have in the office in Berlin.

'Many a true word is spoken in jest,' said Ted hoarsely. 'Yes, your father was like some of those Prussians . . . the ones I liked. When the enquiry was held, it was your father who came to London and gave evidence on my behalf. If it hadn't been for what your dad said, I would have been kicked out of the service without a pension.'

'Is that what happened to Lange?'

'Something like that,' said Ted, as if he didn't want to talk about it.

'Was Lange on the take?'

Ted took his hat from his eyes in order to look at me and smiled. 'Was Lange on the take? Lange was on the way to becoming the king of the Berlin black market by the time they booted him off to Hamburg.'

'And my father didn't know?'

'Now you're comparing me with Lange. That's like comparing a first-time offender with Al Capone. I was just a kid; Lange was an old newspaperman who knew the ways of the world. Did you know that Lange was granted a personal interview with Hitler back in 'thirty-three when the Nazis first came to power? Lange was a mature sophisticated man. He knew how to cover his tracks and he could sweet-talk anyone into anything. Even your father came under his spell. But Lange was frightened of your father. It was only when your dad left Berlin for London that Lange pulled out all the stops. Rumours say he put a million marks into the bank.'

'So much for rumours,' I said. 'Go and visit him now and you won't see much sign of it. He's living in a dilapidated dump off Potsdamerstrasse and drinking homemade wine. I felt so bad about him that I fiddled a small departmental payment for the information he gave me. Rensselaer saw the docket and started quizzing me about what Lange had said.'

'Save your tears, Bernie. Lange did some terrible things in the old days – things I wouldn't like to have on my conscience.'

'What things?'

'Lange's black-market friends were armed, and I don't mean with can openers. People got hurt, some even got killed. Lange stayed clear, but he knew what was happening when those toughs raided warehouses and hijacked Army trucks. And the crime figures prove it. When Lange went to Hamburg, things suddenly improved in Berlin.'

'Was that why Lange was sent to Hamburg?'

'Sure. It was the only way they could prove his guilt. After that he never got a really good job again.'

We sat there in silence, drinking. In an hour it would be finished and done with. I'd be in the car with Ted, roaring down the London road, and we'd be enjoying that slight hysteria that follows risky little games like this one.

I changed the subject. 'So how is Erich Stinnes and his radio?'

'It all worked out just fine, Bernie. He listens to Radio Volga every morning.'

'Radio Volga?'

'For the Soviet Armed Forces in Germany. It broadcasts all day every day up to ten o'clock at night, at which time all good Russian soldiers switch off and go to bed, except Saturday when it goes on until ten-thirty.'

'It doesn't sound likely that the Army would be sending radio messages to a KGB officer.'

'No, but until five o'clock every afternoon Radio Volga is relaying the Moscow Home Service Channel One. That could contain any messages the KGB ordered.'

'What time?'

'As I say, he tunes in each morning. Or perhaps I should say that the timer you put on the electric plug shows electricity being used each morning at eight-thirty. Then he does his exercises and has a couple of cups of coffee before the interrogator comes.'

'Is that the only station he listens to?'

'No, he plays with the buttons. It's a lovely toy, that little shortwave receiver. He amuses himself with it. East and West, Russian language, German language, and all sorts of Spanish-speaking stations, including Cuba. Of course, the only evidence we've got is the way he leaves the radio's tuning memory. Is he on the level, Bernie?'

'What do you think?'

'I've seen quite a few of them over the years that I've worked for the Debriefing Centre.' He sat up, resting his elbow, and drank some of his whiskey. Ted was a serious drinker; he didn't just sip it, he gulped it down. 'They're all a bit nervous. Some were terrified, some were just a little restless, but they were all nervous. But Stinnes is different. He's a cool customer, as calm as anything. The other morning I tried to ruffle his feathers. I put a glass of water and a slice of dry bread in front of him and told him to pack his bag, he was going to the Tower of London. I said we'd tumbled him. He just smiled and said it was bound to happen eventually. He's very cool.'

'You think he is really still working for Moscow? Do you think it could all be an elaborate act to feed us misinformation? And we're swallowing it just the way he wants?'

Ted gave me a very slowly expanding smile, as if I was trying to put one over on him. 'Now you're asking me something. That's what they call the sixty-four-thousand-dollar question. You're the brains now, young Bernard. You're the one who's supposed to be giving me the answers to questions like that one.'

'He's handed us some good stuff,' I said.

'Like the one tonight? Your man said we'll be able to pick up a whole network with the stuff we'll get out of that filing cabinet across the road.'

'I don't like it, Ted. It's not our job, and Five know about it. If we get into hot water, there'll be precious little help from those bastards at the Home Office.'

'Breaking and entering and stealing a couple of files? We've both done it plenty of times over there, Bernie. The only difference is that now we're doing it in England. It will be a piece of cake. I remember the time when you would have done a job like this in half an hour and come back looking for more work.'

'Maybe,' I said. I wasn't sure that I wanted to be reminded.

'Remember when I was sent back to Berlin to break into that big house in Heinersdorf? When you got the maid to let you wait in the front room? A Russian colonel's place it was. The dog took the arse out of your trousers when you climbed down from the bathroom window holding that box of photographs. And you rode the bike all the way back so that no one would see the hole in your pants. Your dad gave me hell for letting you do that.'

'I was the only one thin enough to get through the window.'

'Your dad was right. You were only a child. If those bastards had caught you and found out who your dad was, God knows what might have happened to you.'

'It would have been all right. In those days no one could have guessed I was anything but a German kid.'

'The things we did before they built that Wall! Those were the days, Bernie. I often think what a crazy childhood you had.'

'We should get going,' I said, looking yet again at my watch. I went to the window and opened it. It let cold air into the room but I could see better and hear better that way. I didn't want some squad of Special Branch detectives creeping up to grab Ted and show us what happened to people who poked their noses into Home Office territory.

'We've plenty of time, Bernie. No sense me hanging about in the doorway before the locksmith has got the door open. That's the way accidents happen.'

'You shouldn't be doing this sort of job any more,' I said.

'I can do with the extra money,' said Ted.

'Let me do it, Ted. You do backup!'

He looked at me for a long time, trying to decide if I was serious. 'You know I can't let you do it, old son. Why do you think your boss selected me to do it? Because Ted Riley has no reputation to lose. If the law grabs me, I'll do my act in court and the reporters won't even bother to ask me how I spell my name. If you got caught over there with your hands in the files, it might end up with questions in the House for the Prime Minister. I'd sooner get nabbed for doing it than answer to Mr Rensselaer's fury at letting you do it for me.'

'Then let's go,' I said. I didn't like what he was saying but he was entirely right. 'The locksmith will be standing on the doorstep within three minutes.'

Ted got to his feet and reached for his two-way radio. I did the same thing. 'Is that okay?' I said into the microphone.

Ted had put the earplug in one ear and covered the other ear with his flattened hand. It was too dangerous for the loudspeaker to be switched on while he was working.

I repeated my test and he nodded to tell me he was hearing through the earpiece. Then he said, 'Seems okay, old lad.' His voice came through my handphone.

Then I changed the wavelength and called the car that was to collect him. 'Taxi for two passengers?' I said.

Although I had the volume turned right down, the more powerful transmitter in the car came through loudly. 'Taxi ready and waiting.'

'Have you got everything?' I asked Ted. He was at the sink. The pipes made a loud chugging sound as the water flowed. Without removing his hat, he splashed his face and dried himself on the little towel hanging under the mirror.

Wearily he said, 'Holy Mother of God, we've been all through that at least five times, Bernard.' There were voices in the corridor and then sounds of two people entering the room next door. There was a clatter of the wardrobe door and the harsh swishing sound of coat hangers being pushed along a rail. The wardrobe backing must have been very thin for the sounds were loud. 'Relax, son,' said Ted. 'It's a couple renting the room for an hour or two. It's that sort of hotel.'

Yes, I was even more nervous that he was. I'd seldom played the part of backup man and never before to someone I knew and liked. For the first time I realized that it was worse than actually doing the job. It was that parental agony you suffer every time your children want to bicycle in the traffic or go away to camp.

Still in the dark, Ted buttoned up his coat and straightened his hat. I said, 'If the lock proves difficult, I'll send the big cutters over to you.'

Ted Riley touched my arm as if quietening a frightened horse. 'Don't fuss, Bernard. Our man was in there only two days ago. He's a damned good man, I've worked with him before. He identified the type of filing cabinet and he's opened three of them since then. I watched him. I could almost do it alone.'

'You'd better go now. You call me first, as soon as you're ready for the check calls,' I said. I didn't watch him go, I went to the window to watch the street.

The rendezvous went like a training-school exercise. Our tame locksmith arrived exactly on time and Ted Riley crossed the street and entered the door without a pause in his stride. The locksmith followed him inside, pulled the door closed, and fixed it so that it would remain firm against the test of any passing policeman.

He wouldn't be able to use the lift, so it was a long walk upstairs. But Ted was a pro: he'd make sure he didn't arrive out of breath, just in case there was a reception committee. Even using my pocket binoculars I couldn't see any sign of them entering the office. Ted would make sure they both kept away from the windows as much as possible. It was bad luck that the filing cabinets were on this outer wall.

They'd been inside a couple of minutes when Ted called me up. 'Come back with hair on . . .' he sang softly.

'. . . you bald-headed bastard,' I replied.

There had been no agreed identification, but more than once Ted had used his parody version of 'Come Back to Erin' as recognition.

'It's going to be a piece of cake,' Ted whispered.

'Street clear,' I said.

It was more than three minutes before Ted called again. I was watching the time, otherwise I might have thought it was an hour or more. 'Slight snag . . . but all okay. Add three.'

'Street clear. Departure time add three.'

The car was parked very close by, a few minutes this way or that wouldn't make much difference to them. I decided not to call the car crew until we were nearer to the rendezvous time.

It was five minutes before Ted came on the air again. I wondered what the hell was happening over there, but I knew how annoying such calls could be so I kept silent.

'It's not the same lock,' said Ted. 'The inside has been changed. We'll have to add ten.' He sounded very calm and matter-of-fact, but I didn't like the sound of it.

'Cutters any good?' I offered. They could try going in through the back of the cabinet if all else failed. We had cutters that could go through almost anything.

'Not yet.'

The rain continued. It was what Ted called 'a soft day': steady drizzle that went on without end. There were not many pedestrians on the street and even the cars were infrequent. This was a good night to stay in and watch TV. That bloody Cambridge Constabulary car passed down the street again. Was it the same car showing interest in our target or was I seeing a succession of different cars on their way to and from the police station? I should have noted the registration.

'We've got suddenly lucky,' said Ted's voice. He didn't enlarge on it. He kept the button pressed while he watched the locksmith working at the filing cabinet. I could hear the faint sounds of them working, sweating and straining to shift the cabinet: 'We'll just look at the back of it.' And then Ted was speaking to the locksmith: 'Watch the wiring . . . it's wired! Holy mother of . . .'

I was straining to see through the windows of the dark office. For a moment I thought they'd switched on the lights, for the two windows of the law offices lit up to become bright yellow rectangles. Then came the sound of the explosion. It was a deafening crash and the force of it clawed at me through the open window like a gale.

The law office windows dissolved into a shower of debris that, together with pieces of the two men, was rained out into the street.

'Taxi. Go. Go. Negative.' It was the official way to say to scram to save yourself, and the car crew came back immediately with a reply.

'Please confirm.' The voice was calm but I heard the engine start.

'Go. Go. Negative. Out.'

I heard someone at the other end mutter 'Good luck' as I switched off my radio. It was bad procedure but not one that I'd feel inclined to report: I needed all the well-wishers I could find.

From somewhere over the other side of town I heard a police siren start up. I leaned out of the window and then threw the radio as far as I could towards the office. The windows were now dark again, except for the faint flicker of fire.

I buttoned my coat, put on my cap, and looked quickly around the room to make sure there was nothing there left to compromise us. Then I went downstairs to watch the police and fire service arrive.

The firemen arrived immediately after the first police car. And then an ambulance. The noise of their heavy diesel engines throbbed loudly. Batteries of headlights burned through the continuing drizzle of rain and reflected upon tiny bits of broken glass that were strewn all over the roadway and sparkled like ice. There were black pieces of charred paper and broken bits of wood and things that I didn't care to inspect too closely. The fire engine's ladder moved slowly until it was positioned against the office windows, where a red glow was still to be seen. A fireman climbed it. There was a terrible smell of burning and enough smoke for the firemen to be using breathing gear.

The whole street was brightened as everyone drew back their curtains to watch the activity. By now the front door of the offices had been opened. The ambulance men pushed through the little crowd that had formed and went inside to look around. They didn't take a stretcher with them. They guessed they wouldn't be needing one.

It was three o'clock Sunday morning by the time I'd collected the car and driven back to Bret Rensselaer's place in Berkshire. Bret was fully dressed when he came to answer the door to me – he was quick to tell me that he'd never gone to bed – but he'd changed his clothes; he was now in a roll-neck cashmere sweater and matching blue poplin pants. He'd been waiting for the phone call that would tell him everything had gone smoothly.

But when the phone call came, it told him that an explosion had killed two men in an office in Cambridge. The story was on the wire services. It was too late for the Sunday papers, but the national dailies would probably carry it on Monday. If a TV crew had got pictures, it might be on the evening bulletin.

'We need a break,' said Bret. He'd put a drink in my hand and then devoted a lot of time to getting a second log burning in the fireplace. I crouched over it. I was cold.

'Yes, we need a rise in the price of beer or a bus drivers' strike to grab the headlines,' I said. 'But don't worry; a small explosion in the back streets of Cambridge isn't exactly front-page stuff, Bret.'

Bret pulled a little wheeled trolley over to the fire. On it there was a bottle of single-malt whisky that he'd brought out of the cupboard for me and a full jug of iced water. He sat on the fender seat and warmed his hands. The curtains were closed now, but I could hear the rain still beating on the glass, as it had been not many hours before when I'd sat here with Ted Riley, listening to Bret explaining how easy it was all going to be. 'A booby trap,' said Bret. 'What bastards!'

'Let's not jump to conclusions,' I said. I sat on the other side of the fender. I don't like perching on fender seats; it was like trying to get warm on a barbecue – you cooked one side and froze the other. 'Maybe it wasn't intended to kill.'

'You said it was a booby trap,' said Bret.

'It was a slip of the tongue.'

'So what was it?'

'I don't know. It might have been no more than a device to destroy the secret papers. But a heavy-steel filing cabinet makes it into a bomb.'

'They put a lot of explosive into it. Why not use an incendiary device?' asked Bret.

'We had an explosion like it in Berlin back in the old days. They'd only used a small charge, but the cabinet had some special fireproofing liner. When it went, it blew the side of the building out. It was worse than this one.'

Why is he bugging me about all these details? I thought. Who cares about how big the explosive charge was? Ted Riley was dead.

'There's no chance that . . .'

'No chance at all. Two dead. You said the wire services had the story.'

'They get it wrong sometimes,' said Bret. 'Will they be identified?'

'I didn't go in and look around,' I said.

'Sure, sure,' said Bret. 'Thank Christ it wasn't you.'

'Riley's an old-timer. He emptied his pockets and his clothes had no laundry marks. He made me check it with him. The other man I don't know about.'

'The locksmith came from Duisburg. It was a German make. He was the expert on that sort of safe.'

'They'd changed the inside of the lock,' I said.

'I know,' said Bret. He drank some of his tonic water.

'How could you know unless you had a monitor on the radio?'

Bret smiled. 'I had someone monitoring the radio. There's no secret about that.'

'Then why ask me the questions?'

'The old man is going to ask me a lot of questions and I want to know the answers. And I don't want to read the transcript to him; he can do that for himself. I need to hear what you've got to say.'

'It's simple enough,' I said. 'Stinnes told the interrogator that there was some good stuff in that office. You sent Ted Riley in to get it. The filing cabinet was wired to destroy the evidence – bang. What difficult questions can the D-G ask, except why?'

'I don't blame you for feeling bitter,' said Bret. 'Ted Riley was a friend of your father, wasn't he?'

'Ted Riley was good at his job, Bret. He had the instinct for it. But the poor sod spent his life checking identity cards and making sure the burglar alarms were in working order. Just for one little lapse.'

'He wasn't material for London Central, if that's what you are suggesting.'

'Wasn't he? Who do you have to know to be material for London Central?' I said. 'Jesus, Bret, Ted Riley had more intelligence skills in his little finger than . . .'

'Than I have in my whole body? Or was it going to be Dicky? Or maybe the D-G?'

'Can I have another drink?'

'You won't bring Ted Riley back to life by pouring that stuff down your throat,' said Bret. But he reached for the bottle of Glenlivet and uncapped it before handing it to me. I poured a big one for myself. I didn't offer Bret any; he was quite content with his tonic water.

'I had a talk with Ted Riley last night,' I said. I stopped. The red lights came on in my skull. Everything warned me to be cautious.

'That must have been interesting,' said Bret, keeping his voice just level enough for me not to get up and bust him in the nose.

'Ted told me that Stinnes is tuned to Moscow every morning at eight-thirty. Ted thought he was getting his instructions from them. Maybe one of the instructions they gave him was to tell us about the Cambridge cell and get Ted Riley blown into little pieces.'

'Why are you telling me what Riley thought? Riley was just a security man. I don't need the opinions of security men when the interrogator is doing so well.'

'So why didn't you send the goddamned interrogator to do the break-in last night?'

Bret held up a hand. 'Ah, now I'm reading you loud and clear. You're trying to link the two events. Riley – despite the interrogator's satisfaction – sees through Stinnes and his misinformation scheme. So Riley has to be removed by a Kremlin-planned bomb. Is that what you're trying to sell me?'

'Something along those lines,' I said.

Bret sighed. 'You were the one who's been hyping Stinnes as if he was the greatest thing since sliced bread. Now your friend is killed and everything goes into reverse. Stinnes is the villain. And since Stinnes is virtually under house arrest, Moscow has to be the heavy. You really try my patience at times, Bernard.'

'It fits,' I said.

'So do a million other explanations. First you tell me the bomb was just to destroy the paperwork. Now you want it to be a trap to kill Riley. Make up your mind.'

'Let's not play with words, Bret. The important question is whether Stinnes is playing a double game.'

'Forget it,' said Bret.

'I'm not going to forget it, Bret,' I told him. 'I'm going to pursue it.'

'You landed Erich Stinnes for us. Everyone says that without you he wouldn't have come across to us.'

'I'm not sure that's true,' I said.

'Never mind the modest disclaimers. You got him and everyone gives you the credit for that. Don't start going around the office telling everyone they've got an active KGB agent in position.'

'We'll have to take away the shortwave radio,' I said. 'But that will warn him that we're on to him.'

'Slow down, Bernard. Slow right down. If you're blaming yourself for Ted Riley's death because you agreed to letting Stinnes have the radio, forget it.'

'I can't forget it. It was my suggestion.'

'Even if Stinnes is still active, and even if tonight's fiasco was the result of something arranged between him and Moscow, the radio can't have played a big part in it.'

I drank some of the whisky. I was calmer now; the drink had

helped. I resolved not to fight with Bret to the point where I flounced out and slammed the door, because I didn't feel I was capable of driving back to London.

When I didn't reply, Bret spoke again. 'He couldn't send any messages back to them. Even if by some miracle he smuggled a letter out and posted it, there'd be no time for it to get there and be acted upon. What can they tell him that's worth knowing?'

'Not much, I suppose.'

'If there's any conspiracy, it was all arranged before we got him, before he flew out of Mexico City. The use of that radio means nothing.'

'I suppose you're right,' I said.

'There's a spare bedroom upstairs, Bernard. Have a sleep; you look all in. We'll talk again over breakfast.'

What he said about the radio made sense and I felt a bit better about it. But I noted the way he was going to bat for Stinnes. Was that because Bret was a KGB agent? Or simply because he saw in Stinnes a way of regaining a powerful position in London Central? Or both?

16

As always lately, the D-G was represented by the egregious Morgan. It was a curious fact that although Morgan couldn't always spare time to attend those meetings at which the more banal aspects of departmental administration were discussed, he could always find time to represent the D-G at these Operations discussions. I had always been opposed to the way the top-floor bureaucrats gate-crashed such meetings just to make themselves feel a part of the Operations side, and I particularly objected to pen pushers like Morgan listening in and even offering comments.

We were in Bret Rensselaer's room. Bret was sitting behind his glass-topped desk playing with his pens and pencils. Morgan was standing by the wall studying *The Crucifixion*, a tiny Dürer engraving that Bret had recently inherited from some rich relative. It was the only picture in the room and I doubt if it would have got there if it hadn't fitted in with Bret's black-and-white scheme. Morgan's pose suggested indifference, if not boredom, but his ears were quivering as he listened for every nuance of what was being said.

'This is a time to keep our heads down,' said Dicky. He was wearing his faded jeans and open-necked checked shirt and was sprawled on Bret's black-leather chesterfield, while Frank Harrington was sitting hunched up at the other end of it. 'We've stirred up a hornet's nest and Five will be swarming all over us if they think we're doing any sort of follow-up operation.'

Dicky, of course, had been left out of the fiasco in which Ted Riley was killed and he wasn't happy at the way he'd been bypassed, but Dicky was not a man to hold grudges, he'd told me that a million times. He'd be content to watch Bret Rensselaer crash full length to the floor and bleed to death, but it wouldn't be Dicky who put his dagger in. Dicky was no Brutus; this was a drama in which Dicky would be content with a non-speaking role. But now that Rensselaer wanted to organize a follow-up operation and possibly salvage some measure of success out of the mess, Dicky found his voice. 'I'm against it,' he said.

'It's a perfect opportunity,' said Bret. 'They've lost their records.

It would be natural for Moscow to make contact.' He rearranged the pens, pencils, paper clips, and the big glass paperweight like a miser counting his wealth.

'Is this what Stinnes is saying?' I asked.

Bret looked at me and then at the others. 'I should have told you. . . .' he said. 'Bernard has suddenly decided that Stinnes is here to blow a hole in all of us.' He smiled, but the smile wasn't big enough to completely contradict this contention. He left that to me.

I was forced to modify that wild claim just as Bret knew I would be. 'I didn't exactly say that, Bret,' I said. I was sitting on the hard folding chair. I always seemed to be sitting on hard folding chairs; it was a mark of my low status.

'Then what?' said Frank Harrington. He folded his arms and narrowed his shoulders as if to make himself even smaller.

'I'm not happy with any of it,' I said. I felt like telling them that I had enough evidence to support the idea that Bret should be put straight into one of the Berwick House hard-rooms pending an interior enquiry. But in the present circumstances any attempt to describe my reasoning, and my evidence, could only result in me being put there instead. 'It's just a feeling,' I said lamely.

'So what's your plan?' said Frank, looking at Bret.

'Stinnes says that a courier takes cash to pay the network. We know the KGB rendezvous procedure. We'll contact the network and I'll take them some money.'

'Money? Who'll sign the chit for it?' said Dicky, suddenly sitting up and taking notice. Dicky could be very protective about German-desk funds being spent by anyone other than himself.

'It will come from Central Funding,' said Bret, who was ready for that one.

'It can't come direct from Central Funding,' said Morgan. 'It must have the appropriate signature.' He meant Dicky, of course, and technically he was right.

Bret wiggled his feet a little – his shoes were visible through the glass-topped desk – and ignored him. To the rest of us he said, 'There's sure to have been cash and valuables lost in the explosion. And even if there wasn't, they'll want dough to cover their extra expenses. It's a perfect chance to crack them wide open.'

'It sounds like bloody madness to me,' said Morgan, angry at getting the cold shoulder.

'Do we know any of them?' said Frank vaguely.

Bret had been saving this one, of course, and Frank had fed him just the right cue. 'Damn right we do! We know three of them in considerable detail; one is on the computer. I had a long session with Stinnes yesterday and I know exactly how it should be done.'

Frank still had his arms folded. I realized that he was fighting the temptation to get out his pipe and tobacco; Frank found thinking difficult without the pipe in his hand, but the last time he'd smoked his pungent Balkan Sobranie here, Bret had asked him to put it out. Frank said, 'You're not thinking of trying this yourself, are you, Bret?' He kept his voice level and friendly, but it was impossible to miss the note of incredulity and Bret didn't like it.

'Yes, I am,' said Bret.

'How can you be sure that Bernard's wrong?' said Frank. 'How can you be sure that Stinnes didn't send your two men into that booby trap? And how can you be sure he hasn't got the same kind of thing planned for you?'

'Because I'm taking Stinnes with me,' said Bret.

There was a silence broken only by the sound of the D-G's black Labrador sniffing and scratching at the door. It wanted to get in to Morgan, who took it for walks.

'Whose idea was that?' said Dicky. There was a faint note of admiration and envy there. Like so many of the armchair agents up here on the top floor, Dicky was always saying how much he'd like to do some sort of operational job, although, like all the rest of them until now, he'd never done anything about it.

'Mine,' said Bret. 'It was my idea. Stinnes was doubtful, but my American accent will give me the cover I need. With Stinnes alongside me to give all the usual guarantees they won't possibly suspect me as an agent working for British security.'

I looked at him. It was a good argument. Whatever Bret Rensselaer looked like, it was not one of the ill-groomed spook hunters from MI5, and certainly not one of the Special Branch heavy-glove mob they took along to make their arrests legal.

'It might work,' said Frank Harrington, without putting his heart and soul into it, 'providing Moscow haven't put out an alert for Stinnes.' He looked at me.

'Nothing so far,' I said.

Dicky shifted his weight and nodded. Then he ran his fingers back through his dry curly hair and smiled nervously. I don't know what Dicky was thinking except that anything that kept Bret busy was also keeping him off Dicky's back.

Only Morgan was upset at the idea. He scowled and said, 'There's no chance of the D-G approving this one. Hell, Bret, the phone is still red hot with Five enquiring about the explosion.' The dog, its scent of Morgan supplemented by the sound of Morgan's voice, renewed its scratching at the door. Morgan ignored it.

'You should never have told them,' said Dicky, who could always be relied upon for excellent advice long after it was any use.

But Bret was desperate. He knew his career was at stake. He

needed a scalp, and breaking this network was the only scalp on offer. 'I don't need any special permission. I'm going ahead anyway.'

'I'd not advise that, Bret,' said Morgan. He had both hands in his trouser pockets, and now he slowly walked across the room, staring reflectively at the toes of his shoes.

Bret resented the way in which Morgan used his position as the D-G's hatchet man to address all senior staff by their first name. It wasn't just the use of the first name, but the casual and overfamiliar way in which Morgan spoke that was so annoying. The Welsh accent could be a delight for reciting poetry, but it was an accent that could make even the friendliest greeting sound like a jeer. Bret said, 'I had the backing of the old man for breaking into the law office. This is all part of that same job.'

Morgan swung around and smiled. He had good teeth, and when he smiled he displayed them like someone about to brush them for a dental hygiene demonstration. Or someone about to bite. 'And I say it isn't,' he said.

There was only one way to settle it and Bret knew it. After a little give and take and a phone call, we all trooped down the corridor and into the Director-General's office. He was not very keen to see us, but Bret gently insisted.

The old man's office was in its usual muddle, though some of the clutter had been tidied away. Despite the improvement we all had to stand, for there were books on the chairs and more piled on the floor.

Sir Henry Clevemore, the Director-General, was seated behind a small desk near the window. There wasn't much working space, for its top was occupied by photos of his family, including grown-up children with their offspring, and a vase of cut flowers. The D-G murmured his greetings to all of us in turn and then he listened solemnly to Bret. He didn't invite Morgan to comment although Morgan was bouncing up and down on his toes, as he often did when agitated.

Bret took it very slowly. That was the best way with the D-G, if not to say the only way; he only understood when you explained everything very slowly. And if you could go on long enough you could wear him down until he agreed with whatever the request was, just to get rid of you. In all fairness, the old man needed a guardian like Morgan, but he didn't deserve Morgan. No one did.

It was while Bret was in full flow that a man came in through the door with a bundle of cloth under his arm. The D-G stood up, solemnly removed his jacket, and gave it to the newcomer who hung it on a hanger and put it into the wardrobe that was built into one wall.

Although Bret was disconcerted to the point of drying up, he resumed his pitch rather than let Morgan take over. But he now kept things very vague. 'Don't worry about Bony,' said the D-G, indicating the stranger. 'He was with me in the war. He's vetted.'

'It's rather delicate, sir,' said Bret.

'I'll be gone in three minutes,' said Bony, a short man in a tight-fitting grey worsted three-piece suit. He hung a partly made jacket onto the D-G and, apparently oblivious of us all, stood back to inspect the D-G's appearance. Then he made some chalk marks on the jacket and began to rip pieces off it the way tailors do.

'The lapels were rather wide on the last one,' said the D-G.

'They are wide nowadays,' said Bony. He wrote something into his notebook and, without looking up or interrupting his note taking, he said, 'I've kept yours very narrow compared with what most people are wearing.'

'I like them narrow,' said the D-G, standing upright as if on parade.

'It's just a matter of your okay, Sir Henry,' said Bret, in an effort to squeeze an approval from the old man while he was occupied with the details of his new suit.

'Two pairs of trousers?' said Bony. He put some pins between his lips while he tugged with both hands at the jacket.

'Yes,' said the D-G.

'Isn't that a bit old hat, Sir Henry?' said Frank Harrington, speaking for the first time. Frank was very close to the old man. They'd trained together at some now defunct wartime establishment, and this was a mysterious bond they shared. It gave Frank the right to speak to Sir Henry in a way that no one else in the building dared, not even the Deputy.

'No, always do. Always did, always do,' said the old man, stroking his sleeve.

'Gets damned hot, doesn't it?' said Frank, persisting with his ancient joke. 'Wearing two pairs of trousers.'

The D-G laughed dutifully, a deep resonant sound that might have been a bad cough.

'I feel we must continue,' said Bret, trying now to press the meeting forward without saying anything that Bony might understand. 'We've had a bad start, but we must go on and get something out of it.'

'I'm coming under a great deal of pressure,' said the old man, plucking at his shoulder seam. 'I'll need more room under there, Bony.' He pushed his fist under his arm to show where he wanted it and then stretched an arm high into the air to show that it constricted his movement.

Bony smoothed the material and sniffed. 'You're not supposed to play golf in it, Sir Henry. It's a lounge suit.'

'If we stop now, I fear we'll come out of it badly,' said Bret. 'The trouble we ran into was simply a matter of bad luck. There was no actual operational failure.' The operation was a success but the patient died.

Bony was behind the D-G now, tugging at the remnants of the half-made garment. 'Keep still, sir!' he ordered fiercely, in a voice that shocked us all. Not Bret nor even Frank Harrington would have spoken to the D-G like that.

'I'm sorry, Bony,' said the D-G.

Bony did not graciously accept the apology. 'If we get it wrong, you'll blame me,' he said, with the righteous indignation of the self-employed artisan.

'Have you brought the fabrics?' said the D-G. 'You promised to bring the swatches.' There was a retaliatory petulance in the D-G's voice, as if the swatches were something that Bony had failed to bring more than once in the past.

'I wouldn't advise the synthetics,'.said Bony. 'They're shiny. That wouldn't suit a man of your position, Sir Henry. People would think it was a suit bought off the peg.' Bony did all but shudder at the idea of Sir Henry Clevemore wearing a shiny synthetic ready-made suit.

Bret said, 'We have excellent prospects, Sir Henry. It would be criminal to throw away a chance like this.'

'How long do you want?' said the D-G.

Bony looked at him to see if he was asking about the delivery time of the suit, decided it wasn't a question for him, ana said, 'I want you to look at the wool, Sir Henry. This is the sort of thing for you.' He waved samples of cloth in the air. They all seemed virtually identical to the material of the suit the D-G was wearing when we came in; virtually identical to the fabrics the D-G always wore.

'Two weeks,' said Bret.

'You like it to go quickly,' said the D-G.

Both Bony and Bret denied this, although it appeared that the D-G was addressing this accusation to Bony, for he added, 'If everyone insisted on hard-wearing cloth, it would put you all out of business.'

Bony must have been more indignant than Bret, for he got his rebuttal in first and loudest. 'Now that's nonsense, Sir Henry, and you know it. You have suits you had from me twenty years ago, and they're still good. My reputation depends upon my customers looking their best. If I thought a synthetic material would be best for you, I'd happily supply it.'

'Even one week might be enough,' said Bret, sensing that his first bid was unacceptable.

'If synthetic material was the most expensive, you'd be selling that to me with the same kind of enthusiasm,' said the D-G. He waggled a finger at the tailor like a little child discovering a parent in an untruth.

'Absolutely not,' said Bony. The D-G delivered all his lines as if he'd said them many times before, but Bony responded with a fresh and earnest tone that was near to anger. The D-G seemed to enjoy the exchanges; perhaps this sort of sparring was what made the D-G order his suits from the indomitable Bony.

'I'll hold the barbarians at bay for a week,' conceded the D-G. He didn't have to explain to Bret that the barbarians were at the Home Office or that after a week Bret's head might be handed over to them.

'Thank you, sir,' said Bret, and wisely ended the discussion.

But the D-G was not wholly concerned with the swatches of cloth that he was now fingering close by the window. 'Who are you briefing for this job?' he asked without looking up.

Bony handed him a second batch of materials.

'I'm not very keen on that,' said the D-G. He was still looking at the cloth and there were a few moments of silence while Bony and Bret tried to decide to which of them the remark was addressed. 'But you are in charge so I suppose I'll have to let you decide.'

'Yes, sir. Thank you,' said Bret.

'If you want a shiny cloth, what about that?' said Bony, tapping one of the samples.

'I've no special desire for a shiny cloth,' said the D-G testily. 'But I do want to try one of the synthetic mixtures.'

Bret was edging towards the door.

Bony said, 'They look good in the samples, but some of them don't make up very well.'

'One wool and one mixture. I told you that at the beginning . . . the first fitting.' He looked up to see Bret getting away and added, 'You'll have to take . . .' He nodded his head at me. He knew me well enough. On occasion I'd even had lunch with him. He'd seen me virtually every day at London Central for about six years, but still he couldn't remember my name. It was the same for most of the staff at London Central, yet still I found it irritating.

'Samson,' supplied Bret Rensselaer.

'Samson. Yes.' He smiled at me. 'Take him with you. He knows how these things are done,' said the D-G. The implication was that no one else present did know how such things are done, and he fixed me with a look as if to underline that that's exactly what he meant. He probably liked me; I had, after all, survived quite a few complaints from various members of the senior staff. Or perhaps he was just good at this thing they call management.

But now I wanted to protest. I looked at Bret and saw that he wanted to protest too. But there was no point in saying anything more. The D-G's audience had ended. Seeing us hesitating he waved his cloth sample at us to shoo us away. 'And keep in touch with Morgan,' added the D-G. My heart fell and Bret's jaw tightened in rage. We both knew what that meant; it would give the pasty-faced

Morgan carte blanche to mastermind the operation while using the name of the D-G as his authority.

'Very well, sir,' said Bret.

And so I found myself inextricably linked to Bret Rensselaer's amateur attempt to infiltrate the Cambridge net. And I was the only person who suspected him of treason. For assistance we'd have Stinnes, whose name Bret had craftily kept out of the discussion – the only other person I couldn't trust.

17

'I'm sick to death of hearing what a wonderful man your father was,' said Bret suddenly. He hadn't spoken for a long time. The anger had been brewing up inside him so that even without a cue he had to let me have it.

What had I said about my father that had touched a nerve in him? Only that he hadn't left me any money – hardly a remark to produce such a passionate response.

We were in an all-night launderette. I was pretending to read a newspaper that was resting on my knees. It was 2.30 a.m., and outside the street was very dark. But there was not much to be seen through the windows, for this small shop was a cube of bright blue light suspended in the dark suburban streets of Hampstead. From the loudspeaker fixed in the ceiling came the soft scratchy sounds of pop music too subdued to be recognizable. A dozen big washing machines lined one wall. Their white enamel was chipped and scarred with the initials of the cleaner type of vandal. Detergent was spilled across the floor like yellow snow and there was the pungent smell of boiled coffee from a dispensing machine in the corner. We were sitting at the far end of a line of chairs facing the washing machines. Side by side Bret and I stared at the big cyclops where some dirty linen churned in suds. Customers came and went, so that most of the machines were working. Every few moments the mechanisms made loud clicking noises and sometimes the humming noises modulated to a scream as one of the drums spun.

'My father was a lush,' said Bret. 'His two brothers forced him off the board after he'd punched one of the bank's best customers. I was about ten years old. After that I was the only one to look after him.'

'What about your mother?'

'You have to have an infinity of compassion to look after a drunkard,' said Bret. 'My mother didn't have that gift. And my brother Sheldon only cared about the old man's money. He told me that. Sheldon worked in the bank with my uncles. He would lock his bedroom door and refuse to come out when my father was getting drunk.'

'Didn't he ever try to stop?'

'He tried. He really tried. My mother would never believe he tried, but I knew him. He even went to a clinic in Maine. I went in the car with him. It was a grim-looking place. They wouldn't let me past the entrance lodge. But a few weeks after he came back, he was drinking again. . . . None of them tried to help him. Not Sheldon, not my mother, no one. I hated to leave him when I went into the Navy. He died before I even went to sea.' Bret looked at his watch and at the only other person there: a well-dressed man who'd been sitting near the door reading *Le Monde* and drinking coffee from a paper cup.

Now the man tossed the paper cup onto the floor, got to his feet, and opened the glass door to empty his machine and stuff his damp underwear into a plastic bag. He nodded to us before leaving. Bret looked at me, obviously wondering if that could be their first contact, but he didn't voice this suspicion. He said, 'Maybe they won't buy it. We should have brought Stinnes inside here. Last year he made the cash delivery; that's why he knows exactly how it's done. They'd recognize him. That would be good.'

I'd insisted that Stinnes remain in the second car. I said, 'It's better this way. I want Stinnes where he can be protected. If we need him, we can get him in two minutes. I put Craig in to mind him. Craig's good.'

'I still say we should have used Stinnes to maximum advantage.'

'I don't want him sitting in here under the lights; a target for anyone driving past. I don't want him in here with a bodyguard. And we certainly don't want to give Stinnes a gun.'

'Maybe you're right.'

'If they're on the level, it will be okay.'

'If they think we're on the level, it will be okay,' Bret corrected me. 'But they're bound to be edgy.'

'They're breaking the law and you aren't; remember that. They'll be nervous. Stay cool and it will go smoothly.'

'You don't really believe that; you're just trying to convince yourself,' said Bret. 'You've argued against me all the way.'

'That's right,' I said.

Bret leaned forward to reach inside the bag of laundry that he'd placed between his feet. He was dressed in an old raincoat and a tweed cap. I can't imagine where he'd found them; they weren't the kind of thing Bret would normally consider wearing. It was his first attempt to handle any sort of operation and he couldn't come to terms with the idea that we weren't trying to look like genuine launderette customers; we were trying to look like KGB couriers trying to look like launderette customers.

'Stinnes has been really good,' said Bret. 'The phone call went perfectly. He had the code words – they'll call themselves "Bingo" – and amounts . . . four thousand dollars. They believed I was the regular contact coming through here a week early. No reason for them to be suspicious.' He bent lower to reach deep enough in the bag to finger the money that was in a little parcel under the laundry. According to Stinnes, it was the way it was usually done.

I said nothing.

Bret straightened up and said, 'You don't get too suspicious of a guy who's going to hand you four thousand bucks and no questions asked, right?'

'And that's what you're going to do?'

'It's better that way. We give them the money and say hello. I want to build them up. Next meeting I'll get closer to them.'

'It's very confidence-building, four thousand dollars,' I said.

Bret was too nervous to hear the sarcasm in my voice. He smiled and nodded and stared at the dirty laundry milling round in the machine.

'He got violent, my father. Some guys can drink and just get happy; or amorous. But my father got fighting drunk or else morose. Sometimes, when I was just a child, he'd sit up half the night telling me that he'd ruined my life, ruined my mother's life, and ruined his own life. "You're the only one I've got, Bret," he'd say. Then the next minute he'd be trying to fight me because I was stopping him having another drink. He took no account of my age; he always talked to me the way you'd talk to an adult.'

A man came in through the door. He was young and slim, wearing jeans and a short, dark pea jacket. He had a bright-blue woollen ski mask on his head, the sort that completely hides the face except for eye slots and a hole for the mouth. The pea jacket was unbuttoned and from under it he brought out a sawn-off shotgun. 'Let's go,' he said. He was excited and nervous. He waggled the gun at us and moved his head to show that he wanted us to get going.

'What's this?' said Bret.

'Bingo,' said the man. 'This is Bingo.'

'I've got it here,' said Bret. He seemed to be frozen into position, and because Bret wouldn't move, the boy with the gun was becoming even more agitated.

'Go! go! go!' shouted the boy. His voice was high-pitched and anxious.

Bret got to his feet with the laundry bag in his hand. Another man came in. He was similarly masked, but he was broader and, judging from his movements, older, perhaps forty. He was dressed in a short bulky black-leather overcoat. He stood in the doorway looking first at the man with the shotgun and then back over his shoulder; there must have been three of them. One hand was in his overcoat pocket, in his other hand he had a bouquet of coloured wires. 'What's the delay? I told you . . .'

His words were lost in the muffled bang that made the shop window rattle. Outside in the street there was a blast of flame that for a moment went on burning bright. It was across the road. That could be only one thing; they'd blown up the car. The second man tossed the bundle of coloured wires to the floor. My God! Stinnes was in that car. The bastards!

Bret was standing when the car blew up. He was directly between me and the two men. The explosion gave me the moment's distraction I needed. I leaned forward enough to see round Bret. My silenced pistol was on my lap wrapped in a newspaper. I fired twice at the youngest one. He didn't go down, but he dropped the shotgun and slumped against the washing machines holding his chest. 'Get down, Bret!' I said, and pushed him to the floor before the other joker started firing. 'Hold it right there,' I shouted. Then I ran along the machines, and past the wounded man, kicking the shotgun back towards Bret as I went. I couldn't wait around and play nursemaid to Bret, but if he was a KGB man he might pick up the shotgun and let me have it in the back.

The older one didn't wait to see what I wanted. He went through a door marked STAFF before I could shoot at him. I followed. It was an office – the least amount of office you could get: a small table, one chair, a cheap cashbox, a vacuum flask, a dirty cup and a copy of the *Daily Mirror*.

I went through the next door and found myself at the bottom of a flight of stairs. The door banged behind me and it was suddenly dark. There was a corridor leading to a street door. He hadn't had time to get out into the street that way, but he might have been waiting there in the darkness. Where was he? I remained still for a moment, letting my eyes adjust to the dark.

While I was trying to decide whether to explore the corridor, there was a sound of footsteps from the floor above. Then there was a loud bang. The flash lit the staircase, and lead shot rattled against the wallpaper. So this bastard had a shotgun too. The gun must have been under his buttoned coat; difficult to get at, that's why he'd had to run for it. That shot was just a warning, of course – something to show what was waiting for me if I climbed the stairs.

I wasn't looking for a chance to be a hero, but I heard his feet going up the next flight and I went up the first flight of stairs two at a time. I had rubber-soled shoes. He was making so much noise that he probably couldn't hear me. But as I halted at the next dark landing, his footsteps halted too. In the lexicon of hand-to-hand fighting, going up a dark staircase against a shotgun is high on the list of 'don't-evers'.

I was badly placed. Did he see me or did he guess where I was? He moved across the landing, aimed down the staircase, and pulled the trigger. There was a bang and a flash and the sound of him running. That was nasty; he was trying to kill me now that his warning shot had gone unheeded. Bang! Jesus Christ! Another blast. I felt that one and I jumped back frightened and disoriented. For a moment I thought there must be two of them, but that was just a manifestation of my fear. So was the indigestible lump in my stomach.

I kept still, my heart pounding and my face hot. It was pitch dark except for a glimmer of light escaping from under the door of the office on the floor below me. I fancied I could see a pale blur where he was leaning over the balustrade trying to catch a glimpse of me. He must have taken the woollen mask off; too hot, I suppose. I kept very still, my shoulders pressed flat against the wall, and waited to see if he would do something even more stupid. Come on, come on, come on! Soon the police sirens would be heard and I'd be facing an audience outside in the road. On the other hand, so would he.

Sweat dribbled down my face, but my mouth was dry and rough like sandpaper. It was only with some effort that I breathed slowly and silently. The Department would gloss over the man I'd shot downstairs, especially if I wrote the report to make it sound as if I was protecting Bret. Protecting highly placed top-floor staff at London Central was not something the Department wanted to discourage. But they would not gloss over the inconvenience of untangling me from the clutches of the Metropolitan Police. Particularly not when our present relationship with the Home Office was decidedly turbulent.

Ah . . . keeping very still paid off! This was him. He leaned forward and the glint of light from the hall below caught his forehead. I am not a vindictive man, but I was frightened and angry. I wasn't going to let some hoodlum dynamite one of our cars and push a shotgun under my nose and try to kill me like they'd killed Ted Riley. This one wasn't going to slip away into the night. I raised my gun slowly and took careful aim. Maybe he saw me or the movement of the gun. He ducked back as I started to squeeze the trigger. Too late. I stayed very still, gun uplifted. I counted to ten and I was lucky. My inactivity encouraged him to lean forward again, this time more cautiously, but not cautiously enough. I pumped two shots into him. The silenced gun twisted in my hand and its two thuds were followed by a scream and a crash and the sound of a door banging, as he tumbled back into a room on the landing above me. They must have been using a room here. Maybe one, maybe all of them, had been upstairs waiting for us. That's why we got no warning from our men positioned across the street.

For a moment I hesitated. I wanted to look at their hideout, but time was pressing and the consequences too serious. I ran downstairs, through the office – knocking the cashbox to the floor as I went – and pushed open the swing door into the launderette. Coins and paper money scattered over the floor; perhaps that would convince the cops it was a bungled robbery. It was blindingly bright under the fluorescent lights after the darkness of the stairwell, bright and steamy. I half closed my eyes to try to retain some of their adjustment as I went out onto the street.

The street was lit by the flames from the car. I saw a third man now. He was also dressed in a pea jacket. He was astride a motorbike and got it started as I brought the gun up and fired. But he was quick. And he was strong enough to swing the heavy bike round in a tight curve and open the throttle to roar away. I chanced one more shot at him, but after that I could see him only as a dark smudge against the fronts of the houses. Too dark, too much deflection and too much chance of putting a few rounds into someone's bedroom. So I went back into the launderette to see what Bret was doing.

Bret was doing nothing except holding his bundled-up laundry bag tight under his arm and watching the masked boy bleeding bright red frothy blood. The boy was still clamped over the washing machine, holding it tight as if he was trying to move it to another place. His feet were wide apart and there was blood on the white enamel, blood on the glass, and blood mingling with the spilled soapy water that had leaked onto the floor.

'He's had it,' I said. 'Let's go, Bret.' I stuffed my gun back into my overcoat pocket. Bret was in shock. I gave him a short jab in the ribs to bring him back into the real world. He blinked and shook his head like a boxer trying to clear his brain. Then he got the idea and ran after me to where my car was parked on the corner.

'Stay in the car,' I said, opening the door and pushing him into the front seat. 'I've got to look at the others.'

Bret was still holding the bag with the money and the laundry. He was like a man in a trance. As he settled into the car seat, the bag was on his knees and he had his arms round it tight, as if it was a body. Across the road the Ford Escort in which Stinnes and the minder had arrived was still burning, although the flames were now turning to black smoke as the tyres caught fire. 'He's here,' said Bret, meaning Stinnes.

'Shit,' I said. Because, to my amazement, Bret was right. Stinnes had survived the bomb under the car. He was standing by the door of my Rover waiting to be let in. 'Get in the back seat.' His minder was standing close to him. It was only when they were awkwardly climbing into the back seat that I noticed they were handcuffed together. A minder that cuffs himself to his subject is a minder who takes no chances, but he'd saved Stinnes from certain death. Craig was huge and muscular; shackled to Craig, even King Kong would have to go where Craig went.

I started the car and pulled away before there was any sign of a police car. I suppose that respectable part of Hampstead doesn't attract a big police presence at three o'clock on a Tuesday morning. 'What the hell happened?' I asked.

'I saw them coming,' said Craig. 'They were amateurs, real amateurs.' He was very young, no more than twenty. 'So I put the cuffs on and we got out.' He had a simple outlook: most good minders are like that. And he was right; they'd behaved like amateurs, and that puzzled me. They'd even missed Craig and Stinnes escaping from the car. Amateurs. But the KGB didn't use amateurs in their hit teams and that worried me. We passed a police car at Swiss Cottage. It was doing about seventy on the wrong side of the road, with the blue light flashing and the siren on. They were doing it the way they'd seen it done on late-night TV.

By this time Bret was coming back to life. 'What was that you were saying, about how they would arrive very nervous?' he said. His voice was shaky; suddenly he'd experienced life at the sharp end of the Department and he was shocked.

'Very funny, Bret,' I said. 'Does that crack come before you thank me for saving your life or afterwards?' From behind us I heard young Craig coughing to remind us that the rear seats were occupied by people with ears.

'Saving my life, you son of a bitch?' said Bret in hysterical anger. 'First you shoot, using me as a shield. Then you run out, leaving me to face the music.'

I laughed. 'That's the way it is being a field agent, Bret,' I said. 'If you'd had experience or training, you would have hit the deck. Better still, you would have taken out that second bastard instead of leaving me to deal with all of them.'

'If I'd had experience or training,' said Bret menacingly, 'I would have read to you that section of the Command Rules that applies to the use of firearms in a public place.'

'You don't have to read it to *me*, Bret,' I said. 'You should have read it to that bastard who came at us with the sawn-off shotgun. And to the one who tried to part my hair when I went after him upstairs.'

'You killed him,' said Bret. He was still breathing heavily. He was rattled, really rattled, while I was pumped with adrenalin and ready to say all kinds of things that are better left unsaid. 'He bled to death. I watched him.'

'Why didn't you give him first aid?' I said sarcastically. 'Because that would have meant letting go your four grand? Is that why?'

'You could have winged him,' Bret said.

'That's just for the movies, Bret. That's just for Wyatt Earp and Jesse James. In the real world, no one is shooting guns out of people's hands or giving them flesh wounds in the upper arm. In the real world you hit them or you miss them. It's difficult enough to hit a moving target without selecting tricky bits of anatomy. So don't give me all that crap.'

'We left him to die.'

'That's right. And if you had followed me upstairs with the shotgun I kicked over to you and tried to give me a little cover, you would have seen me kill another of those bastards.'

'Is it going in your report?' said Bret.

'You're damn right it's going in my report. And so is the way you stood there like a goddamned tailor's dummy when I needed backup.'

'You're a maniac, Samson,' said Bret.

Erich Stinnes leaned forward from the back seat and said softly, 'That's the way it is, Mr Rensselaer. What Samson did was just what I would have done. It's what any really good professional would have done.'

Bret said nothing. Bret was clutching his bag and staring into space lost in his own thoughts. I knew what it was; I'd seen it happen to other people. Bret would never be quite the same again. Bret was no longer with us; he'd withdrawn into some inner world into which none of the stinking realities of his job would be allowed to intrude. Then suddenly he spoke, softly, as if just voicing his thoughts: 'And it was Sheldon he really loved. Not me: Sheldon.'

'Well, I don't want any of that in it,' said Dicky. 'It's not a report, it's a diatribe.'

'Whatever you want to call it, it's the truth,' I said. We were sitting side by side in the drawing room of the Cruyers' home. Dicky was wearing his 'I Love New York' sweatshirt, jeans, and jogging shoes, with those special thick white socks that are said to lessen the shocks to the spine. We'd been watching the TV news to see if there was anything about the Hampstead shooting: there wasn't. The gas was hissing in the simulated coal fire and now the TV was displaying a rather unattractive foursome in punk outfits. For a moment Dicky's attention was distracted by them. 'Look at those caterwauling imbeciles,' he said. 'Are we working our guts out just to keep the West safe for that sort of garbage?'

'Not entirely,' I said. 'We're getting paid as well.'

He picked up the remote control and reduced the pop group to a pinpoint of light that disappeared with a soft plop. Then he took up my draft report again and pretended to read it afresh, but actually he was just holding it in front of his face while he thought about what to say next. 'It's your version of the truth,' he said pedantically.

'That's the only one I've got,' I said.

'Try again.'

'It's *anyone*'s version of the truth,' I said. 'Anyone who was there.'

'When are you going to get it through your thick head that I don't want your uncorrupted testimony? I want something that can go to the old man and not get me into hot water.' He tossed the draft of my report onto the table beside him. Then he scratched his curly head. Dicky was worried. He didn't want to be in the middle of a departmental battle. Dicky liked to score his victories by stealth.

I leaned across from the armchair and picked up my carefully typed sheets. But Dicky gently took them from my hand. He folded them up and stuffed them under a paperweight that was handy on the other side of him. 'Better forgotten, Bernard,' he said. 'Start again.'

'Perhaps this time you'd tell me what you want me to say,' I suggested.

'I'll draft something for you,' said Dicky. 'Keep it very short. Just the main essentials will be sufficient.'

'Have you seen Bret's report?' I said.

'There was no report from Bret; just a meeting. Bret had to give a brief account of everything that's happened since he took over the Stinnes business.' Dicky smiled nervously. 'It wasn't the sort of stuff upon which careers are built.'

'I suppose not,' I said. An account of everything that had happened since Bret took responsibility for Stinnes would be one of unremitting disaster. I wondered how much of the blame Bret had unloaded onto me.

'It was decided that Stinnes should go back into Berwick House immediately. And Bret has to keep the old man informed of everything he intends to do about him.'

'Berwick House? What's the panic? Everyone says the interrogation was going well since we moved him.'

'No reflection on you, Bernard. But Stinnes was nearly killed. If it hadn't been for that fellow Craig, they'd have got him. We can't risk that again, Bernard. Stinnes is too precious.'

'Will this affect Bret's appointment to Berlin?'

'They won't consult me on that one, Bernard.' A modest smile to show me that they *might* consult him. In fact, we both knew that Morgan was depending upon Dicky's veto to stop Bret getting Berlin. 'But I'd say Bret will be lucky to escape a suspension.'

'A suspension?'

'It won't be called a suspension. It will be called a posting, or a sabbatical, or a paid leave.'

'Even so.'

'Bret's made a lot of enemies in the Department,' said Dicky.

'You and Morgan, you mean?'

Dicky was flustered at this accusation. He got up from his chair and went to the fireplace so that he could toy with a framed photo of his boat. He looked at it for a moment and wiped the glass with his handkerchief before putting it back alongside the clock. 'I'm no enemy to Bret. I like him. I know he tried to take over my desk, but I don't hold that against him.'

'But?'

'But there are all kinds of loose ends arising out of the Stinnes affair. Bret has gone at it like a bull in a china shop. First there was the fiasco in Cambridge. Now there's the shooting in Hampstead. And what have we got to show for it? Nothing at all.'

'No one tried to stop him,' I said.

'You mean no one listened to your attempts to stop him. Well, you're right, Bernard. You were right and Bret was wrong. But Bret was determined to run it all personally, and with Bret's seniority it wasn't so easy to interfere with him.'

'But now it *is* easy to interfere with him?'

'It's called "a review",' said Dicky.

'Why couldn't it be called a review last week?'

He sank down into the sofa and stretched his legs along it. 'Because a whole assortment of complications came up this week.'

'Concerning Bret?'

'Yes.'

'He's not facing an enquiry?'

'I don't know, Bernard. And even if I did know, I couldn't discuss it with you.'

'Will it affect me?' I asked.

'I don't think so, except inasmuch as you have been working with Bret while all these things have happened.' He fingered his belt buckle. 'Unless of course Bret blames you.'

'And is Bret doing that?' I said. I spoke more loudly than I intended; I hadn't wanted my fears, or my distrust of Bret, to show.

As I said it, Dicky's wife Daphne came in. She smiled. 'And is Bret doing what, Bernard?' she said.

'Dyeing his hair,' improvised Dicky hastily. 'Bernard was wondering if Bret dyes his hair.'

'But his hair is white,' said Daphne.

'Not really white. It's blond and going white,' said Dicky. 'We were just saying that it never seems to go any whiter. What do you think, darling? You ladies know about things like that.'

'He was here the other evening. He had supper with us,' said Daphne. 'He's such a handsome man. . . .' She saw Dicky's face, and maybe mine too. 'For his age, I mean. But I don't think he could be dyeing his hair unless it was being done by some very good hairdresser. It's certainly not obvious.' Daphne stood in front of the fireplace so that we could get a good look at her new outfit. She was dressed in a long gown of striped shiny cotton, an Arab *djellaba* which the neighbours had brought back from their holiday in Cairo. Her hair was plaited, with beads woven into it. She'd been an art student and once worked in an advertising agency. She liked to look artistic.

'He'd have no trouble affording an expensive hairdresser,' said Dicky. 'He inherited a fortune when he was twenty-one. And he certainly knows how to spend it.' Dicky had gone through his college days short of cash, and now he especially resented anyone having been young and rich, whether they were prodigies, divorcees or pop stars. He looked at the clock. 'Is that the time? If we're going to see this video, we'd better get started. Have you got the food ready, darling?' Without waiting to hear her reply he turned to me and said, 'We're eating on trays in here. Better than rushing through our meal.'

Dicky had been determined to get a preview of the report I was preparing for submission to the D-G, but his command to bring it to him had been disguised as an invitation to supper, with a rented video of a Fred Astaire musical as a surprise extra.

'It's only soup and toasted sandwiches,' said Daphne.

Dicky said, 'I bought her one of those sandwich toasters. My God, I rue the day! Now I get everything between toasted bread: salami, cheese, ham, avocado and bacon. . . . What was that mess you served the other day, darling – curried lamb inside a toasted *chapatti*? It was disgusting.'

'It was just an experiment, darling,' said Daphne.

'Yes, well, you didn't have to scrape all the burned pieces off the machine, darling,' said Dicky. 'I thought you'd set the whole kitchen on fire. I burned my finger.'

He showed me the finger. I nodded.

'It's ham and cheese tonight,' said Daphne. 'Onion soup to start with.'

'I hope you chopped the onion really small this time,' said Dicky.

'He hates soup going down his chin,' said Daphne, as though this was a curious aversion for which she could not account.

'It ruined one of my good ties,' said Dicky. 'And in the dark I didn't notice.'

'Bret Rensselaer didn't spill his soup,' said Daphne. 'And he wears beautiful ties.'

'Why don't you get the supper, darling?'

'The trays are all ready.'

'And I'll get the video,' said Dicky. He stood, hitched his trousers up, and retrieved my report from under the paperweight before he strode from the room.

'The video is on the machine,' said Daphne. 'He hates saying he's going to the loo. He's such a prude about some things.'

I nodded.

She stood by the kitchen door and said, 'I'll go and get the food.' But she made no move.

'Can I help you, Daphne?'

To my surprise she said yes. Usually Daphne didn't like visitors to her kitchen. I'd heard her say that many times.

I followed her. The kitchen had all been redecorated since the last time I'd been there. It was like a cupboard shop; there were cupboards on every available piece of wall space. All were made of plastic, patterned to look like oak.

'Dicky is having an affair,' she said.

'Is he?'

She disregarded my feigned surprise. 'Has he spoken with you about her?'

'An affair?'

'He relies on you,' she said. 'Are you sure he hasn't mentioned anything?'

'I've been with Bret Rensselaer a lot of the time lately.'

'I know I'm putting you in a difficult position, Bernard, but I must know.'

'He hasn't discussed it with me, Daphne. To tell you the truth, it's not the sort of thing he'd confide to me, even if it was true.' Her face fell. 'And I'm sure it's not,' I added.

'It's your sister-in-law,' said Daphne. 'She must be as old as I am, perhaps older.' She opened the toasting machine and pried the sandwiches out of it, using the blade of an old knife. Without turning to me she said, 'If it was some very young girl, I'd find it easier to understand.'

I nodded. Was this, I wondered, a concession to my relationship with Gloria? 'Those sandwiches smell good,' I said.

'They're only ham and cheese,' said Daphne. 'Dicky won't eat anything exotic.' She got a big plate of previously prepared sandwiches from the oven. 'Tessa, I mean. Your sister-in-law; Tessa Kosinski.'

'I've only got the one,' I said. And one like Tessa was more than enough, I thought. Why did she have to make everyone's life so bloody complicated?

'And she's a friend,' said Daphne. 'A friend of the family. That's what hurts.'

'Tessa has been kind to me, helping me with the children.'

'Yes, I know.' Daphne sniffed. It wasn't the sort of sniff that fragile ladies used as a prelude to tears – more the sort of sniff Old Bailey judges gave before passing the death sentence. 'I suppose you must feel a debt of loyalty.' She put cutlery on the trays. She did it very carefully and gently, so that I wouldn't think she was angry.

'I'll do anything I can to help,' I said.

'Don't worry about Dicky hearing us. We'll hear the toilet flush.' She began to look for soup bowls and she had to open four of the cupboards before she found them. 'They had an affair before.' She was speaking to the inside of the cupboards. 'Now, don't say you didn't know about that, Bernard. Tessa and I made up after that. I thought it was all finished.'

'And this time?'

'A friend of mine saw them at a little hotel near Deal . . . Kent, you know.'

'That's a strange place to go for . . .' I stopped and tried to rephrase the sentence.

'No, it was chosen as one of the ten best places for a lovers' weekend by one of the women's magazines last month. *Harpers & Queen*, I think. That's why my friend was there.'

'Perhaps Dicky . . .'

'He told me he was in Cologne,' said Daphne. 'He said it was top secret.'

'Is there something you want me to do about it?'

'I want to meet your brother-in-law,' said Daphne. 'I want to talk to him about it. I want him to know how I feel.'

'Would that really be wise?' I said. I wondered how George would react to an approach from Daphne.

'It's what I want. I've thought about it, and it's what I want.'

'It might just blow over.'

'It will. They all blow over,' said Daphne. 'One after another he has these girlfriends, and I wait for it to blow over. Then he goes off with someone else. Or with the same one again.'

'Have you spoken to him about it?' I said.

'He says it's his money he spends, not mine. He says it's the money his uncle left him.' She turned to me. 'It's nothing to do with the money, Bernard. It's the betrayal. He wouldn't betray his country, would he? He's fanatical about loyalty to the Department. So why betray his wife and children?'

'Did you tell him that?'

'Over and over again. I've had enough of it. I'm going to get a divorce. I want George Kosinski to know that I'm naming his wife in a divorce action.'

Poor George, I thought, that's all he needs to complete his misery. 'That's a serious step, Daphne. I know how you feel, but there are your children . . .'

'They're at school. I only see them in the holidays. Sometimes I think that it was a terrible mistake to send them to boarding school. If the children had lived at home, perhaps Dicky would have had more to keep him from straying.'

'Sometimes it works the other way,' I said, more to comfort her than because I believed it. 'Sometimes children at home make husbands want to get out.'

'Will you arrange it?' she said. 'In the next few days?'

'I'll try,' I said. I heard Dicky upstairs.

Daphne had the trays all ready. 'Could you open the wine, Bernard, and bring the paper napkins? The corkscrew is in the drawer.'

As she held the refrigerator door open for me to get the wine, she said, 'Wasn't that a surprise about Mr Rensselaer? I'd always liked him.' She closed the door and I waited for her as she pushed the hot sandwiches onto the serving plate with flicking motions so that she didn't burn her fingers.

'Yes,' I said.

'Stealing a Cabinet memo and giving it to the Russians. And now they're saying he tried to get you all killed.' She saw the surprise in my face. 'Oh, I know it's still the subject of an enquiry, and we mustn't talk about it, but Dicky says Bret is going to have a job talking his way out of this one.' She picked up all three trays after piling them one on top of the other. 'It must be a mistake, don't you think? He couldn't really be a spy, could he? He's such a nice man.'

'Come along, come along,' shouted Dicky from the next room. 'The titles are running.'

'Dicky's such a mean pig,' said Daphne. 'He can't even wait for us before starting the film.'

18

'You said you wouldn't be late.' Gloria was in bed and my coming into the bedroom had wakened her.

'Sorry,' I said. Our relationship had developed – or should I say degenerated? – into that of a married couple. She spent each weekend with me and kept clothes and makeup and jewellery in my house. To say nothing of countless pairs of shoes.

She sat up in bed and switched on the dim bedside light. She was wearing a black chiffon nightdress. Her pale blonde hair was long enough to touch her shoulders. 'Did you go on?'

'No, I didn't "go on", if you mean to a nightclub or fancy-dress party.'

'You don't have to snap at me.' There was enough light for me to see the neat way in which she'd folded her clothes before going to bed. It was a bad sign; such fastidious attention to detail was often a sign of her suppressed bad temper.

'Do you think I like spending the evening with Dicky?' I said.

'Then why stay so late?'

'He'd rented a video. I couldn't leave before it had finished.'

'Did you have dinner there?'

'Supper; a sandwich and a cup of soup.'

'I ate with the children. Doris cooked a meat pie.'

'I wish you'd call her "Nanny",' I said. The nanny was young and I wanted to keep my distance from her. 'She'll start calling me "Bernard" next.'

'You should have told me before. I can't suddenly change now,' said Gloria. 'She'd think she'd upset me or something.' Her hair was falling over her face; she pushed it back with her hand and held her hand to her head as if posing. 'So it wasn't business?'

'Of course it was business. I told you that Dicky insisted that I bring the first draft of my report with me.'

'Who else was there?'

I sat down on the bed. 'Look, darling. If I'd mentioned you, Dicky would have included you in the invitation. We both know that. But

735

didn't we agree that it's better to keep a low profile. We don't want everyone in the office talking.'

'That depends what they're saying,' said Gloria, who felt that we should be together every minute of our free time and especially resented being left alone for any part of the weekends.

I leaned forward and embraced her tightly and kissed her.

'What did you talk about?' she said.

'Bret is in trouble,' I said.

'With the Department?'

'Dicky is the last of the big-time wishful thinkers. But even allowing for Dicky's exaggeration, Bret is facing the music for everything that's gone wrong with the Stinnes debriefing. Now they're going to start saying it's all been done on Moscow's orders.'

'It's Bret's own fault, darling. He thought it was all so easy. You said that yourself.'

'Yes, he's brought it on himself, but now they're going to heap everything they can think of on him. Whether he's KGB or not, they'll make him the scapegoat.'

'Scapegoat's not the word,' she said. 'Scapegoats were released into the wilderness. You mean Bret will be delivered to MI5 as the person who's been usurping all their powers and functions. Not so much a scapegoat as a hostage. Am I right?'

'Perhaps consolation prize is the expression we're looking for,' I said bitterly. I'd seen too many severed heads delivered to the Home Office under similar circumstances to be optimistic about Bret's fate. 'Anyway, Bret is probably going to face more serious charges than that,' I said.

She looked at me quizzically and said, 'He's a KGB mole?'

'I don't know.'

'But that will be the charge?'

'It's too early for charges. Maybe there won't be any. No one's told me anything, but there's been some sort of top-level meeting about Bret. Everyone is beginning to think he's working for Moscow. Dicky seems to have told Daphne. She thought I'd already been told, so she gave the game away.'

'What a bombshell when the newspapers get the story,' said Gloria.

I kissed her again, but she didn't respond.

'They should be shot,' she said. 'Traitors. Bastards.' She didn't raise her voice, but her body stiffened in anger and the depth of her feeling surprised me.

'It's all part of the game.'

'No, it's not. People like Rensselaer are murderers. To appease their social conscience they'll turn over men and women to the torture chambers. What swine they are!'

'Perhaps they do what they think is right,' I said. I didn't exactly believe it but that was the only way I could do my job. I couldn't start thinking I was part of a struggle of good against evil or freedom against tyranny. The only way I could work was to concentrate on the nuts and bolts of the job and do it as well as I could do it.

'Then why don't they go to Russia? They know it's not the kind of world we want or we'd have voted the Communists into power long ago. Why don't they just go to Russia?'

'Well, why don't they?' I said.

'They want to have their cake and eat it. They're always rich and well educated, aren't they? They want their privileged status in a rich West while they're appeasing their guilt about enjoying it.'

'Are you talking about Bret?' I said. I stood up. 'Or are you talking about my wife?'

'I'm talking about traitors,' she said.

I went over to the wardrobe and opened it. Somewhere there was a tweed suit that I hadn't worn for years. I sorted through the clothes until I found it hung inside a plastic bag – Fiona put all my suits into plastic bags – and then I felt through the pockets. 'I suspected Bret of having an affair with my wife. Did I ever tell you about that?'

'If you're looking for cigarettes, I threw them all out.'

'I suddenly remembered leaving a packet in that tweed suit,' I said. The suit brought back memories. The last time I'd worn it I'd been to a horse show with Fiona and my father-in-law. It was a time when I was working very hard at being nice to him. He'd won a prize for jumping over fences, and he took us all to a fancy restaurant on the river near Marlow. I ran out of cigarettes and my father-in-law wouldn't let me pay cash for some more; he insisted they be added to his dinner bill. The incident stuck in my mind because it was in the restaurant that I first heard that he'd set up trust funds for the children. He hadn't told me, and Fiona hadn't told me either. Worse still, he'd told the children but told them not to tell me.

'Yes, I threw them out. If there are cigarettes in the house, you'll start smoking again, you know that. You don't want to, do you?'

I closed the wardrobe door and abandoned the notion of a cigarette. She was right; I didn't want to start smoking again, but given my present level of stress I wasn't sure how long I'd be able to resist the temptation.

'You have to have someone to look after you,' she said in a concili-atory tone.

'Once, I was certain that Bret was having an affair with Fiona. I hated him. My hatred for him influenced everything I thought, said, and did.' My need for a cigarette had abated. Even if I'd found a carton on my pillow, I wouldn't have bothered to open it. 'It was only with great effort that I could listen to anything that was said about him without reprocessing it and distorting it. Now I've got that feeling under control. I don't even care if they *did* have an affair. I can look at Bret Rensselaer with a clear mind. When I tell you I don't know whether he's guilty, I mean exactly that.'

'Jealousy, you mean. You were jealous of Bret Rensselaer because he's rich and successful and maybe had an affair with your wife.'

'Yes,' I said.

'That's natural enough, Bernard. Why shouldn't you be angry and prejudiced? Why should you be impartial to any man who treats you badly?'

'Are you going to tell me why?'

'Because you like to play God, Bernard. You killed two men the other night in the launderette. You didn't gloss over it. You told me. You told Dicky. I have no doubt it's in your report, with you taking unequivocal responsibility for their deaths. You're not an insensitive brute, you're not a thug or a killer. The only way you can cope with the guilt you suffer over those deaths is by convincing yourself that you observe the world around you with total objectivity. That's playing God, darling. And it's not the way to assuage your guilt. Admit that you're fallible, accept the fact that you're only human, admit that if Bret goes to the Old Bailey, you'll be delighted to see him get his comeuppance.'

'But I won't be delighted. Not even a wronged husband wants to see the other man in the Old Bailey. And in Bret's case, I have no real evidence. As far as I know, Fiona was never unfaithful to me.'

'If you don't hate him for betraying you, then hate him for selling out to the Communists. In that sort of hatred I'll join you.'

'Your father was one of our agents, wasn't he?'

'How did you find out?'

'I just guessed. There always has to be some special reason for the daughter of a foreign national to get into the Department.'

'My uncle and my father . . . the secret police took my uncle away. They killed him in the police station. They were looking for my father.'

'You don't have to talk about it,' I said.

'I don't mind talking about it. I'm proud of him. I'm proud of both of them. My father is a dentist. London sent him dental charts – it was part of his regular correspondence with other dentists – and he used the dental charts to identify agents. The dental surgery was a perfect cover for messages to be passed, and the secret police never succeeded in infiltrating the organization. But all the agents had met my father. That was the big disadvantage – everyone in every cell knew my father. The police finally got his name from someone they picked up photographing the frontier. He talked. They made a mistake and arrested my uncle because he had the same name. He managed to keep silent until my father and mother got away. I hate the Communists, Bernard.'

'I'm going to have a drink,' I said. I took off my jacket and tie and kicked off my shoes. 'Whisky. Would you like one?'

'No thanks, darling.'

I went into my study and poured myself a stiff drink. When I got back to the bedroom, Gloria had combed her hair and plumped up the pillows. I went on undressing. I said, 'Dicky is having an affair with Tessa, and Daphne's found out about them.'

'She told you that?'

'A friend of hers saw them in a hotel.'

'There are always wonderful friends who'll bring you bad news.'

'It's difficult, isn't it? You become a party to a secret and suddenly you have a terrible responsibility. Whatever you do is likely to be wrong.'

'You're talking about that Cabinet memo, aren't you?'

'Perhaps I am.'

'You did nothing,' she said.

'It looks as though I didn't have to. The Department knows about Bret. Daphne actually mentioned the Cabinet memo.'

'What does she want you to do?'

'Daphne? She wants to talk to George. She says she's going to name Tessa in a divorce action.'

'Is she serious?'

'You tell me.'

'That would ruin Dicky's career, wouldn't it?'

'It depends. If it looked like becoming the messy sort of divorce that got into the newspapers, then the Department would get rid of Dicky very quickly.'

'Does Daphne know that?'

'She's very bitter.'

'She's put up with a lot.'

'Has she?'

'You told me that Dicky was constantly unfaithful to her.'

'Did I?'

'Of course you did. And everyone in the office has noticed the way he's been dandying up on certain evenings. And his wife is always phoning asking where he is.'

'Everyone knows that?'

'All the girls know.'

'Does his secretary talk about it?'

'You mustn't ask me questions like that, darling. I can't be the office stool pigeon.'

'I don't like the idea of a secretary who talks about her boss. It's a short step from that to official secrets . . . .'

'Don't be pompous, darling. Dicky gives her a rotten time. I think she's wonderfully loyal under the circumstances.'

19

I don't know whether Bret Rensselaer was officially ordered to keep away from Erich Stinnes or even discouraged from doing so, but obviously someone from the Department had to keep in touch with him. Had he been left at Berwick House and neglected, there was always the chance that London Debriefing Centre would encourage the Home Office to take him over.

When Stinnes suddenly stopped talking to the interrogator, the matter became urgent. I was sent to talk with Stinnes. There was a note initialled by Bret waiting on my desk. I don't know who chose me for the job, but I suppose there weren't many on the shortlist of suitable visitors.

It was pouring with rain when I arrived at Berwick House. The formalities that had greeted Bret Rensselaer's Bentley on my previous visit were waived for my second-hand Rover. No pulling to the side after entering the outer gate – just a quick look at my card and a perfunctory salute.

There was no one to see that I parked in the visitors' marked space in the courtyard and no sign of the Governor or his Deputy anywhere. Instead of the main entrance I used the back door. The duty clerk knew me by sight and he swivelled the visitors' book for my signature and offered me his Parker pen. Judging by the blank spaces in the book they didn't have many visitors at Berwick House these days.

Erich Stinnes wasn't locked up. At certain specified hours he was permitted to exercise in the grounds. When it rained he could come down into the great hall and look through the leaded windows at the bare rosebushes. He had the freedom of the first floor, but I had to notify the key-room clerk that I was going up there. The clerk stopped eating his cheese sandwich long enough to write out the chit that permitted me to leave again. When he passed it to me the chit was marked with his greasy fingerprints. I'm glad that hadn't happened to Bret.

'Not like Notting Hill Gate, is it, Erich?' I said.

'It's good enough,' he said. They'd moved him to Number 4, a large comfortable accommodation at the front. He had a sitting room with a sofa and two armchairs, a coloured print of the Battle of Waterloo, and a medieval electric fire. He had a tiny 'kitchen' too, although it was really no more than an alcove equipped with sink, cooking ring, some pans, crockery and an electric kettle.

'Are you going to make me a cup of tea?' I said. 'It's very warm in here – do you want me to open a window?'

'They will bring some tea at four,' he said. 'You must know that by now. No, don't open the window. I think I have a chill.'

'Shall I get the doctor to look at you?'

'No doctors. I have a horror of them.' His voice was flat and cold like his eyes. There was some sort of change in the atmosphere since our last meeting. He was suspicious of me and didn't bother to hide it.

'Still drawing landscapes?' I asked. I took off my raincoat and put it on a hook behind the door.

'There's not much else to do,' he said. The whole building was well heated and it was warm in this room, but the electric fire was fully on, and in addition to his grey flannels and dark-green shirt Stinnes wore a heavy sweater. He was sitting on a big chintz-covered sofa and there were several London newspapers beside him. They'd been folded and refolded as if every word in them had been read.

He was able to be very still. It was not the easy stillness that comes with relaxation or the tense stillness that concentration produces, but something else – some quality that couldn't be defined, something that enabled him to remain always the onlooker no matter how involved he truly felt. He was always the sun; everything moved except him.

I took off my jacket and sat in the chair opposite him. 'The interrogator went home early yesterday,' I said. 'And early the day before that.'

'Some species of bird are born able to sing, but others have to learn to sing from their parents.' There was no jocularity. It sounded like something he had ready to recite for me.

'Is that an ornithological fact or are you trying to tell me something, Erich?' In fact I knew it was true. Stinnes had told me before. He was fond of displaying such expertise.

'It was inevitable that you should try to find some way to blame me,' he said.

'And which sort of bird are you, Erich? And how do we start teaching you how to sing?'

'I accepted your offer in good faith. I didn't promise to run your covert operations department and make it work properly.'

'What *do* you see as your side of the bargain?' I said.

'I give the interrogator full and truthful answers to everything he asks. But I can't tell him things I don't know. I wish you'd explain that to him.'

'Four men have died,' I said. 'You knew one of them: Ted Riley; he was with you in London. He was a personal friend of mine. People are angry.'

'I'm sorry,' said Stinnes. He didn't look very sorry, but then he never did look very anything.

'We were bounced, Erich. Both times we were bounced.'

'I don't know the full details,' he said. It was a very Russian response; he knew all the details.

'Both times we walked into a booby trap,' I said.

'Then both times you were a booby.'

'Don't get too damned smug,' I said, and then regretted that he'd made me angry.

'Are you a professional or have you been behind a desk too long?' He paused, and when I didn't answer he said, 'Don't toy with me, Mr Samson. You know that Rensselaer is an amateur. You know he refused to let your Operations staff plan these meetings. You know that he did it that way because he wanted to show everyone that he could be a wonderful field agent.'

It wasn't the reaction I'd expected. Stinnes showed no anger about Bret Rensselaer's actions even though they'd brought Stinnes near to being killed. In fact his interpretation of the fiasco put Bret into the role of hero – an amateur, blundering hero, but a hero nevertheless. 'Did you criticize these "amateurish" ideas?' I asked.

'Of course I did. Didn't you?'

He had me there. 'Yes,' I admitted. 'I criticized them.'

'So would anyone with half an hour's field experience. Rensselaer is a desk man. Why wasn't he ordered to use your Operations planners? I urged him to do that over and over again.'

'There were problems,' I said.

'And I can guess what the problems were,' said Stinnes. 'Your boss Rensselaer is determined to make his name before the MI5 people take over my interrogation?'

'Something like that,' I said.

'He's at the dangerous age,' said Stinnes with studied contempt. 'It's the age when desk men suddenly want to grab a final chance for glory.'

There was a knock at the door and a middle-aged woman in a green apron brought in a tray of tea with buttered toast and a plate of sliced cake. 'They do you very well in here, Erich,' I said. 'Do you get this sort of stylish tea every day or only when visitors come?'

The woman smiled at me but said nothing. They were all vetted people, of course; some of the domestic help were retired clerical staff from London Central. She set out the cups and teapot and left silently. She knew that even one word can destroy the mood of an interrogation.

'Every day,' said Erich. There was a packet of five small cigars on the tray. I suppose it was his daily ration, but he seemed to have stopped smoking for there was a pile of unopened packets on the mantelpiece.

'But you still don't like it here?' His uncooperative attitude towards the interrogator was what had brought me down here. There was obviously something he didn't like.

'You trust me well enough to act on my information and risk the lives of your agents, but you keep me locked up in case I run away.' He drank some tea. 'Where is it that you think I will run to? Will I run back to Moscow and face trial?'

I was tempted to tell him how vociferously I had opposed his being brought back to Berwick House, but that wasn't the way to do it. And in any case, I didn't want him to know how little effect my opinions had upon London Central's top-floor decisions. 'So what sort of bird are you, Erich? You haven't answered that one yet.'

'Let me out of here and I'll show you,' he said. 'Let me do what Rensselaer failed to do.'

'Penetrate the Cambridge network?'

'They'll trust me.'

'It's risky, Erich.'

'The Cambridge network is the best thing I brought over to you. It's what delayed me in Mexico City. It's what forced me to go back to Berlin before coming over to you. Do you have any idea what risks I took to get enough information to penetrate that network?'

'Tell me.'

It was a sardonic reaction to his plea and he knew it. He said, 'And now you want to throw it away. Well, it's your loss.'

'Then why do you care?'

'Only because you are determined to blame me for disasters of your own making. Why should I be blamed? Why should I be punished? I don't want to spend month after month locked up in this place.'

'I thought you liked it,' I said.

'It's comfortable enough, but I'm a prisoner here. I want to live like a human being. I want to spend some of that money. I want to . . . I want to do all sorts of things.'

'You want to see Zena Volkmann? Is that what you were going to say?'

'Have you seen her?'

'Yes,' I said.

'Did she ask about me?'

'She thinks she did all the work, I got all the credit, and you got all the money.'

'Is that what she said?'

'More or less.'

'I suppose it's true.' He took off his glasses and polished them carefully.

'I don't know that she did all the work, and I certainly didn't get all the credit. Other than that, I suppose it's true.'

He looked at me but didn't smile at my allegation. 'You needn't worry. If I am freed, I won't go rushing off to find her.'

'The love has cooled?'

'I'm fond of her. But she is another man's wife. I no longer have the stamina for that sort of love affair.'

'But you have the stamina to try breaking into the Cambridge net?'

'Because it's the only way I'll ever be able to get free of you people.'

'By giving us proof positive of your loyalty to us?'

'As I've told you, that network is the best prize I can offer you. Surely even you English will not want to keep me locked up after I deliver them to you?' These were his own agents, yet he said it without any sign of emotion. He was a cold-blooded animal.

'There is the problem of protecting you, Erich. You are a big investment. They put a bomb under your car last week.'

'That wasn't intended for me. That was an accident. Surely you don't believe that they identified me?' He leaned back in the sofa and grasped his hands together and cracked the knuckles. It was an old man's gesture that didn't fit my picture of him. Was it this captivity that was ageing him? He was a 'street man' – his whole career had been based upon dealing with people. If he was allowed to try breaking the Cambridge net, at least he'd be doing the thing he was best at. Perhaps all betrayals – marital, professional and political – are motivated by the drive to do what you're best at, no matter whom you're doing it for.

'You seem very certain,' I said.

'I'm not paranoid, if that's what you mean.'

I left it like that for a moment and drank some tea. 'You're not smoking these days, I notice.' I picked up the packet of cheroots from the tray and sniffed them. I hadn't smoked for ages. I put the cheroots down again, but it wasn't easy.

'I don't feel like smoking,' he said. 'It's a good chance for me to give up altogether.'

I poured myself some tea and drank it without milk or sugar the way he drank his; it was awful. 'How would you start?' I didn't have to explain what I meant. The idea of Stinnes trying to crack a Soviet network using his own methods was uppermost in both our minds.

'First, I've got to have my freedom. I can't work if you are going to have someone watching me night and day. I must be able to go to them completely clear of all your strings. You understand?'

'They're alarmed now,' I said. 'They must have been in touch with Moscow. Moscow might have told them about you.'

'You have too much faith in Moscow. Just as we have always had too much faith in the efficiency of London Central.'

'I'd stand very little chance of convincing my masters that you could bring that network home alone. They don't want to believe it; they'd consider it some kind of reflection upon their competence. They'd be afraid of another disaster and this time one in which we lost you too. Moscow are searching for you, Erich. Surely you must know that.'

'Moscow doesn't put out alerts for defectors until there has been publicity about them. The policy is to play down such things in case other Soviet citizens get the same idea.'

'You weren't just a defector,' I said. 'Your going dealt a big blow to them.'

'All the more reason why they would keep quiet. Have your analysts reported anything yet?'

'I'll try and find out,' I promised. Erich knew that my reply was an evasion, and yet there was no way I could keep him from guessing the right answer to that question. The analysts had been monitoring the East Bloc radio and TV and watching the press for anything that could relate to Erich Stinnes. And they'd especially scrutinized the restricted publications and given particular attention to the diplomatic KGB radio traffic by means of which Moscow controlled its embassies and agents throughout the world. So far there had been nothing that could be recognized as a reference to Erich Stinnes or his enrolment by our Department. It was as if he'd disappeared into outer space. He smiled. He knew there had been nothing.

'I'd need only ten days, two weeks at the most. I know this network, and I'd approach it another way. If you were prepared to pick them up without evidence, I could give them to you in less than a week.'

'No. Here on this side of the world we have this inconvenient necessity to provide the courts with clear evidence. Even then, the juries free half the people sent up for trial.'

'Plant something on them. I'll give evidence.'

'We haven't had a clear decision on whether we can use you in court yet,' I said.

'If I agree . . .'

'It's not that easy. There are legal difficulties. My Department isn't empowered to handle this sort of prosecution. If you were cross-questioned in open court, it might become embarrassing.'

'And your Home Office won't help? Why don't you change this

antiquated system? The KGB is centrally controlled to work against the enemies within and the enemies without. Separate agencies – one working to locate foreign agents within Britain and another to penetrate foreign countries – is cumbersome and inefficient.'

'We like it a bit cumbersome and inefficient,' I said. 'An agency like the KGB can take over its government any time it wishes.'

'It hasn't happened yet,' said Stinnes primly. 'And it never will. The Party remains supreme and no one challenges its power.'

'You don't have to proclaim the Party line any more, Erich. We both know the Soviet Union is facing a crisis.'

'A crisis?' he said. He leaned forward, elbows on knees, and hands clasped tight together. His pinched face was very pale and his eyes bright.

'There are urgent demands for incentives to be built into the declining economy. I don't have to tell you all that, Erich.' I smiled but he didn't respond to my smile. I seemed to have touched a nerve.

'And who is fighting against such reforms?' He hunched his shoulders more. I wondered exactly where Stinnes had placed himself in this struggle. Or was he still denying that there was one?

Well, if this was the only way to bring him alive, I'd pursue it. 'The moribund Party officials, who meddle with the economy at grass-roots level and skim the cream from it. They don't want to be replaced by skilled factory managers, technical experts, and trained administrators, the only ones who might be able to create the kind of system of incentives that eventually produces an expanding economy.'

'The Party . . .'

'. . . remains supreme. Yes, you already said that.'

'Is close to the work force,' said Stinnes. He was clearly agitated by my remarks.

'It's close to the work force because of the way in which the Party's come to a tacit agreement with them. The workers stay out of politics and the Party makes sure that no one has to work very hard. That was all right in Lenin's time but it can't go on much longer. The Russian economy is a disaster.'

Stinnes rubbed his cheek, seemingly alarmed at the idea. 'But if they let the factories get rid of the lazy and hire only the hard workers, then they will be reintroducing into the system all the greed, fears, and strife of competitive capitalism. The Revolution will have been for nothing; they will have revived the class war.'

'That's the problem,' I said.

'The Party will stand firm against that kind of reform,' said Stinnes.

'But the economy will continue to decline. And one day the Soviet generals and admirals will encounter resistance to their profligate spending on guns and tanks and ships. The economy won't be able to afford such luxuries.'

'Then the military will throw in their lot with the reformers?' said
Stinnes scornfully. 'Is that your contention?'

'It's possible,' I said.

'Not in your lifetime,' said Stinnes, 'and not in mine.' He'd been
leaning forward, eyes bright and active as he pursued the arguments,
but now he sighed and slumped back in the sofa. Suddenly, for a
brief moment, I glimpsed a different Stinnes. Was it the heaviness
that comes with constant pain? Or was Stinnes regretting the way
he'd let me see a glimpse of what he really was?

'Why do you care, Erich?' I said. 'You're a capitalist now, aren't
you?'

'Of course I am,' he said. He smiled, but the smile was not
reassuring.

From Berwick House I drove straight back to London for a conference that was scheduled for half past five that afternoon. It was a
high-powered departmental meeting that had already been going for
nearly an hour. I waited in the anteroom and was called in just before
six.

The Director-General – wearing one of his baggiest suits – was in
the chair. At the table there were Morgan, Frank Harrington, Dicky
and Bret Rensselaer. It wasn't exactly the full complement. The
Deputy was attending to private business in Nassau and the Controller
Europe was at a meeting in Madrid. Everyone had a glass and there
was a jug of ice on the conference table; also the usual selection of
booze was arranged on the side table, but everyone seemed to be
keeping to Perrier water, except for Frank Harrington who was
nursing a large whisky in both hands and looking into it like a gypsy
consulting a crystal ball. In deference to the D-G no one was smoking.
I could see that this was putting Frank under some strain. He seemed
to guess what I was thinking; he smiled and wetted his lips in the
way he did when about to light his pipe.

'Ah . . .' said the D-G. Twisting round to see me as Morgan
ushered me into the conference room, he knocked his pencil off the
table.

'Samson,' supplied Morgan. It was one of his duties to remind the
D-G of the names of the staff. So was retrieving things the D-G
knocked to the floor without noticing.

'Ah, Samson,' said the D-G. 'You've just been to talk with our
Russian friend. Why don't you pour yourself a drink.'

'Yes, sir.' The fluorescent lights were reflected in the polished table
top. I remembered Fiona saying that fluorescent lighting made gin
taste 'funny'. It was of course an insight into her pampered
upbringing, a rationalization of why she didn't want to drink in

cheap restaurants, corner bars or offices. And yet I was never able to completely shed the suspicion that her theory might be true. I didn't let it interfere with my drinking, though.

While I poured myself a stiff gin and tonic I looked round the room. Sir Henry Clevemore seemed to be in good form today. Despite his wrinkled face and heavy jowls, his eyes were clear under those heavy lids, and his voice was firm. His sparse hair had been carefully arranged to make the most of it, and today there was no sign of the trembling that sometimes made him stutter.

I wondered exactly what they'd been talking about. It was unlikely that Bret had been asked any pointed questions at such a gathering; the D-G wouldn't have Dicky and Morgan along to witness Bret being put through the wringer. If I knew anything about the old man, if things came to the crunch he would stand aside as he had done before. He'd hand the whole business over to Internal Security and let them get their hands dirty. For the old man had a horror of disloyalty and he'd run a mile to get away from any sniff of it.

And certainly Bret showed no sign of strain. He was sitting next to the D-G and being his usual urbane shop-window-dummy self. Dicky was wearing a suede jacket as a sartorial concession to the D-G, Morgan was twitchy, and Frank looked bored. Frank could afford to look bored – he was the only one in the room who would probably remain unaffected if they opened an orange file on Bret. In fact, with Bret put on the back burner, Frank would probably be asked to stay on in Berlin. Knowing Frank and his vociferous requests for retirement, that would mean the offer of a bigger pension and a lot of fringe benefits to keep him happy.

'Did you record your interrogation?' Morgan asked me.

'Yes. But it wasn't exactly an interrogation,' I said, pulling out a chair and sitting down at the other end of the table to face the D-G. 'The recording is being transcribed now.'

'Why wasn't it an interrogation?' said Morgan. 'That was your instruction.' Morgan brandished the notepad and pencil. He had a new suit – dark grey, almost black, and tight fitting, with white shirt and stiff collar – so that he looked like the ambitious junior newspaper reporter that he'd been not so long before.

I didn't reply to Morgan. I stared into the D-G's red-rimmed eyes. 'I went to Berwick House because the senior interrogator was getting nowhere. My task was to find out what the trouble was. I'm not a trained interrogator and I've very little experience.' I spoke loudly, but even so, the D-G cupped his ear.

'What do you make of him?' said the D-G. The others were politely holding back, giving the D-G first go at me.

'He's sick,' I said. 'He seems to be in pain.'

'Is that the most important thing you discovered?' asked Morgan, with more than a touch of sarcasm.

'It's something you aren't likely to get from the tape recording,' I said.

'But is it of any importance?' said Morgan.

'It might be very important,' I said.

'Do we have his medical sheet to hand?' the D-G asked Morgan.

Waiting until after Morgan had registered confusion, Bret answered. 'He has consistently refused a physical. It didn't seem worth getting tough with him about it. But we've been taking it easy with him just in case.'

The D-G nodded. The D-G, like many of the senior staff, was able to nod without making it a gesture of agreement. It was just a sign that he'd heard.

Encouraged by the D-G, I went quickly through my conversation with Stinnes, giving particular attention to his suggestion that he be allowed to break the Cambridge net.

Bret said, 'I'd feel uneasy about releasing him in the new hope that he would pull it off on his own.'

'We're not achieving much by keeping him where he is,' said Morgan. He tapped his pencil on the notepad. The way in which Morgan came to such meetings in the role of note taker for the D-G and then spoke to senior staff as an equal annoyed Bret. It annoyed other people too. I wondered if the D-G failed to understand that or simply failed to care. His ability to play one person off against another was legendary. That was the way the Department had always been run.

'I'm coming under a lot of pressure to transfer him to the Home Office people,' said the D-G, pronouncing the final words with what was almost a shudder of distaste.

'I hope you won't give way to them,' said Bret. He was very polite, but there was an edge in his voice that implied that the D-G would fall from grace if he succumbed to such pressure.

Dicky had consistently resisted any temptation to become involved with the Stinnes debriefing, but now he said what was in everyone's mind. 'I understood that we would hold him for the best part of a year. I understood that the whole idea was to use Stinnes as a way to measure our successes or failures over the past decade. I thought we were going to go through the archives with him.'

Dicky looked at the D-G and Frank Harrington looked at Dicky. Frank Harrington would not emerge shiny bright from any close inspection of the Department's successes and failures. It was a maxim of the German desk that successes were celebrated in Bonn and rewarded in London, but failures were always buried in Berlin. Berlin was the one job you had to do sometimes, but no one had ever built a career upon Berlin.

'That was the original plan,' said Morgan. He looked at the D-G to see if he required more prompting.

The D-G said, 'Yes, that was the original plan but we have had setbacks. More setbacks than you have yet heard about.' Was that, I wondered, a reference to a pending enquiry for Bret? The D-G spoke very slowly and anyone replying immediately was likely to find himself speaking over him. So we all waited, and sure enough he spoke again. 'It's something of a poker game. We have to decide whether to go on with our bluff, trust this Russian, and hope he can deliver the goods that will provide us with a strong bargaining position.' Another long pause. 'Or should we cut our losses and turn him over to MI5?'

'He's a highly experienced Soviet agent,' said Frank Harrington. 'And the KGB is a highly motivated organization. He didn't get to that position by failing to deliver the goods. If he says he can do it, I think we should take that seriously.'

'Let's not just consider his ability, Frank,' I said. 'It's not just a matter of whether he can deliver or might fail to do so. We have to worry whether he's a KGB man still hot and active.'

'Of course we do,' said Frank hastily. 'Only a fool would take him at face value. On the other hand, he's no damned use to us wrapped in tissue paper and stored away on the shelf.'

'And in the long term?' enquired the D-G. I suppose he too realized that Frank couldn't possibly come out well from a systematic review of our activities, and he was curious to see Frank's reaction.

'That's for the historians,' said Frank. 'My concern is last week, this week and next week. The strategy is all yours, Director.'

The D-G smiled at this artful reply. 'I think we are all of one mind,' he said, although I had seen little evidence of that. 'We must go for some sort of compromise.'

'With Stinnes?' said Dicky. I never discovered whether it was supposed to be a joke, but Morgan smiled knowingly so perhaps he'd already told Dicky what was coming.

'A compromise with MI5,' said the D-G. 'I'm proposing that they appoint a couple of people to a committee so that we take joint control of the Stinnes debriefing.'

'And who will be on the committee?' said Bret.

'You, Bret, certainly,' said the D-G. 'And I was going to have Morgan there to represent me. Would that suit you, Frank?'

'Yes indeed, sir. It's an admirable solution,' said Frank.

'And what about German Stations?' said the D-G, looking at Dicky.

'Yes, but I would like to have Samson back working full time for me. He's been devoting a lot of time to the Stinnes business, and someone will have to go to Berlin next week.'

'Of course,' said the D-G.

Bret said, 'We might need him from time to time. He was the file officer on the Stinnes enrolment. The committee are sure to want to see him.'

I suppose Bret now expected Dicky to say yes, of course, but Dicky knew how Bret would exploit such a casual agreement and so he didn't respond. Dicky was going to hold on tight to me. Trying to run his desk all on his own was biting into his social life.

The D-G looked round the table. 'I'm so glad we're all agreed,' he said. He'd obviously made this exact decision before the meeting began. Or Morgan had made it for him.

'Will Stinnes remain at Berwick House?' said Bret.

'Better you work out the details at the first meeting of the whole committee,' said the D-G. 'I don't want them to say we've presented them with a *fait accompli*; it will get things off to a bad start.'

'Of course, sir,' said Bret. 'Who will have the chair?'

'I'll insist that you do,' said the D-G, 'unless you'd prefer not to do it that way. It would limit your voting.'

'I think I should have the chair,' said Bret. Bret was at his smoothest now, his elbows on the polished tabletop, his hands loosely clasped so that we could all see his signet ring and the gold wristwatch. It was all coming out well for him so far, but he wasn't going to enjoy hearing the way Stinnes described him as a blundering amateur when the transcription was sent upstairs. 'How many of them will there be?'

'I'll sound them out,' said the D-G. 'Cabinet Office might want a say in it too.' He looked round the table until he came to me. 'You're looking very stern, young man. Have you any comments?'

I looked at Dicky. Whatever he'd told his wife about Bret being a KGB mole, Dicky was not going to stand up and remind the meeting about it. Dicky looked away from me and grew suddenly interested in the D-G. 'I don't like it,' I said.

'Why not?' interjected Frank, anxious to head off any chance of me being rude to the old man.

'They'll find some damned thing to use against us.' There was no need to say who. They all knew I didn't mean Moscow.

'They're already well provided with things to use against us,' said the D-G. He chuckled. 'It's time for a compromise. I don't want to see us in direct conflict with them.'

I said, 'I still don't like it.'

The D-G nodded. 'No one here likes it,' he said in a soft friendly voice. 'But we have very little choice.' He shook his head so hard that his cheeks wobbled. 'No one here likes it.'

He wasn't quite correct. Behind his lifted glass of Perrier water Morgan was loving every minute of it. He was stepping from office boy to an operational role without the twenty years of experience that usually went with such moves. It was only a matter of time before Morgan would be running the whole Department.

20

'Unmarried men are the best friends, the best masters, and the best servants,' said Tessa Kosinski, my sister-in-law. She was undoing the wire to open a bottle of champagne, careful of her long painted fingernails. She flicked a piece of gold foil from her fingers and swore softly.

'Don't shake the bottle or it will go everywhere,' I said. She smiled and without a word handed the bottle to me. 'Who said that? Was it George?'

'No, Francis Bacon, silly. Why do you always think I'm totally ignorant? I may not have had Fi's brilliant career at Oxford, but I'm not an untutored fool.' Her fair hair was perfect, as if she'd just come from the hairdresser, her pink dress revealed her bare shoulders, and she was wearing a gold necklace and a wristwatch glittering with diamonds. She was waiting for George to come home, and then they were going to the theatre and on to a party at the house of a Greek shipping magnate. That's the sort of life they led.

'I know you're not, Tessa. It's just that it sounded like something George might say.' She was bright when she wanted to be. She knew that I was trying to get the conversation round to the subject of her men friends, but she deftly avoided it. The champagne wasn't so easy to open. I twisted the cork and, despite my warning to her, gave the bottle a little shake to help. The champagne opened with a loud bang.

'George is becoming a religious fanatic since we moved here,' she said. She watched me pouring the champagne and said nothing when some spilled over onto the polished table.

'How did moving here affect him?' I put the bottle back into the silver bucket.

'We're so near the church now. Mass every morning without fail, darling – surely that's rather overwrought?'

'I've learned not to comment on other people's religion,' I said cautiously.

'And he's become awfully friendly with a bishop. You know what a snob George is and he's so easily flattered.'

'How do you know?'

'Now, now.' She grinned. 'I flatter George sometimes. I think he's very clever at business and I'm always telling him so.'

'What's wrong with being friends with a bishop?' I asked.

'Nothing at all; he's an amusing old rogue. He sits up drinking George's best brandy and discussing the nuances of theology.'

'That's not being a fanatic,' I said.

'Even the bishop says that George is zealous. He says he must be trying to compensate for the lives of his two uncles.'

'I thought his uncles were both priests.'

'The bishop knows that; he was joking, darling. Sometimes you're as slow on the uptake as poor old George.'

'Well, I think George is a good husband,' I said, preparing the ground for the subject of her infidelities.

'So do I. He's wonderful.' She got up and looked round the room in which we were sitting. 'And look what he's done with this flat. It was a shambles when we first came to look at it. Most of the furniture was chosen by George. He loves going to the auctions and trying to get a bargain. All I did was to buy some of the fabrics and the carpets.'

'It's a superb result, Tessa,' I said. The cream-coloured sofas and the pale carpet contrasted with the jungle of tropical plants that filled the corner near the far window. The lights were recessed into the ceiling to produce a pink shadowless illumination throughout the whole room. The result was expensive looking and yet austere. It was not exactly what one would expect to be the taste of George, the flashily dressed cockney millionaire. The whole flat was perfect and glossy, like a double-page spread in *House & Garden*. But it was lifeless too. I lived in rooms that bore the imprint of two young children: plastic toys in the bath, odd shoes in the hall, stains on the carpet, and dents in the paintwork. It was nothing less than tragic that George and Tessa had never had children. George desperately wanted to be a father, and Tessa doted on my two kids. Instead, they had this forbiddingly tranquil home in that bleak exclusive part of London – Mayfair. I'm not sure that either of them really belonged there.

'Give me another drink,' said Tessa. She had this preposterous idea that champagne was the only alcohol that would not make her fat. She was like a small child in some matters, and although he grumbled about her behaviour, George indulged her in such ridiculous notions. He was to blame for what he didn't like in her, for to some extent he had created this exasperating creature.

'I didn't intend to stay.'

'George will be back at any time. He phoned from the workshop to say he was leaving.' I took the bottle of vintage Bollinger from the solid-silver wine cooler and poured more for both of us. 'Is the car going well?'

'Yes, thank you.'

'George is sure to ask me if you like the car. He's taken a shine to you. I think he must have guessed the way you bully me about not looking after him properly.' In Tessa's language that meant being unfaithful. Her vocabulary was brutally frank about everything except her infidelity.

'Then there's something we should talk about before he arrives,' I said.

'Your girlfriend was looking absolutely stunning the other night,' said Tessa, getting to her feet. She walked over to the window and looked down at the street. 'If George arrives soon, there's a place for him to park,' she said. She came back to where I was sitting and, standing behind me, ruffled my hair. 'I'm so glad you brought her. Where is she tonight?'

'She's at evening class,' I said. I knew it would produce a hoot of laughter and I wasn't disappointed.

'Evening classes, darling? How old is she? She looks as if you might have kidnapped her from the fifth form.'

'She's studying economics,' I explained. 'She's determined to go to Cambridge.'

'What a coup that would be for an unlettered oaf like you, darling. A wife educated at Oxford and a mistress at Cambridge.' She was still standing behind me, but when I tried to grab her wrist she ducked away.

'It's about you and Dicky,' I said, determined to broach the subject.

'I knew that was coming. I could see it in your face,' she said.

'You've worked hard to avoid talking about it,' I said. 'But there's something you ought to know.'

'Don't tell me Dicky Cruyer is married or something awful like that,' she said. She sank down in the soft chair, kicked off her gold evening shoes, and put her feet on the coffee table in such a way that her toes could touch the ice bucket.

'Daphne is furious,' I said.

'I told him she'd find out about us,' said Tessa calmly. 'He's so careless. It's almost as if he wants everyone to know.'

'A friend of Daphne's saw you at a hotel near Deal.'

'I knew it,' she said. She laughed. 'Dicky packed both bags and forgot that I always leave my nightdress under the pillow . . . in case there's a fire or something. I unpacked when I got home, but at first I didn't notice the nightgown was missing. Then I absolutely panicked.' She drank some champagne. She was enjoying the story, enjoying it more than I was. 'You can imagine what I was thinking. Dicky had put his real address in the hotel register – he's such a chump – and I had visions of the hotel sending my wretched nightie to Daphne with a note saying she'd left it behind or something.'

She looked at me, waiting for me to ask what she did next. 'What did you do next?' I asked.

'I couldn't phone Dicky; he's furious if I phone him at the office. But I couldn't think how to put it to the hotel people. I mean, how can you explain that you don't want them to send your nightie back? Do you tell them to give it to Oxfam or say you've just moved house? It's impossible. So I jumped into my car and trundled all the way back to Deal again.'

'Did you get it back?'

'Darling, it was an absolute riot. This lovely lady in the reception said she'd worked in big hotels all over Europe. No hotel ever returns nightgowns or articles of ladies' underwear to the address in the register, she said. They wait until there is a query about it. Then, darling, she showed me this immense cupboard full of flimsy garments left behind after weekends of illicit passion. You should have seen them, Bernard. I blushed at some of the things in that cupboard.'

'So all was well?' I wanted to talk about her affair with Dicky, but I could see she was trying to spin things out until George got back and so avoid it.

'I said to this amusing lady that we should go into business and buy all these wonderful things from hotels and sell them. I even mentioned it to the people on this committee I'm on – it's a children's charity – but you should have seen their faces. They're all old fogies with tinted hair and fur coats. You'd have thought I'd suggested opening a brothel.'

'You didn't explain to them exactly how you obtained this information?'

'I told them it had happened to a friend of mine.'

'Not a very convincing subterfuge,' I said.

'No, well, I'm not in that world, am I?' she said. That remark was aimed at me.

'It wasn't the nightdress. It was a friend of Daphne who saw you.'

'And my mind has been buzzing ever since you said that just now. I can't think of any familiar face there that weekend.'

'Daphne's talking about a divorce.'

'She always says that,' said Tessa. She flicked her hair back and smiled defensively.

'Always? What do you mean, always?'

'You know very well that I had a little fling with Dandy Dicky last year, or was it the year before? We talked about it one evening. I remember you were very toffee-nosed.'

'If Daphne goes to a lawyer, it could become a rotten business, Tess.'

'It will be all right,' she said. 'I know you mean well, Bernard darling. But it will be all right.'

'If I believed that, I wouldn't be sitting here talking about it. But I know Daphne well enough to think she could be serious.'

'Divorce? What about the children? Where would she live?'

'Never mind Daphne's problems. If she starts making a fuss, you'll have enough of your own. She wants me to introduce her to George.'

'That's ridiculous,' said Tessa.

'Dicky would be the real loser,' I said. 'Publicity such as a nasty divorce action would destroy his career.'

'Don't say they'd fire him – I know that's not true.'

'They probably wouldn't sack him, but he'd be posted to some lousy place on the other side of the world and left there to rot. The Department doesn't like publicity, Tessa. I don't have to draw you a diagram, do I?'

Her flippant attitude had changed now. She took her feet off the table and drank some champagne, frowning deeply as she considered her position. 'George would be furious,' she said, as if he'd be more furious about the publicity than about her infidelity.

'I thought you were trying to put your marriage together again,' I said. 'I remember you talking to me and saying that George was the most wonderful husband in the world and that all you wanted to do was to make him happy.'

'I do, darling, I do. But it won't make him happy to be portrayed as the wronged husband and have his photo in all those lousy newspapers. I'll have to talk to Daphne. I must make her see sense. It would be insane for her to leave Dicky over such a stupid little thing.'

'It's not a "stupid little thing" to her,' I said. 'And if you start talking to her in that fashion, you'll only make things worse.'

'What do you want me to say?'

'Don't make it sound as if you're doing it for me,' I said testily. 'I can't tell you what to say. But the only thing that Daphne will want to hear is that you're not going to see Dicky any more.'

'Then, of course, I'll tell her that.'

'You've got to mean it, Tessa. It's no good just patching it over. . . . You're not in love with him or anything, are you?'

'Good heavens, no. Who could be in love with him? I thought I was doing Daphne a favour, to tell you the truth. I don't know how anyone can bear Dicky round them all the time. He's awfully wearing.'

I listened to her protests with a healthy mistrust. I didn't know much about women, but I knew that such strenuous denials could sometimes be a sign of profound passion. 'Tell her you're sorry. It's time you stopped all this nonsense, Tessa. You're not a child any longer.'

'I'm not old and ugly,' she said.

'No, you're not. Perhaps it would be better if you *were* old and ugly. George would remain loyal, no matter how old and ugly you were, and you'd realize what a good husband you have.'

'You men all stick together,' she said sullenly.

'You make a lot of people unhappy, Tessa. I know you don't see it like that, but you're a troublemaker. You had a rich father who gave you everything you ever asked for, and now you think you can have anything you want, no matter who it belongs to or what the consequences may be.'

'You have a terrible tendency to play the amateur psychologist, Bernard. Did I ever tell you that?'

'I hate amateur psychologists,' I said. She always knew how to needle me. I drank my champagne and stood up.

'Don't give me that injured-pride look, darling. I know you're trying to help.'

'If you want me to talk to Daphne, I will. But I won't do it unless I get a sincere promise from you that the affair is at an end.'

She stood up too. She came close and stroked the lapel of my jacket. Her voice was a purr. 'You're very masterful, Bernard. That's a very attractive quality in a man. I've always said that.'

'Do cut it out, Tessa. Sometimes I think that these love affairs of yours are staged to give you constant reassurance.'

'Fi was always saying that. Father never praised us for anything at all. Fi didn't care, but I wanted a bit of praise now and again.'

There was something in her voice that made me look at her more closely. 'Have you heard from Fiona?' It was a wild guess. 'A letter?'

'I was going to tell you, Bernard. Honestly I was. I was determined to tell you before you left this evening.'

'Tell me what?'

'I saw Fi.'

'Saw Fiona. When?'

'Just a few days ago.'

'Where?'

'I have a dear old aunt who lives in Holland. We used to spend holidays with her. I always go and see her for her birthday. She used to come to us but she's too infirm to travel now.' She gabbled nervously.

'Holland?'

'Near Eindhoven. She lives in a block of tiny flats built specially for elderly people. There's a doctor on call and meals if you want them. The Dutch do that sort of thing so well; it puts us to shame.'

'And Fiona?'

'She came for the birthday meal. I almost fell over with surprise. She was sitting there as if it was the most natural thing in the world.'

'What did you say?'

'What *could* I say, darling? My aunt knew nothing of Fiona going off to the bloody Russians. I didn't want to spoil the birthday for her. I just carried on as I had all the previous years.'

'Was George with you?'

'George doesn't like family gatherings. That is to say, he doesn't like gatherings of my family. When it's *his* family, it's quite a different matter, and there are thousands of them.'

'I see.' If what George didn't like was Tessa's father, it's a feeling that I shared heartily. 'Just you and Fiona and your aunt then?'

'She wants the children, Bernard.'

'Fiona? My children? Billy and Sally?'

'They're her children too,' said Tessa.

'Would you like to see her take them away?'

'Don't be like that, Bernard darling. You know I wouldn't. But she only wants them to spend a few weeks with her.'

'In Moscow? In Berlin?'

'I don't know. For a holiday, she said.'

'And if they go to her for a few weeks, how do we ever get them back?'

'I thought of that,' said Tessa. She sipped her drink. 'But if Fiona promises to send them back, she'll keep to it. It was the same when we were children; she'd never break her word in personal matters.'

'If I was only dealing with Fiona it might be different,' I said. 'But we're dealing with Soviet bureaucracy. And I wouldn't trust British bureaucracy as far as I could throw it, so the idea of delivering my kids to the mercies of the Soviet bureaucrats does not come happily to me.'

'I don't understand.'

'Those bastards want the kids as hostages.'

'For Fiona?'

'Right now she's obviously in the first flush of excitement. The Russians let her out to the West and know she'll come back. But the chances are that feeling won't last. She'll become disillusioned with Soviet society. She'll find it's not the paradise she's been dreaming of all these years.'

'Hostages?'

'When the kids are there, she'll discover that they can't return to the West all together. They'll make sure that she travels alone. She won't have any choice; she'll have to go back to the children.'

'She's prepared to go through the courts to get custody.'

'She told you that?'

'Over and over again.'

'That's because she knows the Department for which I work won't tolerate it going to the courts. They'll press me to let her have custody.'

'That would be disgusting.'

'It's what they would do.'

'The children have rights too. It would be wrong for a court to deliver them to the Russians without giving them a chance.'

'Maybe I shouldn't say what they'd do before they've done it, but I'd say Fiona's chances are good.'

'Bernard darling, do sit down for a moment. I didn't know how badly you'd take it. Do you want a whisky or something?'

'Thanks, Tess. No, I'll have some more champagne,' I said. I sat down while she poured it for me.

'She said she doesn't want to row with you. She's still fond of you, Bernard, I can tell.'

'I don't think so,' I said. But did I really only want to hear myself contradicted?

Tessa sat down next to me. I could feel the warmth of her body and smell the perfume. It was a heavy exotic scent, suited, I suppose, for the sort of evening she had ahead of her. 'I wasn't going to tell you this, but I think Fi is still in love with you. She denied it, but I've always been able to see through her.'

'You're not making it any easier, Tessa.'

'She must miss the children dreadfully. Couldn't it be that she simply wants to be with them for a short time each year?'

'It might be,' I said.

'You don't sound very convinced.'

'Fiona is a very devious person, Tessa. Truthful when it suits her, but devious. Surely I don't have to tell you that. Have you told anyone else about meeting Fiona?'

'Of course not. Fi said not to.'

'Not even George?'

'Not even George. Cross my heart,' she said, and made the children's gesture of running a finger across her throat to swear it was true.

'And there was no one with her?'

'Just Fiona. She stayed the night. My aunt has a spare room. We talked half the night. Fiona had a rented car. She went to Schiphol next morning. She had to fly on to somewhere else . . . Paris, I think.'

'Why couldn't she contact me?'

'She said you'd say that. She said it was better this way. I suppose her own people wouldn't suspect a stopover in Holland the way they would a visit to London to see you.'

For a few minutes we said nothing. Then Tessa said, 'She said she'd seen you.'

'Since leaving?'

'At London airport. She said you had a brief chat.'

'I'll have to ask you to forget that, Tessa. It was a long time back.'

'Didn't you tell Dicky or anyone? That was silly, Bernard. Was that about the children?'

'Yes, it was. No, I didn't tell Dicky or anyone.'

'I didn't tell Dicky about seeing my sister either,' said Tessa.

'I was thinking about that, Tessa. You realize that this has a bearing on your relationship with Dicky?'

'Because I didn't tell him?'

'I don't want to discuss with you what Dicky does for a living, but surely you see that having an affair with you could lead to very bad trouble for him.'

'Because of Fiona?'

'Someone who wanted to make trouble could connect Fiona to Dicky via the affair he's having with you.'

'But equally they could connect Fiona with Dicky via the fact that you work for him.'

'But I'm not regularly seeing Fiona.'

'Neither am I, not regularly.'

'That might be difficult to prove. And it might be that just one meeting with Fiona would be enough to make Dicky's bosses uneasy.'

'My sister went to Russia. That doesn't make me a spy. And it doesn't make everyone I know a suspect.'

'Perhaps it shouldn't, but it does. And in any case, Dicky can't be lumped together with all the other people you know . . . not in this context anyway. Dicky's contacts have to be specially scrutinized.'

'I suppose you're right.'

'I am.'

'So what should I do?'

'I'd hate to see you mixed up in some damned espionage scandal, Tessa. I know you're an innocent, but many innocents get tangled up in these things.'

'You want me to stop seeing Dicky?'

'You should make a clean break without delay.'

'Write him a letter?'

'Absolutely not,' I said. Why did women always feel the need to write letters when ending an affair?

'I can't just stop. I'm having dinner with him the day after tomorrow.'

'You're sure Dicky doesn't know you saw Fiona?'

'I certainly didn't tell him,' said Tessa. She was strident, as if she resented the advice I was giving her – and I suppose she did. 'I told no one, no one at all. But if I just stop seeing him now, perhaps he'll guess there's something more to it.'

'Have dinner with him and tell him it's all over.'

'You don't think he'll ask me about Fiona?'

'I don't think so, but if he brings up the subject, you just say you haven't seen her since she left England and went to Berlin.'

'You've got me worried now, Bernard.'

'It will be all right, Tess.'

'Suppose they know?'

'Deny seeing her. If the worst comes to the worst, you could say you reported it to me and I told you to tell no one. You say you took that instruction literally.'

'Wouldn't that get you into trouble?'

'We'll sort that one out when and if it comes. But I'll only help you if you're really serious about stopping this idiotic affair with Dicky.'

'I am serious, Bernard. I truly am.'

'There's a lot of trouble in the Department right now. There's a lot of suspicion being directed at everyone. It's a bad time to step out of line.'

'For Dicky?'

'For anyone.'

'I suppose they still think you had something to do with Fiona going away?'

'They say they don't, but I believe they do.'

'She said she'd made a lot of trouble for you.'

'Fiona?' I said.

'She said she was sorry about that.'

'She was the one who ran.'

'She said she had to do it.'

'The children never mention her. It worries me sometimes.'

'They're happy children. The nanny is a good girl. You give them a lot of love, Bernard. That's all children really need. It's what we needed from Daddy, but he preferred to give us money. His time was too precious.'

'I'm always away or working late or some damned thing.'

'I didn't mean that, Bernard. I didn't mean that love can be measured in man-hours. You don't clock in for love. The children know you love them. They know you work only in order to look after them; they understand.'

'I hope they do.'

'But what will you do about them? Will you let Fiona take them?'

'I'm damned if I know, Tessa,' I said, and that was the truth. 'But you must stop seeing Dicky.'

21

The newly formed committee that took charge of the Stinnes debriefing lost no time in asserting its importance and demonstrating its energies. For some of the newcomers the committee provided an example of Whitehall's new spirit of intradepartmental cooperation, but those of us with longer memories recognized it as just one more battlefield upon which the Home Office and the Foreign Office could engage forces and try to settle old scores.

The good news was that both Bret Rensselaer and Morgan spent most of each day in Northumberland Avenue, where the committee had its premises. There was a lot for them to do. Like all such well-organized bureaucratic endeavours, it was established regardless of expense. The committee was provided with a staff of six people – for whom heated and carpeted office space was also provided – and all the paraphernalia of administration was installed: desks, typewriters, filing cabinets, and a woman who came in very early to clean and dust, another woman who came in to make tea, and a man to sweep the floor and lock up at night.

'Bret will build himself a nice little empire over there,' said Dicky. 'He's been looking for something to occupy himself with ever since his Economics Intelligence Committee folded.' It was an expression of Dicky's hopes rather than his carefully considered prophecy. Dicky didn't mind if Bret became monarch of all he surveyed over there as long as he didn't come elbowing his way into Dicky's little realm. I looked at him before answering. There had still been no official mention that Bret's loyalty was in question so I played along with what Dicky said. But I was beginning to wonder if I was being deliberately excluded from the Department's suspicions.

'The Stinnes debriefing can't last for ever,' I said.

'Bret will do his best,' said Dicky.

He was wearing a denim waistcoat. He had his arms folded and was pushing his hands out of sight as if he didn't want any flesh to show. It was a neurotic mannerism. Dicky had become very neurotic since the night he'd had dinner with Tessa, the dinner at which she was supposed to tell him that they were through. I wondered exactly what had happened.

'I don't like it,' I said.

'You're not alone there,' said Dicky. 'Thank your lucky stars that you're not running backwards and forwards for Morgan and Bret and the rest of them. I got you out of that one, didn't I?' He was in my miserable little office, watching me work my way through all the trays that he'd failed to cope with during the previous two weeks. He sat on my table and fiddled with the tin lid of paper clips, and the souvenir mug filled with pencils and pens.

'And I'm grateful,' I said. 'But I mean I don't like what's happening over there.'

'What is happening?'

'They're taking evidence from everyone they can think of. There's even talk of the committee going to Berlin to talk to people who can't be brought here.'

'What's wrong with that?'

'They're supposed to be managing the Stinnes debriefing. It's not their business to go poking into everything that happened when we enrolled him.'

'On principle?' said Dicky. He was quick to catch on when it was something to do with office politics.

'Yes, on principle. We don't want Home Office people questioning and passing judgement on our foreign operations. That's our preserve – that's what we've been insisting upon all these years, isn't it?'

'An interdepartmental squabble, is that how you see it?' said Dicky. He unbent a paper clip to make a piece of wire, then he looked round at the cramped little office that I shared with my part-time secretary as if seeing the slums for the first time.

'They'll want to question me, perhaps they'll want to question you. Werner Volkmann is coming over here to give evidence. And his wife. Where's the end of it? We'll have those people crawling all over us before that committee finishes.'

'Zena? Did you authorize Zena Volkmann's trip to London?' He ran a fingernail up the corner of a bundle of papers, so that it made a noise.

'It will come out of committee funds,' I said. 'That's the first thing they got settled – where the money was to come from.'

'Departmental employees going before the committee will not have to answer any question they don't consider relevant.'

'Who said so?'

'That's the form,' said Dicky. He threw the paper clip at my wastepaper basket but missed.

'With other departments, yes. But this committee is chaired by

one of our own senior staff. How many witnesses will tell him to go
to hell?'

'The D-G was obviously in a spot,' said Dicky. 'It's not what he
would have done in the old days. He would have brazened it out and
held on to Stinnes in the hope we'd get something good.'

'I blame Bret,' I said. I was fishing.

'What for?'

'He's let this bloody committee extend its powers too widely.'

'Why would he do that?' Dicky asked.

'I don't know.' There was still no hint that Bret was suspect.

'To make himself more important?' persisted Dicky.

'Perhaps.'

'The committee is stacked against him, Bernard. Bret will be
outvoted if he tries to step out of line. You know who he's got facing
him. He's got no friends around that table.'

'Not even Morgan?' I said.

It was not intended as a serious question, but Dicky answered it
seriously. 'Morgan hates Bret. Sooner or later they'll get into a real
confrontation. It was madness putting them together over there.'

'Especially with an audience to watch them wrangling,' I said.

'That's right,' said Dicky. He looked at me and chewed his fingernail. I tried to get on with some paperwork, but Dicky didn't budge.
All of a sudden he said, 'It's all over.' I looked up. 'Me and your
sister-in-law. *Finito!*'

What was I supposed to say – 'I'm sorry'? Had Tessa told him that
I knew, or was he just guessing? I looked at him to see if he was
serious or smiling. I wanted to react in the way he wanted me to
react. But Dicky wasn't looking at me; he was looking into the
distance, thinking perhaps of his final tête-à-tête with Tessa.

'It had to end,' said Dicky. 'She was upset, of course, but I was
determined. It was making Daphne unhappy. Women can be very
selfish, you know.'

'Yes, I know,' I said.

'Tessa's had a thing about me for years,' said Dicky. 'You could
see that, I'm sure.'

'I did wonder,' I admitted.

'I loved her,' said Dicky. This was all something he was determined
to get off his chest and I was the only suitable audience for him. I
settled back and let him continue. He didn't need encouraging. 'Once
in a lifetime, perhaps, you find yourself in a trap from which there
is no escape. One knows it's wrong, knows people will be hurt, knows
there will be no happy ending. But one can't escape.'

'Is that how it happened with you and Tessa?' I said.

'For a month I couldn't get her out of my mind. She occupied my
every thought. I got no work done.'

'When was that?' Dicky getting no work done was not enough to give me a reference to the date.

'Long ago,' said Dicky. His arms still folded, he hugged himself. 'Did Daphne tell you?'

Careful now. The red-for-danger light was glowing inside my head. 'Daphne? Your Daphne?' He nodded. 'Tell me what?'

'About Tessa, of course.'

'They're friends,' I said.

'I mean did she mention that I was having an affair?'

'With Tessa?'

'Of course with Tessa.' I suppose I was overdoing the innocence. He was getting testy now and I didn't want that either.

'Daphne wouldn't talk to me about such things, Dicky.'

'I thought she might have poured her heart out to you about it. She pestered several other friends of ours. She said she was going to get a divorce.'

'I'm glad it's turned out all right,' I said.

'Even now she's still very moody. You'd think she'd be overjoyed, wouldn't you? Here I've made Tessa unhappy – terribly unhappy – to say nothing of my own sacrifice. *Finito*.' He made a slicing movement of the hand. 'I've given up the woman I truly love. You'd think Daphne would be happy, but no. . . . Do you know what she said last night? She said I was selfish.' Dicky bared his teeth and forced a laugh. 'Selfish. That's a good one, I must say.'

'A divorce would have been terrible,' I said.

'That's what I told her. Think of the kids, I said. If we split, the children would suffer more than either of us. So you never knew that I was having an affair with your sister-in-law?'

'You kept it pretty dark, Dicky,' I said.

He was pleased to hear that. 'There have been a lot of women in my life, Bernard.'

'Is that so?'

'I'm not the sort of man who boasts of his conquests – you know that, Bernard – but one woman could never be enough for me. I have a powerful libido. I should never have got married. I realized that long ago. I remember my old tutor used to say that the trouble with marriage is that while every woman is at heart a mother, every man is at heart a bachelor.' He chuckled.

'I have to see Werner Volkmann at five,' I reminded him.

Dicky looked at his watch. 'Is that the time? How that clock goes round. Every day it's the same.'

'Do you want me to brief him before he sees the Stinnes committee?'

'The Rensselaer committee, you mean. Bret is very keen it's called the Rensselaer committee so that we'll keep control of it.' Dicky said this in such a way as to suggest that we'd already lost control of it.

'Whatever it's called, do you want me to brief Werner Volkmann about what to say to them?'

'Is there something that we don't want him to tell them?'

'Well, obviously I'll warn him he can't reveal operating procedures, codes, safe houses. . . .'

'Jesus Christ!' said Dicky. 'Of course he can't reveal departmental secrets.'

'He won't know that unless someone tells him,' I said.

'You mean we should warn all of our people who are called to give evidence?'

'Either that or you could talk to Bret. You could make sure that each person called to give evidence is told that there are guidelines they must follow.'

'Tell Bret that?'

'One or the other, Dicky.'

Dicky slid off the table and walked up and down, his hands pushed into the pockets of his jeans and his shoulders hunched. 'There's something you'd better know,' he said.

'Yes?' I said.

'Let's go back to one evening just after you came back from Berlin with that transcript . . . the German woman who disappeared into the Havel last Christmas. Remember?'

'How could I forget.'

'You were getting very excited about the radio codes she used. Am I right?'

'Right,' I said.

'Would you like to tell me that over again?'

'The codes?'

'Tell me what you told me that evening.'

'I said she was handling material, selected material, for transmission. I said it was stuff that they didn't want handled by the Embassy.'

'You said it was good. You said it was probably Fiona's stuff that this woman was sending.'

'That was just conjecture.' I wondered what Dicky was trying to get me to say.

'Two codes, you said. And you said two codes was unusual.'

'Unusual for one agent, yes.'

'You're beginning to clam up on me, Bernard. You do this sometimes, and it makes my life very difficult.'

'I'm sorry, but if you told me what you were getting at, I might be able to be more explicit.'

'That's right – make it my fault. You're good at that.'

'There were two codes. What else do you want to know?'

'IRONFOOT and JAKE. You said that Fiona was IRONFOOT. And you said "Who the hell is JAKE?" Right?'

'I found out afterwards that IRONFOOT was a mistranslation for PIG IRON.'

Dicky frowned. 'Did you follow that up, even after I told you to drop it?'

'I was at Silas Gaunt's house. Brahms Four was there. I just casually mentioned the distribution of material and asked him about it.'

'You're bloody insubordinate, Bernard. I told you to drop that one.' He waited for my reply, but I said nothing and that finally forced him to say, 'Okay, okay. What did you find out from him?'

'Nothing I didn't already know, but he confirmed it.'

'That if there were two codes, there were two agents?'

'Normally, yes.'

'Well, you were right, Bernard. Now maybe we see the killing of the Miller woman in another light. The KGB had her killed so that she couldn't spill the beans. Unfortunately for those bastards on the other side of the fence, she'd already spilled the beans . . . to you.'

'I see,' I said. I guessed what was coming, but Dicky liked to squeeze the maximum effect out of everything.

'So who the hell's JAKE, you asked me. Well, maybe I can now tell you the answer to that question. JAKE is Bret Rensselaer! Bret is a double and probably has been for years. We have reports going back to his time in Berlin. Nothing conclusive, nothing that makes firm evidence, but now things are coming together.'

'That's quite a shock,' I said.

'Damned right it's a shock. But I can't say you look very surprised, Bernard. Have you been suspicious of Bret?'

'No, I don't . . .'

'It's not fair to ask you that question. It makes me sound like Joe McCarthy. The fact is that the D-G is dealing with the problem. Now perhaps you realize why Bret is in Northumberland Avenue rubbing shoulders with those MI5 heavies.'

'Has the old man delivered him to MI5 without telling him?'

'Sir Henry wouldn't do anything like that, especially not to one of our own. No, MI5 know nothing of this. But the old man wanted Bret out of this building and working somewhere away from our sensitive day-to-day papers while Internal Security investigate him. . . . Now this is all just between the two of us, Bernard. I don't want a word of this to go out of this room. I don't want you telling Gloria or anyone like that.'

'No,' I said, but I thought that was pretty rich since I'd already got the gist of it from Daphne. Daphne was a wife with no reason to be friendly to him, while Gloria Kent was a vetted employee who was handling the sensitive day-to-day papers that Bret wasn't seeing.

'Bret doesn't realize he's under suspicion. It's essential that he doesn't get wind of it. If he fled the country too, it would look damned bad.'

'Will he face an enquiry?' I asked.

'The old man's dithering.'

'Hell, Dicky, someone should talk to the old man. It can't go on like this. I don't know what evidence there is against Bret, but he's got to be given a chance to answer for his actions. We shouldn't be discussing his fate when the poor sod has been shunted off so that he can't find out what's going on.'

'It's not exactly like that,' said Dicky.

'What is it like then?' I asked. 'How would you like it if it was me telling Bret that you were JAKE?'

'You know that's ridiculous,' said Dicky.

'I don't know anything of the kind,' I said. Dicky's face changed. 'No, no, no . . . I didn't mean you might be a KGB agent. I mean it's not ridiculous to suppose you might be a suspect.'

'I hope you're not going to make a fuss about this,' said Dicky. 'I was in two minds whether to tell you. Perhaps it was an error of judgement.'

'Dicky, it's only fair to the Department and everyone who works here that any uncertainty about Bret be resolved as quickly as possible.'

'Maybe Internal Security need time to collect more evidence.'

'Internal Security always need time to collect more evidence. It's in the nature of the job. But if that's the problem, then Bret should be given leave of absence.'

'Let's assume he's guilty – he'll run.'

'Let's assume he's not guilty – he must have a chance to prepare some sort of defence.'

Dicky now thought I was being very difficult. He moved his lips as he always did when he was agitated. 'Don't get excited, Bernard. I thought you'd be pleased.'

'Pleased to hear you tell me that Bret is a KGB mole?'

'No, of course not that. But I thought you'd be relieved to hear that the real culprit has been uncovered at last.'

'The real culprit?'

'You've been under suspicion. You must have realized that you haven't had a completely clear card ever since Fiona went over to them.'

'You told me that was all past history,' I said. I was being difficult. I knew he'd only told me that to be encouraging.

'Can't you see that if Bret is the one they've been looking for, it will put you in the clear?'

'You talk in riddles, Dicky. What do you mean "the one, they've been looking for"? I wasn't aware they were looking for anyone.'

'An accomplice.'

'I still don't get it,' I said.

'Then you are being deliberately obtuse. If Fiona had an accomplice in the Department, then Bret would be the most natural person for that role. Right?'

'Why wouldn't I be the most natural?'

Dicky slapped his thigh in a gesture of frustrated anger. 'Good God, Bernard, every time anyone suggests that, you bite their head off.'

'If not me, then why Bret?'

Dicky pulled a face and wobbled his head about. 'They were very close, Bernard. Bret and your wife – they were very close. I don't have to tell you the way it was.'

'Would you like to enlarge on that?'

'Don't get touchy. I'm not suggesting that there was anything less than decorous in the relationship, but Bret and Fiona were good friends. I know how comical that sounds in the context of the Department and the way some people talk about each other, but they were friends. They had a lot in common; their background was comparable. I remember one evening Bret was having dinner at your place. Fiona was talking about her childhood . . . they shared memories of places and people.'

'Bret is old enough to be Fiona's father.'

'I'm not denying that.'

'How could they share memories?'

'Of *places*, Bernard. Places and things and facts that only people like them know. Hunting, shooting, and fishing . . . you know. Bret's father loved horses, and so does your father-in-law. Fiona and Bret both learned to ride and to ski before they could walk. They both instinctively know a good horse from a bad one, good snow from bad snow, fresh foie gras from tinned, a good servant from a bad one . . . the rich are different, Bernard.'

I didn't answer. There was nothing to say. Dicky was right, they had had a lot in common. I'd always been frightened of losing her to Bret. My fears were never centred on other younger, more attractive men; always I saw Bret as my rival. Ever since the day I first met her – or at least from the time I went to Bret and suggested that we employ her – I'd feared the attraction that he would have for her. Had that, in some way, brought about the very outcome I most feared? Was it something in my attitude to Bret and to Fiona that provided them with an undefinable thing in common? Was it some factor absent in me that they recognized in each other and shared so happily?

'You see what I mean?' said Dicky, when I hadn't spoken for a long time. 'If there was an accomplice, Bret must be the prime suspect.'

'One per cent motivation and ninety-nine per cent opportunity,' I said, without really intending to say it aloud.

'What's that?' said Dicky.

'One per cent motivation and ninety-nine per cent opportunity. That's what George Kosinski says crime is.'

'I knew I'd heard it before,' said Dicky. 'Tessa says that, but she said it about sex.'

'Maybe they're both right,' I said.

Dicky reached out to touch my shoulder. 'Don't torture yourself about Fiona. There was nothing between her and Bret.'

'I don't care if there was,' I said.

Our conversation seemed to have ended and yet Dicky didn't depart. He fiddled with the typewriter. Finally he said, 'One day I was with Bret. We were in Kiel. Do you know it?'

'I've been there,' I said.

'It's a strange place. Bombed to hell in the war, everything rebuilt after the war ended. New buildings and not the sort that are likely to win prizes for architectural imagination. There's a main street that runs right along the waterfront, remember?'

'Only just.' I tried to guess what was coming, but I couldn't.

'One side of the street consists of department stores and offices and the other side is big seagoing ships. It's unreal, like a stage set, especially at night when the ships are all lit up. I suppose back before it was bombed it was narrow alleys and waterfront bars. Now there are strip-joints and discos, but they're in the new buildings – it's got an atmosphere about as sexy as Fulham High Street.'

'They were after the shipyards,' I said.

'Who were?'

'The bombers. It's where they made the U-boats. Kiel. Half the town worked in the shipyards.'

'I don't know anything about that,' said Dicky. 'All I remember is that Bret had arranged to meet a contact there. We went into the bar about eleven at night, but the place was almost empty. It was elaborately furnished – red velvet and carpet on the floor – but it was empty except for a few regular customers and a line of hostesses and the bartender. I never found out if the nightlife in Kiel starts later than that or doesn't exist at all.'

'It's a beautiful place in summer.'

'That's what Bret said. He knows Kiel. There's a big yachting event there every summer – Kiel Week – and Bret tries not to miss it. He showed me the pictures at the yacht club. There were big yachts with brightly coloured spinnakers billowing. Girls in bikinis. *Kieler Woche* – maybe I'll take my boat there one year. But this time it was my luck to be there in the dead of winter and I've never been so cold in all my life.'

What was all this leading up to, I wondered. 'Why were you and Bret doing it? Don't we have people there? Couldn't the Hamburg office have handled it?'

'There was quite a lot of money involved. It was an official deal: we paid the Russians and they released a prisoner they were holding. It was political. A Cabinet Office request – very hush-hush. You know. It was going to be done in Berlin in the usual way, but Bret argued with Frank Harrington and finally it was decided that Bret would handle it personally. I went along to help.'

'This was when Bret was still running the Economics Intelligence Committee?'

'This was a long time ago, when it was called the European Economics Desk and Bret was officially only Deputy Controller. But there's no reason to think this job was anything directly to do with that desk. I understood that Bret was doing this at the special order of the D-G.'

'European Economics Desk. That's going back a bit.'

'Years and years. Long before Bret got his nice big office and had the decorator in.'

'What are you going to tell me about him?' I said. I had the feeling that Dicky had come to a full stop.

'I was a complete innocent. I was expecting some well-dressed diplomatic official, but the man we met was dressed like a deckhand from one of the Swedish ferries, though I noticed that he arrived in a big black Volvo with a driver. He might just have come across the border – it's an easy enough drive.' Dicky rubbed his face. 'A big bastard he was, an old man. He spoke good English. There was a lot of small talk. He said he'd once lived in Boston.'

'Are we talking about a Soviet official?'

'Yes. He identified himself as a KGB colonel. His documents said his name was Popov. It was such a memorable name that I've remembered it ever since.'

'Go on, Dicky, I'm listening. Popov is a common enough Russian name.'

'He knew Bret.'

'Where from?'

'God knows. But he recognized him – "Good evening, Mr Rensselaer," he said, as bold as brass.'

'You said the place was empty. He could have guessed who you were.'

'There were too many people there for anyone to come in through the door and assume one of them was Mr Rensselaer.'

'How did Bret respond?'

'There was a lot of noise. It was one of these places where they have disco music switched up so loud it bends your eardrums. Bret didn't seem to hear him. But this fellow Popov obviously knew Bret from some other time. He was chatting away, as friendly as can be. Bret went rigid. His face was like one of those Easter Island stone carvings. Then I suppose his friend Popov noticed he was alarmed. Suddenly all the bonhomie was switched off. Bret's name wasn't mentioned after that; it was all very formal. We all went into the washroom and counted the money, tipping all the bundles of bills into a sink and repacking the case. When it was done Popov said good night and departed. No signature, no receipt, no nothing. And no "Good night Mr Rensselaer." This time it was just "Good night, gentlemen". I was worried in case we hadn't handled it right, but they released the man the next day. Have you ever had to do a job like that?'

'Once or twice.'

'They say the KGB keep the cash. Is that true?'

'I don't know, Dicky. No one knows for sure. We can only guess.'

'So how did he know Bret?'

'I don't know that either,' I said. 'You think he knew Bret from somewhere else?'

'Bret's never done any field work.'

'Maybe he'd paid money over in the same way before,' I suggested.

'He said he hadn't. He told me he'd never done anything like that before.'

'Did you ask Bret if he knew the Russian?'

'I was a new boy; Bret was senior staff.'

'Did you report it?'

'That the KGB man had called him "Mr Rensselaer"? No, it didn't seem important. It's only now that it seems important. Do you think I should tell Internal Security?'

'Take your time,' I advised. 'It sounds like Bret has got enough questions to answer for the time being.'

Dicky forced a smile even though he was chewing his nail. Dicky was worried; not about Bret, of course, but about himself.

22

We were celebrating the anniversary of Werner and Zena's marriage. It was not the exact date, but Gloria had offered to cook dinner for the Volkmanns who were in London to appear before the committee.

Gloria was not a great cook. She prepared veal chops followed by a mixed salad and a shop-bought cake that said ZENA AND WERNER CONGRATULATIONS in chocolate.

Not without some misgivings I'd allowed the children to stay up and have dinner with us. I would have preferred them to eat with Nanny upstairs, but it was her night off and she had made arrangements with friends. So the children sat at the table with us and watched Gloria playing hostess in the way their mother had so recently done. Billy seemed relaxed enough – although he only picked at the chocolate cake, which was unusual – but Sally sat through the meal pinch-faced and silent. She watched Gloria's every move and there was tacit criticism in the way she was so reluctant to help pass the dishes down the table. Gloria must have noticed, but she gave no sign of it. She was clever with the children: cheerful, considerate, persuasive, and helpful but never maternal enough to provoke resentment. Gloria took her cue from Nanny, consulting her and deferring to her in such a way that Nanny was forced into Fiona's role while Gloria became a sort of super-nanny and elder sister.

But Gloria's subtle instinct for handling the children let her down when she took the cushioned dining chair that Fiona always used at table. She sat at the end of the table so that she could reach the hotplate and the wine. For the first time the children saw Fiona replaced and perhaps for the first time they faced the idea that their mother was permanently lost to them.

When, after tasting the cake and toasting Zena and Werner in apple juice, Gloria took the children upstairs to change into pyjamas and go to bed, I was half inclined to go with them. But Zena was in the midst of a long story about her wealthy relatives in Mexico City and I let the children go. It was a long time before Gloria returned. Billy was in his new pyjamas and carrying a toy crane that he felt he must demonstrate for Werner.

'Where's Sally?' I asked when I kissed Billy good night.

'She's a little tearful,' said Gloria. 'It's the excitement. She'll be fine after a good night's sleep.'

'Sally says Mummy is never coming back,' said Billy.

'Never is a long time,' I replied. I kissed him again. 'I'll come up and kiss Sally.'

'She's asleep,' said Gloria. 'She'll be all right, Bernie.'

Even after Billy was in bed and Zena had finished her long story, I worried about the children. I suppose Sally felt she had no one she could really confide in. Poor child.

'How did you remember the date of our marriage?' Zena Volkmann asked me.

'I always remember,' I said.

'He's a liar,' said Gloria. 'He made me phone Werner's secretary and ask.'

'You mustn't give away all Bernie's secrets,' Werner told her.

'It was a wonderful surprise,' said Zena. The two women were sitting on the sofa together. They were both very young, but they were as different as two young women could be. Gloria was blonde, fair-skinned, tall and big-boned, with that rather slow tolerant attitude that is often the sign of the scholar. Zena Volkmann was small and dark, with the coil-spring energy and the short fuse of the self-made opportunist. She was dressed expensively and adorned with jewellery; Gloria was in tweed skirt and roll-neck sweater with only a small plain silver brooch.

Werner was in a mood for reminiscence that evening, and he'd related story after story about the times we'd spent together in Berlin. The two women had endured our remembered youthful escapades with fortitude, but now they'd had enough. Gloria got to her feet. 'More coffee? Brandy?' she said. She poured the last of the coffee for me and for Werner. 'You do the brandy, Bernard. I'll make more coffee and tidy away.'

'Let me help you,' said Zena Volkmann.

Gloria said no, but Zena insisted on helping her to clear the table and load the dishwasher. The two women seemed to be getting along well together; I could hear them laughing when they were in the kitchen. When Zena came back to collect the last plates from the table, she was wearing an apron.

'How did it go, Werner?' I asked when finally there was a chance to talk to him. I poured my precious vintage brandy, passed him his coffee, and offered him the jug. But Werner resisted the suggestion of cream in his coffee. I poured the rest of it into my cup. 'Cigar?'

'No thanks. If you can stop smoking, so can I,' said Werner. He drank some coffee. 'It went the way you said it would go.' He had given evidence to the committee.

He slumped back in his chair. Despite his posture, he was looking very trim – Zena's strict diet routine was having an effect – but he looked tired. I suppose anyone would look tired if they were married to Zena as well as giving evidence to the committee. Now Werner pinched his nose between his thumb and forefinger as he always did when he concentrated. But this time his eyes were closed, and I had the feeling he would have liked to go right off to sleep.

'No surprises?' I asked.

'No bad surprises. But I wasn't expecting to see that damned Henry Tiptree on the committee. That's the one who gave you so much trouble. I thought he was attached to Internal Security.'

'These Foreign Office attachments float from department to department. Everyone tries to unload them. The committee is probably a good job for him; it keeps him out of the way.'

'Bret Rensselaer is the chairman.'

'It's Bret's final chance to be the golden boy,' I joked.

'I heard he was in line for Berlin after Frank retires.'

'I heard the same thing, but I could tell you a few people who'll do everything they can to stop him getting it.'

'Dicky, you mean?'

'I think so,' I said.

'Why? Dicky would become Bret's boss. Isn't that what he's always wanted?'

Even Werner didn't fully understand the nuances of London Central's command structure. I suppose it was uniquely British. 'The German desk is senior to Berlin Resident in certain respects, but has to defer to it in others. There is no hard-and-fast rule. Everything depends upon the seniority of the person holding the job. When my dad was Berlin Resident, he was expected to do as he was told. But when Frank Harrington went there, from a senior position in London Central, he wasn't going to be taking orders from Dicky who'd spent a lot of his departmental career attached to the Army.'

'Dicky should never have had his Army service credited to his seniority,' said Werner.

'Don't get me started on that one, Werner,' I said.

'It wasn't fair. It wasn't fair to you, it wasn't fair to the Department, and it wasn't fair to anyone who works for the German desk.'

'I thought you were a supporter of Dicky,' I said.

'Only when you try to tell me he's a complete buffoon. You underrate him, Bernie, and that's where you make a bad mistake.'

'Anyway, Dicky will probably oppose the idea of Bret getting Berlin. Morgan – the D-G's hatchet man – hates Bret and wants Dicky to oppose it. Dicky will do as Morgan wants.'

'Then you'll get it,' said Werner with genuine pleasure.

'No, not a chance.'

'Why? Who else is there?'

'A lot of people will be after that job. I know Frank keeps saying it's the Siberia of the service and the place where careers are buried, and all that may well be true; but everyone wants it, Werner, because it's the one job you've got to be able to say you did.'

'You have enough seniority, and you're the only one who has the right experience. They can't pass you over again, Bernie. It would be absurd.'

'The way I hear it, I'm not even going to be shortlisted.'

'See the D-G,' suggested Werner. 'Get his support.'

'He doesn't even remember my name, Werner.'

'What about Frank Harrington? You can count on him, can't you?'

'They won't listen to what Frank says about who should take over. They'll want a new broom in there. A strong recommendation from Frank would probably be counterproductive.' I smiled; 'counterproductive' was one of Dicky's words, the sort of jargon I used to despise. I was going soft behind that desk.

Werner said, 'Did Frank Harrington oppose the idea of letting MI5 people sit on the Stinnes committee?'

'I was there, Werner. Frank just said, "Yes, sir", without discussion or argument. He said it was "an admirable solution". He's close to the D-G. The D-G must have told Frank what he intended and got his support beforehand.'

'Frank Harrington said okay? Why? It's all a mystery to me,' said Werner. He stopped pinching his nose and looked at me, hoping for a solution.

'The D-G wants Bret out of the Department. There's a lot of discussion about Bret right now. Hysterical discussion.'

Werner looked at me for a long time. He was wearing his plastic inscrutable mask and trying not to look smug. 'This is a new development,' he said, unable to keep the note of triumph out of his voice. 'I seem to remember a Christmas party when you'd come back from Lange – your head was filled with suspicions of Bret Rensselaer.' He was grinning. Only with effort was he able to keep his voice level now, as though he wasn't poking fun at me, just retelling the story.

'I only said that all the leads should be investigated.'

Werner nodded. He knew I was retreating from my former position as prosecutor and it amused him. 'And now you don't think that?'

'Of course I do. But I hate to see the way it's being done. Bret is being railroaded. And I especially don't like the way he's being isolated. I know how it feels, Werner. Not so long ago I was the one whose friends were crossing the street to avoid me.'

'Did you take it any further? Did you report your suspicions?'

'I was with Uncle Silas for the weekend . . . this is some time back

. . . before Christmas. Brahms Four was there. I asked him about the receiving end of the intelligence over there.'

'You told me all that. But what does he know about it?' said Werner scornfully.

'Not much, but as I told you, it was enough to convince me that the Miller woman was running two agents.'

'In London Central? Make up your mind, Bernie. Are you still trying to prove that Bret is a KGB man or not?'

'I don't know. I go round and round in circles. But there *were* two agents: Fiona was coded, PIG IRON, the other was JAKE. Brahms Four confirmed that, Werner.'

'No, no, no. If Bret was feeding material back to Moscow . . . it doesn't bear thinking about. It would mean they knew about all the Brahms Four material as soon as we got it. . . .'

'So we have to find out if Moscow was monitoring the Brahms Four material all the time we were getting it.'

'How would you discover that?'

'I just don't know if we could. It would be the hell of a task to go through the archives, and I'm not sure how the D-G would react to a suggestion that we do it.'

'It would look damned funny if they forbade you going to the archives, wouldn't it?'

'They wouldn't have to say they didn't trust me,' I said. 'They could simply point out how difficult it would be to ascertain that from the archive material. They'd also point out that if the KGB had a good source, they wouldn't compromise it by acting on every damned thing they got. And they'd be right, Werner.'

'I can't believe that Moscow knew what Brahms Four was telling us all those years and let him get away with it. Even if Bret *was* monitoring the stuff for them.'

'Finally they let Brahms Four escape,' I said.

'They didn't exactly let him escape,' said Werner. 'You rescued him.'

'*We* rescued him, Werner, you and me together.'

'If Bret was reporting to Moscow, Brahms Four would still be in East Berlin.'

'They had no warning, Werner. I made sure Bret didn't know what I was going to do. And until the last minute when you came to London and told Dicky, no one at London Central knew I was going to pull Brahms Four out.'

'Your wife knew; she ran. She could have told Bret.'

'Not enough time,' I said. 'I thought of that, but there wasn't enough time for Bret to find out and get a message to Moscow.'

'So Bret is suspect and the D-G has put him on ice while he decides what to do about it?'

'It looks that way,' I said.

'Only the Miller woman knows the truth, I suppose,' said Werner. There was some unusual expression in his face that made me look at him closely.

'And she's in the Havel,' I said.

'Suppose I told you that I'd seen the Miller woman?'

'In the morgue? Did she come out at Spandau locks?'

'She's not dead,' said Werner smugly. 'I saw her looking fit and well. She's a clerk. She works in the *Rote Rathaus*.'

The Red Town Hall was the municipal centre for East Berlin, a massive red-brick building near Alexanderplatz, which, unlike so much around it, had survived for well over a century. 'Alive and well? You're sure?'

'Yes, I'm sure.'

'What's it all about then? Who is she? Was it all a stunt?'

'I found out a little about her – I have a friend who works there. Everything she said about her father living in England and about being married and so on seems to be true. I couldn't actually check her out, of course, but the story she gave you was true, as far as her identity is concerned.'

'She just forgot to mention that she was a resident of the Democratic Republic and worked for the government.'

'Right,' said Werner.

'What luck that you spotted her! I suppose they thought she was tucked well away from us in that place. There wasn't much likelihood of anyone who'd seen her on this side going into an office in the East Berlin town hall.'

'It was a million to one chance that I had to go there again. I remembered her because she once helped me with a tricky problem. An East German truck I use broke down in the West on a delivery trip. I went round in circles trying to find someone who had the necessary permissions to tow it from West to East. That was a year or more ago. Then, last week, I was in there again getting my ration cards.'

'And she didn't recognize you? She must have seen you that night they arrested her and I got her to give me a statement.'

'You did the interrogation. I waited outside. I only caught sight of her very briefly. I knew I'd seen her somewhere before, but I couldn't think where. I mean, it's not the sort of face you never forget. Then, after I'd given up and stopped thinking about her, I walked into the Rathaus and saw her sitting at her desk. This time I took a close look at her.'

'She was no amateur, Werner. She made her suicide attempt convincing enough to get herself slammed into the Steglitz Clinic.'

'Suicides in police cells – cops get very nervous about such things,

Bernie. I looked into it. He was a young cop on duty at night. He played it safe and sent for an ambulance.'

'And then they covered their tracks by taking her from the Steglitz Clinic and running the ambulance into the water.'

'It must have been a diversion while another car took her across to the East.'

'It worked all right,' I said. 'When I remember spending my Christmas Eve standing on that freezing cold wharf, waiting for them to lift that bloody vehicle. . . .'

'I hope you're not going to suggest trying to get hold of her again. We couldn't grab her, Bernie, not there in the Mitte. They'd have us in the bag before we even got her to the car.'

'It would be difficult, wouldn't it?'

'It wouldn't be difficult,' said Werner. 'It would be impossible. Don't even think about it.'

'You'd better put all this in writing, Werner.'

'I've got it drafted out. I thought I'd wait until I came to London so I could check with you first.'

'I appreciate that, Werner. Thanks.'

We sat for a few minutes drinking the coffee and not saying anything. I was fully occupied in trying out all the configurations that this new piece of the jigsaw puzzle presented.

Then Werner said, 'How does this affect Bret?'

'You didn't tell the committee anything about this Miller woman being alive, did you?'

'You said not to tell them departmental secrets. This seemed like a departmental secret.'

'So secret that only you and I know of it,' I said.

'That's right,' said Werner.

'Why, Werner? What the hell was it all about? Why did they use the Miller woman to pick up the material?'

'Suppose everything she told you was exactly true. Suppose she had been a radio operator handling the material from Bret Rensselaer and the stuff from your wife. Suppose Fiona pulled her out when she went over to them. The Miller woman decides she's getting too old for espionage and tells Moscow that she wants to get out of the business – she wants to retire. Fiona encourages her because the Miller woman knows too much. So they find her an easy little job issuing licences in the town hall. It happens all the time, Bernie. Probably she has a small pension and card for the *Valuta* shops so that she can buy Western goods. Everything is lovely, everyone is happy. Then one day, at short notice, they need someone to go to Wannsee and pick up the package. They need someone who has the right sort of papers for coming over to the West side of the city. It seems like a routine task. Little likelihood of danger. She'll only be in the West for a couple of hours, and she won't be searched by anyone on the West side when she goes through with the package.' He fiddled with his coffee spoon, pushing it backwards and forwards. 'Or perhaps it's not a one-off. Perhaps she does a lot of little jobs like that to eke out her salary. Either way, I have no trouble believing it. There's nothing that doesn't fit together.'

'Maybe not. But that's not the way I'd treat someone like her. Imagine that *we* had been running a truly remarkable source in the KGB offices in Moscow. Would we let a case officer or radio operator for that agent go back over there for ten minutes, let alone a couple of hours? You know we wouldn't.'

'The KGB are different,' said Werner. He drove the spoon around the table, cornering recklessly when it came to the fruit bowl.

'Maybe they are, but my supposition isn't complete yet. What if they not only had one remarkable source but *two* remarkable sources? And one of them is still in place, Werner – a source right in London Central still going strong. Are the KGB so different that they'd still let the Miller woman go and put her head in a noose? Would they take a chance on her being arrested and telling us enough to blow their other agent?'

'It's no good trying to think the way they think. That's the first thing I had to learn when I started dealing with them. They don't think like us. And you're being wise after the event. They had no idea that we were going to move in on that party at Wannsee. To them it must have seemed like the most routine and safe assignment possible.' Werner tried to drink from the cup he'd already emptied. Even when he knew it was empty, he tipped his head right back to get the final drips. He hadn't touched his brandy.

'I still find it difficult to believe they'd take the risk,' I said.

'What risk? Our people risk everything when they go through the Wall. They risk the detailed inspection of documents, the guards watching every move they make and listening to everything they say. There are the secret marks made on the passports and travelling papers. Everyone going East is scrutinized under a microscope no matter who they are. But what do their people risk when they come to spy on the West? No one crossing to our side is inspected very closely. Being a KGB agent is one of the safest jobs going. We're a walkover, Bernie. That woman's job was a sinecure. It was a million-to-one chance that she was swept up by the arrest team.'

'And even then she got away with it.'

'Exactly. All she had to do was make some gesture at suicide and she's conveniently moved to the Steglitz Clinic, all ready for the rescue. Damn it, Bernie, why are we so soft?'

'If you are right, Werner, it means that the KGB don't know what she divulged to us about the radio codes.'

Werner turned the cup in the saucer and thought about that and didn't answer.

I pressed him. 'Would they have put her right back into that job at the Rathaus if she'd admitted to giving us a confession?'

'Probably not.'

'She didn't tell them, Werner. I'd bet on that. Perhaps they were impressed by their own efficiency. Maybe they were so pleased at themselves for rescuing her so swiftly and smoothly that it never occurred to them that they were already too late.'

'I know what you're thinking,' said Werner.

'What am I thinking?'

'That she can be turned. You think we should blackmail her, threaten to tell the KGB that she confessed. . . .'

'And get her to work for us? A tired old woman like that? What would she tell us . . . all the latest dope on the ration-card issues? All the town hall gossip? No, Werner, I wasn't thinking of turning her.'

'What then?'

'I don't know.'

Werner changed the subject. 'Do you remember that terrible place under the rubble in Koch Strasse, where the old man made the model planes?'

'The bearded one who built a workshop out of bits of packing cases?' I remembered it well. We were kids; the 'old man' was probably no more than thirty, but there were lots of very elderly thirty-years-olds in Berlin at that time. He'd been a combat engineer in an armoured division, a skilled fitter who scraped a living by selling model aircraft to the conquerors. Even as a child I'd seen the irony of him sitting in the bombed rubble of central Berlin and making so lovingly the model B-17 bombers that the American airmen bought as souvenirs. He was a fierce-looking man with a crippled arm. We called him 'Black Peter' and when we went to watch him working he'd sometimes let us help him with sandpapering or boiling up the smelly animal glue.

'Did you know that the cellar he lived in was part of the prison cells under Prinz-Albrecht Strasse?' Prinz-Albrecht Strasse was the guarded way in which German adults of that time referred to Gestapo headquarters.

'I thought the Gestapo building was on the Eastern side.'

'I was there last week with a friend of mine, a photographer who's doing a magazine article – photos of the graffiti on the Wall. Some of it's very funny.'

'Only from this side,' I said. 'Drink your brandy, Werner. It was a Christmas present from Uncle Silas.'

'Anyway, I walked back to look at the place where we used to visit

Black Peter. It's all been levelled. They're building there. I found a big billboard that had fallen on its face. I picked it up and it was a notice – in four languages, so it must be old – saying YOU ARE NOW STANDING ON THE SITE OF THE GESTAPO PRISON WHERE MANY PATRIOTS DIED.

'Is Black Peter's cellar still there?'

'No, the bulldozers went over it. But there in the middle of the rubble someone had placed a small bunch of flowers, Bernie.'

'Near the sign?'

'The sign was face down. Someone had gone out to that desolate place and put an expensive bunch of flowers on the ground. No one walks across that empty site from one year to the next. How many Berliners know that that heap of rubble is the old Gestapo prison. Can you imagine someone taking flowers out there to remember someone . . .? After all these years. Fancy someone still doing that, Bernie. Like a secret little ritual. It made me shiver.'

'I suppose it would,' I said. I was slightly embarrassed by the depth of Werner's feelings. 'It's a strange city.'

'Don't you ever miss it?'

'Berlin? Yes, sometimes I do,' I admitted.

'It's an amazing town. I've lived there all my life and yet I still discover things that astound me. I wish my father had lived a little longer . . . I couldn't live anywhere else,' said Werner. For him and for me, Berlin represented some part of our fathers' lives that we still hoped to discover.

I said, 'And you're the one who keeps talking about retiring to live in the sun.'

'Because Zena would love it, Bernie. She's always talking about living somewhere warm and sunny. I suppose we will one day. If it made Zena happy, I could put up with it.'

'Talking of bouquets, do you remember that day we trailed Black Peter to see where he was going?'

'I don't know who was more frightened, him or us,' said Werner.

'Us,' I said. 'Remember how he kept getting off his bicycle and looking back?'

'I wonder how much he paid for that big bunch of flowers.'

'A week's work at least,' I said. 'Did you know it was the Jewish cemetery?'

'Didn't you?'

'Not at the time,' I said.

'Every Jew knows it.' For a moment I had forgotten how Werner's Jewish father had survived the Nazi regime by digging graves in a Jewish cemetery, a job no 'Aryan' was permitted to do. 'The Jewish school and the Jewish old-age home were there too. Grosse-Hamburger-Strasse was the heart of Berlin's old Jewish quarter, dating back hundreds of years.'

'Yes, I knew the Jewish old-age home. That was where Berlin Jews were taken and held, prior to being transported to the East.'

'It's strange that they chose such a very public place,' said Werner. 'In other cities the Jews were assembled at railway sidings or empty factory sites. But here they were right in the city centre, a short step from Unter den Linden. From the neighbouring apartment blocks and office buildings the roll calls and loading could be seen by hundreds of local people.'

'He chained his bicycle to the gate, I remember, and you said Black Peter couldn't be a Jew, he was in the Army.'

'Then we saw that the graves were marked with *crosses*,' said Werner. 'There must have been two hundred of them.'

'The way he put the flowers on the grave I guessed it was a relative. He knelt at the grave and said a prayer. He knew we were watching by then.'

'I could tell he wasn't a Jew when he crossed himself,' said Werner, 'but I still didn't realize what it was all about. Who could have guessed that they'd bury all those SS men in the old Jewish cemetery?'

'The bodies were from the fighting round the S-Bahn station Börse. The first orders the Red Army gave, when the fighting stopped, was to start burying the corpses. I suppose the old Jewish cemetery in Grosse-Hamburger-Strasse was the nearest available place.'

'The Russians were frightened of typhus,' said Werner.

'But if the cemetery was very old, it must have been full,' I said.

'No. In 1943 it was all dug up and the graves destroyed. Berlin was declared *judenrein* – cleared of Jews – about that time. The cemetery grounds stood empty from then until the end of the fighting.'

'I thought he was going to kill you when he caught you.' He'd hidden behind some bushes and grabbed Werner as we were leaving.

'I was always a little scared of him; he was so strong. Remember how he used to bend those bits of metal when he was making stands for the planes?'

'We were just kids, Werner. I think we liked to pretend he was dangerous. But Black Peter was miserable and starving, like half the population.'

'He was frightened. I think he must have found out your father was an English officer.'

'Do you think Black Peter was with his brother in the SS?' I asked.

'Do SS men say prayers? I don't know. I just believed everything he told us at the time. But if he wasn't in the fighting with his brother, how would he have known where he was buried.'

I said, 'Remember the evening we went back there and you brought a flashlight to see the name on the grave?'

'They weren't real front-line soldiers . . . clerks from Prinz-Albrecht Strasse and police headquarters, cooks, and Hitler Youth. What terrible luck to be killed when the war was so nearly over.'

'I wonder who decided to give them all proper markers with name, rank and unit.'

'It wasn't the Red Army,' said Werner, 'you can bet on that. I go past there sometimes. It's a memorial park nowadays. Moses Mendelssohn's grave is there and they've given him a new stone.'

'I suppose we shouldn't have followed him. He never forgave us for finding out his little secret. We weren't welcome in his cellar after that.' From the kitchen I heard the sound of the dishwasher starting. It was a very noisy machine and Gloria only switched it on when she was finished. 'The ladies are coming with more coffee,' I said.

'I'll talk to her,' said Werner, as if he'd been thinking of the Miller woman all the time. 'Maybe it will come to nothing, but I'll try.'

'Better do nothing, Werner. It's a departmental problem; let the Department solve it. No sense in you getting into trouble.'

'I'll sound her out,' said Werner.

'No, Werner. And that's an order.'

'Whatever you say, Bernie.'

'I mean it, Werner. Don't go near her.'

Then Gloria came in holding a jug of fresh coffee. She said, 'What have you men been talking about?'

'What we always talk about: naked girls,' I said.

Gloria thumped me between the shoulder blades before she poured out coffee for all four of us.

Zena Volkmann laughed; she was excited. She was hardly into the room before she said, 'Werner, Gloria has been showing me an antique American quilt that Bernard bought for her. Can we buy one, Werner dearest? Appliqué work – a hundred and fifty years old. I've got the address of the shop. They cost an absolute fortune, but it would look wonderful on our bed. It would be a sort of anniversary present for us.'

'Of course, my darling.'

'Isn't he a perfect husband?' said Zena, leaning over and cuddling Werner and planting a kiss on his ear.

'Remember what I said, Werner. For the time being, do nothing.'

'I remember,' said Werner.

'If you don't want that brandy, Werner, I'll drink it.'

23

Gloria expressed her love for me with such desperate intensity that I was frightened by it. Was it, I wondered, the unique passion that she wanted it to be? Was it the one and only chance for us both to find everlasting happiness? Or were these ideas just a measure of her youth? She could be so many different people: amusing companion, shrewd colleague, sulky child, sexy bedmate, and concerned mother to my two children. Sometimes I saw her as the fulfilment of all my hopes and dreams; at others I saw in her just a beautiful young girl balanced on the edge of womanhood and myself as a self-deluding middle-aged lecher.

It is liberating to be in love, and Gloria showed all the exhilaration that dedicated love provides. But to *be* loved is something quite different. To be loved is to suffer a measure of tyranny. For some the sacrifice comes easily, but Gloria could be possessive in a single-minded way that only the very young and the very old inflict upon their loved ones. She couldn't understand why I hadn't invited her to live with me permanently in my home in Duke Street. She resented every evening I didn't spend with her. When she was with me she resented the hours I spent reading, because she felt it was a pleasure we couldn't share. Most of all, she resented the trips abroad I had to make, so that I often deferred telling her about them until the last moment.

'Back to Berlin,' she said peevishly when I told her. We were standing in the kitchen after Zena and Werner had gone back to their hotel.

'It's not my idea,' I said. 'But Berlin is my desk. There's no one else who can go in my place. If I put it off this week, I've have to go next week.'

'What's so urgent in Berlin?'

'Nothing is urgent there. It's all routine, but some of the reports can't be adequately covered in writing.'

'Why not?' There was something, some anxiety in her voice that I didn't recognize. I should have been warned by that but I prattled on.

'It's better to listen at length over a glass of beer. Sometimes the asides are more valuable than the report itself. And I have to see Frank Harrington.'

'One long booze, is it?'

'You know I don't want to go,' I said.

'I don't know anything of the kind. I hear you talking about Berlin with such love and tenderness that it makes me jealous. A woman can't compete with a city, darling.' She smiled a cold and unconvincing smile. She was not good at hiding her emotions; it was one of the things I found attractive about her.

'It's where I grew up, sweetheart. When Werner and I get together, we talk of our childhood. Doesn't everyone reminisce when they see old school friends again? It was my home.'

'Of course they do, darling. You don't have to be so defensive about such a dirty old whore. How can I really be jealous of an ugly, chilly heap of bricks?'

'I'll be back as soon as I can,' I said. Before switching off the hall and kitchen lights, I switched on the lights at the top of the stairs.

It was dark, the glimmer of light just enough to make a halo round her pale yellow hair. As I turned to speak with her she flung her arms round me and kissed me furiously. I could never get used to embracing this young woman who was almost as tall as I am. And when she hugged me there was a strength within her that I found exciting. She whispered, 'You do love me, don't you?' I held her very tight.

'Yes,' I said. I'd given up denying it. The truth was that I didn't know whether I loved her or not; all I knew was that I missed her dreadfully when I wasn't with her. If that wasn't love, I'd settle for it until love arrived. 'Yes, I love you.'

'Oh, Bernard, darling' – her cry of joy was almost a shout.

'You'll wake the children,' I said.

'You're always so frightened of waking the children. We won't wake them, and if we do, they'll go back to sleep again. Come to bed, Bernard. I love you so much.'

We tiptoed upstairs and past the children and the nanny. Once in the bedroom I suppose I should have switched on the overhead light, but I went to the bedside table to switch on that light instead. That's why I stumbled over the large and heavy suitcase that had been left at the foot of the bed. I lost my balance and fell full length to the floor with enough noise to wake up the whole street.

'What the bloody hell is that?' I shouted, sitting on the carpet and rubbing my head where I'd cracked it against the bedstead.

'I'm sorry, darling,' said Gloria. She switched on the bathroom light to see better and helped me to my feet.

'What is it? Did you leave it there?' I didn't want to be helped to my feet; I just wanted her not to make the bedroom into an obstacle course.

'It's mine,' she said in a whisper. For a moment she stood looking at me and then went into the bathroom and began putting cream on her face to remove her makeup.

'Good God, woman! Where did it come from?'

For a long time she didn't reply, then she pushed the door open and said, 'It's some things of mine.' She'd taken off her sweater and her bra. She washed her face and began brushing her teeth, staring at herself in the mirror over the sink as if I wasn't there.

'Things?'

'Clothes and books. I'm not moving in, Bernard, I know you don't want me to move in with you. The case is there only until tomorrow; then it will be gone.' She had taken the toothbrush from her mouth so that she could speak and now she stood looking at herself in the mirror, talking as if to her own image and making the promise to herself.

'Why did you have to leave it in the middle of the bedroom? Why bring it up here at all? Couldn't it go under the stairs?' I started to undress, throwing my clothes on the chair. One shoe hit the wall with more force than I intended.

She finished in the bathroom and reappeared, wearing a new frilly nightdress I hadn't seen before. 'The bathroom is all yours,' she said. And then, 'Mrs Dias, your cleaning woman, has to get into that cupboard under the stairs to get the vacuum cleaner.'

'So what?'

'She'd ask me what it was, wouldn't she? Or ask you what it was? And then you'd fuss about it. I thought it was better in here. I put it under the bed; then I had to get some things from it. I meant to push it back under the bed again. I'm sorry, darling. But you're a difficult man.'

'It's okay,' I said, but I was annoyed and unable to conceal my annoyance.

This silly accident with her suitcase spoiled the mood for both of us. When I came from the bathroom she was curled up in bed, the pillow over her head, and facing away. I got into bed and put an arm around her shoulders and said, 'I'm sorry. I should have looked where I was going.'

She didn't turn to face me. Her face was in the pillow. 'You've changed lately, Bernard. You're very distant. Is it something I've done?'

'Nothing you've done.'

'Is it Dicky? He's been like a bear with a sore head these last few days. They say he's given up his lady friend.'

'You know he was seeing Tessa Kosinski?'

'You told me,' said Gloria. She was still talking to her pillow.
'Did I?'

'A friend of Daphne's saw them in a hotel. You told me all that.
I know you were worried about it.'

'It was madness.'

'Why?' she said. She turned her face towards me. She knew the
answer, but she wanted to talk.

'Tessa is the sister of an intelligence official who is now working
for the KGB. It would be okay for Dicky to have normal social
contact with her. It would be okay for Dicky to be seeing her in the
course of his job. But treason and infidelity have too much in
common. Dicky was meeting Tessa secretly, and that sort of thing
makes Internal Security very very nervous.'

'Is that why he gave her up?'

'Who told you he gave her up?'

'Sometimes I think you don't even trust me, Bernard.'

'Who told you he gave her up?'

A big sigh. 'So *she* gave *him* up.'

'Why did you think it was his idea?'

'Falling over suitcases makes you paranoid, did you know that,
darling?'

'I know that, but answer my question anyway.'

Gloria stroked my face and ran a finger over my mouth. 'You've
just told me that Dicky had everything to lose from the relationship.
Naturally I concluded that he would be the one to end it.'

'And that's the only reason?'

'He's a man; men are selfish. If they have to choose between their
job and a woman, they'll get rid of the woman. Everyone knows how
men are.' It was of course a reference to her fears about me.

'Tessa gave Dicky the push, but Dicky likes to tell it his way:
strong-willed Dicky who knows what's best for both of them and
brokenhearted Tessa trying to put the pieces of her life back together.'

'He is like that, isn't he,' said Gloria. 'He's the worst sort of male
chauvinist pig. Does Tessa really love him?'

'I shouldn't think so. I don't think she knows whether she loves
him or not. I suppose he amuses her; that's all she asks. She'd go to
bed with almost anyone she found amusing. Sometimes I think
perhaps Tessa is incapable of loving anyone.'

'That's a rotten thing to say, darling. She adores you and you've
told me a thousand times that you could never have managed without
all the help she's giving you.'

'That's true, but we were talking about love.'

'I suppose you're right. Love is different.'

'They're not in love, Dicky and Tessa,' I said. 'If they were really
in love, there would be nothing that could keep them apart.'

'Like me pursuing you?' She hugged me.

'Yes, like that.'

'How could your wife have let you go? She must be mad. I adore you so much.'

'Tessa saw Fiona,' I said suddenly. I hadn't meant to tell her, but she was involved. It was better that she knew what was happening. There always came a point at which the job and one's personal life overlapped. It was one of the worst things about the job, telling lies and half-truths about everything. For a womanizer I suppose these things come more easily.

'Your wife came here?'

'They met in Holland, at their aunt's house.'

'What did your wife want?'

'It was the aunt's birthday. Both sisters visit her every year to celebrate it.'

'She didn't go just for that, Bernard; she wanted something.'

'How do you know?'

'I know your wife, Bernard. I think about her all the time. She wouldn't go to Holland to visit her aunt and see her sister except for a very good reason. She must have wanted something. Not a departmental something – there would have been other ways to tackle that; something from you.'

'She wants the children,' I said.

'You mustn't let them go,' said Gloria.

'Just for a holiday, she said. Then she'll send them back.' I was still trying to convince myself that it was as simple as that. I was half hoping that Gloria would encourage that belief, but she didn't.

'What mother could send her children back, not knowing when she'll see them again, if ever? If she goes to such trouble to arrange to see them, she'll never want to give them up again.'

Gloria's opinion didn't make me feel good. I felt like getting up and having another drink, but I resisted the idea; I'd had enough already. 'That's what I think,' I said. 'But if she goes through the courts for custody, she might well get them. I'm going to get a legal opinion about it.'

'Are you going to tell your father-in-law?'

'I just can't decide. She's asking politely, and only asking that they go on holiday with her. If I refuse that request, a court might see that as refusing reasonable access. That would count against me if she pursued the matter and wanted custody.'

'Poor darling, what a worry for you. Tessa told you this last week when you went there for drinks?'

'Yes,' I said.

'You've been in a rotten mood ever since. I wish I'd known. I was worried. I thought perhaps . . .'

'What?'

'You and Tessa,' said Gloria.

'Me and Tessa?'

'You know how much she'd like to get you into bed.'

'But *I* don't want to go to bed with *her*,' I said.

'Now who's shouting loud enough to wake up the children?'

'I like Tessa, but not like that. And anyway, she's married to George. And I've got you.'

'That's what makes you so interesting to her. You're a challenge.'

'Nonsense.'

'Did you tell Werner about Fiona meeting Tessa? Did you tell him she wants the children?'

'No.'

'But Werner's your best friend.'

'He couldn't help. He'd only worry himself sick. I didn't think it was fair to burden him with it.'

'You should have told him. He'll be angry that you haven't confided in him. He's easily hurt, anyone can see that.'

'It's best this way,' I said, without being really sure it was best.

'When are you testifying before the committee?' she said.

'I don't know.'

'There's a rumour that you've refused to go.'

'Oh, yes.'

'Is it true?'

'No, it's not true. Dicky told me that the committee had scheduled a time to hear evidence from me, but I said that I would need written orders.'

'To go before the committee?'

'I want written orders that specify what I can tell them.'

'And Dicky won't give you that?'

'He wouldn't even give Werner guidelines to what he could reveal.'

'He refused?'

'He dithered and changed the subject. You know what Dicky's like. If I'd asked him one more time, he would have developed a head cold and been taken home on a stretcher.'

'Everyone else is giving evidence. Aren't you going rather far, darling?'

'These are not our people on the committee.'

'They are MI5.'

'I am not authorized to tell MI5 anything and everything about our operations.'

'You're just being pigheaded.' She laughed as if pleased I was giving someone else trouble rather than her.

'It's not just a matter of a combined committee: we've had those before, plenty of them. But it looks as if Bret has been shunted off onto that committee while they decide whether he should face an enquiry. If Bret is suspect . . . if Bret might turn out to be a KGB agent, why should I go over there and fill in the blanks for him?'

'If Bret is really suspect, the people on that committee must know,' said Gloria. 'And in that case, they'll make sure that you provide no evidence that would matter if it got back to the Russians.'

'I'm glad you think so,' I said. 'But they're more devious than that. I suspect that the Stinnes committee wants to use me as a blunt instrument to beat Bret across the head. That's the real reason I won't go.'

'What do you mean?'

'That committee isn't called the "Stinnes committee" – it's called the "Rensselaer committee". Was that a Freudian slip? Anyway, it's a good name because that committee isn't primarily interested in Stinnes except as a source of evidence about Bret. And if they finally get me over there, they won't want to know about how we enrolled Stinnes – they'll be asking me questions that might trap Bret.'

'If Bret is guilty, what's wrong with that?'

'Let them provide their own evidence. They think I'll play ball with anything they want. They think I'll cooperate in order to prove that I'm whiter than the driven snow. Dicky more or less told me that. He said I should be pleased that suspicion has fallen on Bret because now they'd be less inclined to believe I was helping Fiona.'

'I'm sure he didn't mean that,' said Gloria.

'He meant it.'

'You're determined to believe that the Department doesn't trust you. But there are no restrictions on you, none at all. I bring the daily sheets up from Registry. If there was any restriction on what you could see, I would know about it.'

'Perhaps you're right,' I said. 'But there's still an undercurrent of suspicion. Perhaps it's just a way of keeping me under pressure, but I don't like it. And I don't like Dicky telling me that Bret's being convicted will let me breathe easy.'

'Do you think the committee was convened by the Director-General as a way to investigate Bret Rensselaer?'

'The committee was the brainchild of someone higher up the ladder. The old man wouldn't be arranging for MI5 to help us wash the dirty linen unless he was ordered to do it that way.'

'Higher up the ladder?'

'I see the hand of the Cabinet Office in this one. The Coordinator of Intelligence and Security is the only man who can tell both us and Five what he wants done. The D-G made it sound like his own idea so that the Department wouldn't feel humiliated.'

'Humiliated by having MI5 investigate one of our people?'

'That's my guess,' I said.

'If Bret is guilty, does it matter how they trap him?'

'If he's guilty. But there's not enough solid evidence for that. Either Bret is a super-agent who never makes a bad mistake or he's being victimized.'

'Victimized by whom?'

'You haven't seen at close quarters the sort of panic that develops when there's talk of an agent infiltrating the Department. There's hysteria. The other day Dicky was remembering all sorts of amazing ramifications of a trip to Kiel he made with Bret. Dicky was turning Bret's reaction to a KGB man into conclusive evidence against Bret. That's how the hysteria builds up.'

'They say that where Bret went wrong was in the launderette,' said Gloria.

'At first I thought so too. But now I'm inclined to see it as evidence in Bret's favour. The kid who came through the door shouted "Go" to us. Why did he do that, unless he thought Bret was Stinnes? He was expecting someone to run off with them. Everyone is trying to believe that it was something Bret arranged to eliminate Stinnes, but that doesn't make sense. It was planned as an escape; I see that now. And don't forget that Bret could have picked up that shotgun and killed me.'

'And the bomb under the car?'

'Because they thought Bret was in the car.'

'And you say that clears Bret?'

'I told you, those hoods were trying to spring Stinnes.'

'Or to kidnap him,' said Gloria.

'Not on a motorcycle. A back-seat passenger has to be willing to go along.'

'If Bret is completely innocent, there's so much else to explain. What about the Cabinet memo that Bret sent to Moscow?'

'There's evidence that Bret's copy got to Moscow. But there was only one copy of that memo in the Department. Why shouldn't Fiona have sent a photocopy to Moscow? She had access.'

'And then used it to frame Bret?'

'I'm only saying that all the evidence against Bret is circumstantial. We aren't certain that Moscow ever got the report that followed the memo. There isn't one really good piece of it that nails Bret beyond doubt.'

'You can't have it both ways, Bernard. You say they put the bomb under the car in which Stinnes was sitting because they thought Bret was inside it. Either Moscow is going to immense trouble to frame Bret or else they tried to kill him. But those two actions are incompatible.'

'Both actions would benefit Moscow. If that bomb had killed Bret, the Department would be in an even worse state of panic. As it is now, they have Bret under observation, they have a measure of control over who he sees and what he does. Everyone feels that if Bret is guilty, he'll fall prey to the interrogator, especially with Stinnes inventing some difficult questions for him. They're comforting themselves with the idea that Bret will cooperate fully with the investigation to avoid a long jail sentence. But if Bret was dead, things wouldn't look so rosy. There'd be no way to pull the chestnuts out of the fire. We'd have to be digging out all the material he'd handled, supervetting all Bret's contacts, and doing the same sort of complicated double-thinking that we did when Fiona went over there.'

'If a dead Bret is worse for us than a live Bret, why haven't they tried again?'

'They don't have hit teams waiting in the Embassy, sweetheart. Such killings have to be planned and authorized. A hit team has to be briefed and provided with false documentation. It all went wrong for them at the launderette, so now there will probably be some KGB officials arguing against trying again. It will take time.' What I didn't say was that Fiona might be one of the people arguing against another attempt on Bret's life, for I suspected that Bret's life might depend upon what she decided.

'Do you think Bret knows he's in danger?'

'This is just one theory, Gloria. It could be wrong; Bret might be the KGB mole that everyone thinks he is.'

'Will they *make* you go before the committee?'

'The D-G won't want to go back to the Cabinet Office and say I'm being difficult, and yet the Coordinator is the only one who can order me to do it. I think the D-G will decide it's better to delay things and hope the committee will decide it can manage without me. In any case, I've got a breathing space. You know what the Department is like; if the committee insists on me attending, they'll have to put it in writing. Then I'll put my objections in writing too. In any case, nothing will happen until I come back from Berlin.'

'When are you going?' said Gloria.

'Tomorrow.'

'Oh, Bernard. Couldn't it wait a week? There's so much I wanted to talk about with you.'

'Is there?' I said, fully alerted. There was something in her voice, a plaintive note I recognized. 'Is it something to do with that suitcase?'

'No,' she said, quickly enough to indicate that she really meant yes.

'What's in it?'

'Clothes. I told you.'

'More clothes? This house is full of your clothes now.'

'It's not.' Her voice was harsh and she was angry. And then, more rueful: 'I knew you'd be beastly.'

'You remember what we agreed, Gloria. We are not going to make this a permanent arrangement.'

'I'm just your weekend girl, aren't I?'

'If that's the way you want to think about it. But there are no other girls, if that's what you mean.'

'You don't care about me.'

'Of course I do, but I must have just a bit of wardrobe space. Couldn't you take a few things back to your parents . . . and maybe rotate things as you need them?'

'I should have known you didn't love me.'

'I do love you, but we can't live together, not all the week.'

'Why?'

'There are all sorts of reasons . . . the children and Nanny and . . . well, I'm just not ready for that sort of permanent domestic scene. I must have breathing space. It's too soon after my wife left.' The words came out in a torrent, none of them providing any real answer for her.

'You're frightened of the word "marriage", aren't you? That really frightens you.'

'I'm not even divorced yet.'

'You say you're worried about your wife getting custody of the children. If we were married, the court would be more sympathetic to the idea of you keeping them.'

'Perhaps you're right, but you can't get married before you're divorced, and the court will not look favourably upon a bigamist.'

'Or look favourably upon a father living with his mistress. So that's the reason?'

'I didn't say that.'

'You treat me like a child. I hate you.'

'We'll talk about it when I come back from Berlin. But there are other people involved in such a decision. Have you considered what your parents are likely to say to you if you moved in here?'

'What they'd say to you, that's what concerns you, isn't it? You're worried about what my parents are going to say to you.'

'Yes, I am concerned about them.'

She began to cry.

'What's wrong, darling?' I said, although of course I knew what was wrong. 'Don't be in such a hurry about everything. You're young.'

'I've left my parents.'

'What's that?'

'All my things are in the suitcase – my books, my pictures, the rest of my clothes. I had a terrible row with my mother, and my father took her side. He had to, I suppose. I understand why he did it. Anyway, I've had enough of them both. I packed my things and left them. I'm never going back.'

I felt sick.

She went on: 'I'm never going back to them. I told them that. My mother called me names. She said awful things about me, Bernard.'

She was crying more seriously now, and her head fell onto my shoulder and I could feel the warm wet tears on my bare skin. 'Go to sleep, sweetheart. We'll talk about it tomorrow,' I said. 'The plane doesn't leave until lunchtime.'

'I'm not staying here. You don't want me, you've told me that.'

'For the time being . . .'

'I'm not staying here. I have someone I can go to. Don't worry, Bernard. By the time you come back from Berlin all my things will be out of here. At last I can see you as you really are.'

She was still limp in my arms, still sobbing with a subdued and desolate weariness, but I could hear the determination in her voice. There was no way she was going to stay except on promise of marriage and that was something I couldn't bring myself to give. She turned over to face away from me and hugged herself. She wouldn't be comforted. I remained awake a long time, but she went on sobbing very quietly. I knew there was nothing I could do. There is no sadness to compare with the grief of the young.

24

Berlin is a sombre city of grey stone. It is an austere Protestant town; the flamboyant excesses of South German baroque never got as far as Prussia's capital. The streets are as wide as the buildings are tall, so that the cityscape dwarfs people hurrying along the windswept streets, in a way that the skyscrapers of Manhattan do not overwhelm the human figure. Even Berlin's modern buildings seem hewn from stone, their glass façades mirroring the grey sky, monolithic and forbidding.

Inside Lisl Hennig's hotel the furniture had the same massive proportions that characterized the city. Solid, stately, and uncompromising, the oak tables, the heavy mahogany wardrobes, and the elegant Biedermeier cupboards and china cabinets of peach and pear wood dominated the house. Even in my little room at the top of the house, the corner cabinet and the chest of drawers, the carved chair and the bed built high upon several mattresses left little space to move from window to door.

I always slept in this room. It was the one I'd occupied as a child, when my family had the top floors assigned to them by the British Army of Occupation. From this window I'd floated my paper aeroplanes, blown soap bubbles, and dropped water bombs into the courtyard far below. Nowadays no one else wanted to use this dark cramped little box room so far from the bath. So the dark-brown floral patterned wallpaper remained, and over the tiny fireplace there still could be seen the framed engraving of medieval Dresden that Lisl Hennig had put there to hide the marks where Werner's air gun had been fired at a drawing of Herr Storch, the fat mathematics teacher. Storch had been a dedicated Nazi, but he had somehow managed to evade the denazification procedures and get his job back after the war.

I moved the picture to show Werner that the marks were still there. 'Spat! spat! spat!' said Werner, firing an imaginary pistol at the place where the drawing of Storch had once been.

'You've got to hand it to him,' I said without mentioning Storch by name. 'He stuck to his views.'

'He was a Nazi bastard,' said Werner without rancour.

'And he did little to hide it,' I said. The sky was black with storm clouds and now the rain began, huge drops of water that hit the glass with loud noises and made patterns on the dirty windowsill.

'Storch was cunning,' said Werner. 'He rephrased all his Nazi claptrap into anti-British and anti-American tirades. They could have put him inside for spreading Nazi ideas, but the British and the Americans kept telling everyone how much they believed in free speech. They couldn't do much about Storch.' Werner was standing by the fireplace, fidgeting with the china figure of William Tell that had been relegated to this room after a maid had dropped it into the sink while cleaning it. The pieces had been stuck together with a glue that had oozed to make brown ridges around the arms and legs.

I'd been trying to find some suitable opportunity to tell Werner about Tessa's meeting with my wife and about her request for the children, but the right moment didn't come. 'Do you ever see him? Herr Storch, do you ever see him?'

'He got married again,' said Werner. 'He married a widow who had a watchmaker's shop in Munich.' Werner was dressed in a dark-grey worsted jacket and the corduroy trousers that the Germans call *Manchesterhosen*. His shirt was green and with it he wore a green polyester tie with little red horses. On the hook behind the door he'd hung a tired old grey raincoat. I knew he had an appointment with some East Bloc bank officials that afternoon, but even if he hadn't told me, I would have guessed he was going over to the East; he always wore such proletarian clothes when going there. His long black coat with its astrakhan collar and the kind of tailored wool suits he preferred, to say nothing of his taste in shoes, would have been too conspicuous in the streets of East Berlin.

'Trust Storch to fall on his feet.'

'He made your life hell,' said Werner.

'No, I wouldn't say that.'

'All that extra homework, and always making you come out to the front of the class and do the geometry at the blackboard.'

'It was good for me. I was top for mathematics two years running. My dad was amazed.' There was a crash of thunder and a blue flash of lightning.

'Even then, old Storch kept on at you.'

'He hated the English. His son was killed fighting in the Libyan Desert. He told the boys in the top class that the English had shot all their prisoners.'

'That was just propaganda,' said Werner.

'You don't have to spare my feelings,' I said. 'There are bastards everywhere, Werner. We both know that.'

'Storch didn't have to take it out on you.'

'I was the only *Engländer* he could get his hands on.'

'I've never heard you say a bad word about old Storch.'

'He was a tough-minded old bastard,' I said. 'He must have known that one word to my dad about him having been a stormtrooper would have got him kicked out of his job, but he didn't seem to care.'

'I would have squealed on him,' said Werner.

'You hated him more than I did.'

'Don't you remember all that poisonous stuff about Jewish profiteers, and the way he stared at me all the time?'

'And you said, "Don't look at me, sir, my father was a gravedigger." '

'That was when old Herr Grossmann was away on sick leave, and Storch did the history lessons.' A long roll of thunder sounded as the storm moved over the city and headed for Poland, such a short drive down the road. Werner scowled. 'All Storch knew about history was what he'd read in his Nazi propaganda – about how the Jewish profiteers had made Germany lose the war and ruined the economy. They should never have let a bigot like that take the history class.'

'I think I know what you're going to say, Werner.'

Werner sat down on the sagging armchair, smiled at me, and, although I knew what was coming, he said it anyway. 'One man was the very worst scoundrel, he told us. Already rich – he amassed a second fortune in a few months. He borrowed from the central bank to buy coal mines, private banks, paper mills and newspapers. And he paid back the loans in money so devalued by inflation that this whole spread cost him almost nothing.'

'It sounds like you've been looking at the encyclopedia, Werner,' I said. Hugo Stinnes. 'Yes, I was thinking of that long passionate lecture from old Storch only the other day.'

'So why would some Russian bastard with a KGB assignment choose a name like Stinnes as an operating name?'

'I wish I knew,' I said.

'Hugo Stinnes was a German capitalist, a class enemy, obsessed by the threat of world Bolshevism. What kind of joke is it for a Russian KGB man to choose that name?'

'What kind of man would choose it?' I said.

'A very, very confident Communist,' said Werner. 'A man who was so trusted by his KGB masters that he could select such a name without fear of being contaminated by it.'

'Did you only think of that now?' I asked.

'Right from the time I first heard the name it seemed a curious choice for a Communist agent. But now – now that so much depends upon his loyalty – I think of it again. And I worry.'

I said. 'Yes, the same with me, Werner.'

Werner paused and, using his little finger, scratched his bushy eyebrows. 'When the Nazi party sent Dr Goebbels to open their first office in Berlin, they used that little back cellar in Potsdamerplatz that belonged to Storch's uncle. It was a filthy hole; the Nazis called it "the opium den". They say Storch's uncle let them have it without paying rent and in return Storch got a nice little job with the Party.'

I looked at the rain as it polished the roofs of the buildings across the courtyard. The roofs were tilted, crippled, and humpbacked, like an illustration from 'Hansel and Gretel'. My mind was not on old Herr Storch any more than Werner's was. I said, 'Why not use his real name – Sadoff – why use a German name at all? And if a German name, why Stinnes?'

'It raises a lot of questions,' said Werner as his mind went another way. 'If Stinnes was planted solely as a way of giving us false information, then the Miller woman was used only to support that trick.'

'That's not difficult to believe, Werner,' I said. 'Now that we know she wasn't drowned in the Havel, now that we know she's safe and well and working for the East German government, I've changed my mind about the whole business.'

'The whole business? Her collecting that material from the car at the big party in Wannsee? Did she want to get arrested that night when we set it up so carefully and were so pleased with ourselves? Was that confession she gave you at some length – was it all set up?'

'To implicate Bret? Yes, the Miller woman made a fool of me, Werner. I believed everything she told me about the two code words. I went back to London convinced that there was another agent in London Central. I disobeyed orders. I went and talked to Brahms Four. I was convinced that someone in London Central – probably Bret – was a prime KGB agent.'

'It looked that way,' said Werner. He was being kind, as always. He could see how upset I was.

'It did to me. But no one else was fooled. You told me again and again. Dicky turned up his nose at the idea, and Silas Gaunt got angry when I suggested it. I even began to wonder if there was a big cover-up. But the truth is that they weren't fooled by her and her story, and I was.'

'Don't blame yourself, Bernard. They didn't see her. She was convincing, I know.'

'She made a fool of me. She had nicotine stains on her fingers and no cigarettes! She had inky fingers and no fountain pen! She drowns, but we find no body. How could I be so stupid! A clerk from East Berlin; yes, of course. Everyone in London Central was right and I was wrong. I feel bad about that, Werner. I have more field experience that any of those people. I should have seen through her. Instead I went around doing exactly what they wanted done.'

'It wasn't like that, Bernie, and you know it. Silas Gaunt and Dicky and the rest of them didn't argue with you or give any reasons. They wouldn't believe your theory because it would have been too inconvenient to believe it.'

'Then Posh Harry gave me documents that supported the idea that there was a mole in London Central.'

'You're not saying Posh Harry was in on it?'

'I don't think so. Posh Harry was a carefully selected go-between. They used him the way we've used him so often. That was probably Fiona's idea.'

'It's the very hell of a complicated scenario they had,' said Werner, rubbing his face. 'Are you sure that you've got it right now? Would it be worth them going to all that trouble? When you got Stinnes out of Mexico City, you nearly got killed doing it. A KGB man from the Embassy was shot.'

'That shooting was an accident, Werner. Pavel Moskvin was the one who gave me a tough time in East Berlin. If Stinnes is a plant, then Moskvin is the man behind it. I can't prove it, of course, but Moskvin is the sort of hard-nosed Party man that Moscow has monitoring and masterminding all their important departments.'

'You think Moskvin planted him without any contacts or case officer or letter drop? You think Stinnes is all on his own?'

' "Solitaries", the Russians call them; agents whose real loyalties are known to only one or two people at the very top of the command structure. The only record of their assignment is a signed contract locked into a safe in Moscow. Sometimes when such people die, despised and unlamented, even their close relatives – wife, husband, children – aren't told the real story.'

'But Stinnes left his wife. He'd even had a fight with her.'

'Yes,' I said, 'and that convinced me that he really wanted to come over to the West. But the fight was genuine – his story false. We should have allowed for that possibility, I suppose.'

'So now you think Stinnes is a solitary?' said Werner.

'For them the solitary isn't so unusual, Werner. Communism has always glamorized secrecy; it's the Communist method; subversion, secret codes, cover names, secret inks, no agent permitted to contact more than two other agents, cells to make sure that one lost secret doesn't lead to the loss of another. All these things are not exclusively Russian, and not peculiar to the KGB; this sort of secrecy comes naturally to *any* Communist. It's part of the appeal that worldwide Communism has for the embittered loner. If my guess is right Moskvin is the only other person who knows the whole story. They probably didn't tell the truth to the snatch team that hit the launderette. The KGB would reason that just one extra person knowing the real story would increase the risk of us discovering that Stinnes was a plant.'

'A man who sacrificed himself? Is Stinnes that sort of man?' said Werner. 'I'd marked him down as a hard-nosed and ambitious opportunist. I'd say Stinnes is the sort of man who sends others off to sacrifice themselves while he stays behind and gets the promotions.'

Werner had hit upon the thing that I found most difficult to reconcile with the facts. Right from the time when Stinnes started talking about coming over to the West I'd found it difficult to believe in his sincerity. The Stinnes of the KGB didn't come West – not as defectors, not as agents, and especially not as solitaries who'd spend the rest of their days unrewarded, unloved, and uninvolved with the job, acting out a role in which they had no belief. As Werner said, Stinnes was the sort who dispatched others to that kind of fate.

'When Moscow wants him back, they'll find a way to get him,' I said.

'I'll go along with your theory,' said Werner grudgingly. 'But you won't convince many others. They like it the way it is. You tell me London Central have practically written Bret off. The Stinnes committee are just getting into their stride. If what you say about Stinnes is correct they're all going to wind up with egg on their faces, a lot of egg on their faces. You'll need some solid evidence before going back there and trying to convince them that Stinnes is a plant. That's a combined-services committee, and they're telling each other that Stinnes is the greatest break they've had in years. You'll have a lot of trouble convincing them that they've fallen for a KGB misinformation stunt.'

'More than just a stunt, Werner,' I said. 'If Stinnes blows a big hole in London Central, forces the Department to compromise with Five, spatters a little blood over me, and has Bret facing a departmental enquiry, I'd call that a KGB triumph of the first order.'

'I've been in front of that committee,' said Werner. 'They'll believe what they want to believe. Rock that boat and you'll be the one who falls into the water and drowns. I'd advise you to keep your theories to yourself. Keep right out of it, Bernie.'

There was more thunder, fainter now as the storm abated, and trickles of sunlight dribbled through the cloud.

'I am keeping out of it,' I said. 'I told Dicky I wouldn't go to the committee without detailed written instructions.'

Werner looked at me wondering, if it was a joke. When he realized it wasn't he said, 'That was silly, Bernie. You should have done what I did. You should have gone through the motions: smiled at their greetings, laughed at their little jokes, accepted one of their cigarettes, and listened to their idiot comments while trying to look enthralled. You refused? They'll regard you as hostile after that. What are they going to think if you go to them now and say that Stinnes is a phoney?'

'What are they going to think?' I said.

'They're going to resurrect all their darkest suspicions of you,' said Werner. 'Someone on that committee is sure to say that you might be a KGB agent trying to rescue Bret and trying to wreck the wonderful job that the Stinnes debriefing is doing.'

'I brought Stinnes in,' I said.

'Because you had no alternative. Don't you remember the way certain people said you were dragging your feet?' He looked at his watch, a stainless-steel one, not his usual gold model. 'I really must be going.'

He had plenty of time, but he was nervous. Werner made a lot of money from his completely legitimate banking deals, but he was always nervous before going East. Sometimes I wondered if it was worth it. 'Where's your car?'

'It's just a quick one. Some signatures to show that goods have arrived over there. The quicker I get the receipts, the quicker I get paid, and with bank charges the way they are . . . I'll go over on the S-Bahn. Once I arrive at Friedrichstrasse, it's only five minutes.'

'I'll walk down to Zoo station and see you onto the train,' I said. I still hadn't told him about Fiona and the children.

'Stay here, Bernie. You'll get wet.'

When we went downstairs, Lisl Hennig was sitting in the dining room. It was a large airy room overlooking the gloomy courtyard. The panelling had been painted cream and so had some of the cupboards. There was an old Oriental rug to cover worn lino just inside the doorway, and there were framed prints on the walls – scenes of German rural life – and one tiny picture that was different from the rest. It was a George Grosz drawing, a picture of a deformed soldier, a war veteran made grotesque by his injuries. It was full of rage and spite and despair so that the artist's lines attacked the paper. Lisl was sitting near the drawing, at a table by the window. She was always there about noon. On the table there was the usual pile of newspapers. She couldn't live without newspapers – she was obsessed by them, and woe betide anyone who interrupted her reading. Her mornings were always spent in going through them all, column by column: news, adverts, gossip, theatre, concert reviews, share prices, and even the classified adverts. Now she had finished her papers; now she was sociable again.

'Werner, darling. Thank you for the beautiful flowers, *Liebchen*. Come and give your Lisl a kiss.' He did so. She looked him up and down. 'It's freezing cold outside. You won't be warm enough in that raincoat, darling. It's terrible weather.' Did she recognize Werner's clothes as those he wore when visiting the East? 'You should be wearing your heavy coat.'

She was a big woman and the old-fashioned black silk dress with a lacy front did nothing to disguise her bulk. Her hair was lacquered, her once-pretty face was heavily but carefully painted, and there was too much mascara on her eyelashes. Backstage in a theatre her appearance would have gone unremarked but in the cold hard light of noon she looked rather grotesque. 'Sit down and have coffee,' she commanded with a regal movement of her hand.

Werner looked at his watch, but he sat down as he was told. Lisl Hennig had protected his Jewish parents, and after Werner was orphaned she brought him up as if he was her one and only son. Although neither of them displayed much sign of deep affection, there was a bond between them that was unbreakable. Lisl commanded; Werner obeyed.

'Coffee, Klara!' she called. '*Zweimal!*' There was a response from some distant part of the kitchen as her 'girl' Klara – only marginally younger than Lisl – acknowledged the imperious command. Lisl was eating her regular lunch: a small piece of cheese, two wholemeal wafers, an apple, and a glass of milk. Except for her, the dining room was empty. There were about a dozen tables, each set with cutlery and wineglasses and a plastic rose, but only one table had linen napkins and this was the only one likely to be used that lunchtime. Not many of Lisl's guests ate lunch; some of them were semipermanent residents, out at work all day, and the rest were the kind of salesmen who couldn't afford lunch at Lisl's or anywhere else. 'Did you bring me what I asked you to bring me?' Lisl asked Werner.

'I forgot, Lisl. I am very sorry.' Werner was embarrassed.

'You have more important things to do,' said Lisl, with that smile of martyrdom that was calculated to twist the knife in poor Werner's wound.

'I'll get it now,' said Werner, rising to his feet.

'What is it?' I said. 'I'll get it for you, Lisl. Werner has an important appointment. I'm walking up to the Zoo station. What can I bring back for you?' In fact, I guessed what it was; it was an eyebrow pencil. Whatever other elements of her makeup Lisl found necessary, none compared with the eyebrow pencil. Ever since her arthritis made shopping difficult for her, Werner had been entrusted with buying her makeup from the KaDeWe department store. But it was a secret, a secret with which even I was not officially entrusted; I knew only because Werner told me.

'Werner will get it for me. It is not important,' said Lisl.

Klara brought a tray with a jug of coffee and the best cups and saucers, the ones with the sunflower pattern, and some *Kipfel* on a silver platter. Klara knew that the little crescent shaped shortcakes were Werner's favourite.

A man in a smart brown-leather jacket and grey slacks came into the dining room and deposited his shoulder bag on a chair. It was at the table where the linen napkins had been arranged. He smiled at Lisl and left without speaking.

'Westies,' explained Lisl, using the Berlin word for tourists from West Germany. 'They eat lunch here every day.'

'The family with the grown-up sons; I saw them in the lobby,' said Werner. Even without hearing an accent, Berliners were always able to recognize such visitors, and yet it was hard to say in what way they were any different from Berliners. The faces were more or less the same, the clothing equally so, but there was something in the manner that distinguished them from 'Islanders', as the West Berliners referred to themselves.

'They hate us,' said Lisl, who was always prone to exaggerate.

'Westies hate us? Don't be silly,' said Werner. He looked at his watch again and drank some coffee.

'They hate us. They blame us for everything bad that happens.'

'They blame you for their high taxes,' I said. 'A lot of West Germans begrudge the subsidies needed to keep Berlin solvent. But all over the world big cities are funded from central government.'

'There is more to it than that,' said Lisl. 'Even the word "Berlin" is disliked and avoided in the Bundesrepublik. If they want a name for a soap or a scent or a radio or a motorcar, they might name such things "New York" or "Rio" or "Paris", but the word "Berlin" is the universal turnoff, the name that no one wants.'

'They don't hate us,' said Werner. 'But they blame us for everything that happens in the cold war. No matter that Bonn and Moscow are making the decisions – Berlin takes the blame.' Werner was diplomat enough to take Lisl's side.

'I don't know about that,' I said. 'Bonn gets more than its fair share of knocks and pays out more than its fair share of money.'

'Does it?' said Lisl. She was unconvinced. She hated to pay her taxes.

I said, 'Conveniently for the DDR, there is only one Germany when someone wants German money. Reparations to Israel didn't come from both halves of Germany – only from the West half. After the war the debts incurred by Hitler's Third Reich were not shared – only the West half settled them. And now, whenever the DDR offers to set free political prisoners in exchange for money, it's the West half that pays the ransoms to the East half. But when anyone anywhere in the world wants to express their prejudice about Germans, they don't tell you how much they hate those Germans in the East – who suffer enough already – all anti-German feeling is directed against the overtaxed, overworked Westies who prop up the overpaid, incompetent bureaucrats of the Common Market and finance its ever-increasing surplus so it can sell more and more bargain-priced wine and butter to the Russians.'

'Bernard has become a Westie,' said Lisl. It was a joke, but there was not much humour there. Werner gobbled the last *Kipfel* and got up and said goodbye to her. Lisl didn't respond to our arguments or to our kisses. She didn't like Westies even when they had lunch every day.

With Werner, I walked along Kantstrasse to Zoo station. The rain had stopped, but the trees dripped disconsolately. There was more rain in the air. The station was busy as usual, the forecourt crowded, a group of Japanese tourists taking photos of each other, a man and woman – both in ankle-length fur coats – buying picture postcards, a boy and girl with stiff dyed hair and shiny leather trousers singing tunelessly to the strumming of a guitar, French soldiers loaded with equipment climbing into a truck, two arty-looking girls selling pictures made from beads, an old man with a pony collecting money for animal welfare, a young bearded man asleep in a doorway, an expensively dressed mother holding a small child at arm's length while it vomited in the gutter, and two young policemen not noticing anything. It was the usual mix for Zoo station. This was the middle of the Old World. Here were Berlin's commuter trains and here too were trains that had come direct from Paris and went on to Warsaw and Moscow.

I went inside with Werner and bought a ticket so that I could accompany him up to the platform. The S-Bahn is Berlin's ancient elevated railway network and the simplest way to get from the centre of West Berlin (Zoo) to the heart of East Berlin (Friedrichstrasse). It was chilly up there on the platform; the trains rattled through, bringing a swirl of damp air and a stirring of wastepaper. The stations are like huge glass aircraft hangars, and like the tracks themselves they are propped up above street level on ornate cast-iron supports.

'Don't worry about Lisl's eyebrow pencil,' I told Werner. 'I'll get that for her on the way back.'

'Do you know the colour she wants?'

'Of course I do. You're always forgetting to get them.'

'I hope you're wrong about Stinnes,' said Werner.

'You forget about all that,' I said. 'You get over there and get your papers signed and get back. Forget about me and the Department. Forget all that stuff until you get back.'

'I think I might stay the night,' said Werner. 'There's someone I must see in the morning, and there are long lines at the passport control if I come through when everyone's coming back from the operas.'

A Friedrichstrasse train came in, but Werner let it go. I had the feeling that he didn't want to go over. That was unusual for Werner; he might get jumpy, but he never seemed to mind going over there. Sometimes I had the feeling that he liked the break it made for him. He got away from Zena and lived his own bachelor life in the comfortable apartment he'd created over a truck garage. Now he lingered. It was a perfect chance for me to tell him how Fiona had gone to Holland and talked to Tessa about having the children with her. But I didn't tell him.

'Where will you eat tonight?' I said, as my contribution to the kind of conversation that takes place on railway stations and airports.

'There are some people I know in Pankow,' said Werner. 'They've invited me.'

'Do I know them?' I said.

'No,' said Werner. 'You don't know them.'

'What time tomorrow?'

'Don't fuss, Bernie. Sometimes you're worse than Lisl.'

The train arrived. 'Take care,' I said as he stepped into it.

'It's all legit, Bernie.'

'But maybe they don't know that,' I said.

Werner grinned and then the doors closed and the train pulled away. It felt very very cold on the platform after the train had departed, but that might just have been my imagination.

25

At midnight the front door to Lisl Hennig's hotel was locked. That had always been the routine, ever since I could remember. Any hotel guest who occasionally returned after that time was given a key on request. Any guest frequently returning after that time was asked to find another hotel.

Guests arriving there after midnight without a key had to tug the old bellpull. You couldn't hear the bell from outside in the street and sometimes guests made a great deal of noise before they got in. I couldn't hear the bell from my little garret room at the very top of the house. Lisl could hear the bell. She slept downstairs – she'd been sleeping downstairs ever since her arthritis had got really bad. Lisl never went down to open the door, of course; just that one flight of stone stairs, from the salon to the front hall, was something she didn't attempt very often. One of the servants opened the door if the bell rang. They took it in turns. Usually it was Klara, but on that night after Werner went over to the East it was Richard, a youngish man from Bremen who worked in the kitchen. Klara was not out that night, of course – she was in bed and asleep and awakened by the bell as always. But when she was off duty, she was off duty, and she just turned over and forgot about it.

So it was Richard who went down to the front door when the bell went at 2:30 a.m. It was dark and still raining, and Richard took with him the wooden bat used for flattening slices of veal to make Wiener schnitzels. As he said afterwards, he knew that there were no guests still not back and he wanted something to defend himself with.

So it was Richard who woke me up out of a deep sleep in which I was dreaming about old Mr Storch who was making me recite a poem about Hitler. It was a silly dream in which I knew no poems about Hitler except a rude one which I was frightened to tell Mr Storch.

'A gentleman to see you, sir,' said Richard, having shaken me by the shoulder and put Storch and my classmates to flight. 'There's a gentleman to see you.' He said it in English. I suspected that he'd got it from one of those film butlers because he had exactly the right accent and inflection whereas the rest of his English was appalling.

'Who?' I said. I switched on the bedside light. Its yellow plastic shade made patterns on the wall and its light made Richard look jaundiced and ferocious.

'It's me.' I put my glasses on and looked towards the doorway. It was Bret Rensselaer. I could hardly believe my eyes. For a moment I thought it was all a part of my dream. I got out of bed and put on my dressing gown.

'My God, Bret, what are you doing in Berlin?' I said. 'It's okay,' I told Richard. 'It's a friend of mine.'

As Richard left and closed the door, Bret stepped into the light. He was hardly recognizable. This wasn't the Bret I knew. His dark overcoat was so soaked with rain that it was dripping pools onto the ancient carpet. There was mud on his shoes. He had no necktie and his shirt was dirty and open at the throat. His staring eyes were deep sunk into his ashen face and he needed a shave badly.

'You look like you could do with a drink,' I said, opening the corner cupboard where I had a bottle of duty-free Johnnie Walker and some glasses. I poured him a big shot of whisky. He almost snatched it from me and drank a couple of gulps.

'I had to find you, Bernard. You're the only one who can help me.'

Was this really Bret Rensselaer? I never thought I'd see the day when Bret was asking anyone for help, let alone asking me. 'What's wrong, Bret?'

'You're the only one I can trust any more.'

'Sit down,' I said. 'Get out of that wet coat and take the weight off your feet.'

He did as I told him, moving with the shambling robotic pace of the sleepwalker. 'They'll go for you too,' said Bret.

'Start at the beginning, Bret,' I said.

But he was too tired to understand. He didn't look up at me, he was slumped on the chair studying his muddy shoes. 'They arrested me.' He said it very quietly so that I had to lean close to him to hear.

'Who did?'

'A team from Five . . . it was all kosher. They had all the documentation . . . even a chit from the Deputy with the two authorized signatures.'

'Morgan had signed?'

'Yes, Morgan had signed. But it's not all Morgan's doing; they've got a whole file on me.'

I poured myself a drink while I pulled my thoughts together. Was Bret admitting to me that he was a KGB mole? Had he come to me convinced that I was a KGB agent too? And how the hell was I going to find out? I sipped the drink and felt the warmth of it slide down my throat. It didn't make my thinking any clearer, but it was waking me up in the best possible way. 'What now?' I said tentatively. 'How can I help?'

'It all began when the committee went down to Berwick House,' said Bret, as if he hadn't heard my question. 'Some of them wanted to be present at an interrogation. There had been a lot of argument about whether Stinnes was really cooperating or just playing us along. Ladbrook was there. Ladbrook's straight, you know that.'

I nodded. Ladbrook was the senior interrogator. He kept out of office politics as much as possible.

'We used one of the big downstairs rooms; there wasn't room for everyone in the recording room.' Bret held out his glass for another drink. I poured him one, a small one this time. He didn't drink it right away. He swirled it round in his hands. Bret said, 'The interrogation was concerned with codes and communications. I wasn't listening all that closely at first; I figured that it was all stuff I'd heard before. But then I realized that Stinnes was offering some goodies. Five had one of their communications boffins assigned to the committee just for that sequence, and he got excited. He didn't jump up and down and sing "Rule, Britannia!" but he might have if there'd been more leg room.'

'Stuff you hadn't heard before?'

'Really good material, Bernard. Stinnes started out by offering us the whole signals procedure at the Embassy, and the boffin from Five asked some questions that Stinnes answered easily and unequivocally. This was a different sort of Stinnes I was seeing; he was smooth and charming and polite and deferential. He cut a hell of a good figure with them. Jokes too. They were even laughing, and Stinnes was more at ease than I'd ever seen him before. Then one of the Five people said it was a pity that he hadn't given us some of this material a few weeks earlier because there were sure to be signals alterations any time now, in the light of Stinnes changing sides. And Stinnes calmly said that he'd told me all this stuff in the first days I saw him.'

'And you denied it?'

Bret's voice was shrill. 'He never gave us any of that hard intelligence. He didn't give it to me, he didn't give it to Ladbrook, and he didn't give it to you.'

'So what was your reaction?'

'I'm the chairman of that lousy committee. What am I supposed to do, call myself to order and appoint a subcommittee? I let it roll. What could I do, except sit there and listen to all that crap.'

'And they swallowed it?'

A thought struck Bret Rensselaer. 'He didn't tell you any of that stuff, did he? Codes and communications? Embassy contact lists?

Foreign country routings? Signals room security? Did he tell you any of that? For God's sake . . .'

'No, he didn't tell me any of that,' I said.

'Thank Christ for that.' He wiped his brow. 'There are moments when I wonder if I'm tipping off my trolley.'

'They arrested you?'

'That wasn't until two days later. From what I heard afterwards, it seems that the people from Five got together that night for some kind of council. They were excited, Bernard, and convinced. They hadn't seen Stinnes before. All they knew about him was this smooth, dynamic guy who's falling over himself trying to give away Soviet secrets. What are they supposed to think except that I've been sitting on him?'

'And Ladbrook?'

'He's a good man, Bernard. Apart from you, Ladbrook is the only person who can see what's really going on. But that won't make any difference. Ladbrook will tell them the truth, but that won't help me.'

'What will he say?'

Bret looked up with alarm and annoyance. I had become the interrogator now, but there was nothing he could do about that; I was his last hope. 'He'll say that Stinnes has given us only operational material.'

'Good operational material,' I said. It wasn't a statement, it wasn't a question; it was a bit of both.

'Wonderful operational material,' said Bret sarcastically. 'But every time we acted on it, things seemed to go unaccountably wrong.'

'They'll say that was your fault,' I said. And to some extent it *was* his fault: Bret had wanted to show everyone what a fine field agent he might have made, and he'd failed.

'Of course they will. That's the brilliance of it. There is just no way of proving whether we did it wrong or if it was material arranged to fail right from the word go.'

I said, 'Stinnes is a plant. A solitary. His briefing must have been lengthy and complex. That's why it took so long to get him to move. That's why he went back to Berlin before coming out to Mexico again.'

'Thanks, buddy,' said Bret. 'Where were you when we needed you?'

'It's easy to see it now,' I admitted. 'But it looked okay at the time. And some of the stuff was good.'

'Those early arrests in Hannover, the dead-letter drops, the kid in our office in Hamburg. Yes, it was good, but it wasn't anything they couldn't spare.'

'How did they arrest you?'

'Five sent two men from K7 who searched my house. That was Tuesday . . . no, maybe Monday . . . I've lost all track of time.'

'They found nothing?'

'What do you think they found?' said Bret angrily. 'A radio transmitter, invisible ink and one-time pads?'

'I just want to get the facts straight,' I said.

'It's a frame-up,' said Bret. 'I thought you were the one person who'd see that.'

'I do see it. I just wanted to know if there was anything planted at the house.'

'Shit,' said Bret. He went pale. 'Now I remember!'

'What?'

'They took a suitcase out of the loft.'

'What was in it?'

'Papers.'

'What papers?'

'I don't know, typewritten paper, reams of it. They took them away to examine them. There were several pieces of baggage in the loft. I thought they were all empty.'

'And now one is full of papers. Any recent visitors to the house?'

'No, none. Not for weeks.'

'No repairmen or telephone wiring?'

'A man came to fix the phone, but that was okay. I had our own engineers out the next day to check the house.'

'Check the house for bugs and wires, not check the house for suitcases full of papers.'

He bit his lip. 'I was a fool.'

'It sounds as if you were, Bret. They would put your phone on the blink and then turn up.'

'That's right. They arrived after I had trouble – they said they were in the street, working on the lines. It was a Saturday. I said I didn't know you guys work on Saturdays.'

'The KGB work a long week, Bret,' I said.

'He can't sustain it,' said Bret, hoping that I would agree. He was talking about Stinnes. I didn't answer. 'It's a bravura performance and the committee are eating out of his hand right now. But he can't sustain it.'

'When did they arrest you?'

'First the senior grade officer from K7 came to my home. He told me I wasn't to leave the house.'

'Your house?'

'I wasn't to go to the office. I wasn't even to go to the shops in the village.'

'What did you say?'

'I couldn't believe my ears. I told him to remain in the room with me while I phoned the office. I tried to get the D-G, but Sir Henry was on a train going to Manchester.'

'Clever Sir Henry,' I said.

'No, it was genuine enough. His secretary tried to reach him with messages at both ends.'

'Are you crazy, Bret? Five send a K7 search and arrest team to pick up a senior officer, and the D-G just happens to have another appointment that he can't break and no contact number? Are you telling me the D-G wasn't in on the secret?'

Bret looked at me. He didn't want to believe they could do that to him. Or that they would want to. Bret didn't just happen to be born in England like the rest of us – Bret was an Anglophile. He loved every blade of bright green grass that Shakespeare might have trodden on. 'I suppose you're right,' he said at last.

'And you skipped?'

'I left a message saying that I urgently wanted an appointment with the D-G and gave my phone number. I said I'd stay by the phone and wait for the call.'

'And then you took off. That was good, Bret,' I said with genuine admiration. 'That's what I would have done. But they'll have you on the airline manifest even if Immigration didn't identify you.'

'I have a friend with a Cessna,' said Bret.

He needn't have told me that, and I felt reassured that he was prepared to fill in the details. 'Did they leave anyone outside the house?' Bret shrugged. 'Do you think they tailed you?'

'I changed cars.'

'And the watchers don't run to anything that could follow a Cessna, so they'll be trying to trace the plane landing.'

'I flew to Hamburg and then came on by car. I rented the car in a false name. Luckily the girl at the counter didn't read the driving licence carefully.'

'You can't win them all, Bret. You forgot about the computer on the autobahn entrance point. They even get traffic violators on that one.'

'I'm innocent, Bernard.'

'I know you are, Bret. But it's going to be tough proving it. Did anyone say anything about a Cabinet memo?'

'Cabinet memo?'

'They're trying to lock you up tight, Bret. There is a Cabinet memo; the numbered copy is the one to which you had access. It's been to Moscow and back again.'

'Are you serious?'

'And a lot of people have been told about it since then.'

'Who?'

'I was singled out to be shown a copy, and so was Dicky Cruyer.

You can bet there were others. The implication is that the full report went to Moscow too.'

'I should have been told.'

'You're not wrestling only with Stinnes,' I said. 'You've got the whole of Moscow Centre to contend with, and they've spent a lot of time working on it.'

He drank a tiny sip of whisky as if he didn't trust himself any longer. He didn't ask what it was all about or anything like that. He'd had a lot of time to think what it was all about. He must have known by that time that his chances of getting out of it and becoming Mr Clean again were very slim. The sea was rough. Bret was going down for the third time and there was every chance he'd take me with him. 'So what do I do, Bernard?'

'Suppose I said, "Turn yourself in"?'

'I wouldn't do that.'

'Suppose *I* turned you in?'

'You wouldn't do that,' said Bret. He looked away from me, as if meeting my eyes would increase the chances of my saying I would turn him in.

'What makes you so sure?' I said.

'Because you're an egomaniac. You're cynical and intractable. You're the only son of a bitch in that Department who'd take the rest of them on single-handed.'

It wasn't exactly what I wanted to hear, but it was sincere enough and that would have to do. 'We don't have a lot of time. They'll trace you right to this room. Getting into Berlin without leaving a track is almost impossible, unless you come in from the East, in which case no records are kept.'

'I never thought of it like that,' said Bret. 'That's crazy, isn't it?'

'Yes, it is, but we don't have time to write to Ripley about it. We don't have time to do anything very much. I'd say that London Central will trace you to Berlin, and maybe to me at this hotel, within two or three days.'

'Are you saying what I think you're saying?'

'Yes. We'll have to talk to Frank. The only other course is for you to leave town very quickly. Why did you come here, Bret?'

'I decided that you were the only person who could help.'

'You'll have to do better than that, Bret,' I said.

'And I have money here,' he said. I continued to stare at him. 'And a gun.'

'Honesty is the best policy, Bret,' I said.

'You knew, did you?'

'Not about the money. But when a senior officer does anything unusual in Berlin I like to know, and there are people who know I like to know.'

'Who the hell told you about the gun?'

'Buying a gun is very unusual, Bret,' I said. 'Especially for a man who can sign a docket and get one across the counter from Frank Harrington.'

'So Frank knows too?'

'I didn't tell him.'

'Will Frank turn me in?'

'Let's not tempt him too much. Suppose I go along and talk to him while you stay out of sight?'

'I'd appreciate that.'

'Frank could defy the Department for weeks, and if Five sent anyone here, Frank has authority enough to have them refused entry at the airport. If we got Frank on our side . . .'

'It would start looking good,' said Bret appreciatively.

'Not good, Bret, but a bit less bloody doomy.'

'So you'll see Frank in the morning?'

'I'll see Frank now. We haven't got enough time for luxuries like night and day. And at night we won't have his secretarial staff to get an eyeful of you and me talking to him. If we see him on his own and he says "No deal", we might persuade him to forget he ever saw us. But once his secretary enters it in the appointment diary, it will be more difficult to deny.'

'He'll be asleep.' Bret obviously thought it would prejudice our chances of success to wake Frank from a deep dreamless slumber.

'Frank never sleeps.'

'He'll be with a girl? Is that what you mean?'

'Now you're getting warmer.'

26

Frank Harrington, Berlin Resident and head of Berlin Field Unit, was not asleep. He was sitting on the floor of the large drawing room of his magnificent house at Grunewald surrounded by records. On every side of him there were piles of Duke Ellington records while music played on his hi-fi. 'Frenesi' – it was a lush orchestral arrangement into which the vocalist sang: 'A long time ago I wandered down into old Mexico. . . .' Or was it something quite different? Was it just that I still felt bad about the way in which I'd contrived that the Stinnes enrolment had taken place in Mexico, rather than in Berlin where Frank would have got a measure of the credit? Whatever the music, I still felt guilty at having deprived Frank of that 'mention' and self-conscious about asking him for help in matters arising from that same event. '. . . Stars were shining bright and I could hear romantic voices in the night. . . .'

Frank's valet, the inscrutable Tarrant, showed me in. He was wearing his dressing gown and his hair was slightly disarranged, but he gave no sign of being surprised by this visit in the small hours of the morning. I suppose Frank's frequent love affairs had provided Tarrant with enough surprises to last a lifetime.

'Bernard,' said Frank very calmly, as if I often visited him in the small hours. 'What about a drink?' He had a record in his hand. Like all the other records it was in a pristine plain-white jacket with a number written in the corner. He hesitated before placing it on one of the piles, then he looked up at me. 'Whisky and water?'

'Yes, please. Shall I help myself?'

There was a cut-glass tumbler on the drinks trolley, some ice cubes in it not yet melted, and traces of bright lipstick on its rim. I picked it up and sniffed at it. 'Campari and orange juice,' said Frank as he watched me. 'Still playing detectives, Bernard?'

There had been another visitor – obviously female – but Frank did not supply her name. 'Force of habit,' I said. Campari and orange juice was one of Zena Volkmann's favourite drinks.

'It must be urgent.' He didn't get up from where he was sitting in the middle of the carpet. He reached for his pipe and tobacco pouch and for the big ashtray that was already half filled with ash and unburned tobacco.

'Yes,' I said. 'It was good of you to let me come right away.'

'You didn't give me much chance to decline.' He said it ruefully. Had he sent her away on my account or was she waiting for him upstairs in the bedroom? Was it Zena Volkmann or just some girl he'd met at a frantic Berlin party as he met so many of the females with whom he got entangled?

'The Stinnes committee have gone mad,' I said.

'Don't sit there!' It was a shout, almost a cry of pain. 'They're my very earliest ones. I'd die if one of those was damaged.'

'This is your Ellington collection, is it?' I asked, looking at the records everywhere.

'The only chance I get is at night. I'm shipping them to England. I have to have them valued for the insurance. It's not easy to put a price on the rare ones.'

I paused politely and then said again, 'The Stinnes committee have gone crazy, Frank.'

'It happens,' said Frank. He was still sitting the way he'd been when I came into the room. Now he charged his pipe, packing the bowl with the shreds of tobacco and pushing them down with his fingertip. He did it very very carefully as if to show me that it was a difficult thing to do.

I said, 'Stinnes seems to have convinced them that Bret Rensselaer is some kind of KGB mole. They put him under house arrest.'

'And what do you want me to do?' said Frank. He didn't light his pipe. He rested it against the ashtray while he read the label on another record, entered details of it into a loose-leaf notebook, and placed it on the appropriate pile.

'Did you know that was going to happen?'

'No, but I should have guessed that something like it was in the wind. I've been against that damned committee right from the start.' He sipped at his drink. 'We should have turned Stinnes over to Five and let it go at that. These combined committees always end in a power struggle. I never saw one that didn't.'

'Stinnes is driving the wedge in deep, Frank.' I didn't remind him that he'd showed no sign of being against the committee when I'd seen him with the D-G.

Frank picked up his pipe while he thought about it. 'House arrest? Bret? Are you quite sure? There was talk of an enquiry, but arrest . . . ?' He lit the pipe with a match, holding the bowl inverted so that the flame could get to the tightly packed tobacco.

'A witch-hunt has started, Frank. It could cause permanent damage to the Department. Bret has a lot of friends, but he has implacable enemies too.'

'Lange?' Was that a gibe at me? He puffed at the pipe as he looked at me, but he didn't smile.

'Some more influential than Lange,' I said. 'And even worse is the way that people – even senior staff – are trying to find evidence to confirm Bret's guilt.'

'Are they?' He didn't believe that.

'Dicky dug up some half-baked story about being in Kiel with Bret when a KGB man recognized him.'

'And it wasn't true?'

'It was entirely true. But if Dicky had taken the trouble to look up Bret's report on the incident, he would have found it completely and adequately explained by Bret. People are jittery, Frank, and that brings out the worst in them.'

'People are jittery since your wife went over. It was the enormity of that that shook the Department to its foundations.'

'If you . . .'

'Don't get angry, Bernard.' He held up a hand and ducked his head as if warding off a blow. It was Frank's pleasure to play the role of vulnerable ancient to my role of bellicose son. 'I'm not putting any blame on you, but I am stating a fact.'

'Bret is here. He's here in Berlin,' I said. 'And he's in bad shape.'

'I rather thought he might be,' said Frank. He puffed his pipe again. He'd lost interest in sorting his record collection now. Even when the Ellington music stopped, he didn't put another one on the player. 'I don't mean in bad shape; I mean I thought he might be in Berlin.'

'How?' If Frank knew officially about Bret's arrival, the report would go through regular channels and be in London by noon the following day.

'Why else would you be here in the middle of the night? It's surely not in response to a phone call from Bret in London. Bret must be here: there's no other explanation.'

'He thinks they'll put out a departmental alert for him.'

'Surely it hasn't come to that,' said Frank calmly.

'I think it might have done, Frank. The old man was not available when Bret was put under house arrest.'

'And you think that's a bad sign?'

'You know the D-G better than anyone, Frank.' Frank puffed his pipe and didn't comment on his possible knowledge of the Director-General's way of going to ground when his senior staff were to be arrested.

Eventually Frank said, 'What could I do for Bret? Supposing I wanted to do anything.'

'We should neutralize Stinnes. Without him the whole action against Bret will collapse.'

'Neutralize him? What do you mean by that?'

'We thought Stinnes was a mediocre agent in a dead-end job. All our records and enquiries pointed to that. But I think that was all cover. I think Stinnes is one of their most reliable people. They might have been grooming him for this one for ages.'

'Or it might be that your wife's arrival over there gave them the necessary extra information that made his job possible.'

'It would be foolish to deny that possibility,' I said without getting angry. 'The timing points to Fiona. She might have been the trigger, but the background must have been started long ago.'

'Neutralize him?'

'How we do it doesn't really matter, but we must persuade Moscow that Stinnes is no longer their man and in place.'

'You're not leading up to an XPD? Because I won't go along with that.'

'I don't want him killed. The best solution would be to make Moscow believe that Stinnes is really turned, and working for us.'

'That might take some time,' said Frank.

'Exactly. So let's not try that. Let's tell them we know about Stinnes, that we have him under lock and key and are giving him a bad time.'

'What sort of bad time?'

'A damned bad sort of bad time,' I said.

'Would they care?'

'How would we feel if it was one of ours?' I said.

'If they were roughing him up, we'd do everything we could to get him out.'

'And that's what they'll want to do,' I said. 'Everything suggests that Stinnes is a sick man. He sits around holding himself as if he's in pain, he resists all attempts to make him have a physical examination, and he's stopped smoking. . . . Of course, that could all be an act.'

'What is it you're expecting me to do?'

'There's something else you should know, Frank,' I said. 'The Miller woman is alive and well and working across the city in the Red Town Hall.'

'Are you sure?'

'Werner spoke with her.'

'He should have reported it.'

'He went back to take another look.'

'So that was it,' said Frank half to himself.

'What?'

'There's something *you*'d better know. They're holding Werner

Volkmann. He was arrested last night in East Berlin and taken to Babelsberg.'

'Babelsberg?'

'It's a part of the old film studios. The Stasis use it when they want to be beyond any possible Protecting Powers jurisdiction that might apply to the inner parts of the city. We can't send a military police patrol into Potsdam the way we can to the rest of Berlin.'

'Poor Werner.'

'You guessed it was Zena: the Campari and orange – that's her drink. I sent for her as soon as I got the report.'

'How is she taking it?' I said.

'The same way Zena takes everything,' said Frank. 'Very, very personally.'

'Where did it happen?'

'The Red Town Hall. He was talking to someone over there and asking too many questions. One of my people saw the van draw up outside the Town Hall and he recognized Volkmann being put in. Later it was confirmed by one of our inside people who saw the police report.'

'Have they charged him?'

'I know nothing except what I've told you. It only happened last evening.'

'We'll have to do something, Frank.'

'I know what you're thinking, Bernard, but that's impossible.'

'What is?'

'Exchanging Werner for Stinnes. London Central would never wear it.'

'Is it better that we deliver Bret back to London and let Stinnes send Five to trample all over him?' I said.

'Bret is innocent. Very well; I believe Bret is innocent too. But let us not overreact. You're not really telling me you think he'll be tried and found guilty and sent to prison?'

'Moscow has produced fake evidence. God knows how much of it there is.'

'Fake evidence or no fake evidence, it won't send Bret to jail and you know it.'

'They won't even send him for trial,' I said. 'They never do send senior staff for trial, no matter what the evidence against them. But Bret will be retired and discredited. Bret has a very exaggerated sense of loyalty – you know what he's like. Bret couldn't live with that.'

'And what if I bring Stinnes here without authority? What will happen to me?'

Well, at least Frank had reached the necessary conclusion without my drawing him a coloured diagram. Frank's authority was confined to Berlin. The only way we could do anything to help Bret in the short term was by bringing Stinnes here. 'You're close to retirement, Frank. If you overstep the mark, they'll get angry but they won't take it out on you. Especially when they realize that you've saved them from a fiasco.'

'I'm not going to lose my bloody pension for some harebrained scheme of yours,' said Frank. 'It's not within my power.'

'See Bret,' I said. 'He's waiting outside in the car. See Bret and you might change your mind.'

'I'll see Bret. But I won't change my mind.'

I wouldn't have convinced him without Bret Rensselaer. It was the mangled patrician figure that moved Frank Harrington to throw the rule book out the window and send two of his heavies to England to get Stinnes. There was paperwork too. Stinnes hadn't yet been given any sort of travel document other than the stateless person's identity card. That was valid for travelling, but it required some hastily done backup with scribbled signatures.

Just to create a smoke screen Frank left a message with the D-G's personal secretary and sent a telex to London that said Stinnes was to be questioned in connection with the detention of a departmental employee in East Berlin. The name of Werner Volkmann was not mentioned and the proposed venue of the Stinnes questioning was left vague.

The other half of the procedure was more straightforward. I found Posh Harry in Frankfurt. When he heard that there was a well-paid job for him he got the next plane for Berlin.

I met him in the Café Leuschner, a big barn of a place near the remains of the Anhalter Bahnhof, that weed-bedecked chunk of railway terminal that has been left standing in the middle of the city like a rich man's folly in some Old-World garden.

The big café was made to look even larger by the row of gilt-framed mirrors. They lined the wall so that the marble countertop with all the glinting bottles and glasses were tilted by the reflections.

As a kid I'd always liked to sit at the counter rather than at the tables. In those days the chairs were old bentwood ones, painted olive green, the only colour of paint that one could get in the city. The furniture at Leuschner's café – like so many other painted things of that time – exactly matched the trucks of the US Army.

Leuschner's used to be my Saturday treat. It was the highpoint of my week. I'd meet my father at his office, and with him in his best uniform we'd walk to Leuschner's for one of Herr Leuschner's ice creams that only kids were allowed to buy. Then one day my father discovered through an informer that the ice cream came from US

Army supplies. He was going to report it, but my mother dissuaded him on account of the way old Herr Leuschner was always feeding hungry kids for nothing. But my father wouldn't take me there after that.

Now it was Leuschner's son Willi behind the bar. We'd been kids together. Not Wilhelm, not Willy, but Willi. I remembered how exasperating he'd always been about adults getting his name right. Willi had the same kind of big moustache his father had worn – the same sort of moustache the Kaiser had worn, and many of his subjects too, until people started thinking that big curly moustaches made you look like a Turk.

The young Leuschner greeted me as I entered. 'How goes it, Bernd?' he said. He had that manner bartenders learn – an arm's-length friendliness that reserved the right to toss you into the street should you get drunk.

'Hello, Willi. Has Posh Harry been in?'

'Not for a long time. He used to come in a lot – he brought some good business too – but he shares an office in Tegel now. He likes to be near the airport, he said, and I don't see him so much.'

It was then that Posh Harry arrived. He arrived at the appointed time; he was a very punctual man. I suppose, like me, he'd learned that it was a necessary part of dealing with Germans.

He was wearing a superb camel-hair overcoat and a grey trilby. They didn't go well together, but Posh Harry had swagger enough to carry off anything. He could have come in wearing a baseball cap and creased pyjamas and Willi Leuschner would still have greeted him with the awed respect I heard in his voice this time. 'I was just saying how much we like to see you here, Herr Harry.' Even Willi didn't know Posh Harry's family name; it was one of Berlin's best-kept secrets. When Posh Harry replied, it was in flawless German and the chirruping Berlin accent.

It was Willi who showed us to a quiet table at the back. Willi was shrewd; he could recognize those customers who wanted to sit near the window and drink wine and those who wanted to sit at the back and drink whisky. And those who wanted to sit somewhere where they couldn't be overheard. To get those seats you had to drink champagne; but German champagne would do.

'We want to set up a meeting, Harry,' I said when Willi had served us our *Sekt*, written the price of it on a beer mat which he slapped on the table, and gone back to his place behind the bar.

'Who's we?' said Posh Harry, toying with the beer mat in such a way as to ensure that I could see what it was costing me.

'Not too many of those big questions, Harry. Let's get the details right and you collect the money, okay?'

'That's the way I like to do it,' said Harry. He smiled. He had the wide toothy smile of the Oriental.

'We're holding a KGB man; he has the working name of Stinnes. We caught him in a red-hot situation.'

'Am I permitted to ask what is a red-hot situation?'

'We caught him mugging a little old lady in a sweet shop.'

'Is this on the level, Bernie?' Now it was the serious face and low sincere voice of the professional. I could see why he did so well at it; he could make you think he really cared.

'No, a lot of it is not on the level, but our KGB friends will know what's what. You tell them that we're holding Stinnes in a hard-room and that we're kicking shit out of him.'

'You want me to say you personally are involved?'

'Yes, you tell them that Bernie Samson is kicking shit out of Erich Stinnes, on account of the way he was held in Normannenstrasse last year by this same individual. Revenge, tell them.'

An old man came in. He was wearing tails complete with top hat, and playing a concertina. He was a famous Berlin character – the 'Gypsy Baron', they called him. In the cafés along the Ku-damm he played the music the foreign tourists liked to hear – Strauss, Lehar, and a selection from *Cabaret* – but this was a place for Berliners, so he kept to their kind of schmalz.

'And?'

'And you felt they should know about it.'

'Okay.' He was a master of inscrutable faces.

'Let them chew it over for five minutes and then say that London Central are finished with this character. London Central will be handing him over to Five unless some better offer came up from somewhere else – like Moscow.'

'When?' said Posh Harry, reaching for the dripping-wet bottle from the ice bucket and pouring more for us both.

'Very soon. Very, very soon. There is no chance that Five would deal with Moscow, so time is vitally important. If they were interested in having Stinnes back, you could get me to a meeting to discuss his release.'

'Here?' He used a paper towel to mop up the ice water he'd dripped over the table.

'His release here in Berlin. But first I want the meeting,' I said.

'With?'

'With my wife. And whoever she wants to bring along.'

'What's the deal, Bernie? You release the Russkie – what do you want in return? Or is kicking shit out of Russkies something you're giving up for Lent?'

'They'll know what I want in return. But I don't want that anywhere on the record, so don't even start guessing,' I said. 'Now, in the course of conversation, you'll make sure they know that Bret Rensselaer has been given an important promotion and a special job. You don't know exactly what it is, but it all came about because he was the one who brought Stinnes down. He was the one who nailed him to the wall. Got it?'

'It's not difficult, Bernie. It's a shame to take the money.'

'Take the money anyway.'

'I shall.'

'The meeting is to be over this side. I suggest the VIP suite on the top floor of the Steigenberger Hotel. It's good security; there's room to move . . . car parking is where you can see it . . . you know.'

'And the food is excellent. That might appeal to them.'

'And the food is excellent.'

'They'll probably want to send someone to inspect the room.'

'No problem,' I said.

'Timing for the exchange?'

'We'll have their man Stinnes available in the city.'

'I mean . . . you'll want to do this immediately the meeting ends, won't you? This is not one of those fancy setups where they come over the bridge for the TV cameras ten days later?'

'Immediate. And complete secrecy; both sides.'

'Your wife, you say? I'll go over there today. Maybe I could wrap up this whole deal by the weekend.'

'Good thinking, Harry. I'll be at Lisl Hennig's this evening. Phone me there anyway; let me know what's happening. Have you got the phone number?'

'Are you kidding? Your wife, eh?' The concertina player finished playing 'Das war in Schöneberg im Monat Mai . . .' and took a bow. Posh Harry eased his chair back and applauded loudly. He smiled at me to show how happy he was. It was a bigger smile this time; I could count his gold teeth.

'She'll be the one to talk to, Harry.'

'I think I can find her.'

'If I know her the way I think I do, she will have planned the whole business; she'll be sitting by the phone waiting for you to call.' I got to my feet. I'd said enough.

'It's like that, is it?'

'The script is all written, Harry. We just have to read our parts.'

Harry pulled a bundle of paper money from his back pocket and paid for the champagne. The tip was far too generous, but the Department would pay.

'That material I gave you – was it good?' he asked.

'It was *Spielmaterial*,' I replied.

'I'm sorry about that,' he said. 'Some you win, some you lose, and some . . .'

'. . . Some get rained out,' I finished for him.

He shrugged. I should have guessed that he had had no real faith in it; he'd given it to me for nothing. That was not Posh Harry's style.

27

Lisl sat where she could see the flowers. It was a vast display of different blooms – more than I could put names to – and arranged in a basket tied with coloured ribbon. The flowers had obviously come from some expensive florist. They were the ones Werner had brought for her. Now the petals were beginning to fall. Werner was not demonstrative, but he was always giving Lisl flowers. Sometimes, according to his mood, he would spend ages choosing them for her. Even his beloved Zena was not treated with such care in the matter of flowers. Lisl loved flowers, especially when they came from Werner.

Sometimes, when she smiled, I could see in Lisl Hennig the beautiful woman I'd met when I first came to Berlin. I was a child then, and Lisl must have already been almost fifty years old. But she was a woman of such beauty that any man would be at her call.

Now she was old, and the commanding manner that had once been a part of her fatal attraction was the petulance of an irritable old woman. But I remembered her as the goddess she'd once been, and so did Lothar Koch, the shrunken little retired bureaucrat who'd regularly played bridge with her.

We were sitting in Lisl's 'study', a small room that had become a museum of her life. Every shelf and cupboard was crammed with mementoes – china ornaments, snuffboxes, and an abundance of souvenir ashtrays. The radio was playing Tchaikovsky from some distant station that faded every now and again. There were only three of us playing bridge. It was more fun this way, Lisl said, whenever we were bidding and deciding which hand would be the dummy. But Lisl liked company, and there were only three of us because Lisl had failed to find a fourth despite all the cajoling of which she was capable.

The counters for which we played were stacked up high. Lisl liked to play for money no matter how tiny the stakes. When she was a young girl she'd been sent to a finishing school in Dresden – a favoured place for wealthy families to send their grown-up daughters – and she liked to affect the manners of that place and time. But now she was content to be the *berlinerisch* old woman she truly was, and there was nothing more *berlinerisch* than playing cards for money.

'It's big business nowadays,' said Herr Koch. 'Since 1963 those East Germans have made almost three billion Deutschemark in ransoms.'

'I bid one spade,' said Lisl, staring at her cards. 'Three billion?'

'No bid,' said Koch. 'Yes, three billion Deutschemark.'

'One heart,' I said.

'You can't do that,' said Lisl.

'Sorry,' I said. 'No bid.' Why had they suddenly started talking about political prisoners held in the Democratic Republic? They couldn't have heard about Werner. Lisl finally bid two spades.

'About fourteen hundred people a year are ransomed by the Bonn government. None of them are criminals. Mostly they are people who have applied for exit permits and then been heard to complain about not getting them.'

'They must be mad to apply for an exit permit,' said Lisl.

'They are desperate,' said Koch. 'Desperate people snatch at any chance however slim.'

Lisl put a queen of hearts on Herr Koch's king. From now on she'd be trumping hearts unless I missed my guess. I knew she didn't have the ace; I had it. I played low; it was Koch's trick. Perhaps they wouldn't exchange Werner for Stinnes. Perhaps we'd have to pay to get Werner back. Would they sell him or would they prefer a big show trial with lots of publicity? Perhaps I'd handled it badly. Perhaps I should have let the KGB think that Stinnes had fooled us completely; then they wouldn't risk spoiling it by publicizing Werner. Could they put Werner on trial without revealing the Miller woman's role in framing Bret Rensselaer?

Koch led with an ace of clubs. I knew Lisl would trump it and she did, using a three. That was the way with cards and with life; the smallest of cards could beat an ace if you chose the right moment.

Lisl picked up the trick and led a four of spades. She must have had a handful of trumps.

'You should have bid a grand slam,' said Herr Koch sarcastically. He was smarting at having his ace trumped.

'The people are priced according to their worth,' said Lisl, continuing with the conversation as if to appease Koch.

'A university don can cost us up to two hundred thousand Deutschemark,' said Koch. 'A skilled worker about thirty thousand.'

'How do you know all this?' I asked him.

'It was in the *Hamburger Abendblatt*,' said Lisl. 'I lent it to him.'

'The government of the Democratic Republic have a bank account in Frankfurt,' said Koch, without acknowledging the loan of Lisl's Hamburg newspaper. 'Prisoners are delivered two weeks after payment is received. It is a slave trade.' Then Lisl led a heart from the dummy hand so she could trump it. My hearts were useless now that Lisl had none. You can only fight in the currency that your opponent shares. I played my jack of hearts.

'Play your ace, Bernard,' she urged. She knew my ace was useless too. Lisl laughed. She loved to win at cards.

Lisl led a small trump and lost the trick to Herr Koch.

'You lost that one,' I said. I couldn't resist it.

Herr Koch said, 'She doesn't care. The dummy has no trumps.'

'You'll never teach him bridge,' said Lisl. 'I've been trying to explain it to him since he was ten years old.'

But Koch persisted. 'She brought out a trump from you and a trump from me.'

'But she lost the trick,' I said. 'You won it with your jack.'

'She removed the potential dangers.' Koch turned over the cards of the trick and showed me the ten and the jack which we'd played. 'Now she knows that you have no trumps and she'll slaughter you whatever you play.'

'Let him play his way,' said Lisl ruthlessly. 'He's not subtle enough for bridge.'

'Don't be fooled by him,' said Herr Koch, talking to Lisl as if I wasn't present. 'The English are all subtle, and this one is subtle in the most dangerous way.'

'And which is that?' said Lisl. She could have simply laid her hand full of trumps on the table and we would have conceded all the remaining tricks to her, but she wouldn't deprive herself of the pleasure of winning the game one trick at a time.

'He doesn't mind us thinking he is a fool. That is Bernard's greatest strength; it always has been.'

'I will never understand the English,' said Lisl. She trumped, picked up the trick, smiled, and led again. Having said she didn't understand the English, she proceeded to explain the English to us. That was *berlinerisch* too; the people of Berlin are reluctant to admit to ignorance of any kind. 'If an Englishman says there's no hurry, that means it must be done immediately. If he says he doesn't mind, it means he minds very much. If he leaves any decision to you by saying "If you like" or "When you like", be on your guard – he means that he's made his requirements clear, and he expects them to be precisely met.'

'Are you going to let this slander go unchallenged, Bernard?' said Koch. He liked a little controversy, providing he could be the referee.

I smiled. I'd heard it all before.

'Then what of us Germans?' persisted Koch. 'Are we so easygoing? Tell me, Bernard, I want your opinion.'

'A German has no greys,' I said, and immediately regretted embarking on such a discussion.

'No greys? What does this mean?' said Koch.

'In Germany two cars collide; one driver is guilty and therefore the other is innocent. Everything is black or white for a German. The weather is good or the weather is bad, a man is sick or he is well, a restaurant is good or it is terrible. At the concert they cheer or they boo.'

'And Werner,' said Koch. 'Is he a man without greys?'

The question was directed at me, but Lisl had to answer. 'Werner is an Englishman,' she said.

It was not true, of course; it was an example of Lisl's impetuous delight in shocking and provoking. Werner was about as un-English as any German could be, and no one knew that better than Lisl.

'You brought him up,' I said. 'How could Werner be English?'

'In spirit,' said Lisl.

'He adored your father,' said Herr Koch, more in order to reconcile the difference of opinion than because it was true.

'He admired him,' I said. 'It's not quite the same thing.'

'It was your mother who first took a liking to Werner,' said Lisl. 'I remember your father complaining that Werner was always upstairs playing with you and making a noise. But your mother encouraged him.'

'She knew you had the hotel to run,' I said. 'You had enough to do without looking after Werner.'

'One day I'll go to England and see her again. She always sends a card at Christmas. Perhaps next year I'll go and see her.'

'She has a spare room,' I said. But I knew in fact that neither Lisl nor my mother would endure the rigours of the aeroplane journey. Only the very fit could cope with the airlines. Lisl had not yet forgotten her uncomfortable trip to Munich five years ago.

'Your father was so formal with little Werner. He always spoke to him as to a grown man.'

'My father spoke to everyone in exactly the same way,' I said. 'It was one of the things I most liked about him.'

'Werner couldn't get over it. "The *Herr Oberst* shook hands with me, Tante Lisl!" It would have been unthinkable for a Wehrmacht colonel to shake hands and talk so solemnly with a small child. You're not listening, Bernard.'

No, I wasn't listening any longer. I'd expected both of them to say I was German, but such an idea had never entered their heads. I was devastated by the rejection so implied. This was where I'd grown up. If I wasn't German in spirit, then what was I? Why didn't they both acknowledge the truth? Berlin was my town. London was a place my English friends lived and where my children were born, but this was where I belonged. I was happy sitting here in Lisl's shabby back room with old Herr Koch. This was the only place I could really call home.

The phone rang. I was sure it was Posh Harry. Lisl was shuffling the cards and Herr Koch was calculating the scores for the hundredth time. The phone rang unanswered several times, then stopped. 'Are you expecting a phone call, Bernard?' enquired Lisl, looking at me closely.

'Possibly,' I said.

'Klara answers if I don't pick it up. It's probably a wrong number. We get a lot of wrong numbers lately.'

What if Posh Harry's approach was rejected? I would be in a very difficult position. Even if Bret Rensselaer was innocent, that didn't prove that the rest of my theory was correct. Stinnes might be genuine. It was then that I began to worry that Stinnes might not be informed about the whole structure of Moscow's plot to discredit Bret Rensselaer. Suppose Stinnes was a kamikaze sent to blow London Central into fragments but had never been told the details of what he was doing? Stinnes was the sort of man who would sacrifice himself for something in which he truly believed. But what did he truly believe? That was the question that had to be answered.

And what would I do in Fiona's position? She was holding all the cards; all she had to do was sacrifice Stinnes. Would she believe that I'd tumbled to their game? Yes, probably. But would she believe that I could convince London Central of the real truth? No, probably not. Bret Rensselaer was the element that would decide the way Fiona jumped. I hoped Posh Harry got that bit of the story right. Maybe Fiona wouldn't believe that I could persuade the fumbling bureaucrats that Stinnes was making a fool of them; but Bret and I together – she'd possibly believe that the two of us combined could do it. Bret and I combined could do anything, in Fiona's opinion. I suppose the kind of man she really wanted was some incongruous and impossible combination of the two of us.

'Drinkies?' said Lisl in what she imagined was English. Without waiting for a reply she poured sherry for all of us. I didn't like sherry, especially the dark sweet variety that Lisl preferred, but I'd been pretending to like it for so long that I didn't have the courage to ask for something else.

It was nine-thirty when the call came through. I was a hundred and fifty points behind Lisl and trying to make two hearts with a hand that wasn't really worth a bid. Lisl answered the phone. She must have realized that I was waiting for my call. She passed it to me. It was Posh Harry.

'Bernard?' They would be monitoring the call, but there was no point in disguising who I was; they would know that already.

'Yes?'

'I've been talking.'

'And?'

'They'll come back to me in one hour.'

'What do you think?'

'She asked me if Bret will be at the meeting.'

'It could be arranged.'

'They might make it a condition.' I looked at Lisl and then at Herr Koch. They were both giving very close attention to their cards in that way people study things when they're trying to look as if they're not eavesdropping.

'Bret's in charge; make that clear,' I said.

'I'll tell them. They will come equipped, you realize that.' That meant armed. There was no way we could prevent that; we had no right to search Russian cars or personnel crossing into West Berlin.

'Okay,' I said.

'Guaranteed safe passage and return for the woman?' That was Fiona, frightened that we might arrest her. But by now they'd no doubt provided her with all the paperwork that made her a Soviet citizen, a colonel in the KGB, and probably a Party member too. It would be a legal nightmare getting her arrested in West Berlin where the USSR was still a Protecting Power with legal rights that compared with the British, French and American ones. In the UK it would be a different matter.

'Guaranteed for the whole party. Do they want it in writing?' I said.

'They don't want it for the whole party – just for the woman,' said Posh Harry. It seemed a strange thing to say, but I gave it no special thought at the time. It was only afterwards that it had any significance.

'Whatever they want, Harry.'

'I'll phone you back,' he said.

'I'll be here,' I said.

I rang off and returned to the bridge game. Lisl and Herr Koch made no reference to my phone call. There was a tacit understanding that I was employed by some international pharmaceutical company.

We played another rubber of bridge before Posh Harry phoned back to tell me that everything was agreed on for the meeting in the Steigenberger Hotel. Even by the end of his negotiations Posh Harry didn't know that they were holding Werner in custody. It was typical of the KGB; nothing was told to anyone except what he needed to know.

I phoned Frank Harrington and told him they'd agreed but would need some kind of written guarantee that the woman would be allowed to return unhindered.

Frank grunted his agreement. He knew the implications, but made no comment about Fiona or the Department's interest in arresting her. 'They are here in saturation levels,' said Frank. 'KGB watchers have been coming through the crossing points for the last two hours. I knew it was going to be an affirmative.'

'KGB? Coming through to the West?'

'Yes, they've been sniffing around ever since you got here. They probably saw our friend arriving.' He meant Bret.

'And their friend too?' I said. I meant Stinnes; he'd arrived that afternoon.

'I hope not,' said Frank.

'But both are secure?'

'Very secure,' said Frank. 'I'm not letting them out.' Frank had both men accommodated at his official mansion in Grunewald. There was half a million pounds' worth of security devices built into that place. Even the KGB would have trouble getting at them there. After a pause Frank said, 'Are you equipped, Bernard?'

I had a Smith & Wesson that I left in Lisl's safe, together with some other personal things. 'Yes,' I said. 'Why?'

'A KGB hit team went through about thirty minutes ago. It was a reliable identification. They don't send a hit team unless they mean business. I can't help worrying that you might be targeted.'

'Thanks, Frank. I'll take the usual precautions.'

'Stay where you are tonight. I'll send a car for you in the morning. Be very careful, Bernard. I don't like the look of it. Eight o'clock okay?'

'Eight o'clock will be very convenient,' I said. 'Good night, Frank. See you in the morning.' I'd turned the radio down while talking on the phone; now I made it louder. It was a Swedish station playing a Bruckner symphony; the opening chords filled the room.

'You people in the pill business work late,' said Lisl sarcastically when I rang off.

Herr Koch had held his ministerial job throughout the Nazi period by not giving way to curiosity or being tempted to such impetuous remarks. He smiled and said, 'I hope everything is in order, Bernard.'

'Everything is just fine,' I told him.

He got up and went to the radio to switch it off.

'Thank you, darling,' said Lisl.

'Bruckner,' explained Herr Koch. 'When they announced the disaster at Stalingrad, the radio played nothing but Beethoven and Bruckner for three whole days.'

'So many fine young boys . . .' said Lisl sadly. 'Put on a record, darling. Something happy – "Bye, bye, Blackbird".'

But when Herr Koch put a record on, it was one of his favourites, *'Das war in Schöneberg im Monat Mai . . .'.*

'Marlene Dietrich,' said Lisl, leaning back and closing her eyes. *'Schön!'*

28

'They're coming through Checkpoint Charlie now.' I recognized the voice that came through the tiny loudspeaker, although I couldn't put a name to it. It was one of the old Berlin Field Unit hands. He was at the checkpoint watching the KGB party coming West for the meeting. 'Three black Volvos.'

I was using my handset radio to monitor the reports. I heard someone at this end say, 'How many of them?'

Standing alongside me in the VIP suite of the Steigenberger Hotel, Frank said, 'Three Volvos! Jesus Christ! It's a bloody invasion!' Frank had committed himself, but now that it was actually happening he was nervous. I'd told him to have a drink, but he'd refused.

'All of a sudden it's green,' said Frank, still looking out of the window to the street far below us. 'Berlin, I mean. The winters always seem as if they'll never end. Then suddenly the sunshine comes and you notice the chestnut trees, magnolias, flowers everywhere. The grey clouds and the snow and ice are gone, and everywhere is green.' That's all he said, but it was enough. I realized then that Frank loved Berlin as I loved it. All his talk of wanting to get away from here, to retire in England and never think about Berlin again, was nonsense. He loved it here. I suppose it was his imminent retirement that had made him face the truth; packing up his Ellington records, separating his personal possessions from the furniture and things that belonged to the residence, had made him miserable.

'Three drivers plus nine passengers,' said the voice.

'Who is that?' I asked Frank. 'I recognize the voice, I think.'

'Old Percy Danvers,' said Frank. It was a man who'd worked here in my father's time. His mother was German from Silesia, father English: a sergeant in the Irish Guards.

'Still working?'

'He retires next year, just a few months after me. But he's remaining here in the city,' said Frank wistfully. 'I don't know how the office will manage without Percy.'

'Who's getting Berlin when you go?' I asked. I sipped the whisky I needed to face them. Would Fiona really come?

'There was talk of Bret taking over.'

'That won't happen now,' I said.

'I don't care who comes here,' said Frank. 'As long as I get away.' I looked at him. Now both of us knew it wasn't true. Frank smiled.

Then Bret Rensselaer came back from the phone, and I said, 'Nine of them; they just came through Checkpoint Charlie. They'll be here at any time.' Behind Bret there was a German kid – Peter – who'd been assigned to provide Bret's personal protection. He was a nice kid, but he took it too seriously, and now he wouldn't let Bret out of his sight.

Bret nodded and joined us for a moment at the window before sinking into one of the soft grey suede armchairs. The VIP suite at the Steigenberger runs the whole length of the building, but the entrance to it is inconspicuous, and many of the hotel's residents don't even know it exists. For that reason the suite is used for top-level meetings both commercial and political and by publicity-shunning tycoons, politicians, and film stars. There's a dining room at one end and an elegant office area at the other. In between there's a TV lounge, sitting room, bedrooms, and even a small room where the waiters can open champagne and prepare canapés.

Champagne and canapés were ready for the KGB party, but higher on the list of priorities were the extra locks, the security devices and doors that close off this part of the top floor, and the suite's private elevator that would enable the KGB delegates to arrive and depart without mixing with the other hotel guests.

'What is their weakest point?' said Bret, speaking from behind us as if talking to himself. Bret had recovered some of his confidence by now. He had the American talent for bouncing back; all he'd needed was a hot shower, clean linen, and the sports pages of the *Herald Tribune*.

I didn't answer, but Frank said, 'Fiona.'

'Fiona?' Did I hear resentment in Bret's voice? Was there a proprietorial tone that came from some affection Bret still had for her? 'Fiona is their weakest point? What do you mean, Frank?'

Frank turned around and went and sat in the armchair opposite Bret. Ever since I'd brought Bret into Frank's house in Grunewald there had been a distance, almost a coldness, between the two men. I couldn't decide to what extent it was a latent hostility and to what extent it was embarrassment, a sign of Frank's concern for the humiliation that Bret was suffering.

Frank said, 'She is a latecomer to their organization. Some of them probably still view her with suspicion; no doubt all of them have some kind of hostility towards her.'

'Is that view based upon received reports?' said Bret.

'She's a foreigner,' said Frank. 'Putting her in charge over there means that everyone's promotion expectations are lessened. Compare her position with ours. We've all known each other many years. We know what we can expect from each other, both in terms of help and hindrance. She is isolated. She has no long-term allies. She has no experience of what actions or opinions can be expected from her colleagues. She is constantly under the microscope; everyone around her will be trying to find fault with what she does. Everything she says will be examined, syllable for syllable, by people who are not in sympathy with what she's doing.'

'She's a Moscow appointment,' said Bret. Again there was some indefinable note of something that might have been affection or even pride. Bret looked at me, but I looked at my drink.

Frank said, 'All the more reason why the staff in her Berlin office will resent her.'

'So what are you proposing?' Bret asked Frank.

'We must give her the opportunity to negotiate while separated from the rest of her people. We must give her a chance to speak without being overheard.'

'That won't be easy, Frank,' I said. 'You know why they send such big teams. They don't trust anyone to be alone with us.'

'We must find a way,' said Frank. 'Bernard must move the chat onto a domestic plane. There must be something he could talk to her about.'

'Talk about the kids,' said Bret. I could cheerfully have throttled him, but I smiled instead.

'She might have thought all this out for herself,' said Frank, who also knew Fiona well. 'She might get time alone with us by some ruse of her own.'

'And what about us?' said Bret. 'What's our weakest point?' Peter, his bodyguard, watched Bret all the time and tried to follow the conversation.

'That's easy,' said Frank. 'Our weakest point is Werner Volkmann.' Frank's dislike of Werner was based upon the affair Frank had had with Werner's wife, Zena. Guilt breeds resentment; Frank disliked Werner because he'd cuckolded him.

'Werner's name hasn't even been mentioned,' said Bret. 'At least, that's what Bernard told us.'

'I'm sure Bernard told us the truth,' said Frank. 'But they're holding Werner Volkmann, and Werner is Bernard's very closest friend. They know what we want in return.'

'What we are *pretending* to want in return, Frank,' I said. 'Our real benefit is revealing to London Central that Stinnes is Moscow's man who's trying to frame Bret and make trouble for everyone else. We have to do that without Moscow realizing what our true purpose is. Making them release Werner is a convenient smokescreen.'

Frank smiled at what he regarded as my rationalization. He thought Werner was my real motive for setting this one up. But Frank was wrong. I wouldn't let either of them discover my real motive. My real motive was my children.

'Bernard!' All of a sudden my wife came walking through the door. 'What a glorious suite. Did you choose it?' A cold smile, just in case anyone thought she was sincere.

She stood there as if expecting the usual kiss, but I hesitated, then extended my hand. She shook it with a mocking grin. 'Hello, Fi,' I said. She was dressed in a grey woollen dress. It was simple but expensive. She was not living like a worker, but like the ones who told the workers what they were allowed to do.

'Hello Frank; hello Bret,' she said. Fiona smiled at them and shook hands. She was in charge of the party and she was determined to show it. This was her first official visit to the West. Looking back afterwards I realized that despite our reassurances, she was wondering if we were going to arrest her. But she carried it off with the same brisk confidence with which she did everything. Her hair was different. She'd let it grow and taken it back into a sort of bun. It was the sort of hair style that Hollywood might provide for a Communist official in the sort of movie where she takes off her glasses, lets her hair down, and becomes a capitalist in the last reel. *Ninotchka*. But I saw no sign of Fiona shedding the chrysalis of Communism. Indeed, if appearances were any guide, it seemed to suit her.

After everyone had shaken hands with everyone, a waiter – that is to say, one of our people, armed but dressed as a waiter – served drinks. Frank offered champagne. He'd bet me five pounds that they wouldn't accept it. He'd got some Russian white wine in the cooler anticipating that they'd ask for something like that, just to be difficult. But Fiona said champagne would be wonderful, and after that, they all said they'd have champagne. Except me; I had another scotch.

There were not nine of them in the room. Two armed KGB men were in the lobby, another was assigned to help the drivers make sure no one tampered with the cars, and someone was supervising the use of the private elevator. There were three actual negotiators and two clerks. The only one I knew, besides Fiona, was Pavel Moskvin, whose path kept crossing mine. He shed his ankle-length black overcoat and dumped it onto the sofa. He stared at me. I smiled and he looked away.

There was a much younger man with their party, a blond man of about twenty-five, wearing the kind of suit that KGB men wore if they couldn't get out of Moscow. He must have been on the teaching machines, for his German and English were perfect and accentless and he even made little jokes. But he was very much in Fiona's pocket and he watched her all the time in case she wanted something done. Alongside him was the third negotiator; a white-haired man who did nothing but frown.

'I hope you agree that time is the vital factor,' said Bret. It was his show; Frank had agreed to that right from the start. Bret had most to lose. If the meeting was going to become a fiasco, then Bret would have only himself to blame. And no doubt Frank would toss him to the wolves in a desperate attempt to save himself. Where would Frank's explanation leave me? I wondered.

'Yes,' said Fiona. 'May we take notes?'

Bret said, 'So we thought we'd break the meeting up into one-to-one discussions. The prime discussion will be about your man Stinnes. We can discuss procedure at the same time, in the hope that we'll reach agreement. Are you the senior officer?'

'Yes,' said Fiona. She drank some champagne. She knew what was coming, of course, but she kept very serious.

'Our senior negotiator is Mr Samson,' said Bret.

There was a long silence. Pavel Moskvin didn't like it. He'd not touched his champagne, which was going flat on the dining table. He showed his hostility by folding his arms and scowling. 'What do you think, Colonel Moskvin?' Fiona asked. *Colonel* Moskvin, was it . . . look out, Major Stinnes, I thought.

'Better we all stay together,' said Moskvin. 'No tricks.'

'Very well,' said Bret. He motioned for them to sit at the circular dining table. The waiter topped up the glasses. The blond youth put his chair behind Fiona so that he could sit with his notepad on his knee.

'What is it you want?' said Moskvin, as if trying to take over from Fiona, who sat back and said nothing. His folded arms strained his jacket across the back and showed where he had a pistol stowed under his armpit.

'We have your man Stinnes,' said Bret. 'It was a good try but it failed. So far we've held the press at bay, but there's a limit to how long we can do that.' The blond youth translated for Moskvin. Moskvin nodded.

'Is that why you brought him to Berlin?' said Fiona.

'Partly. But the Germans have newspapers too. Once the story breaks, we'll have no alternative but to hand him over to the DPP and then it's out of our hands.'

'DPP?' said Moskvin. 'What is this?' Obviously he could understand enough English to follow most of what was said.

'The Director of Public Prosecutions,' said Bret. 'The British state prosecutor. It's another department. We have no control over it.'

'And in return?' said Fiona.

'You've arrested Werner Volkmann,' I said.

'Have we?' said Fiona. It was very Russian.

'I haven't come here to waste time,' I said.

My remark seemed to anger her. 'No,' she said with a quiet voice that throbbed with hatred and resentment. 'You have come here to discuss the fate of Erich Stinnes, a good and loyal comrade who was shamelessly kidnapped by your terrorists, despite his diplomatic status. And who, according to our sources, has been systematically starved and tortured in an attempt to make him betray his country.' Fiona had quickly mastered the syntax of the Party.

It was quite a speech and I was tempted to reply sarcastically, but I didn't. I looked at Frank. We both knew now that I was right, and I could see the relief in Frank's face. If the official KGB line was going to be that Erich Stinnes had been kidnapped, starved, and tortured, Stinnes would be reinstated in his KGB rank and position. Even the most thick-skulled men in London would then have to accept the fact that Stinnes had been planted to make trouble. 'Let's not make this meeting a forum for political bickering,' I said. 'Werner Volkmann for Major Stinnes; straight swap.'

'Where is Comrade Stinnes?' said Fiona.

'Here in Berlin. Where's Werner?'

'Checkpoint Charlie,' said Fiona. It was strange how after all these years the Communists still used the US Army name for it.

'Fit and well?'

'Do you want to send someone over to see him?' she asked.

'We have someone at Checkpoint Charlie. Shall we agree to do that while we go on talking?' I asked. She looked at Moskvin. He gave an almost imperceptible nod.

'Very well. And Comrade Stinnes?' said Fiona. I looked at Bret. The exchange was Bret's worry.

'We have him here in the hotel,' said Bret. 'But you must nominate one of your number to see him. One. I can't let you all go.' Good old Bret. I didn't know he had it in him, but he'd pipped that one on the wing.

'I will go,' said Fiona. Moskvin was not pleased, but there was little he could do about it. If he objected, she'd send him and then she'd still have a chance of speaking to me in private.

Erich Stinnes was in a suite along the corridor. Frank's men had virtually abducted him from Berwick House waving authorizations and a chit signed by Bret in his capacity as chairman of the committee, a position which technically he still held. But I took us to an empty suite next door to the one where Stinnes was being held.

'What's the game?' said Fiona. She looked around the empty

rooms; she even rummaged through the roses looking for a micro-phone. Fiona was very unsophisticated when it came to surveillance electronics. 'What is it?' She seemed anxious.

'Relax,' I said. 'I'm not going to demand my conjugal rights.'

'I came to see Stinnes,' she said.

'You came because you wanted a chance to talk in private.'

'But I still want to see him,' she said.

'He's down the corridor waiting for us.'

'Is he well?'

'What do you care if he's well?'

'Erich Stinnes is a fine man, Bernard. I'll do what I can to prevent his dying in prison.' Stinnes feigning illness was a part of their plan. That became obvious now.

'Don't worry,' I said. 'We both know that Erich Stinnes is as fit as a fiddle. He'll go home and get his chestful of medals.'

'He's a good man,' she said, as if convincing me of it was important to her. She didn't deny that he was fit. His sickness was all part of the scenario – Fiona's touch no doubt; a way to give Stinnes an easier time.

'We haven't got time to waste talking about Stinnes,' I said.

'No, you've come to talk about your precious Werner,' she said. Even now that she'd left me, there was still an edge of resentment in her voice. Did all wives fear and resent the friendships that had come before marriage?

'Wrong again,' I said. 'We have to talk about the children.'

'There's nothing to talk about. I want them for a holiday. It's not much to ask. Did Tessa speak to you?'

'She did. But I don't want you to take the children.'

'They're mine as much as yours. Do you think I'm not human? Do you think I don't love them as much as you do?'

'How can I believe you love them the way I love them when you've left us?'

'Sometimes there are allegiances and aspirations that go beyond family.'

'Is that one of the things you're going to explain to little Billy when you take him round the Moscow electric stations and show him the underground railway?'

'They're my children,' she said.

'Can't you see the danger of taking them with you? Can't you see the way in which they'll become hostages to your good behaviour? Isn't it obvious that once they're there you'll never again be allowed to come West all together? They'll always keep the children there to be sure you do your duty as a good Communist and return East as every good Soviet citizen must.'

'What of their life now? You're always working. Nanny spends her life watching TV. They're shunted from your mother to my father and back again. Soon you'll take up with some other woman and they'll have a stepmother. What sort of life is that? With me they could have a proper home and a stable family life.'

'With a stepfather?'

'There is no other man, Bernard,' she said very softly. 'There will be no other man. That is why I need the children so much. You can have other children, dozens of them if you wish. For a man it's easy – he can have children until he's eighty – but I'll soon be past the suitable age for motherhood. Don't deny me the children.' Like all women she was tyrannized by her biology.

'Don't take them to a country which they won't be able to leave. Fiona! Look at me, Fiona. I'm saying it for your sake, for the children's sake, and for my sake too.'

'I have to see them. I have to.' Nervously she went to the window, looked out, and then came back to me.

'See them in Holland or Sweden or on some other neutral ground. I implore you not to take them to the East.'

'Is this another one of your tricks?' she said harshly.

'You know I'm right, Fi.'

She wrung her hands and twisted the rings on her fingers. Her marriage band was there still and so was the diamond I'd bought with the money from my old Ferrari. 'How are they?' It was a different voice.

'Billy's got a new magic trick and Sally is learning to write with her right hand.'

'How sweet they are. I got their letters and the drawings. Thank you.'

'It was Tessa's idea.'

'Tess has grown up suddenly.'

'Yes, she has.'

'Is she still having those stupid love affairs?'

'Yes, but George is reading the riot act to her. I think she's beginning to wonder if it's worth it.'

'What's the trick?'

'What trick?'

'Billy's.'

'Oh! You cut a piece of rope into two halves and then make it whole again.'

'Is it convincing?'

'Nanny still can't work it out.'

'It's in the family, I suppose.'

'I suppose so,' I said, although I wasn't sure what sort of trickery she was referring to, or whether she meant my sort of trickery or her own.

'Will they arrest me if I come to England on my old passport?' she asked.

'I'll find out,' I promised. 'But why not see the children in Holland?'

'You'd better not become an accessary, Bernard.'

'We are conspiring together right now,' I said. 'Which of our masters would tolerate it?'

'Neither,' she said. It was a concession, a minuscule concession, but the first one she'd made.

'I miss you, Fi,' I said.

'Oh, Bernard,' she said. Tears welled up in her eyes. I was about to take her into my arms but she stepped back from me. 'No,' she said. 'No.'

'I'll do what I can,' I said. I don't know exactly what I meant and she didn't ask; it was no more than an abstract noise that intended comfort and she accepted it as such.

'They won't let Werner go,' she said. She looked around the room, anxious about being recorded.

'I thought it was agreed.'

'Pavel Moskvin has the power of decision. He's in charge of these negotiations, I'm not.'

'Werner did nothing of any importance.'

'I know what he was doing. The Miller woman's been under permanent surveillance since last week. We were waiting for Werner to make contact.'

'The Stinnes operation is all washed up. It's finished, discredited, done for. What Werner said to the Miller woman is of no importance.'

'Keep calm. I know. But I'm under orders.'

'No Werner, no Stinnes,' I said.

She said nothing, but her face was white and tense and she was breathing in that way she did when stress got too much for her.

I said, 'Moskvin killed the little MacKenzie kid in the safe house in Bosham.'

She shrugged.

'What did he have to do that for?' I persisted. 'MacKenzie couldn't swat a fly without reciting the Miranda warnings.'

She looked at me and gave a deep sigh. 'You'll have to take him out, Bernard.'

'What?' I said.

Petulantly and with a gabbled haste that was not typical of her she said, 'You'll have to take him out – Moskvin.'

For a moment I was speechless. Was this my wife speaking? 'How? Where?'

'It's the only way. I've got Werner down to the bus park at Checkpoint Charlie. I told Moskvin that you might want to see him waving to be sure he was fit and well. That was before you got Moskvin's agreement to your sending your man over there.'

'How will you explain it?' I said.

'Rid me of that man and I won't have to explain anything.'

I still wasn't sure. 'Kill him, you mean?'

She was nervous and excited. Her answer was shrill. 'People get killed. It wouldn't be the first time that someone was killed at the Wall, would it?'

'No, but I can't start shooting at a delegation like yours. They're likely to bring up the tanks. I don't want to be the man who starts World War Three. I'm serious, Fi.'

'You must do it personally, Bernard. You mustn't order anyone else to do it. I don't want anyone else to know it was discussed by us.'

'Okay.' I heard myself agreeing to it.

'Promise?' I hesitated. 'It's Werner; your friend,' she said. 'I'm doing everything I can. More than I should.' Because it suited her, I thought. She wasn't doing it for Werner, or even for me. And what was she doing anyway? I was going to be the one putting my neck on the block. And now she wanted to deprive me of the chance of explaining it to my masters.

'I promise,' I said desperately. 'Put him and Stinnes in the last car and let me ride with them. But the children stay with me. That's a condition, Fi.'

'Be careful, Bernard. He's a brute.'

I looked at her. She was very beautiful, more beautiful than I ever remembered. Her eyes were soft and the faint smell of her perfume brought memories. 'Stay here, Fi,' I said. 'Stay here in the West. We could fix everything.'

She shook her head. 'Goodbye for the last time,' she said. 'Don't worry, I'll send Werner back. And I won't take the children from you for the time being.'

'Stay.'

She leaned forward and kissed me in a decorous way that would not smudge her lipstick; I suppose they'd all be looking at her for such signs. 'You don't understand. But one day you will.'

'I don't think so,' I said.

'Let's go and see Comrade Stinnes,' she said. And now her voice was hard and resolute once more.

29

I'd allowed for a lot of varied possibilities arising from my meeting with Fiona, but her demand that I kill Pavel Moskvin, one of her senior staff, caught me unawares. And yet there could be no doubt that she was serious. As Bret and Frank had already agreed just a few minutes before the meeting, my friendship with Werner was damned important to me. If killing a hood like Pavel Moskvin could rescue Werner from a prospect of twenty years in a *gulag*, I wouldn't hesitate. And Fiona knew that.

But there were a lot of unanswered questions. I found it difficult to accept Fiona's explanation at face value. Would she really ask me to kill Moskvin just so she could keep to her side of the bargain? It seemed far more likely that Moskvin was an obstacle to her ambitions. But it was difficult to believe that Fiona would go that far. I preferred to think that her desire to have him dead came from somewhere higher up in the echelons of the KGB – Moscow Centre, in all probability.

But why didn't they try him, sentence him, and execute him for whatever he'd done? The obvious answer to that was *blat*, the Russian all-purpose word for influence, corruption and unofficial power. Was Moskvin the friend or relative of someone that even the KGB would rather not confront? Was getting rid of him in the West – and so attributing his death to the imperialists – a clever scheme whereby Moscow kept their hands clean? Probably.

Werner Volkmann was still in the roadway on the wrong side of Checkpoint Charlie – our man could see him clearly from the observation post on Kochstrasse. According to what was being said on the radiophone, Werner was wearing his grey raincoat and pacing up and down, accompanied by a guard in civilian clothes.

As arranged with Fiona, I was in the last of the three KGB Volvos when they pulled away from the front of the Steigenberger. There were plenty of policemen there, some in civilian clothes, but not so many that the KGB party attracted any more attention than would the departure from the hotel of any minor celebrity. At the front of the line of three black Volvos there was a white VW bus, an unmarked police vehicle, and a motorcycle cop. Behind us there was another white VW bus containing Frank Harrington, Bret Rensselaer, and three members of the Berlin Field Unit. It was our communications van, two whiplash antennas and an FM rod on the roof.

The convoy of cars moved out into the traffic and past the famous black, broken spire of the Memorial Church, incongruously placed amid the flashy shops, outdoor cafés, and swanky restaurants of the Kurfürstendamm. There were no flashing lights or police sirens to clear our way. The cars and their two escorting buses eased into the lanes of slowly moving traffic and halted at the traffic signals.

I turned my head to see the white van behind us. Frank was in the front seat, next to the driver. I couldn't see Bret. The cars followed the motorcycle cop, keeping a distance between them so that it didn't look as if we were all together. We attracted less attention that way.

Along Tauentzienstrasse the traffic thinned, but we were stopped by red lights at the big KaDeWe department store. The lights turned green and we began rolling forward again. Then someone stepping into the road threw a plastic bag of white paint at the car I was in. Whether this was part of Fiona's plan or the action of some demonstrator who'd seen the Volvos – with their DDR registration plates – parked outside the Steigenberger, I never discovered. Neither did I ever find out if Pavel Moskvin had been prepared by stories of danger and possible attempts on his life. But as the bag of white paint hit our car and splashed across the windscreen, the driver hit the brakes. It was then, without any warning, that Pavel Moskvin opened the door and jumped out into the road. I slid across the seat and scrambled out after him as the traffic raced past. A red Merc hooted and almost ran over me; a kid on a motorbike swerved round Moskvin and almost hit me instead.

Moskvin ran for the old U-Bahn station that stands in the middle of the traffic there at Wittenbergplatz. I was a long way behind him. There were cops everywhere. I heard whistles and I noticed that one of the other black Volvos had stopped on the far side of the traffic circus.

Obviously Moskvin didn't know the city well. He ducked into the entrance to the U-Bahn expecting some escape route, but then, realizing he would be trapped, he dashed out again and raced into the fast-moving traffic, jumping between the cars with amazing agility. He ran along the pavement pushing and striking out with his fists to punch people out of his way. He was a violent man whose violence provided a spur for his energy, and, despite his bulk and his middle age, he ran like an athlete. It was a long run. My lungs were bursting and my head spun as I pounded after him.

He turned to see me. He raised an arm. There was a crack and a scream. A woman in front of me doubled up and fell to the ground. I ducked to one side and ran on. Moskvin kept running too. He raced towards Nollendorfplatz. In Kleiststrasse the tracks of the railway emerge from under the roadway and occupy the centre median of the street. He climbed the railings, ran across the tracks, and jumped down the other side. I did the same. I stood on the railings trying to see where he was, thankfully gulping air as my heart pounded with exertion. Bang! There was another shot. I felt the wind of it and jumped down out of sight. Was he, I wondered, heading for the Wall? It wasn't far away; the vast arena of floodlights, barbed wire, mines and machine guns at Potsdamerplatz was close. But how would he try to get across? Were there some secret crossing places which the KGB used and we didn't know about? We'd suspected it for ages but never found one.

I got my second wind and kept pounding after him. He had to go to Nollendorfplatz unless he had a safe house in this street. Then I saw him. And on the other side of the street – the wrong side of the street – one of the VW vans was grinding its way through the oncoming cars. Now there was a blue light flashing on its roof. No siren though. I wondered if Moskvin could see the light. Frank and his BFU detachment were trying to get to the other side of the Platz and cut him off. I saw old Percy Danvers jump out of the white VW bus and start running. But Percy was too old.

Nollendorfplatz was a big traffic intersection, a circus where fast-moving traffic circulates. The centre of the intersection is filled by the ancient iron structure of the station, raised on stilts above the street. The rusty old railway tracks emerge from under Kleiststrasse and slope gently up to it.

I saw Moskvin again. A car flashed its headlights and another one hooted loudly, and then I glimpsed him leaping through the traffic to the middle of the road and the entrance to the station. There were two stations here: the modern underground and the old elevated one it replaced. Had he changed his mind? Was he going to duck down into the U-Bahn, the underground railway, and hope to get aboard a train and leave us behind? A slim hope. But then he raced up the rattling iron steps of the elevated railway station. The bloody fool thought he'd get a train up there. Or perhaps he thought he'd jump down and run along the elevated tracks and cross the Wall the way the elevated trains did from Lehrter Bahnhof to Friedrichstrasse.

I got a clear view of him now. He was halfway up the iron staircase and there was no one in the way. I fired twice. He jumped, but my pistol hand was shaking after the exertions of the chase and I didn't hit him. Across the road Percy Danvers was trying to get ahead of him. Good old Percy. I had to find out what kind of pills he'd been taking.

Then I heard two more shots from the street and I could see the white VW. It bumped as it came riding up onto the pavement. Its doors opened and men jumped out. Frank Harrington was among them, a pistol in his hand. And so was Bret, gung ho and full of fight.

What's Frank doing with a gun? I thought – he doesn't know one end of a gun from the other. Had Frank worried that the Steigenberger meeting might have ended with us all being marched off by the KGB at gunpoint? Frank had always been a bit of a romantic.

I ran into the old elevated station. It was darker in here. I got to the foot of the next staircase and kept close to the wall as I climbed up to the platform. Now there was a volley of shots. They came from across the street. Police perhaps, or people from the other VW bus, but I couldn't see it and I couldn't see any of the three black Volvos either.

Moskvin's feet clattered on the steps. There was a shout as he elbowed someone out of his way. A man carrying a cast-iron bust of the Great Elector fell, the bust hit the stairs with a loud clang, bounced, and broke. I was close behind Moskvin now. At the top of the stairs he stopped. He had realized that the elevated station wasn't a station at all; it had long since been in use as an antique and junk market. This bright yellow train never went anywhere; its doors opened onto little shops and the platform was a line of stalls displaying old clothes, toys, and slightly damaged valuables. The destination boards said BERLINER FLOHMARKT.

He turned and fired at random. I could see the consternation on his face. I fired too. Both of us were being jostled by a terrified crowd. There was a thud and a crash of breaking glass and the bullets zinged off into nowhere.

Moskvin was still hoping that the elevated train tracks would provide him with an escape route. He fought his way through the crowds. There was panic now, screams and shouts. A woman fell and was trampled underfoot. Moskvin turned and fired two shots blindly into the crowd to cause maximum crush that would impede his capture. There was blood spurting. Antique furniture was knocked over, a cut-glass light fell to the floor, a case full of old coins tipped up and the contents went everywhere. A bearded man tried to retrieve the coins and was knocked over.

Through the 'trains' of the *Flohmarkt* I caught a glimpse of the other platform. Frank and his party were there. They were making better progress on that side since they weren't moving in the ferocious and terrible wake of Moskvin. 'Stay back, Bernard!' It was Bret's voice calling from the other platform. 'We'll take him.'

They had marksmen with proper weapons. It made sense to let

them move forward rather than my heading into Moskvin's gun sights.

There was the noise of breaking glass and then I saw that Bret was trying to climb up onto the roof of the train. From there he would see the end of the platform, and Moskvin. But Moskvin saw him first. He fired and Bret lost his balance, slid, toppled, and went to his knees before falling to the ground with a loud scream of pain.

I edged forward, more slowly now. Outside in the street below there was a racket of police sirens and some confused shouting. I saw Moskvin again and again, but he was dodging behind the stalls; there was no way of getting a clear shot at him. His hat had fallen off and his close-cropped hair was little more than stubble. He looked older now, a fierce old man whose eyes gleamed with hatred as he turned once and stared directly at me, daring me to step into the open and do battle with him.

When he got to the end of the platform he was alone. The frightened shoppers had scrambled past him and fled down the steps to shout in the street. He saw the tracks that led to the next elevated station. Did he know that one was a market too? Perhaps he no longer cared. As he turned to face me, he saw Frank and the party that had edged their way down the other side. There was a confusion of shooting, the sound echoing like a drum roll in the confined space.

There was only one way Moskvin could go. He climbed onto a bench and pushed aside old Nazi uniforms and some military helmets adorned with eagles. Then he kicked at the dirty windows using the immense strength that comes to those with nothing to lose. The glass and wooden frames smashed into fragments under the kicks from his heavy boots, and he jumped through the shower of broken glass.

He landed down on the train tracks with a force that made his knees bend, and one hand was stretched out to recover his balance. But in an instant he was upright again and running eastwards. His ankle-length black overcoat was flapping out like the wings of some wounded crow and his pistol was held high in the air, proudly, like the flaming torch of an Olympic runner.

'Hold your fire!' It was Frank Harrington's voice. 'He can't get away, the bloody fool.'

But there was the sound of two shots and the black crow stumbled. Yet he had within him the energy and determination of a dozen ordinary men. He ran: one, two, three, four paces. But when he went down again the wings had flapped for the last time. His gun fell from his hand. His face was screwed up into an expression of rage. He clawed desperately at the rails trying to get up again, but, failing, he rolled over and, face upward, bled.

From the station at the other end of the tracks there came the sound of Oriental music. It was the Türkischer Basar, and today it was crowded.

Everyone kept under cover as training rules demand. But I heard someone shout, 'Where's that bloody doctor!' It was an English voice calling from the other platform. 'Mr Rensselaer is hurt bad.'

Then Frank's voice: 'Everyone stay exactly where they are; everyone!' Then he said it again in German.

I kept under cover too, as Frank commanded. It was his show now: Berlin was Frank's town. I was half inside the entrance to one of the little shops. I put my head out enough to see round the sliding door. I could see Moskvin. He hadn't moved. Frank Harrington went out there alone. He was the first person to get to him. I saw him bend over the body for a moment, take his pulse, and then drag an old fur coat right over him. Pavel Moskvin was dead, just as Fiona wanted him. Everything was quiet now except for the Turkish music and Bret's soft cries of pain.

30

It was night. There was a loud, regular, clicking noise, but it was too dark to see where it was coming from. I could only just see Frank. He was sitting on a hard wooden bench.

'We have to be thankful for small mercies,' said Frank Harrington. 'At least they released Werner Volkmann. They might have kicked up an unholy row when one of their senior staff got killed.'

'Yes, they released Werner.' I'd just come up from the morgue where Pavel Moskvin was in a drawer in a chilled room with a label tied to his toe. I sat down on the bench.

'Even though we didn't guarantee the safety of that party, I was expecting all hell to break loose. I thought there might have been an official protest.'

'Then I've got news for you, Frank,' I said. 'The ballistics report says that Pavel Moskvin was not killed by one of our rounds.' I tossed the mangled piece of metal into the air and caught it.

'What?'

'They said they'd put the report on your desk.'

'I haven't been back to the office.'

'Three of our bullets hit him, but the one that killed him came from a Soviet-calibre gun.' I offered him the round, but he wouldn't take it. Frank was curiously squeamish about firearms.

'What the hell?' said Frank. 'And why use one of their own guns?'

'Someone over there wanted him dead, Frank. And they wanted us to know that.' It was, of course, Fiona's little touch – a way of turning attention away from me, and thus away from her too.

'That's why there's been no protest?'

'And why Werner was released as promised,' I said. I hadn't told Frank about my conversation with Fiona and her request that Pavel Moskvin be 'taken out'. Now it had become evident that the KGB hadn't relied upon us; they'd had their own marksman chasing Moskvin. I suppose they would have had too much to lose had we taken him alive.

'Good grief,' said Frank. 'There's never a clean ending, is there?'

'That's why we have files, Frank.'

'So Moskvin was intended to die,' mused Frank. 'That explains the KGB hit team we identified. I thought they might be after you.'

I said, 'Stinnes will return in triumph. Moskvin represented a threat to him. I overheard a conversation between them once. Moskvin was out to get Stinnes.'

Our voices were hushed. It was night and we were in the Steglitz Clinic, a part of the hospital of the Free University, the same place from which the Miller woman had been rescued after her pretended attempt at suicide. It had been a terrible night and Frank Harrington's lined face showed how badly he was taking it. Old Percy Danvers, one of Frank's best people and his close friend, was dead. Pavel Moskvin had shot him through the head. That happened in Kleistsrasse before they even got to the flea market and the gun battle in the station. Young Peter – Bret's bodyguard – was badly hurt.

We were waiting for Sheldon Rensselaer to arrive. Bret was in the intensive care ward and not expected to live beyond the weekend. His brother Sheldon was flying in from Washington on a US Air Force flight. Sheldon Rensselaer had a lot of influence in Washington.

'And his wife?' I asked. Ex-wife, I meant. Bret's wife had started spending her alimony years ago.

'Yes, they finally found her. Apparently she winters in Monte Carlo.'

'She's coming?'

'She sent three dozen roses.'

'Perhaps she doesn't realize how bad Bret is.'

'Perhaps,' said Frank in a voice that meant she knew.

'Poor Bret,' I said.

'He didn't recognize me,' said Frank. He was waiting to see Bret again and still wearing the white medical gown they'd given him to go into the ward.

'He wasn't really conscious,' I said.

'I should have stopped him getting up on that train. He saw the kid hit and felt he had to do something.'

'I know,' I said. Frank was reproaching himself unnecessarily for what had happened to Bret. 'Did you talk to London?' I asked him, in order to change the subject.

'The old man was not in the best of moods,' said Frank.

'We got him off the hook,' I said. 'We got them all off the hook. Without what you did, those stupid bastards would still be believing all that crap Stinnes was feeding them.'

'But they're not admitting that,' said Frank.

'How can they deny it? Last night the monitoring service picked up an item about Stinnes being honoured in Moscow.'

'We both know we stopped London making complete idiots of themselves, but they're closing ranks and pretending they knew about

Stinnes all the time. Even the old man said that there's valuable information to be obtained even from non-genuine defectors.'

'And what about what they did to Bret?'

'They say he wasn't really under house arrest. They say the man who spoke with him was acting without official intructions.'

'Balls,' I said.

'And now the man in question is on duty somewhere and can't be reached.'

'I bet,' I said.

'I spoke to all of them. They're bastards, Bernard. I've often choked you off for saying so, but I take it all back.' Everywhere was dark. A nurse came through the swing doors wheeling a trolley that was clanking with glass and stainless steel. She walked away slowly and eventually disappeared into the darkness that was at the end of a long corridor.

'And what about you, Frank?'

'I was in line for a K.'

'So I heard.' Frank had set his heart on that knighthood. Even though he pretended not to care, it meant a lot to him.

'The old man says it would be inappropriate to recommend that now, after I've so flagrantly disobeyed orders.'

'But you saved them.'

'You keep saying that,' said Frank peevishly. 'And I keep telling you that they don't see it that way.'

'We couldn't have done it without you, Frank. You risked everything and we were proved right.'

'There was talk of giving the K. to Bret instead,' said Frank. 'I don't know what will happen now.'

'The surgeon said Bret won't live.'

'The surgeon says no one can predict what a bullet wound like that will do. They've wrapped him in some kind of tinfoil trying to preserve his body heat. They're doing everything that can be done.'

'You'll retire anyway?' I said.

'The old man has asked me to stay on here. There is the prospect of a K. in two years' time.'

'What did you say?'

'I said you should have Berlin,' said Frank. 'But the old man said that you were lucky not to be facing grave charges.'

Now that my eyes had become used to the gloom I could see the big electric clock over the door that led to the wards. It was the clock that gave that loud click every second. It was the only sound to be heard. 'What time did they say his brother's plane would arrive?'

'I don't think he can possibly get here before four,' said Frank.

'Sheldon was his father's favourite. Bret resented that. Did he ever tell you?'

'Bret didn't reveal much about his private affairs.'

'Yes. I was surprised he confided in me.'

'He knew he could trust you, Bernard, and he was right. He came to you at a time when there was no one else he could trust.'

'I didn't know him very well,' I said. 'I'd always suspected that he'd had an affair with Fiona.'

'He knew you didn't like him, but he came to you all the same. Bret was grateful for what you did. He told me that. I hope he told you.'

'Neither of us did anything for Bret,' I said. 'It wasn't personal. It wasn't like you doing something for me or me doing something for you . . . '

'Or you doing something for Werner,' said Frank artfully.

'It was for the good of the Department,' I said, ignoring Frank's aside. 'Bret was being framed, and those idiots in London were letting it happen. Something had to be done.'

'There will be a big shake-up,' said Frank. 'Dicky is hoping to get the Europe desk, but there's not much chance of that, thank God. Bret might have got Europe if this hadn't happened. Morgan, the D-G's hatchet man, is getting some sort of promotion too.'

'Is Bret in the clear now?'

'Yes, Bret without this damned bullet in his guts might have ended up as the golden boy all over again. Funny how things happen, isn't it?'

'Yes, very funny.'

'I told the D-G that you should have a recommendation, Bernard. But it was no use. He's against it and I'm not in a position to do much for you at present, I'm afraid.'

'Thanks anyway, Frank.'

'Don't be disappointed, Bernard. This is a disaster averted, a Dunkirk for the Department. There are decorations galore and ennoblements and promotions for victories like Trafalgar and Waterloo; but there are no rewards for Dunkirks, no matter how brave or clever the survivors might be. London Central don't give gold medals to staff who prove they are wrong, and prove it with senior staff from Five looking on. They don't give promotions after finales like the last act of *Hamlet* with blood and gore on every side and the unexplained death of a senior KGB official, even if he wasn't given a safe conduct.'

'But we saved them from making fools of themselves. We saved the D-G's job, Frank.'

'Maybe we did. But there's more to be gained from giving bad advice when the result is a triumph, than from giving good advice when the outcome is a near disaster.'

A doctor came through the door that led down the long corridor to the intensive care unit where a white-faced, motionless, unseeing Bret was wired into a roomful of life-support machinery: heart pumps, oxygen supply and drip feeds. At his side attentive nurses watched dark monitor screens on which little electronic lines jumped, faltered and flickered.

'Would you come?' said the doctor, a Turk with a strong accent and large moustache. 'He might be able to recognize you this time.'

'Thanks,' said Frank to the doctor. To me he said, 'Life is like show business – it's always better to put a fiver into a hit than five grand into a flop.'

'We put five grand into a flop,' I said.

'Give my best wishes to Werner,' said Frank. 'I wouldn't have let him down, Bernard. Even if you hadn't been here, twisting my arm, I wouldn't have let Werner down.'

'He knows that, Frank. Everyone knows!'

Werner was waiting outside in Zena's car. He looked tired, but no more tired that I'd often seen him before. He was still wearing the old jacket and corduroy trousers. 'I got your message,' he said.

'Didn't I tell you not to go near that bloody Miller woman?' I said.

'You didn't know it was a stakeout?'

I let his question hang in the air for a moment; then I said, 'No, I didn't know it was a stakeout, but I had brains enough to guess it might be.'

'I just got back to my apartment here when the phone rang,' said Werner. 'It was your girl. She'd been trying to get you all day.'

'My girl?' I knew he was talking about Gloria, of course, but I was annoyed that she'd phoned, and also that she'd got through to Werner.

'Gloria. She thought you might be staying with us. Rumours were going around in London. She was worried about you.'

'What time was this?'

'Just now.'

'In the middle of the night?'

'She was in some rotten little hotel in Bayswater. She couldn't sleep. She said you'd quarrelled and she'd moved out.'

'That's right.'

'I told her to pack her things and get a cab and move back into your place.'

'You did what?'

'You don't want the poor kid sitting in some crummy little doss house in Bayswater, do you?'

'Are you trying to break my heart, Werner? She's got enough money to check into the Savoy if Bayswater is so terrible.'

'Don't be a bastard, Bernie. She's a nice kid and she loves you.'

'Hold everything, Werner! Did you tell her that this was my idea, this moving back into my place?'

No answer.

'Werner. Did you tell Gloria it was my idea?'

'She thought it was your idea. I thought it was better that you sorted it out when you got back to London.'

'You're a regular bloody matchmaker, aren't you, Werner?'

'You're crazy about her – you know you are. You should grab her while you have the chance, Bernie. It's no good you living in the hope that one day Fiona will come back to you.'

'I know that,' I said.

'You saw her today . . . yesterday, I mean. I saw her too. Fiona's changed, Bernie. She's one of them now. And she beat us at our own game. She's tough and she called the shots. She made fools of us all.'

'What do you mean?' I said. I was weary and irritable. I wasn't asking that Werner thank me for getting him out, but neither was I welcoming his criticism.

'So take Stinnes. Are you still going to tell me he's sick?'

I didn't reply.

'Because I saw him after he arrived over there. I saw him light up a big Havana and make some crack about how pretending to be off tobacco was the worst part of the job. He didn't avoid the physical because he was very sick; he avoided it because he didn't want us to know how strong he was.'

'I know,' I said, but Werner had to go on about it.

'That was just one small part of the deception plan. By letting us think he was sick, he avoided any risk of us giving him intensive interrogation. He was treated with silk gloves . . . '

'Kid gloves,' I corrected him.

'Just the way Fiona knew a sick man would be treated. She outwitted us at every turn. It's game, set and match to Fiona, Bernie. It's no good you trying to pick a quarrel with me – it's game, set and match to Fiona.'

'Don't keep saying the same thing over and over again,' I said.

'Don't keep saying the things *you don't like to hear* over and over again. That's what you mean, isn't it?'

'We came out of it intact,' I said. 'You're here, I'm here, and the Department is still putting our salaries into the bank. . . .'

'Face the truth, Bernie. See how fast her success has come. Do you remember that night we waited at Checkpoint Charlie in my old Audi? Zena was away somewhere and you were sleeping on my sofa. We were expecting Brahms Four to try. Remember? That was only a year ago, Bernie, and that was well before Fiona went over there. Look what she's done since then. Brahms Four is retired, Bret's economic department is closed down. She's smeared you so cleverly that it will take you years to get in the clear again. Bret's been facing some sort of enquiry. Stinnes stirred up all kinds of trouble for us with MI5 so that it may take years before the bad feeling is gone. And they've done it all so cheaply. Fiona is as arrogant and successful as I've ever seen a KGB senior grade officer – and I've seen plenty – while Stinnes is repatriated and will obviously use the knowledge and experience he's acquired to stage more operations against us. Face the facts, Bernie.'

Werner turned the key and started the engine. It was a cold night and the car needed two or three tries before it came to life. He went down the slope and out past the gatekeeper. Berlin never goes to sleep and there was plenty of traffic on Grunewaldstrasse as we headed for his apartment in nearby Dahlem. He took it for granted that I would sleep on his sofa for what was left of the night, just as I took it for granted that Frank Harrington would phone me there to give me any instructions that came from London. It was like that with all of us. We all knew each other very well; too damned well at times. That's why, when we arrived outside his apartment and he switched off the engine, he said, 'Admit it.'

'Look at it another way,' I said. 'Fiona, one of the brightest and best-placed agents they've ever had, was flushed out and had to run for it so hurriedly that we lost little or no data. Brahms Four, a brave old man who for years supplied such good banking data and East Bloc forecasts that the Americans traded with us for it, was brought out safely . . . '

'Because you and I . . .' said Werner.

But I ploughed on. 'I survived their attempts to discredit me and even their loony hope that I'd run. I survived it so well that they had to rejig their resources to turn suspicion onto Bret. Okay, they were smart – I fell for it at first and so eventually did a lot of other people who had more data than I had and should have known better. But at the end of the road, Bret's reputation will have survived, and we proved flexible enough to bend the rules and even break them. The willingness to break rules now and again is what distinguishes free men from robots. And we spiked their guns, Werner. Forget game, set and match. We're not playing tennis; it's a rougher game than that, with more chances to cheat. We bluffed them; we bid a grand slam with a hand full of deuces and jokers, and we fooled them. They were relieved to get Stinnes back and they didn't even try to sustain the fiction that he was really enrolled.'

'Luckily for you,' said Werner.

'Luckily for both of us,' I said. 'Because if they'd stuck to their story that Stinnes was a traitor, I'd now be on a plane to London handcuffed to an Internal Security man and you'd still be on the wrong side of Charlie. Okay, there are wounds, and there will be scars, but it's not game, set and match to Fiona. It's not game, set and match to anyone. It never is.'

Werner opened the door and, as the light inside the car came on, I saw his weary smile. He wasn't convinced.

ABOUT THE AUTHOR

LEN DEIGHTON was born in London, and served with the Special Investigation Branch of the RAF. After his discharge he attended art school, graduating from the Royal College of Art on a scholarship. He later worked as an illustrator and photographer.

In 1960 Deighton went to the Dordogne, where he started work on his first book, *The Ipcress File.* Published in 1962, the book was an instant success. Since then, he has published thirty books of fiction and nonfiction, including spy stories, highly researched war novels, and histories, all of which have appeared to international acclaim. Deighton's most recent novels *Mamista* and *City of Gold* are published by HarperCollins.